THE TARZAN COLLECTION

ROYAL

CLASSICS

The Tarzan Collection: (5 Novels) Tarzan of the Apes, The Return of Tarzan, The Beasts of Tarzan, The Son of Tarzan, and Tarzan and the Jewels of Opar
Burroughs, Edgar Rice 1875 – 1950
Tarzan of the Apes
First Published by A. C. McClurg in 1912
The Return of Tarzan
First Published by A. C. McClurg in 1913
The Beasts of Tarzan
First Published by A. C. McClurg in 1914
The Son of Tarzan
First Published by A. C. McClurg in 1916
Tarzan and the Jewels of Opar
First Published by A. C. McClurg in 1916

Cover design by: A.R. Roumanis

Text set in Minion Pro. Chapter headings set in News Gothic Standard.

ISBN: 978-1-77476-597-5

FIRST EDITION / FIRST PRINTING

Many classics were originally published with inconsistent spellings of the same word, spelling errors, and printer errors. The text of our titles have been edited to give readers the best possible reading experience. Sometimes we can make mistakes, which is why we post "first edition" in all of our titles. This is a standard notice that is historically used by publishers. The above edition notice refers to our edition of this title. If changes are made to correct an error in the text, we will change the wording to "second edition." If we change printers but the text remains the same, the wording will change to "second printing."

LIBRARY AND ARCHIVES CANADA CATALOGUING IN PUBLICATION

Title: The Tarzan collection : Tarzan of the apes, The return of Tarzan, The beasts of Tarzan, The son of Tarzan, Tarzan and the Jewels of Opar / Edgar Rice Burroughs.

Other titles: Novels. Selections (2021) | Tarzan of the apes | Return of Tarzan | Beasts of Tarzan | Son of Tarzan | Jewels of Opar

Names: Burroughs, Edgar Rice, 1875-1950, author. | container of (work): Burroughs, Edgar Rice, 1875-1950. Tarzan of the apes. | container of (work): Burroughs, Edgar Rice, 1875-1950. Return of Tarzan. | container of (work): Burroughs, Edgar Rice, 1875-1950. Beasts of Tarzan. | container of (work): Burroughs, Edgar Rice, 1875-1950. Son of Tarzan. | container of (work): Burroughs, Edgar Rice, 1875-1950. Jewels of Opar.

Description: First edition. | "Tarzan of the apes first published by A.C. McClurg in 1912; The return of Tarzan first published by A.C. McClurg in 1913; The beasts of Tarzan first published by A.C. McClurg in 1914; The son of Tarzan first published by A.C. McClurg in 1916; Tarzan and the Jewels of Opar first published by A.C. McClurg in 1916"--Copyright page.

Identifiers: Canadiana 20210357592 | ISBN 9781774765975 (hardcover)

Classification: LCC PS3503.U687 A6 2022 | DDC 813/.52—DC23

THE TARZAN COLLECTION

EDGAR RICE BURROUGHS

TARZAN OF THE APES
THE RETURN OF TARZAN
THE BEASTS OF TARZAN
THE SON OF TARZAN
TARZAN AND THE JEWELS OF OPAR

VANCOUVER:
ROYAL CLASSICS
2022

CONTENTS

The Return of Tarzan

THE BEASTS OF TARZAN

The Son of Tarzan

Tarzan and the Jewels of Opar

TARZAN
OF THE APES

CHAPTER ONE

Out to Sea

I HAD THIS STORY from one who had no business to tell it to me, or to any other. I may credit the seductive influence of an old vintage upon the narrator for the beginning of it, and my own skeptical incredulity during the days that followed for the balance of the strange tale.

When my convivial host discovered that he had told me so much, and that I was prone to doubtfulness, his foolish pride assumed the task the old vintage had commenced, and so he unearthed written evidence in the form of musty manuscript, and dry official records of the British Colonial Office to support many of the salient features of his remarkable narrative.

I do not say the story is true, for I did not witness the happenings which it portrays, but the fact that in the telling of it to you I have taken fictitious names for the principal characters quite sufficiently evidences the sincerity of my own belief that it *may* be true.

The yellow, mildewed pages of the diary of a man long dead, and the records of the Colonial Office dovetail perfectly with the narrative of my convivial host, and so I give you the story as I painstakingly pieced it out from these several various agencies.

If you do not find it credible you will at least be as one with me in acknowledging that it is unique, remarkable, and interesting.

From the records of the Colonial Office and from the dead man's diary we learn that a certain young English nobleman, whom we shall call John Clayton, Lord Greystoke, was commissioned to make a peculiarly delicate investigation of conditions in a British West Coast African Colony from whose simple native inhabitants another European power was known to be recruiting soldiers for its native army, which it used solely for the forcible collection of rubber and ivory from the savage tribes along the Congo and the Aruwimi. The natives of the British Colony complained that many of their young men were enticed away through the medium of fair and glowing promises, but that few if any ever returned to their families.

The Englishmen in Africa went even further, saying that these poor blacks were held in virtual slavery, since after their terms of enlistment expired their ignorance was imposed upon by their white officers, and they were told that they had yet several years to serve.

And so the Colonial Office appointed John Clayton to a new post in British West Africa, but his confidential instructions centered on a thorough investigation of the unfair treatment of black British subjects by the officers of a friendly European power. Why he was sent, is, however, of little moment to this story, for he never made an investigation, nor, in fact, did he ever reach his destination.

Clayton was the type of Englishman that one likes best to associate with the noblest monuments of historic achievement upon a thousand victorious battlefields – a strong, virile man – mentally, morally, and physically.

In stature he was above the average height; his eyes were gray, his features regular and strong; his carriage that of perfect, robust health influenced by his years of army training.

Political ambition had caused him to seek transference from the army to the Colonial Office and so we find him, still young, entrusted with a delicate and important commission in the service of the Queen.

When he received this appointment he was both elated and appalled. The preferment seemed to him in the nature of a well-merited reward for painstaking and intelligent service, and as a stepping stone to posts of greater importance and responsibility; but, on the other hand, he had been married to the Hon. Alice Rutherford for scarce a three months, and it was the thought of taking this fair young girl into the dangers and isolation of tropical Africa that appalled him.

For her sake he would have refused the appointment, but she would not have it so. Instead she insisted that he accept, and, indeed, take her with him.

There were mothers and brothers and sisters, and aunts and cousins to express various opinions on the subject, but as to what they severally advised history is silent.

We know only that on a bright May morning in 1888, John, Lord Greystoke, and Lady Alice sailed from Dover on their way to Africa.

A month later they arrived at Freetown where they chartered a small sailing vessel, the Fuwalda, which was to bear them to their final destination.

And here John, Lord Greystoke, and Lady Alice, his wife, vanished from the eyes and from the knowledge of men.

Two months after they weighed anchor and cleared from the port of Freetown a half dozen British war vessels were scouring the south Atlantic for trace of them or their little vessel, and it was almost immediately that the wreckage was found upon the shores of St. Helena which convinced the world that the Fuwalda had gone down with all on board, and hence the search was stopped ere it had scarce begun; though hope lingered in longing hearts for many years.

The Fuwalda, a barkentine of about one hundred tons, was a vessel of the type often seen in coastwise trade in the far southern Atlantic, their crews composed of the offscourings of the sea – unhanged murderers and cutthroats of every race and every nation.

The Fuwalda was no exception to the rule. Her officers were swarthy bullies, hating and hated by their crew. The captain, while a competent seaman, was a brute in his treatment of his men. He knew, or at least he used, but two arguments in his dealings with them – a belaying pin and a revolver – nor is it likely that the motley aggregation he signed would have understood aught else.

So it was that from the second day out from Freetown John Clayton and his young wife witnessed scenes upon the deck of the Fuwalda such as they had believed were never enacted outside the covers of printed stories of the sea.

It was on the morning of the second day that the first link was forged in what was destined to form a chain of circumstances ending in a life for one then unborn such as has never been paralleled in the history of man.

Two sailors were washing down the decks of the Fuwalda, the first mate was on duty, and the captain had stopped to speak with John Clayton and Lady Alice.

The men were working backwards toward the little party who were facing away from the sailors. Closer and closer they came, until one of them was directly behind the captain. In another moment he would have passed by and this strange narrative would never have been recorded.

But just that instant the officer turned to leave Lord and Lady Greystoke, and, as he did so, tripped against the sailor and sprawled headlong upon the deck, overturning the water-pail so that he was drenched in its dirty contents.

For an instant the scene was ludicrous; but only for an instant. With a volley of awful oaths, his face suffused with the scarlet of mortification and rage, the captain regained his feet, and with a terrific blow felled the sailor to the deck.

The man was small and rather old, so that the brutality of the act was thus accentuated. The other seaman, however, was neither old nor small – a huge bear of a man, with fierce black mustachios, and a great bull neck set between massive shoulders.

As he saw his mate go down he crouched, and, with a low snarl, sprang upon the captain crushing him to his knees with a single mighty blow.

From scarlet the officer's face went white, for this was mutiny; and mutiny he had met and subdued before in his brutal career. Without waiting to rise he whipped a revolver from his pocket, firing point blank at the great mountain of muscle towering before him; but, quick as he was, John Clayton was almost as quick, so that the bullet which was intended for the sailor's heart lodged in the sailor's leg instead, for Lord Greystoke had struck down the captain's arm as he had seen the weapon flash in the sun.

Words passed between Clayton and the captain, the former making it plain that he was disgusted with the brutality displayed toward the crew, nor would he countenance anything further of the kind while he and Lady Greystoke remained passengers.

The captain was on the point of making an angry reply, but, thinking better of it, turned on his heel and black and scowling, strode aft.

He did not care to antagonize an English official, for the Queen's mighty arm wielded a punitive instrument which he could appreciate, and which he feared – England's far-reaching navy.

The two sailors picked themselves up, the older man assisting his wounded comrade to rise. The big fellow, who was known among his mates as Black Michael, tried his leg gingerly, and, finding that it bore his weight, turned to Clayton with a word of gruff thanks.

Though the fellow's tone was surly, his words were evidently well meant. Ere he had scarce finished his little speech he had turned and was limping off toward the forecastle with the very apparent intention of forestalling any further conversation.

They did not see him again for several days, nor did the captain accord them more than the surliest of grunts when he was forced to speak to them.

They took their meals in his cabin, as they had before the unfortunate occurrence; but the captain was careful to see that his duties never permitted him to eat at the same time.

The other officers were coarse, illiterate fellows, but little above the villainous crew they bullied, and were only too glad to avoid social intercourse with the polished English noble and his lady, so that the Claytons were left very much to themselves.

This in itself accorded perfectly with their desires, but it also rather isolated them from the life of the little ship so that they were unable to keep in touch with the daily happenings which were to culminate so soon in bloody tragedy.

There was in the whole atmosphere of the craft that undefinable something which presages disaster. Outwardly, to the knowledge of the Claytons, all went on as before upon the little vessel; but that there was an undertow leading them toward some unknown danger both felt, though they did not speak of it to each other.

On the second day after the wounding of Black Michael, Clayton came on deck just in time to see the limp body of one of the crew being carried below by four of his fellows while the first mate, a heavy belaying pin in his hand, stood glowering at the little party of sullen sailors.

Clayton asked no questions – he did not need to – and the following day, as the great lines of a British battleship grew out of the distant horizon, he half determined to demand that he and Lady Alice be put aboard her, for his fears were steadily increasing that nothing but harm could result from remaining on the lowering, sullen Fuwalda.

Toward noon they were within speaking distance of the British vessel, but when Clayton had nearly decided to ask the captain to put them aboard her, the obvious ridiculousness of such a request became suddenly apparent. What reason could he give the officer commanding her majesty's ship for desiring to go back in the direction from which he had just come!

What if he told them that two insubordinate seamen had been roughly handled by their officers? They would but laugh in their sleeves and attribute his reason for wishing to leave the ship to but one thing – cowardice.

John Clayton, Lord Greystoke, did not ask to be transferred to the British man-of-war. Late in the afternoon he saw her upper works fade below the far horizon, but not before he learned that which confirmed his greatest fears, and caused him to curse the false pride which had restrained him from seeking safety for his young wife a few short hours before, when safety was within reach – a safety which was now gone forever.

It was mid-afternoon that brought the little old sailor, who had been felled by the captain a few days before, to where Clayton and his wife stood by the ship's side watching the ever diminishing outlines of the great battleship. The old fellow was polishing brasses, and as he came edging along until close to Clayton he said, in an undertone:

"'Ell's to pay, sir, on this 'ere craft, an' mark my word for it, sir. 'Ell's to pay."

"What do you mean, my good fellow?" asked Clayton.

"Wy, hasn't ye seen wats goin' on? Hasn't ye 'eard that devil's spawn of a capting an' is mates knockin' the bloomin' lights outen 'arf the crew?

"Two busted 'eads yeste'day, an' three to-day. Black Michael's as good as new agin an' 'e's not the bully to stand fer it, not 'e; an' mark my word for it, sir."

"You mean, my man, that the crew contemplates mutiny?" asked Clayton.

"Mutiny!" exclaimed the old fellow. "Mutiny! They means murder, sir, an' mark my word for it, sir."

"When?"

"Hit's comin', sir; hit's comin' but I'm not a-sayin' wen, an' I've said too damned much now, but ye was a good sort t'other day an' I thought it no more'n right to warn ye. But keep a still tongue in yer 'ead an' when ye 'ear shootin' git below an' stay there.

"That's all, only keep a still tongue in yer 'ead, or they'll put a pill between yer ribs, an' mark my word for it, sir," and the old fellow went on with his polishing, which carried him away from where the Claytons were standing.

"Deuced cheerful outlook, Alice," said Clayton.

"You should warn the captain at once, John. Possibly the trouble may yet be averted," she said.

"I suppose I should, but yet from purely selfish motives I am almost prompted to 'keep a still tongue in my 'ead.' Whatever they do now they will spare us in recognition of my stand for this fellow Black Michael, but should they find that I had betrayed them there would be no mercy shown us, Alice."

"You have but one duty, John, and that lies in the interest of vested authority. If you do not warn the captain you are as much a party to whatever follows as though you had helped to plot and carry it out with your own head and hands."

"You do not understand, dear," replied Clayton. "It is of you I am thinking – there lies my first duty. The captain has brought this condition upon himself, so why then should I risk subjecting my wife to unthinkable horrors in a probably futile attempt to save him from his own brutal folly? You have no conception, dear, of what would follow were this pack of cutthroats to gain control of the Fuwalda."

"Duty is duty, John, and no amount of sophistries may change it. I would be a poor wife for an English lord were I to be responsible for his shirking a plain duty. I realize the danger which must follow, but I can face it with you."

"Have it as you will then, Alice," he answered, smiling. "Maybe we are borrowing trouble. While I do not like the looks of things on board this ship, they may not be so bad after all, for it is possible that the 'Ancient Mariner' was but voicing the desires of his wicked old heart rather than speaking of real facts.

"Mutiny on the high sea may have been common a hundred years ago, but in this good year 1888 it is the least likely of happenings.

"But there goes the captain to his cabin now. If I am going to warn him I might as well get the beastly job over for I have little stomach to talk with the brute at all."

So saying he strolled carelessly in the direction of the companionway through which the captain had passed, and a moment later was knocking at his door.

"Come in," growled the deep tones of that surly officer.

And when Clayton had entered, and closed the door behind him:

"Well?"

"I have come to report the gist of a conversation I heard to-day, because I feel that, while there may be nothing to it, it is as well that you be forearmed. In short, the men contemplate mutiny and murder."

"It's a lie!" roared the captain. "And if you have been interfering again with the discipline of this ship, or meddling in affairs that don't concern you you can take the consequences, and be damned. I don't care whether you are an English lord or not. I'm captain of this here ship, and from now on you keep your meddling nose out of my business."

The captain had worked himself up to such a frenzy of rage that he was fairly purple of face, and he shrieked the last words at the top of his voice, emphasizing his remarks by a loud thumping of the table with one huge fist, and shaking the other in Clayton's face.

Greystoke never turned a hair, but stood eying the excited man with level gaze.

"Captain Billings," he drawled finally, "if you will pardon my candor, I might remark that you are something of an ass."

Whereupon he turned and left the captain with the same indifferent ease that was habitual with him, and which was more surely calculated to raise the ire of a man of Billings' class than a torrent of invective.

So, whereas the captain might easily have been brought to regret his hasty speech had Clayton attempted to conciliate him, his temper was now irrevocably set in the mold in which Clayton had left it, and the last chance of their working together for their common good was gone.

"Well, Alice," said Clayton, as he rejoined his wife, "I might have saved my breath. The fellow proved most ungrateful. Fairly jumped at me like a mad dog.

"He and his blasted old ship may hang, for aught I care; and until we are safely off the thing I shall spend my energies in looking after our own welfare. And I rather fancy the first step to that end should be to go to our cabin and look over my revolvers. I am sorry now that we packed the larger guns and the ammunition with the stuff below."

They found their quarters in a bad state of disorder. Clothing from their open boxes and bags strewed the little apartment, and even their beds had been torn to pieces.

"Evidently someone was more anxious about our belongings than we," said Clayton. "Let's have a look around, Alice, and see what's missing."

A thorough search revealed the fact that nothing had been taken but Clayton's two revolvers and the small supply of ammunition he had saved out for them.

"Those are the very things I most wish they had left us," said Clayton, "and the fact that they wished for them and them alone is most sinister."

"What are we to do, John?" asked his wife. "Perhaps you were right in that our best chance lies in maintaining a neutral position.

"If the officers are able to prevent a mutiny, we have nothing to fear, while if the mutineers are victorious our one slim hope lies in not having attempted to thwart or antagonize them."

"Right you are, Alice. We'll keep in the middle of the road."

As they started to straighten up their cabin, Clayton and his wife simultaneously noticed the corner of a piece of paper protruding from beneath the door of their quarters. As Clayton stooped to reach for it he was amazed to see it move further into the room, and then he realized that it was being pushed inward by someone from without.

Quickly and silently he stepped toward the door, but, as he reached for the knob to throw it open, his wife's hand fell upon his wrist.

"No, John," she whispered. "They do not wish to be seen, and so we cannot afford to see them. Do not forget that we are keeping to the middle of the road."

Clayton smiled and dropped his hand to his side. Thus they stood watching the little bit of white paper until it finally remained at rest upon the floor just inside the door.

Then Clayton stooped and picked it up. It was a bit of grimy, white paper roughly folded into a ragged square. Opening it they found a crude message printed almost illegibly, and with many evidences of an unaccustomed task.

Translated, it was a warning to the Claytons to refrain from reporting the loss of the revolvers, or from repeating what the old sailor had told them – to refrain on pain of death.

"I rather imagine we'll be good," said Clayton with a rueful smile. "About all we can do is to sit tight and wait for whatever may come."

CHAPTER TWO

The Savage Home

Nor did they have long to wait, for the next morning as Clayton was emerging on deck for his accustomed walk before breakfast, a shot rang out, and then another, and another.

The sight which met his eyes confirmed his worst fears. Facing the little knot of officers was the entire motley crew of the Fuwalda, and at their head stood Black Michael.

At the first volley from the officers the men ran for shelter, and from points of vantage behind masts, wheel-house and cabin they returned the fire of the five men who represented the hated authority of the ship.

Two of their number had gone down before the captain's revolver. They lay where they had fallen between the combatants. But then the first mate lunged forward upon his face, and at a cry of command from Black Michael the mutineers charged the remaining four. The crew had been able to muster but six firearms, so most of them were armed with boat hooks, axes, hatchets and crowbars.

The captain had emptied his revolver and was reloading as the charge was made. The second mate's gun had jammed, and so there were but two weapons opposed to the mutineers as they bore down upon the officers, who now started to give back before the infuriated rush of their men.

Both sides were cursing and swearing in a frightful manner, which, together with the reports of the firearms and the screams and groans of the wounded, turned the deck of the Fuwalda to the likeness of a madhouse.

Before the officers had taken a dozen backward steps the men were upon them. An ax in the hands of a burly Negro cleft the captain from forehead to chin, and an instant later the others were down: dead or wounded from dozens of blows and bullet wounds.

Short and grisly had been the work of the mutineers of the Fuwalda, and through it all John Clayton had stood leaning carelessly beside the companionway puffing meditatively upon his pipe as though he had been but watching an indifferent cricket match.

As the last officer went down he thought it was time that he returned to his wife lest some members of the crew find her alone below.

Though outwardly calm and indifferent, Clayton was inwardly apprehensive and wrought up, for he feared for his wife's safety at the hands of these ignorant, half-brutes into whose hands fate had so remorselessly thrown them.

As he turned to descend the ladder he was surprised to see his wife standing on the steps almost at his side.

"How long have you been here, Alice?"

"Since the beginning," she replied. "How awful, John. Oh, how awful! What can we hope for at the hands of such as those?"

"Breakfast, I hope," he answered, smiling bravely in an attempt to allay her fears.

"At least," he added, "I'm going to ask them. Come with me, Alice. We must not let them think we expect any but courteous treatment."

The men had by this time surrounded the dead and wounded officers, and without either partiality or compassion proceeded to throw both living and dead over the sides of the vessel. With equal heartlessness they disposed of their own dead and dying.

Presently one of the crew spied the approaching Claytons, and with a cry of: "Here's two more for the fishes," rushed toward them with uplifted ax.

But Black Michael was even quicker, so that the fellow went down with a bullet in his back before he had taken a half dozen steps.

With a loud roar, Black Michael attracted the attention of the others, and, pointing to Lord and Lady Greystoke, cried:

"These here are my friends, and they are to be left alone. D'ye understand?

"I'm captain of this ship now, an' what I says goes," he added, turning to Clayton. "Just keep to yourselves, and nobody'll harm ye," and he looked threateningly on his fellows.

The Claytons heeded Black Michael's instructions so well that they saw but little of the crew and knew nothing of the plans the men were making.

Occasionally they heard faint echoes of brawls and quarreling among the mutineers, and on two occasions the vicious bark of firearms rang out on the still air. But Black Michael was a fit leader for this band of cutthroats, and, withal held them in fair subjection to his rule.

On the fifth day following the murder of the ship's officers, land was sighted by the lookout. Whether island or mainland, Black Michael did not know, but he announced to Clayton that if investigation showed that the place was habitable he and Lady Greystoke were to be put ashore with their belongings.

"You'll be all right there for a few months," he explained, "and by that time we'll have been able to make an inhabited coast somewhere and scatter a bit. Then I'll see that yer gover'ment's notified where you be an' they'll soon send a man-o'war to fetch ye off.

"It would be a hard matter to land you in civilization without a lot o' questions being asked, an' none o' us here has any very convincin' answers up our sleeves."

Clayton remonstrated against the inhumanity of landing them upon an unknown shore to be left to the mercies of savage beasts, and, possibly, still more savage men.

But his words were of no avail, and only tended to anger Black Michael, so he was forced to desist and make the best he could of a bad situation.

About three o'clock in the afternoon they came about off a beautiful wooded shore opposite the mouth of what appeared to be a landlocked harbor.

Black Michael sent a small boat filled with men to sound the entrance in an effort to determine if the Fuwalda could be safely worked through the entrance.

In about an hour they returned and reported deep water through the passage as well as far into the little basin.

Before dark the barkentine lay peacefully at anchor upon the bosom of the still, mirror-like surface of the harbor.

The surrounding shores were beautiful with semitropical verdure, while in the distance the country rose from the ocean in hill and tableland, almost uniformly clothed by primeval forest.

No signs of habitation were visible, but that the land might easily support human life was evidenced by the abundant bird and animal life of which the watchers on the Fuwalda's deck caught occasional glimpses, as well as by the shimmer of a little river which emptied into the harbor, insuring fresh water in plenitude.

As darkness settled upon the earth, Clayton and Lady Alice still stood by the ship's rail in silent contemplation of their future abode. From the dark shadows of the mighty forest came the wild calls of savage beasts – the deep roar of the lion, and, occasionally, the shrill scream of a panther.

The woman shrank closer to the man in terror-stricken anticipation of the horrors lying in wait for them in the awful blackness of the nights to come, when they should be alone upon that wild and lonely shore.

Later in the evening Black Michael joined them long enough to instruct them to make their preparations for landing on the morrow. They tried to persuade him to take them to some more hospitable coast near enough to civilization so that they might hope to fall into friendly hands. But no pleas, or threats, or promises of reward could move him.

"I am the only man aboard who would not rather see ye both safely dead, and, while I know that's the sensible way to make sure of our own necks, yet Black Michael's not the man to forget a favor. Ye saved my life once, and in return I'm goin' to spare yours, but that's all I can do.

"The men won't stand for any more, and if we don't get ye landed pretty quick they may even change their minds about giving ye that much show. I'll put all yer stuff ashore with ye as well as cookin' utensils an' some old sails for tents, an' enough grub to last ye until ye can find fruit and game.

"With yer guns for protection, ye ought to be able to live here easy enough until help comes. When I get safely hid away I'll see to it that the British gover'ment learns about where ye be; for the life of me I couldn't tell 'em exactly where, for I don't know myself. But they'll find ye all right."

After he had left them they went silently below, each wrapped in gloomy forebodings.

Clayton did not believe that Black Michael had the slightest intention of notifying the British government of their whereabouts, nor was he any too sure but that some treachery was contemplated for the following day when they should be on shore with the sailors who would have to accompany them with their belongings.

Once out of Black Michael's sight any of the men might strike them down, and still leave Black Michael's conscience clear.

And even should they escape that fate was it not but to be faced with far graver dangers? Alone, he might hope to survive for years; for he was a strong, athletic man.

But what of Alice, and that other little life so soon to be launched amidst the hardships and grave dangers of a primeval world?

The man shuddered as he meditated upon the awful gravity, the fearful helplessness, of their situation. But it was a merciful Providence which prevented him from foreseeing the hideous reality which awaited them in the grim depths of that gloomy wood.

Early next morning their numerous chests and boxes were hoisted on deck and lowered to waiting small boats for transportation to shore.

There was a great quantity and variety of stuff, as the Claytons had expected a possible five to eight years' residence in their new home. Thus, in addition to the many necessities they had brought, there were also many luxuries.

Black Michael was determined that nothing belonging to the Claytons should be left on board. Whether out of compassion for them, or in furtherance of his own self-interests, it would be difficult to say.

There was no question but that the presence of property of a missing British official upon a suspicious vessel would have been a difficult thing to explain in any civilized port in the world.

So zealous was he in his efforts to carry out his intentions that he insisted upon the return of Clayton's revolvers to him by the sailors in whose possession they were.

Into the small boats were also loaded salt meats and biscuit, with a small supply of potatoes and beans, matches, and cooking vessels, a chest of tools, and the old sails which Black Michael had promised them.

As though himself fearing the very thing which Clayton had suspected, Black Michael accompanied them to shore, and was the last to leave them when the small boats, having filled the ship's casks with fresh water, were pushed out toward the waiting Fuwalda.

As the boats moved slowly over the smooth waters of the bay, Clayton and his wife stood silently watching their departure – in the breasts of both a feeling of impending disaster and utter hopelessness.

And behind them, over the edge of a low ridge, other eyes watched – close set, wicked eyes, gleaming beneath shaggy brows.

As the Fuwalda passed through the narrow entrance to the harbor and out of sight behind a projecting point, Lady Alice threw her arms about Clayton's neck and burst into uncontrolled sobs.

Bravely had she faced the dangers of the mutiny; with heroic fortitude she had looked into the terrible future; but now that the horror of absolute solitude was upon them, her overwrought nerves gave way, and the reaction came.

He did not attempt to check her tears. It were better that nature have her way in relieving these long-pent emotions, and it was many minutes before the girl – little more than a child she was – could again gain mastery of herself.

"Oh, John," she cried at last, "the horror of it. What are we to do? What are we to do?"

"There is but one thing to do, Alice," and he spoke as quietly as though they were sitting in their snug living room at home, "and that is work. Work must be our salvation. We must not give ourselves time to think, for in that direction lies madness.

"We must work and wait. I am sure that relief will come, and come quickly, when once it is apparent that the Fuwalda has been lost, even though Black Michael does not keep his word to us."

"But John, if it were only you and I," she sobbed, "we could endure it I know; but – "

"Yes, dear," he answered, gently, "I have been thinking of that, also; but we must face it, as we must face whatever comes, bravely and with the utmost confidence in our ability to cope with circumstances whatever they may be.

"Hundreds of thousands of years ago our ancestors of the dim and distant past faced the same problems which we must face, possibly in these same primeval forests. That we are here today evidences their victory.

"What they did may we not do? And even better, for are we not armed with ages of superior knowledge, and have we not the means of protection, defense, and sustenance which science has given us, but of which they were totally ignorant? What they accomplished, Alice, with instruments and weapons of stone and bone, surely that may we accomplish also."

"Ah, John, I wish that I might be a man with a man's philosophy, but I am but a woman, seeing with my heart rather than my head, and all that I can see is too horrible, too unthinkable to put into words.

"I only hope you are right, John. I will do my best to be a brave primeval woman, a fit mate for the primeval man."

Clayton's first thought was to arrange a sleeping shelter for the night; something which might serve to protect them from prowling beasts of prey.

He opened the box containing his rifles and ammunition, that they might both be armed against possible attack while at work, and then together they sought a location for their first night's sleeping place.

A hundred yards from the beach was a little level spot, fairly free of trees; here they decided eventually to build a permanent house, but for the time being they both thought it best to construct a little platform in the trees out of reach of the larger of the savage beasts in whose realm they were.

To this end Clayton selected four trees which formed a rectangle about eight feet square, and cutting long branches from other trees he constructed a framework around them, about ten feet from the ground, fastening the ends of the branches securely to the trees by means of rope, a quantity of which Black Michael had furnished him from the hold of the Fuwalda.

Across this framework Clayton placed other smaller branches quite close together. This platform he paved with the huge fronds of elephant's ear which grew in profusion about them, and over the fronds he laid a great sail folded into several thicknesses.

Seven feet higher he constructed a similar, though lighter platform to serve as roof, and from the sides of this he suspended the balance of his sailcloth for walls.

When completed he had a rather snug little nest, to which he carried their blankets and some of the lighter luggage.

It was now late in the afternoon, and the balance of the daylight hours were devoted to the building of a rude ladder by means of which Lady Alice could mount to her new home.

All during the day the forest about them had been filled with excited birds of brilliant plumage, and dancing, chattering monkeys, who watched these new arrivals and their wonderful nest building operations with every mark of keenest interest and fascination.

Notwithstanding that both Clayton and his wife kept a sharp lookout they saw nothing of larger animals, though on two occasions they had seen their little simian neighbors come screaming and chattering from the near-by ridge, casting frightened glances back over their little shoulders, and evincing as plainly as though by speech that they were fleeing some terrible thing which lay concealed there.

Just before dusk Clayton finished his ladder, and, filling a great basin with water from the near-by stream, the two mounted to the comparative safety of their aerial chamber.

As it was quite warm, Clayton had left the side curtains thrown back over the roof, and as they sat, like Turks, upon their blankets, Lady Alice, straining her eyes into the darkening shadows of the wood, suddenly reached out and grasped Clayton's arms.

"John," she whispered, "look! What is it, a man?"

As Clayton turned his eyes in the direction she indicated, he saw silhouetted dimly against the shadows beyond, a great figure standing upright upon the ridge.

For a moment it stood as though listening and then turned slowly, and melted into the shadows of the jungle.

"What is it, John?"

"I do not know, Alice," he answered gravely, "it is too dark to see so far, and it may have been but a shadow cast by the rising moon."

"No, John, if it was not a man it was some huge and grotesque mockery of man. Oh, I am afraid."

He gathered her in his arms, whispering words of courage and love into her ears.

Soon after, he lowered the curtain walls, tying them securely to the trees so that, except for a little opening toward the beach, they were entirely enclosed.

As it was now pitch dark within their tiny aerie they lay down upon their blankets to try to gain, through sleep, a brief respite of forgetfulness.

Clayton lay facing the opening at the front, a rifle and a brace of revolvers at his hand.

Scarcely had they closed their eyes than the terrifying cry of a panther rang out from the jungle behind them. Closer and closer it came until they could hear the great beast directly beneath them. For an hour or more they heard it sniffing and clawing at the trees which supported their platform, but at last it roamed away across the beach, where Clayton could see it clearly in the brilliant moonlight – a great, handsome beast, the largest he had ever seen.

During the long hours of darkness they caught but fitful snatches of sleep, for the night noises of a great jungle teeming with myriad animal life kept their overwrought nerves on edge, so that a hundred times they were startled to wakefulness by piercing screams, or the stealthy moving of great bodies beneath them.

CHAPTER THREE

Life and Death

MORNING FOUND them but little, if at all refreshed, though it was with a feeling of intense relief that they saw the day dawn.

As soon as they had made their meager breakfast of salt pork, coffee and biscuit, Clayton commenced work upon their house, for he realized that they could hope for no safety and no peace of mind at night until four strong walls effectually barred the jungle life from them.

The task was an arduous one and required the better part of a month, though he built but one small room. He constructed his cabin of small logs about six inches in diameter, stopping the chinks with clay which he found at the depth of a few feet beneath the surface soil.

At one end he built a fireplace of small stones from the beach. These also he set in clay and when the house had been entirely completed he applied a coating of the clay to the entire outside surface to the thickness of four inches.

In the window opening he set small branches about an inch in diameter both vertically and horizontally, and so woven that they formed a substantial grating that could withstand the strength of a powerful animal. Thus they obtained air and proper ventilation without fear of lessening the safety of their cabin.

The A-shaped roof was thatched with small branches laid close together and over these long jungle grass and palm fronds, with a final coating of clay.

The door he built of pieces of the packing-boxes which had held their belongings, nailing one piece upon another, the grain of contiguous layers running transversely, until he had a solid body some three inches thick and of such great strength that they were both moved to laughter as they gazed upon it.

Here the greatest difficulty confronted Clayton, for he had no means whereby to hang his massive door now that he had built it. After two days' work, however, he succeeded in fashioning two massive hardwood hinges, and with these he hung the door so that it opened and closed easily.

The stuccoing and other final touches were added after they moved into the house, which they had done as soon as the roof was on, piling their boxes before the door at night and thus having a comparatively safe and comfortable habitation.

The building of a bed, chairs, table, and shelves was a relatively easy matter, so that by the end of the second month they were well settled, and, but for the constant dread of attack by wild beasts and the ever growing loneliness, they were not uncomfortable or unhappy.

At night great beasts snarled and roared about their tiny cabin, but, so accustomed may one become to oft repeated noises, that soon they paid little attention to them, sleeping soundly the whole night through.

Thrice had they caught fleeting glimpses of great man-like figures like that of the first night, but never at sufficiently close range to know positively whether the half-seen forms were those of man or brute.

The brilliant birds and the little monkeys had become accustomed to their new acquaintances, and as they had evidently never seen human beings before they presently, after their first fright had worn off, approached closer and closer, impelled by that strange curiosity which dominates the wild creatures of the forest and the jungle and the plain, so that within the first month several of the birds had gone so far as even to accept morsels of food from the friendly hands of the Claytons.

One afternoon, while Clayton was working upon an addition to their cabin, for he contemplated building several more rooms, a number of their grotesque little friends came shrieking and scolding through the trees from the direction of the ridge. Ever as they fled they cast fearful glances back of them, and finally they stopped near Clayton jabbering excitedly to him as though to warn him of approaching danger.

At last he saw it, the thing the little monkeys so feared – the man-brute of which the Claytons had caught occasional fleeting glimpses.

It was approaching through the jungle in a semi-erect position, now and then placing the backs of its closed fists upon the ground – a great anthropoid ape, and, as it advanced, it emitted deep guttural growls and an occasional low barking sound.

Clayton was at some distance from the cabin, having come to fell a particularly perfect tree for his building operations. Grown careless from months of continued safety, during which time he had seen no dangerous animals during the daylight hours, he had left his rifles and revolvers all within the little cabin, and now that he saw the great ape crashing through the underbrush directly toward him, and from a direction which practically cut him off from escape, he felt a vague little shiver play up and down his spine.

He knew that, armed only with an ax, his chances with this ferocious monster were small indeed – and Alice; O God, he thought, what will become of Alice?

There was yet a slight chance of reaching the cabin. He turned and ran toward it, shouting an alarm to his wife to run in and close the great door in case the ape cut off his retreat.

Lady Greystoke had been sitting a little way from the cabin, and when she heard his cry she looked up to see the ape springing with almost incredible swiftness, for so large and awkward an animal, in an effort to head off Clayton.

With a low cry she sprang toward the cabin, and, as she entered, gave a backward glance which filled her soul with terror, for the brute had intercepted her husband, who now stood at bay grasping his ax with both hands ready to swing it upon the infuriated animal when he should make his final charge.

"Close and bolt the door, Alice," cried Clayton. "I can finish this fellow with my ax."

But he knew he was facing a horrible death, and so did she.

The ape was a great bull, weighing probably three hundred pounds. His nasty, close-set eyes gleamed hatred from beneath his shaggy brows, while his great canine fangs were bared in a horrid snarl as he paused a moment before his prey.

Over the brute's shoulder Clayton could see the doorway of his cabin, not twenty paces distant, and a great wave of horror and fear swept over him as he saw his young wife emerge, armed with one of his rifles.

She had always been afraid of firearms, and would never touch them, but now she rushed toward the ape with the fearlessness of a lioness protecting its young.

"Back, Alice," shouted Clayton, "for God's sake, go back."

But she would not heed, and just then the ape charged, so that Clayton could say no more.

The man swung his ax with all his mighty strength, but the powerful brute seized it in those terrible hands, and tearing it from Clayton's grasp hurled it far to one side.

With an ugly snarl he closed upon his defenseless victim, but ere his fangs had reached the throat they thirsted for, there was a sharp report and a bullet entered the ape's back between his shoulders.

Throwing Clayton to the ground the beast turned upon his new enemy. There before him stood the terrified girl vainly trying to fire another bullet into the animal's body; but she did not understand the mechanism of the firearm, and the hammer fell futilely upon an empty cartridge.

Almost simultaneously Clayton regained his feet, and without thought of the utter hopelessness of it, he rushed forward to drag the ape from his wife's prostrate form.

With little or no effort he succeeded, and the great bulk rolled inertly upon the turf before him – the ape was dead. The bullet had done its work.

A hasty examination of his wife revealed no marks upon her, and Clayton decided that the huge brute had died the instant he had sprung toward Alice.

Gently he lifted his wife's still unconscious form, and bore her to the little cabin, but it was fully two hours before she regained consciousness.

Her first words filled Clayton with vague apprehension. For some time after regaining her senses, Alice gazed wonderingly about the interior of the little cabin, and then, with a satisfied sigh, said:

"O, John, it is so good to be really home! I have had an awful dream, dear. I thought we were no longer in London, but in some horrible place where great beasts attacked us."

"There, there, Alice," he said, stroking her forehead, "try to sleep again, and do not worry your head about bad dreams."

That night a little son was born in the tiny cabin beside the primeval forest, while a leopard screamed before the door, and the deep notes of a lion's roar sounded from beyond the ridge.

Lady Greystoke never recovered from the shock of the great ape's attack, and, though she lived for a year after her baby was born, she was never again outside the cabin, nor did she ever fully realize that she was not in England.

Sometimes she would question Clayton as to the strange noises of the nights; the absence of servants and friends, and the strange rudeness of the furnishings within her room, but, though he made no effort to deceive her, never could she grasp the meaning of it all.

In other ways she was quite rational, and the joy and happiness she took in the possession of her little son and the constant attentions of her husband made that year a very happy one for her, the happiest of her young life.

That it would have been beset by worries and apprehension had she been in full command of her mental faculties Clayton well knew; so that while he suffered terribly to see her so, there were times when he was almost glad, for her sake, that she could not understand.

Long since had he given up any hope of rescue, except through accident. With unremitting zeal he had worked to beautify the interior of the cabin.

Skins of lion and panther covered the floor. Cupboards and bookcases lined the walls. Odd vases made by his own hand from the clay of the region held beautiful tropical flowers. Curtains of grass and bamboo covered the windows, and, most arduous task of all, with his meager assortment of tools he had fashioned lumber to neatly seal the walls and ceiling and lay a smooth floor within the cabin.

That he had been able to turn his hands at all to such unaccustomed labor was a source of mild wonder to him. But he loved the work because it was for her and the tiny life that had come to cheer them, though adding a hundredfold to his responsibilities and to the terribleness of their situation.

During the year that followed, Clayton was several times attacked by the great apes which now seemed to continually infest the vicinity of the cabin; but as he never again ventured outside without both rifle and revolvers he had little fear of the huge beasts.

He had strengthened the window protections and fitted a unique wooden lock to the cabin door, so that when he hunted for game and fruits, as it was constantly necessary for him to do to insure sustenance, he had no fear that any animal could break into the little home.

At first he shot much of the game from the cabin windows, but toward the end the animals learned to fear the strange lair from whence issued the terrifying thunder of his rifle.

In his leisure Clayton read, often aloud to his wife, from the store of books he had brought for their new home. Among these were many for little children – picture books, primers, readers – for they had known that their little child would be old enough for such before they might hope to return to England.

At other times Clayton wrote in his diary, which he had always been accustomed to keep in French, and in which he recorded the details of their strange life. This book he kept locked in a little metal box.

A year from the day her little son was born Lady Alice passed quietly away in the night. So peaceful was her end that it was hours before Clayton could awake to a realization that his wife was dead.

The horror of the situation came to him very slowly, and it is doubtful that he ever fully realized the enormity of his sorrow and the fearful responsibility that had devolved upon him with the care of that wee thing, his son, still a nursing babe.

The last entry in his diary was made the morning following her death, and there he recites the sad details in a matter-of-fact way that adds to the pathos of it; for it breathes a tired apathy born of long sorrow and hopelessness, which even this cruel blow could scarcely awake to further suffering:

My little son is crying for nourishment – O Alice, Alice, what shall I do?

And as John Clayton wrote the last words his hand was destined ever to pen, he dropped his head wearily upon his outstretched arms where they rested upon the table he had built for her who lay still and cold in the bed beside him.

For a long time no sound broke the deathlike stillness of the jungle midday save the piteous wailing of the tiny man-child.

CHAPTER FOUR

The Apes

In the forest of the table-land a mile back from the ocean old Kerchak the Ape was on a rampage of rage among his people.

The younger and lighter members of his tribe scampered to the higher branches of the great trees to escape his wrath; risking their lives upon branches that scarce supported their weight rather than face old Kerchak in one of his fits of uncontrolled anger.

The other males scattered in all directions, but not before the infuriated brute had felt the vertebra of one snap between his great, foaming jaws.

A luckless young female slipped from an insecure hold upon a high branch and came crashing to the ground almost at Kerchak's feet.

With a wild scream he was upon her, tearing a great piece from her side with his mighty teeth, and striking her viciously upon her head and shoulders with a broken tree limb until her skull was crushed to a jelly.

And then he spied Kala, who, returning from a search for food with her young babe, was ignorant of the state of the mighty male's temper until suddenly the shrill warnings of her fellows caused her to scamper madly for safety.

But Kerchak was close upon her, so close that he had almost grasped her ankle had she not made a furious leap far into space from one tree to another – a perilous chance which apes seldom if ever take, unless so closely pursued by danger that there is no alternative.

She made the leap successfully, but as she grasped the limb of the further tree the sudden jar loosened the hold of the tiny babe where it clung frantically to her neck, and she saw the little thing hurled, turning and twisting, to the ground thirty feet below.

With a low cry of dismay Kala rushed headlong to its side, thoughtless now of the danger from Kerchak; but when she gathered the wee, mangled form to her bosom life had left it.

With low moans, she sat cuddling the body to her; nor did Kerchak attempt to molest her. With the death of the babe his fit of demoniacal rage passed as suddenly as it had seized him.

Kerchak was a huge king ape, weighing perhaps three hundred and fifty pounds. His forehead was extremely low and receding, his eyes bloodshot, small and close set to his coarse, flat nose; his ears large and thin, but smaller than most of his kind.

His awful temper and his mighty strength made him supreme among the little tribe into which he had been born some twenty years before.

Now that he was in his prime, there was no simian in all the mighty forest through which he roved that dared contest his right to rule, nor did the other and larger animals molest him.

Old Tantor, the elephant, alone of all the wild savage life, feared him not – and he alone did Kerchak fear. When Tantor trumpeted, the great ape scurried with his fellows high among the trees of the second terrace.

The tribe of anthropoids over which Kerchak ruled with an iron hand and bared fangs, numbered some six or eight families, each family consisting of an adult male with his females and their young, numbering in all some sixty or seventy apes.

Kala was the youngest mate of a male called Tublat, meaning broken nose, and the child she had seen dashed to death was her first; for she was but nine or ten years old.

Notwithstanding her youth, she was large and powerful – a splendid, clean-limbed animal, with a round, high forehead, which denoted more intelligence than most of her kind possessed. So, also, she had a great capacity for mother love and mother sorrow.

But she was still an ape, a huge, fierce, terrible beast of a species closely allied to the gorilla, yet more intelligent; which, with the strength of their cousin, made her kind the most fearsome of those awe-inspiring progenitors of man.

When the tribe saw that Kerchak's rage had ceased they came slowly down from their arboreal retreats and pursued again the various occupations which he had interrupted.

The young played and frolicked about among the trees and bushes. Some of the adults lay prone upon the soft mat of dead and decaying vegetation which covered the ground, while others turned over pieces of fallen branches and clods of earth in search of the small bugs and reptiles which formed a part of their food.

Others, again, searched the surrounding trees for fruit, nuts, small birds, and eggs.

They had passed an hour or so thus when Kerchak called them together, and, with a word of command to them to follow him, set off toward the sea.

They traveled for the most part upon the ground, where it was open, following the path of the great elephants whose comings and goings break the only roads through those tangled mazes of bush, vine, creeper, and tree. When they walked it was with a rolling, awkward motion, placing the knuckles of their closed hands upon the ground and swinging their ungainly bodies forward.

But when the way was through the lower trees they moved more swiftly, swinging from branch to branch with the agility of their smaller cousins, the monkeys. And all the way Kala carried her little dead baby hugged closely to her breast.

It was shortly after noon when they reached a ridge overlooking the beach where below them lay the tiny cottage which was Kerchak's goal.

He had seen many of his kind go to their deaths before the loud noise made by the little black stick in the hands of the strange white ape who lived in that wonderful lair, and Kerchak had made up his brute mind to own that death-dealing contrivance, and to explore the interior of the mysterious den.

He wanted, very, very much, to feel his teeth sink into the neck of the queer animal that he had learned to hate and fear, and because of this, he came often with his tribe to reconnoiter, waiting for a time when the white ape should be off his guard.

Of late they had quit attacking, or even showing themselves; for every time they had done so in the past the little stick had roared out its terrible message of death to some member of the tribe.

Today there was no sign of the man about, and from where they watched they could see that the cabin door was open. Slowly, cautiously, and noiselessly they crept through the jungle toward the little cabin.

There were no growls, no fierce screams of rage – the little black stick had taught them to come quietly lest they awaken it.

On, on they came until Kerchak himself slunk stealthily to the very door and peered within. Behind him were two males, and then Kala, closely straining the little dead form to her breast.

Inside the den they saw the strange white ape lying half across a table, his head buried in his arms; and on the bed lay a figure covered by a sailcloth, while from a tiny rustic cradle came the plaintive wailing of a babe.

Noiselessly Kerchak entered, crouching for the charge; and then John Clayton rose with a sudden start and faced them.

The sight that met his eyes must have frozen him with horror, for there, within the door, stood three great bull apes, while behind them crowded many more; how many he never knew, for his revolvers were hanging on the far wall beside his rifle, and Kerchak was charging.

When the king ape released the limp form which had been John Clayton, Lord Greystoke, he turned his attention toward the little cradle; but Kala was there before him, and when he would have grasped the child she snatched it herself, and before he could intercept her she had bolted through the door and taken refuge in a high tree.

As she took up the little live baby of Alice Clayton she dropped the dead body of her own into the empty cradle; for the wail of the living had answered the call of universal motherhood within her wild breast which the dead could not still.

High up among the branches of a mighty tree she hugged the shrieking infant to her bosom, and soon the instinct that was as dominant in this fierce female as it had been in the breast of his tender and beautiful mother – the instinct of mother love – reached out to the tiny man-child's half-formed understanding, and he became quiet.

Then hunger closed the gap between them, and the son of an English lord and an English lady nursed at the breast of Kala, the great ape.

In the meantime the beasts within the cabin were warily examining the contents of this strange lair.

Once satisfied that Clayton was dead, Kerchak turned his attention to the thing which lay upon the bed, covered by a piece of sailcloth.

Gingerly he lifted one corner of the shroud, but when he saw the body of the woman beneath he tore the cloth roughly from her form and seized the still, white throat in his huge, hairy hands.

A moment he let his fingers sink deep into the cold flesh, and then, realizing that she was already dead, he turned from her, to examine the contents of the room; nor did he again molest the body of either Lady Alice or Sir John.

The rifle hanging upon the wall caught his first attention; it was for this strange, death-dealing thunder-stick that he had yearned for months; but now that it was within his grasp he scarcely had the temerity to seize it.

Cautiously he approached the thing, ready to flee precipitately should it speak in its deep roaring tones, as he had heard it speak before, the last words to those of his kind who, through ignorance or rashness, had attacked the wonderful white ape that had borne it.

Deep in the beast's intelligence was something which assured him that the thunder-stick was only dangerous when in the hands of one who could manipulate it, but yet it was several minutes ere he could bring himself to touch it.

Instead, he walked back and forth along the floor before it, turning his head so that never once did his eyes leave the object of his desire.

Using his long arms as a man uses crutches, and rolling his huge carcass from side to side with each stride, the great king ape paced to and fro, uttering deep growls, occasionally punctuated with the ear-piercing scream, than which there is no more terrifying noise in all the jungle.

Presently he halted before the rifle. Slowly he raised a huge hand until it almost touched the shining barrel, only to withdraw it once more and continue his hurried pacing.

It was as though the great brute by this show of fearlessness, and through the medium of his wild voice, was endeavoring to bolster up his courage to the point which would permit him to take the rifle in his hand.

Again he stopped, and this time succeeded in forcing his reluctant hand to the cold steel, only to snatch it away almost immediately and resume his restless beat.

Time after time this strange ceremony was repeated, but on each occasion with increased confidence, until, finally, the rifle was torn from its hook and lay in the grasp of the great brute.

Finding that it harmed him not, Kerchak began to examine it closely. He felt of it from end to end, peered down the black depths of the muzzle, fingered the sights, the breech, the stock, and finally the trigger.

During all these operations the apes who had entered sat huddled near the door watching their chief, while those outside strained and crowded to catch a glimpse of what transpired within.

Suddenly Kerchak's finger closed upon the trigger. There was a deafening roar in the little room and the apes at and beyond the door fell over one another in their wild anxiety to escape.

Kerchak was equally frightened, so frightened, in fact, that he quite forgot to throw aside the author of that fearful noise, but bolted for the door with it tightly clutched in one hand.

As he passed through the opening, the front sight of the rifle caught upon the edge of the inswung door with sufficient force to close it tightly after the fleeing ape.

When Kerchak came to a halt a short distance from the cabin and discovered that he still held the rifle, he dropped it as he might have dropped a red hot iron, nor did he again attempt to recover it – the noise was too much for his brute nerves; but he was now quite convinced that the terrible stick was quite harmless by itself if left alone.

It was an hour before the apes could again bring themselves to approach the cabin to continue their investigations, and when they finally did so, they found to their chagrin that the door was closed and so securely fastened that they could not force it.

The cleverly constructed latch which Clayton had made for the door had sprung as Kerchak passed out; nor could the apes find means of ingress through the heavily barred windows.

After roaming about the vicinity for a short time, they started back for the deeper forests and the higher land from whence they had come.

Kala had not once come to earth with her little adopted babe, but now Kerchak called to her to descend with the rest, and as there was no note of anger in his voice she dropped lightly from branch to branch and joined the others on their homeward march.

Those of the apes who attempted to examine Kala's strange baby were repulsed with bared fangs and low menacing growls, accompanied by words of warning from Kala.

When they assured her that they meant the child no harm she permitted them to come close, but would not allow them to touch her charge.

It was as though she knew that her baby was frail and delicate and feared lest the rough hands of her fellows might injure the little thing.

Another thing she did, and which made traveling an onerous trial for her. Remembering the death of her own little one, she clung desperately to the new babe, with one hand, whenever they were upon the march.

The other young rode upon their mothers' backs; their little arms tightly clasping the hairy necks before them, while their legs were locked beneath their mothers' armpits.

Not so with Kala; she held the small form of the little Lord Greystoke tightly to her breast, where the dainty hands clutched the long black hair which covered that portion of her body. She had seen one child fall from her back to a terrible death, and she would take no further chances with this.

CHAPTER FIVE

The White Ape

Tenderly Kala nursed her little waif, wondering silently why it did not gain strength and agility as did the little apes of other mothers. It was nearly a year from the time the little fellow came into her possession before he would walk alone, and as for climbing – my, but how stupid he was!

Kala sometimes talked with the older females about her young hopeful, but none of them could understand how a child could be so slow and backward in learning to care for itself. Why, it could not even find food alone, and more than twelve moons had passed since Kala had come upon it.

Had they known that the child had seen thirteen moons before it had come into Kala's possession they would have considered its case as absolutely hopeless, for the little apes of their own tribe were as far advanced in two or three moons as was this little stranger after twenty-five.

Tublat, Kala's husband, was sorely vexed, and but for the female's careful watching would have put the child out of the way.

"He will never be a great ape," he argued. "Always will you have to carry him and protect him. What good will he be to the tribe? None; only a burden.

"Let us leave him quietly sleeping among the tall grasses, that you may bear other and stronger apes to guard us in our old age."

"Never, Broken Nose," replied Kala. "If I must carry him forever, so be it."

And then Tublat went to Kerchak to urge him to use his authority with Kala, and force her to give up little Tarzan, which was the name they had given to the tiny Lord Greystoke, and which meant "White-Skin."

But when Kerchak spoke to her about it Kala threatened to run away from the tribe if they did not leave her in peace with the child; and as this is one of the inalienable rights of the jungle folk, if they be dissatisfied among their own people, they bothered her no more, for Kala was a fine clean-limbed young female, and they did not wish to lose her.

As Tarzan grew he made more rapid strides, so that by the time he was ten years old he was an excellent climber, and on the ground could do many wonderful things which were beyond the powers of his little brothers and sisters.

In many ways did he differ from them, and they often marveled at his superior cunning, but in strength and size he was deficient; for at ten the great anthropoids were fully grown, some of them towering over six feet in height, while little Tarzan was still but a half-grown boy.

Yet such a boy!

From early childhood he had used his hands to swing from branch to branch after the manner of his giant mother, and as he grew older he spent hour upon hour daily speeding through the tree tops with his brothers and sisters.

He could spring twenty feet across space at the dizzy heights of the forest top, and grasp with unerring precision, and without apparent jar, a limb waving wildly in the path of an approaching tornado.

He could drop twenty feet at a stretch from limb to limb in rapid descent to the ground, or he could gain the utmost pinnacle of the loftiest tropical giant with the ease and swiftness of a squirrel.

Though but ten years old he was fully as strong as the average man of thirty, and far more agile than the most practiced athlete ever becomes. And day by day his strength was increasing.

His life among these fierce apes had been happy; for his recollection held no other life, nor did he know that there existed within the universe aught else than his little forest and the wild jungle animals with which he was familiar.

He was nearly ten before he commenced to realize that a great difference existed between himself and his fellows. His little body, burned brown by exposure, suddenly caused him feelings of intense shame, for he realized that it was entirely hairless, like some low snake, or other reptile.

He attempted to obviate this by plastering himself from head to foot with mud, but this dried and fell off. Besides it felt so uncomfortable that he quickly decided that he preferred the shame to the discomfort.

In the higher land which his tribe frequented was a little lake, and it was here that Tarzan first saw his face in the clear, still waters of its bosom.

It was on a sultry day of the dry season that he and one of his cousins had gone down to the bank to drink. As they leaned over, both little faces were mirrored on the placid pool; the fierce and terrible features of the ape beside those of the aristocratic scion of an old English house.

Tarzan was appalled. It had been bad enough to be hairless, but to own such a countenance! He wondered that the other apes could look at him at all.

That tiny slit of a mouth and those puny white teeth! How they looked beside the mighty lips and powerful fangs of his more fortunate brothers!

And the little pinched nose of his; so thin was it that it looked half starved. He turned red as he compared it with the beautiful broad nostrils of his companion. Such a generous nose! Why it spread half across his face! It certainly must be fine to be so handsome, thought poor little Tarzan.

But when he saw his own eyes; ah, that was the final blow – a brown spot, a gray circle and then blank whiteness! Frightful! not even the snakes had such hideous eyes as he.

So intent was he upon this personal appraisement of his features that he did not hear the parting of the tall grass behind him as a great body pushed itself stealthily through the jungle; nor did his companion, the ape, hear either, for he was drinking and the noise of his sucking lips and gurgles of satisfaction drowned the quiet approach of the intruder.

Not thirty paces behind the two she crouched – Sabor, the huge lioness – lashing her tail. Cautiously she moved a great padded paw forward, noiselessly placing it before she lifted the next. Thus she advanced; her belly low, almost touching the surface of the ground – a great cat preparing to spring upon its prey.

Now she was within ten feet of the two unsuspecting little playfellows – carefully she drew her hind feet well up beneath her body, the great muscles rolling under the beautiful skin.

So low she was crouching now that she seemed flattened to the earth except for the upward bend of the glossy back as it gathered for the spring.

No longer the tail lashed – quiet and straight behind her it lay.

An instant she paused thus, as though turned to stone, and then, with an awful scream, she sprang.

Sabor, the lioness, was a wise hunter. To one less wise the wild alarm of her fierce cry as she sprang would have seemed a foolish thing, for could she not more surely have fallen upon her victims had she but quietly leaped without that loud shriek?

But Sabor knew well the wondrous quickness of the jungle folk and their almost unbelievable powers of hearing. To them the sudden scraping of one blade of grass across another was as effectual a warning as her loudest cry, and Sabor knew that she could not make that mighty leap without a little noise.

Her wild scream was not a warning. It was voiced to freeze her poor victims in a paralysis of terror for the tiny fraction of an instant which would suffice for her mighty claws to sink into their soft flesh and hold them beyond hope of escape.

So far as the ape was concerned, Sabor reasoned correctly. The little fellow crouched trembling just an instant, but that instant was quite long enough to prove his undoing.

Not so, however, with Tarzan, the man-child. His life amidst the dangers of the jungle had taught him to meet emergencies with self-confidence, and his higher intelligence resulted in a quickness of mental action far beyond the powers of the apes.

So the scream of Sabor, the lioness, galvanized the brain and muscles of little Tarzan into instant action.

Before him lay the deep waters of the little lake, behind him certain death; a cruel death beneath tearing claws and rending fangs.

Tarzan had always hated water except as a medium for quenching his thirst. He hated it because he connected it with the chill and discomfort of the torrential rains, and he feared it for the thunder and lightning and wind which accompanied them.

The deep waters of the lake he had been taught by his wild mother to avoid, and further, had he not seen little Neeta sink beneath its quiet surface only a few short weeks before never to return to the tribe?

But of the two evils his quick mind chose the lesser ere the first note of Sabor's scream had scarce broken the quiet of the jungle, and before the great beast had covered half her leap Tarzan felt the chill waters close above his head.

He could not swim, and the water was very deep; but still he lost no particle of that self-confidence and resourcefulness which were the badges of his superior being.

Rapidly he moved his hands and feet in an attempt to scramble upward, and, possibly more by chance than design, he fell into the stroke that a dog uses when swimming, so that within a few seconds his nose was above water and he found that he could keep it there by continuing his strokes, and also make progress through the water.

He was much surprised and pleased with this new acquirement which had been so suddenly thrust upon him, but he had no time for thinking much upon it.

He was now swimming parallel to the bank and there he saw the cruel beast that would have seized him crouching upon the still form of his little playmate.

The lioness was intently watching Tarzan, evidently expecting him to return to shore, but this the boy had no intention of doing.

Instead he raised his voice in the call of distress common to his tribe, adding to it the warning which would prevent would-be rescuers from running into the clutches of Sabor.

Almost immediately there came an answer from the distance, and presently forty or fifty great apes swung rapidly and majestically through the trees toward the scene of tragedy.

In the lead was Kala, for she had recognized the tones of her best beloved, and with her was the mother of the little ape who lay dead beneath cruel Sabor.

Though more powerful and better equipped for fighting than the apes, the lioness had no desire to meet these enraged adults, and with a snarl of hatred she sprang quickly into the brush and disappeared.

Tarzan now swam to shore and clambered quickly upon dry land. The feeling of freshness and exhilaration which the cool waters had imparted to him, filled his little being with grateful surprise, and ever after he lost no opportunity to take a daily plunge in lake or stream or ocean when it was possible to do so.

For a long time Kala could not accustom herself to the sight; for though her people could swim when forced to it, they did not like to enter water, and never did so voluntarily.

The adventure with the lioness gave Tarzan food for pleasurable memories, for it was such affairs which broke the monotony of his daily life – otherwise but a dull round of searching for food, eating, and sleeping.

The tribe to which he belonged roamed a tract extending, roughly, twenty-five miles along the seacoast and some fifty miles inland. This they traversed almost continually, occasionally remaining for months in one locality; but as they moved through the trees with great speed they often covered the territory in a very few days.

Much depended upon food supply, climatic conditions, and the prevalence of animals of the more dangerous species; though Kerchak often led them on long marches for no other reason than that he had tired of remaining in the same place.

At night they slept where darkness overtook them, lying upon the ground, and sometimes covering their heads, and more seldom their bodies, with the great leaves of the elephant's ear. Two or three might lie cuddled in each other's arms for additional warmth if the night were chill, and thus Tarzan had slept in Kala's arms nightly for all these years.

That the huge, fierce brute loved this child of another race is beyond question, and he, too, gave to the great, hairy beast all the affection that would have belonged to his fair young mother had she lived.

When he was disobedient she cuffed him, it is true, but she was never cruel to him, and was more often caressing him than chastising him.

Tublat, her mate, always hated Tarzan, and on several occasions had come near ending his youthful career.

Tarzan on his part never lost an opportunity to show that he fully reciprocated his foster father's sentiments, and whenever he could safely annoy him or make faces at him or hurl insults upon him from the safety of his mother's arms, or the slender branches of the higher trees, he did so.

His superior intelligence and cunning permitted him to invent a thousand diabolical tricks to add to the burdens of Tublat's life.

Early in his boyhood he had learned to form ropes by twisting and tying long grasses together, and with these he was forever tripping Tublat or attempting to hang him from some overhanging branch.

By constant playing and experimenting with these he learned to tie rude knots, and make sliding nooses; and with these he and the younger apes amused themselves. What Tarzan did they tried to do also, but he alone originated and became proficient.

One day while playing thus Tarzan had thrown his rope at one of his fleeing companions, retaining the other end in his grasp. By accident the noose fell squarely about the running ape's neck, bringing him to a sudden and surprising halt.

Ah, here was a new game, a fine game, thought Tarzan, and immediately he attempted to repeat the trick. And thus, by painstaking and continued practice, he learned the art of roping.

Now, indeed, was the life of Tublat a living nightmare. In sleep, upon the march, night or day, he never knew when that quiet noose would slip about his neck and nearly choke the life out of him.

Kala punished, Tublat swore dire vengeance, and old Kerchak took notice and warned and threatened; but all to no avail.

Tarzan defied them all, and the thin, strong noose continued to settle about Tublat's neck whenever he least expected it.

The other apes derived unlimited amusement from Tublat's discomfiture, for Broken Nose was a disagreeable old fellow, whom no one liked, anyway.

In Tarzan's clever little mind many thoughts revolved, and back of these was his divine power of reason.

If he could catch his fellow apes with his long arm of many grasses, why not Sabor, the lioness?

It was the germ of a thought, which, however, was destined to mull around in his conscious and subconscious mind until it resulted in magnificent achievement.

But that came in later years.

CHAPTER SIX

Jungle Battles

THE WANDERINGS of the tribe brought them often near the closed and silent cabin by the little land-locked harbor. To Tarzan this was always a source of never-ending mystery and pleasure.

He would peek into the curtained windows, or, climbing upon the roof, peer down the black depths of the chimney in vain endeavor to solve the unknown wonders that lay within those strong walls.

His child-like imagination pictured wonderful creatures within, and the very impossibility of forcing entrance added a thousandfold to his desire to do so.

He could clamber about the roof and windows for hours attempting to discover means of ingress, but to the door he paid little attention, for this was apparently as solid as the walls.

It was in the next visit to the vicinity, following the adventure with old Sabor, that, as he approached the cabin, Tarzan noticed that from a distance the door appeared to be an independent part of the wall in which it was set, and for the first time it occurred to him that this might prove the means of entrance which had so long eluded him.

He was alone, as was often the case when he visited the cabin, for the apes had no love for it; the story of the thunder-stick having lost nothing in the telling during these ten years had quite surrounded the white man's deserted abode with an atmosphere of weirdness and terror for the simians.

The story of his own connection with the cabin had never been told him. The language of the apes had so few words that they could talk but little of what they had seen in the cabin, having no words to accurately describe either the strange people or their belongings, and so, long before Tarzan was old enough to understand, the subject had been forgotten by the tribe.

Only in a dim, vague way had Kala explained to him that his father had been a strange white ape, but he did not know that Kala was not his own mother.

On this day, then, he went directly to the door and spent hours examining it and fussing with the hinges, the knob and the latch. Finally he stumbled upon the right combination, and the door swung creakingly open before his astonished eyes.

For some minutes he did not dare venture within, but finally, as his eyes became accustomed to the dim light of the interior he slowly and cautiously entered.

In the middle of the floor lay a skeleton, every vestige of flesh gone from the bones to which still clung the mildewed and moldered remnants of what had once been clothing. Upon the bed lay a similar gruesome thing, but smaller, while in a tiny cradle near-by was a third, a wee mite of a skeleton.

To none of these evidences of a fearful tragedy of a long dead day did little Tarzan give but passing heed. His wild jungle life had inured him to the sight of dead and dying animals, and had he known that he was looking upon the remains of his own father and mother he would have been no more greatly moved.

The furnishings and other contents of the room it was which riveted his attention. He examined many things minutely – strange tools and weapons, books, paper, clothing – what little had withstood the ravages of time in the humid atmosphere of the jungle coast.

He opened chests and cupboards, such as did not baffle his small experience, and in these he found the contents much better preserved.

Among other things he found a sharp hunting knife, on the keen blade of which he immediately proceeded to cut his finger. Undaunted he continued his experiments, finding that he could hack and hew splinters of wood from the table and chairs with this new toy.

For a long time this amused him, but finally tiring he continued his explorations. In a cupboard filled with books he came across one with brightly colored pictures – it was a child's illustrated alphabet –

A is for Archer
Who shoots with a bow.
B is for Boy,
His first name is Joe.

The pictures interested him greatly.

There were many apes with faces similar to his own, and further over in the book he found, under "M," some little monkeys such as he saw daily flitting through the trees of his primeval forest. But nowhere was pictured any of his own people; in all the book was none that resembled Kerchak, or Tublat, or Kala.

At first he tried to pick the little figures from the leaves, but he soon saw that they were not real, though he knew not what they might be, nor had he any words to describe them.

The boats, and trains, and cows and horses were quite meaningless to him, but not quite so baffling as the odd little figures which appeared beneath and between the colored pictures – some strange kind of bug he thought they might be, for many of them had legs though nowhere could he find one with eyes and a mouth. It was his first introduction to the letters of the alphabet, and he was over ten years old.

Of course he had never before seen print, or ever had spoken with any living thing which had the remotest idea that such a thing as a written language existed, nor ever had he seen anyone reading.

So what wonder that the little boy was quite at a loss to guess the meaning of these strange figures.

Near the middle of the book he found his old enemy, Sabor, the lioness, and further on, coiled Histah, the snake.

Oh, it was most engrossing! Never before in all his ten years had he enjoyed anything so much. So absorbed was he that he did not note the approaching dusk, until it was quite upon him and the figures were blurred.

He put the book back in the cupboard and closed the door, for he did not wish anyone else to find and destroy his treasure, and as he went out into the gathering darkness he closed the great door of the cabin behind him as it had been before he discovered the secret of its lock, but before he left he had noticed the hunting knife lying where he had thrown it upon the floor, and this he picked up and took with him to show to his fellows.

He had taken scarce a dozen steps toward the jungle when a great form rose up before him from the shadows of a low bush. At first he thought it was one of his own people but in another instant he realized that it was Bolgani, the huge gorilla.

So close was he that there was no chance for flight and little Tarzan knew that he must stand and fight for his life; for these great beasts were the deadly enemies of his tribe, and neither one nor the other ever asked or gave quarter.

Had Tarzan been a full-grown bull ape of the species of his tribe he would have been more than a match for the gorilla, but being only a little English boy, though enormously muscular for such, he stood no chance against his cruel antagonist. In his veins, though, flowed the blood of the best of a race of mighty fighters, and back of this was the training of his short lifetime among the fierce brutes of the jungle.

He knew no fear, as we know it; his little heart beat the faster but from the excitement and exhilaration of adventure. Had the opportunity presented itself he would have escaped, but solely because his judgment told him he was no match for the great thing which confronted him. And since reason showed him that successful flight was impossible he met the gorilla squarely and bravely without a tremor of a single muscle, or any sign of panic.

In fact he met the brute midway in its charge, striking its huge body with his closed fists and as futilely as he had been a fly attacking an elephant. But in one hand he still clutched the knife he had found in the cabin of his father, and as the brute, striking and biting, closed upon him the boy accidentally turned the point toward the hairy breast. As the knife sank deep into its body the gorilla shrieked in pain and rage.

But the boy had learned in that brief second a use for his sharp and shining toy, so that, as the tearing, striking beast dragged him to earth he plunged the blade repeatedly and to the hilt into its breast.

The gorilla, fighting after the manner of its kind, struck terrific blows with its open hand, and tore the flesh at the boy's throat and chest with its mighty tusks.

For a moment they rolled upon the ground in the fierce frenzy of combat. More and more weakly the torn and bleeding arm struck home with the long sharp blade, then the little figure stiffened with a spasmodic jerk, and Tarzan, the young Lord Greystoke, rolled unconscious upon the dead and decaying vegetation which carpeted his jungle home.

A mile back in the forest the tribe had heard the fierce challenge of the gorilla, and, as was his custom when any danger threatened, Kerchak called his people together, partly for mutual protection against a common enemy, since this gorilla might be but one of a party of several, and also to see that all members of the tribe were accounted for.

It was soon discovered that Tarzan was missing, and Tublat was strongly opposed to sending assistance. Kerchak himself had no liking for the strange little waif, so he listened to Tublat, and, finally, with a shrug of his shoulders, turned back to the pile of leaves on which he had made his bed.

But Kala was of a different mind; in fact, she had not waited but to learn that Tarzan was absent ere she was fairly flying through the matted branches toward the point from which the cries of the gorilla were still plainly audible.

Darkness had now fallen, and an early moon was sending its faint light to cast strange, grotesque shadows among the dense foliage of the forest.

Here and there the brilliant rays penetrated to earth, but for the most part they only served to accentuate the Stygian blackness of the jungle's depths.

Like some huge phantom, Kala swung noiselessly from tree to tree; now running nimbly along a great branch, now swinging through space at the end of another, only to grasp that of a farther tree in her rapid progress toward the scene of the tragedy her knowledge of jungle life told her was being enacted a short distance before her.

The cries of the gorilla proclaimed that it was in mortal combat with some other denizen of the fierce wood. Suddenly these cries ceased, and the silence of death reigned throughout the jungle.

Kala could not understand, for the voice of Bolgani had at last been raised in the agony of suffering and death, but no sound had come to her by which she possibly could determine the nature of his antagonist.

That her little Tarzan could destroy a great bull gorilla she knew to be improbable, and so, as she neared the spot from which the sounds of the struggle had come, she moved more warily and at last slowly and with extreme caution she traversed the lowest branches, peering eagerly into the moon-splashed blackness for a sign of the combatants.

Presently she came upon them, lying in a little open space full under the brilliant light of the moon – little Tarzan's torn and bloody form, and beside it a great bull gorilla, stone dead.

With a low cry Kala rushed to Tarzan's side, and gathering the poor, blood-covered body to her breast, listened for a sign of life. Faintly she heard it – the weak beating of the little heart.

Tenderly she bore him back through the inky jungle to where the tribe lay, and for many days and nights she sat guard beside him, bringing him food and water, and brushing the flies and other insects from his cruel wounds.

Of medicine or surgery the poor thing knew nothing. She could but lick the wounds, and thus she kept them cleansed, that healing nature might the more quickly do her work.

At first Tarzan would eat nothing, but rolled and tossed in a wild delirium of fever. All he craved was water, and this she brought him in the only way she could, bearing it in her own mouth.

No human mother could have shown more unselfish and sacrificing devotion than did this poor, wild brute for the little orphaned waif whom fate had thrown into her keeping.

At last the fever abated and the boy commenced to mend. No word of complaint passed his tight set lips, though the pain of his wounds was excruciating.

A portion of his chest was laid bare to the ribs, three of which had been broken by the mighty blows of the gorilla. One arm was nearly severed by the giant fangs, and a great piece had been torn from his neck, exposing his jugular vein, which the cruel jaws had missed but by a miracle.

With the stoicism of the brutes who had raised him he endured his suffering quietly, preferring to crawl away from the others and lie huddled in some clump of tall grasses rather than to show his misery before their eyes.

Kala, alone, he was glad to have with him, but now that he was better she was gone longer at a time, in search of food; for the devoted animal had scarcely eaten enough to support her own life while Tarzan had been so low, and was in consequence, reduced to a mere shadow of her former self.

CHAPTER SEVEN

The Light of Knowledge

After what seemed an eternity to the little sufferer he was able to walk once more, and from then on his recovery was so rapid that in another month he was as strong and active as ever.

During his convalescence he had gone over in his mind many times the battle with the gorilla, and his first thought was to recover the wonderful little weapon which had transformed him from a hopelessly outclassed weakling to the superior of the mighty terror of the jungle.

Also, he was anxious to return to the cabin and continue his investigations of its wondrous contents.

So, early one morning, he set forth alone upon his quest. After a little search he located the clean-picked bones of his late adversary, and close by, partly buried beneath the fallen leaves, he found the knife, now red with rust from its exposure to the dampness of the ground and from the dried blood of the gorilla.

He did not like the change in its former bright and gleaming surface; but it was still a formidable weapon, and one which he meant to use to advantage whenever the opportunity presented itself. He had in mind that no more would he run from the wanton attacks of old Tublat.

In another moment he was at the cabin, and after a short time had again thrown the latch and entered. His first concern was to learn the mechanism of the lock, and this he did by examining it closely while the door was open, so that he could learn precisely what caused it to hold the door, and by what means it released at his touch.

He found that he could close and lock the door from within, and this he did so that there would be no chance of his being molested while at his investigation.

He commenced a systematic search of the cabin; but his attention was soon riveted by the books which seemed to exert a strange and powerful influence over him, so that he could scarce attend to aught else for the lure of the wondrous puzzle which their purpose presented to him.

Among the other books were a primer, some child's readers, numerous picture books, and a great dictionary. All of these he examined, but the pictures caught his fancy most, though the strange little bugs which covered the pages where there were no pictures excited his wonder and deepest thought.

Squatting upon his haunches on the table top in the cabin his father had built – his smooth, brown, naked little body bent over the book which rested in his strong slender hands, and his great shock of long, black hair falling about his well-shaped head and bright, intelligent eyes – Tarzan of the apes, little primitive man, presented a picture filled, at once, with pathos and with promise – an allegorical figure of the primordial groping through the black night of ignorance toward the light of learning.

His little face was tense in study, for he had partially grasped, in a hazy, nebulous way, the rudiments of a thought which was destined to prove the key and the solution to the puzzling problem of the strange little bugs.

In his hands was a primer opened at a picture of a little ape similar to himself, but covered, except for hands and face, with strange, colored fur, for such he thought the jacket and trousers to be. Beneath the picture were three little bugs –

BOY.

And now he had discovered in the text upon the page that these three were repeated many times in the same sequence.

Another fact he learned – that there were comparatively few individual bugs; but these were repeated many times, occasionally alone, but more often in company with others.

Slowly he turned the pages, scanning the pictures and the text for a repetition of the combination B-O-Y. Presently he found it beneath a picture of another little ape and a strange animal which went upon four legs like the jackal and resembled him not a little. Beneath this picture the bugs appeared as:

A BOY AND A DOG

There they were, the three little bugs which always accompanied the little ape.

And so he progressed very, very slowly, for it was a hard and laborious task which he had set himself without knowing it – a task which might seem to you or me impossible – learning to read without having the slightest knowledge of letters or written language, or the faintest idea that such things existed.

He did not accomplish it in a day, or in a week, or in a month, or in a year; but slowly, very slowly, he learned after he had grasped the possibilities which lay in those little bugs, so that by the time he was fifteen he knew the various combinations of letters which stood for every pictured figure in the little primer and in one or two of the picture books.

Of the meaning and use of the articles and conjunctions, verbs and adverbs and pronouns he had but the faintest conception.

One day when he was about twelve he found a number of lead pencils in a hitherto undiscovered drawer beneath the table, and in scratching upon the table top with one of them he was delighted to discover the black line it left behind it.

He worked so assiduously with this new toy that the table top was soon a mass of scrawly loops and irregular lines and his pencil-point worn down to the wood. Then he took another pencil, but this time he had a definite object in view.

He would attempt to reproduce some of the little bugs that scrambled over the pages of his books.

It was a difficult task, for he held the pencil as one would grasp the hilt of a dagger, which does not add greatly to ease in writing or to the legibility of the results.

But he persevered for months, at such times as he was able to come to the cabin, until at last by repeated experimenting he found a position in which to hold the pencil that best permitted him to guide and control it, so that at last he could roughly reproduce any of the little bugs.

Thus he made a beginning of writing.

Copying the bugs taught him another thing – their number; and though he could not count as we understand it, yet he had an idea of quantity, the base of his calculations being the number of fingers upon one of his hands.

His search through the various books convinced him that he had discovered all the different kinds of bugs most often repeated in combination, and these he arranged in proper order with great ease because of the frequency with which he had perused the fascinating alphabet picture book.

His education progressed; but his greatest finds were in the inexhaustible storehouse of the huge illustrated dictionary, for he learned more through the medium of pictures than text, even after he had grasped the significance of the bugs.

When he discovered the arrangement of words in alphabetical order he delighted in searching for and finding the combinations with which he was familiar, and the words which followed them, their definitions, led him still further into the mazes of erudition.

By the time he was seventeen he had learned to read the simple, child's primer and had fully realized the true and wonderful purpose of the little bugs.

No longer did he feel shame for his hairless body or his human features, for now his reason told him that he was of a different race from his wild and hairy companions. He was a M-A-N, they were A-P-E-S, and the little apes which scurried through the forest top were M-O-N-K-E-Y-S. He knew, too, that old Sabor was a L-I-O-N-E-S-S, and Histah a S-N-A-K-E, and Tantor an E-L-E-P-H-A-N-T. And so he learned to read. From then on his progress was rapid. With the help of the great dictionary and the active intelligence of a healthy mind endowed by inheritance with more than ordinary reasoning powers he shrewdly guessed at much which he could not really understand, and more often than not his guesses were close to the mark of truth.

There were many breaks in his education, caused by the migratory habits of his tribe, but even when removed from his books his active brain continued to search out the mysteries of his fascinating avocation.

Pieces of bark and flat leaves and even smooth stretches of bare earth provided him with copy books whereon to scratch with the point of his hunting knife the lessons he was learning.

Nor did he neglect the sterner duties of life while following the bent of his inclination toward the solving of the mystery of his library.

He practiced with his rope and played with his sharp knife, which he had learned to keep keen by whetting upon flat stones.

The tribe had grown larger since Tarzan had come among them, for under the leadership of Kerchak they had been able to frighten the other tribes from their part of the jungle so that they had plenty to eat and little or no loss from predatory incursions of neighbors.

Hence the younger males as they became adult found it more comfortable to take mates from their own tribe, or if they captured one of another tribe to bring her back to Kerchak's band and live in amity with him rather than attempt to set up new establishments of their own, or fight with the redoubtable Kerchak for supremacy at home.

Occasionally one more ferocious than his fellows would attempt this latter alternative, but none had come yet who could wrest the palm of victory from the fierce and brutal ape.

Tarzan held a peculiar position in the tribe. They seemed to consider him one of them and yet in some way different. The older males either ignored him entirely or else hated him so vindictively that but for his wondrous agility and speed and the fierce protection of the huge Kala he would have been dispatched at an early age.

Tublat was his most consistent enemy, but it was through Tublat that, when he was about thirteen, the persecution of his enemies suddenly ceased and he was left severely alone, except on the occasions when one of them ran amuck in the throes of one of those strange, wild fits of insane rage which attacks the males of many of the fiercer animals of the jungle. Then none was safe.

On the day that Tarzan established his right to respect, the tribe was gathered about a small natural amphitheater which the jungle had left free from its entangling vines and creepers in a hollow among some low hills.

The open space was almost circular in shape. Upon every hand rose the mighty giants of the untouched forest, with the matted undergrowth banked so closely between the huge trunks that the only opening into the little, level arena was through the upper branches of the trees.

Here, safe from interruption, the tribe often gathered. In the center of the amphitheater was one of those strange earthen drums which the anthropoids build for the queer rites the sounds of which men have heard in the fastnesses of the jungle, but which none has ever witnessed.

Many travelers have seen the drums of the great apes, and some have heard the sounds of their beating and the noise of the wild, weird revelry of these first lords of the jungle, but Tarzan, Lord Greystoke, is, doubtless, the only human being who ever joined in the fierce, mad, intoxicating revel of the Dum-Dum.

From this primitive function has arisen, unquestionably, all the forms and ceremonials of modern church and state, for through all the countless ages, back beyond the uttermost ramparts of a dawning humanity our fierce, hairy forebears danced out the rites of the Dum-Dum to the sound of their earthen drums, beneath the bright light of a tropical moon in the depth of a mighty jungle which stands unchanged today as it stood on that long forgotten night in the dim, unthinkable vistas of the long dead past when our first shaggy ancestor swung from a swaying bough and dropped lightly upon the soft turf of the first meeting place.

On the day that Tarzan won his emancipation from the persecution that had followed him remorselessly for twelve of his thirteen years of life, the tribe, now a full hundred strong, trooped silently through the lower terrace of the jungle trees and dropped noiselessly upon the floor of the amphitheater.

The rites of the Dum-Dum marked important events in the life of the tribe – a victory, the capture of a prisoner, the killing of some large fierce denizen of the jungle, the death or accession of a king, and were conducted with set ceremonialism.

Today it was the killing of a giant ape, a member of another tribe, and as the people of Kerchak entered the arena two mighty bulls were seen bearing the body of the vanquished between them.

They laid their burden before the earthen drum and then squatted there beside it as guards, while the other members of the community curled themselves in grassy nooks to sleep until the rising moon should give the signal for the commencement of their savage orgy.

For hours absolute quiet reigned in the little clearing, except as it was broken by the discordant notes of brilliantly feathered parrots, or the screeching and twittering of the thousand jungle birds flitting ceaselessly amongst the vivid orchids and flamboyant blossoms which festooned the myriad, moss-covered branches of the forest kings.

At length as darkness settled upon the jungle the apes commenced to bestir themselves, and soon they formed a great circle about the earthen drum. The females and young squatted in a thin line at the outer periphery of the circle, while just in front of them ranged the adult males. Before the drum sat three old females, each armed with a knotted branch fifteen or eighteen inches in length.

Slowly and softly they began tapping upon the resounding surface of the drum as the first faint rays of the ascending moon silvered the encircling tree tops.

As the light in the amphitheater increased the females augmented the frequency and force of their blows until presently a wild, rhythmic din pervaded the great jungle for miles in every direction. Huge, fierce brutes stopped in their hunting, with up-pricked ears and raised heads, to listen to the dull booming that betokened the Dum-Dum of the apes.

Occasionally one would raise his shrill scream or thunderous roar in answering challenge to the savage din of the anthropoids, but none came near to investigate or attack, for the great apes, assembled in all the power of their numbers, filled the breasts of their jungle neighbors with deep respect.

As the din of the drum rose to almost deafening volume Kerchak sprang into the open space between the squatting males and the drummers.

Standing erect he threw his head far back and looking full into the eye of the rising moon he beat upon his breast with his great hairy paws and emitted his fearful roaring shriek.

One – twice – thrice that terrifying cry rang out across the teeming solitude of that unspeakably quick, yet unthinkably dead, world.

Then, crouching, Kerchak slunk noiselessly around the open circle, veering far away from the dead body lying before the altar-drum, but, as he passed, keeping his little, fierce, wicked, red eyes upon the corpse.

Another male then sprang into the arena, and, repeating the horrid cries of his king, followed stealthily in his wake. Another and another followed in quick succession until the jungle reverberated with the now almost ceaseless notes of their bloodthirsty screams.

It was the challenge and the hunt.

When all the adult males had joined in the thin line of circling dancers the attack commenced.

Kerchak, seizing a huge club from the pile which lay at hand for the purpose, rushed furiously upon the dead ape, dealing the corpse a terrific blow, at the same time emitting the growls and snarls of combat. The din of the drum was now increased, as well as the frequency of the blows, and the warriors, as each approached the victim of the hunt and delivered his bludgeon blow, joined in the mad whirl of the Death Dance.

Tarzan was one of the wild, leaping horde. His brown, sweat-streaked, muscular body, glistening in the moonlight, shone supple and graceful among the uncouth, awkward, hairy brutes about him.

None was more stealthy in the mimic hunt, none more ferocious than he in the wild ferocity of the attack, none who leaped so high into the air in the Dance of Death.

As the noise and rapidity of the drumbeats increased the dancers apparently became intoxicated with the wild rhythm and the savage yells. Their leaps and bounds increased, their bared fangs dripped saliva, and their lips and breasts were flecked with foam.

For half an hour the weird dance went on, until, at a sign from Kerchak, the noise of the drums ceased, the female drummers scampering hurriedly through the line of dancers toward the outer rim of squatting spectators. Then, as one, the males rushed headlong upon the thing which their terrific blows had reduced to a mass of hairy pulp.

Flesh seldom came to their jaws in satisfying quantities, so a fit finale to their wild revel was a taste of fresh killed meat, and it was to the purpose of devouring their late enemy that they now turned their attention.

Great fangs sunk into the carcass tearing away huge hunks, the mightiest of the apes obtaining the choicest morsels, while the weaker circled the outer edge of the fighting, snarling pack awaiting their chance to dodge in and snatch a dropped tidbit or filch a remaining bone before all was gone.

Tarzan, more than the apes, craved and needed flesh. Descended from a race of meat eaters, never in his life, he thought, had he once satisfied his appetite for animal food; and so now his agile little body wormed its way far into the mass of struggling, rending apes in an endeavor to obtain a share which his strength would have been unequal to the task of winning for him.

At his side hung the hunting knife of his unknown father in a sheath self-fashioned in copy of one he had seen among the pictures of his treasure-books.

At last he reached the fast disappearing feast and with his sharp knife slashed off a more generous portion than he had hoped for, an entire hairy forearm, where it protruded from beneath the feet of the mighty Kerchak, who was so busily engaged in perpetuating the royal prerogative of gluttony that he failed to note the act of *lese-majeste.*

So little Tarzan wriggled out from beneath the struggling mass, clutching his grisly prize close to his breast.

Among those circling futilely the outskirts of the banqueters was old Tublat. He had been among the first at the feast, but had retreated with a goodly share to eat in quiet, and was now forcing his way back for more.

So it was that he spied Tarzan as the boy emerged from the clawing, pushing throng with that hairy forearm hugged firmly to his body.

Tublat's little, close-set, bloodshot, pig-eyes shot wicked gleams of hate as they fell upon the object of his loathing. In them, too, was greed for the toothsome dainty the boy carried.

But Tarzan saw his arch enemy as quickly, and divining what the great beast would do he leaped nimbly away toward the females and the young, hoping to hide himself among them. Tublat, however, was close upon his heels, so that he had no opportunity to seek a place of concealment, but saw that he would be put to it to escape at all.

Swiftly he sped toward the surrounding trees and with an agile bound gained a lower limb with one hand, and then, transferring his burden to his teeth, he climbed rapidly upward, closely followed by Tublat.

Up, up he went to the waving pinnacle of a lofty monarch of the forest where his heavy pursuer dared not follow him. There he perched, hurling taunts and insults at the raging, foaming beast fifty feet below him.

And then Tublat went mad.

With horrifying screams and roars he rushed to the ground, among the females and young, sinking his great fangs into a dozen tiny necks and tearing great pieces from the backs and breasts of the females who fell into his clutches.

In the brilliant moonlight Tarzan witnessed the whole mad carnival of rage. He saw the females and the young scamper to the safety of the trees. Then the great bulls in the center of the arena felt the mighty fangs of their demented fellow, and with one accord they melted into the black shadows of the overhanging forest.

There was but one in the amphitheater beside Tublat, a belated female running swiftly toward the tree where Tarzan perched, and close behind her came the awful Tublat.

It was Kala, and as quickly as Tarzan saw that Tublat was gaining on her he dropped with the rapidity of a falling stone, from branch to branch, toward his foster mother.

Now she was beneath the overhanging limbs and close above her crouched Tarzan, waiting the outcome of the race.

She leaped into the air grasping a low-hanging branch, but almost over the head of Tublat, so nearly had he distanced her. She should have been safe now but there was a rending, tearing sound, the branch broke and precipitated her full upon the head of Tublat, knocking him to the ground.

Both were up in an instant, but as quick as they had been Tarzan had been quicker, so that the infuriated bull found himself facing the man-child who stood between him and Kala.

Nothing could have suited the fierce beast better, and with a roar of triumph he leaped upon the little Lord Greystoke. But his fangs never closed in that nut brown flesh.

A muscular hand shot out and grasped the hairy throat, and another plunged a keen hunting knife a dozen times into the broad breast. Like lightning the blows fell, and only ceased when Tarzan felt the limp form crumple beneath him.

As the body rolled to the ground Tarzan of the Apes placed his foot upon the neck of his lifelong enemy and, raising his eyes to the full moon, threw back his fierce young head and voiced the wild and terrible cry of his people.

One by one the tribe swung down from their arboreal retreats and formed a circle about Tarzan and his vanquished foe. When they had all come Tarzan turned toward them.

"I am Tarzan," he cried. "I am a great killer. Let all respect Tarzan of the Apes and Kala, his mother. There be none among you as mighty as Tarzan. Let his enemies beware."

Looking full into the wicked, red eyes of Kerchak, the young Lord Greystoke beat upon his mighty breast and screamed out once more his shrill cry of defiance.

CHAPTER EIGHT

The Tree-top Hunter

The morning after the Dum-Dum the tribe started slowly back through the forest toward the coast.

The body of Tublat lay where it had fallen, for the people of Kerchak do not eat their own dead.

The march was but a leisurely search for food. Cabbage palm and gray plum, pisang and scitamine they found in abundance, with wild pineapple, and occasionally small mammals, birds, eggs, reptiles, and insects. The nuts they cracked between their powerful jaws, or, if too hard, broke by pounding between stones.

Once old Sabor, crossing their path, sent them scurrying to the safety of the higher branches, for if she respected their number and their sharp fangs, they on their part held her cruel and mighty ferocity in equal esteem.

Upon a low-hanging branch sat Tarzan directly above the majestic, supple body as it forged silently through the thick jungle. He hurled a pineapple at the ancient enemy of his people. The great beast stopped and, turning, eyed the taunting figure above her.

With an angry lash of her tail she bared her yellow fangs, curling her great lips in a hideous snarl that wrinkled her bristling snout in serried ridges and closed her wicked eyes to two narrow slits of rage and hatred.

With back-laid ears she looked straight into the eyes of Tarzan of the Apes and sounded her fierce, shrill challenge. And from the safety of his overhanging limb the ape-child sent back the fearsome answer of his kind.

For a moment the two eyed each other in silence, and then the great cat turned into the jungle, which swallowed her as the ocean engulfs a tossed pebble.

But into the mind of Tarzan a great plan sprang. He had killed the fierce Tublat, so was he not therefore a mighty fighter? Now would he track down the crafty Sabor and slay her likewise. He would be a mighty hunter, also.

At the bottom of his little English heart beat the great desire to cover his nakedness with *clothes* for he had learned from his picture books that all *men* were so covered, while *monkeys* and *apes* and every other living thing went naked.

Clothes therefore, must be truly a badge of greatness; the insignia of the superiority of *man* over all other animals, for surely there could be no other reason for wearing the hideous things.

Many moons ago, when he had been much smaller, he had desired the skin of Sabor, the lioness, or Numa, the lion, or Sheeta, the leopard to cover his hairless body that he might no longer resemble hideous Histah, the snake; but now he was proud of his sleek skin for it betokened his descent from a mighty race, and the conflicting desires to go naked in prideful proof of his ancestry, or to conform to the customs of his own kind and wear hideous and uncomfortable apparel found first one and then the other in the ascendency.

As the tribe continued their slow way through the forest after the passing of Sabor, Tarzan's head was filled with his great scheme for slaying his enemy, and for many days thereafter he thought of little else.

On this day, however, he presently had other and more immediate interests to attract his attention.

Suddenly it became as midnight; the noises of the jungle ceased; the trees stood motionless as though in paralyzed expectancy of some great and imminent disaster. All nature waited – but not for long.

Faintly, from a distance, came a low, sad moaning. Nearer and nearer it approached, mounting louder and louder in volume.

The great trees bent in unison as though pressed earthward by a mighty hand. Farther and farther toward the ground they inclined, and still there was no sound save the deep and awesome moaning of the wind.

Then, suddenly, the jungle giants whipped back, lashing their mighty tops in angry and deafening protest. A vivid and blinding light flashed from the whirling, inky clouds above. The deep cannonade of roaring thunder belched forth its fearsome challenge. The deluge came – all hell broke loose upon the jungle.

The tribe shivering from the cold rain, huddled at the bases of great trees. The lightning, darting and flashing through the blackness, showed wildly waving branches, whipping streamers and bending trunks.

Now and again some ancient patriarch of the woods, rent by a flashing bolt, would crash in a thousand pieces among the surrounding trees, carrying down numberless branches and many smaller neighbors to add to the tangled confusion of the tropical jungle.

Branches, great and small, torn away by the ferocity of the tornado, hurtled through the wildly waving verdure, carrying death and destruction to countless unhappy denizens of the thickly peopled world below.

For hours the fury of the storm continued without surcease, and still the tribe huddled close in shivering fear. In constant danger from falling trunks and branches and paralyzed by the vivid flashing of lightning and the bellowing of thunder they crouched in pitiful misery until the storm passed.

The end was as sudden as the beginning. The wind ceased, the sun shone forth – nature smiled once more.

The dripping leaves and branches, and the moist petals of gorgeous flowers glistened in the splendor of the returning day. And, so – as Nature forgot, her children forgot also. Busy life went on as it had been before the darkness and the fright.

But to Tarzan a dawning light had come to explain the mystery of *clothes*. How snug he would have been beneath the heavy coat of Sabor! And so was added a further incentive to the adventure.

For several months the tribe hovered near the beach where stood Tarzan's cabin, and his studies took up the greater portion of his time, but always when journeying through the forest he kept his rope in readiness, and many were the smaller animals that fell into the snare of the quick thrown noose.

Once it fell about the short neck of Horta, the boar, and his mad lunge for freedom toppled Tarzan from the overhanging limb where he had lain in wait and from whence he had launched his sinuous coil.

The mighty tusker turned at the sound of his falling body, and, seeing only the easy prey of a young ape, he lowered his head and charged madly at the surprised youth.

Tarzan, happily, was uninjured by the fall, alighting catlike upon all fours far outspread to take up the shock. He was on his feet in an instant and, leaping with the agility of the monkey he was, he gained the safety of a low limb as Horta, the boar, rushed futilely beneath.

Thus it was that Tarzan learned by experience the limitations as well as the possibilities of his strange weapon.

He lost a long rope on this occasion, but he knew that had it been Sabor who had thus dragged him from his perch the outcome might have been very different, for he would have lost his life, doubtless, into the bargain.

It took him many days to braid a new rope, but when, finally, it was done he went forth purposely to hunt, and lie in wait among the dense foliage of a great branch right above the well-beaten trail that led to water.

Several small animals passed unharmed beneath him. He did not want such insignificant game. It would take a strong animal to test the efficacy of his new scheme.

At last came she whom Tarzan sought, with lithe sinews rolling beneath shimmering hide; fat and glossy came Sabor, the lioness.

Her great padded feet fell soft and noiseless on the narrow trail. Her head was high in ever alert attention; her long tail moved slowly in sinuous and graceful undulations.

Nearer and nearer she came to where Tarzan of the Apes crouched upon his limb, the coils of his long rope poised ready in his hand.

Like a thing of bronze, motionless as death, sat Tarzan. Sabor passed beneath. One stride beyond she took – a second, a third, and then the silent coil shot out above her.

For an instant the spreading noose hung above her head like a great snake, and then, as she looked upward to detect the origin of the swishing sound of the rope, it settled about her neck. With a quick jerk Tarzan snapped the noose tight about the glossy throat, and then he dropped the rope and clung to his support with both hands.

Sabor was trapped.

With a bound the startled beast turned into the jungle, but Tarzan was not to lose another rope through the same cause as the first. He had learned from experience. The lioness had taken but half her second bound when she felt the rope tighten about her neck; her body turned completely over in the air and she fell with a heavy crash upon her back. Tarzan had fastened the end of the rope securely to the trunk of the great tree on which he sat.

Thus far his plan had worked to perfection, but when he grasped the rope, bracing himself behind a crotch of two mighty branches, he found that dragging the mighty, struggling, clawing, biting, screaming mass of iron-muscled fury up to the tree and hanging her was a very different proposition.

The weight of old Sabor was immense, and when she braced her huge paws nothing less than Tantor, the elephant, himself, could have budged her.

The lioness was now back in the path where she could see the author of the indignity which had been placed upon her. Screaming with rage she suddenly charged, leaping high into the air toward Tarzan, but when her huge body struck the limb on which Tarzan had been, Tarzan was no longer there.

Instead he perched lightly upon a smaller branch twenty feet above the raging captive. For a moment Sabor hung half across the branch, while Tarzan mocked, and hurled twigs and branches at her unprotected face.

Presently the beast dropped to the earth again and Tarzan came quickly to seize the rope, but Sabor had now found that it was only a slender cord that held her, and grasping it in her huge jaws severed it before Tarzan could tighten the strangling noose a second time.

Tarzan was much hurt. His well-laid plan had come to naught, so he sat there screaming at the roaring creature beneath him and making mocking grimaces at it.

Sabor paced back and forth beneath the tree for hours; four times she crouched and sprang at the dancing sprite above her, but might as well have clutched at the illusive wind that murmured through the tree tops.

At last Tarzan tired of the sport, and with a parting roar of challenge and a well-aimed ripe fruit that spread soft and sticky over the snarling face of his enemy, he swung rapidly through the trees, a hundred feet above the ground, and in a short time was among the members of his tribe.

Here he recounted the details of his adventure, with swelling chest and so considerable swagger that he quite impressed even his bitterest enemies, while Kala fairly danced for joy and pride.

CHAPTER NINE

Man and Man

Tarzan of the Apes lived on in his wild, jungle existence with little change for several years, only that he grew stronger and wiser, and learned from his books more and more of the strange worlds which lay somewhere outside his primeval forest.

To him life was never monotonous or stale. There was always Pisah, the fish, to be caught in the many streams and the little lakes, and Sabor, with her ferocious cousins to keep one ever on the alert and give zest to every instant that one spent upon the ground.

Often they hunted him, and more often he hunted them, but though they never quite reached him with those cruel, sharp claws of theirs, yet there were times when one could scarce have passed a thick leaf between their talons and his smooth hide.

Quick was Sabor, the lioness, and quick were Numa and Sheeta, but Tarzan of the Apes was lightning.

With Tantor, the elephant, he made friends. How? Ask not. But this is known to the denizens of the jungle, that on many moonlight nights Tarzan of the Apes and Tantor, the elephant, walked together, and where the way was clear Tarzan rode, perched high upon Tantor's mighty back.

Many days during these years he spent in the cabin of his father, where still lay, untouched, the bones of his parents and the skeleton of Kala's baby. At eighteen he read fluently and understood nearly all he read in the many and varied volumes on the shelves.

Also could he write, with printed letters, rapidly and plainly, but script he had not mastered, for though there were several copy books among his treasure, there was so little written English in the cabin that he saw no use for bothering with this other form of writing, though he could read it, laboriously.

Thus, at eighteen, we find him, an English lordling, who could speak no English, and yet who could read and write his native language. Never had he seen a human being other than himself, for the little area traversed by his tribe was watered by no greater river to bring down the savage natives of the interior.

High hills shut it off on three sides, the ocean on the fourth. It was alive with lions and leopards and poisonous snakes. Its untouched mazes of matted jungle had as yet invited no hardy pioneer from the human beasts beyond its frontier.

But as Tarzan of the Apes sat one day in the cabin of his father delving into the mysteries of a new book, the ancient security of his jungle was broken forever.

At the far eastern confine a strange cavalcade strung, in single file, over the brow of a low hill.

In advance were fifty black warriors armed with slender wooden spears with ends hard baked over slow fires, and long bows and poisoned arrows. On their backs were oval shields, in their noses huge rings, while from the kinky wool of their heads protruded tufts of gay feathers.

Across their foreheads were tattooed three parallel lines of color, and on each breast three concentric circles. Their yellow teeth were filed to sharp points, and their great protruding lips added still further to the low and bestial brutishness of their appearance.

Following them were several hundred women and children, the former bearing upon their heads great burdens of cooking pots, household utensils and ivory. In the rear were a hundred warriors, similar in all respects to the advance guard.

That they more greatly feared an attack from the rear than whatever unknown enemies lurked in their advance was evidenced by the formation of the column; and such was the fact, for they were fleeing from the white man's soldiers who had so harassed them for rubber and ivory that they had turned upon their conquerors one day and massacred a white officer and a small detachment of his black troops.

For many days they had gorged themselves on meat, but eventually a stronger body of troops had come and fallen upon their village by night to revenge the death of their comrades.

That night the black soldiers of the white man had had meat a-plenty, and this little remnant of a once powerful tribe had slunk off into the gloomy jungle toward the unknown, and freedom.

But that which meant freedom and the pursuit of happiness to these savage blacks meant consternation and death to many of the wild denizens of their new home.

For three days the little cavalcade marched slowly through the heart of this unknown and untracked forest, until finally, early in the fourth day, they came upon a little spot near the banks of a small river, which seemed less thickly overgrown than any ground they had yet encountered.

Here they set to work to build a new village, and in a month a great clearing had been made, huts and palisades erected, plantains, yams and maize planted, and they had taken up their old life in their new home. Here there were no white men, no soldiers, nor any rubber or ivory to be gathered for cruel and thankless taskmasters.

Several moons passed by ere the blacks ventured far into the territory surrounding their new village. Several had already fallen prey to old Sabor, and because the jungle was so infested with these fierce and bloodthirsty cats, and with lions and leopards, the ebony warriors hesitated to trust themselves far from the safety of their palisades.

But one day, Kulonga, a son of the old king, Mbonga, wandered far into the dense mazes to the west. Warily he stepped, his slender lance ever ready, his long oval shield firmly grasped in his left hand close to his sleek ebony body.

At his back his bow, and in the quiver upon his shield many slim, straight arrows, well smeared with the thick, dark, tarry substance that rendered deadly their tiniest needle prick.

Night found Kulonga far from the palisades of his father's village, but still headed westward, and climbing into the fork of a great tree he fashioned a rude platform and curled himself for sleep.

Three miles to the west slept the tribe of Kerchak.

Early the next morning the apes were astir, moving through the jungle in search of food. Tarzan, as was his custom, prosecuted his search in the direction of the cabin so that by leisurely hunting on the way his stomach was filled by the time he reached the beach.

The apes scattered by ones, and twos, and threes in all directions, but ever within sound of a signal of alarm.

Kala had moved slowly along an elephant track toward the east, and was busily engaged in turning over rotted limbs and logs in search of succulent bugs and fungi, when the faintest shadow of a strange noise brought her to startled attention.

For fifty yards before her the trail was straight, and down this leafy tunnel she saw the stealthy advancing figure of a strange and fearful creature.

It was Kulonga.

Kala did not wait to see more, but, turning, moved rapidly back along the trail. She did not run; but, after the manner of her kind when not aroused, sought rather to avoid than to escape.

Close after her came Kulonga. Here was meat. He could make a killing and feast well this day. On he hurried, his spear poised for the throw.

At a turning of the trail he came in sight of her again upon another straight stretch. His spear hand went far back, the muscles rolled, lightning-like, beneath the sleek hide. Out shot the arm, and the spear sped toward Kala.

A poor cast. It but grazed her side.

With a cry of rage and pain the she-ape turned upon her tormentor. In an instant the trees were crashing beneath the weight of her hurrying fellows, swinging rapidly toward the scene of trouble in answer to Kala's scream.

As she charged, Kulonga unslung his bow and fitted an arrow with almost unthinkable quickness. Drawing the shaft far back he drove the poisoned missile straight into the heart of the great anthropoid.

With a horrid scream Kala plunged forward upon her face before the astonished members of her tribe.

Roaring and shrieking the apes dashed toward Kulonga, but that wary savage was fleeing down the trail like a frightened antelope.

He knew something of the ferocity of these wild, hairy men, and his one desire was to put as many miles between himself and them as he possibly could.

They followed him, racing through the trees, for a long distance, but finally one by one they abandoned the chase and returned to the scene of the tragedy.

None of them had ever seen a man before, other than Tarzan, and so they wondered vaguely what strange manner of creature it might be that had invaded their jungle.

On the far beach by the little cabin Tarzan heard the faint echoes of the conflict and knowing that something was seriously amiss among the tribe he hastened rapidly toward the direction of the sound.

When he arrived he found the entire tribe gathered jabbering about the dead body of his slain mother.

Tarzan's grief and anger were unbounded. He roared out his hideous challenge time and again. He beat upon his great chest with his clenched fists, and then he fell upon the body of Kala and sobbed out the pitiful sorrowing of his lonely heart.

To lose the only creature in all his world who ever had manifested love and affection for him was the greatest tragedy he had ever known.

What though Kala was a fierce and hideous ape! To Tarzan she had been kind, she had been beautiful.

Upon her he had lavished, unknown to himself, all the reverence and respect and love that a normal English boy feels for his own mother. He had never known another, and so to Kala was given, though mutely, all that would have belonged to the fair and lovely Lady Alice had she lived.

After the first outburst of grief Tarzan controlled himself, and questioning the members of the tribe who had witnessed the killing of Kala he learned all that their meager vocabulary could convey.

It was enough, however, for his needs. It told him of a strange, hairless, black ape with feathers growing upon its head, who launched death from a slender branch, and then ran, with the fleetness of Bara, the deer, toward the rising sun.

Tarzan waited no longer, but leaping into the branches of the trees sped rapidly through the forest. He knew the windings of the elephant trail along which Kala's murderer had flown, and so he cut straight through the jungle to intercept the black warrior who was evidently following the tortuous detours of the trail.

At his side was the hunting knife of his unknown sire, and across his shoulders the coils of his own long rope. In an hour he struck the trail again, and coming to earth examined the soil minutely.

In the soft mud on the bank of a tiny rivulet he found footprints such as he alone in all the jungle had ever made, but much larger than his. His heart beat fast. Could it be that he was trailing a *man* – one of his own race?

There were two sets of imprints pointing in opposite directions. So his quarry had already passed on his return along the trail. As he examined the newer spoor a tiny particle of earth toppled from the outer edge of one of the footprints to the bottom of its shallow depression – ah, the trail was very fresh, his prey must have but scarcely passed.

Tarzan swung himself to the trees once more, and with swift noiselessness sped along high above the trail.

He had covered barely a mile when he came upon the black warrior standing in a little open space. In his hand was his slender bow to which he had fitted one of his death dealing arrows.

Opposite him across the little clearing stood Horta, the boar, with lowered head and foam flecked tusks, ready to charge.

Tarzan looked with wonder upon the strange creature beneath him – so like him in form and yet so different in face and color. His books had portrayed the *negro*, but how different had been the dull, dead print to this sleek thing of ebony, pulsing with life.

As the man stood there with taut drawn bow Tarzan recognized him not so much the *negro* as the *archer* of his picture book –

A stands for Archer

How wonderful! Tarzan almost betrayed his presence in the deep excitement of his discovery.

But things were commencing to happen below him. The sinewy black arm had drawn the shaft far back; Horta, the boar, was charging, and then the black released the little poisoned arrow, and Tarzan saw it fly with the quickness of thought and lodge in the bristling neck of the boar.

Scarcely had the shaft left his bow ere Kulonga had fitted another to it, but Horta, the boar, was upon him so quickly that he had no time to discharge it. With a bound the black leaped entirely over the rushing beast and turning with incredible swiftness planted a second arrow in Horta's back.

Then Kulonga sprang into a near-by tree.

Horta wheeled to charge his enemy once more; a dozen steps he took, then he staggered and fell upon his side. For a moment his muscles stiffened and relaxed convulsively, then he lay still.

Kulonga came down from his tree.

With a knife that hung at his side he cut several large pieces from the boar's body, and in the center of the trail he built a fire, cooking and eating as much as he wanted. The rest he left where it had fallen.

Tarzan was an interested spectator. His desire to kill burned fiercely in his wild breast, but his desire to learn was even greater. He would follow this savage creature for a while and know from whence he came. He could kill him at his leisure later, when the bow and deadly arrows were laid aside.

When Kulonga had finished his repast and disappeared beyond a near turning of the path, Tarzan dropped quietly to the ground. With his knife he severed many strips of meat from Horta's carcass, but he did not cook them.

He had seen fire, but only when Ara, the lightning, had destroyed some great tree. That any creature of the jungle could produce the red-and-yellow fangs which devoured wood and left nothing but fine dust surprised Tarzan greatly, and why the black warrior had ruined his delicious repast by plunging it into the blighting heat was quite beyond him. Possibly Ara was a friend with whom the Archer was sharing his food.

But, be that as it may, Tarzan would not ruin good meat in any such foolish manner, so he gobbled down a great quantity of the raw flesh, burying the balance of the carcass beside the trail where he could find it upon his return.

And then Lord Greystoke wiped his greasy fingers upon his naked thighs and took up the trail of Kulonga, the son of Mbonga, the king; while in far-off London another Lord Greystoke, the younger brother of the real Lord Greystoke's father, sent back his chops to the club's *chef* because they were underdone, and when he had finished his repast he dipped his finger-ends into a silver bowl of scented water and dried them upon a piece of snowy damask.

All day Tarzan followed Kulonga, hovering above him in the trees like some malign spirit. Twice more he saw him hurl his arrows of destruction – once at Dango, the hyena, and again at Manu, the monkey. In each instance the animal died almost instantly, for Kulonga's poison was very fresh and very deadly.

Tarzan thought much on this wondrous method of slaying as he swung slowly along at a safe distance behind his quarry. He knew that alone the tiny prick of the arrow could not so quickly dispatch these wild things of the jungle, who were often torn and scratched and gored in a frightful manner as they fought with their jungle neighbors, yet as often recovered as not.

No, there was something mysterious connected with these tiny slivers of wood which could bring death by a mere scratch. He must look into the matter.

That night Kulonga slept in the crotch of a mighty tree and far above him crouched Tarzan of the Apes.

When Kulonga awoke he found that his bow and arrows had disappeared. The black warrior was furious and frightened, but more frightened than furious. He searched the ground below the tree, and he searched the tree above the ground; but there was no sign of either bow or arrows or of the nocturnal marauder.

Kulonga was panic-stricken. His spear he had hurled at Kala and had not recovered; and, now that his bow and arrows were gone, he was defenseless except for a single knife. His only hope lay in reaching the village of Mbonga as quickly as his legs would carry him.

That he was not far from home he was certain, so he took the trail at a rapid trot.

From a great mass of impenetrable foliage a few yards away emerged Tarzan of the Apes to swing quietly in his wake.

Kulonga's bow and arrows were securely tied high in the top of a giant tree from which a patch of bark had been removed by a sharp knife near to the ground, and a branch half cut through and left hanging about fifty feet higher up. Thus Tarzan blazed the forest trails and marked his caches.

As Kulonga continued his journey Tarzan closed on him until he traveled almost over the black's head. His rope he now held coiled in his right hand; he was almost ready for the kill.

The moment was delayed only because Tarzan was anxious to ascertain the black warrior's destination, and presently he was rewarded, for they came suddenly in view of a great clearing, at one end of which lay many strange lairs.

Tarzan was directly over Kulonga, as he made the discovery. The forest ended abruptly and beyond lay two hundred yards of planted fields between the jungle and the village.

Tarzan must act quickly or his prey would be gone; but Tarzan's life training left so little space between decision and action when an emergency confronted him that there was not even room for the shadow of a thought between.

So it was that as Kulonga emerged from the shadow of the jungle a slender coil of rope sped sinuously above him from the lowest branch of a mighty tree directly upon the edge of the fields of Mbonga, and ere the king's son had taken a half dozen steps into the clearing a quick noose tightened about his neck.

So quickly did Tarzan of the Apes drag back his prey that Kulonga's cry of alarm was throttled in his windpipe. Hand over hand Tarzan drew the struggling black until he had him hanging by his neck in midair; then Tarzan climbed to a larger branch drawing the still threshing victim well up into the sheltering verdure of the tree.

Here he fastened the rope securely to a stout branch, and then, descending, plunged his hunting knife into Kulonga's heart. Kala was avenged.

Tarzan examined the black minutely, for he had never seen any other human being. The knife with its sheath and belt caught his eye; he appropriated them. A copper anklet also took his fancy, and this he transferred to his own leg.

He examined and admired the tattooing on the forehead and breast. He marveled at the sharp filed teeth. He investigated and appropriated the feathered headdress, and then he prepared to get down to business, for Tarzan of the Apes was hungry, and here was meat; meat of the kill, which jungle ethics permitted him to eat.

How may we judge him, by what standards, this ape-man with the heart and head and body of an English gentleman, and the training of a wild beast?

Tublat, whom he had hated and who had hated him, he had killed in a fair fight, and yet never had the thought of eating Tublat's flesh entered his head. It would have been as revolting to him as is cannibalism to us.

But who was Kulonga that he might not be eaten as fairly as Horta, the boar, or Bara, the deer? Was he not simply another of the countless wild things of the jungle who preyed upon one another to satisfy the cravings of hunger?

Suddenly, a strange doubt stayed his hand. Had not his books taught him that he was a man? And was not The Archer a man, also?

Did men eat men? Alas, he did not know. Why, then, this hesitancy! Once more he essayed the effort, but a qualm of nausea overwhelmed him. He did not understand.

All he knew was that he could not eat the flesh of this black man, and thus hereditary instinct, ages old, usurped the functions of his untaught mind and saved him from transgressing a worldwide law of whose very existence he was ignorant.

Quickly he lowered Kulonga's body to the ground, removed the noose, and took to the trees again.

CHAPTER TEN

The Fear-Phantom

FROM A LOFTY PERCH Tarzan viewed the village of thatched huts across the intervening plantation.

He saw that at one point the forest touched the village, and to this spot he made his way, lured by a fever of curiosity to behold animals of his own kind, and to learn more of their ways and view the strange lairs in which they lived.

His savage life among the fierce wild brutes of the jungle left no opening for any thought that these could be aught else than enemies. Similarity of form led him into no erroneous conception of the welcome that would be accorded him should he be discovered by these, the first of his own kind he had ever seen.

Tarzan of the Apes was no sentimentalist. He knew nothing of the brotherhood of man. All things outside his own tribe were his deadly enemies, with the few exceptions of which Tantor, the elephant, was a marked example.

And he realized all this without malice or hatred. To kill was the law of the wild world he knew. Few were his primitive pleasures, but the greatest of these was to hunt and kill, and so he accorded to others the right to cherish the same desires as he, even though he himself might be the object of their hunt.

His strange life had left him neither morose nor bloodthirsty. That he joyed in killing, and that he killed with a joyous laugh upon his handsome lips betokened no innate cruelty. He killed for food most often, but, being a man, he sometimes killed for pleasure, a thing which no other animal does; for it has remained for man alone among all creatures to kill senselessly and wantonly for the mere pleasure of inflicting suffering and death.

And when he killed for revenge, or in self-defense, he did that also without hysteria, for it was a very businesslike proceeding which admitted of no levity.

So it was that now, as he cautiously approached the village of Mbonga, he was quite prepared either to kill or be killed should he be discovered. He proceeded with unwonted stealth, for Kulonga had taught him great respect for the little sharp splinters of wood which dealt death so swiftly and unerringly.

At length he came to a great tree, heavy laden with thick foliage and loaded with pendant loops of giant creepers. From this almost impenetrable bower above the village he crouched, looking down upon the scene below him, wondering over every feature of this new, strange life.

There were naked children running and playing in the village street. There were women grinding dried plantain in crude stone mortars, while others were fashioning cakes from the powdered flour. Out in the fields he could see still other women hoeing, weeding, or gathering.

All wore strange protruding girdles of dried grass about their hips and many were loaded with brass and copper anklets, armlets and bracelets. Around many a dusky neck hung curiously coiled strands of wire, while several were further ornamented by huge nose rings.

Tarzan of the Apes looked with growing wonder at these strange creatures. Dozing in the shade he saw several men, while at the extreme outskirts of the clearing he occasionally caught glimpses of armed warriors apparently guarding the village against surprise from an attacking enemy.

He noticed that the women alone worked. Nowhere was there evidence of a man tilling the fields or performing any of the homely duties of the village.

Finally his eyes rested upon a woman directly beneath him.

Before her was a small cauldron standing over a low fire and in it bubbled a thick, reddish, tarry mass. On one side of her lay a quantity of wooden arrows the points of which she dipped into the seething substance, then laying them upon a narrow rack of boughs which stood upon her other side.

Tarzan of the Apes was fascinated. Here was the secret of the terrible destructiveness of The Archer's tiny missiles. He noted the extreme care which the woman took that none of the matter should touch her hands, and once when a particle spattered upon one of her fingers he saw her plunge the member into a vessel of water and quickly rub the tiny stain away with a handful of leaves.

Tarzan knew nothing of poison, but his shrewd reasoning told him that it was this deadly stuff that killed, and not the little arrow, which was merely the messenger that carried it into the body of its victim.

How he should like to have more of those little death-dealing slivers. If the woman would only leave her work for an instant he could drop down, gather up a handful, and be back in the tree again before she drew three breaths.

As he was trying to think out some plan to distract her attention he heard a wild cry from across the clearing. He looked and saw a black warrior standing beneath the very tree in which he had killed the murderer of Kala an hour before.

The fellow was shouting and waving his spear above his head. Now and again he would point to something on the ground before him.

The village was in an uproar instantly. Armed men rushed from the interior of many a hut and raced madly across the clearing toward the excited sentry. After them trooped the old men, and the women and children until, in a moment, the village was deserted.

Tarzan of the Apes knew that they had found the body of his victim, but that interested him far less than the fact that no one remained in the village to prevent his taking a supply of the arrows which lay below him.

Quickly and noiselessly he dropped to the ground beside the cauldron of poison. For a moment he stood motionless, his quick, bright eyes scanning the interior of the palisade.

No one was in sight. His eyes rested upon the open doorway of a nearby hut. He would take a look within, thought Tarzan, and so, cautiously, he approached the low thatched building.

For a moment he stood without, listening intently. There was no sound, and he glided into the semi-darkness of the interior.

Weapons hung against the walls – long spears, strangely shaped knives, a couple of narrow shields. In the center of the room was a cooking pot, and at the far end a litter of dry grasses covered by woven mats which evidently served the owners as beds and bedding. Several human skulls lay upon the floor.

Tarzan of the Apes felt of each article, hefted the spears, smelled of them, for he "saw" largely through his sensitive and highly trained nostrils. He determined to own one of these long, pointed sticks, but he could not take one on this trip because of the arrows he meant to carry.

As he took each article from the walls, he placed it in a pile in the center of the room. On top of all he placed the cooking pot, inverted, and on top of this he laid one of the grinning skulls, upon which he fastened the headdress of the dead Kulonga.

Then he stood back, surveyed his work, and grinned. Tarzan of the Apes enjoyed a joke.

But now he heard, outside, the sounds of many voices, and long mournful howls, and mighty wailing. He was startled. Had he remained too long? Quickly he reached the doorway and peered down the village street toward the village gate.

The natives were not yet in sight, though he could plainly hear them approaching across the plantation. They must be very near.

Like a flash he sprang across the opening to the pile of arrows. Gathering up all he could carry under one arm, he overturned the seething cauldron with a kick, and disappeared into the foliage above just as the first of the returning natives entered the gate at the far end of the village street. Then he turned to watch the proceeding below, poised like some wild bird ready to take swift wing at the first sign of danger.

The natives filed up the street, four of them bearing the dead body of Kulonga. Behind trailed the women, uttering strange cries and weird lamentation. On they came to the portals of Kulonga's hut, the very one in which Tarzan had wrought his depredations.

Scarcely had half a dozen entered the building ere they came rushing out in wild, jabbering confusion. The others hastened to gather about. There was much excited gesticulating, pointing, and chattering; then several of the warriors approached and peered within.

Finally an old fellow with many ornaments of metal about his arms and legs, and a necklace of dried human hands depending upon his chest, entered the hut.

It was Mbonga, the king, father of Kulonga.

For a few moments all was silent. Then Mbonga emerged, a look of mingled wrath and superstitious fear writ upon his hideous countenance. He spoke a few words to the assembled warriors, and in an instant the men were flying through the little village searching minutely every hut and corner within the palisades.

Scarcely had the search commenced than the overturned cauldron was discovered, and with it the theft of the poisoned arrows. Nothing more they found, and it was a thoroughly awed and frightened group of savages which huddled around their king a few moments later.

Mbonga could explain nothing of the strange events that had taken place. The finding of the still warm body of Kulonga – on the very verge of their fields and within easy earshot of the village – knifed and stripped at the door of his father's home, was in itself sufficiently mysterious, but these last awesome discoveries within the village, within the dead Kulonga's own hut, filled their hearts with dismay, and conjured in their poor brains only the most frightful of superstitious explanations.

They stood in little groups, talking in low tones, and ever casting affrighted glances behind them from their great rolling eyes.

Tarzan of the Apes watched them for a while from his lofty perch in the great tree. There was much in their demeanor which he could not understand, for of superstition he was ignorant, and of fear of any kind he had but a vague conception.

The sun was high in the heavens. Tarzan had not broken fast this day, and it was many miles to where lay the toothsome remains of Horta the boar.

So he turned his back upon the village of Mbonga and melted away into the leafy fastness of the forest.

CHAPTER ELEVEN

"King of the Apes"

IT WAS NOT YET DARK when he reached the tribe, though he stopped to exhume and devour the remains of the wild boar he had cached the preceding day, and again to take Kulonga's bow and arrows from the tree top in which he had hidden them.

It was a well-laden Tarzan who dropped from the branches into the midst of the tribe of Kerchak.

With swelling chest he narrated the glories of his adventure and exhibited the spoils of conquest.

Kerchak grunted and turned away, for he was jealous of this strange member of his band. In his little evil brain he sought for some excuse to wreak his hatred upon Tarzan.

The next day Tarzan was practicing with his bow and arrows at the first gleam of dawn. At first he lost nearly every bolt he shot, but finally he learned to guide the little shafts with fair accuracy, and ere a month had passed he was no mean shot; but his proficiency had cost him nearly his entire supply of arrows.

The tribe continued to find the hunting good in the vicinity of the beach, and so Tarzan of the Apes varied his archery practice with further investigation of his father's choice though little store of books.

It was during this period that the young English lord found hidden in the back of one of the cupboards in the cabin a small metal box. The key was in the lock, and a few moments of investigation and experimentation were rewarded with the successful opening of the receptacle.

In it he found a faded photograph of a smooth faced young man, a golden locket studded with diamonds, linked to a small gold chain, a few letters and a small book.

Tarzan examined these all minutely.

The photograph he liked most of all, for the eyes were smiling, and the face was open and frank. It was his father.

The locket, too, took his fancy, and he placed the chain about his neck in imitation of the ornamentation he had seen to be so common among the black men he had visited. The brilliant stones gleamed strangely against his smooth, brown hide.

The letters he could scarcely decipher for he had learned little or nothing of script, so he put them back in the box with the photograph and turned his attention to the book.

This was almost entirely filled with fine script, but while the little bugs were all familiar to him, their arrangement and the combinations in which they occurred were strange, and entirely incomprehensible.

Tarzan had long since learned the use of the dictionary, but much to his sorrow and perplexity it proved of no avail to him in this emergency. Not a word of all that was writ in the book could he find, and so he put it back in the metal box, but with a determination to work out the mysteries of it later on.

Little did he know that this book held between its covers the key to his origin – the answer to the strange riddle of his strange life. It was the diary of John Clayton, Lord Greystoke – kept in French, as had always been his custom.

Tarzan replaced the box in the cupboard, but always thereafter he carried the features of the strong, smiling face of his father in his heart, and in his head a fixed determination to solve the mystery of the strange words in the little black book.

At present he had more important business in hand, for his supply of arrows was exhausted, and he must needs journey to the black men's village and renew it.

Early the following morning he set out, and, traveling rapidly, he came before midday to the clearing. Once more he took up his position in the great tree, and, as before, he saw the women in the fields and the village street, and the cauldron of bubbling poison directly beneath him.

For hours he lay awaiting his opportunity to drop down unseen and gather up the arrows for which he had come; but nothing now occurred to call the villagers away from their homes. The day wore on, and still Tarzan of the Apes crouched above the unsuspecting woman at the cauldron.

Presently the workers in the fields returned. The hunting warriors emerged from the forest, and when all were within the palisade the gates were closed and barred.

Many cooking pots were now in evidence about the village. Before each hut a woman presided over a boiling stew, while little cakes of plantain, and cassava puddings were to be seen on every hand.

Suddenly there came a hail from the edge of the clearing.

Tarzan looked.

It was a party of belated hunters returning from the north, and among them they half led, half carried a struggling animal.

As they approached the village the gates were thrown open to admit them, and then, as the people saw the victim of the chase, a savage cry rose to the heavens, for the quarry was a man.

As he was dragged, still resisting, into the village street, the women and children set upon him with sticks and stones, and Tarzan of the Apes, young and savage beast of the jungle, wondered at the cruel brutality of his own kind.

Sheeta, the leopard, alone of all the jungle folk, tortured his prey. The ethics of all the others meted a quick and merciful death to their victims.

Tarzan had learned from his books but scattered fragments of the ways of human beings.

When he had followed Kulonga through the forest he had expected to come to a city of strange houses on wheels, puffing clouds of black smoke from a huge tree stuck in the roof of one of them – or to a sea covered with mighty floating buildings which he had learned were called, variously, ships and boats and steamers and craft.

He had been sorely disappointed with the poor little village of the blacks, hidden away in his own jungle, and with not a single house as large as his own cabin upon the distant beach.

He saw that these people were more wicked than his own apes, and as savage and cruel as Sabor, herself. Tarzan began to hold his own kind in low esteem.

Now they had tied their poor victim to a great post near the center of the village, directly before Mbonga's hut, and here they formed a dancing, yelling circle of warriors about him, alive with flashing knives and menacing spears.

In a larger circle squatted the women, yelling and beating upon drums. It reminded Tarzan of the Dum-Dum, and so he knew what to expect. He wondered if they would spring upon their meat while it was still alive. The Apes did not do such things as that.

The circle of warriors about the cringing captive drew closer and closer to their prey as they danced in wild and savage abandon to the maddening music of the drums. Presently a spear reached out and pricked the victim. It was the signal for fifty others.

Eyes, ears, arms and legs were pierced; every inch of the poor writhing body that did not cover a vital organ became the target of the cruel lancers.

The women and children shrieked their delight.

The warriors licked their hideous lips in anticipation of the feast to come, and vied with one another in the savagery and loathsomeness of the cruel indignities with which they tortured the still conscious prisoner.

Then it was that Tarzan of the Apes saw his chance. All eyes were fixed upon the thrilling spectacle at the stake. The light of day had given place to the darkness of a moonless night, and only the fires in the immediate vicinity of the orgy had been kept alight to cast a restless glow upon the restless scene.

Gently the lithe boy dropped to the soft earth at the end of the village street. Quickly he gathered up the arrows – all of them this time, for he had brought a number of long fibers to bind them into a bundle.

Without haste he wrapped them securely, and then, ere he turned to leave, the devil of capriciousness entered his heart. He looked about for some hint of a wild prank to play upon these strange, grotesque creatures that they might be again aware of his presence among them.

Dropping his bundle of arrows at the foot of the tree, Tarzan crept among the shadows at the side of the street until he came to the same hut he had entered on the occasion of his first visit.

Inside all was darkness, but his groping hands soon found the object for which he sought, and without further delay he turned again toward the door.

He had taken but a step, however, ere his quick ear caught the sound of approaching footsteps immediately without. In another instant the figure of a woman darkened the entrance of the hut.

Tarzan drew back silently to the far wall, and his hand sought the long, keen hunting knife of his father. The woman came quickly to the center of the hut. There she paused for an instant feeling about with her hands for the thing she sought. Evidently it was not in its accustomed place, for she explored ever nearer and nearer the wall where Tarzan stood.

So close was she now that the ape-man felt the animal warmth of her naked body. Up went the hunting knife, and then the woman turned to one side and soon a guttural "ah" proclaimed that her search had at last been successful.

Immediately she turned and left the hut, and as she passed through the doorway Tarzan saw that she carried a cooking pot in her hand.

He followed closely after her, and as he reconnoitered from the shadows of the doorway he saw that all the women of the village were hastening to and from the various huts with pots and kettles. These they were filling with water and placing over a number of fires near the stake where the dying victim now hung, an inert and bloody mass of suffering.

Choosing a moment when none seemed near, Tarzan hastened to his bundle of arrows beneath the great tree at the end of the village street. As on the former occasion he overthrew the cauldron before leaping, sinuous and catlike, into the lower branches of the forest giant.

Silently he climbed to a great height until he found a point where he could look through a leafy opening upon the scene beneath him.

The women were now preparing the prisoner for their cooking pots, while the men stood about resting after the fatigue of their mad revel. Comparative quiet reigned in the village.

Tarzan raised aloft the thing he had pilfered from the hut, and, with aim made true by years of fruit and coconut throwing, launched it toward the group of savages.

Squarely among them it fell, striking one of the warriors full upon the head and felling him to the ground. Then it rolled among the women and stopped beside the half-butchered thing they were preparing to feast upon.

All gazed in consternation at it for an instant, and then, with one accord, broke and ran for their huts.

It was a grinning human skull which looked up at them from the ground. The dropping of the thing out of the open sky was a miracle well aimed to work upon their superstitious fears.

Thus Tarzan of the Apes left them filled with terror at this new manifestation of the presence of some unseen and unearthly evil power which lurked in the forest about their village.

Later, when they discovered the overturned cauldron, and that once more their arrows had been pilfered, it commenced to dawn upon them that they had offended some great god by placing their village in this part of the jungle without propitiating him. From then on an offering of food was daily placed below the great tree from whence the arrows had disappeared in an effort to conciliate the mighty one.

But the seed of fear was deep sown, and had he but known it, Tarzan of the Apes had laid the foundation for much future misery for himself and his tribe.

That night he slept in the forest not far from the village, and early the next morning set out slowly on his homeward march, hunting as he traveled. Only a few berries and an occasional grub worm rewarded his search, and he was half famished when, looking up from a log he had been rooting beneath, he saw Sabor, the lioness, standing in the center of the trail not twenty paces from him.

The great yellow eyes were fixed upon him with a wicked and baleful gleam, and the red tongue licked the longing lips as Sabor crouched, worming her stealthy way with belly flattened against the earth.

Tarzan did not attempt to escape. He welcomed the opportunity for which, in fact, he had been searching for days past, now that he was armed with something more than a rope of grass.

Quickly he unslung his bow and fitted a well-daubed arrow, and as Sabor sprang, the tiny missile leaped to meet her in mid-air. At the same instant Tarzan of the Apes jumped to one side, and as the great cat struck the ground beyond him another death-tipped arrow sunk deep into Sabor's loin.

With a mighty roar the beast turned and charged once more, only to be met with a third arrow full in one eye; but this time she was too close to the ape-man for the latter to sidestep the onrushing body.

Tarzan of the Apes went down beneath the great body of his enemy, but with gleaming knife drawn and striking home. For a moment they lay there, and then Tarzan realized that the inert mass lying upon him was beyond power ever again to injure man or ape.

With difficulty he wriggled from beneath the great weight, and as he stood erect and gazed down upon the trophy of his skill, a mighty wave of exultation swept over him.

With swelling breast, he placed a foot upon the body of his powerful enemy, and throwing back his fine young head, roared out the awful challenge of the victorious bull ape.

The forest echoed to the savage and triumphant paean. Birds fell still, and the larger animals and beasts of prey slunk stealthily away, for few there were of all the jungle who sought for trouble with the great anthropoids.

And in London another Lord Greystoke was speaking to *his* kind in the House of Lords, but none trembled at the sound of his soft voice.

Sabor proved unsavory eating even to Tarzan of the Apes, but hunger served as a most efficacious disguise to toughness and rank taste, and ere long, with well-filled stomach, the ape-man was ready to sleep again. First, however, he must remove the hide, for it was as much for this as for any other purpose that he had desired to destroy Sabor.

Deftly he removed the great pelt, for he had practiced often on smaller animals. When the task was finished he carried his trophy to the fork of a high tree, and there, curling himself securely in a crotch, he fell into deep and dreamless slumber.

What with loss of sleep, arduous exercise, and a full belly, Tarzan of the Apes slept the sun around, awakening about noon of the following day. He straightway repaired to the carcass of Sabor, but was angered to find the bones picked clean by other hungry denizens of the jungle.

Half an hour's leisurely progress through the forest brought to sight a young deer, and before the little creature knew that an enemy was near a tiny arrow had lodged in its neck.

So quickly the virus worked that at the end of a dozen leaps the deer plunged headlong into the undergrowth, dead. Again did Tarzan feast well, but this time he did not sleep.

Instead, he hastened on toward the point where he had left the tribe, and when he had found them proudly exhibited the skin of Sabor, the lioness.

"Look!" he cried, "Apes of Kerchak. See what Tarzan, the mighty killer, has done. Who else among you has ever killed one of Numa's people? Tarzan is mightiest amongst you for Tarzan is no ape. Tarzan is – " But here he stopped, for in the language of the anthropoids there was no word for man, and Tarzan could only write the word in English; he could not pronounce it.

The tribe had gathered about to look upon the proof of his wondrous prowess, and to listen to his words.

Only Kerchak hung back, nursing his hatred and his rage.

Suddenly something snapped in the wicked little brain of the anthropoid. With a frightful roar the great beast sprang among the assemblage.

Biting, and striking with his huge hands, he killed and maimed a dozen ere the balance could escape to the upper terraces of the forest.

Frothing and shrieking in the insanity of his fury, Kerchak looked about for the object of his greatest hatred, and there, upon a near-by limb, he saw him sitting.

"Come down, Tarzan, great killer," cried Kerchak. "Come down and feel the fangs of a greater! Do mighty fighters fly to the trees at the first approach of danger?" And then Kerchak emitted the volleying challenge of his kind.

Quietly Tarzan dropped to the ground. Breathlessly the tribe watched from their lofty perches as Kerchak, still roaring, charged the relatively puny figure.

Nearly seven feet stood Kerchak on his short legs. His enormous shoulders were bunched and rounded with huge muscles. The back of his short neck was as a single lump of iron sinew which bulged beyond the base of his skull, so that his head seemed like a small ball protruding from a huge mountain of flesh.

His back-drawn, snarling lips exposed his great fighting fangs, and his little, wicked, blood-shot eyes gleamed in horrid reflection of his madness.

Awaiting him stood Tarzan, himself a mighty muscled animal, but his six feet of height and his great rolling sinews seemed pitifully inadequate to the ordeal which awaited them.

His bow and arrows lay some distance away where he had dropped them while showing Sabor's hide to his fellow apes, so that he confronted Kerchak now with only his hunting knife and his superior intellect to offset the ferocious strength of his enemy.

As his antagonist came roaring toward him, Lord Greystoke tore his long knife from its sheath, and with an answering challenge as horrid and bloodcurdling as that of the beast he faced, rushed swiftly to meet the attack. He was too shrewd to allow those long hairy arms to encircle him, and just as their bodies were about to crash together, Tarzan of the Apes grasped one of the huge wrists of his assailant, and, springing lightly to one side, drove his knife to the hilt into Kerchak's body, below the heart.

Before he could wrench the blade free again, the bull's quick lunge to seize him in those awful arms had torn the weapon from Tarzan's grasp.

Kerchak aimed a terrific blow at the ape-man's head with the flat of his hand, a blow which, had it landed, might easily have crushed in the side of Tarzan's skull.

The man was too quick, and, ducking beneath it, himself delivered a mighty one, with clenched fist, in the pit of Kerchak's stomach.

The ape was staggered, and what with the mortal wound in his side had almost collapsed, when, with one mighty effort he rallied for an instant – just long enough to enable him to wrest his arm free from Tarzan's grasp and close in a terrific clinch with his wiry opponent.

Straining the ape-man close to him, his great jaws sought Tarzan's throat, but the young lord's sinewy fingers were at Kerchak's own before the cruel fangs could close on the sleek brown skin.

Thus they struggled, the one to crush out his opponent's life with those awful teeth, the other to close forever the windpipe beneath his strong grasp while he held the snarling mouth from him.

The greater strength of the ape was slowly prevailing, and the teeth of the straining beast were scarce an inch from Tarzan's throat when, with a shuddering tremor, the great body stiffened for an instant and then sank limply to the ground.

Kerchak was dead.

Withdrawing the knife that had so often rendered him master of far mightier muscles than his own, Tarzan of the Apes placed his foot upon the neck of his vanquished enemy, and once again, loud through the forest rang the fierce, wild cry of the conqueror.

And thus came the young Lord Greystoke into the kingship of the Apes.

CHAPTER TWELVE

Man's Reason

There was one of the tribe of Tarzan who questioned his authority, and that was Terkoz, the son of Tublat, but he so feared the keen knife and the deadly arrows of his new lord that he confined the manifestation of his objections to petty disobediences and irritating mannerisms; Tarzan knew, however, that he but waited his opportunity to wrest the kingship from him by some sudden stroke of treachery, and so he was ever on his guard against surprise.

For months the life of the little band went on much as it had before, except that Tarzan's greater intelligence and his ability as a hunter were the means of providing for them more bountifully than ever before. Most of them, therefore, were more than content with the change in rulers.

Tarzan led them by night to the fields of the black men, and there, warned by their chief's superior wisdom, they ate only what they required, nor ever did they destroy what they could not eat, as is the way of Manu, the monkey, and of most apes.

So, while the blacks were wroth at the continued pilfering of their fields, they were not discouraged in their efforts to cultivate the land, as would have been the case had Tarzan permitted his people to lay waste the plantation wantonly.

During this period Tarzan paid many nocturnal visits to the village, where he often renewed his supply of arrows. He soon noticed the food always standing at the foot of the tree which was his avenue into the palisade, and after a little, he commenced to eat whatever the blacks put there.

When the awe-struck savages saw that the food disappeared overnight they were filled with consternation and dread, for it was one thing to put food out to propitiate a god or a devil, but quite another thing to have the spirit really come into the village and eat it. Such a thing was unheard of, and it clouded their superstitious minds with all manner of vague fears.

Nor was this all. The periodic disappearance of their arrows, and the strange pranks perpetrated by unseen hands, had wrought them to such a state that life had become a veritable burden in their new home, and now it was that Mbonga and his head men began to talk of abandoning the village and seeking a site farther on in the jungle.

Presently the black warriors began to strike farther and farther south into the heart of the forest when they went to hunt, looking for a site for a new village.

More often was the tribe of Tarzan disturbed by these wandering huntsmen. Now was the quiet, fierce solitude of the primeval forest broken by new, strange cries. No longer was there safety for bird or beast. Man had come.

Other animals passed up and down the jungle by day and by night – fierce, cruel beasts – but their weaker neighbors only fled from their immediate vicinity to return again when the danger was past.

With man it is different. When he comes many of the larger animals instinctively leave the district entirely, seldom if ever to return; and thus it has always been with the great anthropoids. They flee man as man flees a pestilence.

For a short time the tribe of Tarzan lingered in the vicinity of the beach because their new chief hated the thought of leaving the treasured contents of the little cabin forever. But when one day a member of the tribe discovered the blacks in great numbers on the banks of a little stream that had been their watering place for generations, and in the act of clearing a space in the jungle and erecting many huts, the apes would remain no longer; and so Tarzan led them inland for many marches to a spot as yet undefiled by the foot of a human being.

Once every moon Tarzan would go swinging rapidly back through the swaying branches to have a day with his books, and to replenish his supply of arrows. This latter task was becoming more and more difficult, for the blacks had taken to hiding their supply away at night in granaries and living huts.

This necessitated watching by day on Tarzan's part to discover where the arrows were being concealed.

Twice had he entered huts at night while the inmates lay sleeping upon their mats, and stolen the arrows from the very sides of the warriors. But this method he realized to be too fraught with danger, and so he commenced picking up solitary hunters with his long, deadly noose, stripping them of weapons and ornaments and dropping their bodies from a high tree into the village street during the still watches of the night.

These various escapades again so terrorized the blacks that, had it not been for the monthly respite between Tarzan's visits, in which they had opportunity to renew hope that each fresh incursion would prove the last, they soon would have abandoned their new village.

The blacks had not as yet come upon Tarzan's cabin on the distant beach, but the ape-man lived in constant dread that, while he was away with the tribe, they would discover and despoil his treasure. So it came that he spent more and more time in the vicinity of his father's last home, and less and less with the tribe. Presently the members of his little community began to suffer on account of his neglect, for disputes and quarrels constantly arose which only the king might settle peaceably.

At last some of the older apes spoke to Tarzan on the subject, and for a month thereafter he remained constantly with the tribe.

The duties of kingship among the anthropoids are not many or arduous.

In the afternoon comes Thaka, possibly, to complain that old Mungo has stolen his new wife. Then must Tarzan summon all before him, and if he finds that the wife prefers her new lord he commands that matters remain as they are, or possibly that Mungo give Thaka one of his daughters in exchange.

Whatever his decision, the apes accept it as final, and return to their occupations satisfied.

Then comes Tana, shrieking and holding tight her side from which blood is streaming. Gunto, her husband, has cruelly bitten her! And Gunto, summoned, says that Tana is lazy and will not bring him nuts and beetles, or scratch his back for him.

So Tarzan scolds them both and threatens Gunto with a taste of the death-bearing slivers if he abuses Tana further, and Tana, for her part, is compelled to promise better attention to her wifely duties.

And so it goes, little family differences for the most part, which, if left unsettled would result finally in greater factional strife, and the eventual dismemberment of the tribe.

But Tarzan tired of it, as he found that kingship meant the curtailment of his liberty. He longed for the little cabin and the sun-kissed sea – for the cool interior of the well-built house, and for the never-ending wonders of the many books.

As he had grown older, he found that he had grown away from his people. Their interests and his were far removed. They had not kept pace with him, nor could they understand aught of the many strange and wonderful dreams that passed through the active brain of their human king. So limited was their vocabulary that Tarzan could not even talk with them of the many new truths, and the great fields of thought that his reading had opened up before his longing eyes, or make known ambitions which stirred his soul.

Among the tribe he no longer had friends as of old. A little child may find companionship in many strange and simple creatures, but to a grown man there must be some semblance of equality in intellect as the basis for agreeable association.

Had Kala lived, Tarzan would have sacrificed all else to remain near her, but now that she was dead, and the playful friends of his childhood grown into fierce and surly brutes he felt that he much preferred the peace and solitude of his cabin to the irksome duties of leadership amongst a horde of wild beasts.

The hatred and jealousy of Terkoz, son of Tublat, did much to counteract the effect of Tarzan's desire to renounce his kingship among the apes, for, stubborn young Englishman that he was, he could not bring himself to retreat in the face of so malignant an enemy.

That Terkoz would be chosen leader in his stead he knew full well, for time and again the ferocious brute had established his claim to physical supremacy over the few bull apes who had dared resent his savage bullying.

Tarzan would have liked to subdue the ugly beast without recourse to knife or arrows. So much had his great strength and agility increased in the period following his maturity that he had come to believe that he might master the redoubtable Terkoz in a hand to hand fight were it not for the terrible advantage the anthropoid's huge fighting fangs gave him over the poorly armed Tarzan.

The entire matter was taken out of Tarzan's hands one day by force of circumstances, and his future left open to him, so that he might go or stay without any stain upon his savage escutcheon.

It happened thus:

The tribe was feeding quietly, spread over a considerable area, when a great screaming arose some distance east of where Tarzan lay upon his belly beside a limpid brook, attempting to catch an elusive fish in his quick, brown hands.

With one accord the tribe swung rapidly toward the frightened cries, and there found Terkoz holding an old female by the hair and beating her unmercifully with his great hands.

As Tarzan approached he raised his hand aloft for Terkoz to desist, for the female was not his, but belonged to a poor old ape whose fighting days were long over, and who, therefore, could not protect his family.

Terkoz knew that it was against the laws of his kind to strike this woman of another, but being a bully, he had taken advantage of the weakness of the female's husband to chastise her because she had refused to give up to him a tender young rodent she had captured.

When Terkoz saw Tarzan approaching without his arrows, he continued to belabor the poor woman in a studied effort to affront his hated chieftain.

Tarzan did not repeat his warning signal, but instead rushed bodily upon the waiting Terkoz.

Never had the ape-man fought so terrible a battle since that long-gone day when Bolgani, the great king gorilla had so horribly manhandled him ere the new-found knife had, by accident, pricked the savage heart.

Tarzan's knife on the present occasion but barely offset the gleaming fangs of Terkoz, and what little advantage the ape had over the man in brute strength was almost balanced by the latter's wonderful quickness and agility.

In the sum total of their points, however, the anthropoid had a shade the better of the battle, and had there been no other personal attribute to influence the final outcome, Tarzan of the Apes, the young Lord Greystoke, would have died as he had lived – an unknown savage beast in equatorial Africa.

But there was that which had raised him far above his fellows of the jungle – that little spark which spells the whole vast difference between man and brute – Reason. This it was which saved him from death beneath the iron muscles and tearing fangs of Terkoz.

Scarcely had they fought a dozen seconds ere they were rolling upon the ground, striking, tearing and rending – two great savage beasts battling to the death.

Terkoz had a dozen knife wounds on head and breast, and Tarzan was torn and bleeding – his scalp in one place half torn from his head so that a great piece hung down over one eye, obstructing his vision.

But so far the young Englishman had been able to keep those horrible fangs from his jugular and now, as they fought less fiercely for a moment, to regain their breath, Tarzan formed a cunning plan. He would work his way to the other's back and, clinging there with tooth and nail, drive his knife home until Terkoz was no more.

The maneuver was accomplished more easily than he had hoped, for the stupid beast, not knowing what Tarzan was attempting, made no particular effort to prevent the accomplishment of the design.

But when, finally, he realized that his antagonist was fastened to him where his teeth and fists alike were useless against him, Terkoz hurled himself about upon the ground so violently that Tarzan could but cling desperately to the leaping, turning, twisting body, and ere he had struck a blow the knife was hurled from his hand by a heavy impact against the earth, and Tarzan found himself defenseless.

During the rollings and squirmings of the next few minutes, Tarzan's hold was loosened a dozen times until finally an accidental circumstance of those swift and everchanging evolutions gave him a new hold with his right hand, which he realized was absolutely unassailable.

His arm was passed beneath Terkoz's arm from behind and his hand and forearm encircled the back of Terkoz's neck. It was the half-Nelson of modern wrestling which the untaught ape-man had stumbled upon, but superior reason showed him in an instant the value of the thing he had discovered. It was the difference to him between life and death.

And so he struggled to encompass a similar hold with the left hand, and in a few moments Terkoz's bull neck was creaking beneath a full-Nelson.

There was no more lunging about now. The two lay perfectly still upon the ground, Tarzan upon Terkoz's back. Slowly the bullet head of the ape was being forced lower and lower upon his chest.

Tarzan knew what the result would be. In an instant the neck would break. Then there came to Terkoz's rescue the same thing that had put him in these sore straits – a man's reasoning power.

"If I kill him," thought Tarzan, "what advantage will it be to me? Will it not rob the tribe of a great fighter? And if Terkoz be dead, he will know nothing of my supremacy, while alive he will ever be an example to the other apes."

"*Ka-Goda*?" hissed Tarzan in Terkoz's ear, which, in ape tongue, means, freely translated: "Do you surrender?"

For a moment there was no reply, and Tarzan added a few more ounces of pressure, which elicited a horrified shriek of pain from the great beast.

"*Ka-goda*?" repeated Tarzan.

"*Ka-goda*!" cried Terkoz.

"Listen," said Tarzan, easing up a trifle, but not releasing his hold. "I am Tarzan, King of the Apes, mighty hunter, mighty fighter. In all the jungle there is none so great.

"You have said: '*Ka-goda*' to me. All the tribe have heard. Quarrel no more with your king or your people, for next time I shall kill you. Do you understand?"

"*Huh*," assented Terkoz.

"And you are satisfied?"

"*Huh*," said the ape.

Tarzan let him up, and in a few minutes all were back at their vocations, as though naught had occurred to mar the tranquility of their primeval forest haunts.

But deep in the minds of the apes was rooted the conviction that Tarzan was a mighty fighter and a strange creature. Strange because he had had it in his power to kill his enemy, but had allowed him to live – unharmed.

That afternoon as the tribe came together, as was their wont before darkness settled on the jungle, Tarzan, his wounds washed in the waters of the stream, called the old males about him.

"You have seen again to-day that Tarzan of the Apes is the greatest among you," he said.

"*Huh*," they replied with one voice, "Tarzan is great."

"Tarzan," he continued, "is not an ape. He is not like his people. His ways are not their ways, and so Tarzan is going back to the lair of his own kind by the waters of the great lake which has no farther shore. You must choose another to rule you, for Tarzan will not return."

And thus young Lord Greystoke took the first step toward the goal which he had set – the finding of other white men like himself.

CHAPTER THIRTEEN

His Own Kind

THE FOLLOWING MORNING, Tarzan, lame and sore from the wounds of his battle with Terkoz, set out toward the west and the seacoast.

He traveled very slowly, sleeping in the jungle at night, and reaching his cabin late the following morning.

For several days he moved about but little, only enough to gather what fruits and nuts he required to satisfy the demands of hunger.

In ten days he was quite sound again, except for a terrible, half-healed scar, which, starting above his left eye ran across the top of his head, ending at the right ear. It was the mark left by Terkoz when he had torn the scalp away.

During his convalescence Tarzan tried to fashion a mantle from the skin of Sabor, which had lain all this time in the cabin. But he found the hide had dried as stiff as a board, and as he knew naught of tanning, he was forced to abandon his cherished plan.

Then he determined to filch what few garments he could from one of the black men of Mbonga's village, for Tarzan of the Apes had decided to mark his evolution from the lower orders in every possible manner, and nothing seemed to him a more distinguishing badge of manhood than ornaments and clothing.

To this end, therefore, he collected the various arm and leg ornaments he had taken from the black warriors who had succumbed to his swift and silent noose, and donned them all after the way he had seen them worn.

About his neck hung the golden chain from which depended the diamond encrusted locket of his mother, the Lady Alice. At his back was a quiver of arrows slung from a leathern shoulder belt, another piece of loot from some vanquished black.

About his waist was a belt of tiny strips of rawhide fashioned by himself as a support for the home-made scabbard in which hung his father's hunting knife. The long bow which had been Kulonga's hung over his left shoulder.

The young Lord Greystoke was indeed a strange and war-like figure, his mass of black hair falling to his shoulders behind and cut with his hunting knife to a rude bang upon his forehead, that it might not fall before his eyes.

His straight and perfect figure, muscled as the best of the ancient Roman gladiators must have been muscled, and yet with the soft and sinuous curves of a Greek god, told at a glance the wondrous combination of enormous strength with suppleness and speed.

A personification, was Tarzan of the Apes, of the primitive man, the hunter, the warrior.

With the noble poise of his handsome head upon those broad shoulders, and the fire of life and intelligence in those fine, clear eyes, he might readily have typified some demigod of a wild and warlike bygone people of his ancient forest.

But of these things Tarzan did not think. He was worried because he had not clothing to indicate to all the jungle folks that he was a man and not an ape, and grave doubt often entered his mind as to whether he might not yet become an ape.

Was not hair commencing to grow upon his face? All the apes had hair upon theirs but the black men were entirely hairless, with very few exceptions.

True, he had seen pictures in his books of men with great masses of hair upon lip and cheek and chin, but, nevertheless, Tarzan was afraid. Almost daily he whetted his keen knife and scraped and whittled at his young beard to eradicate this degrading emblem of apehood.

And so he learned to shave – rudely and painfully, it is true – but, nevertheless, effectively.

When he felt quite strong again, after his bloody battle with Terkoz, Tarzan set off one morning towards Mbonga's village. He was moving carelessly along a winding jungle trail, instead of making his progress through the trees, when suddenly he came face to face with a black warrior.

The look of surprise on the savage face was almost comical, and before Tarzan could unsling his bow the fellow had turned and fled down the path crying out in alarm as though to others before him.

Tarzan took to the trees in pursuit, and in a few moments came in view of the men desperately striving to escape.

There were three of them, and they were racing madly in single file through the dense undergrowth.

Tarzan easily distanced them, nor did they see his silent passage above their heads, nor note the crouching figure squatted upon a low branch ahead of them beneath which the trail led them.

Tarzan let the first two pass beneath him, but as the third came swiftly on, the quiet noose dropped about the black throat. A quick jerk drew it taut.

There was an agonized scream from the victim, and his fellows turned to see his struggling body rise as by magic slowly into the dense foliage of the trees above.

With frightened shrieks they wheeled once more and plunged on in their efforts to escape.

Tarzan dispatched his prisoner quickly and silently; removed the weapons and ornaments, and – oh, the greatest joy of all – a handsome deerskin breechcloth, which he quickly transferred to his own person.

Now indeed was he dressed as a man should be. None there was who could now doubt his high origin. How he should have liked to have returned to the tribe to parade before their envious gaze this wondrous finery.

Taking the body across his shoulder, he moved more slowly through the trees toward the little palisaded village, for he again needed arrows.

As he approached quite close to the enclosure he saw an excited group surrounding the two fugitives, who, trembling with fright and exhaustion, were scarce able to recount the uncanny details of their adventure.

Mirando, they said, who had been ahead of them a short distance, had suddenly come screaming toward them, crying that a terrible white and naked warrior was pursuing him. The three of them had hurried toward the village as rapidly as their legs would carry them.

Again Mirando's shrill cry of mortal terror had caused them to look back, and there they had seen the most horrible sight – their companion's body flying upwards into the trees, his arms and legs beating the air and his tongue protruding from his open mouth. No other sound did he utter nor was there any creature in sight about him.

The villagers were worked up into a state of fear bordering on panic, but wise old Mbonga affected to feel considerable skepticism regarding the tale, and attributed the whole fabrication to their fright in the face of some real danger.

"You tell us this great story," he said, "because you do not dare to speak the truth. You do not dare admit that when the lion sprang upon Mirando you ran away and left him. You are cowards."

Scarcely had Mbonga ceased speaking when a great crashing of branches in the trees above them caused the blacks to look up in renewed terror. The sight that met their eyes made even wise old Mbonga shudder, for there, turning and twisting in the air, came the dead body of Mirando, to sprawl with a sickening reverberation upon the ground at their feet.

With one accord the blacks took to their heels; nor did they stop until the last of them was lost in the dense shadows of the surrounding jungle.

Again Tarzan came down into the village and renewed his supply of arrows and ate of the offering of food which the blacks had made to appease his wrath.

Before he left he carried the body of Mirando to the gate of the village, and propped it up against the palisade in such a way that the dead face seemed to be peering around the edge of the gatepost down the path which led to the jungle.

Then Tarzan returned, hunting, always hunting, to the cabin by the beach.

It took a dozen attempts on the part of the thoroughly frightened blacks to reenter their village, past the horrible, grinning face of their dead fellow, and when they found the food and arrows gone they knew, what they had only too well feared, that Mirando had seen the evil spirit of the jungle.

That now seemed to them the logical explanation. Only those who saw this terrible god of the jungle died; for was it not true that none left alive in the village had ever seen him? Therefore, those who had died at his hands must have seen him and paid the penalty with their lives.

As long as they supplied him with arrows and food he would not harm them unless they looked upon him, so it was ordered by Mbonga that in addition to the food offering there should also be laid out an offering of arrows for this Munan-go-Keewati, and this was done from then on.

If you ever chance to pass that far off African village you will still see before a tiny thatched hut, built just without the village, a little iron pot in which is a quantity of food, and beside it a quiver of well-daubed arrows.

When Tarzan came in sight of the beach where stood his cabin, a strange and unusual spectacle met his vision.

On the placid waters of the landlocked harbor floated a great ship, and on the beach a small boat was drawn up.

But, most wonderful of all, a number of white men like himself were moving about between the beach and his cabin.

Tarzan saw that in many ways they were like the men of his picture books. He crept closer through the trees until he was quite close above them.

There were ten men, swarthy, sun-tanned, villainous looking fellows. Now they had congregated by the boat and were talking in loud, angry tones, with much gesticulating and shaking of fists.

Presently one of them, a little, mean-faced, black-bearded fellow with a countenance which reminded Tarzan of Pamba, the rat, laid his hand upon the shoulder of a giant who stood next him, and with whom all the others had been arguing and quarreling.

The little man pointed inland, so that the giant was forced to turn away from the others to look in the direction indicated. As he turned, the little, mean-faced man drew a revolver from his belt and shot the giant in the back.

The big fellow threw his hands above his head, his knees bent beneath him, and without a sound he tumbled forward upon the beach, dead.

The report of the weapon, the first that Tarzan had ever heard, filled him with wonderment, but even this unaccustomed sound could not startle his healthy nerves into even a semblance of panic.

The conduct of the white strangers it was that caused him the greatest perturbation. He puckered his brows into a frown of deep thought. It was well, thought he, that he had not given way to his first impulse to rush forward and greet these white men as brothers.

They were evidently no different from the black men – no more civilized than the apes – no less cruel than Sabor.

For a moment the others stood looking at the little, mean-faced man and the giant lying dead upon the beach.

Then one of them laughed and slapped the little man upon the back. There was much more talk and gesticulating, but less quarreling.

Presently they launched the boat and all jumped into it and rowed away toward the great ship, where Tarzan could see other figures moving about upon the deck.

When they had clambered aboard, Tarzan dropped to earth behind a great tree and crept to his cabin, keeping it always between himself and the ship.

Slipping in at the door he found that everything had been ransacked. His books and pencils strewed the floor. His weapons and shields and other little store of treasures were littered about.

As he saw what had been done a great wave of anger surged through him, and the new made scar upon his forehead stood suddenly out, a bar of inflamed crimson against his tawny hide.

Quickly he ran to the cupboard and searched in the far recess of the lower shelf. Ah! He breathed a sigh of relief as he drew out the little tin box, and, opening it, found his greatest treasures undisturbed.

The photograph of the smiling, strong-faced young man, and the little black puzzle book were safe.

What was that?

His quick ear had caught a faint but unfamiliar sound.

Running to the window Tarzan looked toward the harbor, and there he saw that a boat was being lowered from the great ship beside the one already in the water. Soon he saw many people clambering over the sides of the larger vessel and dropping into the boats. They were coming back in full force.

For a moment longer Tarzan watched while a number of boxes and bundles were lowered into the waiting boats, then, as they shoved off from the ship's side, the ape-man snatched up a piece of paper, and with a pencil printed on it for a few moments until it bore several lines of strong, well-made, almost letter-perfect characters.

This notice he stuck upon the door with a small sharp splinter of wood. Then gathering up his precious tin box, his arrows, and as many bows and spears as he could carry, he hastened through the door and disappeared into the forest.

When the two boats were beached upon the silvery sand it was a strange assortment of humanity that clambered ashore.

Some twenty souls in all there were, fifteen of them rough and villainous appearing seamen.

The others of the party were of different stamp.

One was an elderly man, with white hair and large rimmed spectacles. His slightly stooped shoulders were draped in an ill-fitting, though immaculate, frock coat, and a shiny silk hat added to the incongruity of his garb in an African jungle.

The second member of the party to land was a tall young man in white ducks, while directly behind came another elderly man with a very high forehead and a fussy, excitable manner.

After these came a huge Negress clothed like Solomon as to colors. Her great eyes rolled in evident terror, first toward the jungle and then toward the cursing band of sailors who were removing the bales and boxes from the boats.

The last member of the party to disembark was a girl of about nineteen, and it was the young man who stood at the boat's prow to lift her high and dry upon land. She gave him a brave and pretty smile of thanks, but no words passed between them.

In silence the party advanced toward the cabin. It was evident that whatever their intentions, all had been decided upon before they left the ship; and so they came to the door, the sailors carrying the boxes and bales, followed by the five who were of so different a class. The men put down their burdens, and then one caught sight of the notice which Tarzan had posted.

"Ho, mates!" he cried. "What's here? This sign was not posted an hour ago or I'll eat the cook."

The others gathered about, craning their necks over the shoulders of those before them, but as few of them could read at all, and then only after the most laborious fashion, one finally turned to the little old man of the top hat and frock coat.

"Hi, perfesser," he called, "step for'rd and read the bloomin' notis."

Thus addressed, the old man came slowly to where the sailors stood, followed by the other members of his party. Adjusting his spectacles he looked for a moment at the placard and then, turning away, strolled off muttering to himself: "Most remarkable – most remarkable!"

"Hi, old fossil," cried the man who had first called on him for assistance, "did je think we wanted of you to read the bloomin' notis to yourself? Come back here and read it out loud, you old barnacle."

The old man stopped and, turning back, said: "Oh, yes, my dear sir, a thousand pardons. It was quite thoughtless of me, yes – very thoughtless. Most remarkable – most remarkable!"

Again he faced the notice and read it through, and doubtless would have turned off again to ruminate upon it had not the sailor grasped him roughly by the collar and howled into his ear.

"Read it out loud, you blithering old idiot."

"Ah, yes indeed, yes indeed," replied the professor softly, and adjusting his spectacles once more he read aloud:

THIS IS THE HOUSE OF TARZAN, THE
KILLER OF BEASTS AND MANY BLACK
MEN. DO NOT HARM THE THINGS WHICH
ARE TARZAN'S. TARZAN WATCHES.
TARZAN OF THE APES.

"Who the devil is Tarzan?" cried the sailor who had before spoken.

"He evidently speaks English," said the young man.

"But what does 'Tarzan of the Apes' mean?" cried the girl.

"I do not know, Miss Porter," replied the young man, "unless we have discovered a runaway simian from the London Zoo who has brought back a European education to his jungle home. What do you make of it, Professor Porter?" he added, turning to the old man.

Professor Archimedes Q. Porter adjusted his spectacles.

"Ah, yes, indeed; yes indeed – most remarkable, most remarkable!" said the professor; "but I can add nothing further to what I have already remarked in elucidation of this truly momentous occurrence," and the professor turned slowly in the direction of the jungle.

"But, papa," cried the girl, "you haven't said anything about it yet."

"Tut, tut, child; tut, tut," responded Professor Porter, in a kindly and indulgent tone, "do not trouble your pretty head with such weighty and abstruse problems," and again he wandered slowly off in still another direction, his eyes bent upon the ground at his feet, his hands clasped behind him beneath the flowing tails of his coat.

"I reckon the daffy old bounder don't know no more'n we do about it," growled the rat-faced sailor.

"Keep a civil tongue in your head," cried the young man, his face paling in anger, at the insulting tone of the sailor. "You've murdered our officers and robbed us. We are absolutely in your power, but you'll treat Professor Porter and Miss Porter with respect or I'll break that vile neck of yours with my bare hands – guns or no guns," and the young fellow stepped so close to the rat-faced sailor that the latter, though he bore two revolvers and a villainous looking knife in his belt, slunk back abashed.

"You damned coward," cried the young man. "You'd never dare shoot a man until his back was turned. You don't dare shoot me even then," and he deliberately turned his back full upon the sailor and walked nonchalantly away as if to put him to the test.

The sailor's hand crept slyly to the butt of one of his revolvers; his wicked eyes glared vengefully at the retreating form of the young Englishman. The gaze of his fellows was upon him, but still he hesitated. At heart he was even a greater coward than Mr. William Cecil Clayton had imagined.

Two keen eyes had watched every move of the party from the foliage of a nearby tree. Tarzan had seen the surprise caused by his notice, and while he could understand nothing of the spoken language of these strange people their gestures and facial expressions told him much.

The act of the little rat-faced sailor in killing one of his comrades had aroused a strong dislike in Tarzan, and now that he saw him quarreling with the fine-looking young man his animosity was still further stirred.

Tarzan had never seen the effects of a firearm before, though his books had taught him something of them, but when he saw the rat-faced one fingering the butt of his revolver he thought of the scene he had witnessed so short a time before, and naturally expected to see the young man murdered as had been the huge sailor earlier in the day.

So Tarzan fitted a poisoned arrow to his bow and drew a bead upon the rat-faced sailor, but the foliage was so thick that he soon saw the arrow would be deflected by the leaves or some small branch, and instead he launched a heavy spear from his lofty perch.

Clayton had taken but a dozen steps. The rat-faced sailor had half drawn his revolver; the other sailors stood watching the scene intently.

Professor Porter had already disappeared into the jungle, whither he was being followed by the fussy Samuel T. Philander, his secretary and assistant.

Esmeralda, the Negress, was busy sorting her mistress' baggage from the pile of bales and boxes beside the cabin, and Miss Porter had turned away to follow Clayton, when something caused her to turn again toward the sailor.

And then three things happened almost simultaneously. The sailor jerked out his weapon and leveled it at Clayton's back, Miss Porter screamed a warning, and a long, metal-shod spear shot like a bolt from above and passed entirely through the right shoulder of the rat-faced man.

The revolver exploded harmlessly in the air, and the seaman crumpled up with a scream of pain and terror.

Clayton turned and rushed back toward the scene. The sailors stood in a frightened group, with drawn weapons, peering into the jungle. The wounded man writhed and shrieked upon the ground.

Clayton, unseen by any, picked up the fallen revolver and slipped it inside his shirt, then he joined the sailors in gazing, mystified, into the jungle.

"Who could it have been?" whispered Jane Porter, and the young man turned to see her standing, wide-eyed and wondering, close beside him.

"I dare say Tarzan of the Apes is watching us all right," he answered, in a dubious tone. "I wonder, now, who that spear was intended for. If for Snipes, then our ape friend is a friend indeed.

"By jove, where are your father and Mr. Philander? There's someone or something in that jungle, and it's armed, whatever it is. Ho! Professor! Mr. Philander!" young Clayton shouted. There was no response.

"What's to be done, Miss Porter?" continued the young man, his face clouded by a frown of worry and indecision.

"I can't leave you here alone with these cutthroats, and you certainly can't venture into the jungle with me; yet someone must go in search of your father. He is more than apt to wandering off aimlessly, regardless of danger or direction, and Mr. Philander is only a trifle less impractical than he. You will pardon my bluntness, but our lives are all in jeopardy here, and when we get your father back something must be done to impress upon him the dangers to which he exposes you as well as himself by his absent-mindedness."

"I quite agree with you," replied the girl, "and I am not offended at all. Dear old papa would sacrifice his life for me without an instant's hesitation, provided one could keep his mind on so frivolous a matter for an entire instant. There is only one way to keep him in safety, and that is to chain him to a tree. The poor dear is *so* impractical."

"I have it!" suddenly exclaimed Clayton. "You can use a revolver, can't you?"

"Yes. Why?"

"I have one. With it you and Esmeralda will be comparatively safe in this cabin while I am searching for your father and Mr. Philander. Come, call the woman and I will hurry on. They can't have gone far."

Jane did as he suggested and when he saw the door close safely behind them Clayton turned toward the jungle.

Some of the sailors were drawing the spear from their wounded comrade and, as Clayton approached, he asked if he could borrow a revolver from one of them while he searched the jungle for the professor.

The rat-faced one, finding he was not dead, had regained his composure, and with a volley of oaths directed at Clayton refused in the name of his fellows to allow the young man any firearms.

This man, Snipes, had assumed the role of chief since he had killed their former leader, and so little time had elapsed that none of his companions had as yet questioned his authority.

Clayton's only response was a shrug of the shoulders, but as he left them he picked up the spear which had transfixed Snipes, and thus primitively armed, the son of the then Lord Greystoke strode into the dense jungle.

Every few moments he called aloud the names of the wanderers. The watchers in the cabin by the beach heard the sound of his voice growing ever fainter and fainter, until at last it was swallowed up by the myriad noises of the primeval wood.

When Professor Archimedes Q. Porter and his assistant, Samuel T. Philander, after much insistence on the part of the latter, had finally turned their steps toward camp, they were as completely lost in the wild and tangled labyrinth of the matted jungle as two human beings well could be, though they did not know it.

It was by the merest caprice of fortune that they headed toward the west coast of Africa, instead of toward Zanzibar on the opposite side of the dark continent.

When in a short time they reached the beach, only to find no camp in sight, Philander was positive that they were north of their proper destination, while, as a matter of fact they were about two hundred yards south of it.

It never occurred to either of these impractical theorists to call aloud on the chance of attracting their friends' attention. Instead, with all the assurance that deductive reasoning from a wrong premise induces in one, Mr. Samuel T. Philander grasped Professor Archimedes Q. Porter firmly by the arm and hurried the weakly protesting old gentleman off in the direction of Cape Town, fifteen hundred miles to the south.

When Jane and Esmeralda found themselves safely behind the cabin door the Negress's first thought was to barricade the portal from the inside. With this idea in mind she turned to search for some means of putting it into execution; but her first view of the interior of the cabin brought a shriek of terror to her lips, and like a frightened child the huge woman ran to bury her face on her mistress' shoulder.

Jane, turning at the cry, saw the cause of it lying prone upon the floor before them – the whitened skeleton of a man. A further glance revealed a second skeleton upon the bed.

"What horrible place are we in?" murmured the awe-struck girl. But there was no panic in her fright.

At last, disengaging herself from the frantic clutch of the still shrieking Esmeralda, Jane crossed the room to look into the little cradle, knowing what she should see there even before the tiny skeleton disclosed itself in all its pitiful and pathetic frailty.

What an awful tragedy these poor mute bones proclaimed! The girl shuddered at thought of the eventualities which might lie before herself and her friends in this ill-fated cabin, the haunt of mysterious, perhaps hostile, beings.

Quickly, with an impatient stamp of her little foot, she endeavored to shake off the gloomy forebodings, and turning to Esmeralda bade her cease her wailing.

"Stop, Esmeralda, stop it this minute!" she cried. "You are only making it worse."

She ended lamely, a little quiver in her own voice as she thought of the three men, upon whom she depended for protection, wandering in the depth of that awful forest.

Soon the girl found that the door was equipped with a heavy wooden bar upon the inside, and after several efforts the combined strength of the two enabled them to slip it into place, the first time in twenty years.

Then they sat down upon a bench with their arms about one another, and waited.

CHAPTER FOURTEEN

At the Mercy of the Jungle

After Clayton had plunged into the jungle, the sailors – mutineers of the Arrow – fell into a discussion of their next step; but on one point all were agreed – that they should hasten to put off to the anchored Arrow, where they could at least be safe from the spears of their unseen foe. And so, while Jane Porter and Esmeralda were barricading themselves within the cabin, the cowardly crew of cutthroats were pulling rapidly for their ship in the two boats that had brought them ashore.

So much had Tarzan seen that day that his head was in a whirl of wonder. But the most wonderful sight of all, to him, was the face of the beautiful white girl.

Here at last was one of his own kind; of that he was positive. And the young man and the two old men; they, too, were much as he had pictured his own people to be.

But doubtless they were as ferocious and cruel as other men he had seen. The fact that they alone of all the party were unarmed might account for the fact that they had killed no one. They might be very different if provided with weapons.

Tarzan had seen the young man pick up the fallen revolver of the wounded Snipes and hide it away in his breast; and he had also seen him slip it cautiously to the girl as she entered the cabin door.

He did not understand anything of the motives behind all that he had seen; but, somehow, intuitively he liked the young man and the two old men, and for the girl he had a strange longing which he scarcely understood. As for the big black woman, she was evidently connected in some way to the girl, and so he liked her, also.

For the sailors, and especially Snipes, he had developed a great hatred. He knew by their threatening gestures and by the expression upon their evil faces that they were enemies of the others of the party, and so he decided to watch closely.

Tarzan wondered why the men had gone into the jungle, nor did it ever occur to him that one could become lost in that maze of undergrowth which to him was as simple as is the main street of your own home town to you.

When he saw the sailors row away toward the ship, and knew that the girl and her companion were safe in his cabin, Tarzan decided to follow the young man into the jungle and learn what his errand might be. He swung off rapidly in the direction taken by Clayton, and in a short time heard faintly in the distance the now only occasional calls of the Englishman to his friends.

Presently Tarzan came up with the white man, who, almost fagged, was leaning against a tree wiping the perspiration from his forehead. The ape-man, hiding safe behind a screen of foliage, sat watching this new specimen of his own race intently.

At intervals Clayton called aloud and finally it came to Tarzan that he was searching for the old man.

Tarzan was on the point of going off to look for them himself, when he caught the yellow glint of a sleek hide moving cautiously through the jungle toward Clayton.

It was Sheeta, the leopard. Now, Tarzan heard the soft bending of grasses and wondered why the young white man was not warned. Could it be he had failed to note the loud warning? Never before had Tarzan known Sheeta to be so clumsy.

No, the white man did not hear. Sheeta was crouching for the spring, and then, shrill and horrible, there rose from the stillness of the jungle the awful cry of the challenging ape, and Sheeta turned, crashing into the underbrush.

Clayton came to his feet with a start. His blood ran cold. Never in all his life had so fearful a sound smote upon his ears. He was no coward; but if ever man felt the icy fingers of fear upon his heart, William Cecil Clayton, eldest son of Lord Greystoke of England, did that day in the fastness of the African jungle.

The noise of some great body crashing through the underbrush so close beside him, and the sound of that bloodcurdling shriek from above, tested Clayton's courage to the limit; but he could not know that it was to that very voice he owed his life, nor that the creature who hurled it forth was his own cousin – the real Lord Greystoke.

The afternoon was drawing to a close, and Clayton, disheartened and discouraged, was in a terrible quandary as to the proper course to pursue; whether to keep on in search of Professor Porter, at the almost certain risk of his own death in the jungle by night, or to return to the cabin where he might at least serve to protect Jane from the perils which confronted her on all sides.

He did not wish to return to camp without her father; still more, he shrank from the thought of leaving her alone and unprotected in the hands of the mutineers of the Arrow, or to the hundred unknown dangers of the jungle.

Possibly, too, he thought, the professor and Philander might have returned to camp. Yes, that was more than likely. At least he would return and see, before he continued what seemed to be a most fruitless quest. And so he started, stumbling back through the thick and matted underbrush in the direction that he thought the cabin lay.

To Tarzan's surprise the young man was heading further into the jungle in the general direction of Mbonga's village, and the shrewd young ape-man was convinced that he was lost.

To Tarzan this was scarcely comprehensible; his judgment told him that no man would venture toward the village of the cruel blacks armed only with a spear which, from the awkward way in which he carried it, was evidently an unaccustomed weapon to this white man. Nor was he following the trail of the old men. That, they had crossed and left long since, though it had been fresh and plain before Tarzan's eyes.

Tarzan was perplexed. The fierce jungle would make easy prey of this unprotected stranger in a very short time if he were not guided quickly to the beach.

Yes, there was Numa, the lion, even now, stalking the white man a dozen paces to the right.

Clayton heard the great body paralleling his course, and now there rose upon the evening air the beast's thunderous roar. The man stopped with upraised spear and faced the brush from which issued the awful sound. The shadows were deepening, darkness was settling in.

God! To die here alone, beneath the fangs of wild beasts; to be torn and rended; to feel the hot breath of the brute on his face as the great paw crushed down upon his breast!

For a moment all was still. Clayton stood rigid, with raised spear. Presently a faint rustling of the bush apprised him of the stealthy creeping of the thing behind. It was gathering for the spring. At last he saw it, not twenty feet away – the long, lithe, muscular body and tawny head of a huge black-maned lion.

The beast was upon its belly, moving forward very slowly. As its eyes met Clayton's it stopped, and deliberately, cautiously gathered its hind quarters behind it.

In agony the man watched, fearful to launch his spear, powerless to fly.

He heard a noise in the tree above him. Some new danger, he thought, but he dared not take his eyes from the yellow green orbs before him. There was a sharp twang as of a broken banjo-string, and at the same instant an arrow appeared in the yellow hide of the crouching lion.

With a roar of pain and anger the beast sprang; but, somehow, Clayton stumbled to one side, and as he turned again to face the infuriated king of beasts, he was appalled at the sight which confronted him. Almost simultaneously with the lion's turning to renew the attack a half-naked giant dropped from the tree above squarely on the brute's back.

With lightning speed an arm that was banded layers of iron muscle encircled the huge neck, and the great beast was raised from behind, roaring and pawing the air – raised as easily as Clayton would have lifted a pet dog.

The scene he witnessed there in the twilight depths of the African jungle was burned forever into the Englishman's brain.

The man before him was the embodiment of physical perfection and giant strength; yet it was not upon these he depended in his battle with the great cat, for mighty as were his muscles, they were as nothing by comparison with Numa's. To his agility, to his brain and to his long keen knife he owed his supremacy.

His right arm encircled the lion's neck, while the left hand plunged the knife time and again into the unprotected side behind the left shoulder. The infuriated beast, pulled up and backwards until he stood upon his hind legs, struggled impotently in this unnatural position.

Had the battle been of a few seconds' longer duration the outcome might have been different, but it was all accomplished so quickly that the lion had scarce time to recover from the confusion of its surprise ere it sank lifeless to the ground.

Then the strange figure which had vanquished it stood erect upon the carcass, and throwing back the wild and handsome head, gave out the fearsome cry which a few moments earlier had so startled Clayton.

Before him he saw the figure of a young man, naked except for a loin cloth and a few barbaric ornaments about arms and legs; on the breast a priceless diamond locket gleaming against a smooth brown skin.

The hunting knife had been returned to its homely sheath, and the man was gathering up his bow and quiver from where he had tossed them when he leaped to attack the lion.

Clayton spoke to the stranger in English, thanking him for his brave rescue and complimenting him on the wondrous strength and dexterity he had displayed, but the only answer was a steady stare and a faint shrug of the mighty shoulders, which might betoken either disparagement of the service rendered, or ignorance of Clayton's language.

When the bow and quiver had been slung to his back the wild man, for such Clayton now thought him, once more drew his knife and deftly carved a dozen large strips of meat from the lion's carcass. Then, squatting upon his haunches, he proceeded to eat, first motioning Clayton to join him.

The strong white teeth sank into the raw and dripping flesh in apparent relish of the meal, but Clayton could not bring himself to share the uncooked meat with his strange host; instead he watched him, and presently there dawned upon him the conviction that this was Tarzan of the Apes, whose notice he had seen posted upon the cabin door that morning.

If so he must speak English.

Again Clayton attempted speech with the ape-man; but the replies, now vocal, were in a strange tongue, which resembled the chattering of monkeys mingled with the growling of some wild beast.

No, this could not be Tarzan of the Apes, for it was very evident that he was an utter stranger to English.

When Tarzan had completed his repast he rose and, pointing a very different direction from that which Clayton had been pursuing, started off through the jungle toward the point he had indicated.

Clayton, bewildered and confused, hesitated to follow him, for he thought he was but being led more deeply into the mazes of the forest; but the ape-man, seeing him disinclined to follow, returned, and, grasping him by the coat, dragged him along until he was convinced that Clayton understood what was required of him. Then he left him to follow voluntarily.

The Englishman, finally concluding that he was a prisoner, saw no alternative open but to accompany his captor, and thus they traveled slowly through the jungle while the sable mantle of the impenetrable forest night fell about them, and the stealthy footfalls of padded paws mingled with the breaking of twigs and the wild calls of the savage life that Clayton felt closing in upon him.

Suddenly Clayton heard the faint report of a firearm – a single shot, and then silence.

In the cabin by the beach two thoroughly terrified women clung to each other as they crouched upon the low bench in the gathering darkness.

The Negress sobbed hysterically, bemoaning the evil day that had witnessed her departure from her dear Maryland, while the white girl, dry eyed and outwardly calm, was torn by inward fears and forebodings. She feared not more for herself than for the three men whom she knew to be wandering in the abysmal depths of the savage jungle, from which she now heard issuing the almost incessant shrieks and roars, barkings and growlings of its terrifying and fearsome denizens as they sought their prey.

And now there came the sound of a heavy body brushing against the side of the cabin. She could hear the great padded paws upon the ground outside. For an instant, all was silence; even the bedlam of the forest died to a faint murmur. Then she distinctly heard the beast outside sniffing at the door, not two feet from where she crouched. Instinctively the girl shuddered, and shrank closer to the black woman.

"Hush!" she whispered. "Hush, Esmeralda," for the woman's sobs and groans seemed to have attracted the thing that stalked there just beyond the thin wall.

A gentle scratching sound was heard on the door. The brute tried to force an entrance; but presently this ceased, and again she heard the great pads creeping stealthily around the cabin. Again they stopped – beneath the window on which the terrified eyes of the girl now glued themselves.

"God!" she murmured, for now, silhouetted against the moonlit sky beyond, she saw framed in the tiny square of the latticed window the head of a huge lioness. The gleaming eyes were fixed upon her in intent ferocity.

"Look, Esmeralda!" she whispered. "For God's sake, what shall we do? Look! Quick! The window!"

Esmeralda, cowering still closer to her mistress, took one frightened glance toward the little square of moonlight, just as the lioness emitted a low, savage snarl.

The sight that met the poor woman's eyes was too much for the already overstrung nerves.

"Oh, Gaberelle!" she shrieked, and slid to the floor an inert and senseless mass.

For what seemed an eternity the great brute stood with its forepaws upon the sill, glaring into the little room. Presently it tried the strength of the lattice with its great talons.

The girl had almost ceased to breathe, when, to her relief, the head disappeared and she heard the brute's footsteps leaving the window. But now they came to the door again, and once more the scratching commenced; this time with increasing force until the great beast was tearing at the massive panels in a perfect frenzy of eagerness to seize its defenseless victims.

Could Jane have known the immense strength of that door, built piece by piece, she would have felt less fear of the lioness reaching her by this avenue.

Little did John Clayton imagine when he fashioned that crude but mighty portal that one day, twenty years later, it would shield a fair American girl, then unborn, from the teeth and talons of a man-eater.

For fully twenty minutes the brute alternately sniffed and tore at the door, occasionally giving voice to a wild, savage cry of baffled rage. At length, however, she gave up the attempt, and Jane heard her returning toward the window, beneath which she paused for an instant, and then launched her great weight against the timeworn lattice.

The girl heard the wooden rods groan beneath the impact; but they held, and the huge body dropped back to the ground below.

Again and again the lioness repeated these tactics, until finally the horrified prisoner within saw a portion of the lattice give way, and in an instant one great paw and the head of the animal were thrust within the room.

Slowly the powerful neck and shoulders spread the bars apart, and the lithe body protruded farther and farther into the room.

As in a trance, the girl rose, her hand upon her breast, wide eyes staring horror-stricken into the snarling face of the beast scarce ten feet from her. At her feet lay the prostrate form of the Negress. If she could but arouse her, their combined efforts might possibly avail to beat back the fierce and bloodthirsty intruder.

Jane stooped to grasp the black woman by the shoulder. Roughly she shook her.

"Esmeralda! Esmeralda!" she cried. "Help me, or we are lost."

Esmeralda opened her eyes. The first object they encountered was the dripping fangs of the hungry lioness.

With a horrified scream the poor woman rose to her hands and knees, and in this position scurried across the room, shrieking: "O Gaberelle! O Gaberelle!" at the top of her lungs.

Esmeralda weighed some two hundred and eighty pounds, and her extreme haste, added to her extreme corpulency, produced a most amazing result when Esmeralda elected to travel on all fours.

For a moment the lioness remained quiet with intense gaze directed upon the flitting Esmeralda, whose goal appeared to be the cupboard, into which she attempted to propel her huge bulk; but as the shelves were but nine or ten inches apart, she only succeeded in getting her head in; whereupon, with a final screech, which paled the jungle noises into insignificance, she fainted once again.

With the subsidence of Esmeralda the lioness renewed her efforts to wriggle her huge bulk through the weakening lattice.

The girl, standing pale and rigid against the farther wall, sought with ever-increasing terror for some loophole of escape. Suddenly her hand, tight-pressed against her bosom, felt the hard outline of the revolver that Clayton had left with her earlier in the day.

Quickly she snatched it from its hiding-place, and, leveling it full at the lioness's face, pulled the trigger.

There was a flash of flame, the roar of the discharge, and an answering roar of pain and anger from the beast.

Jane Porter saw the great form disappear from the window, and then she, too, fainted, the revolver falling at her side.

But Sabor was not killed. The bullet had but inflicted a painful wound in one of the great shoulders. It was the surprise at the blinding flash and the deafening roar that had caused her hasty but temporary retreat.

In another instant she was back at the lattice, and with renewed fury was clawing at the aperture, but with lessened effect, since the wounded member was almost useless.

She saw her prey – the two women – lying senseless upon the floor. There was no longer any resistance to be overcome. Her meat lay before her, and Sabor had only to worm her way through the lattice to claim it.

Slowly she forced her great bulk, inch by inch, through the opening. Now her head was through, now one great forearm and shoulder.

Carefully she drew up the wounded member to insinuate it gently beyond the tight pressing bars.

A moment more and both shoulders through, the long, sinuous body and the narrow hips would glide quickly after.

It was on this sight that Jane Porter again opened her eyes.

CHAPTER FIFTEEN

The Forest God

When Clayton heard the report of the firearm he fell into an agony of fear and apprehension. He knew that one of the sailors might be the author of it; but the fact that he had left the revolver with Jane, together with the overwrought condition of his nerves, made him morbidly positive that she was threatened with some great danger. Perhaps even now she was attempting to defend herself against some savage man or beast.

What were the thoughts of his strange captor or guide Clayton could only vaguely conjecture; but that he had heard the shot, and was in some manner affected by it was quite evident, for he quickened his pace so appreciably that Clayton, stumbling blindly in his wake, was down a dozen times in as many minutes in a vain effort to keep pace with him, and soon was left hopelessly behind.

Fearing that he would again be irretrievably lost, he called aloud to the wild man ahead of him, and in a moment had the satisfaction of seeing him drop lightly to his side from the branches above.

For a moment Tarzan looked at the young man closely, as though undecided as to just what was best to do; then, stooping down before Clayton, he motioned him to grasp him about the neck, and, with the white man upon his back, Tarzan took to the trees.

The next few minutes the young Englishman never forgot. High into bending and swaying branches he was borne with what seemed to him incredible swiftness, while Tarzan chafed at the slowness of his progress.

From one lofty branch the agile creature swung with Clayton through a dizzy arc to a neighboring tree; then for a hundred yards maybe the sure feet threaded a maze of interwoven limbs, balancing like a tightrope walker high above the black depths of verdure beneath.

From the first sensation of chilling fear Clayton passed to one of keen admiration and envy of those giant muscles and that wondrous instinct or knowledge which guided this forest god through the inky blackness of the night as easily and safely as Clayton would have strolled a London street at high noon.

Occasionally they would enter a spot where the foliage above was less dense, and the bright rays of the moon lit up before Clayton's wondering eyes the strange path they were traversing.

At such times the man fairly caught his breath at sight of the horrid depths below them, for Tarzan took the easiest way, which often led over a hundred feet above the earth.

And yet with all his seeming speed, Tarzan was in reality feeling his way with comparative slowness, searching constantly for limbs of adequate strength for the maintenance of this double weight.

Presently they came to the clearing before the beach. Tarzan's quick ears had heard the strange sounds of Sabor's efforts to force her way through the lattice, and it seemed to Clayton that they dropped a straight hundred feet to earth, so quickly did Tarzan descend. Yet when they struck the ground it was with scarce a jar; and as Clayton released his hold on the ape-man he saw him dart like a squirrel for the opposite side of the cabin.

The Englishman sprang quickly after him just in time to see the hind quarters of some huge animal about to disappear through the window of the cabin.

As Jane opened her eyes to a realization of the imminent peril which threatened her, her brave young heart gave up at last its final vestige of hope. But then to her surprise she saw the huge animal being slowly drawn back through the window, and in the moonlight beyond she saw the heads and shoulders of two men.

As Clayton rounded the corner of the cabin to behold the animal disappearing within, it was also to see the ape-man seize the long tail in both hands, and, bracing himself with his feet against the side of the cabin, throw all his mighty strength into the effort to draw the beast out of the interior.

Clayton was quick to lend a hand, but the ape-man jabbered to him in a commanding and peremptory tone something which Clayton knew to be orders, though he could not understand them.

At last, under their combined efforts, the great body was slowly dragged farther and farther outside the window, and then there came to Clayton's mind a dawning conception of the rash bravery of his companion's act.

For a naked man to drag a shrieking, clawing man-eater forth from a window by the tail to save a strange white girl, was indeed the last word in heroism.

Insofar as Clayton was concerned it was a very different matter, since the girl was not only of his own kind and race, but was the one woman in all the world whom he loved.

Though he knew that the lioness would make short work of both of them, he pulled with a will to keep it from Jane Porter. And then he recalled the battle between this man and the great, black-maned lion which he had witnessed a short time before, and he commenced to feel more assurance.

Tarzan was still issuing orders which Clayton could not understand.

He was trying to tell the stupid white man to plunge his poisoned arrows into Sabor's back and sides, and to reach the savage heart with the long, thin hunting knife that hung at Tarzan's hip; but the man would not understand, and Tarzan did not dare release his hold to do the things himself, for he knew that the puny white man never could hold mighty Sabor alone, for an instant.

Slowly the lioness was emerging from the window. At last her shoulders were out.

And then Clayton saw an incredible thing. Tarzan, racking his brains for some means to cope single-handed with the infuriated beast, had suddenly recalled his battle with Terkoz; and as the great shoulders came clear of the window, so that the lioness hung upon the sill only by her forepaws, Tarzan suddenly released his hold upon the brute.

With the quickness of a striking rattler he launched himself full upon Sabor's back, his strong young arms seeking and gaining a full-Nelson upon the beast, as he had learned it that other day during his bloody, wrestling victory over Terkoz.

With a roar the lioness turned completely over upon her back, falling full upon her enemy; but the black-haired giant only closed tighter his hold.

Pawing and tearing at earth and air, Sabor rolled and threw herself this way and that in an effort to dislodge this strange antagonist; but ever tighter and tighter drew the iron bands that were forcing her head lower and lower upon her tawny breast.

Higher crept the steel forearms of the ape-man about the back of Sabor's neck. Weaker and weaker became the lioness's efforts.

At last Clayton saw the immense muscles of Tarzan's shoulders and biceps leap into corded knots beneath the silver moonlight. There was a long sustained and supreme effort on the ape-man's part – and the vertebrae of Sabor's neck parted with a sharp snap.

In an instant Tarzan was upon his feet, and for the second time that day Clayton heard the bull ape's savage roar of victory. Then he heard Jane's agonized cry:

"Cecil – Mr. Clayton! Oh, what is it? What is it?"

Running quickly to the cabin door, Clayton called out that all was right, and shouted to her to open the door. As quickly as she could she raised the great bar and fairly dragged Clayton within.

"What was that awful noise?" she whispered, shrinking close to him.

"It was the cry of the kill from the throat of the man who has just saved your life, Miss Porter. Wait, I will fetch him so you may thank him."

The frightened girl would not be left alone, so she accompanied Clayton to the side of the cabin where lay the dead body of the lioness.

Tarzan of the Apes was gone.

Clayton called several times, but there was no reply, and so the two returned to the greater safety of the interior.

"What a frightful sound!" cried Jane, "I shudder at the mere thought of it. Do not tell me that a human throat voiced that hideous and fearsome shriek."

"But it did, Miss Porter," replied Clayton; "or at least if not a human throat that of a forest god."

And then he told her of his experiences with this strange creature – of how twice the wild man had saved his life – of the wondrous strength, and agility, and bravery – of the brown skin and the handsome face.

"I cannot make it out at all," he concluded. "At first I thought he might be Tarzan of the Apes; but he neither speaks nor understands English, so that theory is untenable."

"Well, whatever he may be," cried the girl, "we owe him our lives, and may God bless him and keep him in safety in his wild and savage jungle!"

"Amen," said Clayton, fervently.

"For the good Lord's sake, ain't I dead?"

The two turned to see Esmeralda sitting upright upon the floor, her great eyes rolling from side to side as though she could not believe their testimony as to her whereabouts.

And now, for Jane Porter, the reaction came, and she threw herself upon the bench, sobbing with hysterical laughter.

CHAPTER SIXTEEN

"Most Remarkable"

SEVERAL MILES south of the cabin, upon a strip of sandy beach, stood two old men, arguing.

Before them stretched the broad Atlantic. At their backs was the Dark Continent. Close around them loomed the impenetrable blackness of the jungle.

Savage beasts roared and growled; noises, hideous and weird, assailed their ears. They had wandered for miles in search of their camp, but always in the wrong direction. They were as hopelessly lost as though they suddenly had been transported to another world.

At such a time, indeed, every fiber of their combined intellects must have been concentrated upon the vital question of the minute – the life-and-death question to them of retracing their steps to camp.

Samuel T. Philander was speaking.

"But, my dear professor," he was saying, "I still maintain that but for the victories of Ferdinand and Isabella over the fifteenth-century Moors in Spain the world would be today a thousand years in advance of where we now find ourselves. The Moors were essentially a tolerant, broad-minded, liberal race of agriculturists, artisans and merchants – the very type of people that has made possible such civilization as we find today in America and Europe – while the Spaniards – "

"Tut, tut, dear Mr. Philander," interrupted Professor Porter; "their religion positively precluded the possibilities you suggest. Moslemism was, is, and always will be, a blight on that scientific progress which has marked – "

"Bless me! Professor," interjected Mr. Philander, who had turned his gaze toward the jungle, "there seems to be someone approaching."

Professor Archimedes Q. Porter turned in the direction indicated by the nearsighted Mr. Philander.

"Tut, tut, Mr. Philander," he chided. "How often must I urge you to seek that absolute concentration of your mental faculties which alone may permit you to bring to bear the highest powers of intellectuality upon the momentous problems which naturally fall to the lot of great minds? And now I find you guilty of a most flagrant breach of courtesy in interrupting my learned discourse to call attention to a mere quadruped of the genus *felis*. As I was saying, Mr. – "

"Heavens, Professor, a lion?" cried Mr. Philander, straining his weak eyes toward the dim figure outlined against the dark tropical underbrush.

"Yes, yes, Mr. Philander, if you insist upon employing slang in your discourse, a 'lion.' But as I was saying – "

"Bless me, Professor," again interrupted Mr. Philander; "permit me to suggest that doubtless the Moors who were conquered in the fifteenth century will continue in that most regrettable condition for the time being at least, even though we postpone discussion of that world calamity until we may attain the enchanting view of yon *felis carnivora* which distance proverbially is credited with lending."

In the meantime the lion had approached with quiet dignity to within ten paces of the two men, where he stood curiously watching them.

The moonlight flooded the beach, and the strange group stood out in bold relief against the yellow sand.

"Most reprehensible, most reprehensible," exclaimed Professor Porter, with a faint trace of irritation in his voice. "Never, Mr. Philander, never before in my life have I known one of these animals to be permitted to roam at large from its cage. I shall most certainly report this outrageous breach of ethics to the directors of the adjacent zoological garden."

"Quite right, Professor," agreed Mr. Philander, "and the sooner it is done the better. Let us start now."

Seizing the professor by the arm, Mr. Philander set off in the direction that would put the greatest distance between themselves and the lion.

They had proceeded but a short distance when a backward glance revealed to the horrified gaze of Mr. Philander that the lion was following them. He tightened his grip upon the protesting professor and increased his speed.

"As I was saying, Mr. Philander," repeated Professor Porter.

Mr. Philander took another hasty glance rearward. The lion also had quickened his gait, and was doggedly maintaining an unvarying distance behind them.

"He is following us!" gasped Mr. Philander, breaking into a run.

"Tut, tut, Mr. Philander," remonstrated the professor, "this unseemly haste is most unbecoming to men of letters. What will our friends think of us, who may chance to be upon the street and witness our frivolous antics? Pray let us proceed with more decorum."

Mr. Philander stole another observation astern.

The lion was bounding along in easy leaps scarce five paces behind.

Mr. Philander dropped the professor's arm, and broke into a mad orgy of speed that would have done credit to any varsity track team.

"As I was saying, Mr. Philander – " screamed Professor Porter, as, metaphorically speaking, he himself "threw her into high." He, too, had caught a fleeting backward glimpse of cruel yellow eyes and half open mouth within startling proximity of his person.

With streaming coat tails and shiny silk hat Professor Archimedes Q. Porter fled through the moonlight close upon the heels of Mr. Samuel T. Philander.

Before them a point of the jungle ran out toward a narrow promontory, and it was for the haven of the trees he saw there that Mr. Samuel T. Philander directed his prodigious leaps and bounds; while from the shadows of this same spot peered two keen eyes in interested appreciation of the race.

It was Tarzan of the Apes who watched, with face a-grin, this odd game of follow-the-leader.

He knew the two men were safe enough from attack in so far as the lion was concerned. The very fact that Numa had foregone such easy prey at all convinced the wise forest craft of Tarzan that Numa's belly already was full.

The lion might stalk them until hungry again; but the chances were that if not angered he would soon tire of the sport, and slink away to his jungle lair.

Really, the one great danger was that one of the men might stumble and fall, and then the yellow devil would be upon him in a moment and the joy of the kill would be too great a temptation to withstand.

So Tarzan swung quickly to a lower limb in line with the approaching fugitives; and as Mr. Samuel T. Philander came panting and blowing beneath him, already too spent to struggle up to the safety of the limb, Tarzan reached down and, grasping him by the collar of his coat, yanked him to the limb by his side.

Another moment brought the professor within the sphere of the friendly grip, and he, too, was drawn upward to safety just as the baffled Numa, with a roar, leaped to recover his vanishing quarry.

For a moment the two men clung panting to the great branch, while Tarzan squatted with his back to the stem of the tree, watching them with mingled curiosity and amusement.

It was the professor who first broke the silence.

"I am deeply pained, Mr. Philander, that you should have evinced such a paucity of manly courage in the presence of one of the lower orders, and by your crass timidity have caused me to exert myself to such an unaccustomed degree in order that I might resume my discourse. As I was saying, Mr. Philander, when you interrupted me, the Moors – "

"Professor Archimedes Q. Porter," broke in Mr. Philander, in icy tones, "the time has arrived when patience becomes a crime and mayhem appears garbed in the mantle of virtue. You have accused me of cowardice. You have insinuated that you ran only to overtake me, not to escape the clutches of the lion. Have a care, Professor Archimedes Q. Porter! I am a desperate man. Goaded by long-suffering patience the worm will turn."

"Tut, tut, Mr. Philander, tut, tut!" cautioned Professor Porter; "you forget yourself."

"I forget nothing as yet, Professor Archimedes Q. Porter; but, believe me, sir, I am tottering on the verge of forgetfulness as to your exalted position in the world of science, and your gray hairs."

The professor sat in silence for a few minutes, and the darkness hid the grim smile that wreathed his wrinkled countenance. Presently he spoke.

"Look here, Skinny Philander," he said, in belligerent tones, "if you are lookin' for a scrap, peel off your coat and come on down on the ground, and I'll punch your head just as I did sixty years ago in the alley back of Porky Evans' barn."

"Ark!" gasped the astonished Mr. Philander. "Lordy, how good that sounds! When you're human, Ark, I love you; but somehow it seems as though you had forgotten how to be human for the last twenty years."

The professor reached out a thin, trembling old hand through the darkness until it found his old friend's shoulder.

"Forgive me, Skinny," he said, softly. "It hasn't been quite twenty years, and God alone knows how hard I have tried to be 'human' for Jane's sake, and yours, too, since He took my other Jane away."

Another old hand stole up from Mr. Philander's side to clasp the one that lay upon his shoulder, and no other message could better have translated the one heart to the other.

They did not speak for some minutes. The lion below them paced nervously back and forth. The third figure in the tree was hidden by the dense shadows near the stem. He, too, was silent – motionless as a graven image.

"You certainly pulled me up into this tree just in time," said the professor at last. "I want to thank you. You saved my life."

"But I didn't pull you up here, Professor," said Mr. Philander. "Bless me! The excitement of the moment quite caused me to forget that I myself was drawn up here by some outside agency – there must be someone or something in this tree with us."

"Eh?" ejaculated Professor Porter. "Are you quite positive, Mr. Philander?"

"Most positive, Professor," replied Mr. Philander, "and," he added, "I think we should thank the party. He may be sitting right next to you now, Professor."

"Eh? What's that? Tut, tut, Mr. Philander, tut, tut!" said Professor Porter, edging cautiously nearer to Mr. Philander.

Just then it occurred to Tarzan of the Apes that Numa had loitered beneath the tree for a sufficient length of time, so he raised his young head toward the heavens, and there rang out upon the terrified ears of the two old men the awful warning challenge of the anthropoid.

The two friends, huddled trembling in their precarious position on the limb, saw the great lion halt in his restless pacing as the bloodcurdling cry smote his ears, and then slink quickly into the jungle, to be instantly lost to view.

"Even the lion trembles in fear," whispered Mr. Philander.

"Most remarkable, most remarkable," murmured Professor Porter, clutching frantically at Mr. Philander to regain the balance which the sudden fright had so perilously endangered. Unfortunately for them both, Mr. Philander's center of equilibrium was at that very moment hanging upon the ragged edge of nothing, so that it needed but the gentle impetus supplied by the additional weight of Professor Porter's body to topple the devoted secretary from the limb.

For a moment they swayed uncertainly, and then, with mingled and most unscholarly shrieks, they pitched headlong from the tree, locked in frenzied embrace.

It was quite some moments ere either moved, for both were positive that any such attempt would reveal so many breaks and fractures as to make further progress impossible.

At length Professor Porter made an attempt to move one leg. To his surprise, it responded to his will as in days gone by. He now drew up its mate and stretched it forth again.

"Most remarkable, most remarkable," he murmured.

"Thank God, Professor," whispered Mr. Philander, fervently, "you are not dead, then?"

"Tut, tut, Mr. Philander, tut, tut," cautioned Professor Porter, "I do not know with accuracy as yet."

With infinite solicitude Professor Porter wiggled his right arm – joy! It was intact. Breathlessly he waved his left arm above his prostrate body – it waved!

"Most remarkable, most remarkable," he said.

"To whom are you signaling, Professor?" asked Mr. Philander, in an excited tone.

Professor Porter deigned to make no response to this puerile inquiry. Instead he raised his head gently from the ground, nodding it back and forth a half dozen times.

"Most remarkable," he breathed. "It remains intact."

Mr. Philander had not moved from where he had fallen; he had not dared the attempt. How indeed could one move when one's arms and legs and back were broken?

One eye was buried in the soft loam; the other, rolling sidewise, was fixed in awe upon the strange gyrations of Professor Porter.

"How sad!" exclaimed Mr. Philander, half aloud. "Concussion of the brain, superinducing total mental aberration. How very sad indeed! and for one still so young!"

Professor Porter rolled over upon his stomach; gingerly he bowed his back until he resembled a huge tom cat in proximity to a yelping dog. Then he sat up and felt of various portions of his anatomy.

"They are all here," he exclaimed. "Most remarkable!"

Whereupon he arose, and, bending a scathing glance upon the still prostrate form of Mr. Samuel T. Philander, he said:

"Tut, tut, Mr. Philander; this is no time to indulge in slothful ease. We must be up and doing."

Mr. Philander lifted his other eye out of the mud and gazed in speechless rage at Professor Porter. Then he attempted to rise; nor could there have been any more surprised than he when his efforts were immediately crowned with marked success.

He was still bursting with rage, however, at the cruel injustice of Professor Porter's insinuation, and was on the point of rendering a tart rejoinder when his eyes fell upon a strange figure standing a few paces away, scrutinizing them intently.

Professor Porter had recovered his shiny silk hat, which he had brushed carefully upon the sleeve of his coat and replaced upon his head. When he saw Mr. Philander pointing to something behind him he turned to behold a giant, naked but for a loin cloth and a few metal ornaments, standing motionless before him.

"Good evening, sir!" said the professor, lifting his hat.

For reply the giant motioned them to follow him, and set off up the beach in the direction from which they had recently come.

"I think it the better part of discretion to follow him," said Mr. Philander.

"Tut, tut, Mr. Philander," returned the professor. "A short time since you were advancing a most logical argument in substantiation of your theory that camp lay directly south of us. I was skeptical, but you finally convinced me; so now I am positive that toward the south we must travel to reach our friends. Therefore I shall continue south."

"But, Professor Porter, this man may know better than either of us. He seems to be indigenous to this part of the world. Let us at least follow him for a short distance."

"Tut, tut, Mr. Philander," repeated the professor. "I am a difficult man to convince, but when once convinced my decision is unalterable. I shall continue in the proper direction, if I have to circumambulate the continent of Africa to reach my destination."

Further argument was interrupted by Tarzan, who, seeing that these strange men were not following him, had returned to their side.

Again he beckoned to them; but still they stood in argument.

Presently the ape-man lost patience with their stupid ignorance. He grasped the frightened Mr. Philander by the shoulder, and before that worthy gentleman knew whether he was being killed or merely maimed for life, Tarzan had tied one end of his rope securely about Mr. Philander's neck.

"Tut, tut, Mr. Philander," remonstrated Professor Porter; "it is most unbeseeming in you to submit to such indignities."

But scarcely were the words out of his mouth ere he, too, had been seized and securely bound by the neck with the same rope. Then Tarzan set off toward the north, leading the now thoroughly frightened professor and his secretary.

In deathly silence they proceeded for what seemed hours to the two tired and hopeless old men; but presently as they topped a little rise of ground they were overjoyed to see the cabin lying before them, not a hundred yards distant.

Here Tarzan released them, and, pointing toward the little building, vanished into the jungle beside them.

"Most remarkable, most remarkable!" gasped the professor. "But you see, Mr. Philander, that I was quite right, as usual; and but for your stubborn willfulness we should have escaped a series of most humiliating, not to say dangerous accidents. Pray allow yourself to be guided by a more mature and practical mind hereafter when in need of wise counsel."

Mr. Samuel T. Philander was too much relieved at the happy outcome to their adventure to take umbrage at the professor's cruel fling. Instead he grasped his friend's arm and hastened him forward in the direction of the cabin.

It was a much-relieved party of castaways that found itself once more united. Dawn discovered them still recounting their various adventures and speculating upon the identity of the strange guardian and protector they had found on this savage shore.

Esmeralda was positive that it was none other than an angel of the Lord, sent down especially to watch over them.

"Had you seen him devour the raw meat of the lion, Esmeralda," laughed Clayton, "you would have thought him a very material angel."

"There was nothing heavenly about his voice," said Jane Porter, with a little shudder at recollection of the awful roar which had followed the killing of the lioness.

"Nor did it precisely comport with my preconceived ideas of the dignity of divine messengers," remarked Professor Porter, "when the – ah – gentleman tied two highly respectable and erudite scholars neck to neck and dragged them through the jungle as though they had been cows."

CHAPTER SEVENTEEN

Burials

As it was now quite light, the party, none of whom had eaten or slept since the previous morning, began to bestir themselves to prepare food.

The mutineers of the Arrow had landed a small supply of dried meats, canned soups and vegetables, crackers, flour, tea, and coffee for the five they had marooned, and these were hurriedly drawn upon to satisfy the craving of long-famished appetites.

The next task was to make the cabin habitable, and to this end it was decided to at once remove the gruesome relics of the tragedy which had taken place there on some bygone day.

Professor Porter and Mr. Philander were deeply interested in examining the skeletons. The two larger, they stated, had belonged to a male and female of one of the higher white races.

The smallest skeleton was given but passing attention, as its location, in the crib, left no doubt as to its having been the infant offspring of this unhappy couple.

As they were preparing the skeleton of the man for burial, Clayton discovered a massive ring which had evidently encircled the man's finger at the time of his death, for one of the slender bones of the hand still lay within the golden bauble.

Picking it up to examine it, Clayton gave a cry of astonishment, for the ring bore the crest of the house of Greystoke.

At the same time, Jane discovered the books in the cupboard, and on opening the fly-leaf of one of them saw the name, *John Clayton, London.* In a second book which she hurriedly examined was the single name, *Greystoke.*

"Why, Mr. Clayton," she cried, "what does this mean? Here are the names of some of your own people in these books."

"And here," he replied gravely, "is the great ring of the house of Greystoke which has been lost since my uncle, John Clayton, the former Lord Greystoke, disappeared, presumably lost at sea."

"But how do you account for these things being here, in this savage African jungle?" exclaimed the girl.

"There is but one way to account for it, Miss Porter," said Clayton. "The late Lord Greystoke was not drowned. He died here in this cabin and this poor thing upon the floor is all that is mortal of him."

"Then this must have been Lady Greystoke," said Jane reverently, indicating the poor mass of bones upon the bed.

"The beautiful Lady Alice," replied Clayton, "of whose many virtues and remarkable personal charms I often have heard my mother and father speak. Poor woman," he murmured sadly.

With deep reverence and solemnity the bodies of the late Lord and Lady Greystoke were buried beside their little African cabin, and between them was placed the tiny skeleton of the baby of Kala, the ape.

As Mr. Philander was placing the frail bones of the infant in a bit of sail cloth, he examined the skull minutely. Then he called Professor Porter to his side, and the two argued in low tones for several minutes.

"Most remarkable, most remarkable," said Professor Porter.

"Bless me," said Mr. Philander, "we must acquaint Mr. Clayton with our discovery at once."

"Tut, tut, Mr. Philander, tut, tut!" remonstrated Professor Archimedes Q. Porter. "'Let the dead past bury its dead.'"

And so the white-haired old man repeated the burial service over this strange grave, while his four companions stood with bowed and uncovered heads about him.

From the trees Tarzan of the Apes watched the solemn ceremony; but most of all he watched the sweet face and graceful figure of Jane Porter.

In his savage, untutored breast new emotions were stirring. He could not fathom them. He wondered why he felt so great an interest in these people – why he had gone to such pains to save the three men. But he did not wonder why he had torn Sabor from the tender flesh of the strange girl.

Surely the men were stupid and ridiculous and cowardly. Even Manu, the monkey, was more intelligent than they. If these were creatures of his own kind he was doubtful if his past pride in blood was warranted.

But the girl, ah – that was a different matter. He did not reason here. He knew that she was created to be protected, and that he was created to protect her.

He wondered why they had dug a great hole in the ground merely to bury dry bones. Surely there was no sense in that; no one wanted to steal dry bones.

Had there been meat upon them he could have understood, for thus alone might one keep his meat from Dango, the hyena, and the other robbers of the jungle.

When the grave had been filled with earth the little party turned back toward the cabin, and Esmeralda, still weeping copiously for the two she had never heard of before today, and who had been dead twenty years, chanced to glance toward the harbor. Instantly her tears ceased.

"Look at them low down white trash out there!" she shrilled, pointing toward the Arrow. "They-all's a desecrating us, right here on this here perverted island."

And, sure enough, the Arrow was being worked toward the open sea, slowly, through the harbor's entrance.

"They promised to leave us firearms and ammunition," said Clayton. "The merciless beasts!"

"It is the work of that fellow they call Snipes, I am sure," said Jane. "King was a scoundrel, but he had a little sense of humanity. If they had not killed him I know that he would have seen that we were properly provided for before they left us to our fate."

"I regret that they did not visit us before sailing," said Professor Porter. "I had proposed requesting them to leave the treasure with us, as I shall be a ruined man if that is lost."

Jane looked at her father sadly.

"Never mind, dear," she said. "It wouldn't have done any good, because it is solely for the treasure that they killed their officers and landed us upon this awful shore."

"Tut, tut, child, tut, tut!" replied Professor Porter. "You are a good child, but inexperienced in practical matters," and Professor Porter turned and walked slowly away toward the jungle, his hands clasped beneath his long coat tails and his eyes bent upon the ground.

His daughter watched him with a pathetic smile upon her lips, and then turning to Mr. Philander, she whispered:

"Please don't let him wander off again as he did yesterday. We depend upon you, you know, to keep a close watch upon him."

"He becomes more difficult to handle each day," replied Mr. Philander, with a sigh and a shake of his head. "I presume he is now off to report to the directors of the Zoo that one of their lions was at large last night. Oh, Miss Jane, you don't know what I have to contend with."

"Yes, I do, Mr. Philander; but while we all love him, you alone are best fitted to manage him; for, regardless of what he may say to you, he respects your great learning, and, therefore, has immense confidence in your judgment. The poor dear cannot differentiate between erudition and wisdom."

Mr. Philander, with a mildly puzzled expression on his face, turned to pursue Professor Porter, and in his mind he was revolving the question of whether he should feel complimented or aggrieved at Miss Porter's rather backhanded compliment.

Tarzan had seen the consternation depicted upon the faces of the little group as they witnessed the departure of the Arrow; so, as the ship was a wonderful novelty to him in addition, he determined to hasten out to the point of land at the north of the harbor's mouth and obtain a nearer view of the boat, as well as to learn, if possible, the direction of its flight.

Swinging through the trees with great speed, he reached the point only a moment after the ship had passed out of the harbor, so that he obtained an excellent view of the wonders of this strange, floating house.

There were some twenty men running hither and thither about the deck, pulling and hauling on ropes.

A light land breeze was blowing, and the ship had been worked through the harbor's mouth under scant sail, but now that they had cleared the point every available shred of canvas was being spread that she might stand out to sea as handily as possible.

Tarzan watched the graceful movements of the ship in rapt admiration, and longed to be aboard her. Presently his keen eyes caught the faintest suspicion of smoke on the far northern horizon, and he wondered over the cause of such a thing out on the great water.

About the same time the look-out on the Arrow must have discerned it, for in a few minutes Tarzan saw the sails being shifted and shortened. The ship came about, and presently he knew that she was beating back toward land.

A man at the bows was constantly heaving into the sea a rope to the end of which a small object was fastened. Tarzan wondered what the purpose of this action might be.

At last the ship came up directly into the wind; the anchor was lowered; down came the sails. There was great scurrying about on deck.

A boat was lowered, and in it a great chest was placed. Then a dozen sailors bent to the oars and pulled rapidly toward the point where Tarzan crouched in the branches of a tree.

In the stern of the boat, as it drew nearer, Tarzan saw the rat-faced man.

It was but a few minutes later that the boat touched the beach. The men jumped out and lifted the great chest to the sand. They were on the north side of the point so that their presence was concealed from those at the cabin.

The men argued angrily for a moment. Then the rat-faced one, with several companions, ascended the low bluff on which stood the tree that concealed Tarzan. They looked about for several minutes.

"Here is a good place," said the rat-faced sailor, indicating a spot beneath Tarzan's tree.

"It is as good as any," replied one of his companions. "If they catch us with the treasure aboard it will all be confiscated anyway. We might as well bury it here on the chance that some of us will escape the gallows to come back and enjoy it later."

The rat-faced one now called to the men who had remained at the boat, and they came slowly up the bank carrying picks and shovels.

"Hurry, you!" cried Snipes.

"Stow it!" retorted one of the men, in a surly tone. "You're no admiral, you damned shrimp."

"I'm Cap'n here, though, I'll have you to understand, you swab," shrieked Snipes, with a volley of frightful oaths.

"Steady, boys," cautioned one of the men who had not spoken before. "It ain't goin' to get us nothing by fightin' amongst ourselves."

"Right enough," replied the sailor who had resented Snipes' autocratic tones; "but it ain't a-goin' to get nobody nothin' to put on airs in this bloomin' company neither."

"You fellows dig here," said Snipes, indicating a spot beneath the tree. "And while you're diggin', Peter kin be a-makin' of a map of the location so's we kin find it again. You, Tom, and Bill, take a couple more down and fetch up the chest."

"Wot are you a-goin' to do?" asked he of the previous altercation. "Just boss?"

"Git busy there," growled Snipes. "You didn't think your Cap'n was a-goin' to dig with a shovel, did you?"

The men all looked up angrily. None of them liked Snipes, and this disagreeable show of authority since he had murdered King, the real head and ringleader of the mutineers, had only added fuel to the flames of their hatred.

"Do you mean to say that you don't intend to take a shovel, and lend a hand with this work? Your shoulder's not hurt so all-fired bad as that," said Tarrant, the sailor who had before spoken.

"Not by a damned sight," replied Snipes, fingering the butt of his revolver nervously.

"Then, by God," replied Tarrant, "if you won't take a shovel you'll take a pickax."

With the words he raised his pick above his head, and, with a mighty blow, he buried the point in Snipes' brain.

For a moment the men stood silently looking at the result of their fellow's grim humor. Then one of them spoke.

"Served the skunk jolly well right," he said.

One of the others commenced to ply his pick to the ground. The soil was soft and he threw aside the pick and grasped a shovel; then the others joined him. There was no further comment on the killing, but the men worked in a better frame of mind than they had since Snipes had assumed command.

When they had a trench of ample size to bury the chest, Tarrant suggested that they enlarge it and inter Snipes' body on top of the chest.

"It might 'elp fool any as 'appened to be diggin' 'ereabouts," he explained.

The others saw the cunning of the suggestion, and so the trench was lengthened to accommodate the corpse, and in the center a deeper hole was excavated for the box, which was first wrapped in sailcloth and then lowered to its place, which brought its top about a foot below the bottom of the grave. Earth was shovelled in and tramped down about the chest until the bottom of the grave showed level and uniform.

Two of the men rolled the rat-faced corpse unceremoniously into the grave, after first stripping it of its weapons and various other articles which the several members of the party coveted for their own.

They then filled the grave with earth and tramped upon it until it would hold no more.

The balance of the loose earth was thrown far and wide, and a mass of dead undergrowth spread in as natural a manner as possible over the new-made grave to obliterate all signs of the ground having been disturbed.

Their work done the sailors returned to the small boat, and pulled off rapidly toward the Arrow.

The breeze had increased considerably, and as the smoke upon the horizon was now plainly discernible in considerable volume, the mutineers lost no time in getting under full sail and bearing away toward the southwest.

Tarzan, an interested spectator of all that had taken place, sat speculating on the strange actions of these peculiar creatures.

Men were indeed more foolish and more cruel than the beasts of the jungle! How fortunate was he who lived in the peace and security of the great forest!

Tarzan wondered what the chest they had buried contained. If they did not want it why did they not merely throw it into the water? That would have been much easier.

Ah, he thought, but they do want it. They have hidden it here because they intend returning for it later.

Tarzan dropped to the ground and commenced to examine the earth about the excavation. He was looking to see if these creatures had dropped anything which he might like to own. Soon he discovered a spade hidden by the underbrush which they had laid upon the grave.

He seized it and attempted to use it as he had seen the sailors do. It was awkward work and hurt his bare feet, but he persevered until he had partially uncovered the body. This he dragged from the grave and laid to one side.

Then he continued digging until he had unearthed the chest. This also he dragged to the side of the corpse. Then he filled in the smaller hole below the grave, replaced the body and the earth around and above it, covered it over with underbrush, and returned to the chest.

Four sailors had sweated beneath the burden of its weight – Tarzan of the Apes picked it up as though it had been an empty packing case, and with the spade slung to his back by a piece of rope, carried it off into the densest part of the jungle.

He could not well negotiate the trees with his awkward burden, but he kept to the trails, and so made fairly good time.

For several hours he traveled a little north of east until he came to an impenetrable wall of matted and tangled vegetation. Then he took to the lower branches, and in another fifteen minutes he emerged into the amphitheater of the apes, where they met in council, or to celebrate the rites of the Dum-Dum.

Near the center of the clearing, and not far from the drum, or altar, he commenced to dig. This was harder work than turning up the freshly excavated earth at the grave, but Tarzan of the Apes was persevering and so he kept at his labor until he was rewarded by seeing a hole sufficiently deep to receive the chest and effectually hide it from view.

Why had he gone to all this labor without knowing the value of the contents of the chest?

Tarzan of the Apes had a man's figure and a man's brain, but he was an ape by training and environment. His brain told him that the chest contained something valuable, or the men would not have hidden it. His training had taught him to imitate whatever was new and unusual, and now the natural curiosity, which is as common to men as to apes, prompted him to open the chest and examine its contents.

But the heavy lock and massive iron bands baffled both his cunning and his immense strength, so that he was compelled to bury the chest without having his curiosity satisfied.

By the time Tarzan had hunted his way back to the vicinity of the cabin, feeding as he went, it was quite dark.

Within the little building a light was burning, for Clayton had found an unopened tin of oil which had stood intact for twenty years, a part of the supplies left with the Claytons by Black Michael. The lamps also were still useable, and thus the interior of the cabin appeared as bright as day to the astonished Tarzan.

He had often wondered at the exact purpose of the lamps. His reading and the pictures had told him what they were, but he had no idea of how they could be made to produce the wondrous sunlight that some of his pictures had portrayed them as diffusing upon all surrounding objects.

As he approached the window nearest the door he saw that the cabin had been divided into two rooms by a rough partition of boughs and sailcloth.

In the front room were the three men; the two older deep in argument, while the younger, tilted back against the wall on an improvised stool, was deeply engrossed in reading one of Tarzan's books.

Tarzan was not particularly interested in the men, however, so he sought the other window. There was the girl. How beautiful her features! How delicate her snowy skin!

She was writing at Tarzan's own table beneath the window. Upon a pile of grasses at the far side of the room lay the Negress asleep.

For an hour Tarzan feasted his eyes upon her while she wrote. How he longed to speak to her, but he dared not attempt it, for he was convinced that, like the young man, she would not understand him, and he feared, too, that he might frighten her away.

At length she arose, leaving her manuscript upon the table. She went to the bed upon which had been spread several layers of soft grasses. These she rearranged.

Then she loosened the soft mass of golden hair which crowned her head. Like a shimmering waterfall turned to burnished metal by a dying sun it fell about her oval face; in waving lines, below her waist it tumbled.

Tarzan was spellbound. Then she extinguished the lamp and all within the cabin was wrapped in Cimmerian darkness.

Still Tarzan watched. Creeping close beneath the window he waited, listening, for half an hour. At last he was rewarded by the sounds of the regular breathing within which denotes sleep.

Cautiously he intruded his hand between the meshes of the lattice until his whole arm was within the cabin. Carefully he felt upon the desk. At last he grasped the manuscript upon which Jane Porter had been writing, and as cautiously withdrew his arm and hand, holding the precious treasure.

Tarzan folded the sheets into a small parcel which he tucked into the quiver with his arrows. Then he melted away into the jungle as softly and as noiselessly as a shadow.

CHAPTER EIGHTEEN

The Jungle Toll

EARLY THE FOLLOWING morning Tarzan awoke, and his first thought of the new day, as the last of yesterday, was of the wonderful writing which lay hidden in his quiver.

Hurriedly he brought it forth, hoping against hope that he could read what the beautiful white girl had written there the preceding evening.

At the first glance he suffered a bitter disappointment; never before had he so yearned for anything as now he did for the ability to interpret a message from that golden-haired divinity who had come so suddenly and so unexpectedly into his life.

What did it matter if the message were not intended for him? It was an expression of her thoughts, and that was sufficient for Tarzan of the Apes.

And now to be baffled by strange, uncouth characters the like of which he had never seen before! Why, they even tipped in the opposite direction from all that he had ever examined either in printed books or the difficult script of the few letters he had found.

Even the little bugs of the black book were familiar friends, though their arrangement meant nothing to him; but these bugs were new and unheard of.

For twenty minutes he pored over them, when suddenly they commenced to take familiar though distorted shapes. Ah, they were his old friends, but badly crippled.

Then he began to make out a word here and a word there. His heart leaped for joy. He could read it, and he would.

In another half hour he was progressing rapidly, and, but for an exceptional word now and again, he found it very plain sailing.

Here is what he read:

WEST COAST OF AFRICA, ABOUT 10 DEGREES SOUTH LATITUDE. (So Mr. Clayton says.)
February 3 (?), 1909.

DEAREST HAZEL:

It seems foolish to write you a letter that you may never see, but I simply must tell somebody of our awful experiences since we sailed from Europe on the ill-fated Arrow.

If we never return to civilization, as now seems only too likely, this will at least prove a brief record of the events which led up to our final fate, whatever it may be.

As you know, we were supposed to have set out upon a scientific expedition to the Congo. Papa was presumed to entertain some wondrous theory of an unthinkably ancient civilization, the remains of which lay buried somewhere in the Congo valley. But after we were well under sail the truth came out.

It seems that an old bookworm who has a book and curio shop in Baltimore discovered between the leaves of a very old Spanish manuscript a letter written in 1550 detailing the adventures of a crew of mutineers of a Spanish galleon bound from Spain to South America with a vast treasure of "doubloons" and "pieces of eight," I suppose, for they certainly sound weird and piraty.

The writer had been one of the crew, and the letter was to his son, who was, at the very time the letter was written, master of a Spanish merchantman.

Many years had elapsed since the events the letter narrated had transpired, and the old man had become a respected citizen of an obscure Spanish town, but the love of gold was still so strong upon him that he risked all to acquaint his son with the means of attaining fabulous wealth for them both.

The writer told how when but a week out from Spain the crew had mutinied and murdered every officer and man who opposed them; but they defeated their own ends by this very act, for there was none left competent to navigate a ship at sea.

They were blown hither and thither for two months, until sick and dying of scurvy, starvation, and thirst, they had been wrecked on a small islet.

The galleon was washed high upon the beach where she went to pieces; but not before the survivors, who numbered but ten souls, had rescued one of the great chests of treasure.

This they buried well up on the island, and for three years they lived there in constant hope of being rescued.

One by one they sickened and died, until only one man was left, the writer of the letter.

The men had built a boat from the wreckage of the galleon, but having no idea where the island was located they had not dared to put to sea.

When all were dead except himself, however, the awful loneliness so weighed upon the mind of the sole survivor that he could endure it no longer, and choosing to risk death upon the open sea rather than madness on the lonely isle, he set sail in his little boat after nearly a year of solitude.

Fortunately he sailed due north, and within a week was in the track of the Spanish merchantmen plying between the West Indies and Spain, and was picked up by one of these vessels homeward bound.

The story he told was merely one of shipwreck in which all but a few had perished, the balance, except himself, dying after they reached the island. He did not mention the mutiny or the chest of buried treasure.

The master of the merchantman assured him that from the position at which they had picked him up, and the prevailing winds for the past week he could have been on no other island than one of the Cape Verde group, which lie off the West Coast of Africa in about 16 degrees or 17 degrees north latitude.

His letter described the island minutely, as well as the location of the treasure, and was accompanied by the crudest, funniest little old map you ever saw; with trees and rocks all marked by scrawly X's to show the exact spot where the treasure had been buried.

When papa explained the real nature of the expedition, my heart sank, for I know so well how visionary and impractical the poor dear has always been that I feared that he had again been duped; especially when he told me he had paid a thousand dollars for the letter and map.

To add to my distress, I learned that he had borrowed ten thousand dollars more from Robert Canler, and had given his notes for the amount.

Mr. Canler had asked for no security, and you know, dearie, what that will mean for me if papa cannot meet them. Oh, how I detest that man!

We all tried to look on the bright side of things, but Mr. Philander, and Mr. Clayton – he joined us in London just for the adventure – both felt as skeptical as I.

Well, to make a long story short, we found the island and the treasure – a great iron-bound oak chest, wrapped in many layers of oiled sailcloth, and as strong and firm as when it had been buried nearly two hundred years ago.

It was *simply filled* with gold coin, and was so heavy that four men bent underneath its weight.

The horrid thing seems to bring nothing but murder and misfortune to those who have anything to do with it, for three days after we sailed from the Cape Verde Islands our own crew mutinied and killed every one of their officers.

Oh, it was the most terrifying experience one could imagine – I cannot even write of it.

They were going to kill us too, but one of them, the leader, named King, would not let them, and so they sailed south along the coast to a lonely spot where they found a good harbor, and here they landed and have left us.

They sailed away with the treasure to-day, but Mr. Clayton says they will meet with a fate similar to the mutineers of the ancient galleon, because King, the only man aboard who knew aught of navigation, was murdered on the beach by one of the men the day we landed.

I wish you could know Mr. Clayton; he is the dearest fellow imaginable, and unless I am mistaken he has fallen very much in love with me.

He is the only son of Lord Greystoke, and some day will inherit the title and estates. In addition, he is wealthy in his own right, but the fact that he is going to be an English Lord makes me very sad – you know what my sentiments have always been relative to American girls who married titled foreigners. Oh, if he were only a plain American gentleman!

But it isn't his fault, poor fellow, and in everything except birth he would do credit to my country, and that is the greatest compliment I know how to pay any man.

We have had the most weird experiences since we were landed here. Papa and Mr. Philander lost in the jungle, and chased by a real lion.

Mr. Clayton lost, and attacked twice by wild beasts. Esmeralda and I cornered in an old cabin by a perfectly awful man-eating lioness. Oh, it was simply "terrifical," as Esmeralda would say.

But the strangest part of it all is the wonderful creature who rescued us. I have not seen him, but Mr. Clayton and papa and Mr. Philander have, and they say that he is a perfectly god-like white man tanned to a dusky brown, with the strength of a wild elephant, the agility of a monkey, and the bravery of a lion.

He speaks no English and vanishes as quickly and as mysteriously after he has performed some valorous deed, as though he were a disembodied spirit.

Then we have another weird neighbor, who printed a beautiful sign in English and tacked it on the door of his cabin, which we have preempted, warning us to destroy none of his belongings, and signing himself "Tarzan of the Apes."

We have never seen him, though we think he is about, for one of the sailors, who was going to shoot Mr. Clayton in the back, received a spear in his shoulder from some unseen hand in the jungle.

The sailors left us but a meager supply of food, so, as we have only a single revolver with but three cartridges left in it, we do not know how we can procure meat, though Mr. Philander says that we can exist indefinitely on the wild fruit and nuts which abound in the jungle.

I am very tired now, so I shall go to my funny bed of grasses which Mr. Clayton gathered for me, but will add to this from day to day as things happen.

Lovingly,
JANE PORTER.

TO HAZEL STRONG, BALTIMORE, MD.

Tarzan sat in a brown study for a long time after he finished reading the letter. It was filled with so many new and wonderful things that his brain was in a whirl as he attempted to digest them all.

So they did not know that he was Tarzan of the Apes. He would tell them.

In his tree he had constructed a rude shelter of leaves and boughs, beneath which, protected from the rain, he had placed the few treasures brought from the cabin. Among these were some pencils.

He took one, and beneath Jane Porter's signature he wrote:

I am Tarzan of the Apes

He thought that would be sufficient. Later he would return the letter to the cabin.

In the matter of food, thought Tarzan, they had no need to worry – he would provide, and he did.

The next morning Jane found her missing letter in the exact spot from which it had disappeared two nights before. She was mystified; but when she saw the printed words beneath her signature, she felt a cold, clammy chill run up her spine. She showed the letter, or rather the last sheet with the signature, to Clayton.

"And to think," she said, "that uncanny thing was probably watching me all the time that I was writing – oo! It makes me shudder just to think of it."

"But he must be friendly," reassured Clayton, "for he has returned your letter, nor did he offer to harm you, and unless I am mistaken he left a very substantial memento of his friendship outside the cabin door last night, for I just found the carcass of a wild boar there as I came out."

From then on scarcely a day passed that did not bring its offering of game or other food. Sometimes it was a young deer, again a quantity of strange, cooked food – cassava cakes pilfered from the village of Mbonga – or a boar, or leopard, and once a lion.

Tarzan derived the greatest pleasure of his life in hunting meat for these strangers. It seemed to him that no pleasure on earth could compare with laboring for the welfare and protection of the beautiful white girl.

Some day he would venture into the camp in daylight and talk with these people through the medium of the little bugs which were familiar to them and to Tarzan.

But he found it difficult to overcome the timidity of the wild thing of the forest, and so day followed day without seeing a fulfillment of his good intentions.

The party in the camp, emboldened by familiarity, wandered farther and yet farther into the jungle in search of nuts and fruit.

Scarcely a day passed that did not find Professor Porter straying in his preoccupied indifference toward the jaws of death. Mr. Samuel T. Philander, never what one might call robust, was worn to the shadow of a shadow through the ceaseless worry and mental distraction resultant from his Herculean efforts to safeguard the professor.

A month passed. Tarzan had finally determined to visit the camp by daylight.

It was early afternoon. Clayton had wandered to the point at the harbor's mouth to look for passing vessels. Here he kept a great mass of wood, high piled, ready to be ignited as a signal should a steamer or a sail top the far horizon.

Professor Porter was wandering along the beach south of the camp with Mr. Philander at his elbow, urging him to turn his steps back before the two became again the sport of some savage beast.

The others gone, Jane and Esmeralda had wandered into the jungle to gather fruit, and in their search were led farther and farther from the cabin.

Tarzan waited in silence before the door of the little house until they should return. His thoughts were of the beautiful white girl. They were always of her now. He wondered if she would fear him, and the thought all but caused him to relinquish his plan.

He was rapidly becoming impatient for her return, that he might feast his eyes upon her and be near her, perhaps touch her. The ape-man knew no god, but he was as near to worshipping his divinity as mortal man ever comes to worship. While he waited he passed the time printing a message to her; whether he intended giving it to her he himself could not have told, but he took infinite pleasure in seeing his thoughts expressed in print – in which he was not so uncivilized after all. He wrote:

I am Tarzan of the Apes. I want you. I am yours. You are mine. We live here together always in my house. I will bring you the best of fruits, the tenderest deer, the finest meats that roam the jungle. I will hunt for you. I am the greatest of the jungle fighters. I will fight for you. I am the mightiest of the jungle fighters. You are Jane Porter, I saw it in your letter. When you see this you will know that it is for you and that Tarzan of the Apes loves you.

As he stood, straight as a young Indian, by the door, waiting after he had finished the message, there came to his keen ears a familiar sound. It was the passing of a great ape through the lower branches of the forest.

For an instant he listened intently, and then from the jungle came the agonized scream of a woman, and Tarzan of the Apes, dropping his first love letter upon the ground, shot like a panther into the forest.

Clayton, also, heard the scream, and Professor Porter and Mr. Philander, and in a few minutes they came panting to the cabin, calling out to each other a volley of excited questions as they approached. A glance within confirmed their worst fears.

Jane and Esmeralda were not there.

Instantly, Clayton, followed by the two old men, plunged into the jungle, calling the girl's name aloud. For half an hour they stumbled on, until Clayton, by merest chance, came upon the prostrate form of Esmeralda.

He stopped beside her, feeling for her pulse and then listening for her heartbeats. She lived. He shook her.

"Esmeralda!" he shrieked in her ear. "Esmeralda! For God's sake, where is Miss Porter? What has happened? Esmeralda!"

Slowly Esmeralda opened her eyes. She saw Clayton. She saw the jungle about her.

"Oh, Gaberelle!" she screamed, and fainted again.

By this time Professor Porter and Mr. Philander had come up.

"What shall we do, Mr. Clayton?" asked the old professor. "Where shall we look? God could not have been so cruel as to take my little girl away from me now."

"We must arouse Esmeralda first," replied Clayton. "She can tell us what has happened. Esmeralda!" he cried again, shaking the black woman roughly by the shoulder.

"O Gaberelle, I want to die!" cried the poor woman, but with eyes fast closed. "Let me die, dear Lord, don't let me see that awful face again."

"Come, come, Esmeralda," cried Clayton.

"The Lord isn't here; it's Mr. Clayton. Open your eyes."

Esmeralda did as she was bade.

"O Gaberelle! Thank the Lord," she said.

"Where's Miss Porter? What happened?" questioned Clayton.

"Ain't Miss Jane here?" cried Esmeralda, sitting up with wonderful celerity for one of her bulk. "Oh, Lord, now I remember! It must have took her away," and the Negress commenced to sob, and wail her lamentations.

"What took her away?" cried Professor Porter.

"A great big giant all covered with hair."

"A gorilla, Esmeralda?" questioned Mr. Philander, and the three men scarcely breathed as he voiced the horrible thought.

"I thought it was the devil; but I guess it must have been one of them gorilephants. Oh, my poor baby, my poor little honey," and again Esmeralda broke into uncontrollable sobbing.

Clayton immediately began to look about for tracks, but he could find nothing save a confusion of trampled grasses in the close vicinity, and his woodcraft was too meager for the translation of what he did see.

All the balance of the day they sought through the jungle; but as night drew on they were forced to give up in despair and hopelessness, for they did not even know in what direction the thing had borne Jane.

It was long after dark ere they reached the cabin, and a sad and grief-stricken party it was that sat silently within the little structure.

Professor Porter finally broke the silence. His tones were no longer those of the erudite pedant theorizing upon the abstract and the unknowable; but those of the man of action – determined, but tinged also by a note of indescribable hopelessness and grief which wrung an answering pang from Clayton's heart.

"I shall lie down now," said the old man, "and try to sleep. Early tomorrow, as soon as it is light, I shall take what food I can carry and continue the search until I have found Jane. I will not return without her."

His companions did not reply at once. Each was immersed in his own sorrowful thoughts, and each knew, as did the old professor, what the last words meant – Professor Porter would never return from the jungle.

At length Clayton arose and laid his hand gently upon Professor Porter's bent old shoulder.

"I shall go with you, of course," he said.

"I knew that you would offer – that you would wish to go, Mr. Clayton; but you must not. Jane is beyond human assistance now. What was once my dear little girl shall not lie alone and friendless in the awful jungle.

"The same vines and leaves will cover us, the same rains beat upon us; and when the spirit of her mother is abroad, it will find us together in death, as it has always found us in life.

"No; it is I alone who may go, for she was my daughter – all that was left on earth for me to love."

"I shall go with you," said Clayton simply.

The old man looked up, regarding the strong, handsome face of William Cecil Clayton intently. Perhaps he read there the love that lay in the heart beneath – the love for his daughter.

He had been too preoccupied with his own scholarly thoughts in the past to consider the little occurrences, the chance words, which would have indicated to a more practical man that these young people were being drawn more and more closely to one another. Now they came back to him, one by one.

"As you wish," he said.

"You may count on me, also," said Mr. Philander.

"No, my dear old friend," said Professor Porter. "We may not all go. It would be cruelly wicked to leave poor Esmeralda here alone, and three of us would be no more successful than one.

"There be enough dead things in the cruel forest as it is. Come – let us try to sleep a little."

CHAPTER NINETEEN

The Call of the Primitive

FROM THE TIME Tarzan left the tribe of great anthropoids in which he had been raised, it was torn by continual strife and discord. Terkoz proved a cruel and capricious king, so that, one by one, many of the older and weaker apes, upon whom he was particularly prone to vent his brutish nature, took their families and sought the quiet and safety of the far interior.

But at last those who remained were driven to desperation by the continued truculence of Terkoz, and it so happened that one of them recalled the parting admonition of Tarzan:

"If you have a chief who is cruel, do not do as the other apes do, and attempt, any one of you, to pit yourself against him alone. But, instead, let two or three or four of you attack him together. Then, if you will do this, no chief will dare to be other than he should be, for four of you can kill any chief who may ever be over you."

And the ape who recalled this wise counsel repeated it to several of his fellows, so that when Terkoz returned to the tribe that day he found a warm reception awaiting him.

There were no formalities. As Terkoz reached the group, five huge, hairy beasts sprang upon him.

At heart he was an arrant coward, which is the way with bullies among apes as well as among men; so he did not remain to fight and die, but tore himself away from them as quickly as he could and fled into the sheltering boughs of the forest.

Two more attempts he made to rejoin the tribe, but on each occasion he was set upon and driven away. At last he gave it up, and turned, foaming with rage and hatred, into the jungle.

For several days he wandered aimlessly, nursing his spite and looking for some weak thing on which to vent his pent anger.

It was in this state of mind that the horrible, man-like beast, swinging from tree to tree, came suddenly upon two women in the jungle.

He was right above them when he discovered them. The first intimation Jane Porter had of his presence was when the great hairy body dropped to the earth beside her, and she saw the awful face and the snarling, hideous mouth thrust within a foot of her.

One piercing scream escaped her lips as the brute hand clutched her arm. Then she was dragged toward those awful fangs which yawned at her throat. But ere they touched that fair skin another mood claimed the anthropoid.

The tribe had kept his women. He must find others to replace them. This hairless white ape would be the first of his new household, and so he threw her roughly across his broad, hairy shoulders and leaped back into the trees, bearing Jane away.

Esmeralda's scream of terror had mingled once with that of Jane, and then, as was Esmeralda's manner under stress of emergency which required presence of mind, she swooned.

But Jane did not once lose consciousness. It is true that that awful face, pressing close to hers, and the stench of the foul breath beating upon her nostrils, paralyzed her with terror; but her brain was clear, and she comprehended all that transpired.

With what seemed to her marvelous rapidity the brute bore her through the forest, but still she did not cry out or struggle. The sudden advent of the ape had confused her to such an extent that she thought now that he was bearing her toward the beach.

For this reason she conserved her energies and her voice until she could see that they had approached near enough to the camp to attract the succor she craved.

She could not have known it, but she was being borne farther and farther into the impenetrable jungle.

The scream that had brought Clayton and the two older men stumbling through the undergrowth had led Tarzan of the Apes straight to where Esmeralda lay, but it was not Esmeralda in whom his interest centered, though pausing over her he saw that she was unhurt.

For a moment he scrutinized the ground below and the trees above, until the ape that was in him by virtue of training and environment, combined with the intelligence that was his by right of birth, told his wondrous woodcraft the whole story as plainly as though he had seen the thing happen with his own eyes.

And then he was gone again into the swaying trees, following the high-flung spoor which no other human eye could have detected, much less translated.

At boughs' ends, where the anthropoid swings from one tree to another, there is most to mark the trail, but least to point the direction of the quarry; for there the pressure is downward always, toward the small end of the branch, whether the ape be leaving or entering a tree. Nearer the center of the tree, where the signs of passage are fainter, the direction is plainly marked.

Here, on this branch, a caterpillar has been crushed by the fugitive's great foot, and Tarzan knows instinctively where that same foot would touch in the next stride. Here he looks to find a tiny particle of the demolished larva, ofttimes not more than a speck of moisture.

Again, a minute bit of bark has been upturned by the scraping hand, and the direction of the break indicates the direction of the passage. Or some great limb, or the stem of the tree itself has been brushed by the hairy body, and a tiny shred of hair tells him by the direction from which it is wedged beneath the bark that he is on the right trail.

Nor does he need to check his speed to catch these seemingly faint records of the fleeing beast.

To Tarzan they stand out boldly against all the myriad other scars and bruises and signs upon the leafy way. But strongest of all is the scent, for Tarzan is pursuing up the wind, and his trained nostrils are as sensitive as a hound's.

There are those who believe that the lower orders are specially endowed by nature with better olfactory nerves than man, but it is merely a matter of development.

Man's survival does not hinge so greatly upon the perfection of his senses. His power to reason has relieved them of many of their duties, and so they have, to some extent, atrophied, as have the muscles which move the ears and scalp, merely from disuse.

The muscles are there, about the ears and beneath the scalp, and so are the nerves which transmit sensations to the brain, but they are under-developed because they are not needed.

Not so with Tarzan of the Apes. From early infancy his survival had depended upon acuteness of eyesight, hearing, smell, touch, and taste far more than upon the more slowly developed organ of reason.

The least developed of all in Tarzan was the sense of taste, for he could eat luscious fruits, or raw flesh, long buried with almost equal appreciation; but in that he differed but slightly from more civilized epicures.

Almost silently the ape-man sped on in the track of Terkoz and his prey, but the sound of his approach reached the ears of the fleeing beast and spurred it on to greater speed.

Three miles were covered before Tarzan overtook them, and then Terkoz, seeing that further flight was futile, dropped to the ground in a small open glade, that he might turn and fight for his prize or be free to escape unhampered if he saw that the pursuer was more than a match for him.

He still grasped Jane in one great arm as Tarzan bounded like a leopard into the arena which nature had provided for this primeval-like battle.

When Terkoz saw that it was Tarzan who pursued him, he jumped to the conclusion that this was Tarzan's woman, since they were of the same kind – white and hairless – and so he rejoiced at this opportunity for double revenge upon his hated enemy.

To Jane the strange apparition of this god-like man was as wine to sick nerves.

From the description which Clayton and her father and Mr. Philander had given her, she knew that it must be the same wonderful creature who had saved them, and she saw in him only a protector and a friend.

But as Terkoz pushed her roughly aside to meet Tarzan's charge, and she saw the great proportions of the ape and the mighty muscles and the fierce fangs, her heart quailed. How could any vanquish such a mighty antagonist?

Like two charging bulls they came together, and like two wolves sought each other's throat. Against the long canines of the ape was pitted the thin blade of the man's knife.

Jane – her lithe, young form flattened against the trunk of a great tree, her hands tight pressed against her rising and falling bosom, and her eyes wide with mingled horror, fascination, fear, and admiration – watched the primordial ape battle with the primeval man for possession of a woman – for her.

As the great muscles of the man's back and shoulders knotted beneath the tension of his efforts, and the huge biceps and forearm held at bay those mighty tusks, the veil of centuries of civilization and culture was swept from the blurred vision of the Baltimore girl.

When the long knife drank deep a dozen times of Terkoz' heart's blood, and the great carcass rolled lifeless upon the ground, it was a primeval woman who sprang forward with outstretched arms toward the primeval man who had fought for her and won her.

And Tarzan?

He did what no red-blooded man needs lessons in doing. He took his woman in his arms and smothered her upturned, panting lips with kisses.

For a moment Jane lay there with half-closed eyes. For a moment – the first in her young life – she knew the meaning of love.

But as suddenly as the veil had been withdrawn it dropped again, and an outraged conscience suffused her face with its scarlet mantle, and a mortified woman thrust Tarzan of the Apes from her and buried her face in her hands.

Tarzan had been surprised when he had found the girl he had learned to love after a vague and abstract manner a willing prisoner in his arms. Now he was surprised that she repulsed him.

He came close to her once more and took hold of her arm. She turned upon him like a tigress, striking his great breast with her tiny hands.

Tarzan could not understand it.

A moment ago and it had been his intention to hasten Jane back to her people, but that little moment was lost now in the dim and distant past of things which were but can never be again, and with it the good intentions had gone to join the impossible.

Since then Tarzan of the Apes had felt a warm, lithe form close pressed to his. Hot, sweet breath against his cheek and mouth had fanned a new flame to life within his breast, and perfect lips had clung to his in burning kisses that had seared a deep brand into his soul – a brand which marked a new Tarzan.

Again he laid his hand upon her arm. Again she repulsed him. And then Tarzan of the Apes did just what his first ancestor would have done.

He took his woman in his arms and carried her into the jungle.

Early the following morning the four within the little cabin by the beach were awakened by the booming of a cannon. Clayton was the first to rush out, and there, beyond the harbor's mouth, he saw two vessels lying at anchor.

One was the Arrow and the other a small French cruiser. The sides of the latter were crowded with men gazing shoreward, and it was evident to Clayton, as to the others who had now joined him, that the gun which they had heard had been fired to attract their attention if they still remained at the cabin.

Both vessels lay at a considerable distance from shore, and it was doubtful if their glasses would locate the waving hats of the little party far in between the harbor's points.

Esmeralda had removed her red apron and was waving it frantically above her head; but Clayton, still fearing that even this might not be seen, hurried off toward the northern point where lay his signal pyre ready for the match.

It seemed an age to him, as to those who waited breathlessly behind, ere he reached the great pile of dry branches and underbrush.

As he broke from the dense wood and came in sight of the vessels again, he was filled with consternation to see that the Arrow was making sail and that the cruiser was already under way.

Quickly lighting the pyre in a dozen places, he hurried to the extreme point of the promontory, where he stripped off his shirt, and, tying it to a fallen branch, stood waving it back and forth above him.

But still the vessels continued to stand out; and he had given up all hope, when the great column of smoke, rising above the forest in one dense vertical shaft, attracted the attention of a lookout aboard the cruiser, and instantly a dozen glasses were leveled on the beach.

Presently Clayton saw the two ships come about again; and while the Arrow lay drifting quietly on the ocean, the cruiser steamed slowly back toward shore.

At some distance away she stopped, and a boat was lowered and dispatched toward the beach.

As it was drawn up a young officer stepped out.

"Monsieur Clayton, I presume?" he asked.

"Thank God, you have come!" was Clayton's reply. "And it may be that it is not too late even now."

"What do you mean, Monsieur?" asked the officer.

Clayton told of the abduction of Jane Porter and the need of armed men to aid in the search for her.

"*Mon dieu*!" exclaimed the officer, sadly. "Yesterday and it would not have been too late. Today and it may be better that the poor lady were never found. It is horrible, Monsieur. It is too horrible."

Other boats had now put off from the cruiser, and Clayton, having pointed out the harbor's entrance to the officer, entered the boat with him and its nose was turned toward the little landlocked bay, into which the other craft followed.

Soon the entire party had landed where stood Professor Porter, Mr. Philander and the weeping Esmeralda.

Among the officers in the last boats to put off from the cruiser was the commander of the vessel; and when he had heard the story of Jane's abduction, he generously called for volunteers to accompany Professor Porter and Clayton in their search.

Not an officer or a man was there of those brave and sympathetic Frenchmen who did not quickly beg leave to be one of the expedition.

The commander selected twenty men and two officers, Lieutenant D'Arnot and Lieutenant Charpentier. A boat was dispatched to the cruiser for provisions, ammunition, and carbines; the men were already armed with revolvers.

Then, to Clayton's inquiries as to how they had happened to anchor off shore and fire a signal gun, the commander, Captain Dufranne, explained that a month before they had sighted the Arrow bearing southwest under considerable canvas, and that when they had signaled her to come about she had but crowded on more sail.

They had kept her hull-up until sunset, firing several shots after her, but the next morning she was nowhere to be seen. They had then continued to cruise up and down the coast for several weeks, and had about forgotten the incident of the recent chase, when, early one morning a few days before the lookout had described a vessel laboring in the trough of a heavy sea and evidently entirely out of control.

As they steamed nearer to the derelict they were surprised to note that it was the same vessel that had run from them a few weeks earlier. Her forestaysail and mizzen spanker were set as though an effort had been made to hold her head up into the wind, but the sheets had parted, and the sails were tearing to ribbons in the half gale of wind.

In the high sea that was running it was a difficult and dangerous task to attempt to put a prize crew aboard her; and as no signs of life had been seen above deck, it was decided to stand by until the wind and sea abated; but just then a figure was seen clinging to the rail and feebly waving a mute signal of despair toward them.

Immediately a boat's crew was ordered out and an attempt was successfully made to board the Arrow.

The sight that met the Frenchmen's eyes as they clambered over the ship's side was appalling.

A dozen dead and dying men rolled hither and thither upon the pitching deck, the living intermingled with the dead. Two of the corpses appeared to have been partially devoured as though by wolves.

The prize crew soon had the vessel under proper sail once more and the living members of the ill-starred company carried below to their hammocks.

The dead were wrapped in tarpaulins and lashed on deck to be identified by their comrades before being consigned to the deep.

None of the living was conscious when the Frenchmen reached the Arrow's deck. Even the poor devil who had waved the single despairing signal of distress had lapsed into unconsciousness before he had learned whether it had availed or not.

It did not take the French officer long to learn what had caused the terrible condition aboard; for when water and brandy were sought to restore the men, it was found that there was none, nor even food of any description.

He immediately signalled to the cruiser to send water, medicine, and provisions, and another boat made the perilous trip to the Arrow.

When restoratives had been applied several of the men regained consciousness, and then the whole story was told. That part of it we know up to the sailing of the Arrow after the murder of Snipes, and the burial of his body above the treasure chest.

It seems that the pursuit by the cruiser had so terrorized the mutineers that they had continued out across the Atlantic for several days after losing her; but on discovering the meager supply of water and provisions aboard, they had turned back toward the east.

With no one on board who understood navigation, discussions soon arose as to their whereabouts; and as three days' sailing to the east did not raise land, they bore off to the north, fearing that the high north winds that had prevailed had driven them south of the southern extremity of Africa.

They kept on a north-northeasterly course for two days, when they were overtaken by a calm which lasted for nearly a week. Their water was gone, and in another day they would be without food.

Conditions changed rapidly from bad to worse. One man went mad and leaped overboard. Soon another opened his veins and drank his own blood.

When he died they threw him overboard also, though there were those among them who wanted to keep the corpse on board. Hunger was changing them from human beasts to wild beasts.

Two days before they had been picked up by the cruiser they had become too weak to handle the vessel, and that same day three men died. On the following morning it was seen that one of the corpses had been partially devoured.

All that day the men lay glaring at each other like beasts of prey, and the following morning two of the corpses lay almost entirely stripped of flesh.

The men were but little stronger for their ghoulish repast, for the want of water was by far the greatest agony with which they had to contend. And then the cruiser had come.

When those who could had recovered, the entire story had been told to the French commander; but the men were too ignorant to be able to tell him at just what point on the coast the professor and his party had been marooned, so the cruiser had steamed slowly along within sight of land, firing occasional signal guns and scanning every inch of the beach with glasses.

They had anchored by night so as not to neglect a particle of the shore line, and it had happened that the preceding night had brought them off the very beach where lay the little camp they sought.

The signal guns of the afternoon before had not been heard by those on shore, it was presumed, because they had doubtless been in the thick of the jungle searching for Jane Porter, where the noise of their own crashing through the underbrush would have drowned the report of a far distant gun.

By the time the two parties had narrated their several adventures, the cruiser's boat had returned with supplies and arms for the expedition.

Within a few minutes the little body of sailors and the two French officers, together with Professor Porter and Clayton, set off upon their hopeless and ill-fated quest into the untracked jungle.

CHAPTER TWENTY

Heredity

WHEN JANE REALIZED that she was being borne away a captive by the strange forest creature who had rescued her from the clutches of the ape she struggled desperately to escape, but the strong arms that held her as easily as though she had been but a day-old babe only pressed a little more tightly.

So presently she gave up the futile effort and lay quietly, looking through half-closed lids at the face of the man who strode easily through the tangled undergrowth with her.

The face above her was one of extraordinary beauty.

A perfect type of the strongly masculine, unmarred by dissipation, or brutal or degrading passions. For, though Tarzan of the Apes was a killer of men and of beasts, he killed as the hunter kills, dispassionately, except on those rare occasions when he had killed for hate – though not the brooding, malevolent hate which marks the features of its own with hideous lines.

When Tarzan killed he more often smiled than scowled, and smiles are the foundation of beauty.

One thing the girl had noticed particularly when she had seen Tarzan rushing upon Terkoz – the vivid scarlet band upon his forehead, from above the left eye to the scalp; but now as she scanned his features she noticed that it was gone, and only a thin white line marked the spot where it had been.

As she lay more quietly in his arms Tarzan slightly relaxed his grip upon her.

Once he looked down into her eyes and smiled, and the girl had to close her own to shut out the vision of that handsome, winning face.

Presently Tarzan took to the trees, and Jane, wondering that she felt no fear, began to realize that in many respects she had never felt more secure in her whole life than now as she lay in the arms of this strong, wild creature, being borne, God alone knew where or to what fate, deeper and deeper into the savage fastness of the untamed forest.

When, with closed eyes, she commenced to speculate upon the future, and terrifying fears were conjured by a vivid imagination, she had but to raise her lids and look upon that noble face so close to hers to dissipate the last remnant of apprehension.

No, he could never harm her; of that she was convinced when she translated the fine features and the frank, brave eyes above her into the chivalry which they proclaimed.

On and on they went through what seemed to Jane a solid mass of verdure, yet ever there appeared to open before this forest god a passage, as by magic, which closed behind them as they passed.

Scarce a branch scraped against her, yet above and below, before and behind, the view presented naught but a solid mass of inextricably interwoven branches and creepers.

As Tarzan moved steadily onward his mind was occupied with many strange and new thoughts. Here was a problem the like of which he had never encountered, and he felt rather than reasoned that he must meet it as a man and not as an ape.

The free movement through the middle terrace, which was the route he had followed for the most part, had helped to cool the ardor of the first fierce passion of his new found love.

Now he discovered himself speculating upon the fate which would have fallen to the girl had he not rescued her from Terkoz.

He knew why the ape had not killed her, and he commenced to compare his intentions with those of Terkoz.

True, it was the order of the jungle for the male to take his mate by force; but could Tarzan be guided by the laws of the beasts? Was not Tarzan a Man? But what did men do? He was puzzled; for he did not know.

He wished that he might ask the girl, and then it came to him that she had already answered him in the futile struggle she had made to escape and to repulse him.

But now they had come to their destination, and Tarzan of the Apes with Jane in his strong arms, swung lightly to the turf of the arena where the great apes held their councils and danced the wild orgy of the Dum-Dum.

Though they had come many miles, it was still but midafternoon, and the amphitheater was bathed in the half light which filtered through the maze of encircling foliage.

The green turf looked soft and cool and inviting. The myriad noises of the jungle seemed far distant and hushed to a mere echo of blurred sounds, rising and falling like the surf upon a remote shore.

A feeling of dreamy peacefulness stole over Jane as she sank down upon the grass where Tarzan had placed her, and as she looked up at his great figure towering above her, there was added a strange sense of perfect security.

As she watched him from beneath half-closed lids, Tarzan crossed the little circular clearing toward the trees upon the further side. She noted the graceful majesty of his carriage, the perfect symmetry of his magnificent figure and the poise of his well-shaped head upon his broad shoulders.

What a perfect creature! There could be naught of cruelty or baseness beneath that godlike exterior. Never, she thought had such a man strode the earth since God created the first in his own image.

With a bound Tarzan sprang into the trees and disappeared. Jane wondered where he had gone. Had he left her there to her fate in the lonely jungle?

She glanced nervously about. Every vine and bush seemed but the lurking-place of some huge and horrible beast waiting to bury gleaming fangs into her soft flesh. Every sound she magnified into the stealthy creeping of a sinuous and malignant body.

How different now that he had left her!

For a few minutes that seemed hours to the frightened girl, she sat with tense nerves waiting for the spring of the crouching thing that was to end her misery of apprehension.

She almost prayed for the cruel teeth that would give her unconsciousness and surcease from the agony of fear.

She heard a sudden, slight sound behind her. With a cry she sprang to her feet and turned to face her end.

There stood Tarzan, his arms filled with ripe and luscious fruit.

Jane reeled and would have fallen, had not Tarzan, dropping his burden, caught her in his arms. She did not lose consciousness, but she clung tightly to him, shuddering and trembling like a frightened deer.

Tarzan of the Apes stroked her soft hair and tried to comfort and quiet her as Kala had him, when, as a little ape, he had been frightened by Sabor, the lioness, or Histah, the snake.

Once he pressed his lips lightly upon her forehead, and she did not move, but closed her eyes and sighed.

She could not analyze her feelings, nor did she wish to attempt it. She was satisfied to feel the safety of those strong arms, and to leave her future to fate; for the last few hours had taught her to trust this strange wild creature of the forest as she would have trusted but few of the men of her acquaintance.

As she thought of the strangeness of it, there commenced to dawn upon her the realization that she had, possibly, learned something else which she had never really known before – love. She wondered and then she smiled.

And still smiling, she pushed Tarzan gently away; and looking at him with a half-smiling, half-quizzical expression that made her face wholly entrancing, she pointed to the fruit upon the ground, and seated herself upon the edge of the earthen drum of the anthropoids, for hunger was asserting itself.

Tarzan quickly gathered up the fruit, and, bringing it, laid it at her feet; and then he, too, sat upon the drum beside her, and with his knife opened and prepared the various fruits for her meal.

Together and in silence they ate, occasionally stealing sly glances at one another, until finally Jane broke into a merry laugh in which Tarzan joined.

"I wish you spoke English," said the girl.

Tarzan shook his head, and an expression of wistful and pathetic longing sobered his laughing eyes.

Then Jane tried speaking to him in French, and then in German; but she had to laugh at her own blundering attempt at the latter tongue.

"Anyway," she said to him in English, "you understand my German as well as they did in Berlin."

Tarzan had long since reached a decision as to what his future procedure should be. He had had time to recollect all that he had read of the ways of men and women in the books at the cabin. He would act as he imagined the men in the books would have acted were they in his place.

Again he rose and went into the trees, but first he tried to explain by means of signs that he would return shortly, and he did so well that Jane understood and was not afraid when he had gone.

Only a feeling of loneliness came over her and she watched the point where he had disappeared, with longing eyes, awaiting his return. As before, she was appraised of his presence by a soft sound behind her, and turned to see him coming across the turf with a great armful of branches.

Then he went back again into the jungle and in a few minutes reappeared with a quantity of soft grasses and ferns.

Two more trips he made until he had quite a pile of material at hand.

Then he spread the ferns and grasses upon the ground in a soft flat bed, and above it leaned many branches together so that they met a few feet over its center. Upon these he spread layers of huge leaves of the great elephant's ear, and with more branches and more leaves he closed one end of the little shelter he had built.

Then they sat down together again upon the edge of the drum and tried to talk by signs.

The magnificent diamond locket which hung about Tarzan's neck, had been a source of much wonderment to Jane. She pointed to it now, and Tarzan removed it and handed the pretty bauble to her.

She saw that it was the work of a skilled artisan and that the diamonds were of great brilliancy and superbly set, but the cutting of them denoted that they were of a former day. She noticed too that the locket opened, and, pressing the hidden clasp, she saw the two halves spring apart to reveal in either section an ivory miniature.

One was of a beautiful woman and the other might have been a likeness of the man who sat beside her, except for a subtle difference of expression that was scarcely definable.

She looked up at Tarzan to find him leaning toward her gazing on the miniatures with an expression of astonishment. He reached out his hand for the locket and took it away from her, examining the likenesses within with unmistakable signs of surprise and new interest. His manner clearly denoted that he had never before seen them, nor imagined that the locket opened.

This fact caused Jane to indulge in further speculation, and it taxed her imagination to picture how this beautiful ornament came into the possession of a wild and savage creature of the unexplored jungles of Africa.

Still more wonderful was how it contained the likeness of one who might be a brother, or, more likely, the father of this woodland demigod who was even ignorant of the fact that the locket opened.

Tarzan was still gazing with fixity at the two faces. Presently he removed the quiver from his shoulder, and emptying the arrows upon the ground reached into the bottom of the bag-like receptacle and drew forth a flat object wrapped in many soft leaves and tied with bits of long grass.

Carefully he unwrapped it, removing layer after layer of leaves until at length he held a photograph in his hand.

Pointing to the miniature of the man within the locket he handed the photograph to Jane, holding the open locket beside it.

The photograph only served to puzzle the girl still more, for it was evidently another likeness of the same man whose picture rested in the locket beside that of the beautiful young woman.

Tarzan was looking at her with an expression of puzzled bewilderment in his eyes as she glanced up at him. He seemed to be framing a question with his lips.

The girl pointed to the photograph and then to the miniature and then to him, as though to indicate that she thought the likenesses were of him, but he only shook his head, and then shrugging his great shoulders, he took the photograph from her and having carefully rewrapped it, placed it again in the bottom of his quiver.

For a few moments he sat in silence, his eyes bent upon the ground, while Jane held the little locket in her hand, turning it over and over in an endeavor to find some further clue that might lead to the identity of its original owner.

At length a simple explanation occurred to her.

The locket had belonged to Lord Greystoke, and the likenesses were of himself and Lady Alice.

This wild creature had simply found it in the cabin by the beach. How stupid of her not to have thought of that solution before.

But to account for the strange likeness between Lord Greystoke and this forest god – that was quite beyond her, and it is not strange that she could not imagine that this naked savage was indeed an English nobleman.

At length Tarzan looked up to watch the girl as she examined the locket. He could not fathom the meaning of the faces within, but he could read the interest and fascination upon the face of the live young creature by his side.

She noticed that he was watching her and thinking that he wished his ornament again she held it out to him. He took it from her and taking the chain in his two hands he placed it about her neck, smiling at her expression of surprise at his unexpected gift.

Jane shook her head vehemently and would have removed the golden links from about her throat, but Tarzan would not let her. Taking her hands in his, when she insisted upon it, he held them tightly to prevent her.

At last she desisted and with a little laugh raised the locket to her lips.

Tarzan did not know precisely what she meant, but he guessed correctly that it was her way of acknowledging the gift, and so he rose, and taking the locket in his hand, stooped gravely like some courtier of old, and pressed his lips upon it where hers had rested.

It was a stately and gallant little compliment performed with the grace and dignity of utter unconsciousness of self. It was the hall-mark of his aristocratic birth, the natural outcropping of many generations of fine breeding, an hereditary instinct of graciousness which a lifetime of uncouth and savage training and environment could not eradicate.

It was growing dark now, and so they ate again of the fruit which was both food and drink for them; then Tarzan rose, and leading Jane to the little bower he had erected, motioned her to go within.

For the first time in hours a feeling of fear swept over her, and Tarzan felt her draw away as though shrinking from him.

Contact with this girl for half a day had left a very diferent Tarzan from the one on whom the morning's sun had risen.

Now, in every fiber of his being, heredity spoke louder than training.

He had not in one swift transition become a polished gentleman from a savage ape-man, but at last the instincts of the former predominated, and over all was the desire to please the woman he loved, and to appear well in her eyes.

So Tarzan of the Apes did the only thing he knew to assure Jane of her safety. He removed his hunting knife from its sheath and handed it to her hilt first, again motioning her into the bower.

The girl understood, and taking the long knife she entered and lay down upon the soft grasses while Tarzan of the Apes stretched himself upon the ground across the entrance.

And thus the rising sun found them in the morning.

When Jane awoke, she did not at first recall the strange events of the preceding day, and so she wondered at her odd surroundings – the little leafy bower, the soft grasses of her bed, the unfamiliar prospect from the opening at her feet.

Slowly the circumstances of her position crept one by one into her mind. And then a great wonderment arose in her heart – a mighty wave of thankfulness and gratitude that though she had been in such terrible danger, yet she was unharmed.

She moved to the entrance of the shelter to look for Tarzan. He was gone; but this time no fear assailed her for she knew that he would return.

In the grass at the entrance to her bower she saw the imprint of his body where he had lain all night to guard her. She knew that the fact that he had been there was all that had permitted her to sleep in such peaceful security.

With him near, who could entertain fear? She wondered if there was another man on earth with whom a girl could feel so safe in the heart of this savage African jungle. Even the lions and panthers had no fears for her now.

She looked up to see his lithe form drop softly from a near-by tree. As he caught her eyes upon him his face lighted with that frank and radiant smile that had won her confidence the day before.

As he approached her Jane's heart beat faster and her eyes brightened as they had never done before at the approach of any man.

He had again been gathering fruit and this he laid at the entrance of her bower. Once more they sat down together to eat.

Jane commenced to wonder what his plans were. Would he take her back to the beach or would he keep her here? Suddenly she realized that the matter did not seem to give her much concern. Could it be that she did not care!

She began to comprehend, also, that she was entirely contented sitting here by the side of this smiling giant eating delicious fruit in a sylvan paradise far within the remote depths of an African jungle – that she was contented and very happy.

She could not understand it. Her reason told her that she should be torn by wild anxieties, weighted by dread fears, cast down by gloomy forebodings; but instead, her heart was singing and she was smiling into the answering face of the man beside her.

When they had finished their breakfast Tarzan went to her bower and recovered his knife. The girl had entirely forgotten it. She realized that it was because she had forgotten the fear that prompted her to accept it.

Motioning her to follow, Tarzan walked toward the trees at the edge of the arena, and taking her in one strong arm swung to the branches above.

The girl knew that he was taking her back to her people, and she could not understand the sudden feeling of loneliness and sorrow which crept over her.

For hours they swung slowly along.

Tarzan of the Apes did not hurry. He tried to draw out the sweet pleasure of that journey with those dear arms about his neck as long as possible, and so he went far south of the direct route to the beach.

Several times they halted for brief rests, which Tarzan did not need, and at noon they stopped for an hour at a little brook, where they quenched their thirst, and ate.

So it was nearly sunset when they came to the clearing, and Tarzan, dropping to the ground beside a great tree, parted the tall jungle grass and pointed out the little cabin to her.

She took him by the hand to lead him to it, that she might tell her father that this man had saved her from death and worse than death, that he had watched over her as carefully as a mother might have done.

But again the timidity of the wild thing in the face of human habitation swept over Tarzan of the Apes. He drew back, shaking his head.

The girl came close to him, looking up with pleading eyes. Somehow she could not bear the thought of his going back into the terrible jungle alone.

Still he shook his head, and finally he drew her to him very gently and stooped to kiss her, but first he looked into her eyes and waited to learn if she were pleased, or if she would repulse him.

Just an instant the girl hesitated, and then she realized the truth, and throwing her arms about his neck she drew his face to hers and kissed him – unashamed.

"I love you – I love you," she murmured.

From far in the distance came the faint sound of many guns. Tarzan and Jane raised their heads.

From the cabin came Mr. Philander and Esmeralda.

From where Tarzan and the girl stood they could not see the two vessels lying at anchor in the harbor.

Tarzan pointed toward the sounds, touched his breast and pointed again. She understood. He was going, and something told her that it was because he thought her people were in danger.

Again he kissed her.

"Come back to me," she whispered. "I shall wait for you – always."

He was gone – and Jane turned to walk across the clearing to the cabin.

Mr. Philander was the first to see her. It was dusk and Mr. Philander was very near sighted.

"Quickly, Esmeralda!" he cried. "Let us seek safety within; it is a lioness. Bless me!"

Esmeralda did not bother to verify Mr. Philander's vision. His tone was enough. She was within the cabin and had slammed and bolted the door before he had finished pronouncing her name. The "Bless me" was startled out of Mr. Philander by the discovery that Esmeralda, in the exuberance of her haste, had fastened him upon the same side of the door as was the close-approaching lioness.

He beat furiously upon the heavy portal.

"Esmeralda! Esmeralda!" he shrieked. "Let me in. I am being devoured by a lion."

Esmeralda thought that the noise upon the door was made by the lioness in her attempts to pursue her, so, after her custom, she fainted.

Mr. Philander cast a frightened glance behind him.

Horrors! The thing was quite close now. He tried to scramble up the side of the cabin, and succeeded in catching a fleeting hold upon the thatched roof.

For a moment he hung there, clawing with his feet like a cat on a clothesline, but presently a piece of the thatch came away, and Mr. Philander, preceding it, was precipitated upon his back.

At the instant he fell a remarkable item of natural history leaped to his mind. If one feigns death lions and lionesses are supposed to ignore one, according to Mr. Philander's faulty memory.

So Mr. Philander lay as he had fallen, frozen into the horrid semblance of death. As his arms and legs had been extended stiffly upward as he came to earth upon his back the attitude of death was anything but impressive.

Jane had been watching his antics in mild-eyed surprise. Now she laughed – a little choking gurgle of a laugh; but it was enough. Mr. Philander rolled over upon his side and peered about. At length he discovered her.

"Jane!" he cried. "Jane Porter. Bless me!"

He scrambled to his feet and rushed toward her. He could not believe that it was she, and alive.

"Bless me!" Where did you come from? Where in the world have you been? How – "

"Mercy, Mr. Philander," interrupted the girl, "I can never remember so many questions."

"Well, well," said Mr. Philander. "Bless me! I am so filled with surprise and exuberant delight at seeing you safe and well again that I scarcely know what I am saying, really. But come, tell me all that has happened to you."

CHAPTER TWENTY ONE

The Village of Torture

As THE LITTLE expedition of sailors toiled through the dense jungle searching for signs of Jane Porter, the futility of their venture became more and more apparent, but the grief of the old man and the hopeless eyes of the young Englishman prevented the kind hearted D'Arnot from turning back.

He thought that there might be a bare possibility of finding her body, or the remains of it, for he was positive that she had been devoured by some beast of prey. He deployed his men into a skirmish line from the point where Esmeralda had been found, and in this extended formation they pushed their way, sweating and panting, through the tangled vines and creepers. It was slow work. Noon found them but a few miles inland. They halted for a brief rest then, and after pushing on for a short distance further one of the men discovered a well-marked trail.

It was an old elephant track, and D'Arnot after consulting with Professor Porter and Clayton decided to follow it.

The path wound through the jungle in a northeasterly direction, and along it the column moved in single file.

Lieutenant D'Arnot was in the lead and moving at a quick pace, for the trail was comparatively open. Immediately behind him came Professor Porter, but as he could not keep pace with the younger man D'Arnot was a hundred yards in advance when suddenly a half dozen black warriors arose about him.

D'Arnot gave a warning shout to his column as the blacks closed on him, but before he could draw his revolver he had been pinioned and dragged into the jungle.

His cry had alarmed the sailors and a dozen of them sprang forward past Professor Porter, running up the trail to their officer's aid.

They did not know the cause of his outcry, only that it was a warning of danger ahead. They had rushed past the spot where D'Arnot had been seized when a spear hurled from the jungle transfixed one of the men, and then a volley of arrows fell among them.

Raising their rifles they fired into the underbrush in the direction from which the missiles had come.

By this time the balance of the party had come up, and volley after volley was fired toward the concealed foe. It was these shots that Tarzan and Jane Porter had heard.

Lieutenant Charpentier, who had been bringing up the rear of the column, now came running to the scene, and on hearing the details of the ambush ordered the men to follow him, and plunged into the tangled vegetation.

In an instant they were in a hand-to-hand fight with some fifty black warriors of Mbonga's village. Arrows and bullets flew thick and fast.

Queer African knives and French gun butts mingled for a moment in savage and bloody duels, but soon the natives fled into the jungle, leaving the Frenchmen to count their losses.

Four of the twenty were dead, a dozen others were wounded, and Lieutenant D'Arnot was missing. Night was falling rapidly, and their predicament was rendered doubly worse when they could not even find the elephant trail which they had been following.

There was but one thing to do, make camp where they were until daylight. Lieutenant Charpentier ordered a clearing made and a circular abatis of underbrush constructed about the camp.

This work was not completed until long after dark, the men building a huge fire in the center of the clearing to give them light to work by.

When all was safe as possible against attack of wild beasts and savage men, Lieutenant Charpentier placed sentries about the little camp and the tired and hungry men threw themselves upon the ground to sleep.

The groans of the wounded, mingled with the roaring and growling of the great beasts which the noise and firelight had attracted, kept sleep, except in its most fitful form, from the tired eyes. It was a sad and hungry party that lay through the long night praying for dawn.

The blacks who had seized D'Arnot had not waited to participate in the fight which followed, but instead had dragged their prisoner a little way through the jungle and then struck the trail further on beyond the scene of the fighting in which their fellows were engaged.

They hurried him along, the sounds of battle growing fainter and fainter as they drew away from the contestants until there suddenly broke upon D'Arnot's vision a good-sized clearing at one end of which stood a thatched and palisaded village.

It was now dusk, but the watchers at the gate saw the approaching trio and distinguished one as a prisoner ere they reached the portals.

A cry went up within the palisade. A great throng of women and children rushed out to meet the party.

And then began for the French officer the most terrifying experience which man can encounter upon earth – the reception of a white prisoner into a village of African cannibals.

To add to the fiendishness of their cruel savagery was the poignant memory of still crueler barbarities practiced upon them and theirs by the white officers of that arch hypocrite, Leopold II of Belgium, because of whose atrocities they had fled the Congo Free State – a pitiful remnant of what once had been a mighty tribe.

They fell upon D'Arnot tooth and nail, beating him with sticks and stones and tearing at him with claw-like hands. Every vestige of clothing was torn from him, and the merciless blows fell upon his bare and quivering flesh. But not once did the Frenchman cry out in pain. He breathed a silent prayer that he be quickly delivered from his torture.

But the death he prayed for was not to be so easily had. Soon the warriors beat the women away from their prisoner. He was to be saved for nobler sport than this, and the first wave of their passion having subsided they contented themselves with crying out taunts and insults and spitting upon him.

Presently they reached the center of the village. There D'Arnot was bound securely to the great post from which no live man had ever been released.

A number of the women scattered to their several huts to fetch pots and water, while others built a row of fires on which portions of the feast were to be boiled while the balance would be slowly dried in strips for future use, as they expected the other warriors to return with many prisoners. The festivities were delayed awaiting the return of the warriors who had remained to engage in the skirmish with the white men, so that it was quite late when all were in the village, and the dance of death commenced to circle around the doomed officer.

Half fainting from pain and exhaustion, D'Arnot watched from beneath half-closed lids what seemed but the vagary of delirium, or some horrid nightmare from which he must soon awake.

The bestial faces, daubed with color – the huge mouths and flabby hanging lips – the yellow teeth, sharp filed – the rolling, demon eyes – the shining naked bodies – the cruel spears. Surely no such creatures really existed upon earth – he must indeed be dreaming.

The savage, whirling bodies circled nearer. Now a spear sprang forth and touched his arm. The sharp pain and the feel of hot, trickling blood assured him of the awful reality of his hopeless position.

Another spear and then another touched him. He closed his eyes and held his teeth firm set – he would not cry out.

He was a soldier of France, and he would teach these beasts how an officer and a gentleman died.

Tarzan of the Apes needed no interpreter to translate the story of those distant shots. With Jane Porter's kisses still warm upon his lips he was swinging with incredible rapidity through the forest trees straight toward the village of Mbonga.

He was not interested in the location of the encounter, for he judged that that would soon be over. Those who were killed he could not aid, those who escaped would not need his assistance.

It was to those who had neither been killed or escaped that he hastened. And he knew that he would find them by the great post in the center of Mbonga village.

Many times had Tarzan seen Mbonga's black raiding parties return from the northward with prisoners, and always were the same scenes enacted about that grim stake, beneath the flaring light of many fires.

He knew, too, that they seldom lost much time before consummating the fiendish purpose of their captures. He doubted that he would arrive in time to do more than avenge.

On he sped. Night had fallen and he traveled high along the upper terrace where the gorgeous tropic moon lighted the dizzy pathway through the gently undulating branches of the tree tops.

Presently he caught the reflection of a distant blaze. It lay to the right of his path. It must be the light from the camp fire the two men had built before they were attacked – Tarzan knew nothing of the presence of the sailors.

So sure was Tarzan of his jungle knowledge that he did not turn from his course, but passed the glare at a distance of a half mile. It was the camp fire of the Frenchmen.

In a few minutes more Tarzan swung into the trees above Mbonga's village. Ah, he was not quite too late! Or, was he? He could not tell. The figure at the stake was very still, yet the black warriors were but pricking it.

Tarzan knew their customs. The death blow had not been struck. He could tell almost to a minute how far the dance had gone.

In another instant Mbonga's knife would sever one of the victim's ears – that would mark the beginning of the end, for very shortly after only a writhing mass of mutilated flesh would remain.

There would still be life in it, but death then would be the only charity it craved.

The stake stood forty feet from the nearest tree. Tarzan coiled his rope. Then there rose suddenly above the fiendish cries of the dancing demons the awful challenge of the ape-man.

The dancers halted as though turned to stone.

The rope sped with singing whir high above the heads of the blacks. It was quite invisible in the flaring lights of the camp fires.

D'Arnot opened his eyes. A huge black, standing directly before him, lunged backward as though felled by an invisible hand.

Struggling and shrieking, his body, rolling from side to side, moved quickly toward the shadows beneath the trees.

The blacks, their eyes protruding in horror, watched spellbound.

Once beneath the trees, the body rose straight into the air, and as it disappeared into the foliage above, the terrified negroes, screaming with fright, broke into a mad race for the village gate.

D'Arnot was left alone.

He was a brave man, but he had felt the short hairs bristle upon the nape of his neck when that uncanny cry rose upon the air.

As the writhing body of the black soared, as though by unearthly power, into the dense foliage of the forest, D'Arnot felt an icy shiver run along his spine, as though death had risen from a dark grave and laid a cold and clammy finger on his flesh.

As D'Arnot watched the spot where the body had entered the tree he heard the sounds of movement there.

The branches swayed as though under the weight of a man's body – there was a crash and the black came sprawling to earth again, – to lie very quietly where he had fallen.

Immediately after him came a white body, but this one alighted erect.

D'Arnot saw a clean-limbed young giant emerge from the shadows into the firelight and come quickly toward him.

What could it mean? Who could it be? Some new creature of torture and destruction, doubtless.

D'Arnot waited. His eyes never left the face of the advancing man. Nor did the other's frank, clear eyes waver beneath D'Arnot's fixed gaze.

D'Arnot was reassured, but still without much hope, though he felt that that face could not mask a cruel heart.

Without a word Tarzan of the Apes cut the bonds which held the Frenchman. Weak from suffering and loss of blood, he would have fallen but for the strong arm that caught him.

He felt himself lifted from the ground. There was a sensation as of flying, and then he lost consciousness.

CHAPTER TWENTY TWO

The Search Party

When dawn broke upon the little camp of Frenchmen in the heart of the jungle it found a sad and disheartened group.

As soon as it was light enough to see their surroundings Lieutenant Charpentier sent men in groups of three in several directions to locate the trail, and in ten minutes it was found and the expedition was hurrying back toward the beach.

It was slow work, for they bore the bodies of six dead men, two more having succumbed during the night, and several of those who were wounded required support to move even very slowly.

Charpentier had decided to return to camp for reinforcements, and then make an attempt to track down the natives and rescue D'Arnot.

It was late in the afternoon when the exhausted men reached the clearing by the beach, but for two of them the return brought so great a happiness that all their suffering and heartbreaking grief was forgotten on the instant.

As the little party emerged from the jungle the first person that Professor Porter and Cecil Clayton saw was Jane, standing by the cabin door.

With a little cry of joy and relief she ran forward to greet them, throwing her arms about her father's neck and bursting into tears for the first time since they had been cast upon this hideous and adventurous shore.

Professor Porter strove manfully to suppress his own emotions, but the strain upon his nerves and weakened vitality were too much for him, and at length, burying his old face in the girl's shoulder, he sobbed quietly like a tired child.

Jane led him toward the cabin, and the Frenchmen turned toward the beach from which several of their fellows were advancing to meet them.

Clayton, wishing to leave father and daughter alone, joined the sailors and remained talking with the officers until their boat pulled away toward the cruiser whither Lieutenant Charpentier was bound to report the unhappy outcome of his adventure.

Then Clayton turned back slowly toward the cabin. His heart was filled with happiness. The woman he loved was safe.

He wondered by what manner of miracle she had been spared. To see her alive seemed almost unbelievable.

As he approached the cabin he saw Jane coming out. When she saw him she hurried forward to meet him.

"Jane!" he cried, "God has been good to us, indeed. Tell me how you escaped – what form Providence took to save you for – us."

He had never before called her by her given name. Forty-eight hours before it would have suffused Jane with a soft glow of pleasure to have heard that name from Clayton's lips – now it frightened her.

"Mr. Clayton," she said quietly, extending her hand, "first let me thank you for your chivalrous loyalty to my dear father. He has told me how noble and self-sacrificing you have been. How can we repay you!"

Clayton noticed that she did not return his familiar salutation, but he felt no misgivings on that score. She had been through so much. This was no time to force his love upon her, he quickly realized.

"I am already repaid," he said. "Just to see you and Professor Porter both safe, well, and together again. I do not think that I could much longer have endured the pathos of his quiet and uncomplaining grief.

"It was the saddest experience of my life, Miss Porter; and then, added to it, there was my own grief – the greatest I have ever known. But his was so hopeless – his was pitiful. It taught me that no love, not even that of a man for his wife may be so deep and terrible and self-sacrificing as the love of a father for his daughter."

The girl bowed her head. There was a question she wanted to ask, but it seemed almost sacrilegious in the face of the love of these two men and the terrible suffering they had endured while she sat laughing and happy beside a godlike creature of the forest, eating delicious fruits and looking with eyes of love into answering eyes.

But love is a strange master, and human nature is still stranger, so she asked her question.

"Where is the forest man who went to rescue you? Why did he not return?"

"I do not understand," said Clayton. "Whom do you mean?"

"He who has saved each of us – who saved me from the gorilla."

"Oh," cried Clayton, in surprise. "It was he who rescued you? You have not told me anything of your adventure, you know."

"But the wood man," she urged. "Have you not seen him? When we heard the shots in the jungle, very faint and far away, he left me. We had just reached the clearing, and he hurried off in the direction of the fighting. I know he went to aid you."

Her tone was almost pleading – her manner tense with suppressed emotion. Clayton could not but notice it, and he wondered, vaguely, why she was so deeply moved – so anxious to know the whereabouts of this strange creature.

Yet a feeling of apprehension of some impending sorrow haunted him, and in his breast, unknown to himself, was implanted the first germ of jealousy and suspicion of the ape-man, to whom he owed his life.

"We did not see him," he replied quietly. "He did not join us." And then after a moment of thoughtful pause: "Possibly he joined his own tribe – the men who attacked us." He did not know why he had said it, for he did not believe it.

The girl looked at him wide eyed for a moment.

"No!" she exclaimed vehemently, much too vehemently he thought. "It could not be. They were savages."

Clayton looked puzzled.

"He is a strange, half-savage creature of the jungle, Miss Porter. We know nothing of him. He neither speaks nor understands any European tongue – and his ornaments and weapons are those of the West Coast savages."

Clayton was speaking rapidly.

"There are no other human beings than savages within hundreds of miles, Miss Porter. He must belong to the tribes which attacked us, or to some other equally savage – he may even be a cannibal."

Jane blanched.

"I will not believe it," she half whispered. "It is not true. You shall see," she said, addressing Clayton, "that he will come back and that he will prove that you are wrong. You do not know him as I do. I tell you that he is a gentleman."

Clayton was a generous and chivalrous man, but something in the girl's breathless defense of the forest man stirred him to unreasoning jealousy, so that for the instant he forgot all that they owed to this wild demi-god, and he answered her with a half sneer upon his lip.

"Possibly you are right, Miss Porter," he said, "but I do not think that any of us need worry about our carrion-eating acquaintance. The chances are that he is some half-demented castaway who will forget us more quickly, but no more surely, than we shall forget him. He is only a beast of the jungle, Miss Porter."

The girl did not answer, but she felt her heart shrivel within her.

She knew that Clayton spoke merely what he thought, and for the first time she began to analyze the structure which supported her new-found love, and to subject its object to a critical examination.

Slowly she turned and walked back to the cabin. She tried to imagine her wood-god by her side in the saloon of an ocean liner. She saw him eating with his hands, tearing his food like a beast of prey, and wiping his greasy fingers upon his thighs. She shuddered.

She saw him as she introduced him to her friends – uncouth, illiterate – a boor; and the girl winced.

She had reached her room now, and as she sat upon the edge of her bed of ferns and grasses, with one hand resting upon her rising and falling bosom, she felt the hard outlines of the man's locket.

She drew it out, holding it in the palm of her hand for a moment with tear-blurred eyes bent upon it. Then she raised it to her lips, and crushing it there buried her face in the soft ferns, sobbing.

"Beast?" she murmured. "Then God make me a beast; for, man or beast, I am yours."

She did not see Clayton again that day. Esmeralda brought her supper to her, and she sent word to her father that she was suffering from the reaction following her adventure.

The next morning Clayton left early with the relief expedition in search of Lieutenant D'Arnot. There were two hundred armed men this time, with ten officers and two surgeons, and provisions for a week.

They carried bedding and hammocks, the latter for transporting their sick and wounded.

It was a determined and angry company – a punitive expedition as well as one of relief. They reached the site of the skirmish of the previous expedition shortly after noon, for they were now traveling a known trail and no time was lost in exploring.

From there on the elephant-track led straight to Mbonga's village. It was but two o'clock when the head of the column halted upon the edge of the clearing.

Lieutenant Charpentier, who was in command, immediately sent a portion of his force through the jungle to the opposite side of the village. Another detachment was dispatched to a point before the village gate, while he remained with the balance upon the south side of the clearing.

It was arranged that the party which was to take its position to the north, and which would be the last to gain its station should commence the assault, and that their opening volley should be the signal for a concerted rush from all sides in an attempt to carry the village by storm at the first charge.

For half an hour the men with Lieutenant Charpentier crouched in the dense foliage of the jungle, waiting the signal. To them it seemed like hours. They could see natives in the fields, and others moving in and out of the village gate.

At length the signal came – a sharp rattle of musketry, and like one man, an answering volley tore from the jungle to the west and to the south.

The natives in the field dropped their implements and broke madly for the palisade. The French bullets mowed them down, and the French sailors bounded over their prostrate bodies straight for the village gate.

So sudden and unexpected the assault had been that the whites reached the gates before the frightened natives could bar them, and in another minute the village street was filled with armed men fighting hand to hand in an inextricable tangle.

For a few moments the blacks held their ground within the entrance to the street, but the revolvers, rifles and cutlasses of the Frenchmen crumpled the native spearmen and struck down the black archers with their bows halfdrawn.

Soon the battle turned to a wild rout, and then to a grim massacre; for the French sailors had seen bits of D'Arnot's uniform upon several of the black warriors who opposed them.

They spared the children and those of the women whom they were not forced to kill in self-defense, but when at length they stopped, parting, blood covered and sweating, it was because there lived to oppose them no single warrior of all the savage village of Mbonga.

Carefully they ransacked every hut and corner of the village, but no sign of D'Arnot could they find. They questioned the prisoners by signs, and finally one of the sailors who had served in the French Congo found that he could make them understand the bastard tongue that passes for language between the whites and the more degraded tribes of the coast, but even then they could learn nothing definite regarding the fate of D'Arnot.

Only excited gestures and expressions of fear could they obtain in response to their inquiries concerning their fellow; and at last they became convinced that these were but evidences of the guilt of these demons who had slaughtered and eaten their comrade two nights before.

At length all hope left them, and they prepared to camp for the night within the village. The prisoners were herded into three huts where they were heavily guarded. Sentries were posted at the barred gates, and finally the village was wrapped in the silence of slumber, except for the wailing of the native women for their dead.

The next morning they set out upon the return march. Their original intention had been to burn the village, but this idea was abandoned and the prisoners were left behind, weeping and moaning, but with roofs to cover them and a palisade for refuge from the beasts of the jungle.

Slowly the expedition retraced its steps of the preceding day. Ten loaded hammocks retarded its pace. In eight of them lay the more seriously wounded, while two swung beneath the weight of the dead.

Clayton and Lieutenant Charpentier brought up the rear of the column; the Englishman silent in respect for the other's grief, for D'Arnot and Charpentier had been inseparable friends since boyhood.

Clayton could not but realize that the Frenchman felt his grief the more keenly because D'Arnot's sacrifice had been so futile, since Jane had been rescued before D'Arnot had fallen into the hands of the savages, and again because the service in which he had lost his life had been outside his duty and for strangers and aliens; but when he spoke of it to Lieutenant Charpentier, the latter shook his head.

"No, Monsieur," he said, "D'Arnot would have chosen to die thus. I only grieve that I could not have died for him, or at least with him. I wish that you could have known him better, Monsieur. He was indeed an officer and a gentleman – a title conferred on many, but deserved by so few.

"He did not die futilely, for his death in the cause of a strange American girl will make us, his comrades, face our ends the more bravely, however they may come to us."

Clayton did not reply, but within him rose a new respect for Frenchmen which remained undimmed ever after.

It was quite late when they reached the cabin by the beach. A single shot before they emerged from the jungle had announced to those in camp as well as on the ship that the expedition had been too late – for it had been prearranged that when they came within a mile or two of camp one shot was to be fired to denote failure, or three for success, while two would have indicated that they had found no sign of either D'Arnot or his black captors.

So it was a solemn party that awaited their coming, and few words were spoken as the dead and wounded men were tenderly placed in boats and rowed silently toward the cruiser.

Clayton, exhausted from his five days of laborious marching through the jungle and from the effects of his two battles with the blacks, turned toward the cabin to seek a mouthful of food and then the comparative ease of his bed of grasses after two nights in the jungle.

By the cabin door stood Jane.

"The poor lieutenant?" she asked. "Did you find no trace of him?"

"We were too late, Miss Porter," he replied sadly.

"Tell me. What had happened?" she asked.

"I cannot, Miss Porter, it is too horrible."

"You do not mean that they had tortured him?" she whispered.

"We do not know what they did to him *before* they killed him," he answered, his face drawn with fatigue and the sorrow he felt for poor D'Arnot and he emphasized the word before.

"*Before* they killed him! What do you mean? They are not – ? They are not – ?"

She was thinking of what Clayton had said of the forest man's probable relationship to this tribe and she could not frame the awful word.

"Yes, Miss Porter, they were – cannibals," he said, almost bitterly, for to him too had suddenly come the thought of the forest man, and the strange, unaccountable jealousy he had felt two days before swept over him once more.

And then in sudden brutality that was as unlike Clayton as courteous consideration is unlike an ape, he blurted out:

"When your forest god left you he was doubtless hurrying to the feast."

He was sorry ere the words were spoken though he did not know how cruelly they had cut the girl. His regret was for his baseless disloyalty to one who had saved the lives of every member of his party, and offered harm to none.

The girl's head went high.

"There could be but one suitable reply to your assertion, Mr. Clayton," she said icily, "and I regret that I am not a man, that I might make it." She turned quickly and entered the cabin.

Clayton was an Englishman, so the girl had passed quite out of sight before he deduced what reply a man would have made.

"Upon my word," he said ruefully, "she called me a liar. And I fancy I jolly well deserved it," he added thoughtfully. "Clayton, my boy, I know you are tired out and unstrung, but that's no reason why you should make an ass of yourself. You'd better go to bed."

But before he did so he called gently to Jane upon the opposite side of the sailcloth partition, for he wished to apologize, but he might as well have addressed the Sphinx. Then he wrote upon a piece of paper and shoved it beneath the partition.

Jane saw the little note and ignored it, for she was very angry and hurt and mortified, but – she was a woman, and so eventually she picked it up and read it.

MY DEAR MISS PORTER:

I had no reason to insinuate what I did. My only excuse is that my nerves must be unstrung – which is no excuse at all.

Please try and think that I did not say it. I am very sorry. I would not have hurt YOU, above all others in the world. Say that you forgive me.

WM. CECIL CLAYTON.

"He did think it or he never would have said it," reasoned the girl, "but it cannot be true – oh, I know it is not true!"

One sentence in the letter frightened her: "I would not have hurt *you* above all others in the world."

A week ago that sentence would have filled her with delight, now it depressed her.

She wished she had never met Clayton. She was sorry that she had ever seen the forest god. No, she was glad. And there was that other note she had found in the grass before the cabin the day after her return from the jungle, the love note signed by Tarzan of the Apes.

Who could be this new suitor? If he were another of the wild denizens of this terrible forest what might he not do to claim her?

"Esmeralda! Wake up," she cried.

"You make me so irritable, sleeping there peacefully when you know perfectly well that the world is filled with sorrow."

"Gaberelle!" screamed Esmeralda, sitting up. "What is it now? A hipponocerous? Where is he, Miss Jane?"

"Nonsense, Esmeralda, there is nothing. Go back to sleep. You are bad enough asleep, but you are infinitely worse awake."

"Yes honey, but what's the matter with you, precious? You acts sort of disgranulated this evening."

"Oh, Esmeralda, I'm just plain ugly to-night," said the girl. "Don't pay any attention to me – that's a dear."

"Yes, honey; now you go right to sleep. Your nerves are all on edge. What with all these ripotamuses and man eating geniuses that Mister Philander been telling about – Lord, it ain't no wonder we all get nervous prosecution."

Jane crossed the little room, laughing, and kissing the faithful woman, bid Esmeralda good night.

CHAPTER TWENTY THREE

Brother Men

When D'Arnot regained consciousness, he found himself lying upon a bed of soft ferns and grasses beneath a little "A" shaped shelter of boughs.

At his feet an opening looked out upon a green sward, and at a little distance beyond was the dense wall of jungle and forest.

He was very lame and sore and weak, and as full consciousness returned he felt the sharp torture of many cruel wounds and the dull aching of every bone and muscle in his body as a result of the hideous beating he had received.

Even the turning of his head caused him such excruciating agony that he lay still with closed eyes for a long time.

He tried to piece out the details of his adventure prior to the time he lost consciousness to see if they would explain his present whereabouts – he wondered if he were among friends or foes.

At length he recollected the whole hideous scene at the stake, and finally recalled the strange white figure in whose arms he had sunk into oblivion.

D'Arnot wondered what fate lay in store for him now. He could neither see nor hear any signs of life about him.

The incessant hum of the jungle – the rustling of millions of leaves – the buzz of insects – the voices of the birds and monkeys seemed blended into a strangely soothing purr, as though he lay apart, far from the myriad life whose sounds came to him only as a blurred echo.

At length he fell into a quiet slumber, nor did he awake again until afternoon.

Once more he experienced the strange sense of utter bewilderment that had marked his earlier awakening, but soon he recalled the recent past, and looking through the opening at his feet he saw the figure of a man squatting on his haunches.

The broad, muscular back was turned toward him, but, tanned though it was, D'Arnot saw that it was the back of a white man, and he thanked God.

The Frenchman called faintly. The man turned, and rising, came toward the shelter. His face was very handsome – the handsomest, thought D'Arnot, that he had ever seen.

Stooping, he crawled into the shelter beside the wounded officer, and placed a cool hand upon his forehead.

D'Arnot spoke to him in French, but the man only shook his head – sadly, it seemed to the Frenchman.

Then D'Arnot tried English, but still the man shook his head. Italian, Spanish and German brought similar discouragement.

D'Arnot knew a few words of Norwegian, Russian, Greek, and also had a smattering of the language of one of the West Coast negro tribes – the man denied them all.

After examining D'Arnot's wounds the man left the shelter and disappeared. In half an hour he was back with fruit and a hollow gourd-like vegetable filled with water.

D'Arnot drank and ate a little. He was surprised that he had no fever. Again he tried to converse with his strange nurse, but the attempt was useless.

Suddenly the man hastened from the shelter only to return a few minutes later with several pieces of bark and – wonder of wonders – a lead pencil.

Squatting beside D'Arnot he wrote for a minute on the smooth inner surface of the bark; then he handed it to the Frenchman.

D'Arnot was astonished to see, in plain print-like characters, a message in English:

I am Tarzan of the Apes. Who are you? Can you read this language?

D'Arnot seized the pencil – then he stopped. This strange man wrote English – evidently he was an Englishman.

"Yes," said D'Arnot, "I read English. I speak it also. Now we may talk. First let me thank you for all that you have done for me."

The man only shook his head and pointed to the pencil and the bark.

"*Mon dieu*!" cried D'Arnot. "If you are English why is it then that you cannot speak English?"

And then in a flash it came to him – the man was a mute, possibly a deaf mute.

So D'Arnot wrote a message on the bark, in English.

I am Paul d'Arnot, Lieutenant in the navy of France. I thank you for what you have done for me. You have saved my life, and all that I have is yours. May I ask how it is that one who writes English does not speak it?

Tarzan's reply filled D'Arnot with still greater wonder:

I speak only the language of my tribe – the great apes who were Kerchak's; and a little of the languages of Tantor, the elephant, and Numa, the lion, and of the other folks of the jungle I understand. With a human being I have never spoken, except once with Jane Porter, by signs. This is the first time I have spoken with another of my kind through written words.

D'Arnot was mystified. It seemed incredible that there lived upon earth a full-grown man who had never spoken with a fellow man, and still more preposterous that such a one could read and write.

He looked again at Tarzan's message – "except once, with Jane Porter." That was the American girl who had been carried into the jungle by a gorilla.

A sudden light commenced to dawn on D'Arnot – this then was the "gorilla." He seized the pencil and wrote:

Where is Jane Porter?

And Tarzan replied, below:

Back with her people in the cabin of Tarzan of the Apes.

She is not dead then? Where was she? What happened to her?

She is not dead. She was taken by Terkoz to be his wife; but Tarzan of the Apes took her away from Terkoz and killed him before he could harm her.

None in all the jungle may face Tarzan of the Apes in battle, and live. I am Tarzan of the Apes – mighty fighter.

D'Arnot wrote:

I am glad she is safe. It pains me to write, I will rest a while.

And then Tarzan:

Yes, rest. When you are well I shall take you back to your people.

For many days D'Arnot lay upon his bed of soft ferns. The second day a fever had come and D'Arnot thought that it meant infection and he knew that he would die.

An idea came to him. He wondered why he had not thought of it before.

He called Tarzan and indicated by signs that he would write, and when Tarzan had fetched the bark and pencil, D'Arnot wrote:

Can you go to my people and lead them here? I will write a message that you may take to them, and they will follow you.

Tarzan shook his head and taking the bark, wrote:

I had thought of that – the first day; but I dared not. The great apes come often to this spot, and if they found you here, wounded and alone, they would kill you.

D'Arnot turned on his side and closed his eyes. He did not wish to die; but he felt that he was going, for the fever was mounting higher and higher. That night he lost consciousness.

For three days he was in delirium, and Tarzan sat beside him and bathed his head and hands and washed his wounds.

On the fourth day the fever broke as suddenly as it had come, but it left D'Arnot a shadow of his former self, and very weak. Tarzan had to lift him that he might drink from the gourd.

The fever had not been the result of infection, as D'Arnot had thought, but one of those that commonly attack whites in the jungles of Africa, and either kill or leave them as suddenly as D'Arnot's had left him.

Two days later, D'Arnot was tottering about the amphitheater, Tarzan's strong arm about him to keep him from falling.

They sat beneath the shade of a great tree, and Tarzan found some smooth bark that they might converse.

D'Arnot wrote the first message:

What can I do to repay you for all that you have done for me?

And Tarzan, in reply:

Teach me to speak the language of men.

And so D'Arnot commenced at once, pointing out familiar objects and repeating their names in French, for he thought that it would be easier to teach this man his own language, since he understood it himself best of all.

It meant nothing to Tarzan, of course, for he could not tell one language from another, so when he pointed to the word man which he had printed upon a piece of bark he learned from D'Arnot that it was pronounced *homme*, and in the same way he was taught to pronounce ape, *singe* and tree, *arbre*.

He was a most eager student, and in two more days had mastered so much French that he could speak little sentences such as: "That is a tree," "this is grass," "I am hungry," and the like, but D'Arnot found that it was difficult to teach him the French construction upon a foundation of English.

The Frenchman wrote little lessons for him in English and had Tarzan repeat them in French, but as a literal translation was usually very poor French Tarzan was often confused.

D'Arnot realized now that he had made a mistake, but it seemed too late to go back and do it all over again and force Tarzan to unlearn all that he had learned, especially as they were rapidly approaching a point where they would be able to converse.

On the third day after the fever broke Tarzan wrote a message asking D'Arnot if he felt strong enough to be carried back to the cabin. Tarzan was as anxious to go as D'Arnot, for he longed to see Jane again.

It had been hard for him to remain with the Frenchman all these days for that very reason, and that he had unselfishly done so spoke more glowingly of his nobility of character than even did his rescuing the French officer from Mbonga's clutches.

D'Arnot, only too willing to attempt the journey, wrote:

But you cannot carry me all the distance through this tangled forest.

Tarzan laughed.

"*Mais oui*," he said, and D'Arnot laughed aloud to hear the phrase that he used so often glide from Tarzan's tongue.

So they set out, D'Arnot marveling as had Clayton and Jane at the wondrous strength and agility of the apeman.

Mid-afternoon brought them to the clearing, and as Tarzan dropped to earth from the branches of the last tree his heart leaped and bounded against his ribs in anticipation of seeing Jane so soon again.

No one was in sight outside the cabin, and D'Arnot was perplexed to note that neither the cruiser nor the Arrow was at anchor in the bay.

An atmosphere of loneliness pervaded the spot, which caught suddenly at both men as they strode toward the cabin.

Neither spoke, yet both knew before they opened the closed door what they would find beyond.

Tarzan lifted the latch and pushed the great door in upon its wooden hinges. It was as they had feared. The cabin was deserted.

The men turned and looked at one another. D'Arnot knew that his people thought him dead; but Tarzan thought only of the woman who had kissed him in love and now had fled from him while he was serving one of her people.

A great bitterness rose in his heart. He would go away, far into the jungle and join his tribe. Never would he see one of his own kind again, nor could he bear the thought of returning to the cabin. He would leave that forever behind him with the great hopes he had nursed there of finding his own race and becoming a man among men.

And the Frenchman? D'Arnot? What of him? He could get along as Tarzan had. Tarzan did not want to see him more. He wanted to get away from everything that might remind him of Jane.

As Tarzan stood upon the threshold brooding, D'Arnot had entered the cabin. Many comforts he saw that had been left behind. He recognized numerous articles from the cruiser – a camp oven, some kitchen utensils, a rifle and many rounds of ammunition, canned foods, blankets, two chairs and a cot – and several books and periodicals, mostly American.

"They must intend returning," thought D'Arnot.

He walked over to the table that John Clayton had built so many years before to serve as a desk, and on it he saw two notes addressed to Tarzan of the Apes.

One was in a strong masculine hand and was unsealed. The other, in a woman's hand, was sealed.

"Here are two messages for you, Tarzan of the Apes," cried D'Arnot, turning toward the door; but his companion was not there.

D'Arnot walked to the door and looked out. Tarzan was nowhere in sight. He called aloud but there was no response.

"*Mon dieu*!" exclaimed D'Arnot, "he has left me. I feel it. He has gone back into his jungle and left me here alone."

And then he remembered the look on Tarzan's face when they had discovered that the cabin was empty – such a look as the hunter sees in the eyes of the wounded deer he has wantonly brought down.

The man had been hard hit – D'Arnot realized it now – but why? He could not understand.

The Frenchman looked about him. The loneliness and the horror of the place commenced to get on his nerves – already weakened by the ordeal of suffering and sickness he had passed through.

To be left here alone beside this awful jungle – never to hear a human voice or see a human face – in constant dread of savage beasts and more terribly savage men – a prey to solitude and hopelessness. It was awful.

And far to the east Tarzan of the Apes was speeding through the middle terrace back to his tribe. Never had he traveled with such reckless speed. He felt that he was running away from himself – that by hurtling through the forest like a frightened squirrel he was escaping from his own thoughts. But no matter how fast he went he found them always with him.

He passed above the sinuous body of Sabor, the lioness, going in the opposite direction – toward the cabin, thought Tarzan.

What could D'Arnot do against Sabor – or if Bolgani, the gorilla, should come upon him – or Numa, the lion, or cruel Sheeta?

Tarzan paused in his flight.

"What are you, Tarzan?" he asked aloud. "An ape or a man?"

"If you are an ape you will do as the apes would do – leave one of your kind to die in the jungle if it suited your whim to go elsewhere.

"If you are a man, you will return to protect your kind. You will not run away from one of your own people, because one of them has run away from you."

D'Arnot closed the cabin door. He was very nervous. Even brave men, and D'Arnot was a brave man, are sometimes frightened by solitude.

He loaded one of the rifles and placed it within easy reach. Then he went to the desk and took up the unsealed letter addressed to Tarzan.

Possibly it contained word that his people had but left the beach temporarily. He felt that it would be no breach of ethics to read this letter, so he took the enclosure from the envelope and read:

TO TARZAN OF THE APES:

We thank you for the use of your cabin, and are sorry that you did not permit us the pleasure of seeing and thanking you in person.

We have harmed nothing, but have left many things for you which may add to your comfort and safety here in your lonely home.

If you know the strange white man who saved our lives so many times, and brought us food, and if you can converse with him, thank him, also, for his kindness.

We sail within the hour, never to return; but we wish you and that other jungle friend to know that we shall always thank you for what you did for strangers on your shore, and that we should have done infinitely more to reward you both had you given us the opportunity.

Very respectfully,
WM. CECIL CLAYTON.

"'Never to return,'" muttered D'Arnot, and threw himself face downward upon the cot.

An hour later he started up listening. Something was at the door trying to enter.

D'Arnot reached for the loaded rifle and placed it to his shoulder.

Dusk was falling, and the interior of the cabin was very dark; but the man could see the latch moving from its place.

He felt his hair rising upon his scalp.

Gently the door opened until a thin crack showed something standing just beyond.

D'Arnot sighted along the blue barrel at the crack of the door – and then he pulled the trigger.

CHAPTER TWENTY FOUR

Lost Treasure

When the expedition returned, following their fruitless endeavor to succor D'Arnot, Captain Dufranne was anxious to steam away as quickly as possible, and all save Jane had acquiesced.

"No," she said, determinedly, "I shall not go, nor should you, for there are two friends in that jungle who will come out of it some day expecting to find us awaiting them.

"Your officer, Captain Dufranne, is one of them, and the forest man who has saved the lives of every member of my father's party is the other.

"He left me at the edge of the jungle two days ago to hasten to the aid of my father and Mr. Clayton, as he thought, and he has stayed to rescue Lieutenant D'Arnot; of that you may be sure.

"Had he been too late to be of service to the lieutenant he would have been back before now – the fact that he is not back is sufficient proof to me that he is delayed because Lieutenant D'Arnot is wounded, or he has had to follow his captors further than the village which your sailors attacked."

"But poor D'Arnot's uniform and all his belongings were found in that village, Miss Porter," argued the captain, "and the natives showed great excitement when questioned as to the white man's fate."

"Yes, Captain, but they did not admit that he was dead and as for his clothes and accouterments being in their possession – why more civilized peoples than these poor savage negroes strip their prisoners of every article of value whether they intend killing them or not.

"Even the soldiers of my own dear South looted not only the living but the dead. It is strong circumstantial evidence, I will admit, but it is not positive proof."

"Possibly your forest man, himself was captured or killed by the savages," suggested Captain Dufranne.

The girl laughed.

"You do not know him," she replied, a little thrill of pride setting her nerves a-tingle at the thought that she spoke of her own.

"I admit that he would be worth waiting for, this superman of yours," laughed the captain. "I most certainly should like to see him."

"Then wait for him, my dear captain," urged the girl, "for I intend doing so."

The Frenchman would have been a very much surprised man could he have interpreted the true meaning of the girl's words.

They had been walking from the beach toward the cabin as they talked, and now they joined a little group sitting on camp stools in the shade of a great tree beside the cabin.

Professor Porter was there, and Mr. Philander and Clayton, with Lieutenant Charpentier and two of his brother officers, while Esmeralda hovered in the background, ever and anon venturing opinions and comments with the freedom of an old and much-indulged family servant.

The officers arose and saluted as their superior approached, and Clayton surrendered his camp stool to Jane.

"We were just discussing poor Paul's fate," said Captain Dufranne. "Miss Porter insists that we have no absolute proof of his death – nor have we. And on the other hand she maintains that the continued absence of your omnipotent jungle friend indicates that D'Arnot is still in need of his services, either because he is wounded, or still is a prisoner in a more distant native village."

"It has been suggested," ventured Lieutenant Charpentier, "that the wild man may have been a member of the tribe of blacks who attacked our party – that he was hastening to aid *them* – his own people."

Jane shot a quick glance at Clayton.

"It seems vastly more reasonable," said Professor Porter.

"I do not agree with you," objected Mr. Philander. "He had ample opportunity to harm us himself, or to lead his people against us. Instead, during our long residence here, he has been uniformly consistent in his role of protector and provider."

"That is true," interjected Clayton, "yet we must not overlook the fact that except for himself the only human beings within hundreds of miles are savage cannibals. He was armed precisely as are they, which indicates that he has maintained relations of some nature with them, and the fact that he is but one against possibly thousands suggests that these relations could scarcely have been other than friendly."

"It seems improbable then that he is not connected with them," remarked the captain; "possibly a member of this tribe."

"Otherwise," added another of the officers, "how could he have lived a sufficient length of time among the savage denizens of the jungle, brute and human, to have become proficient in woodcraft, or in the use of African weapons."

"You are judging him according to your own standards, gentlemen," said Jane. "An ordinary white man such as any of you – pardon me, I did not mean just that – rather, a white man above the ordinary in physique and intelligence could never, I grant you, have lived a year alone and naked in this tropical jungle; but this man not only surpasses the average white man in strength and agility, but as far transcends our trained athletes and 'strong men' as they surpass a day-old babe; and his courage and ferocity in battle are those of the wild beast."

"He has certainly won a loyal champion, Miss Porter," said Captain Dufranne, laughing. "I am sure that there be none of us here but would willingly face death a hundred times in its most terrifying forms to deserve the tributes of one even half so loyal – or so beautiful."

"You would not wonder that I defend him," said the girl, "could you have seen him as I saw him, battling in my behalf with that huge hairy brute.

"Could you have seen him charge the monster as a bull might charge a grizzly – absolutely without sign of fear or hesitation – you would have believed him more than human.

"Could you have seen those mighty muscles knotting under the brown skin – could you have seen them force back those awful fangs – you too would have thought him invincible.

"And could you have seen the chivalrous treatment which he accorded a strange girl of a strange race, you would feel the same absolute confidence in him that I feel."

"You have won your suit, my fair pleader," cried the captain. "This court finds the defendant not guilty, and the cruiser shall wait a few days longer that he may have an opportunity to come and thank the divine Portia."

"For the Lord's sake honey," cried Esmeralda. "You all don't mean to tell *me* that you're going to stay right here in this here land of carnivable animals when you all got the opportunity to escapade on that boat? Don't you tell me *that*, honey."

"Why, Esmeralda! You should be ashamed of yourself," cried Jane. "Is this any way to show your gratitude to the man who saved your life twice?"

"Well, Miss Jane, that's all jest as you say; but that there forest man never did save us to stay here. He done save us so we all could get *away* from here. I expect he be mighty peevish when he find we ain't got no more sense than to stay right here after he done give us the chance to get away.

"I hoped I'd never have to sleep in this here geological garden another night and listen to all them lonesome noises that come out of that jumble after dark."

"I don't blame you a bit, Esmeralda," said Clayton, "and you certainly did hit it off right when you called them 'lonesome' noises. I never have been able to find the right word for them but that's it, don't you know, lonesome noises."

"You and Esmeralda had better go and live on the cruiser," said Jane, in fine scorn. "What would you think if you *had* to live all of your life in that jungle as our forest man has done?"

"I'm afraid I'd be a blooming bounder as a wild man," laughed Clayton, ruefully. "Those noises at night make the hair on my head bristle. I suppose that I should be ashamed to admit it, but it's the truth."

"I don't know about that," said Lieutenant Charpentier. "I never thought much about fear and that sort of thing – never tried to determine whether I was a coward or brave man; but the other night as we lay in the jungle there after poor D'Arnot was taken, and those jungle noises rose and fell around us I began to think that I was a coward indeed. It was not the roaring and growling of the big beasts that affected me so much as it was the stealthy noises – the ones that you heard suddenly close by and then listened vainly for a repetition of – the unaccountable sounds as of a great body moving almost noiselessly, and the knowledge that you didn't *know* how close it was, or whether it were creeping closer after you ceased to hear it? It was those noises – and the eyes.

"*Mon dieu*! I shall see them in the dark forever – the eyes that you see, and those that you don't see, but feel – ah, they are the worst."

All were silent for a moment, and then Jane spoke.

"And he is out there," she said, in an awe-hushed whisper. "Those eyes will be glaring at him to-night, and at your comrade Lieutenant D'Arnot. Can you leave them, gentlemen, without at least rendering them the passive succor which remaining here a few days longer might insure them?"

"Tut, tut, child," said Professor Porter. "Captain Dufranne is willing to remain, and for my part I am perfectly willing, perfectly willing – as I always have been to humor your childish whims."

"We can utilize the morrow in recovering the chest, Professor," suggested Mr. Philander.

"Quite so, quite so, Mr. Philander, I had almost forgotten the treasure," exclaimed Professor Porter. "Possibly we can borrow some men from Captain Dufranne to assist us, and one of the prisoners to point out the location of the chest."

"Most assuredly, my dear Professor, we are all yours to command," said the captain.

And so it was arranged that on the next day Lieutenant Charpentier was to take a detail of ten men, and one of the mutineers of the Arrow as a guide, and unearth the treasure; and that the cruiser would remain for a full week in the little harbor. At the end of that time it was to be assumed that D'Arnot was truly dead, and that the forest man would not return while they remained. Then the two vessels were to leave with all the party.

Professor Porter did not accompany the treasure-seekers on the following day, but when he saw them returning empty-handed toward noon, he hastened forward to meet them – his usual preoccupied indifference entirely vanished, and in its place a nervous and excited manner.

"Where is the treasure?" he cried to Clayton, while yet a hundred feet separated them.

Clayton shook his head.

"Gone," he said, as he neared the professor.

"Gone! It cannot be. Who could have taken it?" cried Professor Porter.

"God only knows, Professor," replied Clayton. "We might have thought the fellow who guided us was lying about the location, but his surprise and consternation on finding no chest beneath the body of the murdered Snipes were too real to be feigned. And then our spades showed us that *something* had been buried beneath the corpse, for a hole had been there and it had been filled with loose earth."

"But who could have taken it?" repeated Professor Porter.

"Suspicion might naturally fall on the men of the cruiser," said Lieutenant Charpentier, "but for the fact that sub-lieutenant Janviers here assures me that no men have had shore leave – that none has been on shore since we anchored here except under command of an officer. I do not know that you would suspect our men, but I am glad that there is now no chance for suspicion to fall on them," he concluded.

"It would never have occurred to me to suspect the men to whom we owe so much," replied Professor Porter, graciously. "I would as soon suspect my dear Clayton here, or Mr. Philander."

The Frenchmen smiled, both officers and sailors. It was plain to see that a burden had been lifted from their minds.

"The treasure has been gone for some time," continued Clayton. "In fact the body fell apart as we lifted it, which indicates that whoever removed the treasure did so while the corpse was still fresh, for it was intact when we first uncovered it."

"There must have been several in the party," said Jane, who had joined them. "You remember that it took four men to carry it."

"By jove!" cried Clayton. "That's right. It must have been done by a party of blacks. Probably one of them saw the men bury the chest and then returned immediately after with a party of his friends, and carried it off."

"Speculation is futile," said Professor Porter sadly. "The chest is gone. We shall never see it again, nor the treasure that was in it."

Only Jane knew what the loss meant to her father, and none there knew what it meant to her.

Six days later Captain Dufranne announced that they would sail early on the morrow.

Jane would have begged for a further reprieve, had it not been that she too had begun to believe that her forest lover would return no more.

In spite of herself she began to entertain doubts and fears. The reasonableness of the arguments of these disinterested French officers commenced to convince her against her will.

That he was a cannibal she would not believe, but that he was an adopted member of some savage tribe at length seemed possible to her.

She would not admit that he could be dead. It was impossible to believe that that perfect body, so filled with triumphant life, could ever cease to harbor the vital spark – as soon believe that immortality were dust.

As Jane permitted herself to harbor these thoughts, others equally unwelcome forced themselves upon her.

If he belonged to some savage tribe he had a savage wife – a dozen of them perhaps – and wild, half-caste children. The girl shuddered, and when they told her that the cruiser would sail on the morrow she was almost glad.

It was she, though, who suggested that arms, ammunition, supplies and comforts be left behind in the cabin, ostensibly for that intangible personality who had signed himself Tarzan of the Apes, and for D'Arnot should he still be living, but really, she hoped, for her forest god – even though his feet should prove of clay.

And at the last minute she left a message for him, to be transmitted by Tarzan of the Apes.

She was the last to leave the cabin, returning on some trivial pretext after the others had started for the boat.

She kneeled down beside the bed in which she had spent so many nights, and offered up a prayer for the safety of her primeval man, and crushing his locket to her lips she murmured:

"I love you, and because I love you I believe in you. But if I did not believe, still should I love. Had you come back for me, and had there been no other way, I would have gone into the jungle with you – forever."

CHAPTER TWENTY FIVE

The Outpost of the World

WITH THE REPORT of his gun D'Arnot saw the door fly open and the figure of a man pitch headlong within onto the cabin floor.

The Frenchman in his panic raised his gun to fire again into the prostrate form, but suddenly in the half dusk of the open door he saw that the man was white and in another instant realized that he had shot his friend and protector, Tarzan of the Apes.

With a cry of anguish D'Arnot sprang to the ape-man's side, and kneeling, lifted the latter's head in his arms – calling Tarzan's name aloud.

There was no response, and then D'Arnot placed his ear above the man's heart. To his joy he heard its steady beating beneath.

Carefully he lifted Tarzan to the cot, and then, after closing and bolting the door, he lighted one of the lamps and examined the wound.

The bullet had struck a glancing blow upon the skull. There was an ugly flesh wound, but no signs of a fracture of the skull.

D'Arnot breathed a sigh of relief, and went about bathing the blood from Tarzan's face.

Soon the cool water revived him, and presently he opened his eyes to look in questioning surprise at D'Arnot.

The latter had bound the wound with pieces of cloth, and as he saw that Tarzan had regained consciousness he arose and going to the table wrote a message, which he handed to the ape-man, explaining the terrible mistake he had made and how thankful he was that the wound was not more serious.

Tarzan, after reading the message, sat on the edge of the couch and laughed.

"It is nothing," he said in French, and then, his vocabulary failing him, he wrote:

You should have seen what Bolgani did to me, and Kerchak, and Terkoz, before I killed them – then you would laugh at such a little scratch.

D'Arnot handed Tarzan the two messages that had been left for him.

Tarzan read the first one through with a look of sorrow on his face. The second one he turned over and over, searching for an opening – he had never seen a sealed envelope before. At length he handed it to D'Arnot.

The Frenchman had been watching him, and knew that Tarzan was puzzled over the envelope. How strange it seemed that to a full-grown white man an envelope was a mystery. D'Arnot opened it and handed the letter back to Tarzan.

Sitting on a camp stool the ape-man spread the written sheet before him and read:

TO TARZAN OF THE APES:

Before I leave let me add my thanks to those of Mr. Clayton for the kindness you have shown in permitting us the use of your cabin.

That you never came to make friends with us has been a great regret to us. We should have liked so much to have seen and thanked our host.

There is another I should like to thank also, but he did not come back, though I cannot believe that he is dead.

I do not know his name. He is the great white giant who wore the diamond locket upon his breast.

If you know him and can speak his language carry my thanks to him, and tell him that I waited seven days for him to return.

Tell him, also, that in my home in America, in the city of Baltimore, there will always be a welcome for him if he cares to come.

I found a note you wrote me lying among the leaves beneath a tree near the cabin. I do not know how you learned to love me, who have never spoken to me, and I am very sorry if it is true, for I have already given my heart to another.

But know that I am always your friend,

JANE PORTER.

Tarzan sat with gaze fixed upon the floor for nearly an hour. It was evident to him from the notes that they did not know that he and Tarzan of the Apes were one and the same.

"I have given my heart to another," he repeated over and over again to himself.

Then she did not love him! How could she have pretended love, and raised him to such a pinnacle of hope only to cast him down to such utter depths of despair!

Maybe her kisses were only signs of friendship. How did he know, who knew nothing of the customs of human beings?

Suddenly he arose, and, bidding D'Arnot good night as he had learned to do, threw himself upon the couch of ferns that had been Jane Porter's.

D'Arnot extinguished the lamp, and lay down upon the cot.

For a week they did little but rest, D'Arnot coaching Tarzan in French. At the end of that time the two men could converse quite easily.

One night, as they were sitting within the cabin before retiring, Tarzan turned to D'Arnot.

"Where is America?" he said.

D'Arnot pointed toward the northwest.

"Many thousands of miles across the ocean," he replied. "Why?"

"I am going there."

D'Arnot shook his head.

"It is impossible, my friend," he said.

Tarzan rose, and, going to one of the cupboards, returned with a well-thumbed geography.

Turning to a map of the world, he said:

"I have never quite understood all this; explain it to me, please."

When D'Arnot had done so, showing him that the blue represented all the water on the earth, and the bits of other colors the continents and islands, Tarzan asked him to point out the spot where they now were.

D'Arnot did so.

"Now point out America," said Tarzan.

And as D'Arnot placed his finger upon North America, Tarzan smiled and laid his palm upon the page, spanning the great ocean that lay between the two continents.

"You see it is not so very far," he said; "scarce the width of my hand."

D'Arnot laughed. How could he make the man understand?

Then he took a pencil and made a tiny point upon the shore of Africa.

"This little mark," he said, "is many times larger upon this map than your cabin is upon the earth. Do you see now how very far it is?"

Tarzan thought for a long time.

"Do any white men live in Africa?" he asked.

"Yes."

"Where are the nearest?"

D'Arnot pointed out a spot on the shore just north of them.

"So close?" asked Tarzan, in surprise.

"Yes," said D'Arnot; "but it is not close."

"Have they big boats to cross the ocean?"

"Yes."

"We shall go there to-morrow," announced Tarzan.

Again D'Arnot smiled and shook his head.

"It is too far. We should die long before we reached them."

"Do you wish to stay here then forever?" asked Tarzan.

"No," said D'Arnot.

"Then we shall start to-morrow. I do not like it here longer. I should rather die than remain here."

"Well," answered D'Arnot, with a shrug, "I do not know, my friend, but that I also would rather die than remain here. If you go, I shall go with you."

"It is settled then," said Tarzan. "I shall start for America to-morrow."

"How will you get to America without money?" asked D'Arnot.

"What is money?" inquired Tarzan.

It took a long time to make him understand even imperfectly.

"How do men get money?" he asked at last.

"They work for it."

"Very well. I will work for it, then."

"No, my friend," returned D'Arnot, "you need not worry about money, nor need you work for it. I have enough money for two – enough for twenty. Much more than is good for one man and you shall have all you need if ever we reach civilization."

So on the following day they started north along the shore. Each man carrying a rifle and ammunition, beside bedding and some food and cooking utensils.

The latter seemed to Tarzan a most useless encumbrance, so he threw his away.

"But you must learn to eat cooked food, my friend," remonstrated D'Arnot. "No civilized men eat raw flesh."

"There will be time enough when I reach civilization," said Tarzan. "I do not like the things and they only spoil the taste of good meat."

For a month they traveled north. Sometimes finding food in plenty and again going hungry for days.

They saw no signs of natives nor were they molested by wild beasts. Their journey was a miracle of ease.

Tarzan asked questions and learned rapidly. D'Arnot taught him many of the refinements of civilization – even to the use of knife and fork; but sometimes Tarzan would drop them in disgust and grasp his food in his strong brown hands, tearing it with his molars like a wild beast.

Then D'Arnot would expostulate with him, saying:

"You must not eat like a brute, Tarzan, while I am trying to make a gentleman of you. *Mon dieu*! Gentlemen do not thus – it is terrible."

Tarzan would grin sheepishly and pick up his knife and fork again, but at heart he hated them.

On the journey he told D'Arnot about the great chest he had seen the sailors bury; of how he had dug it up and carried it to the gathering place of the apes and buried it there.

"It must be the treasure chest of Professor Porter," said D'Arnot. "It is too bad, but of course you did not know."

Then Tarzan recalled the letter written by Jane to her friend – the one he had stolen when they first came to his cabin, and now he knew what was in the chest and what it meant to Jane.

"To-morrow we shall go back after it," he announced to D'Arnot.

"Go back?" exclaimed D'Arnot. "But, my dear fellow, we have now been three weeks upon the march. It would require three more to return to the treasure, and then, with that enormous weight which required, you say, four sailors to carry, it would be months before we had again reached this spot."

"It must be done, my friend," insisted Tarzan. "You may go on toward civilization, and I will return for the treasure. I can go very much faster alone."

"I have a better plan, Tarzan," exclaimed D'Arnot. "We shall go on together to the nearest settlement, and there we will charter a boat and sail back down the coast for the treasure and so transport it easily. That will be safer and quicker and also not require us to be separated. What do you think of that plan?"

"Very well," said Tarzan. "The treasure will be there whenever we go for it; and while I could fetch it now, and catch up with you in a moon or two, I shall feel safer for you to know that you are not alone on the trail. When I see how helpless you are, D'Arnot, I often wonder how the human race has escaped annihilation all these ages which you tell me about. Why, Sabor, single handed, could exterminate a thousand of you."

D'Arnot laughed.

"You will think more highly of your genus when you have seen its armies and navies, its great cities, and its mighty engineering works. Then you will realize that it is mind, and not muscle, that makes the human animal greater than the mighty beasts of your jungle.

"Alone and unarmed, a single man is no match for any of the larger beasts; but if ten men were together, they would combine their wits and their muscles against their savage enemies, while the beasts, being unable to reason, would never think of combining against the men. Otherwise, Tarzan of the Apes, how long would you have lasted in the savage wilderness?"

"You are right, D'Arnot," replied Tarzan, "for if Kerchak had come to Tublat's aid that night at the Dum-Dum, there would have been an end of me. But Kerchak could never think far enough ahead to take advantage of any such opportunity. Even Kala, my mother, could never plan ahead. She simply ate what she needed when she needed it, and if the supply was very scarce, even though she found plenty for several meals, she would never gather any ahead.

"I remember that she used to think it very silly of me to burden myself with extra food upon the march, though she was quite glad to eat it with me, if the way chanced to be barren of sustenance."

"Then you knew your mother, Tarzan?" asked D'Arnot, in surprise.

"Yes. She was a great, fine ape, larger than I, and weighing twice as much."

"And your father?" asked D'Arnot.

"I did not know him. Kala told me he was a white ape, and hairless like myself. I know now that he must have been a white man."

D'Arnot looked long and earnestly at his companion.

"Tarzan," he said at length, "it is impossible that the ape, Kala, was your mother. If such a thing can be, which I doubt, you would have inherited some of the characteristics of the ape, but you have not – you are pure man, and, I should say, the offspring of highly bred and intelligent parents. Have you not the slightest clue to your past?"

"Not the slightest," replied Tarzan.

"No writings in the cabin that might have told something of the lives of its original inmates?"

"I have read everything that was in the cabin with the exception of one book which I know now to be written in a language other than English. Possibly you can read it."

Tarzan fished the little black diary from the bottom of his quiver, and handed it to his companion.

D'Arnot glanced at the title page.

"It is the diary of John Clayton, Lord Greystoke, an English nobleman, and it is written in French," he said.

Then he proceeded to read the diary that had been written over twenty years before, and which recorded the details of the story which we already know – the story of adventure, hardships and sorrow of John Clayton and his wife Alice, from the day they left England until an hour before he was struck down by Kerchak.

D'Arnot read aloud. At times his voice broke, and he was forced to stop reading for the pitiful hopelessness that spoke between the lines.

Occasionally he glanced at Tarzan; but the ape-man sat upon his haunches, like a carven image, his eyes fixed upon the ground.

Only when the little babe was mentioned did the tone of the diary alter from the habitual note of despair which had crept into it by degrees after the first two months upon the shore.

Then the passages were tinged with a subdued happiness that was even sadder than the rest.

One entry showed an almost hopeful spirit.

To-day our little boy is six months old. He is sitting in Alice's lap beside the table where I am writing – a happy, healthy, perfect child.

Somehow, even against all reason, I seem to see him a grown man, taking his father's place in the world – the second John Clayton – and bringing added honors to the house of Greystoke.

There – as though to give my prophecy the weight of his endorsement – he has grabbed my pen in his chubby fists and with his inkbegrimed little fingers has placed the seal of his tiny finger prints upon the page.

And there, on the margin of the page, were the partially blurred imprints of four wee fingers and the outer half of the thumb.

When D'Arnot had finished the diary the two men sat in silence for some minutes.

"Well! Tarzan of the Apes, what think you?" asked D'Arnot. "Does not this little book clear up the mystery of your parentage?

"Why man, you are Lord Greystoke."

"The book speaks of but one child," he replied. "Its little skeleton lay in the crib, where it died crying for nourishment, from the first time I entered the cabin until Professor Porter's party buried it, with its father and mother, beside the cabin.

"No, that was the babe the book speaks of – and the mystery of my origin is deeper than before, for I have thought much of late of the possibility of that cabin having been my birthplace. I am afraid that Kala spoke the truth," he concluded sadly.

D'Arnot shook his head. He was unconvinced, and in his mind had sprung the determination to prove the correctness of his theory, for he had discovered the key which alone could unlock the mystery, or consign it forever to the realms of the unfathomable.

A week later the two men came suddenly upon a clearing in the forest.

In the distance were several buildings surrounded by a strong palisade. Between them and the enclosure stretched a cultivated field in which a number of negroes were working.

The two halted at the edge of the jungle.

Tarzan fitted his bow with a poisoned arrow, but D'Arnot placed a hand upon his arm.

"What would you do, Tarzan?" he asked.

"They will try to kill us if they see us," replied Tarzan. "I prefer to be the killer."

"Maybe they are friends," suggested D'Arnot.

"They are black," was Tarzan's only reply.

And again he drew back his shaft.

"You must not, Tarzan!" cried D'Arnot. "White men do not kill wantonly. *Mon dieu*! but you have much to learn.

"I pity the ruffian who crosses you, my wild man, when I take you to Paris. I will have my hands full keeping your neck from beneath the guillotine."

Tarzan lowered his bow and smiled.

"I do not know why I should kill the blacks back there in my jungle, yet not kill them here. Suppose Numa, the lion, should spring out upon us, I should say, then, I presume: Good morning, Monsieur Numa, how is Madame Numa; eh?"

"Wait until the blacks spring upon you," replied D'Arnot, "then you may kill them. Do not assume that men are your enemies until they prove it."

"Come," said Tarzan, "let us go and present ourselves to be killed," and he started straight across the field, his head high held and the tropical sun beating upon his smooth, brown skin.

Behind him came D'Arnot, clothed in some garments which had been discarded at the cabin by Clayton when the officers of the French cruiser had fitted him out in more presentable fashion.

Presently one of the blacks looked up, and beholding Tarzan, turned, shrieking, toward the palisade.

In an instant the air was filled with cries of terror from the fleeing gardeners, but before any had reached the palisade a white man emerged from the enclosure, rifle in hand, to discover the cause of the commotion.

What he saw brought his rifle to his shoulder, and Tarzan of the Apes would have felt cold lead once again had not D'Arnot cried loudly to the man with the leveled gun:

"Do not fire! We are friends!"

"Halt, then!" was the reply.

"Stop, Tarzan!" cried D'Arnot. "He thinks we are enemies."

Tarzan dropped into a walk, and together he and D'Arnot advanced toward the white man by the gate.

The latter eyed them in puzzled bewilderment.

"What manner of men are you?" he asked, in French.

"White men," replied D'Arnot. "We have been lost in the jungle for a long time."

The man had lowered his rifle and now advanced with outstretched hand.

"I am Father Constantine of the French Mission here," he said, "and I am glad to welcome you."

"This is Monsieur Tarzan, Father Constantine," replied D'Arnot, indicating the ape-man; and as the priest extended his hand to Tarzan, D'Arnot added: "and I am Paul D'Arnot, of the French Navy."

Father Constantine took the hand which Tarzan extended in imitation of the priest's act, while the latter took in the superb physique and handsome face in one quick, keen glance.

And thus came Tarzan of the Apes to the first outpost of civilization.

For a week they remained there, and the ape-man, keenly observant, learned much of the ways of men; meanwhile black women sewed white duck garments for himself and D'Arnot so that they might continue their journey properly clothed.

CHAPTER TWENTY SIX

The Height of Civilizations

ANOTHER MONTH brought them to a little group of buildings at the mouth of a wide river, and there Tarzan saw many boats, and was filled with the timidity of the wild thing by the sight of many men.

Gradually he became accustomed to the strange noises and the odd ways of civilization, so that presently none might know that two short months before, this handsome Frenchman in immaculate white ducks, who laughed and chatted with the gayest of them, had been swinging naked through primeval forests to pounce upon some unwary victim, which, raw, was to fill his savage belly.

The knife and fork, so contemptuously flung aside a month before, Tarzan now manipulated as exquisitely as did the polished D'Arnot.

So apt a pupil had he been that the young Frenchman had labored assiduously to make of Tarzan of the Apes a polished gentleman in so far as nicety of manners and speech were concerned.

"God made you a gentleman at heart, my friend," D'Arnot had said; "but we want His works to show upon the exterior also."

As soon as they had reached the little port, D'Arnot had cabled his government of his safety, and requested a three-months' leave, which had been granted.

He had also cabled his bankers for funds, and the enforced wait of a month, under which both chafed, was due to their inability to charter a vessel for the return to Tarzan's jungle after the treasure.

During their stay at the coast town "Monsieur Tarzan" became the wonder of both whites and blacks because of several occurrences which to Tarzan seemed the merest of nothings.

Once a huge black, crazed by drink, had run amuck and terrorized the town, until his evil star had led him to where the black-haired French giant lolled upon the veranda of the hotel.

Mounting the broad steps, with brandished knife, the Negro made straight for a party of four men sitting at a table sipping the inevitable absinthe.

Shouting in alarm, the four took to their heels, and then the black spied Tarzan.

With a roar he charged the ape-man, while half a hundred heads peered from sheltering windows and doorways to witness the butchering of the poor Frenchman by the giant black.

Tarzan met the rush with the fighting smile that the joy of battle always brought to his lips.

As the Negro closed upon him, steel muscles gripped the black wrist of the uplifted knife-hand, and a single swift wrench left the hand dangling below a broken bone.

With the pain and surprise, the madness left the black man, and as Tarzan dropped back into his chair the fellow turned, crying with agony, and dashed wildly toward the native village.

On another occasion as Tarzan and D'Arnot sat at dinner with a number of other whites, the talk fell upon lions and lion hunting.

Opinion was divided as to the bravery of the king of beasts – some maintaining that he was an arrant coward, but all agreeing that it was with a feeling of greater security that they gripped their express rifles when the monarch of the jungle roared about a camp at night.

D'Arnot and Tarzan had agreed that his past be kept secret, and so none other than the French officer knew of the ape-man's familiarity with the beasts of the jungle.

"Monsieur Tarzan has not expressed himself," said one of the party. "A man of his prowess who has spent some time in Africa, as I understand Monsieur Tarzan has, must have had experiences with lions – yes?"

"Some," replied Tarzan, dryly. "Enough to know that each of you are right in your judgment of the characteristics of the lions – you have met. But one might as well judge all blacks by the fellow who ran amuck last week, or decide that all whites are cowards because one has met a cowardly white.

"There is as much individuality among the lower orders, gentlemen, as there is among ourselves. Today we may go out and stumble upon a lion which is over-timid – he runs away from us. To-morrow we may meet his uncle or his twin brother, and our friends wonder why we do not return from the jungle. For myself, I always assume that a lion is ferocious, and so I am never caught off my guard."

"There would be little pleasure in hunting," retorted the first speaker, "if one is afraid of the thing he hunts."

D'Arnot smiled. Tarzan afraid!

"I do not exactly understand what you mean by fear," said Tarzan. "Like lions, fear is a different thing in different men, but to me the only pleasure in the hunt is the knowledge that the hunted thing has power to harm me as much as I have to harm him. If I went out with a couple of rifles and a gun bearer, and twenty or thirty beaters, to hunt a lion, I should not feel that the lion had much chance, and so the pleasure of the hunt would be lessened in proportion to the increased safety which I felt."

"Then I am to take it that Monsieur Tarzan would prefer to go naked into the jungle, armed only with a jackknife, to kill the king of beasts," laughed the other, good naturedly, but with the merest touch of sarcasm in his tone.

"And a piece of rope," added Tarzan.

Just then the deep roar of a lion sounded from the distant jungle, as though to challenge whoever dared enter the lists with him.

"There is your opportunity, Monsieur Tarzan," bantered the Frenchman.

"I am not hungry," said Tarzan simply.

The men laughed, all but D'Arnot. He alone knew that a savage beast had spoken its simple reason through the lips of the ape-man.

"But you are afraid, just as any of us would be, to go out there naked, armed only with a knife and a piece of rope," said the banterer. "Is it not so?"

"No," replied Tarzan. "Only a fool performs any act without reason."

"Five thousand francs is a reason," said the other. "I wager you that amount you cannot bring back a lion from the jungle under the conditions we have named – naked and armed only with a knife and a piece of rope."

Tarzan glanced toward D'Arnot and nodded his head.

"Make it ten thousand," said D'Arnot.

"Done," replied the other.

Tarzan arose.

"I shall have to leave my clothes at the edge of the settlement, so that if I do not return before daylight I shall have something to wear through the streets."

"You are not going now," exclaimed the wagerer – "at night?"

"Why not?" asked Tarzan. "Numa walks abroad at night – it will be easier to find him."

"No," said the other, "I do not want your blood upon my hands. It will be foolhardy enough if you go forth by day."

"I shall go now," replied Tarzan, and went to his room for his knife and rope.

The men accompanied him to the edge of the jungle, where he left his clothes in a small storehouse.

But when he would have entered the blackness of the undergrowth they tried to dissuade him; and the wagerer was most insistent of all that he abandon his foolhardy venture.

"I will accede that you have won," he said, "and the ten thousand francs are yours if you will but give up this foolish attempt, which can only end in your death."

Tarzan laughed, and in another moment the jungle had swallowed him.

The men stood silent for some moments and then slowly turned and walked back to the hotel veranda.

Tarzan had no sooner entered the jungle than he took to the trees, and it was with a feeling of exultant freedom that he swung once more through the forest branches.

This was life! Ah, how he loved it! Civilization held nothing like this in its narrow and circumscribed sphere, hemmed in by restrictions and conventionalities. Even clothes were a hindrance and a nuisance.

At last he was free. He had not realized what a prisoner he had been.

How easy it would be to circle back to the coast, and then make toward the south and his own jungle and cabin.

Now he caught the scent of Numa, for he was traveling up wind. Presently his quick ears detected the familiar sound of padded feet and the brushing of a huge, fur-clad body through the undergrowth.

Tarzan came quietly above the unsuspecting beast and silently stalked him until he came into a little patch of moonlight.

Then the quick noose settled and tightened about the tawny throat, and, as he had done it a hundred times in the past, Tarzan made fast the end to a strong branch and, while the beast fought and clawed for freedom, dropped to the ground behind him, and leaping upon the great back, plunged his long thin blade a dozen times into the fierce heart.

Then with his foot upon the carcass of Numa, he raised his voice in the awesome victory cry of his savage tribe.

For a moment Tarzan stood irresolute, swayed by conflicting emotions of loyalty to D'Arnot and a mighty lust for the freedom of his own jungle. At last the vision of a beautiful face, and the memory of warm lips crushed to his dissolved the fascinating picture he had been drawing of his old life.

The ape-man threw the warm carcass of Numa across his shoulders and took to the trees once more.

The men upon the veranda had sat for an hour, almost in silence.

They had tried ineffectually to converse on various subjects, and always the thing uppermost in the mind of each had caused the conversation to lapse.

"*Mon dieu*," said the wagerer at length, "I can endure it no longer. I am going into the jungle with my express and bring back that mad man."

"I will go with you," said one.

"And I" – "And I" – "And I," chorused the others.

As though the suggestion had broken the spell of some horrid nightmare they hastened to their various quarters, and presently were headed toward the jungle – each one heavily armed.

"God! What was that?" suddenly cried one of the party, an Englishman, as Tarzan's savage cry came faintly to their ears.

"I heard the same thing once before," said a Belgian, "when I was in the gorilla country. My carriers said it was the cry of a great bull ape who has made a kill."

D'Arnot remembered Clayton's description of the awful roar with which Tarzan had announced his kills, and he half smiled in spite of the horror which filled him to think that the uncanny sound could have issued from a human throat – from the lips of his friend.

As the party stood finally near the edge of the jungle, debating as to the best distribution of their forces, they were startled by a low laugh near them, and turning, beheld advancing toward them a giant figure bearing a dead lion upon its broad shoulders.

Even D'Arnot was thunderstruck, for it seemed impossible that the man could have so quickly dispatched a lion with the pitiful weapons he had taken, or that alone he could have borne the huge carcass through the tangled jungle.

The men crowded about Tarzan with many questions, but his only answer was a laughing depreciation of his feat.

To Tarzan it was as though one should eulogize a butcher for his heroism in killing a cow, for Tarzan had killed so often for food and for self-preservation that the act seemed anything but remarkable to him. But he was indeed a hero in the eyes of these men – men accustomed to hunting big game.

Incidentally, he had won ten thousand francs, for D'Arnot insisted that he keep it all.

This was a very important item to Tarzan, who was just commencing to realize the power which lay beyond the little pieces of metal and paper which always changed hands when human beings rode, or ate, or slept, or clothed themselves, or drank, or worked, or played, or sheltered themselves from the rain or cold or sun.

It had become evident to Tarzan that without money one must die. D'Arnot had told him not to worry, since he had more than enough for both, but the ape-man was learning many things and one of them was that people looked down upon one who accepted money from another without giving something of equal value in exchange.

Shortly after the episode of the lion hunt, D'Arnot succeeded in chartering an ancient tub for the coastwise trip to Tarzan's landlocked harbor.

It was a happy morning for them both when the little vessel weighed anchor and made for the open sea.

The trip to the beach was uneventful, and the morning after they dropped anchor before the cabin, Tarzan, garbed once more in his jungle regalia and carrying a spade, set out alone for the amphitheater of the apes where lay the treasure.

Late the next day he returned, bearing the great chest upon his shoulder, and at sunrise the little vessel worked through the harbor's mouth and took up her northward journey.

Three weeks later Tarzan and D'Arnot were passengers on board a French steamer bound for Lyons, and after a few days in that city D'Arnot took Tarzan to Paris.

The ape-man was anxious to proceed to America, but D'Arnot insisted that he must accompany him to Paris first, nor would he divulge the nature of the urgent necessity upon which he based his demand.

One of the first things which D'Arnot accomplished after their arrival was to arrange to visit a high official of the police department, an old friend; and to take Tarzan with him.

Adroitly D'Arnot led the conversation from point to point until the policeman had explained to the interested Tarzan many of the methods in vogue for apprehending and identifying criminals.

Not the least interesting to Tarzan was the part played by finger prints in this fascinating science.

"But of what value are these imprints," asked Tarzan, "when, after a few years the lines upon the fingers are entirely changed by the wearing out of the old tissue and the growth of new?"

"The lines never change," replied the official. "From infancy to senility the fingerprints of an individual change only in size, except as injuries alter the loops and whorls. But if imprints have been taken of the thumb and four fingers of both hands one must needs lose all entirely to escape identification."

"It is marvelous," exclaimed D'Arnot. "I wonder what the lines upon my own fingers may resemble."

"We can soon see," replied the police officer, and ringing a bell he summoned an assistant to whom he issued a few directions.

The man left the room, but presently returned with a little hardwood box which he placed on his superior's desk.

"Now," said the officer, "you shall have your fingerprints in a second."

He drew from the little case a square of plate glass, a little tube of thick ink, a rubber roller, and a few snowy white cards.

Squeezing a drop of ink onto the glass, he spread it back and forth with the rubber roller until the entire surface of the glass was covered to his satisfaction with a very thin and uniform layer of ink.

"Place the four fingers of your right hand upon the glass, thus," he said to D'Arnot. "Now the thumb. That is right. Now place them in just the same position upon this card, here, no – a little to the right. We must leave room for the thumb and the fingers of the left hand. There, that's it. Now the same with the left."

"Come, Tarzan," cried D'Arnot, "let's see what your whorls look like."

Tarzan complied readily, asking many questions of the officer during the operation.

"Do fingerprints show racial characteristics?" he asked. "Could you determine, for example, solely from fingerprints whether the subject was Negro or Caucasian?"

"I think not," replied the officer.

"Could the finger prints of an ape be detected from those of a man?"

"Probably, because the ape's would be far simpler than those of the higher organism."

"But a cross between an ape and a man might show the characteristics of either progenitor?" continued Tarzan.

"Yes, I should think likely," responded the official; "but the science has not progressed sufficiently to render it exact enough in such matters. I should hate to trust its findings further than to differentiate between individuals. There it is absolute. No two people born into the world probably have ever had identical lines upon all their digits. It is very doubtful if any single fingerprint will ever be exactly duplicated by any finger other than the one which originally made it."

"Does the comparison require much time or labor?" asked D'Arnot.

"Ordinarily but a few moments, if the impressions are distinct."

D'Arnot drew a little black book from his pocket and commenced turning the pages.

Tarzan looked at the book in surprise. How did D'Arnot come to have his book?

Presently D'Arnot stopped at a page on which were five tiny little smudges.

He handed the open book to the policeman.

"Are these imprints similar to mine or Monsieur Tarzan's or can you say that they are identical with either?" The officer drew a powerful glass from his desk and examined all three specimens carefully, making notations meanwhile upon a pad of paper.

Tarzan realized now what was the meaning of their visit to the police officer.

The answer to his life's riddle lay in these tiny marks.

With tense nerves he sat leaning forward in his chair, but suddenly he relaxed and dropped back, smiling.

D'Arnot looked at him in surprise.

"You forget that for twenty years the dead body of the child who made those fingerprints lay in the cabin of his father, and that all my life I have seen it lying there," said Tarzan bitterly.

The policeman looked up in astonishment.

"Go ahead, captain, with your examination," said D'Arnot, "we will tell you the story later – provided Monsieur Tarzan is agreeable."

Tarzan nodded his head.

"But you are mad, my dear D'Arnot," he insisted. "Those little fingers are buried on the west coast of Africa."

"I do not know as to that, Tarzan," replied D'Arnot. "It is possible, but if you are not the son of John Clayton then how in heaven's name did you come into that God forsaken jungle where no white man other than John Clayton had ever set foot?"

"You forget – Kala," said Tarzan.

"I do not even consider her," replied D'Arnot.

The friends had walked to the broad window overlooking the boulevard as they talked. For some time they stood there gazing out upon the busy throng beneath, each wrapped in his own thoughts.

"It takes some time to compare finger prints," thought D'Arnot, turning to look at the police officer.

To his astonishment he saw the official leaning back in his chair hastily scanning the contents of the little black diary.

D'Arnot coughed. The policeman looked up, and, catching his eye, raised his finger to admonish silence. D'Arnot turned back to the window, and presently the police officer spoke.

"Gentlemen," he said.

Both turned toward him.

"There is evidently a great deal at stake which must hinge to a greater or lesser extent upon the absolute correctness of this comparison. I therefore ask that you leave the entire matter in my hands until Monsieur Desquerc, our expert returns. It will be but a matter of a few days."

"I had hoped to know at once," said D'Arnot. "Monsieur Tarzan sails for America tomorrow."

"I will promise that you can cable him a report within two weeks," replied the officer; "but what it will be I dare not say. There are resemblances, yet – well, we had better leave it for Monsieur Desquerc to solve."

CHAPTER TWENTY SEVEN

The Giant Again

A TAXICAB DREW UP before an oldfashioned residence upon the outskirts of Baltimore.

A man of about forty, well built and with strong, regular features, stepped out, and paying the chauffeur dismissed him.

A moment later the passenger was entering the library of the old home.

"Ah, Mr. Canler!" exclaimed an old man, rising to greet him.

"Good evening, my dear Professor," cried the man, extending a cordial hand.

"Who admitted you?" asked the professor.

"Esmeralda."

"Then she will acquaint Jane with the fact that you are here," said the old man.

"No, Professor," replied Canler, "for I came primarily to see you."

"Ah, I am honored," said Professor Porter.

"Professor," continued Robert Canler, with great deliberation, as though carefully weighing his words, "I have come this evening to speak with you about Jane.

"You know my aspirations, and you have been generous enough to approve my suit."

Professor Archimedes Q. Porter fidgeted in his armchair. The subject always made him uncomfortable. He could not understand why. Canler was a splendid match.

"But Jane," continued Canler, "I cannot understand her. She puts me off first on one ground and then another. I have always the feeling that she breathes a sigh of relief every time I bid her good-by."

"Tut, tut," said Professor Porter. "Tut, tut, Mr. Canler. Jane is a most obedient daughter. She will do precisely as I tell her."

"Then I can still count on your support?" asked Canler, a tone of relief marking his voice.

"Certainly, sir; certainly, sir," exclaimed Professor Porter. "How could you doubt it?"

"There is young Clayton, you know," suggested Canler. "He has been hanging about for months. I don't know that Jane cares for him; but beside his title they say he has inherited a very considerable estate from his father, and it might not be strange, – if he finally won her, unless – " and Canler paused.

"Tut – tut, Mr. Canler; unless – what?"

"Unless, you see fit to request that Jane and I be married at once," said Canler, slowly and distinctly.

"I have already suggested to Jane that it would be desirable," said Professor Porter sadly, "for we can no longer afford to keep up this house, and live as her associations demand."

"What was her reply?" asked Canler.

"She said she was not ready to marry anyone yet," replied Professor Porter, "and that we could go and live upon the farm in northern Wisconsin which her mother left her.

"It is a little more than self-supporting. The tenants have always made a living from it, and been able to send Jane a trifle beside, each year. She is planning on our going up there the first of the week. Philander and Mr. Clayton have already gone to get things in readiness for us."

"Clayton has gone there?" exclaimed Canler, visibly chagrined. "Why was I not told? I would gladly have gone and seen that every comfort was provided."

"Jane feels that we are already too much in your debt, Mr. Canler," said Professor Porter.

Canler was about to reply, when the sound of footsteps came from the hall without, and Jane entered the room.

"Oh, I beg your pardon!" she exclaimed, pausing on the threshold. "I thought you were alone, papa."

"It is only I, Jane," said Canler, who had risen, "won't you come in and join the family group? We were just speaking of you."

"Thank you," said Jane, entering and taking the chair Canler placed for her. "I only wanted to tell papa that Tobey is coming down from the college tomorrow to pack his books. I want you to be sure, papa, to indicate all that you can do without until fall. Please don't carry this entire library to Wisconsin, as you would have carried it to Africa, if I had not put my foot down."

"Was Tobey here?" asked Professor Porter.

"Yes, I just left him. He and Esmeralda are exchanging religious experiences on the back porch now."

"Tut, tut, I must see him at once!" cried the professor. "Excuse me just a moment, children," and the old man hastened from the room.

As soon as he was out of earshot Canler turned to Jane.

"See here, Jane," he said bluntly. "How long is this thing going on like this? You haven't refused to marry me, but you haven't promised either. I want to get the license tomorrow, so that we can be married quietly before you leave for Wisconsin. I don't care for any fuss or feathers, and I'm sure you don't either."

The girl turned cold, but she held her head bravely.

"Your father wishes it, you know," added Canler.

"Yes, I know."

She spoke scarcely above a whisper.

"Do you realize that you are buying me, Mr. Canler?" she said finally, and in a cold, level voice. "Buying me for a few paltry dollars? Of course you do, Robert Canler, and the hope of just such a contingency was in your mind when you loaned papa the money for that hair-brained escapade, which but for a most mysterious circumstance would have been surprisingly successful.

"But you, Mr. Canler, would have been the most surprised. You had no idea that the venture would succeed. You are too good a businessman for that. And you are too good a businessman to loan money for buried treasure seeking, or to loan money without security – unless you had some special object in view.

"You knew that without security you had a greater hold on the honor of the Porters than with it. You knew the one best way to force me to marry you, without seeming to force me.

"You have never mentioned the loan. In any other man I should have thought that the prompting of a magnanimous and noble character. But you are deep, Mr. Robert Canler. I know you better than you think I know you.

"I shall certainly marry you if there is no other way, but let us understand each other once and for all."

While she spoke Robert Canler had alternately flushed and paled, and when she ceased speaking he arose, and with a cynical smile upon his strong face, said:

"You surprise me, Jane. I thought you had more self-control – more pride. Of course you are right. I am buying you, and I knew that you knew it, but I thought you would prefer to pretend that it was otherwise. I should have thought your self respect and your Porter pride would have shrunk from admitting, even to yourself, that you were a bought woman. But have it your own way, dear girl," he added lightly. "I am going to have you, and that is all that interests me."

Without a word the girl turned and left the room.

Jane was not married before she left with her father and Esmeralda for her little Wisconsin farm, and as she coldly bid Robert Canler good-by as her train pulled out, he called to her that he would join them in a week or two.

At their destination they were met by Clayton and Mr. Philander in a huge touring car belonging to the former, and quickly whirled away through the dense northern woods toward the little farm which the girl had not visited before since childhood.

The farmhouse, which stood on a little elevation some hundred yards from the tenant house, had undergone a complete transformation during the three weeks that Clayton and Mr. Philander had been there.

The former had imported a small army of carpenters and plasterers, plumbers and painters from a distant city, and what had been but a dilapidated shell when they reached it was now a cosy little two-story house filled with every modern convenience procurable in so short a time.

"Why, Mr. Clayton, what have you done?" cried Jane Porter, her heart sinking within her as she realized the probable size of the expenditure that had been made.

"S-sh," cautioned Clayton. "Don't let your father guess. If you don't tell him he will never notice, and I simply couldn't think of him living in the terrible squalor and sordidness which Mr. Philander and I found. It was so little when I would like to do so much, Jane. For his sake, please, never mention it."

"But you know that we can't repay you," cried the girl. "Why do you want to put me under such terrible obligations?"

"Don't, Jane," said Clayton sadly. "If it had been just you, believe me, I wouldn't have done it, for I knew from the start that it would only hurt me in your eyes, but I couldn't think of that dear old man living in the hole we found here. Won't you please believe that I did it just for him and give me that little crumb of pleasure at least?"

"I do believe you, Mr. Clayton," said the girl, "because I know you are big enough and generous enough to have done it just for him – and, oh Cecil, I wish I might repay you as you deserve – as you would wish."

"Why can't you, Jane?"

"Because I love another."

"Canler?"

"No."

"But you are going to marry him. He told me as much before I left Baltimore."

The girl winced.

"I do not love him," she said, almost proudly.

"Is it because of the money, Jane?"

She nodded.

"Then am I so much less desirable than Canler? I have money enough, and far more, for every need," he said bitterly.

"I do not love you, Cecil," she said, "but I respect you. If I must disgrace myself by such a bargain with any man, I prefer that it be one I already despise. I should loathe the man to whom I sold myself without love, whomsoever he might be. You will be happier," she concluded, "alone – with my respect and friendship, than with me and my contempt."

He did not press the matter further, but if ever a man had murder in his heart it was William Cecil Clayton, Lord Greystoke, when, a week later, Robert Canler drew up before the farmhouse in his purring six cylinder.

A week passed; a tense, uneventful, but uncomfortable week for all the inmates of the little Wisconsin farmhouse.

Canler was insistent that Jane marry him at once.

At length she gave in from sheer loathing of the continued and hateful importuning.

It was agreed that on the morrow Canler was to drive to town and bring back the license and a minister.

Clayton had wanted to leave as soon as the plan was announced, but the girl's tired, hopeless look kept him. He could not desert her.

Something might happen yet, he tried to console himself by thinking. And in his heart, he knew that it would require but a tiny spark to turn his hatred for Canler into the blood lust of the killer.

Early the next morning Canler set out for town.

In the east smoke could be seen lying low over the forest, for a fire had been raging for a week not far from them, but the wind still lay in the west and no danger threatened them.

About noon Jane started off for a walk. She would not let Clayton accompany her. She wanted to be alone, she said, and he respected her wishes.

In the house Professor Porter and Mr. Philander were immersed in an absorbing discussion of some weighty scientific problem. Esmeralda dozed in the kitchen, and Clayton, heavy-eyed after a sleepless night, threw himself down upon the couch in the living room and soon dropped into a fitful slumber.

To the east the black smoke clouds rose higher into the heavens, suddenly they eddied, and then commenced to drift rapidly toward the west.

On and on they came. The inmates of the tenant house were gone, for it was market day, and none was there to see the rapid approach of the fiery demon.

Soon the flames had spanned the road to the south and cut off Canler's return. A little fluctuation of the wind now carried the path of the forest fire to the north, then blew back and the flames nearly stood still as though held in leash by some master hand.

Suddenly, out of the northeast, a great black car came careening down the road.

With a jolt it stopped before the cottage, and a black-haired giant leaped out to run up onto the porch. Without a pause he rushed into the house. On the couch lay Clayton. The man started in surprise, but with a bound was at the side of the sleeping man.

Shaking him roughly by the shoulder, he cried:

"My God, Clayton, are you all mad here? Don't you know you are nearly surrounded by fire? Where is Miss Porter?"

Clayton sprang to his feet. He did not recognize the man, but he understood the words and was upon the veranda in a bound.

"Scott!" he cried, and then, dashing back into the house, "Jane! Jane! where are you?"

In an instant Esmeralda, Professor Porter and Mr. Philander had joined the two men.

"Where is Miss Jane?" cried Clayton, seizing Esmeralda by the shoulders and shaking her roughly.

"Oh, Gaberelle, Mister Clayton, she done gone for a walk."

"Hasn't she come back yet?" and, without waiting for a reply, Clayton dashed out into the yard, followed by the others. "Which way did she go?" cried the black-haired giant of Esmeralda.

"Down that road," cried the frightened woman, pointing toward the south where a mighty wall of roaring flames shut out the view.

"Put these people in the other car," shouted the stranger to Clayton. "I saw one as I drove up – and get them out of here by the north road.

"Leave my car here. If I find Miss Porter we shall need it. If I don't, no one will need it. Do as I say," as Clayton hesitated, and then they saw the lithe figure bound away cross the clearing toward the northwest where the forest still stood, untouched by flame.

In each rose the unaccountable feeling that a great responsibility had been raised from their shoulders; a kind of implicit confidence in the power of the stranger to save Jane if she could be saved.

"Who was that?" asked Professor Porter.

"I do not know," replied Clayton. "He called me by name and he knew Jane, for he asked for her. And he called Esmeralda by name."

"There was something most startlingly familiar about him," exclaimed Mr. Philander, "And yet, bless me, I know I never saw him before."

"Tut, tut!" cried Professor Porter. "Most remarkable! Who could it have been, and why do I feel that Jane is safe, now that he has set out in search of her?"

"I can't tell you, Professor," said Clayton soberly, "but I know I have the same uncanny feeling."

"But come," he cried, "we must get out of here ourselves, or we shall be shut off," and the party hastened toward Clayton's car.

When Jane turned to retrace her steps homeward, she was alarmed to note how near the smoke of the forest fire seemed, and as she hastened onward her alarm became almost a panic when she perceived that the rushing flames were rapidly forcing their way between herself and the cottage.

At length she was compelled to turn into the dense thicket and attempt to force her way to the west in an effort to circle around the flames and reach the house.

In a short time the futility of her attempt became apparent and then her one hope lay in retracing her steps to the road and flying for her life to the south toward the town.

The twenty minutes that it took her to regain the road was all that had been needed to cut off her retreat as effectually as her advance had been cut off before.

A short run down the road brought her to a horrified stand, for there before her was another wall of flame. An arm of the main conflagration had shot out a half mile south of its parent to embrace this tiny strip of road in its implacable clutches.

Jane knew that it was useless again to attempt to force her way through the undergrowth.

She had tried it once, and failed. Now she realized that it would be but a matter of minutes ere the whole space between the north and the south would be a seething mass of billowing flames.

Calmly the girl kneeled down in the dust of the roadway and prayed for strength to meet her fate bravely, and for the delivery of her father and her friends from death.

Suddenly she heard her name being called aloud through the forest:

"Jane! Jane Porter!" It rang strong and clear, but in a strange voice.

"Here!" she called in reply. "Here! In the roadway!"

Then through the branches of the trees she saw a figure swinging with the speed of a squirrel.

A veering of the wind blew a cloud of smoke about them and she could no longer see the man who was speeding toward her, but suddenly she felt a great arm about her. Then she was lifted up, and she felt the rushing of the wind and the occasional brush of a branch as she was borne along.

She opened her eyes.

Far below her lay the undergrowth and the hard earth.

About her was the waving foliage of the forest.

From tree to tree swung the giant figure which bore her, and it seemed to Jane that she was living over in a dream the experience that had been hers in that far African jungle.

Oh, if it were but the same man who had borne her so swiftly through the tangled verdure on that other day! but that was impossible! Yet who else in all the world was there with the strength and agility to do what this man was now doing?

She stole a sudden glance at the face close to hers, and then she gave a little frightened gasp. It was he!

"My forest man!" she murmured. "No, I must be delirious!"

"Yes, your man, Jane Porter. Your savage, primeval man come out of the jungle to claim his mate – the woman who ran away from him," he added almost fiercely.

"I did not run away," she whispered. "I would only consent to leave when they had waited a week for you to return."

They had come to a point beyond the fire now, and he had turned back to the clearing.

Side by side they were walking toward the cottage. The wind had changed once more and the fire was burning back upon itself – another hour like that and it would be burned out.

"Why did you not return?" she asked.

"I was nursing D'Arnot. He was badly wounded."

"Ah, I knew it!" she exclaimed.

"They said you had gone to join the blacks – that they were your people."

He laughed.

"But you did not believe them, Jane?"

"No; – what shall I call you?" she asked. "What is your name?"

"I was Tarzan of the Apes when you first knew me," he said.

"Tarzan of the Apes!" she cried – "and that was your note I answered when I left?"

"Yes, whose did you think it was?"

"I did not know; only that it could not be yours, for Tarzan of the Apes had written in English, and you could not understand a word of any language."

Again he laughed.

"It is a long story, but it was I who wrote what I could not speak – and now D'Arnot has made matters worse by teaching me to speak French instead of English.

"Come," he added, "jump into my car, we must overtake your father, they are only a little way ahead."

As they drove along, he said:

"Then when you said in your note to Tarzan of the Apes that you loved another – you might have meant me?"

"I might have," she answered, simply.

"But in Baltimore – Oh, how I have searched for you – they told me you would possibly be married by now. That a man named Canler had come up here to wed you. Is that true?"

"Yes."

"Do you love him?"

"No."

"Do you love me?"

She buried her face in her hands.

"I am promised to another. I cannot answer you, Tarzan of the Apes," she cried.

"You have answered. Now, tell me why you would marry one you do not love."

"My father owes him money."

Suddenly there came back to Tarzan the memory of the letter he had read – and the name Robert Canler and the hinted trouble which he had been unable to understand then.

He smiled.

"If your father had not lost the treasure you would not feel forced to keep your promise to this man Canler?"

"I could ask him to release me."

"And if he refused?"

"I have given my promise."

He was silent for a moment. The car was plunging along the uneven road at a reckless pace, for the fire showed threateningly at their right, and another change of the wind might sweep it on with raging fury across this one avenue of escape.

Finally they passed the danger point, and Tarzan reduced their speed.

"Suppose I should ask him?" ventured Tarzan.

"He would scarcely accede to the demand of a stranger," said the girl. "Especially one who wanted me himself."

"Terkoz did," said Tarzan, grimly.

Jane shuddered and looked fearfully up at the giant figure beside her, for she knew that he meant the great anthropoid he had killed in her defense.

"This is not the African jungle," she said. "You are no longer a savage beast. You are a gentleman, and gentlemen do not kill in cold blood."

"I am still a wild beast at heart," he said, in a low voice, as though to himself.

Again they were silent for a time.

"Jane," said the man, at length, "if you were free, would you marry me?"

She did not reply at once, but he waited patiently.

The girl was trying to collect her thoughts.

What did she know of this strange creature at her side? What did he know of himself? Who was he? Who, his parents?

Why, his very name echoed his mysterious origin and his savage life.

He had no name. Could she be happy with this jungle waif? Could she find anything in common with a husband whose life had been spent in the tree tops of an African wilderness, frolicking and fighting with fierce anthropoids; tearing his food from the quivering flank of fresh-killed prey, sinking his strong teeth into raw flesh, and tearing away his portion while his mates growled and fought about him for their share?

Could he ever rise to her social sphere? Could she bear to think of sinking to his? Would either be happy in such a horrible misalliance?

"You do not answer," he said. "Do you shrink from wounding me?"

"I do not know what answer to make," said Jane sadly. "I do not know my own mind."

"You do not love me, then?" he asked, in a level tone.

"Do not ask me. You will be happier without me. You were never meant for the formal restrictions and conventionalities of society – civilization would become irksome to you, and in a little while you would long for the freedom of your old life – a life to which I am as totally unfitted as you to mine."

"I think I understand you," he replied quietly. "I shall not urge you, for I would rather see you happy than to be happy myself. I see now that you could not be happy with – an ape."

There was just the faintest tinge of bitterness in his voice.

"Don't," she remonstrated. "Don't say that. You do not understand."

But before she could go on a sudden turn in the road brought them into the midst of a little hamlet.

Before them stood Clayton's car surrounded by the party he had brought from the cottage.

CHAPTER TWENTY EIGHT

Conclusion

AT THE SIGHT of Jane, cries of relief and delight broke from every lip, and as Tarzan's car stopped beside the other, Professor Porter caught his daughter in his arms.

For a moment no one noticed Tarzan, sitting silently in his seat.

Clayton was the first to remember, and, turning, held out his hand.

"How can we ever thank you?" he exclaimed. "You have saved us all. You called me by name at the cottage, but I do not seem to recall yours, though there is something very familiar about you. It is as though I had known you well under very different conditions a long time ago."

Tarzan smiled as he took the proffered hand.

"You are quite right, Monsieur Clayton," he said, in French. "You will pardon me if I do not speak to you in English. I am just learning it, and while I understand it fairly well I speak it very poorly."

"But who are you?" insisted Clayton, speaking in French this time himself.

"Tarzan of the Apes."

Clayton started back in surprise.

"By Jove!" he exclaimed. "It is true."

And Professor Porter and Mr. Philander pressed forward to add their thanks to Clayton's, and to voice their surprise and pleasure at seeing their jungle friend so far from his savage home.

The party now entered the modest little hostelry, where Clayton soon made arrangements for their entertainment.

They were sitting in the little, stuffy parlor when the distant chugging of an approaching automobile caught their attention.

Mr. Philander, who was sitting near the window, looked out as the car drew in sight, finally stopping beside the other automobiles.

"Bless me!" said Mr. Philander, a shade of annoyance in his tone. "It is Mr. Canler. I had hoped, er – I had thought or – er – how very happy we should be that he was not caught in the fire," he ended lamely.

"Tut, tut! Mr. Philander," said Professor Porter. "Tut, tut! I have often admonished my pupils to count ten before speaking. Were I you, Mr. Philander, I should count at least a thousand, and then maintain a discreet silence."

"Bless me, yes!" acquiesced Mr. Philander. "But who is the clerical appearing gentleman with him?"

Jane blanched.

Clayton moved uneasily in his chair.

Professor Porter removed his spectacles nervously, and breathed upon them, but replaced them on his nose without wiping.

The ubiquitous Esmeralda grunted.

Only Tarzan did not comprehend.

Presently Robert Canler burst into the room.

"Thank God!" he cried. "I feared the worst, until I saw your car, Clayton. I was cut off on the south road and had to go away back to town, and then strike east to this road. I thought we'd never reach the cottage."

No one seemed to enthuse much. Tarzan eyed Robert Canler as Sabor eyes her prey.

Jane glanced at him and coughed nervously.

"Mr. Canler," she said, "this is Monsieur Tarzan, an old friend."

Canler turned and extended his hand. Tarzan rose and bowed as only D'Arnot could have taught a gentleman to do it, but he did not seem to see Canler's hand.

Nor did Canler appear to notice the oversight.

"This is the Reverend Mr. Tousley, Jane," said Canler, turning to the clerical party behind him. "Mr. Tousley, Miss Porter."

Mr. Tousley bowed and beamed.

Canler introduced him to the others.

"We can have the ceremony at once, Jane," said Canler. "Then you and I can catch the midnight train in town."

Tarzan understood the plan instantly. He glanced out of half-closed eyes at Jane, but he did not move.

The girl hesitated. The room was tense with the silence of taut nerves.

All eyes turned toward Jane, awaiting her reply.

"Can't we wait a few days?" she asked. "I am all unstrung. I have been through so much today."

Canler felt the hostility that emanated from each member of the party. It made him angry.

"We have waited as long as I intend to wait," he said roughly. "You have promised to marry me. I shall be played with no longer. I have the license and here is the preacher. Come Mr. Tousley; come Jane. There are plenty of witnesses – more than enough," he added with a disagreeable inflection; and taking Jane Porter by the arm, he started to lead her toward the waiting minister.

But scarcely had he taken a single step ere a heavy hand closed upon his arm with a grip of steel.

Another hand shot to his throat and in a moment he was being shaken high above the floor, as a cat might shake a mouse.

Jane turned in horrified surprise toward Tarzan.

And, as she looked into his face, she saw the crimson band upon his forehead that she had seen that other day in far distant Africa, when Tarzan of the Apes had closed in mortal combat with the great anthropoid – Terkoz.

She knew that murder lay in that savage heart, and with a little cry of horror she sprang forward to plead with the ape-man. But her fears were more for Tarzan than for Canler. She realized the stern retribution which justice metes to the murderer.

Before she could reach them, however, Clayton had jumped to Tarzan's side and attempted to drag Canler from his grasp.

With a single sweep of one mighty arm the Englishman was hurled across the room, and then Jane laid a firm white hand upon Tarzan's wrist, and looked up into his eyes.

"For my sake," she said.

The grasp upon Canler's throat relaxed.

Tarzan looked down into the beautiful face before him.

"Do you wish this to live?" he asked in surprise.

"I do not wish him to die at your hands, my friend," she replied. "I do not wish you to become a murderer."

Tarzan removed his hand from Canler's throat.

"Do you release her from her promise?" he asked. "It is the price of your life."

Canler, gasping for breath, nodded.

"Will you go away and never molest her further?"

Again the man nodded his head, his face distorted by fear of the death that had been so close.

Tarzan released him, and Canler staggered toward the door. In another moment he was gone, and the terror-stricken preacher with him.

Tarzan turned toward Jane.

"May I speak with you for a moment, alone," he asked.

The girl nodded and started toward the door leading to the narrow veranda of the little hotel. She passed out to await Tarzan and so did not hear the conversation which followed.

"Wait," cried Professor Porter, as Tarzan was about to follow.

The professor had been stricken dumb with surprise by the rapid developments of the past few minutes.

"Before we go further, sir, I should like an explanation of the events which have just transpired. By what right, sir, did you interfere between my daughter and Mr. Canler? I had promised him her hand, sir, and regardless of our personal likes or dislikes, sir, that promise must be kept."

"I interfered, Professor Porter," replied Tarzan, "because your daughter does not love Mr. Canler – she does not wish to marry him. That is enough for me to know."

"You do not know what you have done," said Professor Porter. "Now he will doubtless refuse to marry her."

"He most certainly will," said Tarzan, emphatically.

"And further," added Tarzan, "you need not fear that your pride will suffer, Professor Porter, for you will be able to pay the Canler person what you owe him the moment you reach home."

"Tut, tut, sir!" exclaimed Professor Porter. "What do you mean, sir?"

"Your treasure has been found," said Tarzan.

"What – what is that you are saying?" cried the professor. "You are mad, man. It cannot be."

"It is, though. It was I who stole it, not knowing either its value or to whom it belonged. I saw the sailors bury it, and, ape-like, I had to dig it up and bury it again elsewhere. When D'Arnot told me what it was and what it meant to you I returned to the jungle and recovered it. It had caused so much crime and suffering and sorrow that D'Arnot thought it best not to attempt to bring the treasure itself on here, as had been my intention, so I have brought a letter of credit instead.

"Here it is, Professor Porter," and Tarzan drew an envelope from his pocket and handed it to the astonished professor, "two hundred and forty-one thousand dollars. The treasure was most carefully appraised by experts, but lest there should be any question in your mind, D'Arnot himself bought it and is holding it for you, should you prefer the treasure to the credit."

"To the already great burden of the obligations we owe you, sir," said Professor Porter, with trembling voice, "is now added this greatest of all services. You have given me the means to save my honor."

Clayton, who had left the room a moment after Canler, now returned.

"Pardon me," he said. "I think we had better try to reach town before dark and take the first train out of this forest. A native just rode by from the north, who reports that the fire is moving slowly in this direction."

This announcement broke up further conversation, and the entire party went out to the waiting automobiles.

Clayton, with Jane, the professor and Esmeralda occupied Clayton's car, while Tarzan took Mr. Philander in with him.

"Bless me!" exclaimed Mr. Philander, as the car moved off after Clayton. "Who would ever have thought it possible! The last time I saw you you were a veritable wild man, skipping about among the branches of a tropical African forest, and now you are driving me along a Wisconsin road in a French automobile. Bless me! But it is most remarkable."

"Yes," assented Tarzan, and then, after a pause, "Mr. Philander, do you recall any of the details of the finding and burying of three skeletons found in my cabin beside that African jungle?"

"Very distinctly, sir, very distinctly," replied Mr. Philander.

"Was there anything peculiar about any of those skeletons?"

Mr. Philander eyed Tarzan narrowly.

"Why do you ask?"

"It means a great deal to me to know," replied Tarzan. "Your answer may clear up a mystery. It can do no worse, at any rate, than to leave it still a mystery. I have been entertaining a theory concerning those skeletons for the past two months, and I want you to answer my question to the best of your knowledge – were the three skeletons you buried all human skeletons?"

"No," said Mr. Philander, "the smallest one, the one found in the crib, was the skeleton of an anthropoid ape."

"Thank you," said Tarzan.

In the car ahead, Jane was thinking fast and furiously. She had felt the purpose for which Tarzan had asked a few words with her, and she knew that she must be prepared to give him an answer in the very near future.

He was not the sort of person one could put off, and somehow that very thought made her wonder if she did not really fear him.

And could she love where she feared?

She realized the spell that had been upon her in the depths of that far-off jungle, but there was no spell of enchantment now in prosaic Wisconsin.

Nor did the immaculate young Frenchman appeal to the primal woman in her, as had the stalwart forest god.

Did she love him? She did not know – now.

She glanced at Clayton out of the corner of her eye. Was not here a man trained in the same school of environment in which she had been trained – a man with social position and culture such as she had been taught to consider as the prime essentials to congenial association?

Did not her best judgment point to this young English nobleman, whose love she knew to be of the sort a civilized woman should crave, as the logical mate for such as herself?

Could she love Clayton? She could see no reason why she could not. Jane was not coldly calculating by nature, but training, environment and heredity had all combined to teach her to reason even in matters of the heart.

That she had been carried off her feet by the strength of the young giant when his great arms were about her in the distant African forest, and again today, in the Wisconsin woods, seemed to her only attributable to a temporary mental reversion to type on her part – to the psychological appeal of the primeval man to the primeval woman in her nature.

If he should never touch her again, she reasoned, she would never feel attracted toward him. She had not loved him, then. It had been nothing more than a passing hallucination, super-induced by excitement and by personal contact.

Excitement would not always mark their future relations, should she marry him, and the power of personal contact eventually would be dulled by familiarity.

Again she glanced at Clayton. He was very handsome and every inch a gentleman. She should be very proud of such a husband.

And then he spoke – a minute sooner or a minute later might have made all the difference in the world to three lives – but chance stepped in and pointed out to Clayton the psychological moment.

"You are free now, Jane," he said. "Won't you say yes – I will devote my life to making you very happy."

"Yes," she whispered.

That evening in the little waiting room at the station Tarzan caught Jane alone for a moment.

"You are free now, Jane," he said, "and _I_ have come across the ages out of the dim and distant past from the lair of the primeval man to claim you – for your sake I have become a civilized man – for your sake I have crossed oceans and continents – for your sake I will be whatever you will me to be. I can make you happy, Jane, in the life you know and love best. Will you marry me?"

For the first time she realized the depths of the man's love – all that he had accomplished in so short a time solely for love of her. Turning her head she buried her face in her arms.

What had she done? Because she had been afraid she might succumb to the pleas of this giant, she had burned her bridges behind her – in her groundless apprehension that she might make a terrible mistake, she had made a worse one.

And then she told him all – told him the truth word by word, without attempting to shield herself or condone her error.

"What can we do?" he asked. "You have admitted that you love me. You know that I love you; but I do not know the ethics of society by which you are governed. I shall leave the decision to you, for you know best what will be for your eventual welfare."

"I cannot tell him, Tarzan," she said. "He too, loves me, and he is a good man. I could never face you nor any other honest person if I repudiated my promise to Mr. Clayton. I shall have to keep it – and you must help me bear the burden, though we may not see each other again after tonight."

The others were entering the room now and Tarzan turned toward the little window.

But he saw nothing outside – within he saw a patch of greensward surrounded by a matted mass of gorgeous tropical plants and flowers, and, above, the waving foliage of mighty trees, and, over all, the blue of an equatorial sky.

In the center of the greensward a young woman sat upon a little mound of earth, and beside her sat a young giant. They ate pleasant fruit and looked into each other's eyes and smiled. They were very happy, and they were all alone.

His thoughts were broken in upon by the station agent who entered asking if there was a gentleman by the name of Tarzan in the party.

"I am Monsieur Tarzan," said the ape-man.

"Here is a message for you, forwarded from Baltimore; it is a cablegram from Paris."

Tarzan took the envelope and tore it open. The message was from D'Arnot.

It read:

Fingerprints prove you Greystoke. Congratulations.
D'ARNOT.

As Tarzan finished reading, Clayton entered and came toward him with extended hand.

Here was the man who had Tarzan's title, and Tarzan's estates, and was going to marry the woman whom Tarzan loved – the woman who loved Tarzan. A single word from Tarzan would make a great difference in this man's life.

It would take away his title and his lands and his castles, and – it would take them away from Jane Porter also. "I say, old man," cried Clayton, "I haven't had a chance to thank you for all you've done for us. It seems as though you had your hands full saving our lives in Africa and here.

"I'm awfully glad you came on here. We must get better acquainted. I often thought about you, you know, and the remarkable circumstances of your environment.

"If it's any of my business, how the devil did you ever get into that bally jungle?"

"I was born there," said Tarzan, quietly. "My mother was an Ape, and of course she couldn't tell me much about it. I never knew who my father was."

THE RETURN OF
TARZAN

CHAPTER ONE

The Affair on the Line

"Magnifique!" ejaculated the Countess de Coude, beneath her breath.

"Eh?" questioned the count, turning toward his young wife. "What is it that is magnificent?" and the count bent his eyes in various directions in quest of the object of her admiration.

"Oh, nothing at all, my dear," replied the countess, a slight flush momentarily coloring her already pink cheek. "I was but recalling with admiration those stupendous skyscrapers, as they call them, of New York," and the fair countess settled herself more comfortably in her steamer chair, and resumed the magazine which "nothing at all" had caused her to let fall upon her lap.

Her husband again buried himself in his book, but not without a mild wonderment that three days out from New York his countess should suddenly have realized an admiration for the very buildings she had but recently characterized as horrid.

Presently the count put down his book. "It is very tiresome, Olga," he said. "I think that I shall hunt up some others who may be equally bored, and see if we cannot find enough for a game of cards."

"You are not very gallant, my husband," replied the young woman, smiling, "but as I am equally bored I can forgive you. Go and play at your tiresome old cards, then, if you will."

When he had gone she let her eyes wander slyly to the figure of a tall young man stretched lazily in a chair not far distant.

"MAGNIFIQUE!" she breathed once more.

The Countess Olga de Coude was twenty. Her husband forty. She was a very faithful and loyal wife, but as she had had nothing whatever to do with the selection of a husband, it is not at all unlikely that she was not wildly and passionately in love with the one that fate and her titled Russian father had selected for her. However, simply because she was surprised into a tiny exclamation of approval at sight of a splendid young stranger it must not be inferred therefrom that her thoughts were in any way disloyal to her spouse. She merely admired, as she might have admired a particularly fine specimen of any species. Furthermore, the young man was unquestionably good to look at.

As her furtive glance rested upon his profile he rose to leave the deck. The Countess de Coude beckoned to a passing steward. "Who is that gentleman?" she asked.

"He is booked, madam, as Monsieur Tarzan, of Africa," replied the steward.

"Rather a large estate," thought the girl, but now her interest was still further aroused.

As Tarzan walked slowly toward the smoking-room he came unexpectedly upon two men whispering excitedly just without. He would have vouchsafed them not even a passing thought but for the strangely guilty glance that one of them shot in his direction. They reminded Tarzan of melodramatic villains he had seen at the theaters in Paris. Both were very dark, and this, in connection with the shrugs and stealthy glances that accompanied their palpable intriguing, lent still greater force to the similarity.

Tarzan entered the smoking-room, and sought a chair a little apart from the others who were there. He felt in no mood for conversation, and as he sipped his absinth he let his mind run rather sorrowfully over the past few weeks of his life. Time and again he had wondered if he had acted wisely in renouncing his birthright to a man to whom he owed nothing. It is true that he liked Clayton, but – ah, but that was not the question. It was not for William Cecil Clayton, Lord Greystoke, that he had denied his birth. It was for the woman whom both he and Clayton had loved, and whom a strange freak of fate had given to Clayton instead of to him.

That she loved him made the thing doubly difficult to bear, yet he knew that he could have done nothing less than he did do that night within the little railway station in the far Wisconsin woods. To him her happiness was the first consideration of all, and his brief experience with civilization and civilized men had taught him that without money and position life to most of them was unendurable.

Jane Porter had been born to both, and had Tarzan taken them away from her future husband it would doubtless have plunged her into a life of misery and torture. That she would have spurned Clayton once he had been stripped of both his title and his estates never for once occurred to Tarzan, for he credited to others the same honest loyalty that was so inherent a quality in himself. Nor, in this instance, had he erred. Could any one thing have further bound Jane Porter to her promise to Clayton it would have been in the nature of some such misfortune as this overtaking him.

Tarzan's thoughts drifted from the past to the future. He tried to look forward with pleasurable sensations to his return to the jungle of his birth and boyhood; the cruel, fierce jungle in which he had spent twenty of his twenty-two years. But who or what of all the myriad jungle life would there be to welcome his return? Not one. Only Tantor, the elephant, could he call friend. The others would hunt him or flee from him as had been their way in the past.

Not even the apes of his own tribe would extend the hand of fellowship to him.

If civilization had done nothing else for Tarzan of the Apes, it had to some extent taught him to crave the society of his own kind, and to feel with genuine pleasure the congenial warmth of companionship. And in the same ratio had it made any other life distasteful to him. It was difficult to imagine a world without a friend – without a living thing who spoke the new tongues which Tarzan had learned to love so well. And so it was that Tarzan looked with little relish upon the future he had mapped out for himself.

As he sat musing over his cigarette his eyes fell upon a mirror before him, and in it he saw reflected a table at which four men sat at cards. Presently one of them rose to leave, and then another approached, and Tarzan could see that he courteously offered to fill the vacant chair, that the game might not be interrupted. He was the smaller of the two whom Tarzan had seen whispering just outside the smoking-room.

It was this fact that aroused a faint spark of interest in Tarzan, and so as he speculated upon the future he watched in the mirror the reflection of the players at the table behind him. Aside from the man who had but just entered the game Tarzan knew the name of but one of the other players. It was he who sat opposite the new player, Count Raoul de Coude, whom an over-attentive steward had pointed out as one of the celebrities of the passage, describing him as a man high in the official family of the French minister of war.

Suddenly Tarzan's attention was riveted upon the picture in the glass. The other swarthy plotter had entered, and was standing behind the count's chair. Tarzan saw him turn and glance furtively about the room, but his eyes did not rest for a sufficient time upon the mirror to note the reflection of Tarzan's watchful eyes. Stealthily the man withdrew something from his pocket. Tarzan could not discern what the object was, for the man's hand covered it.

Slowly the hand approached the count, and then, very deftly, the thing that was in it was transferred to the count's pocket. The man remained standing where he could watch the Frenchman's cards. Tarzan was puzzled, but he was all attention now, nor did he permit another detail of the incident to escape him.

The play went on for some ten minutes after this, until the count won a considerable wager from him who had last joined the game, and then Tarzan saw the fellow back of the count's chair nod his head to his confederate. Instantly the player arose and pointed a finger at the count.

"Had I known that monsieur was a professional card sharp I had not been so ready to be drawn into the game," he said.

Instantly the count and the two other players were upon their feet.

De Coude's face went white.

"What do you mean, sir?" he cried. "Do you know to whom you speak?"

"I know that I speak, for the last time, to one who cheats at cards," replied the fellow.

The count leaned across the table, and struck the man full in the mouth with his open palm, and then the others closed in between them.

"There is some mistake, sir," cried one of the other players. "Why, this is Count de Coude, of France." "If I am mistaken," said the accuser, "I shall gladly apologize; but before I do so first let monsieur le count explain the extra cards which I saw him drop into his side pocket."

And then the man whom Tarzan had seen drop them there turned to sneak from the room, but to his annoyance he found the exit barred by a tall, gray-eyed stranger.

"Pardon," said the man brusquely, attempting to pass to one side.

"Wait," said Tarzan.

"But why, monsieur?" exclaimed the other petulantly. "Permit me to pass, monsieur."

"Wait," said Tarzan. "I think that there is a matter in here that you may doubtless be able to explain."

The fellow had lost his temper by this time, and with a low oath seized Tarzan to push him to one side. The ape-man but smiled as he twisted the big fellow about and, grasping him by the collar of his coat, escorted him back to the table, struggling, cursing, and striking in futile remonstrance. It was Nikolas Rokoff's first experience with the muscles that had brought their savage owner victorious through encounters with Numa, the lion, and Terkoz, the great bull ape.

The man who had accused De Coude, and the two others who had been playing, stood looking expectantly at the count. Several other passengers had drawn toward the scene of the altercation, and all awaited the denouement.

"The fellow is crazy," said the count. "Gentlemen, I implore that one of you search me."

"The accusation is ridiculous." This from one of the players.

"You have but to slip your hand in the count's coat pocket and you will see that the accusation is quite serious," insisted the accuser. And then, as the others still hesitated to do so: "Come, I shall do it myself if no other will," and he stepped forward toward the count.

"No, monsieur," said De Coude. "I will submit to a search only at the hands of a gentleman."

"It is unnecessary to search the count. The cards are in his pocket. I myself saw them placed there."

All turned in surprise toward this new speaker, to behold a very well-built young man urging a resisting captive toward them by the scruff of his neck.

"It is a conspiracy," cried De Coude angrily. "There are no cards in my coat," and with that he ran his hand into his pocket. As he did so tense silence reigned in the little group. The count went dead white, and then very slowly he withdrew his hand, and in it were three cards.

He looked at them in mute and horrified surprise, and slowly the red of mortification suffused his face. Expressions of pity and contempt tinged the features of those who looked on at the death of a man's honor.

"It is a conspiracy, monsieur." It was the gray-eyed stranger who spoke. "Gentlemen," he continued, "monsieur le count did not know that those cards were in his pocket. They were placed there without his knowledge as he sat at play. From where I sat in that chair yonder I saw the reflection of it all in the mirror before me. This person whom I just intercepted in an effort to escape placed the cards in the count's pocket."

De Coude had glanced from Tarzan to the man in his grasp.

"MON DIEU, Nikolas!" he cried. "You?"

Then he turned to his accuser, and eyed him intently for a moment.

"And you, monsieur, I did not recognize you without your beard. It quite disguises you, Paulvitch. I see it all now. It is quite clear, gentlemen."

"What shall we do with them, monsieur?" asked Tarzan. "Turn them over to the captain?"

"No, my friend," said the count hastily. "It is a personal matter, and I beg that you will let it drop. It is sufficient that I have been exonerated from the charge. The less we have to do with such fellows, the better. But, monsieur, how can I thank you for the great kindness you have done me? Permit me to offer you my card, and should the time come when I may serve you, remember that I am yours to command."

Tarzan had released Rokoff, who, with his confederate, Paulvitch, had hastened from the smoking-room. Just as he was leaving, Rokoff turned to Tarzan. "Monsieur will have ample opportunity to regret his interference in the affairs of others."

Tarzan smiled, and then, bowing to the count, handed him his own card.

The count read:

M. JEAN C. TARZAN

"Monsieur Tarzan," he said, "may indeed wish that he had never befriended me, for I can assure him that he has won the enmity of two of the most unmitigated scoundrels in all Europe. Avoid them, monsieur, by all means."

"I have had more awe-inspiring enemies, my dear count," replied Tarzan with a quiet smile, "yet I am still alive and unworried. I think that neither of these two will ever find the means to harm me."

"Let us hope not, monsieur," said De Coude; "but yet it will do no harm to be on the alert, and to know that you have made at least one enemy today who never forgets and never forgives, and in whose malignant brain there are always hatching new atrocities to perpetrate upon those who have thwarted or offended him. To say that Nikolas Rokoff is a devil would be to place a wanton affront upon his satanic majesty."

That night as Tarzan entered his cabin he found a folded note upon the floor that had evidently been pushed beneath the door. He opened it and read:

M. TARZAN:

Doubtless you did not realize the gravity of your offense, or you would not have done the thing you did today. I am willing to believe that you acted in ignorance and without any intention to offend a stranger. For this reason I shall gladly permit you to offer an apology, and on receiving your assurances that you will not again interfere in affairs that do not concern you, I shall drop the matter.

Otherwise – but I am sure that you will see the wisdom of adopting the course I suggest.

Very respectfully,
NIKOLAS ROKOFF.

Tarzan permitted a grim smile to play about his lips for a moment, then he promptly dropped the matter from his mind, and went to bed.

In a nearby cabin the Countess de Coude was speaking to her husband.

"Why so grave, my dear Raoul?" she asked. "You have been as glum as could be all evening. What worries you?"

"Olga, Nikolas is on board. Did you know it?"

"Nikolas!" she exclaimed. "But it is impossible, Raoul. It cannot be. Nikolas is under arrest in Germany."

"So I thought myself until I saw him today – him and that other arch scoundrel, Paulvitch. Olga, I cannot endure his persecution much longer. No, not even for you. Sooner or later I shall turn him over to the authorities. In fact, I am half minded to explain all to the captain before we land. On a French liner it were an easy matter, Olga, permanently to settle this Nemesis of ours."

"Oh, no, Raoul!" cried the countess, sinking to her knees before him as he sat with bowed head upon a divan. "Do not do that. Remember your promise to me. Tell me, Raoul, that you will not do that. Do not even threaten him, Raoul."

De Coude took his wife's hands in his, and gazed upon her pale and troubled countenance for some time before he spoke, as though he would wrest from those beautiful eyes the real reason which prompted her to shield this man.

"Let it be as you wish, Olga," he said at length. "I cannot understand. He has forfeited all claim upon your love, loyalty, or respect. He is a menace to your life and honor, and the life and honor of your husband. I trust you may never regret championing him."

"I do not champion him, Raoul," she interrupted vehemently. "I believe that I hate him as much as you do, but – Oh, Raoul, blood is thicker than water."

"I should today have liked to sample the consistency of his," growled De Coude grimly. "The two deliberately attempted to besmirch my honor, Olga," and then he told her of all that had happened in the smoking-room. "Had it not been for this utter stranger, they had succeeded, for who would have accepted my unsupported word against the damning evidence of those cards hidden on my person? I had almost begun to doubt myself when this Monsieur Tarzan dragged your precious Nikolas before us, and explained the whole cowardly transaction."

"Monsieur Tarzan?" asked the countess, in evident surprise.

"Yes. Do you know him, Olga?"

"I have seen him. A steward pointed him out to me."

"I did not know that he was a celebrity," said the count.

Olga de Coude changed the subject. She discovered suddenly that she might find it difficult to explain just why the steward had pointed out the handsome Monsieur Tarzan to her. Perhaps she flushed the least little bit, for was not the count, her husband, gazing at her with a strangely quizzical expression. "Ah," she thought, "a guilty conscience is a most suspicious thing."

CHAPTER TWO

Forging Bonds of Hate and --?

It was not until late the following afternoon that Tarzan saw anything more of the fellow passengers into the midst of whose affairs his love of fair play had thrust him. And then he came most unexpectedly upon Rokoff and Paulvitch at a moment when of all others the two might least appreciate his company.

They were standing on deck at a point which was temporarily deserted, and as Tarzan came upon them they were in heated argument with a woman. Tarzan noted that she was richly appareled, and that her slender, well-modeled figure denoted youth; but as she was heavily veiled he could not discern her features.

The men were standing on either side of her, and the backs of all were toward Tarzan, so that he was quite close to them without their being aware of his presence. He noticed that Rokoff seemed to be threatening, the woman pleading; but they spoke in a strange tongue, and he could only guess from appearances that the girl was afraid.

Rokoff's attitude was so distinctly filled with the threat of physical violence that the ape-man paused for an instant just behind the trio, instinctively sensing an atmosphere of danger. Scarcely had he hesitated ere the man seized the woman roughly by the wrist, twisting it as though to wring a promise from her through torture. What would have happened next had Rokoff had his way we may only conjecture, since he did not have his way at all. Instead, steel fingers gripped his shoulder, and he was swung unceremoniously around, to meet the cold gray eyes of the stranger who had thwarted him on the previous day.

"SAPRISTI!" screamed the infuriated Rokoff. "What do you mean? Are you a fool that you thus again insult Nikolas Rokoff?"

"This is my answer to your note, monsieur," said Tarzan, in a low voice. And then he hurled the fellow from him with such force that Rokoff lunged sprawling against the rail.

"Name of a name!" shrieked Rokoff. "Pig, but you shall die for this," and, springing to his feet, he rushed upon Tarzan, tugging the meanwhile to draw a revolver from his hip pocket. The girl shrank back in terror.

"Nikolas!" she cried. "Do not – oh, do not do that. Quick, monsieur, fly, or he will surely kill you!" But instead of flying Tarzan advanced to meet the fellow. "Do not make a fool of yourself, monsieur," he said.

Rokoff, who was in a perfect frenzy of rage at the humiliation the stranger had put upon him, had at last succeeded in drawing the revolver. He had stopped, and now he deliberately raised it to Tarzan's breast and pulled the trigger. The hammer fell with a futile click on an empty chamber – the ape-man's hand shot out like the head of an angry python; there was a quick wrench, and the revolver sailed far out across the ship's rail, and dropped into the Atlantic.

For a moment the two men stood there facing one another. Rokoff had regained his self-possession. He was the first to speak.

"Twice now has monsieur seen fit to interfere in matters which do not concern him. Twice he has taken it upon himself to humiliate Nikolas Rokoff. The first offense was overlooked on the assumption that monsieur acted through ignorance, but this affair shall not be overlooked. If monsieur does not know who Nikolas Rokoff is, this last piece of effrontery will insure that monsieur later has good reason to remember him."

"That you are a coward and a scoundrel, monsieur," replied Tarzan, "is all that I care to know of you," and he turned to ask the girl if the man had hurt her, but she had disappeared. Then, without even a glance toward Rokoff and his companion, he continued his stroll along the deck.

Tarzan could not but wonder what manner of conspiracy was on foot, or what the scheme of the two men might be. There had been something rather familiar about the appearance of the veiled woman to whose rescue he had just come, but as he had not seen her face he could not be sure that he had ever seen her before. The only thing about her that he had particularly noticed was a ring of peculiar workmanship upon a finger of the hand that Rokoff had seized, and he determined to note the fingers of the women passengers he came upon thereafter, that he might discover the identity of her whom Rokoff was persecuting, and learn if the fellow had offered her further annoyance.

Tarzan had sought his deck chair, where he sat speculating on the numerous instances of human cruelty, selfishness, and spite that had fallen to his lot to witness since that day in the jungle four years since that his eyes had first fallen upon a human being other than himself – the sleek, black Kulonga, whose swift spear had that day found the vitals of Kala, the great she-ape, and robbed the youth, Tarzan, of the only mother he had ever known.

He recalled the murder of King by the rat-faced Snipes; the abandonment of Professor Porter and his party by the mutineers of the ARROW; the cruelty of the black warriors and women of Mbonga to their captives; the petty jealousies of the civil and military officers of the West Coast colony that had afforded him his first introduction to the civilized world.

"MON DIEU!" he soliloquized, "but they are all alike. Cheating, murdering, lying, fighting, and all for things that the beasts of the jungle would not deign to possess – money to purchase the effeminate pleasures of weaklings. And yet withal bound down by silly customs that make them slaves to their unhappy lot while firm in the belief that they be the lords of creation enjoying the only real pleasures of existence. In the jungle one would scarcely stand supinely aside while another took his mate. It is a silly world, an idiotic world, and Tarzan of the Apes was a fool to renounce the freedom and the happiness of his jungle to come into it."

Presently, as he sat there, the sudden feeling came over him that eyes were watching from behind, and the old instinct of the wild beast broke through the thin veneer of civilization, so that Tarzan wheeled about so quickly that the eyes of the young woman who had been surreptitiously regarding him had not even time to drop before the gray eyes of the ape-man shot an inquiring look straight into them. Then, as they fell, Tarzan saw a faint wave of crimson creep swiftly over the now half-averted face.

He smiled to himself at the result of his very uncivilized and ungallant action, for he had not lowered his own eyes when they met those of the young woman. She was very young, and equally good to look upon. Further, there was something rather familiar about her that set Tarzan to wondering where he had seen her before. He resumed his former position, and presently he was aware that she had arisen and was leaving the deck. As she passed, Tarzan turned to watch her, in the hope that he might discover a clew to satisfy his mild curiosity as to her identity.

Nor was he disappointed entirely, for as she walked away she raised one hand to the black, waving mass at the nape of her neck – the peculiarly feminine gesture that admits cognizance of appraising eyes behind her – and Tarzan saw upon a finger of this hand the ring of strange workmanship that he had seen upon the finger of the veiled woman a short time before.

So it was this beautiful young woman Rokoff had been persecuting. Tarzan wondered in a lazy sort of way whom she might be, and what relations one so lovely could have with the surly, bearded Russian.

After dinner that evening Tarzan strolled forward, where he remained until after dark, in conversation with the second officer, and when that gentleman's duties called him elsewhere Tarzan lolled lazily by the rail watching the play of the moonlight upon the gently rolling waters. He was half hidden by a davit, so that two men who approached along the deck did not see him, and as they passed Tarzan caught enough of their conversation to cause him to fall in behind them, to follow and learn what deviltry they were up to. He had recognized the voice as that of Rokoff, and had seen that his companion was Paulvitch.

Tarzan had overheard but a few words: "And if she screams you may choke her until – " But those had been enough to arouse the spirit of adventure within him, and so he kept the two men in sight as they walked, briskly now, along the deck. To the smoking-room he followed them, but they merely halted at the doorway long enough, apparently, to assure themselves that one whose whereabouts they wished to establish was within.

Then they proceeded directly to the first-class cabins upon the promenade deck. Here Tarzan found greater difficulty in escaping detection, but he managed to do so successfully. As they halted before one of the polished hardwood doors, Tarzan slipped into the shadow of a passageway not a dozen feet from them.

To their knock a woman's voice asked in French: "Who is it?"

"It is I, Olga – Nikolas," was the answer, in Rokoff's now familiar guttural. "May I come in?"

"Why do you not cease persecuting me, Nikolas?" came the voice of the woman from beyond the thin panel. "I have never harmed you."

"Come, come, Olga," urged the man, in propitiary tones; "I but ask a half dozen words with you. I shall not harm you, nor shall I enter your cabin; but I cannot shout my message through the door."

Tarzan heard the catch click as it was released from the inside. He stepped out from his hiding-place far enough to see what transpired when the door was opened, for he could not but recall the sinister words he had heard a few moments before upon the deck, "And if she screams you may choke her."

Rokoff was standing directly in front of the door. Paulvitch had flattened himself against the paneled wall of the corridor beyond. The door opened. Rokoff half entered the room, and stood with his back against the door, speaking in a low whisper to the woman, whom Tarzan could not see. Then Tarzan heard the woman's voice, level, but loud enough to distinguish her words.

"No, Nikolas," she was saying, "it is useless. Threaten as you will, I shall never accede to your demands. Leave the room, please; you have no right here. You promised not to enter."

"Very well, Olga, I shall not enter; but before I am done with you, you shall wish a thousand times that you had done at once the favor I have asked. In the end I shall win anyway, so you might as well save trouble and time for me, and disgrace for yourself and your – "

"Never, Nikolas!" interrupted the woman, and then Tarzan saw Rokoff turn and nod to Paulvitch, who sprang quickly toward the doorway of the cabin, rushing in past Rokoff, who held the door open for him. Then the latter stepped quickly out. The door closed. Tarzan heard the click of the lock as Paulvitch turned it from the inside. Rokoff remained standing before the door, with head bent, as though to catch the words of the two within. A nasty smile curled his bearded lip.

Tarzan could hear the woman's voice commanding the fellow to leave her cabin. "I shall send for my husband," she cried. "He will show you no mercy."

Paulvitch's sneering laugh came through the polished panels.

"The purser will fetch your husband, madame," said the man. "In fact, that officer has already been notified that you are entertaining a man other than your husband behind the locked door of your cabin."

"Bah!" cried the woman. "My husband will know!"

"Most assuredly your husband will know, but the purser will not; nor will the newspaper men who shall in some mysterious way hear of it on our landing. But they will think it a fine story, and so will all your friends when they read of it at breakfast on – let me see, this is Tuesday – yes, when they read of it at breakfast next Friday morning. Nor will it detract from the interest they will all feel when they learn that the man whom madame entertained is a Russian servant – her brother's valet, to be quite exact."

"Alexis Paulvitch," came the woman's voice, cold and fearless, "you are a coward, and when I whisper a certain name in your ear you will think better of your demands upon me and your threats against me, and then you will leave my cabin quickly, nor do I think that ever again will you, at least, annoy me," and there came a moment's silence in which Tarzan could imagine the woman leaning toward the scoundrel and whispering the thing she had hinted at into his ear. Only a moment of silence, and then a startled oath from the man – the scuffling of feet – a woman's scream – and silence.

But scarcely had the cry ceased before the ape-man had leaped from his hiding-place. Rokoff started to run, but Tarzan grasped him by the collar and dragged him back. Neither spoke, for both felt instinctively that murder was being done in that room, and Tarzan was confident that Rokoff had had no intention that his confederate should go that far – he felt that the man's aims were deeper than that – deeper and even more sinister than brutal, cold-blooded murder. Without hesitating to question those within, the ape-man threw his giant shoulder against the frail panel, and in a shower of splintered wood he entered the cabin, dragging Rokoff after him. Before him, on a couch, the woman lay, and on top of her was Paulvitch, his fingers gripping the fair throat, while his victim's hands beat futilely at his face, tearing desperately at the cruel fingers that were forcing the life from her.

The noise of his entrance brought Paulvitch to his feet, where he stood glowering menacingly at Tarzan. The girl rose falteringly to a sitting posture upon the couch. One hand was at her throat, and her breath came in little gasps. Although disheveled and very pale, Tarzan recognized her as the young woman whom he had caught staring at him on deck earlier in the day.

"What is the meaning of this?" said Tarzan, turning to Rokoff, whom he intuitively singled out as the instigator of the outrage. The man remained silent, scowling. "Touch the button, please," continued the ape-man; "we will have one of the ship's officers here – this affair has gone quite far enough."

"No, no," cried the girl, coming suddenly to her feet. "Please do not do that. I am sure that there was no real intention to harm me. I angered this person, and he lost control of himself, that is all. I would not care to have the matter go further, please, monsieur," and there was such a note of pleading in her voice that Tarzan could not press the matter, though his better judgment warned him that there was something afoot here of which the proper authorities should be made cognizant.

"You wish me to do nothing, then, in the matter?" he asked.

"Nothing, please," she replied.

"You are content that these two scoundrels should continue persecuting you?"

She did not seem to know what answer to make, and looked very troubled and unhappy. Tarzan saw a malicious grin of triumph curl

Rokoff's lip. The girl evidently was in fear of these two – she dared not express her real desires before them.

"Then," said Tarzan, "I shall act on my own responsibility. To you," he continued, turning to Rokoff, "and this includes your accomplice, I may say that from now on to the end of the voyage I shall take it upon myself to keep an eye on you, and should there chance to come to my notice any act of either one of you that might even remotely annoy this young woman you shall be called to account for it directly to me, nor shall the calling or the accounting be pleasant experiences for either of you.

"Now get out of here," and he grabbed Rokoff and Paulvitch each by the scruff of the neck and thrust them forcibly through the doorway, giving each an added impetus down the corridor with the toe of his boot. Then he turned back to the stateroom and the girl. She was looking at him in wide-eyed astonishment.

"And you, madame, will confer a great favor upon me if you will but let me know if either of those rascals troubles you further."

"Ah, monsieur," she answered, "I hope that you will not suffer for the kind deed you attempted. You have made a very wicked and resourceful enemy, who will stop at nothing to satisfy his hatred. You must be very careful indeed, Monsieur – "

"Pardon me, madame, my name is Tarzan."

"Monsieur Tarzan. And because I would not consent to notify the officers, do not think that I am not sincerely grateful to you for the brave and chivalrous protection you rendered me. Good night, Monsieur Tarzan. I shall never forget the debt I owe you," and, with a most winsome smile that displayed a row of perfect teeth, the girl curtsied to Tarzan, who bade her good night and made his way on deck.

It puzzled the man considerably that there should be two on board – this girl and Count de Coude – who suffered indignities at the hands of Rokoff and his companion, and yet would not permit the offenders to be brought to justice. Before he turned in that night his thoughts reverted many times to the beautiful young woman into the evidently tangled web of whose life fate had so strangely introduced him. It occurred to him that he had not learned her name. That she was married had been evidenced by the narrow gold band that encircled the third finger of her left hand. Involuntarily he wondered who the lucky man might be.

Tarzan saw nothing further of any of the actors in the little drama that he had caught a fleeting glimpse of until late in the afternoon of the last day of the voyage. Then he came suddenly face to face with the young woman as the two approached their deck chairs from opposite directions. She greeted him with a pleasant smile, speaking almost immediately of the affair he had witnessed in her cabin two nights before. It was as though she had been perturbed by a conviction that he might have construed her acquaintance with such men as Rokoff and Paulvitch as a personal reflection upon herself.

"I trust monsieur has not judged me," she said, "by the unfortunate occurrence of Tuesday evening. I have suffered much on account of it – this is the first time that I have ventured from my cabin since; I have been ashamed," she concluded simply.

"One does not judge the gazelle by the lions that attack it," replied Tarzan. "I had seen those two work before – in the smoking-room the day prior to their attack on you, if I recollect it correctly, and so, knowing their methods, I am convinced that their enmity is a sufficient guarantee of the integrity of its object. Men such as they must cleave only to the vile, hating all that is noblest and best."

"It is very kind of you to put it that way," she replied, smiling. "I have already heard of the matter of the card game. My husband told me the entire story. He spoke especially of the strength and bravery of Monsieur Tarzan, to whom he feels that he owes an immense debt of gratitude."

"Your husband?" repeated Tarzan questioningly.

"Yes. I am the Countess de Coude."

"I am already amply repaid, madame, in knowing that I have rendered a service to the wife of the Count de Coude."

"Alas, monsieur, I already am so greatly indebted to you that I may never hope to settle my own account, so pray do not add further to my obligations," and she smiled so sweetly upon him that Tarzan felt that a man might easily attempt much greater things than he had accomplished, solely for the pleasure of receiving the benediction of that smile.

He did not see her again that day, and in the rush of landing on the following morning he missed her entirely, but there had been something in the expression of her eyes as they parted on deck the previous day that haunted him. It had been almost wistful as they had spoken of the strangeness of the swift friendships of an ocean crossing, and of the equal ease with which they are broken forever.

Tarzan wondered if he should ever see her again.

CHAPTER THREE

What Happened in the Rue Maule

On his arrival in Paris, Tarzan had gone directly to the apartments of his old friend, D'Arnot, where the naval lieutenant had scored him roundly for his decision to renounce the title and estates that were rightly his from his father, John Clayton, the late Lord Greystoke.

"You must be mad, my friend," said D'Arnot, "thus lightly to give up not alone wealth and position, but an opportunity to prove beyond doubt to all the world that in your veins flows the noble blood of two of England's most honored houses – instead of the blood of a savage she-ape. It is incredible that they could have believed you – Miss Porter least of all.

"Why, I never did believe it, even back in the wilds of your African jungle, when you tore the raw meat of your kills with mighty jaws, like some wild beast, and wiped your greasy hands upon your thighs. Even then, before there was the slightest proof to the contrary, I knew that you were mistaken in the belief that Kala was your mother.

"And now, with your father's diary of the terrible life led by him and your mother on that wild African shore; with the account of your birth, and, final and most convincing proof of all, your own baby finger prints upon the pages of it, it seems incredible to me that you are willing to remain a nameless, penniless vagabond."

"I do not need any better name than Tarzan," replied the ape-man; "and as for remaining a penniless vagabond, I have no intention of so doing. In fact, the next, and let us hope the last, burden that I shall be forced to put upon your unselfish friendship will be the finding of employment for me."

"Pooh, pooh!" scoffed D'Arnot. "You know that I did not mean that. Have I not told you a dozen times that I have enough for twenty men, and that half of what I have is yours? And if I gave it all to you, would it represent even the tenth part of the value I place upon your friendship, my Tarzan? Would it repay the services you did me in Africa? I do not forget, my friend, that but for you and your wondrous bravery I had died at the stake in the village of Mbonga's cannibals. Nor do I forget that to your self-sacrificing devotion I owe the fact that I recovered from the terrible wounds I received at their hands – I discovered later something of what it meant to you to remain with me in the amphitheater of apes while your heart was urging you on to the coast.

"When we finally came there, and found that Miss Porter and her party had left, I commenced to realize something of what you had done for an utter stranger. Nor am I trying to repay you with money, Tarzan. It is that just at present you need money; were it sacrifice that I might offer you it were the same – my friendship must always be yours, because our tastes are similar, and I admire you. That I cannot command, but the money I can and shall."

"Well," laughed Tarzan, "we shall not quarrel over the money. I must live, and so I must have it; but I shall be more contented with something to do. You cannot show me your friendship in a more convincing manner than to find employment for me – I shall die of inactivity in a short while. As for my birthright – it is in good hands. Clayton is not guilty of robbing me of it. He truly believes that he is the real Lord Greystoke, and the chances are that he will make a better English lord than a man who was born and raised in an African jungle. You know that I am but half civilized even now. Let me see red in anger but for a moment, and all the instincts of the savage beast that I really am, submerge what little I possess of the milder ways of culture and refinement.

"And then again, had I declared myself I should have robbed the woman I love of the wealth and position that her marriage to Clayton will now insure to her. I could not have done that – could I, Paul?

"Nor is the matter of birth of great importance to me," he went on, without waiting for a reply. "Raised as I have been, I see no worth in man or beast that is not theirs by virtue of their own mental or physical prowess. And so I am as happy to think of Kala as my mother as I would be to try to picture the poor, unhappy little English girl who passed away a year after she bore me. Kala was always kind to me in her fierce and savage way. I must have nursed at her hairy breast from the time that my own mother died. She fought for me against the wild denizens of the forest, and against the savage members of our tribe, with the ferocity of real mother love.

"And I, on my part, loved her, Paul. I did not realize how much until after the cruel spear and the poisoned arrow of Mbonga's black warrior had stolen her away from me. I was still a child when that occurred, and I threw myself upon her dead body and wept out my anguish as a child might for his own mother. To you, my friend, she would have appeared a hideous and ugly creature, but to me she was beautiful – so gloriously does love transfigure its object. And so I am perfectly content to remain forever the son of Kala, the she-ape."

"I do not admire you the less for your loyalty," said D'Arnot, "but the time will come when you will be glad to claim your own. Remember what I say, and let us hope that it will be as easy then as it is now. You must bear in mind that Professor Porter and Mr. Philander are the only people in the world who can swear that the little skeleton found in the cabin with those of your father and mother was that of an infant anthropoid ape, and not the offspring of Lord and Lady Greystoke. That evidence is most important. They are both old men. They may not live many years longer. And then, did it not occur to you that once Miss Porter knew the truth she would break her engagement with Clayton? You might easily have your title, your estates, and the woman you love, Tarzan. Had you not thought of that?"

Tarzan shook his head. "You do not know her," he said. "Nothing could bind her closer to her bargain than some misfortune to Clayton. She is from an old southern family in America, and southerners pride themselves upon their loyalty."

Tarzan spent the two following weeks renewing his former brief acquaintance with Paris. In the daytime he haunted the libraries and picture galleries. He had become an omnivorous reader, and the world of possibilities that were opened to him in this seat of culture and learning fairly appalled him when he contemplated the very infinitesimal crumb of the sum total of human knowledge that a single individual might hope to acquire even after a lifetime of study and research; but he learned what he could by day, and threw himself into a search for relaxation and amusement at night. Nor did he find Paris a whit less fertile field for his nocturnal avocation.

If he smoked too many cigarettes and drank too much absinth it was because he took civilization as he found it, and did the things that he found his civilized brothers doing. The life was a new and alluring one, and in addition he had a sorrow in his breast and a great longing which he knew could never be fulfilled, and so he sought in study and in dissipation – the two extremes – to forget the past and inhibit contemplation of the future.

He was sitting in a music hall one evening, sipping his absinth and admiring the art of a certain famous Russian dancer, when he caught a passing glimpse of a pair of evil black eyes upon him. The man turned and was lost in the crowd at the exit before Tarzan could catch a good look at him, but he was confident that he had seen those eyes before and that they had been fastened on him this evening through no passing accident. He had had the uncanny feeling for some time that he was being watched, and it was in response to this animal instinct that was strong within him that he had turned suddenly and surprised the eyes in the very act of watching him.

Before he left the music hall the matter had been forgotten, nor did he notice the swarthy individual who stepped deeper into the shadows of an opposite doorway as Tarzan emerged from the brilliantly lighted amusement hall.

Had Tarzan but known it, he had been followed many times from this and other places of amusement, but seldom if ever had he been alone. Tonight D'Arnot had had another engagement, and Tarzan had come by himself.

As he turned in the direction he was accustomed to taking from this part of Paris to his apartments, the watcher across the street ran from his hiding-place and hurried on ahead at a rapid pace.

Tarzan had been wont to traverse the Rue Maule on his way home at night. Because it was very quiet and very dark it reminded him more of his beloved African jungle than did the noisy and garish streets surrounding it. If you are familiar with your Paris you will recall the narrow, forbidding precincts of the Rue Maule. If you are not, you need but ask the police about it to learn that in all Paris there is no street to which you should give a wider berth after dark.

On this night Tarzan had proceeded some two squares through the dense shadows of the squalid old tenements which line this dismal way when he was attracted by screams and cries for help from the third floor of an opposite building. The voice was a woman's. Before the echoes of her first cries had died Tarzan was bounding up the stairs and through the dark corridors to her rescue.

At the end of the corridor on the third landing a door stood slightly ajar, and from within Tarzan heard again the same appeal that had lured him from the street. Another instant found him in the center of a dimly-lighted room. An oil lamp burned upon a high, old-fashioned mantel, casting its dim rays over a dozen repulsive figures. All but one were men. The other was a woman of about thirty. Her face, marked by low passions and dissipation, might once have been lovely. She stood with one hand at her throat, crouching against the farther wall.

"Help, monsieur," she cried in a low voice as Tarzan entered the room; "they were killing me."

As Tarzan turned toward the men about him he saw the crafty, evil faces of habitual criminals. He wondered that they had made no effort to escape. A movement behind him caused him to turn. Two things his eyes saw, and one of them caused him considerable wonderment. A man was sneaking stealthily from the room, and in the brief glance that Tarzan had of him he saw that it was Rokoff. But the other thing that he saw was of more immediate interest. It was a great brute of a fellow tiptoeing upon him from behind with a huge bludgeon in his hand, and then, as the man and his confederates saw that he was discovered, there was a concerted rush upon Tarzan from all sides. Some of the men drew knives. Others picked up chairs, while the fellow with the bludgeon raised it high above his head in a mighty swing that would have crushed Tarzan's head had it ever descended upon it.

But the brain, and the agility, and the muscles that had coped with the mighty strength and cruel craftiness of Terkoz and Numa in the fastness of their savage jungle were not to be so easily subdued as these apaches of Paris had believed.

Selecting his most formidable antagonist, the fellow with the bludgeon, Tarzan charged full upon him, dodging the falling weapon, and catching the man a terrific blow on the point of the chin that felled him in his tracks.

Then he turned upon the others. This was sport. He was reveling in the joy of battle and the lust of blood. As though it had been but a brittle shell, to break at the least rough usage, the thin veneer of his civilization fell from him, and the ten burly villains found themselves penned in a small room with a wild and savage beast, against whose steel muscles their puny strength was less than futile.

At the end of the corridor without stood Rokoff, waiting the outcome of the affair. He wished to be sure that Tarzan was dead before he left, but it was not a part of his plan to be one of those within the room when the murder occurred.

The woman still stood where she had when Tarzan entered, but her face had undergone a number of changes with the few minutes which had elapsed. From the semblance of distress which it had worn when Tarzan first saw it, it had changed to one of craftiness as he had wheeled to meet the attack from behind; but the change Tarzan had not seen.

Later an expression of surprise and then one of horror superseded the others. And who may wonder. For the immaculate gentleman her cries had lured to what was to have been his death had been suddenly metamorphosed into a demon of revenge. Instead of soft muscles and a weak resistance, she was looking upon a veritable Hercules gone mad.

"MON DIEU!" she cried; "he is a beast!" For the strong, white teeth of the ape-man had found the throat of one of his assailants, and Tarzan fought as he had learned to fight with the great bull apes of the tribe of Kerchak.

He was in a dozen places at once, leaping hither and thither about the room in sinuous bounds that reminded the woman of a panther she had seen at the zoo. Now a wrist-bone snapped in his iron grip, now a shoulder was wrenched from its socket as he forced a victim's arm backward and upward.

With shrieks of pain the men escaped into the hallway as quickly as they could; but even before the first one staggered, bleeding and broken, from the room, Rokoff had seen enough to convince him that Tarzan would not be the one to lie dead in that house this night, and so the Russian had hastened to a nearby den and telephoned the police that a man was committing murder on the third floor of Rue Maule, 27. When the officers arrived they found three men groaning on the floor, a frightened woman lying upon a filthy bed, her face buried in her arms, and what appeared to be a well-dressed young gentleman standing in the center of the room awaiting the reenforcements which he had thought the footsteps of the officers hurrying up the stairway had announced – but they were mistaken in the last; it was a wild beast that looked upon them through those narrowed lids and steel-gray eyes. With the smell of blood the last vestige of civilization had deserted Tarzan, and now he stood at bay, like a lion surrounded by hunters, awaiting the next overt act, and crouching to charge its author.

"What has happened here?" asked one of the policemen.

Tarzan explained briefly, but when he turned to the woman for confirmation of his statement he was appalled by her reply.

"He lies!" she screamed shrilly, addressing the policeman. "He came to my room while I was alone, and for no good purpose. When I repulsed him he would have killed me had not my screams attracted these gentlemen, who were passing the house at the time. He is a devil, monsieurs; alone he has all but killed ten men with his bare hands and his teeth."

So shocked was Tarzan by her ingratitude that for a moment he was struck dumb. The police were inclined to be a little skeptical, for they had

had other dealings with this same lady and her lovely coterie of gentlemen friends. However, they were policemen, not judges, so they decided to place all the inmates of the room under arrest, and let another, whose business it was, separate the innocent from the guilty.

But they found that it was one thing to tell this well-dressed young man that he was under arrest, but quite another to enforce it.

"I am guilty of no offense," he said quietly. "I have but sought to defend myself. I do not know why the woman has told you what she has. She can have no enmity against me, for never until I came to this room in response to her cries for help had I seen her."

"Come, come," said one of the officers; "there are judges to listen to all that," and he advanced to lay his hand upon Tarzan's shoulder. An instant later he lay crumpled in a corner of the room, and then, as his comrades rushed in upon the ape-man, they experienced a taste of what the apaches had but recently gone through. So quickly and so roughly did he handle them that they had not even an opportunity to draw their revolvers.

During the brief fight Tarzan had noted the open window and, beyond, the stem of a tree, or a telegraph pole – he could not tell which. As the last officer went down, one of his fellows succeeded in drawing his revolver and, from where he lay on the floor, fired at Tarzan. The shot missed, and before the man could fire again Tarzan had swept the lamp from the mantel and plunged the room into darkness.

The next they saw was a lithe form spring to the sill of the open window and leap, panther-like, onto the pole across the walk. When the police gathered themselves together and reached the street their prisoner was nowhere to be seen.

They did not handle the woman and the men who had not escaped any too gently when they took them to the station; they were a very sore and humiliated detail of police. It galled them to think that it would be necessary to report that a single unarmed man had wiped the floor with the whole lot of them, and then escaped them as easily as though they had not existed.

The officer who had remained in the street swore that no one had leaped from the window or left the building from the time they entered until they had come out. His comrades thought that he lied, but they could not prove it.

When Tarzan found himself clinging to the pole outside the window, he followed his jungle instinct and looked below for enemies before he ventured down. It was well he did, for just beneath stood a policeman. Above, Tarzan saw no one, so he went up instead of down.

The top of the pole was opposite the roof of the building, so it was but the work of an instant for the muscles that had for years sent him hurtling through the treetops of his primeval forest to carry him across the little space between the pole and the roof. From one building he went to another, and so on, with much climbing, until at a cross street he discovered another pole, down which he ran to the ground.

For a square or two he ran swiftly; then he turned into a little all-night cafe and in the lavatory removed the evidences of his over-roof promenade from hands and clothes. When he emerged a few moments later it was to saunter slowly on toward his apartments.

Not far from them he came to a well-lighted boulevard which it was necessary to cross. As he stood directly beneath a brilliant arc light, waiting for a limousine that was approaching to pass him, he heard his name called in a sweet feminine voice. Looking up, he met the smiling eyes of Olga de Coude as she leaned forward upon the back seat of the machine. He bowed very low in response to her friendly greeting. When he straightened up the machine had borne her away.

"Rokoff and the Countess de Coude both in the same evening," he soliloquized; "Paris is not so large, after all."

CHAPTER FOUR

The Countess Explains

"YOUR PARIS IS MORE dangerous than my savage jungles, Paul," concluded Tarzan, after narrating his adventures to his friend the morning following his encounter with the apaches and police in the Rue Maule. "Why did they lure me there? Were they hungry?"

D'Arnot feigned a horrified shudder, but he laughed at the quaint suggestion.

"It is difficult to rise above the jungle standards and reason by the light of civilized ways, is it not, my friend?" he queried banteringly.

"Civilized ways, forsooth," scoffed Tarzan. "Jungle standards do not countenance wanton atrocities. There we kill for food and for self-preservation, or in the winning of mates and the protection of the young. Always, you see, in accordance with the dictates of some great natural law. But here! Faugh, your civilized man is more brutal than the brutes. He kills wantonly, and, worse than that, he utilizes a noble sentiment, the brotherhood of man, as a lure to entice his unwary victim to his doom. It was in answer to an appeal from a fellow being that I hastened to that room where the assassins lay in wait for me.

"I did not realize, I could not realize for a long time afterward, that any woman could sink to such moral depravity as that one must have to call a would-be rescuer to death. But it must have been so – the sight of Rokoff there and the woman's later repudiation of me to the police make it impossible to place any other construction upon her acts. Rokoff must have known that I frequently passed through the Rue Maule. He lay in wait for me – his entire scheme worked out to the last detail, even to the woman's story in case a hitch should occur in the program such as really did happen. It is all perfectly plain to me."

"Well," said D'Arnot, "among other things, it has taught you what I have been unable to impress upon you – that the Rue Maule is a good place to avoid after dark."

"On the contrary," replied Tarzan, with a smile, "it has convinced me that it is the one worth-while street in all Paris. Never again shall I miss an opportunity to traverse it, for it has given me the first real entertainment I have had since I left Africa."

"It may give you more than you will relish even without another visit," said D'Arnot. "You are not through with the police yet, remember. I know the Paris police well enough to assure you that they will not soon forget what you did to them. Sooner or later they will get you, my dear Tarzan, and then they will lock the wild man of the woods up behind iron bars. How will you like that?"

"They will never lock Tarzan of the Apes behind iron bars," replied he, grimly.

There was something in the man's voice as he said it that caused D'Arnot to look up sharply at his friend. What he saw in the set jaw and the cold, gray eyes made the young Frenchman very apprehensive for this great child, who could recognize no law mightier than his own mighty physical prowess. He saw that something must be done to set Tarzan right with the police before another encounter was possible.

"You have much to learn, Tarzan," he said gravely. "The law of man must be respected, whether you relish it or no. Nothing but trouble can come to you and your friends should you persist in defying the police. I can explain it to them once for you, and that I shall do this very day, but hereafter you must obey the law. If its representatives say 'Come,' you must come; if they say 'Go,' you must go. Now we shall go to my great friend in the department and fix up this matter of the Rue Maule. Come!"

Together they entered the office of the police official a half hour later. He was very cordial. He remembered Tarzan from the visit the two had made him several months prior in the matter of finger prints.

When D'Arnot had concluded the narration of the events which had transpired the previous evening, a grim smile was playing about the lips of the policeman. He touched a button near his hand, and as he waited for the clerk to respond to its summons he searched through the papers on his desk for one which he finally located.

"Here, Joubon," he said as the clerk entered. "Summon these officers – have them come to me at once," and he handed the man the paper he had sought. Then he turned to Tarzan.

"You have committed a very grave offense, monsieur," he said, not unkindly, "and but for the explanation made by our good friend here I should be inclined to judge you harshly. I am, instead, about to do a rather unheard-of-thing. I have summoned the officers whom you maltreated last night. They shall hear Lieutenant D'Arnot's story, and then I shall leave it to their discretion to say whether you shall be prosecuted or not.

"You have much to learn about the ways of civilization. Things that seem strange or unnecessary to you, you must learn to accept until you are able to judge the motives behind them. The officers whom you attacked were but doing their duty. They had no discretion in the matter. Every day they risk their lives in the protection of the lives or property of others. They would do the same for you. They are very brave men, and they are deeply mortified that a single unarmed man bested and beat them.

"Make it easy for them to overlook what you did. Unless I am gravely in error you are yourself a very brave man, and brave men are proverbially magnanimous."

Further conversation was interrupted by the appearance of the four policemen. As their eyes fell on Tarzan, surprise was writ large on each countenance.

"My children," said the official, "here is the gentleman whom you met in the Rue Maule last evening. He has come voluntarily to give himself up. I wish you to listen attentively to Lieutenant D'Arnot, who will tell you a part of the story of monsieur's life. It may explain his attitude toward you of last night. Proceed, my dear lieutenant."

D'Arnot spoke to the policemen for half an hour. He told them something of Tarzan's wild jungle life. He explained the savage training that had taught him to battle like a wild beast in self-preservation. It became plain to them that the man had been guided by instinct rather than reason in his attack upon them. He had not understood their intentions. To him they had been little different from any of the various forms of life he had been accustomed to in his native jungle, where practically all were his enemies.

"Your pride has been wounded," said D'Arnot, in conclusion. "It is the fact that this man overcame you that hurts the most. But you need feel no shame. You would not make apologies for defeat had you been penned in that small room with an African lion, or with the great Gorilla of the jungles.

"And yet you were battling with muscles that have time and time again been pitted, and always victoriously, against these terrors of the dark continent. It is no disgrace to fall beneath the superhuman strength of Tarzan of the Apes."

And then, as the men stood looking first at Tarzan and then at their superior the ape-man did the one thing which was needed to erase the last remnant of animosity which they might have felt for him. With outstretched hand he advanced toward them.

"I am sorry for the mistake I made," he said simply. "Let us be friends." And that was the end of the whole matter, except that Tarzan became a subject of much conversation in the barracks of the police, and increased the number of his friends by four brave men at least.

On their return to D'Arnot's apartments the lieutenant found a letter awaiting him from an English friend, William Cecil Clayton, Lord Greystoke. The two had maintained a correspondence since the birth of their friendship on that ill-fated expedition in search of Jane Porter after her theft by Terkoz, the bull ape.

"They are to be married in London in about two months," said D'Arnot, as he completed his perusal of the letter. Tarzan did not need to be told who was meant by "they." He made no reply, but he was very quiet and thoughtful during the balance of the day.

That evening they attended the opera. Tarzan's mind was still occupied by his gloomy thoughts. He paid little or no attention to what was transpiring upon the stage. Instead he saw only the lovely vision of a beautiful American girl, and heard naught but a sad, sweet voice acknowledging that his love was returned. And she was to marry another!

He shook himself to be rid of his unwelcome thoughts, and at the same instant he felt eyes upon him. With the instinct that was his by virtue of training he looked up squarely into the eyes that were looking at him, to find that they were shining from the smiling face of Olga, Countess de Coude. As Tarzan returned her bow he was positive that there was an invitation in her look, almost a plea. The next intermission found him beside her in her box.

"I have so much wished to see you," she was saying. "It has troubled me not a little to think that after the service you rendered to both my husband and myself no adequate explanation was ever made you of what must have seemed ingratitude on our part in not taking the necessary steps to prevent a repetition of the attacks upon us by those two men."

"You wrong me," replied Tarzan. "My thoughts of you have been only the most pleasant. You must not feel that any explanation is due me. Have they annoyed you further?"

"They never cease," she replied sadly. "I feel that I must tell some one, and I do not know another who so deserves an explanation as you. You must permit me to do so. It may be of service to you, for I know Nikolas Rokoff quite well enough to be positive that you have not seen the last of him. He will find some means to be revenged upon you. What I wish to tell you may be of aid to you in combating any scheme of revenge he may harbor. I cannot tell you here, but tomorrow I shall be at home to Monsieur Tarzan at five."

"It will be an eternity until tomorrow at five," he said, as he bade her good night. From a corner of the theater Rokoff and Paulvitch saw Monsieur Tarzan in the box of the Countess de Coude, and both men smiled.

At four-thirty the following afternoon a swarthy, bearded man rang the bell at the servants' entrance of the palace of the Count de Coude. The footman who opened the door raised his eyebrows in recognition as he saw who stood without. A low conversation passed between the two.

At first the footman demurred from some proposition that the bearded one made, but an instant later something passed from the hand of the caller to the hand of the servant. Then the latter turned and led the visitor by a roundabout way to a little curtained alcove off the apartment in which the countess was wont to serve tea of an afternoon.

A half hour later Tarzan was ushered into the room, and presently his hostess entered, smiling, and with outstretched hands.

"I am so glad that you came," she said.

"Nothing could have prevented," he replied.

For a few moments they spoke of the opera, of the topics that were then occupying the attention of Paris, of the pleasure of renewing their brief acquaintance which had had its inception under such odd circumstances, and this brought them to the subject that was uppermost in the minds of both.

"You must have wondered," said the countess finally, "what the object of Rokoff's persecution could be. It is very simple. The count is intrusted with many of the vital secrets of the ministry of war. He often has in his possession papers that foreign powers would give a fortune to possess – secrets of state that their agents would commit murder and worse than murder to learn.

"There is such a matter now in his possession that would make the fame and fortune of any Russian who could divulge it to his government. Rokoff and Paulvitch are Russian spies. They will stop at nothing to procure this information. The affair on the liner – I mean the matter of the card game – was for the purpose of blackmailing the knowledge they seek from my husband.

"Had he been convicted of cheating at cards, his career would have been blighted. He would have had to leave the war department. He would have been socially ostracized. They intended to hold this club over him – the price of an avowal on their part that the count was but the victim of the plot of enemies who wished to besmirch his name was to have been the papers they seek.

"You thwarted them in this. Then they concocted the scheme whereby my reputation was to be the price, instead of the count's. When Paulvitch entered my cabin he explained it to me. If I would obtain the information for them he promised to go no farther, otherwise Rokoff, who stood without, was to notify the purser that I was entertaining a man other than my husband behind the locked doors of my cabin. He was to tell every one he met on the boat, and when we landed he was to have given the whole story to the newspaper men.

"Was it not too horrible? But I happened to know something of Monsieur Paulvitch that would send him to the gallows in Russia if it were known by the police of St. Petersburg. I dared him to carry out his plan, and then I leaned toward him and whispered a name in his ear. Like that" – and she snapped her fingers – "he flew at my throat as a madman. He would have killed me had you not interfered."

"The brutes!" muttered Tarzan.

"They are worse than that, my friend," she said.

"They are devils. I fear for you because you have gained their hatred. I wish you to be on your guard constantly. Tell me that you will, for my sake, for I should never forgive myself should you suffer through the kindness you did me."

"I do not fear them," he replied. "I have survived grimmer enemies than Rokoff and Paulvitch." He saw that she knew nothing of the occurrence in the Rue Maule, nor did he mention it, fearing that it might distress her.

"For your own safety," he continued, "why do you not turn the scoundrels over to the authorities? They should make quick work of them."

She hesitated for a moment before replying.

"There are two reasons," she said finally. "One of them it is that keeps the count from doing that very thing. The other, my real reason for fearing to expose them, I have never told – only Rokoff and I know it. I wonder," and then she paused, looking intently at him for a long time.

"And what do you wonder?" he asked, smiling.

"I was wondering why it is that I want to tell you the thing that I have not dared tell even to my husband. I believe that you would understand, and that you could tell me the right course to follow. I believe that you would not judge me too harshly."

"I fear that I should prove a very poor judge, madame," Tarzan replied, "for if you had been guilty of murder I should say that the victim should be grateful to have met so sweet a fate."

"Oh, dear, no," she expostulated; "it is not so terrible as that. But first let me tell you the reason the count has for not prosecuting these men; then, if I can hold my courage, I shall tell you the real reason that I dare not. The first is that Nikolas Rokoff is my brother. We are Russians. Nikolas has been a bad man since I can remember. He was cashiered from the Russian army, in which he held a captaincy. There was a scandal for a time, but after a while it was partially forgotten, and my father obtained a position for him in the secret service.

"There have been many terrible crimes laid at Nikolas' door, but he has always managed to escape punishment. Of late he has accomplished it by trumped-up evidence convicting his victims of treason against the czar, and the Russian police, who are always only too ready to fasten guilt of this nature upon any and all, have accepted his version and exonerated him."

"Have not his attempted crimes against you and your husband forfeited whatever rights the bonds of kinship might have accorded him?" asked Tarzan. "The fact that you are his sister has not deterred him from seeking to besmirch your honor. You owe him no loyalty, madame."

"Ah, but there is that other reason. If I owe him no loyalty though he be my brother, I cannot so easily disavow the fear I hold him in because of a certain episode in my life of which he is cognizant.

"I might as well tell you all," she resumed after a pause, "for I see that it is in my heart to tell you sooner or later. I was educated in a convent. While there I met a man whom I supposed to be a gentleman. I knew little or nothing about men and less about love. I got it into my foolish head that I loved this man, and at his urgent request I ran away with him. We were to have been married.

"I was with him just three hours. All in the daytime and in public places – railroad stations and upon a train. When we reached our destination where we were to have been married, two officers stepped up to my escort as we descended from the train, and placed him under arrest. They took me also, but when I had told my story they did not detain me, other than to send me back to the convent under the care of a matron.

It seemed that the man who had wooed me was no gentleman at all, but a deserter from the army as well as a fugitive from civil justice. He had a police record in nearly every country in Europe.

"The matter was hushed up by the authorities of the convent. Not even my parents knew of it. But Nikolas met the man afterward, and learned the whole story. Now he threatens to tell the count if I do not do just as he wishes me to."

Tarzan laughed. "You are still but a little girl. The story that you have told me cannot reflect in any way upon your reputation, and were you not a little girl at heart you would know it. Go to your husband tonight, and tell him the whole story, just as you have told it to me. Unless I am much mistaken he will laugh at you for your fears, and take immediate steps to put that precious brother of yours in prison where he belongs."

"I only wish that I dared," she said; "but I am afraid. I learned early to fear men. First my father, then Nikolas, then the fathers in the convent. Nearly all my friends fear their husbands – why should I not fear mine?"

"It does not seem right that women should fear men," said Tarzan, an expression of puzzlement on his face. "I am better acquainted with the jungle folk, and there it is more often the other way around, except among the black men, and they to my mind are in most ways lower in the scale than the beasts. No, I cannot understand why civilized women should fear men, the beings that are created to protect them. I should hate to think that any woman feared me."

"I do not think that any woman would fear you, my friend," said Olga de Coude softly. "I have known you but a short while, yet though it may seem foolish to say it, you are the only man I have ever known whom I think that I should never fear – it is strange, too, for you are very strong. I wondered at the ease with which you handled Nikolas and Paulvitch that night in my cabin. It was marvellous." As Tarzan was leaving her a short time later he wondered a little at the clinging pressure of her hand at parting, and the firm insistence with which she exacted a promise from him that he would call again on the morrow.

The memory of her half-veiled eyes and perfect lips as she had stood smiling up into his face as he bade her good-by remained with him for the balance of the day. Olga de Coude was a very beautiful woman, and Tarzan of the Apes a very lonely young man, with a heart in him that was in need of the doctoring that only a woman may provide.

As the countess turned back into the room after Tarzan's departure, she found herself face to face with Nikolas Rokoff.

"How long have you been here?" she cried, shrinking away from him.

"Since before your lover came," he answered, with a nasty leer.

"Stop!" she commanded. "How dare you say such a thing to me – your sister!"

"Well, my dear Olga, if he is not your lover, accept my apologies; but it is no fault of yours that he is not. Had he one-tenth the knowledge of women that I have you would be in his arms this minute. He is a stupid fool, Olga. Why, your every word and act was an open invitation to him, and he had not the sense to see it."

The woman put her hands to her ears.

"I will not listen. You are wicked to say such things as that. No matter what you may threaten me with, you know that I am a good woman. After tonight you will not dare to annoy me, for I shall tell Raoul all. He will understand, and then, Monsieur Nikolas, beware!"

"You shall tell him nothing," said Rokoff. "I have this affair now, and with the help of one of your servants whom I may trust it will lack nothing in the telling when the time comes that the details of the sworn evidence shall be poured into your husband's ears. The other affair served its purpose well – we now have something tangible to work on, Olga. A real AFFAIR – and you a trusted wife. Shame, Olga," and the brute laughed.

So the countess told her count nothing, and matters were worse than they had been. From a vague fear her mind was transferred to a very tangible one. It may be, too, that conscience helped to enlarge it out of all proportion.

CHAPTER FIVE

The Plot That Failed

For a month Tarzan was a regular and very welcome devotee at the shrine of the beautiful Countess de Coude. Often he met other members of the select little coterie that dropped in for tea of an afternoon. More often Olga found devices that would give her an hour of Tarzan alone.

For a time she had been frightened by what Nikolas had insinuated. She had not thought of this big, young man as anything more than friend, but with the suggestion implanted by the evil words of her brother she had grown to speculate much upon the strange force which seemed to attract her toward the gray-eyed stranger. She did not wish to love him, nor did she wish his love.

She was much younger than her husband, and without having realized it she had been craving the haven of a friendship with one nearer her own age. Twenty is shy in exchanging confidences with forty. Tarzan was but two years her senior. He could understand her, she felt. Then he was clean and honorable and chivalrous. She was not afraid of him. That she could trust him she had felt instinctively from the first.

From a distance Rokoff had watched this growing intimacy with malicious glee. Ever since he had learned that Tarzan knew that he was a Russian spy there had been added to his hatred for the ape-man a great fear that he would expose him. He was but waiting now until the moment was propitious for a master stroke. He wanted to rid himself forever of Tarzan, and at the same time reap an ample revenge for the humiliations and defeats that he had suffered at his hands.

Tarzan was nearer to contentment than he had been since the peace and tranquility of his jungle had been broken in upon by the advent of the marooned Porter party. He enjoyed the pleasant social intercourse with Olga's friends, while the friendship which had sprung up between the fair countess and himself was a source of never-ending delight. It broke in upon and dispersed his gloomy thoughts, and served as a balm to his lacerated heart.

Sometimes D'Arnot accompanied him on his visits to the De Coude home, for he had long known both Olga and the count. Occasionally De Coude dropped in, but the multitudinous affairs of his official position and the never-ending demands of politics kept him from home usually until late at night.

Rokoff spied upon Tarzan almost constantly, waiting for the time that he should call at the De Coude palace at night, but in this he was doomed to disappointment. On several occasions Tarzan accompanied the countess to her home after the opera, but he invariably left her at the entrance – much to the disgust of the lady's devoted brother.

Finding that it seemed impossible to trap Tarzan through any voluntary act of his own, Rokoff and Paulvitch put their heads together to hatch a plan that would trap the ape-man in all the circumstantial evidence of a compromising position.

For days they watched the papers as well as the movements of De Coude and Tarzan. At length they were rewarded. A morning paper made brief mention of a smoker that was to be given on the following evening by the German minister. De Coude's name was among those of the invited guests. If he attended this meant that he would be absent from his home until after midnight.

On the night of the banquet Paulvitch waited at the curb before the residence of the German minister, where he could scan the face of each guest that arrived. He had not long to wait before De Coude descended from his car and passed him. That was enough. Paulvitch hastened back to his quarters, where Rokoff awaited him. There they waited until after eleven, then Paulvitch took down the receiver of their telephone. He called a number.

"The apartments of Lieutenant D'Arnot?" he asked, when he had obtained his connection.

"A message for Monsieur Tarzan, if he will be so kind as to step to the telephone."

For a minute there was silence.

"Monsieur Tarzan?"

"Ah, yes, monsieur, this is Francois – in the service of the Countess de Coude. Possibly monsieur does poor Francois the honor to recall him – yes?

"Yes, monsieur. I have a message, an urgent message from the countess. She asks that you hasten to her at once – she is in trouble, monsieur.

"No, monsieur, poor Francois does not know. Shall I tell madame that monsieur will be here shortly?

"Thank you, monsieur. The good God will bless you."

Paulvitch hung up the receiver and turned to grin at Rokoff.

"It will take him thirty minutes to get there. If you reach the German minister's in fifteen, De Coude should arrive at his home in about forty-five minutes. It all depends upon whether the fool will remain fifteen minutes after he finds that a trick has been played upon him; but unless I am mistaken Olga will be loath to let him go in so short a time as that. Here is the note for De Coude. Hasten!"

Paulvitch lost no time in reaching the German minister's. At the door he handed the note to a footman. "This is for the Count de Coude. It is very urgent. You must see that it is placed in his hands at once," and he dropped a piece of silver into the willing hand of the servant. Then he returned to his quarters.

A moment later De Coude was apologizing to his host as he tore open the envelope. What he read left his face white and his hand trembling.

MONSIEUR LE COUNT DE COUDE:

One who wishes to save the honor of your name takes this means to warn you that the sanctity of your home is this minute in jeopardy.

A certain man who for months has been a constant visitor there during your absence is now with your wife. If you go at once to your countess' boudoir you will find them together.

A FRIEND.

Twenty minutes after Paulvitch had called Tarzan, Rokoff obtained a connection with Olga's private line. Her maid answered the telephone which was in the countess' boudoir.

"But madame has retired," said the maid, in answer to Rokoff's request to speak with her.

"This is a very urgent message for the countess' ears alone," replied Rokoff. "Tell her that she must arise and slip something about her and come to the telephone. I shall call up again in five minutes." Then he hung up his receiver. A moment later Paulvitch entered.

"The count has the message?" asked Rokoff.

"He should be on his way to his home by now," replied Paulvitch.

"Good! My lady will be sitting in her boudoir, very much in negligee, about now. In a minute the faithful Jacques will escort Monsieur

Tarzan into her presence without announcing him. It will take a few minutes for explanations. Olga will look very alluring in the filmy creation that is her night-dress, and the clinging robe which but half conceals the charms that the former does not conceal at all. Olga will be surprised, but not displeased.

"If there is a drop of red blood in the man the count will break in upon a very pretty love scene in about fifteen minutes from now. I think we have planned marvelously, my dear Alexis. Let us go out and drink to the very good health of Monsieur Tarzan in some of old Plancon's unparalleled absinth; not forgetting that the Count de Coude is one of the best swordsmen in Paris, and by far the best shot in all France."

When Tarzan reached Olga's, Jacques was awaiting him at the entrance.

"This way, Monsieur," he said, and led the way up the broad, marble staircase. In another moment he had opened a door, and, drawing aside a heavy curtain, obsequiously bowed Tarzan into a dimly lighted apartment. Then Jacques vanished.

Across the room from him Tarzan saw Olga seated before a little desk on which stood her telephone. She was tapping impatiently upon the polished surface of the desk. She had not heard him enter.

"Olga," he said, "what is wrong?"

She turned toward him with a little cry of alarm.

"Jean!" she cried. "What are you doing here? Who admitted you? What does it mean?"

Tarzan was thunderstruck, but in an instant he realized a part of the truth.

"Then you did not send for me, Olga?"

"Send for you at this time of night? MON DIEU! Jean, do you think that I am quite mad?"

"Francois telephoned me to come at once; that you were in trouble and wanted me."

"Francois? Who in the world is Francois?"

"He said that he was in your service. He spoke as though I should recall the fact."

"There is no one by that name in my employ. Some one has played a joke upon you, Jean," and Olga laughed.

"I fear that it may be a most sinister 'joke,' Olga," he replied. "There is more back of it than humor."

"What do you mean? You do not think that – "

"Where is the count?" he interrupted.

"At the German ambassador's."

"This is another move by your estimable brother. Tomorrow the count will hear of it. He will question the servants. Everything will point to – to what Rokoff wishes the count to think."

"The scoundrel!" cried Olga. She had arisen, and come close to Tarzan, where she stood looking up into his face. She was very frightened. In her eyes was an expression that the hunter sees in those of a poor, terrified doe – puzzled – questioning. She trembled, and to steady herself raised her hands to his broad shoulders. "What shall we do, Jean?" she whispered. "It is terrible. Tomorrow all Paris will read of it – he will see to that."

Her look, her attitude, her words were eloquent of the age-old appeal of defenseless woman to her natural protector – man. Tarzan took one of the warm little hands that lay on his breast in his own strong one. The act was quite involuntary, and almost equally so was the instinct of protection that threw a sheltering arm around the girl's shoulders.

The result was electrical. Never before had he been so close to her. In startled guilt they looked suddenly into each other's eyes, and where Olga de Coude should have been strong she was weak, for she crept closer into the man's arms, and clasped her own about his neck. And Tarzan of the Apes? He took the panting figure into his mighty arms, and covered the hot lips with kisses.

Raoul de Coude made hurried excuses to his host after he had read the note handed him by the ambassador's butler. Never afterward could he recall the nature of the excuses he made. Everything was quite a blur to him up to the time that he stood on the threshold of his own home. Then he became very cool, moving quietly and with caution. For some inexplicable reason Jacques had the door open before he was halfway to the steps. It did not strike him at the time as being unusual, though afterward he remarked it.

Very softly he tiptoed up the stairs and along the gallery to the door of his wife's boudoir. In his hand was a heavy walking stick – in his heart, murder.

Olga was the first to see him. With a horrified shriek she tore herself from Tarzan's arms, and the ape-man turned just in time to ward with his arm a terrific blow that De Coude had aimed at his head. Once, twice, three times the heavy stick fell with lightning rapidity, and each blow aided in the transition of the ape-man back to the primordial.

With the low, guttural snarl of the bull ape he sprang for the Frenchman. The great stick was torn from his grasp and broken in two as though it had been matchwood, to be flung aside as the now infuriated beast charged for his adversary's throat. Olga de Coude stood a horrified spectator of the terrible scene which ensued during the next brief moment, then she sprang to where Tarzan was murdering her husband – choking the life from him – shaking him as a terrier might shake a rat.

Frantically she tore at his great hands. "Mother of God!" she cried. "You are killing him, you are killing him! Oh, Jean, you are killing my husband!"

Tarzan was deaf with rage. Suddenly he hurled the body to the floor, and, placing his foot upon the upturned breast, raised his head. Then through the palace of the Count de Coude rang the awesome challenge of the bull ape that has made a kill. From cellar to attic the horrid sound searched out the servants, and left them blanched and trembling. The woman in the room sank to her knees beside the body of her husband, and prayed.

Slowly the red mist faded from before Tarzan's eyes. Things began to take form – he was regaining the perspective of civilized man. His eyes fell upon the figure of the kneeling woman. "Olga," he whispered. She looked up, expecting to see the maniacal light of murder in the eyes above her. Instead she saw sorrow and contrition.

"Oh, Jean!" she cried. "See what you have done. He was my husband. I loved him, and you have killed him."

Very gently Tarzan raised the limp form of the Count de Coude and bore it to a couch. Then he put his ear to the man's breast.

"Some brandy, Olga," he said.

She brought it, and together they forced it between his lips. Presently a faint gasp came from the white lips. The head turned, and De Coude groaned.

"He will not die," said Tarzan. "Thank God!"

"Why did you do it, Jean?" she asked.

"I do not know. He struck me, and I went mad. I have seen the apes of my tribe do the same thing. I have never told you my story, Olga. It would have been better had you known it – this might not have happened. I never saw my father. The only mother I knew was a ferocious she-ape. Until I was fifteen I had never seen a human being. I was twenty before I saw a white man. A little more than a year ago I was a naked beast of prey in an African jungle.

"Do not judge me too harshly. Two years is too short a time in which to attempt to work the change in an individual that it has taken countless ages to accomplish in the white race."

"I do not judge at all, Jean. The fault is mine. You must go now – he must not find you here when he regains consciousness. Good-by."

It was a sorrowful Tarzan who walked with bowed head from the palace of the Count de Coude.

Once outside his thoughts took definite shape, to the end that twenty minutes later he entered a police station not far from the Rue Maule. Here he soon found one of the officers with whom he had had the encounter several weeks previous. The policeman was genuinely glad to see again the man who had so roughly handled him. After a moment of conversation Tarzan asked if he had ever heard of Nikolas Rokoff or Alexis Paulvitch.

"Very often, indeed, monsieur. Each has a police record, and while there is nothing charged against them now, we make it a point to know pretty well where they may be found should the occasion demand. It is only the same precaution that we take with every known criminal. Why does monsieur ask?"

"They are known to me," replied Tarzan. "I wish to see Monsieur Rokoff on a little matter of business. If you can direct me to his lodgings I shall appreciate it."

A few minutes later he bade the policeman adieu, and, with a slip of paper in his pocket bearing a certain address in a semirespectable quarter, he walked briskly toward the nearest taxi stand.

Rokoff and Paulvitch had returned to their rooms, and were sitting talking over the probable outcome of the evening's events. They had telephoned to the offices of two of the morning papers from which they momentarily expected representatives to hear the first report of the scandal that was to stir social Paris on the morrow.

A heavy step sounded on the stairway. "Ah, but these newspaper men are prompt," exclaimed Rokoff, and as a knock fell upon the door of their room: "Enter, monsieur."

The smile of welcome froze upon the Russian's face as he looked into the hard, gray eyes of his visitor.

"Name of a name!" he shouted, springing to his feet, "What brings you here!"

"Sit down!" said Tarzan, so low that the men could barely catch the words, but in a tone that brought Rokoff to his chair, and kept Paulvitch in his.

"You know what has brought me here," he continued, in the same low tone. "It should be to kill you, but because you are Olga de Coude's brother I shall not do that – now.

"I shall give you a chance for your lives. Paulvitch does not count much – he is merely a stupid, foolish little tool, and so I shall not kill him so long as I permit you to live. Before I leave you two alive in this room you will have done two things. The first will be to write a full confession of your connection with tonight's plot – and sign it.

"The second will be to promise me upon pain of death that you will permit no word of this affair to get into the newspapers. If you do not do both, neither of you will be alive when I pass next through that doorway. Do you understand?" And, without waiting for a reply: "Make haste; there is ink before you, and paper and a pen."

Rokoff assumed a truculent air, attempting by bravado to show how little he feared Tarzan's threats. An instant later he felt the ape-man's steel fingers at his throat, and Paulvitch, who attempted to dodge them and reach the door, was lifted completely off the floor, and hurled senseless into a corner. When Rokoff commenced to blacken about the face Tarzan released his hold and shoved the fellow back into his chair. After a moment of coughing Rokoff sat sullenly glaring at the man standing opposite him. Presently Paulvitch came to himself, and limped painfully back to his chair at Tarzan's command.

"Now write," said the ape-man. "If it is necessary to handle you again I shall not be so lenient."

Rokoff picked up a pen and commenced to write.

"See that you omit no detail, and that you mention every name," cautioned Tarzan.

Presently there was a knock at the door. "Enter," said Tarzan.

A dapper young man came in. "I am from the MATIN," he announced. "I understand that Monsieur Rokoff has a story for me."

"Then you are mistaken, monsieur," replied Tarzan. "You have no story for publication, have you, my dear Nikolas."

Rokoff looked up from his writing with an ugly scowl upon his face.

"No," he growled, "I have no story for publication – now."

"Nor ever, my dear Nikolas," and the reporter did not see the nasty light in the ape-man's eye; but Nikolas Rokoff did.

"Nor ever," he repeated hastily.

"It is too bad that monsieur has been troubled," said Tarzan, turning to the newspaper man. "I bid monsieur good evening," and he bowed the dapper young man out of the room, and closed the door in his face.

An hour later Tarzan, with a rather bulky manuscript in his coat pocket, turned at the door leading from Rokoff's room.

"Were I you I should leave France," he said, "for sooner or later I shall find an excuse to kill you that will not in any way compromise your sister."

CHAPTER SIX

A Duel

D'Arnot was asleep when Tarzan entered their apartments after leaving Rokoff's. Tarzan did not disturb him, but the following morning he narrated the happenings of the previous evening, omitting not a single detail.

"What a fool I have been," he concluded. "De Coude and his wife were both my friends. How have I returned their friendship? Barely did I escape murdering the count. I have cast a stigma on the name of a good woman. It is very probable that I have broken up a happy home."

"Do you love Olga de Coude?" asked D'Arnot.

"Were I not positive that she does not love me I could not answer your question, Paul; but without disloyalty to her I tell you that I do not love her, nor does she love me. For an instant we were the victims of a sudden madness – it was not love – and it would have left us, unharmed, as suddenly as it had come upon us even though De Coude had not returned. As you know, I have had little experience of women. Olga de Coude is very beautiful; that, and the dim light and the seductive surroundings, and the appeal of the defenseless for protection, might have been resisted by a more civilized man, but my civilization is not even skin deep – it does not go deeper than my clothes.

"Paris is no place for me. I will but continue to stumble into more and more serious pitfalls. The man-made restrictions are irksome. I feel always that I am a prisoner. I cannot endure it, my friend, and so I think that I shall go back to my own jungle, and lead the life that God intended that I should lead when He put me there."

"Do not take it so to heart, Jean," responded D'Arnot. "You have acquitted yourself much better than most 'civilized' men would have under similar circumstances. As to leaving Paris at this time, I rather think that Raoul de Coude may be expected to have something to say on that subject before long."

Nor was D'Arnot mistaken. A week later on Monsieur Flaubert was announced about eleven in the morning, as D'Arnot and Tarzan were breakfasting. Monsieur Flaubert was an impressively polite gentleman. With many low bows he delivered Monsieur le Count de Coude's challenge to Monsieur Tarzan. Would monsieur be so very kind as to arrange to have a friend meet Monsieur Flaubert at as early an hour as convenient, that the details might be arranged to the mutual satisfaction of all concerned?

Certainly. Monsieur Tarzan would be delighted to place his interests unreservedly in the hands of his friend, Lieutenant D'Arnot. And so it was arranged that D'Arnot was to call on Monsieur Flaubert at two that afternoon, and the polite Monsieur Flaubert, with many bows, left them.

When they were again alone D'Arnot looked quizzically at Tarzan.

"Well?" he said.

"Now to my sins I must add murder, or else myself be killed," said Tarzan. "I am progressing rapidly in the ways of my civilized brothers."

"What weapons shall you select?" asked D'Arnot. "De Coude is accredited with being a master with the sword, and a splendid shot."

"I might then choose poisoned arrows at twenty paces, or spears at the same distance," laughed Tarzan. "Make it pistols, Paul."

"He will kill you, Jean."

"I have no doubt of it," replied Tarzan. "I must die some day."

"We had better make it swords," said D'Arnot. "He will be satisfied with wounding you, and there is less danger of a mortal wound." "Pistols," said Tarzan, with finality.

D'Arnot tried to argue him out of it, but without avail, so pistols it was.

D'Arnot returned from his conference with Monsieur Flaubert shortly after four.

"It is all arranged," he said. "Everything is satisfactory. Tomorrow morning at daylight – there is a secluded spot on the road not far from Etamps. For some personal reason Monsieur Flaubert preferred it. I did not demur."

"Good!" was Tarzan's only comment. He did not refer to the matter again even indirectly. That night he wrote several letters before he retired. After sealing and addressing them he placed them all in an envelope addressed to D'Arnot. As he undressed D'Arnot heard him humming a music-hall ditty.

The Frenchman swore under his breath. He was very unhappy, for he was positive that when the sun rose the next morning it would look down upon a dead Tarzan. It grated upon him to see Tarzan so unconcerned.

"This is a most uncivilized hour for people to kill each other," remarked the ape-man when he had been routed out of a comfortable bed in the blackness of the early morning hours. He had slept well, and so it seemed that his head scarcely touched the pillow ere his man deferentially aroused him. His remark was addressed to D'Arnot, who stood fully dressed in the doorway of Tarzan's bedroom.

D'Arnot had scarcely slept at all during the night. He was nervous, and therefore inclined to be irritable.

"I presume you slept like a baby all night," he said.

Tarzan laughed. "From your tone, Paul, I infer that you rather harbor the fact against me. I could not help it, really."

"No, Jean; it is not that," replied D'Arnot, himself smiling. "But you take the entire matter with such infernal indifference – it is exasperating. One would think that you were going out to shoot at a target, rather than to face one of the best shots in France."

Tarzan shrugged his shoulders. "I am going out to expiate a great wrong, Paul. A very necessary feature of the expiation is the marksmanship of my opponent. Wherefore, then, should I be dissatisfied? Have you not yourself told me that Count de Coude is a splendid marksman?"

"You mean that you hope to be killed?" exclaimed D'Arnot, in horror.

"I cannot say that I hope to be; but you must admit that there is little reason to believe that I shall not be killed."

Had D'Arnot known the thing that was in the ape-man's mind – that had been in his mind almost from the first intimation that De Coude would call him to account on the field of honor – he would have been even more horrified than he was.

In silence they entered D'Arnot's great car, and in similar silence they sped over the dim road that leads to Etamps. Each man was occupied with his own thoughts. D'Arnot's were very mournful, for he was genuinely fond of Tarzan. The great friendship which had sprung up between these two men whose lives and training had been so widely different had but been strengthened by association, for they were both men to whom the same high ideals of manhood, of personal courage, and of honor appealed with equal force. They could understand one another, and each could be proud of the friendship of the other.

Tarzan of the Apes was wrapped in thoughts of the past; pleasant memories of the happier occasions of his lost jungle life. He recalled the countless boyhood hours that he had spent cross-legged upon the table in his dead father's cabin, his little brown body bent over one of the fascinating picture books from which, unaided, he had gleaned the secret of the printed language long before the sounds of human speech fell upon his ears. A smile of contentment softened his strong face as he thought of that day of days that he had had alone with Jane Porter in the heart of his primeval forest.

Presently his reminiscences were broken in upon by the stopping of the car – they were at their destination. Tarzan's mind returned to the affairs of the moment. He knew that he was about to die, but there was no fear of death in him. To a denizen of the cruel jungle death is a commonplace. The first law of nature compels them to cling tenaciously to life – to fight for it; but it does not teach them to fear death.

D'Arnot and Tarzan were first upon the field of honor. A moment later De Coude, Monsieur Flaubert, and a third gentleman arrived. The last was introduced to D'Arnot and Tarzan; he was a physician.

D'Arnot and Monsieur Flaubert spoke together in whispers for a brief time. The Count de Coude and Tarzan stood apart at opposite sides of the field. Presently the seconds summoned them. D'Arnot and Monsieur Flaubert had examined both pistols. The two men who were to face each other a moment later stood silently while Monsieur Flaubert recited the conditions they were to observe.

They were to stand back to back. At a signal from Monsieur Flaubert they were to walk in opposite directions, their pistols hanging by their sides. When each had proceeded ten paces D'Arnot was to give the final signal – then they were to turn and fire at will until one fell, or each had expended the three shots allowed.

While Monsieur Flaubert spoke Tarzan selected a cigarette from his case, and lighted it. De Coude was the personification of coolness – was he not the best shot in France?

Presently Monsieur Flaubert nodded to D'Arnot, and each man placed his principal in position.

"Are you quite ready, gentlemen?" asked Monsieur Flaubert.

"Quite," replied De Coude.

Tarzan nodded. Monsieur Flaubert gave the signal. He and D'Arnot stepped back a few paces to be out of the line of fire as the men paced slowly apart. Six! Seven! Eight! There were tears in D'Arnot's eyes. He loved Tarzan very much. Nine! Another pace, and the poor lieutenant gave the signal he so hated to give. To him it sounded the doom of his best friend.

Quickly De Coude wheeled and fired. Tarzan gave a little start. His pistol still dangled at his side. De Coude hesitated, as though waiting to see his antagonist crumple to the ground. The Frenchman was too experienced a marksman not to know that he had scored a hit. Still Tarzan made no move to raise his pistol. De Coude fired once more, but the attitude of the ape-man – the utter indifference that was so apparent in every line of the nonchalant ease of his giant figure, and the even unruffled puffing of his cigarette – had disconcerted the best marksman in France. This time Tarzan did not start, but again De Coude knew that he had hit.

Suddenly the explanation leaped to his mind – his antagonist was coolly taking these terrible chances in the hope that he would receive no staggering wound from any of De Coude's three shots. Then he would take his own time about shooting De Coude down deliberately, coolly, and in cold blood. A little shiver ran up the Frenchman's spine. It was fiendish – diabolical. What manner of creature was this that could stand complacently with two bullets in him, waiting for the third?

And so De Coude took careful aim this time, but his nerve was gone, and he made a clean miss. Not once had Tarzan raised his pistol hand from where it hung beside his leg.

For a moment the two stood looking straight into each other's eyes. On Tarzan's face was a pathetic expression of disappointment. On De Coude's a rapidly growing expression of horror – yes, of terror.

He could endure it no longer.

"Mother of God! Monsieur – shoot!" he screamed.

But Tarzan did not raise his pistol. Instead, he advanced toward De Coude, and when D'Arnot and Monsieur Flaubert, misinterpreting his intention, would have rushed between them, he raised his left hand in a sign of remonstrance.

"Do not fear," he said to them, "I shall not harm him."

It was most unusual, but they halted. Tarzan advanced until he was quite close to De Coude.

"There must have been something wrong with monsieur's pistol," he said. "Or monsieur is unstrung. Take mine, monsieur, and try again," and Tarzan offered his pistol, butt foremost, to the astonished De Coude.

"MON DIEU, monsieur!" cried the latter. "Are you mad?"

"No, my friend," replied the ape-man; "but I deserve to die. It is the only way in which I may atone for the wrong I have done a very good woman. Take my pistol and do as I bid."

"It would be murder," replied De Coude. "But what wrong did you do my wife? She swore to me that – "

"I do not mean that," said Tarzan quickly. "You saw all the wrong that passed between us. But that was enough to cast a shadow upon her name, and to ruin the happiness of a man against whom I had no enmity. The fault was all mine, and so I hoped to die for it this morning. I am disappointed that monsieur is not so wonderful a marksman as I had been led to believe."

"You say that the fault was all yours?" asked De Coude eagerly.

"All mine, monsieur. Your wife is a very pure woman. She loves only you. The fault that you saw was all mine. The thing that brought me there was no fault of either the Countess de Coude or myself. Here is a paper which will quite positively demonstrate that," and Tarzan drew from his pocket the statement Rokoff had written and signed.

De Coude took it and read. D'Arnot and Monsieur Flaubert had drawn near. They were interested spectators of this strange ending of a strange duel. None spoke until De Coude had quite finished, then he looked up at Tarzan.

"You are a very brave and chivalrous gentleman," he said. "I thank God that I did not kill you."

De Coude was a Frenchman. Frenchmen are impulsive. He threw his arms about Tarzan and embraced him. Monsieur Flaubert embraced D'Arnot. There was no one to embrace the doctor. So possibly it was pique which prompted him to interfere, and demand that he be permitted to dress Tarzan's wounds.

"This gentleman was hit once at least," he said. "Possibly thrice."

"Twice," said Tarzan. "Once in the left shoulder, and again in the left side – both flesh wounds, I think." But the doctor insisted upon stretching him upon the sward, and tinkering with him until the wounds were cleansed and the flow of blood checked.

One result of the duel was that they all rode back to Paris together in D'Arnot's car, the best of friends. De Coude was so relieved to have had this double assurance of his wife's loyalty that he felt no rancor at all toward Tarzan. It is true that the latter had assumed much more of the fault than was rightly his, but if he lied a little he may be excused, for he lied in the service of a woman, and he lied like a gentleman.

The ape-man was confined to his bed for several days. He felt that it was foolish and unnecessary, but the doctor and D'Arnot took the matter so to heart that he gave in to please them, though it made him laugh to think of it.

"It is droll," he said to D'Arnot. "To lie abed because of a pin prick! Why, when Bolgani, the king gorilla, tore me almost to pieces, while I was still but a little boy, did I have a nice soft bed to lie on? No, only the damp, rotting vegetation of the jungle. Hidden beneath some friendly bush I lay for days and weeks with only Kala to nurse me – poor, faithful Kala, who kept the insects from my wounds and warned off the beasts of prey.

"When I called for water she brought it to me in her own mouth – the only way she knew to carry it. There was no sterilized gauze, there was no antiseptic bandage – there was nothing that would not have driven our dear doctor mad to have seen. Yet I recovered – recovered to lie in bed because of a tiny scratch that one of the jungle folk would scarce realize unless it were upon the end of his nose."

But the time was soon over, and before he realized it Tarzan found himself abroad again. Several times De Coude had called, and when he found that Tarzan was anxious for employment of some nature he promised to see what could be done to find a berth for him.

It was the first day that Tarzan was permitted to go out that he received a message from De Coude requesting him to call at the count's office that afternoon.

He found De Coude awaiting him with a very pleasant welcome, and a sincere congratulation that he was once more upon his feet. Neither had ever mentioned the duel or the cause of it since that morning upon the field of honor.

"I think that I have found just the thing for you, Monsieur Tarzan," said the count. "It is a position of much trust and responsibility, which also requires considerably physical courage and prowess. I cannot imagine a man better fitted than you, my dear Monsieur Tarzan, for this very position. It will necessitate travel, and later it may lead to a very much better post – possibly in the diplomatic service.

"At first, for a short time only, you will be a special agent in the service of the ministry of war. Come, I will take you to the gentleman who will be your chief. He can explain the duties better than I, and then you will be in a position to judge if you wish to accept or no."

De Coude himself escorted Tarzan to the office of General Rochere, the chief of the bureau to which Tarzan would be attached if he accepted the position. There the count left him, after a glowing description to the general of the many attributes possessed by the ape-man which should fit him for the work of the service.

A half hour later Tarzan walked out of the office the possessor of the first position he had ever held. On the morrow he was to return for further instructions, though General Rochere had made it quite plain that Tarzan might prepare to leave Paris for an almost indefinite period, possibly on the morrow.

It was with feelings of the keenest elation that he hastened home to bear the good news to D'Arnot. At last he was to be of some value in the world. He was to earn money, and, best of all, to travel and see the world.

He could scarcely wait to get well inside D'Arnot's sitting room before he burst out with the glad tidings. D'Arnot was not so pleased.

"It seems to delight you to think that you are to leave Paris, and that we shall not see each other for months, perhaps. Tarzan, you are a most ungrateful beast!" and D'Arnot laughed.

"No, Paul; I am a little child. I have a new toy, and I am tickled to death."

And so it came that on the following day Tarzan left Paris en route for Marseilles and Oran.

CHAPTER SEVEN

The Dancing Girl of Sidi Aissa

TARZAN'S FIRST MISSION did not bid fair to be either exciting or vastly important. There was a certain lieutenant of SPAHIS whom the government had reason to suspect of improper relations with a great European power. This Lieutenant Gernois, who was at present stationed at Sidi-bel-Abbes, had recently been attached to the general staff, where certain information of great military value had come into his possession in the ordinary routine of his duties. It was this information which the government suspected the great power was bartering for with the officer.

It was at most but a vague hint dropped by a certain notorious Parisienne in a jealous mood that had caused suspicion to rest upon the lieutenant. But general staffs are jealous of their secrets, and treason so serious a thing that even a hint of it may not be safely neglected. And so it was that Tarzan had come to Algeria in the guise of an American hunter and traveler to keep a close eye upon Lieutenant Gernois.

He had looked forward with keen delight to again seeing his beloved Africa, but this northern aspect of it was so different from his tropical jungle home that he might as well have been back in Paris for all the heart thrills of homecoming that he experienced. At Oran he spent a day wandering through the narrow, crooked alleys of the Arab quarter enjoying the strange, new sights. The next day found him at Sidi-bel-Abbes, where he presented his letters of introduction to both civil and military authorities – letters which gave no clew to the real significance of his mission.

Tarzan possessed a sufficient command of English to enable him to pass among Arabs and Frenchmen as an American, and that was all that was required of it. When he met an Englishman he spoke French in order that he might not betray himself, but occasionally talked in English to foreigners who understood that tongue, but could not note the slight imperfections of accent and pronunciation that were his.

Here he became acquainted with many of the French officers, and soon became a favorite among them. He met Gernois, whom he found to be a taciturn, dyspeptic-looking man of about forty, having little or no social intercourse with his fellows.

For a month nothing of moment occurred. Gernois apparently had no visitors, nor did he on his occasional visits to the town hold communication with any who might even by the wildest flight of imagination be construed into secret agents of a foreign power. Tarzan was beginning to hope that, after all, the rumor might have been false, when suddenly Gernois was ordered to Bou Saada in the Petit Sahara far to the south.

A company of SPAHIS and three officers were to relieve another company already stationed there. Fortunately one of the officers, Captain Gerard, had become an excellent friend of Tarzan's, and so when the ape-man suggested that he should embrace the opportunity of accompanying him to Bou Saada, where he expected to find hunting, it caused not the slightest suspicion.

At Bouira the detachment detrained, and the balance of the journey was made in the saddle. As Tarzan was dickering at Bouira for a mount he caught a brief glimpse of a man in European clothes eying him from the doorway of a native coffeehouse, but as Tarzan looked the man turned and entered the little, low-ceilinged mud hut, and but for a haunting impression that there had been something familiar about the face or figure of the fellow, Tarzan gave the matter no further thought.

The march to Aumale was fatiguing to Tarzan, whose equestrian experiences hitherto had been confined to a course of riding lessons in a Parisian academy, and so it was that he quickly sought the comforts of a bed in the Hotel Grossat, while the officers and troops took up their quarters at the military post.

Although Tarzan was called early the following morning, the company of SPAHIS was on the march before he had finished his breakfast. He was hurrying through his meal that the soldiers might not get too far in advance of him when he glanced through the door connecting the dining room with the bar.

To his surprise, he saw Gernois standing there in conversation with the very stranger he had seen in the coffee-house at Bouira the day previous. He could not be mistaken, for there was the same strangely familiar attitude and figure, though the man's back was toward him.

As his eyes lingered on the two, Gernois looked up and caught the intent expression on Tarzan's face. The stranger was talking in a low whisper at the time, but the French officer immediately interrupted him, and the two at once turned away and passed out of the range of Tarzan's vision.

This was the first suspicious occurrence that Tarzan had ever witnessed in connection with Gernois' actions, but he was positive that the men had left the barroom solely because Gernois had caught Tarzan's eyes upon them; then there was the persistent impression of familiarity about the stranger to further augment the ape-man's belief that here at length was something which would bear watching.

A moment later Tarzan entered the barroom, but the men had left, nor did he see aught of them in the street beyond, though he found a pretext to ride to various shops before he set out after the column which had now considerable start of him. He did not overtake them until he reached Sidi Aissa shortly after noon, where the soldiers had halted for an hour's rest. Here he found Gernois with the column, but there was no sign of the stranger.

It was market day at Sidi Aissa, and the numberless caravans of camels coming in from the desert, and the crowds of bickering Arabs in the market place, filled Tarzan with a consuming desire to remain for a day that he might see more of these sons of the desert. Thus it was that the company of SPAHIS marched on that afternoon toward Bou Saada without him. He spent the hours until dark wandering about the market in company with a youthful Arab, one Abdul, who had been recommended to him by the innkeeper as a trustworthy servant and interpreter.

Here Tarzan purchased a better mount than the one he had selected at Bouira, and, entering into conversation with the stately Arab to whom the animal had belonged, learned that the seller was Kadour ben Saden, sheik of a desert tribe far south of Djelfa. Through Abdul, Tarzan invited his new acquaintance to dine with him. As the three were making their way through the crowds of marketers, camels, donkeys, and horses that filled the market place with a confusing babel of sounds, Abdul plucked at Tarzan's sleeve.

"Look, master, behind us," and he turned, pointing at a figure which disappeared behind a camel as Tarzan turned. "He has been following us about all afternoon," continued Abdul.

"I caught only a glimpse of an Arab in a dark-blue burnoose and white turban," replied Tarzan. "Is it he you mean?"

"Yes. I suspected him because he seems a stranger here, without other business than following us, which is not the way of the Arab who is honest, and also because he keeps the lower part of his face hidden, only his eyes showing. He must be a bad man, or he would have honest business of his own to occupy his time."

"He is on the wrong scent then, Abdul," replied Tarzan, "for no one here can have any grievance against me. This is my first visit to your country, and none knows me. He will soon discover his error, and cease to follow us."

"Unless he be bent on robbery," returned Abdul.

"Then all we can do is wait until he is ready to try his hand upon us," laughed Tarzan, "and I warrant that he will get his bellyful of robbing now that we are prepared for him," and so he dismissed the subject from his mind, though he was destined to recall it before many hours through a most unlooked-for occurrence.

Kadour ben Saden, having dined well, prepared to take leave of his host. With dignified protestations of friendship, he invited Tarzan to visit him in his wild domain, where the antelope, the stag, the boar, the panther, and the lion might still be found in sufficient numbers to tempt an ardent huntsman.

On his departure the ape-man, with Abdul, wandered again into the streets of Sidi Aissa, where he was soon attracted by the wild din of sound coming from the open doorway of one of the numerous CAFES MAURES. It was after eight, and the dancing was in full swing as Tarzan entered. The room was filled to repletion with Arabs. All were smoking, and drinking their thick, hot coffee.

Tarzan and Abdul found seats near the center of the room, though the terrific noise produced by the musicians upon their Arab drums and pipes would have rendered a seat farther from them more acceptable to the quiet-loving ape-man. A rather good-looking Ouled-Nail was dancing, and, perceiving Tarzan's European clothes, and scenting a generous gratuity, she threw her silken handkerchief upon his shoulder, to be rewarded with a franc.

When her place upon the floor had been taken by another the bright-eyed Abdul saw her in conversation with two Arabs at the far side of the room, near a side door that let upon an inner court, around the gallery of which were the rooms occupied by the girls who danced in this cafe.

At first he thought nothing of the matter, but presently he noticed from the corner of his eye one of the men nod in their direction, and the girl turn and shoot a furtive glance at Tarzan. Then the Arabs melted through the doorway into the darkness of the court.

When it came again the girl's turn to dance she hovered close to Tarzan, and for the ape-man alone were her sweetest smiles. Many an ugly scowl was cast upon the tall European by swarthy, dark-eyed sons of the desert, but neither smiles nor scowls produced any outwardly visible effect upon him. Again the girl cast her handkerchief upon his shoulder, and again was she rewarded with a franc piece. As she was sticking it upon her forehead, after the custom of her kind, she bent low toward Tarzan, whispering a quick word in his ear.

"There are two without in the court," she said quickly, in broken French, "who would harm m'sieur. At first I promised to lure you to them, but you have been kind, and I cannot do it. Go quickly, before they find that I have failed them. I think that they are very bad men."

Tarzan thanked the girl, assuring her that he would be careful, and, having finished her dance, she crossed to the little doorway and went out into the court. But Tarzan did not leave the cafe as she had urged.

For another half hour nothing unusual occurred, then a surly-looking Arab entered the cafe from the street. He stood near Tarzan, where he deliberately made insulting remarks about the European, but as they were in his native tongue Tarzan was entirely innocent of their purport until Abdul took it upon himself to enlighten him.

"This fellow is looking for trouble," warned Abdul. "He is not alone. In fact, in case of a disturbance, nearly every man here would be against you. It would be better to leave quietly, master."

"Ask the fellow what he wants," commanded Tarzan.

"He says that 'the dog of a Christian' insulted the Ouled-Nail, who belongs to him. He means trouble, m'sieur."

"Tell him that I did not insult his or any other Ouled-Nail, that I wish him to go away and leave me alone. That I have no quarrel with him, nor has he any with me."

"He says," replied Abdul, after delivering this message to the Arab, "that besides being a dog yourself that you are the son of one, and that your grandmother was a hyena. Incidentally you are a liar."

The attention of those near by had now been attracted by the altercation, and the sneering laughs that followed this torrent of invective easily indicated the trend of the sympathies of the majority of the audience.

Tarzan did not like being laughed at, neither did he relish the terms applied to him by the Arab, but he showed no sign of anger as he arose from his seat upon the bench. A half smile played about his lips, but of a sudden a mighty fist shot into the face of the scowling Arab, and back of it were the terrible muscles of the ape-man.

At the instant that the man fell a half dozen fierce plainsmen sprang into the room from where they had apparently been waiting for their cue in the street before the cafe. With cries of "Kill the unbeliever!" and "Down with the dog of a Christian!" they made straight for Tarzan. A number of the younger Arabs in the audience sprang to their feet to join in the assault upon the unarmed white man. Tarzan and Abdul were rushed back toward the end of the room by the very force of numbers opposing them. The young Arab remained loyal to his master, and with drawn knife fought at his side.

With tremendous blows the ape-man felled all who came within reach of his powerful hands. He fought quietly and without a word, upon his lips the same half smile they had worn as he rose to strike down the man who had insulted him. It seemed impossible that either he or Abdul could survive the sea of wicked-looking swords and knives that surrounded them, but the very numbers of their assailants proved the best bulwark of their safety. So closely packed was the howling, cursing mob that no weapon could be wielded to advantage, and none of the Arabs dared use a firearm for fear of wounding one of his compatriots.

Finally Tarzan succeeded in seizing one of the most persistent of his attackers. With a quick wrench he disarmed the fellow, and then, holding him before them as a shield, he backed slowly beside Abdul toward the little door which led into the inner courtyard. At the threshold he paused for an instant, and, lifting the struggling Arab above his head, hurled him, as though from a catapult, full in the faces of his on-pressing fellows.

Then Tarzan and Abdul stepped into the semidarkness of the court. The frightened Ouled-Nails were crouching at the tops of the stairs which led to their respective rooms, the only light in the courtyard coming from the sickly candles which each girl had stuck with its own grease to the woodwork of her door-frame, the better to display her charms to those who might happen to traverse the dark inclosure.

Scarcely had Tarzan and Abdul emerged from the room ere a revolver spoke close at their backs from the shadows beneath one of the stairways, and as they turned to meet this new antagonist, two muffled figures sprang toward them, firing as they came. Tarzan leaped to meet these two new assailants. The foremost lay, a second later, in the trampled dirt of the court, disarmed and groaning from a broken wrist. Abdul's knife found the vitals of the second in the instant that the fellow's revolver missed fire as he held it to the faithful Arab's forehead.

The maddened horde within the cafe were now rushing out in pursuit of their quarry. The Ouled-Nails had extinguished their candles at a cry from one of their number, and the only light within the yard came feebly from the open and half-blocked door of the cafe. Tarzan had seized a sword from the man who had fallen before Abdul's knife, and now he stood waiting for the rush of men that was coming in search of them through the darkness.

Suddenly he felt a light hand upon his shoulder from behind, and a woman's voice whispering, "Quick, m'sieur; this way. Follow me."

"Come, Abdul," said Tarzan, in a low tone, to the youth; "we can be no worse off elsewhere than we are here."

The woman turned and led them up the narrow stairway that ended at the door of her quarters. Tarzan was close beside her. He saw the gold and silver bracelets upon her bare arms, the strings of gold coin that depended from her hair ornaments, and the gorgeous colors of her dress. He saw that she was a Ouled-Nail, and instinctively he knew that she was the same who had whispered the warning in his ear earlier in the evening.

As they reached the top of the stairs they could hear the angry crowd searching the yard beneath.

"Soon they will search here," whispered the girl. "They must not find you, for, though you fight with the strength of many men, they will kill you in the end. Hasten; you can drop from the farther window of my room to the street beyond. Before they discover that you are no longer in the court of the buildings you will be safe within the hotel."

But even as she spoke, several men had started up the stairway at the head of which they stood. There was a sudden cry from one of the searchers. They had been discovered. Quickly the crowd rushed for the stairway. The foremost assailant leaped quickly upward, but at the top he met the sudden sword that he had not expected – the quarry had been unarmed before.

With a cry, the man toppled back upon those behind him. Like tenpins they rolled down the stairs. The ancient and rickety structure could not withstand the strain of this unwonted weight and jarring. With a creaking and rending of breaking wood it collapsed beneath the Arabs, leaving Tarzan, Abdul, and the girl alone upon the frail platform at the top.

"Come!" cried the Ouled-Nail. "They will reach us from another stairway through the room next to mine. We have not a moment to spare."

Just as they were entering the room Abdul heard and translated a cry from the yard below for several to hasten to the street and cut off escape from that side.

"We are lost now," said the girl simply.

"We?" questioned Tarzan.

"Yes, m'sieur," she responded; "they will kill me as well. Have I not aided you?"

This put a different aspect on the matter. Tarzan had rather been enjoying the excitement and danger of the encounter. He had not for an instant supposed that either Abdul or the girl could suffer except through accident, and he had only retreated just enough to keep from being killed himself. He had had no intention of running away until he saw that he was hopelessly lost were he to remain.

Alone he could have sprung into the midst of that close-packed mob, and, laying about him after the fashion of Numa, the lion, have struck the Arabs with such consternation that escape would have been easy. Now he must think entirely of these two faithful friends.

He crossed to the window which overlooked the street. In a minute there would be enemies below. Already he could hear the mob clambering the stairway to the next quarters – they would be at the door beside him in another instant. He put a foot upon the sill and leaned out, but he did not look down. Above him, within arm's reach, was the low roof of the building. He called to the girl. She came and stood beside him. He put a great arm about her and lifted her across his shoulder.

"Wait here until I reach down for you from above," he said to Abdul. "In the meantime shove everything in the room against that door – it may delay them long enough." Then he stepped to the sill of the narrow window with the girl upon his shoulders. "Hold tight," he cautioned her. A moment later he had clambered to the roof above with the ease and dexterity of an ape. Setting the girl down, he leaned far over the roof's edge, calling softly to Abdul. The youth ran to the window.

"Your hand," whispered Tarzan. The men in the room beyond were battering at the door. With a sudden crash it fell splintering in, and at the same instant Abdul felt himself lifted like a feather onto the roof above. They were not a moment too soon, for as the men broke into the room which they had just quitted a dozen more rounded the corner in the street below and came running to a spot beneath the girl's window.

CHAPTER EIGHT

The Fight in the Desert

As the three squatted upon the roof above the quarters of the Ouled-Nails they heard the angry cursing of the Arabs in the room beneath. Abdul translated from time to time to Tarzan.

"They are berating those in the street below now," said Abdul, "for permitting us to escape so easily. Those in the street say that we did not come that way – that we are still within the building, and that those above, being too cowardly to attack us, are attempting to deceive them into believing that we have escaped. In a moment they will have fighting of their own to attend to if they continue their brawling."

Presently those in the building gave up the search, and returned to the cafe. A few remained in the street below, smoking and talking.

Tarzan spoke to the girl, thanking her for the sacrifice she had made for him, a total stranger.

"I liked you," she said simply. "You were unlike the others who come to the cafe. You did not speak coarsely to me – the manner in which you gave me money was not an insult."

"What shall you do after tonight?" he asked. "You cannot return to the cafe. Can you even remain with safety in Sidi Aissa?"

"Tomorrow it will be forgotten," she replied. "But I should be glad if it might be that I need never return to this or another cafe. I have not remained because I wished to; I have been a prisoner."

"A prisoner!" ejaculated Tarzan incredulously.

"A slave would be the better word," she answered. "I was stolen in the night from my father's DOUAR by a band of marauders. They brought me here and sold me to the Arab who keeps this cafe. It has been nearly two years now since I saw the last of mine own people. They are very far to the south. They never come to Sidi Aissa."

"You would like to return to your people?" asked Tarzan. "Then I shall promise to see you safely so far as Bou Saada at least. There we can doubtless arrange with the commandant to send you the rest of the way."

"Oh, m'sieur," she cried, "how can I ever repay you! You cannot really mean that you will do so much for a poor Ouled-Nail. But my father can reward you, and he will, for is he not a great sheik? He is Kadour ben Saden."

"Kadour ben Saden!" ejaculated Tarzan. "Why, Kadour ben Saden is in Sidi Aissa this very night. He dined with me but a few hours since."

"My father in Sidi Aissa?" cried the amazed girl. "Allah be praised then, for I am indeed saved."

"Hssh!" cautioned Abdul. "Listen."

From below came the sound of voices, quite distinguishable upon the still night air. Tarzan could not understand the words, but Abdul and the girl translated.

"They have gone now," said the latter. "It is you they want, m'sieur. One of them said that the stranger who had offered money for your slaying lay in the house of Akmed din Soulef with a broken wrist, but that he had offered a still greater reward if some would lay in wait for you upon the road to Bou Saada and kill you."

"It is he who followed m'sieur about the market today," exclaimed Abdul. "I saw him again within the cafe – him and another; and the two went out into the inner court after talking with this girl here. It was they who attacked and fired upon us, as we came out of the cafe. Why do they wish to kill you, m'sieur?"

"I do not know," replied Tarzan, and then, after a pause: "Unless – " But he did not finish, for the thought that had come to his mind, while it seemed the only reasonable solution of the mystery, appeared at the same time quite improbable. Presently the men in the street went away. The courtyard and the cafe were deserted. Cautiously Tarzan lowered himself to the sill of the girl's window. The room was empty. He returned to the roof and let Abdul down, then he lowered the girl to the arms of the waiting Arab.

From the window Abdul dropped the short distance to the street below, while Tarzan took the girl in his arms and leaped down as he had done on so many other occasions in his own forest with a burden in his arms. A little cry of alarm was startled from the girl's lips, but Tarzan landed in the street with but an imperceptible jar, and lowered her in safety to her feet.

She clung to him for a moment.

"How strong m'sieur is, and how active," she cried. "EL ADREA, the black lion, himself is not more so."

"I should like to meet this EL ADREA of yours," he said. "I have heard much about him."

"And you come to the DOUAR of my father you shall see him," said the girl. "He lives in a spur of the mountains north of us, and comes down from his lair at night to rob my father's DOUAR. With a single blow of his mighty paw he crushes the skull of a bull, and woe betide the belated wayfarer who meets EL ADREA abroad at night."

Without further mishap they reached the hotel. The sleepy landlord objected strenuously to instituting a search for Kadour ben Saden until the following morning, but a piece of gold put a different aspect on the matter, so that a few moments later a servant had started to make the rounds of the lesser native hostelries where it might be expected that a desert sheik would find congenial associations. Tarzan had felt it necessary to find the girl's father that night, for fear he might start on his homeward journey too early in the morning to be intercepted.

They had waited perhaps half an hour when the messenger returned with Kadour ben Saden. The old sheik entered the room with a questioning expression upon his proud face.

"Monsieur has done me the honor to – " he commenced, and then his eyes fell upon the girl. With outstretched arms he crossed the room to meet her. "My daughter!" he cried. "Allah is merciful!" and tears dimmed the martial eyes of the old warrior.

When the story of her abduction and her final rescue had been told to Kadour ben Saden he extended his hand to Tarzan.

"All that is Kadour ben Saden's is thine, my friend, even to his life," he said very simply, but Tarzan knew that those were no idle words.

It was decided that although three of them would have to ride after practically no sleep, it would be best to make an early start in the morning, and attempt to ride all the way to Bou Saada in one day. It would have been comparatively easy for the men, but for the girl it was sure to be a fatiguing journey.

She, however, was the most anxious to undertake it, for it seemed to her that she could not quickly enough reach the family and friends from whom she had been separated for two years.

It seemed to Tarzan that he had not closed his eyes before he was awakened, and in another hour the party was on its way south toward Bou Saada. For a few miles the road was good, and they made rapid progress, but suddenly it became only a waste of sand, into which the horses sank fetlock deep at nearly every step. In addition to Tarzan, Abdul, the sheik, and his daughter were four of the wild plainsmen of the sheik's tribe who had accompanied him upon the trip to Sidi Aissa. Thus, seven guns strong, they entertained little fear of attack by day, and if all went well they should reach Bou Saada before nightfall.

A brisk wind enveloped them in the blowing sand of the desert, until Tarzan's lips were parched and cracked. What little he could see of the surrounding country was far from alluring – a vast expanse of rough country, rolling in little, barren hillocks, and tufted here and there with clumps of dreary shrub. Far to the south rose the dim lines of the Saharan Atlas range. How different, thought Tarzan, from the gorgeous Africa of his boyhood!

Abdul, always on the alert, looked backward quite as often as he did ahead. At the top of each hillock that they mounted he would draw in his horse and, turning, scan the country to the rear with utmost care. At last his scrutiny was rewarded.

"Look!" he cried. "There are six horsemen behind us."

"Your friends of last evening, no doubt, monsieur," remarked Kadour ben Saden dryly to Tarzan.

"No doubt," replied the ape-man. "I am sorry that my society should endanger the safety of your journey. At the next village I shall remain and question these gentlemen, while you ride on. There is no necessity for my being at Bou Saada tonight, and less still why you should not ride in peace."

"If you stop we shall stop," said Kadour ben Saden. "Until you are safe with your friends, or the enemy has left your trail, we shall remain with you. There is nothing more to say."

Tarzan nodded his head. He was a man of few words, and possibly it was for this reason as much as any that Kadour ben Saden had taken to him, for if there be one thing that an Arab despises it is a talkative man.

All the balance of the day Abdul caught glimpses of the horsemen in their rear. They remained always at about the same distance. During the occasional halts for rest, and at the longer halt at noon, they approached no closer.

"They are waiting for darkness," said Kadour ben Saden.

And darkness came before they reached Bou Saada. The last glimpse that Abdul had of the grim, white-robed figures that trailed them, just before dusk made it impossible to distinguish them, had made it apparent that they were rapidly closing up the distance that intervened between them and their intended quarry. He whispered this fact to Tarzan, for he did not wish to alarm the girl. The ape-man drew back beside him.

"You will ride ahead with the others, Abdul," said Tarzan. "This is my quarrel. I shall wait at the next convenient spot, and interview these fellows."

"Then Abdul shall wait at thy side," replied the young Arab, nor would any threats or commands move him from his decision.

"Very well, then," replied Tarzan. "Here is as good a place as we could wish. Here are rocks at the top of this hillock. We shall remain hidden here and give an account of ourselves to these gentlemen when they appear."

They drew in their horses and dismounted. The others riding ahead were already out of sight in the darkness. Beyond them shone the lights of Bou Saada. Tarzan removed his rifle from its boot and loosened his revolver in its holster. He ordered Abdul to withdraw behind the rocks with the horses, so that they should be shielded from the enemies' bullets should they fire. The young Arab pretended to do as he was bid, but when he had fastened the two animals securely to a low shrub he crept back to lie on his belly a few paces behind Tarzan.

The ape-man stood erect in the middle of the road, waiting. Nor did he have long to wait. The sound of galloping horses came suddenly out of the darkness below him, and a moment later he discerned the moving blotches of lighter color against the solid background of the night.

"Halt," he cried, "or we fire!"

The white figures came to a sudden stop, and for a moment there was silence. Then came the sound of a whispered council, and like ghosts the phantom riders dispersed in all directions. Again the desert lay still about him, yet it was an ominous stillness that foreboded evil.

Abdul raised himself to one knee. Tarzan cocked his jungle-trained ears, and presently there came to him the sound of horses walking quietly through the sand to the east of him, to the west, to the north, and to the south. They had been surrounded. Then a shot came from the direction in which he was looking, a bullet whirred through the air above his head, and he fired at the flash of the enemy's gun.

Instantly the soundless waste was torn with the quick staccato of guns upon every hand. Abdul and Tarzan fired only at the flashes – they could not yet see their foemen. Presently it became evident that the attackers were circling their position, drawing closer and closer in as they began to realize the paltry numbers of the party which opposed them.

But one came too close, for Tarzan was accustomed to using his eyes in the darkness of the jungle night, than which there is no more utter darkness this side the grave, and with a cry of pain a saddle was emptied.

"The odds are evening, Abdul," said Tarzan, with a low laugh.

But they were still far too one-sided, and when the five remaining horsemen whirled at a signal and charged full upon them it looked as if there would be a sudden ending of the battle. Both Tarzan and Abdul sprang to the shelter of the rocks, that they might keep the enemy in front of them. There was a mad clatter of galloping hoofs, a volley of shots from both sides, and the Arabs withdrew to repeat the maneuver; but there were now only four against the two.

For a few moments there came no sound from out of the surrounding blackness. Tarzan could not tell whether the Arabs, satisfied with their losses, had given up the fight, or were waiting farther along the road to waylay them as they proceeded on toward Bou Saada. But he was not left long in doubt, for now all from one direction came the sound of a new charge. But scarcely had the first gun spoken ere a dozen shots rang out behind the Arabs. There came the wild shouts of a new party to the controversy, and the pounding of the feet of many horses from down the road to Bou Saada.

The Arabs did not wait to learn the identity of the oncomers. With a parting volley as they dashed by the position which Tarzan and Abdul were holding, they plunged off along the road toward Sidi Aissa. A moment later Kadour ben Saden and his men dashed up.

The old sheik was much relieved to find that neither Tarzan nor Abdul had received a scratch. Not even had their horses been wounded. They sought out the two men who had fallen before Tarzan's shots, and, finding that both were dead, left them where they lay.

"Why did you not tell me that you contemplated ambushing those fellows?" asked the sheik in a hurt tone. "We might have had them all if the seven of us had stopped to meet them."

"Then it would have been useless to stop at all," replied Tarzan, "for had we simply ridden on toward Bou Saada they would have been upon us presently, and all could have been engaged. It was to prevent the transfer of my own quarrel to another's shoulders that Abdul and I stopped off to question them. Then there is your daughter – I could not be the cause of exposing her needlessly to the marksmanship of six men."

Kadour ben Saden shrugged his shoulders. He did not relish having been cheated out of a fight.

The little battle so close to Bou Saada had drawn out a company of soldiers. Tarzan and his party met them just outside the town. The officer in charge halted them to learn the significance of the shots.

"A handful of marauders," replied Kadour ben Saden. "They attacked two of our number who had dropped behind, but when we returned to them the fellows soon dispersed. They left two dead. None of my party was injured."

This seemed to satisfy the officer, and after taking the names of the party he marched his men on toward the scene of the skirmish to bring back the dead men for purposes of identification, if possible.

Two days later, Kadour ben Saden, with his daughter and followers, rode south through the pass below Bou Saada, bound for their home in the far wilderness. The sheik had urged Tarzan to accompany him, and the girl had added her entreaties to those of her father; but, though he could not explain it to them, Tarzan's duties loomed particularly large after the happenings of the past few days, so that he could not think of leaving his post for an instant. But he promised to come later if it lay within his power to do so, and they had to content themselves with that assurance.

During these two days Tarzan had spent practically all his time with Kadour ben Saden and his daughter. He was keenly interested in this race of stern and dignified warriors, and embraced the opportunity which their friendship offered to learn what he could of their lives and customs. He even commenced to acquire the rudiments of their language under the pleasant tutorage of the brown-eyed girl. It was with real regret that he saw them depart, and he sat his horse at the opening to the pass, as far as which he had accompanied them, gazing after the little party as long as he could catch a glimpse of them.

Here were people after his own heart! Their wild, rough lives, filled with danger and hardship, appealed to this half-savage man as nothing had appealed to him in the midst of the effeminate civilization of the great cities he had visited. Here was a life that excelled even that of the jungle, for here he might have the society of men – real men whom he could honor and respect, and yet be near to the wild nature that he loved. In his head revolved an idea that when he had completed his mission he would resign and return to live for the remainder of his life with the tribe of Kadour ben Saden.

Then he turned his horse's head and rode slowly back to Bou Saada.

The front of the Hotel du Petit Sahara, where Tarzan stopped in Bou Saada, is taken up with the bar, two dining-rooms, and the kitchens. Both of the dining-rooms open directly off the bar, and one of them is reserved for the use of the officers of the garrison. As you stand in the barroom you may look into either of the dining-rooms if you wish.

It was to the bar that Tarzan repaired after speeding Kadour ben Saden and his party on their way. It was yet early in the morning, for Kadour ben Saden had elected to ride far that day, so that it happened that when Tarzan returned there were guests still at breakfast.

As his casual glance wandered into the officers' dining-room, Tarzan saw something which brought a look of interest to his eyes. Lieutenant Gernois was sitting there, and as Tarzan looked a white-robed Arab approached and, bending, whispered a few words into the lieutenant's ear. Then he passed on out of the building through another door.

In itself the thing was nothing, but as the man had stooped to speak to the officer, Tarzan had caught sight of something which the accidental parting of the man's burnoose had revealed – he carried his left arm in a sling.

CHAPTER NINE

Numa "El Adrea"

On the same day that Kadour ben Saden rode south the diligence from the north brought Tarzan a letter from D'Arnot which had been forwarded from Sidi-bel-Abbes. It opened the old wound that Tarzan would have been glad to have forgotten; yet he was not sorry that D'Arnot had written, for one at least of his subjects could never cease to interest the ape-man. Here is the letter:

MY DEAR JEAN:

Since last I wrote you I have been across to London on a matter of business. I was there but three days. The very first day I came upon an old friend of yours – quite unexpectedly – in Henrietta Street. Now you never in the world would guess whom. None other than Mr. Samuel T. Philander. But it is true. I can see your look of incredulity. Nor is this all. He insisted that I return to the hotel with him, and there I found the others – Professor Archimedes Q. Porter, Miss Porter, and that enormous black woman, Miss Porter's maid – Esmeralda, you will recall. While I was there Clayton came in. They are to be married soon, or rather sooner, for I rather suspect that we shall receive announcements almost any day. On account of his father's death it is to be a very quiet affair – only blood relatives.

While I was alone with Mr. Philander the old fellow became rather confidential. Said Miss Porter had already postponed the wedding on three different occasions. He confided that it appeared to him that she was not particularly anxious to marry Clayton at all; but this time it seems that it is quite likely to go through.

Of course they all asked after you, but I respected your wishes in the matter of your true origin, and only spoke to them of your present affairs.

Miss Porter was especially interested in everything I had to say about you, and asked many questions. I am afraid I took a rather unchivalrous delight in picturing your desire and resolve to go back eventually to your native jungle. I was sorry afterward, for it did seem to cause her real anguish to contemplate the awful dangers to which you wished to return. "And yet," she said, "I do not know. There are more unhappy fates than the grim and terrible jungle presents to Monsieur Tarzan. At least his conscience will be free from remorse. And there are moments of quiet and restfulness by day, and vistas of exquisite beauty. You may find it strange that I should say it, who experienced such terrifying experiences in that frightful forest, yet at times I long to return, for I cannot but feel that the happiest moments of my life were spent there."

There was an expression of ineffable sadness on her face as she spoke, and I could not but feel that she knew that I knew her secret, and that this was her way of transmitting to you a last tender message from a heart that might still enshrine your memory, though its possessor belonged to another.

Clayton appeared nervous and ill at ease while you were the subject of conversation. He wore a worried and harassed expression. Yet he was very kindly in his expressions of interest in you. I wonder if he suspects the truth about you?

Tennington came in with Clayton. They are great friends, you know. He is about to set out upon one of his interminable cruises in that yacht of his, and was urging the entire party to accompany him. Tried to inveigle me into it, too. Is thinking of circumnavigating Africa this time. I told him that his precious toy would take him and some of his friends to the bottom of the ocean one of these days if he didn't get it out of his head that she was a liner or a battleship.

I returned to Paris day before yesterday, and yesterday I met the Count and Countess de Coude at the races. They inquired after you. De Coude really seems quite fond of you. Doesn't appear to harbor the least ill will. Olga is as beautiful as ever, but a trifle subdued. I imagine that she learned a lesson through her acquaintance with you that will serve her in good stead during the balance of her life. It is fortunate for her, and for De Coude as well, that it was you and not another man more sophisticated.

Had you really paid court to Olga's heart I am afraid that there would have been no hope for either of you.

She asked me to tell you that Nikolas had left France. She paid him twenty thousand francs to go away, and stay. She is congratulating herself that she got rid of him before he tried to carry out a threat he recently made her that he should kill you at the first opportunity. She said that she should hate to think that her brother's blood was on your hands, for she is very fond of you, and made no bones in saying so before the count. It never for a moment seemed to occur to her that there might be any possibility of any other outcome of a meeting between you and Nikolas. The count quite agreed with her in that. He added that it would take a regiment of Rokoffs to kill you. He has a most healthy respect for your prowess.

Have been ordered back to my ship. She sails from Havre in two days under sealed orders. If you will address me in her care, the letters will find me eventually. I shall write you as soon as another opportunity presents.

Your sincere friend,
PAUL D'ARNOT.

"I fear," mused Tarzan, half aloud, "that Olga has thrown away her twenty thousand francs."

He read over that part of D'Arnot's letter several times in which he had quoted from his conversation with Jane Porter. Tarzan derived a rather pathetic happiness from it, but it was better than no happiness at all.

The following three weeks were quite uneventful. On several occasions Tarzan saw the mysterious Arab, and once again he had been exchanging words with Lieutenant Gernois; but no amount of espionage or shadowing by Tarzan revealed the Arab's lodgings, the location of which Tarzan was anxious to ascertain.

Gernois, never cordial, had kept more than ever aloof from Tarzan since the episode in the dining-room of the hotel at Aumale. His attitude on the few occasions that they had been thrown together had been distinctly hostile.

That he might keep up the appearance of the character he was playing, Tarzan spent considerable time hunting in the vicinity of Bou Saada. He would spend entire days in the foothills, ostensibly searching for gazelle, but on the few occasions that he came close enough to any of the beautiful little animals to harm them he invariably allowed them to escape without so much as taking his rifle from its boot. The ape-man could see no sport in slaughtering the most harmless and defenseless of God's creatures for the mere pleasure of killing.

In fact, Tarzan had never killed for "pleasure," nor to him was there pleasure in killing. It was the joy of righteous battle that he loved –

the ecstasy of victory. And the keen and successful hunt for food in which he pitted his skill and craftiness against the skill and craftiness of another; but to come out of a town filled with food to shoot down a soft-eyed, pretty gazelle – ah, that was crueller than the deliberate and cold-blooded murder of a fellow man. Tarzan would have none of it, and so he hunted alone that none might discover the sham that he was practicing.

And once, probably because of the fact that he rode alone, he was like to have lost his life. He was riding slowly through a little ravine when a shot sounded close behind him, and a bullet passed through the cork helmet he wore. Although he turned at once and galloped rapidly to the top of the ravine, there was no sign of any enemy, nor did he see aught of another human being until he reached Bou Saada.

"Yes," he soliloquized, in recalling the occurrence, "Olga has indeed thrown away her twenty thousand francs."

That night he was Captain Gerard's guest at a little dinner.

"Your hunting has not been very fortunate?" questioned the officer.

"No," replied Tarzan; "the game hereabout is timid, nor do I care particularly about hunting game birds or antelope. I think I shall move on farther south, and have a try at some of your Algerian lions."

"Good!" exclaimed the captain. "We are marching toward Djelfa on the morrow. You shall have company that far at least. Lieutenant Gernois and I, with a hundred men, are ordered south to patrol a district in which the marauders are giving considerable trouble. Possibly we may have the pleasure of hunting the lion together – what say you?"

Tarzan was more than pleased, nor did he hesitate to say so; but the captain would have been astonished had he known the real reason of Tarzan's pleasure. Gernois was sitting opposite the ape-man. He did not seem so pleased with his captain's invitation.

"You will find lion hunting more exciting than gazelle shooting," remarked Captain Gerard, "and more dangerous."

"Even gazelle shooting has its dangers," replied Tarzan. "Especially when one goes alone. I found it so today. I also found that while the gazelle is the most timid of animals, it is not the most cowardly."

He let his glance rest only casually upon Gernois after he had spoken, for he did not wish the man to know that he was under suspicion, or surveillance, no matter what he might think. The effect of his remark upon him, however, might tend to prove his connection with, or knowledge of, certain recent happenings. Tarzan saw a dull red creep up from beneath Gernois' collar. He was satisfied, and quickly changed the subject.

When the column rode south from Bou Saada the next morning there were half a dozen Arabs bringing up the rear.

"They are not attached to the command," replied Gerard in response to Tarzan's query. "They merely accompany us on the road for companionship."

Tarzan had learned enough about Arab character since he had been in Algeria to know that this was no real motive, for the Arab is never overfond of the companionship of strangers, and especially of French soldiers. So his suspicions were aroused, and he decided to keep a sharp eye on the little party that trailed behind the column at a distance of about a quarter of a mile. But they did not come close enough even during the halts to enable him to obtain a close scrutiny of them.

He had long been convinced that there were hired assassins on his trail, nor was he in great doubt but that Rokoff was at the bottom of the plot. Whether it was to be revenge for the several occasions in the past that Tarzan had defeated the Russian's purposes and humiliated him, or was in some way connected with his mission in the Gernois affair, he could not determine. If the latter, and it seemed probable since the evidence he had had that Gernois suspected him, then he had two rather powerful enemies to contend with, for there would be many opportunities in the wilds of Algeria, for which they were bound, to dispatch a suspected enemy quietly and without attracting suspicion.

After camping at Djelfa for two days the column moved to the southwest, from whence word had come that the marauders were operating against the tribes whose DOUARS were situated at the foot of the mountains.

The little band of Arabs who had accompanied them from Bou Saada had disappeared suddenly the very night that orders had been given to prepare for the morrow's march from Djelfa. Tarzan made casual inquiries among the men, but none could tell him why they had left, or in what direction they had gone. He did not like the looks of it, especially in view of the fact that he had seen Gernois in conversation with one of them some half hour after Captain Gerard had issued his instructions relative to the new move. Only Gernois and Tarzan knew the direction of the proposed march. All the soldiers knew was that they were to be prepared to break camp early the next morning. Tarzan wondered if Gernois could have revealed their destination to the Arabs.

Late that afternoon they went into camp at a little oasis in which was the DOUAR of a sheik whose flocks were being stolen, and whose herdsmen were being killed. The Arabs came out of their goatskin tents, and surrounded the soldiers, asking many questions in the native tongue, for the soldiers were themselves natives. Tarzan, who, by this time, with the assistance of Abdul, had picked up quite a smattering of Arab, questioned one of the younger men who had accompanied the sheik while the latter paid his respects to Captain Gerard.

No, he had seen no party of six horsemen riding from the direction of Djelfa. There were other oases scattered about – possibly they had been journeying to one of these. Then there were the marauders in the mountains above – they often rode north to Bou Saada in small parties, and even as far as Aumale and Bouira. It might indeed have been a few marauders returning to the band from a pleasure trip to one of these cities.

Early the next morning Captain Gerard split his command in two, giving Lieutenant Gernois command of one party, while he headed the other. They were to scour the mountains upon opposite sides of the plain.

"And with which detachment will Monsieur Tarzan ride?" asked the captain. "Or maybe it is that monsieur does not care to hunt marauders?"

"Oh, I shall be delighted to go," Tarzan hastened to explain. He was wondering what excuse he could make to accompany Gernois. His embarrassment was short-lived, and was relieved from a most unexpected source. It was Gernois himself who spoke.

"If my captain will forego the pleasure of Monsieur Tarzan's company for this once, I shall esteem it an honor indeed to have monsieur ride with me today," he said, nor was his tone lacking in cordiality. In fact, Tarzan imagined that he had overdone it a trifle, but, even so, he was both astounded and pleased, hastening to express his delight at the arrangement.

And so it was that Lieutenant Gernois and Tarzan rode off side by side at the head of the little detachment of SPAHIS. Gernois' cordiality was short-lived. No sooner had they ridden out of sight of Captain Gerard and his men than he lapsed once more into his accustomed taciturnity. As they advanced the ground became rougher. Steadily it ascended toward the mountains, into which they filed through a narrow canon close to noon. By the side of a little rivulet Gernois called the midday halt. Here the men prepared and ate their frugal meal, and refilled their canteens.

After an hour's rest they advanced again along the canon, until they presently came to a little valley, from which several rocky gorges diverged. Here they halted, while Gernois minutely examined the surrounding heights from the center of the depression.

"We shall separate here," he said, "several riding into each of these gorges," and then he commenced to detail his various squads and issue instructions to the non-commissioned officers who were to command them. When he had done he turned to Tarzan. "Monsieur will be so good as to remain here until we return."

Tarzan demurred, but the officer cut him short. "There may be fighting for one of these sections," he said, "and troops cannot be embarrassed by civilian noncombatants during action."

"But, my dear lieutenant," expostulated Tarzan, "I am most ready and willing to place myself under command of yourself or any of your sergeants or corporals, and to fight in the ranks as they direct. It is what I came for."

"I should be glad to think so," retorted Gernois, with a sneer he made no attempt to disguise. Then shortly: "You are under my orders, and they are that you remain here until we return. Let that end the matter," and he turned and spurred away at the head of his men. A moment later Tarzan found himself alone in the midst of a desolate mountain fastness.

The sun was hot, so he sought the shelter of a nearby tree, where he tethered his horse, and sat down upon the ground to smoke. Inwardly he swore at Gernois for the trick he had played upon him. A mean little revenge, thought Tarzan, and then suddenly it occurred to him that the man would not be such a fool as to antagonize him through a trivial annoyance of so petty a description. There must be something deeper than this behind it. With the thought he arose and removed his rifle from its boot. He looked to its loads and saw that the magazine was full. Then he inspected his revolver. After this preliminary precaution he scanned the surrounding heights and the mouths of the several gorges – he was determined that he should not be caught napping.

The sun sank lower and lower, yet there was no sign of returning SPAHIS. At last the valley was submerged in shadow Tarzan was too proud to go back to camp until he had given the detachment ample time to return to the valley, which he thought was to have been their rendezvous. With the closing in of night he felt safer from attack, for he was at home in the dark. He knew that none might approach him so cautiously as to elude those alert and sensitive ears of his; then there were his eyes, too, for he could see well at night; and his nose, if they came toward him from up-wind, would apprise him of the approach of an enemy while they were still a great way off.

So he felt that he was in little danger, and thus lulled to a sense of security he fell asleep, with his back against the tree.

He must have slept for several hours, for when he was suddenly awakened by the frightened snorting and plunging of his horse the moon was shining full upon the little valley, and there, not ten paces before him, stood the grim cause of the terror of his mount.

Superb, majestic, his graceful tail extended and quivering, and his two eyes of fire riveted full upon his prey, stood Numa EL ADREA, the black lion. A little thrill of joy tingled through Tarzan's nerves. It was like meeting an old friend after years of separation. For a moment he sat rigid to enjoy the magnificent spectacle of this lord of the wilderness.

But now Numa was crouching for the spring. Very slowly Tarzan raised his gun to his shoulder. He had never killed a large animal with a gun in all his life – heretofore he had depended upon his spear, his poisoned arrows, his rope, his knife, or his bare hands. Instinctively he wished that he had his arrows and his knife – he would have felt surer with them.

Numa was lying quite flat upon the ground now, presenting only his head. Tarzan would have preferred to fire a little from one side, for he knew what terrific damage the lion could do if he lived two minutes, or even a minute after he was hit. The horse stood trembling in terror at Tarzan's back. The ape-man took a cautious step to one side – Numa but followed him with his eyes. Another step he took, and then another. Numa had not moved. Now he could aim at a point between the eye and the ear.

His finger tightened upon the trigger, and as he fired Numa sprang. At the same instant the terrified horse made a last frantic effort to escape – the tether parted, and he went careening down the canon toward the desert.

No ordinary man could have escaped those frightful claws when Numa sprang from so short a distance, but Tarzan was no ordinary man. From earliest childhood his muscles had been trained by the fierce exigencies of his existence to act with the rapidity of thought. As quick as was EL ADREA, Tarzan of the Apes was quicker, and so the great beast crashed against a tree where he had expected to feel the soft flesh of man, while Tarzan, a couple of paces to the right, pumped another bullet into him that brought him clawing and roaring to his side.

Twice more Tarzan fired in quick succession, and then EL ADREA lay still and roared no more. It was no longer Monsieur Jean Tarzan; it was Tarzan of the Apes that put a savage foot upon the body of his savage kill, and, raising his face to the full moon, lifted his mighty voice in the weird and terrible challenge of his kind – a bull ape had made his kill. And the wild things in the wild mountains stopped in their hunting, and trembled at this new and awful voice, while down in the desert the children of the wilderness came out of their goatskin tents and looked toward the mountains, wondering what new and savage scourge had come to devastate their flocks.

A half mile from the valley in which Tarzan stood, a score of white-robed figures, bearing long, wicked-looking guns, halted at the sound, and looked at one another with questioning eyes. But presently, as it was not repeated, they took up their silent, stealthy way toward the valley.

Tarzan was now confident that Gernois had no intention of returning for him, but he could not fathom the object that had prompted the officer to desert him, yet leave him free to return to camp. His horse gone, he decided that it would be foolish to remain longer in the mountains, so he set out toward the desert.

He had scarcely entered the confines of the canon when the first of the white-robed figures emerged into the valley upon the opposite side. For a moment they scanned the little depression from behind sheltering bowlders, but when they had satisfied themselves that it was empty they advanced across it. Beneath the tree at one side they came upon the body of EL ADREA. With muttered exclamations they crowded about it. Then, a moment later, they hurried down the canon which Tarzan was threading a brief distance in advance of them. They moved cautiously and in silence, taking advantage of shelter, as men do who are stalking man.

CHAPTER TEN

Through the Valley of the Shadow

As Tarzan walked down the wild canon beneath the brilliant African moon the call of the jungle was strong upon him. The solitude and the savage freedom filled his heart with life and buoyancy. Again he was Tarzan of the Apes – every sense alert against the chance of surprise by some jungle enemy – yet treading lightly and with head erect, in proud consciousness of his might.

The nocturnal sounds of the mountains were new to him, yet they fell upon his ears like the soft voice of a half-forgotten love. Many he intuitively sensed – ah, there was one that was familiar indeed; the distant coughing of Sheeta, the leopard; but there was a strange note in the final wail which made him doubt. It was a panther he heard.

Presently a new sound – a soft, stealthy sound – obtruded itself among the others. No human ears other than the ape-man's would have detected it. At first he did not translate it, but finally he realized that it came from the bare feet of a number of human beings. They were behind him, and they were coming toward him quietly. He was being stalked.

In a flash he knew why he had been left in that little valley by Gernois; but there had been a hitch in the arrangements – the men had come too late. Closer and closer came the footsteps. Tarzan halted and faced them, his rifle ready in his hand. Now he caught a fleeting glimpse of a white burnoose. He called aloud in French, asking what they would of him. His reply was the flash of a long gun, and with the sound of the shot Tarzan of the Apes plunged forward upon his face.

The Arabs did not rush out immediately; instead, they waited to be sure that their victim did not rise. Then they came rapidly from their concealment, and bent over him. It was soon apparent that he was not dead. One of the men put the muzzle of his gun to the back of Tarzan's head to finish him, but another waved him aside. "If we bring him alive the reward is to be greater," explained the latter. So they bound his hands and feet, and, picking him up, placed him on the shoulders of four of their number. Then the march was resumed toward the desert. When they had come out of the mountains they turned toward the south, and about daylight came to the spot where their horses stood in care of two of their number.

From here on their progress was more rapid. Tarzan, who had regained consciousness, was tied to a spare horse, which they evidently had brought for the purpose. His wound was but a slight scratch, which had furrowed the flesh across his temple. It had stopped bleeding, but the dried and clotted blood smeared his face and clothing. He had said no word since he had fallen into the hands of these Arabs, nor had they addressed him other than to issue a few brief commands to him when the horses had been reached.

For six hours they rode rapidly across the burning desert, avoiding the oases near which their way led. About noon they came to a DOUAR of about twenty tents. Here they halted, and as one of the Arabs was releasing the alfa-grass ropes which bound him to his mount they were surrounded by a mob of men, women, and children. Many of the tribe, and more especially the women, appeared to take delight in heaping insults upon the prisoner, and some had even gone so far as to throw stones at him and strike him with sticks, when an old sheik appeared and drove them away.

"Ali-ben-Ahmed tells me," he said, "that this man sat alone in the mountains and slew EL ADREA. What the business of the stranger who sent us after him may be, I know not, and what he may do with this man when we turn him over to him, I care not; but the prisoner is a brave man, and while he is in our hands he shall be treated with the respect that be due one who hunts THE LORD WITH THE LARGE HEAD alone and by night – and slays him."

Tarzan had heard of the respect in which Arabs held a lion-killer, and he was not sorry that chance had played into his hands thus favorably to relieve him of the petty tortures of the tribe. Shortly after this he was taken to a goat-skin tent upon the upper side of the DOUAR. There he was fed, and then, securely bound, was left lying on a piece of native carpet, alone in the tent.

He could see a guard sitting before the door of his frail prison, but when he attempted to force the stout bonds that held him he realized that any extra precaution on the part of his captors was quite unnecessary; not even his giant muscles could part those numerous strands.

Just before dusk several men approached the tent where he lay, and entered it. All were in Arab dress, but presently one of the number advanced to Tarzan's side, and as he let the folds of cloth that had hidden the lower half of his face fall away the ape-man saw the malevolent features of Nikolas Rokoff. There was a nasty smile on the bearded lips. "Ah, Monsieur Tarzan," he said, "this is indeed a pleasure. But why do you not rise and greet your guest?" Then, with an ugly oath, "Get up, you dog!" and, drawing back his booted foot, he kicked Tarzan heavily in the side. "And here is another, and another, and another," he continued, as he kicked Tarzan about the face and side. "One for each of the injuries you have done me."

The ape-man made no reply – he did not even deign to look upon the Russian again after the first glance of recognition. Finally the sheik, who had been standing a mute and frowning witness of the cowardly attack, intervened.

"Stop!" he commanded. "Kill him if you will, but I will see no brave man subjected to such indignities in my presence. I have half a mind to turn him loose, that I may see how long you would kick him then."

This threat put a sudden end to Rokoff's brutality, for he had no craving to see Tarzan loosed from his bonds while he was within reach of those powerful hands.

"Very well," he replied to the Arab; "I shall kill him presently."

"Not within the precincts of my DOUAR," returned the sheik. "When he leaves here he leaves alive. What you do with him in the desert is none of my concern, but I shall not have the blood of a Frenchman on the hands of my tribe on account of another man's quarrel – they would send soldiers here and kill many of my people, and burn our tents and drive away our flocks."

"As you say," growled Rokoff. "I'll take him out into the desert below the DOUAR, and dispatch him."

"You will take him a day's ride from my country," said the sheik, firmly, "and some of my children shall follow you to see that you do not disobey me – otherwise there may be two dead Frenchmen in the desert."

Rokoff shrugged. "Then I shall have to wait until the morrow – it is already dark."

"As you will," said the sheik. "But by an hour after dawn you must be gone from my DOUAR. I have little liking for unbelievers, and none at all for a coward."

Rokoff would have made some kind of retort, but he checked himself, for he realized that it would require but little excuse for the old man to turn upon him. Together they left the tent. At the door Rokoff could not resist the temptation to turn and fling a parting taunt at Tarzan. "Sleep well, monsieur," he said, "and do not forget to pray well, for when you die tomorrow it will be in such agony that you will be unable to pray for blaspheming."

No one had bothered to bring Tarzan either food or water since noon, and consequently he suffered considerably from thirst. He wondered if it would be worth while to ask his guard for water, but after making two or three requests without receiving any response, he decided that it would not.

Far up in the mountains he heard a lion roar. How much safer one was, he soliloquized, in the haunts of wild beasts than in the haunts of men. Never in all his jungle life had he been more relentlessly tracked down than in the past few months of his experience among civilized men. Never had he been any nearer death.

Again the lion roared. It sounded a little nearer. Tarzan felt the old, wild impulse to reply with the challenge of his kind. His kind? He had almost forgotten that he was a man and not an ape. He tugged at his bonds. God, if he could but get them near those strong teeth of his. He felt a wild wave of madness sweep over him as his efforts to regain his liberty met with failure.

Numa was roaring almost continually now. It was quite evident that he was coming down into the desert to hunt. It was the roar of a hungry lion. Tarzan envied him, for he was free. No one would tie him with ropes and slaughter him like a sheep. It was that which galled the ape-man. He did not fear to die, no – it was the humiliation of defeat before death, without even a chance to battle for his life.

It must be near midnight, thought Tarzan. He had several hours to live. Possibly he would yet find a way to take Rokoff with him on the long journey. He could hear the savage lord of the desert quite close by now. Possibly he sought his meat from among the penned animals within the DOUAR.

For a long time silence reigned, then Tarzan's trained ears caught the sound of a stealthily moving body. It came from the side of the tent nearest the mountains – the back. Nearer and nearer it came. He waited, listening intently, for it to pass. For a time there was silence without, such a terrible silence that Tarzan was surprised that he did not hear the breathing of the animal he felt sure must be crouching close to the back wall of his tent.

There! It is moving again. Closer it creeps. Tarzan turns his head in the direction of the sound. It is very dark within the tent. Slowly the back rises from the ground, forced up by the head and shoulders of a body that looks all black in the semi-darkness. Beyond is a faint glimpse of the dimly starlit desert. A grim smile plays about Tarzan's lips. At least Rokoff will be cheated. How mad he will be! And death will be more merciful than he could have hoped for at the hands of the Russian.

Now the back of the tent drops into place, and all is darkness again – whatever it is is inside the tent with him. He hears it creeping close to him – now it is beside him. He closes his eyes and waits for the mighty paw. Upon his upturned face falls the gentle touch of a soft hand groping in the dark, and then a girl's voice in a scarcely audible whisper pronounces his name.

"Yes, it is I," he whispers in reply. "But in the name of Heaven who are you?"

"The Ouled-Nail of Sisi Aissa," came the answer. While she spoke Tarzan could feel her working about his bonds. Occasionally the cold steel of a knife touched his flesh. A moment later he was free.

"Come!" she whispered.

On hands and knees he followed her out of the tent by the way she had come. She continued crawling thus flat to the ground until she reached a little patch of shrub. There she halted until he gained her side. For a moment he looked at her before he spoke.

"I cannot understand," he said at last. "Why are you here? How did you know that I was a prisoner in that tent? How does it happen that it is you who have saved me?"

She smiled. "I have come a long way tonight," she said, "and we have a long way to go before we shall be out of danger. Come; I shall tell you all about it as we go."

Together they rose and set off across the desert in the direction of the mountains.

"I was not quite sure that I should ever reach you," she said at last. "EL ADREA is abroad tonight, and after I left the horses I think he winded me and was following – I was terribly frightened."

"What a brave girl," he said. "And you ran all that risk for a stranger – an alien – an unbeliever?"

She drew herself up very proudly.

"I am the daughter of the Sheik Kabour ben Saden," she answered. "I should be no fit daughter of his if I would not risk my life to save that of the man who saved mine while he yet thought that I was but a common Ouled-Nail."

"Nevertheless," he insisted, "you are a very brave girl. But how did you know that I was a prisoner back there?"

"Achmet-din-Taieb, who is my cousin on my father's side, was visiting some friends who belong to the tribe that captured you. He was at the DOUAR when you were brought in. When he reached home he was telling us about the big Frenchman who had been captured by Ali-ben-Ahmed for another Frenchman who wished to kill him. From the description I knew that it must be you. My father was away. I tried to persuade some of the men to come and save you, but they would not do it, saying: 'Let the unbelievers kill one another if they wish. It is none of our affair, and if we go and interfere with Ali-ben-Ahmed's plans we shall only stir up a fight with our own people.'

"So when it was dark I came alone, riding one horse and leading another for you. They are tethered not far from here. By morning we shall be within my father's DOUAR. He should be there himself by now – then let them come and try to take Kadour ben Saden's friend."

For a few moments they walked on in silence.

"We should be near the horses," she said. "It is strange that I do not see them here."

Then a moment later she stopped, with a little cry of consternation.

"They are gone!" she exclaimed. "It is here that I tethered them."

Tarzan stooped to examine the ground. He found that a large shrub had been torn up by the roots. Then he found something else. There was a wry smile on his face as he rose and turned toward the girl.

"EL ADREA has been here. From the signs, though, I rather think that his prey escaped him. With a little start they would be safe enough from him in the open."

There was nothing to do but continue on foot. The way led them across a low spur of the mountains, but the girl knew the trail as well as she did her mother's face. They walked in easy, swinging strides, Tarzan keeping a hand's breadth behind the girl's shoulder, that she might set the pace, and thus be less fatigued. As they walked they talked, occasionally stopping to listen for sounds of pursuit.

It was now a beautiful, moonlit night. The air was crisp and invigorating. Behind them lay the interminable vista of the desert, dotted here and there with an occasional oasis. The date palms of the little fertile spot they had just left, and the circle of goatskin tents, stood out in sharp relief against the yellow sand – a phantom paradise upon a phantom sea. Before them rose the grim and silent mountains. Tarzan's blood leaped in his veins. This was life! He looked down upon the girl beside him – a daughter of the desert walking across the face of a dead world with a son of the jungle. He smiled at thc thought. He wished that he had had a sister, and that she had been like this girl. What a bully chum she would have been!

They had entered the mountains now, and were progressing more slowly, for the trail was steeper and very rocky.

For a few minutes they had been silent. The girl was wondering if they would reach her father's DOUAR before the pursuit had overtaken them. Tarzan was wishing that they might walk on thus forever. If the girl were only a man they might. He longed for a friend who loved the same wild life that he loved. He had learned to crave companionship, but it was his misfortune that most of the men he knew preferred immaculate linen and their clubs to nakedness and the jungle. It was, of course, difficult to understand, yet it was very evident that they did.

The two had just turned a projecting rock around which the trail ran when they were brought to a sudden stop. There, before them, directly in the middle of the path, stood Numa, EL ADREA, the black lion. His green eyes looked very wicked, and he bared his teeth, and lashed his bay black sides with his angry tail. Then he roared – the fearsome, terror-inspiring roar of the hungry lion which is also angry.

"Your knife," said Tarzan to the girl, extending his hand. She slipped the hilt of the weapon into his waiting palm. As his fingers closed upon it he drew her back and pushed her behind him. "Walk back to the desert as rapidly as you can. If you hear me call you will know that all is well, and you may return."

"It is useless," she replied, resignedly. "This is the end."

"Do as I tell you," he commanded. "Quickly! He is about to charge." The girl dropped back a few paces, where she stood watching for the terrible sight that she knew she should soon witness.

The lion was advancing slowly toward Tarzan, his nose to the ground, like a challenging bull, his tail extended now and quivering as though with intense excitement.

The ape-man stood, half crouching, the long Arab knife glistening in the moonlight. Behind him the tense figure of the girl, motionless as a carven statue. She leaned slightly forward, her lips parted, her eyes wide. Her only conscious thought was wonder at the bravery of the man who dared face with a puny knife the lord with the large head. A man of her own blood would have knelt in prayer and gone down beneath those awful fangs without resistance. In either case the result would be the same – it was inevitable; but she could not repress a thrill of admiration as her eyes rested upon the heroic figure before her. Not a tremor in the whole giant frame – his attitude as menacing and defiant as that of EL ADREA himself.

The lion was quite close to him now – but a few paces intervened – he crouched, and then, with a deafening roar, he sprang.

CHAPTER ELEVEN

John Caldwell, London

As Numa El Adrea launched himself with widespread paws and bared fangs he looked to find this puny man as easy prey as the score who had gone down beneath him in the past. To him man was a clumsy, slow-moving, defenseless creature – he had little respect for him.

But this time he found that he was pitted against a creature as agile and as quick as himself. When his mighty frame struck the spot where the man had been he was no longer there.

The watching girl was transfixed by astonishment at the ease with which the crouching man eluded the great paws. And now, O Allah! He had rushed in behind EL ADREA'S shoulder even before the beast could turn, and had grasped him by the mane. The lion reared upon his hind legs like a horse – Tarzan had known that he would do this, and he was ready. A giant arm encircled the black-maned throat, and once, twice, a dozen times a sharp blade darted in and out of the bay-black side behind the left shoulder.

Frantic were the leaps of Numa – awful his roars of rage and pain; but the giant upon his back could not be dislodged or brought within reach of fangs or talons in the brief interval of life that remained to the lord with the large head. He was quite dead when Tarzan of the Apes released his hold and arose. Then the daughter of the desert witnessed a thing that terrified her even more than had the presence of EL ADREA. The man placed a foot upon the carcass of his kill, and, with his handsome face raised toward the full moon, gave voice to the most frightful cry that ever had smote upon her ears.

With a little cry of fear she shrank away from him – she thought that the fearful strain of the encounter had driven him mad. As the last note of that fiendish challenge died out in the diminishing echoes of the distance the man dropped his eyes until they rested upon the girl.

Instantly his face was lighted by the kindly smile that was ample assurance of his sanity, and the girl breathed freely once again, smiling in response.

"What manner of man are you?" she asked. "The thing you have done is unheard of. Even now I cannot believe that it is possible for a lone man armed only with a knife to have fought hand to hand with EL ADREA and conquered him, unscathed – to have conquered him at all. And that cry – it was not human. Why did you do that?"

Tarzan flushed. "It is because I forget," he said, "sometimes, that I am a civilized man. When I kill it must be that I am another creature." He did not try to explain further, for it always seemed to him that a woman must look with loathing upon one who was yet so nearly a beast.

Together they continued their journey. The sun was an hour high when they came out into the desert again beyond the mountains. Beside a little rivulet they found the girl's horses grazing. They had come this far on their way home, and with the cause of their fear no longer present had stopped to feed.

With little trouble Tarzan and the girl caught them, and, mounting, rode out into the desert toward the DOUAR of Sheik Kadour ben Saden.

No sign of pursuit developed, and they came in safety about nine o'clock to their destination. The sheik had but just returned. He was frantic with grief at the absence of his daughter, whom he thought had been again abducted by the marauders. With fifty men he was already mounted to go in search of her when the two rode into the DOUAR.

His joy at the safe return of his daughter was only equaled by his gratitude to Tarzan for bringing her safely to him through the dangers of the night, and his thankfulness that she had been in time to save the man who had once saved her.

No honor that Kadour ben Saden could heap upon the ape-man in acknowledgment of his esteem and friendship was neglected. When the girl had recited the story of the slaying of EL ADREA Tarzan was surrounded by a mob of worshiping Arabs – it was a sure road to their admiration and respect.

The old sheik insisted that Tarzan remain indefinitely as his guest. He even wished to adopt him as a member of the tribe, and there was for some time a half-formed resolution in the ape-man's mind to accept and remain forever with these wild people, whom he understood and who seemed to understand him. His friendship and liking for the girl were potent factors in urging him toward an affirmative decision.

Had she been a man, he argued, he should not have hesitated, for it would have meant a friend after his own heart, with whom he could ride and hunt at will; but as it was they would be hedged by the conventionalities that are even more strictly observed by the wild nomads of the desert than by their more civilized brothers and sisters. And in a little while she would be married to one of these swarthy warriors, and there would be an end to their friendship. So he decided against the sheik's proposal, though he remained a week as his guest.

When he left, Kadour ben Saden and fifty white-robed warriors rode with him to Bou Saada. While they were mounting in the DOUAR of Kadour ben Saden the morning of their departure, the girl came to bid farewell to Tarzan.

"I have prayed that you would remain with us," she said simply, as he leaned from his saddle to clasp her hand in farewell, "and now I shall pray that you will return." There was an expression of wistfulness in her beautiful eyes, and a pathetic droop at the corners of her mouth. Tarzan was touched.

"Who knows?" and then he turned and rode after the departing Arabs.

Outside Bou Saada he bade Kadour ben Saden and his men good-by, for there were reasons which made him wish to make his entry into the town as secret as possible, and when he had explained them to the sheik the latter concurred in his decision. The Arabs were to enter Bou Saada ahead of him, saying nothing as to his presence with them. Later Tarzan would come in alone, and go directly to an obscure native inn.

Thus, making his entrance after dark, as he did, he was not seen by any one who knew him, and reached the inn unobserved. After dining with Kadour ben Saden as his guest, he went to his former hotel by a roundabout way, and, coming in by a rear entrance, sought the proprietor, who seemed much surprised to see him alive.

Yes, there was mail for monsieur; he would fetch it. No, he would mention monsieur's return to no one. Presently he returned with a packet of letters. One was an order from his superior to lay off on his present work, and hasten to Cape Town by the first steamer he could get. His further instructions would be awaiting him there in the hands of another agent whose name and address were given. That was all – brief but explicit. Tarzan arranged to leave Bou Saada early the next morning. Then he started for the garrison to see Captain Gerard, whom the hotel man had told him had returned with his detachment the previous day.

He found the officer in his quarters. He was filled with surprise and pleasure at seeing Tarzan alive and well.

"When Lieutenant Gernois returned and reported that he had not found you at the spot that you had chosen to remain while the detachment was scouting, I was filled with alarm. We searched the mountain for days. Then came word that you had been killed and eaten by a lion. As proof your gun was brought to us. Your horse had returned to camp the second day after your disappearance. We could not doubt. Lieutenant Gernois was grief-stricken – he took all the blame upon himself. It was he who insisted on carrying on the search himself. It was he who found the Arab with your gun. He will be delighted to know that you are safe."

"Doubtless," said Tarzan, with a grim smile.

"He is down in the town now, or I should send for him," continued Captain Gerard. "I shall tell him as soon as he returns."

Tarzan let the officer think that he had been lost, wandering finally into the DOUAR of Kadour ben Saden, who had escorted him back to Bou Saada. As soon as possible he bade the good officer adieu, and hastened back into the town. At the native inn he had learned through Kadour ben Saden a piece of interesting information. It told of a black-bearded white man who went always disguised as an Arab. For a time he had nursed a broken wrist. More recently he had been away from Bou Saada, but now he was back, and Tarzan knew his place of concealment. It was for there he headed.

Through narrow, stinking alleys, black as Erebus, he groped, and then up a rickety stairway, at the end of which was a closed door and a tiny, unglazed window. The window was high under the low eaves of the mud building. Tarzan could just reach the sill. He raised himself slowly until his eyes topped it. The room within was lighted, and at a table sat Rokoff and Gernois. Gernois was speaking.

"Rokoff, you are a devil!" he was saying. "You have hounded me until I have lost the last shred of my honor. You have driven me to murder, for the blood of that man Tarzan is on my hands. If it were not that that other devil's spawn, Paulvitch, still knew my secret, I should kill you here tonight with my bare hands."

Rokoff laughed. "You would not do that, my dear lieutenant," he said. "The moment I am reported dead by assassination that dear Alexis will forward to the minister of war full proof of the affair you so ardently long to conceal; and, further, will charge you with my murder. Come, be sensible. I am your best friend. Have I not protected your honor as though it were my own?"

Gernois sneered, and spat out an oath.

"Just one more little payment," continued Rokoff, "and the papers I wish, and you have my word of honor that I shall never ask another cent from you, or further information."

"And a good reason why," growled Gernois. "What you ask will take my last cent, and the only valuable military secret I hold. You ought to be paying me for the information, instead of taking both it and money, too."

"I am paying you by keeping a still tongue in my head," retorted Rokoff. "But let's have done. Will you, or will you not? I give you three minutes to decide. If you are not agreeable I shall send a note to your commandant tonight that will end in the degradation that Dreyfus suffered – the only difference being that he did not deserve it."

For a moment Gernois sat with bowed head. At length he arose. He drew two pieces of paper from his blouse.

"Here," he said hopelessly. "I had them ready, for I knew that there could be but one outcome." He held them toward the Russian.

Rokoff's cruel face lighted in malignant gloating. He seized the bits of paper.

"You have done well, Gernois," he said. "I shall not trouble you again – unless you happen to accumulate some more money or information," and he grinned.

"You never shall again, you dog!" hissed Gernois. "The next time I shall kill you. I came near doing it tonight. For an hour I sat with these two pieces of paper on my table before me ere I came here – beside them lay my loaded revolver. I was trying to decide which I should bring. Next time the choice shall be easier, for I already have decided. You had a close call tonight, Rokoff; do not tempt fate a second time."

Then Gernois rose to leave. Tarzan barely had time to drop to the landing and shrink back into the shadows on the far side of the door. Even then he scarcely hoped to elude detection. The landing was very small, and though he flattened himself against the wall at its far edge he was scarcely more than a foot from the doorway. Almost immediately it opened, and Gernois stepped out. Rokoff was behind him. Neither spoke. Gernois had taken perhaps three steps down the stairway when he halted and half turned, as though to retrace his steps.

Tarzan knew that discovery would be inevitable. Rokoff still stood on the threshold a foot from him, but he was looking in the opposite direction, toward Gernois. Then the officer evidently reconsidered his decision, and resumed his downward course. Tarzan could hear Rokoff's sigh of relief. A moment later the Russian went back into the room and closed the door.

Tarzan waited until Gernois had had time to get well out of hearing, then he pushed open the door and stepped into the room. He was on top of Rokoff before the man could rise from the chair where he sat scanning the paper Gernois had given him. As his eyes turned and fell upon the ape-man's face his own went livid.

"You!" he gasped.

"I," replied Tarzan.

"What do you want?" whispered Rokoff, for the look in the ape-man's eyes frightened him. "Have you come to kill me? You do not dare. They would guillotine you. You do not dare kill me."

"I dare kill you, Rokoff," replied Tarzan, "for no one knows that you are here or that I am here, and Paulvitch would tell them that it was Gernois. I heard you tell Gernois so. But that would not influence me, Rokoff. I would not care who knew that I had killed you; the pleasure of killing you would more than compensate for any punishment they might inflict upon me. You are the most despicable cur of a coward, Rokoff, I have ever heard of. You should be killed. I should love to kill you," and Tarzan approached closer to the man.

Rokoff's nerves were keyed to the breaking point. With a shriek he sprang toward an adjoining room, but the ape-man was upon his back while his leap was yet but half completed. Iron fingers sought his throat – the great coward squealed like a stuck pig, until Tarzan had shut off his wind. Then the ape-man dragged him to his feet, still choking him. The Russian struggled futilely – he was like a babe in the mighty grasp of Tarzan of the Apes.

Tarzan sat him in a chair, and long before there was danger of the man's dying he released his hold upon his throat. When the Russian's coughing spell had abated Tarzan spoke to him again.

"I have given you a taste of the suffering of death," he said. "But I shall not kill – this time. I am sparing you solely for the sake of a very good woman whose great misfortune it was to have been born of the same woman who gave birth to you. But I shall spare you only this once on her account. Should I ever learn that you have again annoyed her or her husband – should you ever annoy me again – should I hear that you have returned to France or to any French possession, I shall make it my sole business to hunt you down and complete the choking I commenced tonight." Then he turned to the table, on which the two pieces of paper still lay. As he picked them up Rokoff gasped in horror.

Tarzan examined both the check and the other. He was amazed at the information the latter contained. Rokoff had partially read it, but Tarzan knew that no one could remember the salient facts and figures it held which made it of real value to an enemy of France.

"These will interest the chief of staff," he said, as he slipped them into his pocket. Rokoff groaned. He did not dare curse aloud.

The next morning Tarzan rode north on his way to Bouira and Algiers. As he had ridden past the hotel Lieutenant Gernois was standing on the veranda. As his eyes discovered Tarzan he went white as chalk. The ape-man would have been glad had the meeting not occurred, but he could not avoid it. He saluted the officer as he rode past. Mechanically Gernois returned the salute, but those terrible, wide eyes followed the horseman, expressionless except for horror. It was as though a dead man looked upon a ghost.

At Sidi Aissa Tarzan met a French officer with whom he had become acquainted on the occasion of his recent sojourn in the town.

"You left Bou Saada early?" questioned the officer. "Then you have not heard about poor Gernois."

"He was the last man I saw as I rode away," replied Tarzan. "What about him?"

"He is dead. He shot himself about eight o'clock this morning."

Two days later Tarzan reached Algiers. There he found that he would have a two days' wait before he could catch a ship bound for Cape Town. He occupied his time in writing out a full report of his mission. The secret papers he had taken from Rokoff he did not inclose, for he did not dare trust them out of his own possession until he had been authorized to turn them over to another agent, or himself return to Paris with them.

As Tarzan boarded his ship after what seemed a most tedious wait to him, two men watched him from an upper deck. Both were fashionably dressed and smooth shaven. The taller of the two had sandy hair, but his eyebrows were very black. Later in the day they chanced to meet Tarzan on deck, but as one hurriedly called his companion's attention to something at sea their faces were turned from Tarzan as he passed, so that he did not notice their features. In fact, he had paid no attention to them at all.

Following the instructions of his chief, Tarzan had booked his passage under an assumed name – John Caldwell, London. He did not understand the necessity of this, and it caused him considerable speculation. He wondered what role he was to play in Cape Town.

"Well," he thought, "thank Heaven that I am rid of Rokoff. He was commencing to annoy me. I wonder if I am really becoming so civilized that presently I shall develop a set of nerves. He would give them to me if any one could, for he does not fight fair. One never knows through what new agency he is going to strike. It is as though Numa, the lion, had induced Tantor, the elephant, and Histah, the snake, to join him in attempting to kill me. I would then never have known what minute, or by whom, I was to be attacked next. But the brutes are more chivalrous than man – they do not stoop to cowardly intrigue."

At dinner that night Tarzan sat next to a young woman whose place was at the captain's left. The officer introduced them.

Miss Strong! Where had he heard the name before? It was very familiar. And then the girl's mother gave him the clew, for when she addressed her daughter she called her Hazel.

Hazel Strong! What memories the name inspired. It had been a letter to this girl, penned by the fair hand of Jane Porter, that had carried to him the first message from the woman he loved. How vividly he recalled the night he had stolen it from the desk in the cabin of his long-dead father, where Jane Porter had sat writing it late into the night, while he crouched in the darkness without. How terror-stricken she would have been that night had she known that the wild jungle beast squatted outside her window, watching her every move.

And this was Hazel Strong – Jane Porter's best friend!

CHAPTER TWELVE

Ships That Pass

Let us go back a few months to the little, windswept platform of a railway station in northern Wisconsin. The smoke of forest fires hangs low over the surrounding landscape, its acrid fumes smarting the eyes of a little party of six who stand waiting the coming of the train that is to bear them away toward the south.

Professor Archimedes Q. Porter, his hands clasped beneath the tails of his long coat, paces back and forth under the ever-watchful eye of his faithful secretary, Mr. Samuel T. Philander. Twice within the past few minutes he has started absent-mindedly across the tracks in the direction of a near-by swamp, only to be rescued and dragged back by the tireless Mr. Philander.

Jane Porter, the professor's daughter, is in strained and lifeless conversation with William Cecil Clayton and Tarzan of the Apes. Within the little waiting room, but a bare moment before, a confession of love and a renunciation had taken place that had blighted the lives and happiness of two of the party, but William Cecil Clayton, Lord Greystoke, was not one of them.

Behind Miss Porter hovered the motherly Esmeralda. She, too, was happy, for was she not returning to her beloved Maryland? Already she could see dimly through the fog of smoke the murky headlight of the oncoming engine. The men began to gather up the hand baggage. Suddenly Clayton exclaimed.

"By Jove! I've left my ulster in the waiting-room," and hastened off to fetch it.

"Good-bye, Jane," said Tarzan, extending his hand. "God bless you!"

"Good-bye," replied the girl faintly. "Try to forget me – no, not that – I could not bear to think that you had forgotten me."

"There is no danger of that, dear," he answered. "I wish to Heaven that I might forget. It would be so much easier than to go through life always remembering what might have been. You will be happy, though; I am sure you shall – you must be. You may tell the others of my decision to drive my car on to New York – I don't feel equal to bidding Clayton good-bye. I want always to remember him kindly, but I fear that I am too much of a wild beast yet to be trusted too long with the man who stands between me and the one person in all the world I want."

As Clayton stooped to pick up his coat in the waiting room his eyes fell on a telegraph blank lying face down upon the floor. He stooped to pick it up, thinking it might be a message of importance which some one had dropped. He glanced at it hastily, and then suddenly he forgot his coat, the approaching train – everything but that terrible little piece of yellow paper in his hand. He read it twice before he could fully grasp the terrific weight of meaning that it bore to him.

When he had picked it up he had been an English nobleman, the proud and wealthy possessor of vast estates – a moment later he had read it, and he knew that he was an untitled and penniless beggar. It was D'Arnot's cablegram to Tarzan, and it read:

Finger prints prove you Greystoke. Congratulations.
D'ARNOT.

He staggered as though he had received a mortal blow. Just then he heard the others calling to him to hurry – the train was coming to a stop at the little platform. Like a man dazed he gathered up his ulster. He would tell them about the cablegram when they were all on board the train. Then he ran out upon the platform just as the engine whistled twice in the final warning that precedes the first rumbling jerk of coupling pins. The others were on board, leaning out from the platform of a Pullman, crying to him to hurry. Quite five minutes elapsed before they were settled in their seats, nor was it until then that Clayton discovered that Tarzan was not with them.

"Where is Tarzan?" he asked Jane Porter. "In another car?"

"No," she replied; "at the last minute he determined to drive his machine back to New York. He is anxious to see more of America than is possible from a car window. He is returning to France, you know."

Clayton did not reply. He was trying to find the right words to explain to Jane Porter the calamity that had befallen him – and her. He wondered just what the effect of his knowledge would be on her. Would she still wish to marry him – to be plain Mrs. Clayton? Suddenly the awful sacrifice which one of them must make loomed large before his imagination. Then came the question: Will Tarzan claim his own? The ape-man had known the contents of the message before he calmly denied knowledge of his parentage! He had admitted that Kala, the ape, was his mother! Could it have been for love of Jane Porter?

There was no other explanation which seemed reasonable. Then, having ignored the evidence of the message, was it not reasonable to assume that he meant never to claim his birthright? If this were so, what right had he, William Cecil Clayton, to thwart the wishes, to balk the self-sacrifice of this strange man? If Tarzan of the Apes could do this thing to save Jane Porter from unhappiness, why should he, to whose care she was intrusting her whole future, do aught to jeopardize her interests?

And so he reasoned until the first generous impulse to proclaim the truth and relinquish his titles and his estates to their rightful owner was forgotten beneath the mass of sophistries which self-interest had advanced. But during the balance of the trip, and for many days thereafter, he was moody and distraught. Occasionally the thought obtruded itself that possibly at some later day Tarzan would regret his magnanimity, and claim his rights.

Several days after they reached Baltimore Clayton broached the subject of an early marriage to Jane.

"What do you mean by early?" she asked.

"Within the next few days. I must return to England at once – I want you to return with me, dear."

"I can't get ready so soon as that," replied Jane. "It will take a whole month, at least."

She was glad, for she hoped that whatever called him to England might still further delay the wedding. She had made a bad bargain, but she intended carrying her part loyally to the bitter end – if she could manage to secure a temporary reprieve, though, she felt that she was warranted in doing so. His reply disconcerted her.

"Very well, Jane," he said. "I am disappointed, but I shall let my trip to England wait a month; then we can go back together."

But when the month was drawing to a close she found still another excuse upon which to hang a postponement, until at last, discouraged and doubting, Clayton was forced to go back to England alone.

The several letters that passed between them brought Clayton no nearer to a consummation of his hopes than he had been before, and so it was that he wrote directly to Professor Porter, and enlisted his services. The old man had always favored the match. He liked Clayton, and, being of an old southern family, he put rather an exaggerated value on the advantages of a title, which meant little or nothing to his daughter.

Clayton urged that the professor accept his invitation to be his guest in London, an invitation which included the professor's entire little family – Mr. Philander, Esmeralda, and all. The Englishman argued that once Jane was there, and home ties had been broken, she would not so dread the step which she had so long hesitated to take.

So the evening that he received Clayton's letter Professor Porter announced that they would leave for London the following week.

But once in London Jane Porter was no more tractable than she had been in Baltimore. She found one excuse after another, and when, finally, Lord Tennington invited the party to cruise around Africa in his yacht, she expressed the greatest delight in the idea, but absolutely refused to be married until they had returned to London. As the cruise was to consume a year at least, for they were to stop for indefinite periods at various points of interest, Clayton mentally anathematized Tennington for ever suggesting such a ridiculous trip.

It was Lord Tennington's plan to cruise through the Mediterranean, and the Red Sea to the Indian Ocean, and thus down the East Coast, putting in at every port that was worth the seeing.

And so it happened that on a certain day two vessels passed in the Strait of Gibraltar. The smaller, a trim white yacht, was speeding toward the east, and on her deck sat a young woman who gazed with sad eyes upon a diamond-studded locket which she idly fingered. Her thoughts were far away, in the dim, leafy fastness of a tropical jungle – and her heart was with her thoughts.

She wondered if the man who had given her the beautiful bauble, that had meant so much more to him than the intrinsic value which he had not even known could ever have meant to him, was back in his savage forest.

And upon the deck of the larger vessel, a passenger steamer passing toward the east, the man sat with another young woman, and the two idly speculated upon the identity of the dainty craft gliding so gracefully through the gentle swell of the lazy sea.

When the yacht had passed the man resumed the conversation that her appearance had broken off.

"Yes," he said, "I like America very much, and that means, of course, that I like Americans, for a country is only what its people make it. I met some very delightful people while I was there. I recall one family from your own city, Miss Strong, whom I liked particularly – Professor Porter and his daughter."

"Jane Porter!" exclaimed the girl. "Do you mean to tell me that you know Jane Porter? Why, she is the very best friend I have in the world. We were little children together – we have known each other for ages."

"Indeed!" he answered, smiling. "You would have difficulty in persuading any one of the fact who had seen either of you."

"I'll qualify the statement, then," she answered, with a laugh. "We have known each other for two ages – hers and mine. But seriously we are as dear to each other as sisters, and now that I am going to lose her I am almost heartbroken."

"Going to lose her?" exclaimed Tarzan. "Why, what do you mean? Oh, yes, I understand. You mean that now that she is married and living in England, you will seldom if ever see her."

"Yes," replied she; "and the saddest part of it all is that she is not marrying the man she loves. Oh, it is terrible. Marrying from a sense of duty! I think it is perfectly wicked, and I told her so. I have felt so strongly on the subject that although I was the only person outside of blood relations who was to have been asked to the wedding I would not let her invite me, for I should not have gone to witness the terrible mockery. But Jane Porter is peculiarly positive. She has convinced herself that she is doing the only honorable thing that she can do, and nothing in the world will ever prevent her from marrying Lord Greystoke except Greystoke himself, or death."

"I am sorry for her," said Tarzan.

"And I am sorry for the man she loves," said the girl, "for he loves her. I never met him, but from what Jane tells me he must be a very wonderful person. It seems that he was born in an African jungle, and brought up by fierce, anthropoid apes. He had never seen a white man or woman until Professor Porter and his party were marooned on the coast right at the threshold of his tiny cabin. He saved them from all manner of terrible beasts, and accomplished the most wonderful feats imaginable, and then to cap the climax he fell in love with Jane and she with him, though she never really knew it for sure until she had promised herself to Lord Greystoke."

"Most remarkable," murmured Tarzan, cudgeling his brain for some pretext upon which to turn the subject. He delighted in hearing Hazel Strong talk of Jane, but when he was the subject of the conversation he was bored and embarrassed. But he was soon given a respite, for the girl's mother joined them, and the talk became general.

The next few days passed uneventfully. The sea was quiet. The sky was clear. The steamer plowed steadily on toward the south without pause. Tarzan spent quite a little time with Miss Strong and her mother. They whiled away their hours on deck reading, talking, or taking pictures with Miss Strong's camera. When the sun had set they walked.

One day Tarzan found Miss Strong in conversation with a stranger, a man he had not seen on board before. As he approached the couple the man bowed to the girl and turned to walk away.

"Wait, Monsieur Thuran," said Miss Strong; "you must meet Mr. Caldwell. We are all fellow passengers, and should be acquainted."

The two men shook hands. As Tarzan looked into the eyes of Monsieur Thuran he was struck by the strange familiarity of their expression.

"I have had the honor of monsieur's acquaintance in the past, I am sure," said Tarzan, "though I cannot recall the circumstances."

Monsieur Thuran appeared ill at ease.

"I cannot say, monsieur," he replied. "It may be so. I have had that identical sensation myself when meeting a stranger."

"Monsieur Thuran has been explaining some of the mysteries of navigation to me," explained the girl.

Tarzan paid little heed to the conversation that ensued – he was attempting to recall where he had met Monsieur Thuran before. That it had been under peculiar circumstances he was positive. Presently the sun reached them, and the girl asked Monsieur Thuran to move her chair farther back into the shade. Tarzan happened to be watching the man at the time, and noticed the awkward manner in which he handled the chair – his left wrist was stiff. That clew was sufficient – a sudden train of associated ideas did the rest.

Monsieur Thuran had been trying to find an excuse to make a graceful departure. The lull in the conversation following the moving of their position gave him an opportunity to make his excuses. Bowing low to Miss Strong, and inclining his head to Tarzan, he turned to leave them.

"Just a moment," said Tarzan. "If Miss Strong will pardon me I will accompany you. I shall return in a moment, Miss Strong."

Monsieur Thuran looked uncomfortable. When the two men had passed out of the girl's sight, Tarzan stopped, laying a heavy hand on the other's shoulder.

"What is your game now, Rokoff?" he asked.

"I am leaving France as I promised you," replied the other, in a surly voice.

"I see you are," said Tarzan; "but I know you so well that I can scarcely believe that your being on the same boat with me is purely a coincidence. If I could believe it the fact that you are in disguise would immediately disabuse my mind of any such idea."

"Well," growled Rokoff, with a shrug, "I cannot see what you are going to do about it. This vessel flies the English flag. I have as much right on board her as you, and from the fact that you are booked under an assumed name I imagine that I have more right."

"We will not discuss it, Rokoff. All I wanted to say to you is that you must keep away from Miss Strong – she is a decent woman."

Rokoff turned scarlet.

"If you don't I shall pitch you overboard," continued Tarzan. "Do not forget that I am just waiting for some excuse." Then he turned on his heel, and left Rokoff standing there trembling with suppressed rage.

He did not see the man again for days, but Rokoff was not idle. In his stateroom with Paulvitch he fumed and swore, threatening the most terrible of revenges.

"I would throw him overboard tonight," he cried, "were I sure that those papers were not on his person. I cannot chance pitching them into the ocean with him. If you were not such a stupid coward, Alexis, you would find a way to enter his stateroom and search for the documents."

Paulvitch smiled. "You are supposed to be the brains of this partnership, my dear Nikolas," he replied. "Why do you not find the means to search Monsieur Caldwell's stateroom – eh?"

Two hours later fate was kind to them, for Paulvitch, who was ever on the watch, saw Tarzan leave his room without locking the door. Five minutes later Rokoff was stationed where he could give the alarm in case Tarzan returned, and Paulvitch was deftly searching the contents of the ape-man's luggage.

He was about to give up in despair when he saw a coat which Tarzan had just removed. A moment later he grasped an official envelope in his hand. A quick glance at its contents brought a broad smile to the Russian's face.

When he left the stateroom Tarzan himself could not have told that an article in it had been touched since he left it – Paulvitch was a past master in his chosen field. When he handed the packet to Rokoff in the seclusion of their stateroom the larger man rang for a steward, and ordered a pint of champagne.

"We must celebrate, my dear Alexis," he said.

"It was luck, Nikolas," explained Paulvitch. "It is evident that he carries these papers always upon his person – just by chance he neglected to transfer them when he changed coats a few minutes since. But there will be the deuce to pay when he discovers his loss. I am afraid that he will immediately connect you with it. Now that he knows that you are on board he will suspect you at once."

"It will make no difference whom he suspects – after to-night," said Rokoff, with a nasty grin.

After Miss Strong had gone below that night Tarzan stood leaning over the rail looking far out to sea. Every night he had done this since he had come on board – sometimes he stood thus for an hour. And the eyes that had been watching his every movement since he had boarded the ship at Algiers knew that this was his habit.

Even as he stood there this night those eyes were on him. Presently the last straggler had left the deck. It was a clear night, but there was no moon – objects on deck were barely discernible.

From the shadows of the cabin two figures crept stealthily upon the ape-man from behind. The lapping of the waves against the ship's sides, the whirring of the propeller, the throbbing of the engines, drowned the almost soundless approach of the two.

They were quite close to him now, and crouching low, like tacklers on a gridiron. One of them raised his hand and lowered it, as though counting off seconds – one – two – three! As one man the two leaped for their victim. Each grasped a leg, and before Tarzan of the Apes, lightning though he was, could turn to save himself he had been pitched over the low rail and was falling into the Atlantic.

Hazel Strong was looking from her darkened port across the dark sea. Suddenly a body shot past her eyes from the deck above. It dropped so quickly into the dark waters below that she could not be sure of what it was – it might have been a man, she could not say. She listened for some outcry from above – for the always-fearsome call, "Man overboard!" but it did not come. All was silence on the ship above – all was silence in the sea below.

The girl decided that she had but seen a bundle of refuse thrown overboard by one of the ship's crew, and a moment later sought her berth.

CHAPTER THIRTEEN

The Wreck of the "Lady Alice"

THE NEXT MORNING AT breakfast Tarzan's place was vacant. Miss Strong was mildly curious, for Mr. Caldwell had always made it a point to wait that he might breakfast with her and her mother. As she was sitting on deck later Monsieur Thuran paused to exchange a half dozen pleasant words with her. He seemed in most excellent spirits – his manner was the extreme of affability. As he passed on Miss Strong thought what a very delightful man was Monsieur Thuran.

The day dragged heavily. She missed the quiet companionship of Mr. Caldwell – there had been something about him that had made the girl like him from the first; he had talked so entertainingly of the places he had seen – the peoples and their customs – the wild beasts; and he had always had a droll way of drawing striking comparisons between savage animals and civilized men that showed a considerable knowledge of the former, and a keen, though somewhat cynical, estimate of the latter.

When Monsieur Thuran stopped again to chat with her in the afternoon she welcomed the break in the day's monotony. But she had begun to become seriously concerned in Mr. Caldwell's continued absence; somehow she constantly associated it with the start she had had the night before, when the dark object fell past her port into the sea. Presently she broached the subject to Monsieur Thuran. Had he seen Mr. Caldwell today? He had not. Why?

"He was not at breakfast as usual, nor have I seen him once since yesterday," explained the girl.

Monsieur Thuran was extremely solicitous.

"I did not have the pleasure of intimate acquaintance with Mr. Caldwell," he said. "He seemed a most estimable gentleman, however.

Can it be that he is indisposed, and has remained in his stateroom? It would not be strange."

"No," replied the girl, "it would not be strange, of course; but for some inexplicable reason I have one of those foolish feminine presentiments that all is not right with Mr. Caldwell. It is the strangest feeling – it is as though I knew that he was not on board the ship."

Monsieur Thuran laughed pleasantly. "Mercy, my dear Miss Strong," he said; "where in the world could he be then? We have not been within sight of land for days."

"Of course, it is ridiculous of me," she admitted. And then: "But I am not going to worry about it any longer; I am going to find out where Mr. Caldwell is," and she motioned to a passing steward.

"That may be more difficult than you imagine, my dear girl," thought Monsieur Thuran, but aloud he said: "By all means."

"Find Mr. Caldwell, please," she said to the steward, "and tell him that his friends are much worried by his continued absence."

"You are very fond of Mr. Caldwell?" suggested Monsieur Thuran.

"I think he is splendid," replied the girl. "And mamma is perfectly infatuated with him. He is the sort of man with whom one has a feeling of perfect security – no one could help but have confidence in Mr. Caldwell."

A moment later the steward returned to say that Mr. Caldwell was not in his stateroom. "I cannot find him, Miss Strong, and" – he hesitated – "I have learned that his berth was not occupied last night. I think that I had better report the matter to the captain."

"Most assuredly," exclaimed Miss Strong. "I shall go with you to the captain myself. It is terrible! I know that something awful has happened. My presentiments were not false, after all."

It was a very frightened young woman and an excited steward who presented themselves before the captain a few moments later. He listened to their stories in silence – a look of concern marking his expression as the steward assured him that he had sought for the missing passenger in every part of the ship that a passenger might be expected to frequent.

"And are you sure, Miss Strong, that you saw a body fall overboard last night?" he asked.

"There is not the slightest doubt about that," she answered. "I cannot say that it was a human body – there was no outcry. It might have been only what I thought it was – a bundle of refuse. But if Mr. Caldwell is not found on board I shall always be positive that it was he whom I saw fall past my port."

The captain ordered an immediate and thorough search of the entire ship from stem to stern – no nook or cranny was to be overlooked. Miss Strong remained in his cabin, waiting the outcome of the quest. The captain asked her many questions, but she could tell him nothing about the missing man other than what she had herself seen during their brief acquaintance on shipboard. For the first time she suddenly realized how very little indeed Mr. Caldwell had told her about himself or his past life. That he had been born in Africa and educated in Paris was about all she knew, and this meager information had been the result of her surprise that an Englishman should speak English with such a marked French accent.

"Did he ever speak of any enemies?" asked the captain.

"Never."

"Was he acquainted with any of the other passengers?"

"Only as he had been with me – through the circumstance of casual meeting as fellow shipmates."

"Er – was he, in your opinion, Miss Strong, a man who drank to excess?"

"I do not know that he drank at all – he certainly had not been drinking up to half an hour before I saw that body fall overboard," she answered, "for I was with him on deck up to that time."

"It is very strange," said the captain. "He did not look to me like a man who was subject to fainting spells, or anything of that sort. And even had he been it is scarcely credible that he should have fallen completely over the rail had he been taken with an attack while leaning upon it – he would rather have fallen inside, upon the deck. If he is not on board, Miss Strong, he was thrown overboard – and the fact that you heard no outcry would lead to the assumption that he was dead before he left the ship's deck – murdered."

The girl shuddered.

It was a full hour later that the first officer returned to report the outcome of the search.

"Mr. Caldwell is not on board, sir," he said.

"I fear that there is something more serious than accident here, Mr. Brently," said the captain. "I wish that you would make a personal and very careful examination of Mr. Caldwell's effects, to ascertain if there is any clew to a motive either for suicide or murder – sift the thing to the bottom."

"Aye, aye, sir!" responded Mr. Brently, and left to commence his investigation.

Hazel Strong was prostrated. For two days she did not leave her cabin, and when she finally ventured on deck she was very wan and white, with great, dark circles beneath her eyes. Waking or sleeping, it seemed that she constantly saw that dark body dropping, swift and silent, into the cold, grim sea.

Shortly after her first appearance on deck following the tragedy, Monsieur Thuran joined her with many expressions of kindly solicitude.

"Oh, but it is terrible, Miss Strong," he said. "I cannot rid my mind of it."

"Nor I," said the girl wearily. "I feel that he might have been saved had I but given the alarm."

"You must not reproach yourself, my dear Miss Strong," urged Monsieur Thuran. "It was in no way your fault. Another would have done as you did. Who would think that because something fell into the sea from a ship that it must necessarily be a man? Nor would the outcome have been different had you given an alarm. For a while they would have doubted your story, thinking it but the nervous hallucination of a woman – had you insisted it would have been too late to have rescued him by the time the ship could have been brought to a stop, and the boats lowered and rowed back miles in search of the unknown spot where the tragedy had occurred. No, you must not censure yourself. You have done more than any other of us for poor Mr. Caldwell – you were the only one to miss him. It was you who instituted the search."

The girl could not help but feel grateful to him for his kind and encouraging words. He was with her often – almost constantly for the remainder of the voyage – and she grew to like him very much indeed. Monsieur Thuran had learned that the beautiful Miss Strong, of Baltimore, was an American heiress – a very wealthy girl in her own right, and with future prospects that quite took his breath away when he contemplated them, and since he spent most of his time in that delectable pastime it is a wonder that he breathed at all.

It had been Monsieur Thuran's intention to leave the ship at the first port they touched after the disappearance of Tarzan. Did he not have in his coat pocket the thing he had taken passage upon this very boat to obtain? There was nothing more to detain him here. He could not return to the Continent fast enough, that he might board the first express for St. Petersburg.

But now another idea had obtruded itself, and was rapidly crowding his original intentions into the background. That American fortune was not to be sneezed at, nor was its possessor a whit less attractive.

"SAPRISTI! but she would cause a sensation in St. Petersburg." And he would, too, with the assistance of her inheritance.

After Monsieur Thuran had squandered a few million dollars, he discovered that the vocation was so entirely to his liking that he would continue on down to Cape Town, where he suddenly decided that he had pressing engagements that might detain him there for some time.

Miss Strong had told him that she and her mother were to visit the latter's brother there – they had not decided upon the duration of their stay, and it would probably run into months.

She was delighted when she found that Monsieur Thuran was to be there also.

"I hope that we shall be able to continue our acquaintance," she said. "You must call upon mamma and me as soon as we are settled."

Monsieur Thuran was delighted at the prospect, and lost no time in saying so. Mrs. Strong was not quite so favorably impressed by him as her daughter.

"I do not know why I should distrust him," she said to Hazel one day as they were discussing him. "He seems a perfect gentleman in every respect, but sometimes there is something about his eyes – a fleeting expression which I cannot describe, but which when I see it gives me a very uncanny feeling."

The girl laughed. "You are a silly dear, mamma," she said.

"I suppose so, but I am sorry that we have not poor Mr. Caldwell for company instead."

"And I, too," replied her daughter.

Monsieur Thuran became a frequent visitor at the home of Hazel Strong's uncle in Cape Town. His attentions were very marked, but they were so punctiliously arranged to meet the girl's every wish that she came to depend upon him more and more. Did she or her mother or a cousin require an escort – was there a little friendly service to be rendered, the genial and ubiquitous Monsieur Thuran was always available. Her uncle and his family grew to like him for his unfailing courtesy and willingness to be of service. Monsieur Thuran was becoming indispensable. At length, feeling the moment propitious, he proposed. Miss Strong was startled. She did not know what to say.

"I had never thought that you cared for me in any such way," she told him. "I have looked upon you always as a very dear friend. I shall not give you my answer now. Forget that you have asked me to be your wife. Let us go on as we have been – then I can consider you from an entirely different angle for a time. It may be that I shall discover that my feeling for you is more than friendship. I certainly have not thought for a moment that I loved you."

This arrangement was perfectly satisfactory to Monsieur Thuran. He deeply regretted that he had been hasty, but he had loved her for so long a time, and so devotedly, that he thought that every one must know it.

"From the first time I saw you, Hazel," he said, "I have loved you. I am willing to wait, for I am certain that so great and pure a love as mine will be rewarded. All that I care to know is that you do not love another. Will you tell me?"

"I have never been in love in my life," she replied, and he was quite satisfied. On the way home that night he purchased a steam yacht, and built a million-dollar villa on the Black Sea.

The next day Hazel Strong enjoyed one of the happiest surprises of her life – she ran face to face upon Jane Porter as she was coming out of a jeweler's shop.

"Why, Jane Porter!" she exclaimed. "Where in the world did you drop from? Why, I can't believe my own eyes."

"Well, of all things!" cried the equally astonished Jane. "And here I have been wasting whole reams of perfectly good imagination picturing you in Baltimore – the very idea!" And she threw her arms about her friend once more, and kissed her a dozen times.

By the time mutual explanations had been made Hazel knew that Lord Tennington's yacht had put in at Cape Town for at least a week's stay, and at the end of that time was to continue on her voyage – this time up the West Coast – and so back to England. "Where," concluded Jane, "I am to be married."

"Then you are not married yet?" asked Hazel.

"Not yet," replied Jane, and then, quite irrelevantly, "I wish England were a million miles from here."

Visits were exchanged between the yacht and Hazel's relatives. Dinners were arranged, and trips into the surrounding country to entertain the visitors. Monsieur Thuran was a welcome guest at every function. He gave a dinner himself to the men of the party, and managed to ingratiate himself in the good will of Lord Tennington by many little acts of hospitality.

Monsieur Thuran had heard dropped a hint of something which might result from this unexpected visit of Lord Tennington's yacht, and he wanted to be counted in on it. Once when he was alone with the Englishman he took occasion to make it quite plain that his engagement to Miss Strong was to be announced immediately upon their return to America. "But not a word of it, my dear Tennington – not a word of it."

"Certainly, I quite understand, my dear fellow," Tennington had replied. "But you are to be congratulated – ripping girl, don't you know – really."

The next day it came. Mrs. Strong, Hazel, and Monsieur Thuran were Lord Tennington's guests aboard his yacht. Mrs. Strong had been telling them how much she had enjoyed her visit at Cape Town, and that she regretted that a letter just received from her attorneys in Baltimore had necessitated her cutting her visit shorter than they had intended.

"When do you sail?" asked Tennington.

"The first of the week, I think," she replied. "Indeed?" exclaimed Monsieur Thuran. "I am very fortunate. I, too, have found that I must return at once, and now I shall have the honor of accompanying and serving you."

"That is nice of you, Monsieur Thuran," replied Mrs. Strong. "I am sure that we shall be glad to place ourselves under your protection." But in the bottom of her heart was the wish that they might escape him. Why, she could not have told.

"By Jove!" ejaculated Lord Tennington, a moment later. "Bully idea, by Jove!"

"Yes, Tennington, of course," ventured Clayton; "it must be a bully idea if you had it, but what the deuce is it? Goin' to steam to China via the south pole?"

"Oh, I say now, Clayton," returned Tennington, "you needn't be so rough on a fellow just because you didn't happen to suggest this trip yourself – you've acted a regular bounder ever since we sailed.

"No, sir," he continued, "it's a bully idea, and you'll all say so. It's to take Mrs. Strong and Miss Strong, and Thuran, too, if he'll come, as far as England with us on the yacht. Now, isn't that a corker?"

"Forgive me, Tenny, old boy," cried Clayton. "It certainly IS a corking idea – I never should have suspected you of it. You're quite sure it's original, are you?"

"And we'll sail the first of the week, or any other time that suits your convenience, Mrs. Strong," concluded the big-hearted Englishman, as though the thing were all arranged except the sailing date.

"Mercy, Lord Tennington, you haven't even given us an opportunity to thank you, much less decide whether we shall be able to accept your generous invitation," said Mrs. Strong.

"Why, of course you'll come," responded Tennington. "We'll make as good time as any passenger boat, and you'll be fully as comfortable; and, anyway, we all want you, and won't take no for an answer."

And so it was settled that they should sail the following Monday.

Two days out the girls were sitting in Hazel's cabin, looking at some prints she had had finished in Cape Town. They represented all the pictures she had taken since she had left America, and the girls were both engrossed in them, Jane asking many questions, and Hazel keeping up a perfect torrent of comment and explanation of the various scenes and people.

"And here," she said suddenly, "here's a man you know. Poor fellow, I have so often intended asking you about him, but I never have been able to think of it when we were together." She was holding the little print so that Jane did not see the face of the man it portrayed.

"His name was John Caldwell," continued Hazel. "Do you recall him? He said that he met you in America. He is an Englishman."

"I do not recollect the name," replied Jane. "Let me see the picture."

"The poor fellow was lost overboard on our trip down the coast," she said, as she handed the print to Jane.

"Lost over – Why, Hazel, Hazel – don't tell me that he is dead – drowned at sea! Hazel! Why don't you say that you are joking!" And before the astonished Miss Strong could catch her Jane Porter had slipped to the floor in a swoon.

After Hazel had restored her chum to consciousness she sat looking at her for a long time before either spoke.

"I did not know, Jane," said Hazel, in a constrained voice, "that you knew Mr. Caldwell so intimately that his death could prove such a shock to you."

"John Caldwell?" questioned Miss Porter. "You do not mean to tell me that you do not know who this man was, Hazel?"

"Why, yes, Jane; I know perfectly well who he was – his name was John Caldwell; he was from London."

"Oh, Hazel, I wish I could believe it," moaned the girl. "I wish I could believe it, but those features are burned so deep into my memory and my heart that I should recognize them anywhere in the world from among a thousand others, who might appear identical to any one but me."

"What do you mean, Jane?" cried Hazel, now thoroughly alarmed. "Who do you think it is?"

"I don't think, Hazel. I know that that is a picture of Tarzan of the Apes."

"Jane!"

"I cannot be mistaken. Oh, Hazel, are you sure that he is dead? Can there be no mistake?"

"I am afraid not, dear," answered Hazel sadly. "I wish I could think that you are mistaken, but now a hundred and one little pieces of corroborative evidence occur to me that meant nothing to me while I thought that he was John Caldwell, of London. He said that he had been born in Africa, and educated in France."

"Yes, that would be true," murmured Jane Porter dully.

"The first officer, who searched his luggage, found nothing to identify John Caldwell, of London. Practically all his belongings had been made, or purchased, in Paris. Everything that bore an initial was marked either with a 'T' alone, or with 'J. C. T.' We thought that he was traveling incognito under his first two names – the J. C. standing for John Caldwell."

"Tarzan of the Apes took the name Jean C. Tarzan," said Jane, in the same lifeless monotone. "And he is dead! Oh! Hazel, it is horrible! He died all alone in this terrible ocean! It is unbelievable that that brave heart should have ceased to beat – that those mighty muscles are quiet and cold forever! That he who was the personification of life and health and manly strength should be the prey of slimy, crawling things, that – " But she could go no further, and with a little moan she buried her head in her arms, and sank sobbing to the floor.

For days Miss Porter was ill, and would see no one except Hazel and the faithful Esmeralda. When at last she came on deck all were struck by the sad change that had taken place in her. She was no longer the alert, vivacious American beauty who had charmed and delighted all who came in contact with her. Instead she was a very quiet and sad little girl – with an expression of hopeless wistfulness that none but Hazel Strong could interpret.

The entire party strove their utmost to cheer and amuse her, but all to no avail. Occasionally the jolly Lord Tennington would wring a wan smile from her, but for the most part she sat with wide eyes looking out across the sea.

With Jane Porter's illness one misfortune after another seemed to attack the yacht. First an engine broke down, and they drifted for two days while temporary repairs were being made. Then a squall struck them unaware, that carried overboard nearly everything above deck that was portable. Later two of the seamen fell to fighting in the forecastle, with the result that one of them was badly wounded with a knife, and the other had to be put in irons. Then, to cap the climax, the mate fell overboard at night, and was drowned before help could reach him. The yacht cruised about the spot for ten hours, but no sign of the man was seen after he disappeared from the deck into the sea.

Every member of the crew and guests was gloomy and depressed after these series of misfortunes. All were apprehensive of worse to come, and this was especially true of the seamen who recalled all sorts of terrible omens and warnings that had occurred during the early part of the voyage, and which they could now clearly translate into the precursors of some grim and terrible tragedy to come.

Nor did the croakers have long to wait. The second night after the drowning of the mate the little yacht was suddenly wracked from stem to stern. About one o'clock in the morning there was a terrific impact that threw the slumbering guests and crew from berth and bunk. A mighty shudder ran through the frail craft; she lay far over to starboard; the engines stopped. For a moment she hung there with her decks at an angle of forty-five degrees – then, with a sullen, rending sound, she slipped back into the sea and righted.

Instantly the men rushed upon deck, followed closely by the women. Though the night was cloudy, there was little wind or sea, nor was it so dark but that just off the port bow a black mass could be discerned floating low in the water.

"A derelict," was the terse explanation of the officer of the watch.

Presently the engineer hurried on deck in search of the captain.

"That patch we put on the cylinder head's blown out, sir," he reported, "and she's makin' water fast for'ard on the port bow."

An instant later a seaman rushed up from below.

"My Gawd!" he cried. "Her whole bleedin' bottom's ripped out. She can't float twenty minutes."

"Shut up!" roared Tennington. "Ladies, go below and get some of your things together. It may not be so bad as that, but we may have to take to the boats. It will be safer to be prepared. Go at once, please. And, Captain Jerrold, send some competent man below, please, to ascertain the exact extent of the damage. In the meantime I might suggest that you have the boats provisioned."

The calm, low voice of the owner did much to reassure the entire party, and a moment later all were occupied with the duties he had suggested. By the time the ladies had returned to the deck the rapid provisioning of the boats had been about completed, and a moment later the officer who had gone below had returned to report. But his opinion was scarcely needed to assure the huddled group of men and women that the end of the LADY ALICE was at hand.

"Well, sir?" said the captain, as his officer hesitated.

"I dislike to frighten the ladies, sir," he said, "but she can't float a dozen minutes, in my opinion. There's a hole in her you could drive a bally cow through, sir."

For five minutes the LADY ALICE had been settling rapidly by the bow. Already her stern loomed high in the air, and foothold on the deck was of the most precarious nature. She carried four boats, and these were all filled and lowered away in safety. As they pulled rapidly from the stricken little vessel Jane Porter turned to have one last look at her. Just then there came a loud crash and an ominous rumbling and pounding from the heart of the ship – her machinery had broken loose, and was dashing its way toward the bow, tearing out partitions and bulkheads as it went – the stern rose rapidly high above them; for a moment she seemed to pause there – a vertical shaft protruding from the bosom of the ocean, and then swiftly she dove headforemost beneath the waves.

In one of the boats the brave Lord Tennington wiped a tear from his eye – he had not seen a fortune in money go down forever into the sea, but a dear, beautiful friend whom he had loved.

At last the long night broke, and a tropical sun smote down upon the rolling water. Jane Porter had dropped into a fitful slumber – the fierce light of the sun upon her upturned face awoke her. She looked about her. In the boat with her were three sailors, Clayton, and Monsieur Thuran. Then she looked for the other boats, but as far as the eye could reach there was nothing to break the fearful monotony of that waste of waters – they were alone in a small boat upon the broad Atlantic.

CHAPTER FOURTEEN

Back to the Primitive

As Tarzan struck the water, his first impulse was to swim clear of the ship and possible danger from her propellers. He knew whom to thank for his present predicament, and as he lay in the sea, just supporting himself by a gentle movement of his hands, his chief emotion was one of chagrin that he had been so easily bested by Rokoff.

He lay thus for some time, watching the receding and rapidly diminishing lights of the steamer without it ever once occurring to him to call for help. He never had called for help in his life, and so it is not strange that he did not think of it now. Always had he depended upon his own prowess and resourcefulness, nor had there ever been since the days of Kala any to answer an appeal for succor. When it did occur to him it was too late.

There was, thought Tarzan, a possible one chance in a hundred thousand that he might be picked up, and an even smaller chance that he would reach land, so he determined that to combine what slight chances there were, he would swim slowly in the direction of the coast – the ship might have been closer in than he had known.

His strokes were long and easy – it would be many hours before those giant muscles would commence to feel fatigue. As he swam, guided toward the east by the stars, he noticed that he felt the weight of his shoes, and so he removed them. His trousers went next, and he would have removed his coat at the same time but for the precious papers in its pocket. To assure himself that he still had them he slipped his hand in to feel, but to his consternation they were gone.

Now he knew that something more than revenge had prompted Rokoff to pitch him overboard – the Russian had managed to obtain possession of the papers Tarzan had wrested from him at Bou Saada. The ape-man swore softly, and let his coat and shirt sink into the Atlantic. Before many hours he had divested himself of his remaining garments, and was swimming easily and unencumbered toward the east.

The first faint evidence of dawn was paling the stars ahead of him when the dim outlines of a low-lying black mass loomed up directly in his track. A few strong strokes brought him to its side – it was the bottom of a wave-washed derelict. Tarzan clambered upon it – he would rest there until daylight at least. He had no intention to remain there inactive – a prey to hunger and thirst. If he must die he preferred dying in action while making some semblance of an attempt to save himself.

The sea was quiet, so that the wreck had only a gently undulating motion, that was nothing to the swimmer who had had no sleep for twenty hours. Tarzan of the Apes curled up upon the slimy timbers, and was soon asleep.

The heat of the sun awoke him early in the forenoon. His first conscious sensation was of thirst, which grew almost to the proportions of suffering with full returning consciousness; but a moment later it was forgotten in the joy of two almost simultaneous discoveries. The first was a mass of wreckage floating beside the derelict in the midst of which, bottom up, rose and fell an overturned lifeboat; the other was the faint, dim line of a far-distant shore showing on the horizon in the east.

Tarzan dove into the water, and swam around the wreck to the lifeboat. The cool ocean refreshed him almost as much as would a draft of water, so that it was with renewed vigor that he brought the smaller boat alongside the derelict, and, after many herculean efforts, succeeded in dragging it onto the slimy ship's bottom. There he righted and examined it – the boat was quite sound, and a moment later floated upright alongside the wreck. Then Tarzan selected several pieces of wreckage that might answer him as paddles, and presently was making good headway toward the far-off shore.

It was late in the afternoon by the time he came close enough to distinguish objects on land, or to make out the contour of the shore line. Before him lay what appeared to be the entrance to a little, landlocked harbor. The wooded point to the north was strangely familiar. Could it be possible that fate had thrown him up at the very threshold of his own beloved jungle! But as the bow of his boat entered the mouth of the harbor the last shred of doubt was cleared away, for there before him upon the farther shore, under the shadows of his primeval forest, stood his own cabin – built before his birth by the hand of his long-dead father, John Clayton, Lord Greystoke.

With long sweeps of his giant muscles Tarzan sent the little craft speeding toward the beach. Its prow had scarcely touched when the ape-man leaped to shore – his heart beat fast in joy and exultation as each long-familiar object came beneath his roving eyes – the cabin, the beach, the little brook, the dense jungle, the black, impenetrable forest. The myriad birds in their brilliant plumage – the gorgeous tropical blooms upon the festooned creepers falling in great loops from the giant trees.

Tarzan of the Apes had come into his own again, and that all the world might know it he threw back his young head, and gave voice to the fierce, wild challenge of his tribe. For a moment silence reigned upon the jungle, and then, low and weird, came an answering challenge – it was the deep roar of Numa, the lion; and from a great distance, faintly, the fearsome answering bellow of a bull ape.

Tarzan went to the brook first, and slaked his thirst. Then he approached his cabin. The door was still closed and latched as he and D'Arnot had left it. He raised the latch and entered. Nothing had been disturbed; there were the table, the bed, and the little crib built by his father – the shelves and cupboards just as they had stood for over twenty-three years – just as he had left them nearly two years before.

His eyes satisfied, Tarzan's stomach began to call aloud for attention – the pangs of hunger suggested a search for food. There was nothing in the cabin, nor had he any weapons; but upon a wall hung one of his old grass ropes. It had been many times broken and spliced, so that he had discarded it for a better one long before. Tarzan wished that he had a knife. Well, unless he was mistaken he should have that and a spear and bows and arrows before another sun had set – the rope would take care of that, and in the meantime it must be made to procure food for him. He coiled it carefully, and, throwing it about his shoulder, went out, closing the door behind him.

Close to the cabin the jungle commenced, and into it Tarzan of the Apes plunged, wary and noiseless – once more a savage beast hunting its food. For a time he kept to the ground, but finally, discovering no spoor indicative of nearby meat, he took to the trees. With the first dizzy swing from tree to tree all the old joy of living swept over him. Vain regrets and dull heartache were forgotten. Now was he living. Now, indeed, was the true happiness of perfect freedom his. Who would go back to the stifling, wicked cities of civilized man when the mighty reaches of the great jungle offered peace and liberty? Not he.

While it was yet light Tarzan came to a drinking place by the side of a jungle river. There was a ford there, and for countless ages the beasts of the forest had come down to drink at this spot. Here of a night might always be found either Sabor or Numa crouching in the dense foliage of the surrounding jungle awaiting an antelope or a water buck for their meal. Here came Horta, the boar, to water, and here came Tarzan of the Apes to make a kill, for he was very empty.

On a low branch he squatted above the trail. For an hour he waited. It was growing dark. A little to one side of the ford in the densest thicket he heard the faint sound of padded feet, and the brushing of a huge body against tall grasses and tangled creepers. None other than Tarzan might have heard it, but the ape-man heard and translated – it was Numa, the lion, on the same errand as himself. Tarzan smiled.

Presently he heard an animal approaching warily along the trail toward the drinking place. A moment more and it came in view – it was Horta, the boar. Here was delicious meat – and Tarzan's mouth watered. The grasses where Numa lay were very still now – ominously still. Horta passed beneath Tarzan – a few more steps and he would be within the radius of Numa's spring. Tarzan could imagine how old Numa's eyes were shining – how he was already sucking in his breath for the awful roar which would freeze his prey for the brief instant between the moment of the spring and the sinking of terrible fangs into splintering bones.

But as Numa gathered himself, a slender rope flew through the air from the low branches of a near-by tree. A noose settled about Horta's neck. There was a frightened grunt, a squeal, and then Numa saw his quarry dragged backward up the trail, and, as he sprang, Horta, the boar, soared upward beyond his clutches into the tree above, and a mocking face looked down and laughed into his own.

Then indeed did Numa roar. Angry, threatening, hungry, he paced back and forth beneath the taunting ape-man. Now he stopped, and, rising on his hind legs against the stem of the tree that held his enemy, sharpened his huge claws upon the bark, tearing out great pieces that laid bare the white wood beneath.

And in the meantime Tarzan had dragged the struggling Horta to the limb beside him. Sinewy fingers completed the work the choking noose had commenced. The ape-man had no knife, but nature had equipped him with the means of tearing his food from the quivering flank of his prey, and gleaming teeth sank into the succulent flesh while the raging lion looked on from below as another enjoyed the dinner that he had thought already his.

It was quite dark by the time Tarzan had gorged himself. Ah, but it had been delicious! Never had he quite accustomed himself to the ruined flesh that civilized men had served him, and in the bottom of his savage heart there had constantly been the craving for the warm meat of the fresh kill, and the rich, red blood.

He wiped his bloody hands upon a bunch of leaves, slung the remains of his kill across his shoulder, and swung off through the middle terrace of the forest toward his cabin, and at the same instant Jane Porter and William Cecil Clayton arose from a sumptuous dinner upon the LADY ALICE, thousands of miles to the east, in the Indian Ocean.

Beneath Tarzan walked Numa, the lion, and when the ape-man deigned to glance downward he caught occasional glimpses of the baleful green eyes following through the darkness. Numa did not roar now – instead, he moved stealthily, like the shadow of a great cat; but yet he took no step that did not reach the sensitive ears of the ape-man.

Tarzan wondered if he would stalk him to his cabin door. He hoped not, for that would mean a night's sleep curled in the crotch of a tree, and he much preferred the bed of grasses within his own abode. But he knew just the tree and the most comfortable crotch, if necessity demanded that he sleep out. A hundred times in the past some great jungle cat had followed him home, and compelled him to seek shelter in this same tree, until another mood or the rising sun had sent his enemy away.

But presently Numa gave up the chase and, with a series of bloodcurdling moans and roars, turned angrily back in search of another and an easier dinner. So Tarzan came to his cabin unattended, and a few moments later was curled up in the mildewed remnants of what had once been a bed of grasses. Thus easily did Monsieur Jean C. Tarzan slough the thin skin of his artificial civilization, and sink happy and contented into the deep sleep of the wild beast that has fed to repletion. Yet a woman's "yes" would have bound him to that other life forever, and made the thought of this savage existence repulsive.

Tarzan slept late into the following forenoon, for he had been very tired from the labors and exertion of the long night and day upon the ocean, and the jungle jaunt that had brought into play muscles that he had scarce used for nearly two years. When he awoke he ran to the brook first to drink. Then he took a plunge into the sea, swimming about for a quarter of an hour. Afterward he returned to his cabin, and breakfasted off the flesh of Horta. This done, he buried the balance of the carcass in the soft earth outside the cabin, for his evening meal.

Once more he took his rope and vanished into the jungle. This time he hunted nobler quarry – man; although had you asked him his own opinion he could have named a dozen other denizens of the jungle which he considered far the superiors in nobility of the men he hunted. Today Tarzan was in quest of weapons. He wondered if the women and children had remained in Mbonga's village after the punitive expedition from the French cruiser had massacred all the warriors in revenge for D'Arnot's supposed death. He hoped that he should find warriors there, for he knew not how long a quest he should have to make were the village deserted.

The ape-man traveled swiftly through the forest, and about noon came to the site of the village, but to his disappointment found that the jungle had overgrown the plantain fields and that the thatched huts had fallen in decay. There was no sign of man. He clambered about among the ruins for half an hour, hoping that he might discover some forgotten weapon, but his search was without fruit, and so he took up his quest once more, following up the stream, which flowed from a southeasterly direction. He knew that near fresh water he would be most likely to find another settlement.

As he traveled he hunted as he had hunted with his ape people in the past, as Kala had taught him to hunt, turning over rotted logs to find some toothsome vermin, running high into the trees to rob a bird's nest, or pouncing upon a tiny rodent with the quickness of a cat. There were other things that he ate, too, but the less detailed the account of an ape's diet, the better – and Tarzan was again an ape, the same fierce, brutal anthropoid that Kala had taught him to be, and that he had been for the first twenty years of his life.

Occasionally he smiled as he recalled some friend who might even at the moment be sitting placid and immaculate within the precincts of his select Parisian club – just as Tarzan had sat but a few months before; and then he would stop, as though turned suddenly to stone as the gentle breeze carried to his trained nostrils the scent of some new prey or a formidable enemy.

That night he slept far inland from his cabin, securely wedged into the crotch of a giant tree, swaying a hundred feet above the ground. He had eaten heartily again – this time from the flesh of Bara, the deer, who had fallen prey to his quick noose.

Early the next morning he resumed his journey, always following the course of the stream. For three days he continued his quest, until he had come to a part of the jungle in which he never before had been. Occasionally upon the higher ground the forest was much thinner, and in the far distance through the trees he could see ranges of mighty mountains, with wide plains in the foreground. Here, in the open spaces, were new game – countless antelope and vast herds of zebra. Tarzan was entranced – he would make a long visit to this new world.

On the morning of the fourth day his nostrils were suddenly surprised by a faint new scent. It was the scent of man, but yet a long way off. The ape-man thrilled with pleasure. Every sense was on the alert as with crafty stealth he moved quickly through the trees, up-wind, in the direction of his prey. Presently he came upon it – a lone warrior treading softly through the jungle.

Tarzan followed close above his quarry, waiting for a clearer space in which to hurl his rope. As he stalked the unconscious man, new thoughts presented themselves to the ape-man – thoughts born of the refining influences of civilization, and of its cruelties. It came to him that seldom if ever did civilized man kill a fellow being without some pretext, however slight. It was true that Tarzan wished this man's weapons and ornaments, but was it necessary to take his life to obtain them?

The longer he thought about it, the more repugnant became the thought of taking human life needlessly; and thus it happened that while he was trying to decide just what to do, they had come to a little clearing, at the far side of which lay a palisaded village of beehive huts.

As the warrior emerged from the forest, Tarzan caught a fleeting glimpse of a tawny hide worming its way through the matted jungle grasses in his wake – it was Numa, the lion. He, too, was stalking the black man. With the instant that Tarzan realized the native's danger his attitude toward his erstwhile prey altered completely – now he was a fellow man threatened by a common enemy.

Numa was about to charge – there was little time in which to compare various methods or weigh the probable results of any. And then a number of things happened, almost simultaneously – the lion sprang from his ambush toward the retreating black – Tarzan cried out in warning – and the black turned just in time to see Numa halted in mid-flight by a slender strand of grass rope, the noosed end of which had fallen cleanly about his neck.

The ape-man had acted so quickly that he had been unable to prepare himself to withstand the strain and shock of Numa's great weight upon the rope, and so it was that though the rope stopped the beast before his mighty talons could fasten themselves in the flesh of the black, the strain overbalanced Tarzan, who came tumbling to the ground not six paces from the infuriated animal. Like lightning Numa turned upon this new enemy, and, defenseless as he was, Tarzan of the Apes was nearer to death that instant than he ever before had been. It was the black who saved him. The warrior realized in an instant that he owed his life to this strange white man, and he also saw that only a miracle could save his preserver from those fierce yellow fangs that had been so near to his own flesh.

With the quickness of thought his spear arm flew back, and then shot forward with all the force of the sinewy muscles that rolled beneath the shimmering ebon hide. True to its mark the iron-shod weapon flew, transfixing Numa's sleek carcass from the right groin to beneath the left shoulder. With a hideous scream of rage and pain the brute turned again upon the black. A dozen paces he had gone when Tarzan's rope brought him to a stand once more – then he wheeled again upon the ape-man, only to feel the painful prick of a barbed arrow as it sank half its length in his quivering flesh. Again he stopped, and by this time Tarzan had run twice around the stem of a great tree with his rope, and made the end fast.

The black saw the trick, and grinned, but Tarzan knew that Numa must be quickly finished before those mighty teeth had found and parted the slender cord that held him. It was a matter of but an instant to reach the black's side and drag his long knife from its scabbard. Then he signed the warrior to continue to shoot arrows into the great beast while he attempted to close in upon him with the knife; so as one tantalized upon one side, the other sneaked cautiously in upon the other. Numa was furious. He raised his voice in a perfect frenzy of shrieks, growls, and hideous moans, the while he reared upon his hind legs in futile attempt to reach first one and then the other of his tormentors.

But at length the agile ape-man saw his chance, and rushed in upon the beast's left side behind the mighty shoulder. A giant arm encircled the tawny throat, and a long blade sank once, true as a die, into the fierce heart. Then Tarzan arose, and the black man and the white looked into each other's eyes across the body of their kill – and the black made the sign of peace and friendship, and Tarzan of the Apes answered in kind.

CHAPTER FIFTEEN

From Ape to Savage

THE NOISE OF THEIR battle with Numa had drawn an excited horde of savages from the nearby village, and a moment after the lion's death the two men were surrounded by lithe, ebon warriors, gesticulating and jabbering – a thousand questions that drowned each ventured reply.

And then the women came, and the children – eager, curious, and, at sight of Tarzan, more questioning than ever. The ape-man's new friend finally succeeded in making himself heard, and when he had done talking the men and women of the village vied with one another in doing honor to the strange creature who had saved their fellow and battled single-handed with fierce Numa.

At last they led him back to their village, where they brought him gifts of fowl, and goats, and cooked food. When he pointed to their weapons the warriors hastened to fetch spear, shield, arrows, and a bow. His friend of the encounter presented him with the knife with which he had killed Numa. There was nothing in all the village he could not have had for the asking.

How much easier this was, thought Tarzan, than murder and robbery to supply his wants. How close he had been to killing this man whom he never had seen before, and who now was manifesting by every primitive means at his command friendship and affection for his would-be slayer. Tarzan of the Apes was ashamed. Hereafter he would at least wait until he knew men deserved it before he thought of killing them.

The idea recalled Rokoff to his mind. He wished that he might have the Russian to himself in the dark jungle for a few minutes. There was a man who deserved killing if ever any one did. And if he could have seen Rokoff at that moment as he assiduously bent every endeavor to the pleasant task of ingratiating himself into the affections of the beautiful

Miss Strong, he would have longed more than ever to mete out to the man the fate he deserved.

Tarzan's first night with the savages was devoted to a wild orgy in his honor. There was feasting, for the hunters had brought in an antelope and a zebra as trophies of their skill, and gallons of the weak native beer were consumed. As the warriors danced in the firelight, Tarzan was again impressed by the symmetry of their figures and the regularity of their features – the flat noses and thick lips of the typical West Coast savage were entirely missing. In repose the faces of the men were intelligent and dignified, those of the women ofttimes prepossessing.

It was during this dance that the ape-man first noticed that some of the men and many of the women wore ornaments of gold – principally anklets and armlets of great weight, apparently beaten out of the solid metal. When he expressed a wish to examine one of these, the owner removed it from her person and insisted, through the medium of signs, that Tarzan accept it as a gift. A close scrutiny of the bauble convinced the ape-man that the article was of virgin gold, and he was surprised, for it was the first time that he had ever seen golden ornaments among the savages of Africa, other than the trifling baubles those near the coast had purchased or stolen from Europeans. He tried to ask them from whence the metal came, but he could not make them understand.

When the dance was done Tarzan signified his intention to leave them, but they almost implored him to accept the hospitality of a great hut which the chief set apart for his sole use. He tried to explain that he would return in the morning, but they could not understand. When he finally walked away from them toward the side of the village opposite the gate, they were still further mystified as to his intentions.

Tarzan, however, knew just what he was about. In the past he had had experience with the rodents and vermin that infest every native village, and, while he was not overscrupulous about such matters, he much preferred the fresh air of the swaying trees to the fetid atmosphere of a hut.

The natives followed him to where a great tree overhung the palisade, and as Tarzan leaped for a lower branch and disappeared into the foliage above, precisely after the manner of Manu, the monkey, there were loud exclamations of surprise and astonishment. For half an hour they called to him to return, but as he did not answer them they at last desisted, and sought the sleeping-mats within their huts.

Tarzan went back into the forest a short distance until he had found a tree suited to his primitive requirements, and then, curling himself in a great crotch, he fell immediately into a deep sleep.

The following morning he dropped into the village street as suddenly as he had disappeared the preceding night. For a moment the natives were startled and afraid, but when they recognized their guest of the night before they welcomed him with shouts and laughter. That day he accompanied a party of warriors to the nearby plains on a great hunt, and so dexterous did they find this white man with their own crude weapons that another bond of respect and admiration was thereby wrought.

For weeks Tarzan lived with his savage friends, hunting buffalo, antelope, and zebra for meat, and elephant for ivory. Quickly he learned their simple speech, their native customs, and the ethics of their wild, primitive tribal life. He found that they were not cannibals – that they looked with loathing and contempt upon men who ate men.

Busuli, the warrior whom he had stalked to the village, told him many of the tribal legends – how, many years before, his people had come many long marches from the north; how once they had been a great and powerful tribe; and how the slave raiders had wrought such havoc among them with their death-dealing guns that they had been reduced to a mere remnant of their former numbers and power.

"They hunted us down as one hunts a fierce beast," said Busuli. "There was no mercy in them. When it was not slaves they sought it was ivory, but usually it was both. Our men were killed and our women driven away like sheep. We fought against them for many years, but our arrows and spears could not prevail against the sticks which spit fire and lead and death to many times the distance that our mightiest warrior could place an arrow. At last, when my father was a young man, the Arabs came again, but our warriors saw them a long way off, and Chowambi, who was chief then, told his people to gather up their belongings and come away with him – that he would lead them far to the south until they found a spot to which the Arab raiders did not come.

"And they did as he bid, carrying all their belongings, including many tusks of ivory. For months they wandered, suffering untold hardships and privations, for much of the way was through dense jungle, and across mighty mountains, but finally they came to this spot, and although they sent parties farther on to search for an even better location, none has ever been found."

"And the raiders have never found you here?" asked Tarzan.

"About a year ago a small party of Arabs and Manyuema stumbled upon us, but we drove them off, killing many. For days we followed them, stalking them for the wild beasts they are, picking them off one by one, until but a handful remained, but these escaped us."

As Busuli talked he fingered a heavy gold armlet that encircled the glossy hide of his left arm. Tarzan's eyes had been upon the ornament, but his thoughts were elsewhere. Presently he recalled the question he had tried to ask when he first came to the tribe – the question he could not at that time make them understand. For weeks he had forgotten so trivial a thing as gold, for he had been for the time a truly primeval man with no thought beyond today. But of a sudden the sight of gold awakened the sleeping civilization that was in him, and with it came the lust for wealth. That lesson Tarzan had learned well in his brief experience of the ways of civilized man. He knew that gold meant power and pleasure. He pointed to the bauble.

"From whence came the yellow metal, Busuli?" he asked.

The black pointed toward the southeast.

"A moon's march away – maybe more," he replied.

"Have you been there?" asked Tarzan.

"No, but some of our people were there years ago, when my father was yet a young man. One of the parties that searched farther for a location for the tribe when first they settled here came upon a strange people who wore many ornaments of yellow metal. Their spears were tipped with it, as were their arrows, and they cooked in vessels made all of solid metal like my armlet.

"They lived in a great village in huts that were built of stone and surrounded by a great wall. They were very fierce, rushing out and falling upon our warriors before ever they learned that their errand was a peaceful one. Our men were few in number, but they held their own at the top of a little rocky hill, until the fierce people went back at sunset into their wicked city. Then our warriors came down from their hill, and, after taking many ornaments of yellow metal from the bodies of those they had slain, they marched back out of the valley, nor have any of us ever returned.

"They are wicked people – neither white like you nor black like me, but covered with hair as is Bolgani, the gorilla. Yes, they are very bad people indeed, and Chowambi was glad to get out of their country."

"And are none of those alive who were with Chowambi, and saw these strange people and their wonderful city?" asked Tarzan.

"Waziri, our chief, was there," replied Busuli. "He was a very young man then, but he accompanied Chowambi, who was his father."

So that night Tarzan asked Waziri about it, and Waziri, who was now an old man, said that it was a long march, but that the way was not difficult to follow. He remembered it well.

"For ten days we followed this river which runs beside our village. Up toward its source we traveled until on the tenth day we came to a little spring far up upon the side of a lofty mountain range. In this little spring our river is born. The next day we crossed over the top of the mountain, and upon the other side we came to a tiny rivulet which we followed down into a great forest. For many days we traveled along the winding banks of the rivulet that had now become a river, until we came to a greater river, into which it emptied, and which ran down the center of a mighty valley.

"Then we followed this large river toward its source, hoping to come to more open land. After twenty days of marching from the time we had crossed the mountains and passed out of our own country we came again to another range of mountains. Up their side we followed the great river, that had now dwindled to a tiny rivulet, until we came to a little cave near the mountain-top. In this cave was the mother of the river.

"I remember that we camped there that night, and that it was very cold, for the mountains were high. The next day we decided to ascend to the top of the mountains, and see what the country upon the other side looked like, and if it seemed no better than that which we had so far traversed we would return to our village and tell them that they had already found the best place in all the world to live.

"And so we clambered up the face of the rocky cliffs until we reached the summit, and there from a flat mountain-top we saw, not far beneath us, a shallow valley, very narrow; and upon the far side of it was a great village of stone, much of which had fallen and crumbled into decay."

The balance of Waziri's story was practically the same as that which Busuli had told.

"I should like to go there and see this strange city," said Tarzan, "and get some of their yellow metal from its fierce inhabitants."

"It is a long march," replied Waziri, "and I am an old man, but if you will wait until the rainy season is over and the rivers have gone down I will take some of my warriors and go with you."

And Tarzan had to be contented with that arrangement, though he would have liked it well enough to have set off the next morning – he was as impatient as a child. Really Tarzan of the Apes was but a child, or a primeval man, which is the same thing in a way.

The next day but one a small party of hunters returned to the village from the south to report a large herd of elephant some miles away. By climbing trees they had had a fairly good view of the herd, which they described as numbering several large tuskers, a great many cows and calves, and full-grown bulls whose ivory would be worth having.

The balance of the day and evening was filled with preparation for a great hunt – spears were overhauled, quivers were replenished, bows were restrung; and all the while the village witch doctor passed through the busy throngs disposing of various charms and amulets designed to protect the possessor from hurt, or bring him good fortune in the morrow's hunt.

At dawn the hunters were off. There were fifty sleek, black warriors, and in their midst, lithe and active as a young forest god, strode Tarzan of the Apes, his brown skin contrasting oddly with the ebony of his companions. Except for color he was one of them. His ornaments and weapons were the same as theirs – he spoke their language – he laughed and joked with them, and leaped and shouted in the brief wild dance that preceded their departure from the village, to all intent and purpose a savage among savages. Nor, had he questioned himself, is it to be doubted that he would have admitted that he was far more closely allied to these people and their life than to the Parisian friends whose ways, apelike, he had successfully mimicked for a few short months.

But he did think of D'Arnot, and a grin of amusement showed his strong white teeth as he pictured the immaculate Frenchman's expression could he by some means see Tarzan as he was that minute. Poor Paul, who had prided himself on having eradicated from his friend the last traces of wild savagery. "How quickly have I fallen!" thought Tarzan; but in his heart he did not consider it a fall – rather, he pitied the poor creatures of Paris, penned up like prisoners in their silly clothes, and watched by policemen all their poor lives, that they might do nothing that was not entirely artificial and tiresome.

A two hours' march brought them close to the vicinity in which the elephants had been seen the previous day. From there on they moved very quietly indeed searching for the spoor of the great beasts. At length they found the well-marked trail along which the herd had passed not many hours before. In single file they followed it for about half an hour. It was Tarzan who first raised his hand in signal that the quarry was at hand – his sensitive nose had warned him that the elephants were not far ahead of them.

The blacks were skeptical when he told them how he knew.

"Come with me," said Tarzan, "and we shall see."

With the agility of a squirrel he sprang into a tree and ran nimbly to the top. One of the blacks followed more slowly and carefully. When he had reached a lofty limb beside the ape-man the latter pointed to the south, and there, some few hundred yards away, the black saw a number of huge black backs swaying back and forth above the top of the lofty jungle grasses. He pointed the direction to the watchers below, indicating with his fingers the number of beasts he could count.

Immediately the hunters started toward the elephants. The black in the tree hastened down, but Tarzan stalked, after his own fashion, along the leafy way of the middle terrace.

It is no child's play to hunt wild elephants with the crude weapons of primitive man. Tarzan knew that few native tribes ever attempted it, and the fact that his tribe did so gave him no little pride – already he was commencing to think of himself as a member of the little community. As Tarzan moved silently through the trees he saw the warriors below creeping in a half circle upon the still unsuspecting elephants. Finally they were within sight of the great beasts. Now they singled out two large tuskers, and at a signal the fifty men rose from the ground where they had lain concealed, and hurled their heavy war spears at the two marked beasts. There was not a single miss; twenty-five spears were embedded in the sides of each of the giant animals. One never moved from the spot where it stood when the avalanche of spears struck it, for two, perfectly aimed, had penetrated its heart, and it lunged forward upon its knees, rolling to the ground without a struggle.

The other, standing nearly head-on toward the hunters, had not proved so good a mark, and though every spear struck not one entered the great heart. For a moment the huge bull stood trumpeting in rage and pain, casting about with its little eyes for the author of its hurt. The blacks had faded into the jungle before the weak eyes of the monster had fallen upon any of them, but now he caught the sound of their retreat, and, amid a terrific crashing of underbrush and branches, he charged in the direction of the noise.

It so happened that chance sent him in the direction of Busuli, whom he was overtaking so rapidly that it was as though the black were standing still instead of racing at full speed to escape the certain death which pursued him. Tarzan had witnessed the entire performance from the branches of a nearby tree, and now that he saw his friend's peril he raced toward the infuriated beast with loud cries, hoping to distract him.

But it had been as well had he saved his breath, for the brute was deaf and blind to all else save the particular object of his rage that raced futilely before him. And now Tarzan saw that only a miracle could save Busuli, and with the same unconcern with which he had once hunted this very man he hurled himself into the path of the elephant to save the black warrior's life.

He still grasped his spear, and while Tantor was yet six or eight paces behind his prey, a sinewy white warrior dropped as from the heavens, almost directly in his path. With a vicious lunge the elephant swerved to the right to dispose of this temerarious foeman who dared intervene between himself and his intended victim; but he had not reckoned on the lightning quickness that could galvanize those steel muscles into action so marvelously swift as to baffle even a keener eyesight than Tantor's.

And so it happened that before the elephant realized that his new enemy had leaped from his path Tarzan had driven his iron-shod spear from behind the massive shoulder straight into the fierce heart, and the colossal pachyderm had toppled to his death at the feet of the ape-man.

Busuli had not beheld the manner of his deliverance, but Waziri, the old chief, had seen, and several of the other warriors, and they hailed Tarzan with delight as they swarmed about him and his great kill. When he leaped upon the mighty carcass, and gave voice to the weird challenge with which he announced a great victory, the blacks shrank back in fear, for to them it marked the brutal Bolgani, whom they feared fully as much as they feared Numa, the lion; but with a fear with which was mixed a certain uncanny awe of the manlike thing to which they attributed supernatural powers.

But when Tarzan lowered his raised head and smiled upon them they were reassured, though they did not understand. Nor did they ever fully understand this strange creature who ran through the trees as quickly as Manu, yet was even more at home upon the ground than themselves; who was except as to color like unto themselves, yet as powerful as ten of them, and singlehanded a match for the fiercest denizens of the fierce jungle.

When the remainder of the warriors had gathered, the hunt was again taken up and the stalking of the retreating herd once more begun; but they had covered a bare hundred yards when from behind them, at a great distance, sounded faintly a strange popping.

For an instant they stood like a group of statuary, intently listening. Then Tarzan spoke.

"Guns!" he said. "The village is being attacked."

"Come!" cried Waziri. "The Arab raiders have returned with their cannibal slaves for our ivory and our women!"

CHAPTER SIXTEEN

The Ivory Raiders

WAZIRI'S WARRIORS MARCHED AT a rapid trot through the jungle in the direction of the village. For a few minutes, the sharp cracking of guns ahead warned them to haste, but finally the reports dwindled to an occasional shot, presently ceasing altogether. Nor was this less ominous than the rattle of musketry, for it suggested but a single solution to the little band of rescuers – that the illy garrisoned village had already succumbed to the onslaught of a superior force.

The returning hunters had covered a little more than three miles of the five that had separated them from the village when they met the first of the fugitives who had escaped the bullets and clutches of the foe. There were a dozen women, youths, and girls in the party, and so excited were they that they could scarce make themselves understood as they tried to relate to Waziri the calamity that had befallen his people.

"They are as many as the leaves of the forest," cried one of the women, in attempting to explain the enemy's force. "There are many Arabs and countless Manyuema, and they all have guns. They crept close to the village before we knew that they were about, and then, with many shouts, they rushed in upon us, shooting down men, and women, and children. Those of us who could fled in all directions into the jungle, but more were killed. I do not know whether they took any prisoners or not – they seemed only bent upon killing us all. The Manyuema called us many names, saying that they would eat us all before they left our country – that this was our punishment for killing their friends last year. I did not hear much, for I ran away quickly."

The march toward the village was now resumed, more slowly and with greater stealth, for Waziri knew that it was too late to rescue – their only mission could be one of revenge. Inside the next mile a hundred more fugitives were met. There were many men among these, and so the fighting strength of the party was augmented.

Now a dozen warriors were sent creeping ahead to reconnoiter. Waziri remained with the main body, which advanced in a thin line that spread in a great crescent through the forest. By the chief's side walked Tarzan.

Presently one of the scouts returned. He had come within sight of the village.

"They are all within the palisade," he whispered.

"Good!" said Waziri. "We shall rush in upon them and slay them all," and he made ready to send word along the line that they were to halt at the edge of the clearing until they saw him rush toward the village – then all were to follow.

"Wait!" cautioned Tarzan. "If there are even fifty guns within the palisade we shall be repulsed and slaughtered. Let me go alone through the trees, so that I may look down upon them from above, and see just how many there be, and what chance we might have were we to charge. It were foolish to lose a single man needlessly if there be no hope of success. I have an idea that we can accomplish more by cunning than by force. Will you wait, Waziri?"

"Yes," said the old chief. "Go!"

So Tarzan sprang into the trees and disappeared in the direction of the village. He moved more cautiously than was his wont, for he knew that men with guns could reach him quite as easily in the treetops as on the ground. And when Tarzan of the Apes elected to adopt stealth, no creature in all the jungle could move so silently or so completely efface himself from the sight of an enemy.

In five minutes he had wormed his way to the great tree that overhung the palisade at one end of the village, and from his point of vantage looked down upon the savage horde beneath. He counted fifty Arabs and estimated that there were five times as many Manyuema. The latter were gorging themselves upon food and, under the very noses of their white masters, preparing the gruesome feast which is the PIECE DE RESISTANCE that follows a victory in which the bodies of their slain enemies fall into their horrid hands.

The ape-man saw that to charge that wild horde, armed as they were with guns, and barricaded behind the locked gates of the village, would be a futile task, and so he returned to Waziri and advised him to wait; that he, Tarzan, had a better plan.

But a moment before one of the fugitives had related to Waziri the story of the atrocious murder of the old chief's wife, and so crazed with rage was the old man that he cast discretion to the winds. Calling his warriors about him, he commanded them to charge, and, with brandishing spears and savage yells, the little force of scarcely more than a hundred dashed madly toward the village gates. Before the clearing had been half crossed the Arabs opened up a withering fire from behind the palisade.

With the first volley Waziri fell. The speed of the chargers slackened. Another volley brought down a half dozen more. A few reached the barred gates, only to be shot in their tracks, without the ghost of a chance to gain the inside of the palisade, and then the whole attack crumpled, and the remaining warriors scampered back into the forest. As they ran the raiders opened the gates, rushing after them, to complete the day's work with the utter extermination of the tribe. Tarzan had been among the last to turn back toward the forest, and now, as he ran slowly, he turned from time to time to speed a well-aimed arrow into the body of a pursuer.

Once within the jungle, he found a little knot of determined blacks waiting to give battle to the oncoming horde, but Tarzan cried to them to scatter, keeping out of harm's way until they could gather in force after dark.

"Do as I tell you," he urged, "and I will lead you to victory over these enemies of yours. Scatter through the forest, picking up as many stragglers as you can find, and at night, if you think that you have been followed, come by roundabout ways to the spot where we killed the elephants today. Then I will explain my plan, and you will find that it is good. You cannot hope to pit your puny strength and simple weapons against the numbers and the guns of the Arabs and the Manyuema."

They finally assented. "When you scatter," explained Tarzan, in conclusion, "your foes will have to scatter to follow you, and so it may happen that if you are watchful you can drop many a Manyuema with your arrows from behind some great trees."

They had barely time to hasten away farther into the forest before the first of the raiders had crossed the clearing and entered it in pursuit of them.

Tarzan ran a short distance along the ground before he took to the trees. Then he raced quickly to the upper terrace, there doubling on his tracks and making his way rapidly back toward the village. Here he found that every Arab and Manyuema had joined in the pursuit, leaving the village deserted except for the chained prisoners and a single guard.

The sentry stood at the open gate, looking in the direction of the forest, so that he did not see the agile giant that dropped to the ground at the far end of the village street. With drawn bow the ape-man crept stealthily toward his unsuspecting victim. The prisoners had already discovered him, and with wide eyes filled with wonder and with hope they watched their would-be rescuer. Now he halted not ten paces from the unconscious Manyuema. The shaft was drawn back its full length at the height of the keen gray eye that sighted along its polished surface. There was a sudden twang as the brown fingers released their hold, and without a sound the raider sank forward upon his face, a wooden shaft transfixing his heart and protruding a foot from his black chest.

Then Tarzan turned his attention to the fifty women and youths chained neck to neck on the long slave chain. There was no releasing of the ancient padlocks in the time that was left him, so the ape-man called to them to follow him as they were, and, snatching the gun and cartridge belt from the dead sentry, he led the now happy band out through the village gate and into the forest upon the far side of the clearing.

It was a slow and arduous march, for the slave chain was new to these people, and there were many delays as one of their number would stumble and fall, dragging others down with her. Then, too, Tarzan had been forced to make a wide detour to avoid any possibility of meeting with returning raiders. He was partially guided by occasional shots which indicated that the Arab horde was still in touch with the villagers; but he knew that if they would but follow his advice there would be but few casualties other than on the side of the marauders.

Toward dusk the firing ceased entirely, and Tarzan knew that the Arabs had all returned to the village. He could scarce repress a smile of triumph as he thought of their rage on discovering that their guard had been killed and their prisoners taken away. Tarzan had wished that he might have taken some of the great store of ivory the village contained, solely for the purpose of still further augmenting the wrath of his enemies; but he knew that that was not necessary for its salvation, since he already had a plan mapped out which would effectually prevent the Arabs leaving the country with a single tusk. And it would have been cruel to have needlessly burdened these poor, overwrought women with the extra weight of the heavy ivory.

It was after midnight when Tarzan, with his slow-moving caravan, approached the spot where the elephants lay. Long before they reached it they had been guided by the huge fire the natives had built in the center of a hastily improvised BOMA, partially for warmth and partially to keep off chance lions.

When they had come close to the encampment Tarzan called aloud to let them know that friends were coming. It was a joyous reception the little party received when the blacks within the BOMA saw the long file of fettered friends and relatives enter the firelight. These had all been given up as lost forever, as had Tarzan as well, so that the happy blacks would have remained awake all night to feast on elephant meat and celebrate the return of their fellows, had not Tarzan insisted that they take what sleep they could, against the work of the coming day.

At that, sleep was no easy matter, for the women who had lost their men or their children in the day's massacre and battle made night hideous with their continued wailing and howling. Finally, however, Tarzan succeeded in silencing them, on the plea that their noise would attract the Arabs to their hiding-place, when all would be slaughtered.

When dawn came Tarzan explained his plan of battle to the warriors, and without demur one and all agreed that it was the safest and surest way in which to rid themselves of their unwelcome visitors and be revenged for the murder of their fellows.

First the women and children, with a guard of some twenty old warriors and youths, were started southward, to be entirely out of the zone of danger. They had instructions to erect temporary shelter and construct a protecting BOMA of thorn bush; for the plan of campaign which Tarzan had chosen was one which might stretch out over many days, or even weeks, during which time the warriors would not return to the new camp.

Two hours after daylight a thin circle of black warriors surrounded the village. At intervals one was perched high in the branches of a tree which could overlook the palisade. Presently a Manyuema within the village fell, pierced by a single arrow. There had been no sound of attack – none of the hideous war-cries or vainglorious waving of menacing spears that ordinarily marks the attack of savages – just a silent messenger of death from out of the silent forest.

The Arabs and their followers were thrown into a fine rage at this unprecedented occurrence. They ran for the gates, to wreak dire vengeance upon the foolhardy perpetrator of the outrage; but they suddenly realized that they did not know which way to turn to find the foe. As they stood debating with many angry shouts and much gesticulating, one of the Arabs sank silently to the ground in their very midst – a thin arrow protruding from his heart.

Tarzan had placed the finest marksmen of the tribe in the surrounding trees, with directions never to reveal themselves while the enemy was faced in their direction. As a black released his messenger of death he would slink behind the sheltering stem of the tree he had selected, nor would he again aim until a watchful eye told him that none was looking toward his tree.

Three times the Arabs started across the clearing in the direction from which they thought the arrows came, but each time another arrow would come from behind to take its toll from among their number. Then they would turn and charge in a new direction. Finally they set out upon a determined search of the forest, but the blacks melted before them, so that they saw no sign of an enemy.

But above them lurked a grim figure in the dense foliage of the mighty trees – it was Tarzan of the Apes, hovering over them as if he had been the shadow of death. Presently a Manyuema forged ahead of his companions; there was none to see from what direction death came, and so it came quickly, and a moment later those behind stumbled over the dead body of their comrade – the inevitable arrow piercing the still heart.

It does not take a great deal of this manner of warfare to get upon the nerves of white men, and so it is little to be wondered at that the Manyuema were soon panic-stricken. Did one forge ahead an arrow found his heart; did one lag behind he never again was seen alive; did one stumble to one side, even for a bare moment from the sight of his fellows, he did not return – and always when they came upon the bodies of their dead they found those terrible arrows driven with the accuracy of superhuman power straight through the victim's heart. But worse than all else was the hideous fact that not once during the morning had they seen or heard the slightest sign of an enemy other than the pitiless arrows.

When finally they returned to the village it was no better. Every now and then, at varying intervals that were maddening in the terrible suspense they caused, a man would plunge forward dead. The blacks besought their masters to leave this terrible place, but the Arabs feared to take up the march through the grim and hostile forest beset by this new and terrible enemy while laden with the great store of ivory they had found within the village; but, worse yet, they hated to leave the ivory behind.

Finally the entire expedition took refuge within the thatched huts – here, at least, they would be free from the arrows. Tarzan, from the tree above the village, had marked the hut into which the chief Arabs had gone, and, balancing himself upon an overhanging limb, he drove his heavy spear with all the force of his giant muscles through the thatched roof. A howl of pain told him that it had found a mark. With this parting salute to convince them that there was no safety for them anywhere within the country, Tarzan returned to the forest, collected his warriors, and withdrew a mile to the south to rest and eat. He kept sentries in several trees that commanded a view of the trail toward the village, but there was no pursuit.

An inspection of his force showed not a single casualty – not even a minor wound; while rough estimates of the enemies' loss convinced the blacks that no fewer than twenty had fallen before their arrows. They were wild with elation, and were for finishing the day in one glorious rush upon the village, during which they would slaughter the last of their foemen. They were even picturing the various tortures they would inflict, and gloating over the suffering of the Manyuema, for whom they entertained a peculiar hatred, when Tarzan put his foot down flatly upon the plan.

"You are crazy!" he cried. "I have shown you the only way to fight these people. Already you have killed twenty of them without the loss of a single warrior, whereas, yesterday, following your own tactics, which you would now renew, you lost at least a dozen, and killed not a single Arab or Manyuema. You will fight just as I tell you to fight, or I shall leave you and go back to my own country."

They were frightened when he threatened this, and promised to obey him scrupulously if he would but promise not to desert them.

"Very well," he said. "We shall return to the elephant BOMA for the night. I have a plan to give the Arabs a little taste of what they may expect if they remain in our country, but I shall need no help. Come! If they suffer no more for the balance of the day they will feel reassured, and the relapse into fear will be even more nerve-racking than as though we continued to frighten them all afternoon."

So they marched back to their camp of the previous night, and, lighting great fires, ate and recounted the adventures of the day until long after dark. Tarzan slept until midnight, then he arose and crept into the Cimmerian blackness of the forest. An hour later he came to the edge of the clearing before the village. There was a camp-fire burning within the palisade. The ape-man crept across the clearing until he stood before the barred gates. Through the interstices he saw a lone sentry sitting before the fire.

Quietly Tarzan went to the tree at the end of the village street. He climbed softly to his place, and fitted an arrow to his bow. For several minutes he tried to sight fairly upon the sentry, but the waving branches and flickering firelight convinced him that the danger of a miss was too great – he must touch the heart full in the center to bring the quiet and sudden death his plan required.

He had brought, besides, his bow, arrows, and rope, the gun he had taken the previous day from the other sentry he had killed. Caching all these in a convenient crotch of the tree, he dropped lightly to the ground within the palisade, armed only with his long knife. The sentry's back was toward him. Like a cat Tarzan crept upon the dozing man. He was within two paces of him now – another instant and the knife would slide silently into the fellow's heart.

Tarzan crouched for a spring, for that is ever the quickest and surest attack of the jungle beast – when the man, warned, by some subtle sense, sprang to his feet and faced the ape-man.

CHAPTER SEVENTEEN

The White Chief of the Waziri

When the eyes of the black Manyuema savage fell upon the strange apparition that confronted him with menacing knife they went wide in horror. He forgot the gun within his hands; he even forgot to cry out – his one thought was to escape this fearsome-looking white savage, this giant of a man upon whose massive rolling muscles and mighty chest the flickering firelight played.

But before he could turn Tarzan was upon him, and then the sentry thought to scream for aid, but it was too late. A great hand was upon his windpipe, and he was being borne to the earth. He battled furiously but futilely – with the grim tenacity of a bulldog those awful fingers were clinging to his throat. Swiftly and surely life was being choked from him. His eyes bulged, his tongue protruded, his face turned to a ghastly purplish hue – there was a convulsive tremor of the stiffening muscles, and the Manyuema sentry lay quite still.

The ape-man threw the body across one of his broad shoulders and, gathering up the fellow's gun, trotted silently up the sleeping village street toward the tree that gave him such easy ingress to the palisaded village. He bore the dead sentry into the midst of the leafy maze above.

First he stripped the body of cartridge belt and such ornaments as he craved, wedging it into a convenient crotch while his nimble fingers ran over it in search of the loot he could not plainly see in the dark. When he had finished he took the gun that had belonged to the man, and walked far out upon a limb, from the end of which he could obtain a better view of the huts. Drawing a careful bead on the beehive structure in which he knew the chief Arabs to be, he pulled the trigger. Almost instantly there was an answering groan. Tarzan smiled. He had made another lucky hit.

Following the shot there was a moment's silence in the camp, and then Manyuema and Arab came pouring from the huts like a swarm of angry hornets; but if the truth were known they were even more frightened than they were angry. The strain of the preceding day had wrought upon the fears of both black and white, and now this single shot in the night conjured all manner of terrible conjectures in their terrified minds.

When they discovered that their sentry had disappeared, their fears were in no way allayed, and as though to bolster their courage by warlike actions, they began to fire rapidly at the barred gates of the village, although no enemy was in sight. Tarzan took advantage of the deafening roar of this fusillade to fire into the mob beneath him.

No one heard his shot above the din of rattling musketry in the street, but some who were standing close saw one of their number crumple suddenly to the earth. When they leaned over him he was dead. They were panic-stricken, and it took all the brutal authority of the Arabs to keep the Manyuema from rushing helter-skelter into the jungle – anywhere to escape from this terrible village.

After a time they commenced to quiet down, and as no further mysterious deaths occurred among them they took heart again. But it was a short-lived respite, for just as they had concluded that they would not be disturbed again Tarzan gave voice to a weird moan, and as the raiders looked up in the direction from which the sound seemed to come, the ape-man, who stood swinging the dead body of the sentry gently to and fro, suddenly shot the corpse far out above their heads.

With howls of alarm the throng broke in all directions to escape this new and terrible creature who seemed to be springing upon them. To their fear-distorted imaginations the body of the sentry, falling with wide-sprawled arms and legs, assumed the likeness of a great beast of prey. In their anxiety to escape, many of the blacks scaled the palisade, while others tore down the bars from the gates and rushed madly across the clearing toward the jungle.

For a time no one turned back toward the thing that had frightened them, but Tarzan knew that they would in a moment, and when they discovered that it was but the dead body of their sentry, while they would doubtless be still further terrified, he had a rather definite idea as to what they would do, and so he faded silently away toward the south, taking the moonlit upper terrace back toward the camp of the Waziri.

Presently one of the Arabs turned and saw that the thing that had leaped from the tree upon them lay still and quiet where it had fallen in the center of the village street. Cautiously he crept back toward it until he saw that it was but a man. A moment later he was beside the figure, and in another had recognized it as the corpse of the Manyuema who had stood on guard at the village gate.

His companions rapidly gathered around at his call, and after a moment's excited conversation they did precisely what Tarzan had reasoned they would. Raising their guns to their shoulders, they poured volley after volley into the tree from which the corpse had been thrown – had Tarzan remained there he would have been riddled by a hundred bullets.

When the Arabs and Manyuema discovered that the only marks of violence upon the body of their dead comrade were giant finger prints upon his swollen throat they were again thrown into deeper apprehension and despair. That they were not even safe within a palisaded village at night came as a distinct shock to them. That an enemy could enter into the midst of their camp and kill their sentry with bare hands seemed outside the bounds of reason, and so the superstitious Manyuema commenced to attribute their ill luck to supernatural causes; nor were the Arabs able to offer any better explanation.

With at least fifty of their number flying through the black jungle, and without the slightest knowledge of when their uncanny foemen might resume the cold-blooded slaughter they had commenced, it was a desperate band of cut-throats that waited sleeplessly for the dawn. Only on the promise of the Arabs that they would leave the village at daybreak, and hasten onward toward their own land, would the remaining Manyuema consent to stay at the village a moment longer. Not even fear of their cruel masters was sufficient to overcome this new terror.

And so it was that when Tarzan and his warriors returned to the attack the next morning they found the raiders prepared to march out of the village. The Manyuema were laden with stolen ivory. As Tarzan saw it he grinned, for he knew that they would not carry it far. Then he saw something which caused him anxiety – a number of the Manyuema were lighting torches in the remnant of the camp-fire. They were about to fire the village.

Tarzan was perched in a tall tree some hundred yards from the palisade. Making a trumpet of his hands, he called loudly in the Arab tongue: "Do not fire the huts, or we shall kill you all! Do not fire the huts, or we shall kill you all!"

A dozen times he repeated it. The Manyuema hesitated, then one of them flung his torch into the campfire. The others were about to do the same when an Arab sprung upon them with a stick, beating them toward the huts. Tarzan could see that he was commanding them to fire the little thatched dwellings. Then he stood erect upon the swaying branch a hundred feet above the ground, and, raising one of the Arab guns to his shoulder, took careful aim and fired. With the report the Arab who was urging on his men to burn the village fell in his tracks, and the Manyuema threw away their torches and fled from the village. The last Tarzan saw of them they were racing toward the jungle, while their former masters knelt upon the ground and fired at them.

But however angry the Arabs might have been at the insubordination of their slaves, they were at least convinced that it would be the better part of wisdom to forego the pleasure of firing the village that had given them two such nasty receptions. In their hearts, however, they swore to return again with such force as would enable them to sweep the entire country for miles around, until no vestige of human life remained.

They had looked in vain for the owner of the voice which had frightened off the men who had been detailed to put the torch to the huts, but not even the keenest eye among them had been able to locate him. They had seen the puff of smoke from the tree following the shot that brought down the Arab, but, though a volley had immediately been loosed into its foliage, there had been no indication that it had been effective.

Tarzan was too intelligent to be caught in any such trap, and so the report of his shot had scarcely died away before the ape-man was on the ground and racing for another tree a hundred yards away. Here he again found a suitable perch from which he could watch the preparations of the raiders. It occurred to him that he might have considerable more fun with them, so again he called to them through his improvised trumpet.

"Leave the ivory!" he cried. "Leave the ivory! Dead men have no use for ivory!"

Some of the Manyuema started to lay down their loads, but this was altogether too much for the avaricious Arabs. With loud shouts and curses they aimed their guns full upon the bearers, threatening instant death to any who might lay down his load. They could give up firing the village, but the thought of abandoning this enormous fortune in ivory was quite beyond their conception – better death than that.

And so they marched out of the village of the Waziri, and on the shoulders of their slaves was the ivory ransom of a score of kings. Toward the north they marched, back toward their savage settlement in the wild and unknown country which lies back from the Kongo in the uttermost depths of The Great Forest, and on either side of them traveled an invisible and relentless foe.

Under Tarzan's guidance the black Waziri warriors stationed themselves along the trail on either side in the densest underbrush. They stood at far intervals, and, as the column passed, a single arrow or a heavy spear, well aimed, would pierce a Manyuema or an Arab. Then the Waziri would melt into the distance and run ahead to take his stand farther on. They did not strike unless success were sure and the danger of detection almost nothing, and so the arrows and the spears were few and far between, but so persistent and inevitable that the slow-moving column of heavy-laden raiders was in a constant state of panic – panic at the uncertainty of who the next would be to fall, and when.

It was with the greatest difficulty that the Arabs prevented their men a dozen times from throwing away their burdens and fleeing like frightened rabbits up the trail toward the north. And so the day wore on – a frightful nightmare of a day for the raiders – a day of weary but well-repaid work for the Waziri. At night the Arabs constructed a rude BOMA in a little clearing by a river, and went into camp.

At intervals during the night a rifle would bark close above their heads, and one of the dozen sentries which they now had posted would tumble to the ground. Such a condition was insupportable, for they saw that by means of these hideous tactics they would be completely wiped out, one by one, without inflicting a single death upon their enemy. But yet, with the persistent avariciousness of the white man, the Arabs clung to their loot, and when morning came forced the demoralized Manyuema to take up their burdens of death and stagger on into the jungle.

For three days the withering column kept up its frightful march. Each hour was marked by its deadly arrow or cruel spear. The nights were made hideous by the barking of the invisible gun that made sentry duty equivalent to a death sentence.

On the morning of the fourth day the Arabs were compelled to shoot two of their blacks before they could compel the balance to take up the hated ivory, and as they did so a voice rang out, clear and strong, from the jungle: "Today you die, oh, Manyuema, unless you lay down the ivory. Fall upon your cruel masters and kill them! You have guns, why do you not use them? Kill the Arabs, and we will not harm you. We will take you back to our village and feed you, and lead you out of our country in safety and in peace. Lay down the ivory, and fall upon your masters – we will help you. Else you die!"

As the voice died down the raiders stood as though turned to stone. The Arabs eyed their Manyuema slaves; the slaves looked first at one of their fellows, and then at another – they were but waiting for some one to take the initiative. There were some thirty Arabs left, and about one hundred and fifty blacks. All were armed – even those who were acting as porters had their rifles slung across their backs.

The Arabs drew together. The sheik ordered the Manyuema to take up the march, and as he spoke he cocked his rifle and raised it. But at the same instant one of the blacks threw down his load, and, snatching his rifle from his back, fired point-blank at the group of Arabs. In an instant the camp was a cursing, howling mass of demons, fighting with guns and knives and pistols. The Arabs stood together, and defended their lives valiantly, but with the rain of lead that poured upon them from their own slaves, and the shower of arrows and spears which now leaped from the surrounding jungle aimed solely at them, there was little question from the first what the outcome would be. In ten minutes from the time the first porter had thrown down his load the last of the Arabs lay dead.

When the firing had ceased Tarzan spoke again to the Manyuema:

"Take up our ivory, and return it to our village, from whence you stole it. We shall not harm you."

For a moment the Manyuema hesitated. They had no stomach to retrace that difficult three days' trail. They talked together in low whispers, and one turned toward the jungle, calling aloud to the voice that had spoken to them from out of the foliage.

"How do we know that when you have us in your village you will not kill us all?" he asked.

"You do not know," replied Tarzan, "other than that we have promised not to harm you if you will return our ivory to us. But this you do know, that it lies within our power to kill you all if you do not return as we direct, and are we not more likely to do so if you anger us than if you do as we bid?"

"Who are you that speaks the tongue of our Arab masters?" cried the Manyuema spokesman. "Let us see you, and then we shall give you our answer."

Tarzan stepped out of the jungle a dozen paces from them.

"Look!" he said. When they saw that he was white they were filled with awe, for never had they seen a white savage before, and at his great muscles and giant frame they were struck with wonder and admiration.

"You may trust me," said Tarzan. "So long as you do as I tell you, and harm none of my people, we shall do you no hurt. Will you take up our ivory and return in peace to our village, or shall we follow along your trail toward the north as we have followed for the past three days?"

The recollection of the horrid days that had just passed was the thing that finally decided the Manyuema, and so, after a short conference, they took up their burdens and set off to retrace their steps toward the village of the Waziri. At the end of the third day they marched into the village gate, and were greeted by the survivors of the recent massacre, to whom Tarzan had sent a messenger in their temporary camp to the south on the day that the raiders had quitted the village, telling them that they might return in safety.

It took all the mastery and persuasion that Tarzan possessed to prevent the Waziri falling on the Manyuema tooth and nail, and tearing them to pieces, but when he had explained that he had given his word that they would not be molested if they carried the ivory back to the spot from which they had stolen it, and had further impressed upon his people that they owed their entire victory to him, they finally acceded to his demands, and allowed the cannibals to rest in peace within their palisade.

That night the village warriors held a big palaver to celebrate their victories, and to choose a new chief. Since old Waziri's death Tarzan had been directing the warriors in battle, and the temporary command had been tacitly conceded to him. There had been no time to choose a new chief from among their own number, and, in fact, so remarkably successful had they been under the ape-man's generalship that they had had no wish to delegate the supreme authority to another for fear that what they already had gained might be lost. They had so recently seen the results of running counter to this savage white man's advice in the disastrous charge ordered by Waziri, in which he himself had died, that it had not been difficult for them to accept Tarzan's authority as final.

The principal warriors sat in a circle about a small fire to discuss the relative merits of whomever might be suggested as old Waziri's successor. It was Busuli who spoke first:

"Since Waziri is dead, leaving no son, there is but one among us whom we know from experience is fitted to make us a good king. There is only one who has proved that he can successfully lead us against the guns of the white man, and bring us easy victory without the loss of a single life. There is only one, and that is the white man who has led us for the past few days," and Busuli sprang to his feet, and with uplifted spear and half-bent, crouching body commenced to dance slowly about Tarzan, chanting in time to his steps: "Waziri, king of the Waziri; Waziri, killer of Arabs; Waziri, king of the Waziri."

One by one the other warriors signified their acceptance of Tarzan as their king by joining in the solemn dance. The women came and squatted about the rim of the circle, beating upon tom-toms, clapping their hands in time to the steps of the dancers, and joining in the chant of the warriors. In the center of the circle sat Tarzan of the Apes – Waziri, king of the Waziri, for, like his predecessor, he was to take the name of his tribe as his own.

Faster and faster grew the pace of the dancers, louder and louder their wild and savage shouts. The women rose and fell in unison, shrieking now at the tops of their voices. The spears were brandishing fiercely, and as the dancers stooped down and beat their shields upon the hard-tramped earth of the village street the whole sight was as terribly primeval and savage as though it were being staged in the dim dawn of humanity, countless ages in the past.

As the excitement waxed the ape-man sprang to his feet and joined in the wild ceremony. In the center of the circle of glittering black bodies he leaped and roared and shook his heavy spear in the same mad abandon that enthralled his fellow savages. The last remnant of his civilization was forgotten – he was a primitive man to the fullest now; reveling in the freedom of the fierce, wild life he loved, gloating in his kingship among these wild blacks.

Ah, if Olga de Coude had but seen him then – could she have recognized the well-dressed, quiet young man whose well-bred face and irreproachable manners had so captivated her but a few short months ago? And Jane Porter! Would she have still loved this savage warrior chieftain, dancing naked among his naked savage subjects? And D'Arnot! Could D'Arnot have believed that this was the same man he had introduced into half a dozen of the most select clubs of Paris? What would his fellow peers in the House of Lords have said had one pointed to this dancing giant, with his barbaric headdress and his metal ornaments, and said: "There, my lords, is John Clayton, Lord Greystoke."

And so Tarzan of the Apes came into a real kingship among men – slowly but surely was he following the evolution of his ancestors, for had he not started at the very bottom?

CHAPTER EIGHTEEN

The Lottery of Death

JANE PORTER HAD BEEN the first of those in the lifeboat to awaken the morning after the wreck of the LADY ALICE. The other members of the party were asleep upon the thwarts or huddled in cramped positions in the bottom of the boat.

When the girl realized that they had become separated from the other boats she was filled with alarm. The sense of utter loneliness and helplessness which the vast expanse of deserted ocean aroused in her was so depressing that, from the first, contemplation of the future held not the slightest ray of promise for her. She was confident that they were lost – lost beyond possibility of succor.

Presently Clayton awoke. It was several minutes before he could gather his senses sufficiently to realize where he was, or recall the disaster of the previous night. Finally his bewildered eyes fell upon the girl.

"Jane!" he cried. "Thank God that we are together!"

"Look," said the girl dully, indicating the horizon with an apathetic gesture. "We are all alone."

Clayton scanned the water in every direction.

"Where can they be?" he cried. "They cannot have gone down, for there has been no sea, and they were afloat after the yacht sank – I saw them all."

He awoke the other members of the party, and explained their plight.

"It is just as well that the boats are scattered, sir," said one of the sailors. "They are all provisioned, so that they do not need each other on that score, and should a storm blow up they could be of no service to one another even if they were together, but scattered about the ocean there is a much better chance that one at least will be picked up, and then a search will be at once started for the others. Were we together there would be but one chance of rescue, where now there may be four."

They saw the wisdom of his philosophy, and were cheered by it, but their joy was short-lived, for when it was decided that they should row steadily toward the east and the continent, it was discovered that the sailors who had been at the only two oars with which the boat had been provided had fallen asleep at their work, and allowed both to slip into the sea, nor were they in sight anywhere upon the water.

During the angry words and recriminations which followed the sailors nearly came to blows, but Clayton succeeded in quieting them; though a moment later Monsieur Thuran almost precipitated another row by making a nasty remark about the stupidity of all Englishmen, and especially English sailors.

"Come, come, mates," spoke up one of the men, Tompkins, who had taken no part in the altercation, "shootin' off our bloomin' mugs won't get us nothin'. As Spider 'ere said afore, we'll all bloody well be picked up, anyway, sez 'e, so wot's the use o' squabblin'? Let's eat, sez I."

"That's not a bad idea," said Monsieur Thuran, and then, turning to the third sailor, Wilson, he said: "Pass one of those tins aft, my good man."

"Fetch it yerself," retorted Wilson sullenly. "I ain't a-takin' no orders from no – furriner – you ain't captain o' this ship yet."

The result was that Clayton himself had to get the tin, and then another angry altercation ensued when one of the sailors accused Clayton and Monsieur Thuran of conspiring to control the provisions so that they could have the lion's share.

"Some one should take command of this boat," spoke up Jane Porter, thoroughly disgusted with the disgraceful wrangling that had marked the very opening of a forced companionship that might last for many days. "It is terrible enough to be alone in a frail boat on the Atlantic, without having the added misery and danger of constant bickering and brawling among the members of our party. You men should elect a leader, and then abide by his decisions in all matters. There is greater need for strict discipline here than there is upon a well-ordered ship."

She had hoped before she voiced her sentiments that it would not be necessary for her to enter into the transaction at all, for she believed that Clayton was amply able to cope with every emergency, but she had to admit that so far at least he had shown no greater promise of successfully handling the situation than any of the others, though he had at least refrained from adding in any way to the unpleasantness, even going so far as to give up the tin to the sailors when they objected to its being opened by him.

The girl's words temporarily quieted the men, and finally it was decided that the two kegs of water and the four tins of food should be divided into two parts, one-half going forward to the three sailors to do with as they saw best, and the balance aft to the three passengers.

Thus was the little company divided into two camps, and when the provisions had been apportioned each immediately set to work to open and distribute food and water. The sailors were the first to get one of the tins of "food" open, and their curses of rage and disappointment caused Clayton to ask what the trouble might be.

"Trouble!" shrieked Spider. "Trouble! It's worse than trouble – it's death! This – -tin is full of coal oil!"

Hastily now Clayton and Monsieur Thuran tore open one of theirs, only to learn the hideous truth that it also contained, not food, but coal oil. One after another the four tins on board were opened. And as the contents of each became known howls of anger announced the grim truth – there was not an ounce of food upon the boat.

"Well, thank Gawd it wasn't the water," cried Thompkins. "It's easier to get along without food than it is without water. We can eat our shoes if worse comes to worst, but we couldn't drink 'em."

As he spoke Wilson had been boring a hole in one of the water kegs, and as Spider held a tin cup he tilted the keg to pour a draft of the precious fluid. A thin stream of blackish, dry particles filtered slowly through the tiny aperture into the bottom of the cup. With a groan Wilson dropped the keg, and sat staring at the dry stuff in the cup, speechless with horror.

"The kegs are filled with gunpowder," said Spider, in a low tone, turning to those aft. And so it proved when the last had been opened.

"Coal oil and gunpowder!" cried Monsieur Thuran. "SAPRISTI! What a diet for shipwrecked mariners!"

With the full knowledge that there was neither food nor water on board, the pangs of hunger and thirst became immediately aggravated, and so on the first day of their tragic adventure real suffering commenced in grim earnest, and the full horrors of shipwreck were upon them.

As the days passed conditions became horrible. Aching eyes scanned the horizon day and night until the weak and weary watchers would sink exhausted to the bottom of the boat, and there wrest in dream-disturbed slumber a moment's respite from the horrors of the waking reality.

The sailors, goaded by the remorseless pangs of hunger, had eaten their leather belts, their shoes, the sweatbands from their caps, although both Clayton and Monsieur Thuran had done their best to convince them that these would only add to the suffering they were enduring.

Weak and hopeless, the entire party lay beneath the pitiless tropic sun, with parched lips and swollen tongues, waiting for the death they were beginning to crave. The intense suffering of the first few days had become deadened for the three passengers who had eaten nothing, but the agony of the sailors was pitiful, as their weak and impoverished stomachs attempted to cope with the bits of leather with which they had filled them. Tompkins was the first to succumb. Just a week from the day the LADY ALICE went down the sailor died horribly in frightful convulsions.

For hours his contorted and hideous features lay grinning back at those in the stern of the little boat, until Jane Porter could endure the sight no longer. "Can you not drop his body overboard, William?" she asked.

Clayton rose and staggered toward the corpse. The two remaining sailors eyed him with a strange, baleful light in their sunken orbs. Futilely the Englishman tried to lift the corpse over the side of the boat, but his strength was not equal to the task.

"Lend me a hand here, please," he said to Wilson, who lay nearest him.

"Wot do you want to throw 'im over for?" questioned the sailor, in a querulous voice.

"We've got to before we're too weak to do it," replied Clayton. "He'd be awful by tomorrow, after a day under that broiling sun."

"Better leave well enough alone," grumbled Wilson. "We may need him before tomorrow."

Slowly the meaning of the man's words percolated into Clayton's understanding. At last he realized the fellow's reason for objecting to the disposal of the dead man.

"God!" whispered Clayton, in a horrified tone. "You don't mean – "

"W'y not?" growled Wilson. "Ain't we gotta live? He's dead," he added, jerking his thumb in the direction of the corpse. "He won't care."

"Come here, Thuran," said Clayton, turning toward the Russian. "We'll have something worse than death aboard us if we don't get rid of this body before dark."

Wilson staggered up menacingly to prevent the contemplated act, but when his comrade, Spider, took sides with Clayton and Monsieur Thuran he gave up, and sat eying the corpse hungrily as the three men, by combining their efforts, succeeded in rolling it overboard.

All the balance of the day Wilson sat glaring at Clayton, in his eyes the gleam of insanity. Toward evening, as the sun was sinking into the sea, he commenced to chuckle and mumble to himself, but his eyes never left Clayton.

After it became quite dark Clayton could still feel those terrible eyes upon him. He dared not sleep, and yet so exhausted was he that it was a constant fight to retain consciousness. After what seemed an eternity of suffering his head dropped upon a thwart, and he slept. How long he was unconscious he did not know – he was awakened by a shuffling noise quite close to him. The moon had risen, and as he opened his startled eyes he saw Wilson creeping stealthily toward him, his mouth open and his swollen tongue hanging out.

The slight noise had awakened Jane Porter at the same time, and as she saw the hideous tableau she gave a shrill cry of alarm, and at the same instant the sailor lurched forward and fell upon Clayton. Like a wild beast his teeth sought the throat of his intended prey, but Clayton, weak though he was, still found sufficient strength to hold the maniac's mouth from him.

At Jane Porter's scream Monsieur Thuran and Spider awoke. On seeing the cause of her alarm, both men crawled to Clayton's rescue, and between the three of them were able to subdue Wilson and hurl him to the bottom of the boat. For a few minutes he lay there chattering and laughing, and then, with an awful scream, and before any of his companions could prevent, he staggered to his feet and leaped overboard.

The reaction from the terrific strain of excitement left the weak survivors trembling and prostrated. Spider broke down and wept; Jane Porter prayed; Clayton swore softly to himself; Monsieur Thuran sat with his head in his hands, thinking. The result of his cogitation developed the following morning in a proposition he made to Spider and Clayton.

"Gentlemen," said Monsieur Thuran, "you see the fate that awaits us all unless we are picked up within a day or two. That there is little hope of that is evidenced by the fact that during all the days we have drifted we have seen no sail, nor the faintest smudge of smoke upon the horizon.

"There might be a chance if we had food, but without food there is none. There remains for us, then, but one of two alternatives, and we must choose at once. Either we must all die together within a few days, or one must be sacrificed that the others may live. Do you quite clearly grasp my meaning?"

Jane Porter, who had overheard, was horrified. If the proposition had come from the poor, ignorant sailor, she might possibly have not been so surprised; but that it should come from one who posed as a man of culture and refinement, from a gentleman, she could scarcely credit.

"It is better that we die together, then," said Clayton.

"That is for the majority to decide," replied Monsieur Thuran. "As only one of us three will be the object of sacrifice, we shall decide. Miss Porter is not interested, since she will be in no danger."

"How shall we know who is to be first?" asked Spider.

"It may be fairly fixed by lot," replied Monsieur Thuran. "I have a number of franc pieces in my pocket. We can choose a certain date from among them – the one to draw this date first from beneath a piece of cloth will be the first."

"I shall have nothing to do with any such diabolical plan," muttered Clayton; "even yet land may be sighted or a ship appear – in time."

"You will do as the majority decide, or you will be 'the first' without the formality of drawing lots," said Monsieur Thuran threateningly. "Come, let us vote on the plan; I for one am in favor of it. How about you, Spider?" "And I," replied the sailor.

"It is the will of the majority," announced Monsieur Thuran, "and now let us lose no time in drawing lots. It is as fair for one as for another. That three may live, one of us must die perhaps a few hours sooner than otherwise."

Then he began his preparation for the lottery of death, while Jane Porter sat wide-eyed and horrified at thought of the thing that she was about to witness. Monsieur Thuran spread his coat upon the bottom of the boat, and then from a handful of money he selected six franc pieces. The other two men bent close above him as he inspected them. Finally he handed them all to Clayton.

"Look at them carefully," he said. "The oldest date is eighteen-seventy-five, and there is only one of that year."

Clayton and the sailor inspected each coin. To them there seemed not the slightest difference that could be detected other than the dates. They were quite satisfied. Had they known that Monsieur Thuran's past experience as a card sharp had trained his sense of touch to so fine a point that he could almost differentiate between cards by the mere feel of them, they would scarcely have felt that the plan was so entirely fair. The 1875 piece was a hair thinner than the other coins, but neither Clayton nor Spider could have detected it without the aid of a micrometer.

"In what order shall we draw?" asked Monsieur Thuran, knowing from past experiencc that the majority of men always prefer last chance in a lottery where the single prize is some distasteful thing – there is always the chance and the hope that another will draw it first. Monsieur Thuran, for reasons of his own, preferred to draw first if the drawing should happen to require a second adventure beneath the coat.

And so when Spider elected to draw last he graciously offered to take the first chance himself. His hand was under the coat for but a moment, yet those quick, deft fingers had felt of each coin, and found and discarded the fatal piece. When he brought forth his hand it contained an 1888 franc piece. Then Clayton drew. Jane Porter leaned forward with a tense and horrified expression on her face as the hand of the man she was to marry groped about beneath the coat. Presently he withdrew it, a franc piece lying in the palm. For an instant he dared not look, but Monsieur Thuran, who had leaned nearer to see the date, exclaimed that he was safe.

Jane Porter sank weak and trembling against the side of the boat. She felt sick and dizzy. And now, if Spider should not draw the 1875 piece she must endure the whole horrid thing again.

The sailor already had his hand beneath the coat. Great beads of sweat were standing upon his brow. He trembled as though with a fit of ague. Aloud he cursed himself for having taken the last draw, for now his chances for escape were but three to one, whereas Monsieur Thuran's had been five to one, and Clayton's four to one.

The Russian was very patient, and did not hurry the man, for he knew that he himself was quite safe whether the 1875 piece came out this time or not. When the sailor withdrew his hand and looked at the piece of money within, he dropped fainting to the bottom of the boat. Both Clayton and Monsieur Thuran hastened weakly to examine the coin, which had rolled from the man's hand and lay beside him. It was not dated 1875. The reaction from the state of fear he had been in had overcome Spider quite as effectually as though he had drawn the fated piece.

But now the whole proceeding must be gone through again. Once more the Russian drew forth a harmless coin. Jane Porter closed her eyes as Clayton reached beneath the coat. Spider bent, wide-eyed, toward the hand that was to decide his fate, for whatever luck was Clayton's on this last draw, the opposite would be Spider's. Then William Cecil Clayton, Lord Greystoke, removed his hand from beneath the coat, and with a coin tight pressed within his palm where none might see it, he looked at Jane Porter. He did not dare open his hand.

"Quick!" hissed Spider. "My Gawd, let's see it."

Clayton opened his fingers. Spider was the first to see the date, and ere any knew what his intention was he raised himself to his feet, and lunged over the side of the boat, to disappear forever into the green depths beneath – the coin had not been the 1875 piece.

The strain had exhausted those who remained to such an extent that they lay half unconscious for the balance of the day, nor was the subject referred to again for several days. Horrible days of increasing weakness and hopelessness. At length Monsieur Thuran crawled to where Clayton lay.

"We must draw once more before we are too weak even to eat," he whispered.

Clayton was in such a state that he was scarcely master of his own will. Jane Porter had not spoken for three days. He knew that she was dying. Horrible as the thought was, he hoped that the sacrifice of either Thuran or himself might be the means of giving her renewed strength, and so he immediately agreed to the Russian's proposal.

They drew under the same plan as before, but there could be but one result – Clayton drew the 1875 piece.

"When shall it be?" he asked Thuran.

The Russian had already drawn a pocketknife from his trousers, and was weakly attempting to open it.

"Now," he muttered, and his greedy eyes gloated upon the Englishman.

"Can't you wait until dark?" asked Clayton. "Miss Porter must not see this thing done. We were to have been married, you know."

A look of disappointment came over Monsieur Thuran's face.

"Very well," he replied hesitatingly. "It will not be long until night. I have waited for many days – I can wait a few hours longer."

"Thank you, my friend," murmured Clayton. "Now I shall go to her side and remain with her until it is time. I would like to have an hour or two with her before I die."

When Clayton reached the girl's side she was unconscious – he knew that she was dying, and he was glad that she should not have to see or know the awful tragedy that was shortly to be enacted. He took her hand and raised it to his cracked and swollen lips. For a long time he lay caressing the emaciated, clawlike thing that had once been the beautiful, shapely white hand of the young Baltimore belle.

It was quite dark before he knew it, but he was recalled to himself by a voice out of the night. It was the Russian calling him to his doom.

"I am coming, Monsieur Thuran," he hastened to reply.

Thrice he attempted to turn himself upon his hands and knees, that he might crawl back to his death, but in the few hours that he had lain there he had become too weak to return to Thuran's side.

"You will have to come to me, monsieur," he called weakly. "I have not sufficient strength to gain my hands and knees."

"SAPRISTI!" muttered Monsieur Thuran. "You are attempting to cheat me out of my winnings."

Clayton heard the man shuffling about in the bottom of the boat. Finally there was a despairing groan. "I cannot crawl," he heard the Russian wail. "It is too late. You have tricked me, you dirty English dog."

"I have not tricked you, monsieur," replied Clayton. "I have done my best to rise, but I shall try again, and if you will try possibly each of us can crawl halfway, and then you shall have your 'winnings.'"

Again Clayton exerted his remaining strength to the utmost, and he heard Thuran apparently doing the same. Nearly an hour later the Englishman succeeded in raising himself to his hands and knees, but at the first forward movement he pitched upon his face.

A moment later he heard an exclamation of relief from Monsieur Thuran.

"I am coming," whispered the Russian.

Again Clayton essayed to stagger on to meet his fate, but once more he pitched headlong to the boat's bottom, nor, try as he would, could he again rise. His last effort caused him to roll over on his back, and there he lay looking up at the stars, while behind him, coming ever nearer and nearer, he could hear the laborious shuffling, and the stertorous breathing of the Russian.

It seemed that he must have lain thus an hour waiting for the thing to crawl out of the dark and end his misery. It was quite close now, but there were longer and longer pauses between its efforts to advance, and each forward movement seemed to the waiting Englishman to be almost imperceptible.

Finally he knew that Thuran was quite close beside him. He heard a cackling laugh, something touched his face, and he lost consciousness.

CHAPTER NINETEEN

The City of Gold

The very night that Tarzan of the Apes became chief of the Waziri the woman he loved lay dying in a tiny boat two hundred miles west of him upon the Atlantic. As he danced among his naked fellow savages, the firelight gleaming against his great, rolling muscles, the personification of physical perfection and strength, the woman who loved him lay thin and emaciated in the last coma that precedes death by thirst and starvation.

The week following the induction of Tarzan into the kingship of the Waziri was occupied in escorting the Manyuema of the Arab raiders to the northern boundary of Waziri in accordance with the promise which Tarzan had made them. Before he left them he exacted a pledge from them that they would not lead any expeditions against the Waziri in the future, nor was it a difficult promise to obtain. They had had sufficient experience with the fighting tactics of the new Waziri chief not to have the slightest desire to accompany another predatory force within the boundaries of his domain.

Almost immediately upon his return to the village Tarzan commenced making preparations for leading an expedition in search of the ruined city of gold which old Waziri had described to him. He selected fifty of the sturdiest warriors of his tribe, choosing only men who seemed anxious to accompany him on the arduous march, and share the dangers of a new and hostile country.

The fabulous wealth of the fabled city had been almost constantly in his mind since Waziri had recounted the strange adventures of the former expedition which had stumbled upon the vast ruins by chance. The lure of adventure may have been quite as powerful a factor in urging Tarzan of the Apes to undertake the journey as the lure of gold, but the lure of gold was there, too, for he had learned among civilized men something of the miracles that may be wrought by the possessor of the magic yellow metal. What he would do with a golden fortune in the heart of savage Africa it had not occurred to him to consider – it would be enough to possess the power to work wonders, even though he never had an opportunity to employ it.

So one glorious tropical morning Waziri, chief of the Waziri, set out at the head of fifty clean-limbed ebon warriors in quest of adventure and of riches. They followed the course which old Waziri had described to Tarzan. For days they marched – up one river, across a low divide; down another river; up a third, until at the end of the twenty-fifth day they camped upon a mountainside, from the summit of which they hoped to catch their first view of the marvelous city of treasure.

Early the next morning they were climbing the almost perpendicular crags which formed the last, but greatest, natural barrier between them and their destination. It was nearly noon before Tarzan, who headed the thin line of climbing warriors, scrambled over the top of the last cliff and stood upon the little flat table-land of the mountaintop.

On either hand towered mighty peaks thousands of feet higher than the pass through which they were entering the forbidden valley. Behind him stretched the wooded valley across which they had marched for many days, and at the opposite side the low range which marked the boundary of their own country.

But before him was the view that centered his attention. Here lay a desolate valley – a shallow, narrow valley dotted with stunted trees and covered with many great bowlders. And on the far side of the valley lay what appeared to be a mighty city, its great walls, its lofty spires, its turrets, minarets, and domes showing red and yellow in the sunlight. Tarzan was yet too far away to note the marks of ruin – to him it appeared a wonderful city of magnificent beauty, and in imagination he peopled its broad avenues and its huge temples with a throng of happy, active people.

For an hour the little expedition rested upon the mountain-top, and then Tarzan led them down into the valley below. There was no trail, but the way was less arduous than the ascent of the opposite face of the mountain had been. Once in the valley their progress was rapid, so that it was still light when they halted before the towering walls of the ancient city.

The outer wall was fifty feet in height where it had not fallen into ruin, but nowhere as far as they could see had more than ten or twenty feet of the upper courses fallen away. It was still a formidable defense. On several occasions Tarzan had thought that he discerned things moving behind the ruined portions of the wall near to them, as though creatures were watching them from behind the bulwarks of the ancient pile. And often he felt the sensation of unseen eyes upon him, but not once could he be sure that it was more than imagination.

That night they camped outside the city. Once, at midnight, they were awakened by a shrill scream from beyond the great wall. It was very high at first, descending gradually until it ended in a series of dismal moans. It had a strange effect upon the blacks, almost paralyzing them with terror while it lasted, and it was an hour before the camp settled down to sleep once more. In the morning the effects of it were still visible in the fearful, sidelong glances that the Waziri continually cast at the massive and forbidding structure which loomed above them.

It required considerable encouragement and urging on Tarzan's part to prevent the blacks from abandoning the venture on the spot and hastening back across the valley toward the cliffs they had scaled the day before. But at length, by dint of commands, and threats that he would enter the city alone, they agreed to accompany him.

For fifteen minutes they marched along the face of the wall before they discovered a means of ingress. Then they came to a narrow cleft about twenty inches wide. Within, a flight of concrete steps, worn hollow by centuries of use, rose before them, to disappear at a sharp turning of the passage a few yards ahead.

Into this narrow alley Tarzan made his way, turning his giant shoulders sideways that they might enter at all. Behind him trailed his black warriors. At the turn in the cleft the stairs ended, and the path was level; but it wound and twisted in a serpentine fashion, until suddenly at a sharp angle it debouched upon a narrow court, across which loomed an inner wall equally as high as the outer. This inner wall was set with little round towers alternating along its entire summit with pointed monoliths. In places these had fallen, and the wall was ruined, but it was in a much better state of preservation than the outer wall.

Another narrow passage led through this wall, and at its end Tarzan and his warriors found themselves in a broad avenue, on the opposite side of which crumbling edifices of hewn granite loomed dark and forbidding. Upon the crumbling debris along the face of the buildings trees had grown, and vines wound in and out of the hollow, staring windows; but the building directly opposite them seemed less overgrown than the others, and in a much better state of preservation. It was a massive pile, surmounted by an enormous dome. At either side of its great entrance stood rows of tall pillars, each capped by a huge, grotesque bird carved from the solid rock of the monoliths.

As the ape-man and his companions stood gazing in varying degrees of wonderment at this ancient city in the midst of savage Africa, several of them became aware of movement within the structure at which they were looking. Dim, shadowy shapes appeared to be moving about in the semi-darkness of the interior. There was nothing tangible that the eye could grasp – only an uncanny suggestion of life where it seemed that there should be no life, for living things seemed out of place in this weird, dead city of the long-dead past.

Tarzan recalled something that he had read in the library at Paris of a lost race of white men that native legend described as living in the heart of Africa. He wondered if he were not looking upon the ruins of the civilization that this strange people had wrought amid the savage surroundings of their strange and savage home. Could it be possible that even now a remnant of that lost race inhabited the ruined grandeur that had once been their progenitor? Again he became conscious of a stealthy movement within the great temple before him. "Come!" he said, to his Waziri. "Let us have a look at what lies behind those ruined walls."

His men were loath to follow him, but when they saw that he was bravely entering the frowning portal they trailed a few paces behind in a huddled group that seemed the personification of nervous terror. A single shriek such as they had heard the night before would have been sufficient to have sent them all racing madly for the narrow cleft that led through the great walls to the outer world.

As Tarzan entered the building he was distinctly aware of many eyes upon him. There was a rustling in the shadows of a near-by corridor, and he could have sworn that he saw a human hand withdrawn from an embrasure that opened above him into the domelike rotunda in which he found himself.

The floor of the chamber was of concrete, the walls of smooth granite, upon which strange figures of men and beasts were carved. In places tablets of yellow metal had been set in the solid masonry of the walls.

When he approached closer to one of these tablets he saw that it was of gold, and bore many hieroglyphics. Beyond this first chamber there were others, and back of them the building branched out into enormous wings. Tarzan passed through several of these chambers, finding many evidences of the fabulous wealth of the original builders. In one room were seven pillars of solid gold, and in another the floor itself was of the precious metal. And all the while that he explored, his blacks huddled close together at his back, and strange shapes hovered upon either hand and before them and behind, yet never close enough that any might say that they were not alone.

The strain, however, was telling upon the nerves of the Waziri. They begged Tarzan to return to the sunlight. They said that no good could come of such an expedition, for the ruins were haunted by the spirits of the dead who had once inhabited them.

"They are watching us, O king," whispered Busuli. "They are waiting until they have led us into the innermost recesses of their stronghold, and then they will fall upon us and tear us to pieces with their teeth. That is the way with spirits. My mother's uncle, who is a great witch doctor, has told me all about it many times."

Tarzan laughed. "Run back into the sunlight, my children," he said. "I will join you when I have searched this old ruin from top to bottom, and found the gold, or found that there is none. At least we may take the tablets from the walls, though the pillars are too heavy for us to handle; but there should be great storerooms filled with gold – gold that we can carry away upon our backs with ease. Run on now, out into the fresh air where you may breathe easier."

Some of the warriors started to obey their chief with alacrity, but Busuli and several others hesitated to leave him – hesitated between love and loyalty for their king, and superstitious fear of the unknown. And then, quite unexpectedly, that occurred which decided the question without the necessity for further discussion. Out of the silence of the ruined temple there rang, close to their ears, the same hideous shriek they had heard the previous night, and with horrified cries the black warriors turned and fled through the empty halls of the age-old edifice.

Behind them stood Tarzan of the Apes where they had left him, a grim smile upon his lips – waiting for the enemy he fully expected was about to pounce upon him. But again silence reigned, except for the faint suggestion of the sound of naked feet moving stealthily in near-by places.

Then Tarzan wheeled and passed on into the depths of the temple. From room to room he went, until he came to one at which a rude, barred door still stood, and as he put his shoulder against it to push it in, again the shriek of warning rang out almost beside him. It was evident that he was being warned to refrain from desecrating this particular room. Or could it be that within lay the secret to the treasure stores?

At any rate, the very fact that the strange, invisible guardians of this weird place had some reason for wishing him not to enter this particular chamber was sufficient to treble Tarzan's desire to do so, and though the shrieking was repeated continuously, he kept his shoulder to the door until it gave before his giant strength to swing open upon creaking wooden hinges.

Within all was black as the tomb. There was no window to let in the faintest ray of light, and as the corridor upon which it opened was itself in semi-darkness, even the open door shed no relieving rays within. Feeling before him upon the floor with the butt of his spear, Tarzan entered the Stygian gloom. Suddenly the door behind him closed, and at the same time hands clutched him from every direction out of the darkness.

The ape-man fought with all the savage fury of self-preservation backed by the herculean strength that was his. But though he felt his blows land, and his teeth sink into soft flesh, there seemed always two new hands to take the place of those that he fought off. At last they dragged him down, and slowly, very slowly, they overcame him by the mere weight of their numbers. And then they bound him – his hands behind his back and his feet trussed up to meet them. He had heard no sound except the heavy breathing of his antagonists, and the noise of the battle. He knew not what manner of creatures had captured him, but that they were human seemed evident from the fact that they had bound him.

Presently they lifted him from the floor, and half dragging, half pushing him, they brought him out of the black chamber through another doorway into an inner courtyard of the temple. Here he saw his captors. There must have been a hundred of them – short, stocky men, with great beards that covered their faces and fell upon their hairy breasts.

The thick, matted hair upon their heads grew low over their receding brows, and hung about their shoulders and their backs. Their crooked legs were short and heavy, their arms long and muscular. About their loins they wore the skins of leopards and lions, and great necklaces of the claws of these same animals depended upon their breasts. Massive circlets of virgin gold adorned their arms and legs. For weapons they carried heavy, knotted bludgeons, and in the belts that confined their single garments each had a long, wicked-looking knife.

But the feature of them that made the most startling impression upon their prisoner was their white skins – neither in color nor feature was there a trace of the negroid about them. Yet, with their receding foreheads, wicked little close-set eyes, and yellow fangs, they were far from prepossessing in appearance.

During the fight within the dark chamber, and while they had been dragging Tarzan to the inner court, no word had been spoken, but now several of them exchanged grunting, monosyllabic conversation in a language unfamiliar to the ape-man, and presently they left him lying upon the concrete floor while they trooped off on their short legs into another part of the temple beyond the court.

As Tarzan lay there upon his back he saw that the temple entirely surrounded the little inclosure, and that on all sides its lofty walls rose high above him. At the top a little patch of blue sky was visible, and, in one direction, through an embrasure, he could see foliage, but whether it was beyond or within the temple he did not know.

About the court, from the ground to the top of the temple, were series of open galleries, and now and then the captive caught glimpses of bright eyes gleaming from beneath masses of tumbling hair, peering down upon him from above.

The ape-man gently tested the strength of the bonds that held him, and while he could not be sure it seemed that they were of insufficient strength to withstand the strain of his mighty muscles when the time came to make a break for freedom; but he did not dare to put them to the crucial test until darkness had fallen, or he felt that no spying eyes were upon him.

He had lain within the court for several hours before the first rays of sunlight penetrated the vertical shaft; almost simultaneously he heard the pattering of bare feet in the corridors about him, and a moment later saw the galleries above fill with crafty faces as a score or more entered the courtyard.

For a moment every eye was bent upon the noonday sun, and then in unison the people in the galleries and those in the court below took up the refrain of a low, weird chant. Presently those about Tarzan began to dance to the cadence of their solemn song. They circled him slowly, resembling in their manner of dancing a number of clumsy, shuffling bears; but as yet they did not look at him, keeping their little eyes fixed upon the sun.

For ten minutes or more they kept up their monotonous chant and steps, and then suddenly, and in perfect unison, they turned toward their victim with upraised bludgeons and emitting fearful howls, the while they contorted their features into the most diabolical expressions, they rushed upon him.

At the same instant a female figure dashed into the midst of the bloodthirsty horde, and, with a bludgeon similar to their own, except that it was wrought from gold, beat back the advancing men.

CHAPTER TWENTY

La

For a moment Tarzan thought that by some strange freak of fate a miracle had saved him, but when he realized the ease with which the girl had, single-handed, beaten off twenty gorilla-like males, and an instant later, as he saw them again take up their dance about him while she addressed them in a singsong monotone, which bore every evidence of rote, he came to the conclusion that it was all but a part of the ceremony of which he was the central figure.

After a moment or two the girl drew a knife from her girdle, and, leaning over Tarzan, cut the bonds from his legs. Then, as the men stopped their dance, and approached, she motioned to him to rise. Placing the rope that had been about his legs around his neck, she led him across the courtyard, the men following in twos.

Through winding corridors she led, farther and farther into the remoter precincts of the temple, until they came to a great chamber in the center of which stood an altar. Then it was that Tarzan translated the strange ceremony that had preceded his introduction into this holy of holies.

He had fallen into the hands of descendants of the ancient sun worshippers. His seeming rescue by a votaress of the high priestess of the sun had been but a part of the mimicry of their heathen ceremony – the sun looking down upon him through the opening at the top of the court had claimed him as his own, and the priestess had come from the inner temple to save him from the polluting hands of worldlings – to save him as a human offering to their flaming deity.

And had he needed further assurance as to the correctness of his theory he had only to cast his eyes upon the brownish-red stains that caked the stone altar and covered the floor in its immediate vicinity, or to the human skulls which grinned from countless niches in the towering walls.

The priestess led the victim to the altar steps. Again the galleries above filled with watchers, while from an arched doorway at the east end of the chamber a procession of females filed slowly into the room. They wore, like the men, only skins of wild animals caught about their waists with rawhide belts or chains of gold; but the black masses of their hair were incrusted with golden headgear composed of many circular and oval pieces of gold ingeniously held together to form a metal cap from which depended at each side of the head, long strings of oval pieces falling to the waist.

The females were more symmetrically proportioned than the males, their features were much more perfect, the shapes of their heads and their large, soft, black eyes denoting far greater intelligence and humanity than was possessed by their lords and masters.

Each priestess bore two golden cups, and as they formed in line along one side of the altar the men formed opposite them, advancing and taking each a cup from the female opposite. Then the chant began once more, and presently from a dark passageway beyond the altar another female emerged from the cavernous depths beneath the chamber.

The high priestess, thought Tarzan. She was a young woman with a rather intelligent and shapely face. Her ornaments were similar to those worn by her votaries, but much more elaborate, many being set with diamonds. Her bare arms and legs were almost concealed by the massive, bejeweled ornaments which covered them, while her single leopard skin was supported by a close-fitting girdle of golden rings set in strange designs with innumerable small diamonds. In the girdle she carried a long, jeweled knife, and in her hand a slender wand in lieu of a bludgeon.

As she advanced to the opposite side of the altar she halted, and the chanting ceased. The priests and priestesses knelt before her, while with wand extended above them she recited a long and tiresome prayer. Her voice was soft and musical – Tarzan could scarce realize that its possessor in a moment more would be transformed by the fanatical ecstasy of religious zeal into a wild-eyed and bloodthirsty executioner, who, with dripping knife, would be the first to drink her victim's red, warm blood from the little golden cup that stood upon the altar.

As she finished her prayer she let her eyes rest for the first time upon Tarzan. With every indication of considerable curiosity she examined him from head to foot. Then she addressed him, and when she had finished stood waiting, as though she expected a reply.

"I do not understand your language," said Tarzan. "Possibly we may speak together in another tongue?" But she could not understand him, though he tried French, English, Arab, Waziri, and, as a last resort, the mongrel tongue of the West Coast.

She shook her head, and it seemed that there was a note of weariness in her voice as she motioned to the priests to continue with the rites. These now circled in a repetition of their idiotic dance, which was terminated finally at a command from the priestess, who had stood throughout, still looking intently upon Tarzan.

At her signal the priests rushed upon the ape-man, and, lifting him bodily, laid him upon his back across the altar, his head hanging over one edge, his legs over the opposite. Then they and the priestesses formed in two lines, with their little golden cups in readiness to capture a share of the victim's lifeblood after the sacrificial knife had accomplished its work.

In the line of priests an altercation arose as to who should have first place. A burly brute with all the refined intelligence of a gorilla stamped upon his bestial face was attempting to push a smaller man to second place, but the smaller one appealed to the high priestess, who in a cold peremptory voice sent the larger to the extreme end of the line. Tarzan could hear him growling and rumbling as he went slowly to the inferior station.

Then the priestess, standing above him, began reciting what Tarzan took to be an invocation, the while she slowly raised her thin, sharp knife aloft. It seemed ages to the ape-man before her arm ceased its upward progress and the knife halted high above his unprotected breast.

Then it started downward, slowly at first, but as the incantation increased in rapidity, with greater speed. At the end of the line Tarzan could still hear the grumbling of the disgruntled priest. The man's voice rose louder and louder. A priestess near him spoke in sharp tones of rebuke. The knife was quite near to Tarzan's breast now, but it halted for an instant as the high priestess raised her eyes to shoot her swift displeasure at the instigator of this sacrilegious interruption.

There was a sudden commotion in the direction of the disputants, and Tarzan rolled his head in their direction in time to see the burly brute of a priest leap upon the woman opposite him, dashing out her brains with a single blow of his heavy cudgel. Then that happened which Tarzan had witnessed a hundred times before among the wild denizens of his own savage jungle. He had seen the thing fall upon Kerchak, and Tublat, and

Terkoz; upon a dozen of the other mighty bull apes of his tribe; and upon Tantor, the elephant; there was scarce any of the males of the forest that did not at times fall prey to it. The priest went mad, and with his heavy bludgeon ran amuck among his fellows.

His screams of rage were frightful as he dashed hither and thither, dealing terrific blows with his giant weapon, or sinking his yellow fangs into the flesh of some luckless victim. And during it the priestess stood with poised knife above Tarzan, her eyes fixed in horror upon the maniacal thing that was dealing out death and destruction to her votaries.

Presently the room was emptied except for the dead and dying on the floor, the victim upon the altar, the high priestess, and the madman. As the cunning eyes of the latter fell upon the woman they lighted with a new and sudden lust. Slowly he crept toward her, and now he spoke; but this time there fell upon Tarzan's surprised ears a language he could understand; the last one that he would ever have thought of employing in attempting to converse with human beings – the low guttural barking of the tribe of great anthropoids – his own mother tongue. And the woman answered the man in the same language.

He was threatening – she attempting to reason with him, for it was quite evident that she saw that he was past her authority. The brute was quite close now – creeping with clawlike hands extended toward her around the end of the altar. Tarzan strained at the bonds which held his arms pinioned behind him. The woman did not see – she had forgotten her prey in the horror of the danger that threatened herself. As the brute leaped past Tarzan to clutch his victim, the ape-man gave one superhuman wrench at the thongs that held him. The effort sent him rolling from the altar to the stone floor on the opposite side from that on which the priestess stood; but as he sprang to his feet the thongs dropped from his freed arms, and at the same time he realized that he was alone in the inner temple – the high priestess and the mad priest had disappeared.

And then a muffled scream came from the cavernous mouth of the dark hole beyond the sacrificial altar through which the priestess had entered the temple. Without even a thought for his own safety, or the possibility for escape which this rapid series of fortuitous circumstances had thrust upon him, Tarzan of the Apes answered the call of the woman in danger. With a little bound he was at the gaping entrance to the subterranean chamber, and a moment later was running down a flight of age-old concrete steps that led he knew not where.

The faint light that filtered in from above showed him a large, low-ceiled vault from which several doorways led off into inky darkness, but there was no need to thread an unknown way, for there before him lay the objects of his search – the mad brute had the girl upon the floor, and gorilla-like fingers were clutching frantically at her throat as she struggled to escape the fury of the awful thing upon her.

As Tarzan's heavy hand fell upon his shoulder the priest dropped his victim, and turned upon her would-be rescuer. With foam-flecked lips and bared fangs the mad sun-worshiper battled with the tenfold power of the maniac. In the blood lust of his fury the creature had undergone a sudden reversion to type, which left him a wild beast, forgetful of the dagger that projected from his belt – thinking only of nature's weapons with which his brute prototype had battled.

But if he could use his teeth and hands to advantage, he found one even better versed in the school of savage warfare to which he had reverted, for Tarzan of the Apes closed with him, and they fell to the floor tearing and rending at one another like two bull apes; while the primitive priestess stood flattened against the wall, watching with wide, fear-fascinated eyes the growling, snapping beasts at her feet.

At last she saw the stranger close one mighty hand upon the throat of his antagonist, and as he forced the bruteman's head far back rain blow after blow upon the upturned face. A moment later he threw the still thing from him, and, arising, shook himself like a lion. He placed a foot upon the carcass before him, and raised his head to give the victory cry of his kind, but as his eyes fell upon the opening above him leading into the temple of human sacrifice he thought better of his intended act.

The girl, who had been half paralyzed by fear as the two men fought, had just commenced to give thought to her probable fate now that, though released from the clutches of a madman, she had fallen into the hands of one whom but a moment before she had been upon the point of killing. She looked about for some means of escape. The black mouth of a diverging corridor was near at hand, but as she turned to dart into it the ape-man's eyes fell upon her, and with a quick leap he was at her side, and a restraining hand was laid upon her arm.

"Wait!" said Tarzan of the Apes, in the language of the tribe of Kerchak.

The girl looked at him in astonishment.

"Who are you," she whispered, "who speaks the language of the first man?"

"I am Tarzan of the Apes," he answered in the vernacular of the anthropoids.

"What do you want of me?" she continued. "For what purpose did you save me from Tha?"

"I could not see a woman murdered?" It was a half question that answered her.

"But what do you intend to do with me now?" she continued.

"Nothing," he replied, "but you can do something for me – you can lead me out of this place to freedom." He made the suggestion without the slightest thought that she would accede. He felt quite sure that the sacrifice would go on from the point where it had been interrupted if the high priestess had her way, though he was equally positive that they would find Tarzan of the Apes unbound and with a long dagger in his hand a much less tractable victim than Tarzan disarmed and bound.

The girl stood looking at him for a long moment before she spoke.

"You are a very wonderful man," she said. "You are such a man as I have seen in my daydreams ever since I was a little girl. You are such a man as I imagine the forbears of my people must have been – the great race of people who built this mighty city in the heart of a savage world that they might wrest from the bowels of the earth the fabulous wealth for which they had sacrificed their far-distant civilization.

"I cannot understand why you came to my rescue in the first place, and now I cannot understand why, having me within your power, you do not wish to be revenged upon me for having sentenced you to death – for having almost put you to death with my own hand."

"I presume," replied the ape-man, "that you but followed the teachings of your religion. I cannot blame YOU for that, no matter what I may think of your creed. But who are you – what people have I fallen among?"

"I am La, high priestess of the Temple of the Sun, in the city of Opar. We are descendants of a people who came to this savage world more than ten thousand years ago in search of gold. Their cities stretched from a great sea under the rising sun to a great sea into which the sun descends at night to cool his flaming brow. They were very rich and very powerful, but they lived only a few months of the year in their magnificent palaces here; the rest of the time they spent in their native land, far, far to the north.

"Many ships went back and forth between this new world and the old. During the rainy season there were but few of the inhabitants remained here, only those who superintended the working of the mines by the black slaves, and the merchants who had to stay to supply their wants, and the soldiers who guarded the cities and the mines.

"It was at one of these times that the great calamity occurred. When the time came for the teeming thousands to return none came. For weeks the people waited. Then they sent out a great galley to learn why no one came from the mother country, but though they sailed about for many months, they were unable to find any trace of the mighty land that had for countless ages borne their ancient civilization – it had sunk into the sea.

"From that day dated the downfall of my people. Disheartened and unhappy, they soon became a prey to the black hordes of the north and the black hordes of the south. One by one the cities were deserted or overcome. The last remnant was finally forced to take shelter within this mighty mountain fortress. Slowly we have dwindled in power, in civilization, in intellect, in numbers, until now we are no more than a small tribe of savage apes.

"In fact, the apes live with us, and have for many ages. We call them the first men – we speak their language quite as much as we do our own; only in the rituals of the temple do we make any attempt to retain our mother tongue. In time it will be forgotten, and we will speak only the language of the apes; in time we will no longer banish those of our people who mate with apes, and so in time we shall descend to the very beasts from which ages ago our progenitors may have sprung."

"But why are you more human than the others?" asked the man.

"For some reason the women have not reverted to savagery so rapidly as the men. It may be because only the lower types of men remained here at the time of the great catastrophe, while the temples were filled with the noblest daughters of the race. My strain has remained clearer than the rest because for countless ages my foremothers were high priestesses – the sacred office descends from mother to daughter. Our husbands are chosen for us from the noblest in the land. The most perfect man, mentally and physically, is selected to be the husband of the high priestess."

"From what I saw of the gentlemen above," said Tarzan, with a grin, "there should be little trouble in choosing from among them."

The girl looked at him quizzically for a moment.

"Do not be sacrilegious," she said. "They are very holy men – they are priests."

"Then there are others who are better to look upon?" he asked.

"The others are all more ugly than the priests," she replied.

Tarzan shuddered at her fate, for even in the dim light of the vault he was impressed by her beauty.

"But how about myself?" he asked suddenly. "Are you going to lead me to liberty?"

"You have been chosen by The Flaming God as his own," she answered solemnly. "Not even I have the power to save you – should they find you again. But I do not intend that they shall find you. You risked your life to save mine. I may do no less for you. It will be no easy matter – it may require days; but in the end I think that I can lead you beyond the walls. Come, they will look here for me presently, and if they find us together we shall both be lost – they would kill me did they think that I had proved false to my god."

"You must not take the risk, then," he said quickly. "I will return to the temple, and if I can fight my way to freedom there will be no suspicion thrown upon you."

But she would not have it so, and finally persuaded him to follow her, saying that they had already remained in the vault too long to prevent suspicion from falling upon her even if they returned to the temple.

"I will hide you, and then return alone," she said, "telling them that I was long unconscious after you killed Tha, and that I do not know whither you escaped."

And so she led him through winding corridors of gloom, until finally they came to a small chamber into which a little light filtered through a stone grating in the ceiling.

"This is the Chamber of the Dead," she said. "None will think of searching here for you – they would not dare. I will return after it is dark. By that time I may have found a plan to effect your escape."

She was gone, and Tarzan of the Apes was left alone in the Chamber of the Dead, beneath the long-dead city of Opar.

CHAPTER TWENTY ONE

The Castaways

CLAYTON DREAMED THAT HE was drinking his fill of water, pure, delightful drafts of fresh water. With a start he gained consciousness to find himself wet through by torrents of rain that were falling upon his body and his upturned face. A heavy tropical shower was beating down upon them. He opened his mouth and drank. Presently he was so revived and strengthened that he was enabled to raise himself upon his hands. Across his legs lay Monsieur Thuran. A few feet aft Jane Porter was huddled in a pitiful little heap in the bottom of the boat – she was quite still. Clayton knew that she was dead.

After infinite labor he released himself from Thuran's pinioning body, and with renewed strength crawled toward the girl. He raised her head from the rough boards of the boat's bottom. There might be life in that poor, starved frame even yet. He could not quite abandon all hope, and so he seized a water-soaked rag and squeezed the precious drops between the swollen lips of the hideous thing that had but a few short days before glowed with the resplendent life of happy youth and glorious beauty.

For some time there was no sign of returning animation, but at last his efforts were rewarded by a slight tremor of the half-closed lids. He chafed the thin hands, and forced a few more drops of water into the parched throat. The girl opened her eyes, looking up at him for a long time before she could recall her surroundings.

"Water?" she whispered. "Are we saved?"

"It is raining," he explained. "We may at least drink. Already it has revived us both."

"Monsieur Thuran?" she asked. "He did not kill you. Is he dead?"

"I do not know," replied Clayton. "If he lives and this rain revives him – " But he stopped there, remembering too late that he must not add further to the horrors which the girl already had endured.

But she guessed what he would have said.

"Where is he?" she asked.

Clayton nodded his head toward the prostrate form of the Russian. For a time neither spoke.

"I will see if I can revive him," said Clayton at length.

"No," she whispered, extending a detaining hand toward him. "Do not do that – he will kill you when the water has given him strength. If he is dying, let him die. Do not leave me alone in this boat with that beast."

Clayton hesitated. His honor demanded that he attempt to revive Thuran, and there was the possibility, too, that the Russian was beyond human aid. It was not dishonorable to hope so. As he sat fighting out his battle he presently raised his eyes from the body of the man, and as they passed above the gunwale of the boat he staggered weakly to his feet with a little cry of joy.

"Land, Jane!" he almost shouted through his cracked lips. "Thank God, land!"

The girl looked, too, and there, not a hundred yards away, she saw a yellow beach, and, beyond, the luxurious foliage of a tropical jungle.

"Now you may revive him," said Jane Porter, for she, too, had been haunted with the pangs of conscience which had resulted from her decision to prevent Clayton from offering succor to their companion.

It required the better part of half an hour before the Russian evinced sufficient symptoms of returning consciousness to open his eyes, and it was some time later before they could bring him to a realization of their good fortune. By this time the boat was scraping gently upon the sandy bottom.

Between the refreshing water that he had drunk and the stimulus of renewed hope, Clayton found strength to stagger through the shallow water to the shore with a line made fast to the boat's bow. This he fastened to a small tree which grew at the top of a low bank, for the tide was at flood, and he feared that the boat might carry them all out to sea again with the ebb, since it was quite likely that it would be beyond his strength to get Jane Porter to the shore for several hours. Next he managed to stagger and crawl toward the near-by jungle, where he had seen evidences of profusion of tropical fruit. His former experience in the jungle of Tarzan of the Apes had taught him which of the many growing things were edible, and after nearly an hour of absence he returned to the beach with a little armful of food.

The rain had ceased, and the hot sun was beating down so mercilessly upon her that Jane Porter insisted on making an immediate attempt to gain the land. Still further invigorated by the food Clayton had brought, the three were able to reach the half shade of the small tree to which their boat was moored. Here, thoroughly exhausted, they threw themselves down to rest, sleeping until dark.

For a month they lived upon the beach in comparative safety. As their strength returned the two men constructed a rude shelter in the branches of a tree, high enough from the ground to insure safety from the larger beasts of prey. By day they gathered fruits and trapped small rodents; at night they lay cowering within their frail shelter while savage denizens of the jungle made hideous the hours of darkness.

They slept upon litters of jungle grasses, and for covering at night Jane Porter had only an old ulster that belonged to Clayton, the same garment that he had worn upon that memorable trip to the Wisconsin woods. Clayton had erected a frail partition of boughs to divide their arboreal shelter into two rooms – one for the girl and the other for Monsieur Thuran and himself.

From the first the Russian had exhibited every trait of his true character – selfishness, boorishness, arrogance, cowardice, and lust. Twice had he and Clayton come to blows because of Thuran's attitude toward the girl. Clayton dared not leave her alone with him for an instant. The existence of the Englishman and his fiancee was one continual nightmare of horror, and yet they lived on in hope of ultimate rescue.

Jane Porter's thoughts often reverted to her other experience on this savage shore. Ah, if the invincible forest god of that dead past were but with them now. No longer would there be aught to fear from prowling beasts, or from the bestial Russian. She could not well refrain from comparing the scant protection afforded her by Clayton with what she might have expected had Tarzan of the Apes been for a single instant confronted by the sinister and menacing attitude of Monsieur Thuran. Once, when Clayton had gone to the little stream for water, and Thuran had spoken coarsely to her, she voiced her thoughts.

"It is well for you, Monsieur Thuran," she said, "that the poor Monsieur Tarzan who was lost from the ship that brought you and Miss Strong to Cape Town is not here now."

"You knew the pig?" asked Thuran, with a sneer.

"I knew the man," she replied. "The only real man, I think, that I have ever known."

There was something in her tone of voice that led the Russian to attribute to her a deeper feeling for his enemy than friendship, and he grasped at the suggestion to be further revenged upon the man whom he supposed dead by besmirching his memory to the girl.

"He was worse than a pig," he cried. "He was a poltroon and a coward. To save himself from the righteous wrath of the husband of a woman he had wronged, he perjured his soul in an attempt to place the blame entirely upon her. Not succeeding in this, he ran away from France to escape meeting the husband upon the field of honor. That is why he was on board the ship that bore Miss Strong and myself to Cape Town. I know whereof I speak, for the woman in the case is my sister. Something more I know that I have never told another – your brave Monsieur Tarzan leaped overboard in an agony of fear because I recognized him, and insisted that he make reparation to me the following morning – we could have fought with knives in my stateroom."

Jane Porter laughed. "You do not for a moment imagine that one who has known both Monsieur Tarzan and you could ever believe such an impossible tale?"

"Then why did he travel under an assumed name?" asked Monsieur Thuran.

"I do not believe you," she cried, but nevertheless the seed of suspicion was sown, for she knew that Hazel Strong had known her forest god only as John Caldwell, of London.

A scant five miles north of their rude shelter, all unknown to them, and practically as remote as though separated by thousands of miles of impenetrable jungle, lay the snug little cabin of Tarzan of the Apes. While farther up the coast, a few miles beyond the cabin, in crude but well-built shelters, lived a little party of eighteen souls – the occupants of the three boats from the LADY ALICE from which Clayton's boat had become separated.

Over a smooth sea they had rowed to the mainland in less than three days. None of the horrors of shipwreck had been theirs, and though depressed by sorrow, and suffering from the shock of the catastrophe and the unaccustomed hardships of their new existence there was none much the worse for the experience.

All were buoyed by the hope that the fourth boat had been picked up, and that a thorough search of the coast would be quickly made. As all the firearms and ammunition on the yacht had been placed in Lord Tennington's boat, the party was well equipped for defense, and for hunting the larger game for food.

Professor Archimedes Q. Porter was their only immediate anxiety. Fully assured in his own mind that his daughter had been picked up by a passing steamer, he gave over the last vestige of apprehension concerning her welfare, and devoted his giant intellect solely to the consideration of those momentous and abstruse scientific problems which he considered the only proper food for thought in one of his erudition. His mind appeared blank to the influence of all extraneous matters.

"Never," said the exhausted Mr. Samuel T. Philander, to Lord Tennington, "never has Professor Porter been more difficult – er – I might say, impossible. Why, only this morning, after I had been forced to relinquish my surveillance for a brief half hour he was entirely missing upon my return. And, bless me, sir, where do you imagine I discovered him? A half mile out in the ocean, sir, in one of the lifeboats, rowing away for dear life. I do not know how he attained even that magnificent distance from shore, for he had but a single oar, with which he was blissfully rowing about in circles.

"When one of the sailors had taken me out to him in another boat the professor became quite indignant at my suggestion that we return at once to land. 'Why, Mr. Philander,' he said, 'I am surprised that you, sir, a man of letters yourself, should have the temerity so to interrupt the progress of science. I had about deduced from certain astronomic phenomena I have had under minute observation during the past several tropic nights an entirely new nebular hypothesis which will unquestionably startle the scientific world. I wish to consult a very excellent monograph on Laplace's hypothesis, which I understand is in a certain private collection in New York City. Your interference, Mr. Philander, will result in an irreparable delay, for I was just rowing over to obtain this pamphlet.' And it was with the greatest difficulty that I persuaded him to return to shore, without resorting to force," concluded Mr. Philander.

Miss Strong and her mother were very brave under the strain of almost constant apprehension of the attacks of savage beasts. Nor were they quite able to accept so readily as the others the theory that Jane, Clayton, and Monsieur Thuran had been picked up safely.

Jane Porter's Esmeralda was in a constant state of tears at the cruel fate which had separated her from her "po, li'le honey."

Lord Tennington's great-hearted good nature never deserted him for a moment. He was still the jovial host, seeking always for the comfort and pleasure of his guests. With the men of his yacht he remained the just but firm commander – there was never any more question in the jungle than there had been on board the LADY ALICE as to who was the final authority in all questions of importance, and in all emergencies requiring cool and intelligent leadership.

Could this well-organized and comparatively secure party of castaways have seen the ragged, fear-haunted trio a few miles south of them they would scarcely have recognized in them the formerly immaculate members of the little company that had laughed and played upon the LADY ALICE. Clayton and Monsieur Thuran were almost naked, so torn had their clothes been by the thorn bushes and tangled vegetation of the matted jungle through which they had been compelled to force their way in search of their ever more difficult food supply.

Jane Porter had of course not been subjected to these strenuous expeditions, but her apparel was, nevertheless, in a sad state of disrepair.

Clayton, for lack of any better occupation, had carefully saved the skin of every animal they had killed. By stretching them upon the stems of trees, and diligently scraping them, he had managed to save them in a fair condition, and now that his clothes were threatening to cover his nakedness no longer, he commenced to fashion a rude garment of them, using a sharp thorn for a needle, and bits of tough grass and animal tendons in lieu of thread.

The result when completed was a sleeveless garment which fell nearly to his knees. As it was made up of numerous small pelts of different species of rodents, it presented a rather strange and wonderful appearance, which, together with the vile stench which permeated it, rendered it anything other than a desirable addition to a wardrobe. But the time came when for the sake of decency he was compelled to don it, and even the misery of their condition could not prevent Jane Porter from laughing heartily at sight of him.

Later, Thuran also found it necessary to construct a similar primitive garment, so that, with their bare legs and heavily bearded faces, they looked not unlike reincarnations of two prehistoric progenitors of the human race. Thuran acted like one.

Nearly two months of this existence had passed when the first great calamity befell them. It was prefaced by an adventure which came near terminating abruptly the sufferings of two of them – terminating them in the grim and horrible manner of the jungle, forever.

Thuran, down with an attack of jungle fever, lay in the shelter among the branches of their tree of refuge. Clayton had been into the jungle a few hundred yards in search of food. As he returned Jane Porter walked to meet him. Behind the man, cunning and crafty, crept an old and mangy lion. For three days his ancient thews and sinews had proved insufficient for the task of providing his cavernous belly with meat. For months he had eaten less and less frequently, and farther and farther had he roamed from his accustomed haunts in search of easier prey. At last he had found nature's weakest and most defenseless creature – in a moment more Numa would dine.

Clayton, all unconscious of the lurking death behind him, strode out into the open toward Jane. He had reached her side, a hundred feet from the tangled edge of jungle when past his shoulder the girl saw the tawny head and the wicked yellow eyes as the grasses parted, and the huge beast, nose to ground, stepped softly into view.

So frozen with horror was she that she could utter no sound, but the fixed and terrified gaze of her fear-widened eyes spoke as plainly to Clayton as words. A quick glance behind him revealed the hopelessness of their situation. The lion was scarce thirty paces from them, and they were equally as far from the shelter. The man was armed with a stout stick – as efficacious against a hungry lion, he realized, as a toy pop-gun charged with a tethered cork.

Numa, ravenous with hunger, had long since learned the futility of roaring and moaning as he searched for prey, but now that it was as surely his as though already he had felt the soft flesh beneath his still mighty paw, he opened his huge jaws, and gave vent to his long-pent rage in a series of deafening roars that made the air tremble.

"Run, Jane!" cried Clayton. "Quick! Run for the shelter!" But her paralyzed muscles refused to respond, and she stood mute and rigid, staring with ghastly countenance at the living death creeping toward them.

Thuran, at the sound of that awful roar, had come to the opening of the shelter, and as he saw the tableau below him he hopped up and down, shrieking to them in Russian.

"Run! Run!" he cried. "Run, or I shall be left all alone in this horrible place," and then he broke down and commenced to weep. For a moment this new voice distracted the attention of the lion, who halted to cast an inquiring glance in the direction of the tree. Clayton could endure the strain no longer. Turning his back upon the beast, he buried his head in his arms and waited.

The girl looked at him in horror. Why did he not do something? If he must die, why not die like a man – bravely; beating at that terrible face with his puny stick, no matter how futile it might be. Would Tarzan of the Apes have done thus? Would he not at least have gone down to his death fighting heroically to the last?

Now the lion was crouching for the spring that would end their young lives beneath cruel, rending, yellow fangs. Jane Porter sank to her knees in prayer, closing her eyes to shut out the last hideous instant. Thuran, weak from fever, fainted.

Seconds dragged into minutes, long minutes into an eternity, and yet the beast did not spring. Clayton was almost unconscious from the prolonged agony of fright – his knees trembled – a moment more and he would collapse.

Jane Porter could endure it no longer. She opened her eyes. Could she be dreaming?

"William," she whispered; "look!"

Clayton mastered himself sufficiently to raise his head and turn toward the lion. An ejaculation of surprise burst from his lips. At their very feet the beast lay crumpled in death. A heavy war spear protruded from the tawny hide. It had entered the great back above the right shoulder, and, passing entirely through the body, had pierced the savage heart.

Jane Porter had risen to her feet; as Clayton turned back to her she staggered in weakness. He put out his arms to save her from falling, and then drew her close to him – pressing her head against his shoulder, he stooped to kiss her in thanksgiving.

Gently the girl pushed him away.

"Please do not do that, William," she said. "I have lived a thousand years in the past brief moments. I have learned in the face of death how to live. I do not wish to hurt you more than is necessary; but I can no longer bear to live out the impossible position I have attempted because of a false sense of loyalty to an impulsive promise I made you.

"The last few seconds of my life have taught me that it would be hideous to attempt further to deceive myself and you, or to entertain for an instant longer the possibility of ever becoming your wife, should we regain civilization."

"Why, Jane," he cried, "what do you mean? What has our providential rescue to do with altering your feelings toward me? You are but unstrung – tomorrow you will be yourself again."

"I am more nearly myself this minute than I have been for over a year," she replied. "The thing that has just happened has again forced to my memory the fact that the bravest man that ever lived honored me with his love. Until it was too late I did not realize that I returned it, and so I sent him away. He is dead now, and I shall never marry. I certainly could not wed another less brave than he without harboring constantly a feeling of contempt for the relative cowardice of my husband. Do you understand me?"

"Yes," he answered, with bowed head, his face mantling with the flush of shame.

And it was the next day that the great calamity befell.

CHAPTER TWENTY TWO

The Treasure Vaults of Opar

IT WAS QUITE DARK before La, the high priestess, returned to the Chamber of the Dead with food and drink for Tarzan. She bore no light, feeling with her hands along the crumbling walls until she gained the chamber. Through the stone grating above, a tropic moon served dimly to illuminate the interior.

Tarzan, crouching in the shadows at the far side of the room as the first sound of approaching footsteps reached him, came forth to meet the girl as he recognized that it was she.

"They are furious," were her first words. "Never before has a human sacrifice escaped the altar. Already fifty have gone forth to track you down. They have searched the temple – all save this single room."

"Why do they fear to come here?" he asked.

"It is the Chamber of the Dead. Here the dead return to worship. See this ancient altar? It is here that the dead sacrifice the living – if they find a victim here. That is the reason our people shun this chamber. Were one to enter he knows that the waiting dead would seize him for their sacrifice."

"But you?" he asked.

"I am high priestess – I alone am safe from the dead. It is I who at rare intervals bring them a human sacrifice from the world above. I alone may enter here in safety."

"Why have they not seized me?" he asked, humoring her grotesque belief.

She looked at him quizzically for a moment. Then she replied:

"It is the duty of a high priestess to instruct, to interpret – according to the creed that others, wiser than herself, have laid down; but there is nothing in the creed which says that she must believe. The more one knows of one's religion the less one believes – no one living knows more of mine than I."

"Then your only fear in aiding me to escape is that your fellow mortals may discover your duplicity?"

"That is all – the dead are dead; they cannot harm – or help. We must therefore depend entirely upon ourselves, and the sooner we act the better it will be. I had difficulty in eluding their vigilance but now in bringing you this morsel of food. To attempt to repeat the thing daily would be the height of folly. Come, let us see how far we may go toward liberty before I must return."

She led him back to the chamber beneath the altar room. Here she turned into one of the several corridors leading from it. In the darkness Tarzan could not see which one. For ten minutes they groped slowly along a winding passage, until at length they came to a closed door. Here he heard her fumbling with a key, and presently came the sound of a metal bolt grating against metal. The door swung in on scraping hinges, and they entered.

"You will be safe here until tomorrow night," she said.

Then she went out, and, closing the door, locked it behind her.

Where Tarzan stood it was dark as Erebus. Not even his trained eyes could penetrate the utter blackness. Cautiously he moved forward until his out-stretched hand touched a wall, then very slowly he traveled around the four walls of the chamber.

Apparently it was about twenty feet square. The floor was of concrete, the walls of the dry masonry that marked the method of construction above ground. Small pieces of granite of various sizes were ingeniously laid together without mortar to construct these ancient foundations.

The first time around the walls Tarzan thought he detected a strange phenomenon for a room with no windows but a single door. Again he crept carefully around close to the wall. No, he could not be mistaken! He paused before the center of the wall opposite the door. For a moment he stood quite motionless, then he moved a few feet to one side. Again he returned, only to move a few feet to the other side.

Once more he made the entire circuit of the room, feeling carefully every foot of the walls. Finally he stopped again before the particular section that had aroused his curiosity. There was no doubt of it! A distinct draft of fresh air was blowing into the chamber through the intersection of the masonry at that particular point – and nowhere else.

Tarzan tested several pieces of the granite which made up the wall at this spot, and finally was rewarded by finding one which lifted out readily. It was about ten inches wide, with a face some three by six inches showing within the chamber. One by one the ape-man lifted out similarly shaped stones. The wall at this point was constructed entirely, it seemed, of these almost perfect slabs. In a short time he had removed some dozen, when he reached in to test the next layer of masonry. To his surprise, he felt nothing behind the masonry he had removed as far as his long arm could reach.

It was a matter of but a few minutes to remove enough of the wall to permit his body to pass through the aperture. Directly ahead of him he thought he discerned a faint glow – scarcely more than a less impenetrable darkness. Cautiously he moved forward on hands and knees, until at about fifteen feet, or the average thickness of the foundation walls, the floor ended abruptly in a sudden drop. As far out as he could reach he felt nothing, nor could he find the bottom of the black abyss that yawned before him, though, clinging to the edge of the floor, he lowered his body into the darkness to its full length.

Finally it occurred to him to look up, and there above him he saw through a round opening a tiny circular patch of starry sky. Feeling up along the sides of the shaft as far as he could reach, the ape-man discovered that so much of the wall as he could feel converged toward the center of the shaft as it rose. This fact precluded possibility of escape in that direction.

As he sat speculating on the nature and uses of this strange passage and its terminal shaft, the moon topped the opening above, letting a flood of soft, silvery light into the shadowy place. Instantly the nature of the shaft became apparent to Tarzan, for far below him he saw the shimmering surface of water. He had come upon an ancient well – but what was the purpose of the connection between the well and the dungeon in which he had been hidden?

As the moon crossed the opening of the shaft its light flooded the whole interior, and then Tarzan saw directly across from him another opening in the opposite wall. He wondered if this might not be the mouth of a passage leading to possible escape. It would be worth investigating, at least, and this he determined to do.

Quickly returning to the wall he had demolished to explore what lay beyond it, he carried the stones into the passageway and replaced them from that side. The deep deposit of dust which he had noticed upon the blocks as he had first removed them from the wall had convinced him that even if the present occupants of the ancient pile had knowledge of this hidden passage they had made no use of it for perhaps generations.

The wall replaced, Tarzan turned to the shaft, which was some fifteen feet wide at this point. To leap across the intervening space was a small matter to the ape-man, and a moment later he was proceeding along a narrow tunnel, moving cautiously for fear of being precipitated into another shaft such as he had just crossed.

He had advanced some hundred feet when he came to a flight of steps leading downward into Stygian gloom. Some twenty feet below, the level floor of the tunnel recommenced, and shortly afterward his progress was stopped by a heavy wooden door which was secured by massive wooden bars upon the side of Tarzan's approach. This fact suggested to the ape-man that he might surely be in a passageway leading to the outer world, for the bolts, barring progress from the opposite side, tended to substantiate this hypothesis, unless it were merely a prison to which it led.

Along the tops of the bars were deep layers of dust – a further indication that the passage had lain long unused. As he pushed the massive obstacle aside, its great hinges shrieked out in weird protest against this unaccustomed disturbance. For a moment Tarzan paused to listen for any responsive note which might indicate that the unusual night noise had alarmed the inmates of the temple; but as he heard nothing he advanced beyond the doorway.

Carefully feeling about, he found himself within a large chamber, along the walls of which, and down the length of the floor, were piled many tiers of metal ingots of an odd though uniform shape. To his groping hands they felt not unlike double-headed bootjacks. The ingots were quite heavy, and but for the enormous number of them he would have been positive that they were gold; but the thought of the fabulous wealth these thousands of pounds of metal would have represented were they in reality gold, almost convinced him that they must be of some baser metal.

At the far end of the chamber he discovered another barred door, and again the bars upon the inside renewed the hope that he was traversing an ancient and forgotten passageway to liberty. Beyond the door the passage ran straight as a war spear, and it soon became evident to the ape-man that it had already led him beyond the outer walls of the temple. If he but knew the direction it was leading him! If toward the west, then he must also be beyond the city's outer walls.

With increasing hopes he forged ahead as rapidly as he dared, until at the end of half an hour he came to another flight of steps leading upward. At the bottom this flight was of concrete, but as he ascended his naked feet felt a sudden change in the substance they were treading. The steps of concrete had given place to steps of granite. Feeling with his hands, the ape-man discovered that these latter were evidently hewed from rock, for there was no crack to indicate a joint.

For a hundred feet the steps wound spirally up, until at a sudden turning Tarzan came into a narrow cleft between two rocky walls. Above him shone the starry sky, and before him a steep incline replaced the steps that had terminated at its foot. Up this pathway Tarzan hastened, and at its upper end came out upon the rough top of a huge granite bowlder.

A mile away lay the ruined city of Opar, its domes and turrets bathed in the soft light of the equatorial moon. Tarzan dropped his eyes to the ingot he had brought away with him. For a moment he examined it by the moon's bright rays, then he raised his head to look out upon the ancient piles of crumbling grandeur in the distance.

"Opar," he mused, "Opar, the enchanted city of a dead and forgotten past. The city of the beauties and the beasts. City of horrors and death; but – city of fabulous riches." The ingot was of virgin gold.

The bowlder on which Tarzan found himself lay well out in the plain between the city and the distant cliffs he and his black warriors had scaled the morning previous. To descend its rough and precipitous face was a task of infinite labor and considerable peril even to the ape-man; but at last he felt the soft soil of the valley beneath his feet, and without a backward glance at Opar he turned his face toward the guardian cliffs, and at a rapid trot set off across the valley.

The sun was just rising as he gained the summit of the flat mountain at the valley's western boundary. Far beneath him he saw smoke arising above the tree-tops of the forest at the base of the foothills.

"Man," he murmured. "And there were fifty who went forth to track me down. Can it be they?"

Swiftly he descended the face of the cliff, and, dropping into a narrow ravine which led down to the far forest, he hastened onward in the direction of the smoke. Striking the forest's edge about a quarter of a mile from the point at which the slender column arose into the still air, he took to the trees. Cautiously he approached until there suddenly burst upon his view a rude BOMA, in the center of which, squatted about their tiny fires, sat his fifty black Waziri. He called to them in their own tongue:

"Arise, my children, and greet thy king!"

With exclamations of surprise and fear the warriors leaped to their feet, scarcely knowing whether to flee or not. Then Tarzan dropped lightly from an overhanging branch into their midst. When they realized that it was indeed their chief in the flesh, and no materialized spirit, they went mad with joy.

"We were cowards, oh, Waziri," cried Busuli. "We ran away and left you to your fate; but when our panic was over we swore to return and save you, or at least take revenge upon your murderers. We were but now preparing to scale the heights once more and cross the desolate valley to the terrible city."

"Have you seen fifty frightful men pass down from the cliffs into this forest, my children?" asked Tarzan.

"Yes, Waziri," replied Busuli. "They passed us late yesterday, as we were about to turn back after you. They had no woodcraft. We heard them coming for a mile before we saw them, and as we had other business in hand we withdrew into the forest and let them pass. They were waddling rapidly along upon short legs, and now and then one would go upon all fours like Bolgani, the gorilla. They were indeed fifty frightful men, Waziri."

When Tarzan had related his adventures and told them of the yellow metal he had found, not one demurred when he outlined a plan to return by night and bring away what they could carry of the vast treasure; and so it was that as dusk fell across the desolate valley of Opar fifty ebon warriors trailed at a smart trot over the dry and dusty ground toward the giant bowlder that loomed before the city.

If it had seemed a difficult task to descend the face of the bowlder, Tarzan soon found that it would be next to impossible to get his fifty warriors to the summit. Finally the feat was accomplished by dint of herculean efforts upon the part of the ape-man. Ten spears were fastened end to end, and with one end of this remarkable chain attached to his waist, Tarzan at last succeeded in reaching the summit.

Once there, he drew up one of his blacks, and in this way the entire party was finally landed in safety upon the bowlder's top. Immediately Tarzan led them to the treasure chamber, where to each was allotted a load of two ingots, for each about eighty pounds.

By midnight the entire party stood once more at the foot of the bowlder, but with their heavy loads it was mid-forenoon ere they reached the summit of the cliffs. From there on the homeward journey was slow, as these proud fighting men were unaccustomed to the duties of porters. But they bore their burdens uncomplainingly, and at the end of thirty days entered their own country.

Here, instead of continuing on toward the northwest and their village, Tarzan guided them almost directly west, until on the morning of the thirty-third day he bade them break camp and return to their own village, leaving the gold where they had stacked it the previous night.

"And you, Waziri?" they asked.

"I shall remain here for a few days, my children," he replied. "Now hasten back to thy wives and children."

When they had gone Tarzan gathered up two of the ingots and, springing into a tree, ran lightly above the tangled and impenetrable mass of undergrowth for a couple of hundred yards, to emerge suddenly upon a circular clearing about which the giants of the jungle forest towered like a guardian host. In the center of this natural amphitheater, was a little flat-topped mound of hard earth.

Hundreds of times before had Tarzan been to this secluded spot, which was so densely surrounded by thorn bushes and tangled vines and creepers of huge girth that not even Sheeta, the leopard, could worm his sinuous way within, nor Tantor, with his giant strength, force the barriers which protected the council chamber of the great apes from all but the harmless denizens of the savage jungle.

Fifty trips Tarzan made before he had deposited all the ingots within the precincts of the amphitheater. Then from the hollow of an ancient, lightning-blasted tree he produced the very spade with which he had uncovered the chest of Professor Archimedes Q. Porter which he had once, apelike, buried in this selfsame spot. With this he dug a long trench, into which he laid the fortune that his blacks had carried from the forgotten treasure vaults of the city of Opar.

That night he slept within the amphitheater, and early the next morning set out to revisit his cabin before returning to his Waziri. Finding things as he had left them, he went forth into the jungle to hunt, intending to bring his prey to the cabin where he might feast in comfort, spending the night upon a comfortable couch.

For five miles toward the south he roamed, toward the banks of a fair-sized river that flowed into the sea about six miles from his cabin. He had gone inland about half a mile when there came suddenly to his trained nostrils the one scent that sets the whole savage jungle aquiver – Tarzan smelled man.

The wind was blowing off the ocean, so Tarzan knew that the authors of the scent were west of him. Mixed with the man scent was the scent of Numa. Man and lion. "I had better hasten," thought the ape-man, for he had recognized the scent of whites. "Numa may be a-hunting."

When he came through the trees to the edge of the jungle he saw a woman kneeling in prayer, and before her stood a wild, primitive-looking white man, his face buried in his arms. Behind the man a mangy lion was advancing slowly toward this easy prey. The man's face was averted; the woman's bowed in prayer. He could not see the features of either.

Already Numa was about to spring. There was not a second to spare. Tarzan could not even unsling his bow and fit an arrow in time to send one of his deadly poisoned shafts into the yellow hide. He was too far away to reach the beast in time with his knife. There was but a single hope – a lone alternative. And with the quickness of thought the ape-man acted.

A brawny arm flew back – for the briefest fraction of an instant a huge spear poised above the giant's shoulder – and then the mighty arm shot out, and swift death tore through the intervening leaves to bury itself in the heart of the leaping lion. Without a sound he rolled over at the very feet of his intended victims – dead.

For a moment neither the man nor the woman moved. Then the latter opened her eyes to look with wonder upon the dead beast behind her companion. As that beautiful head went up Tarzan of the Apes gave a gasp of incredulous astonishment. Was he mad? It could not be the woman he loved! But, indeed, it was none other.

And the woman rose, and the man took her in his arms to kiss her, and of a sudden the ape-man saw red through a bloody mist of murder, and the old scar upon his forehead burned scarlet against his brown hide.

There was a terrible expression upon his savage face as he fitted a poisoned shaft to his bow. An ugly light gleamed in those gray eyes as he sighted full at the back of the unsuspecting man beneath him.

For an instant he glanced along the polished shaft, drawing the bowstring far back, that the arrow might pierce through the heart for which it was aimed.

But he did not release the fatal messenger. Slowly the point of the arrow drooped; the scar upon the brown forehead faded; the bowstring relaxed; and Tarzan of the Apes, with bowed head, turned sadly into the jungle toward the village of the Waziri.

CHAPTER TWENTY THREE

The Fifty Frightful Men

For several long minutes Jane Porter and William Cecil Clayton stood silently looking at the dead body of the beast whose prey they had so narrowly escaped becoming.

The girl was the first to speak again after her outbreak of impulsive avowal.

"Who could it have been?" she whispered.

"God knows!" was the man's only reply.

"If it is a friend, why does he not show himself?" continued Jane. "Wouldn't it be well to call out to him, and at least thank him?"

Mechanically Clayton did her bidding, but there was no response.

Jane Porter shuddered. "The mysterious jungle," she murmured. "The terrible jungle. It renders even the manifestations of friendship terrifying."

"We had best return to the shelter," said Clayton. "You will be at least a little safer there. I am no protection whatever," he added bitterly.

"Do not say that, William," she hastened to urge, acutely sorry for the wound her words had caused. "You have done the best you could. You have been noble, and self-sacrificing, and brave. It is no fault of yours that you are not a superman. There is only one other man I have ever known who could have done more than you. My words were ill chosen in the excitement of the reaction – I did not wish to wound you. All that I wish is that we may both understand once and for all that I can never marry you – that such a marriage would be wicked."

"I think I understand," he replied. "Let us not speak of it again – at least until we are back in civilization."

The next day Thuran was worse. Almost constantly he was in a state of delirium. They could do nothing to relieve him, nor was Clayton over-anxious to attempt anything. On the girl's account he feared the Russian – in the bottom of his heart he hoped the man would die. The thought that something might befall him that would leave her entirely at the mercy of this beast caused him greater anxiety than the probability that almost certain death awaited her should she be left entirely alone upon the outskirts of the cruel forest.

The Englishman had extracted the heavy spear from the body of the lion, so that when he went into the forest to hunt that morning he had a feeling of much greater security than at any time since they had been cast upon the savage shore. The result was that he penetrated farther from the shelter than ever before.

To escape as far as possible from the mad ravings of the fever-stricken Russian, Jane Porter had descended from the shelter to the foot of the tree – she dared not venture farther. Here, beside the crude ladder Clayton had constructed for her, she sat looking out to sea, in the always surviving hope that a vessel might be sighted.

Her back was toward the jungle, and so she did not see the grasses part, or the savage face that peered from between. Little, bloodshot, close-set eyes scanned her intently, roving from time to time about the open beach for indications of the presence of others than herself. Presently another head appeared, and then another and another. The man in the shelter commenced to rave again, and the heads disappeared as silently and as suddenly as they had come. But soon they were thrust forth once more, as the girl gave no sign of perturbation at the continued wailing of the man above.

One by one grotesque forms emerged from the jungle to creep stealthily upon the unsuspecting woman. A faint rustling of the grasses attracted her attention. She turned, and at the sight that confronted her staggered to her feet with a little shriek of fear. Then they closed upon her with a rush. Lifting her bodily in his long, gorilla-like arms, one of the creatures turned and bore her into the jungle. A filthy paw covered her mouth to stifle her screams. Added to the weeks of torture she had already undergone, the shock was more than she could withstand. Shattered nerves collapsed, and she lost consciousness. When she regained her senses she found herself in the thick of the primeval forest. It was night. A huge fire burned brightly in the little clearing in which she lay. About it squatted fifty frightful men. Their heads and faces were covered with matted hair. Their long arms rested upon the bent knees of their short, crooked legs. They were gnawing, like beasts, upon unclean food. A pot boiled upon the edge of the fire, and out of it one of the creatures would occasionally drag a hunk of meat with a sharpened stick.

When they discovered that their captive had regained consciousness, a piece of this repulsive stew was tossed to her from the foul hand of a nearby feaster. It rolled close to her side, but she only closed her eyes as a qualm of nausea surged through her.

For many days they traveled through the dense forest. The girl, footsore and exhausted, was half dragged, half pushed through the long, hot, tedious days. Occasionally, when she would stumble and fall, she was cuffed and kicked by the nearest of the frightful men. Long before they reached their journey's end her shoes had been discarded – the soles entirely gone. Her clothes were torn to mere shreds and tatters, and through the pitiful rags her once white and tender skin showed raw and bleeding from contact with the thousand pitiless thorns and brambles through which she had been dragged.

The last two days of the journey found her in such utter exhaustion that no amount of kicking and abuse could force her to her poor, bleeding feet. Outraged nature had reached the limit of endurance, and the girl was physically powerless to raise herself even to her knees.

As the beasts surrounded her, chattering threateningly the while they goaded her with their cudgels and beat and kicked her with their fists and feet, she lay with closed eyes, praying for the merciful death that she knew alone could give her surcease from suffering; but it did not come, and presently the fifty frightful men realized that their victim was no longer able to walk, and so they picked her up and carried her the balance of the journey.

Late one afternoon she saw the ruined walls of a mighty city looming before them, but so weak and sick was she that it inspired not the faintest shadow of interest. Wherever they were bearing her, there could be but one end to her captivity among these fierce half brutes.

At last they passed through two great walls and came to the ruined city within. Into a crumbling pile they bore her, and here she was surrounded by hundreds more of the same creatures that had brought her; but among them were females who looked less horrible. At sight of them the first faint hope that she had entertained came to mitigate her misery. But it was short-lived, for the women offered her no sympathy, though, on the other hand, neither did they abuse her.

After she had been inspected to the entire satisfaction of the inmates of the building she was borne to a dark chamber in the vaults beneath, and here upon the bare floor she was left, with a metal bowl of water and another of food.

For a week she saw only some of the women whose duty it was to bring her food and water. Slowly her strength was returning – soon she would be in fit condition to offer as a sacrifice to The Flaming God. Fortunate indeed it was that she could not know the fate for which she was destined.

As Tarzan of the Apes moved slowly through the jungle after casting the spear that saved Clayton and Jane Porter from the fangs of Numa, his mind was filled with all the sorrow that belongs to a freshly opened heart wound.

He was glad that he had stayed his hand in time to prevent the consummation of the thing that in the first mad wave of jealous wrath he had contemplated. Only the fraction of a second had stood between Clayton and death at the hands of the ape-man. In the short moment that had elapsed after he had recognized the girl and her companion and the relaxing of the taut muscles that held the poisoned shaft directed at the Englishman's heart, Tarzan had been swayed by the swift and savage impulses of brute life.

He had seen the woman he craved – his woman – his mate – in the arms of another. There had been but one course open to him, according to the fierce jungle code that guided him in this other existence; but just before it had become too late the softer sentiments of his inherent chivalry had risen above the flaming fires of his passion and saved him. A thousand times he gave thanks that they had triumphed before his fingers had released that polished arrow.

As he contemplated his return to the Waziri the idea became repugnant. He did not wish to see a human being again. At least he would range alone through the jungle for a time, until the sharp edge of his sorrow had become blunted. Like his fellow beasts, he preferred to suffer in silence and alone.

That night he slept again in the amphitheater of the apes, and for several days he hunted from there, returning at night. On the afternoon of the third day he returned early. He had lain stretched upon the soft grass of the circular clearing for but a few moments when he heard far to the south a familiar sound. It was the passing through the jungle of a band of great apes – he could not mistake that. For several minutes he lay listening. They were coming in the direction of the amphitheater.

Tarzan arose lazily and stretched himself. His keen ears followed every movement of the advancing tribe. They were upwind, and presently he caught their scent, though he had not needed this added evidence to assure him that he was right.

As they came closer to the amphitheater Tarzan of the Apes melted into the branches upon the other side of the arena. There he waited to inspect the newcomers. Nor had he long to wait.

Presently a fierce, hairy face appeared among the lower branches opposite him. The cruel little eyes took in the clearing at a glance, then there was a chattered report returned to those behind. Tarzan could hear the words. The scout was telling the other members of the tribe that the coast was clear and that they might enter the amphitheater in safety.

First the leader dropped lightly upon the soft carpet of the grassy floor, and then, one by one, nearly a hundred anthropoids followed him. There were the huge adults and several young. A few nursing babes clung close to the shaggy necks of their savage mothers.

Tarzan recognized many members of the tribe. It was the same into which he had come as a tiny babe. Many of the adults had been little apes during his boyhood. He had frolicked and played about this very jungle with them during their brief childhood. He wondered if they would remember him – the memory of some apes is not overlong, and two years may be an eternity to them.

From the talk which he overheard he learned that they had come to choose a new king – their late chief had fallen a hundred feet beneath a broken limb to an untimely end.

Tarzan walked to the end of an overhanging limb in plain view of them. The quick eyes of a female caught sight of him first. With a barking guttural she called the attention of the others. Several huge bulls stood erect to get a better view of the intruder. With bared fangs and bristling necks they advanced slowly toward him, with deep-throated, ominous growls.

"Karnath, I am Tarzan of the Apes," said the ape-man in the vernacular of the tribe. "You remember me. Together we teased Numa when we were still little apes, throwing sticks and nuts at him from the safety of high branches."

The brute he had addressed stopped with a look of half-comprehending, dull wonderment upon his savage face.

"And Magor," continued Tarzan, addressing another, "do you not recall your former king – he who slew the mighty Kerchak? Look at me! Am I not the same Tarzan – mighty hunter – invincible fighter – that you all knew for many seasons?"

The apes all crowded forward now, but more in curiosity than threatening. They muttered among themselves for a few moments.

"What do you want among us now?" asked Karnath.

"Only peace," answered the ape-man.

Again the apes conferred. At length Karnath spoke again.

"Come in peace, then, Tarzan of the Apes," he said.

And so Tarzan of the Apes dropped lightly to the turf into the midst of the fierce and hideous horde – he had completed the cycle of evolution, and had returned to be once again a brute among brutes.

There were no greetings such as would have taken place among men after a separation of two years. The majority of the apes went on about the little activities that the advent of the ape-man had interrupted, paying no further attention to him than as though he had not been gone from the tribe at all.

One or two young bulls who had not been old enough to remember him sidled up on all fours to sniff at him, and one bared his fangs and growled threateningly – he wished to put Tarzan immediately into his proper place. Had Tarzan backed off, growling, the young bull would quite probably have been satisfied, but always after Tarzan's station among his fellow apes would have been beneath that of the bull which had made him step aside.

But Tarzan of the Apes did not back off. Instead, he swung his giant palm with all the force of his mighty muscles, and, catching the young bull alongside the head, sent him sprawling across the turf. The ape was up and at him again in a second, and this time they closed with tearing fingers and rending fangs – or at least that had been the intention of the young bull; but scarcely had they gone down, growling and snapping, than the ape-man's fingers found the throat of his antagonist.

Presently the young bull ceased to struggle, and lay quite still. Then Tarzan released his hold and arose – he did not wish to kill, only to teach the young ape, and others who might be watching, that Tarzan of the Apes was still master.

The lesson served its purpose – the young apes kept out of his way, as young apes should when their betters were about, and the old bulls made no attempt to encroach upon his prerogatives. For several days the she-apes with young remained suspicious of him, and when he ventured too near rushed upon him with wide mouths and hideous roars. Then Tarzan discreetly skipped out of harm's way, for that also is a custom among the apes – only mad bulls will attack a mother. But after a while even they became accustomed to him.

He hunted with them as in days gone by, and when they found that his superior reason guided him to the best food sources, and that his cunning rope ensnared toothsome game that they seldom if ever tasted, they came again to look up to him as they had in the past after he had become their king. And so it was that before they left the amphitheater to return to their wanderings they had once more chosen him as their leader.

The ape-man felt quite contented with his new lot. He was not happy – that he never could be again, but he was at least as far from everything that might remind him of his past misery as he could be. Long since he had given up every intention of returning to civilization, and now he had decided to see no more his black friends of the Waziri. He had foresworn humanity forever. He had started life an ape – as an ape he would die.

He could not, however, erase from his memory the fact that the woman he loved was within a short journey of the stamping-ground of his tribe; nor could he banish the haunting fear that she might be constantly in danger. That she was illy protected he had seen in the brief instant that had witnessed Clayton's inefficiency. The more Tarzan thought of it, the more keenly his conscience pricked him.

Finally he came to loathe himself for permitting his own selfish sorrow and jealousy to stand between Jane Porter and safety. As the days passed the thing preyed more and more upon his mind, and he had about determined to return to the coast and place himself on guard over Jane Porter and Clayton, when news reached him that altered all his plans and sent him dashing madly toward the east in reckless disregard of accident and death.

Before Tarzan had returned to the tribe, a certain young bull, not being able to secure a mate from among his own people, had, according to custom, fared forth through the wild jungle, like some knight-errant of old, to win a fair lady from some neighboring community.

He had but just returned with his bride, and was narrating his adventures quickly before he should forget them. Among other things he told of seeing a great tribe of strange-looking apes.

"They were all hairy-faced bulls but one," he said, "and that one was a she, lighter in color even than this stranger," and he chucked a thumb at Tarzan.

The ape-man was all attention in an instant. He asked questions as rapidly as the slow-witted anthropoid could answer them.

"Were the bulls short, with crooked legs?"

"They were."

"Did they wear the skins of Numa and Sheeta about their loins, and carry sticks and knives?"

"They did."

"And were there many yellow rings about their arms and legs?"

"Yes."

"And the she one – was she small and slender, and very white?"

"Yes."

"Did she seem to be one of the tribe, or was she a prisoner?"

"They dragged her along – sometimes by an arm – sometimes by the long hair that grew upon her head; and always they kicked and beat her. Oh, but it was great fun to watch them."

"God!" muttered Tarzan.

"Where were they when you saw them, and which way were they going?" continued the ape-man.

"They were beside the second water back there," and he pointed to the south. "When they passed me they were going toward the morning, upward along the edge of the water."

"When was this?" asked Tarzan.

"Half a moon since."

Without another word the ape-man sprang into the trees and fled like a disembodied spirit eastward in the direction of the forgotten city of Opar.

CHAPTER TWENTY FOUR

How Tarzan Came Again to Opar

When Clayton returned to the shelter and found Jane Porter was missing, he became frantic with fear and grief. He found Monsieur Thuran quite rational, the fever having left him with the surprising suddenness which is one of its peculiarities. The Russian, weak and exhausted, still lay upon his bed of grasses within the shelter.

When Clayton asked him about the girl he seemed surprised to know that she was not there.

"I have heard nothing unusual," he said. "But then I have been unconscious much of the time."

Had it not been for the man's very evident weakness, Clayton should have suspected him of having sinister knowledge of the girl's whereabouts; but he could see that Thuran lacked sufficient vitality even to descend, unaided, from the shelter. He could not, in his present physical condition, have harmed the girl, nor could he have climbed the rude ladder back to the shelter.

Until dark the Englishman searched the nearby jungle for a trace of the missing one or a sign of the trail of her abductor. But though the spoor left by the fifty frightful men, unversed in woodcraft as they were, would have been as plain to the densest denizen of the jungle as a city street to the Englishman, yet he crossed and recrossed it twenty times without observing the slightest indication that many men had passed that way but a few short hours since.

As he searched, Clayton continued to call the girl's name aloud, but the only result of this was to attract Numa, the lion. Fortunately the man saw the shadowy form worming its way toward him in time to climb into the branches of a tree before the beast was close enough to reach him. This put an end to his search for the balance of the afternoon, as the lion paced back and forth beneath him until dark.

Even after the beast had left, Clayton dared not descend into the awful blackness beneath him, and so he spent a terrifying and hideous night in the tree. The next morning he returned to the beach, relinquishing the last hope of succoring Jane Porter.

During the week that followed, Monsieur Thuran rapidly regained his strength, lying in the shelter while Clayton hunted food for both. The men never spoke except as necessity demanded. Clayton now occupied the section of the shelter which had been reserved for Jane Porter, and only saw the Russian when he took food or water to him, or performed the other kindly offices which common humanity required.

When Thuran was again able to descend in search of food, Clayton was stricken with fever. For days he lay tossing in delirium and suffering, but not once did the Russian come near him. Food the Englishman could not have eaten, but his craving for water amounted practically to torture. Between the recurrent attacks of delirium, weak though he was, he managed to reach the brook once a day and fill a tiny can that had been among the few appointments of the lifeboat.

Thuran watched him on these occasions with an expression of malignant pleasure – he seemed really to enjoy the suffering of the man who, despite the just contempt in which he held him, had ministered to him to the best of his ability while he lay suffering the same agonies. At last Clayton became so weak that he was no longer able to descend from the shelter. For a day he suffered for water without appealing to the Russian, but finally, unable to endure it longer, he asked Thuran to fetch him a drink. The Russian came to the entrance to Clayton's room, a dish of water in his hand. A nasty grin contorted his features.

"Here is water," he said. "But first let me remind you that you maligned me before the girl – that you kept her to yourself, and would not share her with me – "

Clayton interrupted him. "Stop!" he cried. "Stop! What manner of cur are you that you traduce the character of a good woman whom we believe dead! God! I was a fool ever to let you live – you are not fit to live even in this vile land."

"Here is your water," said the Russian. "All you will get," and he raised the basin to his lips and drank; what was left he threw out upon the ground below. Then he turned and left the sick man.

Clayton rolled over, and, burying his face in his arms, gave up the battle.

The next day Thuran determined to set out toward the north along the coast, for he knew that eventually he must come to the habitations of civilized men – at least he could be no worse off than he was here, and, furthermore, the ravings of the dying Englishman were getting on his nerves. So he stole Clayton's spear and set off upon his journey. He would have killed the sick man before he left had it not occurred to him that it would really have been a kindness to do so.

That same day he came to a little cabin by the beach, and his heart filled with renewed hope as he saw this evidence of the proximity of civilization, for he thought it but the outpost of a nearby settlement. Had he known to whom it belonged, and that its owner was at that very moment but a few miles inland, Nikolas Rokoff would have fled the place as he would a pestilence. But he did not know, and so he remained for a few days to enjoy the security and comparative comforts of the cabin. Then he took up his northward journey once more.

In Lord Tennington's camp preparations were going forward to build permanent quarters, and then to send out an expedition of a few men to the north in search of relief.

As the days had passed without bringing the longed-for succor, hope that Jane Porter, Clayton, and Monsieur Thuran had been rescued began to die. No one spoke of the matter longer to Professor Porter, and he was so immersed in his scientific dreaming that he was not aware of the elapse of time.

Occasionally he would remark that within a few days they should certainly see a steamer drop anchor off their shore, and that then they should all be reunited happily. Sometimes he spoke of it as a train, and wondered if it were being delayed by snowstorms.

"If I didn't know the dear old fellow so well by now," Tennington remarked to Miss Strong, "I should be quite certain that he was – er – not quite right, don't you know." "If it were not so pathetic it would be ridiculous," said the girl, sadly. "I, who have known him all my life, know how he worships Jane; but to others it must seem that he is perfectly callous to her fate. It is only that he is so absolutely impractical that he cannot conceive of so real a thing as death unless nearly certain proof of it is thrust upon him."

"You'd never guess what he was about yesterday," continued Tennington. "I was coming in alone from a little hunt when I met him walking rapidly along the game trail that I was following back to camp. His hands were clasped beneath the tails of his long black coat, and his top hat was set firmly down upon his head, as with eyes bent upon the ground he hastened on, probably to some sudden death had I not intercepted him.

"'Why, where in the world are you bound, professor?' I asked him. 'I am going into town, Lord Tennington,' he said, as seriously as possible, 'to complain to the postmaster about the rural free delivery service we are suffering from here. Why, sir, I haven't had a piece of mail in weeks. There should be several letters for me from Jane. The matter must be reported to Washington at once.'

"And would you believe it, Miss Strong," continued Tennington, "I had the very deuce of a job to convince the old fellow that there was not only no rural free delivery, but no town, and that he was not even on the same continent as Washington, nor in the same hemisphere.

"When he did realize he commenced to worry about his daughter – I think it is the first time that he really has appreciated our position here, or the fact that Miss Porter may not have been rescued."

"I hate to think about it," said the girl, "and yet I can think of nothing else than the absent members of our party."

"Let us hope for the best," replied Tennington. "You yourself have set us each a splendid example of bravery, for in a way your loss has been the greatest."

"Yes," she replied; "I could have loved Jane Porter no more had she been my own sister."

Tennington did not show the surprise he felt. That was not at all what he meant. He had been much with this fair daughter of Maryland since the wreck of the LADY ALICE, and it had recently come to him that he had grown much more fond of her than would prove good for the peace of his mind, for he recalled almost constantly now the confidence which Monsieur Thuran had imparted to him that he and Miss Strong were engaged. He wondered if, after all, Thuran had been quite accurate in his statement. He had never seen the slightest indication on the girl's part of more than ordinary friendship.

"And then in Monsieur Thuran's loss, if they are lost, you would suffer a severe bereavement," he ventured.

She looked up at him quickly. "Monsieur Thuran had become a very dear friend," she said. "I liked him very much, though I have known him but a short time."

"Then you were not engaged to marry him?" he blurted out. "Heavens, no!" she cried. "I did not care for him at all in that way."

There was something that Lord Tennington wanted to say to Hazel Strong – he wanted very badly to say it, and to say it at once; but somehow the words stuck in his throat. He started lamely a couple of times, cleared his throat, became red in the face, and finally ended by remarking that he hoped the cabins would be finished before the rainy season commenced.

But, though he did not know it, he had conveyed to the girl the very message he intended, and it left her happy – happier than she had ever before been in all her life.

Just then further conversation was interrupted by the sight of a strange and terrible-looking figure which emerged from the jungle just south of the camp. Tennington and the girl saw it at the same time. The Englishman reached for his revolver, but when the half-naked, bearded creature called his name aloud and came running toward them he dropped his hand and advanced to meet it.

None would have recognized in the filthy, emaciated creature, covered by a single garment of small skins, the immaculate Monsieur Thuran the party had last seen upon the deck of the LADY ALICE.

Before the other members of the little community were apprised of his presence Tennington and Miss Strong questioned him regarding the other occupants of the missing boat.

"They are all dead," replied Thuran. "The three sailors died before we made land. Miss Porter was carried off into the jungle by some wild animal while I was lying delirious with fever. Clayton died of the same fever but a few days since. And to think that all this time we have been separated by but a few miles – scarcely a day's march. It is terrible!"

How long Jane Porter lay in the darkness of the vault beneath the temple in the ancient city of Opar she did not know. For a time she was delirious with fever, but after this passed she commenced slowly to regain her strength. Every day the woman who brought her food beckoned to her to arise, but for many days the girl could only shake her head to indicate that she was too weak.

But eventually she was able to gain her feet, and then to stagger a few steps by supporting herself with one hand upon the wall. Her captors now watched her with increasing interest. The day was approaching, and the victim was gaining in strength.

Presently the day came, and a young woman whom Jane Porter had not seen before came with several others to her dungeon. Here some sort of ceremony was performed – that it was of a religious nature the girl was sure, and so she took new heart, and rejoiced that she had fallen among people upon whom the refining and softening influences of religion evidently had fallen. They would treat her humanely – of that she was now quite sure.

And so when they led her from her dungeon, through long, dark corridors, and up a flight of concrete steps to a brilliant courtyard, she went willingly, even gladly – for was she not among the servants of God? It might be, of course, that their interpretation of the supreme being differed from her own, but that they owned a god was sufficient evidence to her that they were kind and good.

But when she saw a stone altar in the center of the courtyard, and dark-brown stains upon it and the nearby concrete of the floor, she began to wonder and to doubt. And as they stooped and bound her ankles, and secured her wrists behind her, her doubts were turned to fear. A moment later, as she was lifted and placed supine across the altar's top, hope left her entirely, and she trembled in an agony of fright.

During the grotesque dance of the votaries which followed, she lay frozen in horror, nor did she require the sight of the thin blade in the hands of the high priestess as it rose slowly above her to enlighten her further as to her doom.

As the hand began its descent, Jane Porter closed her eyes and sent up a silent prayer to the Maker she was so soon to face – then she succumbed to the strain upon her tired nerves, and swooned.

Day and night Tarzan of the Apes raced through the primeval forest toward the ruined city in which he was positive the woman he loved lay either a prisoner or dead.

In a day and a night he covered the same distance that the fifty frightful men had taken the better part of a week to traverse, for Tarzan of the Apes traveled along the middle terrace high above the tangled obstacles that impede progress upon the ground.

The story the young bull ape had told made it clear to him that the girl captive had been Jane Porter, for there was not another small white "she" in all the jungle. The "bulls" he had recognized from the ape's crude description as the grotesque parodies upon humanity who inhabit the ruins of Opar. And the girl's fate he could picture as plainly as though he were an eyewitness to it. When they would lay her across that trim altar he could not guess, but that her dear, frail body would eventually find its way there he was confident.

But, finally, after what seemed long ages to the impatient ape-man, he topped the barrier cliffs that hemmed the desolate valley, and below him lay the grim and awful ruins of the now hideous city of Opar. At a rapid trot he started across the dry and dusty, bowlder-strewn ground toward the goal of his desires.

Would he be in time to rescue? He hoped against hope. At least he could be revenged, and in his wrath it seemed to him that he was equal to the task of wiping out the entire population of that terrible city. It was nearly noon when he reached the great bowlder at the top of which terminated the secret passage to the pits beneath the city. Like a cat he scaled the precipitous sides of the frowning granite KOPJE. A moment later he was running through the darkness of the long, straight tunnel that led to the treasure vault. Through this he passed, then on and on until at last he came to the well-like shaft upon the opposite side of which lay the dungeon with the false wall.

As he paused a moment upon the brink of the well a faint sound came to him through the opening above. His quick ears caught and translated it – it was the dance of death that preceded a sacrifice, and the singsong ritual of the high priestess. He could even recognize the woman's voice. Could it be that the ceremony marked the very thing he had so hastened to prevent? A wave of horror swept over him. Was he, after all, to be just a moment too late? Like a frightened deer he leaped across the narrow chasm to the continuation of the passage beyond. At the false wall he tore like one possessed to demolish the barrier that confronted him – with giant muscles he forced the opening, thrusting his head and shoulders through the first small hole he made, and carrying the balance of the wall with him, to clatter resoundingly upon the cement floor of the dungeon.

With a single leap he cleared the length of the chamber and threw himself against the ancient door. But here he stopped. The mighty bars upon the other side were proof even against such muscles as his. It needed but a moment's effort to convince him of the futility of endeavoring to force that impregnable barrier. There was but one other way, and that led back through the long tunnels to the bowlder a mile beyond the city's walls, and then back across the open as he had come to the city first with his Waziri.

He realized that to retrace his steps and enter the city from above ground would mean that he would be too late to save the girl, if it were indeed she who lay upon the sacrificial altar above him. But there seemed no other way, and so he turned and ran swiftly back into the passageway beyond the broken wall. At the well he heard again the monotonous voice of the high priestess, and, as he glanced aloft, the opening, twenty feet above, seemed so near that he was tempted to leap for it in a mad endeavor to reach the inner courtyard that lay so near.

If he could but get one end of his grass rope caught upon some projection at the top of that tantalizing aperture! In the instant's pause and thought an idea occurred to him. He would attempt it. Turning back to the tumbled wall, he seized one of the large, flat slabs that had composed it. Hastily making one end of his rope fast to the piece of granite, he returned to the shaft, and, coiling the balance of the rope on the floor beside him, the ape-man took the heavy slab in both hands, and, swinging it several times to get the distance and the direction fixed, he let the weight fly up at a slight angle, so that, instead of falling straight back into the shaft again, it grazed the far edge, tumbling over into the court beyond.

Tarzan dragged for a moment upon the slack end of the rope until he felt that the stone was lodged with fair security at the shaft's top, then he swung out over the black depths beneath. The moment his full weight came upon the rope he felt it slip from above. He waited there in awful suspense as it dropped in little jerks, inch by inch. The stone was being dragged up the outside of the masonry surrounding the top of the shaft – would it catch at the very edge, or would his weight drag it over to fall upon him as he hurtled into the unknown depths below?

CHAPTER TWENTY FIVE

Through the Forest Primeval

For a brief, sickening moment Tarzan felt the slipping of the rope to which he clung, and heard the scraping of the block of stone against the masonry above.

Then of a sudden the rope was still – the stone had caught at the very edge. Gingerly the ape-man clambered up the frail rope. In a moment his head was above the edge of the shaft. The court was empty. The inhabitants of Opar were viewing the sacrifice. Tarzan could hear the voice of La from the nearby sacrificial court. The dance had ceased. It must be almost time for the knife to fall; but even as he thought these things he was running rapidly toward the sound of the high priestess' voice.

Fate guided him to the very doorway of the great roofless chamber. Between him and the altar was the long row of priests and priestesses, awaiting with their golden cups the spilling of the warm blood of their victim. La's hand was descending slowly toward the bosom of the frail, quiet figure that lay stretched upon the hard stone. Tarzan gave a gasp that was almost a sob as he recognized the features of the girl he loved. And then the scar upon his forehead turned to a flaming band of scarlet, a red mist floated before his eyes, and, with the awful roar of the bull ape gone mad, he sprang like a huge lion into the midst of the votaries.

Seizing a cudgel from the nearest priest, he laid about him like a veritable demon as he forged his rapid way toward the altar. The hand of La had paused at the first noise of interruption. When she saw who the author of it was she went white. She had never been able to fathom the secret of the strange white man's escape from the dungeon in which she had locked him. She had not intended that he should ever leave Opar, for she had looked upon his giant frame and handsome face with the eyes of a woman and not those of a priestess.

In her clever mind she had concocted a story of wonderful revelation from the lips of the flaming god himself, in which she had been ordered to receive this white stranger as a messenger from him to his people on earth. That would satisfy the people of Opar, she knew. The man would be satisfied, she felt quite sure, to remain and be her husband rather than to return to the sacrificial altar.

But when she had gone to explain her plan to him he had disappeared, though the door had been tightly locked as she had left it. And now he had returned – materialized from thin air – and was killing her priests as though they had been sheep. For the moment she forgot her victim, and before she could gather her wits together again the huge white man was standing before her, the woman who had lain upon the altar in his arms.

"One side, La," he cried. "You saved me once, and so I would not harm you; but do not interfere or attempt to follow, or I shall have to kill you also."

As he spoke he stepped past her toward the entrance to the subterranean vaults.

"Who is she?" asked the high priestess, pointing at the unconscious woman.

"She is mine," said Tarzan of the Apes.

For a moment the girl of Opar stood wide-eyed and staring. Then a look of hopeless misery suffused her eyes – tears welled into them, and with a little cry she sank to the cold floor, just as a swarm of frightful men dashed past her to leap upon the ape-man.

But Tarzan of the Apes was not there when they reached out to seize him. With a light bound he had disappeared into the passage leading to the pits below, and when his pursuers came more cautiously after they found the chamber empty, they but laughed and jabbered to one another, for they knew that there was no exit from the pits other than the one through which he had entered. If he came out at all he must come this way, and they would wait and watch for him above.

And so Tarzan of the Apes, carrying the unconscious Jane Porter, came through the pits of Opar beneath the temple of The Flaming God without pursuit. But when the men of Opar had talked further about the matter, they recalled to mind that this very man had escaped once before into the pits, and, though they had watched the entrance he had not come forth; and yet today he had come upon them from the outside. They would again send fifty men out into the valley to find and capture this desecrater of their temple.

After Tarzan reached the shaft beyond the broken wall, he felt so positive of the successful issue of his flight that he stopped to replace the tumbled stones, for he was not anxious that any of the inmates should discover this forgotten passage, and through it come upon the treasure chamber. It was in his mind to return again to Opar and bear away a still greater fortune than he had already buried in the amphitheater of the apes.

On through the passageways he trotted, past the first door and through the treasure vault; past the second door and into the long, straight tunnel that led to the lofty hidden exit beyond the city. Jane Porter was still unconscious.

At the crest of the great bowlder he halted to cast a backward glance toward the city. Coming across the plain he saw a band of the hideous men of Opar. For a moment he hesitated. Should he descend and make a race for the distant cliffs, or should he hide here until night? And then a glance at the girl's white face determined him. He could not keep her here and permit her enemies to get between them and liberty. For aught he knew they might have been followed through the tunnels, and to have foes before and behind would result in almost certain capture, since he could not fight his way through the enemy burdened as he was with the unconscious girl.

To descend the steep face of the bowlder with Jane Porter was no easy task, but by binding her across his shoulders with the grass rope he succeeded in reaching the ground in safety before the Oparians arrived at the great rock. As the descent had been made upon the side away from the city, the searching party saw nothing of it, nor did they dream that their prey was so close before them.

By keeping the KOPJE between them and their pursuers, Tarzan of the Apes managed to cover nearly a mile before the men of Opar rounded the granite sentinel and saw the fugitive before them. With loud cries of savage delight, they broke into a mad run, thinking doubtless that they would soon overhaul the burdened runner; but they both underestimated the powers of the ape-man and overestimated the possibilities of their own short, crooked legs.

By maintaining an easy trot, Tarzan kept the distance between them always the same. Occasionally he would glance at the face so near his own. Had it not been for the faint beating of the heart pressed so close against his own, he would not have known that she was alive, so white and drawn was the poor, tired face.

And thus they came to the flat-topped mountain and the barrier cliffs. During the last mile Tarzan had let himself out, running like a deer that he might have ample time to descend the face of the cliffs before the Oparians could reach the summit and hurl rocks down upon them. And so it was that he was half a mile down the mountainside ere the fierce little men came panting to the edge.

With cries of rage and disappointment they ranged along the cliff top shaking their cudgels, and dancing up and down in a perfect passion of anger. But this time they did not pursue beyond the boundary of their own country. Whether it was because they recalled the futility of their former long and irksome search, or after witnessing the ease with which the ape-man swung along before them, and the last burst of speed, they realized the utter hopelessness of further pursuit, it is difficult to say; but as Tarzan reached the woods that began at the base of the foothills which skirted the barrier cliffs they turned their faces once more toward Opar.

Just within the forest's edge, where he could yet watch the cliff tops, Tarzan laid his burden upon the grass, and going to the near-by rivulet brought water with which he bathed her face and hands; but even this did not revive her, and, greatly worried, he gathered the girl into his strong arms once more and hurried on toward the west.

Late in the afternoon Jane Porter regained consciousness. She did not open her eyes at once – she was trying to recall the scenes that she had last witnessed. Ah, she remembered now. The altar, the terrible priestess, the descending knife. She gave a little shudder, for she thought that either this was death or that the knife had buried itself in her heart and she was experiencing the brief delirium preceding death. And when finally she mustered courage to open her eyes, the sight that met them confirmed her fears, for she saw that she was being borne through a leafy paradise in the arms of her dead love. "If this be death," she murmured, "thank God that I am dead."

"You spoke, Jane!" cried Tarzan. "You are regaining consciousness!"

"Yes, Tarzan of the Apes," she replied, and for the first time in months a smile of peace and happiness lighted her face.

"Thank God!" cried the ape-man, coming to the ground in a little grassy clearing beside the stream. "I was in time, after all."

"In time? What do you mean?" she questioned.

"In time to save you from death upon the altar, dear," he replied. "Do you not remember?" "Save me from death?" she asked, in a puzzled tone. "Are we not both dead, my Tarzan?"

He had placed her upon the grass by now, her back resting against the stem of a huge tree. At her question he stepped back where he could the better see her face.

"Dead!" he repeated, and then he laughed. "You are not, Jane; and if you will return to the city of Opar and ask them who dwell there they will tell you that I was not dead a few short hours ago. No, dear, we are both very much alive."

"But both Hazel and Monsieur Thuran told me that you had fallen into the ocean many miles from land," she urged, as though trying to convince him that he must indeed be dead. "They said that there was no question but that it must have been you, and less that you could have survived or been picked up."

"How can I convince you that I am no spirit?" he asked, with a laugh. "It was I whom the delightful Monsieur Thuran pushed overboard, but I did not drown – I will tell you all about it after a while – and here I am very much the same wild man you first knew, Jane Porter."

The girl rose slowly to her feet and came toward him.

"I cannot even yet believe it," she murmured. "It cannot be that such happiness can be true after all the hideous things that I have passed through these awful months since the LADY ALICE went down."

She came close to him and laid a hand, soft and trembling, upon his arm.

"It must be that I am dreaming, and that I shall awaken in a moment to see that awful knife descending toward my heart – kiss me, dear, just once before I lose my dream forever."

Tarzan of the Apes needed no second invitation. He took the girl he loved in his strong arms, and kissed her not once, but a hundred times, until she lay there panting for breath; yet when he stopped she put her arms about his neck and drew his lips down to hers once more.

"Am I alive and a reality, or am I but a dream?" he asked.

"If you are not alive, my man," she answered, "I pray that I may die thus before I awaken to the terrible realities of my last waking moments."

For a while both were silent – gazing into each others' eyes as though each still questioned the reality of the wonderful happiness that had come to them. The past, with all its hideous disappointments and horrors, was forgotten – the future did not belong to them; but the present – ah, it was theirs; none could take it from them. It was the girl who first broke the sweet silence.

"Where are we going, dear?" she asked. "What are we going to do?"

"Where would you like best to go?" he asked. "What would you like best to do?"

"To go where you go, my man; to do whatever seems best to you," she answered.

"But Clayton?" he asked. For a moment he had forgotten that there existed upon the earth other than they two. "We have forgotten your husband."

"I am not married, Tarzan of the Apes," she cried. "Nor am I longer promised in marriage. The day before those awful creatures captured me I spoke to Mr. Clayton of my love for you, and he understood then that I could not keep the wicked promise that I had made. It was after we had been miraculously saved from an attacking lion." She paused suddenly and looked up at him, a questioning light in her eyes. "Tarzan of the Apes," she cried, "it was you who did that thing? It could have been no other."

He dropped his eyes, for he was ashamed.

"How could you have gone away and left me?" she cried reproachfully.

"Don't, Jane!" he pleaded. "Please don't! You cannot know how I have suffered since for the cruelty of that act, or how I suffered then, first in jealous rage, and then in bitter resentment against the fate that I had not deserved. I went back to the apes after that, Jane, intending never again to see a human being." He told her then of his life since he had returned to the jungle – of how he had dropped like a plummet from a civilized Parisian to a savage Waziri warrior, and from there back to the brute that he had been raised.

She asked him many questions, and at last fearfully of the things that Monsieur Thuran had told her – of the woman in Paris. He narrated every detail of his civilized life to her, omitting nothing, for he felt no shame, since his heart always had been true to her. When he had finished he sat looking at her, as though waiting for her judgment, and his sentence.

"I knew that he was not speaking the truth," she said. "Oh, what a horrible creature he is!"

"You are not angry with me, then?" he asked.

And her reply, though apparently most irrelevant, was truly feminine.

"Is Olga de Coude very beautiful?" she asked.

And Tarzan laughed and kissed her again. "Not one-tenth so beautiful as you, dear," he said.

She gave a contented little sigh, and let her head rest against his shoulder. He knew that he was forgiven.

That night Tarzan built a snug little bower high among the swaying branches of a giant tree, and there the tired girl slept, while in a crotch beneath her the ape-man curled, ready, even in sleep, to protect her.

It took them many days to make the long journey to the coast. Where the way was easy they walked hand in hand beneath the arching boughs of the mighty forest, as might in a far-gone past have walked their primeval forbears. When the underbrush was tangled he took her in his great arms, and bore her lightly through the trees, and the days were all too short, for they were very happy. Had it not been for their anxiety to reach and succor Clayton they would have drawn out the sweet pleasure of that wonderful journey indefinitely.

On the last day before they reached the coast Tarzan caught the scent of men ahead of them – the scent of black men. He told the girl, and cautioned her to maintain silence. "There are few friends in the jungle," he remarked dryly.

In half an hour they came stealthily upon a small party of black warriors filing toward the west. As Tarzan saw them he gave a cry of delight – it was a band of his own Waziri. Busuli was there, and others who had accompanied him to Opar. At sight of him they danced and cried out in exuberant joy. For weeks they had been searching for him, they told him.

The blacks exhibited considerable wonderment at the presence of the white girl with him, and when they found that she was to be his woman they vied with one another to do her honor. With the happy Waziri laughing and dancing about them they came to the rude shelter by the shore.

There was no sign of life, and no response to their calls. Tarzan clambered quickly to the interior of the little tree hut, only to emerge a moment later with an empty tin. Throwing it down to Busuli, he told him to fetch water, and then he beckoned Jane Porter to come up.

Together they leaned over the emaciated thing that once had been an English nobleman. Tears came to the girl's eyes as she saw the poor, sunken cheeks and hollow eyes, and the lines of suffering upon the once young and handsome face.

"He still lives," said Tarzan. "We will do all that can be done for him, but I fear that we are too late."

When Busuli had brought the water Tarzan forced a few drops between the cracked and swollen lips. He wetted the hot forehead and bathed the pitiful limbs.

Presently Clayton opened his eyes. A faint, shadowy smile lighted his countenance as he saw the girl leaning over him. At sight of Tarzan the expression changed to one of wonderment.

"It's all right, old fellow," said the ape-man. "We've found you in time. Everything will be all right now, and we'll have you on your feet again before you know it."

The Englishman shook his head weakly. "It's too late," he whispered. "But it's just as well. I'd rather die."

"Where is Monsieur Thuran?" asked the girl.

"He left me after the fever got bad. He is a devil. When I begged for the water that I was too weak to get he drank before me, threw the rest out, and laughed in my face." At the thought of it the man was suddenly animated by a spark of vitality. He raised himself upon one elbow. "Yes," he almost shouted; "I will live. I will live long enough to find and kill that beast!" But the brief effort left him weaker than before, and he sank back again upon the rotting grasses that, with his old ulster, had been the bed of Jane Porter.

"Don't worry about Thuran," said Tarzan of the Apes, laying a reassuring hand on Clayton's forehead. "He belongs to me, and I shall get him in the end, never fear."

For a long time Clayton lay very still. Several times Tarzan had to put his ear quite close to the sunken chest to catch the faint beating of the worn-out heart. Toward evening he aroused again for a brief moment.

"Jane," he whispered. The girl bent her head closer to catch the faint message. "I have wronged you – and him," he nodded weakly toward the ape-man. "I loved you so – it is a poor excuse to offer for injuring you; but I could not bear to think of giving you up. I do not ask your forgiveness. I only wish to do now the thing I should have done over a year ago." He fumbled in the pocket of the ulster beneath him for something that he had discovered there while he lay between the paroxysms of fever. Presently he found it – a crumpled bit of yellow paper. He handed it to the girl, and as she took it his arm fell limply across his chest, his head dropped back, and with a little gasp he stiffened and was still. Then Tarzan of the Apes drew a fold of the ulster across the upturned face.

For a moment they remained kneeling there, the girl's lips moving in silent prayer, and as they rose and stood on either side of the now peaceful form, tears came to the ape-man's eyes, for through the anguish that his own heart had suffered he had learned compassion for the suffering of others.

Through her own tears the girl read the message upon the bit of faded yellow paper, and as she read her eyes went very wide. Twice she read those startling words before she could fully comprehend their meaning.

Finger prints prove you Greystoke. Congratulations.
D'ARNOT.

She handed the paper to Tarzan. "And he has known it all this time," she said, "and did not tell you?"

"I knew it first, Jane," replied the man. "I did not know that he knew it at all. I must have dropped this message that night in the waiting room. It was there that I received it."

"And afterward you told us that your mother was a she-ape, and that you had never known your father?" she asked incredulously.

"The title and the estates meant nothing to me without you, dear," he replied. "And if I had taken them away from him I should have been robbing the woman I love – don't you understand, Jane?" It was as though he attempted to excuse a fault.

She extended her arms toward him across the body of the dead man, and took his hands in hers.

"And I would have thrown away a love like that!" she said.

CHAPTER TWENTY SIX

The Passing of the Ape-Man

THE NEXT MORNING THEY set out upon the short journey to Tarzan's cabin. Four Waziri bore the body of the dead Englishman. It had been the ape-man's suggestion that Clayton be buried beside the former Lord Greystoke near the edge of the jungle against the cabin that the older man had built.

Jane Porter was glad that it was to be so, and in her heart of hearts she wondered at the marvelous fineness of character of this wondrous man, who, though raised by brutes and among brutes, had the true chivalry and tenderness which only associates with the refinements of the highest civilization.

They had proceeded some three miles of the five that had separated them from Tarzan's own beach when the Waziri who were ahead stopped suddenly, pointing in amazement at a strange figure approaching them along the beach. It was a man with a shiny silk hat, who walked slowly with bent head, and hands clasped behind him underneath the tails of his long, black coat.

At sight of him Jane Porter uttered a little cry of surprise and joy, and ran quickly ahead to meet him. At the sound of her voice the old man looked up, and when he saw who it was confronting him he, too, cried out in relief and happiness. As Professor Archimedes Q. Porter folded his daughter in his arms tears streamed down his seamed old face, and it was several minutes before he could control himself sufficiently to speak.

When a moment later he recognized Tarzan it was with difficulty that they could convince him that his sorrow had not unbalanced his mind, for with the other members of the party he had been so thoroughly convinced that the ape-man was dead it was a problem to reconcile the conviction with the very lifelike appearance of Jane's "forest god." The old man was deeply touched at the news of Clayton's death.

"I cannot understand it," he said. "Monsieur Thuran assured us that Clayton passed away many days ago."

"Thuran is with you?" asked Tarzan.

"Yes; he but recently found us and led us to your cabin. We were camped but a short distance north of it. Bless me, but he will be delighted to see you both."

"And surprised," commented Tarzan.

A short time later the strange party came to the clearing in which stood the ape-man's cabin. It was filled with people coming and going, and almost the first whom Tarzan saw was D'Arnot.

"Paul!" he cried. "In the name of sanity what are you doing here? Or are we all insane?"

It was quickly explained, however, as were many other seemingly strange things. D'Arnot's ship had been cruising along the coast, on patrol duty, when at the lieutenant's suggestion they had anchored off the little landlocked harbor to have another look at the cabin and the jungle in which many of the officers and men had taken part in exciting adventures two years before. On landing they had found Lord Tennington's party, and arrangements were being made to take them all on board the following morning, and carry them back to civilization.

Hazel Strong and her mother, Esmeralda, and Mr. Samuel T. Philander were almost overcome by happiness at Jane Porter's safe return. Her escape seemed to them little short of miraculous, and it was the consensus of opinion that it could have been achieved by no other man than Tarzan of the Apes. They loaded the uncomfortable ape-man with eulogies and attentions until he wished himself back in the amphitheater of the apes.

All were interested in his savage Waziri, and many were the gifts the black men received from these friends of their king, but when they learned that he might sail away from them upon the great canoe that lay at anchor a mile off shore they became very sad.

As yet the newcomers had seen nothing of Lord Tennington and Monsieur Thuran. They had gone out for fresh meat early in the day, and had not yet returned.

"How surprised this man, whose name you say is Rokoff, will be to see you," said Jane Porter to Tarzan.

"His surprise will be short-lived," replied the ape-man grimly, and there was that in his tone that made her look up into his face in alarm. What she read there evidently confirmed her fears, for she put her hand upon his arm, and pleaded with him to leave the Russian to the laws of France.

"In the heart of the jungle, dear," she said, "with no other form of right or justice to appeal to other than your own mighty muscles, you would be warranted in executing upon this man the sentence he deserves; but with the strong arm of a civilized government at your disposal it would be murder to kill him now. Even your friends would have to submit to your arrest, or if you resisted it would plunge us all into misery and unhappiness again. I cannot bear to lose you again, my Tarzan. Promise me that you will but turn him over to Captain Dufranne, and let the law take its course – the beast is not worth risking our happiness for."

He saw the wisdom of her appeal, and promised. A half hour later Rokoff and Tennington emerged from the jungle. They were walking side by side. Tennington was the first to note the presence of strangers in the camp. He saw the black warriors palavering with the sailors from the cruiser, and then he saw a lithe, brown giant talking with Lieutenant D'Arnot and Captain Dufranne.

"Who is that, I wonder," said Tennington to Rokoff, and as the Russian raised his eyes and met those of the ape-man full upon him, he staggered and went white.

"SAPRISTI!" he cried, and before Tennington realized what he intended he had thrown his gun to his shoulder, and aiming point-blank at Tarzan pulled the trigger. But the Englishman was close to him – so close that his hand reached the leveled barrel a fraction of a second before the hammer fell upon the cartridge, and the bullet that was intended for Tarzan's heart whirred harmlessly above his head.

Before the Russian could fire again the ape-man was upon him and had wrested the firearm from his grasp. Captain Dufranne, Lieutenant D'Arnot, and a dozen sailors had rushed up at the sound of the shot, and now Tarzan turned the Russian over to them without a word. He had explained the matter to the French commander before Rokoff arrived, and the officer gave immediate orders to place the Russian in irons and confine him on board the cruiser.

Just before the guard escorted the prisoner into the small boat that was to transport him to his temporary prison Tarzan asked permission to search him, and to his delight found the stolen papers concealed upon his person.

The shot had brought Jane Porter and the others from the cabin, and a moment after the excitement had died down she greeted the surprised Lord Tennington. Tarzan joined them after he had taken the papers from Rokoff, and, as he approached, Jane Porter introduced him to Tennington.

"John Clayton, Lord Greystoke, my lord," she said.

The Englishman looked his astonishment in spite of his most herculean efforts to appear courteous, and it required many repetitions of the strange story of the ape-man as told by himself, Jane Porter, and Lieutenant D'Arnot to convince Lord Tennington that they were not all quite mad.

At sunset they buried William Cecil Clayton beside the jungle graves of his uncle and his aunt, the former Lord and Lady Greystoke. And it was at Tarzan's request that three volleys were fired over the last resting place of "a brave man, who met his death bravely."

Professor Porter, who in his younger days had been ordained a minister, conducted the simple services for the dead. About the grave, with bowed heads, stood as strange a company of mourners as the sun ever looked down upon. There were French officers and sailors, two English lords, Americans, and a score of savage African braves.

Following the funeral Tarzan asked Captain Dufranne to delay the sailing of the cruiser a couple of days while he went inland a few miles to fetch his "belongings," and the officer gladly granted the favor.

Late the next afternoon Tarzan and his Waziri returned with the first load of "belongings," and when the party saw the ancient ingots of virgin gold they swarmed upon the ape-man with a thousand questions; but he was smilingly obdurate to their appeals – he declined to give them the slightest clew as to the source of his immense treasure. "There are a thousand that I left behind," he explained, "for every one that I brought away, and when these are spent I may wish to return for more."

The next day he returned to camp with the balance of his ingots, and when they were stored on board the cruiser Captain Dufranne said he felt like the commander of an old-time Spanish galleon returning from the treasure cities of the Aztecs. "I don't know what minute my crew will cut my throat, and take over the ship," he added.

The next morning, as they were preparing to embark upon the cruiser, Tarzan ventured a suggestion to Jane Porter.

"Wild beasts are supposed to be devoid of sentiment," he said, "but nevertheless I should like to be married in the cabin where I was born, beside the graves of my mother and my father, and surrounded by the savage jungle that always has been my home."

"Would it be quite regular, dear?" she asked. "For if it would I know of no other place in which I should rather be married to my forest god than beneath the shade of his primeval forest."

And when they spoke of it to the others they were assured that it would be quite regular, and a most splendid termination of a remarkable romance. So the entire party assembled within the little cabin and about the door to witness the second ceremony that Professor Porter was to solemnize within three days.

D'Arnot was to be best man, and Hazel Strong bridesmaid, until Tennington upset all the arrangements by another of his marvelous "ideas."

"If Mrs. Strong is agreeable," he said, taking the bridesmaid's hand in his, "Hazel and I think it would be ripping to make it a double wedding."

The next day they sailed, and as the cruiser steamed slowly out to sea a tall man, immaculate in white flannel, and a graceful girl leaned against her rail to watch the receding shore line upon which danced twenty naked, black warriors of the Waziri, waving their war spears above their savage heads, and shouting farewells to their departing king.

"I should hate to think that I am looking upon the jungle for the last time, dear," he said, "were it not that I know that I am going to a new world of happiness with you forever," and, bending down, Tarzan of the Apes kissed his mate upon her lips

THE BEASTS OF TARZAN

CHAPTER ONE

Kidnapped

"The entire affair is shrouded in mystery," said D'Arnot. "I have it on the best of authority that neither the police nor the special agents of the general staff have the faintest conception of how it was accomplished. All they know, all that anyone knows, is that Nikolas Rokoff has escaped."

John Clayton, Lord Greystoke – he who had been "Tarzan of the Apes" – sat in silence in the apartments of his friend, Lieutenant Paul D'Arnot, in Paris, gazing meditatively at the toe of his immaculate boot.

His mind revolved many memories, recalled by the escape of his arch-enemy from the French military prison to which he had been sentenced for life upon the testimony of the ape-man.

He thought of the lengths to which Rokoff had once gone to compass his death, and he realized that what the man had already done would doubtless be as nothing by comparison with what he would wish and plot to do now that he was again free.

Tarzan had recently brought his wife and infant son to London to escape the discomforts and dangers of the rainy season upon their vast estate in Uziri – the land of the savage Waziri warriors whose broad African domains the ape-man had once ruled.

He had run across the Channel for a brief visit with his old friend, but the news of the Russian's escape had already cast a shadow upon his outing, so that though he had but just arrived he was already contemplating an immediate return to London.

"It is not that I fear for myself, Paul," he said at last. "Many times in the past have I thwarted Rokoff's designs upon my life; but now there are others to consider. Unless I misjudge the man, he would more quickly strike at me through my wife or son than directly at me, for he doubtless realizes that in no other way could he inflict greater anguish upon me. I must go back to them at once, and remain with them until Rokoff is recaptured – or dead."

As these two talked in Paris, two other men were talking together in a little cottage upon the outskirts of London. Both were dark, sinister-looking men.

One was bearded, but the other, whose face wore the pallor of long confinement within doors, had but a few days' growth of black beard upon his face. It was he who was speaking.

"You must needs shave off that beard of yours, Alexis," he said to his companion. "With it he would recognize you on the instant. We must separate here in the hour, and when we meet again upon the deck of the Kincaid, let us hope that we shall have with us two honoured guests who little anticipate the pleasant voyage we have planned for them.

"In two hours I should be upon my way to Dover with one of them, and by tomorrow night, if you follow my instructions carefully, you should arrive with the other, provided, of course, that he returns to London as quickly as I presume he will.

"There should be both profit and pleasure as well as other good things to reward our efforts, my dear Alexis. Thanks to the stupidity of the French, they have gone to such lengths to conceal the fact of my escape for these many days that I have had ample opportunity to work out every detail of our little adventure so carefully that there is little chance of the slightest hitch occurring to mar our prospects. And now good-bye, and good luck!"

Three hours later a messenger mounted the steps to the apartment of Lieutenant D'Arnot.

"A telegram for Lord Greystoke," he said to the servant who answered his summons. "Is he here?"

The man answered in the affirmative, and, signing for the message, carried it within to Tarzan, who was already preparing to depart for London.

Tarzan tore open the envelope, and as he read his face went white.

"Read it, Paul," he said, handing the slip of paper to D'Arnot. "It has come already."

The Frenchman took the telegram and read:

"Jack stolen from the garden through complicity of new servant. Come at once. – JANE."

As Tarzan leaped from the roadster that had met him at the station and ran up the steps to his London town house he was met at the door by a dry-eyed but almost frantic woman.

Quickly Jane Porter Clayton narrated all that she had been able to learn of the theft of the boy.

The baby's nurse had been wheeling him in the sunshine on the walk before the house when a closed taxicab drew up at the corner of the street. The woman had paid but passing attention to the vehicle, merely noting that it discharged no passenger, but stood at the kerb with the motor running as though waiting for a fare from the residence before which it had stopped.

Almost immediately the new houseman, Carl, had come running from the Greystoke house, saying that the girl's mistress wished to speak with her for a moment, and that she was to leave little Jack in his care until she returned.

The woman said that she entertained not the slightest suspicion of the man's motives until she had reached the doorway of the house, when it occurred to her to warn him not to turn the carriage so as to permit the sun to shine in the baby's eyes.

As she turned about to call this to him she was somewhat surprised to see that he was wheeling the carriage rapidly toward the corner, and at the same time she saw the door of the taxicab open and a swarthy face framed for a moment in the aperture.

Intuitively, the danger to the child flashed upon her, and with a shriek she dashed down the steps and up the walk toward the taxicab, into which Carl was now handing the baby to the swarthy one within.

Just before she reached the vehicle, Carl leaped in beside his confederate, slamming the door behind him. At the same time the chauffeur attempted to start his machine, but it was evident that something had gone wrong, as though the gears refused to mesh, and the delay caused by this, while he pushed the lever into reverse and backed the car a few inches before again attempting to go ahead, gave the nurse time to reach the side of the taxicab.

Leaping to the running-board, she had attempted to snatch the baby from the arms of the stranger, and here, screaming and fighting, she had clung to her position even after the taxicab had got under way; nor was it until the machine had passed the Greystoke residence at good speed that Carl, with a heavy blow to her face, had succeeded in knocking her to the pavement.

Her screams had attracted servants and members of the families from residences near by, as well as from the Greystoke home. Lady Greystoke had witnessed the girl's brave battle, and had herself tried to reach the rapidly passing vehicle, but had been too late.

That was all that anyone knew, nor did Lady Greystoke dream of the possible identity of the man at the bottom of the plot until her husband told her of the escape of Nikolas Rokoff from the French prison where they had hoped he was permanently confined.

As Tarzan and his wife stood planning the wisest course to pursue, the telephone bell rang in the library at their right. Tarzan quickly answered the call in person.

"Lord Greystoke?" asked a man's voice at the other end of the line.

"Yes."

"Your son has been stolen," continued the voice, "and I alone may help you to recover him. I am conversant with the plot of those who took him. In fact, I was a party to it, and was to share in the reward, but now they are trying to ditch me, and to be quits with them I will aid you to recover him on condition that you will not prosecute me for my part in the crime. What do you say?"

"If you lead me to where my son is hidden," replied the ape-man, "you need fear nothing from me."

"Good," replied the other. "But you must come alone to meet me, for it is enough that I must trust you. I cannot take the chance of permitting others to learn my identity."

"Where and when may I meet you?" asked Tarzan.

The other gave the name and location of a public-house on the water-front at Dover – a place frequented by sailors.

"Come," he concluded, "about ten o'clock tonight. It would do no good to arrive earlier. Your son will be safe enough in the meantime, and I can then lead you secretly to where he is hidden. But be sure to come alone, and under no circumstances notify Scotland Yard, for I know you well and shall be watching for you.

"Should any other accompany you, or should I see suspicious characters who might be agents of the police, I shall not meet you, and your last chance of recovering your son will be gone."

Without more words the man rang off.

Tarzan repeated the gist of the conversation to his wife. She begged to be allowed to accompany him, but he insisted that it might result in the man's carrying out his threat of refusing to aid them if Tarzan did not come alone, and so they parted, he to hasten to Dover, and she, ostensibly to wait at home until he should notify her of the outcome of his mission.

Little did either dream of what both were destined to pass through before they should meet again, or the far-distant – but why anticipate?

For ten minutes after the ape-man had left her Jane Clayton walked restlessly back and forth across the silken rugs of the library. Her mother heart ached, bereft of its first-born. Her mind was in an anguish of hopes and fears.

Though her judgment told her that all would be well were her Tarzan to go alone in accordance with the mysterious stranger's summons, her intuition would not permit her to lay aside suspicion of the gravest dangers to both her husband and her son.

The more she thought of the matter, the more convinced she became that the recent telephone message might be but a ruse to keep them inactive until the boy was safely hidden away or spirited out of England. Or it might be that it had been simply a bait to lure Tarzan into the hands of the implacable Rokoff.

With the lodgment of this thought she stopped in wide-eyed terror. Instantly it became a conviction. She glanced at the great clock ticking the minutes in the corner of the library.

It was too late to catch the Dover train that Tarzan was to take. There was another, later, however, that would bring her to the Channel port in time to reach the address the stranger had given her husband before the appointed hour.

Summoning her maid and chauffeur, she issued instructions rapidly. Ten minutes later she was being whisked through the crowded streets toward the railway station.

It was nine-forty-five that night that Tarzan entered the squalid "pub" on the water-front in Dover. As he passed into the evil-smelling room a muffled figure brushed past him toward the street.

"Come, my lord!" whispered the stranger.

The ape-man wheeled about and followed the other into the ill-lit alley, which custom had dignified with the title of thoroughfare. Once outside, the fellow led the way into the darkness, nearer a wharf, where high-piled bales, boxes, and casks cast dense shadows. Here he halted.

"Where is the boy?" asked Greystoke.

"On that small steamer whose lights you can just see yonder," replied the other.

In the gloom Tarzan was trying to peer into the features of his companion, but he did not recognize the man as one whom he had ever before seen. Had he guessed that his guide was Alexis Paulvitch he would have realized that naught but treachery lay in the man's heart, and that danger lurked in the path of every move.

"He is unguarded now," continued the Russian. "Those who took him feel perfectly safe from detection, and with the exception of a couple of members of the crew, whom I have furnished with enough gin to silence them effectually for hours, there is none aboard the Kincaid. We can go aboard, get the child, and return without the slightest fear."

Tarzan nodded.

"Let's be about it, then," he said.

His guide led him to a small boat moored alongside the wharf. The two men entered, and Paulvitch pulled rapidly toward the steamer. The black smoke issuing from her funnel did not at the time make any suggestion to Tarzan's mind. All his thoughts were occupied with the hope that in a few moments he would again have his little son in his arms.

At the steamer's side they found a monkey-ladder dangling close above them, and up this the two men crept stealthily. Once on deck they hastened aft to where the Russian pointed to a hatch.

"The boy is hidden there," he said. "You had better go down after him, as there is less chance that he will cry in fright than should he find himself in the arms of a stranger. I will stand on guard here."

So anxious was Tarzan to rescue the child that he gave not the slightest thought to the strangeness of all the conditions surrounding the Kincaid. That her deck was deserted, though she had steam up, and from the volume of smoke pouring from her funnel was all ready to get under way made no impression upon him.

With the thought that in another instant he would fold that precious little bundle of humanity in his arms, the ape-man swung down into the darkness below. Scarcely had he released his hold upon the edge of the hatch than the heavy covering fell clattering above him.

Instantly he knew that he was the victim of a plot, and that far from rescuing his son he had himself fallen into the hands of his enemies. Though he immediately endeavoured to reach the hatch and lift the cover, he was unable to do so.

Striking a match, he explored his surroundings, finding that a little compartment had been partitioned off from the main hold, with the hatch above his head the only means of ingress or egress. It was evident that the room had been prepared for the very purpose of serving as a cell for himself.

There was nothing in the compartment, and no other occupant. If the child was on board the Kincaid he was confined elsewhere.

For over twenty years, from infancy to manhood, the ape-man had roamed his savage jungle haunts without human companionship of any nature. He had learned at the most impressionable period of his life to take his pleasures and his sorrows as the beasts take theirs.

So it was that he neither raved nor stormed against fate, but instead waited patiently for what might next befall him, though not by any means without an eye to doing the utmost to succour himself. To this end he examined his prison carefully, tested the heavy planking that formed its walls, and measured the distance of the hatch above him.

And while he was thus occupied there came suddenly to him the vibration of machinery and the throbbing of the propeller.

The ship was moving! Where to and to what fate was it carrying him?

And even as these thoughts passed through his mind there came to his ears above the din of the engines that which caused him to go cold with apprehension.

Clear and shrill from the deck above him rang the scream of a frightened woman.

CHAPTER TWO

Maroined

As Tarzan and his guide had disappeared into the shadows upon the dark wharf the figure of a heavily veiled woman had hurried down the narrow alley to the entrance of the drinking-place the two men had just quitted.

Here she paused and looked about, and then as though satisfied that she had at last reached the place she sought, she pushed bravely into the interior of the vile den.

A score of half-drunken sailors and wharf-rats looked up at the unaccustomed sight of a richly gowned woman in their midst. Rapidly she approached the slovenly barmaid who stared half in envy, half in hate, at her more fortunate sister.

"Have you seen a tall, well-dressed man here, but a minute since," she asked, "who met another and went away with him?"

The girl answered in the affirmative, but could not tell which way the two had gone. A sailor who had approached to listen to the conversation vouchsafed the information that a moment before as he had been about to enter the "pub" he had seen two men leaving it who walked toward the wharf.

"Show me the direction they went," cried the woman, slipping a coin into the man's hand.

The fellow led her from the place, and together they walked quickly toward the wharf and along it until across the water they saw a small boat just pulling into the shadows of a nearby steamer.

"There they be," whispered the man.

"Ten pounds if you will find a boat and row me to that steamer," cried the woman.

"Quick, then," he replied, "for we gotta go it if we're goin' to catch the Kincaid afore she sails. She's had steam up for three hours an' jest been a-waitin' fer that one passenger. I was a-talkin' to one of her crew 'arf an hour ago."

As he spoke he led the way to the end of the wharf where he knew another boat lay moored, and, lowering the woman into it, he jumped in after and pushed off. The two were soon scudding over the water.

At the steamer's side the man demanded his pay and, without waiting to count out the exact amount, the woman thrust a handful of bank-notes into his outstretched hand. A single glance at them convinced the fellow that he had been more than well paid. Then he assisted her up the ladder, holding his skiff close to the ship's side against the chance that this profitable passenger might wish to be taken ashore later.

But presently the sound of the donkey engine and the rattle of a steel cable on the hoisting-drum proclaimed the fact that the Kincaid's anchor was being raised, and a moment later the waiter heard the propellers revolving, and slowly the little steamer moved away from him out into the channel.

As he turned to row back to shore he heard a woman's shriek from the ship's deck.

"That's wot I calls rotten luck," he soliloquized. "I might jest as well of 'ad the whole bloomin' wad."

When Jane Clayton climbed to the deck of the Kincaid she found the ship apparently deserted. There was no sign of those she sought nor of any other aboard, and so she went about her search for her husband and the child she hoped against hope to find there without interruption.

Quickly she hastened to the cabin, which was half above and half below deck. As she hurried down the short companion-ladder into the main cabin, on either side of which were the smaller rooms occupied by the officers, she failed to note the quick closing of one of the doors before her. She passed the full length of the main room, and then retracing her steps stopped before each door to listen, furtively trying each latch.

All was silence, utter silence there, in which the throbbing of her own frightened heart seemed to her overwrought imagination to fill the ship with its thunderous alarm.

One by one the doors opened before her touch, only to reveal empty interiors. In her absorption she did not note the sudden activity upon the vessel, the purring of the engines, the throbbing of the propeller. She had reached the last door upon the right now, and as she pushed it open she was seized from within by a powerful, dark-visaged man, and drawn hastily into the stuffy, ill-smelling interior.

The sudden shock of fright which the unexpected attack had upon her drew a single piercing scream from her throat; then the man clapped a hand roughly over the mouth.

"Not until we are farther from land, my dear," he said. "Then you may yell your pretty head off."

Lady Greystoke turned to look into the leering, bearded face so close to hers. The man relaxed the pressure of his fingers upon her lips, and with a little moan of terror as she recognized him the girl shrank away from her captor.

"Nikolas Rokoff! M. Thuran!" she exclaimed.

"Your devoted admirer," replied the Russian, with a low bow.

"My little boy," she said next, ignoring the terms of endearment – "where is he? Let me have him. How could you be so cruel – even as you – Nikolas Rokoff – cannot be entirely devoid of mercy and compassion? Tell me where he is. Is he aboard this ship? Oh, please, if such a thing as a heart beats within your breast, take me to my baby!"

"If you do as you are bid no harm will befall him," replied Rokoff. "But remember that it is your own fault that you are here. You came aboard voluntarily, and you may take the consequences. I little thought," he added to himself, "that any such good luck as this would come to me."

He went on deck then, locking the cabin-door upon his prisoner, and for several days she did not see him. The truth of the matter being that Nikolas Rokoff was so poor a sailor that the heavy seas the Kincaid encountered from the very beginning of her voyage sent the Russian to his berth with a bad attack of sea-sickness.

During this time her only visitor was an uncouth Swede, the Kincaid's unsavoury cook, who brought her meals to her. His name was Sven Anderssen, his one pride being that his patronymic was spelt with a double "s."

The man was tall and raw-boned, with a long yellow moustache, an unwholesome complexion, and filthy nails. The very sight of him with one grimy thumb buried deep in the lukewarm stew, that seemed, from the frequency of its repetition, to constitute the pride of his culinary art, was sufficient to take away the girl's appetite.

His small, blue, close-set eyes never met hers squarely. There was a shiftiness of his whole appearance that even found expression in the cat-like manner of his gait, and to it all a sinister suggestion was added by the long slim knife that always rested at his waist, slipped through the greasy cord that supported his soiled apron. Ostensibly it was but an implement of his calling; but the girl could never free herself of the conviction that it would require less provocation to witness it put to other and less harmless uses.

His manner toward her was surly, yet she never failed to meet him with a pleasant smile and a word of thanks when he brought her food to her, though more often than not she hurled the bulk of it through the tiny cabin port the moment that the door closed behind him.

During the days of anguish that followed Jane Clayton's imprisonment, but two questions were uppermost in her mind – the whereabouts of her husband and her son. She fully believed that the baby was aboard the Kincaid, provided that he still lived, but whether Tarzan had been permitted to live after having been lured aboard the evil craft she could not guess.

She knew, of course, the deep hatred that the Russian felt for the Englishman, and she could think of but one reason for having him brought aboard the ship – to dispatch him in comparative safety in revenge for his having thwarted Rokoff's pet schemes, and for having been at last the means of landing him in a French prison.

Tarzan, on his part, lay in the darkness of his cell, ignorant of the fact that his wife was a prisoner in the cabin almost above his head.

The same Swede that served Jane brought his meals to him, but, though on several occasions Tarzan had tried to draw the man into conversation, he had been unsuccessful. He had hoped to learn through this fellow whether his little son was aboard the Kincaid, but to every question upon this or kindred subjects the fellow returned but one reply, "Ay tank it blow purty soon purty hard." So after several attempts Tarzan gave it up.

For weeks that seemed months to the two prisoners the little steamer forged on they knew not where. Once the Kincaid stopped to coal, only immediately to take up the seemingly interminable voyage.

Rokoff had visited Jane Clayton but once since he had locked her in the tiny cabin. He had come gaunt and hollow-eyed from a long siege of sea-sickness. The object of his visit was to obtain from her her personal cheque for a large sum in return for a guarantee of her personal safety and return to England.

"When you set me down safely in any civilized port, together with my son and my husband," she replied, "I will pay you in gold twice the amount you ask; but until then you shall not have a cent, nor the promise of a cent under any other conditions."

"You will give me the cheque I ask," he replied with a snarl, "or neither you nor your child nor your husband will ever again set foot within any port, civilized or otherwise."

"I would not trust you," she replied. "What guarantee have I that you would not take my money and then do as you pleased with me and mine regardless of your promise?"

"I think you will do as I bid," he said, turning to leave the cabin. "Remember that I have your son – if you chance to hear the agonized wail of a tortured child it may console you to reflect that it is because of your stubbornness that the baby suffers – and that it is your baby."

"You would not do it!" cried the girl. "You would not – could not be so fiendishly cruel!"

"It is not I that am cruel, but you," he returned, "for you permit a paltry sum of money to stand between your baby and immunity from suffering."

The end of it was that Jane Clayton wrote out a cheque of large denomination and handed it to Nikolas Rokoff, who left her cabin with a grin of satisfaction upon his lips.

The following day the hatch was removed from Tarzan's cell, and as he looked up he saw Paulvitch's head framed in the square of light above him.

"Come up," commanded the Russian. "But bear in mind that you will be shot if you make a single move to attack me or any other aboard the ship."

The ape-man swung himself lightly to the deck. About him, but at a respectful distance, stood a half-dozen sailors armed with rifles and revolvers. Facing him was Paulvitch.

Tarzan looked about for Rokoff, who he felt sure must be aboard, but there was no sign of him.

"Lord Greystoke," commenced the Russian, "by your continued and wanton interference with M. Rokoff and his plans you have at last brought yourself and your family to this unfortunate extremity. You have only yourself to thank. As you may imagine, it has cost M. Rokoff a large amount of money to finance this expedition, and, as you are the sole cause of it, he naturally looks to you for reimbursement.

"Further, I may say that only by meeting M. Rokoff's just demands may you avert the most unpleasant consequences to your wife and child, and at the same time retain your own life and regain your liberty."

"What is the amount?" asked Tarzan. "And what assurance have I that you will live up to your end of the agreement? I have little reason to trust two such scoundrels as you and Rokoff, you know."

The Russian flushed.

"You are in no position to deliver insults," he said. "You have no assurance that we will live up to our agreement other than my word, but you have before you the assurance that we can make short work of you if you do not write out the cheque we demand.

"Unless you are a greater fool than I imagine, you should know that there is nothing that would give us greater pleasure than to order these men to fire. That we do not is because we have other plans for punishing you that would be entirely upset by your death."

"Answer one question," said Tarzan. "Is my son on board this ship?"

"No," replied Alexis Paulvitch, "your son is quite safe elsewhere; nor will he be killed until you refuse to accede to our fair demands. If it becomes necessary to kill you, there will be no reason for not killing the child, since with you gone the one whom we wish to punish through the boy will be gone, and he will then be to us only a constant source of danger and embarrassment. You see, therefore, that you may only save the life of your son by saving your own, and you can only save your own by giving us the cheque we ask."

"Very well," replied Tarzan, for he knew that he could trust them to carry out any sinister threat that Paulvitch had made, and there was a bare chance that by conceding their demands he might save the boy.

That they would permit him to live after he had appended his name to the cheque never occurred to him as being within the realms of probability. But he was determined to give them such a battle as they would never forget, and possibly to take Paulvitch with him into eternity. He was only sorry that it was not Rokoff.

He took his pocket cheque-book and fountain-pen from his pocket.

"What is the amount?" he asked.

Paulvitch named an enormous sum. Tarzan could scarce restrain a smile.

Their very cupidity was to prove the means of their undoing, in the matter of the ransom at least. Purposely he hesitated and haggled over the amount, but Paulvitch was obdurate. Finally the ape-man wrote out his cheque for a larger sum than stood to his credit at the bank.

As he turned to hand the worthless slip of paper to the Russian his glance chanced to pass across the starboard bow of the Kincaid. To his surprise he saw that the ship lay within a few hundred yards of land. Almost down to the water's edge ran a dense tropical jungle, and behind was higher land clothed in forest.

Paulvitch noted the direction of his gaze.

"You are to be set at liberty here," he said.

Tarzan's plan for immediate physical revenge upon the Russian vanished. He thought the land before him the mainland of Africa, and he knew that should they liberate him here he could doubtless find his way to civilization with comparative ease.

Paulvitch took the cheque.

"Remove your clothing," he said to the ape-man. "Here you will not need it."

Tarzan demurred.

Paulvitch pointed to the armed sailors. Then the Englishman slowly divested himself of his clothing.

A boat was lowered, and, still heavily guarded, the ape-man was rowed ashore. Half an hour later the sailors had returned to the Kincaid, and the steamer was slowly getting under way.

As Tarzan stood upon the narrow strip of beach watching the departure of the vessel he saw a figure appear at the rail and call aloud to attract his attention.

The ape-man had been about to read a note that one of the sailors had handed him as the small boat that bore him to the shore was on the point of returning to the steamer, but at the hail from the vessel's deck he looked up.

He saw a black-bearded man who laughed at him in derision as he held high above his head the figure of a little child. Tarzan half started as though to rush through the surf and strike out for the already moving steamer; but realizing the futility of so rash an act he halted at the water's edge.

Thus he stood, his gaze riveted upon the Kincaid until it disappeared beyond a projecting promontory of the coast.

From the jungle at his back fierce bloodshot eyes glared from beneath shaggy overhanging brows upon him.

Little monkeys in the tree-tops chattered and scolded, and from the distance of the inland forest came the scream of a leopard.

But still John Clayton, Lord Greystoke, stood deaf and unseeing, suffering the pangs of keen regret for the opportunity that he had wasted because he had been so gullible as to place credence in a single statement of the first lieutenant of his arch-enemy.

"I have at least," he thought, "one consolation – the knowledge that Jane is safe in London. Thank Heaven she, too, did not fall into the clutches of those villains."

Behind him the hairy thing whose evil eyes had been watching him as a cat watches a mouse was creeping stealthily toward him.

Where were the trained senses of the savage ape-man?

Where the acute hearing?

Where the uncanny sense of scent?

CHAPTER THREE

Beasts at Bay

Slowly Tarzan unfolded the note the sailor had thrust into his hand, and read it. At first it made little impression on his sorrow-numbed senses, but finally the full purport of the hideous plot of revenge unfolded itself before his imagination.

"This will explain to you" [the note read] "the exact nature of my intentions relative to your offspring and to you.

"You were born an ape. You lived naked in the jungles – to your own we have returned you; but your son shall rise a step above his sire. It is the immutable law of evolution.

"The father was a beast, but the son shall be a man – he shall take the next ascending step in the scale of progress. He shall be no naked beast of the jungle, but shall wear a loin-cloth and copper anklets, and, perchance, a ring in his nose, for he is to be reared by men – a tribe of savage cannibals.

"I might have killed you, but that would have curtailed the full measure of the punishment you have earned at my hands.

"Dead, you could not have suffered in the knowledge of your son's plight; but living and in a place from which you may not escape to seek or succour your child, you shall suffer worse than death for all the years of your life in contemplation of the horrors of your son's existence.

"This, then, is to be a part of your punishment for having dared to pit yourself against

N. R.

"P.S. – The balance of your punishment has to do with what shall presently befall your wife – that I shall leave to your imagination."

As he finished reading, a slight sound behind him brought him back with a start to the world of present realities.

Instantly his senses awoke, and he was again Tarzan of the Apes.

As he wheeled about, it was a beast at bay, vibrant with the instinct of self-preservation, that faced a huge bull-ape that was already charging down upon him.

The two years that had elapsed since Tarzan had come out of the savage forest with his rescued mate had witnessed slight diminution of the mighty powers that had made him the invincible lord of the jungle. His great estates in Uziri had claimed much of his time and attention, and there he had found ample field for the practical use and retention of his almost superhuman powers; but naked and unarmed to do battle with the shaggy, bull-necked beast that now confronted him was a test that the ape-man would scarce have welcomed at any period of his wild existence.

But there was no alternative other than to meet the rage-maddened creature with the weapons with which nature had endowed him.

Over the bull's shoulder Tarzan could see now the heads and shoulders of perhaps a dozen more of these mighty fore-runners of primitive man.

He knew, however, that there was little chance that they would attack him, since it is not within the reasoning powers of the anthropoid to be able to weigh or appreciate the value of concentrated action against an enemy – otherwise they would long since have become the dominant creatures of their haunts, so tremendous a power of destruction lies in their mighty thews and savage fangs.

With a low snarl the beast now hurled himself at Tarzan, but the ape-man had found, among other things in the haunts of civilized man, certain methods of scientific warfare that are unknown to the jungle folk.

Whereas, a few years since, he would have met the brute rush with brute force, he now sidestepped his antagonist's headlong charge, and as the brute hurtled past him swung a mighty right to the pit of the ape's stomach.

With a howl of mingled rage and anguish the great anthropoid bent double and sank to the ground, though almost instantly he was again struggling to his feet.

Before he could regain them, however, his white-skinned foe had wheeled and pounced upon him, and in the act there dropped from the shoulders of the English lord the last shred of his superficial mantle of civilization.

Once again he was the jungle beast revelling in bloody conflict with his kind. Once again he was Tarzan, son of Kala the she-ape.

His strong, white teeth sank into the hairy throat of his enemy as he sought the pulsing jugular.

Powerful fingers held the mighty fangs from his own flesh, or clenched and beat with the power of a steam-hammer upon the snarling, foam-flecked face of his adversary.

In a circle about them the balance of the tribe of apes stood watching and enjoying the struggle. They muttered low gutturals of approval as bits of white hide or hairy bloodstained skin were torn from one contestant or the other. But they were silent in amazement and expectation when they saw the mighty white ape wriggle upon the back of their king, and, with steel muscles tensed beneath the armpits of his antagonist, bear down mightily with his open palms upon the back of the thick bullneck, so that the king ape could but shriek in agony and flounder helplessly about upon the thick mat of jungle grass.

As Tarzan had overcome the huge Terkoz that time years before when he had been about to set out upon his quest for human beings of his own kind and colour, so now he overcame this other great ape with the same wrestling hold upon which he had stumbled by accident during that other combat. The little audience of fierce anthropoids heard the creaking of their king's neck mingling with his agonized shrieks and hideous roaring.

Then there came a sudden crack, like the breaking of a stout limb before the fury of the wind. The bullet-head crumpled forward upon its flaccid neck against the great hairy chest – the roaring and the shrieking ceased.

The little pig-eyes of the onlookers wandered from the still form of their leader to that of the white ape that was rising to its feet beside the vanquished, then back to their king as though in wonder that he did not arise and slay this presumptuous stranger.

They saw the new-comer place a foot upon the neck of the quiet figure at his feet and, throwing back his head, give vent to the wild, uncanny challenge of the bull-ape that has made a kill. Then they knew that their king was dead.

Across the jungle rolled the horrid notes of the victory cry. The little monkeys in the tree-tops ceased their chattering. The harsh-voiced, brilliant-plumed birds were still. From afar came the answering wail of a leopard and the deep roar of a lion.

It was the old Tarzan who turned questioning eyes upon the little knot of apes before him. It was the old Tarzan who shook his head as though to toss back a heavy mane that had fallen before his face – an old habit dating from the days that his great shock of thick, black hair had fallen about his shoulders, and often tumbled before his eyes when it had meant life or death to him to have his vision unobstructed.

The ape-man knew that he might expect an immediate attack on the part of that particular surviving bull-ape who felt himself best fitted to contend for the kingship of the tribe. Among his own apes he knew that it was not unusual for an entire stranger to enter a community and, after having dispatched the king, assume the leadership of the tribe himself, together with the fallen monarch's mates.

On the other hand, if he made no attempt to follow them, they might move slowly away from him, later to fight among themselves for the supremacy. That he could be king of them, if he so chose, he was confident; but he was not sure he cared to assume the sometimes irksome duties of that position, for he could see no particular advantage to be gained thereby.

One of the younger apes, a huge, splendidly muscled brute, was edging threateningly closer to the ape-man. Through his bared fighting fangs there issued a low, sullen growl.

Tarzan watched his every move, standing rigid as a statue. To have fallen back a step would have been to precipitate an immediate charge; to have rushed forward to meet the other might have had the same result, or it might have put the bellicose one to flight – it all depended upon the young bull's stock of courage.

To stand perfectly still, waiting, was the middle course. In this event the bull would, according to custom, approach quite close to the object of his attention, growling hideously and baring slavering fangs. Slowly he would circle about the other, as though with a chip upon his shoulder; and this he did, even as Tarzan had foreseen.

It might be a bluff royal, or, on the other hand, so unstable is the mind of an ape, a passing impulse might hurl the hairy mass, tearing and rending, upon the man without an instant's warning.

As the brute circled him Tarzan turned slowly, keeping his eyes ever upon the eyes of his antagonist. He had appraised the young bull as one who had never quite felt equal to the task of overthrowing his former king, but who one day would have done so. Tarzan saw that the beast was of wondrous proportions, standing over seven feet upon his short, bowed legs.

His great, hairy arms reached almost to the ground even when he stood erect, and his fighting fangs, now quite close to Tarzan's face, were exceptionally long and sharp. Like the others of his tribe, he differed in several minor essentials from the apes of Tarzan's boyhood.

At first the ape-man had experienced a thrill of hope at sight of the shaggy bodies of the anthropoids – a hope that by some strange freak of fate he had been again returned to his own tribe; but a closer inspection had convinced him that these were another species.

As the threatening bull continued his stiff and jerky circling of the ape-man, much after the manner that you have noted among dogs when a strange canine comes among them, it occurred to Tarzan to discover if the language of his own tribe was identical with that of this other family, and so he addressed the brute in the language of the tribe of Kerchak.

"Who are you," he asked, "who threatens Tarzan of the Apes?"

The hairy brute looked his surprise.

"I am Akut," replied the other in the same simple, primal tongue which is so low in the scale of spoken languages that, as Tarzan had surmised, it was identical with that of the tribe in which the first twenty years of his life had been spent.

"I am Akut," said the ape. "Molak is dead. I am king. Go away or I shall kill you!"

"You saw how easily I killed Molak," replied Tarzan. "So I could kill you if I cared to be king. But Tarzan of the Apes would not be king of the tribe of Akut. All he wishes is to live in peace in this country. Let us be friends. Tarzan of the Apes can help you, and you can help Tarzan of the Apes."

"You cannot kill Akut," replied the other. "None is so great as Akut. Had you not killed Molak, Akut would have done so, for Akut was ready to be king."

For answer the ape-man hurled himself upon the great brute who during the conversation had slightly relaxed his vigilance.

In the twinkling of an eye the man had seized the wrist of the great ape, and before the other could grapple with him had whirled him about and leaped upon his broad back.

Down they went together, but so well had Tarzan's plan worked out that before ever they touched the ground he had gained the same hold upon Akut that had broken Molak's neck.

Slowly he brought the pressure to bear, and then as in days gone by he had given Kerchak the chance to surrender and live, so now he gave to Akut – in whom he saw a possible ally of great strength and resource – the option of living in amity with him or dying as he had just seen his savage and heretofore invincible king die.

"Ka-Goda?" whispered Tarzan to the ape beneath him.

It was the same question that he had whispered to Kerchak, and in the language of the apes it means, broadly, "Do you surrender?"

Akut thought of the creaking sound he had heard just before Molak's thick neck had snapped, and he shuddered.

He hated to give up the kingship, though, so again he struggled to free himself; but a sudden torturing pressure upon his vertebra brought an agonized "ka-goda!" from his lips.

Tarzan relaxed his grip a trifle.

"You may still be king, Akut," he said. "Tarzan told you that he did not wish to be king. If any question your right, Tarzan of the Apes will help you in your battles."

The ape-man rose, and Akut came slowly to his feet. Shaking his bullet head and growling angrily, he waddled toward his tribe, looking first at one and then at another of the larger bulls who might be expected to challenge his leadership.

But none did so; instead, they drew away as he approached, and presently the whole pack moved off into the jungle, and Tarzan was left alone once more upon the beach.

The ape-man was sore from the wounds that Molak had inflicted upon him, but he was inured to physical suffering and endured it with the calm and fortitude of the wild beasts that had taught him to lead the jungle life after the manner of all those that are born to it.

His first need, he realized, was for weapons of offence and defence, for his encounter with the apes, and the distant notes of the savage voices of Numa the lion, and Sheeta, the panther, warned him that his was to be no life of indolent ease and security.

It was but a return to the old existence of constant bloodshed and danger – to the hunting and the being hunted. Grim beasts would stalk him, as they had stalked him in the past, and never would there be a moment, by savage day or by cruel night, that he might not have instant need of such crude weapons as he could fashion from the materials at hand.

Upon the shore he found an out-cropping of brittle, igneous rock. By dint of much labour he managed to chip off a narrow sliver some twelve inches long by a quarter of an inch thick. One edge was quite thin for a few inches near the tip. It was the rudiment of a knife.

With it he went into the jungle, searching until he found a fallen tree of a certain species of hardwood with which he was familiar. From this he cut a small straight branch, which he pointed at one end.

Then he scooped a small, round hole in the surface of the prostrate trunk. Into this he crumbled a few bits of dry bark, minutely shredded, after which he inserted the tip of his pointed stick, and, sitting astride the bole of the tree, spun the slender rod rapidly between his palms.

After a time a thin smoke rose from the little mass of tinder, and a moment later the whole broke into flame. Heaping some larger twigs and sticks upon the tiny fire, Tarzan soon had quite a respectable blaze roaring in the enlarging cavity of the dead tree.

Into this he thrust the blade of his stone knife, and as it became superheated he would withdraw it, touching a spot near the thin edge with a drop of moisture. Beneath the wetted area a little flake of the glassy material would crack and scale away.

Thus, very slowly, the ape-man commenced the tedious operation of putting a thin edge upon his primitive hunting-knife.

He did not attempt to accomplish the feat all in one sitting. At first he was content to achieve a cutting edge of a couple of inches, with which he cut a long, pliable bow, a handle for his knife, a stout cudgel, and a goodly supply of arrows.

These he cached in a tall tree beside a little stream, and here also he constructed a platform with a roof of palm-leaves above it.

When all these things had been finished it was growing dusk, and Tarzan felt a strong desire to eat.

He had noted during the brief incursion he had made into the forest that a short distance up-stream from his tree there was a much-used watering place, where, from the trampled mud of either bank, it was evident beasts of all sorts and in great numbers came to drink. To this spot the hungry ape-man made his silent way.

Through the upper terrace of the tree-tops he swung with the grace and ease of a monkey. But for the heavy burden upon his heart he would have been happy in this return to the old free life of his boyhood.

Yet even with that burden he fell into the little habits and manners of his early life that were in reality more a part of him than the thin veneer of civilization that the past three years of his association with the white men of the outer world had spread lightly over him – a veneer that only hid the crudities of the beast that Tarzan of the Apes had been.

Could his fellow-peers of the House of Lords have seen him then they would have held up their noble hands in holy horror.

Silently he crouched in the lower branches of a great forest giant that overhung the trail, his keen eyes and sensitive ears strained into the distant jungle, from which he knew his dinner would presently emerge.

Nor had he long to wait.

Scarce had he settled himself to a comfortable position, his lithe, muscular legs drawn well up beneath him as the panther draws his hindquarters in preparation for the spring, than Bara, the deer, came daintily down to drink.

But more than Bara was coming. Behind the graceful buck came another which the deer could neither see nor scent, but whose movements were apparent to Tarzan of the Apes because of the elevated position of the ape-man's ambush.

He knew not yet exactly the nature of the thing that moved so stealthily through the jungle a few hundred yards behind the deer; but he was convinced that it was some great beast of prey stalking Bara for the selfsame purpose as that which prompted him to await the fleet animal. Numa, perhaps, or Sheeta, the panther.

In any event, Tarzan could see his repast slipping from his grasp unless Bara moved more rapidly toward the ford than at present.

Even as these thoughts passed through his mind some noise of the stalker in his rear must have come to the buck, for with a sudden start he paused for an instant, trembling, in his tracks, and then with a swift bound dashed straight for the river and Tarzan. It was his intention to flee through the shallow ford and escape upon the opposite side of the river.

Not a hundred yards behind him came Numa.

Tarzan could see him quite plainly now. Below the ape-man Bara was about to pass. Could he do it? But even as he asked himself the question the hungry man launched himself from his perch full upon the back of the startled buck.

In another instant Numa would be upon them both, so if the ape-man were to dine that night, or ever again, he must act quickly.

Scarcely had he touched the sleek hide of the deer with a momentum that sent the animal to its knees than he had grasped a horn in either hand, and with a single quick wrench twisted the animal's neck completely round, until he felt the vertebrae snap beneath his grip.

The lion was roaring in rage close behind him as he swung the deer across his shoulder, and, grasping a foreleg between his strong teeth, leaped for the nearest of the lower branches that swung above his head.

With both hands he grasped the limb, and, at the instant that Numa sprang, drew himself and his prey out of reach of the animal's cruel talons.

There was a thud below him as the baffled cat fell back to earth, and then Tarzan of the Apes, drawing his dinner farther up to the safety of a higher limb, looked down with grinning face into the gleaming yellow eyes of the other wild beast that glared up at him from beneath, and with taunting insults flaunted the tender carcass of his kill in the face of him whom he had cheated of it.

With his crude stone knife he cut a juicy steak from the hindquarters, and while the great lion paced, growling, back and forth below him, Lord Greystoke filled his savage belly, nor ever in the choicest of his exclusive London clubs had a meal tasted more palatable.

The warm blood of his kill smeared his hands and face and filled his nostrils with the scent that the savage carnivora love best.

And when he had finished he left the balance of the carcass in a high fork of the tree where he had dined, and with Numa trailing below him, still keen for revenge, he made his way back to his tree-top shelter, where he slept until the sun was high the following morning.

CHAPTER FOUR

Sheeta

THE NEXT FEW DAYS were occupied by Tarzan in completing his weapons and exploring the jungle. He strung his bow with tendons from the buck upon which he had dined his first evening upon the new shore, and though he would have preferred the gut of Sheeta for the purpose, he was content to wait until opportunity permitted him to kill one of the great cats.

He also braided a long grass rope – such a rope as he had used so many years before to tantalize the ill-natured Tublat, and which later had developed into a wondrous effective weapon in the practised hands of the little ape-boy.

A sheath and handle for his hunting-knife he fashioned, and a quiver for arrows, and from the hide of Bara a belt and loin-cloth. Then he set out to learn something of the strange land in which he found himself. That it was not his old familiar west coast of the African continent he knew from the fact that it faced east – the rising sun came up out of the sea before the threshold of the jungle.

But that it was not the east coast of Africa he was equally positive, for he felt satisfied that the Kincaid had not passed through the Mediterranean, the Suez Canal, and the Red Sea, nor had she had time to round the Cape of Good Hope. So he was quite at a loss to know where he might be.

Sometimes he wondered if the ship had crossed the broad Atlantic to deposit him upon some wild South American shore; but the presence of Numa, the lion, decided him that such could not be the case.

As Tarzan made his lonely way through the jungle paralleling the shore, he felt strong upon him a desire for companionship, so that gradually he commenced to regret that he had not cast his lot with the apes.

He had seen nothing of them since that first day, when the influences of civilization were still paramount within him.

Now he was more nearly returned to the Tarzan of old, and though he appreciated the fact that there could be little in common between himself and the great anthropoids, still they were better than no company at all.

Moving leisurely, sometimes upon the ground and again among the lower branches of the trees, gathering an occasional fruit or turning over a fallen log in search of the larger bugs, which he still found as palatable as of old, Tarzan had covered a mile or more when his attention was attracted by the scent of Sheeta up-wind ahead of him.

Now Sheeta, the panther, was one whom Tarzan was exceptionally glad to fall in with, for he had it in mind not only to utilize the great cat's strong gut for his bow, but also to fashion a new quiver and loin-cloth from pieces of his hide. So, whereas the ape-man had gone carelessly before, he now became the personification of noiseless stealth.

Swiftly and silently he glided through the forest in the wake of the savage cat, nor was the pursuer, for all his noble birth, one whit less savage than the wild, fierce thing he stalked.

As he came closer to Sheeta he became aware that the panther on his part was stalking game of his own, and even as he realized this fact there came to his nostrils, wafted from his right by a vagrant breeze, the strong odour of a company of great apes.

The panther had taken to a large tree as Tarzan came within sight of him, and beyond and below him Tarzan saw the tribe of Akut lolling in a little, natural clearing. Some of them were dozing against the boles of trees, while others roamed about turning over bits of bark from beneath which they transferred the luscious grubs and beetles to their mouths.

Akut was the closest to Sheeta.

The great cat lay crouched upon a thick limb, hidden from the ape's view by dense foliage, waiting patiently until the anthropoid should come within range of his spring.

Tarzan cautiously gained a position in the same tree with the panther and a little above him. In his left hand he grasped his slim stone blade. He would have preferred to use his noose, but the foliage surrounding the huge cat precluded the possibility of an accurate throw with the rope.

Akut had now wandered quite close beneath the tree wherein lay the waiting death. Sheeta slowly edged his hind paws along the branch still further beneath him, and then with a hideous shriek he launched himself toward the great ape. The barest fraction of a second before his spring another beast of prey above him leaped, its weird and savage cry mingling with his.

As the startled Akut looked up he saw the panther almost above him, and already upon the panther's back the white ape that had bested him that day near the great water.

The teeth of the ape-man were buried in the back of Sheeta's neck and his right arm was round the fierce throat, while the left hand, grasping a slender piece of stone, rose and fell in mighty blows upon the panther's side behind the left shoulder.

Akut had just time to leap to one side to avoid being pinioned beneath these battling monsters of the jungle.

With a crash they came to earth at his feet. Sheeta was screaming, snarling, and roaring horribly; but the white ape clung tenaciously and in silence to the thrashing body of his quarry.

Steadily and remorselessly the stone knife was driven home through the glossy hide – time and again it drank deep, until with a final agonized lunge and shriek the great feline rolled over upon its side and, save for the spasmodic jerking of its muscles, lay quiet and still in death.

Then the ape-man raised his head, as he stood over the carcass of his kill, and once again through the jungle rang his wild and savage victory challenge.

Akut and the apes of Akut stood looking in startled wonder at the dead body of Sheeta and the lithe, straight figure of the man who had slain him.

Tarzan was the first to speak.

He had saved Akut's life for a purpose, and, knowing the limitations of the ape intellect, he also knew that he must make this purpose plain to the anthropoid if it were to serve him in the way he hoped.

"I am Tarzan of the Apes," he said, "Mighty hunter. Mighty fighter. By the great water I spared Akut's life when I might have taken it and become king of the tribe of Akut. Now I have saved Akut from death beneath the rending fangs of Sheeta.

"When Akut or the tribe of Akut is in danger, let them call to Tarzan thus" – and the ape-man raised the hideous cry with which the tribe of Kerchak had been wont to summon its absent members in times of peril.

"And," he continued, "when they hear Tarzan call to them, let them remember what he has done for Akut and come to him with great speed. Shall it be as Tarzan says?"

"Huh!" assented Akut, and from the members of his tribe there rose a unanimous "Huh."

Then, presently, they went to feeding again as though nothing had happened, and with them fed John Clayton, Lord Greystoke.

He noticed, however, that Akut kept always close to him, and was often looking at him with a strange wonder in his little bloodshot eyes, and once he did a thing that Tarzan during all his long years among the apes had never before seen an ape do – he found a particularly tender morsel and handed it to Tarzan.

As the tribe hunted, the glistening body of the ape-man mingled with the brown, shaggy hides of his companions. Oftentimes they brushed together in passing, but the apes had already taken his presence for granted, so that he was as much one of them as Akut himself.

If he came too close to a she with a young baby, the former would bare her great fighting fangs and growl ominously, and occasionally a truculent young bull would snarl a warning if Tarzan approached while the former was eating. But in those things the treatment was no different from that which they accorded any other member of the tribe.

Tarzan on his part felt very much at home with these fierce, hairy progenitors of primitive man. He skipped nimbly out of reach of each threatening female – for such is the way of apes, if they be not in one of their occasional fits of bestial rage – and he growled back at the truculent young bulls, baring his canine teeth even as they. Thus easily he fell back into the way of his early life, nor did it seem that he had ever tasted association with creatures of his own kind.

For the better part of a week he roamed the jungle with his new friends, partly because of a desire for companionship and partially through a well-laid plan to impress himself indelibly upon their memories, which at best are none too long; for Tarzan from past experience knew that it might serve him in good stead to have a tribe of these powerful and terrible beasts at his call.

When he was convinced that he had succeeded to some extent in fixing his identity upon them he decided to again take up his exploration. To this end he set out toward the north early one day, and, keeping parallel with the shore, travelled rapidly until almost nightfall.

When the sun rose the next morning he saw that it lay almost directly to his right as he stood upon the beach instead of straight out across the water as heretofore, and so he reasoned that the shore line had trended toward the west. All the second day he continued his rapid course, and when Tarzan of the Apes sought speed, he passed through the middle terrace of the forest with the rapidity of a squirrel.

That night the sun set straight out across the water opposite the land, and then the ape-man guessed at last the truth that he had been suspecting.

Rokoff had set him ashore upon an island.

He might have known it! If there was any plan that would render his position more harrowing he should have known that such would be the one adopted by the Russian, and what could be more terrible than to leave him to a lifetime of suspense upon an uninhabited island?

Rokoff doubtless had sailed directly to the mainland, where it would be a comparatively easy thing for him to find the means of delivering the infant Jack into the hands of the cruel and savage foster-parents, who, as his note had threatened, would have the upbringing of the child.

Tarzan shuddered as he thought of the cruel suffering the little one must endure in such a life, even though he might fall into the hands of individuals whose intentions toward him were of the kindest. The ape-man had had sufficient experience with the lower savages of Africa to know that even there may be found the cruder virtues of charity and humanity; but their lives were at best but a series of terrible privations, dangers, and sufferings.

Then there was the horrid after-fate that awaited the child as he grew to manhood. The horrible practices that would form a part of his life-training would alone be sufficient to bar him forever from association with those of his own race and station in life.

A cannibal! His little boy a savage man-eater! It was too horrible to contemplate.

The filed teeth, the slit nose, the little face painted hideously. Tarzan groaned. Could he but feel the throat of the Russ fiend beneath his steel fingers!

And Jane!

What tortures of doubt and fear and uncertainty she must be suffering. He felt that his position was infinitely less terrible than hers, for he at least knew that one of his loved ones was safe at home, while she had no idea of the whereabouts of either her husband or her son.

It is well for Tarzan that he did not guess the truth, for the knowledge would have but added a hundredfold to his suffering.

As he moved slowly through the jungle his mind absorbed by his gloomy thoughts, there presently came to his ears a strange scratching sound which he could not translate.

Cautiously he moved in the direction from which it emanated, presently coming upon a huge panther pinned beneath a fallen tree.

As Tarzan approached, the beast turned, snarling, toward him, struggling to extricate itself; but one great limb across its back and the smaller entangling branches pinioning its legs prevented it from moving but a few inches in any direction.

The ape-man stood before the helpless cat fitting an arrow to his bow that he might dispatch the beast that otherwise must die of starvation; but even as he drew back the shaft a sudden whim stayed his hand.

Why rob the poor creature of life and liberty, when it would be so easy a thing to restore both to it! He was sure from the fact that the panther moved all its limbs in its futile struggle for freedom that its spine was uninjured, and for the same reason he knew that none of its limbs were broken.

Relaxing his bowstring, he returned the arrow to the quiver and, throwing the bow about his shoulder, stepped closer to the pinioned beast.

On his lips was the soothing, purring sound that the great cats themselves made when contented and happy. It was the nearest approach to a friendly advance that Tarzan could make in the language of Sheeta.

The panther ceased his snarling and eyed the ape-man closely. To lift the tree's great weight from the animal it was necessary to come within reach of those long, strong talons, and when the tree had been removed the man would be totally at the mercy of the savage beast; but to Tarzan of the Apes fear was a thing unknown.

Having decided, he acted promptly.

Unhesitatingly, he stepped into the tangle of branches close to the panther's side, still voicing his friendly and conciliatory purr. The cat turned his head toward the man, eyeing him steadily – questioningly. The long fangs were bared, but more in preparedness than threat.

Tarzan put a broad shoulder beneath the bole of the tree, and as he did so his bare leg pressed against the cat's silken side, so close was the man to the great beast.

Slowly Tarzan extended his giant thews.

The great tree with its entangling branches rose gradually from the panther, who, feeling the encumbering weight diminish, quickly crawled from beneath. Tarzan let the tree fall back to earth, and the two beasts turned to look upon one another.

A grim smile lay upon the ape-man's lips, for he knew that he had taken his life in his hands to free this savage jungle fellow; nor would it have surprised him had the cat sprung upon him the instant that it had been released.

But it did not do so. Instead, it stood a few paces from the tree watching the ape-man clamber out of the maze of fallen branches.

Once outside, Tarzan was not three paces from the panther. He might have taken to the higher branches of the trees upon the opposite side, for Sheeta cannot climb to the heights to which the ape-man can go; but something, a spirit of bravado perhaps, prompted him to approach the panther as though to discover if any feeling of gratitude would prompt the beast to friendliness.

As he approached the mighty cat the creature stepped warily to one side, and the ape-man brushed past him within a foot of the dripping jaws, and as he continued on through the forest the panther followed on behind him, as a hound follows at heel.

For a long time Tarzan could not tell whether the beast was following out of friendly feelings or merely stalking him against the time he should be hungry; but finally he was forced to believe that the former incentive it was that prompted the animal's action.

Later in the day the scent of a deer sent Tarzan into the trees, and when he had dropped his noose about the animal's neck he called to Sheeta, using a purr similar to that which he had utilized to pacify the brute's suspicions earlier in the day, but a trifle louder and more shrill.

It was similar to that which he had heard panthers use after a kill when they had been hunting in pairs.

Almost immediately there was a crashing of the underbrush close at hand, and the long, lithe body of his strange companion broke into view.

At sight of the body of Bara and the smell of blood the panther gave forth a shrill scream, and a moment later two beasts were feeding side by side upon the tender meat of the deer.

For several days this strangely assorted pair roamed the jungle together.

When one made a kill he called the other, and thus they fed well and often.

On one occasion as they were dining upon the carcass of a boar that Sheeta had dispatched, Numa, the lion, grim and terrible, broke through the tangled grasses close beside them.

With an angry, warning roar he sprang forward to chase them from their kill. Sheeta bounded into a near-by thicket, while Tarzan took to the low branches of an overhanging tree.

Here the ape-man unloosed his grass rope from about his neck, and as Numa stood above the body of the boar, challenging head erect, he dropped the sinuous noose about the maned neck, drawing the stout strands taut with a sudden jerk. At the same time he called shrilly to Sheeta, as he drew the struggling lion upward until only his hind feet touched the ground.

Quickly he made the rope fast to a stout branch, and as the panther, in answer to his summons, leaped into sight, Tarzan dropped to the earth beside the struggling and infuriated Numa, and with a long sharp knife sprang upon him at one side even as Sheeta did upon the other.

The panther tore and rent Numa upon the right, while the ape-man struck home with his stone knife upon the other, so that before the mighty clawing of the king of beasts had succeeded in parting the rope he hung quite dead and harmless in the noose.

And then upon the jungle air there rose in unison from two savage throats the victory cry of the bull-ape and the panther, blended into one frightful and uncanny scream.

As the last notes died away in a long-drawn, fearsome wail, a score of painted warriors, drawing their long war-canoe upon the beach, halted to stare in the direction of the jungle and to listen.

CHAPTER FIVE

Mugambi

By the time that Tarzan had travelled entirely about the coast of the island, and made several trips inland from various points, he was sure that he was the only human being upon it.

Nowhere had he found any sign that men had stopped even temporarily upon this shore, though, of course, he knew that so quickly does the rank vegetation of the tropics erase all but the most permanent of human monuments that he might be in error in his deductions.

The day following the killing of Numa, Tarzan and Sheeta came upon the tribe of Akut. At sight of the panther the great apes took to flight, but after a time Tarzan succeeded in recalling them.

It had occurred to him that it would be at least an interesting experiment to attempt to reconcile these hereditary enemies. He welcomed anything that would occupy his time and his mind beyond the filling of his belly and the gloomy thoughts to which he fell prey the moment that he became idle.

To communicate his plan to the apes was not a particularly difficult matter, though their narrow and limited vocabulary was strained in the effort; but to impress upon the little, wicked brain of Sheeta that he was to hunt with and not for his legitimate prey proved a task almost beyond the powers of the ape-man.

Tarzan, among his other weapons, possessed a long, stout cudgel, and after fastening his rope about the panther's neck he used this instrument freely upon the snarling beast, endeavouring in this way to impress upon its memory that it must not attack the great, shaggy manlike creatures that had approached more closely once they had seen the purpose of the rope about Sheeta's neck.

That the cat did not turn and rend Tarzan is something of a miracle which may possibly be accounted for by the fact that twice when it turned growling upon the ape-man he had rapped it sharply upon its sensitive nose, inculcating in its mind thereby a most wholesome fear of the cudgel and the ape-beasts behind it.

It is a question if the original cause of his attachment for Tarzan was still at all clear in the mind of the panther, though doubtless some subconscious suggestion, superinduced by this primary reason and aided and abetted by the habit of the past few days, did much to compel the beast to tolerate treatment at his hands that would have sent it at the throat of any other creature.

Then, too, there was the compelling force of the manmind exerting its powerful influence over this creature of a lower order, and, after all, it may have been this that proved the most potent factor in Tarzan's supremacy over Sheeta and the other beasts of the jungle that had from time to time fallen under his domination.

Be that as it may, for days the man, the panther, and the great apes roamed their savage haunts side by side, making their kills together and sharing them with one another, and of all the fierce and savage band none was more terrible than the smooth-skinned, powerful beast that had been but a few short months before a familiar figure in many a London drawing room.

Sometimes the beasts separated to follow their own inclinations for an hour or a day, and it was upon one of these occasions when the ape-man had wandered through the tree-tops toward the beach, and was stretched in the hot sun upon the sand, that from the low summit of a near-by promontory a pair of keen eyes discovered him.

For a moment the owner of the eyes looked in astonishment at the figure of the savage white man basking in the rays of that hot, tropic sun; then he turned, making a sign to some one behind him. Presently another pair of eyes were looking down upon the ape-man, and then another and another, until a full score of hideously trapped, savage warriors were lying upon their bellies along the crest of the ridge watching the white-skinned stranger.

They were down wind from Tarzan, and so their scent was not carried to him, and as his back was turned half toward them he did not see their cautious advance over the edge of the promontory and down through the rank grass toward the sandy beach where he lay.

Big fellows they were, all of them, their barbaric headdresses and grotesquely painted faces, together with their many metal ornaments and gorgeously coloured feathers, adding to their wild, fierce appearance.

Once at the foot of the ridge, they came cautiously to their feet, and, bent half-double, advanced silently upon the unconscious white man, their heavy war-clubs swinging menacingly in their brawny hands.

The mental suffering that Tarzan's sorrowful thoughts induced had the effect of numbing his keen, perceptive faculties, so that the advancing savages were almost upon him before he became aware that he was no longer alone upon the beach.

So quickly, though, were his mind and muscles wont to react in unison to the slightest alarm that he was upon his feet and facing his enemies, even as he realized that something was behind him. As he sprang to his feet the warriors leaped toward him with raised clubs and savage yells, but the foremost went down to sudden death beneath the long, stout stick of the ape-man, and then the lithe, sinewy figure was among them, striking right and left with a fury, power, and precision that brought panic to the ranks of the blacks.

For a moment they withdrew, those that were left of them, and consulted together at a short distance from the ape-man, who stood with folded arms, a half-smile upon his handsome face, watching them. Presently they advanced upon him once more, this time wielding their heavy war-spears. They were between Tarzan and the jungle, in a little semicircle that closed in upon him as they advanced.

There seemed to the ape-man but slight chance to escape the final charge when all the great spears should be hurled simultaneously at him; but if he had desired to escape there was no way other than through the ranks of the savages except the open sea behind him.

His predicament was indeed most serious when an idea occurred to him that altered his smile to a broad grin. The warriors were still some little distance away, advancing slowly, making, after the manner of their kind, a frightful din with their savage yells and the pounding of their naked feet upon the ground as they leaped up and down in a fantastic war dance.

Then it was that the ape-man lifted his voice in a series of wild, weird screams that brought the blacks to a sudden, perplexed halt. They looked at one another questioningly, for here was a sound so hideous that their own frightful din faded into insignificance beside it. No human throat could have formed those bestial notes, they were sure, and yet with their own eyes they had seen this white man open his mouth to pour forth his awful cry.

But only for a moment they hesitated, and then with one accord they again took up their fantastic advance upon their prey; but even then a sudden crashing in the jungle behind them brought them once more to a halt, and as they turned to look in the direction of this new noise there broke upon their startled visions a sight that may well have frozen the blood of braver men than the Wagambi.

Leaping from the tangled vegetation of the jungle's rim came a huge panther, with blazing eyes and bared fangs, and in his wake a score of mighty, shaggy apes lumbering rapidly toward them, half erect upon their short, bowed legs, and with their long arms reaching to the ground, where their horny knuckles bore the weight of their ponderous bodies as they lurched from side to side in their grotesque advance.

The beasts of Tarzan had come in answer to his call.

Before the Wagambi could recover from their astonishment the frightful horde was upon them from one side and Tarzan of the Apes from the other. Heavy spears were hurled and mighty war-clubs wielded, and though apes went down never to rise, so, too, went down the men of Ugambi.

Sheeta's cruel fangs and tearing talons ripped and tore at the black hides. Akut's mighty yellow tusks found the jugular of more than one sleek-skinned savage, and Tarzan of the Apes was here and there and everywhere, urging on his fierce allies and taking a heavy toll with his long, slim knife.

In a moment the blacks had scattered for their lives, but of the score that had crept down the grassy sides of the promontory only a single warrior managed to escape the horde that had overwhelmed his people.

This one was Mugambi, chief of the Wagambi of Ugambi, and as he disappeared in the tangled luxuriousness of the rank growth upon the ridge's summit only the keen eyes of the ape-man saw the direction of his flight.

Leaving his pack to eat their fill upon the flesh of their victims – flesh that he could not touch – Tarzan of the Apes pursued the single survivor of the bloody fray. Just beyond the ridge he came within sight of the fleeing black, making with headlong leaps for a long war-canoe that was drawn well up upon the beach above the high tide surf.

Noiseless as the fellow's shadow, the ape-man raced after the terror-stricken black. In the white man's mind was a new plan, awakened by sight of the war-canoe. If these men had come to his island from another, or from the mainland, why not utilize their craft to make his way to the country from which they had come? Evidently it was an inhabited country, and no doubt had occasional intercourse with the mainland, if it were not itself upon the continent of Africa.

A heavy hand fell upon the shoulder of the escaping Mugambi before he was aware that he was being pursued, and as he turned to do battle with his assailant giant fingers closed about his wrists and he was hurled to earth with a giant astride him before he could strike a blow in his own defence.

In the language of the West Coast, Tarzan spoke to the prostrate man beneath him.

"Who are you?" he asked.

"Mugambi, chief of the Wagambi," replied the black.

"I will spare your life," said Tarzan, "if you will promise to help me to leave this island. What do you answer?"

"I will help you," replied Mugambi. "But now that you have killed all my warriors, I do not know that even I can leave your country, for there will be none to wield the paddles, and without paddlers we cannot cross the water."

Tarzan rose and allowed his prisoner to come to his feet. The fellow was a magnificent specimen of manhood – a black counterpart in physique of the splendid white man whom he faced.

"Come!" said the ape-man, and started back in the direction from which they could hear the snarling and growling of the feasting pack. Mugambi drew back.

"They will kill us," he said.

"I think not," replied Tarzan. "They are mine."

Still the black hesitated, fearful of the consequences of approaching the terrible creatures that were dining upon the bodies of his warriors; but Tarzan forced him to accompany him, and presently the two emerged from the jungle in full view of the grisly spectacle upon the beach. At sight of the men the beasts looked up with menacing growls, but Tarzan strode in among them, dragging the trembling Wagambi with him.

As he had taught the apes to accept Sheeta, so he taught them to adopt Mugambi as well, and much more easily; but Sheeta seemed quite unable to understand that though he had been called upon to devour Mugambi's warriors he was not to be allowed to proceed after the same fashion with Mugambi. However, being well filled, he contented himself with walking round the terror-stricken savage, emitting low, menacing growls the while he kept his flaming, baleful eyes riveted upon the black.

Mugambi, on his part, clung closely to Tarzan, so that the ape-man could scarce control his laughter at the pitiable condition to which the chief's fear had reduced him; but at length the white took the great cat by the scruff of the neck and, dragging it quite close to the Wagambi, slapped it sharply upon the nose each time that it growled at the stranger.

At the sight of the thing – a man mauling with his bare hands one of the most relentless and fierce of the jungle carnivora – Mugambi's eyes bulged from their sockets, and from entertaining a sullen respect for the giant white man who had made him prisoner, the black felt an almost worshipping awe of Tarzan.

The education of Sheeta progressed so well that in a short time Mugambi ceased to be the object of his hungry attention, and the black felt a degree more of safety in his society.

To say that Mugambi was entirely happy or at ease in his new environment would not be to adhere strictly to the truth. His eyes were constantly rolling apprehensively from side to side as now one and now another of the fierce pack chanced to wander near him, so that for the most of the time it was principally the whites that showed.

Together Tarzan and Mugambi, with Sheeta and Akut, lay in wait at the ford for a deer, and when at a word from the ape-man the four of them leaped out upon the affrighted animal the black was sure that the poor creature died of fright before ever one of the great beasts touched it.

Mugambi built a fire and cooked his portion of the kill; but Tarzan, Sheeta, and Akut tore theirs, raw, with their sharp teeth, growling among themselves when one ventured to encroach upon the share of another.

It was not, after all, strange that the white man's ways should have been so much more nearly related to those of the beasts than were the savage blacks. We are, all of us, creatures of habit, and when the seeming necessity for schooling ourselves in new ways ceases to exist, we fall naturally and easily into the manners and customs which long usage has implanted ineradicably within us.

Mugambi from childhood had eaten no meat until it had been cooked, while Tarzan, on the other hand, had never tasted cooked food of any sort until he had grown almost to manhood, and only within the past three or four years had he eaten cooked meat. Not only did the habit of a lifetime prompt him to eat it raw, but the craving of his palate as well; for to him cooked flesh was spoiled flesh when compared with the rich and juicy meat of a fresh, hot kill.

That he could, with relish, eat raw meat that had been buried by himself weeks before, and enjoy small rodents and disgusting grubs, seems to us who have been always "civilized" a revolting fact; but had we learned in childhood to eat these things, and had we seen all those about us eat them, they would seem no more sickening to us now than do many of our greatest dainties, at which a savage African cannibal would look with repugnance and turn up his nose.

For instance, there is a tribe in the vicinity of Lake Rudolph that will eat no sheep or cattle, though its next neighbors do so. Near by is another tribe that eats donkey-meat – a custom most revolting to the surrounding tribes that do not eat donkey. So who may say that it is nice to eat snails and frogs' legs and oysters, but disgusting to feed upon grubs and beetles, or that a raw oyster, hoof, horns, and tail, is less revolting than the sweet, clean meat of a fresh-killed buck?

The next few days Tarzan devoted to the weaving of a barkcloth sail with which to equip the canoe, for he despaired of being able to teach the apes to wield the paddles, though he did manage to get several of them to embark in the frail craft which he and Mugambi paddled about inside the reef where the water was quite smooth.

During these trips he had placed paddles in their hands, when they attempted to imitate the movements of him and Mugambi, but so difficult is it for them long to concentrate upon a thing that he soon saw that it would require weeks of patient training before they would be able to make any effective use of these new implements, if, in fact, they should ever do so.

There was one exception, however, and he was Akut. Almost from the first he showed an interest in this new sport that revealed a much higher plane of intelligence than that attained by any of his tribe. He seemed to grasp the purpose of the paddles, and when Tarzan saw that this was so he took much pains to explain in the meagre language of the anthropoid how they might be used to the best advantage.

From Mugambi Tarzan learned that the mainland lay but a short distance from the island. It seemed that the Wagambi warriors had ventured too far out in their frail craft, and when caught by a heavy tide and a high wind from off-shore they had been driven out of sight of land. After paddling for a whole night, thinking that they were headed for home, they had seen this land at sunrise, and, still taking it for the mainland, had hailed it with joy, nor had Mugambi been aware that it was an island until Tarzan had told him that this was the fact.

The Wagambi chief was quite dubious as to the sail, for he had never seen such a contrivance used. His country lay far up the broad Ugambi River, and this was the first occasion that any of his people had found their way to the ocean.

Tarzan, however, was confident that with a good west wind he could navigate the little craft to the mainland. At any rate, he decided, it would be preferable to perish on the way than to remain indefinitely upon this evidently uncharted island to which no ships might ever be expected to come.

And so it was that when the first fair wind rose he embarked upon his cruise, and with him he took as strange and fearsome a crew as ever sailed under a savage master.

Mugambi and Akut went with him, and Sheeta, the panther, and a dozen great males of the tribe of Akut.

CHAPTER SIX

A Hideous Crew

THE WAR-CANOE with its savage load moved slowly toward the break in the reef through which it must pass to gain the open sea. Tarzan, Mugambi, and Akut wielded the paddles, for the shore kept the west wind from the little sail.

Sheeta crouched in the bow at the ape-man's feet, for it had seemed best to Tarzan always to keep the wicked beast as far from the other members of the party as possible, since it would require little or no provocation to send him at the throat of any than the white man, whom he evidently now looked upon as his master.

In the stern was Mugambi, and just in front of him squatted Akut, while between Akut and Tarzan the twelve hairy apes sat upon their haunches, blinking dubiously this way and that, and now and then turning their eyes longingly back toward shore.

All went well until the canoe had passed beyond the reef. Here the breeze struck the sail, sending the rude craft lunging among the waves that ran higher and higher as they drew away from the shore.

With the tossing of the boat the apes became panic-stricken. They first moved uneasily about, and then commenced grumbling and whining. With difficulty Akut kept them in hand for a time; but when a particularly large wave struck the dugout simultaneously with a little squall of wind their terror broke all bounds, and, leaping to their feet, they all but overturned the boat before Akut and Tarzan together could quiet them. At last calm was restored, and eventually the apes became accustomed to the strange antics of their craft, after which no more trouble was experienced with them.

The trip was uneventful, the wind held, and after ten hours' steady sailing the black shadows of the coast loomed close before the straining eyes of the ape-man in the bow. It was far too dark to distinguish whether they had approached close to the mouth of the Ugambi or not, so Tarzan ran in through the surf at the closest point to await the dawn.

The dugout turned broadside the instant that its nose touched the sand, and immediately it rolled over, with all its crew scrambling madly for the shore. The next breaker rolled them over and over, but eventually they all succeeded in crawling to safety, and in a moment more their ungainly craft had been washed up beside them.

The balance of the night the apes sat huddled close to one another for warmth; while Mugambi built a fire close to them over which he crouched. Tarzan and Sheeta, however, were of a different mind, for neither of them feared the jungle night, and the insistent craving of their hunger sent them off into the Stygian blackness of the forest in search of prey.

Side by side they walked when there was room for two abreast. At other times in single file, first one and then the other in advance. It was Tarzan who first caught the scent of meat – a bull buffalo – and presently the two came stealthily upon the sleeping beast in the midst of a dense jungle of reeds close to a river.

Closer and closer they crept toward the unsuspecting beast, Sheeta upon his right side and Tarzan upon his left nearest the great heart. They had hunted together now for some time, so that they worked in unison, with only low, purring sounds as signals.

For a moment they lay quite silent near their prey, and then at a sign from the ape-man Sheeta sprang upon the great back, burying his strong teeth in the bull's neck. Instantly the brute sprang to his feet with a bellow of pain and rage, and at the same instant Tarzan rushed in upon his left side with the stone knife, striking repeatedly behind the shoulder.

One of the ape-man's hands clutched the thick mane, and as the bull raced madly through the reeds the thing striking at his life was dragged beside him. Sheeta but clung tenaciously to his hold upon the neck and back, biting deep in an effort to reach the spine.

For several hundred yards the bellowing bull carried his two savage antagonists, until at last the blade found his heart, when with a final bellow that was half-scream he plunged headlong to the earth. Then Tarzan and Sheeta feasted to repletion.

After the meal the two curled up together in a thicket, the man's black head pillowed upon the tawny side of the panther. Shortly after dawn they awoke and ate again, and then returned to the beach that Tarzan might lead the balance of the pack to the kill.

When the meal was done the brutes were for curling up to sleep, so Tarzan and Mugambi set off in search of the Ugambi River. They had proceeded scarce a hundred yards when they came suddenly upon a broad stream, which the Negro instantly recognized as that down which he and his warriors had paddled to the sea upon their ill-starred expedition.

The two now followed the stream down to the ocean, finding that it emptied into a bay not over a mile from the point upon the beach at which the canoe had been thrown the night before.

Tarzan was much elated by the discovery, as he knew that in the vicinity of a large watercourse he should find natives, and from some of these he had little doubt but that he should obtain news of Rokoff and the child, for he felt reasonably certain that the Russian would rid himself of the baby as quickly as possible after having disposed of Tarzan.

He and Mugambi now righted and launched the dugout, though it was a most difficult feat in the face of the surf which rolled continuously in upon the beach; but at last they were successful, and soon after were paddling up the coast toward the mouth of the Ugambi. Here they experienced considerable difficulty in making an entrance against the combined current and ebb tide, but by taking advantage of eddies close in to shore they came about dusk to a point nearly opposite the spot where they had left the pack asleep.

Making the craft fast to an overhanging bough, the two made their way into the jungle, presently coming upon some of the apes feeding upon fruit a little beyond the reeds where the buffalo had fallen. Sheeta was not anywhere to be seen, nor did he return that night, so that Tarzan came to believe that he had wandered away in search of his own kind.

Early the next morning the ape-man led his band down to the river, and as he walked he gave vent to a series of shrill cries. Presently from a great distance and faintly there came an answering scream, and a half-hour later the lithe form of Sheeta bounded into view where the others of the pack were clambering gingerly into the canoe.

The great beast, with arched back and purring like a contented tabby, rubbed his sides against the ape-man, and then at a word from the latter sprang lightly to his former place in the bow of the dugout.

When all were in place it was discovered that two of the apes of Akut were missing, and though both the king ape and Tarzan called to them for the better part of an hour, there was no response, and finally the boat put off without them. As it happened that the two missing ones were the very same who had evinced the least desire to accompany the expedition from the island, and had suffered the most from fright during the voyage, Tarzan was quite sure that they had absented themselves purposely rather than again enter the canoe.

As the party were putting in for the shore shortly after noon to search for food a slender, naked savage watched them for a moment from behind the dense screen of verdure which lined the river's bank, then he melted away up-stream before any of those in the canoe discovered him.

Like a deer he bounded along the narrow trail until, filled with the excitement of his news, he burst into a native village several miles above the point at which Tarzan and his pack had stopped to hunt.

"Another white man is coming!" he cried to the chief who squatted before the entrance to his circular hut. "Another white man, and with him are many warriors. They come in a great war-canoe to kill and rob as did the black-bearded one who has just left us."

Kaviri leaped to his feet. He had but recently had a taste of the white man's medicine, and his savage heart was filled with bitterness and hate. In another moment the rumble of the war-drums rose from the village, calling in the hunters from the forest and the tillers from the fields.

Seven war-canoes were launched and manned by paint-daubed, befeathered warriors. Long spears bristled from the rude battle-ships, as they slid noiselessly over the bosom of the water, propelled by giant muscles rolling beneath glistening, ebony hides.

There was no beating of tom-toms now, nor blare of native horn, for Kaviri was a crafty warrior, and it was in his mind to take no chances, if they could be avoided. He would swoop noiselessly down with his seven canoes upon the single one of the white man, and before the guns of the latter could inflict much damage upon his people he would have overwhelmed the enemy by force of numbers.

Kaviri's own canoe went in advance of the others a short distance, and as it rounded a sharp bend in the river where the swift current bore it rapidly on its way it came suddenly upon the thing that Kaviri sought.

So close were the two canoes to one another that the black had only an opportunity to note the white face in the bow of the oncoming craft before the two touched and his own men were upon their feet, yelling like mad devils and thrusting their long spears at the occupants of the other canoe.

But a moment later, when Kaviri was able to realize the nature of the crew that manned the white man's dugout, he would have given all the beads and iron wire that he possessed to have been safely within his distant village. Scarcely had the two craft come together than the frightful apes of Akut rose, growling and barking, from the bottom of the canoe, and, with long, hairy arms far outstretched, grasped the menacing spears from the hands of Kaviri's warriors.

The blacks were overcome with terror, but there was nothing to do other than to fight. Now came the other war-canoes rapidly down upon the two craft. Their occupants were eager to join the battle, for they thought that their foes were white men and their native porters.

They swarmed about Tarzan's craft; but when they saw the nature of the enemy all but one turned and paddled swiftly up-river. That one came too close to the ape-man's craft before its occupants realized that their fellows were pitted against demons instead of men. As it touched Tarzan spoke a few low words to Sheeta and Akut, so that before the attacking warriors could draw away there sprang upon them with a blood-freezing scream a huge panther, and into the other end of their canoe clambered a great ape.

At one end the panther wrought fearful havoc with his mighty talons and long, sharp fangs, while Akut at the other buried his yellow canines in the necks of those that came within his reach, hurling the terror-stricken blacks overboard as he made his way toward the centre of the canoe.

Kaviri was so busily engaged with the demons that had entered his own craft that he could offer no assistance to his warriors in the other. A giant of a white devil had wrested his spear from him as though he, the mighty Kaviri, had been but a new-born babe. Hairy monsters were overcoming his fighting men, and a black chieftain like himself was fighting shoulder to shoulder with the hideous pack that opposed him.

Kaviri battled bravely against his antagonist, for he felt that death had already claimed him, and so the least that he could do would be to sell his life as dearly as possible; but it was soon evident that his best was quite futile when pitted against the superhuman brawn and agility of the creature that at last found his throat and bent him back into the bottom of the canoe.

Presently Kaviri's head began to whirl – objects became confused and dim before his eyes – there was a great pain in his chest as he struggled for the breath of life that the thing upon him was shutting off for ever. Then he lost consciousness.

When he opened his eyes once more he found, much to his surprise, that he was not dead. He lay, securely bound, in the bottom of his own canoe. A great panther sat upon its haunches, looking down upon him.

Kaviri shuddered and closed his eyes again, waiting for the ferocious creature to spring upon him and put him out of his misery of terror.

After a moment, no rending fangs having buried themselves in his trembling body, he again ventured to open his eyes. Beyond the panther kneeled the white giant who had overcome him.

The man was wielding a paddle, while directly behind him Kaviri saw some of his own warriors similarly engaged. Back of them again squatted several of the hairy apes.

Tarzan, seeing that the chief had regained consciousness, addressed him.

"Your warriors tell me that you are the chief of a numerous people, and that your name is Kaviri," he said.

"Yes," replied the black.

"Why did you attack me? I came in peace."

"Another white man 'came in peace' three moons ago," replied Kaviri; "and after we had brought him presents of a goat and cassava and milk, he set upon us with his guns and killed many of my people, and then went on his way, taking all of our goats and many of our young men and women."

"I am not as this other white man," replied Tarzan. "I should not have harmed you had you not set upon me. Tell me, what was the face of this bad white man like? I am searching for one who has wronged me. Possibly this may be the very one."

"He was a man with a bad face, covered with a great, black beard, and he was very, very wicked – yes, very wicked indeed."

"Was there a little white child with him?" asked Tarzan, his heart almost stopped as he awaited the black's answer.

"No, bwana," replied Kaviri, "the white child was not with this man's party – it was with the other party."

"Other party!" exclaimed Tarzan. "What other party?"

"With the party that the very bad white man was pursuing. There was a white man, woman, and the child, with six Mosula porters. They passed up the river three days ahead of the very bad white man. I think that they were running away from him."

A white man, woman, and child! Tarzan was puzzled. The child must be his little Jack; but who could the woman be – and the man? Was it possible that one of Rokoff's confederates had conspired with some woman – who had accompanied the Russian – to steal the baby from him?

If this was the case, they had doubtless purposed returning the child to civilization and there either claiming a reward or holding the little prisoner for ransom.

But now that Rokoff had succeeded in chasing them far inland, up the savage river, there could be little doubt but that he would eventually overhaul them, unless, as was still more probable, they should be captured and killed by the very cannibals farther up the Ugambi, to whom, Tarzan was now convinced, it had been Rokoff's intention to deliver the baby.

As he talked to Kaviri the canoes had been moving steadily upriver toward the chief's village. Kaviri's warriors plied the paddles in the three canoes, casting sidelong, terrified glances at their hideous passengers. Three of the apes of Akut had been killed in the encounter, but there were, with Akut, eight of the frightful beasts remaining, and there was Sheeta, the panther, and Tarzan and Mugambi.

Kaviri's warriors thought that they had never seen so terrible a crew in all their lives. Momentarily they expected to be pounced upon and torn asunder by some of their captors; and, in fact, it was all that Tarzan and Mugambi and Akut could do to keep the snarling, ill-natured brutes from snapping at the glistening, naked bodies that brushed against them now and then with the movements of the paddlers, whose very fear added incitement to the beasts.

At Kaviri's camp Tarzan paused only long enough to eat the food that the blacks furnished, and arrange with the chief for a dozen men to man the paddles of his canoe.

Kaviri was only too glad to comply with any demands that the ape-man might make if only such compliance would hasten the departure of the horrid pack; but it was easier, he discovered, to promise men than to furnish them, for when his people learned his intentions those that had not already fled into the jungle proceeded to do so without loss of time, so that when Kaviri turned to point out those who were to accompany Tarzan, he discovered that he was the only member of his tribe left within the village.

Tarzan could not repress a smile.

"They do not seem anxious to accompany us," he said; "but just remain quietly here, Kaviri, and presently you shall see your people flocking to your side."

Then the ape-man rose, and, calling his pack about him, commanded that Mugambi remain with Kaviri, and disappeared in the jungle with Sheeta and the apes at his heels.

For half an hour the silence of the grim forest was broken only by the ordinary sounds of the teeming life that but adds to its lowering loneliness. Kaviri and Mugambi sat alone in the palisaded village, waiting.

Presently from a great distance came a hideous sound. Mugambi recognized the weird challenge of the ape-man. Immediately from different points of the compass rose a horrid semicircle of similar shrieks and screams, punctuated now and again by the blood-curdling cry of a hungry panther.

CHAPTER SEVEN

Betrayed

THE TWO SAVAGES, Kaviri and Mugambi, squatting before the entrance to Kaviri's hut, looked at one another – Kaviri with ill-concealed alarm.

"What is it?" he whispered.

"It is Bwana Tarzan and his people," replied Mugambi. "But what they are doing I know not, unless it be that they are devouring your people who ran away."

Kaviri shuddered and rolled his eyes fearfully toward the jungle. In all his long life in the savage forest he had never heard such an awful, fearsome din.

Closer and closer came the sounds, and now with them were mingled the terrified shrieks of women and children and of men. For twenty long minutes the blood-curdling cries continued, until they seemed but a stone's throw from the palisade. Kaviri rose to flee, but Mugambi seized and held him, for such had been the command of Tarzan.

A moment later a horde of terrified natives burst from the jungle, racing toward the shelter of their huts. Like frightened sheep they ran, and behind them, driving them as sheep might be driven, came Tarzan and Sheeta and the hideous apes of Akut.

Presently Tarzan stood before Kaviri, the old quiet smile upon his lips.

"Your people have returned, my brother," he said, "and now you may select those who are to accompany me and paddle my canoe."

Tremblingly Kaviri tottered to his feet, calling to his people to come from their huts; but none responded to his summons.

"Tell them," suggested Tarzan, "that if they do not come I shall send my people in after them."

Kaviri did as he was bid, and in an instant the entire population of the village came forth, their wide and frightened eyes rolling from one to another of the savage creatures that wandered about the village street.

Quickly Kaviri designated a dozen warriors to accompany Tarzan. The poor fellows went almost white with terror at the prospect of close contact with the panther and the apes in the narrow confines of the canoes; but when Kaviri explained to them that there was no escape – that Bwana Tarzan would pursue them with his grim horde should they attempt to run away from the duty – they finally went gloomily down to the river and took their places in the canoe.

It was with a sigh of relief that their chieftain saw the party disappear about a headland a short distance up-river.

For three days the strange company continued farther and farther into the heart of the savage country that lies on either side of the almost unexplored Ugambi. Three of the twelve warriors deserted during that time; but as several of the apes had finally learned the secret of the paddles, Tarzan felt no dismay because of the loss.

As a matter of fact, he could have travelled much more rapidly on shore, but he believed that he could hold his own wild crew together to better advantage by keeping them to the boat as much as possible. Twice a day they landed to hunt and feed, and at night they slept upon the bank of the mainland or on one of the numerous little islands that dotted the river.

Before them the natives fled in alarm, so that they found only deserted villages in their path as they proceeded. Tarzan was anxious to get in touch with some of the savages who dwelt upon the river's banks, but so far he had been unable to do so.

Finally he decided to take to the land himself, leaving his company to follow after him by boat. He explained to Mugambi the thing that he had in mind, and told Akut to follow the directions of the black.

"I will join you again in a few days," he said. "Now I go ahead to learn what has become of the very bad white man whom I seek."

At the next halt Tarzan took to the shore, and was soon lost to the view of his people.

The first few villages he came to were deserted, showing that news of the coming of his pack had travelled rapidly; but toward evening he came upon a distant cluster of thatched huts surrounded by a rude palisade, within which were a couple of hundred natives.

The women were preparing the evening meal as Tarzan of the Apes poised above them in the branches of a giant tree which overhung the palisade at one point.

The ape-man was at a loss as to how he might enter into communication with these people without either frightening them or arousing their savage love of battle. He had no desire to fight now, for he was upon a much more important mission than that of battling with every chance tribe that he should happen to meet with.

At last he hit upon a plan, and after seeing that he was concealed from the view of those below, he gave a few hoarse grunts in imitation of a panther. All eyes immediately turned upward toward the foliage above.

It was growing dark, and they could not penetrate the leafy screen which shielded the ape-man from their view. The moment that he had won their attention he raised his voice to the shriller and more hideous scream of the beast he personated, and then, scarce stirring a leaf in his descent, dropped to the ground once again outside the palisade, and, with the speed of a deer, ran quickly round to the village gate.

Here he beat upon the fibre-bound saplings of which the barrier was constructed, shouting to the natives in their own tongue that he was a friend who wished food and shelter for the night.

Tarzan knew well the nature of the black man. He was aware that the grunting and screaming of Sheeta in the tree above them would set their nerves on edge, and that his pounding upon their gate after dark would still further add to their terror.

That they did not reply to his hail was no surprise, for natives are fearful of any voice that comes out of the night from beyond their palisades, attributing it always to some demon or other ghostly visitor; but still he continued to call.

"Let me in, my friends!" he cried. "I am a white man pursuing the very bad white man who passed this way a few days ago. I follow to punish him for the sins he has committed against you and me.

"If you doubt my friendship, I will prove it to you by going into the tree above your village and driving Sheeta back into the jungle before he leaps among you. If you will not promise to take me in and treat me as a friend I shall let Sheeta stay and devour you."

For a moment there was silence. Then the voice of an old man came out of the quiet of the village street.

"If you are indeed a white man and a friend, we will let you come in; but first you must drive Sheeta away."

"Very well," replied Tarzan. "Listen, and you shall hear Sheeta fleeing before me."

The ape-man returned quickly to the tree, and this time he made a great noise as he entered the branches, at the same time growling ominously after the manner of the panther, so that those below would believe that the great beast was still there.

When he reached a point well above the village street he made a great commotion, shaking the tree violently, crying aloud to the panther to flee or be killed, and punctuating his own voice with the screams and mouthings of an angry beast.

Presently he raced toward the opposite side of the tree and off into the jungle, pounding loudly against the boles of trees as he went, and voicing the panther's diminishing growls as he drew farther and farther away from the village.

A few minutes later he returned to the village gate, calling to the natives within.

"I have driven Sheeta away," he said. "Now come and admit me as you promised."

For a time there was the sound of excited discussion within the palisade, but at length a half-dozen warriors came and opened the gates, peering anxiously out in evident trepidation as to the nature of the creature which they should find waiting there. They were not much relieved at sight of an almost naked white man; but when Tarzan had reassured them in quiet tones, protesting his friendship for them, they opened the barrier a trifle farther and admitted him.

When the gates had been once more secured the self-confidence of the savages returned, and as Tarzan walked up the village street toward the chief's hut he was surrounded by a host of curious men, women, and children.

From the chief he learned that Rokoff had passed up the river a week previous, and that he had horns growing from his forehead, and was accompanied by a thousand devils. Later the chief said that the very bad white man had remained a month in his village.

Though none of these statements agreed with Kaviri's, that the Russian was but three days gone from the chieftain's village and that his following was much smaller than now stated, Tarzan was in no manner surprised at the discrepancies, for he was quite familiar with the savage mind's strange manner of functioning.

What he was most interested in knowing was that he was upon the right trail, and that it led toward the interior. In this circumstance he knew that Rokoff could never escape him.

After several hours of questioning and cross-questioning the ape-man learned that another party had preceded the Russian by several days – three whites – a man, a woman, and a little man-child, with several Mosulas.

Tarzan explained to the chief that his people would follow him in a canoe, probably the next day, and that though he might go on ahead of them the chief was to receive them kindly and have no fear of them, for Mugambi would see that they did not harm the chief's people, if they were accorded a friendly reception.

"And now," he concluded, "I shall lie down beneath this tree and sleep. I am very tired. Permit no one to disturb me."

The chief offered him a hut, but Tarzan, from past experience of native dwellings, preferred the open air, and, further, he had plans of his own that could be better carried out if he remained beneath the tree. He gave as his reason a desire to be close at hand should Sheeta return, and after this explanation the chief was very glad to permit him to sleep beneath the tree.

Tarzan had always found that it stood him in good stead to leave with natives the impression that he was to some extent possessed of more or less miraculous powers. He might easily have entered their village without recourse to the gates, but he believed that a sudden and unaccountable disappearance when he was ready to leave them would result in a more lasting impression upon their childlike minds, and so as soon as the village was quiet in sleep he rose, and, leaping into the branches of the tree above him, faded silently into the black mystery of the jungle night.

All the balance of that night the ape-man swung rapidly through the upper and middle terraces of the forest. When the going was good there he preferred the upper branches of the giant trees, for then his way was better lighted by the moon; but so accustomed were all his senses to the grim world of his birth that it was possible for him, even in the dense, black shadows near the ground, to move with ease and rapidity. You or I walking beneath the arcs of Main Street, or Broadway, or State Street, could not have moved more surely or with a tenth the speed of the agile ape-man through the gloomy mazes that would have baffled us entirely.

At dawn he stopped to feed, and then he slept for several hours, taking up the pursuit again toward noon.

Twice he came upon natives, and, though he had considerable difficulty in approaching them, he succeeded in each instance in quieting both their fears and bellicose intentions toward him, and learned from them that he was upon the trail of the Russian.

Two days later, still following up the Ugambi, he came upon a large village. The chief, a wicked-looking fellow with the sharp-filed teeth that often denote the cannibal, received him with apparent friendliness.

The ape-man was now thoroughly fatigued, and had determined to rest for eight or ten hours that he might be fresh and strong when he caught up with Rokoff, as he was sure he must do within a very short time.

The chief told him that the bearded white man had left his village only the morning before, and that doubtless he would be able to overtake him in a short time. The other party the chief had not seen or heard of, so he said.

Tarzan did not like the appearance or manner of the fellow, who seemed, though friendly enough, to harbour a certain contempt for this half-naked white man who came with no followers and offered no presents; but he needed the rest and food that the village would afford him with less effort than the jungle, and so, as he knew no fear of man, beast, or devil, he curled himself up in the shadow of a hut and was soon asleep.

Scarcely had he left the chief than the latter called two of his warriors, to whom he whispered a few instructions. A moment later the sleek, black bodies were racing along the river path, up-stream, toward the east.

In the village the chief maintained perfect quiet. He would permit no one to approach the sleeping visitor, nor any singing, nor loud talking. He was remarkably solicitous lest his guest be disturbed.

Three hours later several canoes came silently into view from up the Ugambi. They were being pushed ahead rapidly by the brawny muscles of their black crews. Upon the bank before the river stood the chief, his spear raised in a horizontal position above his head, as though in some manner of predetermined signal to those within the boats.

And such indeed was the purpose of his attitude – which meant that the white stranger within his village still slept peacefully.

In the bows of two of the canoes were the runners that the chief had sent forth three hours earlier. It was evident that they had been dispatched to follow and bring back this party, and that the signal from the bank was one that had been determined upon before they left the village.

In a few moments the dugouts drew up to the verdure-clad bank. The native warriors filed out, and with them a half-dozen white men. Sullen, ugly-looking customers they were, and none more so than the evil-faced, black-bearded man who commanded them.

"Where is the white man your messengers report to be with you?" he asked of the chief.

"This way, bwana," replied the native. "Carefully have I kept silence in the village that he might be still asleep when you returned. I do not know that he is one who seeks you to do you harm, but he questioned me closely about your coming and your going, and his appearance is as that of the one you described, but whom you believed safe in the country which you called Jungle Island.

"Had you not told me this tale I should not have recognized him, and then he might have gone after and slain you. If he is a friend and no enemy, then no harm has been done, bwana; but if he proves to be an enemy, I should like very much to have a rifle and some ammunition."

"You have done well," replied the white man, "and you shall have the rifle and ammunition whether he be a friend or enemy, provided that you stand with me."

"I shall stand with you, bwana," said the chief, "and now come and look upon the stranger, who sleeps within my village."

So saying, he turned and led the way toward the hut, in the shadow of which the unconscious Tarzan slept peacefully.

Behind the two men came the remaining whites and a score of warriors; but the raised forefingers of the chief and his companion held them all to perfect silence.

As they turned the corner of the hut, cautiously and upon tiptoe, an ugly smile touched the lips of the white as his eyes fell upon the giant figure of the sleeping ape-man.

The chief looked at the other inquiringly. The latter nodded his head, to signify that the chief had made no mistake in his suspicions. Then he turned to those behind him and, pointing to the sleeping man, motioned for them to seize and bind him.

A moment later a dozen brutes had leaped upon the surprised Tarzan, and so quickly did they work that he was securely bound before he could make half an effort to escape.

Then they threw him down upon his back, and as his eyes turned toward the crowd that stood near, they fell upon the malign face of Nikolas Rokoff.

A sneer curled the Russian's lips. He stepped quite close to Tarzan.

"Pig!" he cried. "Have you not learned sufficient wisdom to keep away from Nikolas Rokoff?"

Then he kicked the prostrate man full in the face.

"That for your welcome," he said.

"Tonight, before my Ethiop friends eat you, I shall tell you what has already befallen your wife and child, and what further plans I have for their futures."

CHAPTER EIGHT

The Dance of Death

THROUGH THE LUXURIANT, tangled vegetation of the Stygian jungle night a great lithe body made its way sinuously and in utter silence upon its soft padded feet. Only two blazing points of yellow-green flame shone occasionally with the reflected light of the equatorial moon that now and again pierced the softly sighing roof rustling in the night wind.

Occasionally the beast would stop with high-held nose, sniffing searchingly. At other times a quick, brief incursion into the branches above delayed it momentarily in its steady journey toward the east. To its sensitive nostrils came the subtle unseen spoor of many a tender four-footed creature, bringing the slaver of hunger to the cruel, drooping jowl.

But steadfastly it kept on its way, strangely ignoring the cravings of appetite that at another time would have sent the rolling, fur-clad muscles flying at some soft throat.

All that night the creature pursued its lonely way, and the next day it halted only to make a single kill, which it tore to fragments and devoured with sullen, grumbling rumbles as though half famished for lack of food.

It was dusk when it approached the palisade that surrounded a large native village. Like the shadow of a swift and silent death it circled the village, nose to ground, halting at last close to the palisade, where it almost touched the backs of several huts. Here the beast sniffed for a moment, and then, turning its head upon one side, listened with up-pricked ears.

What it heard was no sound by the standards of human ears, yet to the highly attuned and delicate organs of the beast a message seemed to be borne to the savage brain. A wondrous transformation was wrought in the motionless mass of statuesque bone and muscle that had an instant before stood as though carved out of the living bronze.

As if it had been poised upon steel springs, suddenly released, it rose quickly and silently to the top of the palisade, disappearing, stealthily and cat-like, into the dark space between the wall and the back of an adjacent hut.

In the village street beyond women were preparing many little fires and fetching cooking-pots filled with water, for a great feast was to be celebrated ere the night was many hours older. About a stout stake near the centre of the circling fires a little knot of black warriors stood conversing, their bodies smeared with white and blue and ochre in broad and grotesque bands. Great circles of colour were drawn about their eyes and lips, their breasts and abdomens, and from their clay-plastered coiffures rose gay feathers and bits of long, straight wire.

The village was preparing for the feast, while in a hut at one side of the scene of the coming orgy the bound victim of their bestial appetites lay waiting for the end. And such an end!

Tarzan of the Apes, tensing his mighty muscles, strained at the bonds that pinioned him; but they had been re-enforced many times at the instigation of the Russian, so that not even the ape-man's giant brawn could budge them.

Death!

Tarzan had looked the Hideous Hunter in the face many a time, and smiled. And he would smile again tonight when he knew the end was coming quickly; but now his thoughts were not of himself, but of those others – the dear ones who must suffer most because of his passing.

Jane would never know the manner of it. For that he thanked Heaven; and he was thankful also that she at least was safe in the heart of the world's greatest city. Safe among kind and loving friends who would do their best to lighten her misery.

But the boy!

Tarzan writhed at the thought of him. His son! And now he – the mighty Lord of the Jungle – he, Tarzan, King of the Apes, the only one in all the world fitted to find and save the child from the horrors that Rokoff's evil mind had planned – had been trapped like a silly, dumb creature. He was to die in a few hours, and with him would go the child's last chance of succour.

Rokoff had been in to see and revile and abuse him several times during the afternoon; but he had been able to wring no word of remonstrance or murmur of pain from the lips of the giant captive.

So at last he had given up, reserving his particular bit of exquisite mental torture for the last moment, when, just before the savage spears of the cannibals should for ever make the object of his hatred immune to further suffering, the Russian planned to reveal to his enemy the true whereabouts of his wife whom he thought safe in England.

Dusk had fallen upon the village, and the ape-man could hear the preparations going forward for the torture and the feast. The dance of death he could picture in his mind's eye – for he had seen the thing many times in the past. Now he was to be the central figure, bound to the stake.

The torture of the slow death as the circling warriors cut him to bits with the fiendish skill, that mutilated without bringing unconsciousness, had no terrors for him. He was inured to suffering and to the sight of blood and to cruel death; but the desire to live was no less strong within him, and until the last spark of life should flicker and go out, his whole being would remain quick with hope and determination. Let them relax their watchfulness but for an instant, he knew that his cunning mind and giant muscles would find a way to escape – escape and revenge.

As he lay, thinking furiously on every possibility of self-salvation, there came to his sensitive nostrils a faint and a familiar scent. Instantly every faculty of his mind was upon the alert. Presently his trained ears caught the sound of the soundless presence without – behind the hut wherein he lay. His lips moved, and though no sound came forth that might have been appreciable to a human ear beyond the walls of his prison, yet he realized that the one beyond would hear. Already he knew who that one was, for his nostrils had told him as plainly as your eyes or mine tell us of the identity of an old friend whom we come upon in broad daylight.

An instant later he heard the soft sound of a fur-clad body and padded feet scaling the outer wall behind the hut and then a tearing at the poles which formed the wall. Presently through the hole thus made slunk a great beast, pressing its cold muzzle close to his neck.

It was Sheeta, the panther.

The beast snuffed round the prostrate man, whining a little. There was a limit to the interchange of ideas which could take place between these two, and so Tarzan could not be sure that Sheeta understood all that he attempted to communicate to him. That the man was tied and helpless Sheeta could, of course, see; but that to the mind of the panther this would carry any suggestion of harm in so far as his master was concerned, Tarzan could not guess.

What had brought the beast to him? The fact that he had come augured well for what he might accomplish; but when Tarzan tried to get Sheeta to gnaw his bonds asunder the great animal could not seem to understand what was expected of him, and, instead, but licked the wrists and arms of the prisoner.

Presently there came an interruption. Some one was approaching the hut. Sheeta gave a low growl and slunk into the blackness of a far corner. Evidently the visitor did not hear the warning sound, for almost immediately he entered the hut – a tall, naked, savage warrior.

He came to Tarzan's side and pricked him with a spear. From the lips of the ape-man came a weird, uncanny sound, and in answer to it there leaped from the blackness of the hut's farthermost corner a bolt of fur-clad death. Full upon the breast of the painted savage the great beast struck, burying sharp talons in the black flesh and sinking great yellow fangs in the ebon throat.

There was a fearful scream of anguish and terror from the black, and mingled with it was the hideous challenge of the killing panther. Then came silence – silence except for the rending of bloody flesh and the crunching of human bones between mighty jaws.

The noise had brought sudden quiet to the village without. Then there came the sound of voices in consultation.

High-pitched, fear-filled voices, and deep, low tones of authority, as the chief spoke. Tarzan and the panther heard the approaching footsteps of many men, and then, to Tarzan's surprise, the great cat rose from across the body of its kill, and slunk noiselessly from the hut through the aperture through which it had entered.

The man heard the soft scraping of the body as it passed over the top of the palisade, and then silence. From the opposite side of the hut he heard the savages approaching to investigate.

He had little hope that Sheeta would return, for had the great cat intended to defend him against all comers it would have remained by his side as it heard the approaching savages without.

Tarzan knew how strange were the workings of the brains of the mighty carnivora of the jungle – how fiendishly fearless they might be in the face of certain death, and again how timid upon the slightest provocation. There was doubt in his mind that some note of the approaching blacks vibrating with fear had struck an answering chord in the nervous system of the panther, sending him slinking through the jungle, his tail between his legs.

The man shrugged. Well, what of it? He had expected to die, and, after all, what might Sheeta have done for him other than to maul a couple of his enemies before a rifle in the hands of one of the whites should have dispatched him!

If the cat could have released him! Ah! that would have resulted in a very different story; but it had proved beyond the understanding of Sheeta, and now the beast was gone and Tarzan must definitely abandon hope.

The natives were at the entrance to the hut now, peering fearfully into the dark interior. Two in advance held lighted torches in their left hands and ready spears in their right. They held back timorously against those behind, who were pushing them forward.

The shrieks of the panther's victim, mingled with those of the great cat, had wrought mightily upon their poor nerves, and now the awful silence of the dark interior seemed even more terribly ominous than had the frightful screaming.

Presently one of those who was being forced unwillingly within hit upon a happy scheme for learning first the precise nature of the danger which menaced him from the silent interior. With a quick movement he flung his lighted torch into the centre of the hut. Instantly all within was illuminated for a brief second before the burning brand was dashed out against the earth floor.

There was the figure of the white prisoner still securely bound as they had last seen him, and in the centre of the hut another figure equally as motionless, its throat and breasts horribly torn and mangled.

The sight that met the eyes of the foremost savages inspired more terror within their superstitious breasts than would the presence of Sheeta, for they saw only the result of a ferocious attack upon one of their fellows.

Not seeing the cause, their fear-ridden minds were free to attribute the ghastly work to supernatural causes, and with the thought they turned, screaming, from the hut, bowling over those who stood directly behind them in the exuberance of their terror.

For an hour Tarzan heard only the murmur of excited voices from the far end of the village. Evidently the savages were once more attempting to work up their flickering courage to a point that would permit them to make another invasion of the hut, for now and then came a savage yell, such as the warriors give to bolster up their bravery upon the field of battle.

But in the end it was two of the whites who first entered, carrying torches and guns. Tarzan was not surprised to discover that neither of them was Rokoff. He would have wagered his soul that no power on earth could have tempted that great coward to face the unknown menace of the hut.

When the natives saw that the white men were not attacked they, too, crowded into the interior, their voices hushed with terror as they looked upon the mutilated corpse of their comrade. The whites tried in vain to elicit an explanation from Tarzan; but to all their queries he but shook his head, a grim and knowing smile curving his lips.

At last Rokoff came.

His face grew very white as his eyes rested upon the bloody thing grinning up at him from the floor, the face set in a death mask of excruciating horror.

"Come!" he said to the chief. "Let us get to work and finish this demon before he has an opportunity to repeat this thing upon more of your people."

The chief gave orders that Tarzan should be lifted and carried to the stake; but it was several minutes before he could prevail upon any of his men to touch the prisoner.

At last, however, four of the younger warriors dragged Tarzan roughly from the hut, and once outside the pall of terror seemed lifted from the savage hearts.

A score of howling blacks pushed and buffeted the prisoner down the village street and bound him to the post in the centre of the circle of little fires and boiling cooking-pots.

When at last he was made fast and seemed quite helpless and beyond the faintest hope of succour, Rokoff's shrivelled wart of courage swelled to its usual proportions when danger was not present.

He stepped close to the ape-man, and, seizing a spear from the hands of one of the savages, was the first to prod the helpless victim. A little stream of blood trickled down the giant's smooth skin from the wound in his side; but no murmur of pain passed his lips.

The smile of contempt upon his face seemed to infuriate the Russian. With a volley of oaths he leaped at the helpless captive, beating him upon the face with his clenched fists and kicking him mercilessly about the legs.

Then he raised the heavy spear to drive it through the mighty heart, and still Tarzan of the Apes smiled contemptuously upon him.

Before Rokoff could drive the weapon home the chief sprang upon him and dragged him away from his intended victim.

"Stop, white man!" he cried. "Rob us of this prisoner and our death-dance, and you yourself may have to take his place."

The threat proved most effective in keeping the Russian from further assaults upon the prisoner, though he continued to stand a little apart and hurl taunts at his enemy. He told Tarzan that he himself was going to eat the ape-man's heart. He enlarged upon the horrors of the future life of Tarzan's son, and intimated that his vengeance would reach as well to Jane Clayton.

"You think your wife safe in England," said Rokoff. "Poor fool! She is even now in the hands of one not even of decent birth, and far from the safety of London and the protection of her friends. I had not meant to tell you this until I could bring to you upon Jungle Island proof of her fate.

"Now that you are about to die the most unthinkably horrid death that it is given a white man to die – let this word of the plight of your wife add to the torments that you must suffer before the last savage spear-thrust releases you from your torture."

The dance had commenced now, and the yells of the circling warriors drowned Rokoff's further attempts to distress his victim.

The leaping savages, the flickering firelight playing upon their painted bodies, circled about the victim at the stake.

To Tarzan's memory came a similar scene, when he had rescued D'Arnot from a like predicament at the last moment before the final spear-thrust should have ended his sufferings. Who was there now to rescue him? In all the world there was none able to save him from the torture and the death.

The thought that these human fiends would devour him when the dance was done caused him not a single qualm of horror or disgust. It did not add to his sufferings as it would have to those of an ordinary white man, for all his life Tarzan had seen the beasts of the jungle devour the flesh of their kills.

Had he not himself battled for the grisly forearm of a great ape at that long-gone Dum-Dum, when he had slain the fierce Tublat and won his niche in the respect of the Apes of Kerchak?

The dancers were leaping more closely to him now. The spears were commencing to find his body in the first torturing pricks that prefaced the more serious thrusts.

It would not be long now. The ape-man longed for the last savage lunge that would end his misery.

And then, far out in the mazes of the weird jungle, rose a shrill scream.

For an instant the dancers paused, and in the silence of the interval there rose from the lips of the fast-bound white man an answering shriek, more fearsome and more terrible than that of the jungle-beast that had roused it.

For several minutes the blacks hesitated; then, at the urging of Rokoff and their chief, they leaped in to finish the dance and the victim; but ere ever another spear touched the brown hide a tawny streak of green-eyed hate and ferocity bounded from the door of the hut in which Tarzan had been imprisoned, and Sheeta, the panther, stood snarling beside his master.

For an instant the blacks and the whites stood transfixed with terror. Their eyes were riveted upon the bared fangs of the jungle cat.

Only Tarzan of the Apes saw what else there was emerging from the dark interior of the hut.

CHAPTER NINE

Chivalry or Villainy

FROM HER CABIN PORT upon the Kincaid, Jane Clayton had seen her husband rowed to the verdure-clad shore of Jungle Island, and then the ship once more proceeded upon its way.

For several days she saw no one other than Sven Anderssen, the Kincaid's taciturn and repellent cook. She asked him the name of the shore upon which her husband had been set.

"Ay tank it blow purty soon purty hard," replied the Swede, and that was all that she could get out of him.

She had come to the conclusion that he spoke no other English, and so she ceased to importune him for information; but never did she forget to greet him pleasantly or to thank him for the hideous, nauseating meals he brought her.

Three days from the spot where Tarzan had been marooned the Kincaid came to anchor in the mouth of a great river, and presently Rokoff came to Jane Clayton's cabin.

"We have arrived, my dear," he said, with a sickening leer. "I have come to offer you safety, liberty, and ease. My heart has been softened toward you in your suffering, and I would make amends as best I may.

"Your husband was a brute – you know that best who found him naked in his native jungle, roaming wild with the savage beasts that were his fellows. Now I am a gentleman, not only born of noble blood, but raised gently as befits a man of quality.

"To you, dear Jane, I offer the love of a cultured man and association with one of culture and refinement, which you must have sorely missed in your relations with the poor ape that through your girlish infatuation you married so thoughtlessly. I love you, Jane. You have but to say the word and no further sorrows shall afflict you – even your baby shall be returned to you unharmed."

Outside the door Sven Anderssen paused with the noonday meal he had been carrying to Lady Greystoke. Upon the end of his long, stringy neck his little head was cocked to one side, his close-set eyes were half closed, his ears, so expressive was his whole attitude of stealthy eavesdropping, seemed truly to be cocked forward – even his long, yellow, straggly moustache appeared to assume a sly droop.

As Rokoff closed his appeal, awaiting the reply he invited, the look of surprise upon Jane Clayton's face turned to one of disgust. She fairly shuddered in the fellow's face.

"I would not have been surprised, M. Rokoff," she said, "had you attempted to force me to submit to your evil desires, but that you should be so fatuous as to believe that I, wife of John Clayton, would come to you willingly, even to save my life, I should never have imagined. I have known you for a scoundrel, M. Rokoff; but until now I had not taken you for a fool."

Rokoff's eyes narrowed, and the red of mortification flushed out the pallor of his face. He took a step toward the girl, threateningly.

"We shall see who is the fool at last," he hissed, "when I have broken you to my will and your plebeian Yankee stubbornness has cost you all that you hold dear – even the life of your baby – for, by the bones of St. Peter, I'll forego all that I had planned for the brat and cut its heart out before your very eyes. You'll learn what it means to insult Nikolas Rokoff."

Jane Clayton turned wearily away.

"What is the use," she said, "of expatiating upon the depths to which your vengeful nature can sink? You cannot move me either by threats or deeds. My baby cannot judge yet for himself, but I, his mother, can foresee that should it have been given him to survive to man's estate he would willingly sacrifice his life for the honour of his mother. Love him as I do, I would not purchase his life at such a price. Did I, he would execrate my memory to the day of his death."

Rokoff was now thoroughly angered because of his failure to reduce the girl to terror. He felt only hate for her, but it had come to his diseased mind that if he could force her to accede to his demands as the price of her life and her child's, the cup of his revenge would be filled to brimming when he could flaunt the wife of Lord Greystoke in the capitals of Europe as his mistress.

Again he stepped closer to her. His evil face was convulsed with rage and desire. Like a wild beast he sprang upon her, and with his strong fingers at her throat forced her backward upon the berth.

At the same instant the door of the cabin opened noisily. Rokoff leaped to his feet, and, turning, faced the Swede cook.

Into the fellow's usually foxy eyes had come an expression of utter stupidity. His lower jaw drooped in vacuous harmony. He busied himself in arranging Lady Greystoke's meal upon the tiny table at one side of her cabin.

The Russian glared at him.

"What do you mean," he cried, "by entering here without permission? Get out!"

The cook turned his watery blue eyes upon Rokoff and smiled vacuously.

"Ay tank it blow purty soon purty hard," he said, and then he began rearranging the few dishes upon the little table.

"Get out of here, or I'll throw you out, you miserable blockhead!" roared Rokoff, taking a threatening step toward the Swede.

Anderssen continued to smile foolishly in his direction, but one ham-like paw slid stealthily to the handle of the long, slim knife that protruded from the greasy cord supporting his soiled apron.

Rokoff saw the move and stopped short in his advance. Then he turned toward Jane Clayton.

"I will give you until tomorrow," he said, "to reconsider your answer to my offer. All will be sent ashore upon one pretext or another except you and the child, Paulvitch and myself. Then without interruption you will be able to witness the death of the baby."

He spoke in French that the cook might not understand the sinister portent of his words. When he had done he banged out of the cabin without another look at the man who had interrupted him in his sorry work.

When he had gone, Sven Anderssen turned toward Lady Greystoke – the idiotic expression that had masked his thoughts had fallen away, and in its place was one of craft and cunning.

"Hay tank Ay ban a fool," he said. "Hay ben the fool. Ay savvy Franch."

Jane Clayton looked at him in surprise.

"You understood all that he said, then?"

Anderssen grinned.

"You bat," he said.

"And you heard what was going on in here and came to protect me?"

"You bane good to me," explained the Swede. "Hay treat me like darty dog. Ay help you, lady. You yust vait – Ay help you. Ay ban Vast Coast lots times."

"But how can you help me, Sven," she asked, "when all these men will be against us?"

"Ay tank," said Sven Anderssen, "it blow purty soon purty hard," and then he turned and left the cabin.

Though Jane Clayton doubted the cook's ability to be of any material service to her, she was nevertheless deeply grateful to him for what he already had done. The feeling that among these enemies she had one friend brought the first ray of comfort that had come to lighten the burden of her miserable apprehensions throughout the long voyage of the Kincaid.

She saw no more of Rokoff that day, nor of any other until Sven came with her evening meal. She tried to draw him into conversation relative to his plans to aid her, but all that she could get from him was his stereotyped prophecy as to the future state of the wind. He seemed suddenly to have relapsed into his wonted state of dense stupidity.

However, when he was leaving her cabin a little later with the empty dishes he whispered very low, "Leave on your clothes an' roll up your blankets. Ay come back after you purty soon."

He would have slipped from the room at once, but Jane laid her hand upon his sleeve.

"My baby?" she asked. "I cannot go without him."

"You do wot Ay tal you," said Anderssen, scowling. "Ay ban halpin' you, so don't you gat too fonny."

When he had gone Jane Clayton sank down upon her berth in utter bewilderment. What was she to do? Suspicions as to the intentions of the Swede swarmed her brain. Might she not be infinitely worse off if she gave herself into his power than she already was?

No, she could be no worse off in company with the devil himself than with Nikolas Rokoff, for the devil at least bore the reputation of being a gentleman.

She swore a dozen times that she would not leave the Kincaid without her baby, and yet she remained clothed long past her usual hour for retiring, and her blankets were neatly rolled and bound with stout cord, when about midnight there came a stealthy scratching upon the panels of her door.

Swiftly she crossed the room and drew the bolt. Softly the door swung open to admit the muffled figure of the Swede. On one arm he carried a bundle, evidently his blankets. His other hand was raised in a gesture commanding silence, a grimy forefinger upon his lips.

He came quite close to her.

"Carry this," he said. "Do not make some noise when you see it. It ban your kid."

Quick hands snatched the bundle from the cook, and hungry mother arms folded the sleeping infant to her breast, while hot tears of joy ran down her cheeks and her whole frame shook with the emotion of the moment.

"Come!" said Anderssen. "We got no time to vaste."

He snatched up her bundle of blankets, and outside the cabin door his own as well. Then he led her to the ship's side, steadied her descent of the monkey-ladder, holding the child for her as she climbed to the waiting boat below. A moment later he had cut the rope that held the small boat to the steamer's side, and, bending silently to the muffled oars, was pulling toward the black shadows up the Ugambi River.

Anderssen rowed on as though quite sure of his ground, and when after half an hour the moon broke through the clouds there was revealed upon their left the mouth of a tributary running into the Ugambi. Up this narrow channel the Swede turned the prow of the small boat.

Jane Clayton wondered if the man knew where he was bound. She did not know that in his capacity as cook he had that day been rowed up this very stream to a little village where he had bartered with the natives for such provisions as they had for sale, and that he had there arranged the details of his plan for the adventure upon which they were now setting forth.

Even though the moon was full, the surface of the small river was quite dark. The giant trees overhung its narrow banks, meeting in a great arch above the centre of the river. Spanish moss dropped from the gracefully bending limbs, and enormous creepers clambered in riotous profusion from the ground to the loftiest branch, falling in curving loops almost to the water's placid breast.

Now and then the river's surface would be suddenly broken ahead of them by a huge crocodile, startled by the splashing of the oars, or, snorting and blowing, a family of hippos would dive from a sandy bar to the cool, safe depths of the bottom.

From the dense jungles upon either side came the weird night cries of the carnivora – the maniacal voice of the hyena, the coughing grunt of the panther, the deep and awful roar of the lion. And with them strange, uncanny notes that the girl could not ascribe to any particular night prowler – more terrible because of their mystery.

Huddled in the stern of the boat she sat with her baby strained close to her bosom, and because of that little tender, helpless thing she was happier tonight than she had been for many a sorrow-ridden day.

Even though she knew not to what fate she was going, or how soon that fate might overtake her, still was she happy and thankful for the moment, however brief, that she might press her baby tightly in her arms. She could scarce wait for the coming of the day that she might look again upon the bright face of her little, black-eyed Jack.

Again and again she tried to strain her eyes through the blackness of the jungle night to have but a tiny peep at those beloved features, but only the dim outline of the baby face rewarded her efforts. Then once more she would cuddle the warm, little bundle close to her throbbing heart.

It must have been close to three o'clock in the morning that Anderssen brought the boat's nose to the shore before a clearing where could be dimly seen in the waning moonlight a cluster of native huts encircled by a thorn boma.

At the village gate they were admitted by a native woman, the wife of the chief whom Anderssen had paid to assist him. She took them to the chief's hut, but Anderssen said that they would sleep without upon the ground, and so, her duty having been completed, she left them to their own devices.

The Swede, after explaining in his gruff way that the huts were doubtless filthy and vermin-ridden, spread Jane's blankets on the ground for her, and at a little distance unrolled his own and lay down to sleep.

It was some time before the girl could find a comfortable position upon the hard ground, but at last, the baby in the hollow of her arm, she dropped asleep from utter exhaustion. When she awoke it was broad daylight.

About her were clustered a score of curious natives – mostly men, for among the aborigines it is the male who owns this characteristic in its most exaggerated form. Instinctively Jane Clayton drew the baby more closely to her, though she soon saw that the blacks were far from intending her or the child any harm.

In fact, one of them offered her a gourd of milk – a filthy, smoke-begrimed gourd, with the ancient rind of long-curdled milk caked in layers within its neck; but the spirit of the giver touched her deeply, and her face lightened for a moment with one of those almost forgotten smiles of radiance that had helped to make her beauty famous both in Baltimore and London.

She took the gourd in one hand, and rather than cause the giver pain raised it to her lips, though for the life of her she could scarce restrain the qualm of nausea that surged through her as the malodorous thing approached her nostrils.

It was Anderssen who came to her rescue, and taking the gourd from her, drank a portion himself, and then returned it to the native with a gift of blue beads.

The sun was shining brightly now, and though the baby still slept, Jane could scarce restrain her impatient desire to have at least a brief glance at the beloved face. The natives had withdrawn at a command from their chief, who now stood talking with Anderssen, a little apart from her.

As she debated the wisdom of risking disturbing the child's slumber by lifting the blanket that now protected its face from the sun, she noted that the cook conversed with the chief in the language of the Negro.

What a remarkable man the fellow was, indeed! She had thought him ignorant and stupid but a short day before, and now, within the past twenty-four hours, she had learned that he spoke not only English but French as well, and the primitive dialect of the West Coast.

She had thought him shifty, cruel, and untrustworthy, yet in so far as she had reason to believe he had proved himself in every way the contrary since the day before. It scarce seemed credible that he could be serving her from motives purely chivalrous. There must be something deeper in his intentions and plans than he had yet disclosed.

She wondered, and when she looked at him – at his close-set, shifty eyes and repulsive features, she shuddered, for she was convinced that no lofty characteristics could be hid behind so foul an exterior.

As she was thinking of these things the while she debated the wisdom of uncovering the baby's face, there came a little grunt from the wee bundle in her lap, and then a gurgling coo that set her heart in raptures.

The baby was awake! Now she might feast her eyes upon him.

Quickly she snatched the blanket from before the infant's face; Anderssen was looking at her as she did so.

He saw her stagger to her feet, holding the baby at arm's length from her, her eyes glued in horror upon the little chubby face and twinkling eyes.

Then he heard her piteous cry as her knees gave beneath her, and she sank to the ground in a swoon.

CHAPTER TEN

The Swede

As THE WARRIORS, clustered thick about Tarzan and Sheeta, realized that it was a flesh-and-blood panther that had interrupted their dance of death, they took heart a trifle, for in the face of all those circling spears even the mighty Sheeta would be doomed.

Rokoff was urging the chief to have his spearmen launch their missiles, and the black was upon the instant of issuing the command, when his eyes strayed beyond Tarzan, following the gaze of the ape-man.

With a yell of terror the chief turned and fled toward the village gate, and as his people looked to see the cause of his fright, they too took to their heels – for there, lumbering down upon them, their huge forms exaggerated by the play of moonlight and camp fire, came the hideous apes of Akut.

The instant the natives turned to flee the ape-man's savage cry rang out above the shrieks of the blacks, and in answer to it Sheeta and the apes leaped growling after the fugitives. Some of the warriors turned to battle with their enraged antagonists, but before the fiendish ferocity of the fierce beasts they went down to bloody death.

Others were dragged down in their flight, and it was not until the village was empty and the last of the blacks had disappeared into the bush that Tarzan was able to recall his savage pack to his side. Then it was that he discovered to his chagrin that he could not make one of them, not even the comparatively intelligent Akut, understand that he wished to be freed from the bonds that held him to the stake.

In time, of course, the idea would filter through their thick skulls, but in the meanwhile many things might happen – the blacks might return in force to regain their village; the whites might readily pick them all off with their rifles from the surrounding trees; he might even starve to death before the dull-witted apes realized that he wished them to gnaw through his bonds.

As for Sheeta – the great cat understood even less than the apes; but yet Tarzan could not but marvel at the remarkable characteristics this beast had evidenced. That it felt real affection for him there seemed little doubt, for now that the blacks were disposed of it walked slowly back and forth about the stake, rubbing its sides against the ape-man's legs and purring like a contented tabby. That it had gone of its own volition to bring the balance of the pack to his rescue, Tarzan could not doubt. His Sheeta was indeed a jewel among beasts.

Mugambi's absence worried the ape-man not a little. He attempted to learn from Akut what had become of the black, fearing that the beasts, freed from the restraint of Tarzan's presence, might have fallen upon the man and devoured him; but to all his questions the great ape but pointed back in the direction from which they had come out of the jungle.

The night passed with Tarzan still fast bound to the stake, and shortly after dawn his fears were realized in the discovery of naked black figures moving stealthily just within the edge of the jungle about the village. The blacks were returning.

With daylight their courage would be equal to the demands of a charge upon the handful of beasts that had routed them from their rightful abodes. The result of the encounter seemed foregone if the savages could curb their superstitious terror, for against their overwhelming numbers, their long spears and poisoned arrows, the panther and the apes could not be expected to survive a really determined attack.

That the blacks were preparing for a charge became apparent a few moments later, when they commenced to show themselves in force upon the edge of the clearing, dancing and jumping about as they waved their spears and shouted taunts and fierce warcries toward the village.

These manoeuvres Tarzan knew would continue until the blacks had worked themselves into a state of hysterical courage sufficient to sustain them for a short charge toward the village, and even though he doubted that they would reach it at the first attempt, he believed that at the second or the third they would swarm through the gateway, when the outcome could not be aught than the extermination of Tarzan's bold, but unarmed and undisciplined, defenders.

Even as he had guessed, the first charge carried the howling warriors but a short distance into the open – a shrill, weird challenge from the ape-man being all that was necessary to send them scurrying back to the bush. For half an hour they pranced and yelled their courage to the sticking-point, and again essayed a charge.

This time they came quite to the village gate, but when Sheeta and the hideous apes leaped among them they turned screaming in terror, and again fled to the jungle.

Again was the dancing and shouting repeated. This time Tarzan felt no doubt they would enter the village and complete the work that a handful of determined white men would have carried to a successful conclusion at the first attempt.

To have rescue come so close only to be thwarted because he could not make his poor, savage friends understand precisely what he wanted of them was most irritating, but he could not find it in his heart to place blame upon them. They had done their best, and now he was sure they would doubtless remain to die with him in a fruitless effort to defend him.

The blacks were already preparing for the charge. A few individuals had advanced a short distance toward the village and were exhorting the others to follow them. In a moment the whole savage horde would be racing across the clearing.

Tarzan thought only of the little child somewhere in this cruel, relentless wilderness. His heart ached for the son that he might no longer seek to save – that and the realization of Jane's suffering were all that weighed upon his brave spirit in these that he thought his last moments of life. Succour, all that he could hope for, had come to him in the instant of his extremity – and failed. There was nothing further for which to hope.

The blacks were half-way across the clearing when Tarzan's attention was attracted by the actions of one of the apes. The beast was glaring toward one of the huts. Tarzan followed his gaze. To his infinite relief and delight he saw the stalwart form of Mugambi racing toward him.

The huge black was panting heavily as though from strenuous physical exertion and nervous excitement. He rushed to Tarzan's side, and as the first of the savages reached the village gate the native's knife severed the last of the cords that bound Tarzan to the stake.

In the street lay the corpses of the savages that had fallen before the pack the night before. From one of these Tarzan seized a spear and knob stick, and with Mugambi at his side and the snarling pack about him, he met the natives as they poured through the gate.

Fierce and terrible was the battle that ensued, but at last the savages were routed, more by terror, perhaps, at sight of a black man and a white fighting in company with a panther and the huge fierce apes of

Akut, than because of their inability to overcome the relatively small force that opposed them.

One prisoner fell into the hands of Tarzan, and him the ape-man questioned in an effort to learn what had become of Rokoff and his party. Promised his liberty in return for the information, the black told all he knew concerning the movements of the Russian.

It seemed that early in the morning their chief had attempted to prevail upon the whites to return with him to the village and with their guns destroy the ferocious pack that had taken possession of it, but Rokoff appeared to entertain even more fears of the giant white man and his strange companions than even the blacks themselves.

Upon no conditions would he consent to returning even within sight of the village. Instead, he took his party hurriedly to the river, where they stole a number of canoes the blacks had hidden there. The last that had been seen of them they had been paddling strongly up-stream, their porters from Kaviri's village wielding the blades.

So once more Tarzan of the Apes with his hideous pack took up his search for the ape-man's son and the pursuit of his abductor.

For weary days they followed through an almost uninhabited country, only to learn at last that they were upon the wrong trail. The little band had been reduced by three, for three of Akut's apes had fallen in the fighting at the village. Now, with Akut, there were five great apes, and Sheeta was there – and Mugambi and Tarzan.

The ape-man no longer heard rumors even of the three who had preceded Rokoff – the white man and woman and the child. Who the man and woman were he could not guess, but that the child was his was enough to keep him hot upon the trail. He was sure that Rokoff would be following this trio, and so he felt confident that so long as he could keep upon the Russian's trail he would be winning so much nearer to the time he might snatch his son from the dangers and horrors that menaced him.

In retracing their way after losing Rokoff's trail Tarzan picked it up again at a point where the Russian had left the river and taken to the brush in a northerly direction. He could only account for this change on the ground that the child had been carried away from the river by the two who now had possession of it.

Nowhere along the way, however, could he gain definite information that might assure him positively that the child was ahead of him. Not a single native they questioned had seen or heard of this other party, though nearly all had had direct experience with the Russian or had talked with others who had.

It was with difficulty that Tarzan could find means to communicate with the natives, as the moment their eyes fell upon his companions they fled precipitately into the bush. His only alternative was to go ahead of his pack and waylay an occasional warrior whom he found alone in the jungle.

One day as he was thus engaged, tracking an unsuspecting savage, he came upon the fellow in the act of hurling a spear at a wounded white man who crouched in a clump of bush at the trail's side. The white was one whom Tarzan had often seen, and whom he recognized at once.

Deep in his memory was implanted those repulsive features – the close-set eyes, the shifty expression, the drooping yellow moustache.

Instantly it occurred to the ape-man that this fellow had not been among those who had accompanied Rokoff at the village where Tarzan had been a prisoner. He had seen them all, and this fellow had not been there. There could be but one explanation – he it was who had fled ahead of the Russian with the woman and the child – and the woman had been Jane Clayton. He was sure now of the meaning of Rokoff's words.

The ape-man's face went white as he looked upon the pasty, vice-marked countenance of the Swede. Across Tarzan's forehead stood out the broad band of scarlet that marked the scar where, years before, Terkoz had torn a great strip of the ape-man's scalp from his skull in the fierce battle in which Tarzan had sustained his fitness to the kingship of the apes of Kerchak.

The man was his prey – the black should not have him, and with the thought he leaped upon the warrior, striking down the spear before it could reach its mark. The black, whipping out his knife, turned to do battle with this new enemy, while the Swede, lying in the bush, witnessed a duel, the like of which he had never dreamed to see – a half-naked white man battling with a half-naked black, hand to hand with the crude weapons of primeval man at first, and then with hands and teeth like the primordial brutes from whose loins their forebears sprung.

For a time Anderssen did not recognize the white, and when at last it dawned upon him that he had seen this giant before, his eyes went wide in surprise that this growling, rending beast could ever have been the well-groomed English gentleman who had been a prisoner aboard the Kincaid.

An English nobleman! He had learned the identity of the Kincaid's prisoners from Lady Greystoke during their flight up the Ugambi. Before, in common with the other members of the crew of the steamer, he had not known who the two might be.

The fight was over. Tarzan had been compelled to kill his antagonist, as the fellow would not surrender.

The Swede saw the white man leap to his feet beside the corpse of his foe, and placing one foot upon the broken neck lift his voice in the hideous challenge of the victorious bull-ape.

Anderssen shuddered. Then Tarzan turned toward him. His face was cold and cruel, and in the grey eyes the Swede read murder.

"Where is my wife?" growled the ape-man. "Where is the child?"

Anderssen tried to reply, but a sudden fit of coughing choked him. There was an arrow entirely through his chest, and as he coughed the blood from his wounded lung poured suddenly from his mouth and nostrils.

Tarzan stood waiting for the paroxysm to pass. Like a bronze image – cold, hard, and relentless – he stood over the helpless man, waiting to wring such information from him as he needed, and then to kill.

Presently the coughing and haemorrhage ceased, and again the wounded man tried to speak. Tarzan knelt near the faintly moving lips.

"The wife and child!" he repeated. "Where are they?"

Anderssen pointed up the trail.

"The Russian – he got them," he whispered.

"How did you come here?" continued Tarzan. "Why are you not with Rokoff?"

"They catch us," replied Anderssen, in a voice so low that the ape-man could just distinguish the words. "They catch us. Ay fight, but my men they all run away. Then they get me when Ay ban vounded. Rokoff he say leave me here for the hyenas. That vas vorse than to kill. He tak your vife and kid."

"What were you doing with them – where were you taking them?" asked Tarzan, and then fiercely, leaping close to the fellow with fierce eyes blazing with the passion of hate and vengeance that he had with difficulty controlled, "What harm did you do to my wife or child? Speak quick before I kill you! Make your peace with God! Tell me the worst, or I will tear you to pieces with my hands and teeth. You have seen that I can do it!"

A look of wide-eyed surprise overspread Anderssen's face.

"Why," he whispered, "Ay did not hurt them. Ay tried to save them from that Russian. Your vife was kind to me on the Kincaid, and Ay hear that little baby cry sometimes. Ay got a vife an' kid for my own by Christiania an' Ay couldn't bear for to see them separated an' in Rokoff's hands any more. That vas all. Do Ay look like Ay ban here to hurt them?" he continued after a pause, pointing to the arrow protruding from his breast.

There was something in the man's tone and expression that convinced Tarzan of the truth of his assertions. More weighty than anything else was the fact that Anderssen evidently seemed more hurt than frightened. He knew he was going to die, so Tarzan's threats had little effect upon him; but it was quite apparent that he wished the Englishman to know the truth and not to wrong him by harbouring the belief that his words and manner indicated that he had entertained.

The ape-man instantly dropped to his knees beside the Swede.

"I am sorry," he said very simply. "I had looked for none but knaves in company with Rokoff. I see that I was wrong. That is past now, and we will drop it for the more important matter of getting you to a place of comfort and looking after your wounds. We must have you on your feet again as soon as possible."

The Swede, smiling, shook his head.

"You go on an' look for the vife an' kid," he said. "Ay ban as gude as dead already; but" – he hesitated – "Ay hate to think of the hyenas. Von't you finish up this job?"

Tarzan shuddered. A moment ago he had been upon the point of killing this man. Now he could no more have taken his life than he could have taken the life of any of his best friends.

He lifted the Swede's head in his arms to change and ease his position.

Again came a fit of coughing and the terrible haemorrhage. After it was over Anderssen lay with closed eyes.

Tarzan thought that he was dead, until he suddenly raised his eyes to those of the ape-man, sighed, and spoke – in a very low, weak whisper.

"Ay tank it blow purty soon purty hard!" he said, and died.

CHAPTER ELEVEN

Tambudza

Tarzan scooped a shallow grave for the Kincaid's cook, beneath whose repulsive exterior had beaten the heart of a chivalrous gentleman. That was all he could do in the cruel jungle for the man who had given his life in the service of his little son and his wife.

Then Tarzan took up again the pursuit of Rokoff. Now that he was positive that the woman ahead of him was indeed Jane, and that she had again fallen into the hands of the Russian, it seemed that with all the incredible speed of his fleet and agile muscles he moved at but a snail's pace.

It was with difficulty that he kept the trail, for there were many paths through the jungle at this point – crossing and crisscrossing, forking and branching in all directions, and over them all had passed natives innumerable, coming and going. The spoor of the white men was obliterated by that of the native carriers who had followed them, and over all was the spoor of other natives and of wild beasts.

It was most perplexing; yet Tarzan kept on assiduously, checking his sense of sight against his sense of smell, that he might more surely keep to the right trail. But, with all his care, night found him at a point where he was positive that he was on the wrong trail entirely.

He knew that the pack would follow his spoor, and so he had been careful to make it as distinct as possible, brushing often against the vines and creepers that walled the jungle-path, and in other ways leaving his scent-spoor plainly discernible.

As darkness settled a heavy rain set in, and there was nothing for the baffled ape-man to do but wait in the partial shelter of a huge tree until morning; but the coming of dawn brought no cessation of the torrential downpour.

For a week the sun was obscured by heavy clouds, while violent rain and wind storms obliterated the last remnants of the spoor Tarzan constantly though vainly sought.

During all this time he saw no signs of natives, nor of his own pack, the members of which he feared had lost his trail during the terrific storm. As the country was strange to him, he had been unable to judge his course accurately, since he had had neither sun by day nor moon nor stars by night to guide him.

When the sun at last broke through the clouds in the fore-noon of the seventh day, it looked down upon an almost frantic ape-man.

For the first time in his life, Tarzan of the Apes had been lost in the jungle. That the experience should have befallen him at such a time seemed cruel beyond expression. Somewhere in this savage land his wife and son lay in the clutches of the arch-fiend Rokoff.

What hideous trials might they not have undergone during those seven awful days that nature had thwarted him in his endeavours to locate them? Tarzan knew the Russian, in whose power they were, so well that he could not doubt but that the man, filled with rage that Jane had once escaped him, and knowing that Tarzan might be close upon his trail, would wreak without further loss of time whatever vengeance his polluted mind might be able to conceive.

But now that the sun shone once more, the ape-man was still at a loss as to what direction to take. He knew that Rokoff had left the river in pursuit of Anderssen, but whether he would continue inland or return to the Ugambi was a question.

The ape-man had seen that the river at the point he had left it was growing narrow and swift, so that he judged that it could not be navigable even for canoes to any great distance farther toward its source. However, if Rokoff had not returned to the river, in what direction had he proceeded?

From the direction of Anderssen's flight with Jane and the child Tarzan was convinced that the man had purposed attempting the tremendous feat of crossing the continent to Zanzibar; but whether Rokoff would dare so dangerous a journey or not was a question.

Fear might drive him to the attempt now that he knew the manner of horrible pack that was upon his trail, and that Tarzan of the Apes was following him to wreak upon him the vengeance that he deserved.

At last the ape-man determined to continue toward the north-east in the general direction of German East Africa until he came upon natives from whom he might gain information as to Rokoff's whereabouts.

The second day following the cessation of the rain Tarzan came upon a native village the inhabitants of which fled into the bush the instant their eyes fell upon him. Tarzan, not to be thwarted in any such manner as this, pursued them, and after a brief chase caught up with a young warrior. The fellow was so badly frightened that he was unable to defend himself, dropping his weapons and falling upon the ground, wide-eyed and screaming as he gazed on his captor.

It was with considerable difficulty that the ape-man quieted the fellow's fears sufficiently to obtain a coherent statement from him as to the cause of his uncalled-for terror.

From him Tarzan learned, by dint of much coaxing, that a party of whites had passed through the village several days before. These men had told them of a terrible white devil that pursued them, warning the natives against it and the frightful pack of demons that accompanied it.

The black had recognized Tarzan as the white devil from the descriptions given by the whites and their black servants. Behind him he had expected to see a horde of demons disguised as apes and panthers.

In this Tarzan saw the cunning hand of Rokoff. The Russian was attempting to make travel as difficult as possible for him by turning the natives against him in superstitious fear.

The native further told Tarzan that the white man who had led the recent expedition had promised them a fabulous reward if they would kill the white devil. This they had fully intended doing should the opportunity present itself; but the moment they had seen Tarzan their blood had turned to water, as the porters of the white men had told them would be the case.

Finding the ape-man made no attempt to harm him, the native at last recovered his grasp upon his courage, and, at Tarzan's suggestion, accompanied the white devil back to the village, calling as he went for his fellows to return also, as "the white devil has promised to do you no harm if you come back right away and answer his questions."

One by one the blacks straggled into the village, but that their fears were not entirely allayed was evident from the amount of white that showed about the eyes of the majority of them as they cast constant and apprehensive sidelong glances at the ape-man.

The chief was among the first to return to the village, and as it was he that Tarzan was most anxious to interview, he lost no time in entering into a palaver with the black.

The fellow was short and stout, with an unusually low and degraded countenance and apelike arms. His whole expression denoted deceitfulness.

Only the superstitious terror engendered in him by the stories poured into his ears by the whites and blacks of the Russian's party kept him from leaping upon Tarzan with his warriors and slaying him forthwith, for he and his people were inveterate maneaters. But the fear that he might indeed be a devil, and that out there in the jungle behind him his fierce demons waited to do his bidding, kept M'ganwazam from putting his desires into action.

Tarzan questioned the fellow closely, and by comparing his statements with those of the young warrior he had first talked with he learned that Rokoff and his safari were in terror-stricken retreat in the direction of the far East Coast.

Many of the Russian's porters had already deserted him. In that very village he had hanged five for theft and attempted desertion. Judging, however, from what the Waganwazam had learned from those of the Russian's blacks who were not too far gone in terror of the brutal Rokoff to fear even to speak of their plans, it was apparent that he would not travel any great distance before the last of his porters, cooks, tent-boys, gun-bearers, askari, and even his headman, would have turned back into the bush, leaving him to the mercy of the merciless jungle.

M'ganwazam denied that there had been any white woman or child with the party of whites; but even as he spoke Tarzan was convinced that he lied. Several times the ape-man approached the subject from different angles, but never was he successful in surprising the wily cannibal into a direct contradiction of his original statement that there had been no women or children with the party.

Tarzan demanded food of the chief, and after considerable haggling on the part of the monarch succeeded in obtaining a meal. He then tried to draw out others of the tribe, especially the young man whom he had captured in the bush, but M'ganwazam's presence sealed their lips.

At last, convinced that these people knew a great deal more than they had told him concerning the whereabouts of the Russian and the fate of Jane and the child, Tarzan determined to remain overnight among them in the hope of discovering something further of importance.

When he had stated his decision to the chief he was rather surprised to note the sudden change in the fellow's attitude toward him. From apparent dislike and suspicion M'ganwazam became a most eager and solicitous host.

Nothing would do but that the ape-man should occupy the best hut in the village, from which M'ganwazam's oldest wife was forthwith summarily ejected, while the chief took up his temporary abode in the hut of one of his younger consorts.

Had Tarzan chanced to recall the fact that a princely reward had been offered the blacks if they should succeed in killing him, he might have more quickly interpreted M'ganwazam's sudden change in front.

To have the white giant sleeping peacefully in one of his own huts would greatly facilitate the matter of earning the reward, and so the chief was urgent in his suggestions that Tarzan, doubtless being very much fatigued after his travels, should retire early to the comforts of the anything but inviting palace.

As much as the ape-man detested the thought of sleeping within a native hut, he had determined to do so this night, on the chance that he might be able to induce one of the younger men to sit and chat with him before the fire that burned in the centre of the smoke-filled dwelling, and from him draw the truths he sought. So Tarzan accepted the invitation of old M'ganwazam, insisting, however, that he much preferred sharing a hut with some of the younger men rather than driving the chief's old wife out in the cold.

The toothless old hag grinned her appreciation of this suggestion, and as the plan still better suited the chief's scheme, in that it would permit him to surround Tarzan with a gang of picked assassins, he readily assented, so that presently Tarzan had been installed in a hut close to the village gate.

As there was to be a dance that night in honour of a band of recently returned hunters, Tarzan was left alone in the hut, the young men, as M'ganwazam explained, having to take part in the festivities.

As soon as the ape-man was safely installed in the trap, M'Ganwazam called about him the young warriors whom he had selected to spend the night with the white devil!

None of them was overly enthusiastic about the plan, since deep in their superstitious hearts lay an exaggerated fear of the strange white giant; but the word of M'ganwazam was law among his people, so not one dared refuse the duty he was called upon to perform.

As M'ganwazam unfolded his plan in whispers to the savages squatting about him the old, toothless hag, to whom Tarzan had saved her hut for the night, hovered about the conspirators ostensibly to replenish the supply of firewood for the blaze about which the men sat, but really to drink in as much of their conversation as possible.

Tarzan had slept for perhaps an hour or two despite the savage din of the revellers when his keen senses came suddenly alert to a suspiciously stealthy movement in the hut in which he lay. The fire had died down to a little heap of glowing embers, which accentuated rather than relieved the darkness that shrouded the interior of the evil-smelling dwelling, yet the trained senses of the ape-man warned him of another presence creeping almost silently toward him through the gloom.

He doubted that it was one of his hut mates returning from the festivities, for he still heard the wild cries of the dancers and the din of the tom-toms in the village street without. Who could it be that took such pains to conceal his approach?

As the presence came within reach of him the ape-man bounded lightly to the opposite side of the hut, his spear poised ready at his side.

"Who is it," he asked, "that creeps upon Tarzan of the Apes, like a hungry lion out of the darkness?"

"Silence, bwana!" replied an old cracked voice. "It is Tambudza – she whose hut you would not take, and thus drive an old woman out into the cold night."

"What does Tambudza want of Tarzan of the Apes?" asked the ape-man.

"You were kind to me to whom none is now kind, and I have come to warn you in payment of your kindness," answered the old hag.

"Warn me of what?"

"M'ganwazam has chosen the young men who are to sleep in the hut with you," replied Tambudza. "I was near as he talked with them, and heard him issuing his instructions to them. When the dance is run well into the morning they are to come to the hut.

"If you are awake they are to pretend that they have come to sleep, but if you sleep it is M'ganwazam's command that you be killed. If you are not then asleep they will wait quietly beside you until you do sleep, and then they will all fall upon you together and slay you. M'ganwazam is determined to win the reward the white man has offered."

"I had forgotten the reward," said Tarzan, half to himself, and then he added, "How may M'ganwazam hope to collect the reward now that the white men who are my enemies have left his country and gone he knows not where?"

"Oh, they have not gone far," replied Tambudza. "M'ganwazam knows where they camp. His runners could quickly overtake them – they move slowly."

"Where are they?" asked Tarzan.

"Do you wish to come to them?" asked Tambudza in way of reply.

Tarzan nodded.

"I cannot tell you where they lie so that you could come to the place yourself, but I could lead you to them, bwana."

In their interest in the conversation neither of the speakers had noticed the little figure which crept into the darkness of the hut behind them, nor did they see it when it slunk noiselessly out again.

It was little Buulaoo, the chief's son by one of his younger wives – a vindictive, degenerate little rascal who hated Tambudza, and was ever seeking opportunities to spy upon her and report her slightest breach of custom to his father.

"Come, then," said Tarzan quickly, "let us be on our way."

This Buulaoo did not hear, for he was already legging it up the village street to where his hideous sire guzzled native beer, and watched the evolutions of the frantic dancers leaping high in the air and cavorting wildly in their hysterical capers.

So it happened that as Tarzan and Tambudza sneaked warily from the village and melted into the Stygian darkness of the jungle two lithe runners took their way in the same direction, though by another trail.

When they had come sufficiently far from the village to make it safe for them to speak above a whisper, Tarzan asked the old woman if she had seen aught of a white woman and a little child.

"Yes, bwana," replied Tambudza, "there was a woman with them and a little child – a little white piccaninny. It died here in our village of the fever and they buried it!"

CHAPTER TWELVE

A Black Scoundrel

WHEN JANE CLAYTON REGAINED consciousness she saw Anderssen standing over her, holding the baby in his arms. As her eyes rested upon them an expression of misery and horror overspread her countenance.

"What is the matter?" he asked. "You ban sick?"

"Where is my baby?" she cried, ignoring his questions.

Anderssen held out the chubby infant, but she shook her head.

"It is not mine," she said. "You knew that it was not mine. You are a devil like the Russian."

Anderssen's blue eyes stretched in surprise.

"Not yours!" he exclaimed. "You tole me the kid aboard the Kincaid ban your kid."

"Not this one," replied Jane dully. "The other. Where is the other? There must have been two. I did not know about this one."

"There vasn't no other kid. Ay tank this ban yours. Ay am very sorry."

Anderssen fidgeted about, standing first on one foot and then upon the other. It was perfectly evident to Jane that he was honest in his protestations of ignorance of the true identity of the child.

Presently the baby commenced to crow, and bounce up and down in the Swede's arms, at the same time leaning forward with little hands outreaching toward the young woman.

She could not withstand the appeal, and with a low cry she sprang to her feet and gathered the baby to her breast.

For a few minutes she wept silently, her face buried in the baby's soiled little dress. The first shock of disappointment that the tiny thing had not been her beloved Jack was giving way to a great hope that after all some miracle had occurred to snatch her baby from Rokoff's hands at the last instant before the Kincaid sailed from England.

Then, too, there was the mute appeal of this wee waif alone and unloved in the midst of the horrors of the savage jungle. It was this thought more than any other that had sent her mother's heart out to the innocent babe, while still she suffered from disappointment that she had been deceived in its identity.

"Have you no idea whose child this is?" she asked Anderssen.

The man shook his head.

"Not now," he said. "If he ain't ban your kid, Ay don' know whose kid he do ban. Rokoff said it was yours. Ay tank he tank so, too.

"What do we do with it now? Ay can't go back to the Kincaid. Rokoff would have me shot; but you can go back. Ay take you to the sea, and then some of these black men they take you to the ship – eh?"

"No! no!" cried Jane. "Not for the world. I would rather die than fall into the hands of that man again. No, let us go on and take this poor little creature with us. If God is willing we shall be saved in one way or another."

So they again took up their flight through the wilderness, taking with them a half-dozen of the Mosulas to carry provisions and the tents that Anderssen had smuggled aboard the small boat in preparation for the attempted escape.

The days and nights of torture that the young woman suffered were so merged into one long, unbroken nightmare of hideousness that she soon lost all track of time. Whether they had been wandering for days or years she could not tell. The one bright spot in that eternity of fear and suffering was the little child whose tiny hands had long since fastened their softly groping fingers firmly about her heart.

In a way the little thing took the place and filled the aching void that the theft of her own baby had left. It could never be the same, of course, but yet, day by day, she found her mother-love, enveloping the waif more closely until she sometimes sat with closed eyes lost in the sweet imagining that the little bundle of humanity at her breast was truly her own.

For some time their progress inland was extremely slow. Word came to them from time to time through natives passing from the coast on hunting excursions that Rokoff had not yet guessed the direction of their flight. This, and the desire to make the journey as light as possible for the gently bred woman, kept Anderssen to a slow advance of short and easy marches with many rests.

The Swede insisted upon carrying the child while they travelled, and in countless other ways did what he could to help Jane Clayton conserve her strength. He had been terribly chagrined on discovering the mistake he had made in the identity of the baby, but once the young woman became convinced that his motives were truly chivalrous she would not permit him longer to upbraid himself for the error that he could not by any means have avoided.

At the close of each day's march Anderssen saw to the erection of a comfortable shelter for Jane and the child. Her tent was always pitched in the most favourable location. The thorn boma round it was the strongest and most impregnable that the Mosula could construct.

Her food was the best that their limited stores and the rifle of the Swede could provide, but the thing that touched her heart the closest was the gentle consideration and courtesy which the man always accorded her.

That such nobility of character could lie beneath so repulsive an exterior never ceased to be a source of wonder and amazement to her, until at last the innate chivalry of the man, and his unfailing kindliness and sympathy transformed his appearance in so far as Jane was concerned until she saw only the sweetness of his character mirrored in his countenance.

They had commenced to make a little better progress when word reached them that Rokoff was but a few marches behind them, and that he had at last discovered the direction of their flight. It was then that Anderssen took to the river, purchasing a canoe from a chief whose village lay a short distance from the Ugambi upon the bank of a tributary.

Thereafter the little party of fugitives fled up the broad Ugambi, and so rapid had their flight become that they no longer received word of their pursuers. At the end of canoe navigation upon the river, they abandoned their canoe and took to the jungle. Here progress became at once arduous, slow, and dangerous.

The second day after leaving the Ugambi the baby fell ill with fever. Anderssen knew what the outcome must be, but he had not the heart to tell Jane Clayton the truth, for he had seen that the young woman had come to love the child almost as passionately as though it had been her own flesh and blood.

As the baby's condition precluded farther advance, Anderssen withdrew a little from the main trail he had been following and built a camp in a natural clearing on the bank of a little river.

Here Jane devoted her every moment to caring for the tiny sufferer, and as though her sorrow and anxiety were not all that she could bear, a further blow came with the sudden announcement of one of the Mosula porters who had been foraging in the jungle adjacent that Rokoff and his party were camped quite close to them, and were evidently upon their trail to this little nook which all had thought so excellent a hiding-place.

This information could mean but one thing, and that they must break camp and fly onward regardless of the baby's condition. Jane Clayton knew the traits of the Russian well enough to be positive that he would separate her from the child the moment that he recaptured them, and she knew that separation would mean the immediate death of the baby.

As they stumbled forward through the tangled vegetation along an old and almost overgrown game trail the Mosula porters deserted them one by one.

The men had been staunch enough in their devotion and loyalty as long as they were in no danger of being overtaken by the Russian and his party. They had heard, however, so much of the atrocious disposition of Rokoff that they had grown to hold him in mortal terror, and now that they knew he was close upon them their timid hearts would fortify them no longer, and as quickly as possible they deserted the three whites.

Yet on and on went Anderssen and the girl. The Swede went ahead, to hew a way through the brush where the path was entirely overgrown, so that on this march it was necessary that the young woman carry the child.

All day they marched. Late in the afternoon they realized that they had failed. Close behind them they heard the noise of a large safari advancing along the trail which they had cleared for their pursuers.

When it became quite evident that they must be overtaken in a short time Anderssen hid Jane behind a large tree, covering her and the child with brush.

"There is a village about a mile farther on," he said to her. "The Mosula told me its location before they deserted us. Ay try to lead the Russian off your trail, then you go on to the village. Ay tank the chief ban friendly to white men – the Mosula tal me he ban. Anyhow, that was all we can do.

"After while you get chief to tak you down by the Mosula village at the sea again, an' after a while a ship is sure to put into the mouth of the Ugambi. Then you be all right. Gude-by an' gude luck to you, lady!"

"But where are you going, Sven?" asked Jane. "Why can't you hide here and go back to the sea with me?"

"Ay gotta tal the Russian you ban dead, so that he don't luke for you no more," and Anderssen grinned.

"Why can't you join me then after you have told him that?" insisted the girl.

Anderssen shook his head.

"Ay don't tank Ay join anybody any more after Ay tal the Russian you ban dead," he said.

"You don't mean that you think he will kill you?" asked Jane, and yet in her heart she knew that that was exactly what the great scoundrel would do in revenge for his having been thwarted by the Swede. Anderssen did not reply, other than to warn her to silence and point toward the path along which they had just come.

"I don't care," whispered Jane Clayton. "I shall not let you die to save me if I can prevent it in any way. Give me your revolver. I can use that, and together we may be able to hold them off until we can find some means of escape."

"It won't work, lady," replied Anderssen. "They would only get us both, and then Ay couldn't do you no good at all. Think of the kid, lady, and what it would be for you both to fall into Rokoff's hands again. For his sake you must do what Ay say. Here, take my rifle and ammunition; you may need them."

He shoved the gun and bandoleer into the shelter beside Jane. Then he was gone.

She watched him as he returned along the path to meet the oncoming safari of the Russian. Soon a turn in the trail hid him from view.

Her first impulse was to follow. With the rifle she might be of assistance to him, and, further, she could not bear the terrible thought of being left alone at the mercy of the fearful jungle without a single friend to aid her.

She started to crawl from her shelter with the intention of running after Anderssen as fast as she could. As she drew the baby close to her she glanced down into its little face.

How red it was! How unnatural the little thing looked. She raised the cheek to hers. It was fiery hot with fever!

With a little gasp of terror Jane Clayton rose to her feet in the jungle path. The rifle and bandoleer lay forgotten in the shelter beside her. Anderssen was forgotten, and Rokoff, and her great peril.

All that rioted through her fear-mad brain was the fearful fact that this little, helpless child was stricken with the terrible jungle-fever, and that she was helpless to do aught to allay its sufferings – sufferings that were sure to come during ensuing intervals of partial consciousness.

Her one thought was to find some one who could help her – some woman who had had children of her own – and with the thought came recollection of the friendly village of which Anderssen had spoken. If she could but reach it – in time!

There was no time to be lost. Like a startled antelope she turned and fled up the trail in the direction Anderssen had indicated.

From far behind came the sudden shouting of men, the sound of shots, and then silence. She knew that Anderssen had met the Russian.

A half-hour later she stumbled, exhausted, into a little thatched village. Instantly she was surrounded by men, women, and children. Eager, curious, excited natives plied her with a hundred questions, no one of which she could understand or answer.

All that she could do was to point tearfully at the baby, now wailing piteously in her arms, and repeat over and over, "Fever – fever – fever."

The blacks did not understand her words, but they saw the cause of her trouble, and soon a young woman had pulled her into a hut and with several others was doing her poor best to quiet the child and allay its agony.

The witch doctor came and built a little fire before the infant, upon which he boiled some strange concoction in a small earthen pot, making weird passes above it and mumbling strange, monotonous chants. Presently he dipped a zebra's tail into the brew, and with further mutterings and incantations sprinkled a few drops of the liquid over the baby's face.

After he had gone the women sat about and moaned and wailed until Jane thought that she should go mad; but, knowing that they were doing it all out of the kindness of their hearts, she endured the frightful waking nightmare of those awful hours in dumb and patient suffering.

It must have been well toward midnight that she became conscious of a sudden commotion in the village. She heard the voices of the natives raised in controversy, but she could not understand the words.

Presently she heard footsteps approaching the hut in which she squatted before a bright fire with the baby on her lap. The little thing lay very still now, its lids, half-raised, showed the pupils horribly upturned.

Jane Clayton looked into the little face with fear-haunted eyes. It was not her baby – not her flesh and blood – but how close, how dear the tiny, helpless thing had become to her. Her heart, bereft of its own, had gone out to this poor, little, nameless waif, and lavished upon it all the love that had been denied her during the long, bitter weeks of her captivity aboard the Kincaid.

She saw that the end was near, and though she was terrified at contemplation of her loss, still she hoped that it would come quickly now and end the sufferings of the little victim.

The footsteps she had heard without the hut now halted before the door. There was a whispered colloquy, and a moment later M'ganwazam, chief of the tribe, entered. She had seen but little of him, as the women had taken her in hand almost as soon as she had entered the village.

M'ganwazam, she now saw, was an evil-appearing savage with every mark of brutal degeneracy writ large upon his bestial countenance. To Jane Clayton he looked more gorilla than human. He tried to converse with her, but without success, and finally he called to some one without.

In answer to his summons another Negro entered – a man of very different appearance from M'ganwazam – so different, in fact, that Jane Clayton immediately decided that he was of another tribe. This man acted as interpreter, and almost from the first question that M'ganwazam put to her, Jane felt an intuitive conviction that the savage was attempting to draw information from her for some ulterior motive.

She thought it strange that the fellow should so suddenly have become interested in her plans, and especially in her intended destination when her journey had been interrupted at his village.

Seeing no reason for withholding the information, she told him the truth; but when he asked if she expected to meet her husband at the end of the trip, she shook her head negatively.

Then he told her the purpose of his visit, talking through the interpreter.

"I have just learned," he said, "from some men who live by the side of the great water, that your husband followed you up the Ugambi for several marches, when he was at last set upon by natives and killed. Therefore I have told you this that you might not waste your time in a long journey if you expected to meet your husband at the end of it; but instead could turn and retrace your steps to the coast."

Jane thanked M'ganwazam for his kindness, though her heart was numb with suffering at this new blow. She who had suffered so much was at last beyond reach of the keenest of misery's pangs, for her senses were numbed and calloused.

With bowed head she sat staring with unseeing eyes upon the face of the baby in her lap. M'ganwazam had left the hut. Sometime later she heard a noise at the entrance – another had entered. One of the women sitting opposite her threw a faggot upon the dying embers of the fire between them.

With a sudden flare it burst into renewed flame, lighting up the hut's interior as though by magic.

The flame disclosed to Jane Clayton's horrified gaze that the baby was quite dead. How long it had been so she could not guess.

A choking lump rose to her throat, her head drooped in silent misery upon the little bundle that she had caught suddenly to her breast.

For a moment the silence of the hut was unbroken. Then the native woman broke into a hideous wail.

A man coughed close before Jane Clayton and spoke her name.

With a start she raised her eyes to look into the sardonic countenance of Nikolas Rokoff.

CHAPTER THIRTEEN

Escape

For a moment Rokoff stood sneering down upon Jane Clayton, then his eyes fell to the little bundle in her lap. Jane had drawn one corner of the blanket over the child's face, so that to one who did not know the truth it seemed but to be sleeping.

"You have gone to a great deal of unnecessary trouble," said Rokoff, "to bring the child to this village. If you had attended to your own affairs I should have brought it here myself.

"You would have been spared the dangers and fatigue of the journey. But I suppose I must thank you for relieving me of the inconvenience of having to care for a young infant on the march.

"This is the village to which the child was destined from the first. M'ganwazam will rear him carefully, making a good cannibal of him, and if you ever chance to return to civilization it will doubtless afford you much food for thought as you compare the luxuries and comforts of your life with the details of the life your son is living in the village of the Waganwazam.

"Again I thank you for bringing him here for me, and now I must ask you to surrender him to me, that I may turn him over to his foster parents." As he concluded Rokoff held out his hands for the child, a nasty grin of vindictiveness upon his lips.

To his surprise Jane Clayton rose and, without a word of protest, laid the little bundle in his arms.

"Here is the child," she said. "Thank God he is beyond your power to harm."

Grasping the import of her words, Rokoff snatched the blanket from the child's face to seek confirmation of his fears. Jane Clayton watched his expression closely.

She had been puzzled for days for an answer to the question of Rokoff's knowledge of the child's identity. If she had been in doubt before the last shred of that doubt was wiped away as she witnessed the terrible anger of the Russian as he looked upon the dead face of the baby and realized that at the last moment his dearest wish for vengeance had been thwarted by a higher power.

Almost throwing the body of the child back into Jane Clayton's arms, Rokoff stamped up and down the hut, pounding the air with his clenched fists and cursing terribly. At last he halted in front of the young woman, bringing his face down close to hers.

"You are laughing at me," he shrieked. "You think that you have beaten me – eh? I'll show you, as I have shown the miserable ape you call 'husband,' what it means to interfere with the plans of Nikolas Rokoff.

"You have robbed me of the child. I cannot make him the son of a cannibal chief, but" – and he paused as though to let the full meaning of his threat sink deep – "I can make the mother the wife of a cannibal, and that I shall do – after I have finished with her myself."

If he had thought to wring from Jane Clayton any sign of terror he failed miserably. She was beyond that. Her brain and nerves were numb to suffering and shock.

To his surprise a faint, almost happy smile touched her lips. She was thinking with thankful heart that this poor little corpse was not that of her own wee Jack, and that – best of all – Rokoff evidently did not know the truth.

She would have liked to have flaunted the fact in his face, but she dared not. If he continued to believe that the child had been hers, so much safer would be the real Jack wherever he might be. She had, of course, no knowledge of the whereabouts of her little son – she did not know, even, that he still lived, and yet there was the chance that he might.

It was more than possible that without Rokoff's knowledge this child had been substituted for hers by one of the Russian's confederates, and that even now her son might be safe with friends in London, where there were many, both able and willing, to have paid any ransom which the traitorous conspirator might have asked for the safe release of Lord Greystoke's son.

She had thought it all out a hundred times since she had discovered that the baby which Anderssen had placed in her arms that night upon the Kincaid was not her own, and it had been a constant and gnawing source of happiness to her to dream the whole fantasy through in its every detail.

No, the Russian must never know that this was not her baby. She realized that her position was hopeless – with Anderssen and her husband dead there was no one in all the world with a desire to succour her who knew where she might be found.

Rokoff's threat, she realized, was no idle one. That he would do, or attempt to do, all that he had promised, she was perfectly sure; but at the worst it meant but a little earlier release from the hideous anguish that she had been enduring. She must find some way to take her own life before the Russian could harm her further.

Just now she wanted time – time to think and prepare herself for the end. She felt that she could not take the last, awful step until she had exhausted every possibility of escape. She did not care to live unless she might find her way back to her own child, but slight as such a hope appeared she would not admit its impossibility until the last moment had come, and she faced the fearful reality of choosing between the final alternatives – Nikolas Rokoff on one hand and self-destruction upon the other.

"Go away!" she said to the Russian. "Go away and leave me in peace with my dead. Have you not brought sufficient misery and anguish upon me without attempting to harm me further? What wrong have I ever done you that you should persist in persecuting me?"

"You are suffering for the sins of the monkey you chose when you might have had the love of a gentleman – of Nikolas Rokoff," he replied. "But where is the use in discussing the matter? We shall bury the child here, and you will return with me at once to my own camp. Tomorrow I shall bring you back and turn you over to your new husband – the lovely M'ganwazam. Come!"

He reached out for the child. Jane, who was on her feet now, turned away from him.

"I shall bury the body," she said. "Send some men to dig a grave outside the village."

Rokoff was anxious to have the thing over and get back to his camp with his victim. He thought he saw in her apathy a resignation to her fate. Stepping outside the hut, he motioned her to follow him, and a moment later, with his men, he escorted Jane beyond the village, where beneath a great tree the blacks scooped a shallow grave.

Wrapping the tiny body in a blanket, Jane laid it tenderly in the black hole, and, turning her head that she might not see the mouldy earth falling upon the pitiful little bundle, she breathed a prayer beside the grave of the nameless waif that had won its way to the innermost recesses of her heart.

Then, dry-eyed but suffering, she rose and followed the Russian through the Stygian blackness of the jungle, along the winding, leafy corridor that led from the village of M'ganwazam, the black cannibal, to the camp of Nikolas Rokoff, the white fiend.

Beside them, in the impenetrable thickets that fringed the path, rising to arch above it and shut out the moon, the girl could hear the stealthy, muffled footfalls of great beasts, and ever round about them rose the deafening roars of hunting lions, until the earth trembled to the mighty sound.

The porters lighted torches now and waved them upon either hand to frighten off the beasts of prey. Rokoff urged them to greater speed, and from the quavering note in his voice Jane Clayton knew that he was weak from terror.

The sounds of the jungle night recalled most vividly the days and nights that she had spent in a similar jungle with her forest god – with the fearless and unconquerable Tarzan of the Apes. Then there had been no thoughts of terror, though the jungle noises were new to her, and the roar of a lion had seemed the most awe-inspiring sound upon the great earth.

How different would it be now if she knew that he was somewhere there in the wilderness, seeking her! Then, indeed, would there be that for which to live, and every reason to believe that succour was close at hand – but he was dead! It was incredible that it should be so.

There seemed no place in death for that great body and those mighty thews. Had Rokoff been the one to tell her of her lord's passing she would have known that he lied. There could be no reason, she thought, why M'ganwazam should have deceived her. She did not know that the Russian had talked with the savage a few minutes before the chief had come to her with his tale.

At last they reached the rude boma that Rokoff's porters had thrown up round the Russian's camp. Here they found all in turmoil. She did not know what it was all about, but she saw that Rokoff was very angry, and from bits of conversation which she could translate she gleaned that there had been further desertions while he had been absent, and that the deserters had taken the bulk of his food and ammunition.

When he had done venting his rage upon those who remained he returned to where Jane stood under guard of a couple of his white sailors. He grasped her roughly by the arm and started to drag her toward his tent. The girl struggled and fought to free herself, while the two sailors stood by, laughing at the rare treat.

Rokoff did not hesitate to use rough methods when he found that he was to have difficulty in carrying out his designs. Repeatedly he struck Jane Clayton in the face, until at last, half-conscious, she was dragged within his tent.

Rokoff's boy had lighted the Russian's lamp, and now at a word from his master he made himself scarce. Jane had sunk to the floor in the middle of the enclosure. Slowly her numbed senses were returning to her and she was commencing to think very fast indeed. Quickly her eyes ran round the interior of the tent, taking in every detail of its equipment and contents.

Now the Russian was lifting her to her feet and attempting to drag her to the camp cot that stood at one side of the tent. At his belt hung a heavy revolver. Jane Clayton's eyes riveted themselves upon it. Her palm itched to grasp the huge butt. She feigned again to swoon, but through her half-closed lids she waited her opportunity.

It came just as Rokoff was lifting her upon the cot. A noise at the tent door behind him brought his head quickly about and away from the girl. The butt of the gun was not an inch from her hand. With a single, lightning-like move she snatched the weapon from its holster, and at the same instant Rokoff turned back toward her, realizing his peril.

She did not dare fire for fear the shot would bring his people about him, and with Rokoff dead she would fall into hands no better than his and to a fate probably even worse than he alone could have imagined. The memory of the two brutes who stood and laughed as Rokoff struck her was still vivid.

As the rage and fear-filled countenance of the Slav turned toward her Jane Clayton raised the heavy revolver high above the pasty face and with all her strength dealt the man a terrific blow between the eyes.

Without a sound he sank, limp and unconscious, to the ground. A moment later the girl stood beside him – for a moment at least free from the menace of his lust.

Outside the tent she again heard the noise that had distracted Rokoff's attention. What it was she did not know, but, fearing the return of the servant and the discovery of her deed, she stepped quickly to the camp table upon which burned the oil lamp and extinguished the smudgy, evil-smelling flame.

In the total darkness of the interior she paused for a moment to collect her wits and plan for the next step in her venture for freedom.

About her was a camp of enemies. Beyond these foes a black wilderness of savage jungle peopled by hideous beasts of prey and still more hideous human beasts.

There was little or no chance that she could survive even a few days of the constant dangers that would confront her there; but the knowledge that she had already passed through so many perils unscathed, and that somewhere out in the faraway world a little child was doubtless at that very moment crying for her, filled her with determination to make the effort to accomplish the seemingly impossible and cross that awful land of horror in search of the sea and the remote chance of succour she might find there.

Rokoff's tent stood almost exactly in the centre of the boma. Surrounding it were the tents and shelters of his white companions and the natives of his safari. To pass through these and find egress through the boma seemed a task too fraught with insurmountable obstacles to warrant even the slightest consideration, and yet there was no other way.

To remain in the tent until she should be discovered would be to set at naught all that she had risked to gain her freedom, and so with stealthy step and every sense alert she approached the back of the tent to set out upon the first stage of her adventure.

Groping along the rear of the canvas wall, she found that there was no opening there. Quickly she returned to the side of the unconscious Russian. In his belt her groping fingers came upon the hilt of a long hunting-knife, and with this she cut a hole in the back wall of the tent.

Silently she stepped without. To her immense relief she saw that the camp was apparently asleep. In the dim and flickering light of the dying fires she saw but a single sentry, and he was dozing upon his haunches at the opposite side of the enclosure.

Keeping the tent between him and herself, she crossed between the small shelters of the native porters to the boma wall beyond.

Outside, in the darkness of the tangled jungle, she could hear the roaring of lions, the laughing of hyenas, and the countless, nameless noises of the midnight jungle.

For a moment she hesitated, trembling. The thought of the prowling beasts out there in the darkness was appalling. Then, with a sudden brave toss of her head, she attacked the thorny boma wall with her delicate hands. Torn and bleeding though they were, she worked on breathlessly until she had made an opening through which she could worm her body, and at last she stood outside the enclosure.

Behind her lay a fate worse than death, at the hands of human beings.

Before her lay an almost certain fate – but it was only death – sudden, merciful, and honourable death.

Without a tremor and without regret she darted away from the camp, and a moment later the mysterious jungle had closed about her.

CHAPTER FOURTEEN

Alone in the Jungle

TAMBUDZA, LEADING TARZAN OF the Apes toward the camp of the Russian, moved very slowly along the winding jungle path, for she was old and her legs stiff with rheumatism.

So it was that the runners dispatched by M'ganwazam to warn Rokoff that the white giant was in his village and that he would be slain that night reached the Russian's camp before Tarzan and his ancient guide had covered half the distance.

The guides found the white man's camp in a turmoil. Rokoff had that morning been discovered stunned and bleeding within his tent. When he had recovered his senses and realized that Jane Clayton had escaped, his rage was boundless.

Rushing about the camp with his rifle, he had sought to shoot down the native sentries who had allowed the young woman to elude their vigilance, but several of the other whites, realizing that they were already in a precarious position owing to the numerous desertions that Rokoff's cruelty had brought about, seized and disarmed him.

Then came the messengers from M'ganwazam, but scarce had they told their story and Rokoff was preparing to depart with them for their village when other runners, panting from the exertions of their swift flight through the jungle, rushed breathless into the firelight, crying that the great white giant had escaped from M'ganwazam and was already on his way to wreak vengeance against his enemies.

Instantly confusion reigned within the encircling boma. The blacks belonging to Rokoff's safari were terror-stricken at the thought of the proximity of the white giant who hunted through the jungle with a fierce pack of apes and panthers at his heels.

Before the whites realized what had happened the superstitious fears of the natives had sent them scurrying into the bush – their own carriers as well as the messengers from M'ganwazam – but even in their haste they had not neglected to take with them every article of value upon which they could lay their hands.

Thus Rokoff and the seven white sailors found themselves deserted and robbed in the midst of a wilderness.

The Russian, following his usual custom, berated his companions, laying all the blame upon their shoulders for the events which had led up to the almost hopeless condition in which they now found themselves; but the sailors were in no mood to brook his insults and his cursing.

In the midst of this tirade one of them drew a revolver and fired point-blank at the Russian. The fellow's aim was poor, but his act so terrified Rokoff that he turned and fled for his tent.

As he ran his eyes chanced to pass beyond the boma to the edge of the forest, and there he caught a glimpse of that which sent his craven heart cold with a fear that almost expunged his terror of the seven men at his back, who by this time were all firing in hate and revenge at his retreating figure.

What he saw was the giant figure of an almost naked white man emerging from the bush.

Darting into his tent, the Russian did not halt in his flight, but kept right on through the rear wall, taking advantage of the long slit that Jane Clayton had made the night before.

The terror-stricken Muscovite scurried like a hunted rabbit through the hole that still gaped in the boma's wall at the point where his own prey had escaped, and as Tarzan approached the camp upon the opposite side Rokoff disappeared into the jungle in the wake of Jane Clayton.

As the ape-man entered the boma with old Tambudza at his elbow the seven sailors, recognizing him, turned and fled in the opposite direction. Tarzan saw that Rokoff was not among them, and so he let them go their way – his business was with the Russian, whom he expected to find in his tent. As to the sailors, he was sure that the jungle would exact from them expiation for their villainies, nor, doubtless, was he wrong, for his were the last white man's eyes to rest upon any of them.

Finding Rokoff's tent empty, Tarzan was about to set out in search of the Russian when Tambudza suggested to him that the departure of the white man could only have resulted from word reaching him from M'ganwazam that Tarzan was in his village.

"He has doubtless hastened there," argued the old woman. "If you would find him let us return at once."

Tarzan himself thought that this would probably prove to be the fact, so he did not waste time in an endeavour to locate the Russian's trail, but, instead, set out briskly for the village of M'ganwazam, leaving Tambudza to plod slowly in his wake.

His one hope was that Jane was still safe and with Rokoff. If this was the case, it would be but a matter of an hour or more before he should be able to wrest her from the Russian.

He knew now that M'ganwazam was treacherous and that he might have to fight to regain possession of his wife. He wished that Mugambi, Sheeta, Akut, and the balance of the pack were with him, for he realized that single-handed it would be no child's play to bring Jane safely from the clutches of two such scoundrels as Rokoff and the wily M'ganwazam.

To his surprise he found no sign of either Rokoff or Jane in the village, and as he could not trust the word of the chief, he wasted no time in futile inquiry. So sudden and unexpected had been his return, and so quickly had he vanished into the jungle after learning that those he sought were not among the Waganwazam, that old M'ganwazam had no time to prevent his going.

Swinging through the trees, he hastened back to the deserted camp he had so recently left, for here, he knew, was the logical place to take up the trail of Rokoff and Jane.

Arrived at the boma, he circled carefully about the outside of the enclosure until, opposite a break in the thorny wall, he came to indications that something had recently passed into the jungle. His acute sense of smell told him that both of those he sought had fled from the camp in this direction, and a moment later he had taken up the trail and was following the faint spoor.

Far ahead of him a terror-stricken young woman was slinking along a narrow game-trail, fearful that the next moment would bring her face to face with some savage beast or equally savage man. As she ran on, hoping against hope that she had hit upon the direction that would lead her eventually to the great river, she came suddenly upon a familiar spot.

At one side of the trail, beneath a giant tree, lay a little heap of loosely piled brush – to her dying day that little spot of jungle would be indelibly impressed upon her memory. It was where Anderssen had hidden her – where he had given up his life in the vain effort to save her from Rokoff.

At sight of it she recalled the rifle and ammunition that the man had thrust upon her at the last moment. Until now she had forgotten them entirely. Still clutched in her hand was the revolver she had snatched from Rokoff's belt, but that could contain at most not over six cartridges – not enough to furnish her with food and protection both on the long journey to the sea.

With bated breath she groped beneath the little mound, scarce daring to hope that the treasure remained where she had left it; but, to her infinite relief and joy, her hand came at once upon the barrel of the heavy weapon and then upon the bandoleer of cartridges.

As she threw the latter about her shoulder and felt the weight of the big game-gun in her hand a sudden sense of security suffused her. It was with new hope and a feeling almost of assured success that she again set forward upon her journey.

That night she slept in the crotch of a tree, as Tarzan had so often told her that he was accustomed to doing, and early the next morning was upon her way again. Late in the afternoon, as she was about to cross a little clearing, she was startled at the sight of a huge ape coming from the jungle upon the opposite side.

The wind was blowing directly across the clearing between them, and Jane lost no time in putting herself downwind from the huge creature. Then she hid in a clump of heavy bush and watched, holding the rifle ready for instant use.

To her consternation she saw that the apes were pausing in the centre of the clearing. They came together in a little knot, where they stood looking backward, as though in expectation of the coming of others of their tribe. Jane wished that they would go on, for she knew that at any moment some little, eddying gust of wind might carry her scent down to their nostrils, and then what would the protection of her rifle amount to in the face of those gigantic muscles and mighty fangs?

Her eyes moved back and forth between the apes and the edge of the jungle toward which they were gazing until at last she perceived the object of their halt and the thing that they awaited. They were being stalked.

Of this she was positive, as she saw the lithe, sinewy form of a panther glide noiselessly from the jungle at the point at which the apes had emerged but a moment before.

Quickly the beast trotted across the clearing toward the anthropoids. Jane wondered at their apparent apathy, and a moment later her wonder turned to amazement as she saw the great cat come quite close to the apes, who appeared entirely unconcerned by its presence, and, squatting down in their midst, fell assiduously to the business of preening, which occupies most of the waking hours of the cat family.

If the young woman was surprised by the sight of these natural enemies fraternizing, it was with emotions little short of fear for her own sanity that she presently saw a tall, muscular warrior enter the clearing and join the group of savage beasts assembled there.

At first sight of the man she had been positive that he would be torn to pieces, and she had half risen from her shelter, raising her rifle to her shoulder to do what she could to avert the man's terrible fate.

Now she saw that he seemed actually conversing with the beasts – issuing orders to them.

Presently the entire company filed on across the clearing and disappeared in the jungle upon the opposite side.

With a gasp of mingled incredulity and relief Jane Clayton staggered to her feet and fled on away from the terrible horde that had just passed her, while a half-mile behind her another individual, following the same trail as she, lay frozen with terror behind an ant-hill as the hideous band passed quite close to him.

This one was Rokoff; but he had recognized the members of the awful aggregation as allies of Tarzan of the Apes. No sooner, therefore, had the beasts passed him than he rose and raced through the jungle as fast as he could go, in order that he might put as much distance as possible between himself and these frightful beasts.

So it happened that as Jane Clayton came to the bank of the river, down which she hoped to float to the ocean and eventual rescue, Nikolas Rokoff was but a short distance in her rear.

Upon the bank the girl saw a great dugout drawn half-way from the water and tied securely to a near-by tree.

This, she felt, would solve the question of transportation to the sea could she but launch the huge, unwieldy craft. Unfastening the rope that had moored it to the tree, Jane pushed frantically upon the bow of the heavy canoe, but for all the results that were apparent she might as well have been attempting to shove the earth out of its orbit.

She was about winded when it occurred to her to try working the dugout into the stream by loading the stern with ballast and then rocking the bow back and forth along the bank until the craft eventually worked itself into the river.

There were no stones or rocks available, but along the shore she found quantities of driftwood deposited by the river at a slightly higher stage. These she gathered and piled far in the stern of the boat, until at last, to her immense relief, she saw the bow rise gently from the mud of the bank and the stern drift slowly with the current until it again lodged a few feet farther down-stream.

Jane found that by running back and forth between the bow and stern she could alternately raise and lower each end of the boat as she shifted her weight from one end to the other, with the result that each time she leaped to the stern the canoe moved a few inches farther into the river.

As the success of her plan approached more closely to fruition she became so wrapped in her efforts that she failed to note the figure of a man standing beneath a huge tree at the edge of the jungle from which he had just emerged.

He watched her and her labours with a cruel and malicious grin upon his swarthy countenance.

The boat at last became so nearly free of the retarding mud and of the bank that Jane felt positive that she could pole it off into deeper water with one of the paddles which lay in the bottom of the rude craft. With this end in view she seized upon one of these implements and had just plunged it into the river bottom close to the shore when her eyes happened to rise to the edge of the jungle.

As her gaze fell upon the figure of the man a little cry of terror rose to her lips. It was Rokoff.

He was running toward her now and shouting to her to wait or he would shoot – though as he was entirely unarmed it was difficult to discover just how he intended making good his threat.

Jane Clayton knew nothing of the various misfortunes that had befallen the Russian since she had escaped from his tent, so she believed that his followers must be close at hand.

However, she had no intention of falling again into the man's clutches. She would rather die at once than that that should happen to her. Another minute and the boat would be free.

Once in the current of the river she would be beyond Rokoff's power to stop her, for there was no other boat upon the shore, and no man, and certainly not the cowardly Rokoff, would dare to attempt to swim the crocodile-infested water in an effort to overtake her.

Rokoff, on his part, was bent more upon escape than aught else. He would gladly have forgone any designs he might have had upon Jane Clayton would she but permit him to share this means of escape that she had discovered. He would promise anything if she would let him come aboard the dugout, but he did not think that it was necessary to do so.

He saw that he could easily reach the bow of the boat before it cleared the shore, and then it would not be necessary to make promises of any sort. Not that Rokoff would have felt the slightest compunction in ignoring any promises he might have made the girl, but he disliked the idea of having to sue for favour with one who had so recently assaulted and escaped him.

Already he was gloating over the days and nights of revenge that would be his while the heavy dugout drifted its slow way to the ocean.

Jane Clayton, working furiously to shove the boat beyond his reach, suddenly realized that she was to be successful, for with a little lurch the dugout swung quickly into the current, just as the Russian reached out to place his hand upon its bow.

His fingers did not miss their goal by a half-dozen inches. The girl almost collapsed with the reaction from the terrific mental, physical, and nervous strain under which she had been labouring for the past few minutes. But, thank Heaven, at last she was safe!

Even as she breathed a silent prayer of thanksgiving, she saw a sudden expression of triumph lighten the features of the cursing Russian, and at the same instant he dropped suddenly to the ground, grasping firmly upon something which wriggled through the mud toward the water.

Jane Clayton crouched, wide-eyed and horror-stricken, in the bottom of the boat as she realized that at the last instant success had been turned to failure, and that she was indeed again in the power of the malignant Rokoff.

For the thing that the man had seen and grasped was the end of the trailing rope with which the dugout had been moored to the tree.

CHAPTER FIFTEEN

Down the Ugambi

HALFWAY BETWEEN THE UGAMBI and the village of the Waganwazam, Tarzan came upon the pack moving slowly along his old spoor. Mugambi could scarce believe that the trail of the Russian and the mate of his savage master had passed so close to that of the pack.

It seemed incredible that two human beings should have come so close to them without having been detected by some of the marvellously keen and alert beasts; but Tarzan pointed out the spoor of the two he trailed, and at certain points the black could see that the man and the woman must have been in hiding as the pack passed them, watching every move of the ferocious creatures.

It had been apparent to Tarzan from the first that Jane and Rokoff were not travelling together. The spoor showed distinctly that the young woman had been a considerable distance ahead of the Russian at first, though the farther the ape-man continued along the trail the more obvious it became that the man was rapidly overhauling his quarry.

At first there had been the spoor of wild beasts over the footprints of Jane Clayton, while upon the top of all Rokoff's spoor showed that he had passed over the trail after the animals had left their records upon the ground. But later there were fewer and fewer animal imprints occurring between those of Jane's and the Russian's feet, until as he approached the river the ape-man became aware that Rokoff could not have been more than a few hundred yards behind the girl.

He felt they must be close ahead of him now, and, with a little thrill of expectation, he leaped rapidly forward ahead of the pack. Swinging swiftly through the trees, he came out upon the river-bank at the very point at which Rokoff had overhauled Jane as she endeavoured to launch the cumbersome dugout.

In the mud along the bank the ape-man saw the footprints of the two he sought, but there was neither boat nor people there when he arrived, nor, at first glance, any sign of their whereabouts.

It was plain that they had shoved off a native canoe and embarked upon the bosom of the stream, and as the ape-man's eye ran swiftly down the course of the river beneath the shadows of the overarching trees he saw in the distance, just as it rounded a bend that shut it off from his view, a drifting dugout in the stern of which was the figure of a man.

Just as the pack came in sight of the river they saw their agile leader racing down the river's bank, leaping from hummock to hummock of the swampy ground that spread between them and a little promontory which rose just where the river curved inward from their sight.

To follow him it was necessary for the heavy, cumbersome apes to make a wide detour, and Sheeta, too, who hated water. Mugambi followed after them as rapidly as he could in the wake of the great white master.

A half-hour of rapid travelling across the swampy neck of land and over the rising promontory brought Tarzan, by a short cut, to the inward bend of the winding river, and there before him upon the bosom of the stream he saw the dugout, and in its stern Nikolas Rokoff.

Jane was not with the Russian.

At sight of his enemy the broad scar upon the ape-man's brow burned scarlet, and there rose to his lips the hideous, bestial challenge of the bull-ape.

Rokoff shuddered as the weird and terrible alarm fell upon his ears. Cowering in the bottom of the boat, his teeth chattering in terror, he watched the man he feared above all other creatures upon the face of the earth as he ran quickly to the edge of the water.

Even though the Russian knew that he was safe from his enemy, the very sight of him threw him into a frenzy of trembling cowardice, which became frantic hysteria as he saw the white giant dive fearlessly into the forbidding waters of the tropical river.

With steady, powerful strokes the ape-man forged out into the stream toward the drifting dugout. Now Rokoff seized one of the paddles lying in the bottom of the craft, and, with terrorwide eyes still glued upon the living death that pursued him, struck out madly in an effort to augment the speed of the unwieldy canoe.

And from the opposite bank a sinister ripple, unseen by either man, moved steadily toward the half-naked swimmer.

Tarzan had reached the stern of the craft at last. One hand upstretched grasped the gunwale. Rokoff sat frozen with fear, unable to move a hand or foot, his eyes riveted upon the face of his Nemesis.

Then a sudden commotion in the water behind the swimmer caught his attention. He saw the ripple, and he knew what caused it.

At the same instant Tarzan felt mighty jaws close upon his right leg. He tried to struggle free and raise himself over the side of the boat. His efforts would have succeeded had not this unexpected interruption galvanized the malign brain of the Russian into instant action with its sudden promise of deliverance and revenge.

Like a venomous snake the man leaped toward the stern of the boat, and with a single swift blow struck Tarzan across the head with the heavy paddle. The ape-man's fingers slipped from their hold upon the gunwale.

There was a short struggle at the surface, and then a swirl of waters, a little eddy, and a burst of bubbles soon smoothed out by the flowing current marked for the instant the spot where Tarzan of the Apes, Lord of the Jungle, disappeared from the sight of men beneath the gloomy waters of the dark and forbidding Ugambi.

Weak from terror, Rokoff sank shuddering into the bottom of the dugout. For a moment he could not realize the good fortune that had befallen him – all that he could see was the figure of a silent, struggling white man disappearing beneath the surface of the river to unthinkable death in the slimy mud of the bottom.

Slowly all that it meant to him filtered into the mind of the Russian, and then a cruel smile of relief and triumph touched his lips; but it was short-lived, for just as he was congratulating himself that he was now comparatively safe to proceed upon his way to the coast unmolested, a mighty pandemonium rose from the river-bank close by.

As his eyes sought the authors of the frightful sound he saw standing upon the shore, glaring at him with hate-filled eyes, a devil-faced panther surrounded by the hideous apes of Akut, and in the forefront of them a giant black warrior who shook his fist at him, threatening him with terrible death.

The nightmare of that flight down the Ugambi with the hideous horde racing after him by day and by night, now abreast of him, now lost in the mazes of the jungle far behind for hours and once for a whole day, only to reappear again upon his trail grim, relentless, and terrible, reduced the Russian from a strong and robust man to an emaciated, white-haired, fear-gibbering thing before ever the bay and the ocean broke upon his hopeless vision.

Past populous villages he had fled. Time and again warriors had put out in their canoes to intercept him, but each time the hideous horde had swept into view to send the terrified natives shrieking back to the shore to lose themselves in the jungle.

Nowhere in his flight had he seen aught of Jane Clayton. Not once had his eyes rested upon her since that moment at the river's brim his hand had closed upon the rope attached to the bow of her dugout and he had believed her safely in his power again, only to be thwarted an instant later as the girl snatched up a heavy express rifle from the bottom of the craft and levelled it full at his breast.

Quickly he had dropped the rope then and seen her float away beyond his reach, but a moment later he had been racing up-stream toward a little tributary in the mouth of which was hidden the canoe in which he and his party had come thus far upon their journey in pursuit of the girl and Anderssen.

What had become of her?

There seemed little doubt in the Russian's mind, however, but that she had been captured by warriors from one of the several villages she would have been compelled to pass on her way down to the sea. Well, he was at least rid of most of his human enemies.

But at that he would gladly have had them all back in the land of the living could he thus have been freed from the menace of the frightful creatures who pursued him with awful relentlessness, screaming and growling at him every time they came within sight of him. The one that filled him with the greatest terror was the panther – the flaming-eyed, devil-faced panther whose grinning jaws gaped wide at him by day, and whose fiery orbs gleamed wickedly out across the water from the Cimmerian blackness of the jungle nights.

The sight of the mouth of the Ugambi filled Rokoff with renewed hope, for there, upon the yellow waters of the bay, floated the Kincaid at anchor. He had sent the little steamer away to coal while he had gone up the river, leaving Paulvitch in charge of her, and he could have cried aloud in his relief as he saw that she had returned in time to save him.

Frantically he alternately paddled furiously toward her and rose to his feet waving his paddle and crying aloud in an attempt to attract the attention of those on board. But loud as he screamed his cries awakened no answering challenge from the deck of the silent craft.

Upon the shore behind him a hurried backward glance revealed the presence of the snarling pack. Even now, he thought, these manlike devils might yet find a way to reach him even upon the deck of the steamer unless there were those there to repel them with firearms.

What could have happened to those he had left upon the Kincaid? Where was Paulvitch? Could it be that the vessel was deserted, and that, after all, he was doomed to be overtaken by the terrible fate that he had been flying from through all these hideous days and nights? He shivered as might one upon whose brow death has already laid his clammy finger.

Yet he did not cease to paddle frantically toward the steamer, and at last, after what seemed an eternity, the bow of the dugout bumped against the timbers of the Kincaid. Over the ship's side hung a monkey-ladder, but as the Russian grasped it to ascend to the deck he heard a warning challenge from above, and, looking up, gazed into the cold, relentless muzzle of a rifle.

After Jane Clayton, with rifle levelled at the breast of Rokoff, had succeeded in holding him off until the dugout in which she had taken refuge had drifted out upon the bosom of the Ugambi beyond the man's reach, she had lost no time in paddling to the swiftest sweep of the channel, nor did she for long days and weary nights cease to hold her craft to the most rapidly moving part of the river, except when during the hottest hours of the day she had been wont to drift as the current would take her, lying prone in the bottom of the canoe, her face sheltered from the sun with a great palm leaf.

Thus only did she gain rest upon the voyage; at other times she continually sought to augment the movement of the craft by wielding the heavy paddle.

Rokoff, on the other hand, had used little or no intelligence in his flight along the Ugambi, so that more often than not his craft had drifted in the slow-going eddies, for he habitually hugged the bank farthest from that along which the hideous horde pursued and menaced him.

Thus it was that, though he had put out upon the river but a short time subsequent to the girl, yet she had reached the bay fully two hours ahead of him. When she had first seen the anchored ship upon the quiet water, Jane Clayton's heart had beat fast with hope and thanksgiving, but as she drew closer to the craft and saw that it was the Kincaid, her pleasure gave place to the gravest misgivings.

It was too late, however, to turn back, for the current that carried her toward the ship was much too strong for her muscles. She could not have forced the heavy dugout up-stream against it, and all that was left her was to attempt either to make the shore without being seen by those upon the deck of the Kincaid, or to throw herself upon their mercy – otherwise she must be swept out to sea.

She knew that the shore held little hope of life for her, as she had no knowledge of the location of the friendly Mosula village to which Anderssen had taken her through the darkness of the night of their escape from the Kincaid.

With Rokoff away from the steamer it might be possible that by offering those in charge a large reward they could be induced to carry her to the nearest civilized port. It was worth risking – if she could make the steamer at all.

The current was bearing her swiftly down the river, and she found that only by dint of the utmost exertion could she direct the awkward craft toward the vicinity of the Kincaid. Having reached the decision to board the steamer, she now looked to it for aid, but to her surprise the decks appeared to be empty and she saw no sign of life aboard the ship.

The dugout was drawing closer and closer to the bow of the vessel, and yet no hail came over the side from any lookout aboard. In a moment more, Jane realized, she would be swept beyond the steamer, and then, unless they lowered a boat to rescue her, she would be carried far out to sea by the current and the swift ebb tide that was running.

The young woman called loudly for assistance, but there was no reply other than the shrill scream of some savage beast upon the jungle-shrouded shore. Frantically Jane wielded the paddle in an effort to carry her craft close alongside the steamer.

For a moment it seemed that she should miss her goal by but a few feet, but at the last moment the canoe swung close beneath the steamer's bow and Jane barely managed to grasp the anchor chain.

Heroically she clung to the heavy iron links, almost dragged from the canoe by the strain of the current upon her craft. Beyond her she saw a monkey-ladder dangling over the steamer's side. To release her hold upon the chain and chance clambering to the ladder as her canoe was swept beneath it seemed beyond the pale of possibility, yet to remain clinging to the anchor chain appeared equally as futile.

Finally her glance chanced to fall upon the rope in the bow of the dugout, and, making one end of this fast to the chain, she succeeded in drifting the canoe slowly down until it lay directly beneath the ladder. A moment later, her rifle slung about her shoulders, she had clambered safely to the deserted deck.

Her first task was to explore the ship, and this she did, her rifle ready for instant use should she meet with any human menace aboard the Kincaid. She was not long in discovering the cause of the apparently deserted condition of the steamer, for in the forecastle she found the sailors, who had evidently been left to guard the ship, deep in drunken slumber.

With a shudder of disgust she clambered above, and to the best of her ability closed and made fast the hatch above the heads of the sleeping guard. Next she sought the galley and food, and, having appeased her hunger, she took her place on deck, determined that none should board the Kincaid without first having agreed to her demands.

For an hour or so nothing appeared upon the surface of the river to cause her alarm, but then, about a bend up-stream, she saw a canoe appear in which sat a single figure. It had not proceeded far in her direction before she recognized the occupant as Rokoff, and when the fellow attempted to board he found a rifle staring him in the face.

When the Russian discovered who it was that repelled his advance he became furious, cursing and threatening in a most horrible manner; but, finding that these tactics failed to frighten or move the girl, he at last fell to pleading and promising.

Jane had but a single reply for his every proposition, and that was that nothing would ever persuade her to permit Rokoff upon the same vessel with her. That she would put her threats into action and shoot him should he persist in his endeavour to board the ship he was convinced.

So, as there was no other alternative, the great coward dropped back into his dugout and, at imminent risk of being swept to sea, finally succeeded in making the shore far down the bay and upon the opposite side from that on which the horde of beasts stood snarling and roaring.

Jane Clayton knew that the fellow could not alone and unaided bring his heavy craft back up-stream to the Kincaid, and so she had no further fear of an attack by him. The hideous crew upon the shore she thought she recognized as the same that had passed her in the jungle far up the Ugambi several days before, for it seemed quite beyond reason that there should be more than one such a strangely assorted pack; but what had brought them down-stream to the mouth of the river she could not imagine.

Toward the day's close the girl was suddenly alarmed by the shouting of the Russian from the opposite bank of the stream, and a moment later, following the direction of his gaze, she was terrified to see a ship's boat approaching from up-stream, in which, she felt assured, there could be only members of the Kincaid's missing crew – only heartless ruffians and enemies.

CHAPTER SIXTEEN

In the Darkness of the Night

When Tarzan of the Apes realized that he was in the grip of the great jaws of a crocodile he did not, as an ordinary man might have done, give up all hope and resign himself to his fate.

Instead, he filled his lungs with air before the huge reptile dragged him beneath the surface, and then, with all the might of his great muscles, fought bitterly for freedom. But out of his native element the ape-man was too greatly handicapped to do more than excite the monster to greater speed as it dragged its prey swiftly through the water.

Tarzan's lungs were bursting for a breath of pure fresh air. He knew that he could survive but a moment more, and in the last paroxysm of his suffering he did what he could to avenge his own death.

His body trailed out beside the slimy carcass of his captor, and into the tough armour the ape-man attempted to plunge his stone knife as he was borne to the creature's horrid den.

His efforts but served to accelerate the speed of the crocodile, and just as the ape-man realized that he had reached the limit of his endurance he felt his body dragged to a muddy bed and his nostrils rise above the water's surface. All about him was the blackness of the pit – the silence of the grave.

For a moment Tarzan of the Apes lay gasping for breath upon the slimy, evil-smelling bed to which the animal had borne him. Close at his side he could feel the cold, hard plates of the creature's coat rising and falling as though with spasmodic efforts to breathe.

For several minutes the two lay thus, and then a sudden convulsion of the giant carcass at the man's side, a tremor, and a stiffening brought Tarzan to his knees beside the crocodile. To his utter amazement he found that the beast was dead. The slim knife had found a vulnerable spot in the scaly armour.

Staggering to his feet, the ape-man groped about the reeking, oozy den. He found that he was imprisoned in a subterranean chamber amply large enough to have accommodated a dozen or more of the huge animals such as the one that had dragged him thither.

He realized that he was in the creature's hidden nest far under the bank of the stream, and that doubtless the only means of ingress or egress lay through the submerged opening through which the crocodile had brought him.

His first thought, of course, was of escape, but that he could make his way to the surface of the river beyond and then to the shore seemed highly improbable. There might be turns and windings in the neck of the passage, or, most to be feared, he might meet another of the slimy inhabitants of the retreat upon his journey outward.

Even should he reach the river in safety, there was still the danger of his being again attacked before he could effect a safe landing. Still there was no alternative, and, filling his lungs with the close and reeking air of the chamber, Tarzan of the Apes dived into the dark and watery hole which he could not see but had felt out and found with his feet and legs.

The leg which had been held within the jaws of the crocodile was badly lacerated, but the bone had not been broken, nor were the muscles or tendons sufficiently injured to render it useless. It gave him excruciating pain, that was all.

But Tarzan of the Apes was accustomed to pain, and gave it no further thought when he found that the use of his legs was not greatly impaired by the sharp teeth of the monster.

Rapidly he crawled and swam through the passage which inclined downward and finally upward to open at last into the river bottom but a few feet from the shore line. As the ape-man reached the surface he saw the heads of two great crocodiles but a short distance from him. They were making rapidly in his direction, and with a superhuman effort the man struck out for the overhanging branches of a near-by tree.

Nor was he a moment too soon, for scarcely had he drawn himself to the safety of the limb than two gaping mouths snapped venomously below him. For a few minutes Tarzan rested in the tree that had proved the means of his salvation. His eyes scanned the river as far downstream as the tortuous channel would permit, but there was no sign of the Russian or his dugout.

When he had rested and bound up his wounded leg he started on in pursuit of the drifting canoe. He found himself upon the opposite of the river to that at which he had entered the stream, but as his quarry was upon the bosom of the water it made little difference to the ape-man upon which side he took up the pursuit.

To his intense chagrin he soon found that his leg was more badly injured than he had thought, and that its condition seriously impeded his progress. It was only with the greatest difficulty that he could proceed faster than a walk upon the ground, and in the trees he discovered that it not only impeded his progress, but rendered travelling distinctly dangerous.

From the old negress, Tambudza, Tarzan had gathered a suggestion that now filled his mind with doubts and misgivings. When the old woman had told him of the child's death she had also added that the white woman, though grief-stricken, had confided to her that the baby was not hers.

Tarzan could see no reason for believing that Jane could have found it advisable to deny her identity or that of the child; the only explanation that he could put upon the matter was that, after all, the white woman who had accompanied his son and the Swede into the jungle fastness of the interior had not been Jane at all.

The more he gave thought to the problem, the more firmly convinced he became that his son was dead and his wife still safe in London, and in ignorance of the terrible fate that had overtaken her first-born.

After all, then, his interpretation of Rokoff's sinister taunt had been erroneous, and he had been bearing the burden of a double apprehension needlessly – at least so thought the ape-man. From this belief he garnered some slight surcease from the numbing grief that the death of his little son had thrust upon him.

And such a death! Even the savage beast that was the real Tarzan, inured to the sufferings and horrors of the grim jungle, shuddered as he contemplated the hideous fate that had overtaken the innocent child.

As he made his way painfully towards the coast, he let his mind dwell so constantly upon the frightful crimes which the Russian had perpetrated against his loved ones that the great scar upon his forehead stood out almost continuously in the vivid scarlet that marked the man's most relentless and bestial moods of rage. At times he startled even himself and sent the lesser creatures of the wild jungle scampering to their hiding places as involuntary roars and growls rumbled from his throat.

Could he but lay his hand upon the Russian!

Twice upon the way to the coast bellicose natives ran threateningly from their villages to bar his further progress, but when the awful cry of the bull-ape thundered upon their affrighted ears, and the great white giant charged bellowing upon them, they had turned and fled into the bush, nor ventured thence until he had safely passed.

Though his progress seemed tantalizingly slow to the ape-man whose idea of speed had been gained by such standards as the lesser apes attain, he made, as a matter of fact, almost as rapid progress as the drifting canoe that bore Rokoff on ahead of him, so that he came to the bay and within sight of the ocean just after darkness had fallen upon the same day that Jane Clayton and the Russian ended their flights from the interior.

The darkness lowered so heavily upon the black river and the encircling jungle that Tarzan, even with eyes accustomed to much use after dark, could make out nothing a few yards from him. His idea was to search the shore that night for signs of the Russian and the woman who he was certain must have preceded Rokoff down the Ugambi. That the Kincaid or other ship lay at anchor but a hundred yards from him he did not dream, for no light showed on board the steamer.

Even as he commenced his search his attention was suddenly attracted by a noise that he had not at first perceived – the stealthy dip of paddles in the water some distance from the shore, and about opposite the point at which he stood. Motionless as a statue he stood listening to the faint sound.

Presently it ceased, to be followed by a shuffling noise that the ape-man's trained ears could interpret as resulting from but a single cause – the scraping of leather-shod feet upon the rounds of a ship's monkey-ladder. And yet, as far as he could see, there was no ship there – nor might there be one within a thousand miles.

As he stood thus, peering out into the darkness of the cloud-enshrouded night, there came to him from across the water, like a slap in the face, so sudden and unexpected was it, the sharp staccato of an exchange of shots and then the scream of a woman.

Wounded though he was, and with the memory of his recent horrible experience still strong upon him, Tarzan of the Apes did not hesitate as the notes of that frightened cry rose shrill and piercing upon the still night air. With a bound he cleared the intervening bush – there was a splash as the water closed about him – and then, with powerful strokes, he swam out into the impenetrable night with no guide save the memory of an illusive cry, and for company the hideous denizens of an equatorial river.

The boat that had attracted Jane's attention as she stood guard upon the deck of the Kincaid had been perceived by Rokoff upon one bank and Mugambi and the horde upon the other. The cries of the Russian had brought the dugout first to him, and then, after a conference, it had been turned toward the Kincaid, but before ever it covered half the distance between the shore and the steamer a rifle had spoken from the latter's deck and one of the sailors in the bow of the canoe had crumpled and fallen into the water.

After that they went more slowly, and presently, when Jane's rifle had found another member of the party, the canoe withdrew to the shore, where it lay as long as daylight lasted.

The savage, snarling pack upon the opposite shore had been directed in their pursuit by the black warrior, Mugambi, chief of the Wagambi. Only he knew which might be foe and which friend of their lost master.

Could they have reached either the canoe or the Kincaid they would have made short work of any whom they found there, but the gulf of black water intervening shut them off from farther advance as effectually as though it had been the broad ocean that separated them from their prey.

Mugambi knew something of the occurrences which had led up to the landing of Tarzan upon Jungle Island and the pursuit of the whites up the Ugambi. He knew that his savage master sought his wife and child who had been stolen by the wicked white man whom they had followed far into the interior and now back to the sea.

He believed also that this same man had killed the great white giant whom he had come to respect and love as he had never loved the greatest chiefs of his own people. And so in the wild breast of Mugambi burned an iron resolve to win to the side of the wicked one and wreak vengeance upon him for the murder of the ape-man.

But when he saw the canoe come down the river and take in Rokoff, when he saw it make for the Kincaid, he realized that only by possessing himself of a canoe could he hope to transport the beasts of the pack within striking distance of the enemy.

So it happened that even before Jane Clayton fired the first shot into Rokoff's canoe the beasts of Tarzan had disappeared into the jungle.

After the Russian and his party, which consisted of Paulvitch and the several men he had left upon the Kincaid to attend to the matter of coaling, had retreated before her fire, Jane realized that it would be but a temporary respite from their attentions which she had gained, and with the conviction came a determination to make a bold and final stroke for freedom from the menacing threat of Rokoff's evil purpose.

With this idea in view she opened negotiations with the two sailors she had imprisoned in the forecastle, and having forced their consent to her plans, upon pain of death should they attempt disloyalty, she released them just as darkness closed about the ship.

With ready revolver to compel obedience, she let them up one by one, searching them carefully for concealed weapons as they stood with hands elevated above their heads. Once satisfied that they were unarmed, she set them to work cutting the cable which held the Kincaid to her anchorage, for her bold plan was nothing less than to set the steamer adrift and float with her out into the open sea, there to trust to the mercy of the elements, which she was confident would be no more merciless than Nikolas Rokoff should he again capture her.

There was, too, the chance that the Kincaid might be sighted by some passing ship, and as she was well stocked with provisions and water – the men had assured her of this fact – and as the season of storm was well over, she had every reason to hope for the eventual success of her plan.

The night was deeply overcast, heavy clouds riding low above the jungle and the water – only to the west, where the broad ocean spread beyond the river's mouth, was there a suggestion of lessening gloom.

It was a perfect night for the purposes of the work in hand.

Her enemies could not see the activity aboard the ship nor mark her course as the swift current bore her outward into the ocean. Before daylight broke the ebb-tide would have carried the Kincaid well into the Benguela current which flows northward along the coast of Africa, and, as a south wind was prevailing, Jane hoped to be out of sight of the mouth of the Ugambi before Rokoff could become aware of the departure of the steamer.

Standing over the labouring seamen, the young woman breathed a sigh of relief as the last strand of the cable parted and she knew that the vessel was on its way out of the maw of the savage Ugambi.

With her two prisoners still beneath the coercing influence of her rifle, she ordered them upon deck with the intention of again imprisoning them in the forecastle; but at length she permitted herself to be influenced by their promises of loyalty and the arguments which they put forth that they could be of service to her, and permitted them to remain above.

For a few minutes the Kincaid drifted rapidly with the current, and then, with a grinding jar, she stopped in midstream. The ship had run upon a low-lying bar that splits the channel about a quarter of a mile from the sea.

For a moment she hung there, and then, swinging round until her bow pointed toward the shore, she broke adrift once more.

At the same instant, just as Jane Clayton was congratulating herself that the ship was once more free, there fell upon her ears from a point up the river about where the Kincaid had been anchored the rattle of musketry and a woman's scream – shrill, piercing, fear-laden.

The sailors heard the shots with certain conviction that they announced the coming of their employer, and as they had no relish for the plan that would consign them to the deck of a drifting derelict, they whispered together a hurried plan to overcome the young woman and hail Rokoff and their companions to their rescue.

It seemed that fate would play into their hands, for with the reports of the guns Jane Clayton's attention had been distracted from her unwilling assistants, and instead of keeping one eye upon them as she had intended doing, she ran to the bow of the Kincaid to peer through the darkness toward the source of the disturbance upon the river's bosom.

Seeing that she was off her guard, the two sailors crept stealthily upon her from behind.

The scraping upon the deck of the shoes of one of them startled the girl to a sudden appreciation of her danger, but the warning had come too late.

As she turned, both men leaped upon her and bore her to the deck, and as she went down beneath them she saw, outlined against the lesser gloom of the ocean, the figure of another man clamber over the side of the Kincaid.

After all her pains her heroic struggle for freedom had failed. With a stifled sob she gave up the unequal battle.

CHAPTER SEVENTEEN

On the Deck of the "Kincaid"

WHEN MUGAMBI HAD TURNED back into the jungle with the pack he had a definite purpose in view. It was to obtain a dugout wherewith to transport the beasts of Tarzan to the side of the Kincaid. Nor was he long in coming upon the object which he sought.

Just at dusk he found a canoe moored to the bank of a small tributary of the Ugambi at a point where he had felt certain that he should find one.

Without loss of time he piled his hideous fellows into the craft and shoved out into the stream. So quickly had they taken possession of the canoe that the warrior had not noticed that it was already occupied. The huddled figure sleeping in the bottom had entirely escaped his observation in the darkness of the night that had now fallen.

But no sooner were they afloat than a savage growling from one of the apes directly ahead of him in the dugout attracted his attention to a shivering and cowering figure that trembled between him and the great anthropoid. To Mugambi's astonishment he saw that it was a native woman. With difficulty he kept the ape from her throat, and after a time succeeded in quelling her fears.

It seemed that she had been fleeing from marriage with an old man she loathed and had taken refuge for the night in the canoe she had found upon the river's edge.

Mugambi did not wish her presence, but there she was, and rather than lose time by returning her to the shore the black permitted her to remain on board the canoe.

As quickly as his awkward companions could paddle the dugout down-stream toward the Ugambi and the Kincaid they moved through the darkness. It was with difficulty that Mugambi could make out the shadowy form of the steamer, but as he had it between himself and the ocean it was much more apparent than to one upon either shore of the river.

As he approached it he was amazed to note that it seemed to be receding from him, and finally he was convinced that the vessel was moving down-stream. Just as he was about to urge his creatures to renewed efforts to overtake the steamer the outline of another canoe burst suddenly into view not three yards from the bow of his own craft.

At the same instant the occupants of the stranger discovered the proximity of Mugambi's horde, but they did not at first recognize the nature of the fearful crew. A man in the bow of the oncoming boat challenged them just as the two dugouts were about to touch.

For answer came the menacing growl of a panther, and the fellow found himself gazing into the flaming eyes of Sheeta, who had raised himself with his forepaws upon the bow of the boat, ready to leap in upon the occupants of the other craft.

Instantly Rokoff realized the peril that confronted him and his fellows. He gave a quick command to fire upon the occupants of the other canoe, and it was this volley and the scream of the terrified native woman in the canoe with Mugambi that both Tarzan and Jane had heard.

Before the slower and less skilled paddlers in Mugambi's canoe could press their advantage and effect a boarding of the enemy the latter had turned swiftly down-stream and were paddling for their lives in the direction of the Kincaid, which was now visible to them.

The vessel after striking upon the bar had swung loose again into a slow-moving eddy, which returns up-stream close to the southern shore of the Ugambi only to circle out once more and join the downward flow a hundred yards or so farther up. Thus the Kincaid was returning Jane Clayton directly into the hands of her enemies.

It so happened that as Tarzan sprang into the river the vessel was not visible to him, and as he swam out into the night he had no idea that a ship drifted so close at hand. He was guided by the sounds which he could hear coming from the two canoes.

As he swam he had vivid recollections of the last occasion upon which he had swum in the waters of the Ugambi, and with them a sudden shudder shook the frame of the giant.

But, though he twice felt something brush his legs from the slimy depths below him, nothing seized him, and of a sudden he quite forgot about crocodiles in the astonishment of seeing a dark mass loom suddenly before him where he had still expected to find the open river.

So close was it that a few strokes brought him up to the thing, when to his amazement his outstretched hand came in contact with a ship's side.

As the agile ape-man clambered over the vessel's rail there came to his sensitive ears the sound of a struggle at the opposite side of the deck.

Noiselessly he sped across the intervening space.

The moon had risen now, and, though the sky was still banked with clouds, a lesser darkness enveloped the scene than that which had blotted out all sight earlier in the night. His keen eyes, therefore, saw the figures of two men grappling with a woman.

That it was the woman who had accompanied Anderssen toward the interior he did not know, though he suspected as much, as he was now quite certain that this was the deck of the Kincaid upon which chance had led him.

But he wasted little time in idle speculation. There was a woman in danger of harm from two ruffians, which was enough excuse for the ape-man to project his giant thews into the conflict without further investigation.

The first that either of the sailors knew that there was a new force at work upon the ship was the falling of a mighty hand upon a shoulder of each. As if they had been in the grip of a fly-wheel, they were jerked suddenly from their prey.

"What means this?" asked a low voice in their ears.

They were given no time to reply, however, for at the sound of that voice the young woman had sprung to her feet and with a little cry of joy leaped toward their assailant.

"Tarzan!" she cried.

The ape-man hurled the two sailors across the deck, where they rolled, stunned and terrified, into the scuppers upon the opposite side, and with an exclamation of incredulity gathered the girl into his arms.

Brief, however, were the moments for their greeting.

Scarcely had they recognized one another than the clouds above them parted to show the figures of a half-dozen men clambering over the side of the Kincaid to the steamer's deck.

Foremost among them was the Russian. As the brilliant rays of the equatorial moon lighted the deck, and he realized that the man before him was Lord Greystoke, he screamed hysterical commands to his followers to fire upon the two.

Tarzan pushed Jane behind the cabin near which they had been standing, and with a quick bound started for Rokoff. The men behind the Russian, at least two of them, raised their rifles and fired at the charging ape-man; but those behind them were otherwise engaged – for up the monkey-ladder in their rear was thronging a hideous horde.

First came five snarling apes, huge, manlike beasts, with bared fangs and slavering jaws; and after them a giant black warrior, his long spear gleaming in the moonlight.

Behind him again scrambled another creature, and of all the horrid horde it was this they most feared – Sheeta, the panther, with gleaming jaws agape and fiery eyes blazing at them in the mightiness of his hate and of his blood lust.

The shots that had been fired at Tarzan missed him, and he would have been upon Rokoff in another instant had not the great coward dodged backward between his two henchmen, and, screaming in hysterical terror, bolted forward toward the forecastle.

For the moment Tarzan's attention was distracted by the two men before him, so that he could not at the time pursue the Russian. About him the apes and Mugambi were battling with the balance of the Russian's party.

Beneath the terrible ferocity of the beasts the men were soon scampering in all directions – those who still lived to scamper, for the great fangs of the apes of Akut and the tearing talons of Sheeta already had found more than a single victim.

Four, however, escaped and disappeared into the forecastle, where they hoped to barricade themselves against further assault. Here they found Rokoff, and, enraged at his desertion of them in their moment of peril, no less than at the uniformly brutal treatment it had been his wont to accord them, they gloated upon the opportunity now offered them to revenge themselves in part upon their hated employer.

Despite his prayers and grovelling pleas, therefore, they hurled him bodily out upon the deck, delivering him to the mercy of the fearful things from which they had themselves just escaped.

Tarzan saw the man emerge from the forecastle – saw and recognized his enemy; but another saw him even as soon.

It was Sheeta, and with grinning jaws the mighty beast slunk silently toward the terror-stricken man.

When Rokoff saw what it was that stalked him his shrieks for help filled the air, as with trembling knees he stood, as one paralyzed, before the hideous death that was creeping upon him.

Tarzan took a step toward the Russian, his brain burning with a raging fire of vengeance. At last he had the murderer of his son at his mercy. His was the right to avenge.

Once Jane had stayed his hand that time that he sought to take the law into his own power and mete to Rokoff the death that he had so long merited; but this time none should stay him.

His fingers clenched and unclenched spasmodically as he approached the trembling Russ, beastlike and ominous as a brute of prey.

Presently he saw that Sheeta was about to forestall him, robbing him of the fruits of his great hate.

He called sharply to the panther, and the words, as if they had broken a hideous spell that had held the Russian, galvanized him into sudden action. With a scream he turned and fled toward the bridge.

After him pounced Sheeta the panther, unmindful of his master's warning voice.

Tarzan was about to leap after the two when he felt a light touch upon his arm. Turning, he found Jane at his elbow.

"Do not leave me," she whispered. "I am afraid."

Tarzan glanced behind her.

All about were the hideous apes of Akut. Some, even, were approaching the young woman with bared fangs and menacing guttural warnings.

The ape-man warned them back. He had forgotten for the moment that these were but beasts, unable to differentiate his friends and his foes. Their savage natures were roused by their recent battle with the sailors, and now all flesh outside the pack was meat to them.

Tarzan turned again toward the Russian, chagrined that he should have to forgo the pleasure of personal revenge – unless the man should escape Sheeta. But as he looked he saw that there could be no hope of that. The fellow had retreated to the end of the bridge, where he now stood trembling and wide-eyed, facing the beast that moved slowly toward him.

The panther crawled with belly to the planking, uttering uncanny mouthings. Rokoff stood as though petrified, his eyes protruding from their sockets, his mouth agape, and the cold sweat of terror clammy upon his brow.

Below him, upon the deck, he had seen the great anthropoids, and so had not dared to seek escape in that direction. In fact, even now one of the brutes was leaping to seize the bridge-rail and draw himself up to the Russian's side.

Before him was the panther, silent and crouched.

Rokoff could not move. His knees trembled. His voice broke in inarticulate shrieks. With a last piercing wail he sank to his knees – and then Sheeta sprang.

Full upon the man's breast the tawny body hurtled, tumbling the Russian to his back.

As the great fangs tore at the throat and chest, Jane Clayton turned away in horror; but not so Tarzan of the Apes. A cold smile of satisfaction touched his lips. The scar upon his forehead that had burned scarlet faded to the normal hue of his tanned skin and disappeared.

Rokoff fought furiously but futilely against the growling, rending fate that had overtaken him. For all his countless crimes he was punished in the brief moment of the hideous death that claimed him at the last.

After his struggles ceased Tarzan approached, at Jane's suggestion, to wrest the body from the panther and give what remained of it decent human burial; but the great cat rose snarling above its kill, threatening even the master it loved in its savage way, so that rather than kill his friend of the jungle, Tarzan was forced to relinquish his intentions.

All that night Sheeta, the panther, crouched upon the grisly thing that had been Nikolas Rokoff. The bridge of the Kincaid was slippery with blood. Beneath the brilliant tropic moon the great beast feasted until, when the sun rose the following morning, there remained of Tarzan's great enemy only gnawed and broken bones.

Of the Russian's party, all were accounted for except Paulvitch. Four were prisoners in the Kincaid's forecastle. The rest were dead.

With these men Tarzan got up steam upon the vessel, and with the knowledge of the mate, who happened to be one of those surviving, he planned to set out in quest of Jungle Island; but as the morning dawned there came with it a heavy gale from the west which raised a sea into which the mate of the Kincaid dared not venture. All that day the ship lay within the shelter of the mouth of the river; for, though night witnessed a lessening of the wind, it was thought safer to wait for daylight before attempting the navigation of the winding channel to the sea.

Upon the deck of the steamer the pack wandered without let or hindrance by day, for they had soon learned through Tarzan and Mugambi that they must harm no one upon the Kincaid; but at night they were confined below.

Tarzan's joy had been unbounded when he learned from his wife that the little child who had died in the village of M'ganwazam was not their son. Who the baby could have been, or what had become of their own, they could not imagine, and as both Rokoff and Paulvitch were gone, there was no way of discovering.

There was, however, a certain sense of relief in the knowledge that they might yet hope. Until positive proof of the baby's death reached them there was always that to buoy them up.

It seemed quite evident that their little Jack had not been brought aboard the Kincaid. Anderssen would have known of it had such been the case, but he had assured Jane time and time again that the little one he had brought to her cabin the night he aided her to escape was the only one that had been aboard the Kincaid since she lay at Dover.

CHAPTER EIGHTEEN

Paulvitch Plots Revenge

As Jane and Tarzan stood upon the vessel's deck recounting to one another the details of the various adventures through which each had passed since they had parted in their London home, there glared at them from beneath scowling brows a hidden watcher upon the shore.

Through the man's brain passed plan after plan whereby he might thwart the escape of the Englishman and his wife, for so long as the vital spark remained within the vindictive brain of Alexander Paulvitch none who had aroused the enmity of the Russian might be entirely safe.

Plan after plan he formed only to discard each either as impracticable, or unworthy the vengeance his wrongs demanded. So warped by faulty reasoning was the criminal mind of Rokoff's lieutenant that he could not grasp the real truth of that which lay between himself and the ape-man and see that always the fault had been, not with the English lord, but with himself and his confederate.

And at the rejection of each new scheme Paulvitch arrived always at the same conclusion – that he could accomplish naught while half the breadth of the Ugambi separated him from the object of his hatred.

But how was he to span the crocodile-infested waters? There was no canoe nearer than the Mosula village, and Paulvitch was none too sure that the Kincaid would still be at anchor in the river when he returned should he take the time to traverse the jungle to the distant village and return with a canoe. Yet there was no other way, and so, convinced that thus alone might he hope to reach his prey, Paulvitch, with a parting scowl at the two figures upon the Kincaid's deck, turned away from the river.

Hastening through the dense jungle, his mind centred upon his one fetich – revenge – the Russian forgot even his terror of the savage world through which he moved.

Baffled and beaten at every turn of Fortune's wheel, reacted upon time after time by his own malign plotting, the principal victim of his own criminality, Paulvitch was yet so blind as to imagine that his greatest happiness lay in a continuation of the plottings and schemings which had ever brought him and Rokoff to disaster, and the latter finally to a hideous death.

As the Russian stumbled on through the jungle toward the Mosula village there presently crystallized within his brain a plan which seemed more feasible than any that he had as yet considered.

He would come by night to the side of the Kincaid, and once aboard, would search out the members of the ship's original crew who had survived the terrors of this frightful expedition, and enlist them in an attempt to wrest the vessel from Tarzan and his beasts.

In the cabin were arms and ammunition, and hidden in a secret receptacle in the cabin table was one of those infernal machines, the construction of which had occupied much of Paulvitch's spare time when he had stood high in the confidence of the Nihilists of his native land.

That was before he had sold them out for immunity and gold to the police of Petrograd. Paulvitch winced as he recalled the denunciation of him that had fallen from the lips of one of his former comrades ere the poor devil expiated his political sins at the end of a hempen rope.

But the infernal machine was the thing to think of now. He could do much with that if he could but get his hands upon it. Within the little hardwood case hidden in the cabin table rested sufficient potential destructiveness to wipe out in the fraction of a second every enemy aboard the Kincaid.

Paulvitch licked his lips in anticipatory joy, and urged his tired legs to greater speed that he might not be too late to the ship's anchorage to carry out his designs.

All depended, of course, upon when the Kincaid departed. The Russian realized that nothing could be accomplished beneath the light of day. Darkness must shroud his approach to the ship's side, for should he be sighted by Tarzan or Lady Greystoke he would have no chance to board the vessel.

The gale that was blowing was, he believed, the cause of the delay in getting the Kincaid under way, and if it continued to blow until night then the chances were all in his favour, for he knew that there was little likelihood of the ape-man attempting to navigate the tortuous channel of the Ugambi while darkness lay upon the surface of the water, hiding the many bars and the numerous small islands which are scattered over the expanse of the river's mouth.

It was well after noon when Paulvitch came to the Mosula village upon the bank of the tributary of the Ugambi. Here he was received with suspicion and unfriendliness by the native chief, who, like all those who came in contact with Rokoff or Paulvitch, had suffered in some manner from the greed, the cruelty, or the lust of the two Muscovites.

When Paulvitch demanded the use of a canoe the chief grumbled a surly refusal and ordered the white man from the village. Surrounded by angry, muttering warriors who seemed to be but waiting some slight pretext to transfix him with their menacing spears the Russian could do naught else than withdraw.

A dozen fighting men led him to the edge of the clearing, leaving him with a warning never to show himself again in the vicinity of their village.

Stifling his anger, Paulvitch slunk into the jungle; but once beyond the sight of the warriors he paused and listened intently. He could hear the voices of his escort as the men returned to the village, and when he was sure that they were not following him he wormed his way through the bushes to the edge of the river, still determined some way to obtain a canoe.

Life itself depended upon his reaching the Kincaid and enlisting the survivors of the ship's crew in his service, for to be abandoned here amidst the dangers of the African jungle where he had won the enmity of the natives was, he well knew, practically equivalent to a sentence of death.

A desire for revenge acted as an almost equally powerful incentive to spur him into the face of danger to accomplish his design, so that it was a desperate man that lay hidden in the foliage beside the little river searching with eager eyes for some sign of a small canoe which might be easily handled by a single paddle.

Nor had the Russian long to wait before one of the awkward little skiffs which the Mosula fashion came in sight upon the bosom of the river. A youth was paddling lazily out into midstream from a point beside the village. When he reached the channel he allowed the sluggish current to carry him slowly along while he lolled indolently in the bottom of his crude canoe.

All ignorant of the unseen enemy upon the river's bank the lad floated slowly down the stream while Paulvitch followed along the jungle path a few yards behind him.

A mile below the village the black boy dipped his paddle into the water and forced his skiff toward the bank. Paulvitch, elated by the chance which had drawn the youth to the same side of the river as that along which he followed rather than to the opposite side where he would have been beyond the stalker's reach, hid in the brush close beside the point at which it was evident the skiff would touch the bank of the slow-moving stream, which seemed jealous of each fleeting instant which drew it nearer to the broad and muddy Ugambi where it must for ever lose its identity in the larger stream that would presently cast its waters into the great ocean.

Equally indolent were the motions of the Mosula youth as he drew his skiff beneath an overhanging limb of a great tree that leaned down to implant a farewell kiss upon the bosom of the departing water, caressing with green fronds the soft breast of its languorous love.

And, snake-like, amidst the concealing foliage lay the malevolent Russ. Cruel, shifty eyes gloated upon the outlines of the coveted canoe, and measured the stature of its owner, while the crafty brain weighed the chances of the white man should physical encounter with the black become necessary.

Only direct necessity could drive Alexander Paulvitch to personal conflict; but it was indeed dire necessity which goaded him on to action now.

There was time, just time enough, to reach the Kincaid by nightfall. Would the black fool never quit his skiff? Paulvitch squirmed and fidgeted. The lad yawned and stretched. With exasperating deliberateness he examined the arrows in his quiver, tested his bow, and looked to the edge upon the hunting-knife in his loin-cloth.

Again he stretched and yawned, glanced up at the river-bank, shrugged his shoulders, and lay down in the bottom of his canoe for a little nap before he plunged into the jungle after the prey he had come forth to hunt.

Paulvitch half rose, and with tensed muscles stood glaring down upon his unsuspecting victim. The boy's lids drooped and closed. Presently his breast rose and fell to the deep breaths of slumber. The time had come!

The Russian crept stealthily nearer. A branch rustled beneath his weight and the lad stirred in his sleep. Paulvitch drew his revolver and levelled it upon the black. For a moment he remained in rigid quiet, and then again the youth relapsed into undisturbed slumber.

The white man crept closer. He could not chance a shot until there was no risk of missing. Presently he leaned close above the Mosula. The cold steel of the revolver in his hand insinuated itself nearer and nearer to the breast of the unconscious lad. Now it stopped but a few inches above the strongly beating heart.

But the pressure of a finger lay between the harmless boy and eternity. The soft bloom of youth still lay upon the brown cheek, a smile half parted the beardless lips. Did any qualm of conscience point its disquieting finger of reproach at the murderer?

To all such was Alexander Paulvitch immune. A sneer curled his bearded lip as his forefinger closed upon the trigger of his revolver. There was a loud report. A little hole appeared above the heart of the sleeping boy, a little hole about which lay a blackened rim of powder-burned flesh.

The youthful body half rose to a sitting posture. The smiling lips tensed to the nervous shock of a momentary agony which the conscious mind never apprehended, and then the dead sank limply back into that deepest of slumbers from which there is no awakening.

The killer dropped quickly into the skiff beside the killed. Ruthless hands seized the dead boy heartlessly and raised him to the low gunwale. A little shove, a splash, some widening ripples broken by the sudden surge of a dark, hidden body from the slimy depths, and the coveted canoe was in the sole possession of the white man – more savage than the youth whose life he had taken.

Casting off the tie rope and seizing the paddle, Paulvitch bent feverishly to the task of driving the skiff downward toward the Ugambi at top speed.

Night had fallen when the prow of the bloodstained craft shot out into the current of the larger stream. Constantly the Russian strained his eyes into the increasing darkness ahead in vain endeavour to pierce the black shadows which lay between him and the anchorage of the Kincaid.

Was the ship still riding there upon the waters of the Ugambi, or had the ape-man at last persuaded himself of the safety of venturing forth into the abating storm? As Paulvitch forged ahead with the current he asked himself these questions, and many more beside, not the least disquieting of which were those which related to his future should it chance that the Kincaid had already steamed away, leaving him to the merciless horrors of the savage wilderness.

In the darkness it seemed to the paddler that he was fairly flying over the water, and he had become convinced that the ship had left her moorings and that he had already passed the spot at which she had lain earlier in the day, when there appeared before him beyond a projecting point which he had but just rounded the flickering light from a ship's lantern.

Alexander Paulvitch could scarce restrain an exclamation of triumph. The Kincaid had not departed! Life and vengeance were not to elude him after all.

He stopped paddling the moment that he descried the gleaming beacon of hope ahead of him. Silently he drifted down the muddy waters of the Ugambi, occasionally dipping his paddle's blade gently into the current that he might guide his primitive craft to the vessel's side.

As he approached more closely the dark bulk of a ship loomed before him out of the blackness of the night. No sound came from the vessel's deck. Paulvitch drifted, unseen, close to the Kincaid's side. Only the momentary scraping of his canoe's nose against the ship's planking broke the silence of the night.

Trembling with nervous excitement, the Russian remained motionless for several minutes; but there was no sound from the great bulk above him to indicate that his coming had been noted.

Stealthily he worked his craft forward until the stays of the bowsprit were directly above him. He could just reach them. To make his canoe fast there was the work of but a minute or two, and then the man raised himself quietly aloft.

A moment later he dropped softly to the deck. Thoughts of the hideous pack which tenanted the ship induced cold tremors along the spine of the cowardly prowler; but life itself depended upon the success of his venture, and so he was enabled to steel himself to the frightful chances which lay before him.

No sound or sign of watch appeared upon the ship's deck. Paulvitch crept stealthily toward the forecastle. All was silence. The hatch was raised, and as the man peered downward he saw one of the Kincaid's crew reading by the light of the smoky lantern depending from the ceiling of the crew's quarters.

Paulvitch knew the man well, a surly cut-throat upon whom he figured strongly in the carrying out of the plan which he had conceived. Gently the Russ lowered himself through the aperture to the rounds of the ladder which led into the forecastle.

He kept his eyes turned upon the reading man, ready to warn him to silence the moment that the fellow discovered him; but so deeply immersed was the sailor in the magazine that the Russian came, unobserved, to the forecastle floor.

There he turned and whispered the reader's name. The man raised his eyes from the magazine – eyes that went wide for a moment as they fell upon the familiar countenance of Rokoff's lieutenant, only to narrow instantly in a scowl of disapproval.

"The devil!" he ejaculated. "Where did you come from? We all thought you were done for and gone where you ought to have gone a long time ago. His lordship will be mighty pleased to see you."

Paulvitch crossed to the sailor's side. A friendly smile lay on the Russian's lips, and his right hand was extended in greeting, as though the other might have been a dear and long lost friend. The sailor ignored the proffered hand, nor did he return the other's smile.

"I've come to help you," explained Paulvitch. "I'm going to help you get rid of the Englishman and his beasts – then there will be no danger from the law when we get back to civilization. We can sneak in on them while they sleep – that is Greystoke, his wife, and that black scoundrel, Mugambi. Afterward it will be a simple matter to clean up the beasts. Where are they?"

"They're below," replied the sailor; "but just let me tell you something, Paulvitch. You haven't got no more show to turn us men against the Englishman than nothing. We had all we wanted of you and that other beast. He's dead, an' if I don't miss my guess a whole lot you'll be dead too before long. You two treated us like dogs, and if you think we got any love for you you better forget it."

"You mean to say that you're going to turn against me?" demanded Paulvitch.

The other nodded, and then after a momentary pause, during which an idea seemed to have occurred to him, he spoke again.

"Unless," he said, "you can make it worth my while to let you go before the Englishman finds you here."

"You wouldn't turn me away in the jungle, would you?" asked Paulvitch. "Why, I'd die there in a week."

"You'd have a chance there," replied the sailor. "Here, you wouldn't have no chance. Why, if I woke up my maties here they'd probably cut your heart out of you before the Englishman got a chance at you at all. It's mighty lucky for you that I'm the one to be awake now and not none of the others."

"You're crazy," cried Paulvitch. "Don't you know that the Englishman will have you all hanged when he gets you back where the law can get hold of you?"

"No, he won't do nothing of the kind," replied the sailor. "He's told us as much, for he says that there wasn't nobody to blame but you and Rokoff – the rest of us was just tools. See?"

For half an hour the Russian pleaded or threatened as the mood seized him. Sometimes he was upon the verge of tears, and again he was promising his listener either fabulous rewards or condign punishment; but the other was obdurate. [condign: of equal value]

He made it plain to the Russian that there were but two plans open to him – either he must consent to being turned over immediately to Lord Greystoke, or he must pay to the sailor, as a price for permission to quit the Kincaid unmolested, every cent of money and article of value upon his person and in his cabin.

"And you'll have to make up your mind mighty quick," growled the man, "for I want to turn in. Come now, choose – his lordship or the jungle?"

"You'll be sorry for this," grumbled the Russian.

"Shut up," admonished the sailor. "If you get funny I may change my mind, and keep you here after all."

Now Paulvitch had no intention of permitting himself to fall into the hands of Tarzan of the Apes if he could possibly avoid it, and while the terrors of the jungle appalled him they were, to his mind, infinitely preferable to the certain death which he knew he merited and for which he might look at the hands of the ape-man.

"Is anyone sleeping in my cabin?" he asked.

The sailor shook his head. "No," he said; "Lord and Lady Greystoke have the captain's cabin. The mate is in his own, and there ain't no one in yours."

"I'll go and get my valuables for you," said Paulvitch.

"I'll go with you to see that you don't try any funny business," said the sailor, and he followed the Russian up the ladder to the deck.

At the cabin entrance the sailor halted to watch, permitting Paulvitch to go alone to his cabin. Here he gathered together his few belongings that were to buy him the uncertain safety of escape, and as he stood for a moment beside the little table on which he had piled them he searched his brain for some feasible plan either to ensure his safety or to bring revenge upon his enemies.

And presently as he thought there recurred to his memory the little black box which lay hidden in a secret receptacle beneath a false top upon the table where his hand rested.

The Russian's face lighted to a sinister gleam of malevolent satisfaction as he stooped and felt beneath the table top. A moment later he withdrew from its hiding-place the thing he sought. He had lighted the lantern swinging from the beams overhead that he might see to collect his belongings, and now he held the black box well in the rays of the lamplight, while he fingered at the clasp that fastened its lid.

The lifted cover revealed two compartments within the box. In one was a mechanism which resembled the works of a small clock. There also was a little battery of two dry cells. A wire ran from the clockwork to one of the poles of the battery, and from the other pole through the partition into the other compartment, a second wire returning directly to the clockwork.

Whatever lay within the second compartment was not visible, for a cover lay over it and appeared to be sealed in place by asphaltum. In the bottom of the box, beside the clockwork, lay a key, and this Paulvitch now withdrew and fitted to the winding stem.

Gently he turned the key, muffling the noise of the winding operation by throwing a couple of articles of clothing over the box. All the time he listened intently for any sound which might indicate that the sailor or another were approaching his cabin; but none came to interrupt his work.

When the winding was completed the Russian set a pointer upon a small dial at the side of the clockwork, then he replaced the cover upon the black box, and returned the entire machine to its hiding-place in the table.

A sinister smile curled the man's bearded lips as he gathered up his valuables, blew out the lamp, and stepped from his cabin to the side of the waiting sailor.

"Here are my things," said the Russian; "now let me go."

"I'll first take a look in your pockets," replied the sailor. "You might have overlooked some trifling thing that won't be of no use to you in the jungle, but that'll come in mighty handy to a poor sailorman in London. Ah! just as I feared," he ejaculated an instant later as he withdrew a roll of bank notes from Paulvitch's inside coat pocket.

The Russian scowled, muttering an imprecation; but nothing could be gained by argument, and so he did his best to reconcile himself to his loss in the knowledge that the sailor would never reach London to enjoy the fruits of his thievery.

It was with difficulty that Paulvitch restrained a consuming desire to taunt the man with a suggestion of the fate that would presently overtake him and the other members of the Kincaid's company; but fearing to arouse the fellow's suspicions, he crossed the deck and lowered himself in silence into his canoe.

A minute or two later he was paddling toward the shore to be swallowed up in the darkness of the jungle night, and the terrors of a hideous existence from which, could he have had even a slight foreknowledge of what awaited him in the long years to come, he would have fled to the certain death of the open sea rather than endure it.

The sailor, having made sure that Paulvitch had departed, returned to the forecastle, where he hid away his booty and turned into his bunk, while in the cabin that had belonged to the Russian there ticked on and on through the silences of the night the little mechanism in the small black box which held for the unconscious sleepers upon the ill-starred Kincaid the coming vengeance of the thwarted Russian.

CHAPTER NINETEEN

The Last of the "Kincaid"

SHORTLY AFTER THE BREAK of day Tarzan was on deck noting the condition of the weather. The wind had abated. The sky was cloudless. Every condition seemed ideal for the commencement of the return voyage to Jungle Island, where the beasts were to be left. And then – home!

The ape-man aroused the mate and gave instructions that the Kincaid sail at the earliest possible moment. The remaining members of the crew, safe in Lord Greystoke's assurance that they would not be prosecuted for their share in the villainies of the two Russians, hastened with cheerful alacrity to their several duties.

The beasts, liberated from the confinement of the hold, wandered about the deck, not a little to the discomfiture of the crew in whose minds there remained a still vivid picture of the savagery of the beasts in conflict with those who had gone to their deaths beneath the fangs and talons which even now seemed itching for the soft flesh of further prey.

Beneath the watchful eyes of Tarzan and Mugambi, however, Sheeta and the apes of Akut curbed their desires, so that the men worked about the deck amongst them in far greater security than they imagined.

At last the Kincaid slipped down the Ugambi and ran out upon the shimmering waters of the Atlantic. Tarzan and Jane Clayton watched the verdure-clad shore-line receding in the ship's wake, and for once the ape-man left his native soil without one single pang of regret.

No ship that sailed the seven seas could have borne him away from Africa to resume his search for his lost boy with half the speed that the Englishman would have desired, and the slow-moving Kincaid seemed scarce to move at all to the impatient mind of the bereaved father.

Yet the vessel made progress even when she seemed to be standing still, and presently the low hills of Jungle Island became distinctly visible upon the western horizon ahead.

In the cabin of Alexander Paulvitch the thing within the black box ticked, ticked, ticked, with apparently unending monotony; but yet, second by second, a little arm which protruded from the periphery of one of its wheels came nearer and nearer to another little arm which projected from the hand which Paulvitch had set at a certain point upon the dial beside the clockwork. When those two arms touched one another the ticking of the mechanism would cease – for ever.

Jane and Tarzan stood upon the bridge looking out toward Jungle Island. The men were forward, also watching the land grow upward out of the ocean. The beasts had sought the shade of the galley, where they were curled up in sleep. All was quiet and peace upon the ship, and upon the waters.

Suddenly, without warning, the cabin roof shot up into the air, a cloud of dense smoke puffed far above the Kincaid, there was a terrific explosion which shook the vessel from stem to stern.

Instantly pandemonium broke loose upon the deck. The apes of Akut, terrified by the sound, ran hither and thither, snarling and growling. Sheeta leaped here and there, screaming out his startled terror in hideous cries that sent the ice of fear straight to the hearts of the Kincaid's crew.

Mugambi, too, was trembling. Only Tarzan of the Apes and his wife retained their composure. Scarce had the debris settled than the ape-man was among the beasts, quieting their fears, talking to them in low, pacific tones, stroking their shaggy bodies, and assuring them, as only he could, that the immediate danger was over.

An examination of the wreckage showed that their greatest danger, now, lay in fire, for the flames were licking hungrily at the splintered wood of the wrecked cabin, and had already found a foothold upon the lower deck through a great jagged hole which the explosion had opened.

By a miracle no member of the ship's company had been injured by the blast, the origin of which remained for ever a total mystery to all but one – the sailor who knew that Paulvitch had been aboard the Kincaid and in his cabin the previous night. He guessed the truth; but discretion sealed his lips. It would, doubtless, fare none too well for the man who had permitted the arch enemy of them all aboard the ship in the watches of the night, where later he might set an infernal machine to blow them all to kingdom come. No, the man decided that he would keep this knowledge to himself.

As the flames gained headway it became apparent to Tarzan that whatever had caused the explosion had scattered some highly inflammable substance upon the surrounding woodwork, for the water which they poured in from the pump seemed rather to spread than to extinguish the blaze.

Fifteen minutes after the explosion great, black clouds of smoke were rising from the hold of the doomed vessel. The flames had reached the engine-room, and the ship no longer moved toward the shore. Her fate was as certain as though the waters had already closed above her charred and smoking remains.

"It is useless to remain aboard her longer," remarked the ape-man to the mate. "There is no telling but there may be other explosions, and as we cannot hope to save her, the safest thing which we can do is to take to the boats without further loss of time and make land."

Nor was there other alternative. Only the sailors could bring away any belongings, for the fire, which had not yet reached the forecastle, had consumed all in the vicinity of the cabin which the explosion had not destroyed.

Two boats were lowered, and as there was no sea the landing was made with infinite ease. Eager and anxious, the beasts of Tarzan sniffed the familiar air of their native island as the small boats drew in toward the beach, and scarce had their keels grated upon the sand than Sheeta and the apes of Akut were over the bows and racing swiftly toward the jungle. A half-sad smile curved the lips of the ape-man as he watched them go.

"Good-bye, my friends," he murmured. "You have been good and faithful allies, and I shall miss you."

"They will return, will they not, dear?" asked Jane Clayton, at his side.

"They may and they may not," replied the ape-man. "They have been ill at ease since they were forced to accept so many human beings into their confidence. Mugambi and I alone affected them less, for he and I are, at best, but half human. You, however, and the members of the crew are far too civilized for my beasts – it is you whom they are fleeing. Doubtless they feel that they cannot trust themselves in the close vicinity of so much perfectly good food without the danger that they may help themselves to a mouthful some time by mistake."

Jane laughed. "I think they are just trying to escape you," she retorted. "You are always making them stop something which they see no reason why they should not do. Like little children they are doubtless delighted at this opportunity to flee from the zone of parental discipline. If they come back, though, I hope they won't come by night."

"Or come hungry, eh?" laughed Tarzan.

For two hours after landing the little party stood watching the burning ship which they had abandoned. Then there came faintly to them from across the water the sound of a second explosion. The Kincaid settled rapidly almost immediately thereafter, and sank within a few minutes.

The cause of the second explosion was less a mystery than that of the first, the mate attributing it to the bursting of the boilers when the flames had finally reached them; but what had caused the first explosion was a subject of considerable speculation among the stranded company.

CHAPTER TWENTY

Jungle Island Again

THE FIRST CONSIDERATION OF the party was to locate fresh water and make camp, for all knew that their term of existence upon Jungle Island might be drawn out to months, or even years.

Tarzan knew the nearest water, and to this he immediately led the party. Here the men fell to work to construct shelters and rude furniture while Tarzan went into the jungle after meat, leaving the faithful Mugambi and the Mosula woman to guard Jane, whose safety he would never trust to any member of the Kincaid's cut-throat crew.

Lady Greystoke suffered far greater anguish than any other of the castaways, for the blow to her hopes and her already cruelly lacerated mother-heart lay not in her own privations but in the knowledge that she might now never be able to learn the fate of her first-born or do aught to discover his whereabouts, or ameliorate his condition – a condition which imagination naturally pictured in the most frightful forms.

For two weeks the party divided the time amongst the various duties which had been allotted to each. A daylight watch was maintained from sunrise to sunset upon a bluff near the camp – a jutting shoulder of rock which overlooked the sea. Here, ready for instant lighting, was gathered a huge pile of dry branches, while from a lofty pole which they had set in the ground there floated an improvised distress signal fashioned from a red undershirt which belonged to the mate of the Kincaid.

But never a speck upon the horizon that might be sail or smoke rewarded the tired eyes that in their endless, hopeless vigil strained daily out across the vast expanse of ocean.

It was Tarzan who suggested, finally, that they attempt to construct a vessel that would bear them back to the mainland. He alone could show them how to fashion rude tools, and when the idea had taken root in the minds of the men they were eager to commence their labours.

But as time went on and the Herculean nature of their task became more and more apparent they fell to grumbling, and to quarrelling among themselves, so that to the other dangers were now added dissension and suspicion.

More than before did Tarzan now fear to leave Jane among the half brutes of the Kincaid's crew; but hunting he must do, for none other could so surely go forth and return with meat as he. Sometimes Mugambi spelled him at the hunting; but the black's spear and arrows were never so sure of results as the rope and knife of the ape-man.

Finally the men shirked their work, going off into the jungle by twos to explore and to hunt. All this time the camp had had no sight of Sheeta, or Akut and the other great apes, though Tarzan had sometimes met them in the jungle as he hunted.

And as matters tended from bad to worse in the camp of the castaways upon the east coast of Jungle Island, another camp came into being upon the north coast.

Here, in a little cove, lay a small schooner, the Cowrie, whose decks had but a few days since run red with the blood of her officers and the loyal members of her crew, for the Cowrie had fallen upon bad days when it had shipped such men as Gust and Momulla the Maori and that arch-fiend Kai Shang of Fachan.

There were others, too, ten of them all told, the scum of the South Sea ports; but Gust and Momulla and Kai Shang were the brains and cunning of the company. It was they who had instigated the mutiny that they might seize and divide the catch of pearls which constituted the wealth of the Cowrie's cargo.

It was Kai Shang who had murdered the captain as he lay asleep in his berth, and it had been Momulla the Maori who had led the attack upon the officer of the watch.

Gust, after his own peculiar habit, had found means to delegate to the others the actual taking of life. Not that Gust entertained any scruples on the subject, other than those which induced in him a rare regard for his own personal safety. There is always a certain element of risk to the assassin, for victims of deadly assault are seldom prone to die quietly and considerately. There is always a certain element of risk to go so far as to dispute the issue with the murderer. It was this chance of dispute which Gust preferred to forgo.

But now that the work was done the Swede aspired to the position of highest command among the mutineers. He had even gone so far as to appropriate and wear certain articles belonging to the murdered captain of the Cowrie – articles of apparel which bore upon them the badges and insignia of authority.

Kai Shang was peeved. He had no love for authority, and certainly not the slightest intention of submitting to the domination of an ordinary Swede sailor.

The seeds of discontent were, therefore, already planted in the camp of the mutineers of the Cowrie at the north edge of Jungle Island. But Kai Shang realized that he must act with circumspection, for Gust alone of the motley horde possessed sufficient knowledge of navigation to get them out of the South Atlantic and around the cape into more congenial waters where they might find a market for their ill-gotten wealth, and no questions asked.

The day before they sighted Jungle Island and discovered the little land-locked harbour upon the bosom of which the Cowrie now rode quietly at anchor, the watch had discovered the smoke and funnels of a warship upon the southern horizon.

The chance of being spoken to and investigated by a man-of-war appealed not at all to any of them, so they put into hiding for a few days until the danger should have passed.

And now Gust did not wish to venture out to sea again. There was no telling, he insisted, but that the ship they had seen was actually searching for them. Kai Shang pointed out that such could not be the case since it was impossible for any human being other than themselves to have knowledge of what had transpired aboard the Cowrie.

But Gust was not to be persuaded. In his wicked heart he nursed a scheme whereby he might increase his share of the booty by something like one hundred per cent. He alone could sail the Cowrie, therefore the others could not leave Jungle Island without him; but what was there to prevent Gust, with just sufficient men to man the schooner, slipping away from Kai Shang, Momulla the Maori, and some half of the crew when opportunity presented?

It was for this opportunity that Gust waited. Some day there would come a moment when Kai Shang, Momulla, and three or four of the others would be absent from camp, exploring or hunting. The Swede racked his brain for some plan whereby he might successfully lure from the sight of the anchored ship those whom he had determined to abandon.

To this end he organized hunting party after hunting party, but always the devil of perversity seemed to enter the soul of Kai Shang, so that wily celestial would never hunt except in the company of Gust himself.

One day Kai Shang spoke secretly with Momulla the Maori, pouring into the brown ear of his companion the suspicions which he harboured concerning the Swede. Momulla was for going immediately and running a long knife through the heart of the traitor.

It is true that Kai Shang had no other evidence than the natural cunning of his own knavish soul – but he imagined in the intentions of Gust what he himself would have been glad to accomplish had the means lain at hand.

But he dared not let Momulla slay the Swede, upon whom they depended to guide them to their destination. They decided, however, that it would do no harm to attempt to frighten Gust into acceding to their demands, and with this purpose in mind the Maori sought out the self-constituted commander of the party.

When he broached the subject of immediate departure Gust again raised his former objection – that the warship might very probably be patrolling the sea directly in their southern path, waiting for them to make the attempt to reach other waters.

Momulla scoffed at the fears of his fellow, pointing out that as no one aboard any warship knew of their mutiny there could be no reason why they should be suspected.

"Ah!" exclaimed Gust, "there is where you are wrong. There is where you are lucky that you have an educated man like me to tell you what to do. You are an ignorant savage, Momulla, and so you know nothing of wireless."

The Maori leaped to his feet and laid his hand upon the hilt of his knife.

"I am no savage," he shouted.

"I was only joking," the Swede hastened to explain. "We are old friends, Momulla; we cannot afford to quarrel, at least not while old Kai Shang is plotting to steal all the pearls from us. If he could find a man to navigate the Cowrie he would leave us in a minute. All his talk about getting away from here is just because he has some scheme in his head to get rid of us."

"But the wireless," asked Momulla. "What has the wireless to do with our remaining here?"

"Oh yes," replied Gust, scratching his head. He was wondering if the Maori were really so ignorant as to believe the preposterous lie he was about to unload upon him. "Oh yes! You see every warship is equipped with what they call a wireless apparatus. It lets them talk to other ships hundreds of miles away, and it lets them listen to all that is said on these other ships. Now, you see, when you fellows were shooting up the Cowrie you did a whole lot of loud talking, and there isn't any doubt but that that warship was a-lyin' off south of us listenin' to it all. Of course they might not have learned the name of the ship, but they heard enough to know that the crew of some ship was mutinying and killin' her officers. So you see they'll be waiting to search every ship they sight for a long time to come, and they may not be far away now."

When he had ceased speaking the Swede strove to assume an air of composure that his listener might not have his suspicions aroused as to the truth of the statements that had just been made.

Momulla sat for some time in silence, eyeing Gust. At last he rose.

"You are a great liar," he said. "If you don't get us on our way by tomorrow you'll never have another chance to lie, for I heard two of the men saying that they'd like to run a knife into you and that if you kept them in this hole any longer they'd do it."

"Go and ask Kai Shang if there is not a wireless," replied Gust. "He will tell you that there is such a thing and that vessels can talk to one another across hundreds of miles of water. Then say to the two men who wish to kill me that if they do so they will never live to spend their share of the swag, for only I can get you safely to any port."

So Momulla went to Kai Shang and asked him if there was such an apparatus as a wireless by means of which ships could talk with each other at great distances, and Kai Shang told him that there was.

Momulla was puzzled; but still he wished to leave the island, and was willing to take his chances on the open sea rather than to remain longer in the monotony of the camp.

"If we only had someone else who could navigate a ship!" wailed Kai Shang.

That afternoon Momulla went hunting with two other Maoris. They hunted toward the south, and had not gone far from camp when they were surprised by the sound of voices ahead of them in the jungle.

They knew that none of their own men had preceded them, and as all were convinced that the island was uninhabited, they were inclined to flee in terror on the hypothesis that the place was haunted – possibly by the ghosts of the murdered officers and men of the Cowrie.

But Momulla was even more curious than he was superstitious, and so he quelled his natural desire to flee from the supernatural. Motioning his companions to follow his example, he dropped to his hands and knees, crawling forward stealthily and with quakings of heart through the jungle in the direction from which came the voices of the unseen speakers.

Presently, at the edge of a little clearing, he halted, and there he breathed a deep sigh of relief, for plainly before him he saw two flesh-and-blood men sitting upon a fallen log and talking earnestly together.

One was Schneider, mate of the Kincaid, and the other was a seaman named Schmidt.

"I think we can do it, Schmidt," Schneider was saying. "A good canoe wouldn't be hard to build, and three of us could paddle it to the mainland in a day if the wind was right and the sea reasonably calm. There ain't no use waiting for the men to build a big enough boat to take the whole party, for they're sore now and sick of working like slaves all day long. It ain't none of our business anyway to save the Englishman. Let him look out for himself, says I." He paused for a moment, and then eyeing the other to note the effect of his next words, he continued, "But we might take the woman. It would be a shame to leave a nice-lookin' piece like she is in such a Gott-forsaken hole as this here island."

Schmidt looked up and grinned.

"So that's how she's blowin', is it?" he asked. "Why didn't you say so in the first place? Wot's in it for me if I help you?"

"She ought to pay us well to get her back to civilization," explained Schneider, "an' I tell you what I'll do. I'll just whack up with the two men that helps me. I'll take half an' they can divide the other half – you an' whoever the other bloke is. I'm sick of this place, an' the sooner I get out of it the better I'll like it. What do you say?"

"Suits me," replied Schmidt. "I wouldn't know how to reach the mainland myself, an' know that none o' the other fellows would, so's you're the only one that knows anything of navigation you're the fellow I'll tie to."

Momulla the Maori pricked up his ears. He had a smattering of every tongue that is spoken upon the seas, and more than a few times had he sailed on English ships, so that he understood fairly well all that had passed between Schneider and Schmidt since he had stumbled upon them.

He rose to his feet and stepped into the clearing. Schneider and his companion started as nervously as though a ghost had risen before them. Schneider reached for his revolver. Momulla raised his right hand, palm forward, as a sign of his pacific intentions.

"I am a friend," he said. "I heard you; but do not fear that I will reveal what you have said. I can help you, and you can help me." He was addressing Schneider. "You can navigate a ship, but you have no ship. We have a ship, but no one to navigate it. If you will come with us and ask no questions we will let you take the ship where you will after you have landed us at a certain port, the name of which we will give you later. You can take the woman of whom you speak, and we will ask no questions either. Is it a bargain?"

Schneider desired more information, and got as much as Momulla thought best to give him. Then the Maori suggested that they speak with Kai Shang. The two members of the Kincaid's company followed Momulla and his fellows to a point in the jungle close by the camp of the mutineers. Here Momulla hid them while he went in search of Kai Shang, first admonishing his Maori companions to stand guard over the two sailors lest they change their minds and attempt to escape. Schneider and Schmidt were virtually prisoners, though they did not know it.

Presently Momulla returned with Kai Shang, to whom he had briefly narrated the details of the stroke of good fortune that had come to them. The Chinaman spoke at length with Schneider, until, notwithstanding his natural suspicion of the sincerity of all men, he became quite convinced that Schneider was quite as much a rogue as himself and that the fellow was anxious to leave the island.

These two premises accepted there could be little doubt that Schneider would prove trustworthy in so far as accepting the command of the Cowrie was concerned; after that Kai Shang knew that he could find means to coerce the man into submission to his further wishes.

When Schneider and Schmidt left them and set out in the direction of their own camp, it was with feelings of far greater relief than they had experienced in many a day. Now at last they saw a feasible plan for leaving the island upon a seaworthy craft. There would be no more hard labour at ship-building, and no risking their lives upon a crudely built makeshift that would be quite as likely to go to the bottom as it would to reach the mainland.

Also, they were to have assistance in capturing the woman, or rather women, for when Momulla had learned that there was a black woman in the other camp he had insisted that she be brought along as well as the white woman.

As Kai Shang and Momulla entered their camp, it was with a realization that they no longer needed Gust. They marched straight to the tent in which they might expect to find him at that hour of the day, for though it would have been more comfortable for the entire party to remain aboard the ship, they had mutually decided that it would be safer for all concerned were they to pitch their camp ashore.

Each knew that in the heart of the others was sufficient treachery to make it unsafe for any member of the party to go ashore leaving the others in possession of the Cowrie, so not more than two or three men at a time were ever permitted aboard the vessel unless all the balance of the company was there too.

As the two crossed toward Gust's tent the Maori felt the edge of his long knife with one grimy, calloused thumb. The Swede would have felt far from comfortable could he have seen this significant action, or read what was passing amid the convolutions of the brown man's cruel brain.

Now it happened that Gust was at that moment in the tent occupied by the cook, and this tent stood but a few feet from his own. So that he heard the approach of Kai Shang and Momulla, though he did not, of course, dream that it had any special significance for him.

Chance had it, though, that he glanced out of the doorway of the cook's tent at the very moment that Kai Shang and Momulla approached the entrance to his, and he thought that he noted a stealthiness in their movements that comported poorly with amicable or friendly intentions, and then, just as they two slunk within the interior, Gust caught a glimpse of the long knife which Momulla the Maori was then carrying behind his back.

The Swede's eyes opened wide, and a funny little sensation assailed the roots of his hairs. Also he turned almost white beneath his tan. Quite precipitately he left the cook's tent. He was not one who required a detailed exposition of intentions that were quite all too obvious.

As surely as though he had heard them plotting, he knew that Kai Shang and Momulla had come to take his life. The knowledge that he alone could navigate the Cowrie had, up to now, been sufficient assurance of his safety; but quite evidently something had occurred of which he had no knowledge that would make it quite worth the while of his co-conspirators to eliminate him.

Without a pause Gust darted across the beach and into the jungle. He was afraid of the jungle; uncanny noises that were indeed frightful came forth from its recesses – the tangled mazes of the mysterious country back of the beach.

But if Gust was afraid of the jungle he was far more afraid of Kai Shang and Momulla. The dangers of the jungle were more or less problematical, while the danger that menaced him at the hands of his companions was a perfectly well-known quantity, which might be expressed in terms of a few inches of cold steel, or the coil of a light rope. He had seen Kai Shang garrotte a man at Pai-sha in a dark alleyway back of Loo Kotai's place. He feared the rope, therefore, more than he did the knife of the Maori; but he feared them both too much to remain within reach of either. Therefore he chose the pitiless jungle.

CHAPTER TWENTY ONE

The Law of the Jungle

In Tarzan's camp, by dint of threats and promised rewards, the ape-man had finally succeeded in getting the hull of a large skiff almost completed. Much of the work he and Mugambi had done with their own hands in addition to furnishing the camp with meat.

Schneider, the mate, had been doing considerable grumbling, and had at last openly deserted the work and gone off into the jungle with Schmidt to hunt. He said that he wanted a rest, and Tarzan, rather than add to the unpleasantness which already made camp life almost unendurable, had permitted the two men to depart without a remonstrance.

Upon the following day, however, Schneider affected a feeling of remorse for his action, and set to work with a will upon the skiff. Schmidt also worked good-naturedly, and Lord Greystoke congratulated himself that at last the men had awakened to the necessity for the labour which was being asked of them and to their obligations to the balance of the party.

It was with a feeling of greater relief than he had experienced for many a day that he set out that noon to hunt deep in the jungle for a herd of small deer which Schneider reported that he and Schmidt had seen there the day before.

The direction in which Schneider had reported seeing the deer was toward the south-west, and to that point the ape-man swung easily through the tangled verdure of the forest.

And as he went there approached from the north a half-dozen ill-featured men who went stealthily through the jungle as go men bent upon the commission of a wicked act.

They thought that they travelled unseen; but behind them, almost from the moment they quitted their own camp, a tall man crept upon their trail. In the man's eyes were hate and fear, and a great curiosity.

Why went Kai Shang and Momulla and the others thus stealthily toward the south? What did they expect to find there? Gust shook his low-browed head in perplexity. But he would know. He would follow them and learn their plans, and then if he could thwart them he would – that went without question.

At first he had thought that they searched for him; but finally his better judgment assured him that such could not be the case, since they had accomplished all they really desired by chasing him out of camp. Never would Kai Shang or Momulla go to such pains to slay him or another unless it would put money into their pockets, and as Gust had no money it was evident that they were searching for someone else.

Presently the party he trailed came to a halt. Its members concealed themselves in the foliage bordering the game trail along which they had come. Gust, that he might the better observe, clambered into the branches of a tree to the rear of them, being careful that the leafy fronds hid him from the view of his erstwhile mates.

He had not long to wait before he saw a strange white man approach carefully along the trail from the south.

At sight of the new-comer Momulla and Kai Shang arose from their places of concealment and greeted him. Gust could not overhear what passed between them. Then the man returned in the direction from which he had come.

He was Schneider. Nearing his camp he circled to the opposite side of it, and presently came running in breathlessly. Excitedly he hastened to Mugambi.

"Quick!" he cried. "Those apes of yours have caught Schmidt and will kill him if we do not hasten to his aid. You alone can call them off. Take Jones and Sullivan – you may need help – and get to him as quick as you can. Follow the game trail south for about a mile. I will remain here. I am too spent with running to go back with you," and the mate of the Kincaid threw himself upon the ground, panting as though he was almost done for.

Mugambi hesitated. He had been left to guard the two women. He did not know what to do, and then Jane Clayton, who had heard Schneider's story, added her pleas to those of the mate.

"Do not delay," she urged. "We shall be all right here. Mr. Schneider will remain with us. Go, Mugambi. The poor fellow must be saved."

Schmidt, who lay hidden in a bush at the edge of the camp, grinned. Mugambi, heeding the commands of his mistress, though still doubtful of the wisdom of his action, started off toward the south, with Jones and Sullivan at his heels.

No sooner had he disappeared than Schmidt rose and darted north into the jungle, and a few minutes later the face of Kai Shang of Fachan appeared at the edge of the clearing. Schneider saw the Chinaman, and motioned to him that the coast was clear.

Jane Clayton and the Mosula woman were sitting at the opening of the former's tent, their backs toward the approaching ruffians. The first intimation that either had of the presence of strangers in camp was the sudden appearance of a half-dozen ragged villains about them.

"Come!" said Kai Shang, motioning that the two arise and follow him.

Jane Clayton sprang to her feet and looked about for Schneider, only to see him standing behind the newcomers, a grin upon his face. At his side stood Schmidt. Instantly she saw that she had been made the victim of a plot.

"What is the meaning of this?" she asked, addressing the mate.

"It means that we have found a ship and that we can now escape from Jungle Island," replied the man.

"Why did you send Mugambi and the others into the jungle?" she inquired.

"They are not coming with us – only you and I, and the Mosula woman."

"Come!" repeated Kai Shang, and seized Jane Clayton's wrist.

One of the Maoris grasped the black woman by the arm, and when she would have screamed struck her across the mouth.

Mugambi raced through the jungle toward the south. Jones and Sullivan trailed far behind. For a mile he continued upon his way to the relief of Schmidt, but no signs saw he of the missing man or of any of the apes of Akut.

At last he halted and called aloud the summons which he and Tarzan had used to hail the great anthropoids. There was no response. Jones and Sullivan came up with the black warrior as the latter stood voicing his weird call. For another half-mile the black searched, calling occasionally.

Finally the truth flashed upon him, and then, like a frightened deer, he wheeled and dashed back toward camp. Arriving there, it was but a moment before full confirmation of his fears was impressed upon him. Lady Greystoke and the Mosula woman were gone. So, likewise, was Schneider.

When Jones and Sullivan joined Mugambi he would have killed them in his anger, thinking them parties to the plot; but they finally succeeded in partially convincing him that they had known nothing of it.

As they stood speculating upon the probable whereabouts of the women and their abductor, and the purpose which Schneider had in mind in taking them from camp, Tarzan of the Apes swung from the branches of a tree and crossed the clearing toward them.

His keen eyes detected at once that something was radically wrong, and when he had heard Mugambi's story his jaws clicked angrily together as he knitted his brows in thought.

What could the mate hope to accomplish by taking Jane Clayton from a camp upon a small island from which there was no escape from the vengeance of Tarzan? The ape-man could not believe the fellow such a fool, and then a slight realization of the truth dawned upon him.

Schneider would not have committed such an act unless he had been reasonably sure that there was a way by which he could quit Jungle Island with his prisoners. But why had he taken the black woman as well? There must have been others, one of whom wanted the dusky female.

"Come," said Tarzan, "there is but one thing to do now, and that is to follow the trail."

As he finished speaking a tall, ungainly figure emerged from the jungle north of the camp. He came straight toward the four men. He was an entire stranger to all of them, not one of whom had dreamed that another human being than those of their own camp dwelt upon the unfriendly shores of Jungle Island.

It was Gust. He came directly to the point.

"Your women were stolen," he said. "If you want ever to see them again, come quickly and follow me. If we do not hurry the Cowrie will be standing out to sea by the time we reach her anchorage."

"Who are you?" asked Tarzan. "What do you know of the theft of my wife and the black woman?"

"I heard Kai Shang and Momulla the Maori plot with two men of your camp. They had chased me from our camp, and would have killed me. Now I will get even with them. Come!"

Gust led the four men of the Kincaid's camp at a rapid trot through the jungle toward the north. Would they come to the sea in time? But a few more minutes would answer the question.

And when at last the little party did break through the last of the screening foliage, and the harbour and the ocean lay before them, they realized that fate had been most cruelly unkind, for the Cowrie was already under sail and moving slowly out of the mouth of the harbour into the open sea.

What were they to do? Tarzan's broad chest rose and fell to the force of his pent emotions. The last blow seemed to have fallen, and if ever in all his life Tarzan of the Apes had had occasion to abandon hope it was now that he saw the ship bearing his wife to some frightful fate moving gracefully over the rippling water, so very near and yet so hideously far away.

In silence he stood watching the vessel. He saw it turn toward the east and finally disappear around a headland on its way he knew not whither. Then he dropped upon his haunches and buried his face in his hands.

It was after dark that the five men returned to the camp on the east shore. The night was hot and sultry. No slightest breeze ruffled the foliage of the trees or rippled the mirror-like surface of the ocean. Only a gentle swell rolled softly in upon the beach.

Never had Tarzan seen the great Atlantic so ominously at peace. He was standing at the edge of the beach gazing out to sea in the direction of the mainland, his mind filled with sorrow and hopelessness, when from the jungle close behind the camp came the uncanny wail of a panther.

There was a familiar note in the weird cry, and almost mechanically Tarzan turned his head and answered. A moment later the tawny figure of Sheeta slunk out into the half-light of the beach. There was no moon, but the sky was brilliant with stars. Silently the savage brute came to the side of the man. It had been long since Tarzan had seen his old fighting companion, but the soft purr was sufficient to assure him that the animal still recalled the bonds which had united them in the past.

The ape-man let his fingers fall upon the beast's coat, and as Sheeta pressed close against his leg he caressed and fondled the wicked head while his eyes continued to search the blackness of the waters.

Presently he started. What was that? He strained his eyes into the night. Then he turned and called aloud to the men smoking upon their blankets in the camp. They came running to his side; but Gust hesitated when he saw the nature of Tarzan's companion.

"Look!" cried Tarzan. "A light! A ship's light! It must be the Cowrie. They are becalmed." And then with an exclamation of renewed hope, "We can reach them! The skiff will carry us easily."

Gust demurred. "They are well armed," he warned. "We could not take the ship – just five of us."

"There are six now," replied Tarzan, pointing to Sheeta, "and we can have more still in a half-hour. Sheeta is the equivalent of twenty men, and the few others I can bring will add full a hundred to our fighting strength. You do not know them."

The ape-man turned and raised his head toward the jungle, while there pealed from his lips, time after time, the fearsome cry of the bull-ape who would summon his fellows.

Presently from the jungle came an answering cry, and then another and another. Gust shuddered. Among what sort of creatures had fate thrown him? Were not Kai Shang and Momulla to be preferred to this great white giant who stroked a panther and called to the beasts of the jungle?

In a few minutes the apes of Akut came crashing through the underbrush and out upon the beach, while in the meantime the five men had been struggling with the unwieldy bulk of the skiff's hull.

By dint of Herculean efforts they had managed to get it to the water's edge. The oars from the two small boats of the Kincaid, which had been washed away by an off-shore wind the very night that the party had landed, had been in use to support the canvas of the sailcloth tents. These were hastily requisitioned, and by the time Akut and his followers came down to the water all was ready for embarkation.

Once again the hideous crew entered the service of their master, and without question took up their places in the skiff. The four men, for Gust could not be prevailed upon to accompany the party, fell to the oars, using them paddle-wise, while some of the apes followed their example, and presently the ungainly skiff was moving quietly out to sea in the direction of the light which rose and fell gently with the swell.

A sleepy sailor kept a poor vigil upon the Cowrie's deck, while in the cabin below Schneider paced up and down arguing with Jane Clayton. The woman had found a revolver in a table drawer in the room in which she had been locked, and now she kept the mate of the Kincaid at bay with the weapon.

The Mosula woman kneeled behind her, while Schneider paced up and down before the door, threatening and pleading and promising, but all to no avail. Presently from the deck above came a shout of warning and a shot. For an instant Jane Clayton relaxed her vigilance, and turned her eyes toward the cabin skylight. Simultaneously Schneider was upon her.

The first intimation the watch had that there was another craft within a thousand miles of the Cowrie came when he saw the head and shoulders of a man poked over the ship's side. Instantly the fellow sprang to his feet with a cry and levelled his revolver at the intruder. It was his cry and the subsequent report of the revolver which threw Jane Clayton off her guard.

Upon deck the quiet of fancied security soon gave place to the wildest pandemonium. The crew of the Cowrie rushed above armed with revolvers, cutlasses, and the long knives that many of them habitually wore; but the alarm had come too late. Already the beasts of Tarzan were upon the ship's deck, with Tarzan and the two men of the Kincaid's crew.

In the face of the frightful beasts the courage of the mutineers wavered and broke. Those with revolvers fired a few scattering shots and then raced for some place of supposed safety. Into the shrouds went some; but the apes of Akut were more at home there than they.

Screaming with terror the Maoris were dragged from their lofty perches. The beasts, uncontrolled by Tarzan who had gone in search of Jane, loosed the full fury of their savage natures upon the unhappy wretches who fell into their clutches.

Sheeta, in the meanwhile, had felt his great fangs sink into but a single jugular. For a moment he mauled the corpse, and then he spied Kai Shang darting down the companionway toward his cabin.

With a shrill scream Sheeta was after him – a scream which awoke an almost equally uncanny cry in the throat of the terror-stricken Chinaman.

But Kai Shang reached his cabin a fraction of a second ahead of the panther, and leaping within slammed the door – just too late. Sheeta's great body hurtled against it before the catch engaged, and a moment later Kai Shang was gibbering and shrieking in the back of an upper berth.

Lightly Sheeta sprang after his victim, and presently the wicked days of Kai Shang of Fachan were ended, and Sheeta was gorging himself upon tough and stringy flesh.

A moment scarcely had elapsed after Schneider leaped upon Jane Clayton and wrenched the revolver from her hand, when the door of the cabin opened and a tall and half-naked white man stood framed within the portal.

Silently he leaped across the cabin. Schneider felt sinewy fingers at his throat. He turned his head to see who had attacked him, and his eyes went wide when he saw the face of the ape-man close above his own.

Grimly the fingers tightened upon the mate's throat. He tried to scream, to plead, but no sound came forth. His eyes protruded as he struggled for freedom, for breath, for life.

Jane Clayton seized her husband's hands and tried to drag them from the throat of the dying man; but Tarzan only shook his head.

"Not again," he said quietly. "Before have I permitted scoundrels to live, only to suffer and to have you suffer for my mercy. This time we shall make sure of one scoundrel – sure that he will never again harm us or another," and with a sudden wrench he twisted the neck of the perfidious mate until there was a sharp crack, and the man's body lay limp and motionless in the ape-man's grasp. With a gesture of disgust Tarzan tossed the corpse aside. Then he returned to the deck, followed by Jane and the Mosula woman.

The battle there was over. Schmidt and Momulla and two others alone remained alive of all the company of the Cowrie, for they had found sanctuary in the forecastle. The others had died, horribly, and as they deserved, beneath the fangs and talons of the beasts of Tarzan, and in the morning the sun rose on a grisly sight upon the deck of the unhappy Cowrie; but this time the blood which stained her white planking was the blood of the guilty and not of the innocent.

Tarzan brought forth the men who had hidden in the forecastle, and without promises of immunity from punishment forced them to help work the vessel – the only alternative was immediate death.

A stiff breeze had risen with the sun, and with canvas spread the Cowrie set in toward Jungle Island, where a few hours later, Tarzan picked up Gust and bid farewell to Sheeta and the apes of Akut, for here he set the beasts ashore to pursue the wild and natural life they loved so well; nor did they lose a moment's time in disappearing into the cool depths of their beloved jungle.

That they knew that Tarzan was to leave them may be doubted – except possibly in the case of the more intelligent Akut, who alone of all the others remained upon the beach as the small boat drew away toward the schooner, carrying his savage lord and master from him.

And as long as their eyes could span the distance, Jane and Tarzan, standing upon the deck, saw the lonely figure of the shaggy anthropoid motionless upon the surf-beaten sands of Jungle Island.

It was three days later that the Cowrie fell in with H.M. sloop-of-war Shorewater, through whose wireless Lord Greystoke soon got in communication with London. Thus he learned that which filled his and his wife's heart with joy and thanksgiving – little Jack was safe at Lord Greystoke's town house.

It was not until they reached London that they learned the details of the remarkable chain of circumstances that had preserved the infant unharmed.

It developed that Rokoff, fearing to take the child aboard the Kincaid by day, had hidden it in a low den where nameless infants were harboured, intending to carry it to the steamer after dark.

His confederate and chief lieutenant, Paulvitch, true to the long years of teaching of his wily master, had at last succumbed to the treachery and greed that had always marked his superior, and, lured by the thoughts of the immense ransom that he might win by returning the child unharmed, had divulged the secret of its parentage to the woman who maintained the foundling asylum. Through her he had arranged for the substitution of another infant, knowing full well that never until it was too late would Rokoff suspect the trick that had been played upon him.

The woman had promised to keep the child until Paulvitch returned to England; but she, in turn, had been tempted to betray her trust by the lure of gold, and so had opened negotiations with Lord Greystoke's solicitors for the return of the child.

Esmeralda, the old Negro nurse whose absence on a vacation in America at the time of the abduction of little Jack had been attributed by her as the cause of the calamity, had returned and positively identified the infant.

The ransom had been paid, and within ten days of the date of his kidnapping the future Lord Greystoke, none the worse for his experience, had been returned to his father's home.

And so that last and greatest of Nikolas Rokoff's many rascalities had not only miserably miscarried through the treachery he had taught his only friend, but it had resulted in the arch-villain's death, and given to Lord and Lady Greystoke a peace of mind that neither could ever have felt so long as the vital spark remained in the body of the Russian and his malign mind was free to formulate new atrocities against them.

Rokoff was dead, and while the fate of Paulvitch was unknown, they had every reason to believe that he had succumbed to the dangers of the jungle where last they had seen him – the malicious tool of his master.

And thus, in so far as they might know, they were to be freed for ever from the menace of these two men – the only enemies which Tarzan of the Apes ever had had occasion to fear, because they struck at him cowardly blows, through those he loved.

It was a happy family party that were reunited in Greystoke House the day that Lord Greystoke and his lady landed upon English soil from the deck of the Shorewater.

Accompanying them were Mugambi and the Mosula woman whom he had found in the bottom of the canoe that night upon the bank of the little tributary of the Ugambi.

The woman had preferred to cling to her new lord and master rather than return to the marriage she had tried to escape.

Tarzan had proposed to them that they might find a home upon his vast African estates in the land of the Waziri, where they were to be sent as soon as opportunity presented itself.

Possibly we shall see them all there amid the savage romance of the grim jungle and the great plains where Tarzan of the Apes loves best to be.

Who knows?

THE SON OF TARZAN

Chapter One

THE LONG BOAT OF the Marjorie W. was floating down the broad Ugambi with ebb tide and current. Her crew were lazily enjoying this respite from the arduous labor of rowing up stream. Three miles below them lay the Marjorie W. herself, quite ready to sail so soon as they should have clambered aboard and swung the long boat to its davits. Presently the attention of every man was drawn from his dreaming or his gossiping to the northern bank of the river. There, screaming at them in a cracked falsetto and with skinny arms outstretched, stood a strange apparition of a man.

"Wot the 'ell?" ejaculated one of the crew.

"A white man!" muttered the mate, and then: "Man the oars, boys, and we'll just pull over an' see what he wants."

When they came close to the shore they saw an emaciated creature with scant white locks tangled and matted. The thin, bent body was naked but for a loin cloth. Tears were rolling down the sunken pock-marked cheeks. The man jabbered at them in a strange tongue.

"Rooshun," hazarded the mate. "Savvy English?" he called to the man.

He did, and in that tongue, brokenly and haltingly, as though it had been many years since he had used it, he begged them to take him with them away from this awful country. Once on board the Marjorie W. the stranger told his rescuers a pitiful tale of privation, hardships, and torture, extending over a period of ten years. How he happened to have come to Africa he did not tell them, leaving them to assume he had forgotten the incidents of his life prior to the frightful ordeals that had wrecked him mentally and physically. He did not even tell them his true name, and so they knew him only as Michael Sabrov, nor was there any resemblance between this sorry wreck and the virile, though unprincipled, Alexis Paulvitch of old.

It had been ten years since the Russian had escaped the fate of his friend, the arch-fiend Rokoff, and not once, but many times during those ten years had Paulvitch cursed the fate that had given to Nicholas Rokoff death and immunity from suffering while it had meted to him the hideous terrors of an existence infinitely worse than the death that persistently refused to claim him.

Paulvitch had taken to the jungle when he had seen the beasts of Tarzan and their savage lord swarm the deck of the Kincaid, and in his terror lest Tarzan pursue and capture him he had stumbled on deep into the jungle, only to fall at last into the hands of one of the savage cannibal tribes that had felt the weight of Rokoff's evil temper and cruel brutality. Some strange whim of the chief of this tribe saved Paulvitch from death only to plunge him into a life of misery and torture. For ten years he had been the butt of the village, beaten and stoned by the women and children, cut and slashed and disfigured by the warriors; a victim of often recurring fevers of the most malignant variety. Yet he did not die. Smallpox laid its hideous clutches upon him; leaving him unspeakably branded with its repulsive marks. Between it and the attentions of the tribe the countenance of Alexis Paulvitch was so altered that his own mother could not have recognized in the pitiful mask he called his face a single familiar feature. A few scraggly, yellow-white locks had supplanted the thick, dark hair that had covered his head. His limbs were bent and twisted, he walked with a shuffling, unsteady gait, his body doubled forward. His teeth were gone – knocked out by his savage masters. Even his mentality was but a sorry mockery of what it once had been.

They took him aboard the Marjorie W., and there they fed and nursed him. He gained a little in strength; but his appearance never altered for the better – a human derelict, battered and wrecked, they had found him; a human derelict, battered and wrecked, he would remain until death claimed him. Though still in his thirties, Alexis Paulvitch could easily have passed for eighty. Inscrutable Nature had demanded of the accomplice a greater penalty than his principal had paid.

In the mind of Alexis Paulvitch there lingered no thoughts of revenge – only a dull hatred of the man whom he and Rokoff had tried to break, and failed. There was hatred, too, of the memory of Rokoff, for Rokoff had led him into the horrors he had undergone. There was hatred of the police of a score of cities from which he had had to flee. There was hatred of law, hatred of order, hatred of everything. Every moment of the man's waking life was filled with morbid thought of hatred – he had become mentally as he was physically in outward appearance, the personification of the blighting emotion of Hate. He had little or nothing to do with the men who had rescued him. He was too weak to work and too morose for company, and so they quickly left him alone to his own devices.

The Marjorie W. had been chartered by a syndicate of wealthy manufacturers, equipped with a laboratory and a staff of scientists, and sent out to search for some natural product which the manufacturers who footed the bills had been importing from South America at an enormous cost. What the product was none on board the Marjorie W. knew except the scientists, nor is it of any moment to us, other than that it led the ship to a certain island off the coast of Africa after Alexis Paulvitch had been taken aboard.

The ship lay at anchor off the coast for several weeks. The monotony of life aboard her became trying for the crew. They went often ashore, and finally Paulvitch asked to accompany them – he too was tiring of the blighting sameness of existence upon the ship.

The island was heavily timbered. Dense jungle ran down almost to the beach. The scientists were far inland, prosecuting their search for the valuable commodity that native rumor upon the mainland had led them to believe might be found here in marketable quantity. The ship's company fished, hunted, and explored. Paulvitch shuffled up and down the beach, or lay in the shade of the great trees that skirted it. One day, as the men were gathered at a little distance inspecting the body of a panther that had fallen to the gun of one of them who had been hunting inland, Paulvitch lay sleeping beneath his tree. He was awakened by the touch of a hand upon his shoulder. With a start he sat up to see a huge, anthropoid ape squatting at his side, inspecting him intently. The Russian was thoroughly frightened. He glanced toward the sailors – they were a couple of hundred yards away. Again the ape plucked at his shoulder, jabbering plaintively. Paulvitch saw no menace in the inquiring gaze, or in the attitude of the beast. He got slowly to his feet. The ape rose at his side.

Half doubled, the man shuffled cautiously away toward the sailors. The ape moved with him, taking one of his arms. They had come almost to the little knot of men before they were seen, and by this time Paulvitch had become assured that the beast meant no harm. The animal evidently was accustomed to the association of human beings. It occurred to the Russian that the ape represented a certain considerable money value, and before they reached the sailors he had decided he should be the one to profit by it.

When the men looked up and saw the oddly paired couple shuffling toward them they were filled with amazement, and started on a run toward the two. The ape showed no sign of fear. Instead he grasped each sailor by the shoulder and peered long and earnestly into his face. Having inspected them all he returned to Paulvitch's side, disappointment written strongly upon his countenance and in his carriage.

The men were delighted with him. They gathered about, asking Paulvitch many questions, and examining his companion. The Russian told them that the ape was his – nothing further would he offer – but kept harping continually upon the same theme, "The ape is mine. The ape is mine." Tiring of Paulvitch, one of the men essayed a pleasantry. Circling about behind the ape he prodded the anthropoid in the back with a pin. Like a flash the beast wheeled upon its tormentor, and, in the briefest instant of turning, the placid, friendly animal was metamorphosed to a frenzied demon of rage. The broad grin that had sat upon the sailor's face as he perpetrated his little joke froze to an expression of terror. He attempted to dodge the long arms that reached for him; but, failing, drew a long knife that hung at his belt. With a single wrench the ape tore the weapon from the man's grasp and flung it to one side, then his yellow fangs were buried in the sailor's shoulder.

With sticks and knives the man's companions fell upon the beast, while Paulvitch danced around the cursing, snarling pack mumbling and screaming pleas and threats. He saw his visions of wealth rapidly dissipating before the weapons of the sailors.

The ape, however, proved no easy victim to the superior numbers that seemed fated to overwhelm him. Rising from the sailor who had precipitated the battle he shook his giant shoulders, freeing himself from two of the men that were clinging to his back, and with mighty blows of his open palms felled one after another of his attackers, leaping hither and thither with the agility of a small monkey.

The fight had been witnessed by the captain and mate who were just landing from the Marjorie W., and Paulvitch saw these two now running forward with drawn revolvers while the two sailors who had brought them ashore trailed at their heels. The ape stood looking about him at the havoc he had wrought, but whether he was awaiting a renewal of the attack or was deliberating which of his foes he should exterminate first Paulvitch could not guess. What he could guess, however, was that the moment the two officers came within firing distance of the beast they would put an end to him in short order unless something were done and done quickly to prevent. The ape had made no move to attack the Russian but even so the man was none too sure of what might happen were he to interfere with the savage beast, now thoroughly aroused to bestial rage, and with the smell of new spilled blood fresh in its nostrils. For an instant he hesitated, and then again there rose before him the dreams of affluence which this great anthropoid would doubtless turn to realities once Paulvitch had landed him safely in some great metropolis like London.

The captain was shouting to him now to stand aside that he might have a shot at the animal; but instead Paulvitch shuffled to the ape's side, and though the man's hair quivered at its roots he mastered his fear and laid hold of the ape's arm.

"Come!" he commanded, and tugged to pull the beast from among the sailors, many of whom were now sitting up in wide eyed fright or crawling away from their conqueror upon hands and knees.

Slowly the ape permitted itself to be led to one side, nor did it show the slightest indication of a desire to harm the Russian. The captain came to a halt a few paces from the odd pair.

"Get aside, Sabrov!" he commanded. "I'll put that brute where he won't chew up any more able seamen."

"It wasn't his fault, captain," pleaded Paulvitch. "Please don't shoot him. The men started it – they attacked him first. You see, he's perfectly gentle – and he's mine – he's mine – he's mine! I won't let you kill him," he concluded, as his half-wrecked mentality pictured anew the pleasure that money would buy in London – money that he could not hope to possess without some such windfall as the ape represented.

The captain lowered his weapon. "The men started it, did they?" he repeated. "How about that?" and he turned toward the sailors who had by this time picked themselves from the ground, none of them much the worse for his experience except the fellow who had been the cause of it, and who would doubtless nurse a sore shoulder for a week or so.

"Simpson done it," said one of the men. "He stuck a pin into the monk from behind, and the monk got him – which served him bloomin' well right – an' he got the rest of us, too, for which I can't blame him, since we all jumped him to once."

The captain looked at Simpson, who sheepishly admitted the truth of the allegation, then he stepped over to the ape as though to discover for himself the sort of temper the beast possessed, but it was noticeable that he kept his revolver cocked and leveled as he did so. However, he spoke soothingly to the animal who squatted at the Russian's side looking first at one and then another of the sailors. As the captain approached him the ape half rose and waddled forward to meet him. Upon his countenance was the same strange, searching expression that had marked his scrutiny of each of the sailors he had first encountered.

He came quite close to the officer and laid a paw upon one of the man's shoulders, studying his face intently for a long moment, then came the expression of disappointment accompanied by what was almost a human sigh, as he turned away to peer in the same curious fashion into the faces of the mate and the two sailors who had arrived with the officers. In each instance he sighed and passed on, returning at length to Paulvitch's side, where he squatted down once more; thereafter evincing little or no interest in any of the other men, and apparently forgetful of his recent battle with them.

When the party returned aboard the Marjorie W., Paulvitch was accompanied by the ape, who seemed anxious to follow him. The captain interposed no obstacles to the arrangement, and so the great anthropoid was tacitly admitted to membership in the ship's company. Once aboard he examined each new face minutely, evincing the same disappointment in each instance that had marked his scrutiny of the others. The officers and scientists aboard often discussed the beast, but they were unable to account satisfactorily for the strange ceremony with which he greeted each new face. Had he been discovered upon the mainland, or any other place than the almost unknown island that had been his home, they would have concluded that he had formerly been a pet of man; but that theory was not tenable in the face of the isolation of his uninhabited island. He seemed continually to be searching for someone, and during the first days of the return voyage from the island he was often discovered nosing about in various parts of the ship; but after he had seen and examined each face of the ship's company, and explored every corner of the vessel he lapsed into utter indifference of all about him. Even the Russian elicited only casual interest when he brought him food. At other times the ape appeared merely to tolerate him. He never showed affection for him, or for anyone else upon the Marjorie W., nor did he at any time evince any indication of the savage temper that had marked his resentment of the attack of the sailors upon him at the time that he had come among them.

Most of his time was spent in the eye of the ship scanning the horizon ahead, as though he were endowed with sufficient reason to know that the vessel was bound for some port where there would be other human beings to undergo his searching scrutiny. All in all, Ajax, as he had been dubbed, was considered the most remarkable and intelligent ape that any one aboard the Marjorie W. ever had seen. Nor was his intelligence the only remarkable attribute he owned. His stature and physique were, for an ape, awe inspiring. That he was old was quite evident, but if his age had impaired his physical or mental powers in the slightest it was not apparent.

And so at length the Marjorie W. came to England, and there the officers and the scientists, filled with compassion for the pitiful wreck of a man they had rescued from the jungles, furnished Paulvitch with funds and bid him and his Ajax Godspeed.

Upon the dock and all through the journey to London the Russian had his hands full with Ajax. Each new face of the thousands that came within the anthropoid's ken must be carefully scrutinized, much to the horror of many of his victims; but at last, failing, apparently, to discover whom he sought, the great ape relapsed into morbid indifference, only occasionally evincing interest in a passing face.

In London, Paulvitch went directly with his prize to a certain famous animal trainer. This man was much impressed with Ajax with the result that he agreed to train him for a lion's share of the profits of exhibiting him, and in the meantime to provide for the keep of both the ape and his owner.

And so came Ajax to London, and there was forged another link in the chain of strange circumstances that were to affect the lives of many people.

Chapter Two

Mr. Harold Moore was a bilious-countenanced, studious young man. He took himself very seriously, and life, and his work, which latter was the tutoring of the young son of a British nobleman. He felt that his charge was not making the progress that his parents had a right to expect, and he was now conscientiously explaining this fact to the boy's mother.

"It's not that he isn't bright," he was saying; "if that were true I should have hopes of succeeding, for then I might bring to bear all my energies in overcoming his obtuseness; but the trouble is that he is exceptionally intelligent, and learns so quickly that I can find no fault in the matter of the preparation of his lessons. What concerns me, however, is the fact that he evidently takes no interest whatever in the subjects we are studying. He merely accomplishes each lesson as a task to be rid of as quickly as possible and I am sure that no lesson ever again enters his mind until the hours of study and recitation once more arrive. His sole interests seem to be feats of physical prowess and the reading of everything that he can get hold of relative to savage beasts and the lives and customs of uncivilized peoples; but particularly do stories of animals appeal to him. He will sit for hours together poring over the work of some African explorer, and upon two occasions I have found him setting up in bed at night reading Carl Hagenbeck's book on men and beasts."

The boy's mother tapped her foot nervously upon the hearth rug.

"You discourage this, of course?" she ventured.

Mr. Moore shuffled embarrassedly.

"I – ah – essayed to take the book from him," he replied, a slight flush mounting his sallow cheek; "but – ah – your son is quite muscular for one so young."

"He wouldn't let you take it?" asked the mother.

"He would not," confessed the tutor. "He was perfectly good natured about it; but he insisted upon pretending that he was a gorilla and that I was a chimpanzee attempting to steal food from him. He leaped upon me with the most savage growls I ever heard, lifted me completely above his head, hurled me upon his bed, and after going through a pantomime indicative of choking me to death he stood upon my prostrate form and gave voice to a most fearsome shriek, which he explained was the victory cry of a bull ape. Then he carried me to the door, shoved me out into the hall and locked me from his room."

For several minutes neither spoke again. It was the boy's mother who finally broke the silence.

"It is very necessary, Mr. Moore," she said, "that you do everything in your power to discourage this tendency in Jack, he – "; but she got no further. A loud "Whoop!" from the direction of the window brought them both to their feet. The room was upon the second floor of the house, and opposite the window to which their attention had been attracted was a large tree, a branch of which spread to within a few feet of the sill. Upon this branch now they both discovered the subject of their recent conversation, a tall, well-built boy, balancing with ease upon the bending limb and uttering loud shouts of glee as he noted the terrified expressions upon the faces of his audience.

The mother and tutor both rushed toward the window but before they had crossed half the room the boy had leaped nimbly to the sill and entered the apartment with them.

"'The wild man from Borneo has just come to town,'" he sang, dancing a species of war dance about his terrified mother and scandalized tutor, and ending up by throwing his arms about the former's neck and kissing her upon either cheek.

"Oh, Mother," he cried, "there's a wonderful, educated ape being shown at one of the music halls. Willie Grimsby saw it last night. He says it can do everything but talk. It rides a bicycle, eats with knife and fork, counts up to ten, and ever so many other wonderful things, and can I go and see it too? Oh, please, Mother – please let me."

Patting the boy's cheek affectionately, the mother shook her head negatively. "No, Jack," she said; "you know I do not approve of such exhibitions."

"I don't see why not, Mother," replied the boy. "All the other fellows go and they go to the Zoo, too, and you'll never let me do even that. Anybody'd think I was a girl – or a mollycoddle. Oh, Father," he exclaimed, as the door opened to admit a tall gray-eyed man. "Oh, Father, can't I go?"

"Go where, my son?" asked the newcomer.

"He wants to go to a music hall to see a trained ape," said the mother, looking warningly at her husband.

"Who, Ajax?" questioned the man.

The boy nodded.

"Well, I don't know that I blame you, my son," said the father, "I wouldn't mind seeing him myself. They say he is very wonderful, and that for an anthropoid he is unusually large. Let's all go, Jane – what do you say?" And he turned toward his wife, but that lady only shook her head in a most positive manner, and turning to Mr. Moore asked him if it was not time that he and Jack were in the study for the morning recitations. When the two had left she turned toward her husband.

"John," she said, "something must be done to discourage Jack's tendency toward anything that may excite the cravings for the savage life which I fear he has inherited from you. You know from your own experience how strong is the call of the wild at times. You know that often it has necessitated a stern struggle on your part to resist the almost insane desire which occasionally overwhelms you to plunge once again into the jungle life that claimed you for so many years, and at the same time you know, better than any other, how frightful a fate it would be for Jack, were the trail to the savage jungle made either alluring or easy to him."

"I doubt if there is any danger of his inheriting a taste for jungle life from me," replied the man, "for I cannot conceive that such a thing may be transmitted from father to son. And sometimes, Jane, I think that in your solicitude for his future you go a bit too far in your restrictive measures. His love for animals – his desire, for example, to see this trained ape – is only natural in a healthy, normal boy of his age. Just because he wants to see Ajax is no indication that he would wish to marry an ape, and even should he, far be it from you Jane to have the right to cry 'shame!'" and John Clayton, Lord Greystoke, put an arm about his wife, laughing good-naturedly down into her upturned face before he bent his head and kissed her. Then, more seriously, he continued: "You have never told Jack anything concerning my early life, nor have you permitted me to, and in this I think that you have made a mistake. Had I been able to tell him of the experiences of Tarzan of the Apes I could doubtless have taken much of the glamour and romance from jungle life that naturally surrounds it in the minds of those who have had no experience of it. He might then have profited by my experience, but now, should the jungle lust ever claim him, he will have nothing to guide him but his own impulses, and I know how powerful these may be in the wrong direction at times."

But Lady Greystoke only shook her head as she had a hundred other times when the subject had claimed her attention in the past.

"No, John," she insisted, "I shall never give my consent to the implanting in Jack's mind of any suggestion of the savage life which we both wish to preserve him from."

It was evening before the subject was again referred to and then it was raised by Jack himself. He had been sitting, curled in a large chair, reading, when he suddenly looked up and addressed his father.

"Why," he asked, coming directly to the point, "can't I go and see Ajax?"

"Your mother does not approve," replied his father.

"Do you?"

"That is not the question," evaded Lord Greystoke. "It is enough that your mother objects."

"I am going to see him," announced the boy, after a few moments of thoughtful silence. "I am not different from Willie Grimsby, or any other of the fellows who have been to see him. It did not harm them and it will not harm me. I could go without telling you; but I would not do that. So I tell you now, beforehand, that I am going to see Ajax."

There was nothing disrespectful or defiant in the boy's tone or manner. His was merely a dispassionate statement of facts. His father could scarce repress either a smile or a show of the admiration he felt for the manly course his son had pursued.

"I admire your candor, Jack," he said. "Permit me to be candid, as well. If you go to see Ajax without permission, I shall punish you. I have never inflicted corporal punishment upon you, but I warn you that should you disobey your mother's wishes in this instance, I shall."

"Yes, sir," replied the boy; and then: "I shall tell you, sir, when I have been to see Ajax."

Mr. Moore's room was next to that of his youthful charge, and it was the tutor's custom to have a look into the boy's each evening as the former was about to retire. This evening he was particularly careful not to neglect his duty, for he had just come from a conference with the boy's father and mother in which it had been impressed upon him that he must exercise the greatest care to prevent Jack visiting the music hall where Ajax was being shown. So, when he opened the boy's door at about half after nine, he was greatly excited, though not entirely surprised to find the future Lord Greystoke fully dressed for the street and about to crawl from his open bed room window.

Mr. Moore made a rapid spring across the apartment; but the waste of energy was unnecessary, for when the boy heard him within the chamber and realized that he had been discovered he turned back as though to relinquish his planned adventure.

"Where were you going?" panted the excited Mr. Moore.

"I am going to see Ajax," replied the boy, quietly.

"I am astonished," cried Mr. Moore; but a moment later he was infinitely more astonished, for the boy, approaching close to him, suddenly seized him about the waist, lifted him from his feet and threw him face downward upon the bed, shoving his face deep into a soft pillow.

"Be quiet," admonished the victor, "or I'll choke you."

Mr. Moore struggled; but his efforts were in vain. Whatever else Tarzan of the Apes may or may not have handed down to his son he had at least bequeathed him almost as marvelous a physique as he himself had possessed at the same age. The tutor was as putty in the boy's hands. Kneeling upon him, Jack tore strips from a sheet and bound the man's hands behind his back. Then he rolled him over and stuffed a gag of the same material between his teeth, securing it with a strip wound about the back of his victim's head. All the while he talked in a low, conversational tone.

"I am Waja, chief of the Waji," he explained, "and you are Mohammed Dubn, the Arab sheik, who would murder my people and steal my ivory," and he dexterously trussed Mr. Moore's hobbled ankles up behind to meet his hobbled wrists. "Ah – ha! Villain! I have you in me power at last. I go; but I shall return!" And the son of Tarzan skipped across the room, slipped through the open window, and slid to liberty by way of the down spout from an eaves trough.

Mr. Moore wriggled and struggled about the bed. He was sure that he should suffocate unless aid came quickly. In his frenzy of terror he managed to roll off the bed. The pain and shock of the fall jolted him back to something like sane consideration of his plight. Where before he had been unable to think intelligently because of the hysterical fear that had claimed him he now lay quietly searching for some means of escape from his dilemma. It finally occurred to him that the room in which Lord and Lady Greystoke had been sitting when he left them was directly beneath that in which he lay upon the floor. He knew that some time had elapsed since he had come up stairs and that they might be gone by this time, for it seemed to him that he had struggled about the bed, in his efforts to free himself, for an eternity. But the best that he could do was to attempt to attract attention from below, and so, after many failures, he managed to work himself into a position in which he could tap the toe of his boot against the floor. This he proceeded to do at short intervals, until, after what seemed a very long time, he was rewarded by hearing footsteps ascending the stairs, and presently a knock upon the door. Mr. Moore tapped vigorously with his toe – he could not reply in any other way. The knock was repeated after a moment's silence. Again Mr. Moore tapped. Would they never open the door! Laboriously he rolled in the direction of succor. If he could get his back against the door he could then tap upon its base, when surely he must be heard. The knocking was repeated a little louder, and finally a voice called: "Mr. Jack!"

It was one of the house men – Mr. Moore recognized the fellow's voice. He came near to bursting a blood vessel in an endeavor to scream "come in" through the stifling gag. After a moment the man knocked again, quite loudly and again called the boy's name. Receiving no reply he turned the knob, and at the same instant a sudden recollection filled the tutor anew with numbing terror – he had, himself, locked the door behind him when he had entered the room.

He heard the servant try the door several times and then depart. Upon which Mr. Moore swooned.

In the meantime Jack was enjoying to the full the stolen pleasures of the music hall. He had reached the temple of mirth just as Ajax's act was commencing, and having purchased a box seat was now leaning breathlessly over the rail watching every move of the great ape, his eyes wide in wonder. The trainer was not slow to note the boy's handsome, eager face, and as one of Ajax's biggest hits consisted in an entry to one or more boxes during his performance, ostensibly in search of a long-lost relative, as the trainer explained, the man realized the effectiveness of sending him into the box with the handsome boy, who, doubtless, would be terror stricken by proximity to the shaggy, powerful beast.

When the time came, therefore, for the ape to return from the wings in reply to an encore the trainer directed its attention to the boy who chanced to be the sole occupant of the box in which he sat. With a spring the huge anthropoid leaped from the stage to the boy's side; but if the trainer had looked for a laughable scene of fright he was mistaken. A broad smile lighted the boy's features as he laid his hand upon the shaggy arm of his visitor. The ape, grasping the boy by either shoulder, peered long and earnestly into his face, while the latter stroked his head and talked to him in a low voice.

Never had Ajax devoted so long a time to an examination of another as he did in this instance. He seemed troubled and not a little excited, jabbering and mumbling to the boy, and now caressing him, as the trainer had never seen him caress a human being before. Presently he clambered over into the box with him and snuggled down close to the boy's side.

The audience was delighted; but they were still more delighted when the trainer, the period of his act having elapsed, attempted to persuade Ajax to leave the box. The ape would not budge. The manager, becoming excited at the delay, urged the trainer to greater haste, but when the latter entered the box to drag away the reluctant Ajax he was met by bared fangs and menacing growls.

The audience was delirious with joy. They cheered the ape. They cheered the boy, and they hooted and jeered at the trainer and the manager, which luckless individual had inadvertently shown himself and attempted to assist the trainer.

Finally, reduced to desperation and realizing that this show of mutiny upon the part of his valuable possession might render the animal worthless for exhibition purposes in the future if not immediately subdued, the trainer had hastened to his dressing room and procured a heavy whip. With this he now returned to the box; but when he had threatened Ajax with it but once he found himself facing two infuriated enemies instead of one, for the boy had leaped to his feet, and seizing a chair was standing ready at the ape's side to defend his new found friend. There was no longer a smile upon his handsome face. In his gray eyes was an expression which gave the trainer pause, and beside him stood the giant anthropoid growling and ready.

What might have happened, but for a timely interruption, may only be surmised; but that the trainer would have received a severe mauling, if nothing more, was clearly indicated by the attitudes of the two who faced him.

It was a pale-faced man who rushed into the Greystoke library to announce that he had found Jack's door locked and had been able to obtain no response to his repeated knocking and calling other than a strange tapping and the sound of what might have been a body moving about upon the floor.

Four steps at a time John Clayton took the stairs that led to the floor above. His wife and the servant hurried after him. Once he called his son's name in a loud voice; but receiving no reply he launched his great weight, backed by all the undiminished power of his giant muscles, against the heavy door. With a snapping of iron butts and a splintering of wood the obstacle burst inward.

At its foot lay the body of the unconscious Mr. Moore, across whom it fell with a resounding thud. Through the opening leaped Tarzan, and a moment later the room was flooded with light from a dozen electric bulbs.

It was several minutes before the tutor was discovered, so completely had the door covered him; but finally he was dragged forth, his gag and bonds cut away, and a liberal application of cold water had hastened returning consciousness.

"Where is Jack?" was John Clayton's first question, and then; "Who did this?" as the memory of Rokoff and the fear of a second abduction seized him.

Slowly Mr. Moore staggered to his feet. His gaze wandered about the room. Gradually he collected his scattered wits. The details of his recent harrowing experience returned to him.

"I tender my resignation, sir, to take effect at once," were his first words. "You do not need a tutor for your son – what he needs is a wild animal trainer."

"But where is he?" cried Lady Greystoke.

"He has gone to see Ajax."

It was with difficulty that Tarzan restrained a smile, and after satisfying himself that the tutor was more scared than injured, he ordered his closed car around and departed in the direction of a certain well-known music hall.

Chapter Three

As the trainer, with raised lash, hesitated an instant at the entrance to the box where the boy and the ape confronted him, a tall broad-shouldered man pushed past him and entered. As his eyes fell upon the newcomer a slight flush mounted the boy's cheeks.

"Father!" he exclaimed.

The ape gave one look at the English lord, and then leaped toward him, calling out in excited jabbering. The man, his eyes going wide in astonishment, stopped as though turned to stone.

"Akut!" he cried.

The boy looked, bewildered, from the ape to his father, and from his father to the ape. The trainer's jaw dropped as he listened to what followed, for from the lips of the Englishman flowed the gutturals of an ape that were answered in kind by the huge anthropoid that now clung to him.

And from the wings a hideously bent and disfigured old man watched the tableau in the box, his pock-marked features working spasmodically in varying expressions that might have marked every sensation in the gamut from pleasure to terror.

"Long have I looked for you, Tarzan," said Akut. "Now that I have found you I shall come to your jungle and live there always."

The man stroked the beast's head. Through his mind there was running rapidly a train of recollection that carried him far into the depths of the primeval African forest where this huge, man-like beast had fought shoulder to shoulder with him years before. He saw the black Mugambi wielding his deadly knob-stick, and beside them, with bared fangs and bristling whiskers, Sheeta the terrible; and pressing close behind the savage and the savage panther, the hideous apes of Akut. The man sighed. Strong within him surged the jungle lust that he had thought dead. Ah! if he could go back even for a brief month of it, to feel again the brush of leafy branches against his naked hide; to smell the musty rot of dead vegetation – frankincense and myrrh to the jungle born; to sense the noiseless coming of the great carnivora upon his trail; to hunt and to be hunted; to kill! The picture was alluring. And then came another picture – a sweet-faced woman, still young and beautiful; friends; a home; a son. He shrugged his giant shoulders.

"It cannot be, Akut," he said; "but if you would return, I shall see that it is done. You could not be happy here – I may not be happy there."

The trainer stepped forward. The ape bared his fangs, growling.

"Go with him, Akut," said Tarzan of the Apes. "I will come and see you tomorrow."

The beast moved sullenly to the trainer's side. The latter, at John Clayton's request, told where they might be found. Tarzan turned toward his son.

"Come!" he said, and the two left the theater. Neither spoke for several minutes after they had entered the limousine. It was the boy who broke the silence.

"The ape knew you," he said, "and you spoke together in the ape's tongue. How did the ape know you, and how did you learn his language?"

And then, briefly and for the first time, Tarzan of the Apes told his son of his early life – of the birth in the jungle, of the death of his parents, and of how Kala, the great she ape had suckled and raised him from infancy almost to manhood. He told him, too, of the dangers and the horrors of the jungle; of the great beasts that stalked one by day and by night; of the periods of drought, and of the cataclysmic rains; of hunger; of cold; of intense heat; of nakedness and fear and suffering. He told him of all those things that seem most horrible to the creature of civilization in the hope that the knowledge of them might expunge from the lad's mind any inherent desire for the jungle. Yet they were the very things that made the memory of the jungle what it was to Tarzan – that made up the composite jungle life he loved. And in the telling he forgot one thing – the principal thing – that the boy at his side, listening with eager ears, was the son of Tarzan of the Apes.

After the boy had been tucked away in bed – and without the threatened punishment – John Clayton told his wife of the events of the evening, and that he had at last acquainted the boy with the facts of his jungle life. The mother, who had long foreseen that her son must some time know of those frightful years during which his father had roamed the jungle, a naked, savage beast of prey, only shook her head, hoping against hope that the lure she knew was still strong in the father's breast had not been transmitted to his son.

Tarzan visited Akut the following day, but though Jack begged to be allowed to accompany him he was refused. This time Tarzan saw the pock-marked old owner of the ape, whom he did not recognize as the wily Paulvitch of former days. Tarzan, influenced by Akut's pleadings, broached the question of the ape's purchase; but Paulvitch would not name any price, saying that he would consider the matter.

When Tarzan returned home Jack was all excitement to hear the details of his visit, and finally suggested that his father buy the ape and bring it home. Lady Greystoke was horrified at the suggestion. The boy was insistent. Tarzan explained that he had wished to purchase Akut and return him to his jungle home, and to this the mother assented. Jack asked to be allowed to visit the ape, but again he was met with flat refusal. He had the address, however, which the trainer had given his father, and two days later he found the opportunity to elude his new tutor – who had replaced the terrified Mr. Moore – and after a considerable search through a section of London which he had never before visited, he found the smelly little quarters of the pock-marked old man. The old fellow himself replied to his knocking, and when he stated that he had come to see Ajax, opened the door and admitted him to the little room which he and the great ape occupied. In former years Paulvitch had been a fastidious scoundrel; but ten years of hideous life among the cannibals of Africa had eradicated the last vestige of niceness from his habits. His apparel was wrinkled and soiled. His hands were unwashed, his few straggling locks uncombed. His room was a jumble of filthy disorder. As the boy entered he saw the great ape squatting upon the bed, the coverlets of which were a tangled wad of filthy blankets and ill-smelling quilts. At sight of the youth the ape leaped to the floor and shuffled forward. The man, not recognizing his visitor and fearing that the ape meant mischief, stepped between them, ordering the ape back to the bed.

"He will not hurt me," cried the boy. "We are friends, and before, he was my father's friend. They knew one another in the jungle. My father is Lord Greystoke. He does not know that I have come here. My mother forbid my coming; but I wished to see Ajax, and I will pay you if you will let me come here often and see him."

At the mention of the boy's identity Paulvitch's eyes narrowed. Since he had first seen Tarzan again from the wings of the theater there had been forming in his deadened brain the beginnings of a desire for revenge. It is a characteristic of the weak and criminal to attribute to others the misfortunes that are the result of their own wickedness, and so now it was that Alexis Paulvitch was slowly recalling the events of his past life and as he did so laying at the door of the man whom he and Rokoff had so assiduously attempted to ruin and murder all the misfortunes that had befallen him in the failure of their various schemes against their intended victim.

He saw at first no way in which he could, with safety to himself, wreak vengeance upon Tarzan through the medium of Tarzan's son; but that great possibilities for revenge lay in the boy was apparent to him, and so he determined to cultivate the lad in the hope that fate would play into his hands in some way in the future. He told the boy all that he knew of his father's past life in the jungle and when he found that the boy had been kept in ignorance of all these things for so many years, and that he had been forbidden visiting the zoological gardens; that he had had to bind and gag his tutor to find an opportunity to come to the music hall and see Ajax, he guessed immediately the nature of the great fear that lay in the hearts of the boy's parents – that he might crave the jungle as his father had craved it.

And so Paulvitch encouraged the boy to come and see him often, and always he played upon the lad's craving for tales of the savage world with which Paulvitch was all too familiar. He left him alone with Akut much, and it was not long until he was surprised to learn that the boy could make the great beast understand him – that he had actually learned many of the words of the primitive language of the anthropoids.

During this period Tarzan came several times to visit Paulvitch. He seemed anxious to purchase Ajax, and at last he told the man frankly that he was prompted not only by a desire upon his part to return the beast to the liberty of his native jungle; but also because his wife feared that in some way her son might learn the whereabouts of the ape and through his attachment for the beast become imbued with the roving instinct which, as Tarzan explained to Paulvitch, had so influenced his own life.

The Russian could scarce repress a smile as he listened to Lord Greystoke's words, since scarce a half hour had passed since the time the future Lord Greystoke had been sitting upon the disordered bed jabbering away to Ajax with all the fluency of a born ape.

It was during this interview that a plan occurred to Paulvitch, and as a result of it he agreed to accept a certain fabulous sum for the ape, and upon receipt of the money to deliver the beast to a vessel that was sailing south from Dover for Africa two days later. He had a double purpose in accepting Clayton's offer. Primarily, the money consideration influenced him strongly, as the ape was no longer a source of revenue to him, having consistently refused to perform upon the stage after having discovered Tarzan. It was as though the beast had suffered himself to be brought from his jungle home and exhibited before thousands of curious spectators for the sole purpose of searching out his long lost friend and master, and, having found him, considered further mingling with the common herd of humans unnecessary. However that may be, the fact remained that no amount of persuasion could influence him even to show himself upon the music hall stage, and upon the single occasion that the trainer attempted force the results were such that the unfortunate man considered himself lucky to have escaped with his life. All that saved him was the accidental presence of Jack Clayton, who had been permitted to visit the animal in the dressing room reserved for him at the music hall, and had immediately interfered when he saw that the savage beast meant serious mischief.

And after the money consideration, strong in the heart of the Russian was the desire for revenge, which had been growing with constant brooding over the failures and miseries of his life, which he attributed to Tarzan; the latest, and by no means the least, of which was Ajax's refusal to longer earn money for him. The ape's refusal he traced directly to Tarzan, finally convincing himself that the ape man had instructed the great anthropoid to refuse to go upon the stage.

Paulvitch's naturally malign disposition was aggravated by the weakening and warping of his mental and physical faculties through torture and privation. From cold, calculating, highly intelligent perversity it had deteriorated into the indiscriminating, dangerous menace of the mentally defective. His plan, however, was sufficiently cunning to at least cast a doubt upon the assertion that his mentality was wandering. It assured him first of the competence which Lord Greystoke had promised to pay him for the deportation of the ape, and then of revenge upon his benefactor through the son he idolized. That part of his scheme was crude and brutal – it lacked the refinement of torture that had marked the master strokes of the Paulvitch of old, when he had worked with that virtuoso of villainy, Nikolas Rokoff – but it at least assured Paulvitch of immunity from responsibility, placing that upon the ape, who would thus also be punished for his refusal longer to support the Russian.

Everything played with fiendish unanimity into Paulvitch's hands. As chance would have it, Tarzan's son overheard his father relating to the boy's mother the steps he was taking to return Akut safely to his jungle home, and having overheard he begged them to bring the ape home that he might have him for a play-fellow. Tarzan would not have been averse to this plan; but Lady Greystoke was horrified at the very thought of it. Jack pleaded with his mother; but all unavailingly. She was obdurate, and at last the lad appeared to acquiesce in his mother's decision that the ape must be returned to Africa and the boy to school, from which he had been absent on vacation.

He did not attempt to visit Paulvitch's room again that day, but instead busied himself in other ways. He had always been well supplied with money, so that when necessity demanded he had no difficulty in collecting several hundred pounds. Some of this money he invested in various strange purchases which he managed to smuggle into the house, undetected, when he returned late in the afternoon.

The next morning, after giving his father time to precede him and conclude his business with Paulvitch, the lad hastened to the Russian's room. Knowing nothing of the man's true character the boy dared not take him fully into his confidence for fear that the old fellow would not only refuse to aid him, but would report the whole affair to his father. Instead, he simply asked permission to take Ajax to Dover. He explained that it would relieve the old man of a tiresome journey, as well as placing a number of pounds in his pocket, for the lad purposed paying the Russian well.

"You see," he went on, "there will be no danger of detection since I am supposed to be leaving on an afternoon train for school. Instead I will come here after they have left me on board the train. Then I can take Ajax to Dover, you see, and arrive at school only a day late. No one will be the wiser, no harm will be done, and I shall have had an extra day with Ajax before I lose him forever."

The plan fitted perfectly with that which Paulvitch had in mind. Had he known what further the boy contemplated he would doubtless have entirely abandoned his own scheme of revenge and aided the boy whole heartedly in the consummation of the lad's, which would have been better for Paulvitch, could he have but read the future but a few short hours ahead.

That afternoon Lord and Lady Greystoke bid their son good-bye and saw him safely settled in a first-class compartment of the railway carriage that would set him down at school in a few hours. No sooner had they left him, however, than he gathered his bags together, descended from the compartment and sought a cab stand outside the station. Here he engaged a cabby to take him to the Russian's address. It was dusk when he arrived. He found Paulvitch awaiting him. The man was pacing the floor nervously. The ape was tied with a stout cord to the bed. It was the first time that Jack had ever seen Ajax thus secured. He looked questioningly at Paulvitch. The man, mumbling, explained that he believed the animal had guessed that he was to be sent away and he feared he would attempt to escape.

Paulvitch carried another piece of cord in his hand. There was a noose in one end of it which he was continually playing with. He walked back and forth, up and down the room. His pock-marked features were working horribly as he talked silent to himself. The boy had never seen him thus – it made him uneasy. At last Paulvitch stopped on the opposite side of the room, far from the ape.

"Come here," he said to the lad. "I will show you how to secure the ape should he show signs of rebellion during the trip."

The lad laughed. "It will not be necessary," he replied. "Ajax will do whatever I tell him to do."

The old man stamped his foot angrily. "Come here, as I tell you," he repeated. "If you do not do as I say you shall not accompany the ape to Dover – I will take no chances upon his escaping."

Still smiling, the lad crossed the room and stood before the Russ.

"Turn around, with your back toward me," directed the latter, "that I may show you how to bind him quickly."

The boy did as he was bid, placing his hands behind him when Paulvitch told him to do so. Instantly the old man slipped the running noose over one of the lad's wrists, took a couple of half hitches about his other wrist, and knotted the cord.

The moment that the boy was secured the attitude of the man changed. With an angry oath he wheeled his prisoner about, tripped him and hurled him violently to the floor, leaping upon his breast as he fell. From the bed the ape growled and struggled with his bonds. The boy did not cry out – a trait inherited from his savage sire whom long years in the jungle following the death of his foster mother, Kala the great ape, had taught that there was none to come to the succor of the fallen.

Paulvitch's fingers sought the lad's throat. He grinned down horribly into the face of his victim.

"Your father ruined me," he mumbled. "This will pay him. He will think that the ape did it. I will tell him that the ape did it. That I left him alone for a few minutes, and that you sneaked in and the ape killed you. I will throw your body upon the bed after I have choked the life from you, and when I bring your father he will see the ape squatting over it," and the twisted fiend cackled in gloating laughter. His fingers closed upon the boy's throat.

Behind them the growling of the maddened beast reverberated against the walls of the little room. The boy paled, but no other sign of fear or panic showed upon his countenance. He was the son of Tarzan. The fingers tightened their grip upon his throat. It was with difficulty that he breathed, gaspingly. The ape lunged against the stout cord that held him. Turning, he wrapped the cord about his hands, as a man might have done, and surged heavily backward. The great muscles stood out beneath his shaggy hide. There was a rending as of splintered wood – the cord held, but a portion of the footboard of the bed came away.

At the sound Paulvitch looked up. His hideous face went white with terror – the ape was free.

With a single bound the creature was upon him. The man shrieked. The brute wrenched him from the body of the boy. Great fingers sunk into the man's flesh. Yellow fangs gaped close to his throat – he struggled, futilely – and when they closed, the soul of Alexis Paulvitch passed into the keeping of the demons who had long been awaiting it.

The boy struggled to his feet, assisted by Akut. For two hours under the instructions of the former the ape worked upon the knots that secured his friend's wrists. Finally they gave up their secret, and the boy was free. Then he opened one of his bags and drew forth some garments. His plans had been well made. He did not consult the beast, which did all that he directed. Together they slunk from the house, but no casual observer might have noted that one of them was an ape.

Chapter Four

The killing of the friendless old Russian, Michael Sabrov, by his great trained ape, was a matter for newspaper comment for a few days. Lord Greystoke read of it, and while taking special precautions not to permit his name to become connected with the affair, kept himself well posted as to the police search for the anthropoid.

As was true of the general public, his chief interest in the matter centered about the mysterious disappearance of the slayer. Or at least this was true until he learned, several days subsequent to the tragedy, that his son Jack had not reported at the public school en route for which they had seen him safely ensconced in a railway carriage. Even then the father did not connect the disappearance of his son with the mystery surrounding the whereabouts of the ape. Nor was it until a month later that careful investigation revealed the fact that the boy had left the train before it pulled out of the station at London, and the cab driver had been found who had driven him to the address of the old Russian, that Tarzan of the Apes realized that Akut had in some way been connected with the disappearance of the boy.

Beyond the moment that the cab driver had deposited his fare beside the curb in front of the house in which the Russian had been quartered there was no clue. No one had seen either the boy or the ape from that instant – at least no one who still lived. The proprietor of the house identified the picture of the lad as that of one who had been a frequent visitor in the room of the old man. Aside from this he knew nothing. And there, at the door of a grimy, old building in the slums of London, the searchers came to a blank wall – baffled.

The day following the death of Alexis Paulvitch a youth accompanying his invalid grandmother, boarded a steamer at Dover. The old lady was heavily veiled, and so weakened by age and sickness that she had to be wheeled aboard the vessel in an invalid chair.

The boy would permit none but himself to wheel her, and with his own hands assisted her from the chair to the interior of their stateroom – and that was the last that was seen of the old lady by the ship's company until the pair disembarked. The boy even insisted upon doing the work of their cabin steward, since, as he explained, his grandmother was suffering from a nervous disposition that made the presence of strangers extremely distasteful to her.

Outside the cabin – and none there was aboard who knew what he did in the cabin – the lad was just as any other healthy, normal English boy might have been. He mingled with his fellow passengers, became a prime favorite with the officers, and struck up numerous friendships among the common sailors. He was generous and unaffected, yet carried an air of dignity and strength of character that inspired his many new friends with admiration as well as affection for him.

Among the passengers there was an American named Condon, a noted blackleg and crook who was "wanted" in a half dozen of the larger cities of the United States. He had paid little attention to the boy until on one occasion he had seen him accidentally display a roll of bank notes. From then on Condon cultivated the youthful Briton. He learned, easily, that the boy was traveling alone with his invalid grandmother, and that their destination was a small port on the west coast of Africa, a little below the equator; that their name was Billings, and that they had no friends in the little settlement for which they were bound. Upon the point of their purpose in visiting the place Condon found the boy reticent, and so he did not push the matter – he had learned all that he cared to know as it was.

Several times Condon attempted to draw the lad into a card game; but his victim was not interested, and the black looks of several of the other men passengers decided the American to find other means of transferring the boy's bank roll to his own pocket.

At last came the day that the steamer dropped anchor in the lee of a wooded promontory where a score or more of sheet-iron shacks making an unsightly blot upon the fair face of nature proclaimed the fact that civilization had set its heel. Straggling upon the outskirts were the thatched huts of natives, picturesque in their primeval savagery, harmonizing with the background of tropical jungle and accentuating the squalid hideousness of the white man's pioneer architecture.

The boy, leaning over the rail, was looking far beyond the man-made town deep into the God-made jungle. A little shiver of anticipation tingled his spine, and then, quite without volition, he found himself gazing into the loving eyes of his mother and the strong face of the father which mirrored, beneath its masculine strength, a love no less than the mother's eyes proclaimed. He felt himself weakening in his resolve. Nearby one of the ship's officers was shouting orders to a flotilla of native boats that was approaching to lighter the consignment of the steamer's cargo destined for this tiny post.

"When does the next steamer for England touch here?" the boy asked.

"The Emanuel ought to be along most any time now," replied the officer. "I figgered we'd find her here," and he went on with his bellowing remarks to the dusty horde drawing close to the steamer's side.

The task of lowering the boy's grandmother over the side to a waiting canoe was rather difficult. The lad insisted on being always at her side, and when at last she was safely ensconced in the bottom of the craft that was to bear them shoreward her grandson dropped catlike after her. So interested was he in seeing her comfortably disposed that he failed to notice the little package that had worked from his pocket as he assisted in lowering the sling that contained the old woman over the steamer's side, nor did he notice it even as it slipped out entirely and dropped into the sea.

Scarcely had the boat containing the boy and the old woman started for the shore than Condon hailed a canoe upon the other side of the ship, and after bargaining with its owner finally lowered his baggage and himself aboard. Once ashore he kept out of sight of the two-story atrocity that bore the legend "Hotel" to lure unsuspecting wayfarers to its multitudinous discomforts. It was quite dark before he ventured to enter and arrange for accommodations.

In a back room upon the second floor the lad was explaining, not without considerable difficulty, to his grandmother that he had decided to return to England upon the next steamer. He was endeavoring to make it plain to the old lady that she might remain in Africa if she wished but that for his part his conscience demanded that he return to his father and mother, who doubtless were even now suffering untold sorrow because of his absence; from which it may be assumed that his parents had not been acquainted with the plans that he and the old lady had made for their adventure into African wilds.

Having come to a decision the lad felt a sense of relief from the worry that had haunted him for many sleepless nights. When he closed his eyes in sleep it was to dream of a happy reunion with those at home. And as he dreamed, Fate, cruel and inexorable, crept stealthily upon him through the dark corridor of the squalid building in which he slept – Fate in the form of the American crook, Condon.

Cautiously the man approached the door of the lad's room. There he crouched listening until assured by the regular breathing of those within that both slept. Quietly he inserted a slim, skeleton key in the lock of the door. With deft fingers, long accustomed to the silent manipulation of the bars and bolts that guarded other men's property, Condon turned the key and the knob simultaneously. Gentle pressure upon the door swung it slowly inward upon its hinges. The man entered the room, closing the door behind him. The moon was temporarily overcast by heavy clouds. The interior of the apartment was shrouded in gloom. Condon groped his way toward the bed. In the far corner of the room something moved – moved with a silent stealthiness which transcended even the trained silence of the burglar. Condon heard nothing. His attention was riveted upon the bed in which he thought to find a young boy and his helpless, invalid grandmother.

The American sought only the bank roll. If he could possess himself of this without detection, well and good; but were he to meet resistance he was prepared for that too. The lad's clothes lay across a chair beside the bed. The American's fingers felt swiftly through them – the pockets contained no roll of crisp, new notes. Doubtless they were beneath the pillows of the bed. He stepped closer toward the sleeper; his hand was already half way beneath the pillow when the thick cloud that had obscured the moon rolled aside and the room was flooded with light. At the same instant the boy opened his eyes and looked straight into those of Condon. The man was suddenly conscious that the boy was alone in the bed. Then he clutched for his victim's throat. As the lad rose to meet him Condon heard a low growl at his back, then he felt his wrists seized by the boy, and realized that beneath those tapering, white fingers played muscles of steel.

He felt other hands at his throat, rough hairy hands that reached over his shoulders from behind. He cast a terrified glance backward, and the hairs of his head stiffened at the sight his eyes revealed, for grasping him from the rear was a huge, man-like ape. The bared fighting fangs of the anthropoid were close to his throat. The lad pinioned his wrists. Neither uttered a sound. Where was the grandmother? Condon's eyes swept the room in a single all-inclusive glance. His eyes bulged in horror at the realization of the truth which that glance revealed. In the power of what creatures of hideous mystery had he placed himself! Frantically he fought to beat off the lad that he might turn upon the fearsome thing at his back. Freeing one hand he struck a savage blow at the lad's face. His act seemed to unloose a thousand devils in the hairy creature clinging to his throat. Condon heard a low and savage snarl. It was the last thing that the American ever heard in this life. Then he was dragged backward upon the floor, a heavy body fell upon him, powerful teeth fastened themselves in his jugular, his head whirled in the sudden blackness which rims eternity – a moment later the ape rose from his prostrate form; but Condon did not know – he was quite dead.

The lad, horrified, sprang from the bed to lean over the body of the man. He knew that Akut had killed in his defense, as he had killed Michael Sabrov; but here, in savage Africa, far from home and friends what would they do to him and his faithful ape? The lad knew that the penalty of murder was death. He even knew that an accomplice might suffer the death penalty with the principal. Who was there who would plead for them? All would be against them. It was little more than a half-civilized community, and the chances were that they would drag Akut and him forth in the morning and hang them both to the nearest tree – he had read of such things being done in America, and Africa was worse even and wilder than the great West of his mother's native land. Yes, they would both be hanged in the morning!

Was there no escape? He thought in silence for a few moments, and then, with an exclamation of relief, he struck his palms together and turned toward his clothing upon the chair. Money would do anything! Money would save him and Akut! He felt for the bank roll in the pocket in which he had been accustomed to carry it. It was not there! Slowly at first and at last frantically he searched through the remaining pockets of his clothing. Then he dropped upon his hands and knees and examined the floor. Lighting the lamp he moved the bed to one side and, inch by inch, he felt over the entire floor. Beside the body of Condon he hesitated, but at last he nerved himself to touch it. Rolling it over he sought beneath it for the money. Nor was it there. He guessed that Condon had entered their room to rob; but he did not believe that the man had had time to possess himself of the money; however, as it was nowhere else, it must be upon the body of the dead man. Again and again he went over the room, only to return each time to the corpse; but no where could he find the money.

He was half-frantic with despair. What were they to do? In the morning they would be discovered and killed. For all his inherited size and strength he was, after all, only a little boy – a frightened, homesick little boy – reasoning faultily from the meager experience of childhood. He could think of but a single glaring fact – they had killed a fellow man, and they were among savage strangers, thirsting for the blood of the first victim whom fate cast into their clutches. This much he had gleaned from penny-dreadfuls.

And they must have money!

Again he approached the corpse. This time resolutely. The ape squatted in a corner watching his young companion. The youth commenced to remove the American's clothing piece by piece, and, piece by piece, he examined each garment minutely. Even to the shoes he searched with painstaking care, and when the last article had been removed and scrutinized he dropped back upon the bed with dilated eyes that saw nothing in the present – only a grim tableau of the future in which two forms swung silently from the limb of a great tree.

How long he sat thus he did not know; but finally he was aroused by a noise coming from the floor below. Springing quickly to his feet he blew out the lamp, and crossing the floor silently locked the door. Then he turned toward the ape, his mind made up.

Last evening he had been determined to start for home at the first opportunity, to beg the forgiveness of his parents for this mad adventure. Now he knew that he might never return to them. The blood of a fellow man was upon his hands – in his morbid reflections he had long since ceased to attribute the death of Condon to the ape. The hysteria of panic had fastened the guilt upon himself. With money he might have bought justice; but penniless! – ah, what hope could there be for strangers without money here?

But what had become of the money? He tried to recall when last he had seen it. He could not, nor, could he, would he have been able to account for its disappearance, for he had been entirely unconscious of the falling of the little package from his pocket into the sea as he clambered over the ship's side into the waiting canoe that bore him to shore.

Now he turned toward Akut. "Come!" he said, in the language of the great apes.

Forgetful of the fact that he wore only a thin pajama suit he led the way to the open window. Thrusting his head out he listened attentively. A single tree grew a few feet from the window. Nimbly the lad sprang to its bole, clinging cat-like for an instant before he clambered quietly to the ground below. Close behind him came the great ape. Two hundred yards away a spur of the jungle ran close to the straggling town. Toward this the lad led the way. None saw them, and a moment later the jungle swallowed them, and John Clayton, future Lord Greystoke, passed from the eyes and the knowledge of men.

It was late the following morning that a native houseman knocked upon the door of the room that had been assigned to Mrs. Billings and her grandson. Receiving no response he inserted his pass key in the lock, only to discover that another key was already there, but from the inside. He reported the fact to Herr Skopf, the proprietor, who at once made his way to the second floor where he, too, pounded vigorously upon the door. Receiving no reply he bent to the key hole in an attempt to look through into the room beyond. In so doing, being portly, he lost his balance, which necessitated putting a palm to the floor to maintain his equilibrium. As he did so he felt something soft and thick and wet beneath his fingers. He raised his open palm before his eyes in the dim light of the corridor and peered at it. Then he gave a little shudder, for even in the semi-darkness he saw a dark red stain upon his hand. Leaping to his feet he hurled his shoulder against the door. Herr Skopf is a heavy man – or at least he was then – I have not seen him for several years. The frail door collapsed beneath his weight, and Herr Skopf stumbled precipitately into the room beyond.

Before him lay the greatest mystery of his life. Upon the floor at his feet was the dead body of a strange man. The neck was broken and the jugular severed as by the fangs of a wild beast. The body was entirely naked, the clothing being strewn about the corpse. The old lady and her grandson were gone. The window was open. They must have disappeared through the window for the door had been locked from the inside.

But how could the boy have carried his invalid grandmother from a second story window to the ground? It was preposterous. Again Herr Skopf searched the small room. He noticed that the bed was pulled well away from the wall – why? He looked beneath it again for the third or fourth time. The two were gone, and yet his judgment told him that the old lady could not have gone without porters to carry her down as they had carried her up the previous day.

Further search deepened the mystery. All the clothing of the two was still in the room – if they had gone then they must have gone naked or in their night clothes. Herr Skopf shook his head; then he scratched it. He was baffled. He had never heard of Sherlock Holmes or he would have lost no time in invoking the aid of that celebrated sleuth, for here was a real mystery: An old woman – an invalid who had to be carried from the ship to her room in the hotel – and a handsome lad, her grandson, had entered a room on the second floor of his hostelry the day before. They had had their evening meal served in their room – that was the last that had been seen of them. At nine the following morning the corpse of a strange man had been the sole occupant of that room. No boat had left the harbor in the meantime – there was not a railroad within hundreds of miles – there was no other white settlement that the two could reach under several days of arduous marching accompanied by a well-equipped safari. They had simply vanished into thin air, for the native he had sent to inspect the ground beneath the open window had just returned to report that there was no sign of a footstep there, and what sort of creatures were they who could have dropped that distance to the soft turf without leaving spoor? Herr Skopf shuddered. Yes, it was a great mystery – there was something uncanny about the whole thing – he hated to think about it, and he dreaded the coming of night.

It was a great mystery to Herr Skopf – and, doubtless, still is.

Chapter Five

Captain Armand Jacot of the Foreign Legion sat upon an outspread saddle blanket at the foot of a stunted palm tree. His broad shoulders and his close-cropped head rested in luxurious ease against the rough bole of the palm. His long legs were stretched straight before him overlapping the meager blanket, his spurs buried in the sandy soil of the little desert oasis. The captain was taking his ease after a long day of weary riding across the shifting sands of the desert.

Lazily he puffed upon his cigarette and watched his orderly who was preparing his evening meal. Captain Armand Jacot was well satisfied with himself and the world. A little to his right rose the noisy activity of his troop of sun-tanned veterans, released for the time from the irksome trammels of discipline, relaxing tired muscles, laughing, joking, and smoking as they, too, prepared to eat after a twelve-hour fast. Among them, silent and taciturn, squatted five white-robed Arabs, securely bound and under heavy guard.

It was the sight of these that filled Captain Armand Jacot with the pleasurable satisfaction of a duty well-performed. For a long, hot, gaunt month he and his little troop had scoured the places of the desert waste in search of a band of marauders to the sin-stained account of which were charged innumerable thefts of camels, horses, and goats, as well as murders enough to have sent the whole unsavory gang to the guillotine several times over.

A week before, he had come upon them. In the ensuing battle he had lost two of his own men, but the punishment inflicted upon the marauders had been severe almost to extinction. A half dozen, perhaps, had escaped; but the balance, with the exception of the five prisoners, had expiated their crimes before the nickel jacketed bullets of the legionaries. And, best of all, the ring leader, Achmet ben Houdin, was among the prisoners.

From the prisoners Captain Jacot permitted his mind to traverse the remaining miles of sand to the little garrison post where, upon the morrow, he should find awaiting him with eager welcome his wife and little daughter. His eyes softened to the memory of them, as they always did. Even now he could see the beauty of the mother reflected in the childish lines of little Jeanne's face, and both those faces would be smiling up into his as he swung from his tired mount late the following afternoon. Already he could feel a soft cheek pressed close to each of his – velvet against leather.

His reverie was broken in upon by the voice of a sentry summoning a non-commissioned officer. Captain Jacot raised his eyes. The sun had not yet set; but the shadows of the few trees huddled about the water hole and of his men and their horses stretched far away into the east across the now golden sand. The sentry was pointing in this direction, and the corporal, through narrowed lids, was searching the distance. Captain Jacot rose to his feet. He was not a man content to see through the eyes of others. He must see for himself. Usually he saw things long before others were aware that there was anything to see – a trait that had won for him the sobriquet of Hawk. Now he saw, just beyond the long shadows, a dozen specks rising and falling among the sands. They disappeared and reappeared, but always they grew larger. Jacot recognized them immediately. They were horsemen – horsemen of the desert. Already a sergeant was running toward him. The entire camp was straining its eyes into the distance. Jacot gave a few terse orders to the sergeant who saluted, turned upon his heel and returned to the men. Here he gathered a dozen who saddled their horses, mounted and rode out to meet the strangers. The remaining men disposed themselves in readiness for instant action. It was not entirely beyond the range of possibilities that the horsemen riding thus swiftly toward the camp might be friends of the prisoners bent upon the release of their kinsmen by a sudden attack. Jacot doubted this, however, since the strangers were evidently making no attempt to conceal their presence. They were galloping rapidly toward the camp in plain view of all. There might be treachery lurking beneath their fair appearance; but none who knew The Hawk would be so gullible as to hope to trap him thus.

The sergeant with his detail met the Arabs two hundred yards from the camp. Jacot could see him in conversation with a tall, white-robed figure – evidently the leader of the band. Presently the sergeant and this Arab rode side by side toward camp. Jacot awaited them. The two reined in and dismounted before him.

"Sheik Amor ben Khatour," announced the sergeant by way of introduction.

Captain Jacot eyed the newcomer. He was acquainted with nearly every principal Arab within a radius of several hundred miles. This man he never had seen. He was a tall, weather beaten, sour looking man of sixty or more. His eyes were narrow and evil. Captain Jacot did not relish his appearance.

"Well?" he asked, tentatively.

The Arab came directly to the point.

"Achmet ben Houdin is my sister's son," he said. "If you will give him into my keeping I will see that he sins no more against the laws of the French."

Jacot shook his head. "That cannot be," he replied. "I must take him back with me. He will be properly and fairly tried by a civil court. If he is innocent he will be released."

"And if he is not innocent?" asked the Arab.

"He is charged with many murders. For any one of these, if he is proved guilty, he will have to die."

The Arab's left hand was hidden beneath his burnous. Now he withdrew it disclosing a large goatskin purse, bulging and heavy with coins. He opened the mouth of the purse and let a handful of the contents trickle into the palm of his right hand – all were pieces of good French gold. From the size of the purse and its bulging proportions Captain Jacot concluded that it must contain a small fortune. Sheik Amor ben Khatour dropped the spilled gold pieces one by one back into the purse. Jacot was eyeing him narrowly. They were alone. The sergeant, having introduced the visitor, had withdrawn to some little distance – his back was toward them. Now the sheik, having returned all the gold pieces, held the bulging purse outward upon his open palm toward Captain Jacot.

"Achmet ben Houdin, my sister's son, MIGHT escape tonight," he said. "Eh?"

Captain Armand Jacot flushed to the roots of his close-cropped hair. Then he went very white and took a half-step toward the Arab. His fists were clenched. Suddenly he thought better of whatever impulse was moving him.

"Sergeant!" he called. The non-commissioned officer hurried toward him, saluting as his heels clicked together before his superior.

"Take this black dog back to his people," he ordered. "See that they leave at once. Shoot the first man who comes within range of camp tonight."

Sheik Amor ben Khatour drew himself up to his full height. His evil eyes narrowed. He raised the bag of gold level with the eyes of the French officer.

"You will pay more than this for the life of Achmet ben Houdin, my sister's son," he said. "And as much again for the name that you have called me and a hundred fold in sorrow in the bargain."

"Get out of here!" growled Captain Armand Jacot, "before I kick you out."

All of this happened some three years before the opening of this tale. The trail of Achmet ben Houdin and his accomplices is a matter of record – you may verify it if you care to. He met the death he deserved, and he met it with the stoicism of the Arab.

A month later little Jeanne Jacot, the seven-year-old daughter of Captain Armand Jacot, mysteriously disappeared. Neither the wealth of her father and mother, or all the powerful resources of the great republic were able to wrest the secret of her whereabouts from the inscrutable desert that had swallowed her and her abductor.

A reward of such enormous proportions was offered that many adventurers were attracted to the hunt. This was no case for the modern detective of civilization, yet several of these threw themselves into the search – the bones of some are already bleaching beneath the African sun upon the silent sands of the Sahara.

Two Swedes, Carl Jenssen and Sven Malbihn, after three years of following false leads at last gave up the search far to the south of the Sahara to turn their attention to the more profitable business of ivory poaching. In a great district they were already known for their relentless cruelty and their greed for ivory. The natives feared and hated them. The European governments in whose possessions they worked had long sought them; but, working their way slowly out of the north they had learned many things in the no-man's-land south of the Sahara which gave them immunity from capture through easy avenues of escape that were unknown to those who pursued them. Their raids were sudden and swift. They seized ivory and retreated into the trackless wastes of the north before the guardians of the territory they raped could be made aware of their presence. Relentlessly they slaughtered elephants themselves as well as stealing ivory from the natives. Their following consisted of a hundred or more renegade Arabs and Negro slaves – a fierce, relentless band of cut-throats. Remember them – Carl Jenssen and Sven Malbihn, yellow-bearded, Swedish giants – for you will meet them later.

In the heart of the jungle, hidden away upon the banks of a small unexplored tributary of a large river that empties into the Atlantic not so far from the equator, lay a small, heavily palisaded village. Twenty palm-thatched, beehive huts sheltered its black population, while a half-dozen goat skin tents in the center of the clearing housed the score of Arabs who found shelter here while, by trading and raiding, they collected the cargoes which their ships of the desert bore northward twice each year to the market of Timbuktu.

Playing before one of the Arab tents was a little girl of ten – a black-haired, black-eyed little girl who, with her nut-brown skin and graceful carriage looked every inch a daughter of the desert. Her little fingers were busily engaged in fashioning a skirt of grasses for a much-disheveled doll which a kindly disposed slave had made for her a year or two before. The head of the doll was rudely chipped from ivory, while the body was a rat skin stuffed with grass. The arms and legs were bits of wood, perforated at one end and sewn to the rat skin torso. The doll was quite hideous and altogether disreputable and soiled, but Meriem thought it the most beautiful and adorable thing in the whole world, which is not so strange in view of the fact that it was the only object within that world upon which she might bestow her confidence and her love.

Everyone else with whom Meriem came in contact was, almost without exception, either indifferent to her or cruel. There was, for example, the old black hag who looked after her, Mabunu – toothless, filthy and ill tempered. She lost no opportunity to cuff the little girl, or even inflict minor tortures upon her, such as pinching, or, as she had twice done, searing the tender flesh with hot coals. And there was The Sheik, her father. She feared him more than she did Mabunu. He often scolded her for nothing, quite habitually terminating his tirades by cruelly beating her, until her little body was black and blue.

But when she was alone she was happy, playing with Geeka, or decking her hair with wild flowers, or making ropes of grasses. She was always busy and always singing – when they left her alone. No amount of cruelty appeared sufficient to crush the innate happiness and sweetness from her full little heart. Only when The Sheik was near was she quiet and subdued. Him she feared with a fear that was at times almost hysterical terror. She feared the gloomy jungle too – the cruel jungle that surrounded the little village with chattering monkeys and screaming birds by day and the roaring and coughing and moaning of the carnivora by night. Yes, she feared the jungle; but so much more did she fear The Sheik that many times it was in her childish head to run away, out into the terrible jungle forever rather than longer to face the ever present terror of her father.

As she sat there this day before The Sheik's goatskin tent, fashioning a skirt of grasses for Geeka, The Sheik appeared suddenly approaching. Instantly the look of happiness faded from the child's face. She shrunk aside in an attempt to scramble from the path of the leathern-faced old Arab; but she was not quick enough. With a brutal kick the man sent her sprawling upon her face, where she lay quite still, tearless but trembling. Then, with an oath at her, the man passed into the tent. The old, black hag shook with appreciative laughter, disclosing an occasional and lonesome yellow fang.

When she was sure The Sheik had gone, the little girl crawled to the shady side of the tent, where she lay quite still, hugging Geeka close to her breast, her little form racked at long intervals with choking sobs. She dared not cry aloud, since that would have brought The Sheik upon her again. The anguish in her little heart was not alone the anguish of physical pain; but that infinitely more pathetic anguish – of love denied a childish heart that yearns for love.

Little Meriem could scarce recall any other existence than that of the stern cruelty of The Sheik and Mabunu. Dimly, in the back of her childish memory there lurked a blurred recollection of a gentle mother; but Meriem was not sure but that even this was but a dream picture induced by her own desire for the caresses she never received, but which she lavished upon the much loved Geeka. Never was such a spoiled child as Geeka. Its little mother, far from fashioning her own conduct after the example set her by her father and nurse, went to the extreme of indulgence. Geeka was kissed a thousand times a day. There was play in which Geeka was naughty; but the little mother never punished. Instead, she caressed and fondled; her attitude influenced solely by her own pathetic desire for love.

Now, as she pressed Geeka close to her, her sobs lessened gradually, until she was able to control her voice, and pour out her misery into the ivory ear of her only confidante.

"Geeka loves Meriem," she whispered. "Why does The Sheik, my father, not love me, too? Am I so naughty? I try to be good; but I never know why he strikes me, so I cannot tell what I have done which displeases him. Just now he kicked me and hurt me so, Geeka; but I was only sitting before the tent making a skirt for you. That must be wicked, or he would not have kicked me for it. But why is it wicked, Geeka? Oh dear! I do not know, I do not know. I wish, Geeka, that I were dead. Yesterday the hunters brought in the body of El Adrea. El Adrea was quite dead.

No more will he slink silently upon his unsuspecting prey. No more will his great head and his maned shoulders strike terror to the hearts of the grass eaters at the drinking ford by night. No more will his thundering roar shake the ground. El Adrea is dead. They beat his body terribly when it was brought into the village; but El Adrea did not mind. He did not feel the blows, for he was dead. When I am dead, Geeka, neither shall I feel the blows of Mabunu, or the kicks of The Sheik, my father. Then shall I be happy. Oh, Geeka, how I wish that I were dead!"

If Geeka contemplated a remonstrance it was cut short by sounds of altercation beyond the village gates. Meriem listened. With the curiosity of childhood she would have liked to have run down there and learn what it was that caused the men to talk so loudly. Others of the village were already trooping in the direction of the noise. But Meriem did not dare. The Sheik would be there, doubtless, and if he saw her it would be but another opportunity to abuse her, so Meriem lay still and listened.

Presently she heard the crowd moving up the street toward The Sheik's tent. Cautiously she stuck her little head around the edge of the tent. She could not resist the temptation, for the sameness of the village life was monotonous, and she craved diversion. What she saw was two strangers – white men. They were alone, but as they approached she learned from the talk of the natives that surrounded them that they possessed a considerable following that was camped outside the village. They were coming to palaver with The Sheik.

The old Arab met them at the entrance to his tent. His eyes narrowed wickedly when they had appraised the newcomers. They stopped before him, exchanging greetings. They had come to trade for ivory they said. The Sheik grunted. He had no ivory. Meriem gasped. She knew that in a near-by hut the great tusks were piled almost to the roof. She poked her little head further forward to get a better view of the strangers. How white their skins! How yellow their great beards!

Suddenly one of them turned his eyes in her direction. She tried to dodge back out of sight, for she feared all men; but he saw her. Meriem noticed the look of almost shocked surprise that crossed his face. The Sheik saw it too, and guessed the cause of it.

"I have no ivory," he repeated. "I do not wish to trade. Go away. Go now."

He stepped from his tent and almost pushed the strangers about in the direction of the gates. They demurred, and then The Sheik threatened. It would have been suicide to have disobeyed, so the two men turned and left the village, making their way immediately to their own camp.

The Sheik returned to his tent; but he did not enter it. Instead he walked to the side where little Meriem lay close to the goat skin wall, very frightened. The Sheik stooped and clutched her by the arm. Viciously he jerked her to her feet, dragged her to the entrance of the tent, and shoved her viciously within. Following her he again seized her, beating her ruthlessly.

"Stay within!" he growled. "Never let the strangers see thy face. Next time you show yourself to strangers I shall kill you!"

With a final vicious cuff he knocked the child into a far corner of the tent, where she lay stifling her moans, while The Sheik paced to and fro muttering to himself. At the entrance sat Mabunu, muttering and chuckling.

In the camp of the strangers one was speaking rapidly to the other.

"There is no doubt of it, Malbihn," he was saying. "Not the slightest; but why the old scoundrel hasn't claimed the reward long since is what puzzles me."

"There are some things dearer to an Arab, Jenssen, than money," returned the first speaker – "revenge is one of them."

"Anyhow it will not harm to try the power of gold," replied Jenssen.

Malbihn shrugged.

"Not on The Sheik," he said. "We might try it on one of his people; but The Sheik will not part with his revenge for gold. To offer it to him would only confirm his suspicions that we must have awakened when we were talking to him before his tent. If we got away with our lives, then, we should be fortunate."

"Well, try bribery, then," assented Jenssen.

But bribery failed – grewsomely. The tool they selected after a stay of several days in their camp outside the village was a tall, old headman of The Sheik's native contingent. He fell to the lure of the shining metal, for he had lived upon the coast and knew the power of gold. He promised to bring them what they craved, late that night.

Immediately after dark the two white men commenced to make arrangements to break camp. By midnight all was prepared. The porters lay beside their loads, ready to swing them aloft at a moment's notice. The armed askaris loitered between the balance of the safari and the Arab village, ready to form a rear guard for the retreat that was to begin the moment that the head man brought that which the white masters awaited.

Presently there came the sound of footsteps along the path from the village. Instantly the askaris and the whites were on the alert. More than a single man was approaching. Jenssen stepped forward and challenged the newcomers in a low whisper.

"Who comes?" he queried.

"Mbeeda," came the reply.

Mbeeda was the name of the traitorous head man. Jenssen was satisfied, though he wondered why Mbeeda had brought others with him. Presently he understood. The thing they fetched lay upon a litter borne by two men. Jenssen cursed beneath his breath. Could the fool be bringing them a corpse? They had paid for a living prize!

The bearers came to a halt before the white men.

"This has your gold purchased," said one of the two. They set the litter down, turned and vanished into the darkness toward the village. Malbihn looked at Jenssen, a crooked smile twisting his lips. The thing upon the litter was covered with a piece of cloth.

"Well?" queried the latter. "Raise the covering and see what you have bought. Much money shall we realize on a corpse – especially after the six months beneath the burning sun that will be consumed in carrying it to its destination!"

"The fool should have known that we desired her alive," grumbled Malbihn, grasping a corner of the cloth and jerking the cover from the thing that lay upon the litter.

At sight of what lay beneath both men stepped back – involuntary oaths upon their lips – for there before them lay the dead body of Mbeeda, the faithless head man.

Five minutes later the safari of Jenssen and Malbihn was forcing its way rapidly toward the west, nervous askaris guarding the rear from the attack they momentarily expected.

Chapter Six

His first night in the jungle was one which the son of Tarzan held longest in his memory. No savage carnivora menaced him. There was never a sign of hideous barbarian. Or, if there were, the boy's troubled mind took no cognizance of them. His conscience was harassed by the thought of his mother's suffering. Self-blame plunged him into the depths of misery. The killing of the American caused him little or no remorse. The fellow had earned his fate. Jack's regret on this score was due mainly to the effect which the death of Condon had had upon his own plans. Now he could not return directly to his parents as he had planned. Fear of the primitive, borderland law, of which he had read highly colored, imaginary tales, had thrust him into the jungle a fugitive. He dared not return to the coast at this point – not that he was so greatly influenced through personal fear as from a desire to shield his father and mother from further sorrow and from the shame of having their honored name dragged through the sordid degradation of a murder trial.

With returning day the boy's spirits rose. With the rising sun rose new hope within his breast. He would return to civilization by another way. None would guess that he had been connected with the killing of the stranger in the little out-of-the-way trading post upon a remote shore.

Crouched close to the great ape in the crotch of a tree the boy had shivered through an almost sleepless night. His light pajamas had been but little protection from the chill dampness of the jungle, and only that side of him which was pressed against the warm body of his shaggy companion approximated to comfort. And so he welcomed the rising sun with its promise of warmth as well as light – the blessed sun, dispeller of physical and mental ills.

He shook Akut into wakefulness.

"Come," he said. "I am cold and hungry. We will search for food, out there in the sunlight," and he pointed to an open plain, dotted with stunted trees and strewn with jagged rock.

The boy slid to the ground as he spoke, but the ape first looked carefully about, sniffing the morning air. Then, satisfied that no danger lurked near, he descended slowly to the ground beside the boy.

"Numa, and Sabor his mate, feast upon those who descend first and look afterward, while those who look first and descend afterward live to feast themselves." Thus the old ape imparted to the son of Tarzan the boy's first lesson in jungle lore. Side by side they set off across the rough plain, for the boy wished first to be warm. The ape showed him the best places to dig for rodents and worms; but the lad only gagged at the thought of devouring the repulsive things. Some eggs they found, and these he sucked raw, as also he ate roots and tubers which Akut unearthed. Beyond the plain and across a low bluff they came upon water – brackish, ill-smelling stuff in a shallow water hole, the sides and bottom of which were trampled by the feet of many beasts. A herd of zebra galloped away as they approached.

The lad was too thirsty by now to cavil at anything even remotely resembling water, so he drank his fill while Akut stood with raised head, alert for any danger. Before the ape drank he cautioned the boy to be watchful; but as he drank he raised his head from time to time to cast a quick glance toward a clump of bushes a hundred yards away upon the opposite side of the water hole. When he had done he rose and spoke to the boy, in the language that was their common heritage – the tongue of the great apes.

"There is no danger near?" he asked.

"None," replied the boy. "I saw nothing move while you drank."

"Your eyes will help you but little in the jungle," said the ape.

"Here, if you would live, you must depend upon your ears and your nose but most upon your nose. When we came down to drink I knew that no danger lurked near upon this side of the water hole, for else the zebras would have discovered it and fled before we came; but upon the other side toward which the wind blows danger might lie concealed. We could not smell it for its scent is being blown in the other direction, and so I bent my ears and eyes down wind where my nose cannot travel."

"And you found – nothing?" asked the lad, with a laugh.

"I found Numa crouching in that clump of bushes where the tall grasses grow," and Akut pointed.

"A lion?" exclaimed the boy. "How do you know? I can see nothing."

"Numa is there, though," replied the great ape. "First I heard him sigh. To you the sigh of Numa may sound no different from the other noises which the wind makes among the grasses and the trees; but later you must learn to know the sigh of Numa. Then I watched and at last I saw the tall grasses moving at one point to a force other than the force of the wind. See, they are spread there upon either side of Numa's great body, and as he breathes – you see? You see the little motion at either side that is not caused by the wind – the motion that none of the other grasses have?"

The boy strained his eyes – better eyes than the ordinary boy inherits – and at last he gave a little exclamation of discovery.

"Yes," he said, "I see. He lies there," and he pointed. "His head is toward us. Is he watching us?"

"Numa is watching us," replied Akut, "but we are in little danger, unless we approach too close, for he is lying upon his kill. His belly is almost full, or we should hear him crunching the bones. He is watching us in silence merely from curiosity. Presently he will resume his feeding or he will rise and come down to the water for a drink. As he neither fears or desires us he will not try to hide his presence from us; but now is an excellent time to learn to know Numa, for you must learn to know him well if you would live long in the jungle. Where the great apes are many Numa leaves us alone. Our fangs are long and strong, and we can fight; but when we are alone and he is hungry we are no match for him. Come, we will circle him and catch his scent. The sooner you learn to know it the better; but keep close to the trees, as we go around him, for Numa often does that which he is least expected to do. And keep your ears and your eyes and your nose open. Remember always that there may be an enemy behind every bush, in every tree and amongst every clump of jungle grass. While you are avoiding Numa do not run into the jaws of Sabor, his mate. Follow me," and Akut set off in a wide circle about the water hole and the crouching lion.

The boy followed close upon his heels, his every sense upon the alert, his nerves keyed to the highest pitch of excitement. This was life! For the instant he forgot his resolutions of a few minutes past to hasten to the coast at some other point than that at which he had landed and make his way immediately back to London. He thought now only of the savage joy of living, and of pitting one's wits and prowess against the wiles and might of the savage jungle brood which haunted the broad plains and the gloomy forest aisles of the great, untamed continent. He knew no fear. His father had had none to transmit to him; but honor and conscience he did have and these were to trouble him many times as they battled with his inherent love of freedom for possession of his soul.

They had passed but a short distance to the rear of Numa when the boy caught the unpleasant odor of the carnivore. His face lighted with a smile. Something told him that he would have known that scent among a myriad of others even if Akut had not told him that a lion lay near. There was a strange familiarity – a weird familiarity in it that made the short hairs rise at the nape of his neck, and brought his upper lip into an involuntary snarl that bared his fighting fangs. There was a sense of stretching of the skin about his ears, for all the world as though those members were flattening back against his skull in preparation for deadly combat. His skin tingled. He was aglow with a pleasurable sensation that he never before had known. He was, upon the instant, another creature – wary, alert, ready. Thus did the scent of Numa, the lion, transform the boy into a beast.

He had never seen a lion – his mother had gone to great pains to prevent it. But he had devoured countless pictures of them, and now he was ravenous to feast his eyes upon the king of beasts in the flesh. As he trailed Akut he kept an eye cocked over one shoulder, rearward, in the hope that Numa might rise from his kill and reveal himself. Thus it happened that he dropped some little way behind Akut, and the next he knew he was recalled suddenly to a contemplation of other matters than the hidden Numa by a shrill scream of warning from the Ape. Turning his eyes quickly in the direction of his companion, the boy saw that, standing in the path directly before him, which sent tremors of excitement racing along every nerve of his body. With body half-merging from a clump of bushes in which she must have lain hidden stood a sleek and beautiful lioness. Her yellow-green eyes were round and staring, boring straight into the eyes of the boy. Not ten paces separated them. Twenty paces behind the lioness stood the great ape, bellowing instructions to the boy and hurling taunts at the lioness in an evident effort to attract her attention from the lad while he gained the shelter of a near-by tree.

But Sabor was not to be diverted. She had her eyes upon the lad. He stood between her and her mate, between her and the kill. It was suspicious. Probably he had ulterior designs upon her lord and master or upon the fruits of their hunting. A lioness is short tempered. Akut's bellowing annoyed her. She uttered a little rumbling growl, taking a step toward the boy.

"The tree!" screamed Akut.

The boy turned and fled, and at the same instant the lioness charged. The tree was but a few paces away. A limb hung ten feet from the ground, and as the boy leaped for it the lioness leaped for him. Like a monkey he pulled himself up and to one side. A great forepaw caught him a glancing blow at the hips – just grazing him. One curved talon hooked itself into the waist band of his pajama trousers, ripping them from him as the lioness sped by. Half-naked the lad drew himself to safety as the beast turned and leaped for him once more.

Akut, from a near-by tree, jabbered and scolded, calling the lioness all manner of foul names. The boy, patterning his conduct after that of his preceptor, unstoppered the vials of his invective upon the head of the enemy, until in realization of the futility of words as weapons he bethought himself of something heavier to hurl. There was nothing but dead twigs and branches at hand, but these he flung at the upturned, snarling face of Sabor just as his father had before him twenty years ago, when as a boy he too had taunted and tantalized the great cats of the jungle.

The lioness fretted about the bole of the tree for a short time; but finally, either realizing the uselessness of her vigil, or prompted by the pangs of hunger, she stalked majestically away and disappeared in the brush that hid her lord, who had not once shown himself during the altercation.

Freed from their retreats Akut and the boy came to the ground, to take up their interrupted journey once more. The old ape scolded the lad for his carelessness.

"Had you not been so intent upon the lion behind you you might have discovered the lioness much sooner than you did."

"But you passed right by her without seeing her," retorted the boy.

Akut was chagrined.

"It is thus," he said, "that jungle folk die. We go cautiously for a lifetime, and then, just for an instant, we forget, and – " he ground his teeth in mimicry of the crunching of great jaws in flesh. "It is a lesson," he resumed. "You have learned that you may not for too long keep your eyes and your ears and your nose all bent in the same direction."

That night the son of Tarzan was colder than he ever had been in all his life. The pajama trousers had not been heavy; but they had been much heavier than nothing. And the next day he roasted in the hot sun, for again their way led much across wide and treeless plains.

It was still in the boy's mind to travel to the south, and circle back to the coast in search of another outpost of civilization. He had said nothing of this plan to Akut, for he knew that the old ape would look with displeasure upon any suggestion that savored of separation.

For a month the two wandered on, the boy learning rapidly the laws of the jungle; his muscles adapting themselves to the new mode of life that had been thrust upon them. The thews of the sire had been transmitted to the son – it needed only the hardening of use to develop them. The lad found that it came quite naturally to him to swing through the trees. Even at great heights he never felt the slightest dizziness, and when he had caught the knack of the swing and the release, he could hurl himself through space from branch to branch with even greater agility than the heavier Akut.

And with exposure came a toughening and hardening of his smooth, white skin, browning now beneath the sun and wind. He had removed his pajama jacket one day to bathe in a little stream that was too small to harbor crocodiles, and while he and Akut had been disporting themselves in the cool waters a monkey had dropped down from the over hanging trees, snatched up the boy's single remaining article of civilized garmenture, and scampered away with it.

For a time Jack was angry; but when he had been without the jacket for a short while he began to realize that being half-clothed is infinitely more uncomfortable than being entirely naked. Soon he did not miss his clothing in the least, and from that he came to revel in the freedom of his unhampered state. Occasionally a smile would cross his face as he tried to imagine the surprise of his schoolmates could they but see him now. They would envy him. Yes, how they would envy him. He felt sorry for them at such times, and again as he thought of them amid luxuries and comforts of their English homes, happy with their fathers and mothers, a most uncomfortable lump would arise into the boy's throat, and he would see a vision of his mother's face through a blur of mist that came unbidden to his eyes. Then it was that he urged Akut onward, for now they were headed westward toward the coast. The old ape thought that they were searching for a tribe of his own kind, nor did the boy disabuse his mind of this belief. It would do to tell Akut of his real plans when they had come within sight of civilization.

One day as they were moving slowly along beside a river they came unexpectedly upon a native village. Some children were playing beside the water. The boy's heart leaped within his breast at sight of them – for over a month he had seen no human being. What if these were naked savages? What if their skins were black? Were they not creatures fashioned in the mold of their Maker, as was he? They were his brothers and sisters! He started toward them. With a low warning Akut laid a hand upon his arm to hold him back. The boy shook himself free, and with a shout of greeting ran forward toward the ebon players.

The sound of his voice brought every head erect. Wide eyes viewed him for an instant, and then, with screams of terror, the children turned and fled toward the village. At their heels ran their mothers, and from the village gate, in response to the alarm, came a score of warriors, hastily snatched spears and shields ready in their hands.

At sight of the consternation he had wrought the boy halted. The glad smile faded from his face as with wild shouts and menacing gestures the warriors ran toward him. Akut was calling to him from behind to turn and flee, telling him that the blacks would kill him. For a moment he stood watching them coming, then he raised his hand with the palm toward them in signal for them to halt, calling out at the same time that he came as a friend – that he had only wanted to play with their children. Of course they did not understand a word that he addressed to them, and their answer was what any naked creature who had run suddenly out of the jungle upon their women and children might have expected – a shower of spears. The missiles struck all about the boy, but none touched him. Again his spine tingled and the short hairs lifted at the nape of his neck and along the top of his scalp. His eyes narrowed. Sudden hatred flared in them to wither the expression of glad friendliness that had lighted them but an instant before. With a low snarl, quite similar to that of a baffled beast, he turned and ran into the jungle. There was Akut awaiting him in a tree. The ape urged him to hasten in flight, for the wise old anthropoid knew that they two, naked and unarmed, were no match for the sinewy black warriors who would doubtless make some sort of search for them through the jungle.

But a new power moved the son of Tarzan. He had come with a boy's glad and open heart to offer his friendship to these people who were human beings like himself. He had been met with suspicion and spears. They had not even listened to him. Rage and hatred consumed him. When Akut urged speed he held back. He wanted to fight, yet his reason made it all too plain that it would be but a foolish sacrifice of his life to meet these armed men with his naked hands and his teeth – already the boy thought of his teeth, of his fighting fangs, when possibility of combat loomed close.

Moving slowly through the trees he kept his eyes over his shoulder, though he no longer neglected the possibilities of other dangers which might lurk on either hand or ahead – his experience with the lioness did not need a repetition to insure the permanency of the lesson it had taught. Behind he could hear the savages advancing with shouts and cries. He lagged further behind until the pursuers were in sight. They did not see him, for they were not looking among the branches of the trees for human quarry. The lad kept just ahead of them. For a mile perhaps they continued the search, and then they turned back toward the village. Here was the boy's opportunity, that for which he had been waiting, while the hot blood of revenge coursed through his veins until he saw his pursuers through a scarlet haze.

When they turned back he turned and followed them. Akut was no longer in sight. Thinking that the boy followed he had gone on further ahead. He had no wish to tempt fate within range of those deadly spears. Slinking silently from tree to tree the boy dogged the footsteps of the returning warriors. At last one dropped behind his fellows as they followed a narrow path toward the village. A grim smile lit the lad's face. Swiftly he hurried forward until he moved almost above the unconscious black – stalking him as Sheeta, the panther, stalked his prey, as the boy had seen Sheeta do on many occasions.

Suddenly and silently he leaped forward and downward upon the broad shoulders of his prey. In the instant of contact his fingers sought and found the man's throat. The weight of the boy's body hurled the black heavily to the ground, the knees in his back knocking the breath from him as he struck. Then a set of strong, white teeth fastened themselves in his neck, and muscular fingers closed tighter upon his windpipe. For a time the warrior struggled frantically, throwing himself about in an effort to dislodge his antagonist; but all the while he was weakening and all the while the grim and silent thing he could not see clung tenaciously to him, and dragged him slowly into the bush to one side of the trail.

Hidden there at last, safe from the prying eyes of searchers, should they miss their fellow and return for him, the lad choked the life from the body of his victim. At last he knew by the sudden struggle, followed by limp relaxation, that the warrior was dead. Then a strange desire seized him. His whole being quivered and thrilled. Involuntarily he leaped to his feet and placed one foot upon the body of his kill. His chest expanded. He raised his face toward the heavens and opened his mouth to voice a strange, weird cry that seemed screaming within him for outward expression, but no sound passed his lips – he just stood there for a full minute, his face turned toward the sky, his breast heaving to the pent emotion, like an animate statue of vengeance.

The silence which marked the first great kill of the son of Tarzan was to typify all his future kills, just as the hideous victory cry of the bull ape had marked the kills of his mighty sire.

Chapter Seven

Akut, discovering that the boy was not close behind him, turned back to search for him. He had gone but a short distance in return when he was brought to a sudden and startled halt by sight of a strange figure moving through the trees toward him. It was the boy, yet could it be? In his hand was a long spear, down his back hung an oblong shield such as the black warriors who had attacked them had worn, and upon ankle and arm were bands of iron and brass, while a loin cloth was twisted about the youth's middle. A knife was thrust through its folds.

When the boy saw the ape he hastened forward to exhibit his trophies. Proudly he called attention to each of his newly won possessions. Boastfully he recounted the details of his exploit.

"With my bare hands and my teeth I killed him," he said. "I would have made friends with them but they chose to be my enemies. And now that I have a spear I shall show Numa, too, what it means to have me for a foe. Only the white men and the great apes, Akut, are our friends. Them we shall seek, all others must we avoid or kill. This have I learned of the jungle."

They made a detour about the hostile village, and resumed their journey toward the coast. The boy took much pride in his new weapons and ornaments. He practiced continually with the spear, throwing it at some object ahead hour by hour as they traveled their loitering way, until he gained a proficiency such as only youthful muscles may attain to speedily. All the while his training went on under the guidance of Akut. No longer was there a single jungle spoor but was an open book to the keen eyes of the lad, and those other indefinite spoor that elude the senses of civilized man and are only partially appreciable to his savage cousin came to be familiar friends of the eager boy. He could differentiate the innumerable species of the herbivora by scent, and he could tell, too, whether an animal was approaching or departing merely by the waxing or waning strength of its effluvium. Nor did he need the evidence of his eyes to tell him whether there were two lions or four up wind, – a hundred yards away or half a mile.

Much of this had Akut taught him, but far more was instinctive knowledge – a species of strange intuition inherited from his father. He had come to love the jungle life. The constant battle of wits and senses against the many deadly foes that lurked by day and by night along the pathway of the wary and the unwary appealed to the spirit of adventure which breathes strong in the heart of every red-blooded son of primordial Adam. Yet, though he loved it, he had not let his selfish desires outweigh the sense of duty that had brought him to a realization of the moral wrong which lay beneath the adventurous escapade that had brought him to Africa. His love of father and mother was strong within him, too strong to permit unalloyed happiness which was undoubtedly causing them days of sorrow. And so he held tight to his determination to find a port upon the coast where he might communicate with them and receive funds for his return to London. There he felt sure that he could now persuade his parents to let him spend at least a portion of his time upon those African estates which from little careless remarks dropped at home he knew his father possessed. That would be something, better at least than a lifetime of the cramped and cloying restrictions of civilization.

And so he was rather contented than otherwise as he made his way in the direction of the coast, for while he enjoyed the liberty and the savage pleasures of the wild his conscience was at the same time clear, for he knew that he was doing all that lay in his power to return to his parents. He rather looked forward, too, to meeting white men again – creatures of his own kind – for there had been many occasions upon which he had longed for other companionship than that of the old ape. The affair with the blacks still rankled in his heart. He had approached them in such innocent good fellowship and with such childlike assurance of a hospitable welcome that the reception which had been accorded him had proved a shock to his boyish ideals. He no longer looked upon the black man as his brother; but rather as only another of the innumerable foes of the bloodthirsty jungle – a beast of prey which walked upon two feet instead of four.

But if the blacks were his enemies there were those in the world who were not. There were those who always would welcome him with open arms; who would accept him as a friend and brother, and with whom he might find sanctuary from every enemy. Yes, there were always white men. Somewhere along the coast or even in the depths of the jungle itself there were white men. To them he would be a welcome visitor. They would befriend him. And there were also the great apes – the friends of his father and of Akut. How glad they would be to receive the son of Tarzan of the Apes! He hoped that he could come upon them before he found a trading post upon the coast. He wanted to be able to tell his father that he had known his old friends of the jungle, that he had hunted with them, that he had joined with them in their savage life, and their fierce, primeval ceremonies – the strange ceremonies of which Akut had tried to tell him. It cheered him immensely to dwell upon these happy meetings. Often he rehearsed the long speech which he would make to the apes, in which he would tell them of the life of their former king since he had left them.

At other times he would play at meeting with white men. Then he would enjoy their consternation at sight of a naked white boy trapped in the war togs of a black warrior and roaming the jungle with only a great ape as his companion.

And so the days passed, and with the traveling and the hunting and the climbing the boy's muscles developed and his agility increased until even phlegmatic Akut marvelled at the prowess of his pupil. And the boy, realizing his great strength and revelling in it, became careless. He strode through the jungle, his proud head erect, defying danger. Where Akut took to the trees at the first scent of Numa, the lad laughed in the face of the king of beasts and walked boldly past him. Good fortune was with him for a long time. The lions he met were well-fed, perhaps, or the very boldness of the strange creature which invaded their domain so filled them with surprise that thoughts of attack were banished from their minds as they stood, round-eyed, watching his approach and his departure. Whatever the cause, however, the fact remains that on many occasions the boy passed within a few paces of some great lion without arousing more than a warning growl.

But no two lions are necessarily alike in character or temper. They differ as greatly as do individuals of the human family. Because ten lions act similarly under similar conditions one cannot say that the eleventh lion will do likewise – the chances are that he will not. The lion is a creature of high nervous development. He thinks, therefore he reasons. Having a nervous system and brains he is the possessor of temperament, which is affected variously by extraneous causes. One day the boy met the eleventh lion. The former was walking across a small plain upon which grew little clumps of bushes. Akut was a few yards to the left of the lad who was the first to discover the presence of Numa.

"Run, Akut," called the boy, laughing. "Numa lies hid in the bushes to my right. Take to the trees. Akut! I, the son of Tarzan, will protect you," and the boy, laughing, kept straight along his way which led close beside the brush in which Numa lay concealed.

The ape shouted to him to come away, but the lad only flourished his spear and executed an improvised war dance to show his contempt for the king of beasts. Closer and closer to the dread destroyer he came, until, with a sudden, angry growl, the lion rose from his bed not ten paces from the youth. A huge fellow he was, this lord of the jungle and the desert. A shaggy mane clothed his shoulders. Cruel fangs armed his great jaws. His yellow-green eyes blazed with hatred and challenge.

The boy, with his pitifully inadequate spear ready in his hand, realized quickly that this lion was different from the others he had met; but he had gone too far now to retreat. The nearest tree lay several yards to his left – the lion could be upon him before he had covered half the distance, and that the beast intended to charge none could doubt who looked upon him now. Beyond the lion was a thorn tree – only a few feet beyond him. It was the nearest sanctuary but Numa stood between it and his prey.

The feel of the long spear shaft in his hand and the sight of the tree beyond the lion gave the lad an idea – a preposterous idea – a ridiculous, forlorn hope of an idea; but there was no time now to weigh chances – there was but a single chance, and that was the thorn tree. If the lion charged it would be too late – the lad must charge first, and to the astonishment of Akut and none the less of Numa, the boy leaped swiftly toward the beast. Just for a second was the lion motionless with surprise and in that second Jack Clayton put to the crucial test an accomplishment which he had practiced at school.

Straight for the savage brute he ran, his spear held butt foremost across his body. Akut shrieked in terror and amazement. The lion stood with wide, round eyes awaiting the attack, ready to rear upon his hind feet and receive this rash creature with blows that could crush the skull of a buffalo.

Just in front of the lion the boy placed the butt of his spear upon the ground, gave a mighty spring, and, before the bewildered beast could guess the trick that had been played upon him, sailed over the lion's head into the rending embrace of the thorn tree – safe but lacerated.

Akut had never before seen a pole-vault. Now he leaped up and down within the safety of his own tree, screaming taunts and boasts at the discomfited Numa, while the boy, torn and bleeding, sought some position in his thorny retreat in which he might find the least agony. He had saved his life; but at considerable cost in suffering. It seemed to him that the lion would never leave, and it was a full hour before the angry brute gave up his vigil and strode majestically away across the plain. When he was at a safe distance the boy extricated himself from the thorn tree; but not without inflicting new wounds upon his already tortured flesh.

It was many days before the outward evidence of the lesson he had learned had left him; while the impression upon his mind was one that was to remain with him for life. Never again did he uselessly tempt fate.

He took long chances often in his after life; but only when the taking of chances might further the attainment of some cherished end – and, always thereafter, he practiced pole-vaulting.

For several days the boy and the ape lay up while the former recovered from the painful wounds inflicted by the sharp thorns. The great anthropoid licked the wounds of his human friend, nor, aside from this, did they receive other treatment, but they soon healed, for healthy flesh quickly replaces itself.

When the lad felt fit again the two continued their journey toward the coast, and once more the boy's mind was filled with pleasurable anticipation.

And at last the much dreamed of moment came. They were passing through a tangled forest when the boy's sharp eyes discovered from the lower branches through which he was traveling an old but well-marked spoor – a spoor that set his heart to leaping – the spoor of man, of white men, for among the prints of naked feet were the well defined outlines of European made boots. The trail, which marked the passage of a good-sized company, pointed north at right angles to the course the boy and the ape were taking toward the coast.

Doubtless these white men knew the nearest coast settlement. They might even be headed for it now. At any rate it would be worth while overtaking them if even only for the pleasure of meeting again creatures of his own kind. The lad was all excitement; palpitant with eagerness to be off in pursuit. Akut demurred. He wanted nothing of men. To him the lad was a fellow ape, for he was the son of the king of apes. He tried to dissuade the boy, telling him that soon they should come upon a tribe of their own folk where some day when he was older the boy should be king as his father had before him. But Jack was obdurate. He insisted that he wanted to see white men again. He wanted to send a message to his parents. Akut listened and as he listened the intuition of the beast suggested the truth to him – the boy was planning to return to his own kind.

The thought filled the old ape with sorrow. He loved the boy as he had loved the father, with the loyalty and faithfulness of a hound for its master. In his ape brain and his ape heart he had nursed the hope that he and the lad would never be separated. He saw all his fondly cherished plans fading away, and yet he remained loyal to the lad and to his wishes. Though disconsolate he gave in to the boy's determination to pursue the safari of the white men, accompanying him upon what he believed would be their last journey together.

The spoor was but a couple of days old when the two discovered it, which meant that the slow-moving caravan was but a few hours distant from them whose trained and agile muscles could carry their bodies swiftly through the branches above the tangled undergrowth which had impeded the progress of the laden carriers of the white men.

The boy was in the lead, excitement and anticipation carrying him ahead of his companion to whom the attainment of their goal meant only sorrow. And it was the boy who first saw the rear guard of the caravan and the white men he had been so anxious to overtake.

Stumbling along the tangled trail of those ahead a dozen heavily laden blacks who, from fatigue or sickness, had dropped behind were being prodded by the black soldiers of the rear guard, kicked when they fell, and then roughly jerked to their feet and hustled onward. On either side walked a giant white man, heavy blonde beards almost obliterating their countenances. The boy's lips formed a glad cry of salutation as his eyes first discovered the whites – a cry that was never uttered, for almost immediately he witnessed that which turned his happiness to anger as he saw that both the white men were wielding heavy whips brutally upon the naked backs of the poor devils staggering along beneath loads that would have overtaxed the strength and endurance of strong men at the beginning of a new day.

Every now and then the rear guard and the white men cast apprehensive glances rearward as though momentarily expecting the materialization of some long expected danger from that quarter. The boy had paused after his first sight of the caravan, and now was following slowly in the wake of the sordid, brutal spectacle. Presently Akut came up with him. To the beast there was less of horror in the sight than to the lad, yet even the great ape growled beneath his breath at useless torture being inflicted upon the helpless slaves. He looked at the boy. Now that he had caught up with the creatures of his own kind, why was it that he did not rush forward and greet them? He put the question to his companion.

"They are fiends," muttered the boy. "I would not travel with such as they, for if I did I should set upon them and kill them the first time they beat their people as they are beating them now; but," he added, after a moment's thought, "I can ask them the whereabouts of the nearest port, and then, Akut, we can leave them."

The ape made no reply, and the boy swung to the ground and started at a brisk walk toward the safari. He was a hundred yards away, perhaps, when one of the whites caught sight of him. The man gave a shout of alarm, instantly levelling his rifle upon the boy and firing. The bullet struck just in front of its mark, scattering turf and fallen leaves against the lad's legs. A second later the other white and the black soldiers of the rear guard were firing hysterically at the boy.

Jack leaped behind a tree, unhit. Days of panic ridden flight through the jungle had filled Carl Jenssen and Sven Malbihn with jangling nerves and their native boys with unreasoning terror. Every new note from behind sounded to their frightened ears the coming of The Sheik and his bloodthirsty entourage. They were in a blue funk, and the sight of the naked white warrior stepping silently out of the jungle through which they had just passed had been sufficient shock to let loose in action all the pent nerve energy of Malbihn, who had been the first to see the strange apparition. And Malbihn's shout and shot had set the others going.

When their nervous energy had spent itself and they came to take stock of what they had been fighting it developed that Malbihn alone had seen anything clearly. Several of the blacks averred that they too had obtained a good view of the creature but their descriptions of it varied so greatly that Jenssen, who had seen nothing himself, was inclined to be a trifle skeptical. One of the blacks insisted that the thing had been eleven feet tall, with a man's body and the head of an elephant. Another had seen THREE immense Arabs with huge, black beards; but when, after conquering their nervousness, the rear guard advanced upon the enemy's position to investigate they found nothing, for Akut and the boy had retreated out of range of the unfriendly guns.

Jack was disheartened and sad. He had not entirely recovered from the depressing effect of the unfriendly reception he had received at the hands of the blacks, and now he had found an even more hostile one accorded him by men of his own color.

"The lesser beasts flee from me in terror," he murmured, half to himself, "the greater beasts are ready to tear me to pieces at sight. Black men would kill me with their spears or arrows. And now white men, men of my own kind, have fired upon me and driven me away. Are all the creatures of the world my enemies? Has the son of Tarzan no friend other than Akut?"

The old ape drew closer to the boy.

"There are the great apes," he said. "They only will be the friends of Akut's friend. Only the great apes will welcome the son of Tarzan. You have seen that men want nothing of you. Let us go now and continue our search for the great apes – our people."

The language of the great apes is a combination of monosyllabic gutturals, amplified by gestures and signs. It may not be literally translated into human speech; but as near as may be this is what Akut said to the boy.

The two proceeded in silence for some time after Akut had spoken. The boy was immersed in deep thought – bitter thoughts in which hatred and revenge predominated. Finally he spoke: "Very well, Akut," he said, "we will find our friends, the great apes."

The anthropoid was overjoyed; but he gave no outward demonstration of his pleasure. A low grunt was his only response, and a moment later he had leaped nimbly upon a small and unwary rodent that had been surprised at a fatal distance from its burrow. Tearing the unhappy creature in two Akut handed the lion's share to the lad.

Chapter Eight

A YEAR HAD PASSED since the two Swedes had been driven in terror from the savage country where The Sheik held sway. Little Meriem still played with Geeka, lavishing all her childish love upon the now almost hopeless ruin of what had never, even in its palmiest days, possessed even a slight degree of loveliness. But to Meriem, Geeka was all that was sweet and adorable. She carried to the deaf ears of the battered ivory head all her sorrows all her hopes and all her ambitions, for even in the face of hopelessness, in the clutches of the dread authority from which there was no escape, little Meriem yet cherished hopes and ambitions. It is true that her ambitions were rather nebulous in form, consisting chiefly of a desire to escape with Geeka to some remote and unknown spot where there were no Sheiks, no Mabunus – where El Adrea could find no entrance, and where she might play all day surrounded only by flowers and birds and the harmless little monkeys playing in the tree tops.

The Sheik had been away for a long time, conducting a caravan of ivory, skins, and rubber far into the north. The interim had been one of great peace for Meriem. It is true that Mabunu had still been with her, to pinch or beat her as the mood seized the villainous old hag; but Mabunu was only one. When The Sheik was there also there were two of them, and The Sheik was stronger and more brutal even than Mabunu. Little Meriem often wondered why the grim old man hated her so. It is true that he was cruel and unjust to all with whom he came in contact, but to Meriem he reserved his greatest cruelties, his most studied injustices.

Today Meriem was squatting at the foot of a large tree which grew inside the palisade close to the edge of the village. She was fashioning a tent of leaves for Geeka. Before the tent were some pieces of wood and small leaves and a few stones. These were the household utensils. Geeka was cooking dinner. As the little girl played she prattled continuously to her companion, propped in a sitting position with a couple of twigs. She was totally absorbed in the domestic duties of Geeka – so much so that she did not note the gentle swaying of the branches of the tree above her as they bent to the body of the creature that had entered them stealthily from the jungle.

In happy ignorance the little girl played on, while from above two steady eyes looked down upon her – unblinking, unwavering. There was none other than the little girl in this part of the village, which had been almost deserted since The Sheik had left long months before upon his journey toward the north.

And out in the jungle, an hour's march from the village, The Sheik was leading his returning caravan homeward.

A year had passed since the white men had fired upon the lad and driven him back into the jungle to take up his search for the only remaining creatures to whom he might look for companionship – the great apes. For months the two had wandered eastward, deeper and deeper into the jungle. The year had done much for the boy – turning his already mighty muscles to thews of steel, developing his woodcraft to a point where it verged upon the uncanny, perfecting his arboreal instincts, and training him in the use of both natural and artificial weapons.

He had become at last a creature of marvelous physical powers and mental cunning. He was still but a boy, yet so great was his strength that the powerful anthropoid with which he often engaged in mimic battle was no match for him. Akut had taught him to fight as the bull ape fights, nor ever was there a teacher better fitted to instruct in the savage warfare of primordial man, or a pupil better equipped to profit by the lessons of a master.

As the two searched for a band of the almost extinct species of ape to which Akut belonged they lived upon the best the jungle afforded. Antelope and zebra fell to the boy's spear, or were dragged down by the two powerful beasts of prey who leaped upon them from some overhanging limb or from the ambush of the undergrowth beside the trail to the water hole or the ford.

The pelt of a leopard covered the nakedness of the youth; but the wearing of it had not been dictated by any prompting of modesty. With the rifle shots of the white men showering about him he had reverted to the savagery of the beast that is inherent in each of us, but that flamed more strongly in this boy whose father had been raised a beast of prey. He wore his leopard skin at first in response to a desire to parade a trophy of his prowess, for he had slain the leopard with his knife in a hand-to-hand combat. He saw that the skin was beautiful, which appealed to his barbaric sense of ornamentation, and when it stiffened and later commenced to decompose because of his having no knowledge of how to cure or tan it was with sorrow and regret that he discarded it. Later, when he chanced upon a lone, black warrior wearing the counterpart of it, soft and clinging and beautiful from proper curing, it required but an instant to leap from above upon the shoulders of the unsuspecting black, sink a keen blade into his heart and possess the rightly preserved hide.

There were no after-qualms of conscience. In the jungle might is right, nor does it take long to inculcate this axiom in the mind of a jungle dweller, regardless of what his past training may have been. That the black would have killed him had he had the chance the boy knew full well. Neither he nor the black were any more sacred than the lion, or the buffalo, the zebra or the deer, or any other of the countless creatures who roamed, or slunk, or flew, or wriggled through the dark mazes of the forest. Each had but a single life, which was sought by many. The greater number of enemies slain the better chance to prolong that life. So the boy smiled and donned the finery of the vanquished, and went his way with Akut, searching, always searching for the elusive anthropoids who were to welcome them with open arms.

And at last they found them. Deep in the jungle, buried far from sight of man, they came upon such another little natural arena as had witnessed the wild ceremony of the Dum-Dum in which the boy's father had taken part long years before.

First, at a great distance, they heard the beating of the drum of the great apes. They were sleeping in the safety of a huge tree when the booming sound smote upon their ears. Both awoke at once. Akut was the first to interpret the strange cadence.

"The great apes!" he growled. "They dance the Dum-Dum. Come, Korak, son of Tarzan, let us go to our people."

Months before Akut had given the boy a name of his own choosing, since he could not master the man given name of Jack. Korak is as near as it may be interpreted into human speech. In the language of the apes it means Killer. Now the Killer rose upon the branch of the great tree where he had been sleeping with his back braced against the stem. He stretched his lithe young muscles, the moonlight filtering through the foliage from above dappling his brown skin with little patches of light.

The ape, too, stood up, half squatting after the manner of his kind. Low growls rumbled from the bottom of his deep chest – growls of excited anticipation. The boy growled in harmony with the ape. Then the anthropoid slid softly to the ground. Close by, in the direction of the booming drum, lay a clearing which they must cross. The moon flooded it with silvery light. Half-erect, the great ape shuffled into the full glare of the moon. At his side, swinging gracefully along in marked contrast to the awkwardness of his companion, strode the boy, the dark, shaggy coat of the one brushing against the smooth, clear hide of the other. The lad was humming now, a music hall air that had found its way to the forms of the great English public school that was to see him no more. He was happy and expectant. The moment he had looked forward to for so long was about to be realized. He was coming into his own. He was coming home. As the months had dragged or flown along, retarded or spurred on as privation or adventure predominated, thoughts of his own home, while oft recurring, had become less vivid. The old life had grown to seem more like a dream than a reality, and the balking of his determination to reach the coast and return to London had finally thrown the hope of realization so remotely into the future that it too now seemed little more than a pleasant but hopeless dream.

Now all thoughts of London and civilization were crowded so far into the background of his brain that they might as well have been non-existent. Except for form and mental development he was as much an ape as the great, fierce creature at his side.

In the exuberance of his joy he slapped his companion roughly on the side of the head. Half in anger, half in play the anthropoid turned upon him, his fangs bared and glistening. Long, hairy arms reached out to seize him, and, as they had done a thousand times before, the two clinched in mimic battle, rolling upon the sward, striking, growling and biting, though never closing their teeth in more than a rough pinch. It was wondrous practice for them both. The boy brought into play wrestling tricks that he had learned at school, and many of these Akut learned to use and to foil. And from the ape the boy learned the methods that had been handed down to Akut from some common ancestor of them both, who had roamed the teeming earth when ferns were trees and crocodiles were birds.

But there was one art the boy possessed which Akut could not master, though he did achieve fair proficiency in it for an ape – boxing. To have his bull-like charges stopped and crumpled with a suddenly planted fist upon the end of his snout, or a painful jolt in the short ribs, always surprised Akut. It angered him too, and at such times his mighty jaws came nearer to closing in the soft flesh of his friend than at any other, for he was still an ape, with an ape's short temper and brutal instincts; but the difficulty was in catching his tormentor while his rage lasted, for when he lost his head and rushed madly into close quarters with the boy he discovered that the stinging hail of blows released upon him always found their mark and effectually stopped him – effectually and painfully. Then he would withdraw growling viciously, backing away with grinning jaws distended, to sulk for an hour or so.

Tonight they did not box. Just for a moment or two they wrestled playfully, until the scent of Sheeta, the panther, brought them to their feet, alert and wary. The great cat was passing through the jungle in front of them. For a moment it paused, listening. The boy and the ape growled menacingly in chorus and the carnivore moved on.

Then the two took up their journey toward the sound of the Dum-Dum. Louder and louder came the beating of the drum. Now, at last, they could hear the growling of the dancing apes, and strong to their nostrils came the scent of their kind. The lad trembled with excitement. The hair down Akut's spine stiffened – the symptoms of happiness and anger are often similar.

Silently they crept through the jungle as they neared the meeting place of the apes. Now they were in the trees, worming their way forward, alert for sentinels. Presently through a break in the foliage the scene burst upon the eager eyes of the boy. To Akut it was a familiar one; but to Korak it was all new. His nerves tingled at the savage sight. The great bulls were dancing in the moonlight, leaping in an irregular circle about the flat-topped earthen drum about which three old females sat beating its resounding top with sticks worn smooth by long years of use.

Akut, knowing the temper and customs of his kind, was too wise to make their presence known until the frenzy of the dance had passed. After the drum was quiet and the bellies of the tribe well-filled he would hail them. Then would come a parley, after which he and Korak would be accepted into membership by the community. There might be those who would object; but such could be overcome by brute force, of which he and the lad had an ample surplus. For weeks, possibly months, their presence might cause ever decreasing suspicion among others of the tribe; but eventually they would become as born brothers to these strange apes.

He hoped that they had been among those who had known Tarzan, for that would help in the introduction of the lad and in the consummation of Akut's dearest wish, that Korak should become king of the apes. It was with difficulty, however, that Akut kept the boy from rushing into the midst of the dancing anthropoids – an act that would have meant the instant extermination of them both, since the hysterical frenzy into which the great apes work themselves during the performance of their strange rites is of such a nature that even the most ferocious of the carnivora give them a wide berth at such times.

As the moon declined slowly toward the lofty, foliaged horizon of the amphitheater the booming of the drum decreased and lessened were the exertions of the dancers, until, at last, the final note was struck and the huge beasts turned to fall upon the feast they had dragged hither for the orgy.

From what he had seen and heard Akut was able to explain to Korak that the rites proclaimed the choosing of a new king, and he pointed out to the boy the massive figure of the shaggy monarch, come into his kingship, no doubt, as many human rulers have come into theirs – by the murder of his predecessor.

When the apes had filled their bellies and many of them had sought the bases of the trees to curl up in sleep Akut plucked Korak by the arm.

"Come," he whispered. "Come slowly. Follow me. Do as Akut does."

Then he advanced slowly through the trees until he stood upon a bough overhanging one side of the amphitheater. Here he stood in silence for a moment. Then he uttered a low growl. Instantly a score of apes leaped to their feet. Their savage little eyes sped quickly around the periphery of the clearing. The king ape was the first to see the two figures upon the branch. He gave voice to an ominous growl. Then he took a few lumbering steps in the direction of the intruders. His hair was bristling. His legs were stiff, imparting a halting, jerky motion to his gait. Behind him pressed a number of bulls.

He stopped just a little before he came beneath the two – just far enough to be beyond their spring. Wary king! Here he stood rocking himself to and fro upon his short legs, baring his fangs in hideous grinnings, rumbling out an ever increasing volume of growls, which were slowly but steadily increasing to the proportions of roars. Akut knew that he was planning an attack upon them. The old ape did not wish to fight. He had come with the boy to cast his lot with the tribe.

"I am Akut," he said. "This is Korak. Korak is the son of Tarzan who was king of the apes. I, too, was king of the apes who dwelt in the midst of the great waters. We have come to hunt with you, to fight with you. We are great hunters. We are mighty fighters. Let us come in peace."

The king ceased his rocking. He eyed the pair from beneath his beetling brows. His bloodshot eyes were savage and crafty. His kingship was very new and he was jealous of it. He feared the encroachments of two strange apes. The sleek, brown, hairless body of the lad spelled "man," and man he feared and hated.

"Go away!" he growled. "Go away, or I will kill you."

The eager lad, standing behind the great Akut, had been pulsing with anticipation and happiness. He wanted to leap down among these hairy monsters and show them that he was their friend, that he was one of them. He had expected that they would receive him with open arms, and now the words of the king ape filled him with indignation and sorrow. The blacks had set upon him and driven him away. Then he had turned to the white men – to those of his own kind – only to hear the ping of bullets where he had expected words of cordial welcome. The great apes had remained his final hope. To them he looked for the companionship man had denied him. Suddenly rage overwhelmed him.

The king ape was almost directly beneath him. The others were formed in a half circle several yards behind the king. They were watching events interestedly. Before Akut could guess his intention, or prevent, the boy leaped to the ground directly in the path of the king, who had now succeeded in stimulating himself to a frenzy of fury.

"I am Korak!" shouted the boy. "I am the Killer. I came to live among you as a friend. You want to drive me away. Very well, then, I shall go; but before I go I shall show you that the son of Tarzan is your master, as his father was before him – that he is not afraid of your king or you."

For an instant the king ape had stood motionless with surprise. He had expected no such rash action upon the part of either of the intruders. Akut was equally surprised. Now he shouted excitedly for Korak to come back, for he knew that in the sacred arena the other bulls might be expected to come to the assistance of their king against an outsider, though there was small likelihood that the king would need assistance. Once those mighty jaws closed upon the boy's soft neck the end would come quickly. To leap to his rescue would mean death for Akut, too; but the brave old ape never hesitated. Bristling and growling, he dropped to the sward just as the king ape charged.

The beast's hands clutched for their hold as the animal sprang upon the lad. The fierce jaws were wide distended to bury the yellow fangs deeply in the brown hide. Korak, too, leaped forward to meet the attack; but leaped crouching, beneath the outstretched arms. At the instant of contact the lad pivoted on one foot, and with all the weight of his body and the strength of his trained muscles drove a clenched fist into the bull's stomach. With a gasping shriek the king ape collapsed, clutching futilely for the agile, naked creature nimbly sidestepping from his grasp.

Howls of rage and dismay broke from the bull apes behind the fallen king, as with murder in their savage little hearts they rushed forward upon Korak and Akut; but the old ape was too wise to court any such unequal encounter. To have counseled the boy to retreat now would have been futile, and Akut knew it. To delay even a second in argument would have sealed the death warrants of them both. There was but a single hope and Akut seized it. Grasping the lad around the waist he lifted him bodily from the ground, and turning ran swiftly toward another tree which swung low branches above the arena. Close upon their heels swarmed the hideous mob; but Akut, old though he was and burdened by the weight of the struggling Korak, was still fleeter than his pursuers.

With a bound he grasped a low limb, and with the agility of a little monkey swung himself and the boy to temporary safety. Nor did he hesitate even here; but raced on through the jungle night, bearing his burden to safety. For a time the bulls pursued; but presently, as the swifter outdistanced the slower and found themselves separated from their fellows they abandoned the chase, standing roaring and screaming until the jungle reverberated to their hideous noises. Then they turned and retraced their way to the amphitheater.

When Akut felt assured that they were no longer pursued he stopped and released Korak. The boy was furious.

"Why did you drag me away?" he cried. "I would have taught them! I would have taught them all! Now they will think that I am afraid of them."

"What they think cannot harm you," said Akut. "You are alive. If I had not brought you away you would be dead now and so would I. Do you not know that even Numa slinks from the path of the great apes when there are many of them and they are mad?"

Chapter Nine

It was an unhappy Korak who wandered aimlessly through the jungle the day following his inhospitable reception by the great apes. His heart was heavy from disappointment. Unsatisfied vengeance smoldered in his breast. He looked with hatred upon the denizens of his jungle world, baring his fighting fangs and growling at those that came within radius of his senses. The mark of his father's early life was strong upon him and enhanced by months of association with beasts, from whom the imitative faculty of youth had absorbed a countless number of little mannerisms of the predatory creatures of the wild.

He bared his fangs now as naturally and upon as slight provocation as Sheeta, the panther, bared his. He growled as ferociously as Akut himself. When he came suddenly upon another beast his quick crouch bore a strange resemblance to the arching of a cat's back. Korak, the killer, was looking for trouble. In his heart of hearts he hoped to meet the king ape who had driven him from the amphitheater. To this end he insisted upon remaining in the vicinity; but the exigencies of the perpetual search for food led them several miles further away during day.

They were moving slowly down wind, and warily because the advantage was with whatever beast might chance to be hunting ahead of them, where their scent-spoor was being borne by the light breeze. Suddenly the two halted simultaneously. Two heads were cocked upon one side. Like creatures hewn from solid rock they stood immovable, listening. Not a muscle quivered. For several seconds they remained thus, then Korak advanced cautiously a few yards and leaped nimbly into a tree. Akut followed close upon his heels. Neither had made a noise that would have been appreciable to human ears at a dozen paces.

Stopping often to listen they crept forward through the trees. That both were greatly puzzled was apparent from the questioning looks they cast at one another from time to time. Finally the lad caught a glimpse of a palisade a hundred yards ahead, and beyond it the tops of some goat-skin tents and a number of thatched huts. His lip upcurled in a savage snarl. Blacks! How he hated them. He signed to Akut to remain where he was while he advanced to reconnoiter.

Woe betide the unfortunate villager whom The Killer came upon now. Slinking through the lower branches of the trees, leaping lightly from one jungle giant to its neighbor where the distance was not too great, or swinging from one hand hold to another Korak came silently toward the village. He heard a voice beyond the palisade and toward that he made his way. A great tree overhung the enclosure at the very point from which the voice came. Into this Korak crept. His spear was ready in his hand. His ears told him of the proximity of a human being. All that his eyes required was a single glance to show him his target. Then, lightning like, the missile would fly to its goal. With raised spear he crept among the branches of the tree glaring narrowly downward in search of the owner of the voice which rose to him from below.

At last he saw a human back. The spear hand flew to the limit of the throwing position to gather the force that would send the iron shod missile completely through the body of the unconscious victim. And then The Killer paused. He leaned forward a little to get a better view of the target. Was it to insure more perfect aim, or had there been that in the graceful lines and the childish curves of the little body below him that had held in check the spirit of murder running riot in his veins?

He lowered his spear cautiously that it might make no noise by scraping against foliage or branches. Quietly he crouched in a comfortable position along a great limb and there he lay with wide eyes looking down in wonder upon the creature he had crept upon to kill – looking down upon a little girl, a little nut brown maiden. The snarl had gone from his lip. His only expression was one of interested attention – he was trying to discover what the girl was doing. Suddenly a broad grin overspread his face, for a turn of the girl's body had revealed Geeka of the ivory head and the rat skin torso – Geeka of the splinter limbs and the disreputable appearance. The little girl raised the marred face to hers and rocking herself backward and forward crooned a plaintive Arab lullaby to the doll. A softer light entered the eyes of The Killer. For a long hour that passed very quickly to him Korak lay with gaze riveted upon the playing child. Not once had he had a view of the girl's full face. For the most part he saw only a mass of wavy, black hair, one brown little shoulder exposed upon the side from where her single robe was caught beneath her arm, and a shapely knee protruding from beneath her garment as she sat cross legged upon the ground. A tilt of the head as she emphasized some maternal admonition to the passive Geeka revealed occasionally a rounded cheek or a piquant little chin. Now she was shaking a slim finger at Geeka, reprovingly, and again she crushed to her heart this only object upon which she might lavish the untold wealth of her childish affections.

Korak, momentarily forgetful of his bloody mission, permitted the fingers of his spear hand to relax a little their grasp upon the shaft of his formidable weapon. It slipped, almost falling; but the occurrence recalled The Killer to himself. It reminded him of his purpose in slinking stealthily upon the owner of the voice that had attracted his vengeful attention. He glanced at the spear, with its well-worn grip and cruel, barbed head. Then he let his eyes wander again to the dainty form below him. In imagination he saw the heavy weapon shooting downward. He saw it pierce the tender flesh, driving its way deep into the yielding body. He saw the ridiculous doll drop from its owner's arms to lie sprawled and pathetic beside the quivering body of the little girl. The Killer shuddered, scowling at the inanimate iron and wood of the spear as though they constituted a sentient being endowed with a malignant mind.

Korak wondered what the girl would do were he to drop suddenly from the tree to her side. Most likely she would scream and run away. Then would come the men of the village with spears and guns and set upon him. They would either kill him or drive him away. A lump rose in the boy's throat. He craved the companionship of his own kind, though he scarce realized how greatly. He would have liked to slip down beside the little girl and talk with her, though he knew from the words he had overheard that she spoke a language with which he was unfamiliar. They could have talked by signs a little. That would have been better than nothing. Too, he would have been glad to see her face. What he had glimpsed assured him that she was pretty; but her strongest appeal to him lay in the affectionate nature revealed by her gentle mothering of the grotesque doll.

At last he hit upon a plan. He would attract her attention, and reassure her by a smiling greeting from a greater distance. Silently he wormed his way back into the tree. It was his intention to hail her from beyond the palisade, giving her the feeling of security which he imagined the stout barricade would afford.

He had scarcely left his position in the tree when his attention was attracted by a considerable noise upon the opposite side of the village. By moving a little he could see the gate at the far end of the main street. A number of men, women and children were running toward it. It swung open, revealing the head of a caravan upon the opposite side. In trooped the motley organization – black slaves and dark hued Arabs of the northern deserts; cursing camel drivers urging on their vicious charges; overburdened donkeys, waving sadly pendulous ears while they endured with stoic patience the brutalities of their masters; goats, sheep and horses. Into the village they all trooped behind a tall, sour, old man, who rode without greetings to those who shrunk from his path directly to a large goatskin tent in the center of the village. Here he spoke to a wrinkled hag.

Korak, from his vantage spot, could see it all. He saw the old man asking questions of the black woman, and then he saw the latter point toward a secluded corner of the village which was hidden from the main street by the tents of the Arabs and the huts of the natives in the direction of the tree beneath which the little girl played. This was doubtless her father, thought Korak. He had been away and his first thought upon returning was of his little daughter. How glad she would be to see him! How she would run and throw herself into his arms, to be crushed to his breast and covered with his kisses. Korak sighed. He thought of his own father and mother far away in London.

He returned to his place in the tree above the girl. If he couldn't have happiness of this sort himself he wanted to enjoy the happiness of others. Possibly if he made himself known to the old man he might be permitted to come to the village occasionally as a friend. It would be worth trying. He would wait until the old Arab had greeted his daughter, then he would make his presence known with signs of peace.

The Arab was striding softly toward the girl. In a moment he would be beside her, and then how surprised and delighted she would be! Korak's eyes sparkled in anticipation – and now the old man stood behind the little girl. His stern old face was still unrelaxed. The child was yet unconscious of his presence. She prattled on to the unresponsive Geeka. Then the old man coughed. With a start the child glanced quickly up over her shoulder. Korak could see her full face now. It was very beautiful in its sweet and innocent childishness – all soft and lovely curves. He could see her great, dark eyes. He looked for the happy love light that would follow recognition; but it did not come. Instead, terror, stark, paralyzing terror, was mirrored in her eyes, in the expression of her mouth, in the tense, cowering attitude of her body. A grim smile curved the thin, cruel lip of the Arab. The child essayed to crawl away; but before she could get out of his reach the old man kicked her brutally, sending her sprawling upon the grass. Then he followed her up to seize and strike her as was his custom.

Above them, in the tree, a beast crouched where a moment before had been a boy – a beast with dilating nostrils and bared fangs – a beast that trembled with rage.

The Sheik was stooping to reach for the girl when The Killer dropped to the ground at his side. His spear was still in his left hand but he had forgotten it. Instead his right fist was clenched and as The Sheik took a backward step, astonished by the sudden materialization of this strange apparition apparently out of clear air, the heavy fist landed full upon his mouth backed by the weight of the young giant and the terrific power of his more than human muscles.

Bleeding and senseless The Sheik sank to earth. Korak turned toward the child. She had regained her feet and stood wide eyed and frightened, looking first into his face and then, horror struck, at the recumbent figure of The Sheik. In an involuntary gesture of protection The Killer threw an arm about the girl's shoulders and stood waiting for the Arab to regain consciousness. For a moment they remained thus, when the girl spoke.

"When he regains his senses he will kill me," she said, in Arabic.

Korak could not understand her. He shook his head, speaking to her first in English and then in the language of the great apes; but neither of these was intelligible to her. She leaned forward and touched the hilt of the long knife that the Arab wore. Then she raised her clasped hand above her head and drove an imaginary blade into her breast above her heart. Korak understood. The old man would kill her. The girl came to his side again and stood there trembling. She did not fear him. Why should she? He had saved her from a terrible beating at the hands of The Sheik. Never, in her memory, had another so befriended her. She looked up into his face. It was a boyish, handsome face, nut-brown like her own. She admired the spotted leopard skin that circled his lithe body from one shoulder to his knees. The metal anklets and armlets adorning him aroused her envy. Always had she coveted something of the kind; but never had The Sheik permitted her more than the single cotton garment that barely sufficed to cover her nakedness. No furs or silks or jewelry had there ever been for little Meriem.

And Korak looked at the girl. He had always held girls in a species of contempt. Boys who associated with them were, in his estimation, mollycoddles. He wondered what he should do. Could he leave her here to be abused, possibly murdered, by the villainous old Arab? No! But, on the other hand, could he take her into the jungle with him? What could he accomplish burdened by a weak and frightened girl? She would scream at her own shadow when the moon came out upon the jungle night and the great beasts roamed, moaning and roaring, through the darkness.

He stood for several minutes buried in thought. The girl watched his face, wondering what was passing in his mind. She, too, was thinking of the future. She feared to remain and suffer the vengeance of The Sheik. There was no one in all the world to whom she might turn, other than this half-naked stranger who had dropped miraculously from the clouds to save her from one of The Sheik's accustomed beatings. Would her new friend leave her now? Wistfully she gazed at his intent face. She moved a little closer to him, laying a slim, brown hand upon his arm. The contact awakened the lad from his absorption. He looked down at her, and then his arm went about her shoulder once more, for he saw tears upon her lashes.

"Come," he said. "The jungle is kinder than man. You shall live in the jungle and Korak and Akut will protect you."

She did not understand his words, but the pressure of his arm drawing her away from the prostrate Arab and the tents was quite intelligible. One little arm crept about his waist and together they walked toward the palisade. Beneath the great tree that had harbored Korak while he watched the girl at play he lifted her in his arms and throwing her lightly across his shoulder leaped nimbly into the lower branches. Her arms were about his neck and from one little hand Geeka dangled down his straight young back.

And so Meriem entered the jungle with Korak, trusting, in her childish innocence, the stranger who had befriended her, and perhaps influenced in her belief in him by that strange intuitive power possessed by woman. She had no conception of what the future might hold. She did not know, nor could she have guessed the manner of life led by her protector. Possibly she pictured a distant village similar to that of The Sheik in which lived other white men like the stranger. That she was to be taken into the savage, primeval life of a jungle beast could not have occurred to her. Had it, her little heart would have palpitated with fear. Often had she wished to run away from the cruelties of The Sheik and Mabunu; but the dangers of the jungle always had deterred her.

The two had gone but a short distance from the village when the girl spied the huge proportions of the great Akut. With a half-stifled scream she clung more closely to Korak, and pointed fearfully toward the ape.

Akut, thinking that The Killer was returning with a prisoner, came growling toward them – a little girl aroused no more sympathy in the beast's heart than would a full-grown bull ape. She was a stranger and therefore to be killed. He bared his yellow fangs as he approached, and to his surprise The Killer bared his likewise, but he bared them at Akut, and snarled menacingly.

"Ah," thought Akut, "The Killer has taken a mate," and so, obedient to the tribal laws of his kind, he left them alone, becoming suddenly absorbed in a fuzzy caterpillar of peculiarly succulent appearance. The larva disposed of, he glanced from the corner of an eye at Korak. The youth had deposited his burden upon a large limb, where she clung desperately to keep from falling.

"She will accompany us," said Korak to Akut, jerking a thumb in the direction of the girl. "Do not harm her. We will protect her."

Akut shrugged. To be burdened by the young of man was in no way to his liking. He could see from her evident fright at her position on the branch, and from the terrified glances she cast in his direction that she was hopelessly unfit. By all the ethics of Akut's training and inheritance the unfit should be eliminated; but if The Killer wished this there was nothing to be done about it but to tolerate her. Akut certainly didn't want her – of that he was quite positive. Her skin was too smooth and hairless. Quite snake-like, in fact, and her face was most unattractive. Not at all like that of a certain lovely she he had particularly noticed among the apes in the amphitheater the previous night. Ah, there was true feminine beauty for one! – a great, generous mouth; lovely, yellow fangs, and the cutest, softest side whiskers! Akut sighed. Then he rose, expanded his great chest and strutted back and forth along a substantial branch, for even a puny thing like this she of Korak's might admire his fine coat and his graceful carriage.

But poor little Meriem only shrank closer to Korak and almost wished that she were back in the village of The Sheik where the terrors of existence were of human origin, and so more or less familiar. The hideous ape frightened her. He was so large and so ferocious in appearance. His actions she could only interpret as a menace, for how could she guess that he was parading to excite admiration? Nor could she know of the bond of fellowship which existed between this great brute and the godlike youth who had rescued her from the Sheik.

Meriem spent an evening and a night of unmitigated terror. Korak and Akut led her along dizzy ways as they searched for food. Once they hid her in the branches of a tree while they stalked a near-by buck. Even her natural terror of being left alone in the awful jungle was submerged in a greater horror as she saw the man and the beast spring simultaneously upon their prey and drag it down, as she saw the handsome face of her preserver contorted in a bestial snarl; as she saw his strong, white teeth buried in the soft flesh of the kill.

When he came back to her blood smeared his face and hands and breast and she shrank from him as he offered her a huge hunk of hot, raw meat. He was evidently much disturbed by her refusal to eat, and when, a moment later, he scampered away into the forest to return with fruit for her she was once more forced to alter her estimation of him. This time she did not shrink, but acknowledged his gift with a smile that, had she known it, was more than ample payment to the affection starved boy.

The sleeping problem vexed Korak. He knew that the girl could not balance herself in safety in a tree crotch while she slept, nor would it be safe to permit her to sleep upon the ground open to the attacks of prowling beasts of prey. There was but a single solution that presented itself – he must hold her in his arms all night. And that he did, with Akut braced upon one side of her and he upon the other, so that she was warmed by the bodies of them both.

She did not sleep much until the night was half spent; but at last Nature overcame her terrors of the black abyss beneath and the hairy body of the wild beast at her side, and she fell into a deep slumber which outlasted the darkness. When she opened her eyes the sun was well up. At first she could not believe in the reality of her position. Her head had rolled from Korak's shoulder so that her eyes were directed upon the hairy back of the ape. At sight of it she shrank away. Then she realized that someone was holding her, and turning her head she saw the smiling eyes of the youth regarding her. When he smiled she could not fear him, and now she shrank closer against him in natural revulsion toward the rough coat of the brute upon her other side.

Korak spoke to her in the language of the apes; but she shook her head, and spoke to him in the language of the Arab, which was as unintelligible to him as was ape speech to her. Akut sat up and looked at them. He could understand what Korak said but the girl made only foolish noises that were entirely unintelligible and ridiculous. Akut could not understand what Korak saw in her to attract him. He looked at her long and steadily, appraising her carefully, then he scratched his head, rose and shook himself.

His movement gave the girl a little start – she had forgotten Akut for the moment. Again she shrank from him. The beast saw that she feared him, and being a brute enjoyed the evidence of the terror his brutishness inspired. Crouching, he extended his huge hand stealthily toward her, as though to seize her. She shrank still further away.

Akut's eyes were busy drinking in the humor of the situation – he did not see the narrowing eyes of the boy upon him, nor the shortening neck as the broad shoulders rose in a characteristic attitude of preparation for attack. As the ape's fingers were about to close upon the girl's arm the youth rose suddenly with a short, vicious growl. A clenched fist flew before Meriem's eyes to land full upon the snout of the astonished Akut. With an explosive bellow the anthropoid reeled backward and tumbled from the tree.

Korak stood glaring down upon him when a sudden swish in the bushes close by attracted his attention. The girl too was looking down; but she saw nothing but the angry ape scrambling to his feet. Then, like a bolt from a cross bow, a mass of spotted, yellow fur shot into view straight for Akut's back. It was Sheeta, the leopard.

Chapter Ten

As THE LEOPARD LEAPED for the great ape Meriem gasped in surprise and horror – not for the impending fate of the anthropoid, but at the act of the youth who but an instant before had angrily struck his strange companion; for scarce had the carnivore burst into view than with drawn knife the youth had leaped far out above him, so that as Sheeta was almost in the act of sinking fangs and talons in Akut's broad back The Killer landed full upon the leopard's shoulders.

The cat halted in mid air, missed the ape by but a hair's breadth, and with horrid snarlings rolled over upon its back, clutching and clawing in an effort to reach and dislodge the antagonist biting at its neck and knifing it in the side.

Akut, startled by the sudden rush from his rear, and following hoary instinct, was in the tree beside the girl with an agility little short of marvelous in so heavy a beast. But the moment that he turned to see what was going on below him brought him as quickly to the ground again. Personal differences were quickly forgotten in the danger which menaced his human companion, nor was he a whit less eager to jeopardize his own safety in the service of his friend than Korak had been to succor him.

The result was that Sheeta presently found two ferocious creatures tearing him to ribbons. Shrieking, snarling and growling, the three rolled hither and thither among the underbrush, while with staring eyes the sole spectator of the battle royal crouched trembling in the tree above them hugging Geeka frantically to her breast.

It was the boy's knife which eventually decided the battle, and as the fierce feline shuddered convulsively and rolled over upon its side the youth and the ape rose and faced one another across the prostrate carcass. Korak jerked his head in the direction of the little girl in the tree.

"Leave her alone," he said; "she is mine."

Akut grunted, blinked his blood-shot eyes, and turned toward the body of Sheeta. Standing erect upon it he threw out his great chest, raised his face toward the heavens and gave voice to so horrid a scream that once again the little girl shuddered and shrank. It was the victory cry of the bull ape that has made a kill. The boy only looked on for a moment in silence; then he leaped into the tree again to the girl's side. Akut presently rejoined them. For a few minutes he busied himself licking his wounds, then he wandered off to hunt his breakfast.

For many months the strange life of the three went on unmarked by any unusual occurrences. At least without any occurrences that seemed unusual to the youth or the ape; but to the little girl it was a constant nightmare of horrors for days and weeks, until she too became accustomed to gazing into the eyeless sockets of death and to the feel of the icy wind of his shroud-like mantle. Slowly she learned the rudiments of the only common medium of thought exchange which her companions possessed – the language of the great apes. More quickly she perfected herself in jungle craft, so that the time soon came when she was an important factor in the chase, watching while the others slept, or helping them to trace the spoor of whatever prey they might be stalking. Akut accepted her on a footing which bordered upon equality when it was necessary for them to come into close contact; but for the most part he avoided her. The youth always was kind to her, and if there were many occasions upon which he felt the burden of her presence he hid it from her. Finding that the night damp and chill caused her discomfort and even suffering, Korak constructed a tight little shelter high among the swaying branches of a giant tree. Here little Meriem slept in comparative warmth and safety, while The Killer and the ape perched upon near-by branches, the former always before the entrance to the lofty domicile, where he best could guard its inmate from the dangers of arboreal enemies. They were too high to feel much fear of Sheeta; but there was always Histah, the snake, to strike terror to one's soul, and the great baboons who lived near-by, and who, while never attacking always bared their fangs and barked at any of the trio when they passed near them.

After the construction of the shelter the activities of the three became localized. They ranged less widely, for there was always the necessity of returning to their own tree at nightfall. A river flowed near by. Game and fruit were plentiful, as were fish also. Existence had settled down to the daily humdrum of the wild – the search for food and the sleeping upon full bellies. They looked no further ahead than today. If the youth thought of his past and of those who longed for him in the distant metropolis it was in a detached and impersonal sort of way as though that other life belonged to another creature than himself. He had given up hope of returning to civilization, for since his various rebuffs at the hands of those to whom he had looked for friendship he had wandered so far inland as to realize that he was completely lost in the mazes of the jungle.

Then, too, since the coming of Meriem he had found in her that one thing which he had most missed before in his savage, jungle life – human companionship. In his friendship for her there was appreciable no trace of sex influence of which he was cognizant. They were friends – companions – that was all. Both might have been boys, except for the half tender and always masterful manifestation of the protective instinct which was apparent in Korak's attitude.

The little girl idolized him as she might have idolized an indulgent brother had she had one. Love was a thing unknown to either; but as the youth neared manhood it was inevitable that it should come to him as it did to every other savage, jungle male.

As Meriem became proficient in their common language the pleasures of their companionship grew correspondingly, for now they could converse and aided by the mental powers of their human heritage they amplified the restricted vocabulary of the apes until talking was transformed from a task into an enjoyable pastime. When Korak hunted, Meriem usually accompanied him, for she had learned the fine art of silence, when silence was desirable. She could pass through the branches of the great trees now with all the agility and stealth of The Killer himself. Great heights no longer appalled her. She swung from limb to limb, or she raced through the mighty branches, surefooted, lithe, and fearless. Korak was very proud of her, and even old Akut grunted in approval where before he had growled in contempt.

A distant village of blacks had furnished her with a mantle of fur and feathers, with copper ornaments, and weapons, for Korak would not permit her to go unarmed, or unversed in the use of the weapons he stole for her. A leather thong over one shoulder supported the ever present Geeka who was still the recipient of her most sacred confidences. A light spear and a long knife were her weapons of offense or defense. Her body, rounding into the fulness of an early maturity, followed the lines of a Greek goddess; but there the similarity ceased, for her face was beautiful.

As she grew more accustomed to the jungle and the ways of its wild denizens fear left her. As time wore on she even hunted alone when

Korak and Akut were prowling at a great distance, as they were sometimes forced to do when game was scarce in their immediate vicinity. Upon these occasions she usually confined her endeavors to the smaller animals though sometimes she brought down a deer, and once even Horta, the boar – a great tusker that even Sheeta might have thought twice before attacking.

In their stamping grounds in the jungle the three were familiar figures. The little monkeys knew them well, often coming close to chatter and frolic about them. When Akut was by, the small folk kept their distance, but with Korak they were less shy and when both the males were gone they would come close to Meriem, tugging at her ornaments or playing with Geeka, who was a never ending source of amusement to them. The girl played with them and fed them, and when she was alone they helped her to pass the long hours until Korak's return.

Nor were they worthless as friends. In the hunt they helped her locate her quarry. Often they would come racing through the trees to her side to announce the near presence of antelope or giraffe, or with excited warnings of the proximity of Sheeta or Numa. Luscious, sun-kissed fruits which hung far out upon the frail bough of the jungle's waving crest were brought to her by these tiny, nimble allies. Sometimes they played tricks upon her; but she was always kind and gentle with them and in their wild, half-human way they were kind to her and affectionate. Their language being similar to that of the great apes Meriem could converse with them though the poverty of their vocabulary rendered these exchanges anything but feasts of reason. For familiar objects they had names, as well as for those conditions which induced pain or pleasure, joy, sorrow, or rage. These root words were so similar to those in use among the great anthropoids as to suggest that the language of the Manus was the mother tongue. At best it lent itself to but material and sordid exchange. Dreams, aspirations, hopes, the past, the future held no place in the conversation of Manu, the monkey. All was of the present – particularly of filling his belly and catching lice.

Poor food was this to nourish the mental appetite of a girl just upon the brink of womanhood. And so, finding Manu only amusing as an occasional playfellow or pet, Meriem poured out her sweetest soul thoughts into the deaf ears of Geeka's ivory head. To Geeka she spoke in Arabic, knowing that Geeka, being but a doll, could not understand the language of Korak and Akut, and that the language of Korak and Akut being that of male apes contained nothing of interest to an Arab doll.

Geeka had undergone a transformation since her little mother had left the village of The Sheik. Her garmenture now reflected in miniature that of Meriem. A tiny bit of leopard skin covered her ratskin torso from shoulder to splinter knee. A band of braided grasses about her brow held in place a few gaudy feathers from the parakeet, while other bits of grass were fashioned into imitations of arm and leg ornaments of metal. Geeka was a perfect little savage; but at heart she was unchanged, being the same omnivorous listener as of yore. An excellent trait in Geeka was that she never interrupted in order to talk about herself. Today was no exception. She had been listening attentively to Meriem for an hour, propped against the bole of a tree while her lithe, young mistress stretched catlike and luxurious along a swaying branch before her.

"Little Geeka," said Meriem, "our Korak has been gone for a long time today. We miss him, little Geeka, do we not? It is dull and lonesome in the great jungle when our Korak is away. What will he bring us this time, eh? Another shining band of metal for Meriem's ankle? Or a soft, doeskin loin cloth from the body of a black she? He tells me that it is harder to get the possessions of the shes, for he will not kill them as he does the males, and they fight savagely when he leaps upon them to wrest their ornaments from them. Then come the males with spears and arrows and Korak takes to the trees. Sometimes he takes the she with him and high among the branches divests her of the things he wishes to bring home to Meriem. He says that the blacks fear him now, and at first sight of him the women and children run shrieking to their huts; but he follows them within, and it is not often that he returns without arrows for himself and a present for Meriem. Korak is mighty among the jungle people – our Korak, Geeka – no, MY Korak!"

Meriem's conversation was interrupted by the sudden plunge of an excited little monkey that landed upon her shoulders in a flying leap from a neighboring tree.

"Climb!" he cried. "Climb! The Mangani are coming."

Meriem glanced lazily over her shoulder at the excited disturber of her peace.

"Climb, yourself, little Manu," she said. "The only Mangani in our jungle are Korak and Akut. It is they you have seen returning from the hunt. Some day you will see your own shadow, little Manu, and then you will be frightened to death."

But the monkey only screamed his warning more lustily before he raced upward toward the safety of the high terrace where Mangani, the great ape, could not follow. Presently Meriem heard the sound of approaching bodies swinging through the trees. She listened attentively. There were two and they were great apes – Korak and Akut. To her Korak was an ape – a Mangani, for as such the three always described themselves. Man was an enemy, so they did not think of themselves as belonging any longer to the same genus. Tarmangani, or great white ape, which described the white man in their language, did not fit them all. Gomangani – great black ape, or Negro – described none of them so they called themselves plain Mangani.

Meriem decided that she would feign slumber and play a joke on Korak. So she lay very still with eyes tightly closed. She heard the two approaching closer and closer. They were in the adjoining tree now and must have discovered her, for they had halted. Why were they so quiet? Why did not Korak call out his customary greeting? The quietness was ominous. It was followed presently by a very stealthy sound – one of them was creeping upon her. Was Korak planning a joke upon his own account? Well, she would fool him. Cautiously she opened her eyes the tiniest bit, and as she did so her heart stood still. Creeping silently toward her was a huge bull ape that she never before had seen. Behind him was another like him.

With the agility of a squirrel Meriem was upon her feet and at the same instant the great bull lunged for her. Leaping from limb to limb the girl fled through the jungle while close behind her came the two great apes. Above them raced a bevy of screaming, chattering monkeys, hurling taunts and insults at the Mangani, and encouragement and advice to the girl.

From tree to tree swung Meriem working ever upward toward the smaller branches which would not bear the weight of her pursuers. Faster and faster came the bull apes after her. The clutching fingers of the foremost were almost upon her again and again, but she eluded them by sudden bursts of speed or reckless chances as she threw herself across dizzy spaces.

Slowly she was gaining her way to the greater heights where safety lay, when, after a particularly daring leap, the swaying branch she grasped bent low beneath her weight, nor whipped upward again as it should have done. Even before the rending sound which followed Meriem knew that she had misjudged the strength of the limb. It gave slowly at first. Then there was a ripping as it parted from the trunk. Releasing her hold Meriem dropped among the foliage beneath, clutching for a new support. She found it a dozen feet below the broken limb. She had fallen thus many times before, so that she had no particular terror of a fall – it was the delay which appalled her most, and rightly, for scarce had she scrambled to a place of safety than the body of the huge ape dropped at her side and a great, hairy arm went about her waist.

Almost at once the other ape reached his companion's side. He made a lunge at Meriem; but her captor swung her to one side, bared his fighting fangs and growled ominously. Meriem struggled to escape. She struck at the hairy breast and bearded cheek. She fastened her strong, white teeth in one shaggy forearm. The ape cuffed her viciously across the face, then he had to turn his attention to his fellow who quite evidently desired the prize for his own.

The captor could not fight to advantage upon the swaying bough, burdened as he was by a squirming, struggling captive, so he dropped quickly to the ground beneath. The other followed him, and here they fought, occasionally abandoning their duel to pursue and recapture the girl who took every advantage of her captors' preoccupation in battle to break away in attempted escape; but always they overtook her, and first one and then the other possessed her as they struggled to tear one another to pieces for the prize.

Often the girl came in for many blows that were intended for a hairy foe, and once she was felled, lying unconscious while the apes, relieved of the distraction of detaining her by force, tore into one another in fierce and terrible combat.

Above them screamed the little monkeys, racing hither and thither in a frenzy of hysterical excitement. Back and forth over the battle field flew countless birds of gorgeous plumage, squawking their hoarse cries of rage and defiance. In the distance a lion roared.

The larger bull was slowly tearing his antagonist to pieces. They rolled upon the ground biting and striking. Again, erect upon their hind legs they pulled and tugged like human wrestlers; but always the giant fangs found their bloody part to play until both combatants and the ground about them were red with gore.

Meriem, through it all, lay still and unconscious upon the ground. At last one found a permanent hold upon the jugular of the other and thus they went down for the last time. For several minutes they lay with scarce a struggle. It was the larger bull who arose alone from the last embrace. He shook himself. A deep growl rumbled from his hairy throat. He waddled back and forth between the body of the girl and that of his vanquished foe. Then he stood upon the latter and gave tongue to his hideous challenge. The little monkeys broke, screaming, in all directions as the terrifying noise broke upon their ears. The gorgeous birds took wing and fled. Once again the lion roared, this time at a greater distance.

The great ape waddled once more to the girl's side. He turned her over upon her back, and stooping commenced to sniff and listen about her face and breast. She lived. The monkeys were returning. They came in swarms, and from above hurled down insults upon the victor.

The ape showed his displeasure by baring his teeth and growling up at them. Then he stooped and lifting the girl to his shoulder waddled off through the jungle. In his wake followed the angry mob.

Chapter Eleven

Korak, returning from the hunt, heard the jabbering of the excited monkeys. He knew that something was seriously amiss. Histah, the snake, had doubtless coiled his slimy folds about some careless Manu. The youth hastened ahead. The monkeys were Meriem's friends. He would help them if he could. He traveled rapidly along the middle terrace. In the tree by Meriem's shelter he deposited his trophies of the hunt and called aloud to her. There was no answer. He dropped quickly to a lower level. She might be hiding from him.

Upon a great branch where Meriem often swung at indolent ease he saw Geeka propped against the tree's great bole. What could it mean? Meriem had never left Geeka thus alone before. Korak picked up the doll and tucked it in his belt. He called again, more loudly; but no Meriem answered his summons. In the distance the jabbering of the excited Manus was growing less distinct.

Could their excitement be in any way connected with Meriem's disappearance? The bare thought was enough. Without waiting for Akut who was coming slowly along some distance in his rear, Korak swung rapidly in the direction of the chattering mob. But a few minutes sufficed to overtake the rearmost. At sight of him they fell to screaming and pointing downward ahead of them, and a moment later Korak came within sight of the cause of their rage.

The youth's heart stood still in terror as he saw the limp body of the girl across the hairy shoulders of a great ape. That she was dead he did not doubt, and in that instant there arose within him a something which he did not try to interpret nor could have had he tried; but all at once the whole world seemed centered in that tender, graceful body, that frail little body, hanging so pitifully limp and helpless across the bulging shoulders of the brute.

He knew then that little Meriem was his world – his sun, his moon, his stars – with her going had gone all light and warmth and happiness. A groan escaped his lips, and after that a series of hideous roars, more bestial than the beasts', as he dropped plummet-like in mad descent toward the perpetrator of this hideous crime.

The bull ape turned at the first note of this new and menacing voice, and as he turned a new flame was added to the rage and hatred of The Killer, for he saw that the creature before him was none other than the king ape which had driven him away from the great anthropoids to whom he had looked for friendship and asylum.

Dropping the body of the girl to the ground the bull turned to battle anew for possession of his expensive prize; but this time he looked for an easy conquest. He too recognized Korak. Had he not chased him away from the amphitheater without even having to lay a fang or paw upon him? With lowered head and bulging shoulders he rushed headlong for the smooth-skinned creature who was daring to question his right to his prey.

They met head on like two charging bulls, to go down together tearing and striking. Korak forgot his knife. Rage and bloodlust such as his could be satisfied only by the feel of hot flesh between rending fangs, by the gush of new life blood against his bare skin, for, though he did not realize it, Korak, The Killer, was fighting for something more compelling than hate or revenge – he was a great male fighting another male for a she of his own kind.

So impetuous was the attack of the man-ape that he found his hold before the anthropoid could prevent him – a savage hold, with strong jaws closed upon a pulsing jugular, and there he clung, with closed eyes, while his fingers sought another hold upon the shaggy throat.

It was then that Meriem opened her eyes. At the sight before her they went wide.

"Korak!" she cried. "Korak! My Korak! I knew that you would come. Kill him, Korak! Kill him!" And with flashing eyes and heaving bosom the girl, coming to her feet, ran to Korak's side to encourage him. Nearby lay The Killer's spear, where he had flung it as he charged the ape. The girl saw it and snatched it up. No faintness overcame her in the face of this battle primeval at her feet. For her there was no hysterical reaction from the nerve strain of her own personal encounter with the bull. She was excited; but cool and entirely unafraid. Her Korak was battling with another Mangani that would have stolen her; but she did not seek the safety of an overhanging bough there to watch the battle from afar, as would a she Mangani. Instead she placed the point of Korak's spear against the bull ape's side and plunged the sharp point deep into the savage heart. Korak had not needed her aid, for the great bull had been already as good as dead, with the blood gushing from his torn jugular; but Korak rose smiling with a word of approbation for his helper.

How tall and fine she was! Had she changed suddenly within the few hours of his absence, or had his battle with the ape affected his vision? He might have been looking at Meriem through new eyes for the many startling and wonderful surprises his gaze revealed. How long it had been since he had found her in her father's village, a little Arab girl, he did not know, for time is of no import in the jungle and so he had kept no track of the passing days. But he realized, as he looked upon her now, that she was no longer such a little girl as he had first seen playing with Geeka beneath the great tree just within the palisade. The change must have been very gradual to have eluded his notice until now. And what was it that had caused him to realize it so suddenly? His gaze wandered from the girl to the body of the dead bull. For the first time there flashed to his understanding the explanation of the reason for the girl's attempted abduction. Korak's eyes went wide and then they closed to narrow slits of rage as he stood glaring down upon the abysmal brute at his feet. When next his glance rose to Meriem's face a slow flush suffused his own. Now, indeed, was he looking upon her through new eyes – the eyes of a man looking upon a maid.

Akut had come up just as Meriem had speared Korak's antagonist. The exultation of the old ape was keen. He strutted, stiff-legged and truculent about the body of the fallen enemy. He growled and upcurved his long, flexible lip. His hair bristled. He was paying no attention to Meriem and Korak. Back in the uttermost recesses of his little brain something was stirring – something which the sight and smell of the great bull had aroused. The outward manifestation of the germinating idea was one of bestial rage; but the inner sensations were pleasurable in the extreme. The scent of the great bull and the sight of his huge and hairy figure had wakened in the heart of Akut a longing for the companionship of his own kind. So Korak was not alone undergoing a change.

And Meriem? She was a woman. It is woman's divine right to love. Always she had loved Korak. He was her big brother. Meriem alone underwent no change. She was still happy in the companionship of her Korak. She still loved him – as a sister loves an indulgent brother – and she was very, very proud of him. In all the jungle there was no other creature so strong, so handsome, or so brave.

Korak came close to her. There was a new light in his eyes as she looked up into them; but she did not understand it. She did not realize how close they were to maturity, nor aught of all the difference in their lives the look in Korak's eyes might mean.

"Meriem," he whispered and his voice was husky as he laid a brown hand upon her bare shoulder. "Meriem!" Suddenly he crushed her to him. She looked up into his face, laughing, and then he bent and kissed her full upon the mouth. Even then she did not understand. She did not recall ever having been kissed before. It was very nice. Meriem liked it. She thought it was Korak's way of showing how glad he was that the great ape had not succeeded in running away with her. She was glad too, so she put her arms about The Killer's neck and kissed him again and again. Then, discovering the doll in his belt she transferred it to her own possession, kissing it as she had kissed Korak.

Korak wanted her to say something. He wanted to tell her how he loved her; but the emotion of his love choked him and the vocabulary of the Mangani was limited.

There came a sudden interruption. It was from Akut – a sudden, low growl, no louder than those he had been giving vent to the while he pranced about the dead bull, nor half so loud in fact; but of a timbre that bore straight to the perceptive faculties of the jungle beast ingrained in Korak. It was a warning. Korak looked quickly up from the glorious vision of the sweet face so close to his. Now his other faculties awoke. His ears, his nostrils were on the alert. Something was coming!

The Killer moved to Akut's side. Meriem was just behind them. The three stood like carved statues gazing into the leafy tangle of the jungle. The noise that had attracted their attention increased, and presently a great ape broke through the underbrush a few paces from where they stood. The beast halted at sight of them. He gave a warning grunt back over his shoulder, and a moment later coming cautiously another bull appeared. He was followed by others – both bulls and females with young, until two score hairy monsters stood glaring at the three. It was the tribe of the dead king ape. Akut was the first to speak. He pointed to the body of the dead bull.

"Korak, mighty fighter, has killed your king," he grunted. "There is none greater in all the jungle than Korak, son of Tarzan. Now Korak is king. What bull is greater than Korak?" It was a challenge to any bull who might care to question Korak's right to the kingship. The apes jabbered and chattered and growled among themselves for a time. At last a young bull came slowly forward rocking upon his short legs, bristling, growling, terrible.

The beast was enormous, and in the full prime of his strength. He belonged to that almost extinct species for which white men have long sought upon the information of the natives of the more inaccessible jungles. Even the natives seldom see these great, hairy, primordial men.

Korak advanced to meet the monster. He, too, was growling. In his mind a plan was revolving. To close with this powerful, untired brute after having just passed through a terrific battle with another of his kind would have been to tempt defeat. He must find an easier way to victory. Crouching, he prepared to meet the charge which he knew would soon come, nor did he have long to wait. His antagonist paused only for sufficient time to permit him to recount for the edification of the audience and the confounding of Korak a brief resume of his former victories, of his prowess, and of what he was about to do to this puny Tarmangani. Then he charged.

With clutching fingers and wide opened jaws he came down upon the waiting Korak with the speed of an express train. Korak did not move until the great arms swung to embrace him, then he dropped low beneath them, swung a terrific right to the side of the beast's jaw as he sidestepped his rushing body, and swinging quickly about stood ready over the fallen ape where he sprawled upon the ground.

It was a surprised anthropoid that attempted to scramble to its feet. Froth flecked its hideous lips. Red were the little eyes. Blood curdling roars tumbled from the deep chest. But it did not reach its feet. The Killer stood waiting above it, and the moment that the hairy chin came upon the proper level another blow that would have felled an ox sent the ape over backward.

Again and again the beast struggled to arise, but each time the mighty Tarmangani stood waiting with ready fist and pile driver blow to bowl him over. Weaker and weaker became the efforts of the bull. Blood smeared his face and breast. A red stream trickled from nose and mouth. The crowd that had cheered him on at first with savage yells, now jeered him – their approbation was for the Tarmangani.

"Kagoda?" inquired Korak, as he sent the bull down once more.

Again the stubborn bull essayed to scramble to his feet. Again The Killer struck him a terrific blow. Again he put the question, kagoda – have you had enough?

For a moment the bull lay motionless. Then from between battered lips came the single word: "Kagoda!"

"Then rise and go back among your people," said Korak. "I do not wish to be king among people who once drove me from them. Keep your own ways, and we will keep ours. When we meet we may be friends, but we shall not live together."

An old bull came slowly toward The Killer.

"You have killed our king," he said. "You have defeated him who would have been king. You could have killed him had you wished. What shall we do for a king?"

Korak turned toward Akut.

"There is your king," he said. But Akut did not want to be separated from Korak, although he was anxious enough to remain with his own kind. He wanted Korak to remain, too. He said as much.

The youth was thinking of Meriem – of what would be best and safest for her. If Akut went away with the apes there would be but one to watch over and protect her. On the other hand were they to join the tribe he would never feel safe to leave Meriem behind when he went out to hunt, for the passions of the ape-folk are not ever well controlled. Even a female might develop an insane hatred for the slender white girl and kill her during Korak's absence.

"We will live near you," he said, at last. "When you change your hunting ground we will change ours, Meriem and I, and so remain near you; but we shall not dwell among you."

Akut raised objections to this plan. He did not wish to be separated from Korak. At first he refused to leave his human friend for the companionship of his own kind; but when he saw the last of the tribe wandering off into the jungle again and his glance rested upon the lithe figure of the dead king's young mate as she cast admiring glances at her lord's successor the call of blood would not be denied. With a farewell glance toward his beloved Korak he turned and followed the she ape into the labyrinthine mazes of the wood.

After Korak had left the village of the blacks following his last thieving expedition, the screams of his victim and those of the other women and children had brought the warriors in from the forest and the river. Great was the excitement and hot was the rage of the men when they learned that the white devil had again entered their homes, frightened their women and stolen arrows and ornaments and food.

Even their superstitious fear of this weird creature who hunted with a huge bull ape was overcome in their desire to wreak vengeance upon him and rid themselves for good and all of the menace of his presence in the jungle.

And so it was that a score of the fleetest and most doughty warriors of the tribe set out in pursuit of Korak and Akut but a few minutes after they had left the scene of The Killer's many depredations.

The youth and the ape had traveled slowly and with no precautions against a successful pursuit. Nor was their attitude of careless indifference to the blacks at all remarkable. So many similar raids had gone unpunished that the two had come to look upon the Negroes with contempt. The return journey led them straight up wind. The result being that the scent of their pursuers was borne away from them, so they proceeded upon their way in total ignorance of the fact that tireless trackers but little less expert in the mysteries of woodcraft than themselves were dogging their trail with savage insistence.

The little party of warriors was led by Kovudoo, the chief; a middle-aged savage of exceptional cunning and bravery. It was he who first came within sight of the quarry which they had followed for hours by the mysterious methods of their almost uncanny powers of observation, intuition, and even scent.

Kovudoo and his men came upon Korak, Akut and Meriem after the killing of the king ape, the noise of the combat having led them at last straight to their quarry. The sight of the slender white girl had amazed the savage chief and held him gazing at the trio for a moment before ordering his warriors to rush out upon their prey. In that moment it was that the great apes came and again the blacks remained awestruck witnesses to the palaver, and the battle between Korak and the young bull.

But now the apes had gone, and the white youth and the white maid stood alone in the jungle. One of Kovudoo's men leaned close to the ear of his chief. "Look!" he whispered, and pointed to something that dangled at the girl's side. "When my brother and I were slaves in the village of The Sheik my brother made that thing for The Sheik's little daughter – she played with it always and called it after my brother, whose name is Geeka. Just before we escaped some one came and struck down The Sheik, stealing his daughter away. If this is she The Sheik will pay you well for her return."

Korak's arm had again gone around the shoulders of Meriem. Love raced hot through his young veins. Civilization was but a half-remembered state – London as remote as ancient Rome. In all the world there were but they two – Korak, The Killer, and Meriem, his mate. Again he drew her close to him and covered her willing lips with his hot kisses. And then from behind him broke a hideous bedlam of savage war cries and a score of shrieking blacks were upon them.

Korak turned to give battle. Meriem with her own light spear stood by his side. An avalanche of barbed missiles flew about them. One pierced Korak's shoulder, another his leg, and he went down.

Meriem was unscathed for the blacks had intentionally spared her. Now they rushed forward to finish Korak and make good the girl's capture; but as they came there came also from another point in the jungle the great Akut and at his heels the huge bulls of his new kingdom.

Snarling and roaring they rushed upon the black warriors when they saw the mischief they had already wrought. Kovudoo, realizing the danger of coming to close quarters with these mighty ape-men, seized Meriem and called upon his warriors to retreat. For a time the apes followed them, and several of the blacks were badly mauled and one killed before they succeeded in escaping. Nor would they have gotten off thus easily had Akut not been more concerned with the condition of the wounded Korak than with the fate of the girl upon whom he had always looked as more or less of an interloper and an unquestioned burden.

Korak lay bleeding and unconscious when Akut reached his side. The great ape tore the heavy spears from his flesh, licked the wounds and then carried his friend to the lofty shelter that Korak had constructed for Meriem. Further than this the brute could do nothing. Nature must accomplish the rest unaided or Korak must die.

He did not die, however. For days he lay helpless with fever, while Akut and the apes hunted close by that they might protect him from such birds and beasts as might reach his lofty retreat. Occasionally Akut brought him juicy fruits which helped to slake his thirst and allay his fever, and little by little his powerful constitution overcame the effects of the spear thrusts. The wounds healed and his strength returned. All during his rational moments as he had lain upon the soft furs which lined Meriem's nest he had suffered more acutely from fears for Meriem than from the pain of his own wounds. For her he must live. For her he must regain his strength that he might set out in search of her. What had the blacks done to her? Did she still live, or had they sacrificed her to their lust for torture and human flesh? Korak almost trembled with terror as the most hideous possibilities of the girl's fate suggested themselves to him out of his knowledge of the customs of Kovudoo's tribe.

The days dragged their weary lengths along, but at last he had sufficiently regained his strength to crawl from the shelter and make his way unaided to the ground. Now he lived more upon raw meat, for which he was entirely dependent on Akut's skill and generosity. With the meat diet his strength returned more rapidly, and at last he felt that he was fit to undertake the journey to the village of the blacks.

Chapter Twelve

Two tall, bearded white men moved cautiously through the jungle from their camp beside a wide river. They were Carl Jenssen and Sven Malbihn, but little altered in appearance since the day, years before, that they and their safari had been so badly frightened by Korak and Akut as the former sought haven with them.

Every year had they come into the jungle to trade with the natives, or to rob them; to hunt and trap; or to guide other white men in the land they knew so well. Always since their experience with The Sheik had they operated at a safe distance from his territory.

Now they were closer to his village than they had been for years, yet safe enough from discovery owing to the uninhabited nature of the intervening jungle and the fear and enmity of Kovudoo's people for The Sheik, who, in time past, had raided and all but exterminated the tribe.

This year they had come to trap live specimens for a European zoological garden, and today they were approaching a trap which they had set in the hope of capturing a specimen of the large baboons that frequented the neighborhood. As they approached the trap they became aware from the noises emanating from its vicinity that their efforts had been crowned with success. The barking and screaming of hundreds of baboons could mean naught else than that one or more of their number had fallen a victim to the allurements of the bait.

The extreme caution of the two men was prompted by former experiences with the intelligent and doglike creatures with which they had to deal. More than one trapper has lost his life in battle with enraged baboons who will hesitate to attack nothing upon one occasion, while upon another a single gun shot will disperse hundreds of them.

Heretofore the Swedes had always watched near-by their trap, for as a rule only the stronger bulls are thus caught, since in their greediness they prevent the weaker from approaching the covered bait, and when once within the ordinary rude trap woven on the spot of interlaced branches they are able, with the aid of their friends upon the outside, to demolish their prison and escape. But in this instance the trappers had utilized a special steel cage which could withstand all the strength and cunning of a baboon. It was only necessary, therefore, to drive away the herd which they knew were surrounding the prison and wait for their boys who were even now following them to the trap.

As they came within sight of the spot they found conditions precisely as they had expected. A large male was battering frantically against the steel wires of the cage that held him captive. Upon the outside several hundred other baboons were tearing and tugging in his aid, and all were roaring and jabbering and barking at the top of their lungs.

But what neither the Swedes nor the baboons saw was the half-naked figure of a youth hidden in the foliage of a nearby tree. He had come upon the scene at almost the same instant as Jenssen and Malbihn, and was watching the activities of the baboons with every mark of interest.

Korak's relations with the baboons had never been over friendly. A species of armed toleration had marked their occasional meetings. The baboons and Akut had walked stiff legged and growling past one another, while Korak had maintained a bared fang neutrality. So now he was not greatly disturbed by the predicament of their king. Curiosity prompted him to tarry a moment, and in that moment his quick eyes caught the unfamiliar coloration of the clothing of the two Swedes behind a bush not far from him. Now he was all alertness. Who were these interlopers? What was their business in the jungle of the Mangani? Korak slunk noiselessly around them to a point where he might get their scent as well as a better view of them, and scarce had he done so when he recognized them – they were the men who had fired upon him years before. His eyes blazed. He could feel the hairs upon his scalp stiffen at the roots. He watched them with the intentness of a panther about to spring upon its prey.

He saw them rise and, shouting, attempt to frighten away the baboons as they approached the cage. Then one of them raised his rifle and fired into the midst of the surprised and angry herd. For an instant Korak thought that the baboons were about to charge, but two more shots from the rifles of the white men sent them scampering into the trees. Then the two Europeans advanced upon the cage. Korak thought that they were going to kill the king. He cared nothing for the king but he cared less for the two white men. The king had never attempted to kill him – the white men had. The king was a denizen of his own beloved jungle – the white men were aliens. His loyalty therefore was to the baboon against the human. He could speak the language of the baboon – it was identical to that of the great apes. Across the clearing he saw the jabbering horde watching.

Raising his voice he shouted to them. The white men turned at the sound of this new factor behind them. They thought it was another baboon that had circled them; but though they searched the trees with their eyes they saw nothing of the now silent figure hidden by the foliage. Again Korak shouted.

"I am The Killer," he cried. "These men are my enemies and yours. I will help you free your king. Run out upon the strangers when you see me do so, and together we will drive them away and free your king."

And from the baboons came a great chorus: "We will do what you say, Korak."

Dropping from his tree Korak ran toward the two Swedes, and at the same instant three hundred baboons followed his example. At sight of the strange apparition of the half-naked white warrior rushing upon them with uplifted spear Jenssen and Malbihn raised their rifles and fired at Korak; but in the excitement both missed and a moment later the baboons were upon them. Now their only hope of safety lay in escape, and dodging here and there, fighting off the great beasts that leaped upon their backs, they ran into the jungle. Even then they would have died but for the coming of their men whom they met a couple of hundred yards from the cage.

Once the white men had turned in flight Korak gave them no further attention, turning instead to the imprisoned baboon. The fastenings of the door that had eluded the mental powers of the baboons, yielded their secret immediately to the human intelligence of The Killer, and a moment later the king baboon stepped forth to liberty. He wasted no breath in thanks to Korak, nor did the young man expect thanks. He knew that none of the baboons would ever forget his service, though as a matter of fact he did not care if they did. What he had done had been prompted by a desire to be revenged upon the two white men. The baboons could never be of service to him. Now they were racing in the direction of the battle that was being waged between their fellows and the followers of the two Swedes, and as the din of battle subsided in the distance, Korak turned and resumed his journey toward the village of Kovudoo.

On the way he came upon a herd of elephants standing in an open forest glade. Here the trees were too far apart to permit Korak to travel through the branches – a trail he much preferred not only because of its freedom from dense underbrush and the wider field of vision it gave him but from pride in his arboreal ability. It was exhilarating to swing from tree to tree; to test the prowess of his mighty muscles; to reap the pleasurable fruits of his hard won agility. Korak joyed in the thrills of the highflung upper terraces of the great forest, where, unhampered and unhindered, he might laugh down upon the great brutes who must keep forever to the darkness and the gloom of the musty soil.

But here, in this open glade where Tantor flapped his giant ears and swayed his huge bulk from side to side, the ape-man must pass along the surface of the ground – a pygmy amongst giants. A great bull raised his trunk to rattle a low warning as he sensed the coming of an intruder. His weak eyes roved hither and thither but it was his keen scent and acute hearing which first located the ape-man. The herd moved restlessly, prepared for fight, for the old bull had caught the scent of man.

"Peace, Tantor," called The Killer. "It is I, Korak, Tarmangani."

The bull lowered his trunk and the herd resumed their interrupted meditations. Korak passed within a foot of the great bull. A sinuous trunk undulated toward him, touching his brown hide in a half caress. Korak slapped the great shoulder affectionately as he went by. For years he had been upon good terms with Tantor and his people. Of all the jungle folk he loved best the mighty pachyderm – the most peaceful and at the same time the most terrible of them all. The gentle gazelle feared him not, yet Numa, lord of the jungle, gave him a wide berth. Among the younger bulls, the cows and the calves Korak wound his way. Now and then another trunk would run out to touch him, and once a playful calf grasped his legs and upset him.

The afternoon was almost spent when Korak arrived at the village of Kovudoo. There were many natives lolling in shady spots beside the conical huts or beneath the branches of the several trees which had been left standing within the enclosure. Warriors were in evidence upon hand. It was not a good time for a lone enemy to prosecute a search through the village. Korak determined to await the coming of darkness. He was a match for many warriors; but he could not, unaided, overcome an entire tribe – not even for his beloved Meriem. While he waited among the branches and foliage of a near-by tree he searched the village constantly with his keen eyes, and twice he circled it, sniffing the vagrant breezes which puffed erratically from first one point of the compass and then another. Among the various stenches peculiar to a native village the ape-man's sensitive nostrils were finally rewarded by cognizance of the delicate aroma which marked the presence of her he sought. Meriem was there – in one of those huts! But which one he could not know without closer investigation, and so he waited, with the dogged patience of a beast of prey, until night had fallen.

The camp fires of the blacks dotted the gloom with little points of light, casting their feeble rays in tiny circles of luminosity that brought into glistening relief the naked bodies of those who lay or squatted about them. It was then that Korak slid silently from the tree that had hidden him and dropped lightly to the ground within the enclosure.

Keeping well in the shadows of the huts he commenced a systematic search of the village – ears, eyes and nose constantly upon the alert for the first intimation of the near presence of Meriem. His progress must of necessity be slow since not even the keen-eared curs of the savages must guess the presence of a stranger within the gates. How close he came to a detection on several occasions The Killer well knew from the restless whining of several of them.

It was not until he reached the back of a hut at the head of the wide village street that Korak caught again, plainly, the scent of Meriem. With nose close to the thatched wall Korak sniffed eagerly about the structure – tense and palpitant as a hunting hound. Toward the front and the door he made his way when once his nose had assured him that Meriem lay within; but as he rounded the side and came within view of the entrance he saw a burly Negro armed with a long spear squatting at the portal of the girl's prison. The fellow's back was toward him, his figure outlined against the glow of cooking fires further down the street. He was alone. The nearest of his fellows were beside a fire sixty or seventy feet beyond. To enter the hut Korak must either silence the sentry or pass him unnoticed. The danger in the accomplishment of the former alternative lay in the practical certainty of alarming the warriors near by and bringing them and the balance of the village down upon him. To achieve the latter appeared practically impossible. To you or me it would have been impossible; but Korak, The Killer, was not as you or I.

There was a good twelve inches of space between the broad back of the black and the frame of the doorway. Could Korak pass through behind the savage warrior without detection? The light that fell upon the glistening ebony of the sentry's black skin fell also upon the light brown of Korak's. Should one of the many further down the street chance to look long in this direction they must surely note the tall, light-colored, moving figure; but Korak depended upon their interest in their own gossip to hold their attention fast where it already lay, and upon the firelight near them to prevent them seeing too plainly at a distance into the darkness at the village end where his work lay.

Flattened against the side of the hut, yet not arousing a single warning rustle from its dried thatching, The Killer came closer and closer to the watcher. Now he was at his shoulder. Now he had wormed his sinuous way behind him. He could feel the heat of the naked body against his knees. He could hear the man breathe. He marveled that the dull-witted creature had not long since been alarmed; but the fellow sat there as ignorant of the presence of another as though that other had not existed.

Korak moved scarcely more than an inch at a time, then he would stand motionless for a moment. Thus was he worming his way behind the guard when the latter straightened up, opened his cavernous mouth in a wide yawn, and stretched his arms above his head. Korak stood rigid as stone. Another step and he would be within the hut. The black lowered his arms and relaxed. Behind him was the frame work of the doorway. Often before had it supported his sleepy head, and now he leaned back to enjoy the forbidden pleasure of a cat nap.

But instead of the door frame his head and shoulders came in contact with the warm flesh of a pair of living legs. The exclamation of surprise that almost burst from his lips was throttled in his throat by steel-thewed fingers that closed about his windpipe with the suddenness of thought. The black struggled to arise – to turn upon the creature that had seized him – to wriggle from its hold; but all to no purpose. As he had been held in a mighty vise of iron he could not move. He could not scream. Those awful fingers at his throat but closed more and more tightly. His eyes bulged from their sockets. His face turned an ashy blue. Presently he relaxed once more – this time in the final dissolution from which there is no quickening. Korak propped the dead body against the door frame. There it sat, lifelike in the gloom. Then the ape-man turned and glided into the Stygian darkness of the hut's interior.

"Meriem!" he whispered.

"Korak! My Korak!" came an answering cry, subdued by fear of alarming her captors, and half stifled by a sob of joyful welcome.

The youth knelt and cut the bonds that held the girl's wrists and ankles. A moment later he had lifted her to her feet, and grasping her by the hand led her towards the entrance. Outside the grim sentinel of death kept his grisly vigil. Sniffing at his dead feet whined a mangy native cur. At sight of the two emerging from the hut the beast gave an ugly snarl and an instant later as it caught the scent of the strange white man it raised a series of excited yelps. Instantly the warriors at the near-by fire were attracted. They turned their heads in the direction of the commotion. It was impossible that they should fail to see the white skins of the fugitives.

Korak slunk quickly into the shadows at the hut's side, drawing Meriem with him; but he was too late. The blacks had seen enough to arouse their suspicions and a dozen of them were now running to investigate. The yapping cur was still at Korak's heels leading the searchers unerringly in pursuit. The youth struck viciously at the brute with his long spear; but, long accustomed to dodging blows, the wily creature made a most uncertain target.

Other blacks had been alarmed by the running and shouting of their companions and now the entire population of the village was swarming up the street to assist in the search. Their first discovery was the dead body of the sentry, and a moment later one of the bravest of them had entered the hut and discovered the absence of the prisoner. These startling announcements filled the blacks with a combination of terror and rage; but, seeing no foe in evidence they were enabled to permit their rage to get the better of their terror, and so the leaders, pushed on by those behind them, ran rapidly around the hut in the direction of the yapping of the mangy cur. Here they found a single white warrior making away with their captive, and recognizing him as the author of numerous raids and indignities and believing that they had him cornered and at a disadvantage, they charged savagely upon him.

Korak, seeing that they were discovered, lifted Meriem to his shoulders and ran for the tree which would give them egress from the village. He was handicapped in his flight by the weight of the girl whose legs would but scarce bear her weight, to say nothing of maintaining her in rapid flight, for the tightly drawn bonds that had been about her ankles for so long had stopped circulation and partially paralyzed her extremities.

Had this not been the case the escape of the two would have been a feat of little moment, since Meriem was scarcely a whit less agile than Korak, and fully as much at home in the trees as he. But with the girl on his shoulder Korak could not both run and fight to advantage, and the result was that before he had covered half the distance to the tree a score of native curs attracted by the yelping of their mate and the yells and shouts of their masters had closed in upon the fleeing white man, snapping at his legs and at last succeeding in tripping him. As he went down the hyena-like brutes were upon him, and as he struggled to his feet the blacks closed in.

A couple of them seized the clawing, biting Meriem, and subdued her – a blow upon the head was sufficient. For the ape-man they found more drastic measures would be necessary.

Weighted down as he was by dogs and warriors he still managed to struggle to his feet. To right and left he swung crushing blows to the faces of his human antagonists – to the dogs he paid not the slightest attention other than to seize the more persistent and wring their necks with a single quick movement of the wrist.

A knob stick aimed at him by an ebon Hercules he caught and wrested from his antagonist, and then the blacks experienced to the full the possibilities for punishment that lay within those smooth flowing muscles beneath the velvet brown skin of the strange, white giant. He rushed among them with all the force and ferocity of a bull elephant gone mad. Hither and thither he charged striking down the few who had the temerity to stand against him, and it was evident that unless a chance spear thrust brought him down he would rout the entire village and regain his prize. But old Kovudoo was not to be so easily robbed of the ransom which the girl represented, and seeing that their attack which had up to now resulted in a series of individual combats with the white warrior, he called his tribesmen off, and forming them in a compact body about the girl and the two who watched over her bid them do nothing more than repel the assaults of the ape-man.

Again and again Korak rushed against this human barricade bristling with spear points. Again and again he was repulsed, often with severe wounds to caution him to greater wariness. From head to foot he was red with his own blood, and at last, weakening from the loss of it, he came to the bitter realization that alone he could do no more to succor his Meriem.

Presently an idea flashed through his brain. He called aloud to the girl. She had regained consciousness now and replied.

"Korak goes," he shouted; "but he will return and take you from the Gomangani. Good-bye, my Meriem. Korak will come for you again."

"Good-bye!" cried the girl. "Meriem will look for you until you come."

Like a flash, and before they could know his intention or prevent him, Korak wheeled, raced across the village and with a single leap disappeared into the foliage of the great tree that was his highroad to the village of Kovudoo. A shower of spears followed him, but their only harvest was a taunting laugh flung back from out the darkness of the jungle.

Chapter Thirteen

Meriem, again bound and under heavy guard in Kovudoo's own hut, saw the night pass and the new day come without bringing the momentarily looked for return of Korak. She had no doubt but that he would come back and less still that he would easily free her from her captivity. To her Korak was little short of omnipotent. He embodied for her all that was finest and strongest and best in her savage world. She gloried in his prowess and worshipped him for the tender thoughtfulness that always had marked his treatment of her. No other within the ken of her memory had ever accorded her the love and gentleness that was his daily offering to her. Most of the gentler attributes of his early childhood had long since been forgotten in the fierce battle for existence which the customs of the mysterious jungle had forced upon him. He was more often savage and bloodthirsty than tender and kindly. His other friends of the wild looked for no gentle tokens of his affection. That he would hunt with them and fight for them was sufficient. If he growled and showed his fighting fangs when they trespassed upon his inalienable rights to the fruits of his kills they felt no anger toward him – only greater respect for the efficient and the fit – for him who could not only kill but protect the flesh of his kill.

But toward Meriem he always had shown more of his human side. He killed primarily for her. It was to the feet of Meriem that he brought the fruits of his labors. It was for Meriem more than for himself that he squatted beside his flesh and growled ominously at whosoever dared sniff too closely to it. When he was cold in the dark days of rain, or thirsty in a prolonged drouth, his discomfort engendered first of all thoughts of Meriem's welfare – after she had been made warm, after her thirst had been slaked, then he turned to the affair of ministering to his own wants.

The softest skins fell gracefully from the graceful shoulders of his Meriem. The sweetest-scented grasses lined her bower where other soft, furry pelts made hers the downiest couch in all the jungle.

What wonder then that Meriem loved her Korak? But she loved him as a little sister might love a big brother who was very good to her. As yet she knew naught of the love of a maid for a man.

So now as she lay waiting for him she dreamed of him and of all that he meant to her. She compared him with The Sheik, her father, and at thought of the stern, grizzled, old Arab she shuddered. Even the savage blacks had been less harsh to her than he. Not understanding their tongue she could not guess what purpose they had in keeping her a prisoner. She knew that man ate man, and she had expected to be eaten; but she had been with them for some time now and no harm had befallen her. She did not know that a runner had been dispatched to the distant village of The Sheik to barter with him for a ransom. She did not know, nor did Kovudoo, that the runner had never reached his destination – that he had fallen in with the safari of Jenssen and Malbihn and with the talkativeness of a native to other natives had unfolded his whole mission to the black servants of the two Swedes. These had not been long in retailing the matter to their masters, and the result was that when the runner left their camp to continue his journey he had scarce passed from sight before there came the report of a rifle and he rolled lifeless into the underbrush with a bullet in his back.

A few moments later Malbihn strolled back into the encampment, where he went to some pains to let it be known that he had had a shot at a fine buck and missed. The Swedes knew that their men hated them, and that an overt act against Kovudoo would quickly be carried to the chief at the first opportunity. Nor were they sufficiently strong in either guns or loyal followers to risk antagonizing the wily old chief.

Following this episode came the encounter with the baboons and the strange, white savage who had allied himself with the beasts against the humans. Only by dint of masterful maneuvering and the expenditure of much power had the Swedes been able to repulse the infuriated apes, and even for hours afterward their camp was constantly besieged by hundreds of snarling, screaming devils.

The Swedes, rifles in hand, repelled numerous savage charges which lacked only efficient leadership to have rendered them as effective in results as they were terrifying in appearance. Time and time again the two men thought they saw the smooth-skinned body of the wild ape-man moving among the baboons in the forest, and the belief that he might head a charge upon them proved most disquieting. They would have given much for a clean shot at him, for to him they attributed the loss of their specimen and the ugly attitude of the baboons toward them.

"The fellow must be the same we fired on several years ago," said Malbihn. "That time he was accompanied by a gorilla. Did you get a good look at him, Carl?"

"Yes," replied Jenssen. "He was not five paces from me when I fired at him. He appears to be an intelligent looking European – and not much more than a lad. There is nothing of the imbecile or degenerate in his features or expression, as is usually true in similar cases, where some lunatic escapes into the woods and by living in filth and nakedness wins the title of wild man among the peasants of the neighborhood. No, this fellow is of different stuff – and so infinitely more to be feared. As much as I should like a shot at him I hope he stays away. Should he ever deliberately lead a charge against us I wouldn't give much for our chances if we happened to fail to bag him at the first rush."

But the white giant did not appear again to lead the baboons against them, and finally the angry brutes themselves wandered off into the jungle leaving the frightened safari in peace.

The next day the Swedes set out for Kovudoo's village bent on securing possession of the person of the white girl whom Kovudoo's runner had told them lay captive in the chief's village. How they were to accomplish their end they did not know. Force was out of the question, though they would not have hesitated to use it had they possessed it. In former years they had marched rough shod over enormous areas, taking toll by brute force even when kindliness or diplomacy would have accomplished more; but now they were in bad straits – so bad that they had shown their true colors scarce twice in a year and then only when they came upon an isolated village, weak in numbers and poor in courage.

Kovudoo was not as these, and though his village was in a way remote from the more populous district to the north his power was such that he maintained an acknowledged suzerainty over the thin thread of villages which connected him with the savage lords to the north. To have antagonized him would have spelled ruin for the Swedes. It would have meant that they might never reach civilization by the northern route. To the west, the village of The Sheik lay directly in their path, barring them effectually. To the east the trail was unknown to them, and to the south there was no trail. So the two Swedes approached the village of Kovudoo with friendly words upon their tongues and deep craft in their hearts.

Their plans were well made. There was no mention of the white prisoner – they chose to pretend that they were not aware that Kovudoo had a white prisoner. They exchanged gifts with the old chief, haggling with his plenipotentiaries over the value of what they were to receive for what they gave, as is customary and proper when one has no ulterior motives. Unwarranted generosity would have aroused suspicion.

During the palaver which followed they retailed the gossip of the villages through which they had passed, receiving in exchange such news as Kovudoo possessed. The palaver was long and tiresome, as these native ceremonies always are to Europeans. Kovudoo made no mention of his prisoner and from his generous offers of guides and presents seemed anxious to assure himself of the speedy departure of his guests. It was Malbihn who, quite casually, near the close of their talk, mentioned the fact that The Sheik was dead. Kovudoo evinced interest and surprise.

"You did not know it?" asked Malbihn. "That is strange. It was during the last moon. He fell from his horse when the beast stepped in a hole. The horse fell upon him. When his men came up The Sheik was quite dead."

Kovudoo scratched his head. He was much disappointed. No Sheik meant no ransom for the white girl. Now she was worthless, unless he utilized her for a feast or – a mate. The latter thought aroused him. He spat at a small beetle crawling through the dust before him. He eyed Malbihn appraisingly. These white men were peculiar. They traveled far from their own villages without women. Yet he knew they cared for women. But how much did they care for them? – that was the question that disturbed Kovudoo.

"I know where there is a white girl," he said, unexpectedly. "If you wish to buy her she may be had cheap."

Malbihn shrugged. "We have troubles enough, Kovudoo," he said, "without burdening ourselves with an old she-hyena, and as for paying for one – " Malbihn snapped his fingers in derision.

"She is young," said Kovudoo, "and good looking."

The Swedes laughed. "There are no good looking white women in the jungle, Kovudoo," said Jenssen. "You should be ashamed to try to make fun of old friends."

Kovudoo sprang to his feet. "Come," he said, "I will show you that she is all I say."

Malbihn and Jenssen rose to follow him and as they did so their eyes met, and Malbihn slowly drooped one of his lids in a sly wink. Together they followed Kovudoo toward his hut. In the dim interior they discerned the figure of a woman lying bound upon a sleeping mat.

Malbihn took a single glance and turned away. "She must be a thousand years old, Kovudoo," he said, as he left the hut.

"She is young," cried the savage. "It is dark in here. You cannot see. Wait, I will have her brought out into the sunlight," and he commanded the two warriors who watched the girl to cut the bonds from her ankles and lead her forth for inspection.

Malbihn and Jenssen evinced no eagerness, though both were fairly bursting with it – not to see the girl but to obtain possession of her. They cared not if she had the face of a marmoset, or the figure of potbellied Kovudoo himself. All that they wished to know was that she was the girl who had been stolen from The Sheik several years before. They thought that they would recognize her for such if she was indeed the same, but even so the testimony of the runner Kovudoo had sent to The Sheik was such as to assure them that the girl was the one they had once before attempted to abduct.

As Meriem was brought forth from the darkness of the hut's interior the two men turned with every appearance of disinterestedness to glance at her. It was with difficulty that Malbihn suppressed an ejaculation of astonishment. The girl's beauty fairly took his breath from him; but instantly he recovered his poise and turned to Kovudoo.

"Well?" he said to the old chief.

"Is she not both young and good looking?" asked Kovudoo.

"She is not old," replied Malbihn; "but even so she will be a burden. We did not come from the north after wives – there are more than enough there for us."

Meriem stood looking straight at the white men. She expected nothing from them – they were to her as much enemies as the black men. She hated and feared them all. Malbihn spoke to her in Arabic.

"We are friends," he said. "Would you like to have us take you away from here?"

Slowly and dimly as though from a great distance recollection of the once familiar tongue returned to her.

"I should like to go free," she said, "and go back to Korak."

"You would like to go with us?" persisted Malbihn.

"No," said Meriem.

Malbihn turned to Kovudoo. "She does not wish to go with us," he said.

"You are men," returned the black. "Can you not take her by force?"

"It would only add to our troubles," replied the Swede. "No, Kovudoo, we do not wish her; though, if you wish to be rid of her, we will take her away because of our friendship for you."

Now Kovudoo knew that he had made a sale. They wanted her. So he commenced to bargain, and in the end the person of Meriem passed from the possession of the black chieftain into that of the two Swedes in consideration of six yards of Amerikan, three empty brass cartridge shells and a shiny, new jack knife from New Jersey. And all but Meriem were more than pleased with the bargain.

Kovudoo stipulated but a single condition and that was that the Europeans were to leave his village and take the girl with them as early the next morning as they could get started. After the sale was consummated he did not hesitate to explain his reasons for this demand. He told them of the strenuous attempt of the girl's savage mate to rescue her, and suggested that the sooner they got her out of the country the more likely they were to retain possession of her.

Meriem was again bound and placed under guard, but this time in the tent of the Swedes. Malbihn talked to her, trying to persuade her to accompany them willingly. He told her that they would return her to her own village; but when he discovered that she would rather die than go back to the old sheik, he assured her that they would not take her there, nor, as a matter of fact, had they had an intention of so doing. As he talked with the girl the Swede feasted his eyes upon the beautiful lines of her face and figure. She had grown tall and straight and slender toward maturity since he had seen her in The Sheik's village on that long gone day. For years she had represented to him a certain fabulous reward. In his thoughts she had been but the personification of the pleasures and luxuries that many francs would purchase. Now as she stood before him pulsing with life and loveliness she suggested other seductive and alluring possibilities. He came closer to her and laid his hand upon her. The girl shrank from him. He seized her and she struck him heavily in the mouth as he sought to kiss her. Then Jenssen entered the tent.

"Malbihn!" he almost shouted. "You fool!"

Sven Malbihn released his hold upon the girl and turned toward his companion. His face was red with mortification.

"What the devil are you trying to do?" growled Jenssen. "Would you throw away every chance for the reward? If we maltreat her we not only couldn't collect a sou, but they'd send us to prison for our pains. I thought you had more sense, Malbihn."

"I'm not a wooden man," growled Malbihn.

"You'd better be," rejoined Jenssen, "at least until we have delivered her over in safety and collected what will be coming to us."

"Oh, hell," cried Malbihn. "What's the use? They'll be glad enough to have her back, and by the time we get there with her she'll be only too glad to keep her mouth shut. Why not?"

"Because I say not," growled Jenssen. "I've always let you boss things, Sven; but here's a case where what I say has got to go – because I'm right and you're wrong, and we both know it."

"You're getting damned virtuous all of a sudden," growled Malbihn. "Perhaps you think I have forgotten about the inn keeper's daughter, and little Celella, and that nigger at – "

"Shut up!" snapped Jenssen. "It's not a matter of virtue and you are as well aware of that as I. I don't want to quarrel with you, but so help me God, Sven, you're not going to harm this girl if I have to kill you to prevent it. I've suffered and slaved and been nearly killed forty times in the last nine or ten years trying to accomplish what luck has thrown at our feet at last, and now I'm not going to be robbed of the fruits of success because you happen to be more of a beast than a man. Again I warn you, Sven – " and he tapped the revolver that swung in its holster at his hip.

Malbihn gave his friend an ugly look, shrugged his shoulders, and left the tent. Jenssen turned to Meriem.

"If he bothers you again, call me," he said. "I shall always be near."

The girl had not understood the conversation that had been carried on by her two owners, for it had been in Swedish; but what Jenssen had just said to her in Arabic she understood and from it grasped an excellent idea of what had passed between the two. The expressions upon their faces, their gestures, and Jenssen's final tapping of his revolver before Malbihn had left the tent had all been eloquent of the seriousness of their altercation. Now, toward Jenssen she looked for friendship, and with the innocence of youth she threw herself upon his mercy, begging him to set her free, that she might return to Korak and her jungle life; but she was doomed to another disappointment, for the man only laughed at her roughly and told her that if she tried to escape she would be punished by the very thing that he had just saved her from.

All that night she lay listening for a signal from Korak. All about the jungle life moved through the darkness. To her sensitive ears came sounds that the others in the camp could not hear – sounds that she interpreted as we might interpret the speech of a friend, but not once came a single note that reflected the presence of Korak. But she knew that he would come. Nothing short of death itself could prevent her Korak from returning for her. What delayed him though?

When morning came again and the night had brought no succoring Korak, Meriem's faith and loyalty were still unshaken though misgivings began to assail her as to the safety of her friend. It seemed unbelievable that serious mishap could have overtaken her wonderful Korak who daily passed unscathed through all the terrors of the jungle. Yet morning came, the morning meal was eaten, the camp broken and the disreputable safari of the Swedes was on the move northward with still no sign of the rescue the girl momentarily expected.

All that day they marched, and the next and the next, nor did Korak even so much as show himself to the patient little waiter moving, silently and stately, beside her hard captors.

Malbihn remained scowling and angry. He replied to Jenssen's friendly advances in curt monosyllables. To Meriem he did not speak, but on several occasions she discovered him glaring at her from beneath half closed lids – greedily. The look sent a shudder through her. She hugged Geeka closer to her breast and doubly regretted the knife that they had taken from her when she was captured by Kovudoo.

It was on the fourth day that Meriem began definitely to give up hope. Something had happened to Korak. She knew it. He would never come now, and these men would take her far away. Presently they would kill her. She would never see her Korak again.

On this day the Swedes rested, for they had marched rapidly and their men were tired. Malbihn and Jenssen had gone from camp to hunt, taking different directions. They had been gone about an hour when the door of Meriem's tent was lifted and Malbihn entered. The look of a beast was on his face.

Chapter Fourteen

WITH WIDE EYES FIXED upon him, like a trapped creature horrified beneath the mesmeric gaze of a great serpent, the girl watched the approach of the man. Her hands were free, the Swedes having secured her with a length of ancient slave chain fastened at one end to an iron collar padlocked about her neck and at the other to a long stake driven deep into the ground.

Slowly Meriem shrank inch by inch toward the opposite end of the tent. Malbihn followed her. His hands were extended and his fingers half-opened – claw-like – to seize her. His lips were parted, and his breath came quickly, pantingly.

The girl recalled Jenssen's instructions to call him should Malbihn molest her; but Jenssen had gone into the jungle to hunt. Malbihn had chosen his time well. Yet she screamed, loud and shrill, once, twice, a third time, before Malbihn could leap across the tent and throttle her alarming cries with his brute fingers. Then she fought him, as any jungle she might fight, with tooth and nail. The man found her no easy prey. In that slender, young body, beneath the rounded curves and the fine, soft skin, lay the muscles of a young lioness. But Malbihn was no weakling. His character and appearance were brutal, nor did they belie his brawn. He was of giant stature and of giant strength. Slowly he forced the girl back upon the ground, striking her in the face when she hurt him badly either with teeth or nails. Meriem struck back, but she was growing weaker from the choking fingers at her throat.

Out in the jungle Jenssen had brought down two bucks. His hunting had not carried him far afield, nor was he prone to permit it to do so. He was suspicious of Malbihn. The very fact that his companion had refused to accompany him and elected instead to hunt alone in another direction would not, under ordinary circumstances, have seemed fraught with sinister suggestion; but Jenssen knew Malbihn well, and so, having secured meat, he turned immediately back toward camp, while his boys brought in his kill.

He had covered about half the return journey when a scream came faintly to his ears from the direction of camp. He halted to listen. It was repeated twice. Then silence. With a muttered curse Jenssen broke into a rapid run. He wondered if he would be too late. What a fool Malbihn was indeed to thus chance jeopardizing a fortune!

Further away from camp than Jenssen and upon the opposite side another heard Meriem's screams – a stranger who was not even aware of the proximity of white men other than himself – a hunter with a handful of sleek, black warriors. He, too, listened intently for a moment. That the voice was that of a woman in distress he could not doubt, and so he also hastened at a run in the direction of the affrighted voice; but he was much further away than Jenssen so that the latter reached the tent first. What the Swede found there roused no pity within his calloused heart, only anger against his fellow scoundrel. Meriem was still fighting off her attacker. Malbihn still was showering blows upon her. Jenssen, streaming foul curses upon his erstwhile friend, burst into the tent. Malbihn, interrupted, dropped his victim and turned to meet Jenssen's infuriated charge. He whipped a revolver from his hip. Jenssen, anticipating the lightning move of the other's hand, drew almost simultaneously, and both men fired at once. Jenssen was still moving toward Malbihn at the time, but at the flash of the explosion he stopped. His revolver dropped from nerveless fingers. For a moment he staggered drunkenly. Deliberately Malbihn put two more bullets into his friend's body at close range. Even in the midst of the excitement and her terror Meriem found herself wondering at the tenacity of life which the hit man displayed. His eyes were closed, his head dropped forward upon his breast, his hands hung limply before him. Yet still he stood there upon his feet, though he reeled horribly. It was not until the third bullet had found its mark within his body that he lunged forward upon his face. Then Malbihn approached him, and with an oath kicked him viciously. Then he returned once more to Meriem. Again he seized her, and at the same instant the flaps of the tent opened silently and a tall white man stood in the aperture. Neither Meriem or Malbihn saw the newcomer. The latter's back was toward him while his body hid the stranger from Meriem's eyes.

He crossed the tent quickly, stepping over Jenssen's body. The first intimation Malbihn had that he was not to carry out his design without further interruption was a heavy hand upon his shoulder. He wheeled to face an utter stranger – a tall, black-haired, gray-eyed stranger clad in khaki and pith helmet. Malbihn reached for his gun again, but another hand had been quicker than his and he saw the weapon tossed to the ground at the side of the tent – out of reach.

"What is the meaning of this?" the stranger addressed his question to Meriem in a tongue she did not understand. She shook her head and spoke in Arabic. Instantly the man changed his question to that language.

"These men are taking me away from Korak," explained the girl. "This one would have harmed me. The other, whom he had just killed, tried to stop him. They were both very bad men; but this one is the worse. If my Korak were here he would kill him. I suppose you are like them, so you will not kill him."

The stranger smiled. "He deserves killing," he said. "There is no doubt of that. Once I should have killed him; but not now. I will see, though, that he does not bother you any more."

He was holding Malbihn in a grasp the giant Swede could not break, though he struggled to do so, and he was holding him as easily as Malbihn might have held a little child, yet Malbihn was a huge man, mightily thewed. The Swede began to rage and curse. He struck at his captor, only to be twisted about and held at arm's length. Then he shouted to his boys to come and kill the stranger. In response a dozen strange blacks entered the tent. They, too, were powerful, clean-limbed men, not at all like the mangy crew that followed the Swedes.

"We have had enough foolishness," said the stranger to Malbihn. "You deserve death, but I am not the law. I know now who you are. I have heard of you before. You and your friend here bear a most unsavory reputation. We do not want you in our country. I shall let you go this time; but should you ever return I shall take the law into my own hands. You understand?"

Malbihn blustered and threatened, finishing by applying a most uncomplimentary name to his captor. For this he received a shaking that rattled his teeth. Those who know say that the most painful punishment that can be inflicted upon an adult male, short of injuring him, is a good, old fashioned shaking. Malbihn received such a shaking.

"Now get out," said the stranger, "and next time you see me remember who I am," and he spoke a name in the Swede's ear – a name that more effectually subdued the scoundrel than many beatings – then he gave him a push that carried him bodily through the tent doorway to sprawl upon the turf beyond.

"Now," he said, turning toward Meriem, "who has the key to this thing about your neck?"

The girl pointed to Jenssen's body. "He carried it always," she said.

The stranger searched the clothing on the corpse until he came upon the key. A moment more Meriem was free.

"Will you let me go back to my Korak?" she asked.

"I will see that you are returned to your people," he replied. "Who are they and where is their village?"

He had been eyeing her strange, barbaric garmenture wonderingly. From her speech she was evidently an Arab girl; but he had never before seen one thus clothed.

"Who are your people? Who is Korak?" he asked again.

"Korak! Why Korak is an ape. I have no other people. Korak and I live in the jungle alone since A'ht went to be king of the apes." She had always thus pronounced Akut's name, for so it had sounded to her when first she came with Korak and the ape. "Korak could have been kind, but he would not."

A questioning expression entered the stranger's eyes. He looked at the girl closely.

"So Korak is an ape?" he said. "And what, pray, are you?"

"I am Meriem. I, also, am an ape."

"M-m," was the stranger's only oral comment upon this startling announcement; but what he thought might have been partially interpreted through the pitying light that entered his eyes. He approached the girl and started to lay his hand upon her forehead. She drew back with a savage little growl. A smile touched his lips.

"You need not fear me," he said. "I shall not harm you. I only wish to discover if you have fever – if you are entirely well. If you are we will set forth in search of Korak."

Meriem looked straight into the keen gray eyes. She must have found there an unquestionable assurance of the honorableness of their owner, for she permitted him to lay his palm upon her forehead and feel her pulse. Apparently she had no fever.

"How long have you been an ape?" asked the man.

"Since I was a little girl, many, many years ago, and Korak came and took me from my father who was beating me. Since then I have lived in the trees with Korak and A'ht."

"Where in the jungle lives Korak?" asked the stranger.

Meriem pointed with a sweep of her hand that took in, generously, half the continent of Africa.

"Could you find your way back to him?"

"I do not know," she replied; "but he will find his way to me."

"Then I have a plan," said the stranger. "I live but a few marches from here. I shall take you home where my wife will look after you and care for you until we can find Korak or Korak finds us. If he could find you here he can find you at my village. Is it not so?"

Meriem thought that it was so; but she did not like the idea of not starting immediately back to meet Korak. On the other hand the man had no intention of permitting this poor, insane child to wander further amidst the dangers of the jungle. From whence she had come, or what she had undergone he could not guess, but that her Korak and their life among the apes was but a figment of a disordered mind he could not doubt. He knew the jungle well, and he knew that men have lived alone and naked among the savage beasts for years; but a frail and slender girl! No, it was not possible.

Together they went outside. Malbihn's boys were striking camp in preparation for a hasty departure. The stranger's blacks were conversing with them. Malbihn stood at a distance, angry and glowering. The stranger approached one of his own men.

"Find out where they got this girl," he commanded.

The Negro thus addressed questioned one of Malbihn's followers. Presently he returned to his master.

"They bought her from old Kovudoo," he said. "That is all that this fellow will tell me. He pretends that he knows nothing more, and I guess that he does not. These two white men were very bad men. They did many things that their boys knew not the meanings of. It would be well, Bwana, to kill the other."

"I wish that I might; but a new law is come into this part of the jungle. It is not as it was in the old days, Muviri," replied the master.

The stranger remained until Malbihn and his safari had disappeared into the jungle toward the north. Meriem, trustful now, stood at his side, Geeka clutched in one slim, brown hand. They talked together, the man wondering at the faltering Arabic of the girl, but attributing it finally to her defective mentality. Could he have known that years had elapsed since she had used it until she was taken by the Swedes he would not have wondered that she had half forgotten it. There was yet another reason why the language of The Sheik had thus readily eluded her; but of that reason she herself could not have guessed the truth any better than could the man.

He tried to persuade her to return with him to his "village" as he called it, or douar, in Arabic; but she was insistent upon searching immediately for Korak. As a last resort he determined to take her with him by force rather than sacrifice her life to the insane hallucination which haunted her; but, being a wise man, he determined to humor her first and then attempt to lead her as he would have her go. So when they took up their march it was in the direction of the south, though his own ranch lay almost due east.

By degrees he turned the direction of their way more and more eastward, and greatly was he pleased to note that the girl failed to discover that any change was being made. Little by little she became more trusting. At first she had had but her intuition to guide her belief that this big Tarmangani meant her no harm, but as the days passed and she saw that his kindness and consideration never faltered she came to compare him with Korak, and to be very fond of him; but never did her loyalty to her apeman flag.

On the fifth day they came suddenly upon a great plain and from the edge of the forest the girl saw in the distance fenced fields and many buildings. At the sight she drew back in astonishment.

"Where are we?" she asked, pointing.

"We could not find Korak," replied the man, "and as our way led near my douar I have brought you here to wait and rest with my wife until my men can find your ape, or he finds you. It is better thus, little one. You will be safer with us, and you will be happier."

"I am afraid, Bwana," said the girl. "In thy douar they will beat me as did The Sheik, my father. Let me go back into the jungle. There Korak will find me. He would not think to look for me in the douar of a white man."

"No one will beat you, child," replied the man. "I have not done so, have I? Well, here all belong to me. They will treat you well. Here no one is beaten. My wife will be very good to you, and at last Korak will come, for I shall send men to search for him."

The girl shook her head. "They could not bring him, for he would kill them, as all men have tried to kill him. I am afraid. Let me go, Bwana."

"You do not know the way to your own country. You would be lost. The leopards or the lions would get you the first night, and after all you would not find your Korak. It is better that you stay with us. Did I not save you from the bad man? Do you not owe me something for that? Well, then remain with us for a few weeks at least until we can determine what is best for you. You are only a little girl – it would be wicked to permit you to go alone into the jungle."

Meriem laughed. "The jungle," she said, "is my father and my mother. It has been kinder to me than have men. I am not afraid of the jungle. Nor am I afraid of the leopard or the lion. When my time comes I shall die.

It may be that a leopard or a lion shall kill me, or it may be a tiny bug no bigger than the end of my littlest finger. When the lion leaps upon me, or the little bug stings me I shall be afraid – oh, then I shall be terribly afraid, I know; but life would be very miserable indeed were I to spend it in terror of the thing that has not yet happened. If it be the lion my terror shall be short of life; but if it be the little bug I may suffer for days before I die. And so I fear the lion least of all. He is great and noisy. I can hear him, or see him, or smell him in time to escape; but any moment I may place a hand or foot on the little bug, and never know that he is there until I feel his deadly sting. No, I do not fear the jungle. I love it. I should rather die than leave it forever; but your douar is close beside the jungle. You have been good to me. I will do as you wish, and remain here for a while to wait the coming of my Korak."

"Good!" said the man, and he led the way down toward the flower-covered bungalow behind which lay the barns and out-houses of a well-ordered African farm.

As they came nearer a dozen dogs ran barking toward them – gaunt wolf hounds, a huge great Dane, a nimble-footed collie and a number of yapping, quarrelsome fox terriers. At first their appearance was savage and unfriendly in the extreme; but once they recognized the foremost black warriors, and the white man behind them their attitude underwent a remarkable change. The collie and the fox terriers became frantic with delirious joy, and while the wolf hounds and the great Dane were not a whit less delighted at the return of their master their greetings were of a more dignified nature. Each in turn sniffed at Meriem who displayed not the slightest fear of any of them.

The wolf hounds bristled and growled at the scent of wild beasts that clung to her garment; but when she laid her hand upon their heads and her soft voice murmured caressingly they half-closed their eyes, lifting their upper lips in contented canine smiles. The man was watching them and he too smiled, for it was seldom that these savage brutes took thus kindly to strangers. It was as though in some subtile way the girl had breathed a message of kindred savagery to their savage hearts.

With her slim fingers grasping the collar of a wolf hound upon either side of her Meriem walked on toward the bungalow upon the porch of which a woman dressed in white waved a welcome to her returning lord. There was more fear in the girl's eyes now than there had been in the presence of strange men or savage beasts. She hesitated, turning an appealing glance toward the man.

"This is my wife," he said. "She will be glad to welcome you."

The woman came down the path to meet them. The man kissed her, and turning toward Meriem introduced them, speaking in the Arab tongue the girl understood.

"This is Meriem, my dear," he said, and he told the story of the jungle waif in so far as he knew it.

Meriem saw that the woman was beautiful. She saw that sweetness and goodness were stamped indelibly upon her countenance. She no longer feared her, and when her brief story had been narrated and the woman came and put her arms about her and kissed her and called her "poor little darling" something snapped in Meriem's little heart. She buried her face on the bosom of this new friend in whose voice was the mother tone that Meriem had not heard for so many years that she had forgotten its very existence. She buried her face on the kindly bosom and wept as she had not wept before in all her life – tears of relief and joy that she could not fathom.

And so came Meriem, the savage little Mangani, out of her beloved jungle into the midst of a home of culture and refinement. Already "Bwana" and "My Dear," as she first heard them called and continued to call them, were as father and mother to her. Once her savage fears allayed, she went to the opposite extreme of trustfulness and love. Now she was willing to wait here until they found Korak, or Korak found her. She did not give up that thought – Korak, her Korak always was first.

Chapter Fifteen

AND OUT IN THE jungle, far away, Korak, covered with wounds, stiff with clotted blood, burning with rage and sorrow, swung back upon the trail of the great baboons. He had not found them where he had last seen them, nor in any of their usual haunts; but he sought them along the well-marked spoor they had left behind them, and at last he overtook them. When first he came upon them they were moving slowly but steadily southward in one of those periodic migrations the reasons for which the baboon himself is best able to explain. At sight of the white warrior who came upon them from down wind the herd halted in response to the warning cry of the sentinel that had discovered him. There was much growling and muttering; much stiff-legged circling on the part of the bulls. The mothers, in nervous, high pitched tones, called their young to their sides, and with them moved to safety behind their lords and masters.

Korak called aloud to the king, who, at the familiar voice, advanced slowly, warily, and still stiff-legged. He must have the confirmatory evidence of his nose before venturing to rely too implicitly upon the testimony of his ears and eyes. Korak stood perfectly still. To have advanced then might have precipitated an immediate attack, or, as easily, a panic of flight. Wild beasts are creatures of nerves. It is a relatively simple thing to throw them into a species of hysteria which may induce either a mania for murder, or symptoms of apparent abject cowardice – it is a question, however, if a wild animal ever is actually a coward.

The king baboon approached Korak. He walked around him in an ever decreasing circle – growling, grunting, sniffing. Korak spoke to him.

"I am Korak," he said. "I opened the cage that held you. I saved you from the Tarmangani. I am Korak, The Killer. I am your friend."

"Huh," grunted the king. "Yes, you are Korak. My ears told me that you were Korak. My eyes told me that you were Korak. Now my nose tells me that you are Korak. My nose is never wrong. I am your friend. Come, we shall hunt together."

"Korak cannot hunt now," replied the ape-man. "The Gomangani have stolen Meriem. They have tied her in their village. They will not let her go. Korak, alone, was unable to set her free. Korak set you free. Now will you bring your people and set Korak's Meriem free?"

"The Gomangani have many sharp sticks which they throw. They pierce the bodies of my people. They kill us. The gomangani are bad people. They will kill us all if we enter their village."

"The Tarmangani have sticks that make a loud noise and kill at a great distance," replied Korak. "They had these when Korak set you free from their trap. If Korak had run away from them you would now be a prisoner among the Tarmangani."

The baboon scratched his head. In a rough circle about him and the ape-man squatted the bulls of his herd. They blinked their eyes, shouldered one another about for more advantageous positions, scratched in the rotting vegetation upon the chance of unearthing a toothsome worm, or sat listlessly eyeing their king and the strange Mangani, who called himself thus but who more closely resembled the hated Tarmangani. The king looked at some of the older of his subjects, as though inviting suggestion.

"We are too few," grunted one.

"There are the baboons of the hill country," suggested another. "They are as many as the leaves of the forest. They, too, hate the Gomangani. They love to fight. They are very savage. Let us ask them to accompany us. Then can we kill all the Gomangani in the jungle." He rose and growled horribly, bristling his stiff hair.

"That is the way to talk," cried The Killer, "but we do not need the baboons of the hill country. We are enough. It will take a long time to fetch them. Meriem may be dead and eaten before we could free her. Let us set out at once for the village of the Gomangani. If we travel very fast it will not take long to reach it. Then, all at the same time, we can charge into the village, growling and barking. The Gomangani will be very frightened and will run away. While they are gone we can seize Meriem and carry her off. We do not have to kill or be killed – all that Korak wishes is his Meriem."

"We are too few," croaked the old ape again.

"Yes, we are too few," echoed others.

Korak could not persuade them. They would help him, gladly; but they must do it in their own way and that meant enlisting the services of their kinsmen and allies of the hill country. So Korak was forced to give in. All he could do for the present was to urge them to haste, and at his suggestion the king baboon with a dozen of his mightiest bulls agreed to go to the hill country with Korak, leaving the balance of the herd behind.

Once enlisted in the adventure the baboons became quite enthusiastic about it. The delegation set off immediately. They traveled swiftly; but the ape-man found no difficulty in keeping up with them. They made a tremendous racket as they passed through the trees in an endeavor to suggest to enemies in their front that a great herd was approaching, for when the baboons travel in large numbers there is no jungle creature who cares to molest them. When the nature of the country required much travel upon the level, and the distance between trees was great, they moved silently, knowing that the lion and the leopard would not be fooled by noise when they could see plainly for themselves that only a handful of baboons were on the trail.

For two days the party raced through the savage country, passing out of the dense jungle into an open plain, and across this to timbered mountain slopes. Here Korak never before had been. It was a new country to him and the change from the monotony of the circumscribed view in the jungle was pleasing. But he had little desire to enjoy the beauties of nature at this time. Meriem, his Meriem was in danger. Until she was freed and returned to him he had little thought for aught else.

Once in the forest that clothed the mountain slopes the baboons advanced more slowly. Constantly they gave tongue to a plaintive note of calling. Then would follow silence while they listened. At last, faintly from the distance straight ahead came an answer.

The baboons continued to travel in the direction of the voices that floated through the forest to them in the intervals of their own silence. Thus, calling and listening, they came closer to their kinsmen, who, it was evident to Korak, were coming to meet them in great numbers; but when, at last, the baboons of the hill country came in view the ape-man was staggered at the reality that broke upon his vision.

What appeared a solid wall of huge baboons rose from the ground through the branches of the trees to the loftiest terrace to which they dared entrust their weight. Slowly they were approaching, voicing their weird, plaintive call, and behind them, as far as Korak's eyes could pierce the verdure, rose solid walls of their fellows treading close upon their heels. There were thousands of them. The ape-man could not but think of the fate of his little party should some untoward incident arouse even momentarily the rage of fear of a single one of all these thousands.

But nothing such befell. The two kings approached one another, as was their custom, with much sniffing and bristling. They satisfied themselves of each other's identity. Then each scratched the other's back. After a moment they spoke together. Korak's friend explained the nature of their visit, and for the first time Korak showed himself. He had been hiding behind a bush. The excitement among the hill baboons was intense at sight of him. For a moment Korak feared that he should be torn to pieces; but his fear was for Meriem. Should he die there would be none to succor her.

The two kings, however, managed to quiet the multitude, and Korak was permitted to approach. Slowly the hill baboons came closer to him. They sniffed at him from every angle. When he spoke to them in their own tongue they were filled with wonder and delight. They talked to him and listened while he spoke. He told them of Meriem, and of their life in the jungle where they were the friends of all the ape folk from little Manu to Mangani, the great ape.

"The Gomangani, who are keeping Meriem from me, are no friends of yours," he said. "They kill you. The baboons of the low country are too few to go against them. They tell me that you are very many and very brave – that your numbers are as the numbers of the grasses upon the plains or the leaves within the forest, and that even Tantor, the elephant, fears you, so brave you are. They told me that you would be happy to accompany us to the village of the Gomangani and punish these bad people while I, Korak, The Killer, carry away my Meriem."

The king ape puffed out his chest and strutted about very stiff-legged indeed. So also did many of the other great bulls of his nation. They were pleased and flattered by the words of the strange Tarmangani, who called himself Mangani and spoke the language of the hairy progenitors of man.

"Yes," said one, "we of the hill country are mighty fighters. Tantor fears us. Numa fears us. Sheeta fears us. The Gomangani of the hill country are glad to pass us by in peace. I, for one, will come with you to the village of the Gomangani of the low places. I am the king's first he-child. Alone can I kill all the Gomangani of the low country," and he swelled his chest and strutted proudly back and forth, until the itching back of a comrade commanded his industrious attention.

"I am Goob," cried another. "My fighting fangs are long. They are sharp. They are strong. Into the soft flesh of many a Gomangani have they been buried. Alone I slew the sister of Sheeta. Goob will go to the low country with you and kill so many of the Gomangani that there will be none left to count the dead," and then he, too, strutted and pranced before the admiring eyes of the shes and the young.

Korak looked at the king, questioningly.

"Your bulls are very brave," he said; "but braver than any is the king."

Thus addressed, the shaggy bull, still in his prime – else he had been no longer king – growled ferociously. The forest echoed to his lusty challenges. The little baboons clutched fearfully at their mothers' hairy necks. The bulls, electrified, leaped high in air and took up the roaring challenge of their king. The din was terrific.

Korak came close to the king and shouted in his ear, "Come." Then he started off through the forest toward the plain that they must cross on their long journey back to the village of Kovudoo, the Gomangani. The king, still roaring and shrieking, wheeled and followed him. In their wake came the handful of low country baboons and the thousands of the hill clan – savage, wiry, dog-like creatures, athirst for blood.

And so they came, upon the second day, to the village of Kovudoo. It was mid-afternoon. The village was sunk in the quiet of the great equatorial sun-heat. The mighty herd traveled quietly now. Beneath the thousands of padded feet the forest gave forth no greater sound than might have been produced by the increased soughing of a stronger breeze through the leafy branches of the trees.

Korak and the two kings were in the lead. Close beside the village they halted until the stragglers had closed up. Now utter silence reigned. Korak, creeping stealthily, entered the tree that overhung the palisade. He glanced behind him. The pack were close upon his heels. The time had come. He had warned them continuously during the long march that no harm must befall the white she who lay a prisoner within the village. All others were their legitimate prey. Then, raising his face toward the sky, he gave voice to a single cry. It was the signal.

In response three thousand hairy bulls leaped screaming and barking into the village of the terrified blacks. Warriors poured from every hut. Mothers gathered their babies in their arms and fled toward the gates as they saw the horrid horde pouring into the village street. Kovudoo marshaled his fighting men about him and, leaping and yelling to arouse their courage, offered a bristling, spear tipped front to the charging horde.

Korak, as he had led the march, led the charge. The blacks were struck with horror and dismay at the sight of this white-skinned youth at the head of a pack of hideous baboons. For an instant they held their ground, hurling their spears once at the advancing multitude; but before they could fit arrows to their bows they wavered, gave, and turned in terrified rout. Into their ranks, upon their backs, sinking strong fangs into the muscles of their necks sprang the baboons and first among them, most ferocious, most blood-thirsty, most terrible was Korak, The Killer.

At the village gates, through which the blacks poured in panic, Korak left them to the tender mercies of his allies and turned himself eagerly toward the hut in which Meriem had been a prisoner. It was empty. One after another the filthy interiors revealed the same disheartening fact – Meriem was in none of them. That she had not been taken by the blacks in their flight from the village Korak knew for he had watched carefully for a glimpse of her among the fugitives.

To the mind of the ape-man, knowing as he did the proclivities of the savages, there was but a single explanation – Meriem had been killed and eaten. With the conviction that Meriem was dead there surged through Korak's brain a wave of blood red rage against those he believed to be her murderer. In the distance he could hear the snarling of the baboons mixed with the screams of their victims, and towards this he made his way. When he came upon them the baboons had commenced to tire of the sport of battle, and the blacks in a little knot were making a new stand, using their knob sticks effectively upon the few bulls who still persisted in attacking them.

Among these broke Korak from the branches of a tree above them – swift, relentless, terrible, he hurled himself upon the savage warriors of Kovudoo. Blind fury possessed him. Too, it protected him by its very ferocity. Like a wounded lioness he was here, there, everywhere, striking terrific blows with hard fists and with the precision and timeliness of the trained fighter. Again and again he buried his teeth in the flesh of a foeman. He was upon one and gone again to another before an effective blow could be dealt him. Yet, though great was the weight of his execution in determining the result of the combat, it was outweighed by the terror which he inspired in the simple, superstitious minds of his foeman. To them this white warrior, who consorted with the great apes and the fierce baboons, who growled and snarled and snapped like a beast, was not human. He was a demon of the forest – a fearsome god of evil whom they had offended, and who had come out of his lair deep in the jungle to punish them. And because of this belief there were many who offered but little defense, feeling as they did the futility of pitting their puny mortal strength against that of a deity.

Those who could fled, until at last there were no more to pay the penalty for a deed, which, while not beyond them, they were, nevertheless, not guilty of. Panting and bloody, Korak paused for want of further victims. The baboons gathered about him, sated themselves with blood and battle. They lolled upon the ground, fagged.

In the distance Kovudoo was gathering his scattered tribesmen, and taking account of injuries and losses. His people were panic stricken. Nothing could prevail upon them to remain longer in this country. They would not even return to the village for their belongings. Instead they insisted upon continuing their flight until they had put many miles between themselves and the stamping ground of the demon who had so bitterly attacked them. And thus it befell that Korak drove from their homes the only people who might have aided him in a search for Meriem, and cut off the only connecting link between him and her from whomsoever might come in search of him from the douar of the kindly Bwana who had befriended his little jungle sweetheart.

It was a sour and savage Korak who bade farewell to his baboon allies upon the following morning. They wished him to accompany him; but the ape-man had no heart for the society of any. Jungle life had encouraged taciturnity in him. His sorrow had deepened this to a sullen moroseness that could not brook even the savage companionship of the ill-natured baboons.

Brooding and despondent he took his solitary way into the deepest jungle. He moved along the ground when he knew that Numa was abroad and hungry. He took to the same trees that harbored Sheeta, the panther. He courted death in a hundred ways and a hundred forms. His mind was ever occupied with reminiscences of Meriem and the happy years that they had spent together. He realized now to the full what she had meant to him. The sweet face, the tanned, supple, little body, the bright smile that always had welcomed his return from the hunt haunted him continually.

Inaction soon threatened him with madness. He must be on the go. He must fill his days with labor and excitement that he might forget – that night might find him so exhausted that he should sleep in blessed unconsciousness of his misery until a new day had come.

Had he guessed that by any possibility Meriem might still live he would at least have had hope. His days could have been devoted to searching for her; but he implicitly believed that she was dead.

For a long year he led his solitary, roaming life. Occasionally he fell in with Akut and his tribe, hunting with them for a day or two; or he might travel to the hill country where the baboons had come to accept him as a matter of course; but most of all was he with Tantor, the elephant – the great gray battle ship of the jungle – the super-dreadnaught of his savage world.

The peaceful quiet of the monster bulls, the watchful solicitude of the mother cows, the awkward playfulness of the calves rested, interested, and amused Korak. The life of the huge beasts took his mind, temporarily from his own grief. He came to love them as he loved not even the great apes, and there was one gigantic tusker in particular of which he was very fond – the lord of the herd – a savage beast that was wont to charge a stranger upon the slightest provocation, or upon no provocation whatsoever. And to Korak this mountain of destruction was docile and affectionate as a lap dog.

He came when Korak called. He wound his trunk about the ape-man's body and lifted him to his broad neck in response to a gesture, and there would Korak lie at full length kicking his toes affectionately into the thick hide and brushing the flies from about the tender ears of his colossal chum with a leafy branch torn from a nearby tree by Tantor for the purpose.

And all the while Meriem was scarce a hundred miles away.

Chapter Sixteen

To Meriem, in her new home, the days passed quickly. At first she was all anxiety to be off into the jungle searching for her Korak. Bwana, as she insisted upon calling her benefactor, dissuaded her from making the attempt at once by dispatching a head man with a party of blacks to Kovudoo's village with instructions to learn from the old savage how he came into possession of the white girl and as much of her antecedents as might be culled from the black chieftain. Bwana particularly charged his head man with the duty of questioning Kovudoo relative to the strange character whom the girl called Korak, and of searching for the ape-man if he found the slightest evidence upon which to ground a belief in the existence of such an individual. Bwana was more than fully convinced that Korak was a creature of the girl's disordered imagination. He believed that the terrors and hardships she had undergone during captivity among the blacks and her frightful experience with the two Swedes had unbalanced her mind but as the days passed and he became better acquainted with her and able to observe her under the ordinary conditions of the quiet of his African home he was forced to admit that her strange tale puzzled him not a little, for there was no other evidence whatever that Meriem was not in full possession of her normal faculties.

The white man's wife, whom Meriem had christened "My Dear" from having first heard her thus addressed by Bwana, took not only a deep interest in the little jungle waif because of her forlorn and friendless state, but grew to love her as well for her sunny disposition and natural charm of temperament. And Meriem, similarly impressed by little attributes in the gentle, cultured woman, reciprocated the other's regard and affection.

And so the days flew by while Meriem waited the return of the head man and his party from the country of Kovudoo. They were short days, for into them were crowded many hours of insidious instruction of the unlettered child by the lonely woman. She commenced at once to teach the girl English without forcing it upon her as a task. She varied the instruction with lessons in sewing and deportment, nor once did she let Meriem guess that it was not all play. Nor was this difficult, since the girl was avid to learn. Then there were pretty dresses to be made to take the place of the single leopard skin and in this she found the child as responsive and enthusiastic as any civilized miss of her acquaintance.

A month passed before the head man returned – a month that had transformed the savage, half-naked little tarmangani into a daintily frocked girl of at least outward civilization. Meriem had progressed rapidly with the intricacies of the English language, for Bwana and My Dear had persistently refused to speak Arabic from the time they had decided that Meriem must learn English, which had been a day or two after her introduction into their home.

The report of the head man plunged Meriem into a period of despondency, for he had found the village of Kovudoo deserted nor, search as he would, could he discover a single native anywhere in the vicinity. For some time he had camped near the village, spending the days in a systematic search of the environs for traces of Meriem's Korak; but in this quest, too, had he failed. He had seen neither apes nor ape-man. Meriem at first insisted upon setting forth herself in search of Korak, but Bwana prevailed upon her to wait. He would go himself, he assured her, as soon as he could find the time, and at last Meriem consented to abide by his wishes; but it was months before she ceased to mourn almost hourly for her Korak.

My Dear grieved with the grieving girl and did her best to comfort and cheer her. She told her that if Korak lived he would find her; but all the time she believed that Korak had never existed beyond the child's dreams. She planned amusements to distract Meriem's attention from her sorrow, and she instituted a well-designed campaign to impress upon the child the desirability of civilized life and customs. Nor was this difficult, as she was soon to learn, for it rapidly became evident that beneath the uncouth savagery of the girl was a bed rock of innate refinement – a nicety of taste and predilection that quite equaled that of her instructor.

My Dear was delighted. She was lonely and childless, and so she lavished upon this little stranger all the mother love that would have gone to her own had she had one. The result was that by the end of the first year none might have guessed that Meriem ever had existed beyond the lap of culture and luxury.

She was sixteen now, though she easily might have passed for nineteen, and she was very good to look upon, with her black hair and her tanned skin and all the freshness and purity of health and innocence. Yet she still nursed her secret sorrow, though she no longer mentioned it to My Dear. Scarce an hour passed that did not bring its recollection of Korak, and its poignant yearning to see him again.

Meriem spoke English fluently now, and read and wrote it as well. One day My Dear spoke jokingly to her in French and to her surprise Meriem replied in the same tongue – slowly, it is true, and haltingly; but none the less in excellent French, such, though, as a little child might use. Thereafter they spoke a little French each day, and My Dear often marveled that the girl learned this language with a facility that was at times almost uncanny. At first Meriem had puckered her narrow, arched, little eye brows as though trying to force recollection of something all but forgotten which the new words suggested, and then, to her own astonishment as well as to that of her teacher she had used other French words than those in the lessons – used them properly and with a pronunciation that the English woman knew was more perfect than her own; but Meriem could neither read nor write what she spoke so well, and as My Dear considered a knowledge of correct English of the first importance, other than conversational French was postponed for a later day.

"You doubtless heard French spoken at times in your father's douar," suggested My Dear, as the most reasonable explanation.

Meriem shook her head.

"It may be," she said, "but I do not recall ever having seen a Frenchman in my father's company – he hated them and would have nothing whatever to do with them, and I am quite sure that I never heard any of these words before, yet at the same time I find them all familiar. I cannot understand it."

"Neither can I," agreed My Dear.

It was about this time that a runner brought a letter that, when she learned the contents, filled Meriem with excitement. Visitors were coming! A number of English ladies and gentlemen had accepted My Dear's invitation to spend a month of hunting and exploring with them. Meriem was all expectancy. What would these strangers be like? Would they be as nice to her as had Bwana and My Dear, or would they be like the other white folk she had known – cruel and relentless. My Dear assured her that they all were gentle folk and that she would find them kind, considerate and honorable.

To My Dear's surprise there was none of the shyness of the wild creature in Meriem's anticipation of the visit of strangers.

She looked forward to their coming with curiosity and with a certain pleasurable anticipation when once she was assured that they would not bite her. In fact she appeared no different than would any pretty young miss who had learned of the expected coming of company.

Korak's image was still often in her thoughts, but it aroused now a less well-defined sense of bereavement. A quiet sadness pervaded Meriem when she thought of him; but the poignant grief of her loss when it was young no longer goaded her to desperation. Yet she was still loyal to him. She still hoped that some day he would find her, nor did she doubt for a moment but that he was searching for her if he still lived. It was this last suggestion that caused her the greatest perturbation. Korak might be dead. It scarce seemed possible that one so well-equipped to meet the emergencies of jungle life should have succumbed so young; yet when she had last seen him he had been beset by a horde of armed warriors, and should he have returned to the village again, as she well knew he must have, he may have been killed. Even her Korak could not, single handed, slay an entire tribe.

At last the visitors arrived. There were three men and two women – the wives of the two older men. The youngest member of the party was Hon. Morison Baynes, a young man of considerable wealth who, having exhausted all the possibilities for pleasure offered by the capitals of Europe, had gladly seized upon this opportunity to turn to another continent for excitement and adventure.

He looked upon all things un-European as rather more than less impossible, still he was not at all averse to enjoying the novelty of unaccustomed places, and making the most of strangers indigenous thereto, however unspeakable they might have seemed to him at home. In manner he was suave and courteous to all – if possible a trifle more punctilious toward those he considered of meaner clay than toward the few he mentally admitted to equality.

Nature had favored him with a splendid physique and a handsome face, and also with sufficient good judgment to appreciate that while he might enjoy the contemplation of his superiority to the masses, there was little likelihood of the masses being equally entranced by the same cause. And so he easily maintained the reputation of being a most democratic and likeable fellow, and indeed he was likable. Just a shade of his egotism was occasionally apparent – never sufficient to become a burden to his associates. And this, briefly, was the Hon. Morison Baynes of luxurious European civilization. What would be the Hon. Morison Baynes of central Africa it were difficult to guess.

Meriem, at first, was shy and reserved in the presence of the strangers. Her benefactors had seen fit to ignore mention of her strange past, and so she passed as their ward whose antecedents not having been mentioned were not to be inquired into. The guests found her sweet and unassuming, laughing, vivacious and a never exhausted storehouse of quaint and interesting jungle lore.

She had ridden much during her year with Bwana and My Dear. She knew each favorite clump of concealing reeds along the river that the buffalo loved best. She knew a dozen places where lions laired, and every drinking hole in the drier country twenty-five miles back from the river. With unerring precision that was almost uncanny she could track the largest or the smallest beast to his hiding place. But the thing that baffled them all was her instant consciousness of the presence of carnivora that others, exerting their faculties to the utmost, could neither see nor hear.

The Hon. Morison Baynes found Meriem a most beautiful and charming companion. He was delighted with her from the first. Particularly so, it is possible, because he had not thought to find companionship of this sort upon the African estate of his London friends. They were together a great deal as they were the only unmarried couple in the little company. Meriem, entirely unaccustomed to the companionship of such as Baynes, was fascinated by him. His tales of the great, gay cities with which he was familiar filled her with admiration and with wonder. If the Hon. Morison always shone to advantage in these narratives Meriem saw in that fact but a most natural consequence to his presence upon the scene of his story – wherever Morison might be he must be a hero; so thought the girl.

With the actual presence and companionship of the young Englishman the image of Korak became less real. Where before it had been an actuality to her she now realized that Korak was but a memory. To that memory she still was loyal; but what weight has a memory in the presence of a fascinating reality?

Meriem had never accompanied the men upon a hunt since the arrival of the guests. She never had cared particularly for the sport of killing. The tracking she enjoyed; but the mere killing for the sake of killing she could not find pleasure in – little savage that she had been, and still, to some measure, was. When Bwana had gone forth to shoot for meat she had always been his enthusiastic companion; but with the coming of the London guests the hunting had deteriorated into mere killing. Slaughter the host would not permit; yet the purpose of the hunts were for heads and skins and not for food. So Meriem remained behind and spent her days either with My Dear upon the shaded verandah, or riding her favorite pony across the plains or to the forest edge. Here she would leave him untethered while she took to the trees for the moment's unalloyed pleasures of a return to the wild, free existence of her earlier childhood.

Then would come again visions of Korak, and, tired at last of leaping and swinging through the trees, she would stretch herself comfortably upon a branch and dream. And presently, as today, she found the features of Korak slowly dissolve and merge into those of another, and the figure of a tanned, half-naked tarmangani become a khaki clothed Englishman astride a hunting pony.

And while she dreamed there came to her ears from a distance, faintly, the terrified bleating of a kid. Meriem was instantly alert. You or I, even had we been able to hear the pitiful wail at so great distance, could not have interpreted it; but to Meriem it meant a species of terror that afflicts the ruminant when a carnivore is near and escape impossible.

It had been both a pleasure and a sport of Korak's to rob Numa of his prey whenever possible, and Meriem too had often joyed in the thrill of snatching some dainty morsel almost from the very jaws of the king of beasts. Now, at the sound of the kid's bleat, all the well remembered thrills recurred. Instantly she was all excitement to play again the game of hide and seek with death.

Quickly she loosened her riding skirt and tossed it aside – it was a heavy handicap to successful travel in the trees. Her boots and stockings followed the skirt, for the bare sole of the human foot does not slip upon dry or even wet bark as does the hard leather of a boot. She would have liked to discard her riding breeches also, but the motherly admonitions of My Dear had convinced Meriem that it was not good form to go naked through the world.

At her hip hung a hunting knife. Her rifle was still in its boot at her pony's withers. Her revolver she had not brought.

The kid was still bleating as Meriem started rapidly in its direction, which she knew was straight toward a certain water hole which had once been famous as a rendezvous for lions. Of late there had been no evidence of carnivora in the neighborhood of this drinking place; but Meriem was positive that the bleating of the kid was due to the presence of either lion or panther.

But she would soon know, for she was rapidly approaching the terrified animal. She wondered as she hastened onward that the sounds continued to come from the same point. Why did the kid not run away? And then she came in sight of the little animal and knew. The kid was tethered to a stake beside the waterhole.

Meriem paused in the branches of a near-by tree and scanned the surrounding clearing with quick, penetrating eyes. Where was the hunter?

Bwana and his people did not hunt thus. Who could have tethered this poor little beast as a lure to Numa? Bwana never countenanced such acts in his country and his word was law among those who hunted within a radius of many miles of his estate.

Some wandering savages, doubtless, thought Meriem; but where were they? Not even her keen eyes could discover them. And where was Numa? Why had he not long since sprung upon this delicious and defenseless morsel? That he was close by was attested by the pitiful crying of the kid. Ah! Now she saw him. He was lying close in a clump of brush a few yards to her right. The kid was down wind from him and getting the full benefit of his terrorizing scent, which did not reach Meriem.

To circle to the opposite side of the clearing where the trees approached closer to the kid. To leap quickly to the little animal's side and cut the tether that held him would be the work of but a moment. In that moment Numa might charge, and then there would be scarce time to regain the safety of the trees, yet it might be done. Meriem had escaped from closer quarters than that many times before.

The doubt that gave her momentary pause was caused by fear of the unseen hunters more than by fear of Numa. If they were stranger blacks the spears that they held in readiness for Numa might as readily be loosed upon whomever dared release their bait as upon the prey they sought thus to trap. Again the kid struggled to be free. Again his piteous wail touched the tender heart strings of the girl. Tossing discretion aside, she commenced to circle the clearing. Only from Numa did she attempt to conceal her presence. At last she reached the opposite trees. An instant she paused to look toward the great lion, and at the same moment she saw the huge beast rise slowly to his full height. A low roar betokened that he was ready.

Meriem loosened her knife and leaped to the ground. A quick run brought her to the side of the kid. Numa saw her. He lashed his tail against his tawny sides. He roared terribly; but, for an instant, he remained where he stood – surprised into inaction, doubtless, by the strange apparition that had sprung so unexpectedly from the jungle.

Other eyes were upon Meriem, too – eyes in which were no less surprise than that reflected in the yellow-green orbs of the carnivore. A white man, hiding in a thorn boma, half rose as the young girl leaped into the clearing and dashed toward the kid. He saw Numa hesitate. He raised his rifle and covered the beast's breast. The girl reached the kid's side. Her knife flashed, and the little prisoner was free. With a parting bleat it dashed off into the jungle. Then the girl turned to retreat toward the safety of the tree from which she had dropped so suddenly and unexpectedly into the surprised view of the lion, the kid and the man.

As she turned the girl's face was turned toward the hunter. His eyes went wide as he saw her features. He gave a little gasp of surprise; but now the lion demanded all his attention – the baffled, angry beast was charging. His breast was still covered by the motionless rifle. The man could have fired and stopped the charge at once; but for some reason, since he had seen the girl's face, he hesitated. Could it be that he did not care to save her? Or, did he prefer, if possible, to remain unseen by her? It must have been the latter cause which kept the trigger finger of the steady hand from exerting the little pressure that would have brought the great beast to at least a temporary pause.

Like an eagle the man watched the race for life the girl was making. A second or two measured the time which the whole exciting event consumed from the moment that the lion broke into his charge. Nor once did the rifle sights fail to cover the broad breast of the tawny sire as the lion's course took him a little to the man's left. Once, at the very last moment, when escape seemed impossible, the hunter's finger tightened ever so little upon the trigger, but almost coincidentally the girl leaped for an over hanging branch and seized it. The lion leaped too; but the nimble Meriem had swung herself beyond his reach without a second or an inch to spare.

The man breathed a sigh of relief as he lowered his rifle. He saw the girl fling a grimace at the angry, roaring, maneater beneath her, and then, laughing, speed away into the forest. For an hour the lion remained about the water hole. A hundred times could the hunter have bagged his prey. Why did he fail to do so? Was he afraid that the shot might attract the girl and cause her to return?

At last Numa, still roaring angrily, strode majestically into the jungle. The hunter crawled from his boma, and half an hour later was entering a little camp snugly hidden in the forest. A handful of black followers greeted his return with sullen indifference. He was a great bearded man, a huge, yellow-bearded giant, when he entered his tent. Half an hour later he emerged smooth shaven.

His blacks looked at him in astonishment.

"Would you know me?" he asked.

"The hyena that bore you would not know you, Bwana," replied one.

The man aimed a heavy fist at the black's face; but long experience in dodging similar blows saved the presumptuous one.

Chapter Seventeen

Meriem returned slowly toward the tree in which she had left her skirt, her shoes and her stockings. She was singing blithely; but her song came to a sudden stop when she came within sight of the tree, for there, disporting themselves with glee and pulling and hauling upon her belongings, were a number of baboons. When they saw her they showed no signs of terror. Instead they bared their fangs and growled at her. What was there to fear in a single she-Tarmangani? Nothing, absolutely nothing.

In the open plain beyond the forest the hunters were returning from the day's sport. They were widely separated, hoping to raise a wandering lion on the homeward journey across the plain. The Hon. Morison Baynes rode closest to the forest. As his eyes wandered back and forth across the undulating, shrub sprinkled ground they fell upon the form of a creature close beside the thick jungle where it terminated abruptly at the plain's edge.

He reined his mount in the direction of his discovery. It was yet too far away for his untrained eyes to recognize it; but as he came closer he saw that it was a horse, and was about to resume the original direction of his way when he thought that he discerned a saddle upon the beast's back. He rode a little closer. Yes, the animal was saddled. The Hon. Morison approached yet nearer, and as he did so his eyes expressed a pleasurable emotion of anticipation, for they had now recognized the pony as the special favorite of Meriem.

He galloped to the animal's side. Meriem must be within the wood. The man shuddered a little at the thought of an unprotected girl alone in the jungle that was still, to him, a fearful place of terrors and stealthily stalking death. He dismounted and left his horse beside Meriem's. On foot he entered the jungle. He knew that she was probably safe enough and he wished to surprise her by coming suddenly upon her.

He had gone but a short distance into the wood when he heard a great jabbering in a near-by tree. Coming closer he saw a band of baboons snarling over something. Looking intently he saw that one of them held a woman's riding skirt and that others had boots and stockings. His heart almost ceased to beat as he quite naturally placed the most direful explanation upon the scene. The baboons had killed Meriem and stripped this clothing from her body. Morison shuddered.

He was about to call aloud in the hope that after all the girl still lived when he saw her in a tree close beside that was occupied by the baboons, and now he saw that they were snarling and jabbering at her. To his amazement he saw the girl swing, ape-like, into the tree below the huge beasts. He saw her pause upon a branch a few feet from the nearest baboon. He was about to raise his rifle and put a bullet through the hideous creature that seemed about to leap upon her when he heard the girl speak. He almost dropped his rifle from surprise as a strange jabbering, identical with that of the apes, broke from Meriem's lips.

The baboons stopped their snarling and listened. It was quite evident that they were as much surprised as the Hon. Morison Baynes. Slowly and one by one they approached the girl. She gave not the slightest evidence of fear of them. They quite surrounded her now so that Baynes could not have fired without endangering the girl's life; but he no longer desired to fire. He was consumed with curiosity.

For several minutes the girl carried on what could be nothing less than a conversation with the baboons, and then with seeming alacrity every article of her apparel in their possession was handed over to her. The baboons still crowded eagerly about her as she donned them. They chattered to her and she chattered back. The Hon. Morison Baynes sat down at the foot of a tree and mopped his perspiring brow. Then he rose and made his way back to his mount.

When Meriem emerged from the forest a few minutes later she found him there, and he eyed her with wide eyes in which were both wonder and a sort of terror.

"I saw your horse here," he explained, "and thought that I would wait and ride home with you – you do not mind?"

"Of course not," she replied. "It will be lovely."

As they made their way stirrup to stirrup across the plain the Hon. Morison caught himself many times watching the girl's regular profile and wondering if his eyes had deceived him or if, in truth, he really had seen this lovely creature consorting with grotesque baboons and conversing with them as fluently as she conversed with him. The thing was uncanny – impossible; yet he had seen it with his own eyes.

And as he watched her another thought persisted in obtruding itself into his mind. She was most beautiful and very desirable; but what did he know of her? Was she not altogether impossible? Was the scene that he had but just witnessed not sufficient proof of her impossibility? A woman who climbed trees and conversed with the baboons of the jungle! It was quite horrible!

Again the Hon. Morison mopped his brow. Meriem glanced toward him.

"You are warm," she said. "Now that the sun is setting I find it quite cool. Why do you perspire now?"

He had not intended to let her know that he had seen her with the baboons; but quite suddenly, before he realized what he was saying, he had blurted it out.

"I perspire from emotion," he said. "I went into the jungle when I discovered your pony. I wanted to surprise you; but it was I who was surprised. I saw you in the trees with the baboons."

"Yes?" she said quite unemotionally, as though it was a matter of little moment that a young girl should be upon intimate terms with savage jungle beasts.

"It was horrible!" ejaculated the Hon. Morison.

"Horrible?" repeated Meriem, puckering her brows in bewilderment. "What was horrible about it? They are my friends. Is it horrible to talk with one's friends?"

"You were really talking with them, then?" cried the Hon. Morison. "You understood them and they understood you?"

"Certainly."

"But they are hideous creatures – degraded beasts of a lower order. How could you speak the language of beasts?"

"They are not hideous, and they are not degraded," replied Meriem. "Friends are never that. I lived among them for years before Bwana found me and brought me here. I scarce knew any other tongue than that of the mangani. Should I refuse to know them now simply because I happen, for the present, to live among humans?"

"For the present!" ejaculated the Hon. Morison. "You cannot mean that you expect to return to live among them? Come, come, what foolishness are we talking! The very idea! You are spoofing me, Miss Meriem. You have been kind to these baboons here and they know you and do not molest you; but that you once lived among them – no, that is preposterous."

"But I did, though," insisted the girl, seeing the real horror that the man felt in the presence of such an idea reflected in his tone and manner, and rather enjoying baiting him still further. "Yes, I lived, almost naked, among the great apes and the lesser apes. I dwelt among the branches of the trees. I pounced upon the smaller prey and devoured it – raw. With Korak and A'ht I hunted the antelope and the boar, and I sat upon a tree limb and made faces at Numa, the lion, and threw sticks at him and annoyed him until he roared so terribly in his rage that the earth shook.

"And Korak built me a lair high among the branches of a mighty tree. He brought me fruits and flesh. He fought for me and was kind to me – until I came to Bwana and My Dear I do not recall that any other than Korak was ever kind to me." There was a wistful note in the girl's voice now and she had forgotten that she was bantering the Hon. Morison. She was thinking of Korak. She had not thought of him a great deal of late.

For a time both were silently absorbed in their own reflections as they rode on toward the bungalow of their host. The girl was thinking of a god-like figure, a leopard skin half concealing his smooth, brown hide as he leaped nimbly through the trees to lay an offering of food before her on his return from a successful hunt. Behind him, shaggy and powerful, swung a huge anthropoid ape, while she, Meriem, laughing and shouting her welcome, swung upon a swaying limb before the entrance to her sylvan bower. It was a pretty picture as she recalled it. The other side seldom obtruded itself upon her memory – the long, black nights – the chill, terrible jungle nights – the cold and damp and discomfort of the rainy season – the hideous mouthings of the savage carnivora as they prowled through the Stygian darkness beneath – the constant menace of Sheeta, the panther, and Histah, the snake – the stinging insects – the loathesome vermin. For, in truth, all these had been outweighed by the happiness of the sunny days, the freedom of it all, and, most, the companionship of Korak.

The man's thoughts were rather jumbled. He had suddenly realized that he had come mighty near falling in love with this girl of whom he had known nothing up to the previous moment when she had voluntarily revealed a portion of her past to him. The more he thought upon the matter the more evident it became to him that he had given her his love – that he had been upon the verge of offering her his honorable name. He trembled a little at the narrowness of his escape. Yet, he still loved her. There was no objection to that according to the ethics of the Hon. Morison Baynes and his kind. She was a meaner clay than he. He could no more have taken her in marriage than he could have taken one of her baboon friends, nor would she, of course, expect such an offer from him. To have his love would be sufficient honor for her – his name he would, naturally, bestow upon one in his own elevated social sphere.

A girl who had consorted with apes, who, according to her own admission, had lived almost naked among them, could have no considerable sense of the finer qualities of virtue. The love that he would offer her, then, would, far from offending her, probably cover all that she might desire or expect.

The more the Hon. Morison Baynes thought upon the subject the more fully convinced he became that he was contemplating a most chivalrous and unselfish act. Europeans will better understand his point of view than Americans, poor, benighted provincials, who are denied a true appreciation of caste and of the fact that "the king can do no wrong." He did not even have to argue the point that she would be much happier amidst the luxuries of a London apartment, fortified as she would be by both his love and his bank account, than lawfully wed to such a one as her social position warranted. There was one question however, which he wished to have definitely answered before he committed himself even to the program he was considering.

"Who were Korak and A'ht?" he asked.

"A'ht was a Mangani," replied Meriem, "and Korak a Tarmangani."

"And what, pray, might a Mangani be, and a Tarmangani?"

The girl laughed.

"You are a Tarmangani," she replied. "The Mangani are covered with hair – you would call them apes."

"Then Korak was a white man?" he asked.

"Yes."

"And he was – ah – your – er – your – ?" He paused, for he found it rather difficult to go on with that line of questioning while the girl's clear, beautiful eyes were looking straight into his.

"My what?" insisted Meriem, far too unsophisticated in her unspoiled innocence to guess what the Hon. Morison was driving at.

"Why – ah – your brother?" he stumbled.

"No, Korak was not my brother," she replied.

"Was he your husband, then?" he finally blurted.

Far from taking offense, Meriem broke into a merry laugh.

"My husband!" she cried. "Why how old do you think I am? I am too young to have a husband. I had never thought of such a thing. Korak was – why – ," and now she hesitated, too, for she never before had attempted to analyse the relationship that existed between herself and Korak – "why, Korak was just Korak," and again she broke into a gay laugh as she realized the illuminating quality of her description.

Looking at her and listening to her the man beside her could not believe that depravity of any sort or degree entered into the girl's nature, yet he wanted to believe that she had not been virtuous, for otherwise his task was less a sinecure – the Hon. Morison was not entirely without conscience.

For several days the Hon. Morison made no appreciable progress toward the consummation of his scheme. Sometimes he almost abandoned it for he found himself time and again wondering how slight might be the provocation necessary to trick him into making a bona-fide offer of marriage to Meriem if he permitted himself to fall more deeply in love with her, and it was difficult to see her daily and not love her. There was a quality about her which, all unknown to the Hon. Morison, was making his task an extremely difficult one – it was that quality of innate goodness and cleanness which is a good girl's stoutest bulwark and protection – an impregnable barrier that only degeneracy has the effrontery to assail. The Hon. Morison Baynes would never be considered a degenerate.

He was sitting with Meriem upon the verandah one evening after the others had retired. Earlier they had been playing tennis – a game in which the Hon. Morison shone to advantage, as, in truth, he did in most all manly sports. He was telling Meriem stories of London and Paris, of balls and banquets, of the wonderful women and their wonderful gowns, of the pleasures and pastimes of the rich and powerful. The Hon. Morison was a past master in the art of insidious boasting. His egotism was never flagrant or tiresome – he was never crude in it, for crudeness was a plebeianism that the Hon. Morison studiously avoided, yet the impression derived by a listener to the Hon. Morison was one that was not at all calculated to detract from the glory of the house of Baynes, or from that of its representative.

Meriem was entranced. His tales were like fairy stories to this little jungle maid. The Hon. Morison loomed large and wonderful and magnificent in her mind's eye. He fascinated her, and when he drew closer to her after a short silence and took her hand she thrilled as one might thrill beneath the touch of a deity – a thrill of exaltation not unmixed with fear.

He bent his lips close to her ear.

"Meriem!" he whispered. "My little Meriem! May I hope to have the right to call you 'my little Meriem'?"

The girl turned wide eyes upward to his face; but it was in shadow. She trembled but she did not draw away. The man put an arm about her and drew her closer.

"I love you!" he whispered.

She did not reply. She did not know what to say. She knew nothing of love. She had never given it a thought; but she did know that it was very nice to be loved, whatever it meant. It was nice to have people kind to one. She had known so little of kindness or affection.

"Tell me," he said, "that you return my love."

His lips came steadily closer to hers. They had almost touched when a vision of Korak sprang like a miracle before her eyes. She saw Korak's face close to hers, she felt his lips hot against hers, and then for the first time in her life she guessed what love meant. She drew away, gently.

"I am not sure," she said, "that I love you. Let us wait. There is plenty of time. I am too young to marry yet, and I am not sure that I should be happy in London or Paris – they rather frighten me."

How easily and naturally she had connected his avowal of love with the idea of marriage! The Hon. Morison was perfectly sure that he had not mentioned marriage – he had been particularly careful not to do so. And then she was not sure that she loved him! That, too, came rather in the nature of a shock to his vanity. It seemed incredible that this little barbarian should have any doubts whatever as to the desirability of the Hon. Morison Baynes.

The first flush of passion cooled, the Hon. Morison was enabled to reason more logically. The start had been all wrong. It would be better now to wait and prepare her mind gradually for the only proposition which his exalted estate would permit him to offer her. He would go slow. He glanced down at the girl's profile. It was bathed in the silvery light of the great tropic moon. The Hon. Morison Baynes wondered if it were to be so easy a matter to "go slow." She was most alluring.

Meriem rose. The vision of Korak was still before her.

"Good night," she said. "It is almost too beautiful to leave," she waved her hand in a comprehensive gesture which took in the starry heavens, the great moon, the broad, silvered plain, and the dense shadows in the distance, that marked the jungle. "Oh, how I love it!"

"You would love London more," he said earnestly. "And London would love you. You would be a famous beauty in any capital of Europe. You would have the world at your feet, Meriem."

"Good night!" she repeated, and left him.

The Hon. Morison selected a cigarette from his crested case, lighted it, blew a thin line of blue smoke toward the moon, and smiled.

Chapter Eighteen

Meriem and Bwana were sitting on the verandah together the following day when a horseman appeared in the distance riding across the plain toward the bungalow. Bwana shaded his eyes with his hand and gazed out toward the oncoming rider. He was puzzled. Strangers were few in Central Africa. Even the blacks for a distance of many miles in every direction were well known to him. No white man came within a hundred miles that word of his coming did not reach Bwana long before the stranger. His every move was reported to the big Bwana – just what animals he killed and how many of each species, how he killed them, too, for Bwana would not permit the use of prussic acid or strychnine; and how he treated his "boys."

Several European sportsmen had been turned back to the coast by the big Englishman's orders because of unwarranted cruelty to their black followers, and one, whose name had long been heralded in civilized communities as that of a great sportsman, was driven from Africa with orders never to return when Bwana found that his big bag of fourteen lions had been made by the diligent use of poisoned bait.

The result was that all good sportsmen and all the natives loved and respected him. His word was law where there had never been law before. There was scarce a head man from coast to coast who would not heed the big Bwana's commands in preference to those of the hunters who employed them, and so it was easy to turn back any undesirable stranger – Bwana had simply to threaten to order his boys to desert him.

But there was evidently one who had slipped into the country unheralded. Bwana could not imagine who the approaching horseman might be. After the manner of frontier hospitality the globe round he met the newcomer at the gate, welcoming him even before he had dismounted. He saw a tall, well knit man of thirty or over, blonde of hair and smooth shaven. There was a tantalizing familiarity about him that convinced

Bwana that he should be able to call the visitor by name, yet he was unable to do so. The newcomer was evidently of Scandinavian origin – both his appearance and accent denoted that. His manner was rough but open. He made a good impression upon the Englishman, who was wont to accept strangers in this wild and savage country at their own valuation, asking no questions and assuming the best of them until they proved themselves undeserving of his friendship and hospitality.

"It is rather unusual that a white man comes unheralded," he said, as they walked together toward the field into which he had suggested that the traveler might turn his pony. "My friends, the natives, keep us rather well-posted."

"It is probably due to the fact that I came from the south," explained the stranger, "that you did not hear of my coming. I have seen no village for several marches."

"No, there are none to the south of us for many miles," replied Bwana. "Since Kovudoo deserted his country I rather doubt that one could find a native in that direction under two or three hundred miles."

Bwana was wondering how a lone white man could have made his way through the savage, unhospitable miles that lay toward the south. As though guessing what must be passing through the other's mind, the stranger vouchsafed an explanation.

"I came down from the north to do a little trading and hunting," he said, "and got way off the beaten track. My head man, who was the only member of the safari who had ever before been in the country, took sick and died. We could find no natives to guide us, and so I simply swung back straight north. We have been living on the fruits of our guns for over a month. Didn't have an idea there was a white man within a thousand miles of us when we camped last night by a water hole at the edge of the plain. This morning I started out to hunt and saw the smoke from your chimney, so I sent my gun bearer back to camp with the good news and rode straight over here myself. Of course I've heard of you – everybody who comes into Central Africa does – and I'd be mighty glad of permission to rest up and hunt around here for a couple of weeks."

"Certainly," replied Bwana. "Move your camp up close to the river below my boys' camp and make yourself at home."

They had reached the verandah now and Bwana was introducing the stranger to Meriem and My Dear, who had just come from the bungalow's interior.

"This is Mr. Hanson," he said, using the name the man had given him. "He is a trader who has lost his way in the jungle to the south."

My Dear and Meriem bowed their acknowledgments of the introduction. The man seemed rather ill at ease in their presence. His host attributed this to the fact that his guest was unaccustomed to the society of cultured women, and so found a pretext to quickly extricate him from his seemingly unpleasant position and lead him away to his study and the brandy and soda which were evidently much less embarrassing to Mr. Hanson.

When the two had left them Meriem turned toward My Dear.

"It is odd," she said, "but I could almost swear that I had known Mr. Hanson in the past. It is odd, but quite impossible," and she gave the matter no further thought.

Hanson did not accept Bwana's invitation to move his camp closer to the bungalow. He said his boys were inclined to be quarrelsome, and so were better off at a distance; and he, himself, was around but little, and then always avoided coming into contact with the ladies. A fact which naturally aroused only laughing comment on the rough trader's bashfulness. He accompanied the men on several hunting trips where they found him perfectly at home and well versed in all the finer points of big game hunting. Of an evening he often spent much time with the white foreman of the big farm, evidently finding in the society of this rougher man more common interests than the cultured guests of Bwana possessed for him. So it came that his was a familiar figure about the premises by night. He came and went as he saw fit, often wandering along in the great flower garden that was the especial pride and joy of My Dear and Meriem. The first time that he had been surprised there he apologized gruffly, explaining that he had always been fond of the good old blooms of northern Europe which My Dear had so successfully transplanted in African soil.

Was it, though, the ever beautiful blossoms of hollyhocks and phlox that drew him to the perfumed air of the garden, or that other infinitely more beautiful flower who wandered often among the blooms beneath the great moon – the black-haired, suntanned Meriem?

For three weeks Hanson had remained. During this time he said that his boys were resting and gaining strength after their terrible ordeals in the untracked jungle to the south; but he had not been as idle as he appeared to have been. He divided his small following into two parties, entrusting the leadership of each to men whom he believed that he could trust. To them he explained his plans and the rich reward that they would win from him if they carried his designs to a successful conclusion. One party he moved very slowly northward along the trail that connects with the great caravan routes entering the Sahara from the south. The other he ordered straight westward with orders to halt and go into permanent camp just beyond the great river which marks the natural boundary of the country that the big Bwana rightfully considers almost his own.

To his host he explained that he was moving his safari slowly toward the north – he said nothing of the party moving westward. Then, one day, he announced that half his boys had deserted, for a hunting party from the bungalow had come across his northerly camp and he feared that they might have noticed the reduced numbers of his following.

And thus matters stood when, one hot night, Meriem, unable to sleep, rose and wandered out into the garden. The Hon. Morison had been urging his suit once more that evening, and the girl's mind was in such a turmoil that she had been unable to sleep.

The wide heavens about her seemed to promise a greater freedom from doubt and questioning. Baynes had urged her to tell him that she loved him. A dozen times she thought that she might honestly give him the answer that he demanded. Korak fast was becoming but a memory. That he was dead she had come to believe, since otherwise he would have sought her out. She did not know that he had even better reason to believe her dead, and that it was because of that belief he had made no effort to find her after his raid upon the village of Kovudoo.

Behind a great flowering shrub Hanson lay gazing at the stars and waiting. He had lain thus and there many nights before. For what was he waiting, or for whom? He heard the girl approaching, and half raised himself to his elbow. A dozen paces away, the reins looped over a fence post, stood his pony.

Meriem, walking slowly, approached the bush behind which the waiter lay. Hanson drew a large bandanna handkerchief from his pocket and rose stealthily to his knees. A pony neighed down at the corrals. Far out across the plain a lion roared. Hanson changed his position until he squatted upon both feet, ready to come erect quickly.

Again the pony neighed – this time closer. There was the sound of his body brushing against shrubbery. Hanson heard and wondered how the animal had gotten from the corral, for it was evident that he was already in the garden. The man turned his head in the direction of the beast. What he saw sent him to the ground, huddled close beneath the shrubbery – a man was coming, leading two ponies.

Meriem heard now and stopped to look and listen. A moment later the Hon. Morison Baynes drew near, the two saddled mounts at his heels.

Meriem looked up at him in surprise. The Hon. Morison grinned sheepishly.

"I couldn't sleep," he explained, "and was going for a bit of a ride when I chanced to see you out here, and I thought you'd like to join me. Ripping good sport, you know, night riding. Come on."

Meriem laughed. The adventure appealed to her.

"All right," she said.

Hanson swore beneath his breath. The two led their horses from the garden to the gate and through it. There they discovered Hanson's mount.

"Why here's the trader's pony," remarked Baynes.

"He's probably down visiting with the foreman," said Meriem.

"Pretty late for him, isn't it?" remarked the Hon. Morison. "I'd hate to have to ride back through that jungle at night to his camp."

As though to give weight to his apprehensions the distant lion roared again. The Hon. Morison shivered and glanced at the girl to note the effect of the uncanny sound upon her. She appeared not to have noticed it.

A moment later the two had mounted and were moving slowly across the moon-bathed plain. The girl turned her pony's head straight toward the jungle. It was in the direction of the roaring of the hungry lion.

"Hadn't we better steer clear of that fellow?" suggested the Hon. Morison. "I guess you didn't hear him."

"Yes, I heard him," laughed Meriem. "Let's ride over and call on him."

The Hon. Morison laughed uneasily. He didn't care to appear at a disadvantage before this girl, nor did he care, either, to approach a hungry lion too closely at night. He carried his rifle in his saddle boot; but moonlight is an uncertain light to shoot by, nor ever had he faced a lion alone – even by day. The thought gave him a distinct nausea. The beast ceased his roaring now. They heard him no more and the Hon. Morison gained courage accordingly. They were riding down wind toward the jungle. The lion lay in a little swale to their right. He was old. For two nights he had not fed, for no longer was his charge as swift or his spring as mighty as in the days of his prime when he spread terror among the creatures of his wild domain. For two nights and days he had gone empty, and for long time before that he had fed only upon carrion. He was old; but he was yet a terrible engine of destruction.

At the edge of the forest the Hon. Morison drew rein. He had no desire to go further. Numa, silent upon his padded feet, crept into the jungle beyond them. The wind, now, was blowing gently between him and his intended prey. He had come a long way in search of man, for even in his youth he had tasted human flesh and while it was poor stuff by comparison with eland and zebra it was less difficult to kill. In Numa's estimation man was a slow-witted, slow-footed creature which commanded no respect unless accompanied by the acrid odor which spelled to the monarch's sensitive nostrils the great noise and the blinding flash of an express rifle.

He caught the dangerous scent tonight; but he was ravenous to madness. He would face a dozen rifles, if necessary, to fill his empty belly. He circled about into the forest that he might again be down wind from his victims, for should they get his scent he could not hope to overtake them. Numa was famished; but he was old and crafty.

Deep in the jungle another caught faintly the scent of man and of Numa both. He raised his head and sniffed. He cocked it upon one side and listened.

"Come on," said Meriem, "let's ride in a way – the forest is wonderful at night. It is open enough to permit us to ride."

The Hon. Morison hesitated. He shrank from revealing his fear in the presence of the girl. A braver man, sure of his own position, would have had the courage to have refused uselessly to expose the girl to danger. He would not have thought of himself at all; but the egotism of the Hon. Morison required that he think always of self first. He had planned the ride to get Meriem away from the bungalow. He wanted to talk to her alone and far enough away so should she take offense at his purposed suggestion he would have time in which to attempt to right himself in her eyes before they reached home. He had little doubt, of course, but that he should succeed; but it is to his credit that he did have some slight doubts.

"You needn't be afraid of the lion," said Meriem, noting his slight hesitancy. "There hasn't been a man eater around here for two years, Bwana says, and the game is so plentiful that there is no necessity to drive Numa to human flesh. Then, he has been so often hunted that he rather keeps out of man's way."

"Oh, I'm not afraid of lions," replied the Hon. Morison. "I was just thinking what a beastly uncomfortable place a forest is to ride in. What with the underbrush and the low branches and all that, you know, it's not exactly cut out for pleasure riding."

"Let's go a-foot then," suggested Meriem, and started to dismount.

"Oh, no," cried the Hon. Morison, aghast at this suggestion. "Let's ride," and he reined his pony into the dark shadows of the wood. Behind him came Meriem and in front, prowling ahead waiting a favorable opportunity, skulked Numa, the lion.

Out upon the plain a lone horseman muttered a low curse as he saw the two disappear from sight. It was Hanson. He had followed them from the bungalow. Their way led in the direction of his camp, so he had a ready and plausible excuse should they discover him; but they had not seen him for they had not turned their eyes behind.

Now he turned directly toward the spot at which they had entered the jungle. He no longer cared whether he was observed or not. There were two reasons for his indifference. The first was that he saw in Baynes' act a counterpart of his own planned abduction of the girl. In some way he might turn the thing to his own purposes. At least he would keep in touch with them and make sure that Baynes did not get her. His other reason was based on his knowledge of an event that had transpired at his camp the previous night – an event which he had not mentioned at the bungalow for fear of drawing undesired attention to his movements and bringing the blacks of the big Bwana into dangerous intercourse with his own boys. He had told at the bungalow that half his men had deserted. That story might be quickly disproved should his boys and Bwana's grow confidential.

The event that he had failed to mention and which now urged him hurriedly after the girl and her escort had occurred during his absence early the preceding evening. His men had been sitting around their camp fire, entirely encircled by a high, thorn boma, when, without the slightest warning, a huge lion had leaped amongst them and seized one of their number. It had been solely due to the loyalty and courage of his comrades that his life had been saved, and then only after a battle royal with the hunger-enraged beast had they been able to drive him off with burning brands, spears, and rifles.

From this Hanson knew that a man eater had wandered into the district or been developed by the aging of one of the many lions who ranged the plains and hills by night, or lay up in the cool wood by day. He had heard the roaring of a hungry lion not half an hour before, and there was little doubt in his mind but that the man eater was stalking Meriem and Baynes. He cursed the Englishman for a fool, and spurred rapidly after them.

Meriem and Baynes had drawn up in a small, natural clearing. A hundred yards beyond them Numa lay crouching in the underbrush, his yellow-green eyes fixed upon his prey, the tip of his sinuous tail jerking spasmodically. He was measuring the distance between him and them. He was wondering if he dared venture a charge, or should he wait yet a little longer in the hope that they might ride straight into his jaws. He was very hungry; but also was he very crafty. He could not chance losing his meat by a hasty and ill-considered rush. Had he waited the night before until the blacks slept he would not have been forced to go hungry for another twenty-four hours.

Behind him the other that had caught his scent and that of man together came to a sitting posture upon the branch of a tree in which he had reposed himself for slumber. Beneath him a lumbering gray hulk swayed to and fro in the darkness. The beast in the tree uttered a low guttural and dropped to the back of the gray mass. He whispered a word in one of the great ears and Tantor, the elephant, raised his trunk aloft, swinging it high and low to catch the scent that the word had warned him of. There was another whispered word – was it a command? – and the lumbering beast wheeled into an awkward, yet silent shuffle, in the direction of Numa, the lion, and the stranger Tarmangani his rider had scented.

Onward they went, the scent of the lion and his prey becoming stronger and stronger. Numa was becoming impatient. How much longer must he wait for his meat to come his way? He lashed his tail viciously now. He almost growled. All unconscious of their danger the man and the girl sat talking in the little clearing.

Their horses were pressed side by side. Baynes had found Meriem's hand and was pressing it as he poured words of love into her ear, and Meriem was listening.

"Come to London with me," urged the Hon. Morison. "I can gather a safari and we can be a whole day upon the way to the coast before they guess that we have gone."

"Why must we go that way?" asked the girl. "Bwana and My Dear would not object to our marriage."

"I cannot marry you just yet," explained the Hon. Morison, "there are some formalities to be attended to first – you do not understand. It will be all right. We will go to London. I cannot wait. If you love me you will come. What of the apes you lived with? Did they bother about marriage? They love as we love. Had you stayed among them you would have mated as they mate. It is the law of nature – no man-made law can abrogate the laws of God. What difference does it make if we love one another? What do we care for anyone in the world besides ourselves? I would give my life for you – will you give nothing for me?"

"You love me?" she said. "You will marry me when we have reached London?"

"I swear it," he cried.

"I will go with you," she whispered, "though I do not understand why it is necessary." She leaned toward him and he took her in his arms and bent to press his lips to hers.

At the same instant the head of a huge tusker poked through the trees that fringed the clearing. The Hon. Morison and Meriem, with eyes and ears for one another alone, did not see or hear; but Numa did. The man upon Tantor's broad head saw the girl in the man's arms. It was Korak; but in the trim figure of the neatly garbed girl he did not recognize his Meriem. He only saw a Tarmangani with his she. And then Numa charged.

With a frightful roar, fearful lest Tantor had come to frighten away his prey, the great beast leaped from his hiding place. The earth trembled to his mighty voice. The ponies stood for an instant transfixed with terror. The Hon. Morison Baynes went white and cold. The lion was charging toward them full in the brilliant light of the magnificent moon. The muscles of the Hon. Morison no longer obeyed his will – they flexed to the urge of a greater power – the power of Nature's first law. They drove his spurred heels deep into his pony's flanks, they bore the rein against the brute's neck that wheeled him with an impetuous drive toward the plain and safety.

The girl's pony, squealing in terror, reared and plunged upon the heels of his mate. The lion was close upon him. Only the girl was cool – the girl and the half-naked savage who bestrode the neck of his mighty mount and grinned at the exciting spectacle chance had staked for his enjoyment.

To Korak here were but two strange Tarmangani pursued by Numa, who was empty. It was Numa's right to prey; but one was a she. Korak felt an intuitive urge to rush to her protection. Why, he could not guess. All Tarmangani were enemies now. He had lived too long a beast to feel strongly the humanitarian impulses that were inherent in him – yet feel them he did, for the girl at least.

He urged Tantor forward. He raised his heavy spear and hurled it at the flying target of the lion's body. The girl's pony had reached the trees upon the opposite side of the clearing. Here he would become easy prey to the swiftly moving lion; but Numa, infuriated, preferred the woman upon his back. It was for her he leaped.

Korak gave an exclamation of astonishment and approval as Numa landed upon the pony's rump and at the same instant the girl swung free of her mount to the branches of a tree above her.

Korak's spear struck Numa in the shoulder, knocking him from his precarious hold upon the frantically plunging horse. Freed of the weight of both girl and lion the pony raced ahead toward safety. Numa tore and struck at the missile in his shoulder but could not dislodge it. Then he resumed the chase.

Korak guided Tantor into the seclusion of the jungle. He did not wish to be seen, nor had he.

Hanson had almost reached the wood when he heard the lion's terrific roars, and knew that the charge had come. An instant later the Hon. Morison broke upon his vision, racing like mad for safety. The man lay flat upon his pony's back hugging the animal's neck tightly with both arms and digging the spurs into his sides. An instant later the second pony appeared – riderless.

Hanson groaned as he guessed what had happened out of sight in the jungle. With an oath he spurred on in the hope of driving the lion from his prey – his rifle was ready in his hand. And then the lion came into view behind the girl's pony. Hanson could not understand. He knew that if Numa had succeeded in seizing the girl he would not have continued in pursuit of the others.

He drew in his own mount, took quick aim and fired. The lion stopped in his tracks, turned and bit at his side, then rolled over dead. Hanson rode on into the forest, calling aloud to the girl.

"Here I am," came a quick response from the foliage of the trees just ahead. "Did you hit him?"

"Yes," replied Hanson. "Where are you? You had a mighty narrow escape. It will teach you to keep out of the jungle at night."

Together they returned to the plain where they found the Hon. Morison riding slowly back toward them. He explained that his pony had bolted and that he had had hard work stopping him at all. Hanson grinned, for he recalled the pounding heels that he had seen driving sharp spurs into the flanks of Baynes' mount; but he said nothing of what he had seen. He took Meriem up behind him and the three rode in silence toward the bungalow.

Chapter Nineteen

Behind them Korak emerged from the jungle and recovered his spear from Numa's side. He still was smiling. He had enjoyed the spectacle exceedingly. There was one thing that troubled him – the agility with which the she had clambered from her pony's back into the safety of the tree ABOVE her. That was more like mangani – more like his lost Meriem. He sighed. His lost Meriem! His little, dead Meriem! He wondered if this she stranger resembled his Meriem in other ways. A great longing to see her overwhelmed him. He looked after the three figures moving steadily across the plain. He wondered where might lie their destination. A desire to follow them came over him, but he only stood there watching until they had disappeared in the distance. The sight of the civilized girl and the dapper, khaki clad Englishman had aroused in Korak memories long dormant.

Once he had dreamed of returning to the world of such as these; but with the death of Meriem hope and ambition seemed to have deserted him. He cared now only to pass the remainder of his life in solitude, as far from man as possible. With a sigh he turned slowly back into the jungle.

Tantor, nervous by nature, had been far from reassured by close proximity to the three strange whites, and with the report of Hanson's rifle had turned and ambled away at his long, swinging shuffle. He was nowhere in sight when Korak returned to look for him. The ape-man, however, was little concerned by the absence of his friend. Tantor had a habit of wandering off unexpectedly. For a month they might not see one another, for Korak seldom took the trouble to follow the great pachyderm, nor did he upon this occasion. Instead he found a comfortable perch in a large tree and was soon asleep.

At the bungalow Bwana had met the returning adventurers on the verandah. In a moment of wakefulness he had heard the report of Hanson's rifle far out across the plain, and wondered what it might mean. Presently it had occurred to him that the man whom he considered in the light of a guest might have met with an accident on his way back to camp, so he had arisen and gone to his foreman's quarters where he had learned that Hanson had been there earlier in the evening but had departed several hours before. Returning from the foreman's quarters Bwana had noticed that the corral gate was open and further investigation revealed the fact that Meriem's pony was gone and also the one most often used by Baynes. Instantly Bwana assumed that the shot had been fired by Hon. Morison, and had again aroused his foreman and was making preparations to set forth in investigation when he had seen the party approaching across the plain.

Explanation on the part of the Englishman met a rather chilly reception from his host. Meriem was silent. She saw that Bwana was angry with her. It was the first time and she was heart broken.

"Go to your room, Meriem," he said; "and Baynes, if you will step into my study, I'd like to have a word with you in a moment."

He stepped toward Hanson as the others turned to obey him. There was something about Bwana even in his gentlest moods that commanded instant obedience.

"How did you happen to be with them, Hanson?" he asked.

"I'd been sitting in the garden," replied the trader, "after leaving Jervis' quarters. I have a habit of doing that as your lady probably knows. Tonight I fell asleep behind a bush, and was awakened by them two spooning. I couldn't hear what they said, but presently Baynes brings two ponies and they ride off. I didn't like to interfere for it wasn't any of my business, but I knew they hadn't ought to be ridin' about that time of night, leastways not the girl – it wasn't right and it wasn't safe. So I follows them and it's just as well I did. Baynes was gettin' away from the lion as fast as he could, leavin' the girl to take care of herself, when I got a lucky shot into the beast's shoulder that fixed him."

Hanson paused. Both men were silent for a time. Presently the trader coughed in an embarrassed manner as though there was something on his mind he felt in duty bound to say, but hated to.

"What is it, Hanson?" asked Bwana. "You were about to say something weren't you?"

"Well, you see it's like this," ventured Hanson. "Bein' around here evenings a good deal I've seen them two together a lot, and, beggin' your pardon, sir, but I don't think Mr. Baynes means the girl any good. I've overheard enough to make me think he's tryin' to get her to run off with him." Hanson, to fit his own ends, hit nearer the truth than he knew. He was afraid that Baynes would interfere with his own plans, and he had hit upon a scheme to both utilize the young Englishman and get rid of him at the same time.

"And I thought," continued the trader, "that inasmuch as I'm about due to move you might like to suggest to Mr. Baynes that he go with me. I'd be willin' to take him north to the caravan trails as a favor to you, sir."

Bwana stood in deep thought for a moment. Presently he looked up.

"Of course, Hanson, Mr. Baynes is my guest," he said, a grim twinkle in his eye. "Really I cannot accuse him of planning to run away with Meriem on the evidence that we have, and as he is my guest I should hate to be so discourteous as to ask him to leave; but, if I recall his words correctly, it seems to me that he has spoken of returning home, and I am sure that nothing would delight him more than going north with you – you say you start tomorrow? I think Mr. Baynes will accompany you. Drop over in the morning, if you please, and now good night, and thank you for keeping a watchful eye on Meriem."

Hanson hid a grin as he turned and sought his saddle. Bwana stepped from the verandah to his study, where he found the Hon. Morison pacing back and forth, evidently very ill at ease.

"Baynes," said Bwana, coming directly to the point, "Hanson is leaving for the north tomorrow. He has taken a great fancy to you, and just asked me to say to you that he'd be glad to have you accompany him. Good night, Baynes."

At Bwana's suggestion Meriem kept to her room the following morning until after the Hon. Morison Baynes had departed. Hanson had come for him early – in fact he had remained all night with the foreman, Jervis, that they might get an early start.

The farewell exchanges between the Hon. Morison and his host were of the most formal type, and when at last the guest rode away Bwana breathed a sigh of relief. It had been an unpleasant duty and he was glad that it was over; but he did not regret his action. He had not been blind to Baynes' infatuation for Meriem, and knowing the young man's pride in caste he had never for a moment believed that his guest would offer his name to this nameless Arab girl, for, extremely light in color though she was for a full blood Arab, Bwana believed her to be such.

He did not mention the subject again to Meriem, and in this he made a mistake, for the young girl, while realizing the debt of gratitude she owed Bwana and My Dear, was both proud and sensitive, so that Bwana's action in sending Baynes away and giving her no opportunity to explain or defend hurt and mortified her. Also it did much toward making a martyr of Baynes in her eyes and arousing in her breast a keen feeling of loyalty toward him.

What she had half-mistaken for love before, she now wholly mistook for love. Bwana and My Dear might have told her much of the social barriers that they only too well knew Baynes must feel existed between Meriem and himself, but they hesitated to wound her. It would have been better had they inflicted this lesser sorrow, and saved the child the misery that was to follow because of her ignorance.

As Hanson and Baynes rode toward the former's camp the Englishman maintained a morose silence. The other was attempting to formulate an opening that would lead naturally to the proposition he had in mind. He rode a neck behind his companion, grinning as he noted the sullen scowl upon the other's patrician face.

"Rather rough on you, wasn't he?" he ventured at last, jerking his head back in the direction of the bungalow as Baynes turned his eyes upon him at the remark. "He thinks a lot of the girl," continued Hanson, "and don't want nobody to marry her and take her away; but it looks to me as though he was doin' her more harm than good in sendin' you away. She ought to marry some time, and she couldn't do better than a fine young gentleman like you."

Baynes, who had at first felt inclined to take offense at the mention of his private affairs by this common fellow, was mollified by Hanson's final remark, and immediately commenced to see in him a man of fine discrimination.

"He's a darned bounder," grumbled the Hon. Morison; "but I'll get even with him. He may be the whole thing in Central Africa but I'm as big as he is in London, and he'll find it out when he comes home."

"If I was you," said Hanson, "I wouldn't let any man keep me from gettin' the girl I want. Between you and me I ain't got no use for him either, and if I can help you any way just call on me."

"It's mighty good of you, Hanson," replied Baynes, warming up a bit; "but what can a fellow do here in this God-forsaken hole?"

"I know what I'd do," said Hanson. "I'd take the girl along with me. If she loves you she'll go, all right."

"It can't be done," said Baynes. "He bosses this whole blooming country for miles around. He'd be sure to catch us."

"No, he wouldn't, not with me running things," said Hanson. "I've been trading and hunting here for ten years and I know as much about the country as he does. If you want to take the girl along I'll help you, and I'll guarantee that there won't nobody catch up with us before we reach the coast. I'll tell you what, you write her a note and I'll get it to her by my head man. Ask her to meet you to say goodbye – she won't refuse that. In the meantime we can be movin' camp a little further north all the time and you can make arrangements with her to be all ready on a certain night. Tell her I'll meet her then while you wait for us in camp. That'll be better for I know the country well and can cover it quicker than you. You can take care of the safari and be movin' along slow toward the north and the girl and I'll catch up to you."

"But suppose she won't come?" suggested Baynes.

"Then make another date for a last good-bye," said Hanson, "and instead of you I'll be there and I'll bring her along anyway. She'll have to come, and after it's all over she won't feel so bad about it – especially after livin' with you for two months while we're makin' the coast."

A shocked and angry protest rose to Baynes' lips; but he did not utter it, for almost simultaneously came the realization that this was practically the same thing he had been planning upon himself. It had sounded brutal and criminal from the lips of the rough trader; but nevertheless the young Englishman saw that with Hanson's help and his knowledge of African travel the possibilities of success would be much greater than as though the Hon. Morison were to attempt the thing single handed. And so he nodded a glum assent.

The balance of the long ride to Hanson's northerly camp was made in silence, for both men were occupied with their own thoughts, most of which were far from being either complimentary or loyal to the other. As they rode through the wood the sounds of their careless passage came to the ears of another jungle wayfarer. The Killer had determined to come back to the place where he had seen the white girl who took to the trees with the ability of long habitude. There was a compelling something in the recollection of her that drew him irresistibly toward her. He wished to see her by the light of day, to see her features, to see the color of her eyes and hair. It seemed to him that she must bear a strong resemblance to his lost Meriem, and yet he knew that the chances were that she did not. The fleeting glimpse that he had had of her in the moonlight as she swung from the back of her plunging pony into the branches of the tree above her had shown him a girl of about the same height as his Meriem; but of a more rounded and developed femininity.

Now he was moving lazily back in the direction of the spot where he had seen the girl when the sounds of the approaching horsemen came to his sharp ears. He moved stealthily through the branches until he came within sight of the riders. The younger man he instantly recognized as the same he had seen with his arms about the girl in the moonlit glade just the instant before Numa charged. The other he did not recognize though there was a familiarity about his carriage and figure that puzzled Korak.

The ape-man decided that to find the girl again he would but have to keep in touch with the young Englishman, and so he fell in behind the pair, following them to Hanson's camp. Here the Hon. Morison penned a brief note, which Hanson gave into the keeping of one of his boys who started off forthwith toward the south.

Korak remained in the vicinity of the camp, keeping a careful watch upon the Englishman. He had half expected to find the girl at the destination of the two riders and had been disappointed when no sign of her materialized about the camp.

Baynes was restless, pacing back and forth beneath the trees when he should have been resting against the forced marches of the coming flight. Hanson lay in his hammock and smoked. They spoke but little. Korak lay stretched upon a branch among the dense foliage above them. Thus passed the balance of the afternoon. Korak became hungry and thirsty. He doubted that either of the men would leave camp now before morning, so he withdrew, but toward the south, for there it seemed most likely the girl still was.

In the garden beside the bungalow Meriem wandered thoughtfully in the moonlight. She still smarted from Bwana's, to her, unjust treatment of the Hon. Morison Baynes. Nothing had been explained to her, for both Bwana and My Dear had wished to spare her the mortification and sorrow of the true explanation of Baynes' proposal. They knew, as Meriem did not, that the man had no intention of marrying her, else he would have come directly to Bwana, knowing full well that no objection would be interposed if Meriem really cared for him.

Meriem loved them both and was grateful to them for all that they had done for her; but deep in her little heart surged the savage love of liberty that her years of untrammeled freedom in the jungle had made part and parcel of her being. Now, for the first time since she had come to them, Meriem felt like a prisoner in the bungalow of Bwana and My Dear.

Like a caged tigress the girl paced the length of the enclosure. Once she paused near the outer fence, her head upon one side – listening. What was it she had heard? The pad of naked human feet just beyond the garden. She listened for a moment. The sound was not repeated. Then she resumed her restless walking. Down to the opposite end of the garden she passed, turned and retraced her steps toward the upper end. Upon the sward near the bushes that hid the fence, full in the glare of the moonlight, lay a white envelope that had not been there when she had turned almost upon the very spot a moment before.

Meriem stopped short in her tracks, listening again, and sniffing – more than ever the tigress; alert, ready. Beyond the bushes a naked black runner squatted, peering through the foliage. He saw her take a step closer to the letter. She had seen it. He rose quietly and following the shadows of the bushes that ran down to the corral was soon gone from sight.

Meriem's trained ears heard his every move. She made no attempt to seek closer knowledge of his identity. Already she had guessed that he was a messenger from the Hon. Morison. She stooped and picked up the envelope. Tearing it open she easily read the contents by the moon's brilliant light. It was, as she had guessed, from Baynes.

"I cannot go without seeing you again," it read. "Come to the clearing early tomorrow morning and say good-bye to me. Come alone."

There was a little more – words that made her heart beat faster and a happy flush mount her cheek.

Chapter Twenty

It was still dark when the Hon. Morison Baynes set forth for the trysting place. He insisted upon having a guide, saying that he was not sure that he could find his way back to the little clearing. As a matter of fact the thought of that lonely ride through the darkness before the sun rose had been too much for his courage, and he craved company. A black, therefore, preceded him on foot. Behind and above him came Korak, whom the noise in the camp had awakened.

It was nine o'clock before Baynes drew rein in the clearing. Meriem had not yet arrived. The black lay down to rest. Baynes lolled in his saddle. Korak stretched himself comfortably upon a lofty limb, where he could watch those beneath him without being seen.

An hour passed. Baynes gave evidence of nervousness. Korak had already guessed that the young Englishman had come here to meet another, nor was he at all in doubt as to the identity of that other. The Killer was perfectly satisfied that he was soon again to see the nimble she who had so forcefully reminded him of Meriem.

Presently the sound of an approaching horse came to Korak's ears. She was coming! She had almost reached the clearing before Baynes became aware of her presence, and then as he looked up, the foliage parted to the head and shoulders of her mount and Meriem rode into view. Baynes spurred to meet her. Korak looked searchingly down upon her, mentally anathematizing the broad-brimmed hat that hid her features from his eyes. She was abreast the Englishman now. Korak saw the man take both her hands and draw her close to his breast. He saw the man's face concealed for a moment beneath the same broad brim that hid the girl's. He could imagine their lips meeting, and a twinge of sorrow and sweet recollection combined to close his eyes for an instant in that involuntary muscular act with which we attempt to shut out from the mind's eye harrowing reflections.

When he looked again they had drawn apart and were conversing earnestly. Korak could see the man urging something. It was equally evident that the girl was holding back. There were many of her gestures, and the way in which she tossed her head up and to the right, tip-tilting her chin, that reminded Korak still more strongly of Meriem. And then the conversation was over and the man took the girl in his arms again to kiss her good-bye. She turned and rode toward the point from which she had come. The man sat on his horse watching her. At the edge of the jungle she turned to wave him a final farewell.

"Tonight!" she cried, throwing back her head as she called the words to him across the little distance which separated them – throwing back her head and revealing her face for the first time to the eyes of The Killer in the tree above. Korak started as though pierced through the heart with an arrow. He trembled and shook like a leaf. He closed his eyes, pressing his palms across them, and then he opened them again and looked but the girl was gone – only the waving foliage of the jungle's rim marked where she had disappeared. It was impossible! It could not be true! And yet, with his own eyes he had seen his Meriem – older a little, with figure more rounded by nearer maturity, and subtly changed in other ways; more beautiful than ever, yet still his little Meriem. Yes, he had seen the dead alive again; he had seen his Meriem in the flesh. She lived! She had not died! He had seen her – he had seen his Meriem – IN THE ARMS OF ANOTHER MAN! And that man sat below him now, within easy reach. Korak, The Killer, fondled his heavy spear. He played with the grass rope dangling from his gee-string. He stroked the hunting knife at his hip. And the man beneath him called to his drowsy guide, bent the rein to his pony's neck and moved off toward the north. Still sat Korak, The Killer, alone among the trees. Now his hands hung idly at his sides. His weapons and what he had intended were forgotten for the moment. Korak was thinking. He had noted that subtle change in Meriem. When last he had seen her she had been his little, half-naked Mangani – wild, savage, and uncouth. She had not seemed uncouth to him then; but now, in the change that had come over her, he knew that such she had been; yet no more uncouth than he, and he was still uncouth.

In her had taken place the change. In her he had just seen a sweet and lovely flower of refinement and civilization, and he shuddered as he recalled the fate that he himself had planned for her – to be the mate of an ape-man, his mate, in the savage jungle. Then he had seen no wrong in it, for he had loved her, and the way he had planned had been the way of the jungle which they two had chosen as their home; but now, after having seen the Meriem of civilized attire, he realized the hideousness of his once cherished plan, and he thanked God that chance and the blacks of Kovudoo had thwarted him.

Yet he still loved her, and jealousy seared his soul as he recalled the sight of her in the arms of the dapper young Englishman. What were his intentions toward her? Did he really love her? How could one not love her? And she loved him, of that Korak had had ample proof. Had she not loved him she would not have accepted his kisses. His Meriem loved another! For a long time he let that awful truth sink deep, and from it he tried to reason out his future plan of action. In his heart was a great desire to follow the man and slay him; but ever there rose in his consciousness the thought: She loves him. Could he slay the creature Meriem loved? Sadly he shook his head. No, he could not. Then came a partial decision to follow Meriem and speak with her. He half started, and then glanced down at his nakedness and was ashamed. He, the son of a British peer, had thus thrown away his life, had thus degraded himself to the level of a beast that he was ashamed to go to the woman he loved and lay his love at her feet. He was ashamed to go to the little Arab maid who had been his jungle playmate, for what had he to offer her?

For years circumstances had prevented a return to his father and mother, and at last pride had stepped in and expunged from his mind the last vestige of any intention to return. In a spirit of boyish adventure he had cast his lot with the jungle ape. The killing of the crook in the coast inn had filled his childish mind with terror of the law, and driven him deeper into the wilds. The rebuffs that he had met at the hands of men, both black and white, had had their effect upon his mind while yet it was in a formative state, and easily influenced.

He had come to believe that the hand of man was against him, and then he had found in Meriem the only human association he required or craved. When she had been snatched from him his sorrow had been so deep that the thought of ever mingling again with human beings grew still more unutterably distasteful. Finally and for all time, he thought, the die was cast. Of his own volition he had become a beast, a beast he had lived, a beast he would die.

Now that it was too late, he regretted it. For now Meriem, still living, had been revealed to him in a guise of progress and advancement that had carried her completely out of his life. Death itself could not have further removed her from him. In her new world she loved a man of her own kind. And Korak knew that it was right. She was not for him – not for the naked, savage ape. No, she was not for him; but he still was hers. If he could not have her and happiness, he would at least do all that lay in his power to assure happiness to her. He would follow the young Englishman. In the first place he would know that he meant Meriem no harm, and after that, though jealousy wrenched his heart, he would watch over the man Meriem loved, for Meriem's sake; but God help that man if he thought to wrong her!

Slowly he aroused himself. He stood erect and stretched his great frame, the muscles of his arms gliding sinuously beneath his tanned skin as he bent his clenched fists behind his head. A movement on the ground beneath caught his eye. An antelope was entering the clearing. Immediately Korak became aware that he was empty – again he was a beast. For a moment love had lifted him to sublime heights of honor and renunciation.

The antelope was crossing the clearing. Korak dropped to the ground upon the opposite side of the tree, and so lightly that not even the sensitive ears of the antelope apprehended his presence. He uncoiled his grass rope – it was the latest addition to his armament, yet he was proficient with it. Often he traveled with nothing more than his knife and his rope – they were light and easy to carry. His spear and bow and arrows were cumbersome and he usually kept one or all of them hidden away in a private cache.

Now he held a single coil of the long rope in his right hand, and the balance in his left. The antelope was but a few paces from him. Silently Korak leaped from his hiding place swinging the rope free from the entangling shrubbery. The antelope sprang away almost instantly; but instantly, too, the coiled rope, with its sliding noose, flew through the air above him. With unerring precision it settled about the creature's neck. There was a quick wrist movement of the thrower, the noose tightened. The Killer braced himself with the rope across his hip, and as the antelope tautened the singing strands in a last frantic bound for liberty he was thrown over upon his back.

Then, instead of approaching the fallen animal as a roper of the western plains might do, Korak dragged his captive to himself, pulling him in hand over hand, and when he was within reach leaping upon him even as Sheeta the panther might have done, and burying his teeth in the animal's neck while he found its heart with the point of his hunting knife. Recoiling his rope, he cut a few generous strips from his kill and took to the trees again, where he ate in peace. Later he swung off in the direction of a nearby water hole, and then he slept.

In his mind, of course, was the suggestion of another meeting between Meriem and the young Englishman that had been borne to him by the girl's parting: "Tonight!"

He had not followed Meriem because he knew from the direction from which she had come and in which she returned that wheresoever she had found an asylum it lay out across the plains and not wishing to be discovered by the girl he had not cared to venture into the open after her. It would do as well to keep in touch with the young man, and that was precisely what he intended doing.

To you or me the possibility of locating the Hon. Morison in the jungle after having permitted him to get such a considerable start might have seemed remote; but to Korak it was not at all so. He guessed that the white man would return to his camp; but should he have done otherwise it would be a simple matter to The Killer to trail a mounted man accompanied by another on foot. Days might pass and still such a spoor would be sufficiently plain to lead Korak unfalteringly to its end; while a matter of a few hours only left it as clear to him as though the makers themselves were still in plain sight.

And so it came that a few minutes after the Hon. Morison Baynes entered the camp to be greeted by Hanson, Korak slipped noiselessly into a near-by tree. There he lay until late afternoon and still the young Englishman made no move to leave camp. Korak wondered if Meriem were coming there. A little later Hanson and one of his black boys rode out of camp. Korak merely noted the fact. He was not particularly interested in what any other member of the company than the young Englishman did.

Darkness came and still the young man remained. He ate his evening meal, afterward smoking numerous cigarettes. Presently he began to pace back and forth before his tent. He kept his boy busy replenishing the fire. A lion coughed and he went into his tent to reappear with an express rifle. Again he admonished the boy to throw more brush upon the fire. Korak saw that he was nervous and afraid, and his lip curled in a sneer of contempt.

Was this the creature who had supplanted him in the heart of his Meriem? Was this a man, who trembled when Numa coughed? How could such as he protect Meriem from the countless dangers of the jungle? Ah, but he would not have to. They would live in the safety of European civilization, where men in uniforms were hired to protect them. What need had a European of prowess to protect his mate? Again the sneer curled Korak's lip.

Hanson and his boy had ridden directly to the clearing. It was already dark when they arrived. Leaving the boy there Hanson rode to the edge of the plain, leading the boy's horse. There he waited. It was nine o'clock before he saw a solitary figure galloping toward him from the direction of the bungalow. A few moments later Meriem drew in her mount beside him. She was nervous and flushed. When she recognized Hanson she drew back, startled.

"Mr. Baynes' horse fell on him and sprained his ankle," Hanson hastened to explain. "He couldn't very well come so he sent me to meet you and bring you to camp."

The girl could not see in the darkness the gloating, triumphant expression on the speaker's face.

"We had better hurry," continued Hanson, "for we'll have to move along pretty fast if we don't want to be overtaken."

"Is he hurt badly?" asked Meriem.

"Only a little sprain," replied Hanson. "He can ride all right; but we both thought he'd better lie up tonight, and rest, for he'll have plenty hard riding in the next few weeks."

"Yes," agreed the girl.

Hanson swung his pony about and Meriem followed him. They rode north along the edge of the jungle for a mile and then turned straight into it toward the west. Meriem, following, payed little attention to directions. She did not know exactly where Hanson's camp lay and so she did not guess that he was not leading her toward it. All night they rode, straight toward the west. When morning came, Hanson permitted a short halt for breakfast, which he had provided in well-filled saddle bags before leaving his camp. Then they pushed on again, nor did they halt a second time until in the heat of the day he stopped and motioned the girl to dismount.

"We will sleep here for a time and let the ponies graze," he said.

"I had no idea the camp was so far away," said Meriem.

"I left orders that they were to move on at day break," explained the trader, "so that we could get a good start. I knew that you and I could easily overtake a laden safari. It may not be until tomorrow that we'll catch up with them."

But though they traveled part of the night and all the following day no sign of the safari appeared ahead of them. Meriem, an adept in jungle craft, knew that none had passed ahead of them for many days. Occasionally she saw indications of an old spoor, a very old spoor, of many men. For the most part they followed this well-marked trail along elephant paths and through park-like groves. It was an ideal trail for rapid traveling.

Meriem at last became suspicious. Gradually the attitude of the man at her side had begun to change. Often she surprised him devouring her with his eyes. Steadily the former sensation of previous acquaintanceship urged itself upon her. Somewhere, sometime before she had known this man. It was evident that he had not shaved for several days. A blonde stubble had commenced to cover his neck and cheeks and chin, and with it the assurance that he was no stranger continued to grow upon the girl.

It was not until the second day, however, that Meriem rebelled. She drew in her pony at last and voiced her doubts. Hanson assured her that the camp was but a few miles further on.

"We should have overtaken them yesterday," he said. "They must have marched much faster than I had believed possible."

"They have not marched here at all," said Meriem. "The spoor that we have been following is weeks old."

Hanson laughed.

"Oh, that's it, is it?" he cried. "Why didn't you say so before? I could have easily explained. We are not coming by the same route; but we'll pick up their trail sometime today, even if we don't overtake them."

Now, at last, Meriem knew the man was lying to her. What a fool he must be to think that anyone could believe such a ridiculous explanation? Who was so stupid as to believe that they could have expected to overtake another party, and he had certainly assured her that momentarily he expected to do so, when that party's route was not to meet theirs for several miles yet?

She kept her own counsel however, planning to escape at the first opportunity when she might have a sufficient start of her captor, as she now considered him, to give her some assurance of outdistancing him. She watched his face continually when she could without being observed. Tantalizingly the placing of his familiar features persisted in eluding her. Where had she known him? Under what conditions had they met before she had seen him about the farm of Bwana? She ran over in her mind all the few white men she ever had known. There were some who had come to her father's douar in the jungle. Few it is true, but there had been some. Ah, now she had it! She had seen him there! She almost seized upon his identity and then in an instant, it had slipped from her again.

It was mid afternoon when they suddenly broke out of the jungle upon the banks of a broad and placid river. Beyond, upon the opposite shore, Meriem described a camp surrounded by a high, thorn boma.

"Here we are at last," said Hanson. He drew his revolver and fired in the air. Instantly the camp across the river was astir. Black men ran down the river's bank. Hanson hailed them. But there was no sign of the Hon. Morison Baynes.

In accordance with their master's instructions the blacks manned a canoe and rowed across. Hanson placed Meriem in the little craft and entered it himself, leaving two boys to watch the horses, which the canoe was to return for and swim across to the camp side of the river.

Once in the camp Meriem asked for Baynes. For the moment her fears had been allayed by the sight of the camp, which she had come to look upon as more or less a myth. Hanson pointed toward the single tent that stood in the center of the enclosure.

"There," he said, and preceded her toward it. At the entrance he held the flap aside and motioned her within. Meriem entered and looked about. The tent was empty. She turned toward Hanson. There was a broad grin on his face.

"Where is Mr. Baynes?" she demanded.

"He ain't here," replied Hanson. "Leastwise I don't see him, do you? But I'm here, and I'm a damned sight better man than that thing ever was. You don't need him no more – you got me," and he laughed uproariously and reached for her.

Meriem struggled to free herself. Hanson encircled her arms and body in his powerful grip and bore her slowly backward toward the pile of blankets at the far end of the tent. His face was bent close to hers. His eyes were narrowed to two slits of heat and passion and desire. Meriem was looking full into his face as she fought for freedom when there came over her a sudden recollection of a similar scene in which she had been a participant and with it full recognition of her assailant. He was the Swede Malbihn who had attacked her once before, who had shot his companion who would have saved her, and from whom she had been rescued by Bwana. His smooth face had deceived her; but now with the growing beard and the similarity of conditions recognition came swift and sure.

But today there would be no Bwana to save her.

Chapter Twenty One

The black boy whom Malbihn had left awaiting him in the clearing with instructions to remain until he returned sat crouched at the foot of a tree for an hour when he was suddenly startled by the coughing grunt of a lion behind him. With celerity born of the fear of death the boy clambered into the branches of the tree, and a moment later the king of beasts entered the clearing and approached the carcass of an antelope which, until now, the boy had not seen.

Until daylight the beast fed, while the black clung, sleepless, to his perch, wondering what had become of his master and the two ponies. He had been with Malbihn for a year, and so was fairly conversant with the character of the white. His knowledge presently led him to believe that he had been purposely abandoned. Like the balance of Malbihn's followers, this boy hated his master cordially – fear being the only bond that held him to the white man. His present uncomfortable predicament but added fuel to the fires of his hatred.

As the sun rose the lion withdrew into the jungle and the black descended from his tree and started upon his long journey back to camp. In his primitive brain revolved various fiendish plans for a revenge that he would not have the courage to put into effect when the test came and he stood face to face with one of the dominant race.

A mile from the clearing he came upon the spoor of two ponies crossing his path at right angles. A cunning look entered the black's eyes. He laughed uproariously and slapped his thighs.

Negroes are tireless gossipers, which, of course, is but a roundabout way of saying that they are human. Malbihn's boys had been no exception to the rule and as many of them had been with him at various times during the past ten years there was little about his acts and life in the African wilds that was not known directly or by hearsay to them all.

And so, knowing his master and many of his past deeds, knowing, too, a great deal about the plans of Malbihn and Baynes that had been overheard by himself, or other servants; and knowing well from the gossip of the head-men that half of Malbihn's party lay in camp by the great river far to the west, it was not difficult for the boy to put two and two together and arrive at four as the sum – the four being represented by a firm conviction that his master had deceived the other white man and taken the latter's woman to his western camp, leaving the other to suffer capture and punishment at the hands of the Big Bwana whom all feared. Again the boy bared his rows of big, white teeth and laughed aloud. Then he resumed his northward way, traveling at a dogged trot that ate up the miles with marvelous rapidity.

In the Swede's camp the Hon. Morison had spent an almost sleepless night of nervous apprehension and doubts and fears. Toward morning he had slept, utterly exhausted. It was the headman who awoke him shortly after sun rise to remind him that they must at once take up their northward journey. Baynes hung back. He wanted to wait for "Hanson" and Meriem. The headman urged upon him the danger that lay in loitering. The fellow knew his master's plans sufficiently well to understand that he had done something to arouse the ire of the Big Bwana and that it would fare ill with them all if they were overtaken in Big Bwana's country. At the suggestion Baynes took alarm.

What if the Big Bwana, as the head-man called him, had surprised "Hanson" in his nefarious work. Would he not guess the truth and possibly be already on the march to overtake and punish him? Baynes had heard much of his host's summary method of dealing out punishment to malefactors great and small who transgressed the laws or customs of his savage little world which lay beyond the outer ramparts of what men are pleased to call frontiers. In this savage world where there was no law the Big Bwana was law unto himself and all who dwelt about him. It was even rumored that he had extracted the death penalty from a white man who had maltreated a native girl.

Baynes shuddered at the recollection of this piece of gossip as he wondered what his host would exact of the man who had attempted to steal his young, white ward. The thought brought him to his feet.

"Yes," he said, nervously, "we must get away from here at once. Do you know the trail to the north?"

The head-man did, and he lost no time in getting the safari upon the march.

It was noon when a tired and sweat-covered runner overtook the trudging little column. The man was greeted with shouts of welcome from his fellows, to whom he imparted all that he knew and guessed of the actions of their master, so that the entire safari was aware of matters before Baynes, who marched close to the head of the column, was reached and acquainted with the facts and the imaginings of the black boy whom Malbihn had deserted in the clearing the night before.

When the Hon. Morison had listened to all that the boy had to say and realized that the trader had used him as a tool whereby he himself might get Meriem into his possession, his blood ran hot with rage and he trembled with apprehension for the girl's safety.

That another contemplated no worse a deed than he had contemplated in no way palliated the hideousness of the other's offense. At first it did not occur to him that he would have wronged Meriem no less than he believed "Hanson" contemplated wronging her. Now his rage was more the rage of a man beaten at his own game and robbed of the prize that he had thought already his.

"Do you know where your master has gone?" he asked the black.

"Yes, Bwana," replied the boy. "He has gone to the other camp beside the big afi that flows far toward the setting sun.

"Can you take me to him?" demanded Baynes.

The boy nodded affirmatively. Here he saw a method of revenging himself upon his hated Bwana and at the same time of escaping the wrath of the Big Bwana whom all were positive would first follow after the northerly safari.

"Can you and I, alone, reach his camp?" asked the Hon. Morison.

"Yes, Bwana," assured the black.

Baynes turned toward the head-man. He was conversant with "Hanson's" plans now. He understood why he had wished to move the northern camp as far as possible toward the northern boundary of the Big Bwana's country – it would give him far more time to make his escape toward the West Coast while the Big Bwana was chasing the northern contingent. Well, he would utilize the man's plans to his own end. He, too, must keep out of the clutches of his host.

"You may take the men north as fast as possible," he said to the head-man. "I shall return and attempt to lead the Big Bwana to the west."

The Negro assented with a grunt. He had no desire to follow this strange white man who was afraid at night; he had less to remain at the tender mercies of the Big Bwana's lusty warriors, between whom and his people there was long-standing blood feud; and he was more than delighted, into the bargain, for a legitimate excuse for deserting his much hated Swede master. He knew a way to the north and his own country that the white men did not know – a short cut across an arid plateau where lay water holes of which the white hunters and explorers that had passed from time to time the fringe of the dry country had never dreamed. He might even elude the Big Bwana should he follow them, and with this thought uppermost in his mind he gathered the remnants of Malbihn's safari into a semblance of order and moved off toward the north. And toward the southwest the black boy led the Hon. Morison Baynes into the jungles.

Korak had waited about the camp, watching the Hon. Morison until the safari had started north. Then, assured that the young Englishman was going in the wrong direction to meet Meriem he had abandoned him and returned slowly to the point where he had seen the girl, for whom his heart yearned, in the arms of another.

So great had been his happiness at seeing Meriem alive that, for the instant, no thought of jealousy had entered his mind. Later these thoughts had come – dark, bloody thoughts that would have made the flesh of the Hon. Morison creep could he have guessed that they were revolving in the brain of a savage creature creeping stealthily among the branches of the forest giant beneath which he waited the coming of "Hanson" and the girl.

And with passing of the hours had come subdued reflection in which he had weighed himself against the trimly clad English gentleman and – found that he was wanting. What had he to offer her by comparison with that which the other man might offer? What was his "mess of pottage" to the birthright that the other had preserved? How could he dare go, naked and unkempt, to that fair thing who had once been his jungle-fellow and propose the thing that had been in his mind when first the realization of his love had swept over him? He shuddered as he thought of the irreparable wrong that his love would have done the innocent child but for the chance that had snatched her from him before it was too late. Doubtless she knew now the horror that had been in his mind. Doubtless she hated and loathed him as he hated and loathed himself when he let his mind dwell upon it. He had lost her. No more surely had she been lost when he thought her dead than she was in reality now that he had seen her living – living in the guise of a refinement that had transfigured and sanctified her.

He had loved her before, now he worshipped her. He knew that he might never possess her now, but at least he might see her. From a distance he might look upon her. Perhaps he might serve her; but never must she guess that he had found her or that he lived.

He wondered if she ever thought of him – if the happy days that they had spent together never recurred to her mind. It seemed unbelievable that such could be the case, and yet, too, it seemed almost equally unbelievable that this beautiful girl was the same disheveled, half naked, little sprite who skipped nimbly among the branches of the trees as they ran and played in the lazy, happy days of the past. It could not be that her memory held more of the past than did her new appearance.

It was a sad Korak who ranged the jungle near the plain's edge waiting for the coming of his Meriem – the Meriem who never came.

But there came another – a tall, broad-shouldered man in khaki at the head of a swarthy crew of ebon warriors. The man's face was set in hard, stern lines and the marks of sorrow were writ deep about his mouth and eyes – so deep that the set expression of rage upon his features could not obliterate them.

Korak saw the man pass beneath him where he hid in the great tree that had harbored him before upon the edge of that fateful little clearing. He saw him come and he set rigid and frozen and suffering above him. He saw him search the ground with his keen eyes, and he only sat there watching with eyes that glazed from the intensity of his gaze. He saw him sign to his men that he had come upon that which he sought and he saw him pass out of sight toward the north, and still Korak sat like a graven image, with a heart that bled in dumb misery. An hour later Korak moved slowly away, back into the jungle toward the west. He went listlessly, with bent head and stooped shoulders, like an old man who bore upon his back the weight of a great sorrow.

Baynes, following his black guide, battled his way through the dense underbrush, riding stooped low over his horse's neck, or often he dismounted where the low branches swept too close to earth to permit him to remain in the saddle. The black was taking him the shortest way, which was no way at all for a horseman, and after the first day's march the young Englishman was forced to abandon his mount, and follow his nimble guide entirely on foot.

During the long hours of marching the Hon. Morison had much time to devote to thought, and as he pictured the probable fate of Meriem at the hands of the Swede his rage against the man became the greater. But presently there came to him a realization of the fact that his own base plans had led the girl into this terrible predicament, and that even had she escaped "Hanson" she would have found but little better deserts awaiting her with him.

There came too, the realization that Meriem was infinitely more precious to him than he had imagined. For the first time he commenced to compare her with other women of his acquaintance – women of birth and position – and almost to his surprise – he discovered that the young Arab girl suffered less than they by the comparison. And then from hating "Hanson" he came to look upon himself with hate and loathing – to see himself and his perfidious act in all their contemptible hideousness.

Thus, in the crucible of shame amidst the white heat of naked truths, the passion that the man had felt for the girl he had considered his social inferior was transmuted into love. And as he staggered on there burned within him beside his newborn love another great passion – the passion of hate urging him on to the consummation of revenge.

A creature of ease and luxury, he had never been subjected to the hardships and tortures which now were his constant companionship, yet, his clothing torn, his flesh scratched and bleeding, he urged the black to greater speed, though with every dozen steps he himself fell from exhaustion.

It was revenge which kept him going – that and a feeling that in his suffering he was partially expiating the great wrong he had done the girl he loved – for hope of saving her from the fate into which he had trapped her had never existed. "Too late! Too late!" was the dismal accompaniment of thought to which he marched. "Too late! Too late to save; but not too late to avenge!" That kept him up.

Only when it became too dark to see would he permit of a halt. A dozen times in the afternoon he had threatened the black with instant death when the tired guide insisted upon resting. The fellow was terrified. He could not understand the remarkable change that had so suddenly come over the white man who had been afraid in the dark the night before. He would have deserted this terrifying master had he had the opportunity; but Baynes guessed that some such thought might be in the other's mind, and so gave the fellow none. He kept close to him by day and slept touching him at night in the rude thorn boma they constructed as a slight protection against prowling carnivora.

That the Hon. Morison could sleep at all in the midst of the savage jungle was sufficient indication that he had changed considerably in the past twenty-four hours, and that he could lie close beside a none-too-fragrant black man spoke of possibilities for democracy within him yet all undreamed of.

Morning found him stiff and lame and sore, but none the less determined to push on in pursuit of "Hanson" as rapidly as possible. With his rifle he brought down a buck at a ford in a small stream shortly after they broke camp, breakfastless. Begrudgingly he permitted a halt while they cooked and ate, and then on again through the wilderness of trees and vines and underbrush.

And in the meantime Korak wandered slowly westward, coming upon the trail of Tantor, the elephant, whom he overtook browsing in the deep shade of the jungle. The ape-man, lonely and sorrowing, was glad of the companionship of his huge friend. Affectionately the sinuous trunk encircled him, and he was swung to the mighty back where so often before he had lolled and dreamed the long afternoon away.

Far to the north the Big Bwana and his black warriors clung tenaciously to the trail of the fleeing safari that was luring them further and further from the girl they sought to save, while back at the bungalow the woman who had loved Meriem as though she had been her own waited impatiently and in sorrow for the return of the rescuing party and the girl she was positive her invincible lord and master would bring back with him.

Chapter Twenty Two

As Meriem struggled with Malbihn, her hands pinioned to her sides by his brawny grip, hope died within her. She did not utter a sound for she knew that there was none to come to her assistance, and, too, the jungle training of her earlier life had taught her the futility of appeals for succor in the savage world of her up-bringing.

But as she fought to free herself one hand came in contact with the butt of Malbihn's revolver where it rested in the holster at his hip. Slowly he was dragging her toward the blankets, and slowly her fingers encircled the coveted prize and drew it from its resting place.

Then, as Malbihn stood at the edge of the disordered pile of blankets, Meriem suddenly ceased to draw away from him, and as quickly hurled her weight against him with the result that he was thrown backward, his feet stumbled against the bedding and he was hurled to his back. Instinctively his hands flew out to save himself and at the same instant Meriem leveled the revolver at his breast and pulled the trigger.

But the hammer fell futilely upon an empty shell, and Malbihn was again upon his feet clutching at her. For a moment she eluded him, and ran toward the entrance to the tent, but at the very doorway his heavy hand fell upon her shoulder and dragged her back. Wheeling upon him with the fury of a wounded lioness Meriem grasped the long revolver by the barrel, swung it high above her head and crashed it down full in Malbihn's face.

With an oath of pain and rage the man staggered backward, releasing his hold upon her and then sank unconscious to the ground. Without a backward look Meriem turned and fled into the open. Several of the blacks saw her and tried to intercept her flight, but the menace of the empty weapon kept them at a distance. And so she won beyond the encircling boma and disappeared into the jungle to the south.

Straight into the branches of a tree she went, true to the arboreal instincts of the little mangani she had been, and here she stripped off her riding skirt, her shoes and her stockings, for she knew that she had before her a journey and a flight which would not brook the burden of these garments. Her riding breeches and jacket would have to serve as protection from cold and thorns, nor would they hamper her over much; but a skirt and shoes were impossible among the trees.

She had not gone far before she commenced to realize how slight were her chances for survival without means of defense or a weapon to bring down meat. Why had she not thought to strip the cartridge belt from Malbihn's waist before she had left his tent! With cartridges for the revolver she might hope to bag small game, and to protect herself from all but the most ferocious of the enemies that would beset her way back to the beloved hearthstone of Bwana and My Dear.

With the thought came determination to return and obtain the coveted ammunition. She realized that she was taking great chances of recapture; but without means of defense and of obtaining meat she felt that she could never hope to reach safety. And so she turned her face back toward the camp from which she had but just escaped.

She thought Malbihn dead, so terrific a blow had she dealt him, and she hoped to find an opportunity after dark to enter the camp and search his tent for the cartridge belt; but scarcely had she found a hiding place in a great tree at the edge of the boma where she could watch without danger of being discovered, when she saw the Swede emerge from his tent, wiping blood from his face, and hurling a volley of oaths and questions at his terrified followers.

Shortly after the entire camp set forth in search of her and when Meriem was positive that all were gone she descended from her hiding place and ran quickly across the clearing to Malbihn's tent. A hasty survey of the interior revealed no ammunition; but in one corner was a box in which were packed the Swede's personal belongings that he had sent along by his headman to this westerly camp.

Meriem seized the receptacle as the possible container of extra ammunition. Quickly she loosed the cords that held the canvas covering about the box, and a moment later had raised the lid and was rummaging through the heterogeneous accumulation of odds and ends within. There were letters and papers and cuttings from old newspapers, and among other things the photograph of a little girl upon the back of which was pasted a cutting from a Paris daily – a cutting that she could not read, yellowed and dimmed by age and handling – but something about the photograph of the little girl which was also reproduced in the newspaper cutting held her attention. Where had she seen that picture before? And then, quite suddenly, it came to her that this was a picture of herself as she had been years and years before.

Where had it been taken? How had it come into the possession of this man? Why had it been reproduced in a newspaper? What was the story that the faded type told of it?

Meriem was baffled by the puzzle that her search for ammunition had revealed. She stood gazing at the faded photograph for a time and then bethought herself of the ammunition for which she had come. Turning again to the box she rummaged to the bottom and there in a corner she came upon a little box of cartridges. A single glance assured her that they were intended for the weapon she had thrust inside the band of her riding breeches, and slipping them into her pocket she turned once more for an examination of the baffling likeness of herself that she held in her hand.

As she stood thus in vain endeavor to fathom this inexplicable mystery the sound of voices broke upon her ears. Instantly she was all alert. They were coming closer! A second later she recognized the lurid profanity of the Swede. Malbihn, her persecutor, was returning! Meriem ran quickly to the opening of the tent and looked out. It was too late! She was fairly cornered! The white man and three of his black henchmen were coming straight across the clearing toward the tent. What was she to do? She slipped the photograph into her waist. Quickly she slipped a cartridge into each of the chambers of the revolver. Then she backed toward the end of the tent, keeping the entrance covered by her weapon. The man stopped outside, and Meriem could hear Malbihn profanely issuing instructions. He was a long time about it, and while he talked in his bellowing, brutish voice, the girl sought some avenue of escape. Stooping, she raised the bottom of the canvas and looked beneath and beyond. There was no one in sight upon that side. Throwing herself upon her stomach she wormed beneath the tent wall just as Malbihn, with a final word to his men, entered the tent.

Meriem heard him cross the floor, and then she rose and, stooping low, ran to a native hut directly behind. Once inside this she turned and glanced back. There was no one in sight. She had not been seen. And now from Malbihn's tent she heard a great cursing. The Swede had discovered the rifling of his box. He was shouting to his men, and as she heard them reply Meriem darted from the hut and ran toward the edge of the boma furthest from Malbihn's tent. Overhanging the boma at this point was a tree that had been too large, in the eyes of the rest-loving blacks, to cut down. So they had terminated the boma just short of it. Meriem was thankful for whatever circumstance had resulted in the leaving of that particular tree where it was, since it gave her the much-needed avenue of escape which she might not otherwise have had.

From her hiding place she saw Malbihn again enter the jungle, this time leaving a guard of three of his boys in the camp. He went toward the south, and after he had disappeared, Meriem skirted the outside of the enclosure and made her way to the river. Here lay the canoes that had been used in bringing the party from the opposite shore. They were unwieldy things for a lone girl to handle, but there was no other way and she must cross the river.

The landing place was in full view of the guard at the camp. To risk the crossing under their eyes would have meant undoubted capture. Her only hope lay in waiting until darkness had fallen, unless some fortuitous circumstance should arise before. For an hour she lay watching the guard, one of whom seemed always in a position where he would immediately discover her should she attempt to launch one of the canoes.

Presently Malbihn appeared, coming out of the jungle, hot and puffing. He ran immediately to the river where the canoes lay and counted them. It was evident that it had suddenly occurred to him that the girl must cross here if she wished to return to her protectors. The expression of relief on his face when he found that none of the canoes was gone was ample evidence of what was passing in his mind. He turned and spoke hurriedly to the head man who had followed him out of the jungle and with whom were several other blacks.

Following Malbihn's instructions they launched all the canoes but one. Malbihn called to the guards in the camp and a moment later the entire party had entered the boats and were paddling up stream.

Meriem watched them until a bend in the river directly above the camp hid them from her sight. They were gone! She was alone, and they had left a canoe in which lay a paddle! She could scarce believe the good fortune that had come to her. To delay now would be suicidal to her hopes. Quickly she ran from her hiding place and dropped to the ground. A dozen yards lay between her and the canoe.

Up stream, beyond the bend, Malbihn ordered his canoes in to shore. He landed with his head man and crossed the little point slowly in search of a spot where he might watch the canoe he had left at the landing place. He was smiling in anticipation of the almost certain success of his stratagem – sooner or later the girl would come back and attempt to cross the river in one of their canoes. It might be that the idea would not occur to her for some time. They might have to wait a day, or two days; but that she would come if she lived or was not captured by the men he had scouting the jungle for her Malbihn was sure. That she would come so soon, however, he had not guessed, and so when he topped the point and came again within sight of the river he saw that which drew an angry oath from his lips – his quarry already was half way across the river.

Turning, he ran rapidly back to his boats, the head man at his heels. Throwing themselves in, Malbihn urged his paddlers to their most powerful efforts. The canoes shot out into the stream and down with the current toward the fleeing quarry. She had almost completed the crossing when they came in sight of her. At the same instant she saw them, and redoubled her efforts to reach the opposite shore before they should overtake her. Two minutes' start of them was all Meriem cared for. Once in the trees she knew that she could outdistance and elude them. Her hopes were high – they could not overtake her now – she had had too good a start of them.

Malbihn, urging his men onward with a stream of hideous oaths and blows from his fists, realized that the girl was again slipping from his clutches. The leading canoe, in the bow of which he stood, was yet a hundred yards behind the fleeing Meriem when she ran the point of her craft beneath the overhanging trees on the shore of safety.

Malbihn screamed to her to halt. He seemed to have gone mad with rage at the realization that he could not overtake her, and then he threw his rifle to his shoulder, aimed carefully at the slim figure scrambling into the trees, and fired.

Malbihn was an excellent shot. His misses at so short a distance were practically non-existent, nor would he have missed this time but for an accident occurring at the very instant that his finger tightened upon the trigger – an accident to which Meriem owed her life – the providential presence of a water-logged tree trunk, one end of which was embedded in the mud of the river bottom and the other end of which floated just beneath the surface where the prow of Malbihn's canoe ran upon it as he fired. The slight deviation of the boat's direction was sufficient to throw the muzzle of the rifle out of aim. The bullet whizzed harmlessly by Meriem's head and an instant later she had disappeared into the foliage of the tree.

There was a smile on her lips as she dropped to the ground to cross a little clearing where once had stood a native village surrounded by its fields. The ruined huts still stood in crumbling decay. The rank vegetation of the jungle overgrew the cultivated ground. Small trees already had sprung up in what had been the village street; but desolation and loneliness hung like a pall above the scene. To Meriem, however, it presented but a place denuded of large trees which she must cross quickly to regain the jungle upon the opposite side before Malbihn should have landed.

The deserted huts were, to her, all the better because they were deserted – she did not see the keen eyes watching her from a dozen points, from tumbling doorways, from behind tottering granaries. In utter unconsciousness of impending danger she started up the village street because it offered the clearest pathway to the jungle.

A mile away toward the east, fighting his way through the jungle along the trail taken by Malbihn when he had brought Meriem to his camp, a man in torn khaki – filthy, haggard, unkempt – came to a sudden stop as the report of Malbihn's rifle resounded faintly through the tangled forest. The black man just ahead of him stopped, too.

"We are almost there, Bwana," he said. There was awe and respect in his tone and manner.

The white man nodded and motioned his ebon guide forward once more. It was the Hon. Morison Baynes – the fastidious – the exquisite. His face and hands were scratched and smeared with dried blood from the wounds he had come by in thorn and thicket. His clothes were tatters. But through the blood and the dirt and the rags a new Baynes shone forth – a handsomer Baynes than the dandy and the fop of yore.

In the heart and soul of every son of woman lies the germ of manhood and honor. Remorse for a scurvy act, and an honorable desire to right the wrong he had done the woman he now knew he really loved had excited these germs to rapid growth in Morison Baynes – and the metamorphosis had taken place.

Onward the two stumbled toward the point from which the single rifle shot had come. The black was unarmed – Baynes, fearing his loyalty had not dared trust him even to carry the rifle which the white man would have been glad to be relieved of many times upon the long march; but now that they were approaching their goal, and knowing as he did that hatred of Malbihn burned hot in the black man's brain, Baynes handed him the rifle, for he guessed that there would be fighting – he intended that there should, for he had come to avenge. Himself, an excellent revolver shot, would depend upon the smaller weapon at his side.

As the two forged ahead toward their goal they were startled by a volley of shots ahead of them. Then came a few scattering reports, some savage yells, and silence. Baynes was frantic in his endeavors to advance more rapidly, but there the jungle seemed a thousand times more tangled than before. A dozen times he tripped and fell. Twice the black followed a blind trail and they were forced to retrace their steps; but at last they came out into a little clearing near the big afi – a clearing that once held a thriving village, but lay somber and desolate in decay and ruin.

In the jungle vegetation that overgrew what had once been the main village street lay the body of a black man, pierced through the heart with a bullet, and still warm. Baynes and his companion looked about in all directions; but no sign of living being could they discover. They stood in silence listening intently.

What was that! Voices and the dip of paddles out upon the river?

Baynes ran across the dead village toward the fringe of jungle upon the river's brim. The black was at his side. Together they forced their way through the screening foliage until they could obtain a view of the river, and there, almost to the other shore, they saw Malbihn's canoes making rapidly for camp. The black recognized his companions immediately.

"How can we cross?" asked Baynes.

The black shook his head. There was no canoe and the crocodiles made it equivalent to suicide to enter the water in an attempt to swim across. Just then the fellow chanced to glance downward. Beneath him, wedged among the branches of a tree, lay the canoe in which Meriem had escaped. The Negro grasped Baynes' arm and pointed toward his find. The Hon. Morison could scarce repress a shout of exultation. Quickly the two slid down the drooping branches into the boat. The black seized the paddle and Baynes shoved them out from beneath the tree. A second later the canoe shot out upon the bosom of the river and headed toward the opposite shore and the camp of the Swede. Baynes squatted in the bow, straining his eyes after the men pulling the other canoes upon the bank across from him. He saw Malbihn step from the bow of the foremost of the little craft. He saw him turn and glance back across the river. He could see his start of surprise as his eyes fell upon the pursuing canoe, and called the attention of his followers to it.

Then he stood waiting, for there was but one canoe and two men – little danger to him and his followers in that. Malbihn was puzzled. Who was this white man? He did not recognize him though Baynes' canoe was now in mid stream and the features of both its occupants plainly discernible to those on shore. One of Malbihn's blacks it was who first recognized his fellow black in the person of Baynes' companion. Then

Malbihn guessed who the white man must be, though he could scarce believe his own reasoning. It seemed beyond the pale of wildest conjecture to suppose that the Hon. Morison Baynes had followed him through the jungle with but a single companion – and yet it was true. Beneath the dirt and dishevelment he recognized him at last, and in the necessity of admitting that it was he, Malbihn was forced to recognize the incentive that had driven Baynes, the weakling and coward, through the savage jungle upon his trail.

The man had come to demand an accounting and to avenge. It seemed incredible, and yet there could be no other explanation. Malbihn shrugged. Well, others had sought Malbihn for similar reasons in the course of a long and checkered career. He fingered his rifle, and waited.

Now the canoe was within easy speaking distance of the shore.

"What do you want?" yelled Malbihn, raising his weapon threateningly.

The Hon. Morison Baynes leaped to his feet.

"You, damn you!" he shouted, whipping out his revolver and firing almost simultaneously with the Swede.

As the two reports rang out Malbihn dropped his rifle, clutched frantically at his breast, staggered, fell first to his knees and then lunged upon his face. Baynes stiffened. His head flew back spasmodically. For an instant he stood thus, and then crumpled very gently into the bottom of the boat.

The black paddler was at a loss as to what to do. If Malbihn really were dead he could continue on to join his fellows without fear; but should the Swede only be wounded he would be safer upon the far shore. Therefore he hesitated, holding the canoe in mid stream. He had come to have considerable respect for his new master and was not unmoved by his death. As he sat gazing at the crumpled body in the bow of the boat he saw it move. Very feebly the man essayed to turn over. He still lived. The black moved forward and lifted him to a sitting position. He was standing in front of him, his paddle in one hand, asking Baynes where he was hit when there was another shot from shore and the Negro pitched head-long overboard, his paddle still clutched in his dead fingers – shot through the forehead.

Baynes turned weakly in the direction of the shore to see Malbihn drawn up upon his elbows levelling his rifle at him. The Englishman slid to the bottom of the canoe as a bullet whizzed above him. Malbihn, sore hit, took longer in aiming, nor was his aim as sure as formerly. With difficulty Baynes turned himself over on his belly and grasping his revolver in his right hand drew himself up until he could look over the edge of the canoe.

Malbihn saw him instantly and fired; but Baynes did not flinch or duck. With painstaking care he aimed at the target upon the shore from which he now was drifting with the current. His finger closed upon the trigger – there was a flash and a report, and Malbihn's giant frame jerked to the impact of another bullet.

But he was not yet dead. Again he aimed and fired, the bullet splintering the gunwale of the canoe close by Baynes' face. Baynes fired again as his canoe drifted further down stream and Malbihn answered from the shore where he lay in a pool of his own blood. And thus, doggedly, the two wounded men continued to carry on their weird duel until the winding African river had carried the Hon. Morison Baynes out of sight around a wooded point.

Chapter Twenty Three

Meriem had traversed half the length of the village street when a score of white-robed Negroes and half-castes leaped out upon her from the dark interiors of surrounding huts. She turned to flee, but heavy hands seized her, and when she turned at last to plead with them her eyes fell upon the face of a tall, grim, old man glaring down upon her from beneath the folds of his burnous.

At sight of him she staggered back in shocked and terrified surprise. It was The Sheik!

Instantly all the old fears and terrors of her childhood returned upon her. She stood trembling before this horrible old man, as a murderer before the judge about to pass sentence of death upon him. She knew that The Sheik recognized her. The years and the changed raiment had not altered her so much but what one who had known her features so well in childhood would know her now.

"So you have come back to your people, eh?" snarled The Sheik. "Come back begging for food and protection, eh?"

"Let me go," cried the girl. "I ask nothing of you, but that you let me go back to the Big Bwana."

"The Big Bwana?" almost screamed The Sheik, and then followed a stream of profane, Arabic invective against the white man whom all the transgressors of the jungle feared and hated. "You would go back to the Big Bwana, would you? So that is where you have been since you ran away from me, is it? And who comes now across the river after you – the Big Bwana?"

"The Swede whom you once chased away from your country when he and his companion conspired with Nbeeda to steal me from you," replied Meriem.

The Sheik's eyes blazed, and he called his men to approach the shore and hide among the bushes that they might ambush and annihilate

Malbihn and his party; but Malbihn already had landed and crawling through the fringe of jungle was at that very moment looking with wide and incredulous eyes upon the scene being enacted in the street of the deserted village. He recognized The Sheik the moment his eyes fell upon him. There were two men in the world that Malbihn feared as he feared the devil. One was the Big Bwana and the other The Sheik. A single glance he took at that gaunt, familiar figure and then he turned tail and scurried back to his canoe calling his followers after him. And so it happened that the party was well out in the stream before The Sheik reached the shore, and after a volley and a few parting shots that were returned from the canoes the Arab called his men off and securing his prisoner set off toward the South.

One of the bullets from Malbihn's force had struck a black standing in the village street where he had been left with another to guard Meriem, and his companions had left him where he had fallen, after appropriating his apparel and belongings. His was the body that Baynes had discovered when he had entered the village.

The Sheik and his party had been marching southward along the river when one of them, dropping out of line to fetch water, had seen Meriem paddling desperately from the opposite shore. The fellow had called The Sheik's attention to the strange sight – a white woman alone in Central Africa and the old Arab had hidden his men in the deserted village to capture her when she landed, for thoughts of ransom were always in the mind of The Sheik. More than once before had glittering gold filtered through his fingers from a similar source. It was easy money and The Sheik had none too much easy money since the Big Bwana had so circumscribed the limits of his ancient domain that he dared not even steal ivory from natives within two hundred miles of the Big Bwana's douar. And when at last the woman had walked into the trap he had set for her and he had recognized her as the same little girl he had brutalized and mal-treated years before his gratification had been huge. Now he lost no time in establishing the old relations of father and daughter that had existed between them in the past. At the first opportunity he struck her a heavy blow across the face. He forced her to walk when he might have dismounted one of his men instead, or had her carried on a horse's rump. He seemed to revel in the discovery of new methods for torturing or humiliating her, and among all his followers she found no single one to offer her sympathy, or who dared defend her, even had they had the desire to do so.

A two days' march brought them at last to the familiar scenes of her childhood, and the first face upon which she set her eyes as she was driven through the gates into the strong stockade was that of the toothless, hideous Mabunu, her one time nurse. It was as though all the years that had intervened were but a dream. Had it not been for her clothing and the fact that she had grown in stature she might well have believed it so. All was there as she had left it – the new faces which supplanted some of the old were of the same bestial, degraded type. There were a few young Arabs who had joined The Sheik since she had been away. Otherwise all was the same – all but one. Geeka was not there, and she found herself missing Geeka as though the ivory-headed one had been a flesh and blood intimate and friend. She missed her ragged little confidante, into whose deaf ears she had been wont to pour her many miseries and her occasional joys – Geeka, of the splinter limbs and the ratskin torso – Geeka the disreputable – Geeka the beloved.

For a time the inhabitants of The Sheik's village who had not been upon the march with him amused themselves by inspecting the strangely clad white girl, whom some of them had known as a little child. Mabunu pretended great joy at her return, baring her toothless gums in a hideous grimace that was intended to be indicative of rejoicing. But Meriem could but shudder as she recalled the cruelties of this terrible old hag in the years gone by.

Among the Arabs who had come in her absence was a tall young fellow of twenty – a handsome, sinister looking youth – who stared at her in open admiration until The Sheik came and ordered him away, and Abdul Kamak went, scowling.

At last, their curiosity satisfied, Meriem was alone. As of old, she was permitted the freedom of the village, for the stockade was high and strong and the only gates were well-guarded by day and by night; but as of old she cared not for the companionship of the cruel Arabs and the degraded blacks who formed the following of The Sheik, and so, as had been her wont in the sad days of her childhood, she slunk down to an unfrequented corner of the enclosure where she had often played at house-keeping with her beloved Geeka beneath the spreading branches of the great tree that had overhung the palisade; but now the tree was gone, and Meriem guessed the reason. It was from this tree that Korak had descended and struck down The Sheik the day that he had rescued her from the life of misery and torture that had been her lot for so long that she could remember no other.

There were low bushes growing within the stockade, however, and in the shade of these Meriem sat down to think. A little glow of happiness warmed her heart as she recalled her first meeting with Korak and then the long years that he had cared for and protected her with the solicitude and purity of an elder brother. For months Korak had not so occupied her thoughts as he did today. He seemed closer and dearer now than ever he had before, and she wondered that her heart had drifted so far from loyalty to his memory. And then came the image of the Hon. Morison, the exquisite, and Meriem was troubled. Did she really love the flawless young Englishman? She thought of the glories of London, of which he had told her in such glowing language. She tried to picture herself admired and honored in the midst of the gayest society of the great capital. The pictures she drew were the pictures that the Hon. Morison had drawn for her. They were alluring pictures, but through them all the brawny, half-naked figure of the giant Adonis of the jungle persisted in obtruding itself.

Meriem pressed her hand above her heart as she stifled a sigh, and as she did so she felt the hard outlines of the photograph she had hidden there as she slunk from Malbihn's tent. Now she drew it forth and commenced to re-examine it more carefully than she had had time to do before. She was sure that the baby face was hers. She studied every detail of the picture. Half hidden in the lace of the dainty dress rested a chain and locket. Meriem puckered her brows. What tantalizing half-memories it awakened! Could this flower of evident civilization be the little Arab Meriem, daughter of The Sheik? It was impossible, and yet that locket? Meriem knew it. She could not refute the conviction of her memory. She had seen that locket before and it had been hers. What strange mystery lay buried in her past?

As she sat gazing at the picture she suddenly became aware that she was not alone – that someone was standing close behind her – some one who had approached her noiselessly. Guiltily she thrust the picture back into her waist. A hand fell upon her shoulder. She was sure that it was The Sheik and she awaited in dumb terror the blow that she knew would follow.

No blow came and she looked upward over her shoulder – into the eyes of Abdul Kamak, the young Arab.

"I saw," he said, "the picture that you have just hidden. It is you when you were a child – a very young child. May I see it again?"

Meriem drew away from him.

"I will give it back," he said. "I have heard of you and I know that you have no love for The Sheik, your father. Neither have I. I will not betray you. Let me see the picture."

Friendless among cruel enemies, Meriem clutched at the straw that Abdul Kamak held out to her. Perhaps in him she might find the friend she needed. Anyway he had seen the picture and if he was not a friend he could tell The Sheik about it and it would be taken away from her. So she might as well grant his request and hope that he had spoken fairly, and would deal fairly. She drew the photograph from its hiding place and handed it to him.

Abdul Kamak examined it carefully, comparing it, feature by feature with the girl sitting on the ground looking up into his face. Slowly he nodded his head.

"Yes," he said, "it is you, but where was it taken? How does it happen that The Sheik's daughter is clothed in the garments of the unbeliever?"

"I do not know," replied Meriem. "I never saw the picture until a couple of days ago, when I found it in the tent of the Swede, Malbihn."

Abdul Kamak raised his eyebrows. He turned the picture over and as his eyes fell upon the old newspaper cutting they went wide. He could read French, with difficulty, it is true; but he could read it. He had been to Paris. He had spent six months there with a troupe of his desert fellows, upon exhibition, and he had improved his time, learning many of the customs, some of the language, and most of the vices of his conquerors. Now he put his learning to use. Slowly, laboriously he read the yellowed cutting. His eyes were no longer wide. Instead they narrowed to two slits of cunning. When he had done he looked at the girl.

"You have read this?" he asked.

"It is French," she replied, "and I do not read French."

Abdul Kamak stood long in silence looking at the girl. She was very beautiful. He desired her, as had many other men who had seen her. At last he dropped to one knee beside her.

A wonderful idea had sprung to Abdul Kamak's mind. It was an idea that might be furthered if the girl were kept in ignorance of the contents of that newspaper cutting. It would certainly be doomed should she learn its contents.

"Meriem," he whispered, "never until today have my eyes beheld you, yet at once they told my heart that it must ever be your servant. You do not know me, but I ask that you trust me. I can help you. You hate The Sheik – so do I. Let me take you away from him. Come with me, and we will go back to the great desert where my father is a sheik mightier than is yours. Will you come?"

Meriem sat in silence. She hated to wound the only one who had offered her protection and friendship; but she did not want Abdul Kamak's love. Deceived by her silence the man seized her and strained her to him; but Meriem struggled to free herself.

"I do not love you," she cried. "Oh, please do not make me hate you. You are the only one who has shown kindness toward me, and I want to like you, but I cannot love you."

Abdul Kamak drew himself to his full height.

"You will learn to love me," he said, "for I shall take you whether you will or no. You hate The Sheik and so you will not tell him, for if you do I will tell him of the picture. I hate The Sheik, and – "

"You hate The Sheik?" came a grim voice from behind them.

Both turned to see The Sheik standing a few paces from them. Abdul still held the picture in his hand. Now he thrust it within his burnous.

"Yes," he said, "I hate the Sheik," and as he spoke he sprang toward the older man, felled him with a blow and dashed on across the village to the line where his horse was picketed, saddled and ready, for Abdul Kamak had been about to ride forth to hunt when he had seen the stranger girl alone by the bushes.

Leaping into the saddle Abdul Kamak dashed for the village gates. The Sheik, momentarily stunned by the blow that had felled him, now staggered to his feet, shouting lustily to his followers to stop the escaped Arab. A dozen blacks leaped forward to intercept the horseman, only to be ridden down or brushed aside by the muzzle of Abdul Kamak's long musket, which he lashed from side to side about him as he spurred on toward the gate. But here he must surely be intercepted. Already the two blacks stationed there were pushing the unwieldy portals to. Up flew the barrel of the fugitive's weapon. With reins flying loose and his horse at a mad gallop the son of the desert fired once – twice; and both the keepers of the gate dropped in their tracks. With a wild whoop of exultation, twirling his musket high above his head and turning in his saddle to laugh back into the faces of his pursuers Abdul Kamak dashed out of the village of The Sheik and was swallowed up by the jungle.

Foaming with rage The Sheik ordered immediate pursuit, and then strode rapidly back to where Meriem sat huddled by the bushes where he had left her.

"The picture!" he cried. "What picture did the dog speak of? Where is it? Give it to me at once!"

"He took it," replied Meriem, dully.

"What was it?" again demanded The Sheik, seizing the girl roughly by the hair and dragging her to her feet, where he shook her venomously. "What was it a picture of?"

"Of me," said Meriem, "when I was a little girl. I stole it from Malbihn, the Swede – it had printing on the back cut from an old newspaper."

The Sheik went white with rage.

"What said the printing?" he asked in a voice so low that she but barely caught his words.

"I do not know. It was in French and I cannot read French."

The Sheik seemed relieved. He almost smiled, nor did he again strike Meriem before he turned and strode away with the parting admonition that she speak never again to any other than Mabunu and himself. And along the caravan trail galloped Abdul Kamak toward the north.

As his canoe drifted out of sight and range of the wounded Swede the Hon. Morison sank weakly to its bottom where he lay for long hours in partial stupor.

It was night before he fully regained consciousness. And then he lay for a long time looking up at the stars and trying to recollect where he was, what accounted for the gently rocking motion of the thing upon which he lay, and why the position of the stars changed so rapidly and miraculously. For a while he thought he was dreaming, but when he would have moved to shake sleep from him the pain of his wound recalled to him the events that had led up to his present position. Then it was that he realized that he was floating down a great African river in a native canoe – alone, wounded, and lost.

Painfully he dragged himself to a sitting position. He noticed that the wound pained him less than he had imagined it would. He felt of it gingerly – it had ceased to bleed. Possibly it was but a flesh wound after all, and nothing serious. If it totally incapacitated him even for a few days it would mean death, for by that time he would be too weakened by hunger and pain to provide food for himself.

From his own troubles his mind turned to Meriem's. That she had been with the Swede at the time he had attempted to reach the fellow's camp he naturally believed; but he wondered what would become of her now. Even if Hanson died of his wounds would Meriem be any better off? She was in the power of equally villainous men – brutal savages of the lowest order. Baynes buried his face in his hands and rocked back and forth as the hideous picture of her fate burned itself into his consciousness. And it was he who had brought this fate upon her! His wicked desire had snatched a pure and innocent girl from the protection of those who loved her to hurl her into the clutches of the bestial Swede and his outcast following! And not until it had become too late had he realized the magnitude of the crime he himself had planned and contemplated. Not until it had become too late had he realized that greater than his desire, greater than his lust, greater than any passion he had ever felt before was the newborn love that burned within his breast for the girl he would have ruined.

The Hon. Morison Baynes did not fully realize the change that had taken place within him. Had one suggested that he ever had been aught than the soul of honor and chivalry he would have taken umbrage forthwith. He knew that he had done a vile thing when he had plotted to carry Meriem away to London, yet he excused it on the ground of his great passion for the girl having temporarily warped his moral standards by the intensity of its heat. But, as a matter of fact, a new Baynes had been born. Never again could this man be bent to dishonor by the intensity of a desire. His moral fiber had been strengthened by the mental suffering he had endured. His mind and his soul had been purged by sorrow and remorse.

His one thought now was to atone – win to Meriem's side and lay down his life, if necessary, in her protection. His eyes sought the length of the canoe in search of the paddle, for a determination had galvanized him to immediate action despite his weakness and his wound. But the paddle was gone. He turned his eyes toward the shore. Dimly through the darkness of a moonless night he saw the awful blackness of the jungle, yet it touched no responsive chord of terror within him now as it had done in the past. He did not even wonder that he was unafraid, for his mind was entirely occupied with thoughts of another's danger.

Drawing himself to his knees he leaned over the edge of the canoe and commenced to paddle vigorously with his open palm. Though it tired and hurt him he kept assiduously at his self imposed labor for hours. Little by little the drifting canoe moved nearer and nearer the shore. The Hon. Morison could hear a lion roaring directly opposite him and so close that he felt he must be almost to the shore. He drew his rifle closer to his side; but he did not cease to paddle.

After what seemed to the tired man an eternity of time he felt the brush of branches against the canoe and heard the swirl of the water about them. A moment later he reached out and clutched a leafy limb. Again the lion roared – very near it seemed now, and Baynes wondered if the brute could have been following along the shore waiting for him to land.

He tested the strength of the limb to which he clung. It seemed strong enough to support a dozen men. Then he reached down and lifted his rifle from the bottom of the canoe, slipping the sling over his shoulder. Again he tested the branch, and then reaching upward as far as he could for a safe hold he drew himself painfully and slowly upward until his feet swung clear of the canoe, which, released, floated silently from beneath him to be lost forever in the blackness of the dark shadows down stream.

He had burned his bridges behind him. He must either climb aloft or drop back into the river; but there had been no other way. He struggled to raise one leg over the limb, but found himself scarce equal to the effort, for he was very weak. For a time he hung there feeling his strength ebbing. He knew that he must gain the branch above at once or it would be too late.

Suddenly the lion roared almost in his ear. Baynes glanced up. He saw two spots of flame a short distance from and above him. The lion was standing on the bank of the river glaring at him, and – waiting for him. Well, thought the Hon. Morison, let him wait. Lions can't climb trees, and if I get into this one I shall be safe enough from him.

The young Englishman's feet hung almost to the surface of the water – closer than he knew, for all was pitch dark below as above him. Presently he heard a slight commotion in the river beneath him and something banged against one of his feet, followed almost instantly by a sound that he felt he could not have mistaken – the click of great jaws snapping together.

"By George!" exclaimed the Hon. Morison, aloud. "The beggar nearly got me," and immediately he struggled again to climb higher and to comparative safety; but with that final effort he knew that it was futile. Hope that had survived persistently until now began to wane. He felt his tired, numbed fingers slipping from their hold – he was dropping back into the river – into the jaws of the frightful death that awaited him there.

And then he heard the leaves above him rustle to the movement of a creature among them. The branch to which he clung bent beneath an added weight – and no light weight, from the way it sagged; but still Baynes clung desperately – he would not give up voluntarily either to the death above or the death below.

He felt a soft, warm pad upon the fingers of one of his hands where they circled the branch to which he clung, and then something reached down out of the blackness above and dragged him up among the branches of the tree.

Chapter Twenty Four

Sometimes lolling upon Tantor's back, sometimes roaming the jungle in solitude, Korak made his way slowly toward the West and South. He made but a few miles a day, for he had a whole lifetime before him and no place in particular to go. Possibly he would have moved more rapidly but for the thought which continually haunted him that each mile he traversed carried him further and further away from Meriem – no longer his Meriem, as of yore, it is true! but still as dear to him as ever.

Thus he came upon the trail of The Sheik's band as it traveled down river from the point where The Sheik had captured Meriem to his own stockaded village. Korak pretty well knew who it was that had passed, for there were few in the great jungle with whom he was not familiar, though it had been years since he had come this far north. He had no particular business, however, with the old Sheik and so he did not propose following him – the further from men he could stay the better pleased he would be – he wished that he might never see a human face again. Men always brought him sorrow and misery.

The river suggested fishing and so he dawdled upon its shores, catching fish after a fashion of his own devising and eating them raw. When night came he curled up in a great tree beside the stream – the one from which he had been fishing during the afternoon – and was soon asleep. Numa, roaring beneath him, awoke him. He was about to call out in anger to his noisy neighbor when something else caught his attention. He listened. Was there something in the tree beside himself? Yes, he heard the noise of something below him trying to clamber upward. Presently he heard the click of a crocodile's jaws in the waters beneath, and then, low but distinct: "By George! The beggar nearly got me." The voice was familiar.

Korak glanced downward toward the speaker. Outlined against the faint luminosity of the water he saw the figure of a man clinging to a lower branch of the tree. Silently and swiftly the ape-man clambered downward. He felt a hand beneath his foot. He reached down and clutched the figure beneath him and dragged it up among the branches. It struggled weakly and struck at him; but Korak paid no more attention than Tantor to an ant. He lugged his burden to the higher safety and greater comfort of a broad crotch, and there he propped it in a sitting position against the bole of the tree. Numa still was roaring beneath them, doubtless in anger that he had been robbed of his prey. Korak shouted down at him, calling him, in the language of the great apes, "Old green-eyed eater of carrion," "Brother of Dango," the hyena, and other choice appellations of jungle opprobrium.

The Hon. Morison Baynes, listening, felt assured that a gorilla had seized upon him. He felt for his revolver, and as he was drawing it stealthily from its holster a voice asked in perfectly good English, "Who are you?"

Baynes started so that he nearly fell from the branch.

"My God!" he exclaimed. "Are you a man?"

"What did you think I was?" asked Korak.

"A gorilla," replied Baynes, honestly.

Korak laughed.

"Who are you?" he repeated.

"I'm an Englishman by the name of Baynes; but who the devil are you?" asked the Hon. Morison.

"They call me The Killer," replied Korak, giving the English translation of the name that Akut had given him. And then after a pause during which the Hon. Morison attempted to pierce the darkness and catch a glimpse of the features of the strange being into whose hands he had fallen, "You are the same whom I saw kissing the girl at the edge of the great plain to the East, that time that the lion charged you?"

"Yes," replied Baynes.

"What are you doing here?"

"The girl was stolen – I am trying to rescue her."

"Stolen!" The word was shot out like a bullet from a gun. "Who stole her?"

"The Swede trader, Hanson," replied Baynes.

"Where is he?"

Baynes related to Korak all that had transpired since he had come upon Hanson's camp. Before he was done the first gray dawn had relieved the darkness. Korak made the Englishman comfortable in the tree. He filled his canteen from the river and fetched him fruits to eat. Then he bid him good-bye.

"I am going to the Swede's camp," he announced. "I will bring the girl back to you here."

"I shall go, too, then," insisted Baynes. "It is my right and my duty, for she was to have become my wife."

Korak winced. "You are wounded. You could not make the trip," he said. "I can go much faster alone."

"Go, then," replied Baynes; "but I shall follow. It is my right and duty."

"As you will," replied Korak, with a shrug. If the man wanted to be killed it was none of his affair. He wanted to kill him himself, but for Meriem's sake he would not. If she loved him then he must do what he could to preserve him, but he could not prevent his following him, more than to advise him against it, and this he did, earnestly.

And so Korak set out rapidly toward the North, and limping slowly and painfully along, soon far to the rear, came the tired and wounded Baynes. Korak had reached the river bank opposite Malbihn's camp before Baynes had covered two miles. Late in the afternoon the Englishman was still plodding wearily along, forced to stop often for rest when he heard the sound of the galloping feet of a horse behind him. Instinctively he drew into the concealing foliage of the underbrush and a moment later a white-robed Arab dashed by. Baynes did not hail the rider. He had heard of the nature of the Arabs who penetrate thus far to the South, and what he had heard had convinced him that a snake or a panther would as quickly befriend him as one of these villainous renegades from the Northland.

When Abdul Kamak had passed out of sight toward the North Baynes resumed his weary march. A half hour later he was again surprised by the unmistakable sound of galloping horses. This time there were many. Once more he sought a hiding place; but it chanced that he was crossing a clearing which offered little opportunity for concealment. He broke into a slow trot – the best that he could do in his weakened condition; but it did not suffice to carry him to safety and before he reached the opposite side of the clearing a band of white-robed horsemen dashed into view behind him.

At sight of him they shouted in Arabic, which, of course, he could not understand, and then they closed about him, threatening and angry. Their questions were unintelligible to him, and no more could they interpret his English. At last, evidently out of patience, the leader ordered two of his men to seize him, which they lost no time in doing.

They disarmed him and ordered him to climb to the rump of one of the horses, and then the two who had been detailed to guard him turned and rode back toward the South, while the others continued their pursuit of Abdul Kamak.

As Korak came out upon the bank of the river across from which he could see the camp of Malbihn he was at a loss as to how he was to cross. He could see men moving about among the huts inside the boma – evidently Hanson was still there. Korak did not know the true identity of Meriem's abductor.

How was he to cross. Not even he would dare the perils of the river – almost certain death. For a moment he thought, then wheeled and sped away into the jungle, uttering a peculiar cry, shrill and piercing. Now and again he would halt to listen as though for an answer to his weird call, then on again, deeper and deeper into the wood.

At last his listening ears were rewarded by the sound they craved – the trumpeting of a bull elephant, and a few moments later Korak broke through the trees into the presence of Tantor, standing with upraised trunk, waving his great ears.

"Quick, Tantor!" shouted the ape-man, and the beast swung him to his head. "Hurry!" and the mighty pachyderm lumbered off through the jungle, guided by kicking of naked heels against the sides of his head.

Toward the northwest Korak guided his huge mount, until they came out upon the river a mile or more above the Swede's camp, at a point where Korak knew that there was an elephant ford. Never pausing the ape-man urged the beast into the river, and with trunk held high Tantor forged steadily toward the opposite bank. Once an unwary crocodile attacked him but the sinuous trunk dove beneath the surface and grasping the amphibian about the middle dragged it to light and hurled it a hundred feet down stream. And so, in safety, they made the opposite shore, Korak perched high and dry above the turgid flood.

Then back toward the South Tantor moved, steadily, relentlessly, and with a swinging gait which took no heed of any obstacle other than the larger jungle trees. At times Korak was forced to abandon the broad head and take to the trees above, so close the branches raked the back of the elephant; but at last they came to the edge of the clearing where lay the camp of the renegade Swede, nor even then did they hesitate or halt. The gate lay upon the east side of the camp, facing the river. Tantor and Korak approached from the north. There was no gate there; but what cared Tantor or Korak for gates.

At a word from the ape man and raising his tender trunk high above the thorns Tantor breasted the boma, walking through it as though it had not existed. A dozen blacks squatted before their huts looked up at the noise of his approach. With sudden howls of terror and amazement they leaped to their feet and fled for the open gates. Tantor would have pursued. He hated man, and he thought that Korak had come to hunt these; but the ape man held him back, guiding him toward a large, canvas tent that rose in the center of the clearing – there should be the girl and her abductor.

Malbihn lay in a hammock beneath canopy before his tent. His wounds were painful and he had lost much blood. He was very weak. He looked up in surprise as he heard the screams of his men and saw them running toward the gate. And then from around the corner of his tent loomed a huge bulk, and Tantor, the great tusker, towered above him. Malbihn's boy, feeling neither affection nor loyalty for his master, broke and ran at the first glimpse of the beast, and Malbihn was left alone and helpless.

The elephant stopped a couple of paces from the wounded man's hammock. Malbihn cowered, moaning. He was too weak to escape. He could only lie there with staring eyes gazing in horror into the blood rimmed, angry little orbs fixed upon him, and await his death.

Then, to his astonishment, a man slid to the ground from the elephant's back. Almost at once Malbihn recognized the strange figure as that of the creature who consorted with apes and baboons – the white warrior of the jungle who had freed the king baboon and led the whole angry horde of hairy devils upon him and Jenssen. Malbihn cowered still lower.

"Where is the girl?" demanded Korak, in English.

"What girl?" asked Malbihn. "There is no girl here – only the women of my boys. Is it one of them you want?"

"The white girl," replied Korak. "Do not lie to me – you lured her from her friends. You have her. Where is she?"

"It was not I," cried Malbihn. "It was an Englishman who hired me to steal her. He wished to take her to London with him. She was willing to go. His name is Baynes. Go to him, if you want to know where the girl is."

"I have just come from him," said Korak. "He sent me to you. The girl is not with him. Now stop your lying and tell me the truth. Where is she?" Korak took a threatening step toward the Swede.

Malbihn shrank from the anger in the other's face.

"I will tell you," he cried. "Do not harm me and I will tell you all that I know. I had the girl here; but it was Baynes who persuaded her to leave her friends – he had promised to marry her. He does not know who she is; but I do, and I know that there is a great reward for whoever takes her back to her people. It was the only reward I wanted. But she escaped and crossed the river in one of my canoes. I followed her, but The Sheik was there, God knows how, and he captured her and attacked me and drove me back. Then came Baynes, angry because he had lost the girl, and shot me. If you want her, go to The Sheik and ask him for her – she has passed as his daughter since childhood."

"She is not The Sheik's daughter?" asked Korak.

"She is not," replied Malbihn.

"Who is she then?" asked Korak.

Here Malbihn saw his chance. Possibly he could make use of his knowledge after all – it might even buy back his life for him. He was not so credulous as to believe that this savage ape-man would have any compunctions about slaying him.

"When you find her I will tell you," he said, "if you will promise to spare my life and divide the reward with me. If you kill me you will never know, for only The Sheik knows and he will never tell. The girl herself is ignorant of her origin."

"If you have told me the truth I will spare you," said Korak. "I shall go now to The Sheik's village and if the girl is not there I shall return and slay you. As for the other information you have, if the girl wants it when we have found her we will find a way to purchase it from you."

The look in the Killer's eyes and his emphasis of the word "purchase" were none too reassuring to Malbihn. Evidently, unless he found means to escape, this devil would have both his secret and his life before he was done with him. He wished he would be gone and take his evil-eyed companion away with him. The swaying bulk towering high above him, and the ugly little eyes of the elephant watching his every move made Malbihn nervous.

Korak stepped into the Swede's tent to assure himself that Meriem was not hid there. As he disappeared from view Tantor, his eyes still fixed upon Malbihn, took a step nearer the man. An elephant's eyesight is none too good; but the great tusker evidently had harbored suspicions of this yellow-bearded white man from the first. Now he advanced his snake-like trunk toward the Swede, who shrank still deeper into his hammock.

The sensitive member felt and smelled back and forth along the body of the terrified Malbihn. Tantor uttered a low, rumbling sound. His little eyes blazed. At last he had recognized the creature who had killed his mate long years before. Tantor, the elephant, never forgets and never forgives. Malbihn saw in the demoniacal visage above him the murderous purpose of the beast. He shrieked aloud to Korak. "Help! Help! The devil is going to kill me!"

Korak ran from the tent just in time to see the enraged elephant's trunk encircle the beast's victim, and then hammock, canopy and man were swung high over Tantor's head. Korak leaped before the animal, commanding him to put down his prey unharmed; but as well might he have ordered the eternal river to reverse its course. Tantor wheeled around like a cat, hurled Malbihn to the earth and kneeled upon him with the quickness of a cat. Then he gored the prostrate thing through and through with his mighty tusks, trumpeting and roaring in his rage, and at last, convinced that no slightest spark of life remained in the crushed and lacerated flesh, he lifted the shapeless clay that had been Sven Malbihn far aloft and hurled the bloody mass, still entangled in canopy and hammock, over the boma and out into the jungle.

Korak stood looking sorrowfully on at the tragedy he gladly would have averted. He had no love for the Swede, in fact only hatred; but he would have preserved the man for the sake of the secret he possessed. Now that secret was gone forever unless The Sheik could be made to divulge it; but in that possibility Korak placed little faith.

The ape-man, as unafraid of the mighty Tantor as though he had not just witnessed his shocking murder of a human being, signalled the beast to approach and lift him to its head, and Tantor came as he was bid, docile as a kitten, and hoisted The Killer tenderly aloft.

From the safety of their hiding places in the jungle Malbihn's boys had witnessed the killing of their master, and now, with wide, frightened eyes, they saw the strange white warrior, mounted upon the head of his ferocious charger, disappear into the jungle at the point from which he had emerged upon their terrified vision.

Chapter Twenty Five

The Sheik glowered at the prisoner which his two men brought back to him from the North. He had sent the party after Abdul Kamak, and he was wroth that instead of his erstwhile lieutenant they had sent back a wounded and useless Englishman. Why had they not dispatched him where they had found him? He was some penniless beggar of a trader who had wandered from his own district and became lost. He was worthless. The Sheik scowled terribly upon him.

"Who are you?" he asked in French.

"I am the Hon. Morison Baynes of London," replied his prisoner.

The title sounded promising, and at once the wily old robber had visions of ransom. His intentions, if not his attitude toward the prisoner underwent a change – he would investigate further.

"What were you doing poaching in my country?" growled he.

"I was not aware that you owned Africa," replied the Hon. Morison. "I was searching for a young woman who had been abducted from the home of a friend. The abductor wounded me and I drifted down river in a canoe – I was on my way back to his camp when your men seized me."

"A young woman?" asked The Sheik. "Is that she?" and he pointed to his left over toward a clump of bushes near the stockade.

Baynes looked in the direction indicated and his eyes went wide, for there, sitting cross-legged upon the ground, her back toward them, was Meriem.

"Meriem!" he shouted, starting toward her; but one of his guards grasped his arm and jerked him back. The girl leaped to her feet and turned toward him as she heard her name.

"Morison!" she cried.

"Be still, and stay where you are," snapped The Sheik, and then to Baynes. "So you are the dog of a Christian who stole my daughter from me?"

"Your daughter?" ejaculated Baynes. "She is your daughter?"

"She is my daughter," growled the Arab, "and she is not for any unbeliever. You have earned death, Englishman, but if you can pay for your life I will give it to you."

Baynes' eyes were still wide at the unexpected sight of Meriem here in the camp of the Arab when he had thought her in Hanson's power. What had happened? How had she escaped the Swede? Had the Arab taken her by force from him, or had she escaped and come voluntarily back to the protection of the man who called her "daughter"? He would have given much for a word with her. If she was safe here he might only harm her by antagonizing the Arab in an attempt to take her away and return her to her English friends. No longer did the Hon. Morison harbor thoughts of luring the girl to London.

"Well?" asked The Sheik.

"Oh," exclaimed Baynes; "I beg your pardon – I was thinking of something else. Why yes, of course, glad to pay, I'm sure. How much do you think I'm worth?"

The Sheik named a sum that was rather less exorbitant than the Hon. Morison had anticipated. The latter nodded his head in token of his entire willingness to pay. He would have promised a sum far beyond his resources just as readily, for he had no intention of paying anything – his one reason for seeming to comply with The Sheik's demands was that the wait for the coming of the ransom money would give him the time and the opportunity to free Meriem if he found that she wished to be freed. The Arab's statement that he was her father naturally raised the question in the Hon. Morison's mind as to precisely what the girl's attitude toward escape might be. It seemed, of course, preposterous that this fair and beautiful young woman should prefer to remain in the filthy douar of an illiterate old Arab rather than return to the comforts, luxuries, and congenial associations of the hospitable African bungalow from which the Hon. Morison had tricked her. The man flushed at the thought of his duplicity which these recollections aroused – thoughts which were interrupted by The Sheik, who instructed the Hon. Morison to write a letter to the British consul at Algiers, dictating the exact phraseology of it with a fluency that indicated to his captive that this was not the first time the old rascal had had occasion to negotiate with English relatives for the ransom of a kinsman. Baynes demurred when he saw that the letter was addressed to the consul at Algiers, saying that it would require the better part of a year to get the money back to him; but The Sheik would not listen to Baynes' plan to send a messenger directly to the nearest coast town, and from there communicate with the nearest cable station, sending the Hon. Morison's request for funds straight to his own solicitors. No, The Sheik was cautious and wary. He knew his own plan had worked well in the past. In the other were too many untried elements. He was in no hurry for the money – he could wait a year, or two years if necessary; but it should not require over six months. He turned to one of the Arabs who had been standing behind him and gave the fellow instructions in relation to the prisoner.

Baynes could not understand the words, spoken in Arabic, but the jerk of the thumb toward him showed that he was the subject of conversation. The Arab addressed by The Sheik bowed to his master and beckoned Baynes to follow him. The Englishman looked toward The Sheik for confirmation. The latter nodded impatiently, and the Hon. Morison rose and followed his guide toward a native hut which lay close beside one of the outside goatskin tents. In the dark, stifling interior his guard led him, then stepped to the doorway and called to a couple of black boys squatting before their own huts. They came promptly and in accordance with the Arab's instructions bound Baynes' wrists and ankles securely. The Englishman objected strenuously; but as neither the blacks nor the Arab could understand a word he said his pleas were wasted. Having bound him they left the hut. The Hon. Morison lay for a long time contemplating the frightful future which awaited him during the long months which must intervene before his friends learned of his predicament and could get succor to him. Now he hoped that they would send the ransom – he would gladly pay all that he was worth to be out of this hole. At first it had been his intention to cable his solicitors to send no money but to communicate with the British West African authorities and have an expedition sent to his aid.

His patrician nose wrinkled in disgust as his nostrils were assailed by the awful stench of the hut. The nasty grasses upon which he lay exuded the effluvium of sweaty bodies, of decayed animal matter and of offal. But worse was yet to come. He had lain in the uncomfortable position in which they had thrown him but for a few minutes when he became distinctly conscious of an acute itching sensation upon his hands, his neck and scalp. He wriggled to a sitting posture horrified and disgusted. The itching rapidly extended to other parts of his body – it was torture, and his hands were bound securely at his back!

He tugged and pulled at his bonds until he was exhausted; but not entirely without hope, for he was sure that he was working enough slack out of the knot to eventually permit of his withdrawing one of his hands. Night came. They brought him neither food nor drink. He wondered if they expected him to live on nothing for a year. The bites of the vermin grew less annoying though not less numerous. The Hon. Morison saw a ray of hope in this indication of future immunity through inoculation. He still worked weakly at his bonds, and then the rats came. If the vermin were disgusting the rats were terrifying. They scurried over his body, squealing and fighting. Finally one commenced to chew at one of his ears. With an oath, the Hon. Morison struggled to a sitting posture. The rats retreated. He worked his legs beneath him and came to his knees, and then, by superhuman effort, rose to his feet. There he stood, reeling drunkenly, dripping with cold sweat.

"God!" he muttered, "what have I done to deserve – " He paused. What had he done? He thought of the girl in another tent in that accursed village. He was getting his deserts. He set his jaws firmly with the realization. He would never complain again! At that moment he became aware of voices raised angrily in the goatskin tent close beside the hut in which he lay. One of them was a woman's. Could it be Meriem's? The language was probably Arabic – he could not understand a word of it; but the tones were hers.

He tried to think of some way of attracting her attention to his near presence. If she could remove his bonds they might escape together – if she wished to escape. That thought bothered him. He was not sure of her status in the village. If she were the petted child of the powerful Sheik then she would probably not care to escape. He must know, definitely.

At the bungalow he had often heard Meriem sing God Save the King, as My Dear accompanied her on the piano. Raising his voice he now hummed the tune. Immediately he heard Meriem's voice from the tent. She spoke rapidly.

"Good bye, Morison," she cried. "If God is good I shall be dead before morning, for if I still live I shall be worse than dead after tonight."

Then he heard an angry exclamation in a man's voice, followed by the sounds of a scuffle. Baynes went white with horror. He struggled frantically again with his bonds. They were giving. A moment later one hand was free. It was but the work of an instant then to loose the other. Stooping, he untied the rope from his ankles, then he straightened and started for the hut doorway bent on reaching Meriem's side. As he stepped out into the night the figure of a huge black rose and barred his progress.

When speed was required of him Korak depended upon no other muscles than his own, and so it was that the moment Tantor had landed him safely upon the same side of the river as lay the village of The Sheik, the ape-man deserted his bulky comrade and took to the trees in a rapid race toward the south and the spot where the Swede had told him Meriem might be. It was dark when he came to the palisade, strengthened considerably since the day that he had rescued Meriem from her pitiful life within its cruel confines. No longer did the giant tree spread its branches above the wooden rampart; but ordinary man-made defenses were scarce considered obstacles by Korak. Loosening the rope at his waist he tossed the noose over one of the sharpened posts that composed the palisade. A moment later his eyes were above the level of the obstacle taking in all within their range beyond. There was no one in sight close by, and Korak drew himself to the top and dropped lightly to the ground within the enclosure.

Then he commenced his stealthy search of the village. First toward the Arab tents he made his way, sniffing and listening. He passed behind them searching for some sign of Meriem. Not even the wild Arab curs heard his passage, so silently he went – a shadow passing through shadows. The odor of tobacco told him that the Arabs were smoking before their tents. The sound of laughter fell upon his ears, and then from the opposite side of the village came the notes of a once familiar tune: God Save the King. Korak halted in perplexity. Who might it be – the tones were those of a man. He recalled the young Englishman he had left on the river trail and who had disappeared before he returned. A moment later there came to him a woman's voice in reply – it was Meriem's, and The Killer, quickened into action, slunk rapidly in the direction of these two voices.

The evening meal over Meriem had gone to her pallet in the women's quarters of The Sheik's tent, a little corner screened off in the rear by a couple of priceless Persian rugs to form a partition. In these quarters she had dwelt with Mabunu alone, for The Sheik had no wives. Nor were conditions altered now after the years of her absence – she and Mabunu were alone in the women's quarters.

Presently The Sheik came and parted the rugs. He glared through the dim light of the interior.

"Meriem!" he called. "Come hither."

The girl arose and came into the front of the tent. There the light of a fire illuminated the interior. She saw Ali ben Kadin, The Sheik's half brother, squatted upon a rug, smoking. The Sheik was standing. The Sheik and Ali ben Kadin had had the same father, but Ali ben Kadin's mother had been a slave – a West Coast Negress. Ali ben Kadin was old and hideous and almost black. His nose and part of one cheek were eaten away by disease. He looked up and grinned as Meriem entered.

The Sheik jerked his thumb toward Ali ben Kadin and addressed Meriem.

"I am getting old," he said, "I shall not live much longer. Therefore I have given you to Ali ben Kadin, my brother."

That was all. Ali ben Kadin rose and came toward her. Meriem shrank back, horrified. The man seized her wrist.

"Come!" he commanded, and dragged her from The Sheik's tent and to his own.

After they had gone The Sheik chuckled. "When I send her north in a few months," he soliloquized, "they will know the reward for slaying the son of the sister of Amor ben Khatour."

And in Ali ben Kadin's tent Meriem pleaded and threatened, but all to no avail. The hideous old halfcaste spoke soft words at first, but when Meriem loosed upon him the vials of her horror and loathing he became enraged, and rushing upon her seized her in his arms. Twice she tore away from him, and in one of the intervals during which she managed to elude him she heard Baynes' voice humming the tune that she knew was meant for her ears. At her reply Ali ben Kadin rushed upon her once again. This time he dragged her back into the rear apartment of his tent where three Negresses looked up in stolid indifference to the tragedy being enacted before them.

As the Hon. Morison saw his way blocked by the huge frame of the giant black his disappointment and rage filled him with a bestial fury that transformed him into a savage beast. With an oath he leaped upon the man before him, the momentum of his body hurling the black to the ground. There they fought, the black to draw his knife, the white to choke the life from the black.

Baynes' fingers shut off the cry for help that the other would have been glad to voice; but presently the Negro succeeded in drawing his weapon and an instant later Baynes felt the sharp steel in his shoulder. Again and again the weapon fell. The white man removed one hand from its choking grip upon the black throat. He felt around upon the ground beside him searching for some missile, and at last his fingers touched a stone and closed upon it. Raising it above his antagonist's head the Hon. Morison drove home a terrific blow. Instantly the black relaxed – stunned. Twice more Baynes struck him. Then he leaped to his feet and ran for the goat skin tent from which he had heard the voice of Meriem in distress.

But before him was another. Naked but for his leopard skin and his loin cloth, Korak, The Killer, slunk into the shadows at the back of Ali ben Kadin's tent. The half-caste had just dragged Meriem into the rear chamber as Korak's sharp knife slit a six foot opening in the tent wall, and Korak, tall and mighty, sprang through upon the astonished visions of the inmates.

Meriem saw and recognized him the instant that he entered the apartment. Her heart leaped in pride and joy at the sight of the noble figure for which it had hungered for so long.

"Korak!" she cried.

"Meriem!" He uttered the single word as he hurled himself upon the astonished Ali ben Kadin. The three Negresses leaped from their sleeping mats, screaming. Meriem tried to prevent them from escaping; but before she could succeed the terrified blacks had darted through the hole in the tent wall made by Korak's knife, and were gone screaming through the village.

The Killer's fingers closed once upon the throat of the hideous Ali. Once his knife plunged into the putrid heart – and Ali ben Kadin lay dead upon the floor of his tent. Korak turned toward Meriem and at the same moment a bloody and disheveled apparition leaped into the apartment.

"Morison!" cried the girl.

Korak turned and looked at the new comer. He had been about to take Meriem in his arms, forgetful of all that might have transpired since last he had seen her. Then the coming of the young Englishman recalled the scene he had witnessed in the little clearing, and a wave of misery swept over the ape man.

Already from without came the sounds of the alarm that the three Negresses had started. Men were running toward the tent of Ali ben Kadin. There was no time to be lost.

"Quick!" cried Korak, turning toward Baynes, who had scarce yet realized whether he was facing a friend or foe. "Take her to the palisade, following the rear of the tents. Here is my rope. With it you can scale the wall and make your escape."

"But you, Korak?" cried Meriem.

"I will remain," replied the ape-man. "I have business with The Sheik."

Meriem would have demurred, but The Killer seized them both by the shoulders and hustled them through the slit wall and out into the shadows beyond.

"Now run for it," he admonished, and turned to meet and hold those who were pouring into the tent from the front.

The ape-man fought well – fought as he had never fought before; but the odds were too great for victory, though he won that which he most craved – time for the Englishman to escape with Meriem. Then he was overwhelmed by numbers, and a few minutes later, bound and guarded, he was carried to The Sheik's tent.

The old men eyed him in silence for a long time. He was trying to fix in his own mind some form of torture that would gratify his rage and hatred toward this creature who twice had been the means of his losing possession of Meriem. The killing of Ali ben Kadin caused him little anger – always had he hated the hideous son of his father's hideous slave. The blow that this naked white warrior had once struck him added fuel to his rage. He could think of nothing adequate to the creature's offense.

And as he sat there looking upon Korak the silence was broken by the trumpeting of an elephant in the jungle beyond the palisade. A half smile touched Korak's lips. He turned his head a trifle in the direction from which the sound had come and then there broke from his lips, a low, weird call. One of the blacks guarding him struck him across the mouth with the haft of his spear; but none there knew the significance of his cry.

In the jungle Tantor cocked his ears as the sound of Korak's voice fell upon them. He approached the palisade and lifting his trunk above it, sniffed. Then he placed his head against the wooden logs and pushed; but the palisade was strong and only gave a little to the pressure.

In The Sheik's tent The Sheik rose at last, and, pointing toward the bound captive, turned to one of his lieutenants.

"Burn him," he commanded. "At once. The stake is set."

The guard pushed Korak from The Sheik's presence. They dragged him to the open space in the center of the village, where a high stake was set in the ground. It had not been intended for burnings, but offered a convenient place to tie up refractory slaves that they might be beaten – ofttimes until death relieved their agonies.

To this stake they bound Korak. Then they brought brush and piled about him, and The Sheik came and stood by that he might watch the agonies of his victim. But Korak did not wince even after they had fetched a brand and the flames had shot up among the dry tinder.

Once, then, he raised his voice in the low call that he had given in The Sheik's tent, and now, from beyond the palisade, came again the trumpeting of an elephant.

Old Tantor had been pushing at the palisade in vain. The sound of Korak's voice calling him, and the scent of man, his enemy, filled the great beast with rage and resentment against the dumb barrier that held him back. He wheeled and shuffled back a dozen paces, then he turned, lifted his trunk and gave voice to a mighty roaring, trumpet-call of anger, lowered his head and charged like a huge battering ram of flesh and bone and muscle straight for the mighty barrier.

The palisade sagged and splintered to the impact, and through the breach rushed the infuriated bull. Korak heard the sounds that the others heard, and he interpreted them as the others did not. The flames were creeping closer to him when one of the blacks, hearing a noise behind him turned to see the enormous bulk of Tantor lumbering toward them. The man screamed and fled, and then the bull elephant was among them tossing Negroes and Arabs to right and left as he tore through the flames he feared to the side of the comrade he loved.

The Sheik, calling orders to his followers, ran to his tent to get his rifle. Tantor wrapped his trunk about the body of Korak and the stake to which it was bound, and tore it from the ground. The flames were searing his sensitive hide – sensitive for all its thickness – so that in his frenzy to both rescue his friend and escape the hated fire he had all but crushed the life from the ape-man.

Lifting his burden high above his head the giant beast wheeled and raced for the breach that he had just made in the palisade. The Sheik, rifle in hand, rushed from his tent directly into the path of the maddened brute. He raised his weapon and fired once, the bullet missed its mark, and Tantor was upon him, crushing him beneath those gigantic feet as he raced over him as you and I might crush out the life of an ant that chanced to be in our pathway.

And then, bearing his burden carefully, Tantor, the elephant, entered the blackness of the jungle.

Chapter Twenty Six

Meriem, dazed by the unexpected sight of Korak whom she had long given up as dead, permitted herself to be led away by Baynes. Among the tents he guided her safely to the palisade, and there, following Korak's instructions, the Englishman pitched a noose over the top of one of the upright logs that formed the barrier. With difficulty he reached the top and then lowered his hand to assist Meriem to his side.

"Come!" he whispered. "We must hurry." And then, as though she had awakened from a sleep, Meriem came to herself. Back there, fighting her enemies, alone, was Korak – her Korak. Her place was by his side, fighting with him and for him. She glanced up at Baynes.

"Go!" she called. "Make your way back to Bwana and bring help. My place is here. You can do no good remaining. Get away while you can and bring the Big Bwana back with you."

Silently the Hon. Morison Baynes slid to the ground inside the palisade to Meriem's side.

"It was only for you that I left him," he said, nodding toward the tents they had just left. "I knew that he could hold them longer than I and give you a chance to escape that I might not be able to have given you. It was I though who should have remained. I heard you call him Korak and so I know now who he is. He befriended you. I would have wronged you. No – don't interrupt. I'm going to tell you the truth now and let you know just what a beast I have been. I planned to take you to London, as you know; but I did not plan to marry you. Yes, shrink from me – I deserve it. I deserve your contempt and loathing; but I didn't know then what love was. Since I have learned that I have learned something else – what a cad and what a coward I have been all my life. I looked down upon those whom I considered my social inferiors. I did not think you good enough to bear my name. Since Hanson tricked me and took you for himself I have been through hell; but it has made a man of me, though too late. Now I can come to you with an offer of honest love, which will realize the honor of having such as you share my name with me."

For a moment Meriem was silent, buried in thought. Her first question seemed irrelevant.

"How did you happen to be in this village?" she asked.

He told her all that had transpired since the black had told him of Hanson's duplicity.

"You say that you are a coward," she said, "and yet you have done all this to save me? The courage that it must have taken to tell me the things that you told me but a moment since, while courage of a different sort, proves that you are no moral coward, and the other proves that you are not a physical coward. I could not love a coward."

"You mean that you love me?" he gasped in astonishment, taking a step toward her as though to gather her into his arms; but she placed her hand against him and pushed him gently away, as much as to say, not yet. What she did mean she scarcely knew. She thought that she loved him, of that there can be no question; nor did she think that love for this young Englishman was disloyalty to Korak, for her love for Korak was undiminished – the love of a sister for an indulgent brother. As they stood there for the moment of their conversation the sounds of tumult in the village subsided.

"They have killed him," whispered Meriem.

The statement brought Baynes to a realization of the cause of their return.

"Wait here," he said. "I will go and see. If he is dead we can do him no good. If he lives I will do my best to free him."

"We will go together," replied Meriem. "Come!" And she led the way back toward the tent in which they last had seen Korak. As they went they were often forced to throw themselves to the ground in the shadow of a tent or hut, for people were passing hurriedly to and fro now – the whole village was aroused and moving about. The return to the tent of Ali ben Kadin took much longer than had their swift flight to the palisade. Cautiously they crept to the slit that Korak's knife had made in the rear wall. Meriem peered within – the rear apartment was empty. She crawled through the aperture, Baynes at her heels, and then silently crossed the space to the rugs that partitioned the tent into two rooms. Parting the hangings Meriem looked into the front room. It, too, was deserted. She crossed to the door of the tent and looked out. Then she gave a little gasp of horror. Baynes at her shoulder looked past her to the sight that had startled her, and he, too, exclaimed; but his was an oath of anger.

A hundred feet away they saw Korak bound to a stake – the brush piled about him already alight. The Englishman pushed Meriem to one side and started to run for the doomed man. What he could do in the face of scores of hostile blacks and Arabs he did not stop to consider. At the same instant Tantor broke through the palisade and charged the group. In the face of the maddened beast the crowd turned and fled, carrying Baynes backward with them. In a moment it was all over, and the elephant had disappeared with his prize; but pandemonium reigned throughout the village. Men, women and children ran helter skelter for safety. Curs fled, yelping. The horses and camels and donkeys, terrorized by the trumpeting of the pachyderm, kicked and pulled at their tethers. A dozen or more broke loose, and it was the galloping of these past him that brought a sudden idea into Baynes' head. He turned to search for Meriem only to find her at his elbow.

"The horses!" he cried. "If we can get a couple of them!"

Filled with the idea Meriem led him to the far end of the village.

"Loosen two of them," she said, "and lead them back into the shadows behind those huts. I know where there are saddles. I will bring them and the bridles," and before he could stop her she was gone.

Baynes quickly untied two of the restive animals and led them to the point designated by Meriem. Here he waited impatiently for what seemed an hour; but was, in reality, but a few minutes. Then he saw the girl approaching beneath the burden of two saddles. Quickly they placed these upon the horses. They could see by the light of the torture fire that still burned that the blacks and Arabs were recovering from their panic. Men were running about gathering in the loose stock, and two or three were already leading their captives back to the end of the village where Meriem and Baynes were busy with the trappings of their mounts.

Now thc girl flung herself into the saddle.

"Hurry!" she whispered. "We shall have to run for it. Ride through the gap that Tantor made," and as she saw Baynes swing his leg over the back of his horse, she shook the reins free over her mount's neck. With a lunge, the nervous beast leaped forward. The shortest path led straight through the center of the village, and this Meriem took. Baynes was close behind her, their horses running at full speed.

So sudden and impetuous was their dash for escape that it carried them half-way across the village before the surprised inhabitants were aware of what was happening. Then an Arab recognized them, and, with a cry of alarm, raised his rifle and fired. The shot was a signal for a volley, and amid the rattle of musketry Meriem and Baynes leaped their flying mounts through the breach in the palisade and were gone up the well-worn trail toward the north.

And Korak?

Tantor carried him deep into the jungle, nor paused until no sound from the distant village reached his keen ears. Then he laid his burden gently down. Korak struggled to free himself from his bonds, but even his great strength was unable to cope with the many strands of hard-knotted cord that bound him. While he lay there, working and resting by turns, the elephant stood guard above him, nor was there jungle enemy with the hardihood to tempt the sudden death that lay in that mighty bulk.

Dawn came, and still Korak was no nearer freedom than before. He commenced to believe that he should die there of thirst and starvation with plenty all about him, for he knew that Tantor could not unloose the knots that held him.

And while he struggled through the night with his bonds, Baynes and Meriem were riding rapidly northward along the river. The girl had assured Baynes that Korak was safe in the jungle with Tantor. It had not occurred to her that the ape-man might not be able to burst his bonds. Baynes had been wounded by a shot from the rifle of one of the Arabs, and the girl wanted to get him back to Bwana's home, where he could be properly cared for.

"Then," she said, "I shall get Bwana to come with me and search for Korak. He must come and live with us."

All night they rode, and the day was still young when they came suddenly upon a party hurrying southward. It was Bwana himself and his sleek, black warriors. At sight of Baynes the big Englishman's brows contracted in a scowl; but he waited to hear Meriem's story before giving vent to the long anger in his breast. When she had finished he seemed to have forgotten Baynes. His thoughts were occupied with another subject.

"You say that you found Korak?" he asked. "You really saw him?"

"Yes," replied Meriem; "as plainly as I see you, and I want you to come with me, Bwana, and help me find him again."

"Did you see him?" He turned toward the Hon. Morison.

"Yes, sir," replied Baynes; "very plainly."

"What sort of appearing man is he?" continued Bwana. "About how old, should you say?"

"I should say he was an Englishman, about my own age," replied Baynes; "though he might be older. He is remarkably muscled, and exceedingly tanned."

"His eyes and hair, did you notice them?" Bwana spoke rapidly, almost excitedly. It was Meriem who answered him.

"Korak's hair is black and his eyes are gray," she said.

Bwana turned to his headman.

"Take Miss Meriem and Mr. Baynes home," he said. "I am going into the jungle."

"Let me go with you, Bwana," cried Meriem. "You are going to search for Korak. Let me go, too."

Bwana turned sadly but firmly upon the girl.

"Your place," he said, "is beside the man you love."

Then he motioned to his head-man to take his horse and commence the return journey to the farm. Meriem slowly mounted the tired Arab that had brought her from the village of The Sheik. A litter was rigged for the now feverish Baynes, and the little cavalcade was soon slowly winding off along the river trail.

Bwana stood watching them until they were out of sight. Not once had Meriem turned her eyes backward. She rode with bowed head and drooping shoulders. Bwana sighed. He loved the little Arab girl as he might have loved an own daughter. He realized that Baynes had redeemed himself, and so he could interpose no objections now if Meriem really loved the man; but, somehow, some way, Bwana could not convince himself that the Hon. Morison was worthy of his little Meriem. Slowly he turned toward a nearby tree. Leaping upward he caught a lower branch and drew himself up among the branches. His movements were cat-like and agile. High into the trees he made his way and there commenced to divest himself of his clothing. From the game bag slung across one shoulder he drew a long strip of doe-skin, a neatly coiled rope, and a wicked looking knife. The doe-skin, he fashioned into a loin cloth, the rope he looped over one shoulder, and the knife he thrust into the belt formed by his gee string.

When he stood erect, his head thrown back and his great chest expanded a grim smile touched his lips for a moment. His nostrils dilated as he sniffed the jungle odors. His gray eyes narrowed. He crouched and leaped to a lower limb and was away through the trees toward the southeast, bearing away from the river. He moved swiftly, stopping only occasionally to raise his voice in a weird and piercing scream, and to listen for a moment after for a reply.

He had traveled thus for several hours when, ahead of him and a little to his left, he heard, far off in the jungle, a faint response – the cry of a bull ape answering his cry. His nerves tingled and his eyes lighted as the sound fell upon his ears. Again he voiced his hideous call, and sped forward in the new direction.

Korak, finally becoming convinced that he must die if he remained where he was, waiting for the succor that could not come, spoke to Tantor in the strange tongue that the great beast understood. He commanded the elephant to lift him and carry him toward the northeast. There, recently, Korak had seen both white men and black. If he could come upon one of the latter it would be a simple matter to command Tantor to capture the fellow, and then Korak could get him to release him from the stake. It was worth trying at least – better than lying there in the jungle until he died. As Tantor bore him along through the forest Korak called aloud now and then in the hope of attracting Akut's band of anthropoids, whose wanderings often brought them into their neighborhood. Akut, he thought, might possibly be able to negotiate the knots – he had done so upon that other occasion when the Russian had bound Korak years before; and Akut, to the south of him, heard his calls faintly, and came. There was another who heard them, too.

After Bwana had left his party, sending them back toward the farm, Meriem had ridden for a short distance with bowed head. What thoughts passed through that active brain who may say? Presently she seemed to come to a decision. She called the headman to her side.

"I am going back with Bwana," she announced.

The black shook his head. "No!" he announced. "Bwana says I take you home. So I take you home."

"You refuse to let me go?" asked the girl.

The black nodded, and fell to the rear where he might better watch her. Meriem half smiled. Presently her horse passed beneath a low-hanging branch, and the black headman found himself gazing at the girl's empty saddle. He ran forward to the tree into which she had disappeared. He could see nothing of her. He called; but there was no response, unless it might have been a low, taunting laugh far to the right. He sent his men into the jungle to search for her; but they came back empty handed. After a while he resumed his march toward the farm, for Baynes, by this time, was delirious with fever.

Meriem raced straight back toward the point she imagined Tantor would make for – a point where she knew the elephants often gathered deep in the forest due east of The Sheik's village. She moved silently and swiftly. From her mind she had expunged all thoughts other than that she must reach Korak and bring him back with her. It was her place to do that. Then, too, had come the tantalizing fear that all might not be well with him. She upbraided herself for not thinking of that before – of letting her desire to get the wounded Morison back to the bungalow blind her to the possibilities of Korak's need for her. She had been traveling rapidly for several hours without rest when she heard ahead of her the familiar cry of a great ape calling to his kind.

She did not reply, only increased her speed until she almost flew. Now there came to her sensitive nostrils the scent of Tantor and she knew that she was on the right trail and close to him she sought. She did not call out because she wished to surprise him, and presently she did, breaking into sight of them as the great elephant shuffled ahead balancing the man and the heavy stake upon his head, holding them there with his upcurled trunk.

"Korak!" cried Meriem from the foliage above him.

Instantly the bull swung about, lowered his burden to the ground and, trumpeting savagely, prepared to defend his comrade. The ape-man, recognizing the girl's voice, felt a sudden lump in his throat.

"Meriem!" he called back to her.

Happily the girl clambered to the ground and ran forward to release Korak; but Tantor lowered his head ominously and trumpeted a warning.

"Go back! Go back!" cried Korak. "He will kill you."

Meriem paused. "Tantor!" she called to the huge brute. "Don't you remember me? I am little Meriem. I used to ride on your broad back;" but the bull only rumbled in his throat and shook his tusks in angry defiance. Then Korak tried to placate him. Tried to order him away, that the girl might approach and release him; but Tantor would not go. He saw in every human being other than Korak an enemy. He thought the girl bent upon harming his friend and he would take no chances. For an hour the girl and the man tried to find some means whereby they might circumvent the beast's ill directed guardianship, but all to no avail; Tantor stood his ground in grim determination to let no one approach Korak.

Presently the man hit upon a scheme. "Pretend to go away," he called to the girl. "Keep down wind from us so that Tantor won't get your scent, then follow us. After a while I'll have him put me down, and find some pretext for sending him away. While he is gone you can slip up and cut my bonds – have you a knife?"

"Yes, I have a knife," she replied. "I'll go now – I think we may be able to fool him; but don't be too sure – Tantor invented cunning."

Korak smiled, for he knew that the girl was right. Presently she had disappeared. The elephant listened, and raised his trunk to catch her scent. Korak commanded him to raise him to his head once more and proceed upon their way. After a moment's hesitation he did as he was bid. It was then that Korak heard the distant call of an ape.

"Akut!" he thought. "Good! Tantor knew Akut well. He would let him approach." Raising his voice Korak replied to the call of the ape; but he let Tantor move off with him through the jungle; it would do no harm to try the other plan. They had come to a clearing and plainly Korak smelled water. Here was a good place and a good excuse. He ordered Tantor to lay him down, and go and fetch him water in his trunk. The big beast deposited him upon the grass in the center of the clearing, then he stood with cocked ears and attentive trunk, searching for the slightest indication of danger – there seemed to be none and he moved away in the direction of the little brook that Korak knew was some two or three hundred yards away. The ape-man could scarce help smiling as he thought how cleverly he had tricked his friend; but well as he knew Tantor he little guessed the guile of his cunning brain. The animal ambled off across the clearing and disappeared in the jungle beyond in the direction of the stream; but scarce had his great bulk been screened by the dense foliage than he wheeled about and came cautiously back to the edge of the clearing where he could see without being seen. Tantor, by nature, is suspicious. Now he still feared the return of the she Tarmangani who had attempted to attack his Korak. He would just stand there for a moment and assure himself that all was well before he continued on toward the water. Ah! It was well that he did! There she was now dropping from the branches of a tree across the clearing and running swiftly toward the ape-man. Tantor waited. He would let her reach Korak before he charged – that would ensure that she had no chance of escape. His little eyes blazed savagely. His tail was elevated stiffly. He could scarce restrain a desire to trumpet forth his rage to the world. Meriem was almost at Korak's side when Tantor saw the long knife in her hand, and then he broke forth from the jungle, bellowing horribly, and charged down upon the frail girl.

Chapter Twenty Seven

Korak screamed commands to his huge protector, in an effort to halt him; but all to no avail. Meriem raced toward the bordering trees with all the speed that lay in her swift, little feet; but Tantor, for all his huge bulk, drove down upon her with the rapidity of an express train.

Korak lay where he could see the whole frightful tragedy. The cold sweat broke out upon his body. His heart seemed to have stopped its beating. Meriem might reach the trees before Tantor overtook her, but even her agility would not carry her beyond the reach of that relentless trunk - she would be dragged down and tossed. Korak could picture the whole frightful scene. Then Tantor would follow her up, goring the frail, little body with his relentless tusks, or trampling it into an unrecognizable mass beneath his ponderous feet.

He was almost upon her now. Korak wanted to close his eyes, but could not. His throat was dry and parched. Never in all his savage existence had he suffered such blighting terror - never before had he known what terror meant. A dozen more strides and the brute would seize her. What was that? Korak's eyes started from their sockets. A strange figure had leaped from the tree the shade of which Meriem already had reached - leaped beyond the girl straight into the path of the charging elephant. It was a naked white giant. Across his shoulder a coil of rope was looped. In the band of his gee string was a hunting knife. Otherwise he was unarmed. With naked hands he faced the maddening Tantor. A sharp command broke from the stranger's lips - the great beast halted in his tracks - and Meriem swung herself upward into the tree to safety. Korak breathed a sigh of relief not unmixed with wonder. He fastened his eyes upon the face of Meriem's deliverer and as recognition slowly filtered into his understanding they went wide in incredulity and surprise.

Tantor, still rumbling angrily, stood swaying to and fro close before the giant white man. Then the latter stepped straight beneath the upraised trunk and spoke a low word of command. The great beast ceased his muttering. The savage light died from his eyes, and as the stranger stepped forward toward Korak, Tantor trailed docilely at his heels.

Meriem was watching, too, and wondering. Suddenly the man turned toward her as though recollecting her presence after a moment of forgetfulness. "Come! Meriem," he called, and then she recognized him with a startled: "Bwana!" Quickly the girl dropped from the tree and ran to his side. Tantor cocked a questioning eye at the white giant, but receiving a warning word let Meriem approach. Together the two walked to where Korak lay, his eyes wide with wonder and filled with a pathetic appeal for forgiveness, and, mayhap, a glad thankfulness for the miracle that had brought these two of all others to his side.

"Jack!" cried the white giant, kneeling at the ape-man's side.

"Father!" came chokingly from The Killer's lips. "Thank God that it was you. No one else in all the jungle could have stopped Tantor."

Quickly the man cut the bonds that held Korak, and as the youth leaped to his feet and threw his arms about his father, the older man turned toward Meriem.

"I thought," he said, sternly, "that I told you to return to the farm."

Korak was looking at them wonderingly. In his heart was a great yearning to take the girl in his arms; but in time he remembered the other – the dapper young English gentleman – and that he was but a savage, uncouth ape-man.

Meriem looked up pleadingly into Bwana's eyes.

"You told me," she said, in a very small voice, "that my place was beside the man I loved," and she turned her eyes toward Korak all filled with the wonderful light that no other man had yet seen in them, and that none other ever would.

The Killer started toward her with outstretched arms; but suddenly he fell upon one knee before her, instead, and lifting her hand to his lips kissed it more reverently than he could have kissed the hand of his country's queen.

A rumble from Tantor brought the three, all jungle bred, to instant alertness. Tantor was looking toward the trees behind them, and as their eyes followed his gaze the head and shoulders of a great ape appeared amidst the foliage. For a moment the creature eyed them, and then from its throat rose a loud scream of recognition and of joy, and a moment later the beast had leaped to the ground, followed by a score of bulls like himself, and was waddling toward them, shouting in the primordial tongue of the anthropoid:

"Tarzan has returned! Tarzan, Lord of the Jungle!"

It was Akut, and instantly he commenced leaping and bounding about the trio, uttering hideous shrieks and mouthings that to any other human beings might have indicated the most ferocious rage; but these three knew that the king of the apes was doing homage to a king greater than himself. In his wake leaped his shaggy bulls, vying with one another as to which could spring the highest and which utter the most uncanny sounds.

Korak laid his hand affectionately upon his father's shoulder.

"There is but one Tarzan," he said. "There can never be another."

Two days later the three dropped from the trees on the edge of the plain across which they could see the smoke rising from the bungalow and the cook house chimneys. Tarzan of the Apes had regained his civilized clothing from the tree where he had hidden it, and as Korak refused to enter the presence of his mother in the savage half-raiment that he had worn so long and as Meriem would not leave him, for fear, as she explained, that he would change his mind and run off into the jungle again, the father went on ahead to the bungalow for horses and clothes.

My Dear met him at the gate, her eyes filled with questioning and sorrow, for she saw that Meriem was not with him.

"Where is she?" she asked, her voice trembling. "Muviri told me that she disobeyed your instructions and ran off into the jungle after you had left them. Oh, John, I cannot bear to lose her, too!" And Lady Greystoke broke down and wept, as she pillowed her head upon the broad breast where so often before she had found comfort in the great tragedies of her life.

Lord Greystoke raised her head and looked down into her eyes, his own smiling and filled with the light of happiness.

"What is it, John?" she cried. "You have good news – do not keep me waiting for it."

"I want to be quite sure that you can stand hearing the best news that ever came to either of us," he said.

"Joy never kills," she cried. "You have found – her?" She could not bring herself to hope for the impossible.

"Yes, Jane," he said, and his voice was husky with emotion; "I have found her, and – HIM!"

"Where is he? Where are they?" she demanded.

"Out there at the edge of the jungle. He wouldn't come to you in his savage leopard skin and his nakedness – he sent me to fetch him civilized clothing."

She clapped her hands in ecstasy, and turned to run toward the bungalow. "Wait!" she cried over her shoulder. "I have all his little suits – I have saved them all. I will bring one to you."

Tarzan laughed and called to her to stop.

"The only clothing on the place that will fit him," he said, "is mine – if it isn't too small for him – your little boy has grown, Jane."

She laughed, too; she felt like laughing at everything, or at nothing. The world was all love and happiness and joy once more – the world that had been shrouded in the gloom of her great sorrow for so many years. So great was her joy that for the moment she forgot the sad message that awaited Meriem. She called to Tarzan after he had ridden away to prepare her for it, but he did not hear and rode on without knowing himself what the event was to which his wife referred.

And so, an hour later, Korak, The Killer, rode home to his mother – the mother whose image had never faded in his boyish heart – and found in her arms and her eyes the love and forgiveness that he plead for.

And then the mother turned toward Meriem, an expression of pitying sorrow erasing the happiness from her eyes.

"My little girl," she said, "in the midst of our happiness a great sorrow awaits you – Mr. Baynes did not survive his wound."

The expression of sorrow in Meriem's eyes expressed only what she sincerely felt; but it was not the sorrow of a woman bereft of her best beloved.

"I am sorry," she said, quite simply. "He would have done me a great wrong; but he amply atoned before he died. Once I thought that I loved him. At first it was only fascination for a type that was new to me – then it was respect for a brave man who had the moral courage to admit a sin and the physical courage to face death to right the wrong he had committed. But it was not love. I did not know what love was until I knew that Korak lived," and she turned toward The Killer with a smile.

Lady Greystoke looked quickly up into the eyes of her son – the son who one day would be Lord Greystoke. No thought of the difference in the stations of the girl and her boy entered her mind. To her Meriem was fit for a king. She only wanted to know that Jack loved the little Arab waif. The look in his eyes answered the question in her heart, and she threw her arms about them both and kissed them each a dozen times.

"Now," she cried, "I shall really have a daughter!"

It was several weary marches to the nearest mission; but they only waited at the farm a few days for rest and preparation for the great event before setting out upon the journey, and after the marriage ceremony had been performed they kept on to the coast to take passage for England. Those days were the most wonderful of Meriem's life. She had not dreamed even vaguely of the marvels that civilization held in store for her. The great ocean and the commodious steamship filled her with awe. The noise, and bustle and confusion of the English railway station frightened her.

"If there was a good-sized tree at hand," she confided to Korak, "I know that I should run to the very top of it in terror of my life."

"And make faces and throw twigs at the engine?" he laughed back.

"Poor old Numa," sighed the girl. "What will he do without us?"

"Oh, there are others to tease him, my little Mangani," assured Korak.

The Greystoke town house quite took Meriem's breath away; but when strangers were about none might guess that she had not been to the manner born.

They had been home but a week when Lord Greystoke received a message from his friend of many years, D'Arnot.

It was in the form of a letter of introduction brought by one General Armand Jacot. Lord Greystoke recalled the name, as who familiar with modern French history would not, for Jacot was in reality the Prince de Cadrenet – that intense republican who refused to use, even by courtesy, a title that had belonged to his family for four hundred years.

"There is no place for princes in a republic," he was wont to say.

Lord Greystoke received the hawk-nosed, gray mustached soldier in his library, and after a dozen words the two men had formed a mutual esteem that was to endure through life.

"I have come to you," explained General Jacot, "because our dear Admiral tells me that there is no one in all the world who is more intimately acquainted with Central Africa than you.

"Let me tell you my story from the beginning. Many years ago my little daughter was stolen, presumably by Arabs, while I was serving with the Foreign Legion in Algeria. We did all that love and money and even government resources could do to discover her; but all to no avail. Her picture was published in the leading papers of every large city in the world, yet never did we find a man or woman who ever had seen her since the day she mysteriously disappeared.

"A week since there came to me in Paris a swarthy Arab, who called himself Abdul Kamak. He said that he had found my daughter and could lead me to her. I took him at once to Admiral d'Arnot, whom I knew had traveled some in Central Africa. The man's story led the Admiral to believe that the place where the white girl the Arab supposed to be my daughter was held in captivity was not far from your African estates, and he advised that I come at once and call upon you – that you would know if such a girl were in your neighborhood."

"What proof did the Arab bring that she was your daughter?" asked Lord Greystoke.

"None," replied the other. "That is why we thought best to consult you before organizing an expedition. The fellow had only an old photograph of her on the back of which was pasted a newspaper cutting describing her and offering a reward. We feared that having found this somewhere it had aroused his cupidity and led him to believe that in some way he could obtain the reward, possibly by foisting upon us a white girl on the chance that so many years had elapsed that we would not be able to recognize an imposter as such."

"Have you the photograph with you?" asked Lord Greystoke.

The General drew an envelope from his pocket, took a yellowed photograph from it and handed it to the Englishman.

Tears dimmed the old warrior's eyes as they fell again upon the pictured features of his lost daughter.

Lord Greystoke examined the photograph for a moment. A queer expression entered his eyes. He touched a bell at his elbow, and an instant later a footman entered.

"Ask my son's wife if she will be so good as to come to the library," he directed.

The two men sat in silence. General Jacot was too well bred to show in any way the chagrin and disappointment he felt in the summary manner in which Lord Greystoke had dismissed the subject of his call. As soon as the young lady had come and he had been presented he would make his departure. A moment later Meriem entered.

Lord Greystoke and General Jacot rose and faced her. The Englishman spoke no word of introduction – he wanted to mark the effect of the first sight of the girl's face on the Frenchman, for he had a theory – a heaven-born theory that had leaped into his mind the moment his eyes had rested on the baby face of Jeanne Jacot.

General Jacot took one look at Meriem, then he turned toward Lord Greystoke.

"How long have you known it?" he asked, a trifle accusingly.

"Since you showed me that photograph a moment ago," replied the Englishman.

"It is she," said Jacot, shaking with suppressed emotion; "but she does not recognize me – of course she could not." Then he turned to Meriem. "My child," he said, "I am your – "

But she interrupted him with a quick, glad cry, as she ran toward him with outstretched arms.

"I know you! I know you!" she cried. "Oh, now I remember," and the old man folded her in his arms.

Jack Clayton and his mother were summoned, and when the story had been told them they were only glad that little Meriem had found a father and a mother.

"And really you didn't marry an Arab waif after all," said Meriem. "Isn't it fine!"

"You are fine," replied The Killer. "I married my little Meriem, and I don't care, for my part, whether she is an Arab, or just a little Tarmangani."

"She is neither, my son," said General Armand Jacot. "She is a princess in her own right."

TARZAN
AND THE JEWELS OF OPAR

CHAPTER ONE

Belgian and Arab

Lieutenant Albert Werper had only the prestige of the name he had dishonored to thank for his narrow escape from being cashiered. At first he had been humbly thankful, too, that they had sent him to this Godforsaken Congo post instead of court-martialing him, as he had so justly deserved; but now six months of the monotony, the frightful isolation and the loneliness had wrought a change. The young man brooded continually over his fate. His days were filled with morbid self-pity, which eventually engendered in his weak and vacillating mind a hatred for those who had sent him here – for the very men he had at first inwardly thanked for saving him from the ignominy of degradation.

He regretted the gay life of Brussels as he never had regretted the sins which had snatched him from that gayest of capitals, and as the days passed he came to center his resentment upon the representative in Congo land of the authority which had exiled him – his captain and immediate superior.

This officer was a cold, taciturn man, inspiring little love in those directly beneath him, yet respected and feared by the black soldiers of his little command.

Werper was accustomed to sit for hours glaring at his superior as the two sat upon the veranda of their common quarters, smoking their evening cigarets in a silence which neither seemed desirous of breaking. The senseless hatred of the lieutenant grew at last into a form of mania. The captain's natural taciturnity he distorted into a studied attempt to insult him because of his past shortcomings. He imagined that his superior held him in contempt, and so he chafed and fumed inwardly until one evening his madness became suddenly homicidal. He fingered the butt of the revolver at his hip, his eyes narrowed and his brows contracted. At last he spoke.

"You have insulted me for the last time!" he cried, springing to his feet. "I am an officer and a gentleman, and I shall put up with it no longer without an accounting from you, you pig."

The captain, an expression of surprise upon his features, turned toward his junior. He had seen men before with the jungle madness upon them – the madness of solitude and unrestrained brooding, and perhaps a touch of fever.

He rose and extended his hand to lay it upon the other's shoulder. Quiet words of counsel were upon his lips; but they were never spoken. Werper construed his superior's action into an attempt to close with him. His revolver was on a level with the captain's heart, and the latter had taken but a step when Werper pulled the trigger. Without a moan the man sank to the rough planking of the veranda, and as he fell the mists that had clouded Werper's brain lifted, so that he saw himself and the deed that he had done in the same light that those who must judge him would see them.

He heard excited exclamations from the quarters of the soldiers and he heard men running in his direction. They would seize him, and if they didn't kill him they would take him down the Congo to a point where a properly ordered military tribunal would do so just as effectively, though in a more regular manner.

Werper had no desire to die. Never before had he so yearned for life as in this moment that he had so effectively forfeited his right to live. The men were nearing him. What was he to do? He glanced about as though searching for the tangible form of a legitimate excuse for his crime; but he could find only the body of the man he had so causelessly shot down.

In despair, he turned and fled from the oncoming soldiery. Across the compound he ran, his revolver still clutched tightly in his hand. At the gates a sentry halted him. Werper did not pause to parley or to exert the influence of his commission – he merely raised his weapon and shot down the innocent black. A moment later the fugitive had torn open the gates and vanished into the blackness of the jungle, but not before he had transferred the rifle and ammunition belts of the dead sentry to his own person.

All that night Werper fled farther and farther into the heart of the wilderness. Now and again the voice of a lion brought him to a listening halt; but with cocked and ready rifle he pushed ahead again, more fearful of the human huntsmen in his rear than of the wild carnivora ahead.

Dawn came at last, but still the man plodded on. All sense of hunger and fatigue were lost in the terrors of contemplated capture. He could think only of escape. He dared not pause to rest or eat until there was no further danger from pursuit, and so he staggered on until at last he fell and could rise no more. How long he had fled he did not know, or try to know. When he could flee no longer the knowledge that he had reached his limit was hidden from him in the unconsciousness of utter exhaustion.

And thus it was that Achmet Zek, the Arab, found him. Achmet's followers were for running a spear through the body of their hereditary enemy; but Achmet would have it otherwise. First he would question the Belgian. It were easier to question a man first and kill him afterward, than kill him first and then question him.

So he had Lieutenant Albert Werper carried to his own tent, and there slaves administered wine and food in small quantities until at last the prisoner regained consciousness. As he opened his eyes he saw the faces of strange black men about him, and just outside the tent the figure of an Arab. Nowhere was the uniform of his soldiers to be seen.

The Arab turned and seeing the open eyes of the prisoner upon him, entered the tent.

"I am Achmet Zek," he announced. "Who are you, and what were you doing in my country? Where are your soldiers?"

Achmet Zek! Werper's eyes went wide, and his heart sank. He was in the clutches of the most notorious of cut-throats – a hater of all Europeans, especially those who wore the uniform of Belgium. For years the military forces of Belgian Congo had waged a fruitless war upon this man and his followers – a war in which quarter had never been asked nor expected by either side.

But presently in the very hatred of the man for Belgians, Werper saw a faint ray of hope for himself. He, too, was an outcast and an outlaw. So far, at least, they possessed a common interest, and Werper decided to play upon it for all that it might yield.

"I have heard of you," he replied, "and was searching for you. My people have turned against me. I hate them. Even now their soldiers are searching for me, to kill me. I knew that you would protect me from them, for you, too, hate them. In return I will take service with you. I am a trained soldier. I can fight, and your enemies are my enemies."

Achmet Zek eyed the European in silence. In his mind he revolved many thoughts, chief among which was that the unbeliever lied. Of course there was the chance that he did not lie, and if he told the truth then his proposition was one well worthy of consideration, since fighting men were never over plentiful – especially white men with the training and knowledge of military matters that a European officer must possess.

Achmet Zek scowled and Werper's heart sank; but Werper did not know Achmet Zek, who was quite apt to scowl where another would smile, and smile where another would scowl.

"And if you have lied to me," said Achmet Zek, "I will kill you at any time. What return, other than your life, do you expect for your services?"

"My keep only, at first," replied Werper. "Later, if I am worth more, we can easily reach an understanding." Werper's only desire at the moment was to preserve his life. And so the agreement was reached and Lieutenant Albert Werper became a member of the ivory and slave raiding band of the notorious Achmet Zek.

For months the renegade Belgian rode with the savage raider. He fought with a savage abandon, and a vicious cruelty fully equal to that of his fellow desperadoes. Achmet Zek watched his recruit with eagle eye, and with a growing satisfaction which finally found expression in a greater confidence in the man, and resulted in an increased independence of action for Werper.

Achmet Zek took the Belgian into his confidence to a great extent, and at last unfolded to him a pet scheme which the Arab had long fostered, but which he never had found an opportunity to effect. With the aid of a European, however, the thing might be easily accomplished. He sounded Werper.

"You have heard of the man men call Tarzan?" he asked.

Werper nodded. "I have heard of him; but I do not know him."

"But for him we might carry on our 'trading' in safety and with great profit," continued the Arab. "For years he has fought us, driving us from the richest part of the country, harassing us, and arming the natives that they may repel us when we come to 'trade.' He is very rich. If we could find some way to make him pay us many pieces of gold we should not only be avenged upon him; but repaid for much that he has prevented us from winning from the natives under his protection."

Werper withdrew a cigaret from a jeweled case and lighted it.

"And you have a plan to make him pay?" he asked.

"He has a wife," replied Achmet Zek, "whom men say is very beautiful. She would bring a great price farther north, if we found it too difficult to collect ransom money from this Tarzan."

Werper bent his head in thought. Achmet Zek stood awaiting his reply. What good remained in Albert Werper revolted at the thought of selling a white woman into the slavery and degradation of a Moslem harem. He looked up at Achmet Zek. He saw the Arab's eyes narrow, and he guessed that the other had sensed his antagonism to the plan. What would it mean to Werper to refuse? His life lay in the hands of this semi-barbarian, who esteemed the life of an unbeliever less highly than that of a dog. Werper loved life. What was this woman to him, anyway? She was a European, doubtless, a member of organized society. He was an outcast. The hand of every white man was against him. She was his natural enemy, and if he refused to lend himself to her undoing, Achmet Zek would have him killed.

"You hesitate," murmured the Arab.

"I was but weighing the chances of success," lied Werper, "and my reward. As a European I can gain admittance to their home and table. You have no other with you who could do so much. The risk will be great. I should be well paid, Achmet Zek."

A smile of relief passed over the raider's face.

"Well said, Werper," and Achmet Zek slapped his lieutenant upon the shoulder. "You should be well paid and you shall. Now let us sit together and plan how best the thing may be done," and the two men squatted upon a soft rug beneath the faded silks of Achmet's once gorgeous tent, and talked together in low voices well into the night. Both were tall and bearded, and the exposure to sun and wind had given an almost Arab hue to the European's complexion. In every detail of dress, too, he copied the fashions of his chief, so that outwardly he was as much an Arab as the other. It was late when he arose and retired to his own tent.

The following day Werper spent in overhauling his Belgian uniform, removing from it every vestige of evidence that might indicate its military purposes. From a heterogeneous collection of loot, Achmet Zek procured a pith helmet and a European saddle, and from his black slaves and followers a party of porters, askaris and tent boys to make up a modest safari for a big game hunter. At the head of this party Werper set out from camp.

CHAPTER TWO

On the Road To Opar

It was two weeks later that John Clayton, Lord Greystoke, riding in from a tour of inspection of his vast African estate, glimpsed the head of a column of men crossing the plain that lay between his bungalow and the forest to the north and west.

He reined in his horse and watched the little party as it emerged from a concealing swale. His keen eyes caught the reflection of the sun upon the white helmet of a mounted man, and with the conviction that a wandering European hunter was seeking his hospitality, he wheeled his mount and rode slowly forward to meet the newcomer.

A half hour later he was mounting the steps leading to the veranda of his bungalow, and introducing M. Jules Frecoult to Lady Greystoke.

"I was completely lost," M. Frecoult was explaining. "My head man had never before been in this part of the country and the guides who were to have accompanied me from the last village we passed knew even less of the country than we. They finally deserted us two days since. I am very fortunate indeed to have stumbled so providentially upon succor. I do not know what I should have done, had I not found you."

It was decided that Frecoult and his party should remain several days, or until they were thoroughly rested, when Lord Greystoke would furnish guides to lead them safely back into country with which Frecoult's head man was supposedly familiar.

In his guise of a French gentleman of leisure, Werper found little difficulty in deceiving his host and in ingratiating himself with both Tarzan and Jane Clayton; but the longer he remained the less hopeful he became of an easy accomplishment of his designs.

Lady Greystoke never rode alone at any great distance from the bungalow, and the savage loyalty of the ferocious Waziri warriors who formed a great part of Tarzan's followers seemed to preclude the possibility of a successful attempt at forcible abduction, or of the bribery of the Waziri themselves.

A week passed, and Werper was no nearer the fulfillment of his plan, in so far as he could judge, than upon the day of his arrival, but at that very moment something occurred which gave him renewed hope and set his mind upon an even greater reward than a woman's ransom.

A runner had arrived at the bungalow with the weekly mail, and Lord Greystoke had spent the afternoon in his study reading and answering letters. At dinner he seemed distraught, and early in the evening he excused himself and retired, Lady Greystoke following him very soon after. Werper, sitting upon the veranda, could hear their voices in earnest discussion, and having realized that something of unusual moment was afoot, he quietly rose from his chair, and keeping well in the shadow of the shrubbery growing profusely about the bungalow, made his silent way to a point beneath the window of the room in which his host and hostess slept.

Here he listened, and not without result, for almost the first words he overheard filled him with excitement. Lady Greystoke was speaking as Werper came within hearing.

"I always feared for the stability of the company," she was saying; "but it seems incredible that they should have failed for so enormous a sum – unless there has been some dishonest manipulation."

"That is what I suspect," replied Tarzan; "but whatever the cause, the fact remains that I have lost everything, and there is nothing for it but to return to Opar and get more."

"Oh, John," cried Lady Greystoke, and Werper could feel the shudder through her voice, "is there no other way? I cannot bear to think of you returning to that frightful city. I would rather live in poverty always than to have you risk the hideous dangers of Opar."

"You need have no fear," replied Tarzan, laughing. "I am pretty well able to take care of myself, and were I not, the Waziri who will accompany me will see that no harm befalls me."

"They ran away from Opar once, and left you to your fate," she reminded him.

"They will not do it again," he answered. "They were very much ashamed of themselves, and were coming back when I met them."

"But there must be some other way," insisted the woman.

"There is no other way half so easy to obtain another fortune, as to go to the treasure vaults of Opar and bring it away," he replied. "I shall be very careful, Jane, and the chances are that the inhabitants of Opar will never know that I have been there again and despoiled them of another portion of the treasure, the very existence of which they are as ignorant of as they would be of its value."

The finality in his tone seemed to assure Lady Greystoke that further argument was futile, and so she abandoned the subject.

Werper remained, listening, for a short time, and then, confident that he had overheard all that was necessary and fearing discovery, returned to the veranda, where he smoked numerous cigarets in rapid succession before retiring.

The following morning at breakfast, Werper announced his intention of making an early departure, and asked Tarzan's permission to hunt big game in the Waziri country on his way out – permission which Lord Greystoke readily granted.

The Belgian consumed two days in completing his preparations, but finally got away with his safari, accompanied by a single Waziri guide whom Lord Greystoke had loaned him. The party made but a single short march when Werper simulated illness, and announced his intention of remaining where he was until he had fully recovered. As they had gone but a short distance from the Greystoke bungalow, Werper dismissed the Waziri guide, telling the warrior that he would send for him when he was able to proceed. The Waziri gone, the Belgian summoned one of Achmet Zek's trusted blacks to his tent, and dispatched him to watch for the departure of Tarzan, returning immediately to advise Werper of the event and the direction taken by the Englishman.

The Belgian did not have long to wait, for the following day his emissary returned with word that Tarzan and a party of fifty Waziri warriors had set out toward the southeast early in the morning.

Werper called his head man to him, after writing a long letter to Achmet Zek. This letter he handed to the head man.

"Send a runner at once to Achmet Zek with this," he instructed the head man. "Remain here in camp awaiting further instructions from him or from me. If any come from the bungalow of the Englishman, tell them that I am very ill within my tent and can see no one. Now, give me six porters and six askaris – the strongest and bravest of the safari – and I will march after the Englishman and discover where his gold is hidden."

And so it was that as Tarzan, stripped to the loin cloth and armed after the primitive fashion he best loved, led his loyal Waziri toward the dead city of Opar, Werper, the renegade, haunted his trail through the long, hot days, and camped close behind him by night.

And as they marched, Achmet Zek rode with his entire following southward toward the Greystoke farm.

To Tarzan of the Apes the expedition was in the nature of a holiday outing. His civilization was at best but an outward veneer which he gladly peeled off with his uncomfortable European clothes whenever any reasonable pretext presented itself. It was a woman's love which kept Tarzan even to the semblance of civilization – a condition for which familiarity had bred contempt. He hated the shams and the hypocrisies of it and with the clear vision of an unspoiled mind he had penetrated to the rotten core of the heart of the thing – the cowardly greed for peace and ease and the safe-guarding of property rights. That the fine things of life – art, music and literature – had thriven upon such enervating ideals he strenuously denied, insisting, rather, that they had endured in spite of civilization.

"Show me the fat, opulent coward," he was wont to say, "who ever originated a beautiful ideal. In the clash of arms, in the battle for survival, amid hunger and death and danger, in the face of God as manifested in the display of Nature's most terrific forces, is born all that is finest and best in the human heart and mind."

And so Tarzan always came back to Nature in the spirit of a lover keeping a long deferred tryst after a period behind prison walls. His Waziri, at marrow, were more civilized than he. They cooked their meat before they ate it and they shunned many articles of food as unclean that Tarzan had eaten with gusto all his life and so insidious is the virus of hypocrisy that even the stalwart ape-man hesitated to give rein to his natural longings before them. He ate burnt flesh when he would have preferred it raw and unspoiled, and he brought down game with arrow or spear when he would far rather have leaped upon it from ambush and sunk his strong teeth in its jugular; but at last the call of the milk of the savage mother that had suckled him in infancy rose to an insistent demand – he craved the hot blood of a fresh kill and his muscles yearned to pit themselves against the savage jungle in the battle for existence that had been his sole birthright for the first twenty years of his life.

CHAPTER THREE

The Call of the Jungle

MOVED BY THESE VAGUE yet all-powerful urgings the ape-man lay awake one night in the little thorn boma that protected, in a way, his party from the depredations of the great carnivora of the jungle. A single warrior stood sleepy guard beside the fire that yellow eyes out of the darkness beyond the camp made imperative. The moans and the coughing of the big cats mingled with the myriad noises of the lesser denizens of the jungle to fan the savage flame in the breast of this savage English lord. He tossed upon his bed of grasses, sleepless, for an hour and then he rose, noiseless as a wraith, and while the Waziri's back was turned, vaulted the boma wall in the face of the flaming eyes, swung silently into a great tree and was gone.

For a time in sheer exuberance of animal spirit he raced swiftly through the middle terrace, swinging perilously across wide spans from one jungle giant to the next, and then he clambered upward to the swaying, lesser boughs of the upper terrace where the moon shone full upon him and the air was stirred by little breezes and death lurked ready in each frail branch. Here he paused and raised his face to Goro, the moon. With uplifted arm he stood, the cry of the bull ape quivering upon his lips, yet he remained silent lest he arouse his faithful Waziri who were all too familiar with the hideous challenge of their master.

And then he went on more slowly and with greater stealth and caution, for now Tarzan of the Apes was seeking a kill. Down to the ground he came in the utter blackness of the close-set boles and the overhanging verdure of the jungle. He stooped from time to time and put his nose close to earth. He sought and found a wide game trail and at last his nostrils were rewarded with the scent of the fresh spoor of Bara, the deer. Tarzan's mouth watered and a low growl escaped his patrician lips. Sloughed from him was the last vestige of artificial caste – once again he was the primeval hunter – the first man – the highest caste type of the human race. Up wind he followed the elusive spoor with a sense of perception so transcending that of ordinary man as to be inconceivable to us. Through counter currents of the heavy stench of meat eaters he traced the trail of Bara; the sweet and cloying stink of Horta, the boar, could not drown his quarry's scent – the permeating, mellow musk of the deer's foot.

Presently the body scent of the deer told Tarzan that his prey was close at hand. It sent him into the trees again – into the lower terrace where he could watch the ground below and catch with ears and nose the first intimation of actual contact with his quarry. Nor was it long before the ape-man came upon Bara standing alert at the edge of a moon-bathed clearing. Noiselessly Tarzan crept through the trees until he was directly over the deer. In the ape-man's right hand was the long hunting knife of his father and in his heart the blood lust of the carnivore. Just for an instant he poised above the unsuspecting Bara and then he launched himself downward upon the sleek back. The impact of his weight carried the deer to its knees and before the animal could regain its feet the knife had found its heart. As Tarzan rose upon the body of his kill to scream forth his hideous victory cry into the face of the moon the wind carried to his nostrils something which froze him to statuesque immobility and silence. His savage eyes blazed into the direction from which the wind had borne down the warning to him and a moment later the grasses at one side of the clearing parted and Numa, the lion, strode majestically into view. His yellow-green eyes were fastened upon Tarzan as he halted just within the clearing and glared enviously at the successful hunter, for Numa had had no luck this night.

From the lips of the ape-man broke a rumbling growl of warning. Numa answered but he did not advance. Instead he stood waving his tail gently to and fro, and presently Tarzan squatted upon his kill and cut a generous portion from a hind quarter. Numa eyed him with growing resentment and rage as, between mouthfuls, the ape-man growled out his savage warnings. Now this particular lion had never before come in contact with Tarzan of the Apes and he was much mystified. Here was the appearance and the scent of a man-thing and Numa had tasted of human flesh and learned that though not the most palatable it was certainly by far the easiest to secure, yet there was that in the bestial growls of the strange creature which reminded him of formidable antagonists and gave him pause, while his hunger and the odor of the hot flesh of Bara goaded him almost to madness. Always Tarzan watched him, guessing what was passing in the little brain of the carnivore and well it was that he did watch him, for at last Numa could stand it no longer. His tail shot suddenly erect and at the same instant the wary ape-man, knowing all too well what the signal portended, grasped the remainder of the deer's hind quarter between his teeth and leaped into a nearby tree as Numa charged him with all the speed and a sufficient semblance of the weight of an express train.

Tarzan's retreat was no indication that he felt fear. Jungle life is ordered along different lines than ours and different standards prevail. Had Tarzan been famished he would, doubtless, have stood his ground and met the lion's charge. He had done the thing before upon more than one occasion, just as in the past he had charged lions himself; but tonight he was far from famished and in the hind quarter he had carried off with him was more raw flesh than he could eat; yet it was with no equanimity that he looked down upon Numa rending the flesh of Tarzan's kill. The presumption of this strange Numa must be punished! And forthwith Tarzan set out to make life miserable for the big cat. Close by were many trees bearing large, hard fruits and to one of these the ape-man swung with the agility of a squirrel. Then commenced a bombardment which brought forth earthshaking roars from Numa. One after another as rapidly as he could gather and hurl them, Tarzan pelted the hard fruit down upon the lion. It was impossible for the tawny cat to eat under that hail of missiles – he could but roar and growl and dodge and eventually he was driven away entirely from the carcass of Bara, the deer. He went roaring and resentful; but in the very center of the clearing his voice was suddenly hushed and Tarzan saw the great head lower and flatten out, the body crouch and the long tail quiver, as the beast slunk cautiously toward the trees upon the opposite side.

Immediately Tarzan was alert. He lifted his head and sniffed the slow, jungle breeze. What was it that had attracted Numa's attention and taken him soft-footed and silent away from the scene of his discomfiture? Just as the lion disappeared among the trees beyond the clearing Tarzan caught upon the down-coming wind the explanation of his new interest – the scent spoor of man was wafted strongly to the sensitive nostrils. Caching the remainder of the deer's hind quarter in the crotch of a tree the ape-man wiped his greasy palms upon his naked thighs and swung off in pursuit of Numa. A broad, well-beaten elephant path led into the forest from the clearing. Parallel to this slunk Numa, while above him Tarzan moved through the trees, the shadow of a wraith. The savage cat and the savage man saw Numa's quarry almost simultaneously, though both had known before it came within the vision of their eyes that it was a black man. Their sensitive nostrils had told them this much and Tarzan's had told him that the scent spoor was that of a stranger – old and a male, for race and sex and age each has its own distinctive scent. It was an old man that made his way alone through the gloomy jungle, a wrinkled, dried up, little old man hideously scarred and tattooed and strangely garbed, with the skin of a hyena about his shoulders and the dried head mounted upon his grey pate. Tarzan recognized the ear-marks of the witch-doctor and awaited Numa's charge with a feeling of pleasurable anticipation, for the ape-man had no love for witch-doctors; but in the instant that Numa did charge, the white man suddenly recalled that the lion had stolen his kill a few minutes before and that revenge is sweet.

The first intimation the black man had that he was in danger was the crash of twigs as Numa charged through the bushes into the game trail not twenty yards behind him. Then he turned to see a huge, black-maned lion racing toward him and even as he turned, Numa seized him. At the same instant the ape-man dropped from an overhanging limb full upon the lion's back and as he alighted he plunged his knife into the tawny side behind the left shoulder, tangled the fingers of his right hand in the long mane, buried his teeth in Numa's neck and wound his powerful legs about the beast's torso. With a roar of pain and rage, Numa reared up and fell backward upon the ape-man; but still the mighty man-thing clung to his hold and repeatedly the long knife plunged rapidly into his side. Over and over rolled Numa, the lion, clawing and biting at the air, roaring and growling horribly in savage attempt to reach the thing upon its back. More than once was Tarzan almost brushed from his hold. He was battered and bruised and covered with blood from Numa and dirt from the trail, yet not for an instant did he lessen the ferocity of his mad attack nor his grim hold upon the back of his antagonist. To have loosened for an instant his grip there, would have been to bring him within reach of those tearing talons or rending fangs, and have ended forever the grim career of this jungle-bred English lord. Where he had fallen beneath the spring of the lion the witch-doctor lay, torn and bleeding, unable to drag himself away and watched the terrific battle between these two lords of the jungle. His sunken eyes glittered and his wrinkled lips moved over toothless gums as he mumbled weird incantations to the demons of his cult.

For a time he felt no doubt as to the outcome – the strange white man must certainly succumb to terrible Simba – whoever heard of a lone man armed only with a knife slaying so mighty a beast! Yet presently the old black man's eyes went wider and he commenced to have his doubts and misgivings. What wonderful sort of creature was this that battled with Simba and held his own despite the mighty muscles of the king of beasts and slowly there dawned in those sunken eyes, gleaming so brightly from the scarred and wrinkled face, the light of a dawning recollection. Gropingly backward into the past reached the fingers of memory, until at last they seized upon a faint picture, faded and yellow with the passing years. It was the picture of a lithe, white-skinned youth swinging through the trees in company with a band of huge apes, and the old eyes blinked and a great fear came into them – the superstitious fear of one who believes in ghosts and spirits and demons.

And came the time once more when the witch-doctor no longer doubted the outcome of the duel, yet his first judgment was reversed, for now he knew that the jungle god would slay Simba and the old black was even more terrified of his own impending fate at the hands of the victor than he had been by the sure and sudden death which the triumphant lion would have meted out to him. He saw the lion weaken from loss of blood. He saw the mighty limbs tremble and stagger and at last he saw the beast sink down to rise no more. He saw the forest god or demon rise from the vanquished foe, and placing a foot upon the still quivering carcass, raise his face to the moon and bay out a hideous cry that froze the ebbing blood in the veins of the witch-doctor.

CHAPTER FOUR

Prophecy and Fulfillment

THEN TARZAN TURNED HIS attention to the man. He had not slain Numa to save the Negro – he had merely done it in revenge upon the lion; but now that he saw the old man lying helpless and dying before him something akin to pity touched his savage heart. In his youth he would have slain the witch-doctor without the slightest compunction; but civilization had had its softening effect upon him even as it does upon the nations and races which it touches, though it had not yet gone far enough with Tarzan to render him either cowardly or effeminate. He saw an old man suffering and dying, and he stooped and felt of his wounds and stanched the flow of blood.

"Who are you?" asked the old man in a trembling voice.

"I am Tarzan – Tarzan of the Apes," replied the ape-man and not without a greater touch of pride than he would have said, "I am John Clayton, Lord Greystoke."

The witch-doctor shook convulsively and closed his eyes. When he opened them again there was in them a resignation to whatever horrible fate awaited him at the hands of this feared demon of the woods. "Why do you not kill me?" he asked.

"Why should I kill you?" inquired Tarzan. "You have not harmed me, and anyway you are already dying. Numa, the lion, has killed you."

"You would not kill me?" Surprise and incredulity were in the tones of the quavering old voice.

"I would save you if I could," replied Tarzan, "but that cannot be done. Why did you think I would kill you?"

For a moment the old man was silent. When he spoke it was evidently after some little effort to muster his courage. "I knew you of old," he said, "when you ranged the jungle in the country of Mbonga, the chief.

I was already a witch-doctor when you slew Kulonga and the others, and when you robbed our huts and our poison pot. At first I did not remember you; but at last I did – the white-skinned ape that lived with the hairy apes and made life miserable in the village of Mbonga, the chief – the forest god – the Munango-Keewati for whom we set food outside our gates and who came and ate it. Tell me before I die – are you man or devil?"

Tarzan laughed. "I am a man," he said.

The old fellow sighed and shook his head. "You have tried to save me from Simba," he said. "For that I shall reward you. I am a great witch-doctor. Listen to me, white man! I see bad days ahead of you. It is writ in my own blood which I have smeared upon my palm. A god greater even than you will rise up and strike you down. Turn back, Munango-Keewati! Turn back before it is too late. Danger lies ahead of you and danger lurks behind; but greater is the danger before. I see – " He paused and drew a long, gasping breath. Then he crumpled into a little, wrinkled heap and died. Tarzan wondered what else he had seen.

It was very late when the ape-man re-entered the boma and lay down among his black warriors. None had seen him go and none saw him return. He thought about the warning of the old witch-doctor before he fell asleep and he thought of it again after he awoke; but he did not turn back for he was unafraid, though had he known what lay in store for one he loved most in all the world he would have flown through the trees to her side and allowed the gold of Opar to remain forever hidden in its forgotten storehouse.

Behind him that morning another white man pondered something he had heard during the night and very nearly did he give up his project and turn back upon his trail. It was Werper, the murderer, who in the still of the night had heard far away upon the trail ahead of him a sound that had filled his cowardly soul with terror – a sound such as he never before had heard in all his life, nor dreamed that such a frightful thing could emanate from the lungs of a God-created creature. He had heard the victory cry of the bull ape as Tarzan had screamed it forth into the face of Goro, the moon, and he had trembled then and hidden his face; and now in the broad light of a new day he trembled again as he recalled it, and would have turned back from the nameless danger the echo of that frightful sound seemed to portend, had he not stood in even greater fear of Achmet Zek, his master.

And so Tarzan of the Apes forged steadily ahead toward Opar's ruined ramparts and behind him slunk Werper, jackal-like, and only God knew what lay in store for each.

At the edge of the desolate valley, overlooking the golden domes and minarets of Opar, Tarzan halted. By night he would go alone to the treasure vault, reconnoitering, for he had determined that caution should mark his every move upon this expedition.

With the coming of night he set forth, and Werper, who had scaled the cliffs alone behind the ape-man's party, and hidden through the day among the rough boulders of the mountain top, slunk stealthily after him. The boulder-strewn plain between the valley's edge and the mighty granite kopje, outside the city's walls, where lay the entrance to the passage-way leading to the treasure vault, gave the Belgian ample cover as he followed Tarzan toward Opar.

He saw the giant ape-man swing himself nimbly up the face of the great rock. Werper, clawing fearfully during the perilous ascent, sweating in terror, almost palsied by fear, but spurred on by avarice, following upward, until at last he stood upon the summit of the rocky hill.

Tarzan was nowhere in sight. For a time Werper hid behind one of the lesser boulders that were scattered over the top of the hill, but, seeing or hearing nothing of the Englishman, he crept from his place of concealment to undertake a systematic search of his surroundings, in the hope that he might discover the location of the treasure in ample time to make his escape before Tarzan returned, for it was the Belgian's desire merely to locate the gold, that, after Tarzan had departed, he might come in safety with his followers and carry away as much as he could transport.

He found the narrow cleft leading downward into the heart of the kopje along well-worn, granite steps. He advanced quite to the dark mouth of the tunnel into which the runway disappeared; but here he halted, fearing to enter, lest he meet Tarzan returning.

The ape-man, far ahead of him, groped his way along the rocky passage, until he came to the ancient wooden door. A moment later he stood within the treasure chamber, where, ages since, long-dead hands had ranged the lofty rows of precious ingots for the rulers of that great continent which now lies submerged beneath the waters of the Atlantic.

No sound broke the stillness of the subterranean vault. There was no evidence that another had discovered the forgotten wealth since last the ape-man had visited its hiding place.

Satisfied, Tarzan turned and retraced his steps toward the summit of the kopje. Werper, from the concealment of a jutting, granite shoulder, watched him pass up from the shadows of the stairway and advance toward the edge of the hill which faced the rim of the valley where the

Waziri awaited the signal of their master. Then Werper, slipping stealthily from his hiding place, dropped into the somber darkness of the entrance and disappeared.

Tarzan, halting upon the kopje's edge, raised his voice in the thunderous roar of a lion. Twice, at regular intervals, he repeated the call, standing in attentive silence for several minutes after the echoes of the third call had died away. And then, from far across the valley, faintly, came an answering roar – once, twice, thrice. Basuli, the Waziri chieftain, had heard and replied.

Tarzan again made his way toward the treasure vault, knowing that in a few hours his blacks would be with him, ready to bear away another fortune in the strangely shaped, golden ingots of Opar. In the meantime he would carry as much of the precious metal to the summit of the kopje as he could.

Six trips he made in the five hours before Basuli reached the kopje, and at the end of that time he had transported forty-eight ingots to the edge of the great boulder, carrying upon each trip a load which might well have staggered two ordinary men, yet his giant frame showed no evidence of fatigue, as he helped to raise his ebon warriors to the hill top with the rope that had been brought for the purpose.

Six times he had returned to the treasure chamber, and six times Werper, the Belgian, had cowered in the black shadows at the far end of the long vault. Once again came the ape-man, and this time there came with him fifty fighting men, turning porters for love of the only creature in the world who might command of their fierce and haughty natures such menial service. Fifty-two more ingots passed out of the vaults, making the total of one hundred which Tarzan intended taking away with him.

As the last of the Waziri filed from the chamber, Tarzan turned back for a last glimpse of the fabulous wealth upon which his two inroads had made no appreciable impression. Before he extinguished the single candle he had brought with him for the purpose, and the flickering light of which had cast the first alleviating rays into the impenetrable darkness of the buried chamber, that it had known for the countless ages since it had lain forgotten of man, Tarzan's mind reverted to that first occasion upon which he had entered the treasure vault, coming upon it by chance as he fled from the pits beneath the temple, where he had been hidden by La, the High Priestess of the Sun Worshipers.

He recalled the scene within the temple when he had lain stretched upon the sacrificial altar, while La, with high-raised dagger, stood above him, and the rows of priests and priestesses awaited, in the ecstatic hysteria of fanaticism, the first gush of their victim's warm blood, that they might fill their golden goblets and drink to the glory of their Flaming God.

The brutal and bloody interruption by Tha, the mad priest, passed vividly before the ape-man's recollective eyes, the flight of the votaries before the insane blood lust of the hideous creature, the brutal attack upon La, and his own part of the grim tragedy when he had battled with the infuriated Oparian and left him dead at the feet of the priestess he would have profaned.

This and much more passed through Tarzan's memory as he stood gazing at the long tiers of dull-yellow metal. He wondered if La still ruled the temples of the ruined city whose crumbling walls rose upon the very foundations about him. Had she finally been forced into a union with one of her grotesque priests? It seemed a hideous fate, indeed, for one so beautiful. With a shake of his head, Tarzan stepped to the flickering candle, extinguished its feeble rays and turned toward the exit.

Behind him the spy waited for him to be gone. He had learned the secret for which he had come, and now he could return at his leisure to his waiting followers, bring them to the treasure vault and carry away all the gold that they could stagger under.

The Waziri had reached the outer end of the tunnel, and were winding upward toward the fresh air and the welcome starlight of the kopje's summit, before Tarzan shook off the detaining hand of reverie and started slowly after them.

Once again, and, he thought, for the last time, he closed the massive door of the treasure room. In the darkness behind him Werper rose and stretched his cramped muscles. He stretched forth a hand and lovingly caressed a golden ingot on the nearest tier. He raised it from its immemorial resting place and weighed it in his hands. He clutched it to his bosom in an ecstasy of avarice.

Tarzan dreamed of the happy homecoming which lay before him, of dear arms about his neck, and a soft cheek pressed to his; but there rose to dispel that dream the memory of the old witch-doctor and his warning.

And then, in the span of a few brief seconds, the hopes of both these men were shattered. The one forgot even his greed in the panic of terror – the other was plunged into total forgetfulness of the past by a jagged fragment of rock which gashed a deep cut upon his head.

CHAPTER FIVE

The Altar of the Flaming God

It was at the moment that Tarzan turned from the closed door to pursue his way to the outer world. The thing came without warning. One instant all was quiet and stability – the next, and the world rocked, the tortured sides of the narrow passageway split and crumbled, great blocks of granite, dislodged from the ceiling, tumbled into the narrow way, choking it, and the walls bent inward upon the wreckage. Beneath the blow of a fragment of the roof, Tarzan staggered back against the door to the treasure room, his weight pushed it open and his body rolled inward upon the floor.

In the great apartment where the treasure lay less damage was wrought by the earthquake. A few ingots toppled from the higher tiers, a single piece of the rocky ceiling splintered off and crashed downward to the floor, and the walls cracked, though they did not collapse.

There was but the single shock, no other followed to complete the damage undertaken by the first. Werper, thrown to his length by the suddenness and violence of the disturbance, staggered to his feet when he found himself unhurt. Groping his way toward the far end of the chamber, he sought the candle which Tarzan had left stuck in its own wax upon the protruding end of an ingot.

By striking numerous matches the Belgian at last found what he sought, and when, a moment later, the sickly rays relieved the Stygian darkness about him, he breathed a nervous sigh of relief, for the impenetrable gloom had accentuated the terrors of his situation.

As they became accustomed to the light the man turned his eyes toward the door – his one thought now was of escape from this frightful tomb – and as he did so he saw the body of the naked giant lying stretched upon the floor just within the doorway. Werper drew back in sudden fear of detection; but a second glance convinced him that the Englishman was dead. From a great gash in the man's head a pool of blood had collected upon the concrete floor.

Quickly, the Belgian leaped over the prostrate form of his erstwhile host, and without a thought of succor for the man in whom, for aught he knew, life still remained, he bolted for the passageway and safety.

But his renewed hopes were soon dashed. Just beyond the doorway he found the passage completely clogged and choked by impenetrable masses of shattered rock. Once more he turned and re-entered the treasure vault. Taking the candle from its place he commenced a systematic search of the apartment, nor had he gone far before he discovered another door in the opposite end of the room, a door which gave upon creaking hinges to the weight of his body. Beyond the door lay another narrow passageway. Along this Werper made his way, ascending a flight of stone steps to another corridor twenty feet above the level of the first. The flickering candle lighted the way before him, and a moment later he was thankful for the possession of this crude and antiquated luminant, which, a few hours before he might have looked upon with contempt, for it showed him, just in time, a yawning pit, apparently terminating the tunnel he was traversing.

Before him was a circular shaft. He held the candle above it and peered downward. Below him, at a great distance, he saw the light reflected back from the surface of a pool of water. He had come upon a well. He raised the candle above his head and peered across the black void, and there upon the opposite side he saw the continuation of the tunnel; but how was he to span the gulf?

As he stood there measuring the distance to the opposite side and wondering if he dared venture so great a leap, there broke suddenly upon his startled ears a piercing scream which diminished gradually until it ended in a series of dismal moans. The voice seemed partly human, yet so hideous that it might well have emanated from the tortured throat of a lost soul, writhing in the fires of hell.

The Belgian shuddered and looked fearfully upward, for the scream had seemed to come from above him. As he looked he saw an opening far overhead, and a patch of sky pinked with brilliant stars.

His half-formed intention to call for help was expunged by the terrifying cry – where such a voice lived, no human creatures could dwell. He dared not reveal himself to whatever inhabitants dwelt in the place above him. He cursed himself for a fool that he had ever embarked upon such a mission. He wished himself safely back in the camp of Achmet Zek, and would almost have embraced an opportunity to give himself up to the military authorities of the Congo if by so doing he might be rescued from the frightful predicament in which he now was.

He listened fearfully, but the cry was not repeated, and at last spurred to desperate means, he gathered himself for the leap across the chasm. Going back twenty paces, he took a running start, and at the edge of the well, leaped upward and outward in an attempt to gain the opposite side.

In his hand he clutched the sputtering candle, and as he took the leap the rush of air extinguished it. In utter darkness he flew through space, clutching outward for a hold should his feet miss the invisible ledge.

He struck the edge of the door of the opposite terminus of the rocky tunnel with his knees, slipped backward, clutched desperately for a moment, and at last hung half within and half without the opening; but he was safe. For several minutes he dared not move; but clung, weak and sweating, where he lay. At last, cautiously, he drew himself well within the tunnel, and again he lay at full length upon the floor, fighting to regain control of his shattered nerves.

When his knees struck the edge of the tunnel he had dropped the candle. Presently, hoping against hope that it had fallen upon the floor of the passageway, rather than back into the depths of the well, he rose upon all fours and commenced a diligent search for the little tallow cylinder, which now seemed infinitely more precious to him than all the fabulous wealth of the hoarded ingots of Opar.

And when, at last, he found it, he clasped it to him and sank back sobbing and exhausted. For many minutes he lay trembling and broken; but finally he drew himself to a sitting posture, and taking a match from his pocket, lighted the stump of the candle which remained to him. With the light he found it easier to regain control of his nerves, and presently he was again making his way along the tunnel in search of an avenue of escape. The horrid cry that had come down to him from above through the ancient well-shaft still haunted him, so that he trembled in terror at even the sounds of his own cautious advance.

He had gone forward but a short distance, when, to his chagrin, a wall of masonry barred his farther progress, closing the tunnel completely from top to bottom and from side to side. What could it mean? Werper was an educated and intelligent man. His military training had taught him to use his mind for the purpose for which it was intended. A blind tunnel such as this was senseless. It must continue beyond the wall. Someone, at some time in the past, had had it blocked for an unknown purpose of his own. The man fell to examining the masonry by the light of his candle. To his delight he discovered that the thin blocks of hewn stone of which it was constructed were fitted in loosely without mortar or cement. He tugged upon one of them, and to his joy found that it was easily removable. One after another he pulled out the blocks until he had opened an aperture large enough to admit his body, then he crawled through into a large, low chamber. Across this another door barred his way; but this, too, gave before his efforts, for it was not barred. A long, dark corridor showed before him, but before he had followed it far, his candle burned down until it scorched his fingers. With an oath he dropped it to the floor, where it sputtered for a moment and went out.

Now he was in total darkness, and again terror rode heavily astride his neck. What further pitfalls and dangers lay ahead he could not guess; but that he was as far as ever from liberty he was quite willing to believe, so depressing is utter absence of light to one in unfamiliar surroundings.

Slowly he groped his way along, feeling with his hands upon the tunnel's walls, and cautiously with his feet ahead of him upon the floor before he could take a single forward step. How long he crept on thus he could not guess; but at last, feeling that the tunnel's length was interminable, and exhausted by his efforts, by terror, and loss of sleep, he determined to lie down and rest before proceeding farther.

When he awoke there was no change in the surrounding blackness. He might have slept a second or a day – he could not know; but that he had slept for some time was attested by the fact that he felt refreshed and hungry.

Again he commenced his groping advance; but this time he had gone but a short distance when he emerged into a room, which was lighted through an opening in the ceiling, from which a flight of concrete steps led downward to the floor of the chamber.

Above him, through the aperture, Werper could see sunlight glancing from massive columns, which were twined about by clinging vines. He listened; but he heard no sound other than the soughing of the wind through leafy branches, the hoarse cries of birds, and the chattering of monkeys.

Boldly he ascended the stairway, to find himself in a circular court. Just before him stood a stone altar, stained with rusty-brown discolorations. At the time Werper gave no thought to an explanation of these stains – later their origin became all too hideously apparent to him.

Beside the opening in the floor, just behind the altar, through which he had entered the court from the subterranean chamber below, the Belgian discovered several doors leading from the enclosure upon the level of the floor. Above, and circling the courtyard, was a series of open balconies. Monkeys scampered about the deserted ruins, and gaily plumaged birds flitted in and out among the columns and the galleries far above; but no sign of human presence was discernible. Werper felt relieved. He sighed, as though a great weight had been lifted from his shoulders. He took a step toward one of the exits, and then he halted, wide-eyed in astonishment and terror, for almost at the same instant a dozen doors opened in the courtyard wall and a horde of frightful men rushed in upon him.

They were the priests of the Flaming God of Opar – the same, shaggy, knotted, hideous little men who had dragged Jane Clayton to the sacrificial altar at this very spot years before. Their long arms, their short and crooked legs, their close-set, evil eyes, and their low, receding foreheads gave them a bestial appearance that sent a qualm of paralyzing fright through the shaken nerves of the Belgian.

With a scream he turned to flee back into the lesser terrors of the gloomy corridors and apartments from which he had just emerged, but the frightful men anticipated his intentions. They blocked the way; they seized him, and though he fell, groveling upon his knees before them, begging for his life, they bound him and hurled him to the floor of the inner temple.

The rest was but a repetition of what Tarzan and Jane Clayton had passed through. The priestesses came, and with them La, the High Priestess. Werper was raised and laid across the altar. Cold sweat exuded from his every pore as La raised the cruel, sacrificial knife above him. The death chant fell upon his tortured ears. His staring eyes wandered to the golden goblets from which the hideous votaries would soon quench their inhuman thirst in his own, warm life-blood.

He wished that he might be granted the brief respite of unconsciousness before the final plunge of the keen blade – and then there was a frightful roar that sounded almost in his ears. The High Priestess lowered her dagger. Her eyes went wide in horror. The priestesses, her votaresses, screamed and fled madly toward the exits. The priests roared out their rage and terror according to the temper of their courage. Werper strained his neck about to catch a sight of the cause of their panic, and when, at last he saw it, he too went cold in dread, for what his eyes beheld was the figure of a huge lion standing in the center of the temple, and already a single victim lay mangled beneath his cruel paws.

Again the lord of the wilderness roared, turning his baleful gaze upon the altar. La staggered forward, reeled, and fell across Werper in a swoon.

CHAPTER SIX

The Arab Raid

AFTER THEIR FIRST TERROR had subsided subsequent to the shock of the earthquake, Basuli and his warriors hastened back into the passageway in search of Tarzan and two of their own number who were also missing.

They found the way blocked by jammed and distorted rock. For two days they labored to tear a way through to their imprisoned friends; but when, after Herculean efforts, they had unearthed but a few yards of the choked passage, and discovered the mangled remains of one of their fellows they were forced to the conclusion that Tarzan and the second Waziri also lay dead beneath the rock mass farther in, beyond human aid, and no longer susceptible of it.

Again and again as they labored they called aloud the names of their master and their comrade; but no answering call rewarded their listening ears. At last they gave up the search. Tearfully they cast a last look at the shattered tomb of their master, shouldered the heavy burden of gold that would at least furnish comfort, if not happiness, to their bereaved and beloved mistress, and made their mournful way back across the desolate valley of Opar, and downward through the forests beyond toward the distant bungalow.

And as they marched what sorry fate was already drawing down upon that peaceful, happy home!

From the north came Achmet Zek, riding to the summons of his lieutenant's letter. With him came his horde of renegade Arabs, outlawed marauders, these, and equally degraded blacks, garnered from the more debased and ignorant tribes of savage cannibals through whose countries the raider passed to and fro with perfect impunity.

Mugambi, the ebon Hercules, who had shared the dangers and vicissitudes of his beloved Bwana, from Jungle Island, almost to the headwaters of the Ugambi, was the first to note the bold approach of the sinister caravan.

He it was whom Tarzan had left in charge of the warriors who remained to guard Lady Greystoke, nor could a braver or more loyal guardian have been found in any clime or upon any soil. A giant in stature, a savage, fearless warrior, the huge black possessed also soul and judgment in proportion to his bulk and his ferocity.

Not once since his master had departed had he been beyond sight or sound of the bungalow, except when Lady Greystoke chose to canter across the broad plain, or relieve the monotony of her loneliness by a brief hunting excursion. On such occasions Mugambi, mounted upon a wiry Arab, had ridden close at her horse's heels.

The raiders were still a long way off when the warrior's keen eyes discovered them. For a time he stood scrutinizing the advancing party in silence, then he turned and ran rapidly in the direction of the native huts which lay a few hundred yards below the bungalow.

Here he called out to the lolling warriors. He issued orders rapidly. In compliance with them the men seized upon their weapons and their shields. Some ran to call in the workers from the fields and to warn the tenders of the flocks and herds. The majority followed Mugambi back toward the bungalow.

The dust of the raiders was still a long distance away. Mugambi could not know positively that it hid an enemy; but he had spent a lifetime of savage life in savage Africa, and he had seen parties before come thus unheralded. Sometimes they had come in peace and sometimes they had come in war – one could never tell. It was well to be prepared. Mugambi did not like the haste with which the strangers advanced.

The Greystoke bungalow was not well adapted for defense. No palisade surrounded it, for, situated as it was, in the heart of loyal Waziri, its master had anticipated no possibility of an attack in force by any enemy. Heavy, wooden shutters there were to close the window apertures against hostile arrows, and these Mugambi was engaged in lowering when Lady Greystoke appeared upon the veranda.

"Why, Mugambi!" she exclaimed. "What has happened? Why are you lowering the shutters?"

Mugambi pointed out across the plain to where a white-robed force of mounted men was now distinctly visible.

"Arabs," he explained. "They come for no good purpose in the absence of the Great Bwana."

Beyond the neat lawn and the flowering shrubs, Jane Clayton saw the glistening bodies of her Waziri. The sun glanced from the tips of their metal-shod spears, picked out the gorgeous colors in the feathers of their war bonnets, and reflected the high-lights from the glossy skins of their broad shoulders and high cheek bones.

Jane Clayton surveyed them with unmixed feelings of pride and affection. What harm could befall her with such as these to protect her?

The raiders had halted now, a hundred yards out upon the plain. Mugambi had hastened down to join his warriors. He advanced a few yards before them and raising his voice hailed the strangers. Achmet Zek sat straight in his saddle before his henchmen.

"Arab!" cried Mugambi. "What do you here?"

"We come in peace," Achmet Zek called back.

"Then turn and go in peace," replied Mugambi. "We do not want you here. There can be no peace between Arab and Waziri."

Mugambi, although not born in Waziri, had been adopted into the tribe, which now contained no member more jealous of its traditions and its prowess than he.

Achmet Zek drew to one side of his horde, speaking to his men in a low voice. A moment later, without warning, a ragged volley was poured into the ranks of the Waziri. A couple of warriors fell, the others were for charging the attackers; but Mugambi was a cautious as well as a brave leader. He knew the futility of charging mounted men armed with muskets. He withdrew his force behind the shrubbery of the garden. Some he dispatched to various other parts of the grounds surrounding the bungalow. Half a dozen he sent to the bungalow itself with instructions to keep their mistress within doors, and to protect her with their lives.

Adopting the tactics of the desert fighters from which he had sprung, Achmet Zek led his followers at a gallop in a long, thin line, describing a great circle which drew closer and closer in toward the defenders.

At that part of the circle closest to the Waziri, a constant fusillade of shots was poured into the bushes behind which the black warriors had concealed themselves. The latter, on their part, loosed their slim shafts at the nearest of the enemy.

The Waziri, justly famed for their archery, found no cause to blush for their performance that day. Time and again some swarthy horseman threw hands above his head and toppled from his saddle, pierced by a deadly arrow; but the contest was uneven. The Arabs outnumbered the Waziri; their bullets penetrated the shrubbery and found marks that the Arab riflemen had not even seen; and then Achmet Zek circled inward a half mile above the bungalow, tore down a section of the fence, and led his marauders within the grounds.

Across the fields they charged at a mad run. Not again did they pause to lower fences, instead, they drove their wild mounts straight for them, clearing the obstacles as lightly as winged gulls.

Mugambi saw them coming, and, calling those of his warriors who remained, ran for the bungalow and the last stand. Upon the veranda Lady Greystoke stood, rifle in hand. More than a single raider had accounted to her steady nerves and cool aim for his outlawry; more than a single pony raced, riderless, in the wake of the charging horde.

Mugambi pushed his mistress back into the greater security of the interior, and with his depleted force prepared to make a last stand against the foe.

On came the Arabs, shouting and waving their long guns above their heads. Past the veranda they raced, pouring a deadly fire into the kneeling Waziri who discharged their volley of arrows from behind their long, oval shields – shields well adapted, perhaps, to stop a hostile arrow, or deflect a spear; but futile, quite, before the leaden missiles of the riflemen.

From beneath the half-raised shutters of the bungalow other bowmen did effective service in greater security, and after the first assault, Mugambi withdrew his entire force within the building.

Again and again the Arabs charged, at last forming a stationary circle about the little fortress, and outside the effective range of the defenders' arrows. From their new position they fired at will at the windows. One by one the Waziri fell. Fewer and fewer were the arrows that replied to the guns of the raiders, and at last Achmet Zek felt safe in ordering an assault.

Firing as they ran, the bloodthirsty horde raced for the veranda. A dozen of them fell to the arrows of the defenders; but the majority reached the door. Heavy gun butts fell upon it. The crash of splintered wood mingled with the report of a rifle as Jane Clayton fired through the panels upon the relentless foe.

Upon both sides of the door men fell; but at last the frail barrier gave to the vicious assaults of the maddened attackers; it crumpled inward and a dozen swarthy murderers leaped into the living-room. At the far end stood Jane Clayton surrounded by the remnant of her devoted guardians. The floor was covered by the bodies of those who already had given up their lives in her defense. In the forefront of her protectors stood the giant Mugambi. The Arabs raised their rifles to pour in the last volley that would effectually end all resistance; but Achmet Zek roared out a warning order that stayed their trigger fingers.

"Fire not upon the woman!" he cried. "Who harms her, dies. Take the woman alive!"

The Arabs rushed across the room; the Waziri met them with their heavy spears. Swords flashed, long-barreled pistols roared out their sullen death dooms. Mugambi launched his spear at the nearest of the enemy with a force that drove the heavy shaft completely through the Arab's body, then he seized a pistol from another, and grasping it by the barrel brained all who forced their way too near his mistress.

Emulating his example the few warriors who remained to him fought like demons; but one by one they fell, until only Mugambi remained to defend the life and honor of the ape-man's mate.

From across the room Achmet Zek watched the unequal struggle and urged on his minions. In his hands was a jeweled musket. Slowly he raised it to his shoulder, waiting until another move should place Mugambi at his mercy without endangering the lives of the woman or any of his own followers.

At last the moment came, and Achmet Zek pulled the trigger. Without a sound the brave Mugambi sank to the floor at the feet of Jane Clayton.

An instant later she was surrounded and disarmed. Without a word they dragged her from the bungalow. A giant Negro lifted her to the pommel of his saddle, and while the raiders searched the bungalow and outhouses for plunder he rode with her beyond the gates and waited the coming of his master.

Jane Clayton saw the raiders lead the horses from the corral, and drive the herds in from the fields. She saw her home plundered of all that represented intrinsic worth in the eyes of the Arabs, and then she saw the torch applied, and the flames lick up what remained.

And at last, when the raiders assembled after glutting their fury and their avarice, and rode away with her toward the north, she saw the smoke and the flames rising far into the heavens until the winding of the trail into the thick forests hid the sad view from her eyes.

As the flames ate their way into the living-room, reaching out forked tongues to lick up the bodies of the dead, one of that gruesome company whose bloody welterings had long since been stilled, moved again. It was a huge black who rolled over upon his side and opened blood-shot, suffering eyes. Mugambi, whom the Arabs had left for dead, still lived. The hot flames were almost upon him as he raised himself painfully upon his hands and knees and crawled slowly toward the doorway.

Again and again he sank weakly to the floor; but each time he rose again and continued his pitiful way toward safety. After what seemed to him an interminable time, during which the flames had become a veritable fiery furnace at the far side of the room, the great black managed to reach the veranda, roll down the steps, and crawl off into the cool safety of some nearby shrubbery.

All night he lay there, alternately unconscious and painfully sentient; and in the latter state watching with savage hatred the lurid flames which still rose from burning crib and hay cock. A prowling lion roared close at hand; but the giant black was unafraid. There was place for but a single thought in his savage mind – revenge! revenge! revenge!

CHAPTER SEVEN

The Arab Raid

For some time Tarzan lay where he had fallen upon the floor of the treasure chamber beneath the ruined walls of Opar. He lay as one dead; but he was not dead. At length he stirred. His eyes opened upon the utter darkness of the room. He raised his hand to his head and brought it away sticky with clotted blood. He sniffed at his fingers, as a wild beast might sniff at the life-blood upon a wounded paw.

Slowly he rose to a sitting posture – listening. No sound reached to the buried depths of his sepulcher. He staggered to his feet, and groped his way about among the tiers of ingots. What was he? Where was he? His head ached; but otherwise he felt no ill effects from the blow that had felled him. The accident he did not recall, nor did he recall aught of what had led up to it.

He let his hands grope unfamiliarly over his limbs, his torso, and his head. He felt of the quiver at his back, the knife in his loin cloth. Something struggled for recognition within his brain. Ah! he had it. There was something missing. He crawled about upon the floor, feeling with his hands for the thing that instinct warned him was gone. At last he found it – the heavy war spear that in past years had formed so important a feature of his daily life, almost of his very existence, so inseparably had it been connected with his every action since the long-gone day that he had wrested his first spear from the body of a black victim of his savage training.

Tarzan was sure that there was another and more lovely world than that which was confined to the darkness of the four stone walls surrounding him. He continued his search and at last found the doorway leading inward beneath the city and the temple. This he followed, most incautiously. He came to the stone steps leading upward to the higher level. He ascended them and continued onward toward the well.

Nothing spurred his hurt memory to a recollection of past familiarity with his surroundings. He blundered on through the darkness as though he were traversing an open plain under the brilliance of a noonday sun, and suddenly there happened that which had to happen under the circumstances of his rash advance.

He reached the brink of the well, stepped outward into space, lunged forward, and shot downward into the inky depths below. Still clutching his spear, he struck the water, and sank beneath its surface, plumbing the depths.

The fall had not injured him, and when he rose to the surface, he shook the water from his eyes, and found that he could see. Daylight was filtering into the well from the orifice far above his head. It illumined the inner walls faintly. Tarzan gazed about him. On the level with the surface of the water he saw a large opening in the dark and slimy wall. He swam to it, and drew himself out upon the wet floor of a tunnel.

Along this he passed; but now he went warily, for Tarzan of the Apes was learning. The unexpected pit had taught him care in the traversing of dark passageways – he needed no second lesson.

For a long distance the passage went straight as an arrow. The floor was slippery, as though at times the rising waters of the well overflowed and flooded it. This, in itself, retarded Tarzan's pace, for it was with difficulty that he kept his footing.

The foot of a stairway ended the passage. Up this he made his way. It turned back and forth many times, leading, at last, into a small, circular chamber, the gloom of which was relieved by a faint light which found ingress through a tubular shaft several feet in diameter which rose from the center of the room's ceiling, upward to a distance of a hundred feet or more, where it terminated in a stone grating through which Tarzan could see a blue and sun-lit sky.

Curiosity prompted the ape-man to investigate his surroundings. Several metal-bound, copper-studded chests constituted the sole furniture of the round room. Tarzan let his hands run over these. He felt of the copper studs, he pulled upon the hinges, and at last, by chance, he raised the cover of one.

An exclamation of delight broke from his lips at sight of the pretty contents. Gleaming and glistening in the subdued light of the chamber, lay a great tray full of brilliant stones. Tarzan, reverted to the primitive by his accident, had no conception of the fabulous value of his find. To him they were but pretty pebbles. He plunged his hands into them and let the priceless gems filter through his fingers. He went to others of the chests, only to find still further stores of precious stones. Nearly all were cut, and from these he gathered a handful and filled the pouch which dangled at his side – the uncut stones he tossed back into the chests.

Unwittingly, the ape-man had stumbled upon the forgotten jewel-room of Opar. For ages it had lain buried beneath the temple of the Flaming God, midway of one of the many inky passages which the superstitious descendants of the ancient Sun Worshipers had either dared not or cared not to explore.

Tiring at last of this diversion, Tarzan took up his way along the corridor which led upward from the jewel-room by a steep incline. Winding and twisting, but always tending upward, the tunnel led him nearer and nearer to the surface, ending finally in a low-ceiled room, lighter than any that he had as yet discovered.

Above him an opening in the ceiling at the upper end of a flight of concrete steps revealed a brilliant sunlit scene. Tarzan viewed the vine-covered columns in mild wonderment. He puckered his brows in an attempt to recall some recollection of similar things. He was not sure of himself. There was a tantalizing suggestion always present in his mind that something was eluding him – that he should know many things which he did not know.

His earnest cogitation was rudely interrupted by a thunderous roar from the opening above him. Following the roar came the cries and screams of men and women. Tarzan grasped his spear more firmly and ascended the steps. A strange sight met his eyes as he emerged from the semi-darkness of the cellar to the brilliant light of the temple.

The creatures he saw before him he recognized for what they were – men and women, and a huge lion. The men and women were scuttling for the safety of the exits. The lion stood upon the body of one who had been less fortunate than the others. He was in the center of the temple. Directly before Tarzan, a woman stood beside a block of stone. Upon the top of the stone lay stretched a man, and as the ape-man watched the scene, he saw the lion glare terribly at the two who remained within the temple. Another thunderous roar broke from the savage throat, the woman screamed and swooned across the body of the man stretched prostrate upon the stone altar before her.

The lion advanced a few steps and crouched. The tip of his sinuous tail twitched nervously. He was upon the point of charging when his eyes were attracted toward the ape-man.

Werper, helpless upon the altar, saw the great carnivore preparing to leap upon him. He saw the sudden change in the beast's expression as his eyes wandered to something beyond the altar and out of the Belgian's view. He saw the formidable creature rise to a standing position. A figure darted past Werper. He saw a mighty arm upraised, and a stout spear shoot forward toward the lion, to bury itself in the broad chest.

He saw the lion snapping and tearing at the weapon's shaft, and he saw, wonder of wonders, the naked giant who had hurled the missile charging upon the great beast, only a long knife ready to meet those ferocious fangs and talons.

The lion reared up to meet this new enemy. The beast was growling frightfully, and then upon the startled ears of the Belgian, broke a similar savage growl from the lips of the man rushing upon the beast.

By a quick side step, Tarzan eluded the first swinging clutch of the lion's paws. Darting to the beast's side, he leaped upon the tawny back. His arms encircled the maned neck, his teeth sank deep into the brute's flesh. Roaring, leaping, rolling and struggling, the giant cat attempted to dislodge this savage enemy, and all the while one great, brown fist was driving a long keen blade repeatedly into the beast's side.

During the battle, La regained consciousness. Spellbound, she stood above her victim watching the spectacle. It seemed incredible that a human being could best the king of beasts in personal encounter and yet before her very eyes there was taking place just such an improbability.

At last Tarzan's knife found the great heart, and with a final, spasmodic struggle the lion rolled over upon the marble floor, dead. Leaping to his feet the conqueror placed a foot upon the carcass of his kill, raised his face toward the heavens, and gave voice to so hideous a cry that both La and Werper trembled as it reverberated through the temple.

Then the ape-man turned, and Werper recognized him as the man he had left for dead in the treasure room.

CHAPTER EIGHT

The Escape from Opar

Werper was astounded. Could this creature be the same dignified Englishman who had entertained him so graciously in his luxurious African home? Could this wild beast, with blazing eyes, and bloody countenance, be at the same time a man? Could the horrid, victory cry he had but just heard have been formed in human throat?

Tarzan was eyeing the man and the woman, a puzzled expression in his eyes, but there was no faintest tinge of recognition. It was as though he had discovered some new species of living creature and was marveling at his find.

La was studying the ape-man's features. Slowly her large eyes opened very wide.

"Tarzan!" she exclaimed, and then, in the vernacular of the great apes which constant association with the anthropoids had rendered the common language of the Oparians: "You have come back to me! La has ignored the mandates of her religion, waiting, always waiting for Tarzan – for her Tarzan. She has taken no mate, for in all the world there was but one with whom La would mate. And now you have come back! Tell me, O Tarzan, that it is for me you have returned."

Werper listened to the unintelligible jargon. He looked from La to Tarzan. Would the latter understand this strange tongue? To the Belgian's surprise, the Englishman answered in a language evidently identical to hers.

"Tarzan," he repeated, musingly. "Tarzan. The name sounds familiar."

"It is your name – you are Tarzan," cried La.

"I am Tarzan?" The ape-man shrugged. "Well, it is a good name – I know no other, so I will keep it; but I do not know you. I did not come hither for you. Why I came, I do not know at all; neither do I know from whence I came. Can you tell me?"

La shook her head. "I never knew," she replied.

Tarzan turned toward Werper and put the same question to him; but in the language of the great apes. The Belgian shook his head.

"I do not understand that language," he said in French.

Without effort, and apparently without realizing that he made the change, Tarzan repeated his question in French. Werper suddenly came to a full realization of the magnitude of the injury of which Tarzan was a victim. The man had lost his memory – no longer could he recollect past events. The Belgian was upon the point of enlightening him, when it suddenly occurred to him that by keeping Tarzan in ignorance, for a time at least, of his true identity, it might be possible to turn the ape-man's misfortune to his own advantage.

"I cannot tell you from whence you came," he said; "but this I can tell you – if we do not get out of this horrible place we shall both be slain upon this bloody altar. The woman was about to plunge her knife into my heart when the lion interrupted the fiendish ritual. Come! Before they recover from their fright and reassemble, let us find a way out of their damnable temple."

Tarzan turned again toward La.

"Why," he asked, "would you have killed this man? Are you hungry?"

The High Priestess cried out in disgust.

"Did he attempt to kill you?" continued Tarzan.

The woman shook her head.

"Then why should you have wished to kill him?" Tarzan was determined to get to the bottom of the thing.

La raised her slender arm and pointed toward the sun.

"We were offering up his soul as a gift to the Flaming God," she said.

Tarzan looked puzzled. He was again an ape, and apes do not understand such matters as souls and Flaming Gods.

"Do you wish to die?" he asked Werper.

The Belgian assured him, with tears in his eyes, that he did not wish to die.

"Very well then, you shall not," said Tarzan. "Come! We will go. This SHE would kill you and keep me for herself. It is no place anyway for a Mangani. I should soon die, shut up behind these stone walls."

He turned toward La. "We are going now," he said.

The woman rushed forward and seized the ape-man's hands in hers.

"Do not leave me!" she cried. "Stay, and you shall be High Priest. La loves you. All Opar shall be yours. Slaves shall wait upon you. Stay, Tarzan of the Apes, and let love reward you."

The ape-man pushed the kneeling woman aside. "Tarzan does not desire you," he said, simply, and stepping to Werper's side he cut the Belgian's bonds and motioned him to follow.

Panting – her face convulsed with rage, La sprang to her feet.

"Stay, you shall!" she screamed. "La will have you – if she cannot have you alive, she will have you dead," and raising her face to the sun she gave voice to the same hideous shriek that Werper had heard once before and Tarzan many times.

In answer to her cry a babel of voices broke from the surrounding chambers and corridors.

"Come, Guardian Priests!" she cried. "The infidels have profaned the holiest of the holies. Come! Strike terror to their hearts; defend La and her altar; wash clean the temple with the blood of the polluters."

Tarzan understood, though Werper did not. The former glanced at the Belgian and saw that he was unarmed. Stepping quickly to La's side the ape-man seized her in his strong arms and though she fought with all the mad savagery of a demon, he soon disarmed her, handing her long, sacrificial knife to Werper.

"You will need this," he said, and then from each doorway a horde of the monstrous, little men of Opar streamed into the temple.

They were armed with bludgeons and knives, and fortified in their courage by fanatical hate and frenzy. Werper was terrified. Tarzan stood eyeing the foe in proud disdain. Slowly he advanced toward the exit he had chosen to utilize in making his way from the temple. A burly priest barred his way. Behind the first was a score of others. Tarzan swung his heavy spear, clublike, down upon the skull of the priest. The fellow collapsed, his head crushed.

Again and again the weapon fell as Tarzan made his way slowly toward the doorway. Werper pressed close behind, casting backward glances toward the shrieking, dancing mob menacing their rear. He held the sacrificial knife ready to strike whoever might come within its reach; but none came. For a time he wondered that they should so bravely battle with the giant ape-man, yet hesitate to rush upon him, who was relatively so weak. Had they done so he knew that he must have fallen at the first charge. Tarzan had reached the doorway over the corpses of all that had stood to dispute his way, before Werper guessed at the reason for his immunity. The priests feared the sacrificial knife! Willingly would they face death and welcome it if it came while they defended their High Priestess and her altar; but evidently there were deaths, and deaths. Some strange superstition must surround that polished blade, that no Oparian cared to chance a death thrust from it, yet gladly rushed to the slaughter of the ape-man's flaying spear.

Once outside the temple court, Werper communicated his discovery to Tarzan. The ape-man grinned, and let Werper go before him, brandishing the jeweled and holy weapon. Like leaves before a gale, the Oparians scattered in all directions and Tarzan and the Belgian found a clear passage through the corridors and chambers of the ancient temple.

The Belgian's eyes went wide as they passed through the room of the seven pillars of solid gold. With ill-concealed avarice he looked upon the age-old, golden tablets set in the walls of nearly every room and down the sides of many of the corridors. To the ape-man all this wealth appeared to mean nothing.

On the two went, chance leading them toward the broad avenue which lay between the stately piles of the half-ruined edifices and the inner wall of the city. Great apes jabbered at them and menaced them; but Tarzan answered them after their own kind, giving back taunt for taunt, insult for insult, challenge for challenge.

Werper saw a hairy bull swing down from a broken column and advance, stiff-legged and bristling, toward the naked giant. The yellow fangs were bared, angry snarls and barkings rumbled threateningly through the thick and hanging lips.

The Belgian watched his companion. To his horror, he saw the man stoop until his closed knuckles rested upon the ground as did those of the anthropoid. He saw him circle, stiff-legged about the circling ape. He heard the same bestial barkings and growlings issue from the human throat that were coming from the mouth of the brute. Had his eyes been closed he could not have known but that two giant apes were bridling for combat.

But there was no battle. It ended as the majority of such jungle encounters end – one of the boasters loses his nerve, and becomes suddenly interested in a blowing leaf, a beetle, or the lice upon his hairy stomach.

In this instance it was the anthropoid that retired in stiff dignity to inspect an unhappy caterpillar, which he presently devoured. For a moment Tarzan seemed inclined to pursue the argument. He swaggered truculently, stuck out his chest, roared and advanced closer to the bull. It was with difficulty that Werper finally persuaded him to leave well enough alone and continue his way from the ancient city of the Sun Worshipers.

The two searched for nearly an hour before they found the narrow exit through the inner wall. From there the well-worn trail led them beyond the outer fortification to the desolate valley of Opar.

Tarzan had no idea, in so far as Werper could discover, as to where he was or whence he came. He wandered aimlessly about, searching for food, which he discovered beneath small rocks, or hiding in the shade of the scant brush which dotted the ground.

The Belgian was horrified by the hideous menu of his companion. Beetles, rodents and caterpillars were devoured with seeming relish. Tarzan was indeed an ape again.

At last Werper succeeded in leading his companion toward the distant hills which mark the northwestern boundary of the valley, and together the two set out in the direction of the Greystoke bungalow.

What purpose prompted the Belgian in leading the victim of his treachery and greed back toward his former home it is difficult to guess, unless it was that without Tarzan there could be no ransom for Tarzan's wife.

That night they camped in the valley beyond the hills, and as they sat before a little fire where cooked a wild pig that had fallen to one of Tarzan's arrows, the latter sat lost in speculation. He seemed continually to be trying to grasp some mental image which as constantly eluded him.

At last he opened the leathern pouch which hung at his side. From it he poured into the palm of his hand a quantity of glittering gems. The firelight playing upon them conjured a multitude of scintillating rays, and as the wide eyes of the Belgian looked on in rapt fascination, the man's expression at last acknowledged a tangible purpose in courting the society of the ape-man.

CHAPTER NINE

The Theft of the Jewels

For two days Werper sought for the party that had accompanied him from the camp to the barrier cliffs; but not until late in the afternoon of the second day did he find clew to its whereabouts, and then in such gruesome form that he was totally unnerved by the sight.

In an open glade he came upon the bodies of three of the blacks, terribly mutilated, nor did it require considerable deductive power to explain their murder. Of the little party only these three had not been slaves. The others, evidently tempted to hope for freedom from their cruel Arab master, had taken advantage of their separation from the main camp, to slay the three representatives of the hated power which held them in slavery, and vanish into the jungle.

Cold sweat exuded from Werper's forehead as he contemplated the fate which chance had permitted him to escape, for had he been present when the conspiracy bore fruit, he, too, must have been of the garnered.

Tarzan showed not the slightest surprise or interest in the discovery. Inherent in him was a calloused familiarity with violent death. The refinements of his recent civilization expunged by the force of the sad calamity which had befallen him, left only the primitive sensibilities which his childhood's training had imprinted indelibly upon the fabric of his mind.

The training of Kala, the examples and precepts of Kerchak, of Tublat, and of Terkoz now formed the basis of his every thought and action. He retained a mechanical knowledge of French and English speech. Werper had spoken to him in French, and Tarzan had replied in the same tongue without conscious realization that he had departed from the anthropoidal speech in which he had addressed La. Had Werper used English, the result would have been the same.

Again, that night, as the two sat before their camp fire, Tarzan played with his shining baubles. Werper asked him what they were and where he had found them. The ape-man replied that they were gay-colored stones, with which he purposed fashioning a necklace, and that he had found them far beneath the sacrificial court of the temple of the Flaming God.

Werper was relieved to find that Tarzan had no conception of the value of the gems. This would make it easier for the Belgian to obtain possession of them. Possibly the man would give them to him for the asking. Werper reached out his hand toward the little pile that Tarzan had arranged upon a piece of flat wood before him.

"Let me see them," said the Belgian.

Tarzan placed a large palm over his treasure. He bared his fighting fangs, and growled. Werper withdrew his hand more quickly than he had advanced it. Tarzan resumed his playing with the gems, and his conversation with Werper as though nothing unusual had occurred. He had but exhibited the beast's jealous protective instinct for a possession. When he killed he shared the meat with Werper; but had Werper ever, by accident, laid a hand upon Tarzan's share, he would have aroused the same savage, and resentful warning.

From that occurrence dated the beginning of a great fear in the breast of the Belgian for his savage companion. He had never understood the transformation that had been wrought in Tarzan by the blow upon his head, other than to attribute it to a form of amnesia. That Tarzan had once been, in truth, a savage, jungle beast, Werper had not known, and so, of course, he could not guess that the man had reverted to the state in which his childhood and young manhood had been spent.

Now Werper saw in the Englishman a dangerous maniac, whom the slightest untoward accident might turn upon him with rending fangs. Not for a moment did Werper attempt to delude himself into the belief that he could defend himself successfully against an attack by the ape-man. His one hope lay in eluding him, and making for the far distant camp of Achmet Zek as rapidly as he could; but armed only with the sacrificial knife, Werper shrank from attempting the journey through the jungle. Tarzan constituted a protection that was by no means despicable, even in the face of the larger carnivora, as Werper had reason to acknowledge from the evidence he had witnessed in the Oparian temple.

Too, Werper had his covetous soul set upon the pouch of gems, and so he was torn between the various emotions of avarice and fear.

But avarice it was that burned most strongly in his breast, to the end that he dared the dangers and suffered the terrors of constant association with him he thought a mad man, rather than give up the hope of obtaining possession of the fortune which the contents of the little pouch represented.

Achmet Zek should know nothing of these – these would be for Werper alone, and so soon as he could encompass his design he would reach the coast and take passage for America, where he could conceal himself beneath the veil of a new identity and enjoy to some measure the fruits of his theft. He had it all planned out, did Lieutenant Albert Werper, living in anticipation the luxurious life of the idle rich. He even found himself regretting that America was so provincial, and that nowhere in the new world was a city that might compare with his beloved Brussels.

It was upon the third day of their progress from Opar that the keen ears of Tarzan caught the sound of men behind them. Werper heard nothing above the humming of the jungle insects, and the chattering life of the lesser monkeys and the birds.

For a time Tarzan stood in statuesque silence, listening, his sensitive nostrils dilating as he assayed each passing breeze. Then he withdrew Werper into the concealment of thick brush, and waited. Presently, along the game trail that Werper and Tarzan had been following, there came in sight a sleek, black warrior, alert and watchful.

In single file behind him, there followed, one after another, near fifty others, each burdened with two dull-yellow ingots lashed upon his back. Werper recognized the party immediately as that which had accompanied Tarzan on his journey to Opar. He glanced at the ape-man; but in the savage, watchful eyes he saw no recognition of Basuli and those other loyal Waziri.

When all had passed, Tarzan rose and emerged from concealment. He looked down the trail in the direction the party had gone. Then he turned to Werper.

"We will follow and slay them," he said.

"Why?" asked the Belgian.

"They are black," explained Tarzan. "It was a black who killed Kala. They are the enemies of the Manganis."

Werper did not relish the idea of engaging in a battle with Basuli and his fierce fighting men. And, again, he had welcomed the sight of them returning toward the Greystoke bungalow, for he had begun to have doubts as to his ability to retrace his steps to the Waziri country. Tarzan, he knew, had not the remotest idea of whither they were going.

By keeping at a safe distance behind the laden warriors, they would have no difficulty in following them home. Once at the bungalow, Werper knew the way to the camp of Achmet Zek. There was still another reason why he did not wish to interfere with the Waziri – they were bearing the great burden of treasure in the direction he wished it borne. The farther they took it, the less the distance that he and Achmet Zek would have to transport it.

He argued with the ape-man therefore, against the latter's desire to exterminate the blacks, and at last he prevailed upon Tarzan to follow them in peace, saying that he was sure they would lead them out of the forest into a rich country, teeming with game.

It was many marches from Opar to the Waziri country; but at last came the hour when Tarzan and the Belgian, following the trail of the warriors, topped the last rise, and saw before them the broad Waziri plain, the winding river, and the distant forests to the north and west.

A mile or more ahead of them, the line of warriors was creeping like a giant caterpillar through the tall grasses of the plain. Beyond, grazing herds of zebra, hartebeest, and topi dotted the level landscape, while closer to the river a bull buffalo, his head and shoulders protruding from the reeds watched the advancing blacks for a moment, only to turn at last and disappear into the safety of his dank and gloomy retreat.

Tarzan looked out across the familiar vista with no faintest gleam of recognition in his eyes. He saw the game animals, and his mouth watered; but he did not look in the direction of his bungalow. Werper, however, did. A puzzled expression entered the Belgian's eyes. He shaded them with his palms and gazed long and earnestly toward the spot where the bungalow had stood. He could not credit the testimony of his eyes – there was no bungalow – no barns – no out-houses. The corrals, the hay stacks – all were gone. What could it mean?

And then, slowly there filtered into Werper's consciousness an explanation of the havoc that had been wrought in that peaceful valley since last his eyes had rested upon it – Achmet Zek had been there!

Basuli and his warriors had noted the devastation the moment they had come in sight of the farm. Now they hastened on toward it talking excitedly among themselves in animated speculation upon the cause and meaning of the catastrophe.

When, at last they crossed the trampled garden and stood before the charred ruins of their master's bungalow, their greatest fears became convictions in the light of the evidence about them.

Remnants of human dead, half devoured by prowling hyenas and others of the carnivora which infested the region, lay rotting upon the ground, and among the corpses remained sufficient remnants of their clothing and ornaments to make clear to Basuli the frightful story of the disaster that had befallen his master's house.

"The Arabs," he said, as his men clustered about him.

The Waziri gazed about in mute rage for several minutes. Everywhere they encountered only further evidence of the ruthlessness of the cruel enemy that had come during the Great Bwana's absence and laid waste his property.

"What did they with 'Lady'?" asked one of the blacks.

They had always called Lady Greystoke thus.

"The women they would have taken with them," said Basuli. "Our women and his."

A giant black raised his spear above his head, and gave voice to a savage cry of rage and hate. The others followed his example. Basuli silenced them with a gesture.

"This is no time for useless noises of the mouth," he said. "The Great Bwana has taught us that it is acts by which things are done, not words. Let us save our breath – we shall need it all to follow up the Arabs and slay them. If 'Lady' and our women live the greater the need of haste, and warriors cannot travel fast upon empty lungs."

From the shelter of the reeds along the river, Werper and Tarzan watched the blacks. They saw them dig a trench with their knives and fingers. They saw them lay their yellow burdens in it and scoop the overturned earth back over the tops of the ingots.

Tarzan seemed little interested, after Werper had assured him that that which they buried was not good to eat; but Werper was intensely interested. He would have given much had he had his own followers with him, that he might take away the treasure as soon as the blacks left, for he was sure that they would leave this scene of desolation and death as soon as possible.

The treasure buried, the blacks removed themselves a short distance up wind from the fetid corpses, where they made camp, that they might rest before setting out in pursuit of the Arabs. It was already dusk. Werper and Tarzan sat devouring some pieces of meat they had brought from their last camp. The Belgian was occupied with his plans for the immediate future. He was positive that the Waziri would pursue Achmet Zek, for he knew enough of savage warfare, and of the characteristics of the Arabs and their degraded followers to guess that they had carried the Waziri women off into slavery. This alone would assure immediate pursuit by so warlike a people as the Waziri.

Werper felt that he should find the means and the opportunity to push on ahead, that he might warn Achmet Zek of the coming of Basuli, and also of the location of the buried treasure. What the Arab would now do with Lady Greystoke, in view of the mental affliction of her husband, Werper neither knew nor cared. It was enough that the golden treasure buried upon the site of the burned bungalow was infinitely more valuable than any ransom that would have occurred even to the avaricious mind of the Arab, and if Werper could persuade the raider to share even a portion of it with him he would be well satisfied.

But by far the most important consideration, to Werper, at least, was the incalculably valuable treasure in the little leathern pouch at Tarzan's side. If he could but obtain possession of this! He must! He would!

His eyes wandered to the object of his greed. They measured Tarzan's giant frame, and rested upon the rounded muscles of his arms. It was hopeless. What could he, Werper, hope to accomplish, other than his own death, by an attempt to wrest the gems from their savage owner?

Disconsolate, Werper threw himself upon his side. His head was pillowed on one arm, the other rested across his face in such a way that his eyes were hidden from the ape-man, though one of them was fastened upon him from beneath the shadow of the Belgian's forearm. For a time he lay thus, glowering at Tarzan, and originating schemes for plundering him of his treasure – schemes that were discarded as futile as rapidly as they were born.

Tarzan presently let his own eyes rest upon Werper. The Belgian saw that he was being watched, and lay very still. After a few moments he simulated the regular breathing of deep slumber.

Tarzan had been thinking. He had seen the Waziri bury their belongings. Werper had told him that they were hiding them lest some one find them and take them away. This seemed to Tarzan a splendid plan for safeguarding valuables. Since Werper had evinced a desire to possess his glittering pebbles, Tarzan, with the suspicions of a savage, had guarded the baubles, of whose worth he was entirely ignorant, as zealously as though they spelled life or death to him.

For a long time the ape-man sat watching his companion. At last, convinced that he slept, Tarzan withdrew his hunting knife and commenced to dig a hole in the ground before him. With the blade he loosened up the earth, and with his hands he scooped it out until he had excavated a little cavity a few inches in diameter, and five or six inches in depth. Into this he placed the pouch of jewels. Werper almost forgot to breathe after the fashion of a sleeper as he saw what the ape-man was doing – he scarce repressed an ejaculation of satisfaction.

Tarzan become suddenly rigid as his keen ears noted the cessation of the regular inspirations and expirations of his companion. His narrowed eyes bored straight down upon the Belgian. Werper felt that he was lost – he must risk all on his ability to carry on the deception. He sighed, threw both arms outward, and turned over on his back mumbling as though in the throes of a bad dream. A moment later he resumed the regular breathing.

Now he could not watch Tarzan, but he was sure that the man sat for a long time looking at him. Then, faintly, Werper heard the other's hands scraping dirt, and later patting it down. He knew then that the jewels were buried.

It was an hour before Werper moved again, then he rolled over facing Tarzan and opened his eyes. The ape-man slept. By reaching out his hand Werper could touch the spot where the pouch was buried.

For a long time he lay watching and listening. He moved about, making more noise than necessary, yet Tarzan did not awaken. He drew the sacrificial knife from his belt, and plunged it into the ground. Tarzan did not move. Cautiously the Belgian pushed the blade downward through the loose earth above the pouch. He felt the point touch the soft, tough fabric of the leather. Then he pried down upon the handle. Slowly the little mound of loose earth rose and parted. An instant later a corner of the pouch came into view. Werper pulled it from its hiding place, and tucked it in his shirt. Then he refilled the hole and pressed the dirt carefully down as it had been before.

Greed had prompted him to an act, the discovery of which by his companion could lead only to the most frightful consequences for Werper. Already he could almost feel those strong, white fangs burying themselves in his neck. He shuddered. Far out across the plain a leopard screamed, and in the dense reeds behind him some great beast moved on padded feet.

Werper feared these prowlers of the night; but infinitely more he feared the just wrath of the human beast sleeping at his side. With utmost caution the Belgian arose. Tarzan did not move. Werper took a few steps toward the plain and the distant forest to the northwest, then he paused and fingered the hilt of the long knife in his belt. He turned and looked down upon the sleeper.

"Why not?" he mused. "Then I should be safe."

He returned and bent above the ape-man. Clutched tightly in his hand was the sacrificial knife of the High Priestess of the Flaming God!

CHAPTER TEN

Achmet Zek Sees the Jewels

Mugambi, weak and suffering, had dragged his painful way along the trail of the retreating raiders. He could move but slowly, resting often; but savage hatred and an equally savage desire for vengeance kept him to his task. As the days passed his wounds healed and his strength returned, until at last his giant frame had regained all of its former mighty powers. Now he went more rapidly; but the mounted Arabs had covered a great distance while the wounded black had been painfully crawling after them.

They had reached their fortified camp, and there Achmet Zek awaited the return of his lieutenant, Albert Werper. During the long, rough journey, Jane Clayton had suffered more in anticipation of her impending fate than from the hardships of the road.

Achmet Zek had not deigned to acquaint her with his intentions regarding her future. She prayed that she had been captured in the hope of ransom, for if such should prove the case, no great harm would befall her at the hands of the Arabs; but there was the chance, the horrid chance, that another fate awaited her. She had heard of many women, among whom were white women, who had been sold by outlaws such as Achmet Zek into the slavery of black harems, or taken farther north into the almost equally hideous existence of some Turkish seraglio.

Jane Clayton was of sterner stuff than that which bends in spineless terror before danger. Until hope proved futile she would not give it up; nor did she entertain thoughts of self-destruction only as a final escape from dishonor. So long as Tarzan lived there was every reason to expect succor. No man nor beast who roamed the savage continent could boast the cunning and the powers of her lord and master. To her, he was little short of omnipotent in his native world – this world of savage beasts and savage men. Tarzan would come, and she would be rescued and avenged, of that she was certain. She counted the days that must elapse before he would return from Opar and discover what had transpired during his absence. After that it would be but a short time before he had surrounded the Arab stronghold and punished the motley crew of wrongdoers who inhabited it.

That he could find her she had no slightest doubt. No spoor, however faint, could elude the keen vigilance of his senses. To him, the trail of the raiders would be as plain as the printed page of an open book to her.

And while she hoped, there came through the dark jungle another. Terrified by night and by day, came Albert Werper. A dozen times he had escaped the claws and fangs of the giant carnivora only by what seemed a miracle to him. Armed with nothing more than the knife he had brought with him from Opar, he had made his way through as savage a country as yet exists upon the face of the globe.

By night he had slept in trees. By day he had stumbled fearfully on, often taking refuge among the branches when sight or sound of some great cat warned him from danger. But at last he had come within sight of the palisade behind which were his fierce companions.

At almost the same time Mugambi came out of the jungle before the walled village. As he stood in the shadow of a great tree, reconnoitering, he saw a man, ragged and disheveled, emerge from the jungle almost at his elbow. Instantly he recognized the newcomer as he who had been a guest of his master before the latter had departed for Opar.

The black was upon the point of hailing the Belgian when something stayed him. He saw the white man walking confidently across the clearing toward the village gate. No sane man thus approached a village in this part of Africa unless he was sure of a friendly welcome. Mugambi waited. His suspicions were aroused.

He heard Werper halloo; he saw the gates swing open, and he witnessed the surprised and friendly welcome that was accorded the erstwhile guest of Lord and Lady Greystoke. A light broke upon the understanding of Mugambi. This white man had been a traitor and a spy. It was to him they owed the raid during the absence of the Great Bwana. To his hate for the Arabs, Mugambi added a still greater hate for the white spy.

Within the village Werper passed hurriedly toward the silken tent of Achmet Zek. The Arab arose as his lieutenant entered. His face showed surprise as he viewed the tattered apparel of the Belgian.

"What has happened?" he asked.

Werper narrated all, save the little matter of the pouch of gems which were now tightly strapped about his waist, beneath his clothing. The Arab's eyes narrowed greedily as his henchman described the treasure that the Waziri had buried beside the ruins of the Greystoke bungalow.

"It will be a simple matter now to return and get it," said Achmet Zek. "First we will await the coming of the rash Waziri, and after we have slain them we may take our time to the treasure – none will disturb it where it lies, for we shall leave none alive who knows of its existence.

"And the woman?" asked Werper.

"I shall sell her in the north," replied the raider. "It is the only way, now. She should bring a good price."

The Belgian nodded. He was thinking rapidly. If he could persuade Achmet Zek to send him in command of the party which took Lady Greystoke north it would give him the opportunity he craved to make his escape from his chief. He would forego a share of the gold, if he could but get away unscathed with the jewels.

He knew Achmet Zek well enough by this time to know that no member of his band ever was voluntarily released from the service of Achmet Zek. Most of the few who deserted were recaptured. More than once had Werper listened to their agonized screams as they were tortured before being put to death. The Belgian had no wish to take the slightest chance of recapture.

"Who will go north with the woman," he asked, "while we are returning for the gold that the Waziri buried by the bungalow of the Englishman?"

Achmet Zek thought for a moment. The buried gold was of much greater value than the price the woman would bring. It was necessary to rid himself of her as quickly as possible and it was also well to obtain the gold with the least possible delay. Of all his followers, the Belgian was the most logical lieutenant to intrust with the command of one of the parties. An Arab, as familiar with the trails and tribes as Achmet Zek himself, might collect the woman's price and make good his escape into the far north. Werper, on the other hand, could scarce make his escape alone through a country hostile to Europeans while the men he would send with the Belgian could be carefully selected with a view to preventing Werper from persuading any considerable portion of his command to accompany him should he contemplate desertion of his chief.

At last the Arab spoke: "It is not necessary that we both return for the gold. You shall go north with the woman, carrying a letter to a friend of mine who is always in touch with the best markets for such merchandise, while I return for the gold. We can meet again here when our business is concluded."

Werper could scarce disguise the joy with which he received this welcome decision. And that he did entirely disguise it from the keen and suspicious eyes of Achmet Zek is open to question. However, the decision reached, the Arab and his lieutenant discussed the details of their forthcoming ventures for a short time further, when Werper made his excuses and returned to his own tent for the comforts and luxury of a long-desired bath and shave.

Having bathed, the Belgian tied a small hand mirror to a cord sewn to the rear wall of his tent, placed a rude chair beside an equally rude table that stood beside the glass, and proceeded to remove the rough stubble from his face.

In the catalog of masculine pleasures there is scarce one which imparts a feeling of greater comfort and refreshment than follows a clean shave, and now, with weariness temporarily banished, Albert Werper sprawled in his rickety chair to enjoy a final cigaret before retiring. His thumbs, tucked in his belt in lazy support of the weight of his arms, touched the belt which held the jewel pouch about his waist. He tingled with excitement as he let his mind dwell upon the value of the treasure, which, unknown to all save himself, lay hidden beneath his clothing.

What would Achmet Zek say, if he knew? Werper grinned. How the old rascal's eyes would pop could he but have a glimpse of those scintillating beauties! Werper had never yet had an opportunity to feast his eyes for any great length of time upon them. He had not even counted them – only roughly had he guessed at their value.

He unfastened the belt and drew the pouch from its hiding place. He was alone. The balance of the camp, save the sentries, had retired – none would enter the Belgian's tent. He fingered the pouch, feeling out the shapes and sizes of the precious, little nodules within. He hefted the bag, first in one palm, then in the other, and at last he wheeled his chair slowly around before the table, and in the rays of his small lamp let the glittering gems roll out upon the rough wood.

The refulgent rays transformed the interior of the soiled and squalid canvas to the splendor of a palace in the eyes of the dreaming man. He saw the gilded halls of pleasure that would open their portals to the possessor of the wealth which lay scattered upon this stained and dented table top. He dreamed of joys and luxuries and power which always had been beyond his grasp, and as he dreamed his gaze lifted from the table, as the gaze of a dreamer will, to a far distant goal above the mean horizon of terrestrial commonplaceness.

Unseeing, his eyes rested upon the shaving mirror which still hung upon the tent wall above the table; but his sight was focused far beyond. And then a reflection moved within the polished surface of the tiny glass, the man's eyes shot back out of space to the mirror's face, and in it he saw reflected the grim visage of Achmet Zek, framed in the flaps of the tent doorway behind him.

Werper stifled a gasp of dismay. With rare self-possession he let his gaze drop, without appearing to have halted upon the mirror until it rested again upon the gems. Without haste, he replaced them in the pouch, tucked the latter into his shirt, selected a cigaret from his case, lighted it and rose. Yawning, and stretching his arms above his head, he turned slowly toward the opposite end of the tent. The face of Achmet Zek had disappeared from the opening.

To say that Albert Werper was terrified would be putting it mildly. He realized that he not only had sacrificed his treasure; but his life as well. Achmet Zek would never permit the wealth that he had discovered to slip through his fingers, nor would he forgive the duplicity of a lieutenant who had gained possession of such a treasure without offering to share it with his chief.

Slowly the Belgian prepared for bed. If he were being watched, he could not know; but if so the watcher saw no indication of the nervous excitement which the European strove to conceal. When ready for his blankets, the man crossed to the little table and extinguished the light.

It was two hours later that the flaps at the front of the tent separated silently and gave entrance to a dark-robed figure, which passed noiselessly from the darkness without to the darkness within. Cautiously the prowler crossed the interior. In one hand was a long knife. He came at last to the pile of blankets spread upon several rugs close to one of the tent walls.

Lightly, his fingers sought and found the bulk beneath the blankets – the bulk that should be Albert Werper. They traced out the figure of a man, and then an arm shot upward, poised for an instant and descended. Again and again it rose and fell, and each time the long blade of the knife buried itself in the thing beneath the blankets. But there was an initial lifelessness in the silent bulk that gave the assassin momentary wonder. Feverishly he threw back the coverlets, and searched with nervous hands for the pouch of jewels which he expected to find concealed upon his victim's body.

An instant later he rose with a curse upon his lips. It was Achmet Zek, and he cursed because he had discovered beneath the blankets of his lieutenant only a pile of discarded clothing arranged in the form and semblance of a sleeping man – Albert Werper had fled.

Out into the village ran the chief, calling in angry tones to the sleepy Arabs, who tumbled from their tents in answer to his voice. But though they searched the village again and again they found no trace of the Belgian. Foaming with anger, Achmet Zek called his followers to horse, and though the night was pitchy black they set out to scour the adjoining forest for their quarry.

As they galloped from the open gates, Mugambi, hiding in a nearby bush, slipped, unseen, within the palisade. A score of blacks crowded about the entrance to watch the searchers depart, and as the last of them passed out of the village the blacks seized the portals and drew them to, and Mugambi lent a hand in the work as though the best of his life had been spent among the raiders.

In the darkness he passed, unchallenged, as one of their number, and as they returned from the gates to their respective tents and huts, Mugambi melted into the shadows and disappeared.

For an hour he crept about in the rear of the various huts and tents in an effort to locate that in which his master's mate was imprisoned. One there was which he was reasonably assured contained her, for it was the only hut before the door of which a sentry had been posted. Mugambi was crouching in the shadow of this structure, just around the corner from the unsuspecting guard, when another approached to relieve his comrade.

"The prisoner is safe within?" asked the newcomer.

"She is," replied the other, "for none has passed this doorway since I came."

The new sentry squatted beside the door, while he whom he had relieved made his way to his own hut. Mugambi slunk closer to the corner of the building. In one powerful hand he gripped a heavy knob-stick. No sign of elation disturbed his phlegmatic calm, yet inwardly he was aroused to joy by the proof he had just heard that "Lady" really was within.

The sentry's back was toward the corner of the hut which hid the giant black. The fellow did not see the huge form which silently loomed behind him. The knob-stick swung upward in a curve, and downward again. There was the sound of a dull thud, the crushing of heavy bone, and the sentry slumped into a silent, inanimate lump of clay.

A moment later Mugambi was searching the interior of the hut. At first slowly, calling, "Lady!" in a low whisper, and finally with almost frantic haste, until the truth presently dawned upon him – the hut was empty!

CHAPTER ELEVEN

Tarzan Becomes a Beast Again

For a moment Werper had stood above the sleeping ape-man, his murderous knife poised for the fatal thrust; but fear stayed his hand. What if the first blow should fail to drive the point to his victim's heart? Werper shuddered in contemplation of the disastrous consequences to himself. Awakened, and even with a few moments of life remaining, the giant could literally tear his assailant to pieces should he choose, and the Belgian had no doubt but that Tarzan would so choose.

Again came the soft sound of padded footsteps in the reeds – closer this time. Werper abandoned his design. Before him stretched the wide plain and escape. The jewels were in his possession. To remain longer was to risk death at the hands of Tarzan, or the jaws of the hunter creeping ever nearer. Turning, he slunk away through the night, toward the distant forest.

Tarzan slept on. Where were those uncanny, guardian powers that had formerly rendered him immune from the dangers of surprise? Could this dull sleeper be the alert, sensitive Tarzan of old?

Perhaps the blow upon his head had numbed his senses, temporarily – who may say? Closer crept the stealthy creature through the reeds. The rustling curtain of vegetation parted a few paces from where the sleeper lay, and the massive head of a lion appeared. The beast surveyed the ape-man intently for a moment, then he crouched, his hind feet drawn well beneath him, his tail lashing from side to side.

It was the beating of the beast's tail against the reeds which awakened Tarzan. Jungle folk do not awaken slowly – instantly, full consciousness and full command of their every faculty returns to them from the depth of profound slumber.

Even as Tarzan opened his eyes he was upon his feet, his spear grasped firmly in his hand and ready for attack. Again was he Tarzan of the Apes, sentient, vigilant, ready.

No two lions have identical characteristics, nor does the same lion invariably act similarly under like circumstances. Whether it was surprise, fear or caution which prompted the lion crouching ready to spring upon the man, is immaterial – the fact remains that he did not carry out his original design, he did not spring at the man at all, but, instead, wheeled and sprang back into the reeds as Tarzan arose and confronted him.

The ape-man shrugged his broad shoulders and looked about for his companion. Werper was nowhere to be seen. At first Tarzan suspected that the man had been seized and dragged off by another lion, but upon examination of the ground he soon discovered that the Belgian had gone away alone out into the plain.

For a moment he was puzzled; but presently came to the conclusion that Werper had been frightened by the approach of the lion, and had sneaked off in terror. A sneer touched Tarzan's lips as he pondered the man's act – the desertion of a comrade in time of danger, and without warning. Well, if that was the sort of creature Werper was, Tarzan wished nothing more of him. He had gone, and for all the ape-man cared, he might remain away – Tarzan would not search for him.

A hundred yards from where he stood grew a large tree, alone upon the edge of the reedy jungle. Tarzan made his way to it, clambered into it, and finding a comfortable crotch among its branches, reposed himself for uninterrupted sleep until morning.

And when morning came Tarzan slept on long after the sun had risen. His mind, reverted to the primitive, was untroubled by any more serious obligations than those of providing sustenance, and safeguarding his life. Therefore, there was nothing to awaken for until danger threatened, or the pangs of hunger assailed. It was the latter which eventually aroused him.

Opening his eyes, he stretched his giant thews, yawned, rose and gazed about him through the leafy foliage of his retreat. Across the wasted meadowlands and fields of John Clayton, Lord Greystoke, Tarzan of the Apes looked, as a stranger, upon the moving figures of Basuli and his braves as they prepared their morning meal and made ready to set out upon the expedition which Basuli had planned after discovering the havoc and disaster which had befallen the estate of his dead master.

The ape-man eyed the blacks with curiosity. In the back of his brain loitered a fleeting sense of familiarity with all that he saw, yet he could not connect any of the various forms of life, animate and inanimate, which had fallen within the range of his vision since he had emerged from the darkness of the pits of Opar, with any particular event of the past.

Hazily he recalled a grim and hideous form, hairy, ferocious. A vague tenderness dominated his savage sentiments as this phantom memory struggled for recognition. His mind had reverted to his childhood days – it was the figure of the giant she-ape, Kala, that he saw; but only half recognized. He saw, too, other grotesque, manlike forms. They were of Terkoz, Tublat, Kerchak, and a smaller, less ferocious figure, that was Neeta, the little playmate of his boyhood.

Slowly, very slowly, as these visions of the past animated his lethargic memory, he came to recognize them. They took definite shape and form, adjusting themselves nicely to the various incidents of his life with which they had been intimately connected. His boyhood among the apes spread itself in a slow panorama before him, and as it unfolded it induced within him a mighty longing for the companionship of the shaggy, low-browed brutes of his past.

He watched the blacks scatter their cook fire and depart; but though the face of each of them had but recently been as familiar to him as his own, they awakened within him no recollections whatsoever.

When they had gone, he descended from the tree and sought food. Out upon the plain grazed numerous herds of wild ruminants. Toward a sleek, fat bunch of zebra he wormed his stealthy way. No intricate process of reasoning caused him to circle widely until he was down wind from his prey – he acted instinctively. He took advantage of every form of cover as he crawled upon all fours and often flat upon his stomach toward them.

A plump young mare and a fat stallion grazed nearest to him as he neared the herd. Again it was instinct which selected the former for his meat. A low bush grew but a few yards from the unsuspecting two. The ape-man reached its shelter. He gathered his spear firmly in his grasp. Cautiously he drew his feet beneath him. In a single swift move he rose and cast his heavy weapon at the mare's side. Nor did he wait to note the effect of his assault, but leaped cat-like after his spear, his hunting knife in his hand.

For an instant the two animals stood motionless. The tearing of the cruel barb into her side brought a sudden scream of pain and fright from the mare, and then they both wheeled and broke for safety; but Tarzan of the Apes, for a distance of a few yards, could equal the speed of even these, and the first stride of the mare found her overhauled, with a savage beast at her shoulder. She turned, biting and kicking at her foe. Her mate hesitated for an instant, as though about to rush to her assistance; but a backward glance revealed to him the flying heels of the balance of the herd, and with a snort and a shake of his head he wheeled and dashed away.

Clinging with one hand to the short mane of his quarry, Tarzan struck again and again with his knife at the unprotected heart. The result had, from the first, been inevitable. The mare fought bravely, but hopelessly, and presently sank to the earth, her heart pierced. The ape-man placed a foot upon her carcass and raised his voice in the victory call of the Mangani. In the distance, Basuli halted as the faint notes of the hideous scream broke upon his ears.

"The great apes," he said to his companion. "It has been long since I have heard them in the country of the Waziri. What could have brought them back?"

Tarzan grasped his kill and dragged it to the partial seclusion of the bush which had hidden his own near approach, and there he squatted upon it, cut a huge hunk of flesh from the loin and proceeded to satisfy his hunger with the warm and dripping meat.

Attracted by the shrill screams of the mare, a pair of hyenas slunk presently into view. They trotted to a point a few yards from the gorging ape-man, and halted. Tarzan looked up, bared his fighting fangs and growled. The hyenas returned the compliment, and withdrew a couple of paces. They made no move to attack; but continued to sit at a respectful distance until Tarzan had concluded his meal. After the ape-man had cut a few strips from the carcass to carry with him, he walked slowly off in the direction of the river to quench his thirst. His way lay directly toward the hyenas, nor did he alter his course because of them.

With all the lordly majesty of Numa, the lion, he strode straight toward the growling beasts. For a moment they held their ground, bristling and defiant; but only for a moment, and then slunk away to one side while the indifferent ape-man passed them on his lordly way. A moment later they were tearing at the remains of the zebra.

Back to the reeds went Tarzan, and through them toward the river. A herd of buffalo, startled by his approach, rose ready to charge or to fly. A great bull pawed the ground and bellowed as his bloodshot eyes discovered the intruder; but the ape-man passed across their front as though ignorant of their existence. The bull's bellowing lessened to a low rumbling, he turned and scraped a horde of flies from his side with his muzzle, cast a final glance at the ape-man and resumed his feeding. His numerous family either followed his example or stood gazing after Tarzan in mild-eyed curiosity, until the opposite reeds swallowed him from view.

At the river, Tarzan drank his fill and bathed. During the heat of the day he lay up under the shade of a tree near the ruins of his burned barns. His eyes wandered out across the plain toward the forest, and a longing for the pleasures of its mysterious depths possessed his thoughts for a considerable time. With the next sun he would cross the open and enter the forest! There was no hurry – there lay before him an endless vista of tomorrows with naught to fill them but the satisfying of the appetites and caprices of the moment.

The ape-man's mind was untroubled by regret for the past, or aspiration for the future. He could lie at full length along a swaying branch, stretching his giant limbs, and luxuriating in the blessed peace of utter thoughtlessness, without an apprehension or a worry to sap his nervous energy and rob him of his peace of mind. Recalling only dimly any other existence, the ape-man was happy. Lord Greystoke had ceased to exist.

For several hours Tarzan lolled upon his swaying, leafy couch until once again hunger and thirst suggested an excursion. Stretching lazily he dropped to the ground and moved slowly toward the river. The game trail down which he walked had become by ages of use a deep, narrow trench, its walls topped on either side by impenetrable thicket and dense-growing trees closely interwoven with thick-stemmed creepers and lesser vines inextricably matted into two solid ramparts of vegetation. Tarzan had almost reached the point where the trail debouched upon the open river bottom when he saw a family of lions approaching along the path from the direction of the river. The ape-man counted seven – a male and two lionesses, full grown, and four young lions as large and quite as formidable as their parents. Tarzan halted, growling, and the lions paused, the great male in the lead baring his fangs and rumbling forth a warning roar. In his hand the ape-man held his heavy spear; but he had no intention of pitting his puny weapon against seven lions; yet he stood there growling and roaring and the lions did likewise. It was purely an exhibition of jungle bluff. Each was trying to frighten off the other. Neither wished to turn back and give way, nor did either at first desire to precipitate an encounter. The lions were fed sufficiently so as not to be goaded by pangs of hunger and as for Tarzan he seldom ate the meat of the carnivores; but a point of ethics was at stake and neither side wished to back down. So they stood there facing one another, making all sorts of hideous noises the while they hurled jungle invective back and forth. How long this bloodless duel would have persisted it is difficult to say, though eventually Tarzan would have been forced to yield to superior numbers.

There came, however, an interruption which put an end to the deadlock and it came from Tarzan's rear. He and the lions had been making so much noise that neither could hear anything above their concerted bedlam, and so it was that Tarzan did not hear the great bulk bearing down upon him from behind until an instant before it was upon him, and then he turned to see Buto, the rhinoceros, his little, pig eyes blazing, charging madly toward him and already so close that escape seemed impossible; yet so perfectly were mind and muscles coordinated in this unspoiled, primitive man that almost simultaneously with the sense perception of the threatened danger he wheeled and hurled his spear at Buto's chest. It was a heavy spear shod with iron, and behind it were the giant muscles of the ape-man, while coming to meet it was the enormous weight of Buto and the momentum of his rapid rush. All that happened in the instant that Tarzan turned to meet the charge of the irascible rhinoceros might take long to tell, and yet would have taxed the swiftest lens to record. As his spear left his hand the ape-man was looking down upon the mighty horn lowered to toss him, so close was Buto to him. The spear entered the rhinoceros' neck at its junction with the left shoulder and passed almost entirely through the beast's body, and at the instant that he launched it, Tarzan leaped straight into the air alighting upon Buto's back but escaping the mighty horn.

Then Buto espied the lions and bore madly down upon them while Tarzan of the Apes leaped nimbly into the tangled creepers at one side of the trail. The first lion met Buto's charge and was tossed high over the back of the maddened brute, torn and dying, and then the six remaining lions were upon the rhinoceros, rending and tearing the while they were being gored or trampled. From the safety of his perch Tarzan watched the royal battle with the keenest interest, for the more intelligent of the jungle folk are interested in such encounters. They are to them what the racetrack and the prize ring, the theater and the movies are to us. They see them often; but always they enjoy them for no two are precisely alike.

For a time it seemed to Tarzan that Buto, the rhinoceros, would prove victor in the gory battle. Already had he accounted for four of the seven lions and badly wounded the three remaining when in a momentary lull in the encounter he sank limply to his knees and rolled over upon his side. Tarzan's spear had done its work. It was the man-made weapon which killed the great beast that might easily have survived the assault of seven mighty lions, for Tarzan's spear had pierced the great lungs, and Buto, with victory almost in sight, succumbed to internal hemorrhage.

Then Tarzan came down from his sanctuary and as the wounded lions, growling, dragged themselves away, the ape-man cut his spear from the body of Buto, hacked off a steak and vanished into the jungle. The episode was over. It had been all in the day's work – something which you and I might talk about for a lifetime Tarzan dismissed from his mind the moment that the scene passed from his sight.

CHAPTER TWELVE

La Seeks Vengeance

Swinging back through the jungle in a wide circle the ape-man came to the river at another point, drank and took to the trees again and while he hunted, all oblivious of his past and careless of his future, there came through the dark jungles and the open, parklike places and across the wide meadows, where grazed the countless herbivora of the mysterious continent, a weird and terrible caravan in search of him. There were fifty frightful men with hairy bodies and gnarled and crooked legs. They were armed with knives and great bludgeons and at their head marched an almost naked woman, beautiful beyond compare. It was La of Opar, High Priestess of the Flaming God, and fifty of her horrid priests searching for the purloiner of the sacred sacrificial knife.

Never before had La passed beyond the crumbling outer walls of Opar; but never before had need been so insistent. The sacred knife was gone! Handed down through countless ages it had come to her as a heritage and an insignia of her religious office and regal authority from some long-dead progenitor of lost and forgotten Atlantis. The loss of the crown jewels or the Great Seal of England could have brought no greater consternation to a British king than did the pilfering of the sacred knife bring to La, the Oparian, Queen and High Priestess of the degraded remnants of the oldest civilization upon earth. When Atlantis, with all her mighty cities and her cultivated fields and her great commerce and culture and riches sank into the sea long ages since, she took with her all but a handful of her colonists working the vast gold mines of Central Africa. From these and their degraded slaves and a later intermixture of the blood of the anthropoids sprung the gnarled men of Opar; but by some queer freak of fate, aided by natural selection, the old Atlantean strain had remained pure and undegraded in the females descended from a single princess of the royal house of Atlantis who had been in Opar at the time of the great catastrophe. Such was La.

Burning with white-hot anger was the High Priestess, her heart a seething, molten mass of hatred for Tarzan of the Apes. The zeal of the religious fanatic whose altar has been desecrated was triply enhanced by the rage of a woman scorned. Twice had she thrown her heart at the feet of the godlike ape-man and twice had she been repulsed. La knew that she was beautiful – and she was beautiful, not by the standards of prehistoric Atlantis alone, but by those of modern times was La physically a creature of perfection. Before Tarzan came that first time to Opar, La had never seen a human male other than the grotesque and knotted men of her clan. With one of these she must mate sooner or later that the direct line of high priestesses might not be broken, unless Fate should bring other men to Opar. Before Tarzan came upon his first visit, La had had no thought that such men as he existed, for she knew only her hideous little priests and the bulls of the tribe of great anthropoids that had dwelt from time immemorial in and about Opar, until they had come to be looked upon almost as equals by the Oparians. Among the legends of Opar were tales of godlike men of the olden time and of black men who had come more recently; but these latter had been enemies who killed and robbed. And, too, these legends always held forth the hope that some day that nameless continent from which their race had sprung, would rise once more out of the sea and with slaves at the long sweeps would send her carven, gold-picked galleys forth to succor the long-exiled colonists.

The coming of Tarzan had aroused within La's breast the wild hope that at last the fulfillment of this ancient prophecy was at hand; but more strongly still had it aroused the hot fires of love in a heart that never otherwise would have known the meaning of that all-consuming passion, for such a wondrous creature as La could never have felt love for any of the repulsive priests of Opar. Custom, duty and religious zeal might have commanded the union; but there could have been no love on La's part. She had grown to young womanhood a cold and heartless creature, daughter of a thousand other cold, heartless, beautiful women who had never known love. And so when love came to her it liberated all the pent passions of a thousand generations, transforming La into a pulsing, throbbing volcano of desire, and with desire thwarted this great force of love and gentleness and sacrifice was transmuted by its own fires into one of hatred and revenge.

It was in a state of mind superinduced by these conditions that La led forth her jabbering company to retrieve the sacred emblem of her high office and wreak vengeance upon the author of her wrongs. To Werper she gave little thought. The fact that the knife had been in his hand when it departed from Opar brought down no thoughts of vengeance upon his head. Of course, he should be slain when captured; but his death would give La no pleasure – she looked for that in the contemplated death agonies of Tarzan. He should be tortured. His should be a slow and frightful death. His punishment should be adequate to the immensity of his crime. He had wrested the sacred knife from La; he had lain sacrilegious hands upon the High Priestess of the Flaming God; he had desecrated the altar and the temple. For these things he should die; but he had scorned the love of La, the woman, and for this he should die horribly with great anguish.

The march of La and her priests was not without its adventures. Unused were these to the ways of the jungle, since seldom did any venture forth from behind Opar's crumbling walls, yet their very numbers protected them and so they came without fatalities far along the trail of Tarzan and Werper. Three great apes accompanied them and to these was delegated the business of tracking the quarry, a feat beyond the senses of the Oparians. La commanded. She arranged the order of march, she selected the camps, she set the hour for halting and the hour for resuming and though she was inexperienced in such matters, her native intelligence was so far above that of the men or the apes that she did better than they could have done. She was a hard taskmaster, too, for she looked down with loathing and contempt upon the misshapen creatures amongst which cruel Fate had thrown her and to some extent vented upon them her dissatisfaction and her thwarted love. She made them build her a strong protection and shelter each night and keep a great fire burning before it from dusk to dawn. When she tired of walking they were forced to carry her upon an improvised litter, nor did one dare to question her authority or her right to such services. In fact they did not question either. To them she was a goddess and each loved her and each hoped that he would be chosen as her mate, so they slaved for her and bore the stinging lash of her displeasure and the habitually haughty disdain of her manner without a murmur.

For many days they marched, the apes following the trail easily and going a little distance ahead of the body of the caravan that they might warn the others of impending danger. It was during a noonday halt while all were lying resting after a tiresome march that one of the apes rose suddenly and sniffed the breeze. In a low guttural he cautioned the others to silence and a moment later was swinging quietly up wind into the jungle. La and the priests gathered silently together, the hideous little men fingering their knives and bludgeons, and awaited the return of the shaggy anthropoid.

Nor had they long to wait before they saw him emerge from a leafy thicket and approach them. Straight to La he came and in the language of the great apes which was also the language of decadent Opar he addressed her.

"The great Tarmangani lies asleep there," he said, pointing in the direction from which he had just come. "Come and we can kill him."

"Do not kill him," commanded La in cold tones. "Bring the great Tarmangani to me alive and unhurt. The vengeance is La's. Go; but make no sound!" and she waved her hands to include all her followers.

Cautiously the weird party crept through the jungle in the wake of the great ape until at last he halted them with a raised hand and pointed upward and a little ahead. There they saw the giant form of the ape-man stretched along a low bough and even in sleep one hand grasped a stout limb and one strong, brown leg reached out and overlapped another. At ease lay Tarzan of the Apes, sleeping heavily upon a full stomach and dreaming of Numa, the lion, and Horta, the boar, and other creatures of the jungle. No intimation of danger assailed the dormant faculties of the ape-man – he saw no crouching hairy figures upon the ground beneath him nor the three apes that swung quietly into the tree beside him.

The first intimation of danger that came to Tarzan was the impact of three bodies as the three apes leaped upon him and hurled him to the ground, where he alighted half stunned beneath their combined weight and was immediately set upon by the fifty hairy men or as many of them as could swarm upon his person. Instantly the ape-man became the center of a whirling, striking, biting maelstrom of horror. He fought nobly but the odds against him were too great. Slowly they overcame him though there was scarce one of them that did not feel the weight of his mighty fist or the rending of his fangs.

CHAPTER THIRTEEN

Condemned to Torture and Death

La had followed her company and when she saw them clawing and biting at Tarzan, she raised her voice and cautioned them not to kill him. She saw that he was weakening and that soon the greater numbers would prevail over him, nor had she long to wait before the mighty jungle creature lay helpless and bound at her feet.

"Bring him to the place at which we stopped," she commanded and they carried Tarzan back to the little clearing and threw him down beneath a tree.

"Build me a shelter!" ordered La. "We shall stop here tonight and tomorrow in the face of the Flaming God, La will offer up the heart of this defiler of the temple. Where is the sacred knife? Who took it from him?"

But no one had seen it and each was positive in his assurance that the sacrificial weapon had not been upon Tarzan's person when they captured him. The ape-man looked upon the menacing creatures which surrounded him and snarled his defiance. He looked upon La and smiled. In the face of death he was unafraid.

"Where is the knife?" La asked him.

"I do not know," replied Tarzan. "The man took it with him when he slipped away during the night. Since you are so desirous for its return I would look for him and get it back for you, did you not hold me prisoner; but now that I am to die I cannot get it back. Of what good was your knife, anyway? You can make another. Did you follow us all this way for nothing more than a knife? Let me go and find him and I will bring it back to you."

La laughed a bitter laugh, for in her heart she knew that Tarzan's sin was greater than the purloining of the sacrificial knife of Opar; yet as she looked at him lying bound and helpless before her, tears rose to her eyes so that she had to turn away to hide them; but she remained inflexible in her determination to make him pay in frightful suffering and in eventual death for daring to spurn the love of La.

When the shelter was completed La had Tarzan transferred to it. "All night I shall torture him," she muttered to her priests, "and at the first streak of dawn you may prepare the flaming altar upon which his heart shall be offered up to the Flaming God. Gather wood well filled with pitch, lay it in the form and size of the altar at Opar in the center of the clearing that the Flaming God may look down upon our handiwork and be pleased."

During the balance of the day the priests of Opar were busy erecting an altar in the center of the clearing, and while they worked they chanted weird hymns in the ancient tongue of that lost continent that lies at the bottom of the Atlantic. They knew not the meanings of the words they mouthed; they but repeated the ritual that had been handed down from preceptor to neophyte since that long-gone day when the ancestors of the Piltdown man still swung by their tails in the humid jungles that are England now.

And in the shelter of the hut, La paced to and fro beside the stoic ape-man. Resigned to his fate was Tarzan. No hope of succor gleamed through the dead black of the death sentence hanging over him. He knew that his giant muscles could not part the many strands that bound his wrists and ankles, for he had strained often, but ineffectually for release. He had no hope of outside help and only enemies surrounded him within the camp, and yet he smiled at La as she paced nervously back and forth the length of the shelter.

And La? She fingered her knife and looked down upon her captive. She glared and muttered but she did not strike. "Tonight!" she thought. "Tonight, when it is dark I will torture him." She looked upon his perfect, godlike figure and upon his handsome, smiling face and then she steeled her heart again by thoughts of her love spurned; by religious thoughts that damned the infidel who had desecrated the holy of holies; who had taken from the blood-stained altar of Opar the offering to the Flaming God – and not once but thrice. Three times had Tarzan cheated the god of her fathers. At the thought La paused and knelt at his side. In her hand was a sharp knife. She placed its point against the ape-man's side and pressed upon the hilt; but Tarzan only smiled and shrugged his shoulders.

How beautiful he was! La bent low over him, looking into his eyes. How perfect was his figure. She compared it with those of the knurled and knotted men from whom she must choose a mate, and La shuddered at the thought. Dusk came and after dusk came night. A great fire blazed within the little thorn boma about the camp. The flames played upon the new altar erected in the center of the clearing, arousing in the mind of the High Priestess of the Flaming God a picture of the event of the coming dawn. She saw this giant and perfect form writhing amid the flames of the burning pyre. She saw those smiling lips, burned and blackened, falling away from the strong, white teeth. She saw the shock of black hair tousled upon Tarzan's well-shaped head disappear in a spurt of flame. She saw these and many other frightful pictures as she stood with closed eyes and clenched fists above the object of her hate – ah! was it hate that La of Opar felt?

The darkness of the jungle night had settled down upon the camp, relieved only by the fitful flarings of the fire that was kept up to warn off the man-eaters. Tarzan lay quietly in his bonds. He suffered from thirst and from the cutting of the tight strands about his wrists and ankles; but he made no complaint. A jungle beast was Tarzan with the stoicism of the beast and the intelligence of man. He knew that his doom was sealed – that no supplications would avail to temper the severity of his end and so he wasted no breath in pleadings; but waited patiently in the firm conviction that his sufferings could not endure forever.

In the darkness La stooped above him. In her hand was a sharp knife and in her mind the determination to initiate his torture without further delay. The knife was pressed against his side and La's face was close to his when a sudden burst of flame from new branches thrown upon the fire without, lighted up the interior of the shelter. Close beneath her lips La saw the perfect features of the forest god and into her woman's heart welled all the great love she had felt for Tarzan since first she had seen him, and all the accumulated passion of the years that she had dreamed of him.

Dagger in hand, La, the High Priestess, towered above the helpless creature that had dared to violate the sanctuary of her deity. There should be no torture – there should be instant death. No longer should the defiler of the temple pollute the sight of the lord god almighty. A single stroke of the heavy blade and then the corpse to the flaming pyre without. The knife arm stiffened ready for the downward plunge, and then La, the woman, collapsed weakly upon the body of the man she loved.

She ran her hands in mute caress over his naked flesh; she covered his forehead, his eyes, his lips with hot kisses; she covered him with her body as though to protect him from the hideous fate she had ordained for him, and in trembling, piteous tones she begged him for his love. For hours the frenzy of her passion possessed the burning handmaiden of the Flaming God, until at last sleep overpowered her and she lapsed into unconsciousness beside the man she had sworn to torture and to slay. And Tarzan, untroubled by thoughts of the future, slept peacefully in La's embrace.

At the first hint of dawn the chanting of the priests of Opar brought Tarzan to wakefulness. Initiated in low and subdued tones, the sound soon rose in volume to the open diapason of barbaric blood lust. La stirred. Her perfect arm pressed Tarzan closer to her – a smile parted her lips and then she awoke, and slowly the smile faded and her eyes went wide in horror as the significance of the death chant impinged upon her understanding.

"Love me, Tarzan!" she cried. "Love me, and you shall be saved."

Tarzan's bonds hurt him. He was suffering the tortures of long-restricted circulation. With an angry growl he rolled over with his back toward La. That was her answer! The High Priestess leaped to her feet. A hot flush of shame mantled her cheek and then she went dead white and stepped to the shelter's entrance.

"Come, Priests of the Flaming God!" she cried, "and make ready the sacrifice."

The warped things advanced and entered the shelter. They laid hands upon Tarzan and bore him forth, and as they chanted they kept time with their crooked bodies, swaying to and fro to the rhythm of their song of blood and death. Behind them came La, swaying too; but not in unison with the chanted cadence. White and drawn was the face of the High Priestess – white and drawn with unrequited love and hideous terror of the moments to come. Yet stern in her resolve was La. The infidel should die! The scorner of her love should pay the price upon the fiery altar. She saw them lay the perfect body there upon the rough branches. She saw the High Priest, he to whom custom would unite her – bent, crooked, gnarled, stunted, hideous – advance with the flaming torch and stand awaiting her command to apply it to the faggots surrounding the sacrificial pyre. His hairy, bestial face was distorted in a yellow-fanged grin of anticipatory enjoyment. His hands were cupped to receive the life blood of the victim – the red nectar that at Opar would have filled the golden sacrificial goblets.

La approached with upraised knife, her face turned toward the rising sun and upon her lips a prayer to the burning deity of her people. The High Priest looked questioningly toward her – the brand was burning close to his hand and the faggots lay temptingly near. Tarzan closed his eyes and awaited the end. He knew that he would suffer, for he recalled the faint memories of past burns. He knew that he would suffer and die; but he did not flinch. Death is no great adventure to the jungle bred who walk hand-in-hand with the grim specter by day and lie down at his side by night through all the years of their lives. It is doubtful that the ape-man even speculated upon what came after death. As a matter of fact as his end approached, his mind was occupied by thoughts of the pretty pebbles he had lost, yet his every faculty still was open to what passed around him.

He felt La lean over him and he opened his eyes. He saw her white, drawn face and he saw tears blinding her eyes. "Tarzan, my Tarzan!" she moaned, "tell me that you love me – that you will return to Opar with me – and you shall live. Even in the face of the anger of my people I will save you. This last chance I give you. What is your answer?"

At the last moment the woman in La had triumphed over the High Priestess of a cruel cult. She saw upon the altar the only creature that ever had aroused the fires of love within her virgin breast; she saw the beast-faced fanatic who would one day be her mate, unless she found another less repulsive, standing with the burning torch ready to ignite the pyre; yet with all her mad passion for the ape-man she would give the word to apply the flame if Tarzan's final answer was unsatisfactory. With heaving bosom she leaned close above him. "Yes or no?" she whispered.

Through the jungle, out of the distance, came faintly a sound that brought a sudden light of hope to Tarzan's eyes. He raised his voice in a weird scream that sent La back from him a step or two. The impatient priest grumbled and switched the torch from one hand to the other at the same time holding it closer to the tinder at the base of the pyre.

"Your answer!" insisted La. "What is your answer to the love of La of Opar?"

Closer came the sound that had attracted Tarzan's attention and now the others heard it – the shrill trumpeting of an elephant. As La looked wide-eyed into Tarzan's face, there to read her fate for happiness or heartbreak, she saw an expression of concern shadow his features. Now, for the first time, she guessed the meaning of Tarzan's shrill scream – he had summoned Tantor, the elephant, to his rescue! La's brows contracted in a savage scowl. "You refuse La!" she cried. "Then die! The torch!" she commanded, turning toward the priest.

Tarzan looked up into her face. "Tantor is coming," he said. "I thought that he would rescue me; but I know now from his voice that he will slay me and you and all that fall in his path, searching out with the cunning of Sheeta, the panther, those who would hide from him, for Tantor is mad with the madness of love."

La knew only too well the insane ferocity of a bull elephant in MUST. She knew that Tarzan had not exaggerated. She knew that the devil in the cunning, cruel brain of the great beast might send it hither and thither hunting through the forest for those who escaped its first charge, or the beast might pass on without returning – no one might guess which.

"I cannot love you, La," said Tarzan in a low voice. "I do not know why, for you are very beautiful. I could not go back and live in Opar – I who have the whole broad jungle for my range. No, I cannot love you but I cannot see you die beneath the goring tusks of mad Tantor. Cut my bonds before it is too late. Already he is almost upon us. Cut them and I may yet save you."

A little spiral of curling smoke rose from one corner of the pyre – the flames licked upward, crackling. La stood there like a beautiful statue of despair gazing at Tarzan and at the spreading flames. In a moment they would reach out and grasp him. From the tangled forest came the sound of cracking limbs and crashing trunks – Tantor was coming down upon them, a huge Juggernaut of the jungle. The priests were becoming uneasy. They cast apprehensive glances in the direction of the approaching elephant and then back at La.

"Fly!" she commanded them and then she stooped and cut the bonds securing her prisoner's feet and hands. In an instant Tarzan was upon the ground. The priests screamed out their rage and disappointment. He with the torch took a menacing step toward La and the ape-man. "Traitor!" He shrieked at the woman. "For this you too shall die!" Raising his bludgeon he rushed upon the High Priestess; but Tarzan was there before her. Leaping in to close quarters the ape-man seized the upraised weapon and wrenched it from the hands of the frenzied fanatic and then the priest closed upon him with tooth and nail. Seizing the stocky, stunted body in his mighty hands Tarzan raised the creature high above his head, hurling him at his fellows who were now gathered ready to bear down upon their erstwhile captive. La stood proudly with ready knife behind the ape-man. No faint sign of fear marked her perfect brow – only haughty disdain for her priests and admiration for the man she loved so hopelessly filled her thoughts.

Suddenly upon this scene burst the mad bull – a huge tusker, his little eyes inflamed with insane rage. The priests stood for an instant paralyzed with terror; but Tarzan turned and gathering La in his arms raced for the nearest tree. Tantor bore down upon him trumpeting shrilly. La clung with both white arms about the ape-man's neck. She felt him leap into the air and marveled at his strength and his ability as, burdened with her weight, he swung nimbly into the lower branches of a large tree and quickly bore her upward beyond reach of the sinuous trunk of the pachyderm.

Momentarily baffled here, the huge elephant wheeled and bore down upon the hapless priests who had now scattered, terror-stricken, in every direction. The nearest he gored and threw high among the branches of a tree. One he seized in the coils of his trunk and broke upon a huge bole, dropping the mangled pulp to charge, trumpeting, after another. Two he trampled beneath his huge feet and by then the others had disappeared into the jungle. Now Tantor turned his attention once more to Tarzan for one of the symptoms of madness is a revulsion of affection – objects of sane love become the objects of insane hatred. Peculiar in the unwritten annals of the jungle was the proverbial love that had existed between the ape-man and the tribe of Tantor. No elephant in all the jungle would harm the Tarmangani – the white-ape; but with the madness of MUST upon him the great bull sought to destroy his long-time play-fellow.

Back to the tree where La and Tarzan perched came Tantor, the elephant. He reared up with his forefeet against the bole and reached high toward them with his long trunk; but Tarzan had foreseen this and clambered beyond the bull's longest reach. Failure but tended to further enrage the mad creature. He bellowed and trumpeted and screamed until the earth shook to the mighty volume of his noise. He put his head against the tree and pushed and the tree bent before his mighty strength; yet still it held.

The actions of Tarzan were peculiar in the extreme. Had Numa, or Sabor, or Sheeta, or any other beast of the jungle been seeking to destroy him, the ape-man would have danced about hurling missiles and invectives at his assailant. He would have insulted and taunted them, reviling in the jungle Billingsgate he knew so well; but now he sat silent out of Tantor's reach and upon his handsome face was an expression of deep sorrow and pity, for of all the jungle folk Tarzan loved Tantor the best. Could he have slain him he would not have thought of doing so. His one idea was to escape, for he knew that with the passing of the MUST Tantor would be sane again and that once more he might stretch at full length upon that mighty back and make foolish speech into those great, flapping ears.

Finding that the tree would not fall to his pushing, Tantor was but enraged the more. He looked up at the two perched high above him, his red-rimmed eyes blazing with insane hatred, and then he wound his trunk about the bole of the tree, spread his giant feet wide apart and tugged to uproot the jungle giant. A huge creature was Tantor, an enormous bull in the full prime of all his stupendous strength. Mightily he strove until presently, to Tarzan's consternation, the great tree gave slowly at the roots. The ground rose in little mounds and ridges about the base of the bole, the tree tilted – in another moment it would be uprooted and fall.

The ape-man whirled La to his back and just as the tree inclined slowly in its first movement out of the perpendicular, before the sudden rush of its final collapse, he swung to the branches of a lesser neighbor. It was a long and perilous leap. La closed her eyes and shuddered; but when she opened them again she found herself safe and Tarzan whirling onward through the forest. Behind them the uprooted tree crashed heavily to the ground, carrying with it the lesser trees in its path and then Tantor, realizing that his prey had escaped him, set up once more his hideous trumpeting and followed at a rapid charge upon their trail.

CHAPTER FOURTEEN

A Priestess But Yet a Woman

At first La closed her eyes and clung to Tarzan in terror, though she made no outcry; but presently she gained sufficient courage to look about her, to look down at the ground beneath and even to keep her eyes open during the wide, perilous swings from tree to tree, and then there came over her a sense of safety because of her confidence in the perfect physical creature in whose strength and nerve and agility her fate lay. Once she raised her eyes to the burning sun and murmured a prayer of thanks to her pagan god that she had not been permitted to destroy this godlike man, and her long lashes were wet with tears. A strange anomaly was La of Opar – a creature of circumstance torn by conflicting emotions. Now the cruel and bloodthirsty creature of a heartless god and again a melting woman filled with compassion and tenderness. Sometimes the incarnation of jealousy and revenge and sometimes a sobbing maiden, generous and forgiving; at once a virgin and a wanton; but always – a woman. Such was La.

She pressed her cheek close to Tarzan's shoulder. Slowly she turned her head until her hot lips were pressed against his flesh. She loved him and would gladly have died for him; yet within an hour she had been ready to plunge a knife into his heart and might again within the coming hour.

A hapless priest seeking shelter in the jungle chanced to show himself to enraged Tantor. The great beast turned to one side, bore down upon the crooked, little man, snuffed him out and then, diverted from his course, blundered away toward the south. In a few minutes even the noise of his trumpeting was lost in the distance.

Tarzan dropped to the ground and La slipped to her feet from his back. "Call your people together," said Tarzan.

"They will kill me," replied La.

"They will not kill you," contradicted the ape-man. "No one will kill you while Tarzan of the Apes is here. Call them and we will talk with them."

La raised her voice in a weird, flutelike call that carried far into the jungle on every side. From near and far came answering shouts in the barking tones of the Oparian priests: "We come! We come!" Again and again, La repeated her summons until singly and in pairs the greater portion of her following approached and halted a short distance away from the High Priestess and her savior. They came with scowling brows and threatening mien. When all had come Tarzan addressed them.

"Your La is safe," said the ape-man. "Had she slain me she would now herself be dead and many more of you; but she spared me that I might save her. Go your way with her back to Opar, and Tarzan will go his way into the jungle. Let there be peace always between Tarzan and La. What is your answer?"

The priests grumbled and shook their heads. They spoke together and La and Tarzan could see that they were not favorably inclined toward the proposition. They did not wish to take La back and they did wish to complete the sacrifice of Tarzan to the Flaming God. At last the ape-man became impatient.

"You will obey the commands of your queen," he said, "and go back to Opar with her or Tarzan of the Apes will call together the other creatures of the jungle and slay you all. La saved me that I might save you and her. I have served you better alive than I could have dead. If you are not all fools you will let me go my way in peace and you will return to Opar with La. I know not where the sacred knife is; but you can fashion another. Had I not taken it from La you would have slain me and now your god must be glad that I took it since I have saved his priestess from love-mad Tantor. Will you go back to Opar with La, promising that no harm shall befall her?"

The priests gathered together in a little knot arguing and discussing. They pounded upon their breasts with their fists; they raised their hands and eyes to their fiery god; they growled and barked among themselves until it became evident to Tarzan that one of their number was preventing the acceptance of his proposal. This was the High Priest whose heart was filled with jealous rage because La openly acknowledged her love for the stranger, when by the worldly customs of their cult she should have belonged to him. Seemingly there was to be no solution of the problem until another priest stepped forth and, raising his hand, addressed La.

"Cadj, the High Priest," he announced, "would sacrifice you both to the Flaming God; but all of us except Cadj would gladly return to Opar with our queen."

"You are many against one," spoke up Tarzan. "Why should you not have your will? Go your way with La to Opar and if Cadj interferes slay him."

The priests of Opar welcomed this suggestion with loud cries of approval. To them it appeared nothing short of divine inspiration. The influence of ages of unquestioning obedience to high priests had made it seem impossible to them to question his authority; but when they realized that they could force him to their will they were as happy as children with new toys.

They rushed forward and seized Cadj. They talked in loud menacing tones into his ear. They threatened him with bludgeon and knife until at last he acquiesced in their demands, though sullenly, and then Tarzan stepped close before Cadj.

"Priest," he said, "La goes back to her temple under the protection of her priests and the threat of Tarzan of the Apes that whoever harms her shall die. Tarzan will go again to Opar before the next rains and if harm has befallen La, woe betide Cadj, the High Priest."

Sullenly Cadj promised not to harm his queen.

"Protect her," cried Tarzan to the other Oparians. "Protect her so that when Tarzan comes again he will find La there to greet him."

"La will be there to greet thee," exclaimed the High Priestess, "and La will wait, longing, always longing, until you come again. Oh, tell me that you will come!"

"Who knows?" asked the ape-man as he swung quickly into the trees and raced off toward the east.

For a moment La stood looking after him, then her head drooped, a sigh escaped her lips and like an old woman she took up the march toward distant Opar.

Through the trees raced Tarzan of the Apes until the darkness of night had settled upon the jungle, then he lay down and slept, with no thought beyond the morrow and with even La but the shadow of a memory within his consciousness.

But a few marches to the north Lady Greystoke looked forward to the day when her mighty lord and master should discover the crime of Achmet Zek, and be speeding to rescue and avenge, and even as she pictured the coming of John Clayton, the object of her thoughts squatted almost naked, beside a fallen log, beneath which he was searching with grimy fingers for a chance beetle or a luscious grub.

Two days elapsed following the theft of the jewels before Tarzan gave them a thought. Then, as they chanced to enter his mind, he conceived a desire to play with them again, and, having nothing better to do than satisfy the first whim which possessed him, he rose and started across the plain from the forest in which he had spent the preceding day.

Though no mark showed where the gems had been buried, and though the spot resembled the balance of an unbroken stretch several miles in length, where the reeds terminated at the edge of the meadowland, yet the ape-man moved with unerring precision directly to the place where he had hid his treasure.

With his hunting knife he upturned the loose earth, beneath which the pouch should be; but, though he excavated to a greater distance than the depth of the original hole there was no sign of pouch or jewels. Tarzan's brow clouded as he discovered that he had been despoiled. Little or no reasoning was required to convince him of the identity of the guilty party, and with the same celerity that had marked his decision to unearth the jewels, he set out upon the trail of the thief.

Though the spoor was two days old, and practically obliterated in many places, Tarzan followed it with comparative ease. A white man could not have followed it twenty paces twelve hours after it had been made, a black man would have lost it within the first mile; but Tarzan of the Apes had been forced in childhood to develop senses that an ordinary mortal scarce ever uses.

We may note the garlic and whisky on the breath of a fellow strap hanger, or the cheap perfume emanating from the person of the wondrous lady sitting in front of us, and deplore the fact of our sensitive noses; but, as a matter of fact, we cannot smell at all, our olfactory organs are practically atrophied, by comparison with the development of the sense among the beasts of the wild.

Where a foot is placed an effluvium remains for a considerable time. It is beyond the range of our sensibilities; but to a creature of the lower orders, especially to the hunters and the hunted, as interesting and ofttimes more lucid than is the printed page to us.

Nor was Tarzan dependent alone upon his sense of smell. Vision and hearing had been brought to a marvelous state of development by the necessities of his early life, where survival itself depended almost daily upon the exercise of the keenest vigilance and the constant use of all his faculties.

And so he followed the old trail of the Belgian through the forest and toward the north; but because of the age of the trail he was constrained to a far from rapid progress. The man he followed was two days ahead of him when Tarzan took up the pursuit, and each day he gained upon the ape-man. The latter, however, felt not the slightest doubt as to the outcome. Some day he would overhaul his quarry – he could bide his time in peace until that day dawned. Doggedly he followed the faint spoor, pausing by day only to kill and eat, and at night only to sleep and refresh himself.

Occasionally he passed parties of savage warriors; but these he gave a wide berth, for he was hunting with a purpose that was not to be distracted by the minor accidents of the trail.

These parties were of the collecting hordes of the Waziri and their allies which Basuli had scattered his messengers broadcast to summon. They were marching to a common rendezvous in preparation for an assault upon the stronghold of Achmet Zek; but to Tarzan they were enemies – he retained no conscious memory of any friendship for the black men.

It was night when he halted outside the palisaded village of the Arab raider. Perched in the branches of a great tree he gazed down upon the life within the enclosure. To this place had the spoor led him. His quarry must be within; but how was he to find him among so many huts? Tarzan, although cognizant of his mighty powers, realized also his limitations. He knew that he could not successfully cope with great numbers in open battle. He must resort to the stealth and trickery of the wild beast, if he were to succeed.

Sitting in the safety of his tree, munching upon the leg bone of Horta, the boar, Tarzan waited a favorable opportunity to enter the village. For awhile he gnawed at the bulging, round ends of the large bone, splintering off small pieces between his strong jaws, and sucking at the delicious marrow within; but all the time he cast repeated glances into the village. He saw white-robed figures, and half-naked blacks; but not once did he see one who resembled the stealer of the gems.

Patiently he waited until the streets were deserted by all save the sentries at the gates, then he dropped lightly to the ground, circled to the opposite side of the village and approached the palisade.

At his side hung a long, rawhide rope – a natural and more dependable evolution from the grass rope of his childhood. Loosening this, he spread the noose upon the ground behind him, and with a quick movement of his wrist tossed the coils over one of the sharpened projections of the summit of the palisade.

Drawing the noose taut, he tested the solidity of its hold. Satisfied, the ape-man ran nimbly up the vertical wall, aided by the rope which he clutched in both hands. Once at the top it required but a moment to gather the dangling rope once more into its coils, make it fast again at his waist, take a quick glance downward within the palisade, and, assured that no one lurked directly beneath him, drop softly to the ground.

Now he was within the village. Before him stretched a series of tents and native huts. The business of exploring each of them would be fraught with danger; but danger was only a natural factor of each day's life – it never appalled Tarzan. The chances appealed to him – the chances of life and death, with his prowess and his faculties pitted against those of a worthy antagonist.

It was not necessary that he enter each habitation – through a door, a window or an open chink, his nose told him whether or not his prey lay within. For some time he found one disappointment following upon the heels of another in quick succession. No spoor of the Belgian was discernible. But at last he came to a tent where the smell of the thief was strong. Tarzan listened, his ear close to the canvas at the rear, but no sound came from within.

At last he cut one of the pin ropes, raised the bottom of the canvas, and intruded his head within the interior. All was quiet and dark. Tarzan crawled cautiously within – the scent of the Belgian was strong; but it was not live scent. Even before he had examined the interior minutely, Tarzan knew that no one was within it.

In one corner he found a pile of blankets and clothing scattered about; but no pouch of pretty pebbles. A careful examination of the balance of the tent revealed nothing more, at least nothing to indicate the presence of the jewels; but at the side where the blankets and clothing lay, the ape-man discovered that the tent wall had been loosened at the bottom, and presently he sensed that the Belgian had recently passed out of the tent by this avenue.

Tarzan was not long in following the way that his prey had fled. The spoor led always in the shadow and at the rear of the huts and tents of the village – it was quite evident to Tarzan that the Belgian had gone alone and secretly upon his mission. Evidently he feared the inhabitants of the village, or at least his work had been of such a nature that he dared not risk detection.

At the back of a native hut the spoor led through a small hole recently cut in the brush wall and into the dark interior beyond. Fearlessly, Tarzan followed the trail. On hands and knees, he crawled through the small aperture. Within the hut his nostrils were assailed by many odors; but clear and distinct among them was one that half aroused a latent memory of the past – it was the faint and delicate odor of a woman. With the cognizance of it there rose in the breast of the ape-man a strange uneasiness – the result of an irresistible force which he was destined to become acquainted with anew – the instinct which draws the male to his mate.

In the same hut was the scent spoor of the Belgian, too, and as both these assailed the nostrils of the ape-man, mingling one with the other, a jealous rage leaped and burned within him, though his memory held before the mirror of recollection no image of the she to which he had attached his desire.

Like the tent he had investigated, the hut, too, was empty, and after satisfying himself that his stolen pouch was secreted nowhere within, he left, as he had entered, by the hole in the rear wall.

Here he took up the spoor of the Belgian, followed it across the clearing, over the palisade, and out into the dark jungle beyond.

CHAPTER FIFTEEN

The Flight of Werper

After Werper had arranged the dummy in his bed, and sneaked out into the darkness of the village beneath the rear wall of his tent, he had gone directly to the hut in which Jane Clayton was held captive.

Before the doorway squatted a black sentry. Werper approached him boldly, spoke a few words in his ear, handed him a package of tobacco, and passed into the hut. The black grinned and winked as the European disappeared within the darkness of the interior.

The Belgian, being one of Achmet Zek's principal lieutenants, might naturally go where he wished within or without the village, and so the sentry had not questioned his right to enter the hut with the white, woman prisoner.

Within, Werper called in French and in a low whisper: "Lady Greystoke! It is I, M. Frecoult. Where are you?" But there was no response. Hastily the man felt around the interior, groping blindly through the darkness with outstretched hands. There was no one within!

Werper's astonishment surpassed words. He was on the point of stepping without to question the sentry, when his eyes, becoming accustomed to the dark, discovered a blotch of lesser blackness near the base of the rear wall of the hut. Examination revealed the fact that the blotch was an opening cut in the wall. It was large enough to permit the passage of his body, and assured as he was that Lady Greystoke had passed out through the aperture in an attempt to escape the village, he lost no time in availing himself of the same avenue; but neither did he lose time in a fruitless search for Jane Clayton.

His own life depended upon the chance of his eluding, or outdistancing Achmet Zek, when that worthy should have discovered that he had escaped. His original plan had contemplated connivance in the escape of

Lady Greystoke for two very good and sufficient reasons. The first was that by saving her he would win the gratitude of the English, and thus lessen the chance of his extradition should his identity and his crime against his superior officer be charged against him.

The second reason was based upon the fact that only one direction of escape was safely open to him. He could not travel to the west because of the Belgian possessions which lay between him and the Atlantic. The south was closed to him by the feared presence of the savage ape-man he had robbed. To the north lay the friends and allies of Achmet Zek. Only toward the east, through British East Africa, lay reasonable assurance of freedom.

Accompanied by a titled Englishwoman whom he had rescued from a frightful fate, and his identity vouched for by her as that of a Frenchman by the name of Frecoult, he had looked forward, and not without reason, to the active assistance of the British from the moment that he came in contact with their first outpost.

But now that Lady Greystoke had disappeared, though he still looked toward the east for hope, his chances were lessened, and another, subsidiary design completely dashed. From the moment that he had first laid eyes upon Jane Clayton he had nursed within his breast a secret passion for the beautiful American wife of the English lord, and when Achmet Zek's discovery of the jewels had necessitated flight, the Belgian had dreamed, in his planning, of a future in which he might convince Lady Greystoke that her husband was dead, and by playing upon her gratitude win her for himself.

At that part of the village farthest from the gates, Werper discovered that two or three long poles, taken from a nearby pile which had been collected for the construction of huts, had been leaned against the top of the palisade, forming a precarious, though not impossible avenue of escape.

Rightly, he inferred that thus had Lady Greystoke found the means to scale the wall, nor did he lose even a moment in following her lead. Once in the jungle he struck out directly eastward.

A few miles south of him, Jane Clayton lay panting among the branches of a tree in which she had taken refuge from a prowling and hungry lioness.

Her escape from the village had been much easier than she had anticipated. The knife which she had used to cut her way through the brush wall of the hut to freedom she had found sticking in the wall of her prison, doubtless left there by accident when a former tenant had vacated the premises.

To cross the rear of the village, keeping always in the densest shadows, had required but a few moments, and the fortunate circumstance of the discovery of the hut poles lying so near the palisade had solved for her the problem of the passage of the high wall.

For an hour she had followed the old game trail toward the south, until there fell upon her trained hearing the stealthy padding of a stalking beast behind her. The nearest tree gave her instant sanctuary, for she was too wise in the ways of the jungle to chance her safety for a moment after discovering that she was being hunted.

Werper, with better success, traveled slowly onward until dawn, when, to his chagrin, he discovered a mounted Arab upon his trail. It was one of Achmet Zek's minions, many of whom were scattered in all directions through the forest, searching for the fugitive Belgian.

Jane Clayton's escape had not yet been discovered when Achmet Zek and his searchers set forth to overhaul Werper. The only man who had seen the Belgian after his departure from his tent was the black sentry before the doorway of Lady Greystoke's prison hut, and he had been silenced by the discovery of the dead body of the man who had relieved him, the sentry that Mugambi had dispatched.

The bribe taker naturally inferred that Werper had slain his fellow and dared not admit that he had permitted him to enter the hut, fearing as he did, the anger of Achmet Zek. So, as chance directed that he should be the one to discover the body of the sentry when the first alarm had been given following Achmet Zek's discovery that Werper had outwitted him, the crafty black had dragged the dead body to the interior of a nearby tent, and himself resumed his station before the doorway of the hut in which he still believed the woman to be.

With the discovery of the Arab close behind him, the Belgian hid in the foliage of a leafy bush. Here the trail ran straight for a considerable distance, and down the shady forest aisle, beneath the overarching branches of the trees, rode the white-robed figure of the pursuer.

Nearer and nearer he came. Werper crouched closer to the ground behind the leaves of his hiding place. Across the trail a vine moved. Werper's eyes instantly centered upon the spot. There was no wind to stir the foliage in the depths of the jungle. Again the vine moved. In the mind of the Belgian only the presence of a sinister and malevolent force could account for the phenomenon.

The man's eyes bored steadily into the screen of leaves upon the opposite side of the trail. Gradually a form took shape beyond them – a tawny form, grim and terrible, with yellow-green eyes glaring fearsomely across the narrow trail straight into his.

Werper could have screamed in fright, but up the trail was coming the messenger of another death, equally sure and no less terrible. He remained silent, almost paralyzed by fear. The Arab approached. Across the trail from Werper the lion crouched for the spring, when suddenly his attention was attracted toward the horseman.

The Belgian saw the massive head turn in the direction of the raider and his heart all but ceased its beating as he awaited the result of this interruption. At a walk the horseman approached. Would the nervous animal he rode take fright at the odor of the carnivore, and, bolting, leave Werper still to the mercies of the king of beasts?

But he seemed unmindful of the near presence of the great cat. On he came, his neck arched, champing at the bit between his teeth. The Belgian turned his eyes again toward the lion. The beast's whole attention now seemed riveted upon the horseman. They were abreast the lion now, and still the brute did not spring. Could he be but waiting for them to pass before returning his attention to the original prey? Werper shuddered and half rose. At the same instant the lion sprang from his place of concealment, full upon the mounted man. The horse, with a shrill neigh of terror, shrank sideways almost upon the Belgian, the lion dragged the helpless Arab from his saddle, and the horse leaped back into the trail and fled away toward the west.

But he did not flee alone. As the frightened beast had pressed in upon him, Werper had not been slow to note the quickly emptied saddle and the opportunity it presented. Scarcely had the lion dragged the Arab down from one side, than the Belgian, seizing the pommel of the saddle and the horse's mane, leaped upon the horse's back from the other.

A half hour later a naked giant, swinging easily through the lower branches of the trees, paused, and with raised head, and dilating nostrils sniffed the morning air. The smell of blood fell strong upon his senses, and mingled with it was the scent of Numa, the lion. The giant cocked his head upon one side and listened.

From a short distance up the trail came the unmistakable noises of the greedy feeding of a lion. The crunching of bones, the gulping of great pieces, the contented growling, all attested the nearness of the king at table.

Tarzan approached the spot, still keeping to the branches of the trees. He made no effort to conceal his approach, and presently he had evidence that Numa had heard him, from the ominous, rumbling warning that broke from a thicket beside the trail.

Halting upon a low branch just above the lion Tarzan looked down upon the grisly scene. Could this unrecognizable thing be the man he had been trailing? The ape-man wondered. From time to time he had descended to the trail and verified his judgment by the evidence of his scent that the Belgian had followed this game trail toward the east.

Now he proceeded beyond the lion and his feast, again descended and examined the ground with his nose. There was no scent spoor here of the man he had been trailing. Tarzan returned to the tree. With keen eyes he searched the ground about the mutilated corpse for a sign of the missing pouch of pretty pebbles; but naught could he see of it.

He scolded Numa and tried to drive the great beast away; but only angry growls rewarded his efforts. He tore small branches from a nearby limb and hurled them at his ancient enemy. Numa looked up with bared fangs, grinning hideously, but he did not rise from his kill.

Then Tarzan fitted an arrow to his bow, and drawing the slim shaft far back let drive with all the force of the tough wood that only he could bend. As the arrow sank deeply into his side, Numa leaped to his feet with a roar of mingled rage and pain. He leaped futilely at the grinning ape-man, tore at the protruding end of the shaft, and then, springing into the trail, paced back and forth beneath his tormentor. Again Tarzan loosed a swift bolt. This time the missile, aimed with care, lodged in the lion's spine. The great creature halted in its tracks, and lurched awkwardly forward upon its face, paralyzed.

Tarzan dropped to the trail, ran quickly to the beast's side, and drove his spear deep into the fierce heart, then after recovering his arrows turned his attention to the mutilated remains of the animal's prey in the nearby thicket.

The face was gone. The Arab garments aroused no doubt as to the man's identity, since he had trailed him into the Arab camp and out again, where he might easily have acquired the apparel. So sure was Tarzan that the body was that of he who had robbed him that he made no effort to verify his deductions by scent among the conglomerate odors of the great carnivore and the fresh blood of the victim.

He confined his attentions to a careful search for the pouch, but nowhere upon or about the corpse was any sign of the missing article or its contents. The ape-man was disappointed – possibly not so much because of the loss of the colored pebbles as with Numa for robbing him of the pleasures of revenge.

Wondering what could have become of his possessions, the ape-man turned slowly back along the trail in the direction from which he had come. In his mind he revolved a plan to enter and search the Arab camp, after darkness had again fallen. Taking to the trees, he moved directly south in search of prey, that he might satisfy his hunger before midday, and then lie up for the afternoon in some spot far from the camp, where he might sleep without fear of discovery until it came time to prosecute his design.

Scarcely had he quitted the trail when a tall, black warrior, moving at a dogged trot, passed toward the east. It was Mugambi, searching for his mistress. He continued along the trail, halting to examine the body of the dead lion. An expression of puzzlement crossed his features as he bent to search for the wounds which had caused the death of the jungle lord. Tarzan had removed his arrows, but to Mugambi the proof of death was as strong as though both the lighter missiles and the spear still protruded from the carcass.

The black looked furtively about him. The body was still warm, and from this fact he reasoned that the killer was close at hand, yet no sign of living man appeared. Mugambi shook his head, and continued along the trail, but with redoubled caution.

All day he traveled, stopping occasionally to call aloud the single word, "Lady," in the hope that at last she might hear and respond; but in the end his loyal devotion brought him to disaster.

From the northeast, for several months, Abdul Mourak, in command of a detachment of Abyssinian soldiers, had been assiduously searching for the Arab raider, Achmet Zek, who, six months previously, had affronted the majesty of Abdul Mourak's emperor by conducting a slave raid within the boundaries of Menelek's domain.

And now it happened that Abdul Mourak had halted for a short rest at noon upon this very day and along the same trail that Werper and Mugambi were following toward the east.

It was shortly after the soldiers had dismounted that the Belgian, unaware of their presence, rode his tired mount almost into their midst, before he had discovered them. Instantly he was surrounded, and a volley of questions hurled at him, as he was pulled from his horse and led toward the presence of the commander.

Falling back upon his European nationality, Werper assured Abdul Mourak that he was a Frenchman, hunting in Africa, and that he had been attacked by strangers, his safari killed or scattered, and himself escaping only by a miracle.

From a chance remark of the Abyssinian, Werper discovered the purpose of the expedition, and when he realized that these men were the enemies of Achmet Zek, he took heart, and immediately blamed his predicament upon the Arab.

Lest, however, he might again fall into the hands of the raider, he discouraged Abdul Mourak in the further prosecution of his pursuit, assuring the Abyssinian that Achmet Zek commanded a large and dangerous force, and also that he was marching rapidly toward the south.

Convinced that it would take a long time to overhaul the raider, and that the chances of engagement made the outcome extremely questionable, Mourak, none too unwillingly, abandoned his plan and gave the necessary orders for his command to pitch camp where they were, preparatory to taking up the return march toward Abyssinia the following morning.

It was late in the afternoon that the attention of the camp was attracted toward the west by the sound of a powerful voice calling a single word, repeated several times: "Lady! Lady! Lady!"

True to their instincts of precaution, a number of Abyssinians, acting under orders from Abdul Mourak, advanced stealthily through the jungle toward the author of the call.

A half hour later they returned, dragging Mugambi among them. The first person the big black's eyes fell upon as he was hustled into the presence of the Abyssinian officer, was M. Jules Frecoult, the Frenchman who had been the guest of his master and whom he last had seen entering the village of Achmet Zek under circumstances which pointed to his familiarity and friendship for the raiders.

Between the disasters that had befallen his master and his master's house, and the Frenchman, Mugambi saw a sinister relationship, which kept him from recalling to Werper's attention the identity which the latter evidently failed to recognize.

Pleading that he was but a harmless hunter from a tribe farther south, Mugambi begged to be allowed to go upon his way; but Abdul Mourak, admiring the warrior's splendid physique, decided to take him back to Adis Abeba and present him to Menelek. A few moments later Mugambi and Werper were marched away under guard, and the Belgian learned for the first time, that he too was a prisoner rather than a guest. In vain he protested against such treatment, until a strapping soldier struck him across the mouth and threatened to shoot him if he did not desist.

Mugambi took the matter less to heart, for he had not the slightest doubt but that during the course of the journey he would find ample opportunity to elude the vigilance of his guards and make good his escape. With this idea always uppermost in his mind, he courted the good opinion of the Abyssinians, asked them many questions about their emperor and their country, and evinced a growing desire to reach their destination, that he might enjoy all the good things which they assured him the city of Adis Abeba contained. Thus he disarmed their suspicions, and each day found a slight relaxation of their watchfulness over him.

By taking advantage of the fact that he and Werper always were kept together, Mugambi sought to learn what the other knew of the whereabouts of Tarzan, or the authorship of the raid upon the bungalow, as well as the fate of Lady Greystoke; but as he was confined to the accidents of conversation for this information, not daring to acquaint Werper with his true identity, and as Werper was equally anxious to conceal from the world his part in the destruction of his host's home and happiness, Mugambi learned nothing – at least in this way.

But there came a time when he learned a very surprising thing, by accident.

The party had camped early in the afternoon of a sultry day, upon the banks of a clear and beautiful stream. The bottom of the river was gravelly, there was no indication of crocodiles, those menaces to promiscuous bathing in the rivers of certain portions of the dark continent, and so the Abyssinians took advantage of the opportunity to perform long-deferred, and much needed, ablutions.

As Werper, who, with Mugambi, had been given permission to enter the water, removed his clothing, the black noted the care with which he unfastened something which circled his waist, and which he took off with his shirt, keeping the latter always around and concealing the object of his suspicious solicitude.

It was this very carefulness which attracted the black's attention to the thing, arousing a natural curiosity in the warrior's mind, and so it chanced that when the Belgian, in the nervousness of overcaution, fumbled the hidden article and dropped it, Mugambi saw it as it fell upon the ground, spilling a portion of its contents on the sward.

Now Mugambi had been to London with his master. He was not the unsophisticated savage that his apparel proclaimed him. He had mingled with the cosmopolitan hordes of the greatest city in the world; he had visited museums and inspected shop windows; and, besides, he was a shrewd and intelligent man.

The instant that the jewels of Opar rolled, scintillating, before his astonished eyes, he recognized them for what they were; but he recognized something else, too, that interested him far more deeply than the value of the stones. A thousand times he had seen the leathern pouch which dangled at his master's side, when Tarzan of the Apes had, in a spirit of play and adventure, elected to return for a few hours to the primitive manners and customs of his boyhood, and surrounded by his naked warriors hunt the lion and the leopard, the buffalo and the elephant after the manner he loved best.

Werper saw that Mugambi had seen the pouch and the stones. Hastily he gathered up the precious gems and returned them to their container, while Mugambi, assuming an air of indifference, strolled down to the river for his bath.

The following morning Abdul Mourak was enraged and chagrined to discover that his huge, black prisoner had escaped during the night, while Werper was terrified for the same reason, until his trembling fingers discovered the pouch still in its place beneath his shirt, and within it the hard outlines of its contents.

CHAPTER SIXTEEN

Tarzan Again Leads the Mangani

ACHMET ZEK WITH TWO of his followers had circled far to the south to intercept the flight of his deserting lieutenant, Werper. Others had spread out in various directions, so that a vast circle had been formed by them during the night, and now they were beating in toward the center.

Achmet and the two with him halted for a short rest just before noon. They squatted beneath the trees upon the southern edge of a clearing. The chief of the raiders was in ill humor. To have been outwitted by an unbeliever was bad enough; but to have, at the same time, lost the jewels upon which he had set his avaricious heart was altogether too much – Allah must, indeed be angry with his servant.

Well, he still had the woman. She would bring a fair price in the north, and there was, too, the buried treasure beside the ruins of the Englishman's house.

A slight noise in the jungle upon the opposite side of the clearing brought Achmet Zek to immediate and alert attention. He gathered his rifle in readiness for instant use, at the same time motioning his followers to silence and concealment. Crouching behind the bushes the three waited, their eyes fastened upon the far side of the open space.

Presently the foliage parted and a woman's face appeared, glancing fearfully from side to side. A moment later, evidently satisfied that no immediate danger lurked before her, she stepped out into the clearing in full view of the Arab.

Achmet Zek caught his breath with a muttered exclamation of incredulity and an imprecation. The woman was the prisoner he had thought safely guarded at his camp!

Apparently she was alone, but Achmet Zek waited that he might make sure of it before seizing her. Slowly Jane Clayton started across the clearing. Twice already since she had quitted the village of the raiders had she barely escaped the fangs of carnivora, and once she had almost stumbled into the path of one of the searchers. Though she was almost despairing of ever reaching safety she still was determined to fight on, until death or success terminated her endeavors.

As the Arabs watched her from the safety of their concealment, and Achmet Zek noted with satisfaction that she was walking directly into his clutches, another pair of eyes looked down upon the entire scene from the foliage of an adjacent tree.

Puzzled, troubled eyes they were, for all their gray and savage glint, for their owner was struggling with an intangible suggestion of the familiarity of the face and figure of the woman below him.

A sudden crashing of the bushes at the point from which Jane Clayton had emerged into the clearing brought her to a sudden stop and attracted the attention of the Arabs and the watcher in the tree to the same point.

The woman wheeled about to see what new danger menaced her from behind, and as she did so a great, anthropoid ape waddled into view. Behind him came another and another; but Lady Greystoke did not wait to learn how many more of the hideous creatures were so close upon her trail.

With a smothered scream she rushed toward the opposite jungle, and as she reached the bushes there, Achmet Zek and his two henchmen rose up and seized her. At the same instant a naked, brown giant dropped from the branches of a tree at the right of the clearing.

Turning toward the astonished apes he gave voice to a short volley of low gutturals, and without waiting to note the effect of his words upon them, wheeled and charged for the Arabs.

Achmet Zek was dragging Jane Clayton toward his tethered horse. His two men were hastily unfastening all three mounts. The woman, struggling to escape the Arab, turned and saw the ape-man running toward her. A glad light of hope illuminated her face.

"John!" she cried. "Thank God that you have come in time."

Behind Tarzan came the great apes, wondering, but obedient to his summons. The Arabs saw that they would not have time to mount and make their escape before the beasts and the man were upon them. Achmet Zek recognized the latter as the redoubtable enemy of such as he, and he saw, too, in the circumstance an opportunity to rid himself forever of the menace of the ape-man's presence.

Calling to his men to follow his example he raised his rifle and leveled it upon the charging giant. His followers, acting with no less alacrity than himself, fired almost simultaneously, and with the reports of the rifles, Tarzan of the Apes and two of his hairy henchmen pitched forward among the jungle grasses.

The noise of the rifle shots brought the balance of the apes to a wondering pause, and, taking advantage of their momentary distraction, Achmet Zek and his fellows leaped to their horses' backs and galloped away with the now hopeless and grief-stricken woman.

Back to the village they rode, and once again Lady Greystoke found herself incarcerated in the filthy, little hut from which she had thought to have escaped for good. But this time she was not only guarded by an additional sentry, but bound as well.

Singly and in twos the searchers who had ridden out with Achmet Zek upon the trail of the Belgian, returned empty handed. With the report of each the raider's rage and chagrin increased, until he was in such a transport of ferocious anger that none dared approach him. Threatening and cursing, Achmet Zek paced up and down the floor of his silken tent; but his temper served him naught – Werper was gone and with him the fortune in scintillating gems which had aroused the cupidity of his chief and placed the sentence of death upon the head of the lieutenant.

With the escape of the Arabs the great apes had turned their attention to their fallen comrades. One was dead, but another and the great white ape still breathed. The hairy monsters gathered about these two, grumbling and muttering after the fashion of their kind.

Tarzan was the first to regain consciousness. Sitting up, he looked about him. Blood was flowing from a wound in his shoulder. The shock had thrown him down and dazed him; but he was far from dead. Rising slowly to his feet he let his eyes wander toward the spot where last he had seen the she, who had aroused within his savage breast such strange emotions.

"Where is she?" he asked.

"The Tarmangani took her away," replied one of the apes. "Who are you who speak the language of the Mangani?"

"I am Tarzan," replied the ape-man; "mighty hunter, greatest of fighters. When I roar, the jungle is silent and trembles with terror. I am Tarzan of the Apes. I have been away; but now I have come back to my people."

"Yes," spoke up an old ape, "he is Tarzan. I know him. It is well that he has come back. Now we shall have good hunting."

The other apes came closer and sniffed at the ape-man. Tarzan stood very still, his fangs half bared, and his muscles tense and ready for action; but there was none there to question his right to be with them, and presently, the inspection satisfactorily concluded, the apes again returned their attention to the other survivor.

He too was but slightly wounded, a bullet, grazing his skull, having stunned him, so that when he regained consciousness he was apparently as fit as ever.

The apes told Tarzan that they had been traveling toward the east when the scent spoor of the she had attracted them and they had stalked her. Now they wished to continue upon their interrupted march; but Tarzan preferred to follow the Arabs and take the woman from them. After a considerable argument it was decided that they should first hunt toward the east for a few days and then return and search for the Arabs, and as time is of little moment to the ape folk, Tarzan acceded to their demands, he, himself, having reverted to a mental state but little superior to their own.

Another circumstance which decided him to postpone pursuit of the Arabs was the painfulness of his wound. It would be better to wait until that had healed before he pitted himself again against the guns of the Tarmangani.

And so, as Jane Clayton was pushed into her prison hut and her hands and feet securely bound, her natural protector roamed off toward the east in company with a score of hairy monsters, with whom he rubbed shoulders as familiarly as a few months before he had mingled with his immaculate fellow-members of one of London's most select and exclusive clubs.

But all the time there lurked in the back of his injured brain a troublesome conviction that he had no business where he was – that he should be, for some unaccountable reason, elsewhere and among another sort of creature. Also, there was the compelling urge to be upon the scent of the Arabs, undertaking the rescue of the woman who had appealed so strongly to his savage sentiments; though the thought-word which naturally occurred to him in the contemplation of the venture, was "capture," rather than "rescue."

To him she was as any other jungle she, and he had set his heart upon her as his mate. For an instant, as he had approached closer to her in the clearing where the Arabs had seized her, the subtle aroma which had first aroused his desires in the hut that had imprisoned her had fallen upon his nostrils, and told him that he had found the creature for whom he had developed so sudden and inexplicable a passion.

The matter of the pouch of jewels also occupied his thoughts to some extent, so that he found a double urge for his return to the camp of the raiders. He would obtain possession of both his pretty pebbles and the she. Then he would return to the great apes with his new mate and his baubles, and leading his hairy companions into a far wilderness beyond the ken of man, live out his life, hunting and battling among the lower orders after the only manner which he now recollected.

He spoke to his fellow-apes upon the matter, in an attempt to persuade them to accompany him; but all except Taglat and Chulk refused. The latter was young and strong, endowed with a greater intelligence than his fellows, and therefore the possessor of better developed powers of imagination. To him the expedition savored of adventure, and so appealed, strongly. With Taglat there was another incentive – a secret and sinister incentive, which, had Tarzan of the Apes had knowledge of it, would have sent him at the other's throat in jealous rage.

Taglat was no longer young; but he was still a formidable beast, mightily muscled, cruel, and, because of his greater experience, crafty and cunning. Too, he was of giant proportions, the very weight of his huge bulk serving ofttimes to discount in his favor the superior agility of a younger antagonist.

He was of a morose and sullen disposition that marked him even among his frowning fellows, where such characteristics are the rule rather than the exception, and, though Tarzan did not guess it, he hated the ape-man with a ferocity that he was able to hide only because the dominant spirit of the nobler creature had inspired within him a species of dread which was as powerful as it was inexplicable to him.

These two, then, were to be Tarzan's companions upon his return to the village of Achmet Zek. As they set off, the balance of the tribe vouchsafed them but a parting stare, and then resumed the serious business of feeding.

Tarzan found difficulty in keeping the minds of his fellows set upon the purpose of their adventure, for the mind of an ape lacks the power of long-sustained concentration. To set out upon a long journey, with a definite destination in view, is one thing, to remember that purpose and keep it uppermost in one's mind continually is quite another. There are so many things to distract one's attention along the way.

Chulk was, at first, for rushing rapidly ahead as though the village of the raiders lay but an hour's march before them instead of several days; but within a few minutes a fallen tree attracted his attention with its suggestion of rich and succulent forage beneath, and when Tarzan, missing him, returned in search, he found Chulk squatting beside the rotting bole, from beneath which he was assiduously engaged in digging out the grubs and beetles, whose kind form a considerable proportion of the diet of the apes.

Unless Tarzan desired to fight there was nothing to do but wait until Chulk had exhausted the storehouse, and this he did, only to discover that Taglat was now missing. After a considerable search, he found that worthy gentleman contemplating the sufferings of an injured rodent he had pounced upon. He would sit in apparent indifference, gazing in another direction, while the crippled creature wriggled slowly and painfully away from him, and then, just as his victim felt assured of escape, he would reach out a giant palm and slam it down upon the fugitive. Again and again he repeated this operation, until, tiring of the sport, he ended the sufferings of his plaything by devouring it.

Such were the exasperating causes of delay which retarded Tarzan's return journey toward the village of Achmet Zek; but the ape-man was patient, for in his mind was a plan which necessitated the presence of Chulk and Taglat when he should have arrived at his destination.

It was not always an easy thing to maintain in the vacillating minds of the anthropoids a sustained interest in their venture. Chulk was wearying of the continued marching and the infrequency and short duration of the rests. He would gladly have abandoned this search for adventure had not Tarzan continually filled his mind with alluring pictures of the great stores of food which were to be found in the village of Tarmangani.

Taglat nursed his secret purpose to better advantage than might have been expected of an ape, yet there were times when he, too, would have abandoned the adventure had not Tarzan cajoled him on.

It was mid-afternoon of a sultry, tropical day when the keen senses of the three warned them of the proximity of the Arab camp. Stealthily they approached, keeping to the dense tangle of growing things which made concealment easy to their uncanny jungle craft.

First came the giant ape-man, his smooth, brown skin glistening with the sweat of exertion in the close, hot confines of the jungle. Behind him crept Chulk and Taglat, grotesque and shaggy caricatures of their godlike leader.

Silently they made their way to the edge of the clearing which surrounded the palisade, and here they clambered into the lower branches of a large tree overlooking the village occupied by the enemy, the better to spy upon his goings and comings.

A horseman, white burnoosed, rode out through the gateway of the village. Tarzan, whispering to Chulk and Taglat to remain where they were, swung, monkey-like, through the trees in the direction of the trail the Arab was riding. From one jungle giant to the next he sped with the rapidity of a squirrel and the silence of a ghost.

The Arab rode slowly onward, unconscious of the danger hovering in the trees behind him. The ape-man made a slight detour and increased his speed until he had reached a point upon the trail in advance of the horseman. Here he halted upon a leafy bough which overhung the narrow, jungle trail. On came the victim, humming a wild air of the great desert land of the north. Above him poised the savage brute that was today bent upon the destruction of a human life – the same creature who a few months before, had occupied his seat in the House of Lords at London, a respected and distinguished member of that august body.

The Arab passed beneath the overhanging bough, there was a slight rustling of the leaves above, the horse snorted and plunged as a brown-skinned creature dropped upon its rump. A pair of mighty arms encircled the Arab and he was dragged from his saddle to the trail.

Ten minutes later the ape-man, carrying the outer garments of an Arab bundled beneath an arm, rejoined his companions. He exhibited his trophies to them, explaining in low gutturals the details of his exploit. Chulk and Taglat fingered the fabrics, smelled of them, and, placing them to their ears, tried to listen to them.

Then Tarzan led them back through the jungle to the trail, where the three hid themselves and waited. Nor had they long to wait before two of Achmet Zek's blacks, clothed in habiliments similar to their master's, came down the trail on foot, returning to the camp.

One moment they were laughing and talking together – the next they lay stretched in death upon the trail, three mighty engines of destruction bending over them. Tarzan removed their outer garments as he had removed those of his first victim, and again retired with Chulk and Taglat to the greater seclusion of the tree they had first selected.

Here the ape-man arranged the garments upon his shaggy fellows and himself, until, at a distance, it might have appeared that three white-robed Arabs squatted silently among the branches of the forest.

Until dark they remained where they were, for from his point of vantage, Tarzan could view the enclosure within the palisade. He marked the position of the hut in which he had first discovered the scent spoor of the she he sought. He saw the two sentries standing before its doorway, and he located the habitation of Achmet Zek, where something told him he would most likely find the missing pouch and pebbles.

Chulk and Taglat were, at first, greatly interested in their wonderful raiment. They fingered the fabric, smelled of it, and regarded each other intently with every mark of satisfaction and pride. Chulk, a humorist in his way, stretched forth a long and hairy arm, and grasping the hood of Taglat's burnoose pulled it down over the latter's eyes, extinguishing him, snuffer-like, as it were.

The older ape, pessimistic by nature, recognized no such thing as humor. Creatures laid their paws upon him for but two things – to search for fleas and to attack. The pulling of the Tarmangani-scented thing about his head and eyes could not be for the performance of the former act; therefore it must be the latter. He was attacked! Chulk had attacked him.

With a snarl he was at the other's throat, not even waiting to lift the woolen veil which obscured his vision. Tarzan leaped upon the two, and swaying and toppling upon their insecure perch the three great beasts tussled and snapped at one another until the ape-man finally succeeded in separating the enraged anthropoids.

As apology is unknown to these savage progenitors of man, and explanation a laborious and usually futile process, Tarzan bridged the dangerous gulf by distracting their attention from their altercation to a consideration of their plans for the immediate future. Accustomed to frequent arguments in which more hair than blood is wasted, the apes speedily forget such trivial encounters, and presently Chulk and Taglat were again squatting in close proximity to each other and peaceful repose, awaiting the moment when the ape-man should lead them into the village of the Tarmangani.

It was long after darkness had fallen, that Tarzan led his companions from their hiding place in the tree to the ground and around the palisade to the far side of the village.

Gathering the skirts of his burnoose, beneath one arm, that his legs might have free action, the ape-man took a short running start, and scrambled to the top of the barrier. Fearing lest the apes should rend their garments to shreds in a similar attempt, he had directed them to wait below for him, and himself securely perched upon the summit of the palisade he unslung his spear and lowered one end of it to Chulk.

The ape seized it, and while Tarzan held tightly to the upper end, the anthropoid climbed quickly up the shaft until with one paw he grasped the top of the wall. To scramble then to Tarzan's side was the work of but an instant. In like manner Taglat was conducted to their sides, and a moment later the three dropped silently within the enclosure.

Tarzan led them first to the rear of the hut in which Jane Clayton was confined, where, through the roughly repaired aperture in the wall, he sought with his sensitive nostrils for proof that the she he had come for was within.

Chulk and Taglat, their hairy faces pressed close to that of the patrician, sniffed with him. Each caught the scent spoor of the woman within, and each reacted according to his temperament and his habits of thought.

It left Chulk indifferent. The she was for Tarzan – all that he desired was to bury his snout in the foodstuffs of the Tarmangani. He had come to eat his fill without labor – Tarzan had told him that that should be his reward, and he was satisfied.

But Taglat's wicked, bloodshot eyes, narrowed to the realization of the nearing fulfillment of his carefully nursed plan. It is true that sometimes during the several days that had elapsed since they had set out upon their expedition it had been difficult for Taglat to hold his idea uppermost in his mind, and on several occasions he had completely forgotten it, until Tarzan, by a chance word, had recalled it to him, but, for an ape, Taglat had done well.

Now, he licked his chops, and he made a sickening, sucking noise with his flabby lips as he drew in his breath.

Satisfied that the she was where he had hoped to find her, Tarzan led his apes toward the tent of Achmet Zek. A passing Arab and two slaves saw them, but the night was dark and the white burnooses hid the hairy limbs of the apes and the giant figure of their leader, so that the three, by squatting down as though in conversation, were passed by, unsuspected. To the rear of the tent they made their way. Within, Achmet Zek conversed with several of his lieutenants. Without, Tarzan listened.

CHAPTER SEVENTEEN

The Deadly Peril of Jane Clayton

Lieutenant Albert Werper, terrified by contemplation of the fate which might await him at Adis Abeba, cast about for some scheme of escape, but after the black Mugambi had eluded their vigilance the Abyssinians redoubled their precautions to prevent Werper following the lead of the Negro.

For some time Werper entertained the idea of bribing Abdul Mourak with a portion of the contents of the pouch; but fearing that the man would demand all the gems as the price of liberty, the Belgian, influenced by avarice, sought another avenue from his dilemma.

It was then that there dawned upon him the possibility of the success of a different course which would still leave him in possession of the jewels, while at the same time satisfying the greed of the Abyssinian with the conviction that he had obtained all that Werper had to offer.

And so it was that a day or so after Mugambi had disappeared, Werper asked for an audience with Abdul Mourak. As the Belgian entered the presence of his captor the scowl upon the features of the latter boded ill for any hope which Werper might entertain, still he fortified himself by recalling the common weakness of mankind, which permits the most inflexible of natures to bend to the consuming desire for wealth.

Abdul Mourak eyed him, frowningly. "What do you want now?" he asked.

"My liberty," replied Werper.

The Abyssinian sneered. "And you disturbed me thus to tell me what any fool might know," he said.

"I can pay for it," said Werper.

Abdul Mourak laughed loudly. "Pay for it?" he cried. "What with – the rags that you have upon your back? Or, perhaps you are concealing beneath your coat a thousand pounds of ivory. Get out! You are a fool. Do not bother me again or I shall have you whipped."

But Werper persisted. His liberty and perhaps his life depended upon his success.

"Listen to me," he pleaded. "If I can give you as much gold as ten men may carry will you promise that I shall be conducted in safety to the nearest English commissioner?"

"As much gold as ten men may carry!" repeated Abdul Mourak. "You are crazy. Where have you so much gold as that?"

"I know where it is hid," said Werper. "Promise, and I will lead you to it – if ten loads is enough?"

Abdul Mourak had ceased to laugh. He was eyeing the Belgian intently. The fellow seemed sane enough – yet ten loads of gold! It was preposterous. The Abyssinian thought in silence for a moment.

"Well, and if I promise," he said. "How far is this gold?"

"A long week's march to the south," replied Werper.

"And if we do not find it where you say it is, do you realize what your punishment will be?"

"If it is not there I will forfeit my life," replied the Belgian. "I know it is there, for I saw it buried with my own eyes. And more – there are not only ten loads, but as many as fifty men may carry. It is all yours if you will promise to see me safely delivered into the protection of the English."

"You will stake your life against the finding of the gold?" asked Abdul.

Werper assented with a nod.

"Very well," said the Abyssinian, "I promise, and even if there be but five loads you shall have your freedom; but until the gold is in my possession you remain a prisoner."

"I am satisfied," said Werper. "Tomorrow we start?"

Abdul Mourak nodded, and the Belgian returned to his guards. The following day the Abyssinian soldiers were surprised to receive an order which turned their faces from the northeast to the south. And so it happened that upon the very night that Tarzan and the two apes entered the village of the raiders, the Abyssinians camped but a few miles to the east of the same spot.

While Werper dreamed of freedom and the unmolested enjoyment of the fortune in his stolen pouch, and Abdul Mourak lay awake in greedy contemplation of the fifty loads of gold which lay but a few days farther to the south of him, Achmet Zek gave orders to his lieutenants that they should prepare a force of fighting men and carriers to proceed to the ruins of the Englishman's DOUAR on the morrow and bring back the fabulous fortune which his renegade lieutenant had told him was buried there.

And as he delivered his instructions to those within, a silent listener crouched without his tent, waiting for the time when he might enter in safety and prosecute his search for the missing pouch and the pretty pebbles that had caught his fancy.

At last the swarthy companions of Achmet Zek quitted his tent, and the leader went with them to smoke a pipe with one of their number, leaving his own silken habitation unguarded. Scarcely had they left the interior when a knife blade was thrust through the fabric of the rear wall, some six feet above the ground, and a swift downward stroke opened an entrance to those who waited beyond.

Through the opening stepped the ape-man, and close behind him came the huge Chulk; but Taglat did not follow them. Instead he turned and slunk through the darkness toward the hut where the she who had arrested his brutish interest lay securely bound. Before the doorway the sentries sat upon their haunches, conversing in monotones. Within, the young woman lay upon a filthy sleeping mat, resigned, through utter hopelessness to whatever fate lay in store for her until the opportunity arrived which would permit her to free herself by the only means which now seemed even remotely possible – the hitherto detested act of self-destruction.

Creeping silently toward the sentries, a white-burnoosed figure approached the shadows at one end of the hut. The meager intellect of the creature denied it the advantage it might have taken of its disguise. Where it could have walked boldly to the very sides of the sentries, it chose rather to sneak upon them, unseen, from the rear.

It came to the corner of the hut and peered around. The sentries were but a few paces away; but the ape did not dare expose himself, even for an instant, to those feared and hated thunder-sticks which the Tarmangani knew so well how to use, if there were another and safer method of attack.

Taglat wished that there was a tree nearby from the over-hanging branches of which he might spring upon his unsuspecting prey; but, though there was no tree, the idea gave birth to a plan. The eaves of the hut were just above the heads of the sentries – from them he could leap upon the Tarmangani, unseen. A quick snap of those mighty jaws would dispose of one of them before the other realized that they were attacked, and the second would fall an easy prey to the strength, agility and ferocity of a second quick charge.

Taglat withdrew a few paces to the rear of the hut, gathered himself for the effort, ran quickly forward and leaped high into the air. He struck the roof directly above the rear wall of the hut, and the structure, reinforced by the wall beneath, held his enormous weight for an instant, then he moved forward a step, the roof sagged, the thatching parted and the great anthropoid shot through into the interior.

The sentries, hearing the crashing of the roof poles, leaped to their feet and rushed into the hut. Jane Clayton tried to roll aside as the great form lit upon the floor so close to her that one foot pinned her clothing to the ground.

The ape, feeling the movement beside him, reached down and gathered the girl in the hollow of one mighty arm. The burnoose covered the hairy body so that Jane Clayton believed that a human arm supported her, and from the extremity of hopelessness a great hope sprang into her breast that at last she was in the keeping of a rescuer.

The two sentries were now within the hut, but hesitating because of doubt as to the nature of the cause of the disturbance. Their eyes, not yet accustomed to the darkness of the interior, told them nothing, nor did they hear any sound, for the ape stood silently awaiting their attack.

Seeing that they stood without advancing, and realizing that, handicapped as he was by the weight of the she, he could put up but a poor battle, Taglat elected to risk a sudden break for liberty. Lowering his head, he charged straight for the two sentries who blocked the doorway. The impact of his mighty shoulders bowled them over upon their backs, and before they could scramble to their feet, the ape was gone, darting in the shadows of the huts toward the palisade at the far end of the village.

The speed and strength of her rescuer filled Jane Clayton with wonder. Could it be that Tarzan had survived the bullet of the Arab? Who else in all the jungle could bear the weight of a grown woman as lightly as he who held her? She spoke his name; but there was no response. Still she did not give up hope.

At the palisade the beast did not even hesitate. A single mighty leap carried it to the top, where it poised but for an instant before dropping to the ground upon the opposite side. Now the girl was almost positive that she was safe in the arms of her husband, and when the ape took to the trees and bore her swiftly into the jungle, as Tarzan had done at other times in the past, belief became conviction.

In a little moonlit glade, a mile or so from the camp of the raiders, her rescuer halted and dropped her to the ground. His roughness surprised her, but still she had no doubts. Again she called him by name, and at the same instant the ape, fretting under the restraints of the unaccustomed garments of the Tarmangani, tore the burnoose from him, revealing to the eyes of the horror-struck woman the hideous face and hairy form of a giant anthropoid.

With a piteous wail of terror, Jane Clayton swooned, while, from the concealment of a nearby bush, Numa, the lion, eyed the pair hungrily and licked his chops.

Tarzan, entering the tent of Achmet Zek, searched the interior thoroughly. He tore the bed to pieces and scattered the contents of box and bag about the floor. He investigated whatever his eyes discovered, nor did those keen organs overlook a single article within the habitation of the raider chief; but no pouch or pretty pebbles rewarded his thoroughness.

Satisfied at last that his belongings were not in the possession of Achmet Zek, unless they were on the person of the chief himself, Tarzan decided to secure the person of the she before further prosecuting his search for the pouch.

Motioning for Chulk to follow him, he passed out of the tent by the same way that he had entered it, and walking boldly through the village, made directly for the hut where Jane Clayton had been imprisoned.

He noted with surprise the absence of Taglat, whom he had expected to find awaiting him outside the tent of Achmet Zek; but, accustomed as he was to the unreliability of apes, he gave no serious attention to the present defection of his surly companion. So long as Taglat did not cause interference with his plans, Tarzan was indifferent to his absence.

As he approached the hut, the ape-man noticed that a crowd had collected about the entrance. He could see that the men who composed it were much excited, and fearing lest Chulk's disguise should prove inadequate to the concealment of his true identity in the face of so many observers, he commanded the ape to betake himself to the far end of the village, and there await him.

As Chulk waddled off, keeping to the shadows, Tarzan advanced boldly toward the excited group before the doorway of the hut. He mingled with the blacks and the Arabs in an endeavor to learn the cause of the commotion, in his interest forgetting that he alone of the assemblage carried a spear, a bow and arrows, and thus might become an object of suspicious attention.

Shouldering his way through the crowd he approached the doorway, and had almost reached it when one of the Arabs laid a hand upon his shoulder, crying: "Who is this?" at the same time snatching back the hood from the ape-man's face.

Tarzan of the Apes in all his savage life had never been accustomed to pause in argument with an antagonist. The primitive instinct of self-preservation acknowledges many arts and wiles; but argument is not one of them, nor did he now waste precious time in an attempt to convince the raiders that he was not a wolf in sheep's clothing. Instead he had his unmasker by the throat ere the man's words had scarce quitted his lips, and hurling him from side to side brushed away those who would have swarmed upon him.

Using the Arab as a weapon, Tarzan forced his way quickly to the doorway, and a moment later was within the hut. A hasty examination revealed the fact that it was empty, and his sense of smell discovered, too, the scent spoor of Taglat, the ape. Tarzan uttered a low, ominous growl. Those who were pressing forward at the doorway to seize him, fell back as the savage notes of the bestial challenge smote upon their ears. They looked at one another in surprise and consternation. A man had entered the hut alone, and yet with their own ears they had heard the voice of a wild beast within. What could it mean? Had a lion or a leopard sought sanctuary in the interior, unbeknown to the sentries?

Tarzan's quick eyes discovered the opening in the roof, through which Taglat had fallen. He guessed that the ape had either come or gone by way of the break, and while the Arabs hesitated without, he sprang, catlike, for the opening, grasped the top of the wall and clambered out upon the roof, dropping instantly to the ground at the rear of the hut.

When the Arabs finally mustered courage to enter the hut, after firing several volleys through the walls, they found the interior deserted. At the same time Tarzan, at the far end of the village, sought for Chulk; but the ape was nowhere to be found.

Robbed of his she, deserted by his companions, and as much in ignorance as ever as to the whereabouts of his pouch and pebbles, it was an angry Tarzan who climbed the palisade and vanished into the darkness of the jungle.

For the present he must give up the search for his pouch, since it would be paramount to self-destruction to enter the Arab camp now while all its inhabitants were aroused and upon the alert.

In his escape from the village, the ape-man had lost the spoor of the fleeing Taglat, and now he circled widely through the forest in an endeavor to again pick it up.

Chulk had remained at his post until the cries and shots of the Arabs had filled his simple soul with terror, for above all things the ape folk fear the thunder-sticks of the Tarmangani; then he had clambered nimbly over the palisade, tearing his burnoose in the effort, and fled into the depths of the jungle, grumbling and scolding as he went.

Tarzan, roaming the jungle in search of the trail of Taglat and the she, traveled swiftly. In a little moonlit glade ahead of him the great ape was bending over the prostrate form of the woman Tarzan sought. The beast was tearing at the bonds that confined her ankles and wrists, pulling and gnawing upon the cords.

The course the ape-man was taking would carry him but a short distance to the right of them, and though he could not have seen them the wind was bearing down from them to him, carrying their scent spoor strongly toward him.

A moment more and Jane Clayton's safety might have been assured, even though Numa, the lion, was already gathering himself in preparation for a charge; but Fate, already all too cruel, now outdid herself – the wind veered suddenly for a few moments, the scent spoor that would have led the ape-man to the girl's side was wafted in the opposite direction; Tarzan passed within fifty yards of the tragedy that was being enacted in the glade, and the opportunity was gone beyond recall.

CHAPTER EIGHTEEN

The Fight for the Treasure

It was morning before Tarzan could bring himself to a realization of the possibility of failure of his quest, and even then he would only admit that success was but delayed. He would eat and sleep, and then set forth again. The jungle was wide; but wide too were the experience and cunning of Tarzan. Taglat might travel far; but Tarzan would find him in the end, though he had to search every tree in the mighty forest.

Soliloquizing thus, the ape-man followed the spoor of Bara, the deer, the unfortunate upon which he had decided to satisfy his hunger. For half an hour the trail led the ape-man toward the east along a well-marked game path, when suddenly, to the stalker's astonishment, the quarry broke into sight, racing madly back along the narrow way straight toward the hunter.

Tarzan, who had been following along the trail, leaped so quickly to the concealing verdure at the side that the deer was still unaware of the presence of an enemy in this direction, and while the animal was still some distance away, the ape-man swung into the lower branches of the tree which overhung the trail. There he crouched, a savage beast of prey, awaiting the coming of its victim.

What had frightened the deer into so frantic a retreat, Tarzan did not know – Numa, the lion, perhaps, or Sheeta, the panther; but whatsoever it was mattered little to Tarzan of the Apes – he was ready and willing to defend his kill against any other denizen of the jungle. If he were unable to do it by means of physical prowess, he had at his command another and a greater power – his shrewd intelligence.

And so, on came the running deer, straight into the jaws of death. The ape-man turned so that his back was toward the approaching animal. He poised with bent knees upon the gently swaying limb above the trail, timing with keen ears the nearing hoof beats of frightened Bara.

In a moment the victim flashed beneath the limb and at the same instant the ape-man above sprang out and down upon its back. The weight of the man's body carried the deer to the ground. It stumbled forward once in a futile effort to rise, and then mighty muscles dragged its head far back, gave the neck a vicious wrench, and Bara was dead.

Quick had been the killing, and equally quick were the ape-man's subsequent actions, for who might know what manner of killer pursued Bara, or how close at hand he might be? Scarce had the neck of the victim snapped than the carcass was hanging over one of Tarzan's broad shoulders, and an instant later the ape-man was perched once more among the lower branches of a tree above the trail, his keen, gray eyes scanning the pathway down which the deer had fled.

Nor was it long before the cause of Bara's fright became evident to Tarzan, for presently came the unmistakable sounds of approaching horsemen. Dragging his kill after him the ape-man ascended to the middle terrace, and settling himself comfortably in the crotch of a tree where he could still view the trail beneath, cut a juicy steak from the deer's loin, and burying his strong, white teeth in the hot flesh proceeded to enjoy the fruits of his prowess and his cunning.

Nor did he neglect the trail beneath while he satisfied his hunger. His sharp eyes saw the muzzle of the leading horse as it came into view around a bend in the tortuous trail, and one by one they scrutinized the riders as they passed beneath him in single file.

Among them came one whom Tarzan recognized, but so schooled was the ape-man in the control of his emotions that no slightest change of expression, much less any hysterical demonstration that might have revealed his presence, betrayed the fact of his inward excitement.

Beneath him, as unconscious of his presence as were the Abyssinians before and behind him, rode Albert Werper, while the ape-man scrutinized the Belgian for some sign of the pouch which he had stolen.

As the Abyssinians rode toward the south, a giant figure hovered ever upon their trail – a huge, almost naked white man, who carried the bloody carcass of a deer upon his shoulders, for Tarzan knew that he might not have another opportunity to hunt for some time if he were to follow the Belgian.

To endeavor to snatch him from the midst of the armed horsemen, not even Tarzan would attempt other than in the last extremity, for the way of the wild is the way of caution and cunning, unless they be aroused to rashness by pain or anger.

So the Abyssinians and the Belgian marched southward and Tarzan of the Apes swung silently after them through the swaying branches of the middle terrace.

A two days' march brought them to a level plain beyond which lay mountains – a plain which Tarzan remembered and which aroused within him vague half memories and strange longings. Out upon the plain the horsemen rode, and at a safe distance behind them crept the ape-man, taking advantage of such cover as the ground afforded.

Beside a charred pile of timbers the Abyssinians halted, and Tarzan, sneaking close and concealing himself in nearby shrubbery, watched them in wonderment. He saw them digging up the earth, and he wondered if they had hidden meat there in the past and now had come for it. Then he recalled how he had buried his pretty pebbles, and the suggestion that had caused him to do it. They were digging for the things the blacks had buried here!

Presently he saw them uncover a dirty, yellow object, and he witnessed the joy of Werper and of Abdul Mourak as the grimy object was exposed to view. One by one they unearthed many similar pieces, all of the same uniform, dirty yellow, until a pile of them lay upon the ground, a pile which Abdul Mourak fondled and petted in an ecstasy of greed.

Something stirred in the ape-man's mind as he looked long upon the golden ingots. Where had he seen such before? What were they? Why did these Tarmangani covet them so greatly? To whom did they belong?

He recalled the black men who had buried them. The things must be theirs. Werper was stealing them as he had stolen Tarzan's pouch of pebbles. The ape-man's eyes blazed in anger. He would like to find the black men and lead them against these thieves. He wondered where their village might be.

As all these things ran through the active mind, a party of men moved out of the forest at the edge of the plain and advanced toward the ruins of the burned bungalow.

Abdul Mourak, always watchful, was the first to see them, but already they were halfway across the open. He called to his men to mount and hold themselves in readiness, for in the heart of Africa who may know whether a strange host be friend or foe?

Werper, swinging into his saddle, fastened his eyes upon the newcomers, then, white and trembling he turned toward Abdul Mourak.

"It is Achmet Zek and his raiders," he whispered. "They are come for the gold."

It must have been at about the same instant that Achmet Zek discovered the pile of yellow ingots and realized the actuality of what he had already feared since first his eyes had alighted upon the party beside the ruins of the Englishman's bungalow. Someone had forestalled him – another had come for the treasure ahead of him.

The Arab was crazed by rage. Recently everything had gone against him. He had lost the jewels, the Belgian, and for the second time he had lost the Englishwoman. Now some one had come to rob him of this treasure which he had thought as safe from disturbance here as though it never had been mined.

He cared not whom the thieves might be. They would not give up the gold without a battle, of that he was certain, and with a wild whoop and a command to his followers, Achmet Zek put spurs to his horse and dashed down upon the Abyssinians, and after him, waving their long guns above their heads, yelling and cursing, came his motley horde of cut-throat followers.

The men of Abdul Mourak met them with a volley which emptied a few saddles, and then the raiders were among them, and sword, pistol and musket, each was doing its most hideous and bloody work.

Achmet Zek, spying Werper at the first charge, bore down upon the Belgian, and the latter, terrified by contemplation of the fate he deserved, turned his horse's head and dashed madly away in an effort to escape. Shouting to a lieutenant to take command, and urging him upon pain of death to dispatch the Abyssinians and bring the gold back to his camp, Achmet Zek set off across the plain in pursuit of the Belgian, his wicked nature unable to forego the pleasures of revenge, even at the risk of sacrificing the treasure.

As the pursued and the pursuer raced madly toward the distant forest the battle behind them raged with bloody savageness. No quarter was asked or given by either the ferocious Abyssinians or the murderous cut-throats of Achmet Zek.

From the concealment of the shrubbery Tarzan watched the sanguinary conflict which so effectually surrounded him that he found no loop-hole through which he might escape to follow Werper and the Arab chief.

The Abyssinians were formed in a circle which included Tarzan's position, and around and into them galloped the yelling raiders, now darting away, now charging in to deliver thrusts and cuts with their curved swords.

Numerically the men of Achmet Zek were superior, and slowly but surely the soldiers of Menelek were being exterminated. To Tarzan the result was immaterial. He watched with but a single purpose – to escape the ring of blood-mad fighters and be away after the Belgian and his pouch.

When he had first discovered Werper upon the trail where he had slain Bara, he had thought that his eyes must be playing him false, so certain had he been that the thief had been slain and devoured by Numa; but after following the detachment for two days, with his keen eyes always upon the Belgian, he no longer doubted the identity of the man, though he was put to it to explain the identity of the mutilated corpse he had supposed was the man he sought.

As he crouched in hiding among the unkempt shrubbery which so short a while since had been the delight and pride of the wife he no longer recalled, an Arab and an Abyssinian wheeled their mounts close to his position as they slashed at each other with their swords.

Step by step the Arab beat back his adversary until the latter's horse all but trod upon the ape-man, and then a vicious cut clove the black warrior's skull, and the corpse toppled backward almost upon Tarzan.

As the Abyssinian tumbled from his saddle the possibility of escape which was represented by the riderless horse electrified the ape-man to instant action. Before the frightened beast could gather himself for flight a naked giant was astride his back. A strong hand had grasped his bridle rein, and the surprised Arab discovered a new foe in the saddle of him, whom he had slain.

But this enemy wielded no sword, and his spear and bow remained upon his back. The Arab, recovered from his first surprise, dashed in with raised sword to annihilate this presumptuous stranger. He aimed a mighty blow at the ape-man's head, a blow which swung harmlessly through thin air as Tarzan ducked from its path, and then the Arab felt the other's horse brushing his leg, a great arm shot out and encircled his waist, and before he could recover himself he was dragged from his saddle, and forming a shield for his antagonist was borne at a mad run straight through the encircling ranks of his fellows.

Just beyond them he was tossed aside upon the ground, and the last he saw of his strange foeman the latter was galloping off across the plain in the direction of the forest at its farther edge.

For another hour the battle raged nor did it cease until the last of the Abyssinians lay dead upon the ground, or had galloped off toward the north in flight. But a handful of men escaped, among them Abdul Mourak.

The victorious raiders collected about the pile of golden ingots which the Abyssinians had uncovered, and there awaited the return of their leader. Their exultation was slightly tempered by the glimpse they had had of the strange apparition of the naked white man galloping away upon the horse of one of their foemen and carrying a companion who was now among them expatiating upon the superhuman strength of the ape-man. None of them there but was familiar with the name and fame of Tarzan of the Apes, and the fact that they had recognized the white giant as the ferocious enemy of the wrongdoers of the jungle, added to their terror, for they had been assured that Tarzan was dead.

Naturally superstitious, they fully believed that they had seen the disembodied spirit of the dead man, and now they cast fearful glances about them in expectation of the ghost's early return to the scene of the ruin they had inflicted upon him during their recent raid upon his home, and discussed in affrighted whispers the probable nature of the vengeance which the spirit would inflict upon them should he return to find them in possession of his gold.

As they conversed their terror grew, while from the concealment of the reeds along the river below them a small party of naked, black warriors watched their every move. From the heights beyond the river these black men had heard the noise of the conflict, and creeping warily down to the stream had forded it and advanced through the reeds until they were in a position to watch every move of the combatants.

For a half hour the raiders awaited Achmet Zek's return, their fear of the earlier return of the ghost of Tarzan constantly undermining their loyalty to and fear of their chief. Finally one among them voiced the desires of all when he announced that he intended riding forth toward the forest in search of Achmet Zek. Instantly every man of them sprang to his mount.

"The gold will be safe here," cried one. "We have killed the Abyssinians and there are no others to carry it away. Let us ride in search of Achmet Zek!"

And a moment later, amidst a cloud of dust, the raiders were galloping madly across the plain, and out from the concealment of the reeds along the river, crept a party of black warriors toward the spot where the golden ingots of Opar lay piled on the ground.

Werper had still been in advance of Achmet Zek when he reached the forest; but the latter, better mounted, was gaining upon him. Riding with the reckless courage of desperation the Belgian urged his mount to greater speed even within the narrow confines of the winding, game trail that the beast was following.

Behind him he could hear the voice of Achmet Zek crying to him to halt; but Werper only dug the spurs deeper into the bleeding sides of his panting mount. Two hundred yards within the forest a broken branch lay across the trail. It was a small thing that a horse might ordinarily take in his natural stride without noticing its presence; but Werper's horse was jaded, his feet were heavy with weariness, and as the branch caught between his front legs he stumbled, was unable to recover himself, and went down, sprawling in the trail.

Werper, going over his head, rolled a few yards farther on, scrambled to his feet and ran back. Seizing the reins he tugged to drag the beast to his feet; but the animal would not or could not rise, and as the Belgian cursed and struck at him, Achmet Zek appeared in view.

Instantly the Belgian ceased his efforts with the dying animal at his feet, and seizing his rifle, dropped behind the horse and fired at the oncoming Arab.

His bullet, going low, struck Achmet Zek's horse in the breast, bringing him down a hundred yards from where Werper lay preparing to fire a second shot.

The Arab, who had gone down with his mount, was standing astride him, and seeing the Belgian's strategic position behind his fallen horse, lost no time in taking up a similar one behind his own.

And there the two lay, alternately firing at and cursing each other, while from behind the Arab, Tarzan of the Apes approached to the edge of the forest. Here he heard the occasional shots of the duelists, and choosing the safer and swifter avenue of the forest branches to the uncertain transportation afforded by a half-broken Abyssinian pony, took to the trees.

Keeping to one side of the trail, the ape-man came presently to a point where he could look down in comparative safety upon the fighters. First one and then the other would partially raise himself above his breastwork of horseflesh, fire his weapon and immediately drop flat behind his shelter, where he would reload and repeat the act a moment later.

Werper had but little ammunition, having been hastily armed by Abdul Mourak from the body of one of the first of the Abyssinians who had fallen in the fight about the pile of ingots, and now he realized that soon he would have used his last bullet, and be at the mercy of the Arab – a mercy with which he was well acquainted.

Facing both death and despoilment of his treasure, the Belgian cast about for some plan of escape, and the only one that appealed to him as containing even a remote possibility of success hinged upon the chance of bribing Achmet Zek.

Werper had fired all but a single cartridge, when, during a lull in the fighting, he called aloud to his opponent.

"Achmet Zek," he cried, "Allah alone knows which one of us may leave our bones to rot where he lies upon this trail today if we keep up our foolish battle. You wish the contents of the pouch I wear about my waist, and I wish my life and my liberty even more than I do the jewels. Let us each, then, take that which he most desires and go our separate ways in peace. I will lay the pouch upon the carcass of my horse, where you may see it, and you, in turn, will lay your gun upon your horse, with butt toward me. Then I will go away, leaving the pouch to you, and you will let me go in safety. I want only my life, and my freedom."

The Arab thought in silence for a moment. Then he spoke. His reply was influenced by the fact that he had expended his last shot.

"Go your way, then," he growled, "leaving the pouch in plain sight behind you. See, I lay my gun thus, with the butt toward you. Go."

Werper removed the pouch from about his waist. Sorrowfully and affectionately he let his fingers press the hard outlines of the contents. Ah, if he could extract a little handful of the precious stones! But Achmet Zek was standing now, his eagle eyes commanding a plain view of the Belgian and his every act.

Regretfully Werper laid the pouch, its contents undisturbed, upon the body of his horse, rose, and taking his rifle with him, backed slowly down the trail until a turn hid him from the view of the watchful Arab.

Even then Achmet Zek did not advance, fearful as he was of some such treachery as he himself might have been guilty of under like circumstances; nor were his suspicions groundless, for the Belgian, no sooner had he passed out of the range of the Arab's vision, halted behind the bole of a tree, where he still commanded an unobstructed view of his dead horse and the pouch, and raising his rifle covered the spot where the other's body must appear when he came forward to seize the treasure.

But Achmet Zek was no fool to expose himself to the blackened honor of a thief and a murderer. Taking his long gun with him, he left the trail, entering the rank and tangled vegetation which walled it, and crawling slowly forward on hands and knees he paralleled the trail; but never for an instant was his body exposed to the rifle of the hidden assassin.

Thus Achmet Zek advanced until he had come opposite the dead horse of his enemy. The pouch lay there in full view, while a short distance along the trail, Werper waited in growing impatience and nervousness, wondering why the Arab did not come to claim his reward.

Presently he saw the muzzle of a rifle appear suddenly and mysteriously a few inches above the pouch, and before he could realize the cunning trick that the Arab had played upon him the sight of the weapon was adroitly hooked into the rawhide thong which formed the carrying strap of the pouch, and the latter was drawn quickly from his view into the dense foliage at the trail's side.

Not for an instant had the raider exposed a square inch of his body, and Werper dared not fire his one remaining shot unless every chance of a successful hit was in his favor.

Chuckling to himself, Achmet Zek withdrew a few paces farther into the jungle, for he was as positive that Werper was waiting nearby for a chance to pot him as though his eyes had penetrated the jungle trees to the figure of the hiding Belgian, fingering his rifle behind the bole of the buttressed giant.

Werper did not dare advance – his cupidity would not permit him to depart, and so he stood there, his rifle ready in his hands, his eyes watching the trail before him with catlike intensity.

But there was another who had seen the pouch and recognized it, who did advance with Achmet Zek, hovering above him, as silent and as sure as death itself, and as the Arab, finding a little spot less overgrown with bushes than he had yet encountered, prepared to gloat his eyes upon the contents of the pouch, Tarzan paused directly above him, intent upon the same object.

Wetting his thin lips with his tongue, Achmet Zek loosened the tie strings which closed the mouth of the pouch, and cupping one claw-like hand poured forth a portion of the contents into his palm.

A single look he took at the stones lying in his hand. His eyes narrowed, a curse broke from his lips, and he hurled the small objects upon the ground, disdainfully. Quickly he emptied the balance of the contents until he had scanned each separate stone, and as he dumped them all upon the ground and stamped upon them his rage grew until the muscles of his face worked in demon-like fury, and his fingers clenched until his nails bit into the flesh.

Above, Tarzan watched in wonderment. He had been curious to discover what all the pow-wow about his pouch had meant. He wanted to see what the Arab would do after the other had gone away, leaving the pouch behind him, and, having satisfied his curiosity, he would then have pounced upon Achmet Zek and taken the pouch and his pretty pebbles away from him, for did they not belong to Tarzan?

He saw the Arab now throw aside the empty pouch, and grasping his long gun by the barrel, clublike, sneak stealthily through the jungle beside the trail along which Werper had gone.

As the man disappeared from his view, Tarzan dropped to the ground and commenced gathering up the spilled contents of the pouch, and the moment that he obtained his first near view of the scattered pebbles he understood the rage of the Arab, for instead of the glittering and scintillating gems which had first caught and held the attention of the ape-man, the pouch now contained but a collection of ordinary river pebbles.

CHAPTER NINETEEN

Jane Clayton and the Beasts of the Jungle

MUGAMBI, AFTER HIS SUCCESSFUL break for liberty, had fallen upon hard times. His way had led him through a country with which he was unfamiliar, a jungle country in which he could find no water, and but little food, so that after several days of wandering he found himself so reduced in strength that he could barely drag himself along.

It was with growing difficulty that he found the strength necessary to construct a shelter by night wherein he might be reasonably safe from the large carnivora, and by day he still further exhausted his strength in digging for edible roots, and searching for water.

A few stagnant pools at considerable distances apart saved him from death by thirst; but his was a pitiable state when finally he stumbled by accident upon a large river in a country where fruit was abundant, and small game which he might bag by means of a combination of stealth, cunning, and a crude knob-stick which he had fashioned from a fallen limb.

Realizing that he still had a long march ahead of him before he could reach even the outskirts of the Waziri country, Mugambi wisely decided to remain where he was until he had recuperated his strength and health. A few days' rest would accomplish wonders for him, he knew, and he could ill afford to sacrifice his chances for a safe return by setting forth handicapped by weakness.

And so it was that he constructed a substantial thorn boma, and rigged a thatched shelter within it, where he might sleep by night in security, and from which he sallied forth by day to hunt the flesh which alone could return to his giant thews their normal prowess.

One day, as he hunted, a pair of savage eyes discovered him from the concealment of the branches of a great tree beneath which the black warrior passed. Bloodshot, wicked eyes they were, set in a fierce and hairy face.

They watched Mugambi make his little kill of a small rodent, and they followed him as he returned to his hut, their owner moving quietly through the trees upon the trail of the Negro.

The creature was Chulk, and he looked down upon the unconscious man more in curiosity than in hate. The wearing of the Arab burnoose which Tarzan had placed upon his person had aroused in the mind of the anthropoid a desire for similar mimicry of the Tarmangani. The burnoose, though, had obstructed his movements and proven such a nuisance that the ape had long since torn it from him and thrown it away.

Now, however, he saw a Gomangani arrayed in less cumbersome apparel – a loin cloth, a few copper ornaments and a feather headdress. These were more in line with Chulk's desires than a flowing robe which was constantly getting between one's legs, and catching upon every limb and bush along the leafy trail.

Chulk eyed the pouch, which, suspended over Mugambi's shoulder, swung beside his black hip. This took his fancy, for it was ornamented with feathers and a fringe, and so the ape hung about Mugambi's boma, waiting an opportunity to seize either by stealth or might some object of the black's apparel.

Nor was it long before the opportunity came. Feeling safe within his thorny enclosure, Mugambi was wont to stretch himself in the shade of his shelter during the heat of the day, and sleep in peaceful security until the declining sun carried with it the enervating temperature of midday.

Watching from above, Chulk saw the black warrior stretched thus in the unconsciousness of sleep one sultry afternoon. Creeping out upon an overhanging branch the anthropoid dropped to the ground within the boma. He approached the sleeper upon padded feet which gave forth no sound, and with an uncanny woodcraft that rustled not a leaf or a grass blade.

Pausing beside the man, the ape bent over and examined his belongings. Great as was the strength of Chulk there lay in the back of his little brain a something which deterred him from arousing the man to combat – a sense that is inherent in all the lower orders, a strange fear of man, that rules even the most powerful of the jungle creatures at times.

To remove Mugambi's loin cloth without awakening him would be impossible, and the only detachable things were the knob-stick and the pouch, which had fallen from the black's shoulder as he rolled in sleep.

Seizing these two articles, as better than nothing at all, Chulk retreated with haste, and every indication of nervous terror, to the safety of the tree from which he had dropped, and, still haunted by that indefinable terror which the close proximity of man awakened in his breast, fled precipitately through the jungle. Aroused by attack, or supported by the presence of another of his kind, Chulk could have braved the presence of a score of human beings, but alone – ah, that was a different matter – alone, and unenraged.

It was some time after Mugambi awoke that he missed the pouch. Instantly he was all excitement. What could have become of it? It had been at his side when he lay down to sleep – of that he was certain, for had he not pushed it from beneath him when its bulging bulk, pressing against his ribs, caused him discomfort? Yes, it had been there when he lay down to sleep. How then had it vanished?

Mugambi's savage imagination was filled with visions of the spirits of departed friends and enemies, for only to the machinations of such as these could he attribute the disappearance of his pouch and knob-stick in the first excitement of the discovery of their loss; but later and more careful investigation, such as his woodcraft made possible, revealed indisputable evidence of a more material explanation than his excited fancy and superstition had at first led him to accept.

In the trampled turf beside him was the faint impress of huge, manlike feet. Mugambi raised his brows as the truth dawned upon him. Hastily leaving the boma he searched in all directions about the enclosure for some further sign of the tell-tale spoor. He climbed trees and sought for evidence of the direction of the thief's flight; but the faint signs left by a wary ape who elects to travel through the trees eluded the woodcraft of Mugambi. Tarzan might have followed them; but no ordinary mortal could perceive them, or perceiving, translate.

The black, now strengthened and refreshed by his rest, felt ready to set out again for Waziri, and finding himself another knob-stick, turned his back upon the river and plunged into the mazes of the jungle.

As Taglat struggled with the bonds which secured the ankles and wrists of his captive, the great lion that eyed the two from behind a near-by clump of bushes wormed closer to his intended prey.

The ape's back was toward the lion. He did not see the broad head, fringed by its rough mane, protruding through the leafy wall. He could not know that the powerful hind paws were gathering close beneath the tawny belly preparatory to a sudden spring, and his first intimation of impending danger was the thunderous and triumphant roar which the charging lion could no longer suppress.

Scarce pausing for a backward glance, Taglat abandoned the unconscious woman and fled in the opposite direction from the horrid sound which had broken in so unexpected and terrifying a manner upon his startled ears; but the warning had come too late to save him, and the lion, in his second bound, alighted full upon the broad shoulders of the anthropoid.

As the great bull went down there was awakened in him to the full all the cunning, all the ferocity, all the physical prowess which obey the mightiest of the fundamental laws of nature, the law of self-preservation, and turning upon his back he closed with the carnivore in a death struggle so fearless and abandoned, that for a moment the great Numa himself may have trembled for the outcome.

Seizing the lion by the mane, Taglat buried his yellowed fangs deep in the monster's throat, growling hideously through the muffled gag of blood and hair. Mixed with the ape's voice the lion's roars of rage and pain reverberated through the jungle, till the lesser creatures of the wild, startled from their peaceful pursuits, scurried fearfully away.

Rolling over and over upon the turf the two battled with demoniac fury, until the colossal cat, by doubling his hind paws far up beneath his belly sank his talons deep into Taglat's chest, then, ripping downward with all his strength, Numa accomplished his design, and the disemboweled anthropoid, with a last spasmodic struggle, relaxed in limp and bloody dissolution beneath his titanic adversary.

Scrambling to his feet, Numa looked about quickly in all directions, as though seeking to detect the possible presence of other foes; but only the still and unconscious form of the girl, lying a few paces from him met his gaze, and with an angry growl he placed a forepaw upon the body of his kill and raising his head gave voice to his savage victory cry.

For another moment he stood with fierce eyes roving to and fro about the clearing. At last they halted for a second time upon the girl. A low growl rumbled from the lion's throat. His lower jaw rose and fell, and the slaver drooled and dripped upon the dead face of Taglat.

Like two yellow-green augurs, wide and unblinking, the terrible eyes remained fixed upon Jane Clayton. The erect and majestic pose of the great frame shrank suddenly into a sinister crouch as, slowly and gently as one who treads on eggs, the devil-faced cat crept forward toward the girl.

Beneficent Fate maintained her in happy unconsciousness of the dread presence sneaking stealthily upon her. She did not know when the lion paused at her side. She did not hear the sniffing of his nostrils as he smelled about her. She did not feel the heat of the fetid breath upon her face, nor the dripping of the saliva from the frightful jaws half opened so close above her.

Finally the lion lifted a forepaw and turned the body of the girl half over, then he stood again eyeing her as though still undetermined whether life was extinct or not. Some noise or odor from the nearby jungle attracted his attention for a moment. His eyes did not again return to Jane Clayton, and presently he left her, walked over to the remains of Taglat, and crouching down upon his kill with his back toward the girl, proceeded to devour the ape.

It was upon this scene that Jane Clayton at last opened her eyes. Inured to danger, she maintained her self-possession in the face of the startling surprise which her new-found consciousness revealed to her. She neither cried out nor moved a muscle, until she had taken in every detail of the scene which lay within the range of her vision.

She saw that the lion had killed the ape, and that he was devouring his prey less than fifty feet from where she lay; but what could she do? Her hands and feet were bound. She must wait then, in what patience she could command, until Numa had eaten and digested the ape, when, without doubt, he would return to feast upon her, unless, in the meantime, the dread hyenas should discover her, or some other of the numerous prowling carnivora of the jungle.

As she lay tormented by these frightful thoughts, she suddenly became conscious that the bonds at her wrists and ankles no longer hurt her, and then of the fact that her hands were separated, one lying upon either side of her, instead of both being confined at her back.

Wonderingly she moved a hand. What miracle had been performed? It was not bound! Stealthily and noiselessly she moved her other limbs, only to discover that she was free. She could not know how the thing had happened, that Taglat, gnawing upon them for sinister purposes of his own, had cut them through but an instant before Numa had frightened him from his victim.

For a moment Jane Clayton was overwhelmed with joy and thanksgiving; but only for a moment. What good was her new-found liberty in the face of the frightful beast crouching so close beside her? If she could have had this chance under different conditions, how happily she would have taken advantage of it; but now it was given to her when escape was practically impossible.

The nearest tree was a hundred feet away, the lion less than fifty. To rise and attempt to reach the safety of those tantalizing branches would be but to invite instant destruction, for Numa would doubtless be too jealous of this future meal to permit it to escape with ease. And yet, too, there was another possibility – a chance which hinged entirely upon the unknown temper of the great beast.

His belly already partially filled, he might watch with indifference the departure of the girl; yet could she afford to chance so improbable a contingency? She doubted it. Upon the other hand she was no more minded to allow this frail opportunity for life to entirely elude her without taking or attempting to take some advantage from it.

She watched the lion narrowly. He could not see her without turning his head more than halfway around. She would attempt a ruse. Silently she rolled over in the direction of the nearest tree, and away from the lion, until she lay again in the same position in which Numa had left her, but a few feet farther from him.

Here she lay breathless watching the lion; but the beast gave no indication that he had heard aught to arouse his suspicions. Again she rolled over, gaining a few more feet and again she lay in rigid contemplation of the beast's back.

During what seemed hours to her tense nerves, Jane Clayton continued these tactics, and still the lion fed on in apparent unconsciousness that his second prey was escaping him. Already the girl was but a few paces from the tree – a moment more and she would be close enough to chance springing to her feet, throwing caution aside and making a sudden, bold dash for safety. She was halfway over in her turn, her face away from the lion, when he suddenly turned his great head and fastened his eyes upon her. He saw her roll over upon her side away from him, and then her eyes were turned again toward him, and the cold sweat broke from the girl's every pore as she realized that with life almost within her grasp, death had found her out.

For a long time neither the girl nor the lion moved. The beast lay motionless, his head turned upon his shoulders and his glaring eyes fixed upon the rigid victim, now nearly fifty yards away. The girl stared back straight into those cruel orbs, daring not to move even a muscle.

The strain upon her nerves was becoming so unbearable that she could scarcely restrain a growing desire to scream, when Numa deliberately turned back to the business of feeding; but his back-layed ears attested a sinister regard for the actions of the girl behind him.

Realizing that she could not again turn without attracting his immediate and perhaps fatal attention, Jane Clayton resolved to risk all in one last attempt to reach the tree and clamber to the lower branches.

Gathering herself stealthily for the effort, she leaped suddenly to her feet, but almost simultaneously the lion sprang up, wheeled and with wide-distended jaws and terrific roars, charged swiftly down upon her.

Those who have spent lifetimes hunting the big game of Africa will tell you that scarcely any other creature in the world attains the speed of a charging lion. For the short distance that the great cat can maintain it, it resembles nothing more closely than the onrushing of a giant locomotive under full speed, and so, though the distance that Jane Clayton must cover was relatively small, the terrific speed of the lion rendered her hopes of escape almost negligible.

Yet fear can work wonders, and though the upward spring of the lion as he neared the tree into which she was scrambling brought his talons in contact with her boots she eluded his raking grasp, and as he hurtled against the bole of her sanctuary, the girl drew herself into the safety of the branches above his reach.

For some time the lion paced, growling and moaning, beneath the tree in which Jane Clayton crouched, panting and trembling. The girl was a prey to the nervous reaction from the frightful ordeal through which she had so recently passed, and in her overwrought state it seemed that never again should she dare descend to the ground among the fearsome dangers which infested the broad stretch of jungle that she knew must lie between herself and the nearest village of her faithful Waziri.

It was almost dark before the lion finally quit the clearing, and even had his place beside the remnants of the mangled ape not been immediately usurped by a pack of hyenas, Jane Clayton would scarcely have dared venture from her refuge in the face of impending night, and so she composed herself as best she could for the long and tiresome wait, until daylight might offer some means of escape from the dread vicinity in which she had witnessed such terrifying adventures.

Tired nature at last overcame even her fears, and she dropped into a deep slumber, cradled in a comparatively safe, though rather uncomfortable, position against the bole of the tree, and supported by two large branches which grew outward, almost horizontally, but a few inches apart.

The sun was high in the heavens when she at last awoke, and beneath her was no sign either of Numa or the hyenas. Only the clean-picked bones of the ape, scattered about the ground, attested the fact of what had transpired in this seemingly peaceful spot but a few hours before.

Both hunger and thirst assailed her now, and realizing that she must descend or die of starvation, she at last summoned courage to undertake the ordeal of continuing her journey through the jungle.

Descending from the tree, she set out in a southerly direction, toward the point where she believed the plains of Waziri lay, and though she knew that only ruin and desolation marked the spot where once her happy home had stood, she hoped that by coming to the broad plain she might eventually reach one of the numerous Waziri villages that were scattered over the surrounding country, or chance upon a roving band of these indefatigable huntsmen.

The day was half spent when there broke unexpectedly upon her startled ears the sound of a rifle shot not far ahead of her. As she paused to listen, this first shot was followed by another and another and another. What could it mean? The first explanation which sprung to her mind attributed the firing to an encounter between the Arab raiders and a party of Waziri; but as she did not know upon which side victory might rest, or whether she were behind friend or foe, she dared not advance nearer on the chance of revealing herself to an enemy.

After listening for several minutes she became convinced that no more than two or three rifles were engaged in the fight, since nothing approximating the sound of a volley reached her ears; but still she hesitated to approach, and at last, determining to take no chance, she climbed into the concealing foliage of a tree beside the trail she had been following and there fearfully awaited whatever might reveal itself.

As the firing became less rapid she caught the sound of men's voices, though she could distinguish no words, and at last the reports of the guns ceased, and she heard two men calling to each other in loud tones. Then there was a long silence which was finally broken by the stealthy padding of footfalls on the trail ahead of her, and in another moment a man appeared in view backing toward her, a rifle ready in his hands, and his eyes directed in careful watchfulness along the way that he had come.

Almost instantly Jane Clayton recognized the man as M. Jules Frecoult, who so recently had been a guest in her home. She was upon the point of calling to him in glad relief when she saw him leap quickly to one side and hide himself in the thick verdure at the trail's side. It was evident that he was being followed by an enemy, and so Jane Clayton kept silent, lest she distract Frecoult's attention, or guide his foe to his hiding place.

Scarcely had Frecoult hidden himself than the figure of a white-robed Arab crept silently along the trail in pursuit. From her hiding place, Jane Clayton could see both men plainly. She recognized Achmet Zek as the leader of the band of ruffians who had raided her home and made her a prisoner, and as she saw Frecoult, the supposed friend and ally, raise his gun and take careful aim at the Arab, her heart stood still and every power of her soul was directed upon a fervent prayer for the accuracy of his aim.

Achmet Zek paused in the middle of the trail. His keen eyes scanned every bush and tree within the radius of his vision. His tall figure presented a perfect target to the perfidious assassin. There was a sharp report, and a little puff of smoke arose from the bush that hid the Belgian, as Achmet Zek stumbled forward and pitched, face down, upon the trail.

As Werper stepped back into the trail, he was startled by the sound of a glad cry from above him, and as he wheeled about to discover the author of this unexpected interruption, he saw Jane Clayton drop lightly from a nearby tree and run forward with outstretched hands to congratulate him upon his victory.

CHAPTER TWENTY

Jane Clayton Again a Prisoner

Though her clothes were torn and her hair disheveled, Albert Werper realized that he never before had looked upon such a vision of loveliness as that which Lady Greystoke presented in the relief and joy which she felt in coming so unexpectedly upon a friend and rescuer when hope had seemed so far away.

If the Belgian had entertained any doubts as to the woman's knowledge of his part in the perfidious attack upon her home and herself, it was quickly dissipated by the genuine friendliness of her greeting. She told him quickly of all that had befallen her since he had departed from her home, and as she spoke of the death of her husband her eyes were veiled by the tears which she could not repress.

"I am shocked," said Werper, in well-simulated sympathy; "but I am not surprised. That devil there," and he pointed toward the body of Achmet Zek, "has terrorized the entire country. Your Waziri are either exterminated, or have been driven out of their country, far to the south. The men of Achmet Zek occupy the plain about your former home – there is neither sanctuary nor escape in that direction. Our only hope lies in traveling northward as rapidly as we may, of coming to the camp of the raiders before the knowledge of Achmet Zek's death reaches those who were left there, and of obtaining, through some ruse, an escort toward the north.

"I think that the thing can be accomplished, for I was a guest of the raider's before I knew the nature of the man, and those at the camp are not aware that I turned against him when I discovered his villainy.

"Come! We will make all possible haste to reach the camp before those who accompanied Achmet Zek upon his last raid have found his body and carried the news of his death to the cut-throats who remained behind. It is our only hope, Lady Greystoke, and you must place your entire faith in me if I am to succeed. Wait for me here a moment while I take from the Arab's body the wallet that he stole from me," and Werper stepped quickly to the dead man's side, and, kneeling, sought with quick fingers the pouch of jewels. To his consternation, there was no sign of them in the garments of Achmet Zek. Rising, he walked back along the trail, searching for some trace of the missing pouch or its contents; but he found nothing, even though he searched carefully the vicinity of his dead horse, and for a few paces into the jungle on either side. Puzzled, disappointed and angry, he at last returned to the girl. "The wallet is gone," he explained, crisply, "and I dare not delay longer in search of it. We must reach the camp before the returning raiders."

Unsuspicious of the man's true character, Jane Clayton saw nothing peculiar in his plans, or in his specious explanation of his former friendship for the raider, and so she grasped with alacrity the seeming hope for safety which he proffered her, and turning about she set out with Albert Werper toward the hostile camp in which she so lately had been a prisoner.

It was late in the afternoon of the second day before they reached their destination, and as they paused upon the edge of the clearing before the gates of the walled village, Werper cautioned the girl to accede to whatever he might suggest by his conversation with the raiders.

"I shall tell them," he said, "that I apprehended you after you escaped from the camp, that I took you to Achmet Zek, and that as he was engaged in a stubborn battle with the Waziri, he directed me to return to camp with you, to obtain here a sufficient guard, and to ride north with you as rapidly as possible and dispose of you at the most advantageous terms to a certain slave broker whose name he gave me."

Again the girl was deceived by the apparent frankness of the Belgian. She realized that desperate situations required desperate handling, and though she trembled inwardly at the thought of again entering the vile and hideous village of the raiders she saw no better course than that which her companion had suggested.

Calling aloud to those who tended the gates, Werper, grasping Jane Clayton by the arm, walked boldly across the clearing. Those who opened the gates to him permitted their surprise to show clearly in their expressions. That the discredited and hunted lieutenant should be thus returning fearlessly of his own volition, seemed to disarm them quite as effectually as his manner toward Lady Greystoke had deceived her.

The sentries at the gate returned Werper's salutations, and viewed with astonishment the prisoner whom he brought into the village with him.

Immediately the Belgian sought the Arab who had been left in charge of the camp during Achmet Zek's absence, and again his boldness disarmed suspicion and won the acceptance of his false explanation of his return. The fact that he had brought back with him the woman prisoner who had escaped, added strength to his claims, and Mohammed Beyd soon found himself fraternizing good-naturedly with the very man whom he would have slain without compunction had he discovered him alone in the jungle a half hour before.

Jane Clayton was again confined to the prison hut she had formerly occupied, but as she realized that this was but a part of the deception which she and Frecoult were playing upon the credulous raiders, it was with quite a different sensation that she again entered the vile and filthy interior, from that which she had previously experienced, when hope was so far away.

Once more she was bound and sentries placed before the door of her prison; but before Werper left her he whispered words of cheer into her ear. Then he left, and made his way back to the tent of Mohammed Beyd. He had been wondering how long it would be before the raiders who had ridden out with Achmet Zek would return with the murdered body of their chief, and the more he thought upon the matter the greater his fears became, that without accomplices his plan would fail.

What, even, if he got away from the camp in safety before any returned with the true story of his guilt – of what value would this advantage be other than to protract for a few days his mental torture and his life? These hard riders, familiar with every trail and bypath, would get him long before he could hope to reach the coast.

As these thoughts passed through his mind he entered the tent where Mohammed Beyd sat cross-legged upon a rug, smoking. The Arab looked up as the European came into his presence.

"Greetings, O Brother!" he said.

"Greetings!" replied Werper.

For a while neither spoke further. The Arab was the first to break the silence.

"And my master, Achmet Zek, was well when last you saw him?" he asked.

"Never was he safer from the sins and dangers of mortality," replied the Belgian.

"It is well," said Mohammed Beyd, blowing a little puff of blue smoke straight out before him.

Again there was silence for several minutes.

"And if he were dead?" asked the Belgian, determined to lead up to the truth, and attempt to bribe Mohammed Beyd into his service.

The Arab's eyes narrowed and he leaned forward, his gaze boring straight into the eyes of the Belgian.

"I have been thinking much, Werper, since you returned so unexpectedly to the camp of the man whom you had deceived, and who sought you with death in his heart. I have been with Achmet Zek for many years – his own mother never knew him so well as I. He never forgives – much less would he again trust a man who had once betrayed him; that I know.

"I have thought much, as I said, and the result of my thinking has assured me that Achmet Zek is dead – for otherwise you would never have dared return to his camp, unless you be either a braver man or a bigger fool than I have imagined. And, if this evidence of my judgment is not sufficient, I have but just now received from your own lips even more confirmatory witness – for did you not say that Achmet Zek was never more safe from the sins and dangers of mortality?

"Achmet Zek is dead – you need not deny it. I was not his mother, or his mistress, so do not fear that my wailings shall disturb you. Tell me why you have come back here. Tell me what you want, and, Werper, if you still possess the jewels of which Achmet Zek told me, there is no reason why you and I should not ride north together and divide the ransom of the white woman and the contents of the pouch you wear about your person. Eh?"

The evil eyes narrowed, a vicious, thin-lipped smile tortured the villainous face, as Mohammed Beyd grinned knowingly into the face of the Belgian.

Werper was both relieved and disturbed by the Arab's attitude. The complacency with which he accepted the death of his chief lifted a considerable burden of apprehension from the shoulders of Achmet Zek's assassin; but his demand for a share of the jewels boded ill for Werper when Mohammed Beyd should have learned that the precious stones were no longer in the Belgian's possession.

To acknowledge that he had lost the jewels might be to arouse the wrath or suspicion of the Arab to such an extent as would jeopardize his new-found chances of escape. His one hope seemed, then, to lie in fostering Mohammed Beyd's belief that the jewels were still in his possession, and depend upon the accidents of the future to open an avenue of escape.

Could he contrive to tent with the Arab upon the march north, he might find opportunity in plenty to remove this menace to his life and liberty – it was worth trying, and, further, there seemed no other way out of his difficulty.

"Yes," he said, "Achmet Zek is dead. He fell in battle with a company of Abyssinian cavalry that held me captive. During the fighting I escaped; but I doubt if any of Achmet Zek's men live, and the gold they sought is in the possession of the Abyssinians. Even now they are doubtless marching on this camp, for they were sent by Menelek to punish Achmet Zek and his followers for a raid upon an Abyssinian village. There are many of them, and if we do not make haste to escape we shall all suffer the same fate as Achmet Zek."

Mohammed Beyd listened in silence. How much of the unbeliever's story he might safely believe he did not know; but as it afforded him an excuse for deserting the village and making for the north he was not inclined to cross-question the Belgian too minutely.

"And if I ride north with you," he asked, "half the jewels and half the ransom of the woman shall be mine?"

"Yes," replied Werper.

"Good," said Mohammed Beyd. "I go now to give the order for the breaking of camp early on the morrow," and he rose to leave the tent.

Werper laid a detaining hand upon his arm.

"Wait," he said, "let us determine how many shall accompany us. It is not well that we be burdened by the women and children, for then indeed we might be overtaken by the Abyssinians. It would be far better to select a small guard of your bravest men, and leave word behind that we are riding WEST. Then, when the Abyssinians come they will be put upon the wrong trail should they have it in their hearts to pursue us, and if they do not they will at least ride north with less rapidity than as though they thought that we were ahead of them."

"The serpent is less wise than thou, Werper," said Mohammed Beyd with a smile. "It shall be done as you say. Twenty men shall accompany us, and we shall ride WEST – when we leave the village."

"Good," cried the Belgian, and so it was arranged.

Early the next morning Jane Clayton, after an almost sleepless night, was aroused by the sound of voices outside her prison, and a moment later, M. Frecoult, and two Arabs entered. The latter unbound her ankles and lifted her to her feet. Then her wrists were loosed, she was given a handful of dry bread, and led out into the faint light of dawn.

She looked questioningly at Frecoult, and at a moment that the Arab's attention was attracted in another direction the man leaned toward her and whispered that all was working out as he had planned. Thus assured, the young woman felt a renewal of the hope which the long and miserable night of bondage had almost expunged.

Shortly after, she was lifted to the back of a horse, and surrounded by Arabs, was escorted through the gateway of the village and off into the jungle toward the west. Half an hour later the party turned north, and northerly was their direction for the balance of the march.

M. Frecoult spoke with her but seldom, and she understood that in carrying out his deception he must maintain the semblance of her captor, rather than protector, and so she suspected nothing though she saw the friendly relations which seemed to exist between the European and the Arab leader of the band.

If Werper succeeded in keeping himself from conversation with the young woman, he failed signally to expel her from his thoughts. A hundred times a day he found his eyes wandering in her direction and feasting themselves upon her charms of face and figure. Each hour his infatuation for her grew, until his desire to possess her gained almost the proportions of madness.

If either the girl or Mohammed Beyd could have guessed what passed in the mind of the man which each thought a friend and ally, the apparent harmony of the little company would have been rudely disturbed.

Werper had not succeeded in arranging to tent with Mohammed Beyd, and so he revolved many plans for the assassination of the Arab that would have been greatly simplified had he been permitted to share the other's nightly shelter.

Upon the second day out Mohammed Beyd reined his horse to the side of the animal on which the captive was mounted. It was, apparently, the first notice which the Arab had taken of the girl; but many times during these two days had his cunning eyes peered greedily from beneath the hood of his burnoose to gloat upon the beauties of the prisoner.

Nor was this hidden infatuation of any recent origin. He had conceived it when first the wife of the Englishman had fallen into the hands of Achmet Zek; but while that austere chieftain lived, Mohammed Beyd had not even dared hope for a realization of his imaginings.

Now, though, it was different – only a despised dog of a Christian stood between himself and possession of the girl. How easy it would be to slay the unbeliever, and take unto himself both the woman and the jewels! With the latter in his possession, the ransom which might be obtained for the captive would form no great inducement to her relinquishment in the face of the pleasures of sole ownership of her. Yes, he would kill Werper, retain all the jewels and keep the Englishwoman.

He turned his eyes upon her as she rode along at his side. How beautiful she was! His fingers opened and closed – skinny, brown talons itching to feel the soft flesh of the victim in their remorseless clutch.

"Do you know," he asked leaning toward her, "where this man would take you?"

Jane Clayton nodded affirmatively.

"And you are willing to become the plaything of a black sultan?"

The girl drew herself up to her full height, and turned her head away; but she did not reply. She feared lest her knowledge of the ruse that M. Frecoult was playing upon the Arab might cause her to betray herself through an insufficient display of terror and aversion.

"You can escape this fate," continued the Arab; "Mohammed Beyd will save you," and he reached out a brown hand and seized the fingers of her right hand in a grasp so sudden and so fierce that his brutal passion was revealed as clearly in the act as though his lips had confessed it in words. Jane Clayton wrenched herself from his grasp.

"You beast!" she cried. "Leave me or I shall call M. Frecoult."

Mohammed Beyd drew back with a scowl. His thin, upper lip curled upward, revealing his smooth, white teeth.

"M. Frecoult?" he jeered. "There is no such person. The man's name is Werper. He is a liar, a thief, and a murderer. He killed his captain in the Congo country and fled to the protection of Achmet Zek. He led Achmet Zek to the plunder of your home. He followed your husband, and planned to steal his gold from him. He has told me that you think him your protector, and he has played upon this to win your confidence that it might be easier to carry you north and sell you into some black sultan's harem. Mohammed Beyd is your only hope," and with this assertion to provide the captive with food for thought, the Arab spurred forward toward the head of the column.

Jane Clayton could not know how much of Mohammed Beyd's indictment might be true, or how much false; but at least it had the effect of dampening her hopes and causing her to review with suspicion every past act of the man upon whom she had been looking as her sole protector in the midst of a world of enemies and dangers.

On the march a separate tent had been provided for the captive, and at night it was pitched between those of Mohammed Beyd and Werper. A sentry was posted at the front and another at the back, and with these precautions it had not been thought necessary to confine the prisoner to bonds. The evening following her interview with Mohammed Beyd, Jane

Clayton sat for some time at the opening of her tent watching the rough activities of the camp. She had eaten the meal that had been brought her by Mohammed Beyd's Negro slave – a meal of cassava cakes and a nondescript stew in which a new-killed monkey, a couple of squirrels and the remains of a zebra, slain the previous day, were impartially and unsavorily combined; but the one-time Baltimore belle had long since submerged in the stern battle for existence, an estheticism which formerly revolted at much slighter provocation.

As the girl's eyes wandered across the trampled jungle clearing, already squalid from the presence of man, she no longer apprehended either the nearer objects of the foreground, the uncouth men laughing or quarreling among themselves, or the jungle beyond, which circumscribed the extreme range of her material vision. Her gaze passed through all these, unseeing, to center itself upon a distant bungalow and scenes of happy security which brought to her eyes tears of mingled joy and sorrow. She saw a tall, broad-shouldered man riding in from distant fields; she saw herself waiting to greet him with an armful of fresh-cut roses from the bushes which flanked the little rustic gate before her. All this was gone, vanished into the past, wiped out by the torches and bullets and hatred of these hideous and degenerate men. With a stifled sob, and a little shudder, Jane Clayton turned back into her tent and sought the pile of unclean blankets which were her bed. Throwing herself face downward upon them she sobbed forth her misery until kindly sleep brought her, at least temporary, relief.

And while she slept a figure stole from the tent that stood to the right of hers. It approached the sentry before the doorway and whispered a few words in the man's ear. The latter nodded, and strode off through the darkness in the direction of his own blankets. The figure passed to the rear of Jane Clayton's tent and spoke again to the sentry there, and this man also left, following in the trail of the first.

Then he who had sent them away stole silently to the tent flap and untying the fastenings entered with the noiselessness of a disembodied spirit.

CHAPTER TWENTY ONE

The Flight to the Jungle

Sleepless upon his blankets, Albert Werper let his evil mind dwell upon the charms of the woman in the nearby tent. He had noted Mohammed Beyd's sudden interest in the girl, and judging the man by his own standards, had guessed at the basis of the Arab's sudden change of attitude toward the prisoner.

And as he let his imaginings run riot they aroused within him a bestial jealousy of Mohammed Beyd, and a great fear that the other might encompass his base designs upon the defenseless girl. By a strange process of reasoning, Werper, whose designs were identical with the Arab's, pictured himself as Jane Clayton's protector, and presently convinced himself that the attentions which might seem hideous to her if proffered by Mohammed Beyd, would be welcomed from Albert Werper.

Her husband was dead, and Werper fancied that he could replace in the girl's heart the position which had been vacated by the act of the grim reaper. He could offer Jane Clayton marriage – a thing which Mohammed Beyd would not offer, and which the girl would spurn from him with as deep disgust as she would his unholy lust.

It was not long before the Belgian had succeeded in convincing himself that the captive not only had every reason for having conceived sentiments of love for him; but that she had by various feminine methods acknowledged her new-born affection.

And then a sudden resolution possessed him. He threw the blankets from him and rose to his feet. Pulling on his boots and buckling his cartridge belt and revolver about his hips he stepped to the flap of his tent and looked out. There was no sentry before the entrance to the prisoner's tent! What could it mean? Fate was indeed playing into his hands.

Stepping outside he passed to the rear of the girl's tent. There was no sentry there, either! And now, boldly, he walked to the entrance and stepped within.

Dimly the moonlight illumined the interior. Across the tent a figure bent above the blankets of a bed. There was a whispered word, and another figure rose from the blankets to a sitting position. Slowly Albert Werper's eyes were becoming accustomed to the half darkness of the tent. He saw that the figure leaning over the bed was that of a man, and he guessed at the truth of the nocturnal visitor's identity.

A sullen, jealous rage enveloped him. He took a step in the direction of the two. He heard a frightened cry break from the girl's lips as she recognized the features of the man above her, and he saw Mohammed Beyd seize her by the throat and bear her back upon the blankets.

Cheated passion cast a red blur before the eyes of the Belgian. No! The man should not have her. She was for him and him alone. He would not be robbed of his rights.

Quickly he ran across the tent and threw himself upon the back of Mohammed Beyd. The latter, though surprised by this sudden and unexpected attack, was not one to give up without a battle. The Belgian's fingers were feeling for his throat, but the Arab tore them away, and rising wheeled upon his adversary. As they faced each other Werper struck the Arab a heavy blow in the face, sending him staggering backward. If he had followed up his advantage he would have had Mohammed Beyd at his mercy in another moment; but instead he tugged at his revolver to draw it from its holster, and Fate ordained that at that particular moment the weapon should stick in its leather scabbard.

Before he could disengage it, Mohammed Beyd had recovered himself and was dashing upon him. Again Werper struck the other in the face, and the Arab returned the blow. Striking at each other and ceaselessly attempting to clinch, the two battled about the small interior of the tent, while the girl, wide-eyed in terror and astonishment, watched the duel in frozen silence.

Again and again Werper struggled to draw his weapon. Mohammed Beyd, anticipating no such opposition to his base desires, had come to the tent unarmed, except for a long knife which he now drew as he stood panting during the first brief rest of the encounter.

"Dog of a Christian," he whispered, "look upon this knife in the hands of Mohammed Beyd! Look well, unbeliever, for it is the last thing in life that you shall see or feel. With it Mohammed Beyd will cut out your black heart. If you have a God pray to him now – in a minute more you shall be dead," and with that he rushed viciously upon the Belgian, his knife raised high above his head.

Werper was still dragging futilely at his weapon. The Arab was almost upon him. In desperation the European waited until Mohammed Beyd was all but against him, then he threw himself to one side to the floor of the tent, leaving a leg extended in the path of the Arab.

The trick succeeded. Mohammed Beyd, carried on by the momentum of his charge, stumbled over the projecting obstacle and crashed to the ground. Instantly he was up again and wheeling to renew the battle; but Werper was on foot ahead of him, and now his revolver, loosened from its holster, flashed in his hand.

The Arab dove headfirst to grapple with him, there was a sharp report, a lurid gleam of flame in the darkness, and Mohammed Beyd rolled over and over upon the floor to come to a final rest beside the bed of the woman hc had sought to dishonor.

Almost immediately following the report came the sound of excited voices in the camp without. Men were calling back and forth to one another asking the meaning of the shot. Werper could hear them running hither and thither, investigating.

Jane Clayton had risen to her feet as the Arab died, and now she came forward with outstretched hands toward Werper.

"How can I ever thank you, my friend?" she asked. "And to think that only today I had almost believed the infamous story which this beast told me of your perfidy and of your past. Forgive me, M. Frecoult. I might have known that a white man and a gentleman could be naught else than the protector of a woman of his own race amid the dangers of this savage land."

Werper's hands dropped limply at his sides. He stood looking at the girl; but he could find no words to reply to her. Her innocent arraignment of his truc purposcs was unanswerable.

Outside, the Arabs were searching for the author of the disturbing shot. The two sentries who had been relieved and sent to their blankets by Mohammed Beyd were the first to suggest going to the tent of the prisoner. It occurred to them that possibly the woman had successfully defended herself against their leader.

Werper heard the men approaching. To be apprehended as the slayer of Mohammed Beyd would be equivalent to a sentence of immediate death. The fierce and brutal raiders would tear to pieces a Christian who had dared spill the blood of their leader. He must find some excuse to delay the finding of Mohammed Beyd's dead body.

Returning his revolver to its holster, he walked quickly to the entrance of the tent. Parting the flaps he stepped out and confronted the men, who were rapidly approaching. Somehow he found within him the necessary bravado to force a smile to his lips, as he held up his hand to bar their farther progress.

"The woman resisted," he said, "and Mohammed Beyd was forced to shoot her. She is not dead – only slightly wounded. You may go back to your blankets. Mohammed Beyd and I will look after the prisoner;" then he turned and re-entered the tent, and the raiders, satisfied by this explanation, gladly returned to their broken slumbers.

As he again faced Jane Clayton, Werper found himself animated by quite different intentions than those which had lured him from his blankets but a few minutes before. The excitement of his encounter with Mohammed Beyd, as well as the dangers which he now faced at the hands of the raiders when morning must inevitably reveal the truth of what had occurred in the tent of the prisoner that night, had naturally cooled the hot passion which had dominated him when he entered the tent.

But another and stronger force was exerting itself in the girl's favor. However low a man may sink, honor and chivalry, has he ever possessed them, are never entirely eradicated from his character, and though Albert Werper had long since ceased to evidence the slightest claim to either the one or the other, the spontaneous acknowledgment of them which the girl's speech had presumed had reawakened them both within him.

For the first time he realized the almost hopeless and frightful position of the fair captive, and the depths of ignominy to which he had sunk, that had made it possible for him, a well-born, European gentleman, to have entertained even for a moment the part that he had taken in the ruin of her home, happiness, and herself.

Too much of baseness already lay at the threshold of his conscience for him ever to hope entirely to redeem himself; but in the first, sudden burst of contrition the man conceived an honest intention to undo, in so far as lay within his power, the evil that his criminal avarice had brought upon this sweet and unoffending woman.

As he stood apparently listening to the retreating footsteps – Jane Clayton approached him.

"What are we to do now?" she asked. "Morning will bring discovery of this," and she pointed to the still body of Mohammed Beyd. "They will kill you when they find him."

For a time Werper did not reply, then he turned suddenly toward the woman.

"I have a plan," he cried. "It will require nerve and courage on your part; but you have already shown that you possess both. Can you endure still more?"

"I can endure anything," she replied with a brave smile, "that may offer us even a slight chance for escape."

"You must simulate death," he explained, "while I carry you from the camp. I will explain to the sentries that Mohammed Beyd has ordered me to take your body into the jungle. This seemingly unnecessary act I shall explain upon the grounds that Mohammed Beyd had conceived a violent passion for you and that he so regretted the act by which he had become your slayer that he could not endure the silent reproach of your lifeless body."

The girl held up her hand to stop. A smile touched her lips.

"Are you quite mad?" she asked. "Do you imagine that the sentries will credit any such ridiculous tale?"

"You do not know them," he replied. "Beneath their rough exteriors, despite their calloused and criminal natures, there exists in each a well-defined strain of romantic emotionalism – you will find it among such as these throughout the world. It is romance which lures men to lead wild lives of outlawry and crime. The ruse will succeed – never fear."

Jane Clayton shrugged. "We can but try it – and then what?"

"I shall hide you in the jungle," continued the Belgian, "coming for you alone and with two horses in the morning."

"But how will you explain Mohammed Beyd's death?" she asked. "It will be discovered before ever you can escape the camp in the morning."

"I shall not explain it," replied Werper. "Mohammed Beyd shall explain it himself – we must leave that to him. Are you ready for the venture?"

"Yes."

"But wait, I must get you a weapon and ammunition," and Werper walked quickly from the tent.

Very shortly he returned with an extra revolver and ammunition belt strapped about his waist.

"Are you ready?" he asked.

"Quite ready," replied the girl.

"Then come and throw yourself limply across my left shoulder," and Werper knelt to receive her.

"There," he said, as he rose to his feet. "Now, let your arms, your legs and your head hang limply. Remember that you are dead."

A moment later the man walked out into the camp, the body of the woman across his shoulder.

A thorn boma had been thrown up about the camp, to discourage the bolder of the hungry carnivora. A couple of sentries paced to and fro in the light of a fire which they kept burning brightly. The nearer of these looked up in surprise as he saw Werper approaching.

"Who are you?" he cried. "What have you there?"

Werper raised the hood of his burnoose that the fellow might see his face.

"This is the body of the woman," he explained. "Mohammed Beyd has asked me to take it into the jungle, for he cannot bear to look upon the face of her whom he loved, and whom necessity compelled him to slay. He suffers greatly – he is inconsolable. It was with difficulty that I prevented him taking his own life."

Across the speaker's shoulder, limp and frightened, the girl waited for the Arab's reply. He would laugh at this preposterous story; of that she was sure. In an instant he would unmask the deception that M. Frecoult was attempting to practice upon him, and they would both be lost. She tried to plan how best she might aid her would-be rescuer in the fight which must most certainly follow within a moment or two.

Then she heard the voice of the Arab as he replied to M. Frecoult.

"Are you going alone, or do you wish me to awaken someone to accompany you?" he asked, and his tone denoted not the least surprise that Mohammed Beyd had suddenly discovered such remarkably sensitive characteristics.

"I shall go alone," replied Werper, and he passed on and out through the narrow opening in the boma, by which the sentry stood.

A moment later he had entered among the boles of the trees with his burden, and when safely hidden from the sentry's view lowered the girl to her feet, with a low, "sh-sh," when she would have spoken.

Then he led her a little farther into the forest, halted beneath a large tree with spreading branches, buckled a cartridge belt and revolver about her waist, and assisted her to clamber into the lower branches.

"Tomorrow," he whispered, "as soon as I can elude them, I will return for you. Be brave, Lady Greystoke – we may yet escape."

"Thank you," she replied in a low tone. "You have been very kind, and very brave."

Werper did not reply, and the darkness of the night hid the scarlet flush of shame which swept upward across his face. Quickly he turned and made his way back to camp. The sentry, from his post, saw him enter his own tent; but he did not see him crawl under the canvas at the rear and sneak cautiously to the tent which the prisoner had occupied, where now lay the dead body of Mohammed Beyd.

Raising the lower edge of the rear wall, Werper crept within and approached the corpse. Without an instant's hesitation he seized the dead wrists and dragged the body upon its back to the point where he had just entered. On hands and knees he backed out as he had come in, drawing the corpse after him. Once outside the Belgian crept to the side of the tent and surveyed as much of the camp as lay within his vision – no one was watching.

Returning to the body, he lifted it to his shoulder, and risking all on a quick sally, ran swiftly across the narrow opening which separated the prisoner's tent from that of the dead man. Behind the silken wall he halted and lowered his burden to the ground, and there he remained motionless for several minutes, listening.

Satisfied, at last, that no one had seen him, he stooped and raised the bottom of the tent wall, backed in and dragged the thing that had been Mohammed Beyd after him. To the sleeping rugs of the dead raider he drew the corpse, then he fumbled about in the darkness until he had found Mohammed Beyd's revolver. With the weapon in his hand he returned to the side of the dead man, kneeled beside the bedding, and inserted his right hand with the weapon beneath the rugs, piled a number of thicknesses of the closely woven fabric over and about the revolver with his left hand. Then he pulled the trigger, and at the same time he coughed.

The muffled report could not have been heard above the sound of his cough by one directly outside the tent. Werper was satisfied. A grim smile touched his lips as he withdrew the weapon from the rugs and placed it carefully in the right hand of the dead man, fixing three of the fingers around the grip and the index finger inside the trigger guard.

A moment longer he tarried to rearrange the disordered rugs, and then he left as he had entered, fastening down the rear wall of the tent as it had been before he had raised it.

Going to the tent of the prisoner he removed there also the evidence that someone might have come or gone beneath the rear wall. Then he returned to his own tent, entered, fastened down the canvas, and crawled into his blankets.

The following morning he was awakened by the excited voice of Mohammed Beyd's slave calling to him at the entrance of his tent.

"Quick! Quick!" cried the black in a frightened tone. "Come! Mohammed Beyd is dead in his tent – dead by his own hand."

Werper sat up quickly in his blankets at the first alarm, a startled expression upon his countenance; but at the last words of the black a sigh of relief escaped his lips and a slight smile replaced the tense lines upon his face.

"I come," he called to the slave, and drawing on his boots, rose and went out of his tent.

Excited Arabs and blacks were running from all parts of the camp toward the silken tent of Mohammed Beyd, and when Werper entered he found a number of the raiders crowded about the corpse, now cold and stiff.

Shouldering his way among them, the Belgian halted beside the dead body of the raider. He looked down in silence for a moment upon the still face, then he wheeled upon the Arabs.

"Who has done this thing?" he cried. His tone was both menacing and accusing. "Who has murdered Mohammed Beyd?"

A sudden chorus of voices arose in tumultuous protest.

"Mohammed Beyd was not murdered," they cried. "He died by his own hand. This, and Allah, are our witnesses," and they pointed to a revolver in the dead man's hand.

For a time Werper pretended to be skeptical; but at last permitted himself to be convinced that Mohammed Beyd had indeed killed himself in remorse for the death of the white woman he had, all unknown to his followers, loved so devotedly.

Werper himself wrapped the blankets of the dead man about the corpse, taking care to fold inward the scorched and bullet-torn fabric that had muffled the report of the weapon he had fired the night before. Then six husky blacks carried the body out into the clearing where the camp stood, and deposited it in a shallow grave. As the loose earth fell upon the silent form beneath the tell-tale blankets, Albert Werper heaved another sigh of relief – his plan had worked out even better than he had dared hope.

With Achmet Zek and Mohammed Beyd both dead, the raiders were without a leader, and after a brief conference they decided to return into the north on visits to the various tribes to which they belonged. Werper, after learning the direction they intended taking, announced that for his part, he was going east to the coast, and as they knew of nothing he possessed which any of them coveted, they signified their willingness that he should go his way.

As they rode off, he sat his horse in the center of the clearing watching them disappear one by one into the jungle, and thanked his God that he had at last escaped their villainous clutches.

When he could no longer hear any sound of them, he turned to the right and rode into the forest toward the tree where he had hidden

Lady Greystoke, and drawing rein beneath it, called up in a gay and hopeful voice a pleasant, "Good morning!"

There was no reply, and though his eyes searched the thick foliage above him, he could see no sign of the girl. Dismounting, he quickly climbed into the tree, where he could obtain a view of all its branches. The tree was empty – Jane Clayton had vanished during the silent watches of the jungle night.

CHAPTER TWENTY TWO

Tarzan Recovers his Reason

As Tarzan let the pebbles from the recovered pouch run through his fingers, his thoughts returned to the pile of yellow ingots about which the Arabs and the Abyssinians had waged their relentless battle.

What was there in common between that pile of dirty metal and the beautiful, sparkling pebbles that had formerly been in his pouch? What was the metal? From whence had it come? What was that tantalizing half-conviction which seemed to demand the recognition of his memory that the yellow pile for which these men had fought and died had been intimately connected with his past – that it had been his?

What had been his past? He shook his head. Vaguely the memory of his apish childhood passed slowly in review – then came a strangely tangled mass of faces, figures and events which seemed to have no relation to Tarzan of the Apes, and yet which were, even in their fragmentary form, familiar.

Slowly and painfully, recollection was attempting to reassert itself, the hurt brain was mending, as the cause of its recent failure to function was being slowly absorbed or removed by the healing processes of perfect circulation.

The people who now passed before his mind's eye for the first time in weeks wore familiar faces; but yet he could neither place them in the niches they had once filled in his past life, nor call them by name. One was a fair she, and it was her face which most often moved through the tangled recollections of his convalescing brain. Who was she? What had she been to Tarzan of the Apes? He seemed to see her about the very spot upon which the pile of gold had been unearthed by the Abyssinians; but the surroundings were vastly different from those which now obtained.

There was a building – there were many buildings – and there were hedges, fences, and flowers. Tarzan puckered his brow in puzzled study of the wonderful problem. For an instant he seemed to grasp the whole of a true explanation, and then, just as success was within his grasp, the picture faded into a jungle scene where a naked, white youth danced in company with a band of hairy, primordial ape-things.

Tarzan shook his head and sighed. Why was it that he could not recollect? At least he was sure that in some way the pile of gold, the place where it lay, the subtle aroma of the elusive she he had been pursuing, the memory figure of the white woman, and he himself, were inextricably connected by the ties of a forgotten past.

If the woman belonged there, what better place to search or await her than the very spot which his broken recollections seemed to assign to her? It was worth trying. Tarzan slipped the thong of the empty pouch over his shoulder and started off through the trees in the direction of the plain.

At the outskirts of the forest he met the Arabs returning in search of Achmet Zek. Hiding, he let them pass, and then resumed his way toward the charred ruins of the home he had been almost upon the point of recalling to his memory.

His journey across the plain was interrupted by the discovery of a small herd of antelope in a little swale, where the cover and the wind were well combined to make stalking easy. A fat yearling rewarded a half hour of stealthy creeping and a sudden, savage rush, and it was late in the afternoon when the ape-man settled himself upon his haunches beside his kill to enjoy the fruits of his skill, his cunning, and his prowess.

His hunger satisfied, thirst next claimed his attention. The river lured him by the shortest path toward its refreshing waters, and when he had drunk, night already had fallen and he was some half mile or more down stream from the point where he had seen the pile of yellow ingots, and where he hoped to meet the memory woman, or find some clew to her whereabouts or her identity.

To the jungle bred, time is usually a matter of small moment, and haste, except when engendered by terror, by rage, or by hunger, is distasteful. Today was gone. Therefore tomorrow, of which there was an infinite procession, would answer admirably for Tarzan's further quest. And, besides, the ape-man was tired and would sleep.

A tree afforded him the safety, seclusion and comforts of a well-appointed bedchamber, and to the chorus of the hunters and the hunted of the wild river bank he soon dropped off into deep slumber.

Morning found him both hungry and thirsty again, and dropping from his tree he made his way to the drinking place at the river's edge. There he found Numa, the lion, ahead of him. The big fellow was lapping the water greedily, and at the approach of Tarzan along the trail in his rear, he raised his head, and turning his gaze backward across his maned shoulders glared at the intruder. A low growl of warning rumbled from his throat; but Tarzan, guessing that the beast had but just quitted his kill and was well filled, merely made a slight detour and continued to the river, where he stopped a few yards above the tawny cat, and dropping upon his hands and knees plunged his face into the cool water. For a moment the lion continued to eye the man; then he resumed his drinking, and man and beast quenched their thirst side by side each apparently oblivious of the other's presence.

Numa was the first to finish. Raising his head, he gazed across the river for a few minutes with that stony fixity of attention which is a characteristic of his kind. But for the ruffling of his black mane to the touch of the passing breeze he might have been wrought from golden bronze, so motionless, so statuesque his pose.

A deep sigh from the cavernous lungs dispelled the illusion. The mighty head swung slowly around until the yellow eyes rested upon the man. The bristled lip curved upward, exposing yellow fangs. Another warning growl vibrated the heavy jowls, and the king of beasts turned majestically about and paced slowly up the trail into the dense reeds.

Tarzan of the Apes drank on, but from the corners of his gray eyes he watched the great brute's every move until he had disappeared from view, and, after, his keen ears marked the movements of the carnivore.

A plunge in the river was followed by a scant breakfast of eggs which chance discovered to him, and then he set off up river toward the ruins of the bungalow where the golden ingots had marked the center of yesterday's battle.

And when he came upon the spot, great was his surprise and consternation, for the yellow metal had disappeared. The earth, trampled by the feet of horses and men, gave no clew. It was as though the ingots had evaporated into thin air.

The ape-man was at a loss to know where to turn or what next to do. There was no sign of any spoor which might denote that the she had been here. The metal was gone, and if there was any connection between the she and the metal it seemed useless to wait for her now that the latter had been removed elsewhere.

Everything seemed to elude him – the pretty pebbles, the yellow metal, the she, his memory. Tarzan was disgusted. He would go back into the jungle and look for Chulk, and so he turned his steps once more toward the forest. He moved rapidly, swinging across the plain in a long, easy trot, and at the edge of the forest, taking to the trees with the agility and speed of a small monkey.

His direction was aimless – he merely raced on and on through the jungle, the joy of unfettered action his principal urge, with the hope of stumbling upon some clew to Chulk or the she, a secondary incentive.

For two days he roamed about, killing, eating, drinking and sleeping wherever inclination and the means to indulge it occurred simultaneously. It was upon the morning of the third day that the scent spoor of horse and man were wafted faintly to his nostrils. Instantly he altered his course to glide silently through the branches in the direction from which the scent came.

It was not long before he came upon a solitary horseman riding toward the east. Instantly his eyes confirmed what his nose had previously suspected – the rider was he who had stolen his pretty pebbles. The light of rage flared suddenly in the gray eyes as the ape-man dropped lower among the branches until he moved almost directly above the unconscious Werper.

There was a quick leap, and the Belgian felt a heavy body hurtle onto the rump of his terror-stricken mount. The horse, snorting, leaped forward. Giant arms encircled the rider, and in the twinkling of an eye he was dragged from his saddle to find himself lying in the narrow trail with a naked, white giant kneeling upon his breast.

Recognition came to Werper with the first glance at his captor's face, and a pallor of fear overspread his features. Strong fingers were at his throat, fingers of steel. He tried to cry out, to plead for his life; but the cruel fingers denied him speech, as they were as surely denying him life.

"The pretty pebbles?" cried the man upon his breast. "What did you with the pretty pebbles – with Tarzan's pretty pebbles?"

The fingers relaxed to permit a reply. For some time Werper could only choke and cough – at last he regained the powers of speech.

"Achmet Zek, the Arab, stole them from me," he cried; "he made me give up the pouch and the pebbles."

"I saw all that," replied Tarzan; "but the pebbles in the pouch were not the pebbles of Tarzan – they were only such pebbles as fill the bottoms of the rivers, and the shelving banks beside them. Even the Arab would not have them, for he threw them away in anger when he had looked upon them. It is my pretty pebbles that I want – where are they?"

"I do not know, I do not know," cried Werper. "I gave them to Achmet Zek or he would have killed me. A few minutes later he followed me along the trail to slay me, although he had promised to molest me no further, and I shot and killed him; but the pouch was not upon his person and though I searched about the jungle for some time I could not find it."

"I found it, I tell you," growled Tarzan, "and I also found the pebbles which Achmet Zek had thrown away in disgust. They were not Tarzan's pebbles. You have hidden them! Tell me where they are or I will kill you," and the brown fingers of the ape-man closed a little tighter upon the throat of his victim.

Werper struggled to free himself. "My God, Lord Greystoke," he managed to scream, "would you commit murder for a handful of stones?"

The fingers at his throat relaxed, a puzzled, far-away expression softened the gray eyes.

"Lord Greystoke!" repeated the ape-man. "Lord Greystoke! Who is Lord Greystoke? Where have I heard that name before?"

"Why man, you are Lord Greystoke," cried the Belgian. "You were injured by a falling rock when the earthquake shattered the passage to the underground chamber to which you and your black Waziri had come to fetch golden ingots back to your bungalow. The blow shattered your memory. You are John Clayton, Lord Greystoke – don't you remember?"

"John Clayton, Lord Greystoke!" repeated Tarzan. Then for a moment he was silent. Presently his hand went falteringly to his forehead, an expression of wonderment filled his eyes – of wonderment and sudden understanding. The forgotten name had reawakened the returning memory that had been struggling to reassert itself. The ape-man relinquished his grasp upon the throat of the Belgian, and leaped to his feet.

"God!" he cried, and then, "Jane!" Suddenly he turned toward Werper. "My wife?" he asked. "What has become of her? The farm is in ruins. You know. You have had something to do with all this. You followed me to Opar, you stole the jewels which I thought but pretty pebbles. You are a crook! Do not try to tell me that you are not."

"He is worse than a crook," said a quiet voice close behind them.

Tarzan turned in astonishment to see a tall man in uniform standing in the trail a few paces from him. Back of the man were a number of black soldiers in the uniform of the Congo Free State.

"He is a murderer, Monsieur," continued the officer. "I have followed him for a long time to take him back to stand trial for the killing of his superior officer."

Werper was upon his feet now, gazing, white and trembling, at the fate which had overtaken him even in the fastness of the labyrinthine jungle. Instinctively he turned to flee; but Tarzan of the Apes reached out a strong hand and grasped him by the shoulder.

"Wait!" said the ape-man to his captive. "This gentleman wishes you, and so do I. When I am through with you, he may have you. Tell me what has become of my wife."

The Belgian officer eyed the almost naked, white giant with curiosity. He noted the strange contrast of primitive weapons and apparel, and the easy, fluent French which the man spoke. The former denoted the lowest, the latter the highest type of culture. He could not quite determine the social status of this strange creature; but he knew that he did not relish the easy assurance with which the fellow presumed to dictate when he might take possession of the prisoner.

"Pardon me," he said, stepping forward and placing his hand on Werper's other shoulder; "but this gentleman is my prisoner. He must come with me."

"When I am through with him," replied Tarzan, quietly.

The officer turned and beckoned to the soldiers standing in the trail behind him. A company of uniformed blacks stepped quickly forward and pushing past the three, surrounded the ape-man and his captive.

"Both the law and the power to enforce it are upon my side," announced the officer. "Let us have no trouble. If you have a grievance against this man you may return with me and enter your charge regularly before an authorized tribunal."

"Your legal rights are not above suspicion, my friend," replied Tarzan, "and your power to enforce your commands are only apparent – not real. You have presumed to enter British territory with an armed force. Where is your authority for this invasion? Where are the extradition papers which warrant the arrest of this man? And what assurance have you that I cannot bring an armed force about you that will prevent your return to the Congo Free State?"

The Belgian lost his temper. "I have no disposition to argue with a naked savage," he cried. "Unless you wish to be hurt you will not interfere with me. Take the prisoner, Sergeant!"

Werper raised his lips close to Tarzan's ear. "Keep me from them, and I can show you the very spot where I saw your wife last night," he whispered. "She cannot be far from here at this very minute."

The soldiers, following the signal from their sergeant, closed in to seize Werper. Tarzan grabbed the Belgian about the waist, and bearing him beneath his arm as he might have borne a sack of flour, leaped forward in an attempt to break through the cordon. His right fist caught the nearest soldier upon the jaw and sent him hurtling backward upon his fellows. Clubbed rifles were torn from the hands of those who barred his way, and right and left the black soldiers stumbled aside in the face of the ape-man's savage break for liberty.

So completely did the blacks surround the two that they dared not fire for fear of hitting one of their own number, and Tarzan was already through them and upon the point of dodging into the concealing mazes of the jungle when one who had sneaked upon him from behind struck him a heavy blow upon the head with a rifle.

In an instant the ape-man was down and a dozen black soldiers were upon his back. When he regained consciousness he found himself securely bound, as was Werper also. The Belgian officer, success having crowned his efforts, was in good humor, and inclined to chaff his prisoners about the ease with which they had been captured; but from Tarzan of the Apes he elicited no response. Werper, however, was voluble in his protests. He explained that Tarzan was an English lord; but the officer only laughed at the assertion, and advised his prisoner to save his breath for his defense in court.

As soon as Tarzan regained his senses and it was found that he was not seriously injured, the prisoners were hastened into line and the return march toward the Congo Free State boundary commenced.

Toward evening the column halted beside a stream, made camp and prepared the evening meal. From the thick foliage of the nearby jungle a pair of fierce eyes watched the activities of the uniformed blacks with silent intensity and curiosity. From beneath beetling brows the creature saw the boma constructed, the fires built, and the supper prepared.

Tarzan and Werper had been lying bound behind a small pile of knapsacks from the time that the company had halted; but with the preparation of the meal completed, their guard ordered them to rise and come forward to one of the fires where their hands would be unfettered that they might eat.

As the giant ape-man rose, a startled expression of recognition entered the eyes of the watcher in the jungle, and a low guttural broke from the savage lips. Instantly Tarzan was alert, but the answering growl died upon his lips, suppressed by the fear that it might arouse the suspicions of the soldiers.

Suddenly an inspiration came to him. He turned toward Werper.

"I am going to speak to you in a loud voice and in a tongue which you do not understand. Appear to listen intently to what I say, and occasionally mumble something as though replying in the same language – our escape may hinge upon the success of your efforts."

Werper nodded in assent and understanding, and immediately there broke from the lips of his companion a strange jargon which might have been compared with equal propriety to the barking and growling of a dog and the chattering of monkeys.

The nearer soldiers looked in surprise at the ape-man. Some of them laughed, while others drew away in evident superstitious fear. The officer approached the prisoners while Tarzan was still jabbering, and halted behind them, listening in perplexed interest. When Werper mumbled some ridiculous jargon in reply his curiosity broke bounds, and he stepped forward, demanding to know what language it was that they spoke.

Tarzan had gauged the measure of the man's culture from the nature and quality of his conversation during the march, and he rested the success of his reply upon the estimate he had made.

"Greek," he explained.

"Oh, I thought it was Greek," replied the officer; "but it has been so many years since I studied it that I was not sure. In future, however, I will thank you to speak in a language which I am more familiar with."

Werper turned his head to hide a grin, whispering to Tarzan: "It was Greek to him all right – and to me, too."

But one of the black soldiers mumbled in a low voice to a companion: "I have heard those sounds before – once at night when I was lost in the jungle, I heard the hairy men of the trees talking among themselves, and their words were like the words of this white man. I wish that we had not found him. He is not a man at all – he is a bad spirit, and we shall have bad luck if we do not let him go," and the fellow rolled his eyes fearfully toward the jungle.

His companion laughed nervously, and moved away, to repeat the conversation, with variations and exaggerations, to others of the black soldiery, so that it was not long before a frightful tale of black magic and sudden death was woven about the giant prisoner, and had gone the rounds of the camp.

And deep in the gloomy jungle amidst the darkening shadows of the falling night a hairy, manlike creature swung swiftly southward upon some secret mission of his own.

CHAPTER TWENTY THREE

A Night of Terror

To Jane Clayton, waiting in the tree where Werper had placed her, it seemed that the long night would never end, yet end it did at last, and within an hour of the coming of dawn her spirits leaped with renewed hope at sight of a solitary horseman approaching along the trail.

The flowing burnoose, with its loose hood, hid both the face and the figure of the rider; but that it was M. Frecoult the girl well knew, since he had been garbed as an Arab, and he alone might be expected to seek her hiding place.

That which she saw relieved the strain of the long night vigil; but there was much that she did not see. She did not see the black face beneath the white hood, nor the file of ebon horsemen beyond the trail's bend riding slowly in the wake of their leader. These things she did not see at first, and so she leaned downward toward the approaching rider, a cry of welcome forming in her throat.

At the first word the man looked up, reining in in surprise, and as she saw the black face of Abdul Mourak, the Abyssinian, she shrank back in terror among the branches; but it was too late. The man had seen her, and now he called to her to descend. At first she refused; but when a dozen black cavalrymen drew up behind their leader, and at Abdul Mourak's command one of them started to climb the tree after her she realized that resistance was futile, and came slowly down to stand upon the ground before this new captor and plead her cause in the name of justice and humanity.

Angered by recent defeat, and by the loss of the gold, the jewels, and his prisoners, Abdul Mourak was in no mood to be influenced by any appeal to those softer sentiments to which, as a matter of fact, he was almost a stranger even under the most favourable conditions.

He looked for degradation and possible death in punishment for his failures and his misfortunes when he should have returned to his native land and made his report to Menelek; but an acceptable gift might temper the wrath of the emperor, and surely this fair flower of another race should be gratefully received by the black ruler!

When Jane Clayton had concluded her appeal, Abdul Mourak replied briefly that he would promise her protection; but that he must take her to his emperor. The girl did not need ask him why, and once again hope died within her breast. Resignedly she permitted herself to be lifted to a seat behind one of the troopers, and again, under new masters, her journey was resumed toward what she now began to believe was her inevitable fate.

Abdul Mourak, bereft of his guides by the battle he had waged against the raiders, and himself unfamiliar with the country, had wandered far from the trail he should have followed, and as a result had made but little progress toward the north since the beginning of his flight. Today he was beating toward the west in the hope of coming upon a village where he might obtain guides; but night found him still as far from a realization of his hopes as had the rising sun.

It was a dispirited company which went into camp, waterless and hungry, in the dense jungle. Attracted by the horses, lions roared about the boma, and to their hideous din was added the shrill neighs of the terror-stricken beasts they hunted. There was little sleep for man or beast, and the sentries were doubled that there might be enough on duty both to guard against the sudden charge of an overbold, or overhungry lion, and to keep the fire blazing which was an even more effectual barrier against them than the thorny boma.

It was well past midnight, and as yet Jane Clayton, notwithstanding that she had passed a sleepless night the night before, had scarcely more than dozed. A sense of impending danger seemed to hang like a black pall over the camp. The veteran troopers of the black emperor were nervous and ill at ease. Abdul Mourak left his blankets a dozen times to pace restlessly back and forth between the tethered horses and the crackling fire. The girl could see his great frame silhouetted against the lurid glare of the flames, and she guessed from the quick, nervous movements of the man that he was afraid.

The roaring of the lions rose in sudden fury until the earth trembled to the hideous chorus. The horses shrilled their neighs of terror as they lay back upon their halter ropes in their mad endeavors to break loose. A trooper, braver than his fellows, leaped among the kicking, plunging, fear-maddened beasts in a futile attempt to quiet them. A lion, large, and fierce, and courageous, leaped almost to the boma, full in the bright light from the fire. A sentry raised his piece and fired, and the little leaden pellet unstoppered the vials of hell upon the terror-stricken camp.

The shot ploughed a deep and painful furrow in the lion's side, arousing all the bestial fury of the little brain; but abating not a whit the power and vigor of the great body.

Unwounded, the boma and the flames might have turned him back; but now the pain and the rage wiped caution from his mind, and with a loud, and angry roar he topped the barrier with an easy leap and was among the horses.

What had been pandemonium before became now an indescribable tumult of hideous sound. The stricken horse upon which the lion leaped shrieked out its terror and its agony. Several about it broke their tethers and plunged madly about the camp. Men leaped from their blankets and with guns ready ran toward the picket line, and then from the jungle beyond the boma a dozen lions, emboldened by the example of their fellow charged fearlessly upon the camp.

Singly and in twos and threes they leaped the boma, until the little enclosure was filled with cursing men and screaming horses battling for their lives with the green-eyed devils of the jungle.

With the charge of the first lion, Jane Clayton had scrambled to her feet, and now she stood horror-struck at the scene of savage slaughter that swirled and eddied about her. Once a bolting horse knocked her down, and a moment later a lion, leaping in pursuit of another terror-stricken animal, brushed her so closely that she was again thrown from her feet.

Amidst the cracking of the rifles and the growls of the carnivora rose the death screams of stricken men and horses as they were dragged down by the blood-mad cats. The leaping carnivora and the plunging horses, prevented any concerted action by the Abyssinians – it was every man for himself – and in the melee, the defenseless woman was either forgotten or ignored by her black captors. A score of times was her life menaced by charging lions, by plunging horses, or by the wildly fired bullets of the frightened troopers, yet there was no chance of escape, for now with the fiendish cunning of their kind, the tawny hunters commenced to circle about their prey, hemming them within a ring of mighty, yellow fangs, and sharp, long talons. Again and again an individual lion would dash suddenly among the frightened men and horses, and occasionally a horse, goaded to frenzy by pain or terror, succeeded in racing safely through the circling lions, leaping the boma, and escaping into the jungle; but for the men and the woman no such escape was possible.

A horse, struck by a stray bullet, fell beside Jane Clayton, a lion leaped across the expiring beast full upon the breast of a black trooper just beyond. The man clubbed his rifle and struck futilely at the broad head, and then he was down and the carnivore was standing above him.

Shrieking out his terror, the soldier clawed with puny fingers at the shaggy breast in vain endeavor to push away the grinning jaws. The lion lowered his head, the gaping fangs closed with a single sickening crunch upon the fear-distorted face, and turning strode back across the body of the dead horse dragging his limp and bloody burden with him.

Wide-eyed the girl stood watching. She saw the carnivore step upon the corpse, stumblingly, as the grisly thing swung between its forepaws, and her eyes remained fixed in fascination while the beast passed within a few paces of her.

The interference of the body seemed to enrage the lion. He shook the inanimate clay venomously. He growled and roared hideously at the dead, insensate thing, and then he dropped it and raised his head to look about in search of some living victim upon which to wreak his ill temper. His yellow eyes fastened themselves balefully upon the figure of the girl, the bristling lips raised, disclosing the grinning fangs. A terrific roar broke from the savage throat, and the great beast crouched to spring upon this new and helpless victim.

Quiet had fallen early upon the camp where Tarzan and Werper lay securely bound. Two nervous sentries paced their beats, their eyes rolling often toward the impenetrable shadows of the gloomy jungle. The others slept or tried to sleep – all but the ape-man. Silently and powerfully he strained at the bonds which fettered his wrists.

The muscles knotted beneath the smooth, brown skin of his arms and shoulders, the veins stood out upon his temples from the force of his exertions – a strand parted, another and another, and one hand was free. Then from the jungle came a low guttural, and the ape-man became suddenly a silent, rigid statue, with ears and nostrils straining to span the black void where his eyesight could not reach.

Again came the uncanny sound from the thick verdure beyond the camp. A sentry halted abruptly, straining his eyes into the gloom. The kinky wool upon his head stiffened and raised. He called to his comrade in a hoarse whisper.

"Did you hear it?" he asked.

The other came closer, trembling.

"Hear what?"

Again was the weird sound repeated, followed almost immediately by a similar and answering sound from the camp. The sentries drew close together, watching the black spot from which the voice seemed to come.

Trees overhung the boma at this point which was upon the opposite side of the camp from them. They dared not approach. Their terror even prevented them from arousing their fellows – they could only stand in frozen fear and watch for the fearsome apparition they momentarily expected to see leap from the jungle.

Nor had they long to wait. A dim, bulky form dropped lightly from the branches of a tree into the camp. At sight of it one of the sentries recovered command of his muscles and his voice. Screaming loudly to awaken the sleeping camp, he leaped toward the flickering watch fire and threw a mass of brush upon it.

The white officer and the black soldiers sprang from their blankets. The flames leaped high upon the rejuvenated fire, lighting the entire camp, and the awakened men shrank back in superstitious terror from the sight that met their frightened and astonished vision.

A dozen huge and hairy forms loomed large beneath the trees at the far side of the enclosure. The white giant, one hand freed, had struggled to his knees and was calling to the frightful, nocturnal visitors in a hideous medley of bestial gutturals, barkings and growlings.

Werper had managed to sit up. He, too, saw the savage faces of the approaching anthropoids and scarcely knew whether to be relieved or terror-stricken.

Growling, the great apes leaped forward toward Tarzan and Werper. Chulk led them. The Belgian officer called to his men to fire upon the intruders; but the Negroes held back, filled as they were with superstitious terror of the hairy treemen, and with the conviction that the white giant who could thus summon the beasts of the jungle to his aid was more than human.

Drawing his own weapon, the officer fired, and Tarzan fearing the effect of the noise upon his really timid friends called to them to hasten and fulfill his commands.

A couple of the apes turned and fled at the sound of the firearm; but Chulk and a half dozen others waddled rapidly forward, and, following the ape-man's directions, seized both him and Werper and bore them off toward the jungle.

By dint of threats, reproaches and profanity the Belgian officer succeeded in persuading his trembling command to fire a volley after the retreating apes. A ragged, straggling volley it was, but at least one of its bullets found a mark, for as the jungle closed about the hairy rescuers, Chulk, who bore Werper across one broad shoulder, staggered and fell.

In an instant he was up again; but the Belgian guessed from his unsteady gait that he was hard hit. He lagged far behind the others, and it was several minutes after they had halted at Tarzan's command before he came slowly up to them, reeling from side to side, and at last falling again beneath the weight of his burden and the shock of his wound.

As Chulk went down he dropped Werper, so that the latter fell face downward with the body of the ape lying half across him. In this position the Belgian felt something resting against his hands, which were still bound at his back – something that was not a part of the hairy body of the ape.

Mechanically the man's fingers felt of the object resting almost in their grasp – it was a soft pouch, filled with small, hard particles. Werper gasped in wonderment as recognition filtered through the incredulity of his mind. It was impossible, and yet – it was true!

Feverishly he strove to remove the pouch from the ape and transfer it to his own possession; but the restricted radius to which his bonds held his hands prevented this, though he did succeed in tucking the pouch with its precious contents inside the waist band of his trousers.

Tarzan, sitting at a short distance, was busy with the remaining knots of the cords which bound him. Presently he flung aside the last of them and rose to his feet. Approaching Werper he knelt beside him. For a moment he examined the ape.

"Quite dead," he announced. "It is too bad – he was a splendid creature," and then he turned to the work of liberating the Belgian.

He freed his hands first, and then commenced upon the knots at his ankles.

"I can do the rest," said the Belgian. "I have a small pocketknife which they overlooked when they searched me," and in this way he succeeded in ridding himself of the ape-man's attentions that he might find and open his little knife and cut the thong which fastened the pouch about Chulk's shoulder, and transfer it from his waist band to the breast of his shirt. Then he rose and approached Tarzan.

Once again had avarice claimed him. Forgotten were the good intentions which the confidence of Jane Clayton in his honor had awakened. What she had done, the little pouch had undone. How it had come upon the person of the great ape, Werper could not imagine, unless it had been that the anthropoid had witnessed his fight with Achmet Zek, seen the Arab with the pouch and taken it away from him; but that this pouch contained the jewels of Opar, Werper was positive, and that was all that interested him greatly.

"Now," said the ape-man, "keep your promise to me. Lead me to the spot where you last saw my wife."

It was slow work pushing through the jungle in the dead of night behind the slow-moving Belgian. The ape-man chafed at the delay, but the European could not swing through the trees as could his more agile and muscular companions, and so the speed of all was limited to that of the slowest.

The apes trailed out behind the two white men for a matter of a few miles; but presently their interest lagged, the foremost of them halted in a little glade and the others stopped at his side. There they sat peering from beneath their shaggy brows at the figures of the two men forging steadily ahead, until the latter disappeared in the leafy trail beyond the clearing. Then an ape sought a comfortable couch beneath a tree, and one by one the others followed his example, so that Werper and Tarzan continued their journey alone; nor was the latter either surprised or concerned.

The two had gone but a short distance beyond the glade where the apes had deserted them, when the roaring of distant lions fell upon their ears. The ape-man paid no attention to the familiar sounds until the crack of a rifle came faintly from the same direction, and when this was followed by the shrill neighing of horses, and an almost continuous fusillade of shots intermingled with increased and savage roaring of a large troop of lions, he became immediately concerned.

"Someone is having trouble over there," he said, turning toward Werper. "I'll have to go to them – they may be friends."

"Your wife might be among them," suggested the Belgian, for since he had again come into possession of the pouch he had become fearful and suspicious of the ape-man, and in his mind had constantly revolved many plans for eluding this giant Englishman, who was at once his savior and his captor.

At the suggestion Tarzan started as though struck with a whip.

"God!" he cried, "she might be, and the lions are attacking them – they are in the camp. I can tell from the screams of the horses – and there! that was the cry of a man in his death agonies. Stay here man – I will come back for you. I must go first to them," and swinging into a tree the lithe figure swung rapidly off into the night with the speed and silence of a disembodied spirit.

For a moment Werper stood where the ape-man had left him. Then a cunning smile crossed his lips. "Stay here?" he asked himself. "Stay here and wait until you return to find and take these jewels from me? Not I, my friend, not I," and turning abruptly eastward Albert Werper passed through the foliage of a hanging vine and out of the sight of his fellow-man – forever.

CHAPTER TWENTY FOUR

Home

As Tarzan of the Apes hurtled through the trees the discordant sounds of the battle between the Abyssinians and the lions smote more and more distinctly upon his sensitive ears, redoubling his assurance that the plight of the human element of the conflict was critical indeed.

At last the glare of the camp fire shone plainly through the intervening trees, and a moment later the giant figure of the ape-man paused upon an overhanging bough to look down upon the bloody scene of carnage below.

His quick eye took in the whole scene with a single comprehending glance and stopped upon the figure of a woman standing facing a great lion across the carcass of a horse.

The carnivore was crouching to spring as Tarzan discovered the tragic tableau. Numa was almost beneath the branch upon which the ape-man stood, naked and unarmed. There was not even an instant's hesitation upon the part of the latter – it was as though he had not even paused in his swift progress through the trees, so lightning-like his survey and comprehension of the scene below him – so instantaneous his consequent action.

So hopeless had seemed her situation to her that Jane Clayton but stood in lethargic apathy awaiting the impact of the huge body that would hurl her to the ground – awaiting the momentary agony that cruel talons and grisly fangs may inflict before the coming of the merciful oblivion which would end her sorrow and her suffering.

What use to attempt escape? As well face the hideous end as to be dragged down from behind in futile flight. She did not even close her eyes to shut out the frightful aspect of that snarling face, and so it was that as she saw the lion preparing to charge she saw, too, a bronzed and mighty figure leap from an overhanging tree at the instant that Numa rose in his spring.

Wide went her eyes in wonder and incredulity, as she beheld this seeming apparition risen from the dead. The lion was forgotten – her own peril – everything save the wondrous miracle of this strange recrudescence. With parted lips, with palms tight pressed against her heaving bosom, the girl leaned forward, large-eyed, enthralled by the vision of her dead mate.

She saw the sinewy form leap to the shoulder of the lion, hurtling against the leaping beast like a huge, animate battering ram. She saw the carnivore brushed aside as he was almost upon her, and in the instant she realized that no substanceless wraith could thus turn the charge of a maddened lion with brute force greater than the brute's.

Tarzan, her Tarzan, lived! A cry of unspeakable gladness broke from her lips, only to die in terror as she saw the utter defenselessness of her mate, and realized that the lion had recovered himself and was turning upon Tarzan in mad lust for vengeance.

At the ape-man's feet lay the discarded rifle of the dead Abyssinian whose mutilated corpse sprawled where Numa had abandoned it. The quick glance which had swept the ground for some weapon of defense discovered it, and as the lion reared upon his hind legs to seize the rash man-thing who had dared interpose its puny strength between Numa and his prey, the heavy stock whirred through the air and splintered upon the broad forehead.

Not as an ordinary mortal might strike a blow did Tarzan of the Apes strike; but with the maddened frenzy of a wild beast backed by the steel thews which his wild, arboreal boyhood had bequeathed him. When the blow ended the splintered stock was driven through the splintered skull into the savage brain, and the heavy iron barrel was bent into a rude V.

In the instant that the lion sank, lifeless, to the ground, Jane Clayton threw herself into the eager arms of her husband. For a brief instant he strained her dear form to his breast, and then a glance about him awakened the ape-man to the dangers which still surrounded them.

Upon every hand the lions were still leaping upon new victims. Fear-maddened horses still menaced them with their erratic bolting from one side of the enclosure to the other. Bullets from the guns of the defenders who remained alive but added to the perils of their situation.

To remain was to court death. Tarzan seized Jane Clayton and lifted her to a broad shoulder. The blacks who had witnessed his advent looked on in amazement as they saw the naked giant leap easily into the branches of the tree from whence he had dropped so uncannily upon the scene, and vanish as he had come, bearing away their prisoner with him.

They were too well occupied in self-defense to attempt to halt him, nor could they have done so other than by the wasting of a precious bullet which might be needed the next instant to turn the charge of a savage foe.

And so, unmolested, Tarzan passed from the camp of the Abyssinians, from which the din of conflict followed him deep into the jungle until distance gradually obliterated it entirely.

Back to the spot where he had left Werper went the ape-man, joy in his heart now, where fear and sorrow had so recently reigned; and in his mind a determination to forgive the Belgian and aid him in making good his escape. But when he came to the place, Werper was gone, and though Tarzan called aloud many times he received no reply. Convinced that the man had purposely eluded him for reasons of his own, John Clayton felt that he was under no obligations to expose his wife to further danger and discomfort in the prosecution of a more thorough search for the missing Belgian.

"He has acknowledged his guilt by his flight, Jane," he said. "We will let him go to lie in the bed that he has made for himself."

Straight as homing pigeons, the two made their way toward the ruin and desolation that had once been the center of their happy lives, and which was soon to be restored by the willing black hands of laughing laborers, made happy again by the return of the master and mistress whom they had mourned as dead.

Past the village of Achmet Zek their way led them, and there they found but the charred remains of the palisade and the native huts, still smoking, as mute evidence of the wrath and vengeance of a powerful enemy.

"The Waziri," commented Tarzan with a grim smile.

"God bless them!" cried Jane Clayton.

"They cannot be far ahead of us," said Tarzan, "Basuli and the others. The gold is gone and the jewels of Opar, Jane; but we have each other and the Waziri – and we have love and loyalty and friendship. And what are gold and jewels to these?"

"If only poor Mugambi lived," she replied, "and those other brave fellows who sacrificed their lives in vain endeavor to protect me!"

In the silence of mingled joy and sorrow they passed along through the familiar jungle, and as the afternoon was waning there came faintly to the ears of the ape-man the murmuring cadence of distant voices.

"We are nearing the Waziri, Jane," he said. "I can hear them ahead of us. They are going into camp for the night, I imagine."

A half hour later the two came upon a horde of ebon warriors which Basuli had collected for his war of vengeance upon the raiders. With them were the captured women of the tribe whom they had found in the village of Achmet Zek, and tall, even among the giant Waziri, loomed a familiar black form at the side of Basuli. It was Mugambi, whom Jane had thought dead amidst the charred ruins of the bungalow.

Ah, such a reunion! Long into the night the dancing and the singing and the laughter awoke the echoes of the somber wood. Again and again were the stories of their various adventures retold. Again and once again they fought their battles with savage beast and savage man, and dawn was already breaking when Basuli, for the fortieth time, narrated how he and a handful of his warriors had watched the battle for the golden ingots which the Abyssinians of Abdul Mourak had waged against the Arab raiders of Achmet Zek, and how, when the victors had ridden away they had sneaked out of the river reeds and stolen away with the precious ingots to hide them where no robber eye ever could discover them.

Pieced out from the fragments of their various experiences with the Belgian the truth concerning the malign activities of Albert Werper became apparent. Only Lady Greystoke found aught to praise in the conduct of the man, and it was difficult even for her to reconcile his many heinous acts with this one evidence of chivalry and honor.

"Deep in the soul of every man," said Tarzan, "must lurk the germ of righteousness. It was your own virtue, Jane, rather even than your helplessness which awakened for an instant the latent decency of this degraded man. In that one act he retrieved himself, and when he is called to face his Maker may it outweigh in the balance, all the sins he has committed."

And Jane Clayton breathed a fervent, "Amen!"

Months had passed. The labor of the Waziri and the gold of Opar had rebuilt and refurnished the wasted homestead of the Greystokes. Once more the simple life of the great African farm went on as it had before the coming of the Belgian and the Arab. Forgotten were the sorrows and dangers of yesterday.

For the first time in months Lord Greystoke felt that he might indulge in a holiday, and so a great hunt was organized that the faithful laborers might feast in celebration of the completion of their work.

In itself the hunt was a success, and ten days after its inauguration, a well-laden safari took up its return march toward the Waziri plain. Lord and Lady Greystoke with Basuli and Mugambi rode together at the head of the column, laughing and talking together in that easy familiarity which common interests and mutual respect breed between honest and intelligent men of any races.

Jane Clayton's horse shied suddenly at an object half hidden in the long grasses of an open space in the jungle. Tarzan's keen eyes sought quickly for an explanation of the animal's action.

"What have we here?" he cried, swinging from his saddle, and a moment later the four were grouped about a human skull and a little litter of whitened human bones.

Tarzan stooped and lifted a leathern pouch from the grisly relics of a man. The hard outlines of the contents brought an exclamation of surprise to his lips.

"The jewels of Opar!" he cried, holding the pouch aloft, "and," pointing to the bones at his feet, "all that remains of Werper, the Belgian."

Mugambi laughed. "Look within, Bwana," he cried, "and you will see what are the jewels of Opar – you will see what the Belgian gave his life for," and the black laughed aloud.

"Why do you laugh?" asked Tarzan.

"Because," replied Mugambi, "I filled the Belgian's pouch with river gravel before I escaped the camp of the Abyssinians whose prisoners we were. I left the Belgian only worthless stones, while I brought away with me the jewels he had stolen from you. That they were afterward stolen from me while I slept in the jungle is my shame and my disgrace; but at least the Belgian lost them – open his pouch and you will see."

Tarzan untied the thong which held the mouth of the leathern bag closed, and permitted the contents to trickle slowly forth into his open palm. Mugambi's eyes went wide at the sight, and the others uttered exclamations of surprise and incredulity, for from the rusty and weather-worn pouch ran a stream of brilliant, scintillating gems.

"The jewels of Opar!" cried Tarzan. "But how did Werper come by them again?"

None could answer, for both Chulk and Werper were dead, and no other knew.

"Poor devil!" said the ape-man, as he swung back into his saddle. "Even in death he has made restitution – let his sins lie with his bones."

ROYAL CLASSICS

20,000 Leagues Under the Sea by Jules Verne
A Christmas Carol by Charles Dickens
A Portrait of the Artist as a Young Man by James Joyce
A Princess of Mars by Edgar Rice Burroughs
A Room with a View by E. M. Forster
A Study in Scarlet by Arthur Conan Doyle
A Tale of Two Cities by Charles Dickens
Aesop's Fables by Aesop
Alice in Wonderland by Lewis Carroll
Anna Karenina by Leo Tolstoy
Anne of Green Gables by Lucy Maud Montgomery
Around the World in 80 Days by Jules Verne
Black Beauty by Anna Sewell
Bleak House by Charles Dickens
Candide by Voltaire
Common Sense by Thomas Paine
Crime and Punishment by Fyodor Dostoevsky
Don Quixote by Miguel de Cervantes
Dracula by Bram Stoker
Dubliners by James Joyce
Emma by Jane Austen
Far from the Madding Crowd by Thomas Hardy
Frankenstein by Mary Shelley
From the Earth to the Moon by Jules Verne
Great Expectations by Charles Dickens
Grimm's Fairy Tales by Jakob and Wilhelm Grimm
Gulliver's Travels by Jonathan Swift
Hamlet by William Shakespeare
Hard Times by Charles Dickens
Heart of Darkness by Joseph Conrad
Howards End by E. M. Forster
Jane Eyre by Charlotte Brontë
Journey to the Center of the Earth by Jules Verne
Kidnapped by Robert Louis Stevenson
Kim by Rudyard Kipling
Les Misérables by Victor Hugo
Little Men by Louisa May Alcott
Little Women by Louisa May Alcott
Macbeth by William Shakespeare
Madame Bovary by Gustave Flaubert
Mansfield Park by Jane Austen
Meditations by Marcus Aurelius
Middlemarch by George Eliot
Moby Dick by Herman Melville
My Ántonia by Willa Cather
Nicomachean Ethics by Aristotle

ROYAL CLASSICS

North and South BY ELIZABETH GASKELL
Northanger Abbey BY JANE AUSTEN
Notes from the Underground BY FYODOR DOSTOYEVSKY
Oliver Twist BY CHARLES DICKENS
On War BY CARL VON CLAUSEWITZ
Persuasion BY JANE AUSTEN
Plato: Five Dialogues BY PLATO
Plutarch's Lives BY PLUTARCH
Politics BY ARISTOTLE
Pollyanna BY ELEANOR H. PORTER
Pride & Prejudice BY JANE AUSTEN
Raggedy Ann Stories BY JOHNNY GRUELLE
Robinson Crusoe BY DANIEL DEFOE
Sense & Sensibility BY JANE AUSTEN
Sons and Lovers BY D. H. LAWRENCE
Swann's Way, In Search of Lost Time BY MARCEL PROUST
Tarzan of the Apes BY EDGAR RICE BURROUGHS
Tess of the d'Urbervilles BY THOMAS HARDY
The Adventures of Huckleberry Finn BY MARK TWAIN
The Adventures of Sherlock Holmes BY ARTHUR CONAN DOYLE
The Adventures of Tom Sawyer BY MARK TWAIN
The Age of Innocence BY EDITH WHARTON
The Art of War BY SUN TZU
The Awakening BY KATE CHOPIN
The Beautiful and the Damned BY F. SCOTT FITZGERALD
The Brothers Karamazov BY FYODOR DOSTOEVSKY
The Call of the Wild BY JACK LONDON
The Communist Manifesto BY KARL MARX & FRIEDRICH ENGELS
The Count of Monte Cristo BY ALEXANDRE DUMAS
The First Men in the Moon BY H. G. WELLS
The Histories BY HERODOTUS
The History of the Peloponnesian War BY THUCYDIDES
The Hound of the Baskervilles BY ARTHUR CONAN DOYLE
The Hunchback of Notre-Dame BY VICTOR HUGO
The Idiot BY FYODOR DOSTOEVSKY
The Iliad BY HOMER
The Importance of Being Earnest BY OSCAR WILDE
The Innocents Abroad BY MARK TWAIN
The Invisible Man BY H. G. WELLS
The Island of Doctor Moreau BY H. G. WELLS
The Jungle BY UPTON SINCLAIR
The Jungle Book BY RUDYARD KIPLING
The Kama Sutra BY VĀTSYĀYANA
The Last of the Mohicans BY JAMES FENIMORE COOPER
The Legend of Sleepy Hollow BY WASHINGTON IRVING
The Life and Opinions of Tristram Shandy BY LAURENCE STERNE

ROYAL

CLASSICS

The Lost World BY ARTHUR CONAN DOYLE
The Memoirs of Sherlock Holmes BY ARTHUR CONAN DOYLE
The Merry Adventures of Robin Hood BY HOWARD PYLE
The Metamorphosis BY FRANZ KAFKA
The Mill on the Floss BY GEORGE ELIOT
The Murder on the Links BY AGATHA CHRISTIE
The Mysterious Affair at Styles BY AGATHA CHRISTIE
The Odyssey BY HOMER
The Old Curiosity Shop BY CHARLES DICKENS
The Origin of Species BY CHARLES DARWIN
The Picture of Dorian Gray BY OSCAR WILDE
The Portrait of a Lady BY HENRY JAMES
The Prince BY NICCOLÒ MACHIAVELLI
The Prince and the Pauper BY MARK TWAIN
The Prophet BY KAHLIL GIBRAN
The Republic BY PLATO
The Return of the Native BY THOMAS HARDY
The Scarlet Letter BY NATHANIEL HAWTHORNE
The Secret Garden BY FRANCES HODGSON BURNETT
The Sign of the Four BY ARTHUR CONAN DOYLE
The Souls of Black Folk BY W. E. B. DU BOIS
The Strange Case of Dr. Jekyll & Mr. Hyde BY ROBERT LOUIS STEVENSON
The Swiss Family Robinson BY JOHANN DAVID WYSS
The Tale of Peter Rabbit BY BEATRIX POTTER
The Tenant of Wildfell Hall BY ANNE BRONTË
The Three Musketeers BY ALEXANDRE DUMAS
The Time Machine BY H. G. WELLS
The Valley of Fear BY ARTHUR CONAN DOYLE
The War of the Worlds BY H. G. WELLS
The Wealth of Nations BY ADAM SMITH
The Wind in the Willows BY KENNETH GRAHAME
The Wizard of Oz BY L. FRANK BAUM
The Woman in White BY WILKIE COLLINS
This Side of Paradise BY F. SCOTT FITZGERALD
Through the Looking-Glass BY LEWIS CARROLL
Tom Jones BY HENRY FIELDING
Treasure Island BY ROBERT LOUIS STEVENSON
Twelve Years a Slave BY SOLOMON NORTHUP
Ulysses BY JAMES JOYCE
Uncle Tom's Cabin BY HARRIET BEECHER STOWE
Vanity Fair BY WILLIAM MAKEPEACE THACKERAY
Villette BY CHARLOTTE BRONTË
Walden BY HENRY DAVID THOREAU
War and Peace BY LEO TOLSTOY
White Fang BY JACK LONDON
Wuthering Heights BY EMILY BRONTË

www.ingramcontent.com/pod-product-compliance
Lightning Source LLC
Chambersburg PA
CBHW020920310726
48980CB00011B/969/J

* 9 7 8 1 7 7 4 7 6 5 9 7 5 *